KINGDOM HEARTS II ②

SHIRO AMANO

ORIGINAL CONCEPT:
TETSUYA NOMURA

Translation: Alethea and Athena Nibley • Lettering: Lys Blakeslee, Terri Delgado

KINGDOM HEARTS © Disney Enterprises, Inc. Characters from FINAL FANTASY video game series © 1990, 1997, 1999, 2001, 2002 Square Enix Co., Ltd. All rights reserved.

Translation © 2013 by Disney Enterprises, Inc.

Yen Press
Hachette Book Group
1290 Avenue of the Americas, New York, NY 10104

www.HachetteBookGroup.com
www.YenPress.com

Yen Press is an imprint of Hachette Book Group, Inc. The Yen Press name and logo are trademarks of Hachette Book Group, Inc.

First Yen Press Edition: August 2013

ISBN: 978-0-316-40115-9

10 9 8 7 6

BVG

Printed in the United States of America

KINGDOM HEARTS II

A scattered dream that's like a far-off memory. A far-off memory that's like a scattered dream.
I want to line the pieces up, yours and mine.

SHIRO AMANO
ORIGINAL CONCEPT:
TETSUYA NOMURA

2

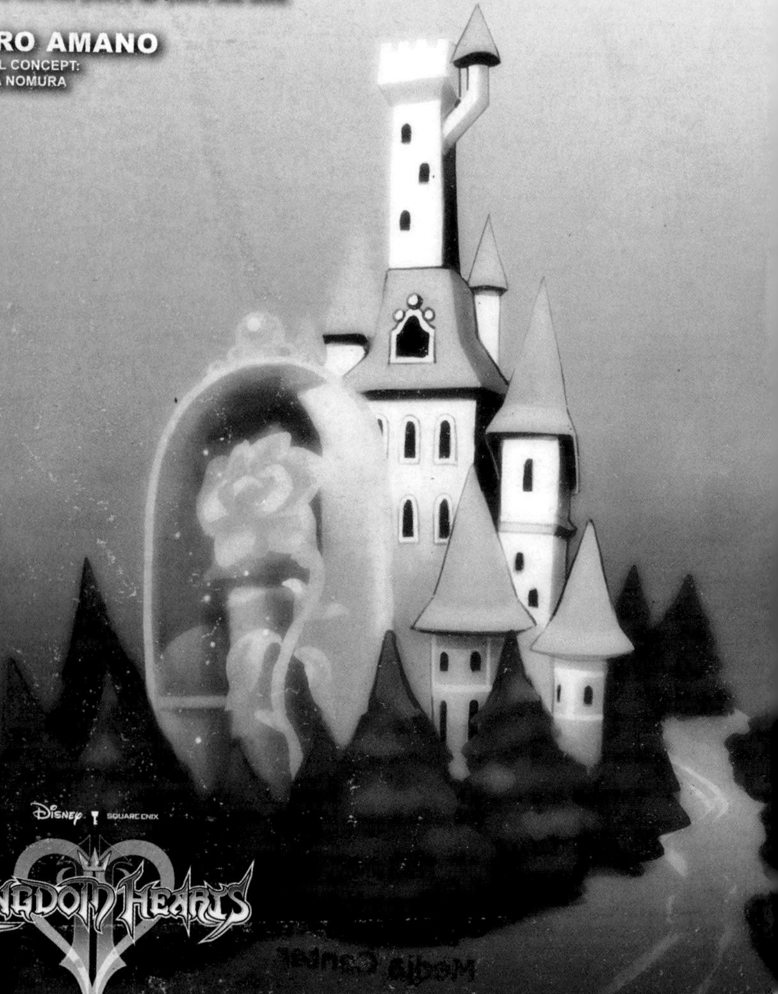

DISNEY SQUARE ENIX

KINGDOM HEARTS

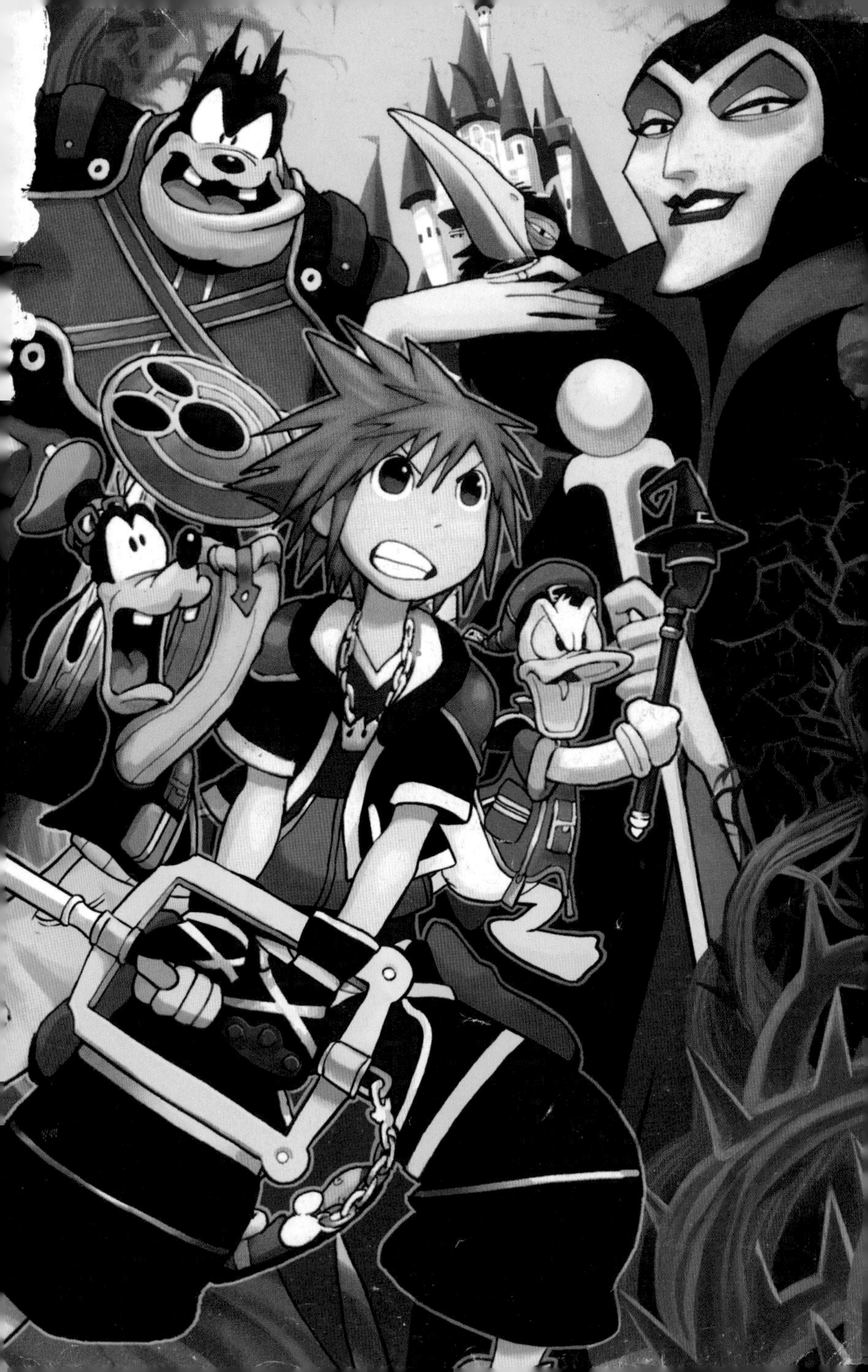

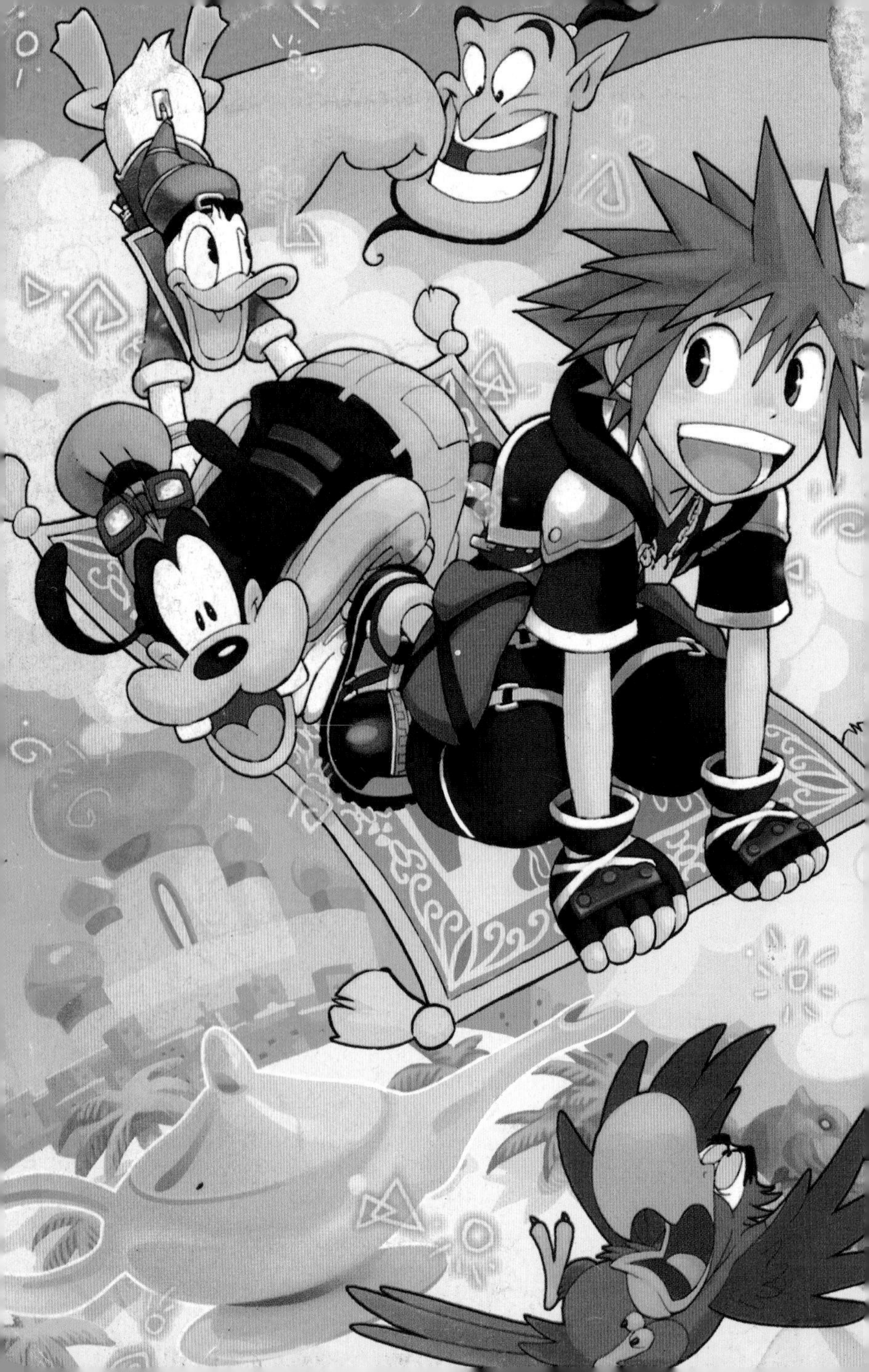

CONTENTS

KINGDOM HEARTS II

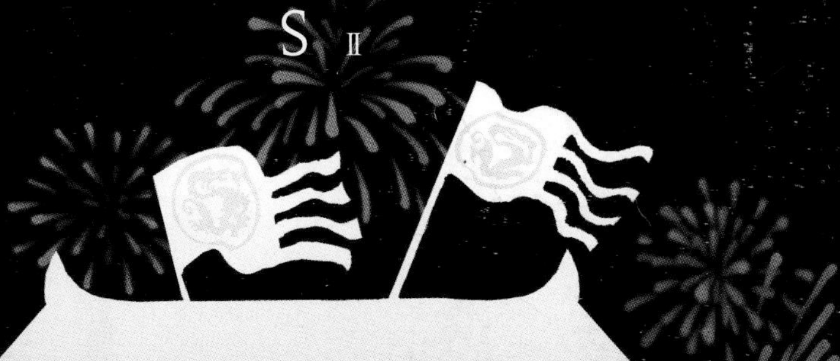

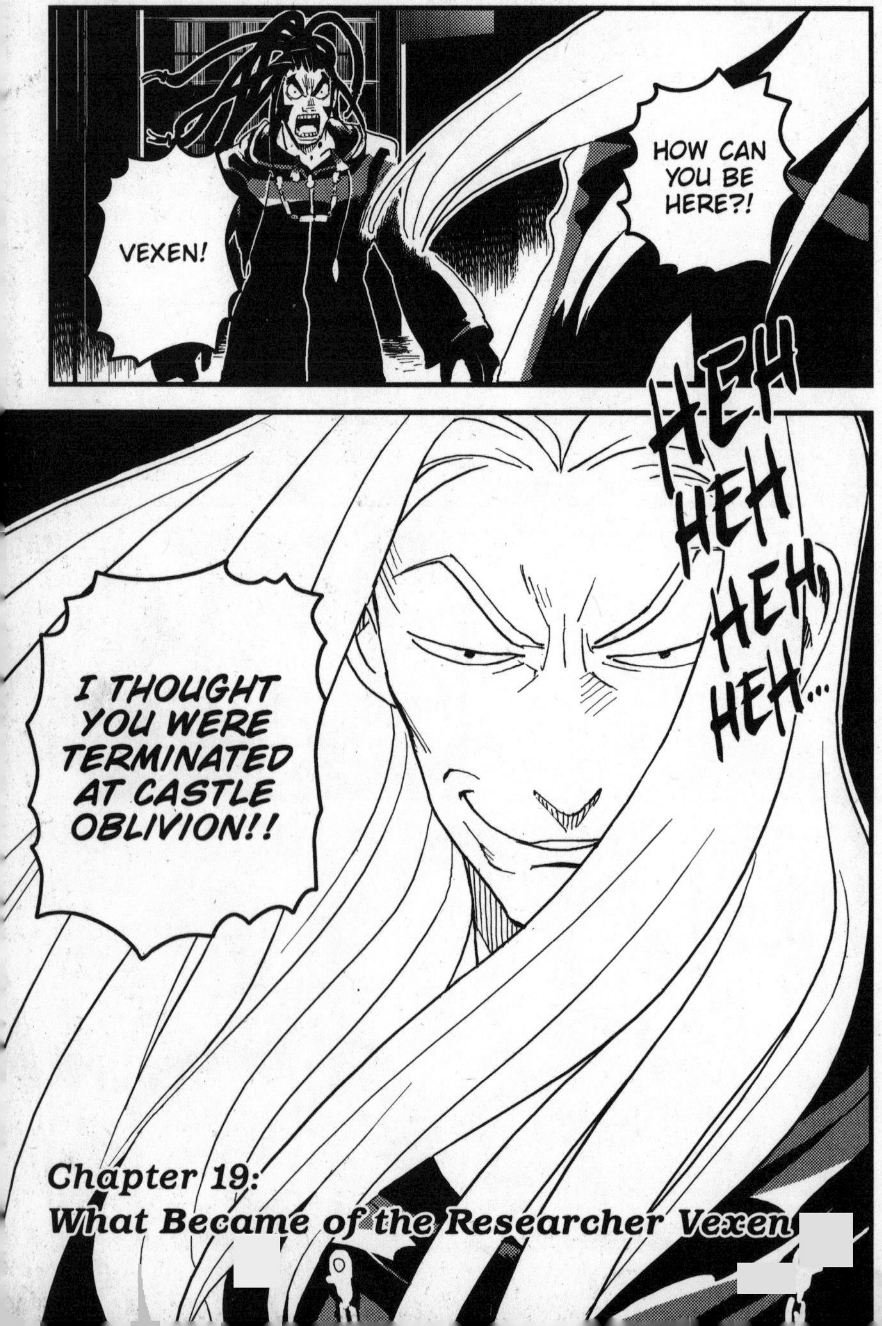
HOW CAN YOU BE HERE?!
VEXEN!
HEH HEH HEH HEH...
I THOUGHT YOU WERE TERMINATED AT CASTLE OBLIVION!!

Chapter 19: What Became of the Researcher Vexen

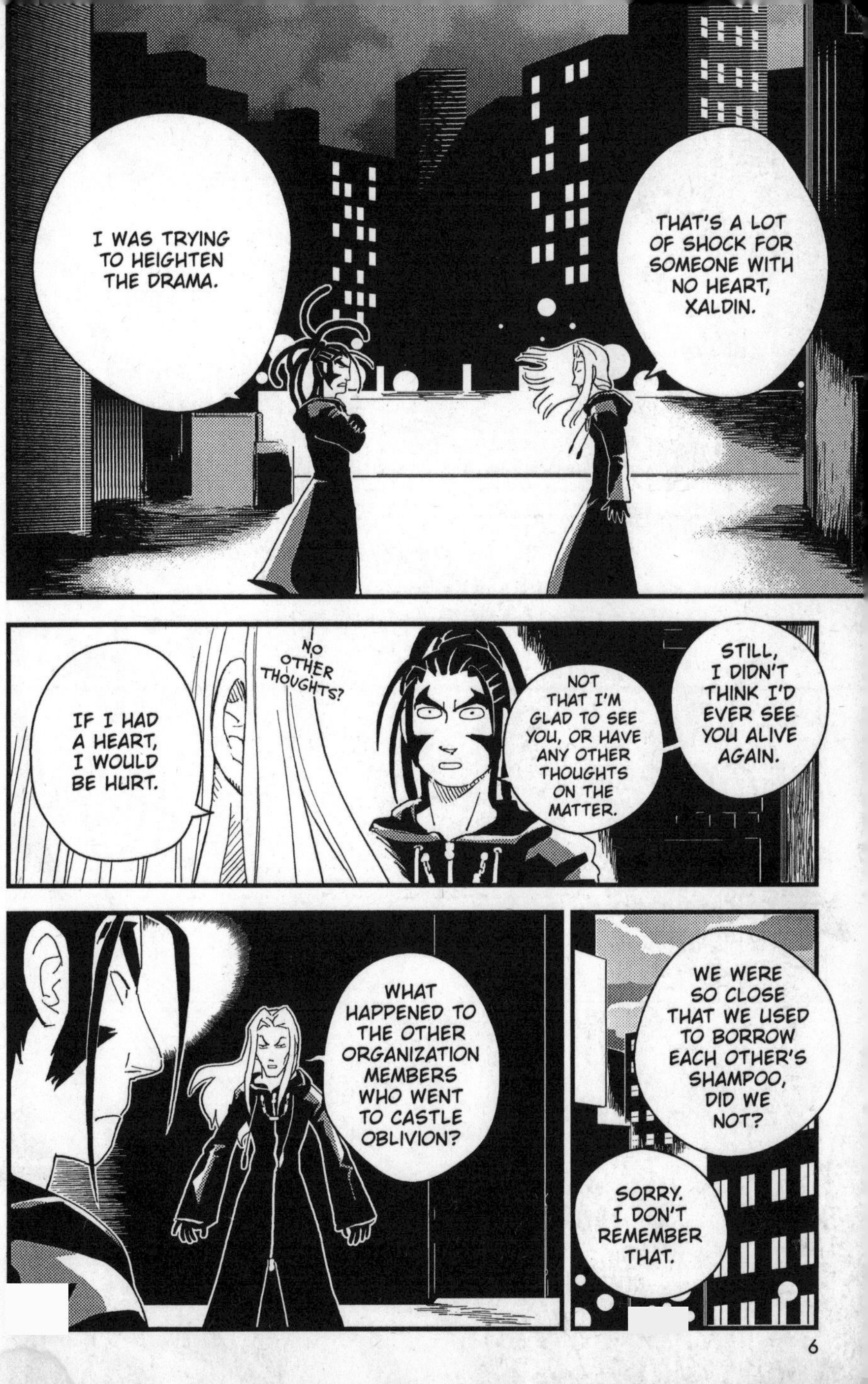
THAT'S A LOT OF SHOCK FOR SOMEONE WITH NO HEART, XALDIN.
I WAS TRYING TO HEIGHTEN THE DRAMA.
STILL, I DIDN'T THINK I'D EVER SEE YOU ALIVE AGAIN.
NOT THAT I'M GLAD TO SEE YOU, OR HAVE ANY OTHER THOUGHTS ON THE MATTER.
NO OTHER THOUGHTS?
IF I HAD A HEART, I WOULD BE HURT.
WE WERE SO CLOSE THAT WE USED TO BORROW EACH OTHER'S SHAMPOO, DID WE NOT?
SORRY. I DON'T REMEMBER THAT.
WHAT HAPPENED TO THE OTHER ORGANIZATION MEMBERS WHO WENT TO CASTLE OBLIVION?

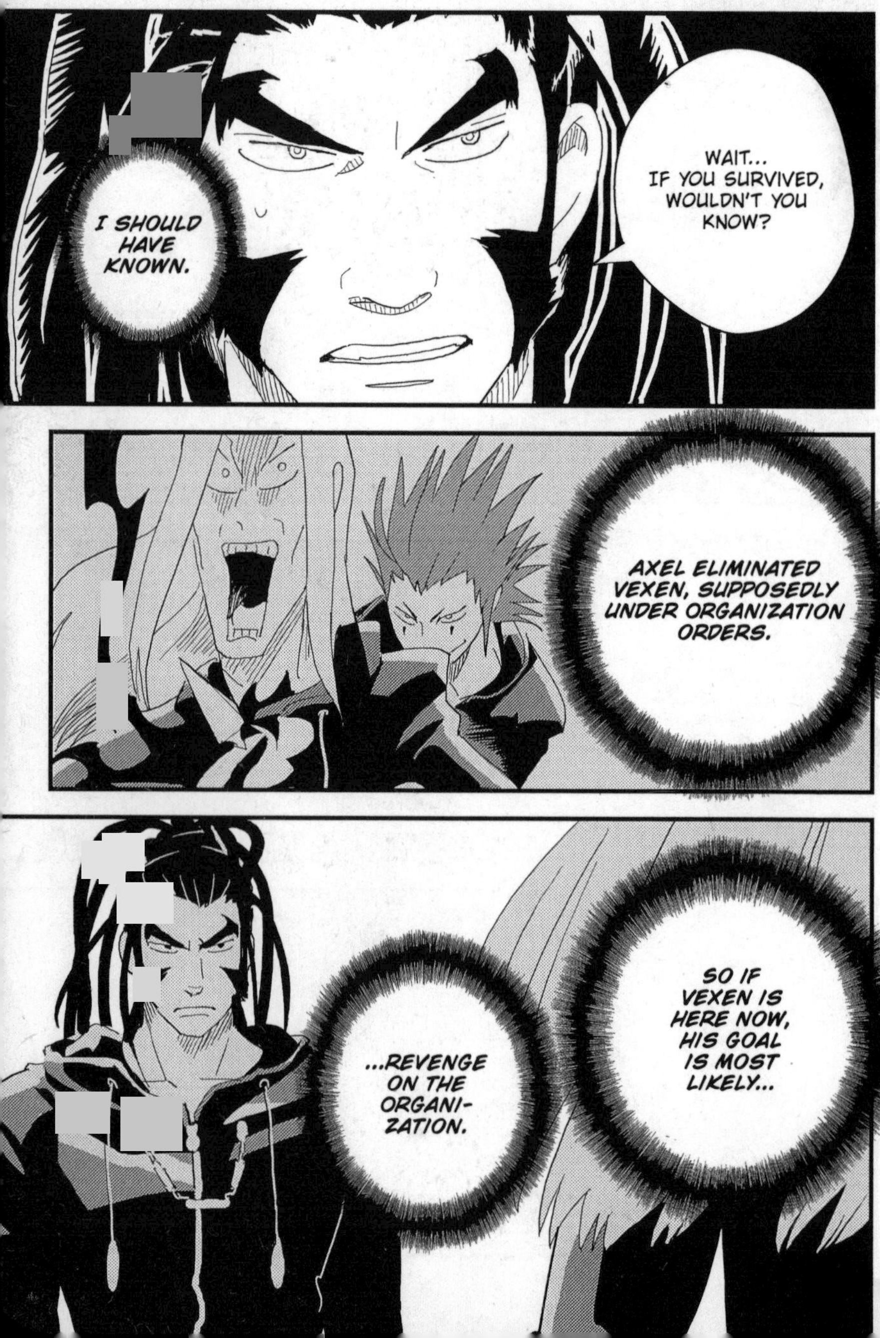
WAIT... IF YOU SURVIVED, WOULDN'T YOU KNOW?
I SHOULD HAVE KNOWN.
AXEL ELIMINATED VEXEN, SUPPOSEDLY UNDER ORGANIZATION ORDERS.
SO IF VEXEN IS HERE NOW, HIS GOAL IS MOST LIKELY...
...REVENGE ON THE ORGANI-ZATION.

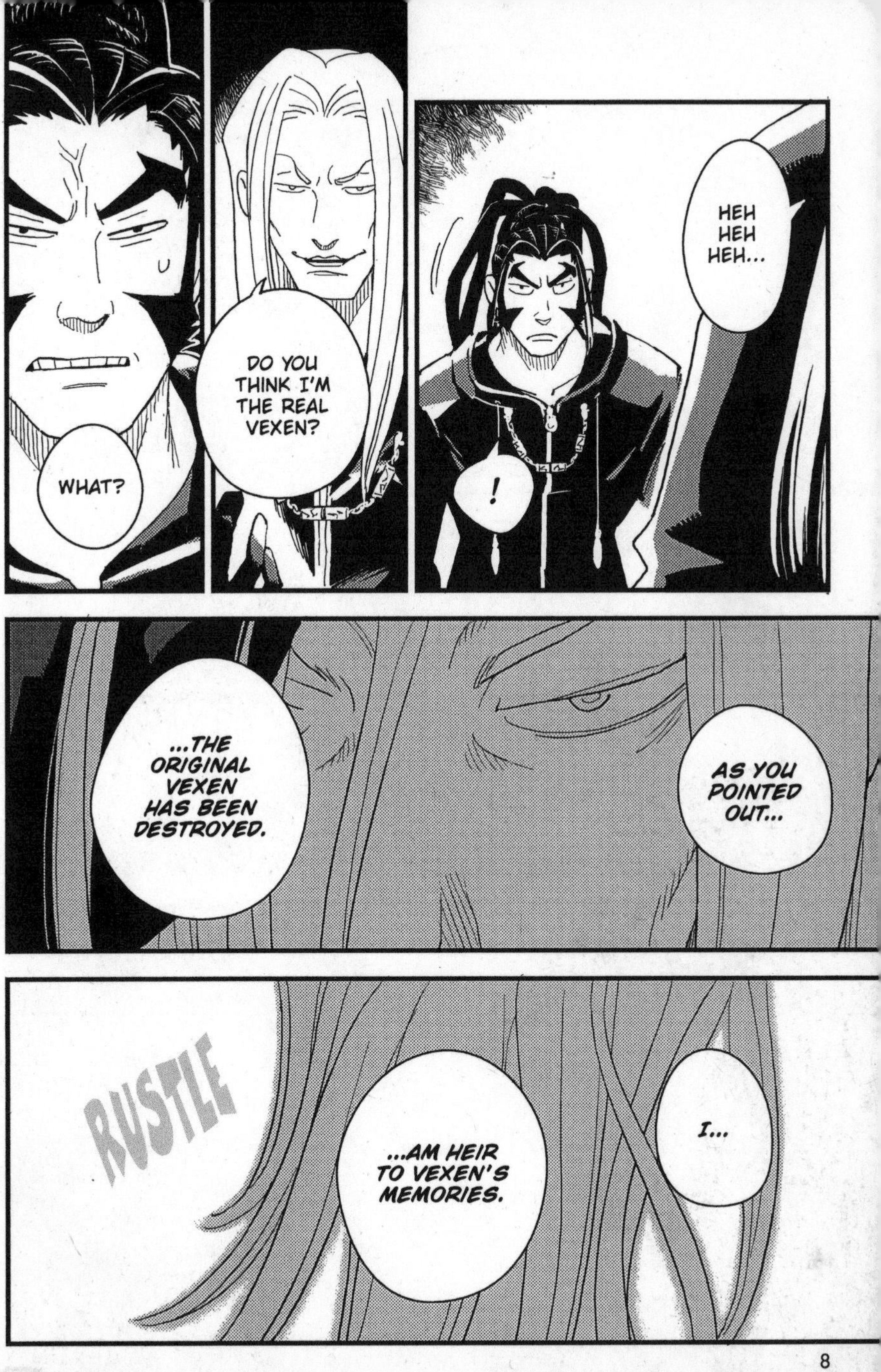
HEH HEH HEH...
!
DO YOU THINK I'M THE REAL VEXEN?
WHAT?
AS YOU POINTED OUT...
...THE ORIGINAL VEXEN HAS BEEN DESTROYED.
I...
...AM HEIR TO VEXEN'S MEMORIES.
RUSTLE

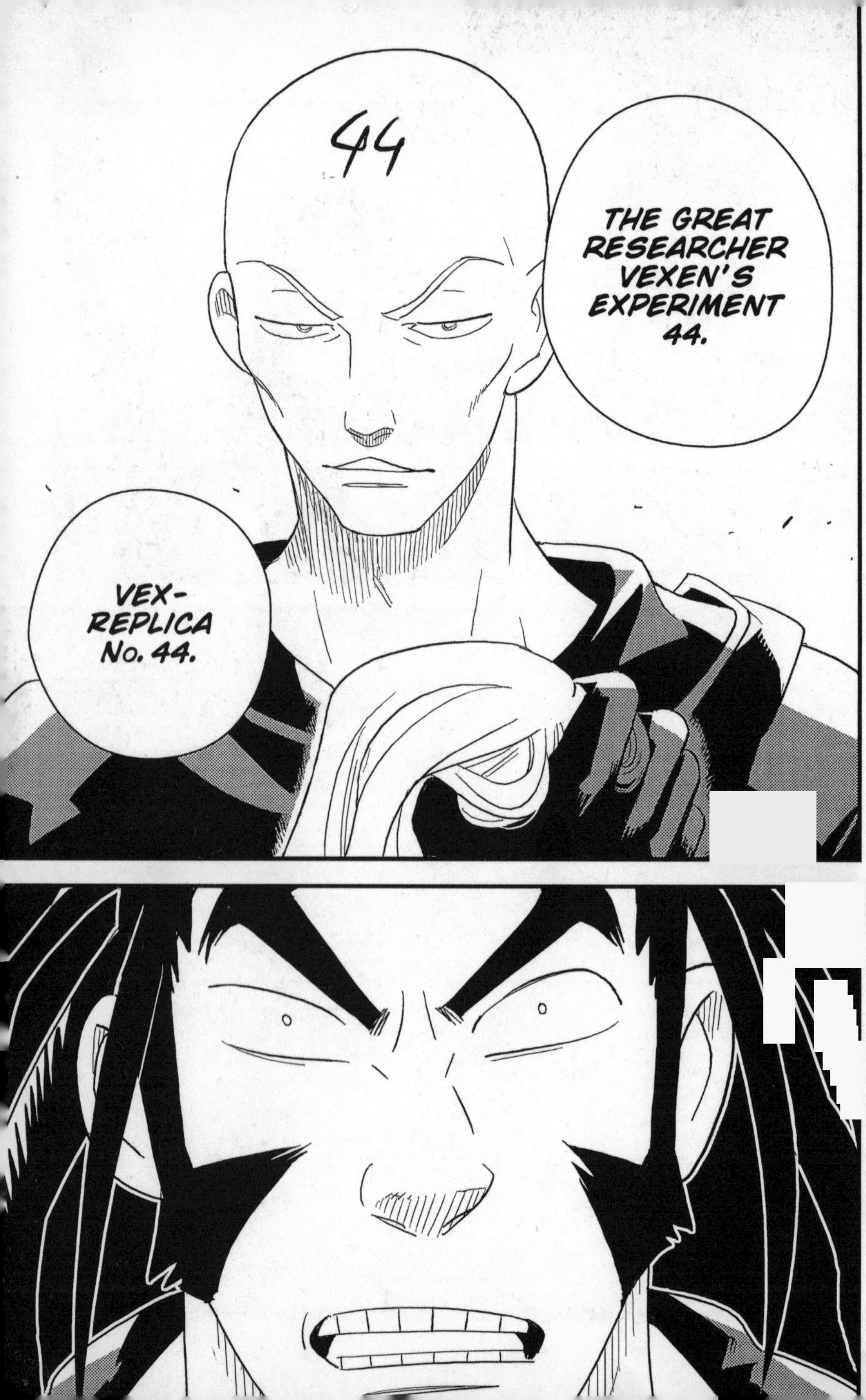
44
THE GREAT RESEARCHER VEXEN'S EXPERIMENT 44.
VEX-REPLICA No. 44.

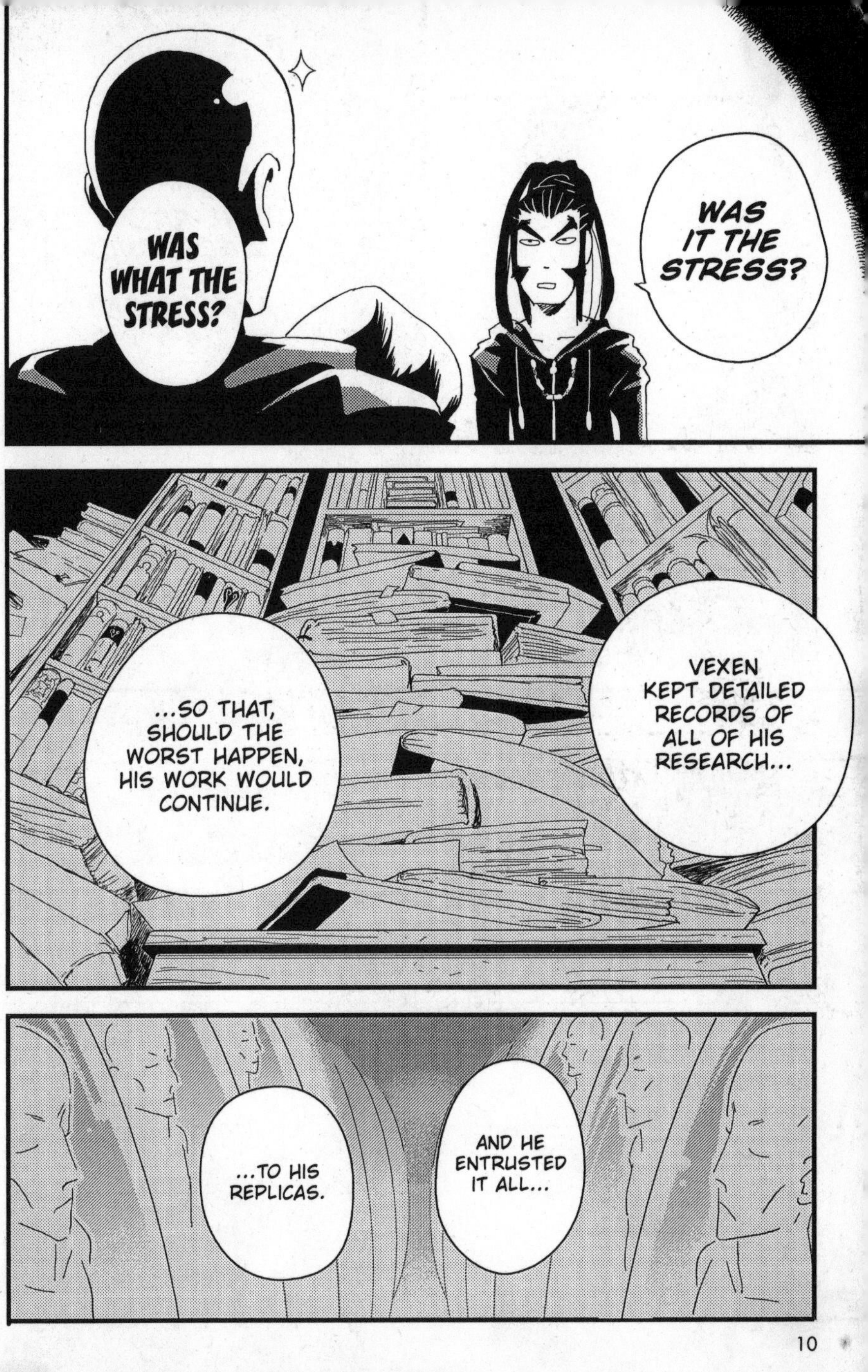
WAS IT THE STRESS?
WAS WHAT THE STRESS?
VEXEN KEPT DETAILED RECORDS OF ALL OF HIS RESEARCH...
...SO THAT, SHOULD THE WORST HAPPEN, HIS WORK WOULD CONTINUE.
AND HE ENTRUSTED IT ALL...
...TO HIS REPLICAS.

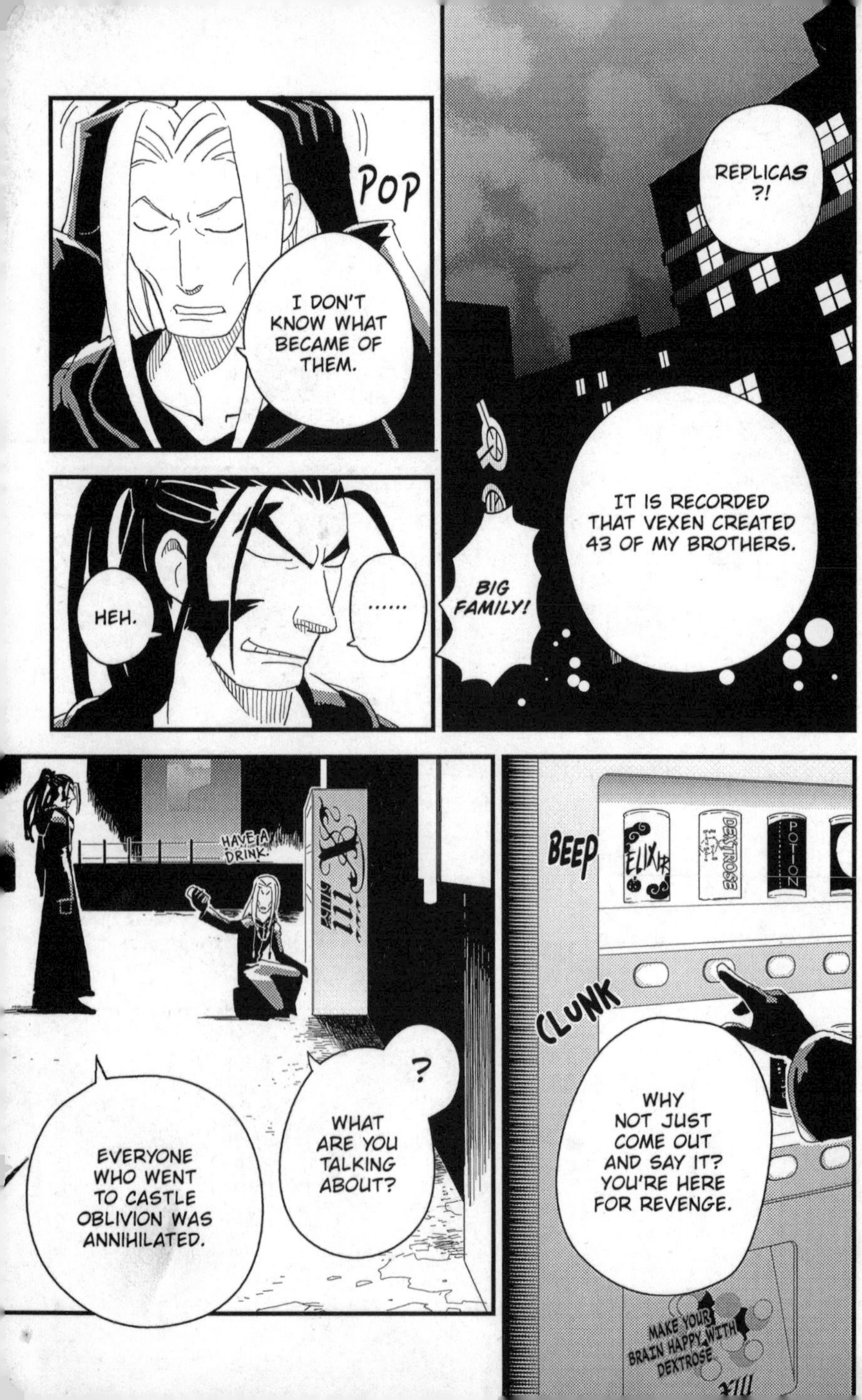

REPLICAS ?!
IT IS RECORDED THAT VEXEN CREATED 43 OF MY BROTHERS.
BIG FAMILY!
POP
I DON'T KNOW WHAT BECAME OF THEM.
......
HEH.
ELIXIR
DEXTROSE
POTION
BEEP
CLUNK
WHY NOT JUST COME OUT AND SAY IT? YOU'RE HERE FOR REVENGE.
MAKE YOUR BRAIN HAPPY WITH DEXTROSE
HAVE A DRINK.
?
WHAT ARE YOU TALKING ABOUT?
EVERYONE WHO WENT TO CASTLE OBLIVION WAS ANNIHILATED.

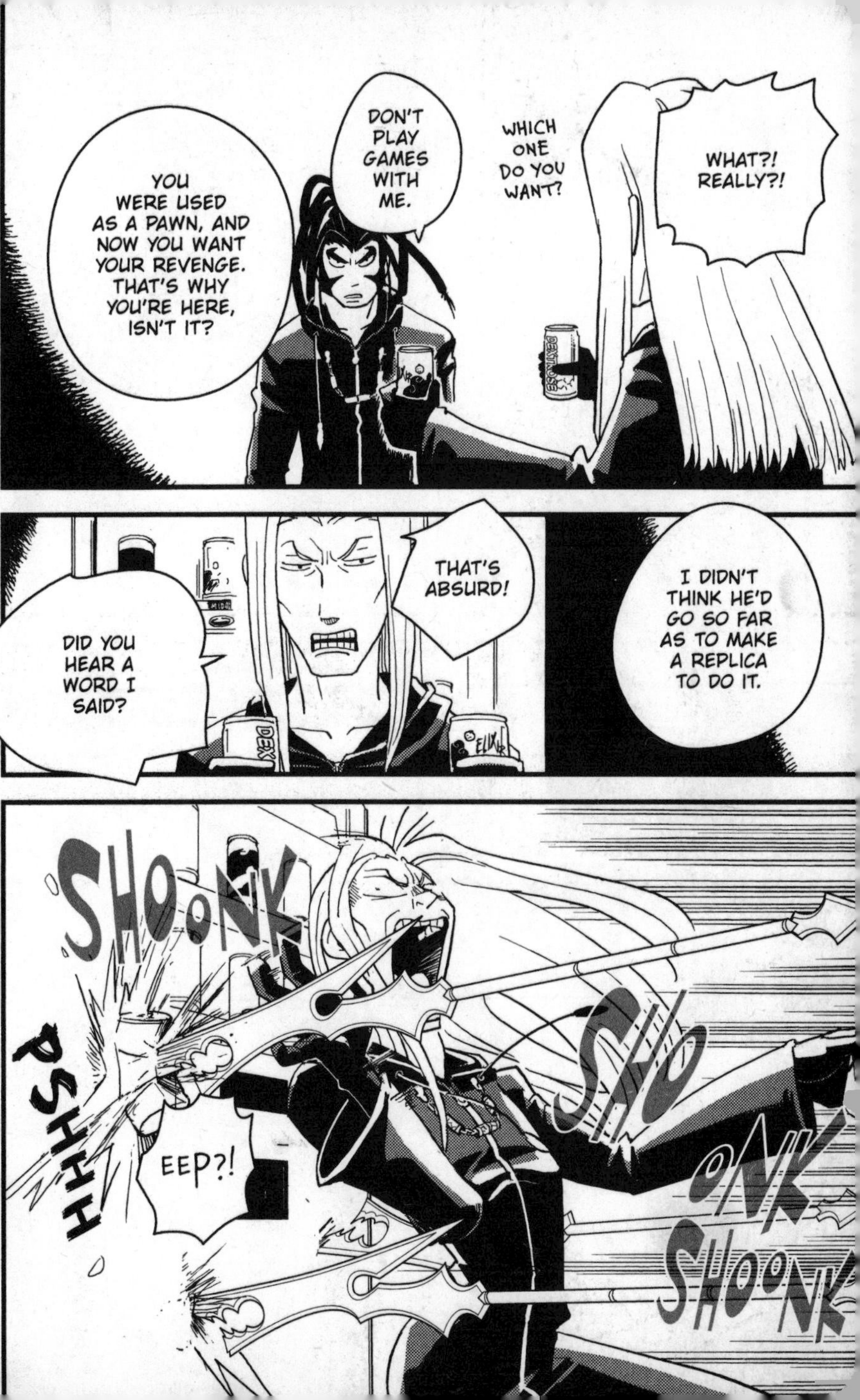
WHAT?! REALLY?!
WHICH ONE DO YOU WANT?
DON'T PLAY GAMES WITH ME.
YOU WERE USED AS A PAWN, AND NOW YOU WANT YOUR REVENGE. THAT'S WHY YOU'RE HERE, ISN'T IT?
I DIDN'T THINK HE'D GO SO FAR AS TO MAKE A REPLICA TO DO IT.
THAT'S ABSURD!
DID YOU HEAR A WORD I SAID?
SHOONK
SHOONK
SHOONK
EEP?!
PSHHH

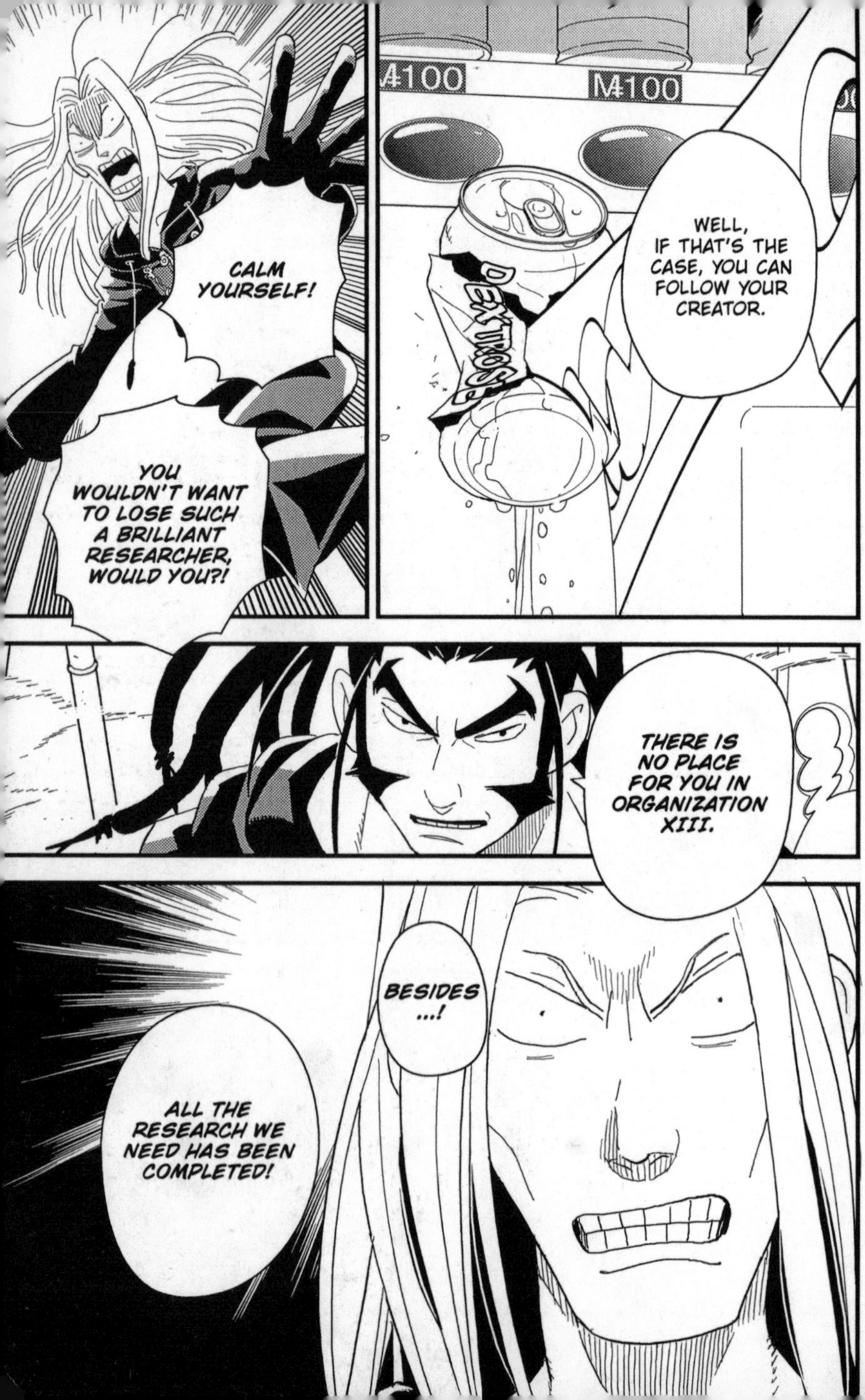
M100
M100
WELL, IF THAT'S THE CASE, YOU CAN FOLLOW YOUR CREATOR.
DEXTROSE
CALM YOURSELF!
YOU WOULDN'T WANT TO LOSE SUCH A BRILLIANT RESEARCHER, WOULD YOU?!
THERE IS NO PLACE FOR YOU IN ORGANIZATION XIII.
BESIDES ...!
ALL THE RESEARCH WE NEED HAS BEEN COMPLETED!

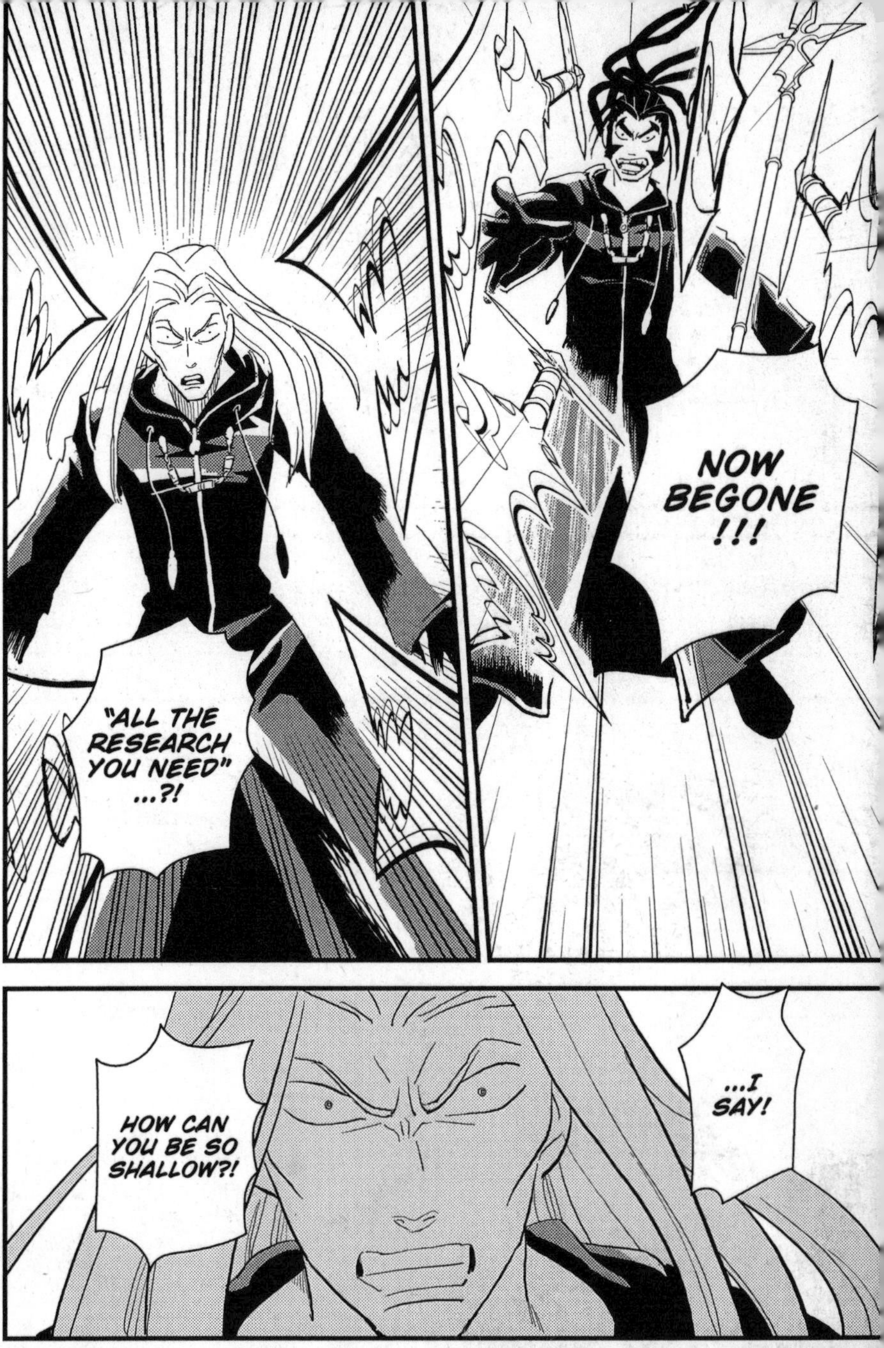
NOW BEGONE!!!
"ALL THE RESEARCH YOU NEED" ...?!
...I SAY!
HOW CAN YOU BE SO SHALLOW?!

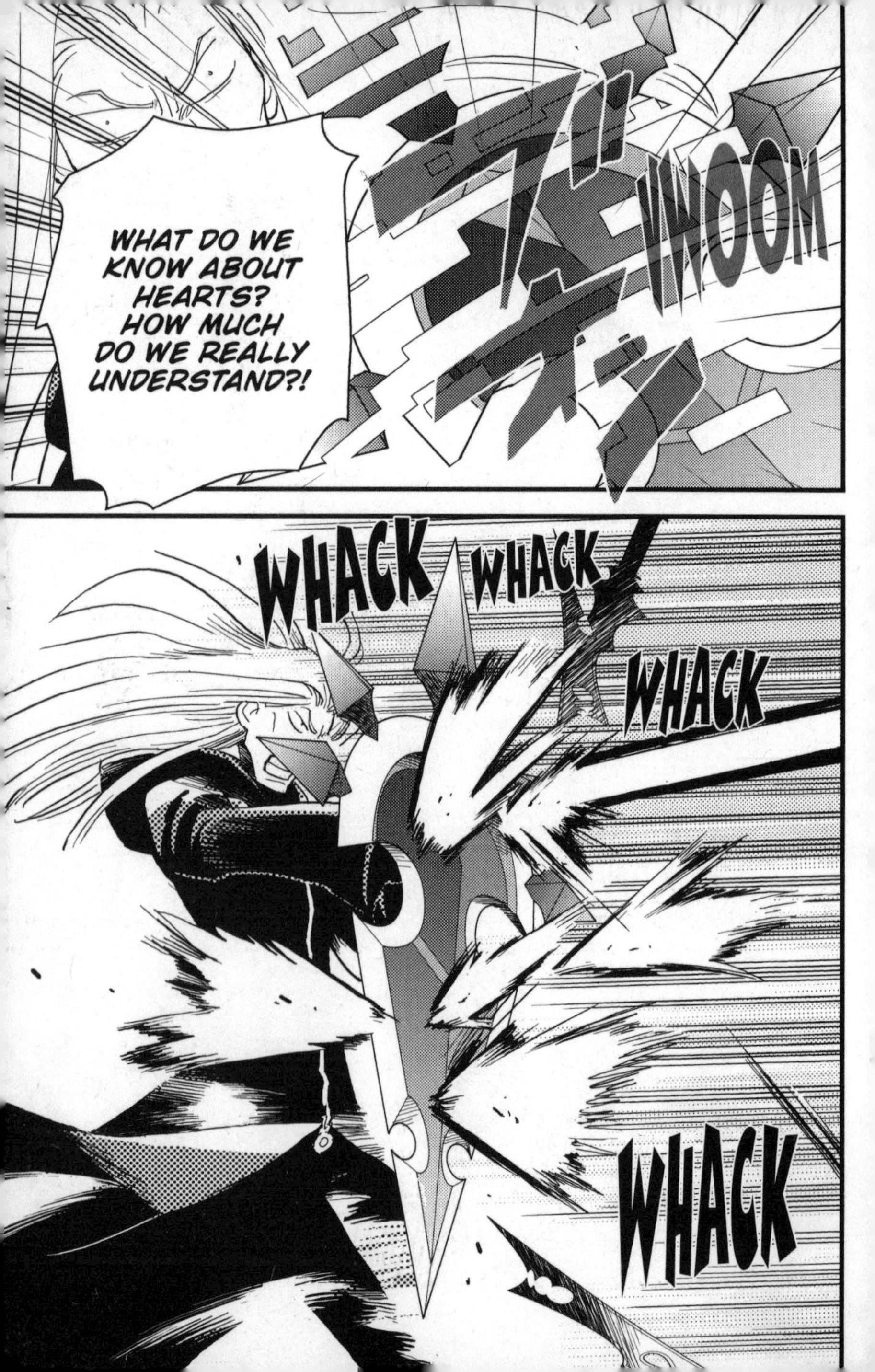
VWOOM
WHAT DO WE KNOW ABOUT HEARTS? HOW MUCH DO WE REALLY UNDERSTAND?!
WHACK
WHACK
WHACK
WHACK

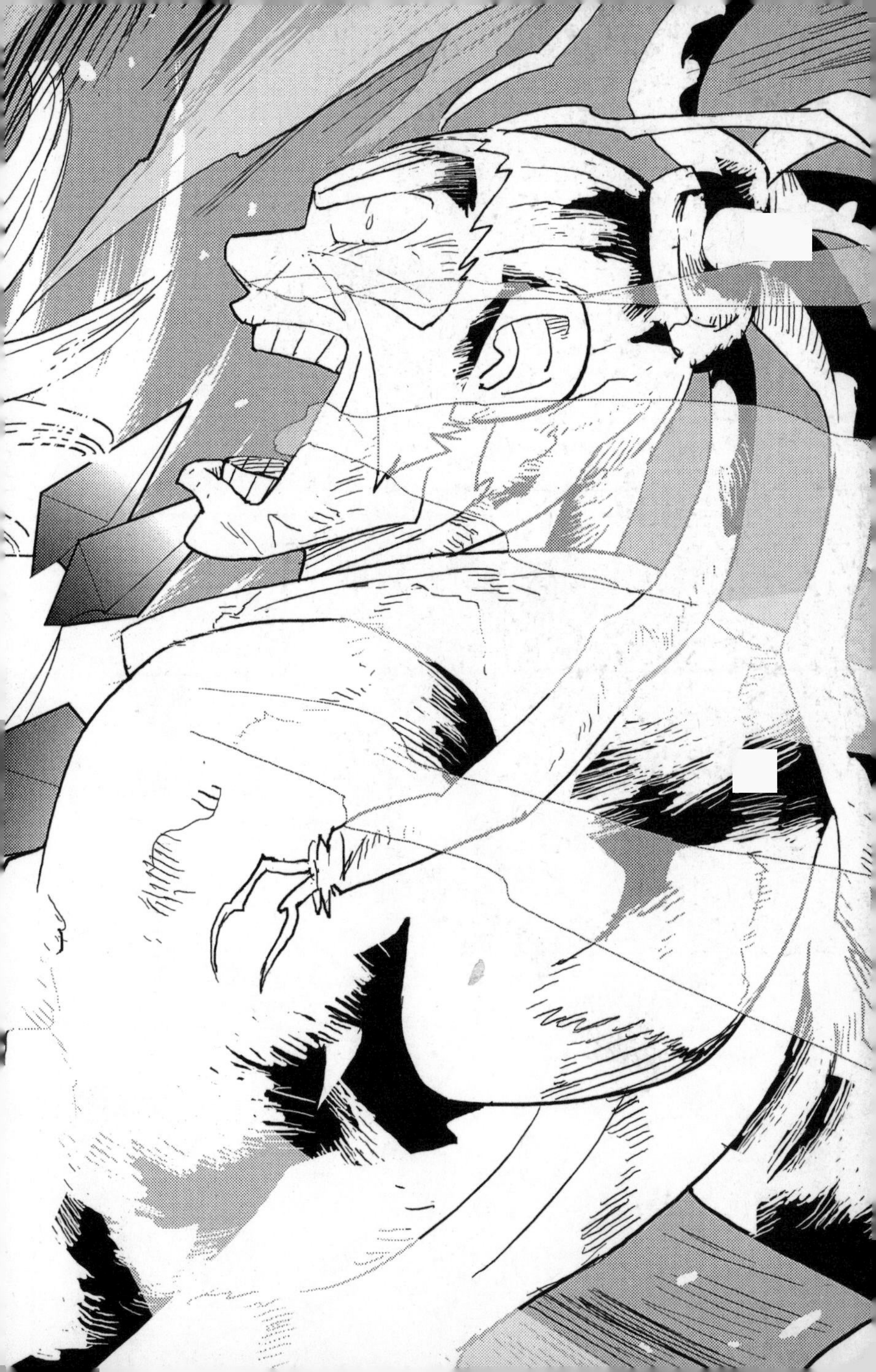

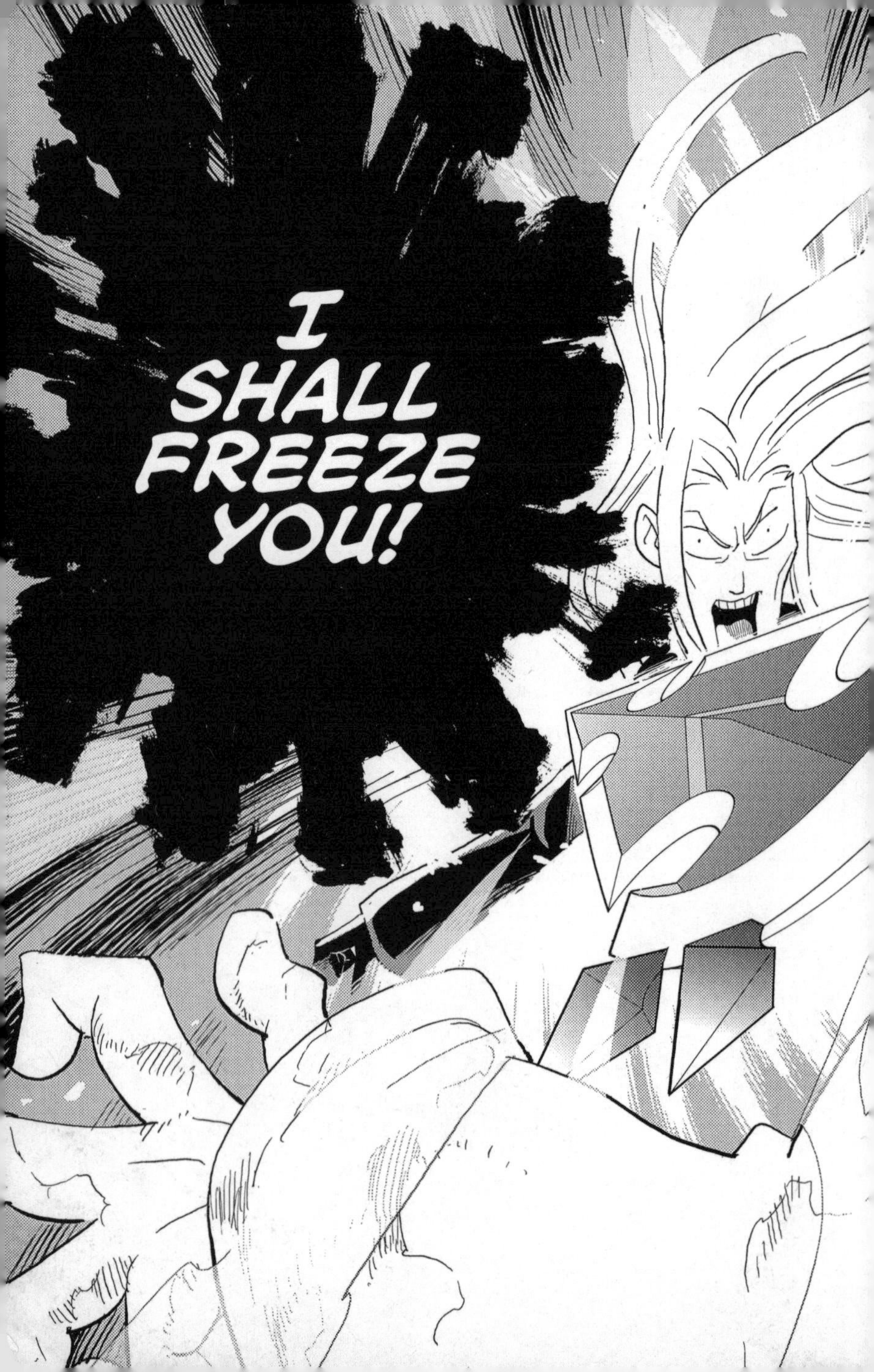
I SHALL FREEZE YOU!

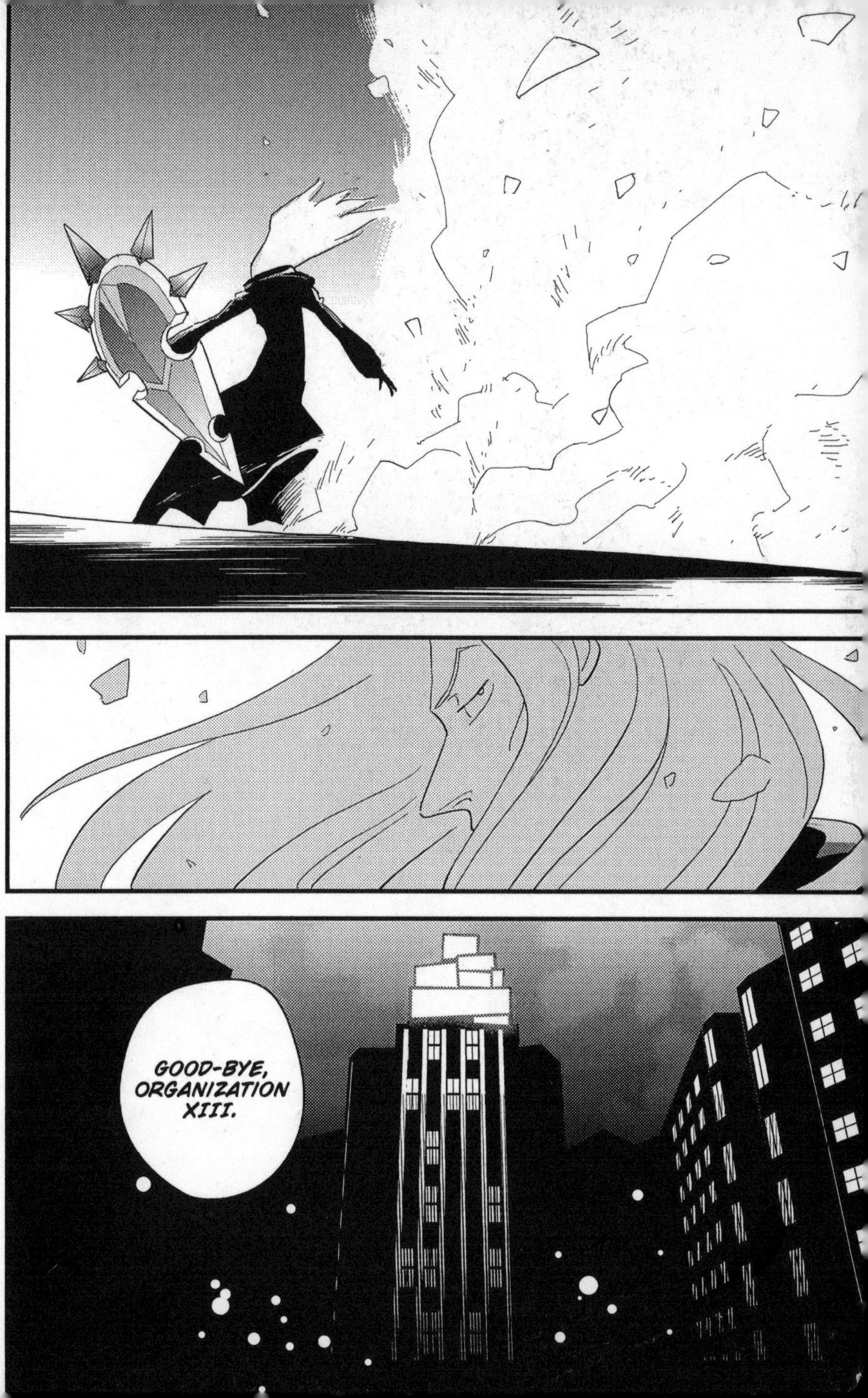
GOOD-BYE, ORGANIZATION XIII.

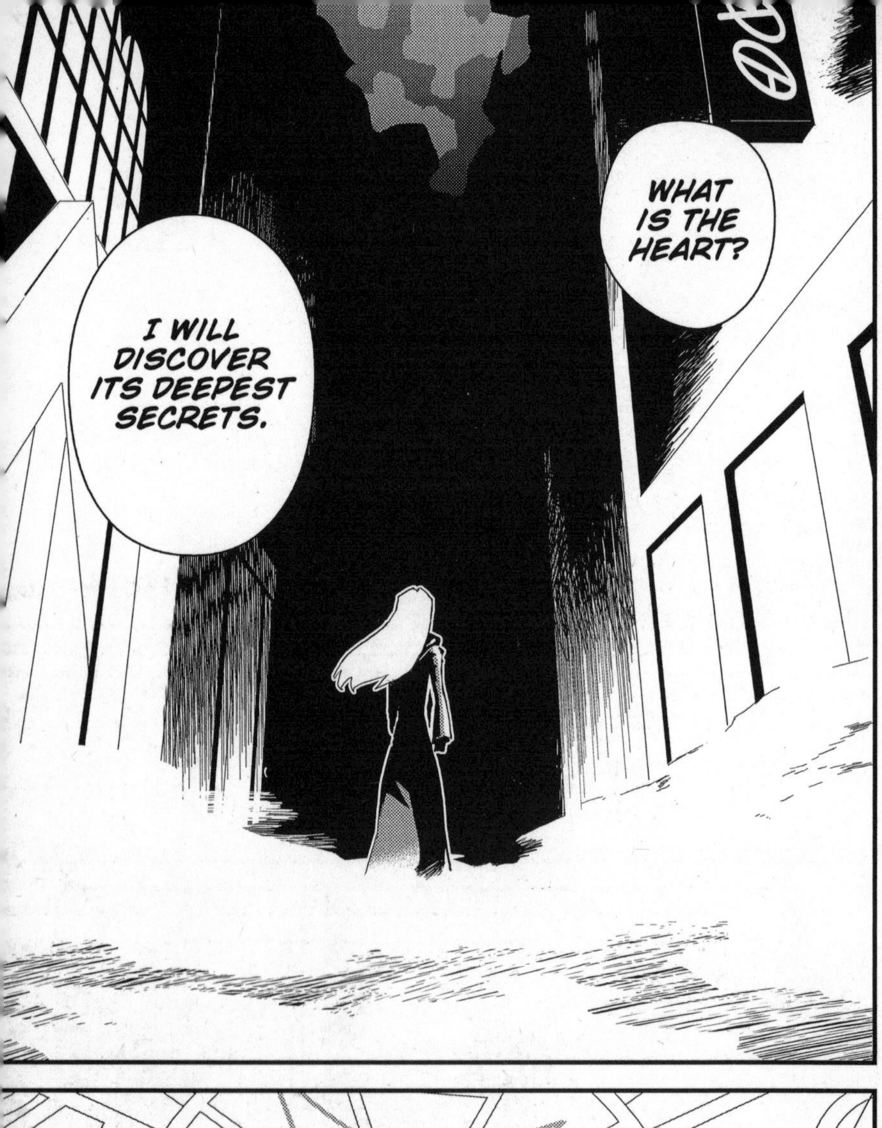
WHAT IS THE HEART?
I WILL DISCOVER ITS DEEPEST SECRETS.
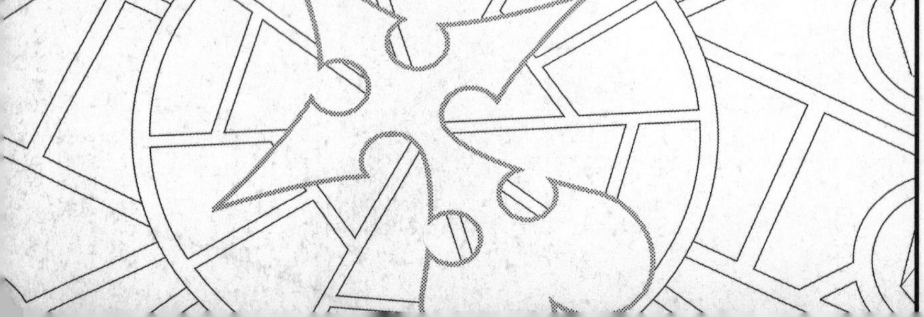

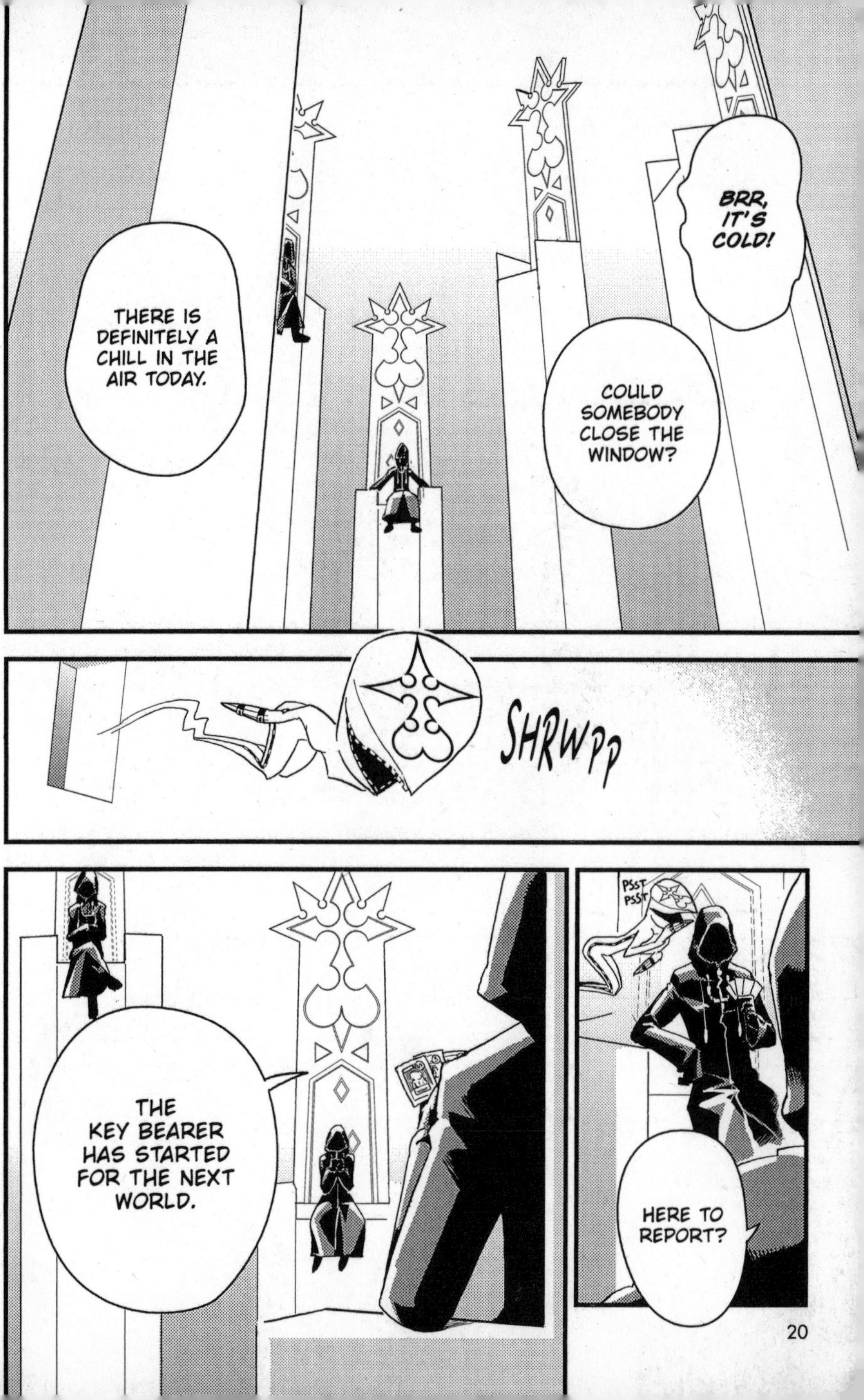
BRR, IT'S COLD!
COULD SOMEBODY CLOSE THE WINDOW?
THERE IS DEFINITELY A CHILL IN THE AIR TODAY.
SHRWPP
PSST PSST
HERE TO REPORT?
THE KEY BEARER HAS STARTED FOR THE NEXT WORLD.

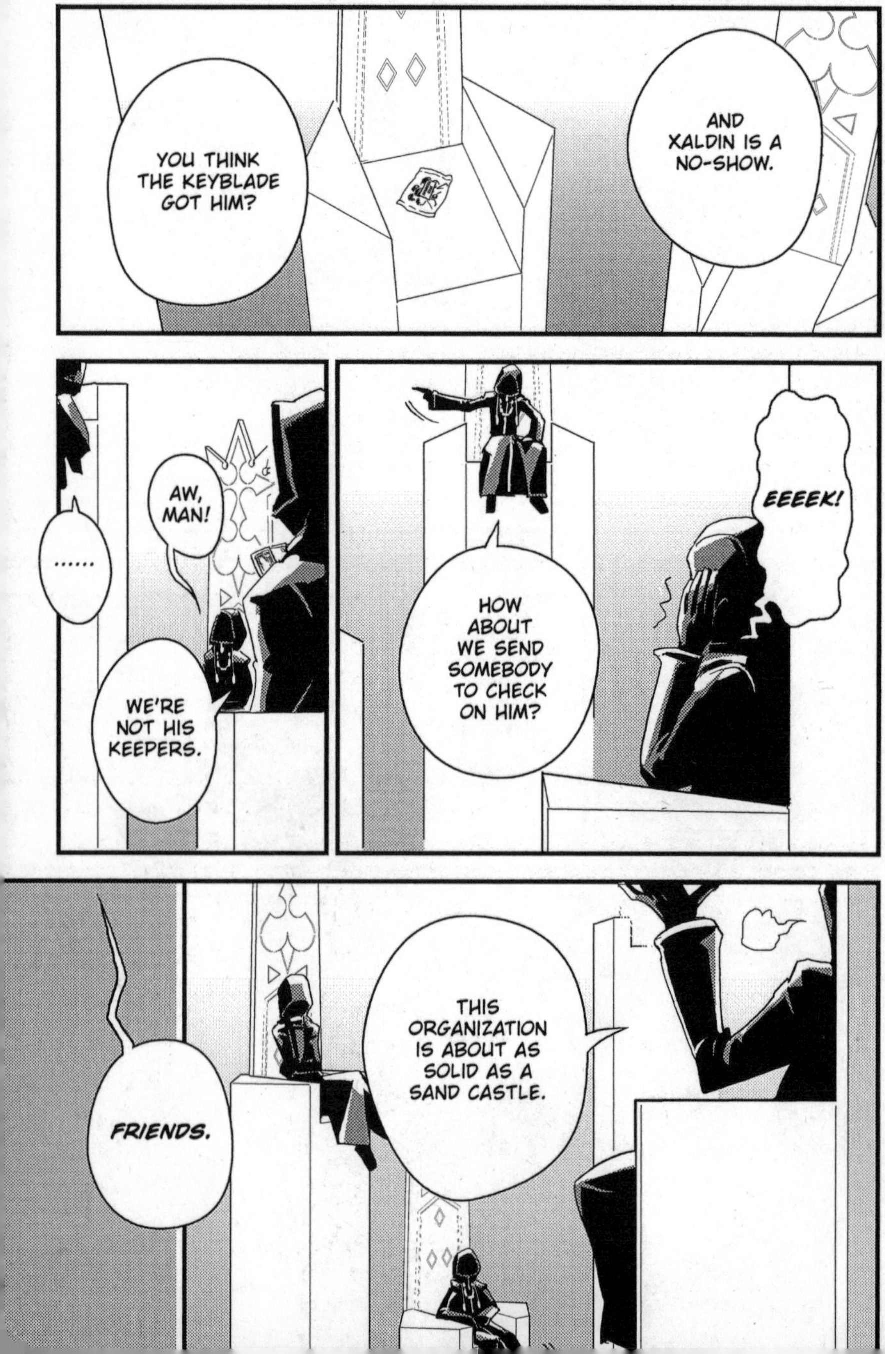
AND XALDIN IS A NO-SHOW.
YOU THINK THE KEYBLADE GOT HIM?
EEEEK!
HOW ABOUT WE SEND SOMEBODY TO CHECK ON HIM?
AW, MAN!
......
WE'RE NOT HIS KEEPERS.
THIS ORGANIZATION IS ABOUT AS SOLID AS A SAND CASTLE.
FRIENDS.

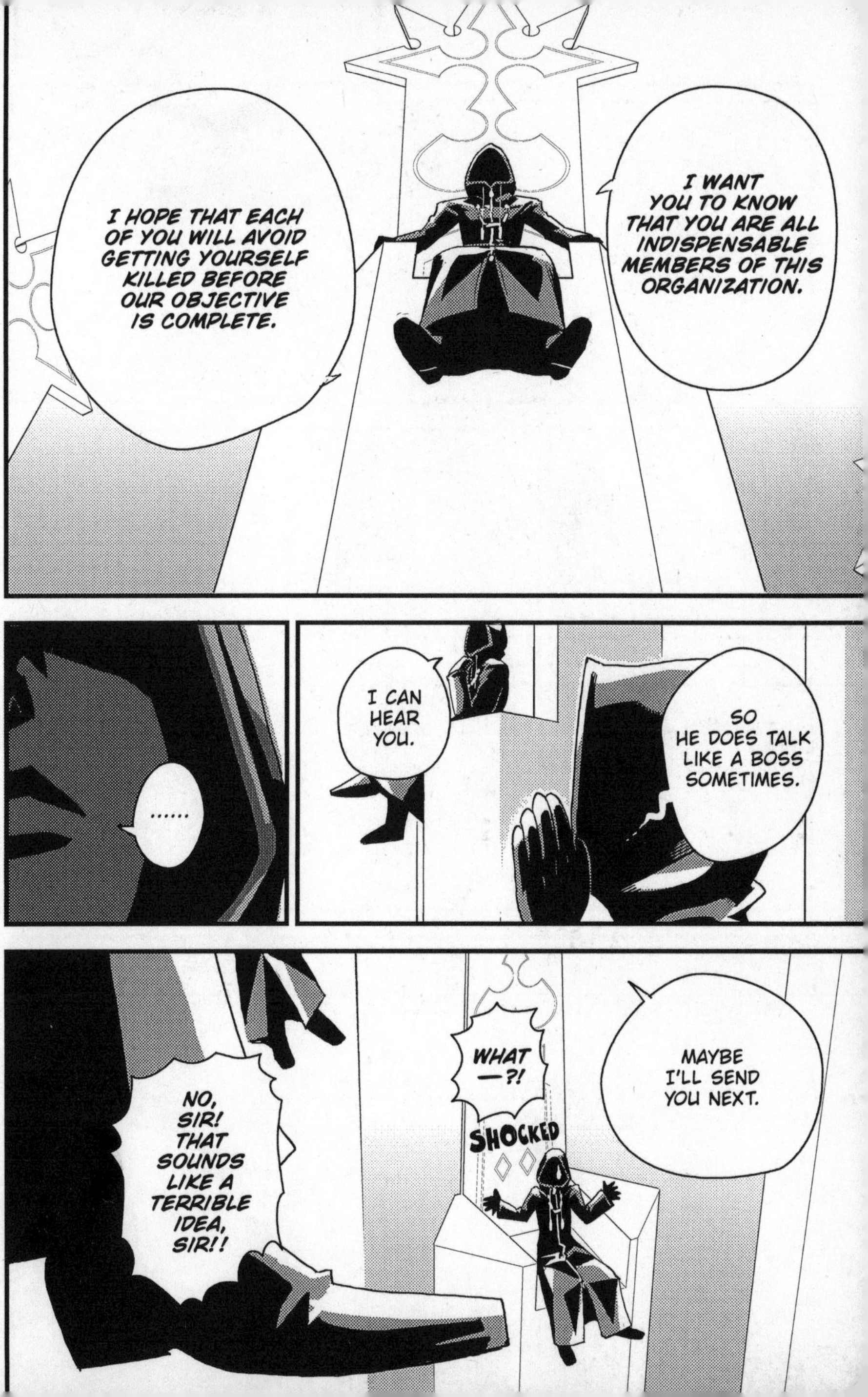
I WANT YOU TO KNOW THAT YOU ARE ALL INDISPENSABLE MEMBERS OF THIS ORGANIZATION.
I HOPE THAT EACH OF YOU WILL AVOID GETTING YOURSELF KILLED BEFORE OUR OBJECTIVE IS COMPLETE.
SO HE DOES TALK LIKE A BOSS SOMETIMES.
I CAN HEAR YOU.
......
MAYBE I'LL SEND YOU NEXT.
WHAT—?!
SHOCKED
NO, SIR! THAT SOUNDS LIKE A TERRIBLE IDEA, SIR!!

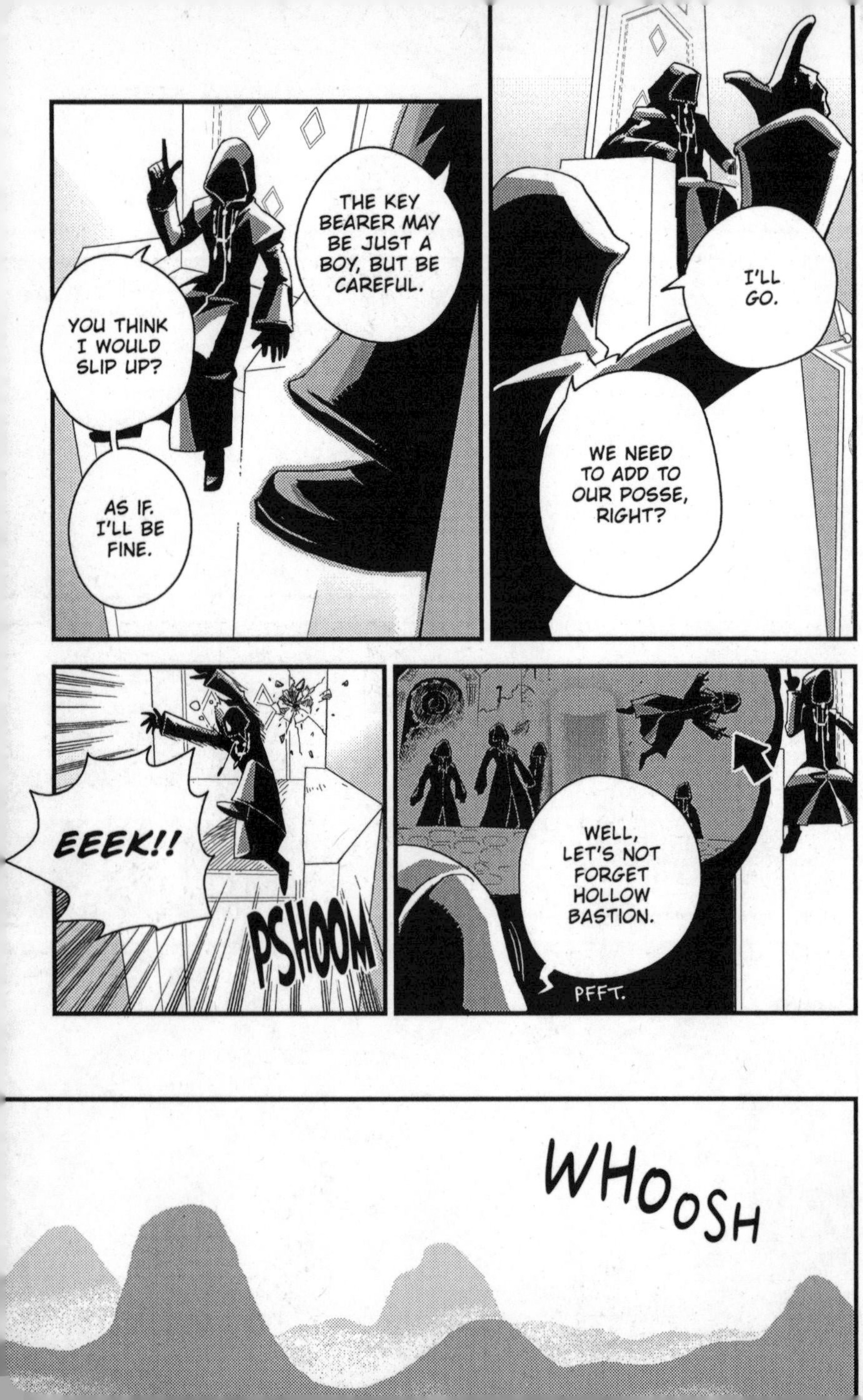
I'LL GO.
WE NEED TO ADD TO OUR POSSE, RIGHT?
THE KEY BEARER MAY BE JUST A BOY, BUT BE CAREFUL.
YOU THINK I WOULD SLIP UP?
AS IF. I'LL BE FINE.
WELL, LET'S NOT FORGET HOLLOW BASTION.
PFFT.
EEEK!!
PSHOOM
WHOOSH

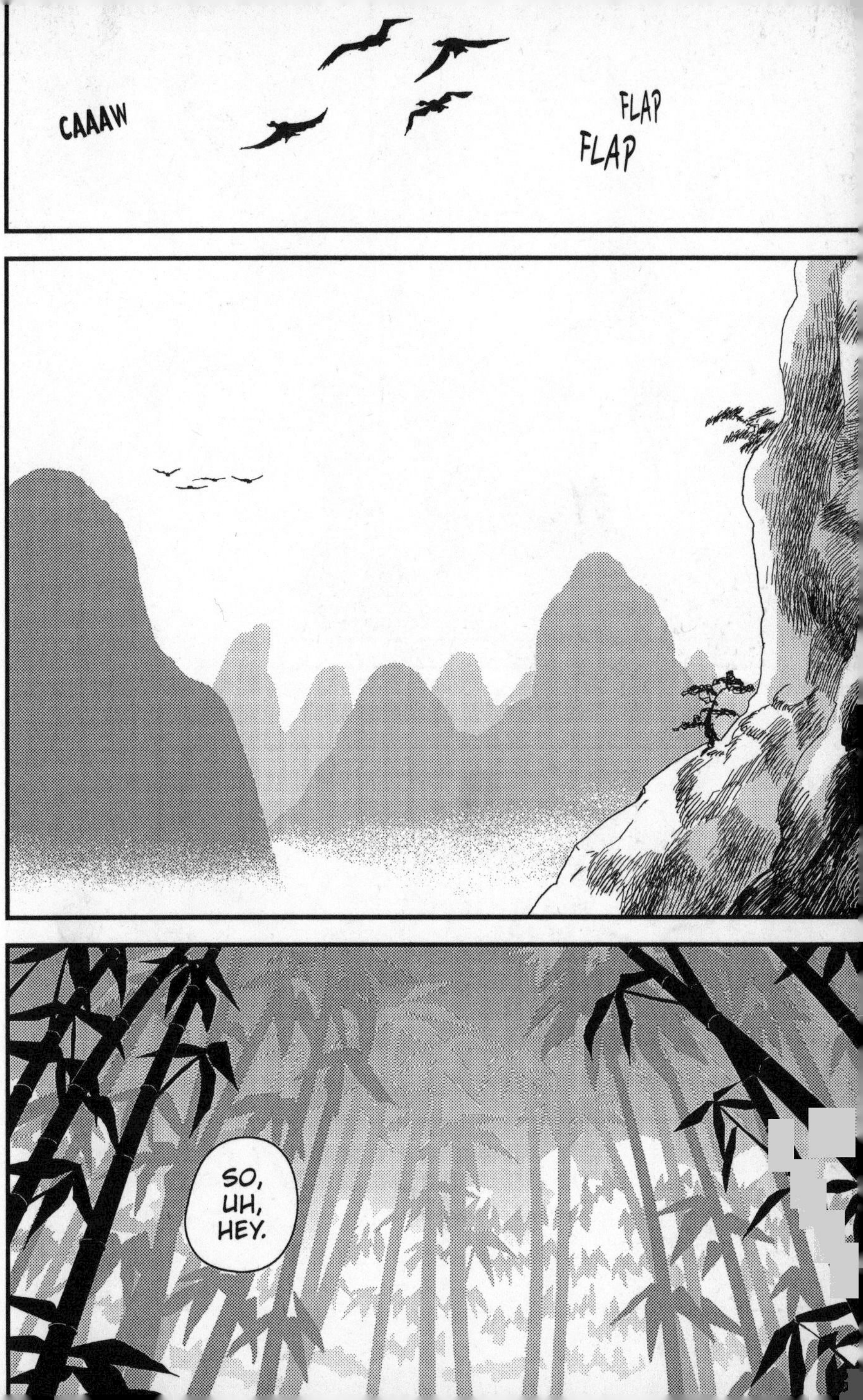
FLAP
FLAP
CAAAW
SO, UH, HEY.

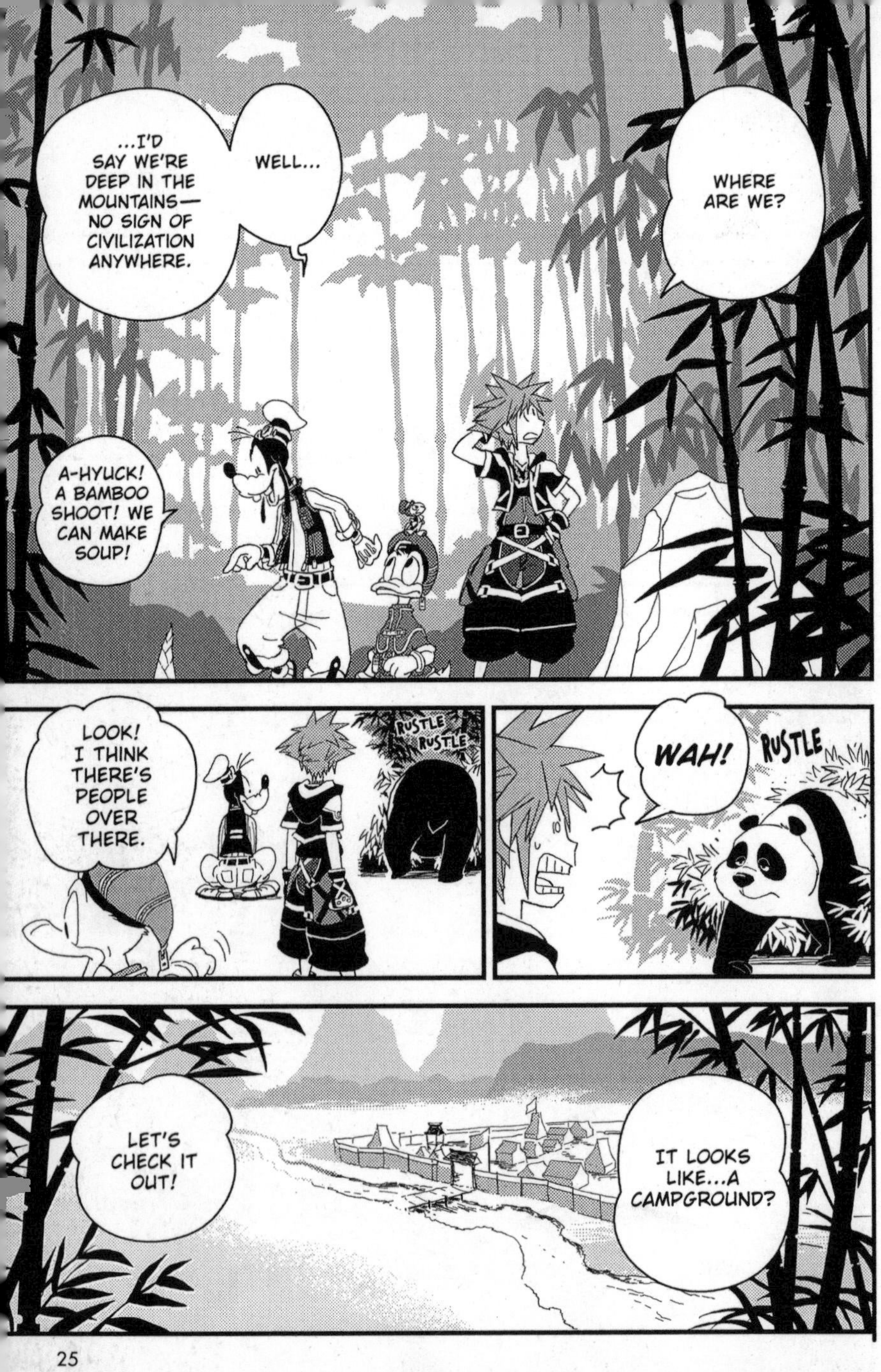
WHERE ARE WE?
WELL...
...I'D SAY WE'RE DEEP IN THE MOUNTAINS—NO SIGN OF CIVILIZATION ANYWHERE.
A-HYUCK! A BAMBOO SHOOT! WE CAN MAKE SOUP!
RUSTLE
WAH!
RUSTLE RUSTLE
LOOK! I THINK THERE'S PEOPLE OVER THERE.
IT LOOKS LIKE...A CAMPGROUND?
LET'S CHECK IT OUT!

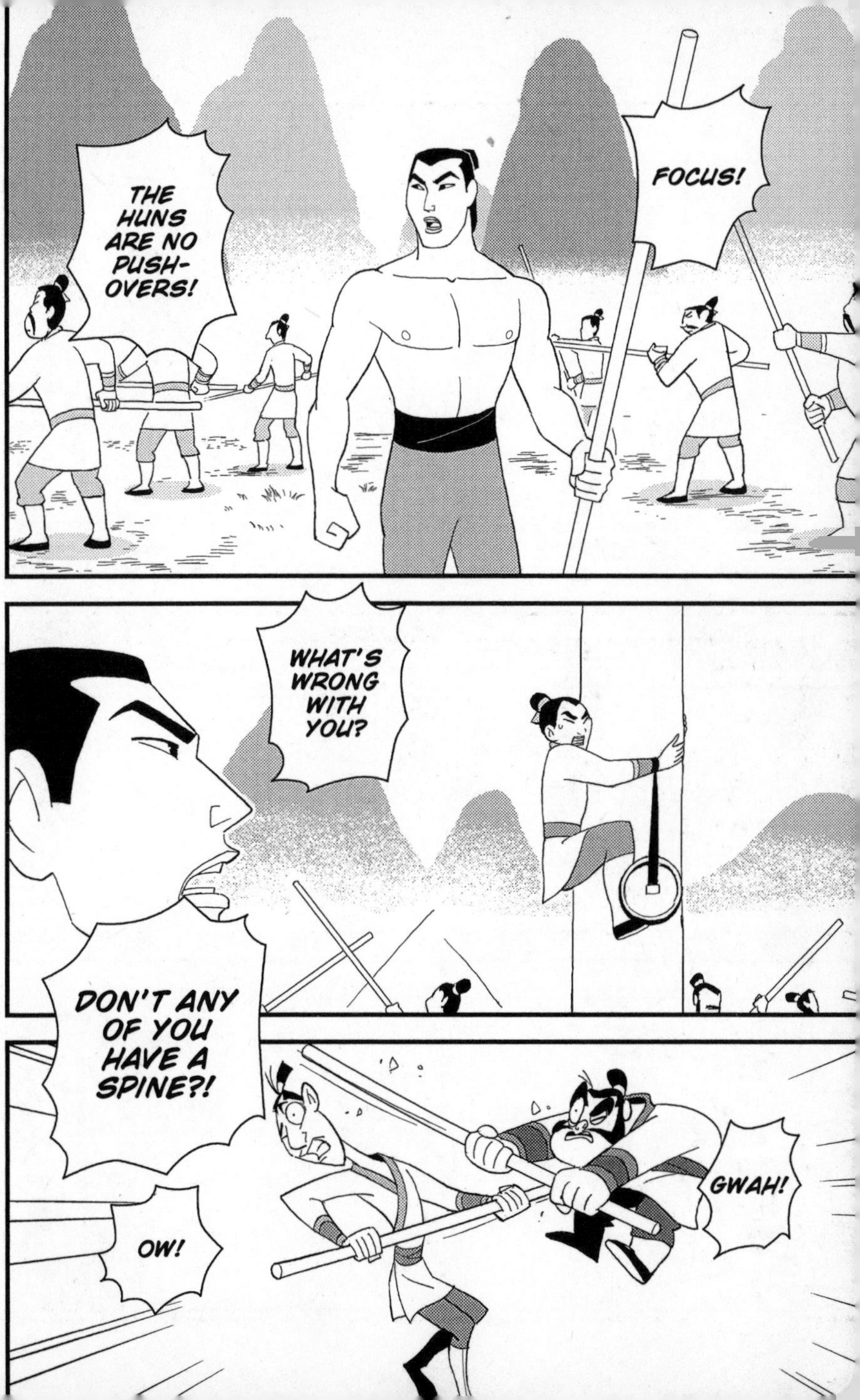
FOCUS!
THE HUNS ARE NO PUSH-OVERS!
WHAT'S WRONG WITH YOU?
DON'T ANY OF YOU HAVE A SPINE?!
GWAH!
OW!

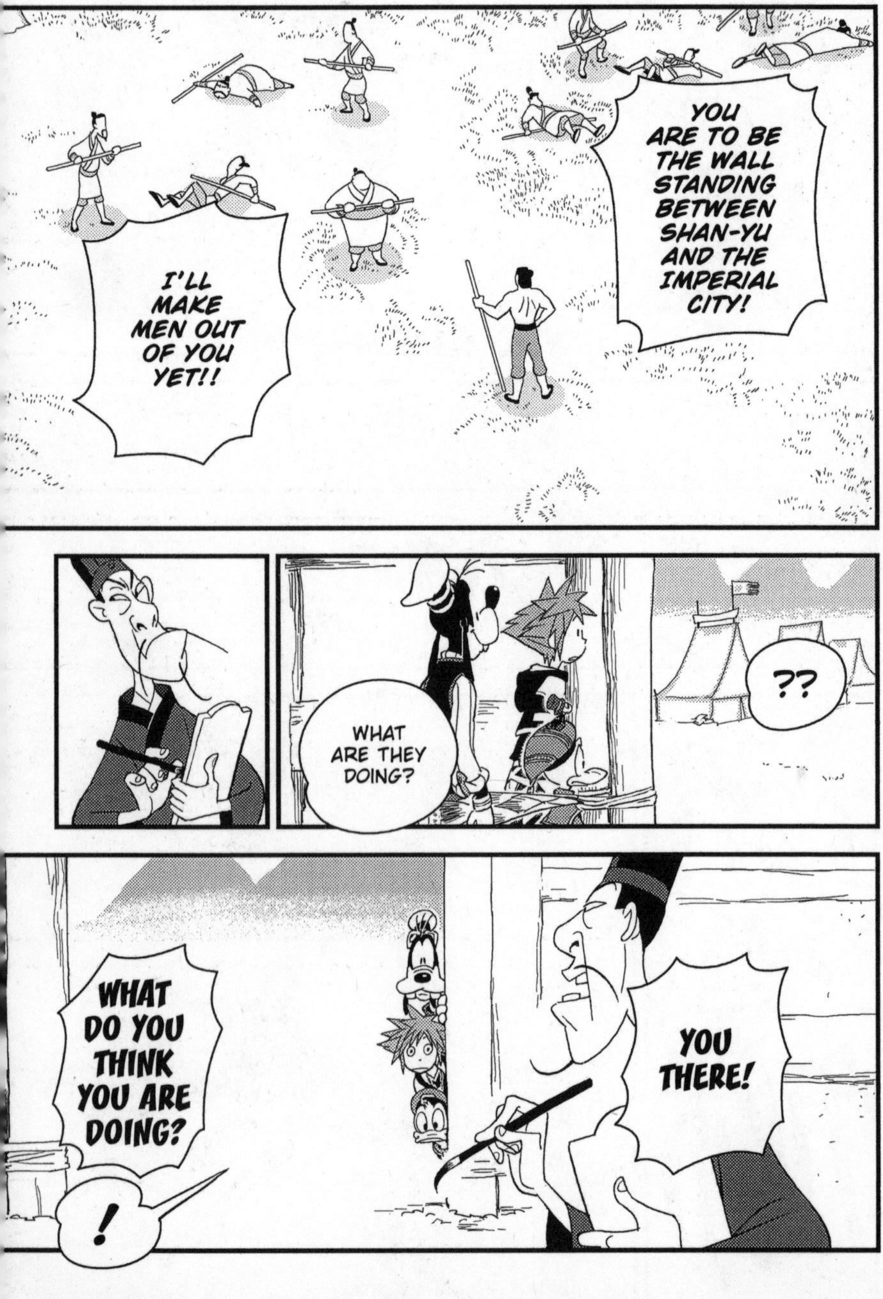
YOU ARE TO BE THE WALL STANDING BETWEEN SHAN-YU AND THE IMPERIAL CITY!
I'LL MAKE MEN OUT OF YOU YET!!
??
WHAT ARE THEY DOING?
YOU THERE!
WHAT DO YOU THINK YOU ARE DOING?
!

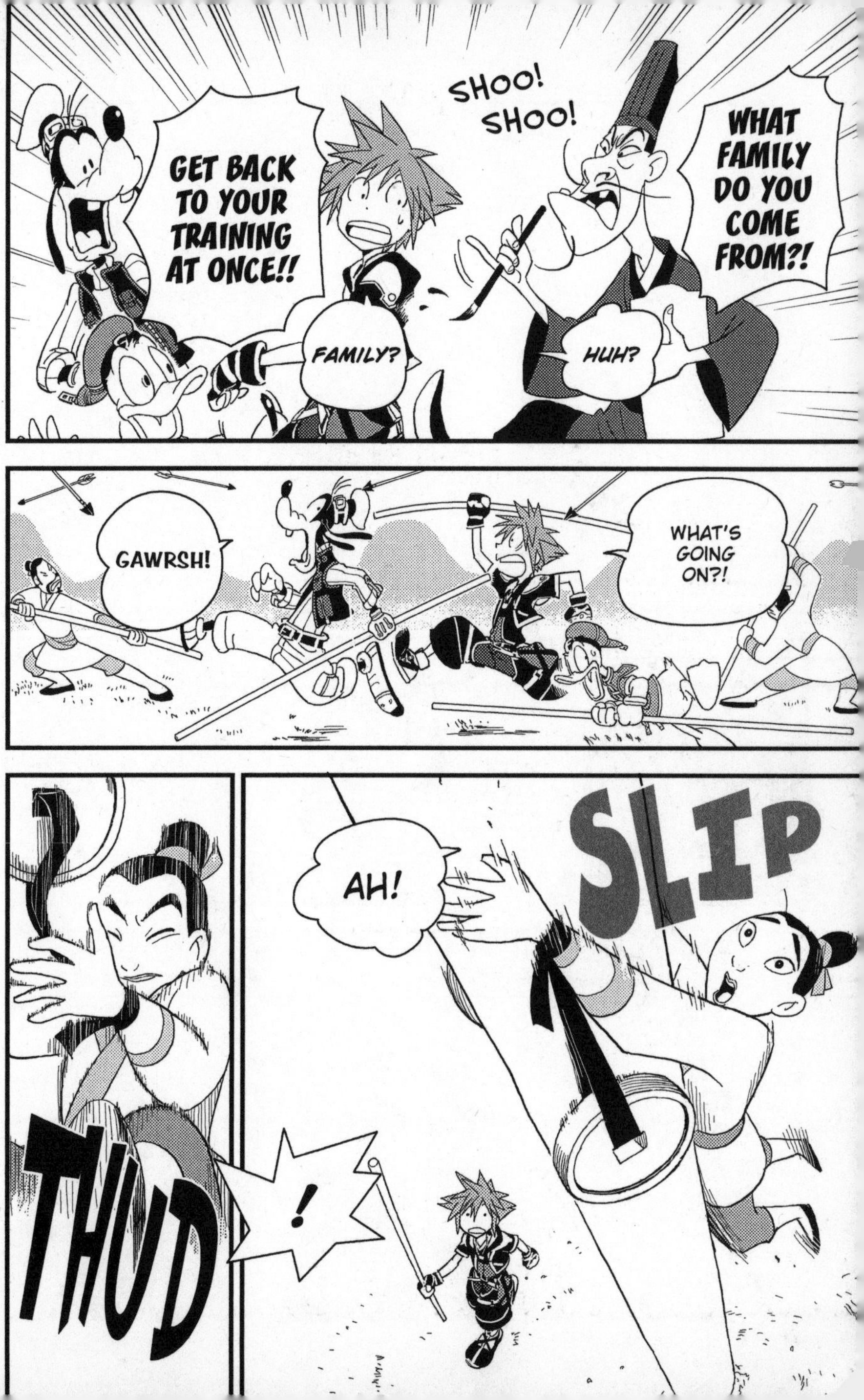
WHAT FAMILY DO YOU COME FROM?!
SHOO! SHOO!
GET BACK TO YOUR TRAINING AT ONCE!!
HUH?
FAMILY?
WHAT'S GOING ON?!
GAWRSH!
SLIP
AH!
!
THUD

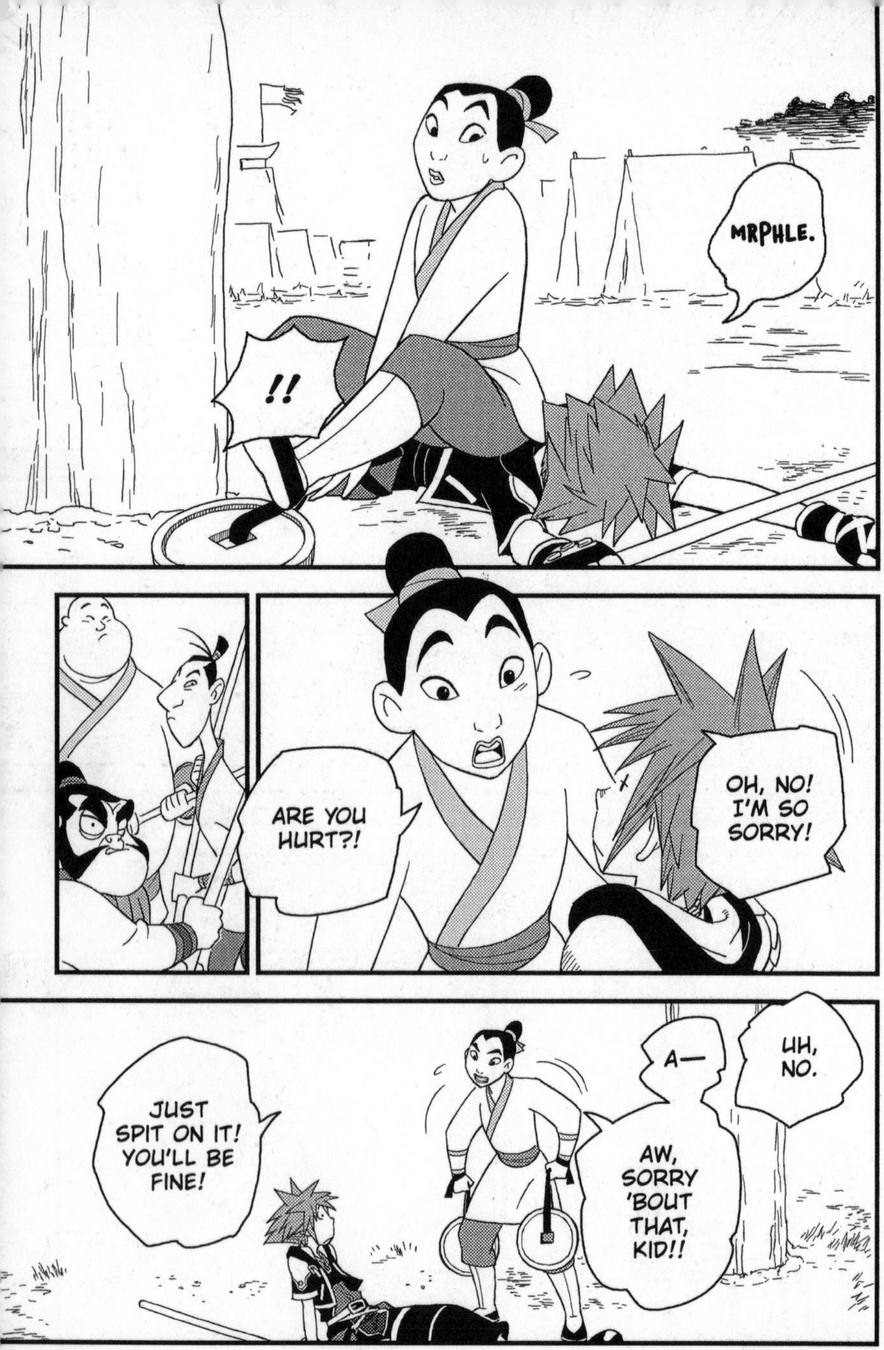
MRPHLE.
!!
OH, NO! I'M SO SORRY!
ARE YOU HURT?!
UH, NO.
A—
AW, SORRY 'BOUT THAT, KID!!
JUST SPIT ON IT! YOU'LL BE FINE!

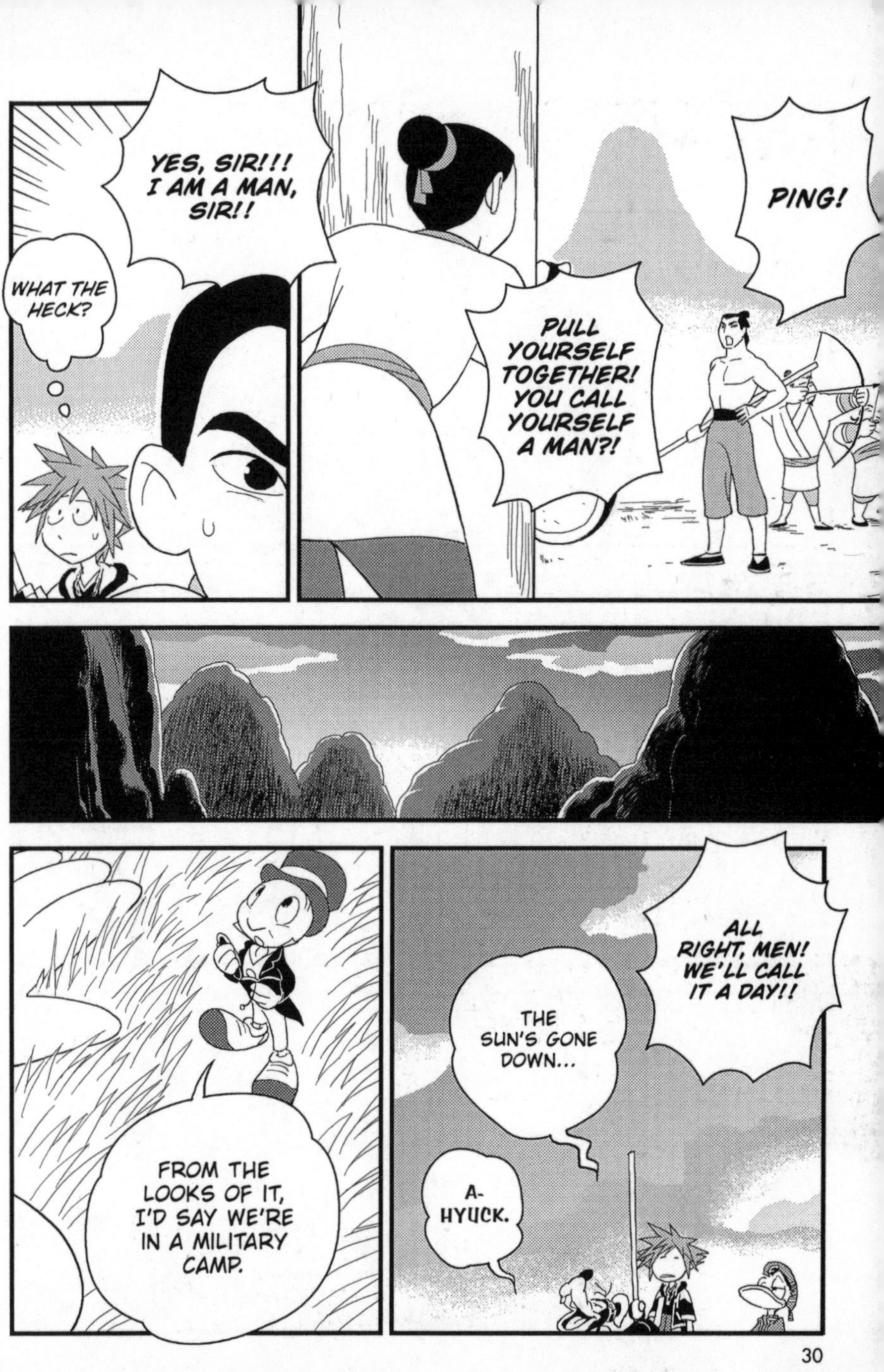
PING!
PULL YOURSELF TOGETHER! YOU CALL YOURSELF A MAN?!
YES, SIR!!! I AM A MAN, SIR!!
WHAT THE HECK?
ALL RIGHT, MEN! WE'LL CALL IT A DAY!!
THE SUN'S GONE DOWN...
A-HYUCK.
FROM THE LOOKS OF IT, I'D SAY WE'RE IN A MILITARY CAMP.

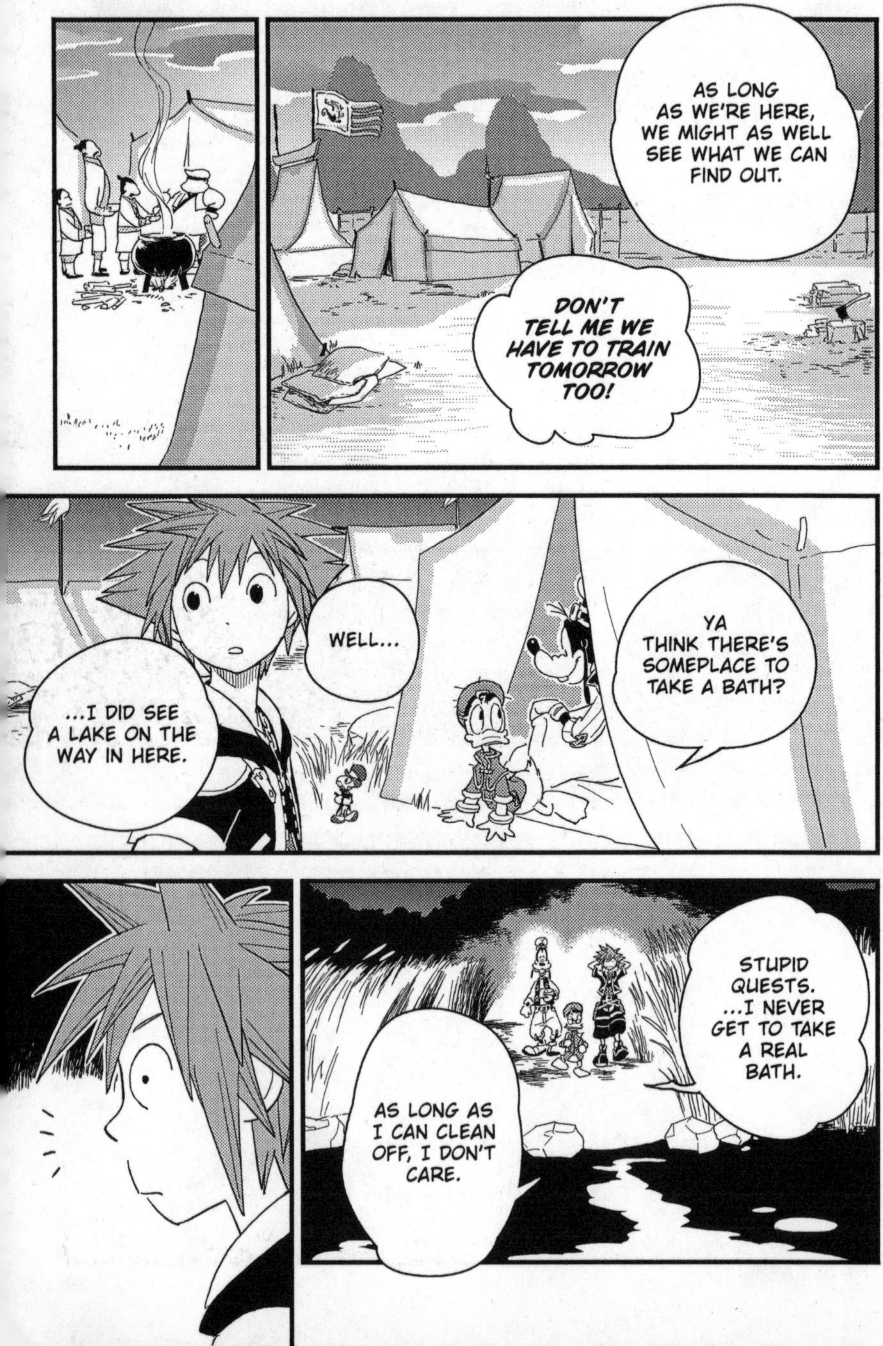
AS LONG AS WE'RE HERE, WE MIGHT AS WELL SEE WHAT WE CAN FIND OUT.
DON'T TELL ME WE HAVE TO TRAIN TOMORROW TOO!
YA THINK THERE'S SOMEPLACE TO TAKE A BATH?
WELL...
...I DID SEE A LAKE ON THE WAY IN HERE.
STUPID QUESTS. ...I NEVER GET TO TAKE A REAL BATH.
AS LONG AS I CAN CLEAN OFF, I DON'T CARE.

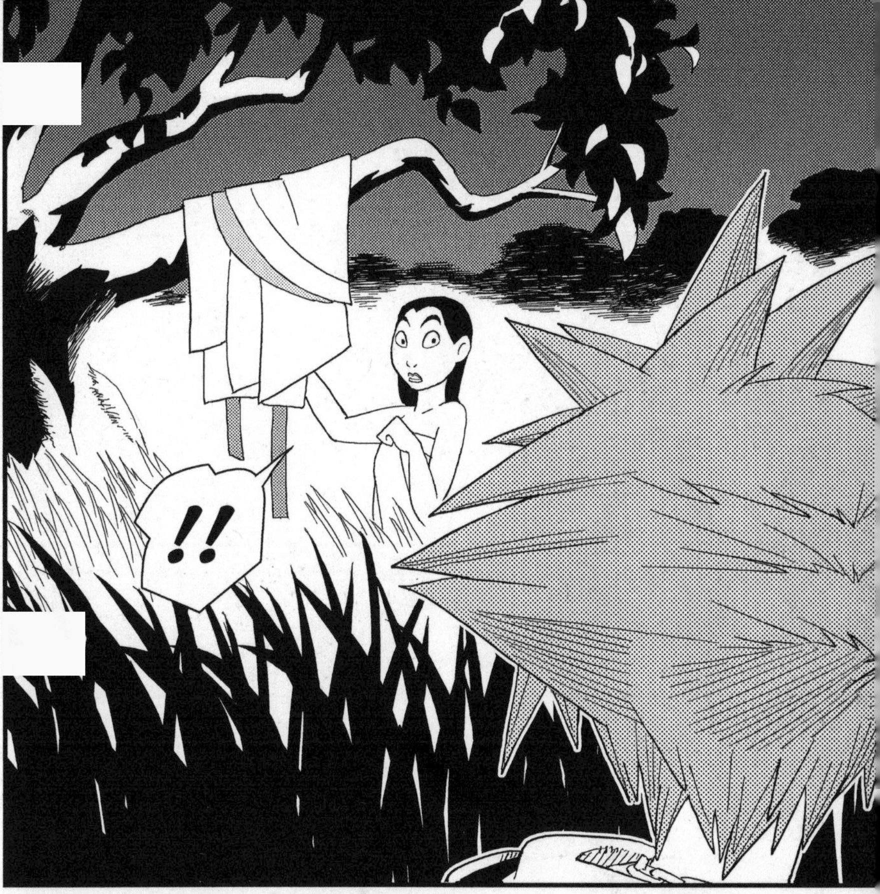
!!

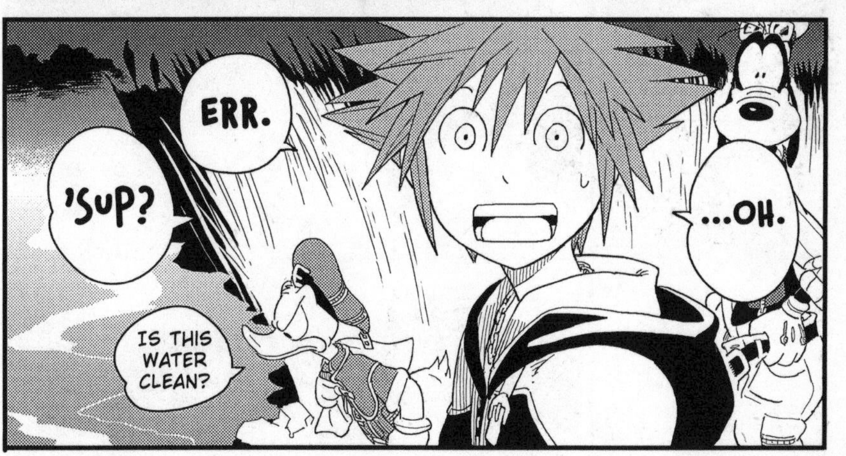
...OH.
ERR.
'SUP?
IS THIS WATER CLEAN?

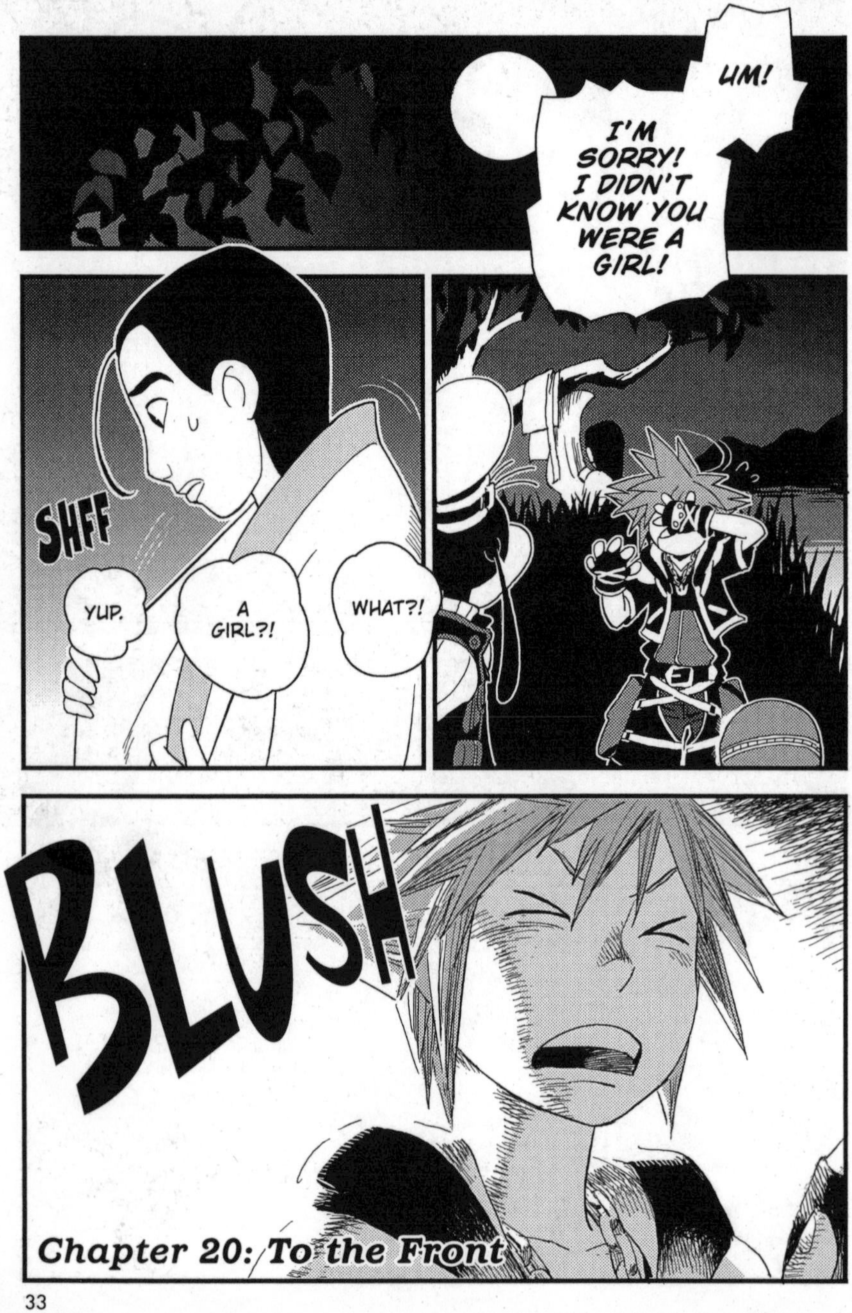
UM!
I'M SORRY! I DIDN'T KNOW YOU WERE A GIRL!
WHAT?!
A GIRL?!
SHFF
YUP.
BLUSH
Chapter 20: To the Front

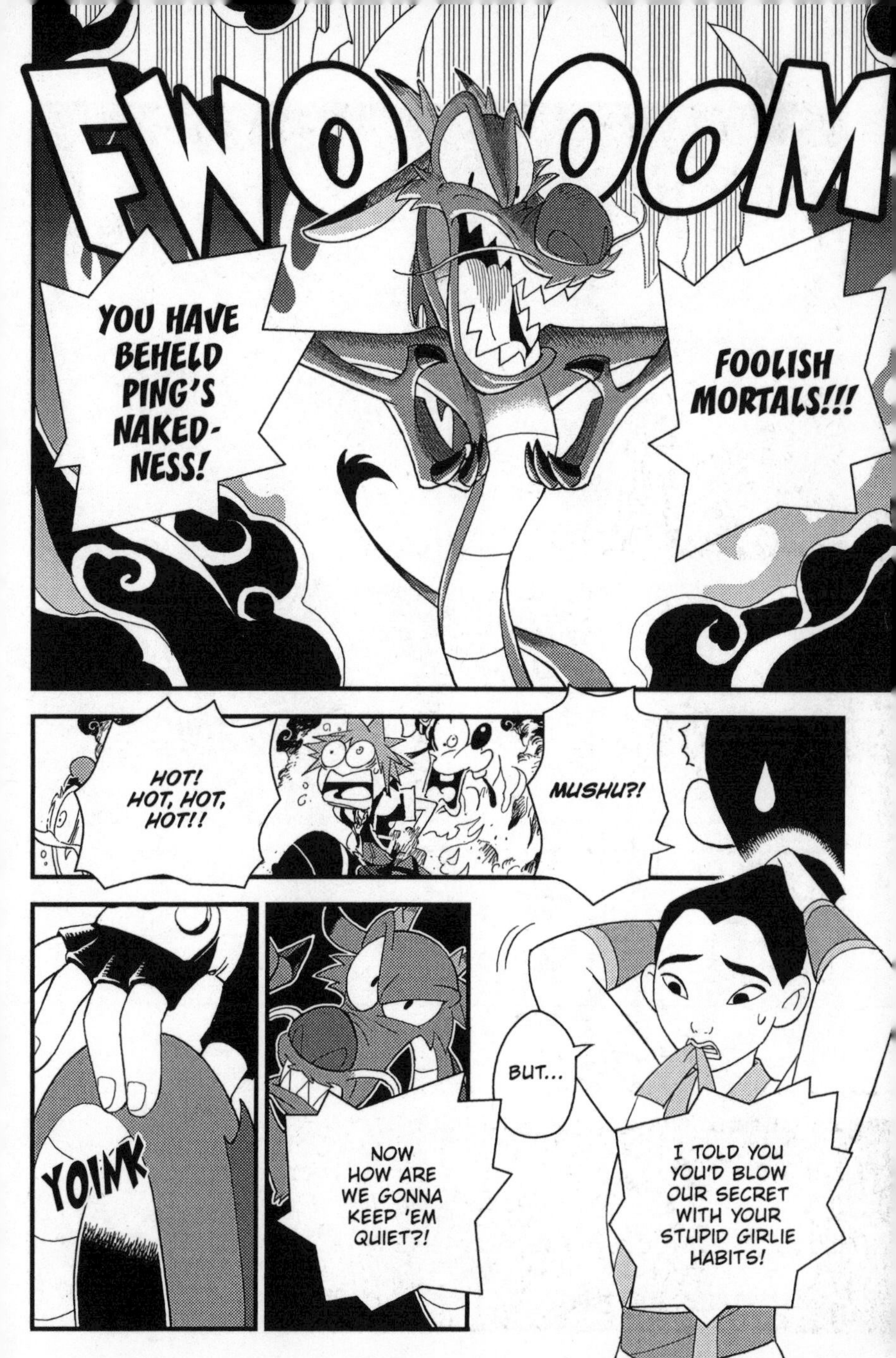
FWOOOOM
FOOLISH MORTALS!!!
YOU HAVE BEHELD PING'S NAKED-NESS!
MUSHU?!
HOT! HOT, HOT, HOT!!
BUT...
I TOLD YOU YOU'D BLOW OUR SECRET WITH YOUR STUPID GIRLIE HABITS!
NOW HOW ARE WE GONNA KEEP 'EM QUIET?!
YOINK

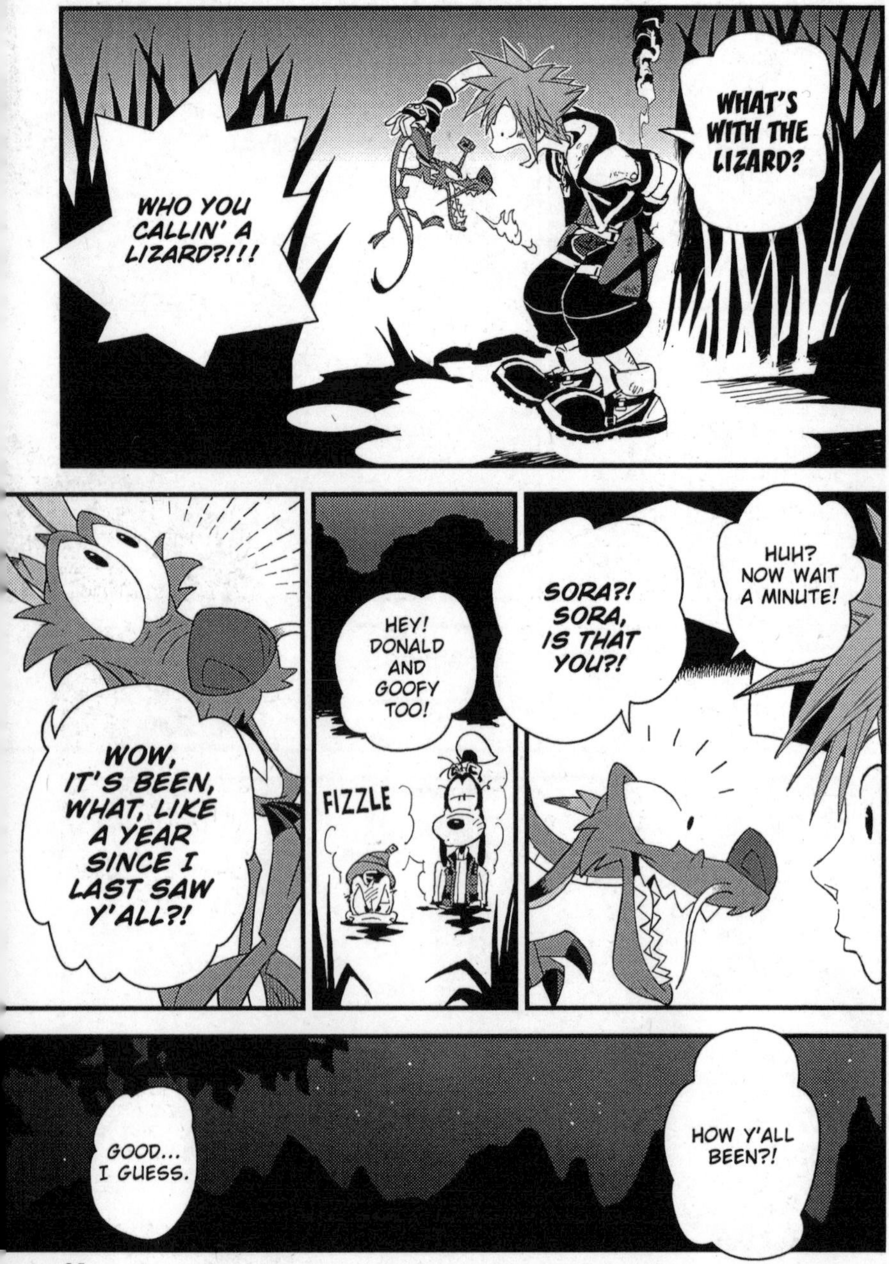
WHAT'S WITH THE LIZARD?
WHO YOU CALLIN' A LIZARD?!!!
HUH? NOW WAIT A MINUTE!
SORA?! SORA, IS THAT YOU?!
HEY! DONALD AND GOOFY TOO!
FIZZLE
WOW, IT'S BEEN, WHAT, LIKE A YEAR SINCE I LAST SAW Y'ALL?!
HOW Y'ALL BEEN?!
GOOD... I GUESS.

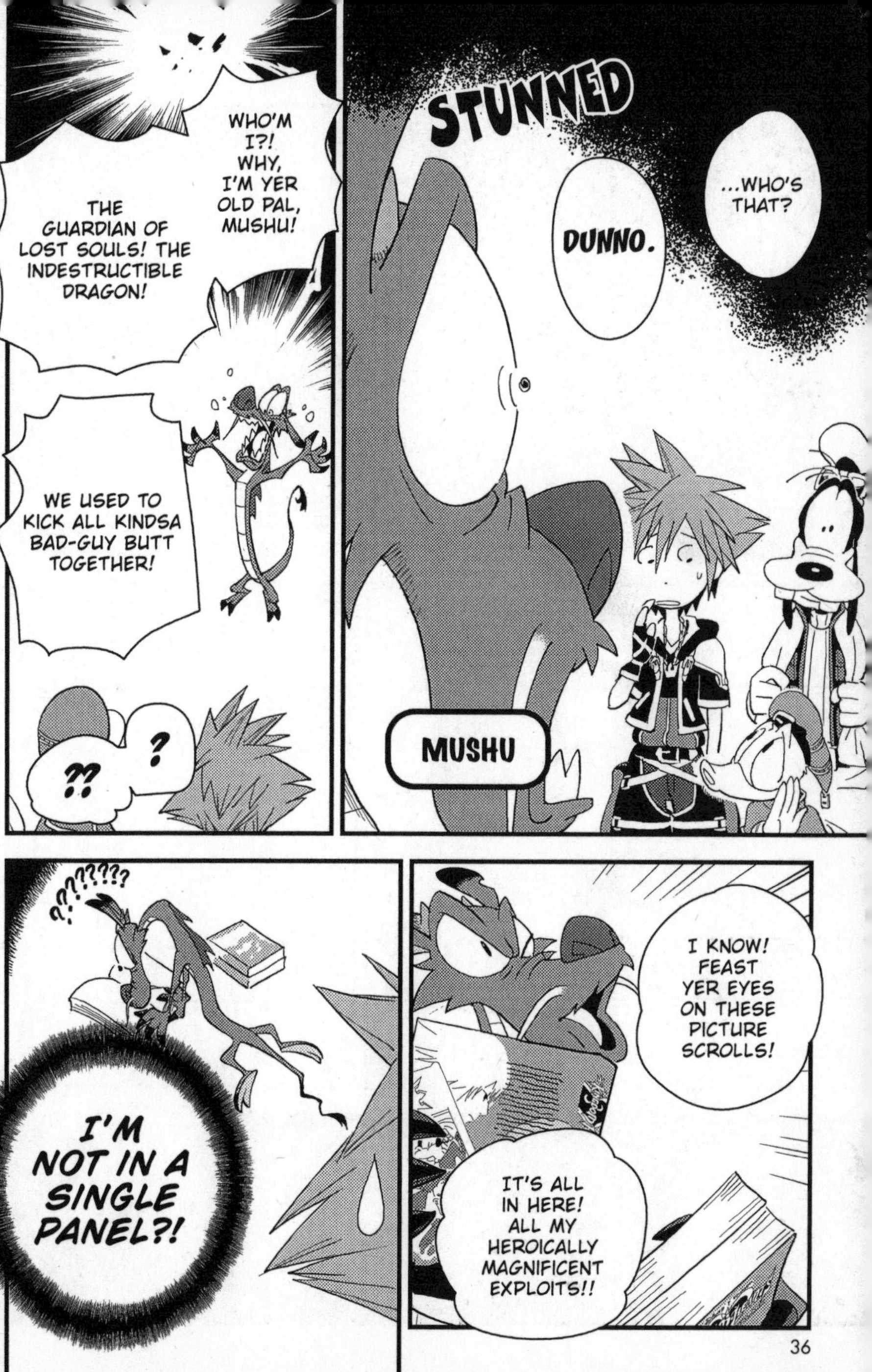
STUNNED
...WHO'S THAT?
DUNNO.
MUSHU
WHO'M I?! WHY, I'M YER OLD PAL, MUSHU!
THE GUARDIAN OF LOST SOULS! THE INDESTRUCTIBLE DRAGON!
WE USED TO KICK ALL KINDSA BAD-GUY BUTT TOGETHER!
?
??
I KNOW! FEAST YER EYES ON THESE PICTURE SCROLLS!
IT'S ALL IN HERE! ALL MY HEROICALLY MAGNIFICENT EXPLOITS!!
????????
I'M NOT IN A SINGLE PANEL?!

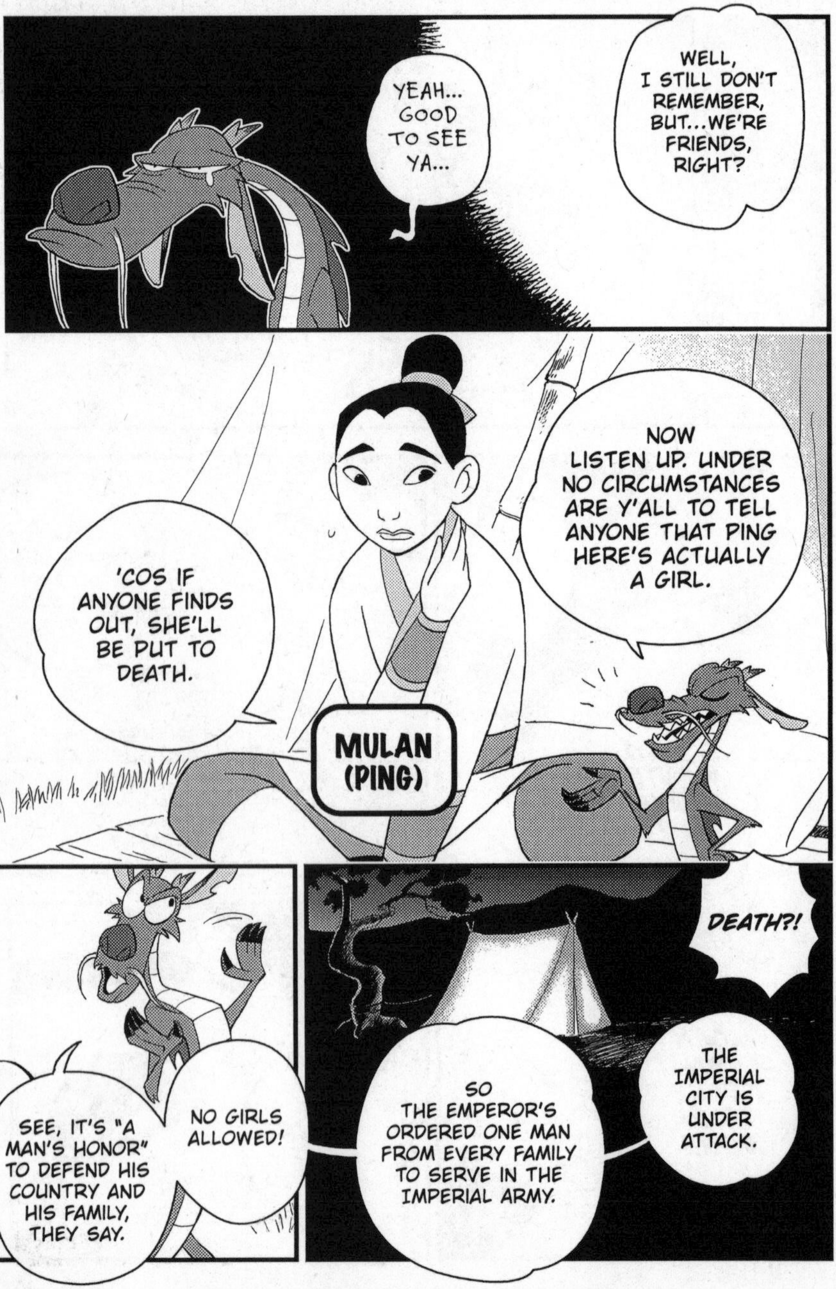
WELL, I STILL DON'T REMEMBER, BUT...WE'RE FRIENDS, RIGHT?
YEAH... GOOD TO SEE YA...
NOW LISTEN UP. UNDER NO CIRCUMSTANCES ARE Y'ALL TO TELL ANYONE THAT PING HERE'S ACTUALLY A GIRL.
'COS IF ANYONE FINDS OUT, SHE'LL BE PUT TO DEATH.
MULAN (PING)
DEATH?!
THE IMPERIAL CITY IS UNDER ATTACK.
SO THE EMPEROR'S ORDERED ONE MAN FROM EVERY FAMILY TO SERVE IN THE IMPERIAL ARMY.
NO GIRLS ALLOWED!
SEE, IT'S "A MAN'S HONOR" TO DEFEND HIS COUNTRY AND HIS FAMILY, THEY SAY.

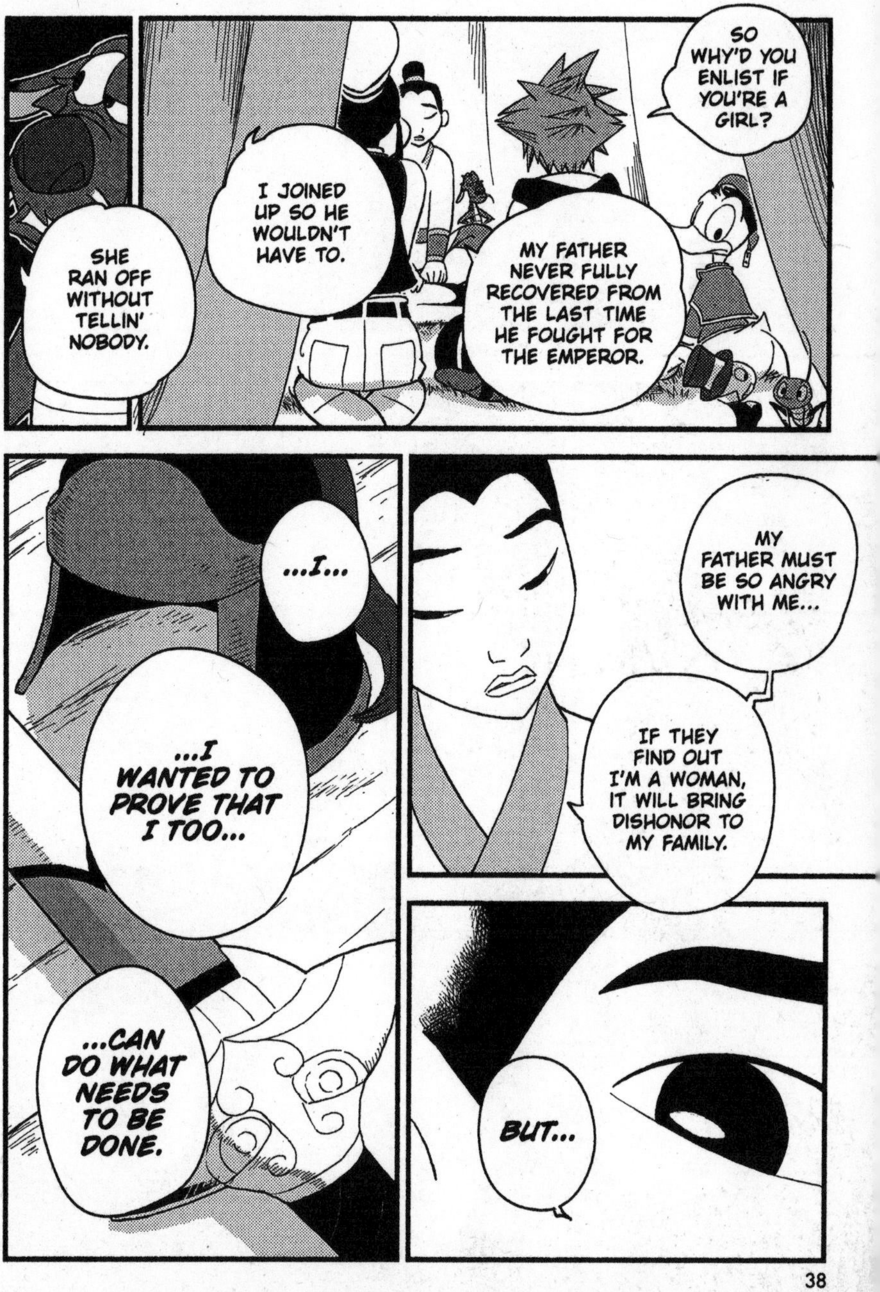
SO WHY'D YOU ENLIST IF YOU'RE A GIRL?
MY FATHER NEVER FULLY RECOVERED FROM THE LAST TIME HE FOUGHT FOR THE EMPEROR.
I JOINED UP SO HE WOULDN'T HAVE TO.
SHE RAN OFF WITHOUT TELLIN' NOBODY.
MY FATHER MUST BE SO ANGRY WITH ME...
IF THEY FIND OUT I'M A WOMAN, IT WILL BRING DISHONOR TO MY FAMILY.
BUT...
...I...
...I WANTED TO PROVE THAT I TOO...
...CAN DO WHAT NEEDS TO BE DONE.

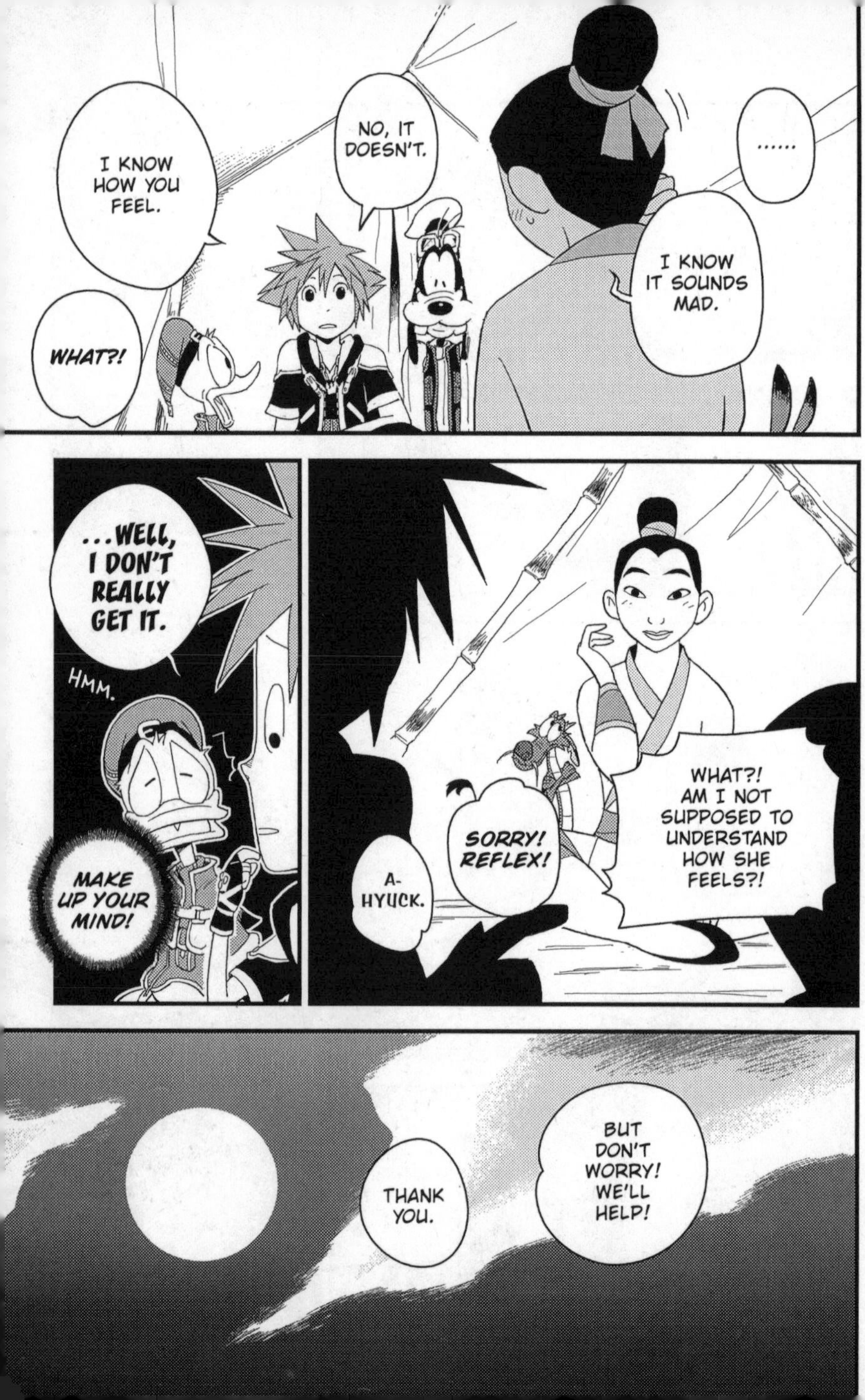
......
I KNOW IT SOUNDS MAD.
NO, IT DOESN'T.
I KNOW HOW YOU FEEL.
WHAT?!
WHAT?! AM I NOT SUPPOSED TO UNDERSTAND HOW SHE FEELS?!
SORRY! REFLEX!
A-HYUCK.
...WELL, I DON'T REALLY GET IT.
HMM.
MAKE UP YOUR MIND!
BUT DON'T WORRY! WE'LL HELP!
THANK YOU.

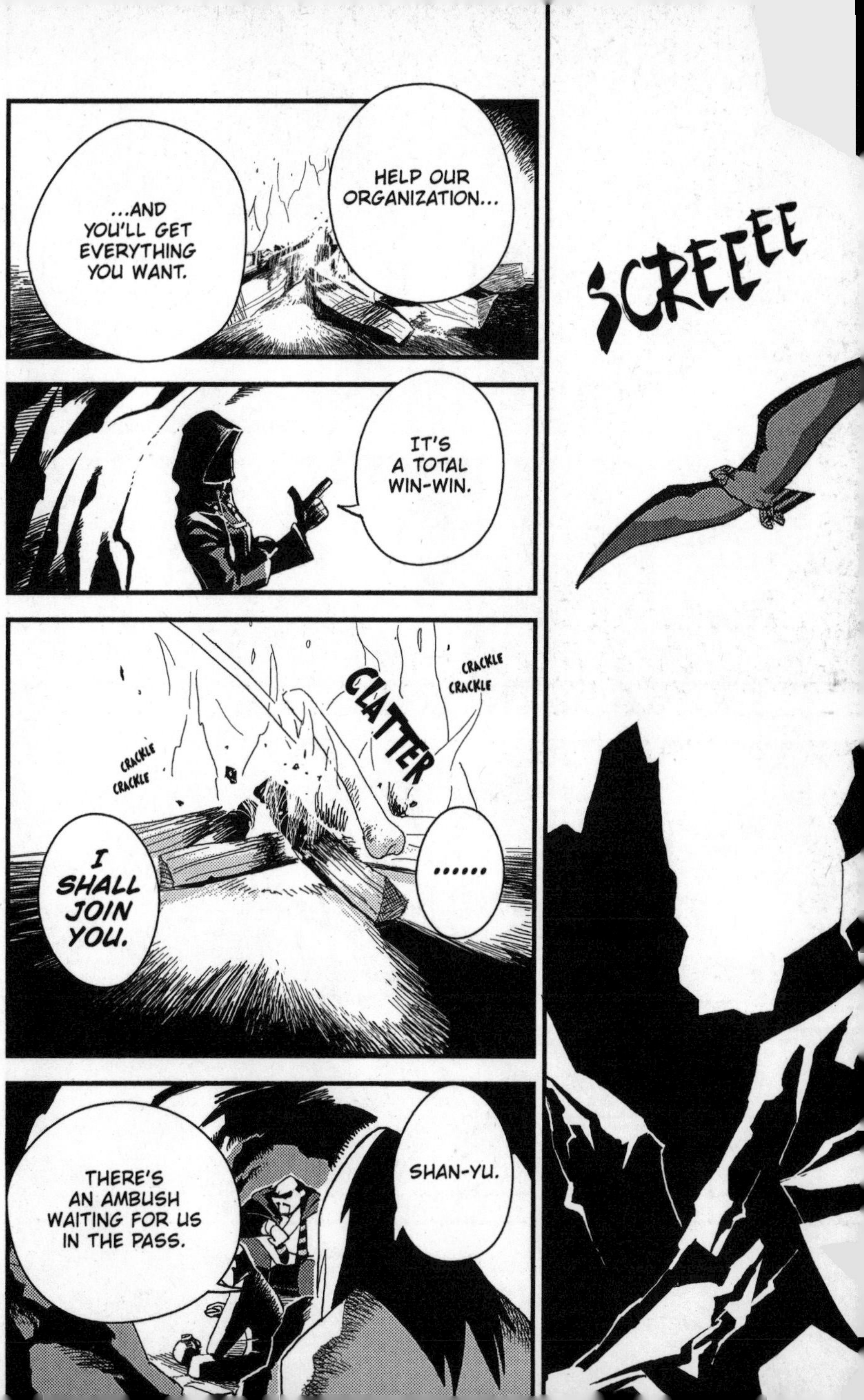
SCREEEE
HELP OUR ORGANIZATION...
...AND YOU'LL GET EVERYTHING YOU WANT.
IT'S A TOTAL WIN-WIN.
CRACKLE CRACKLE
CLATTER
......
CRACKLE CRACKLE
I SHALL JOIN YOU.
SHAN-YU.
THERE'S AN AMBUSH WAITING FOR US IN THE PASS.

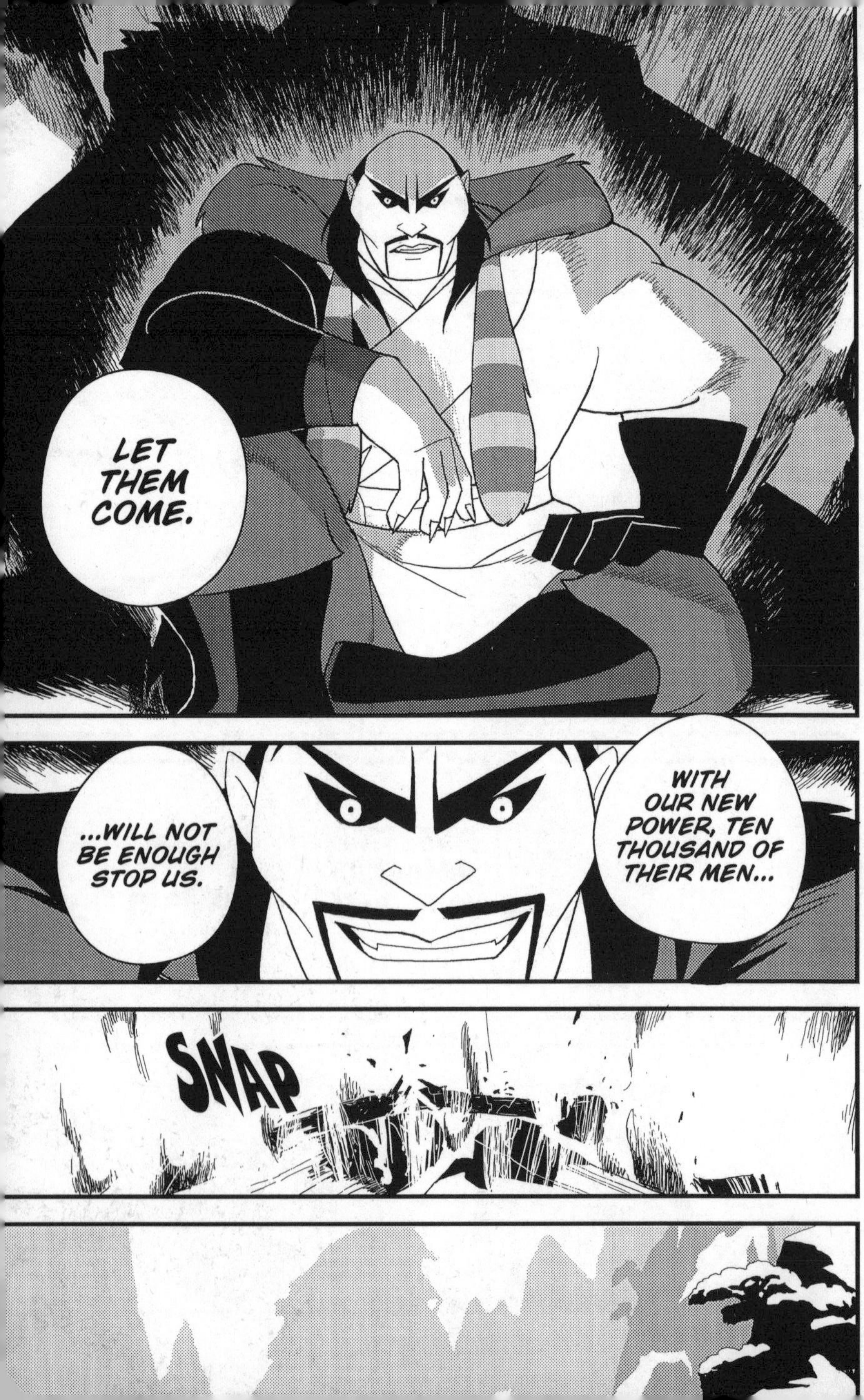
LET THEM COME.
WITH OUR NEW POWER, TEN THOUSAND OF THEIR MEN...
...WILL NOT BE ENOUGH STOP US.
SNAP

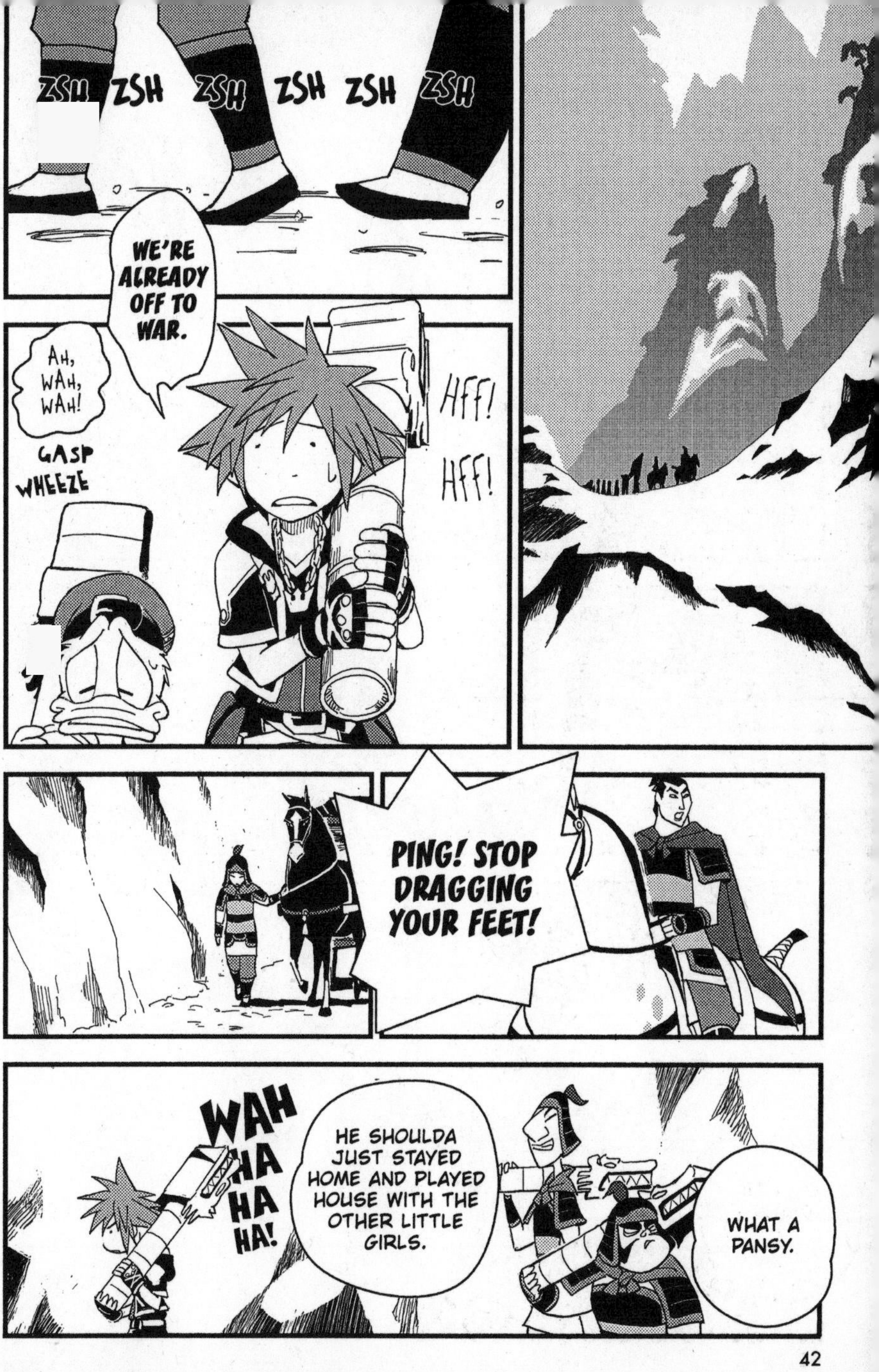
ZSH ZSH ZSH ZSH ZSH ZSH
WE'RE ALREADY OFF TO WAR.
HFF!
HFF!
AH, WAH, WAH!
GASP WHEEZE
PING! STOP DRAGGING YOUR FEET!
WHAT A PANSY.
HE SHOULDA JUST STAYED HOME AND PLAYED HOUSE WITH THE OTHER LITTLE GIRLS.
WAH HA HA HA!

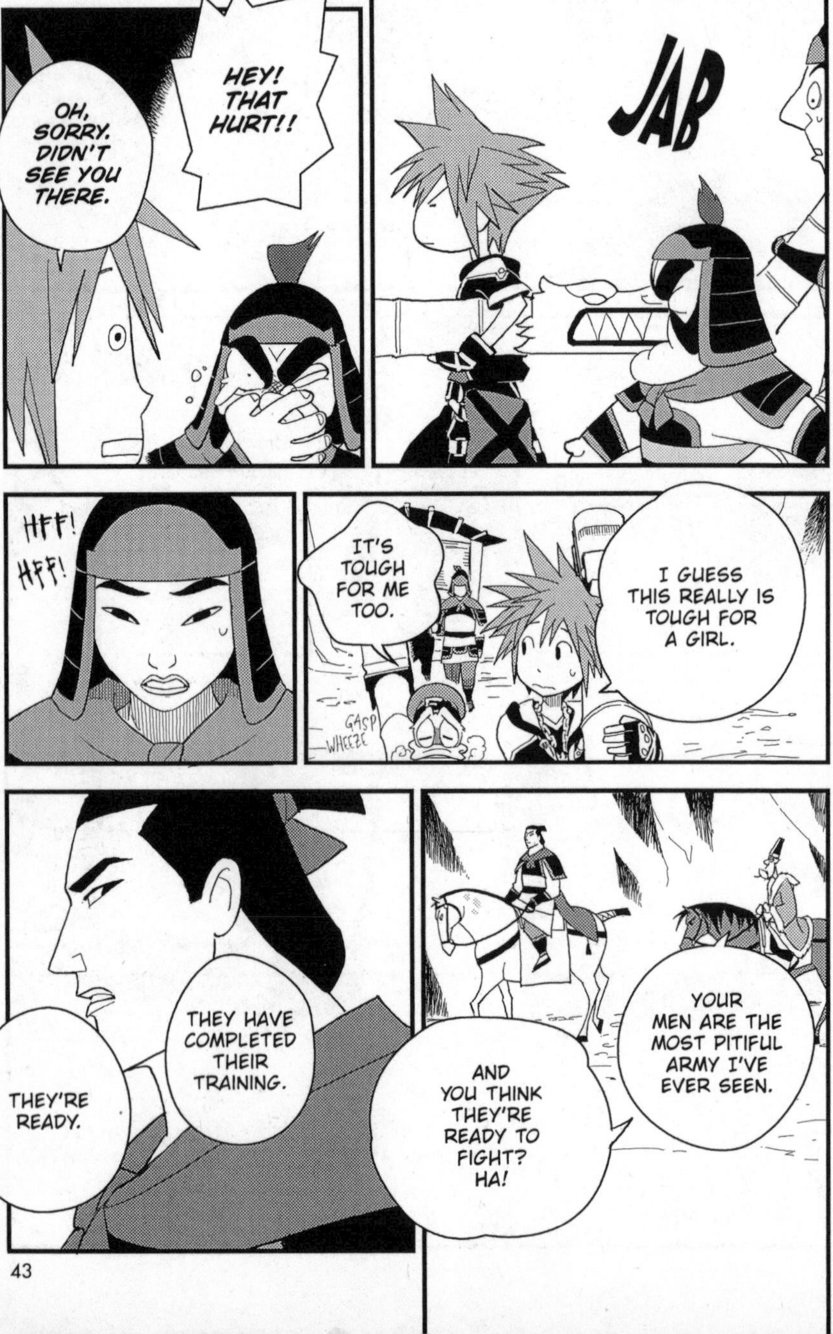
JAB
HEY! THAT HURT!!
OH, SORRY. DIDN'T SEE YOU THERE.
I GUESS THIS REALLY IS TOUGH FOR A GIRL.
IT'S TOUGH FOR ME TOO.
GASP
WHEEZE
HFF!
HFF!
YOUR MEN ARE THE MOST PITIFUL ARMY I'VE EVER SEEN.
AND YOU THINK THEY'RE READY TO FIGHT? HA!
THEY HAVE COMPLETED THEIR TRAINING.
THEY'RE READY.

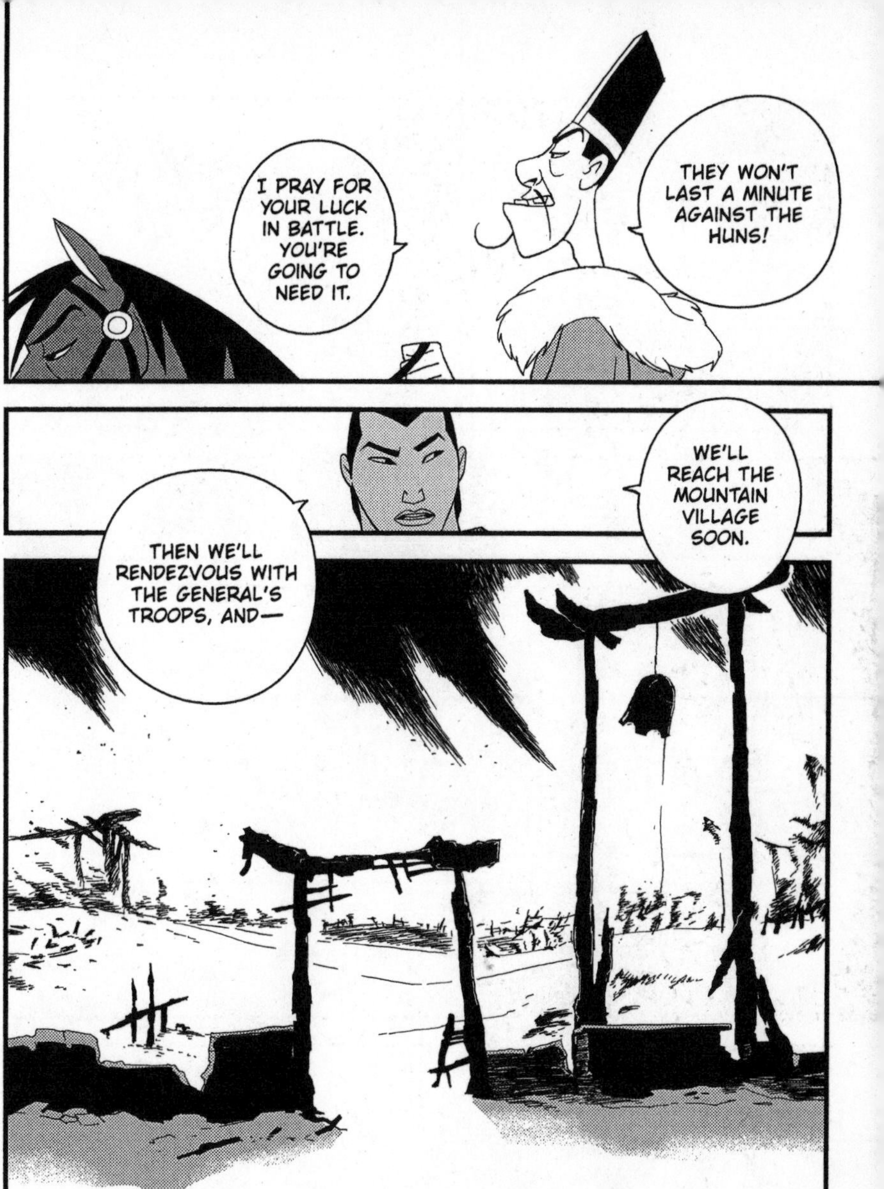
THEY WON'T LAST A MINUTE AGAINST THE HUNS!
I PRAY FOR YOUR LUCK IN BATTLE. YOU'RE GOING TO NEED IT.
WE'LL REACH THE MOUNTAIN VILLAGE SOON.
THEN WE'LL RENDEZVOUS WITH THE GENERAL'S TROOPS, AND—

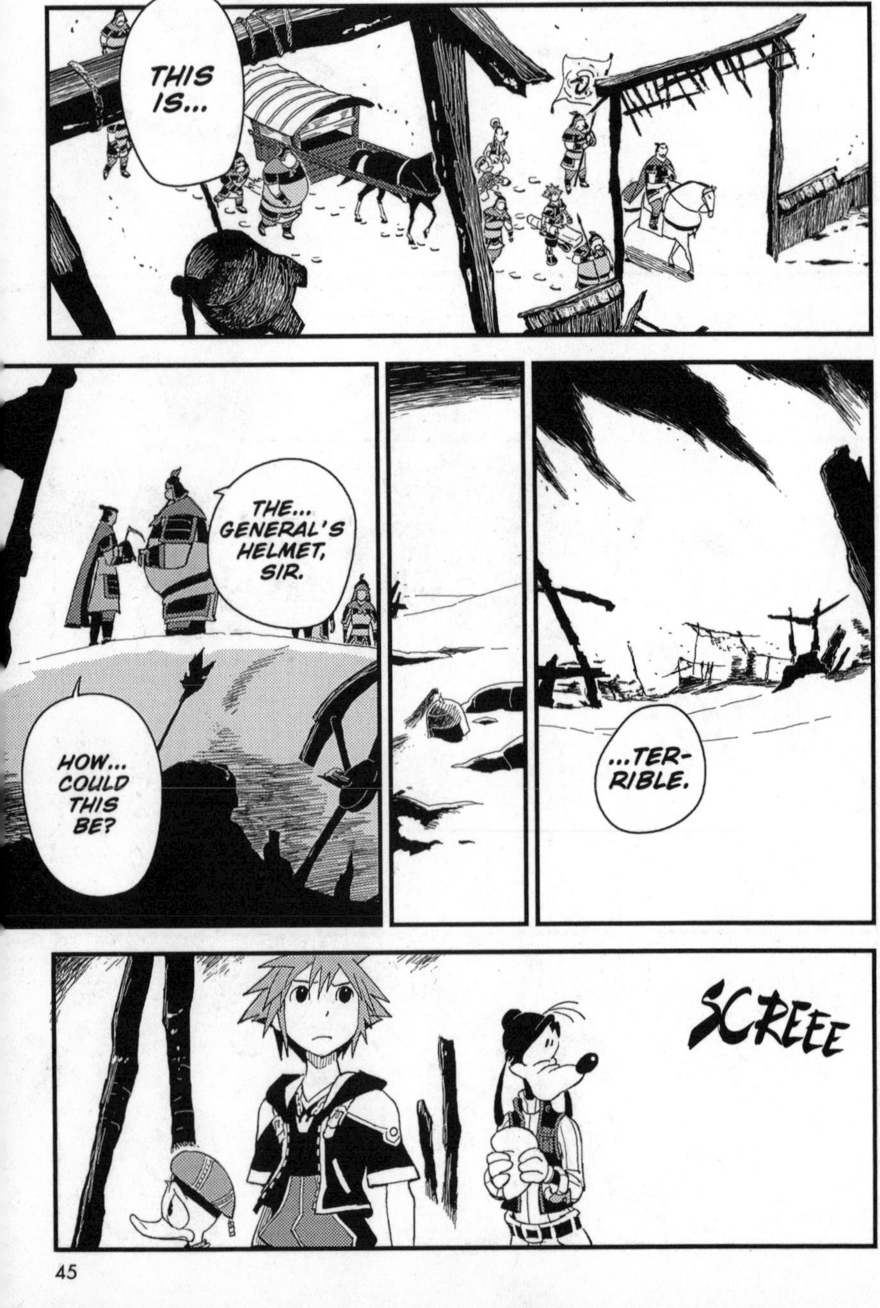
THIS IS...
...TER-RIBLE.
THE... GENERAL'S HELMET, SIR.
HOW... COULD THIS BE?
SCREEE

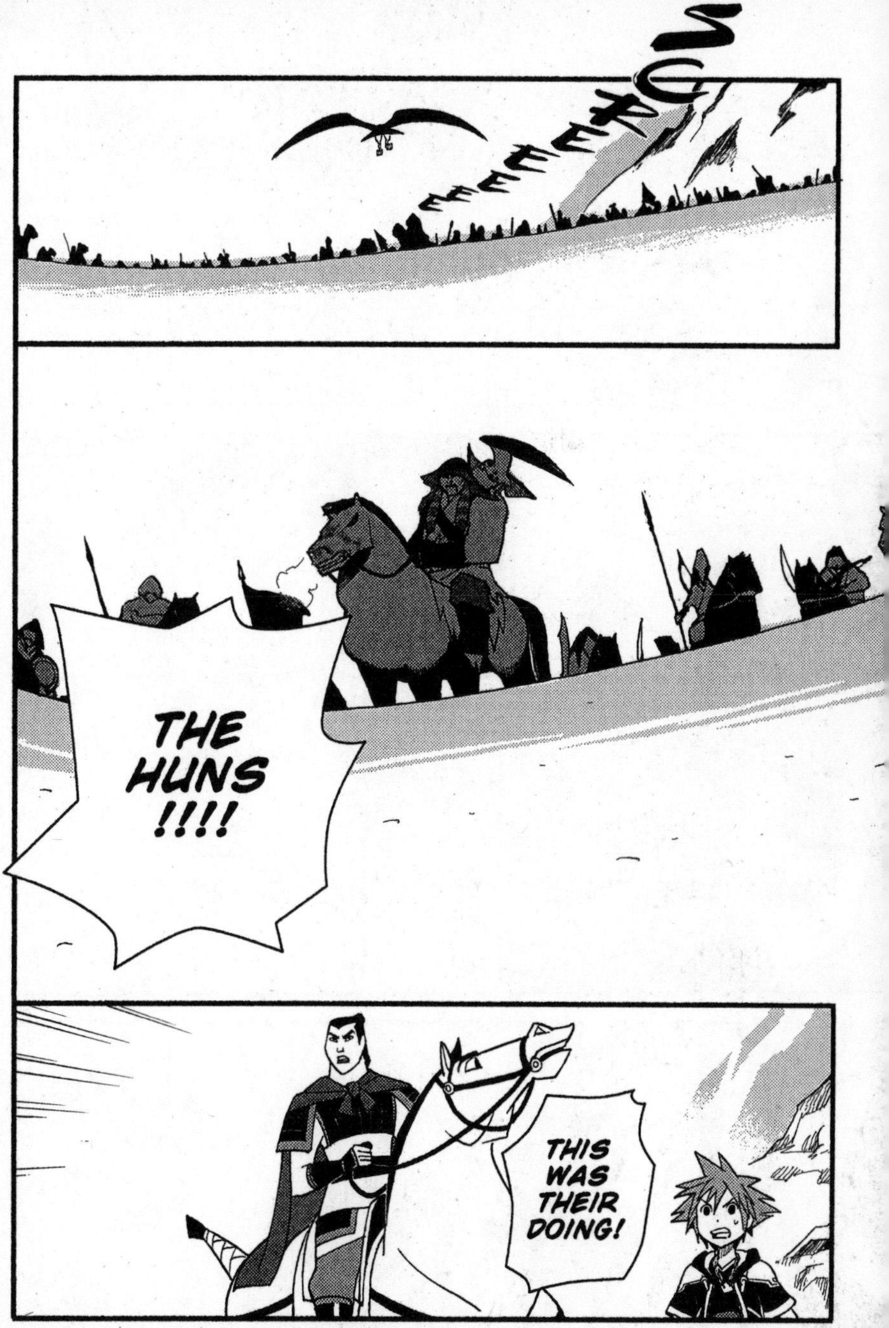
SCREEEEE
THE HUNS !!!!
THIS WAS THEIR DOING!

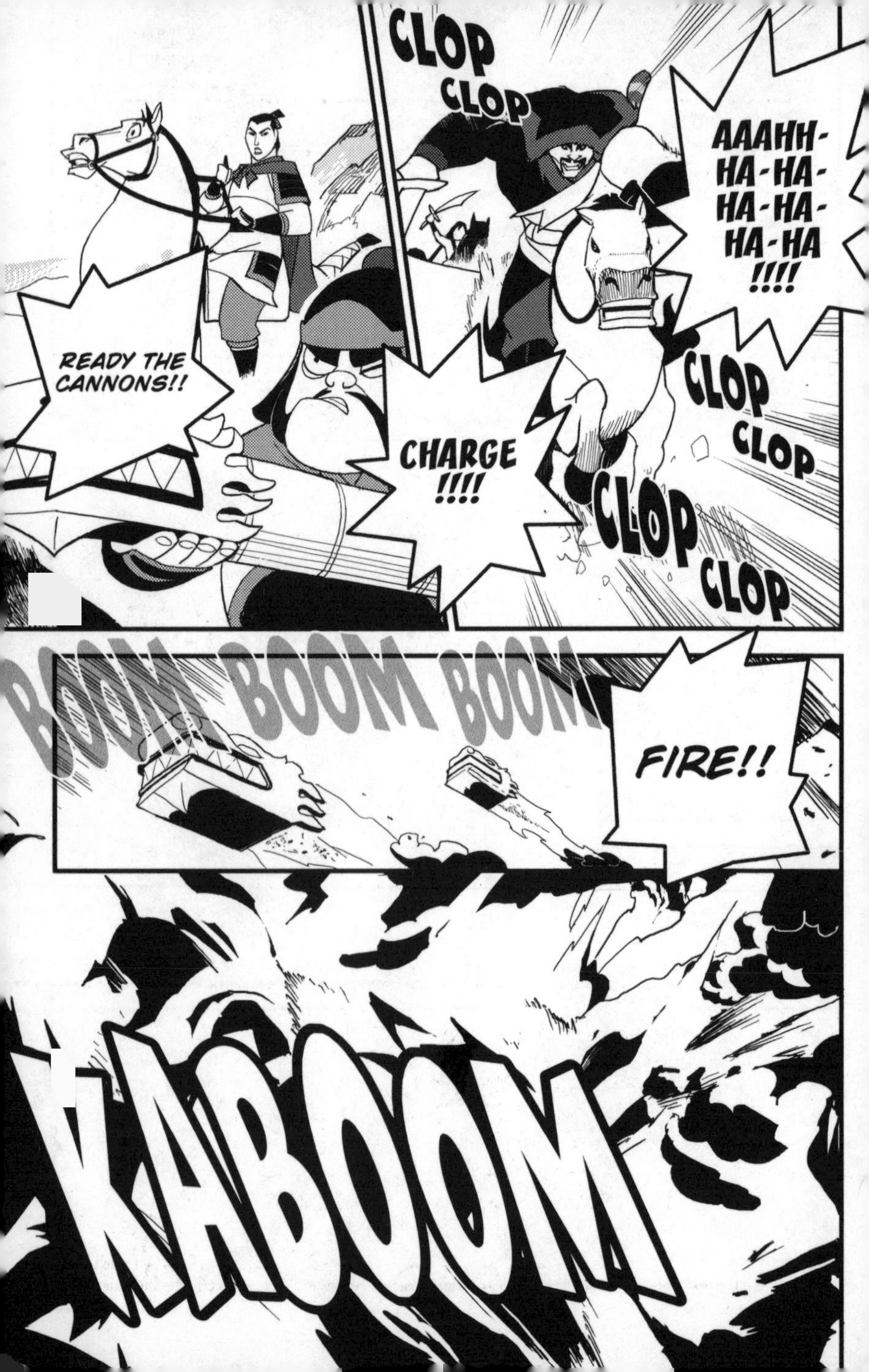

CLOP CLOP
AAAHH-HA-HA-HA-HA-HA-HA!!!!
CHARGE!!!!
CLOP CLOP
CLOP CLOP
READY THE CANNONS!!
FIRE!!
BOOM BOOM BOOM
KABOOM

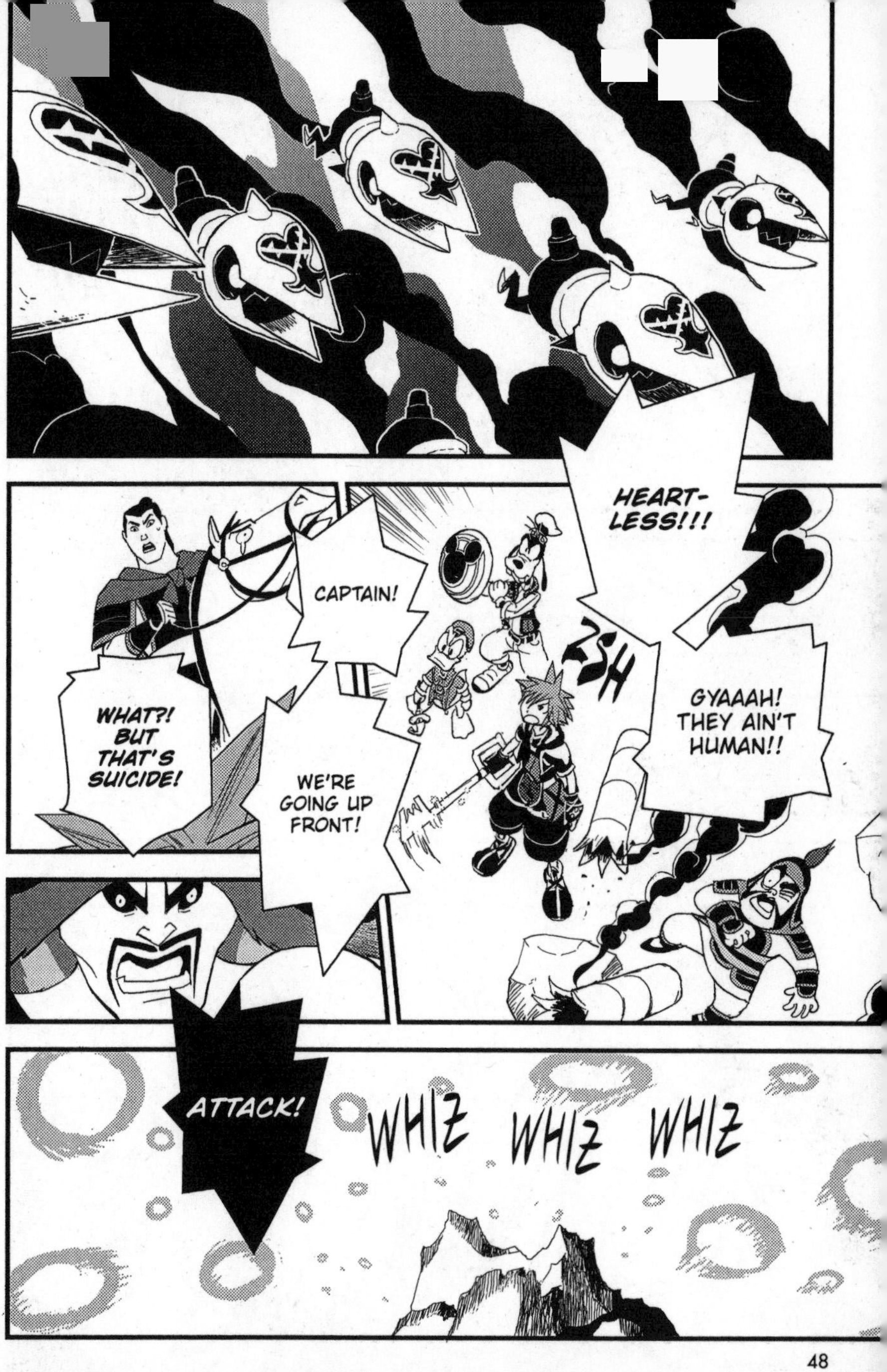
HEART-LESS!!!
ZSH
GYAAAH! THEY AIN'T HUMAN!!
CAPTAIN!
WE'RE GOING UP FRONT!
WHAT?! BUT THAT'S SUICIDE!
ATTACK!
WHIZ WHIZ WHIZ

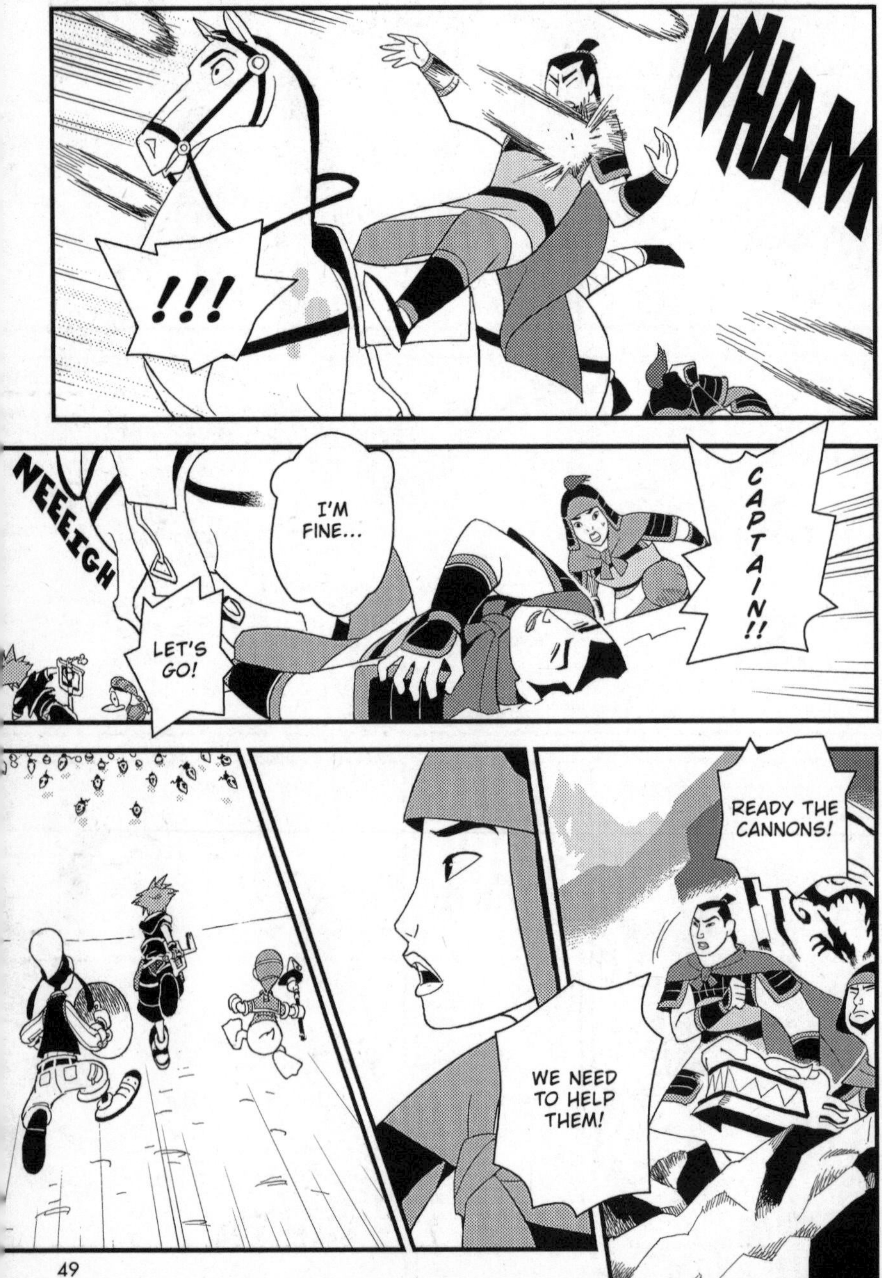
WHAM
!!!
CAPTAIN!!
I'M FINE...
LET'S GO!
NEEEIGH
READY THE CANNONS!
WE NEED TO HELP THEM!

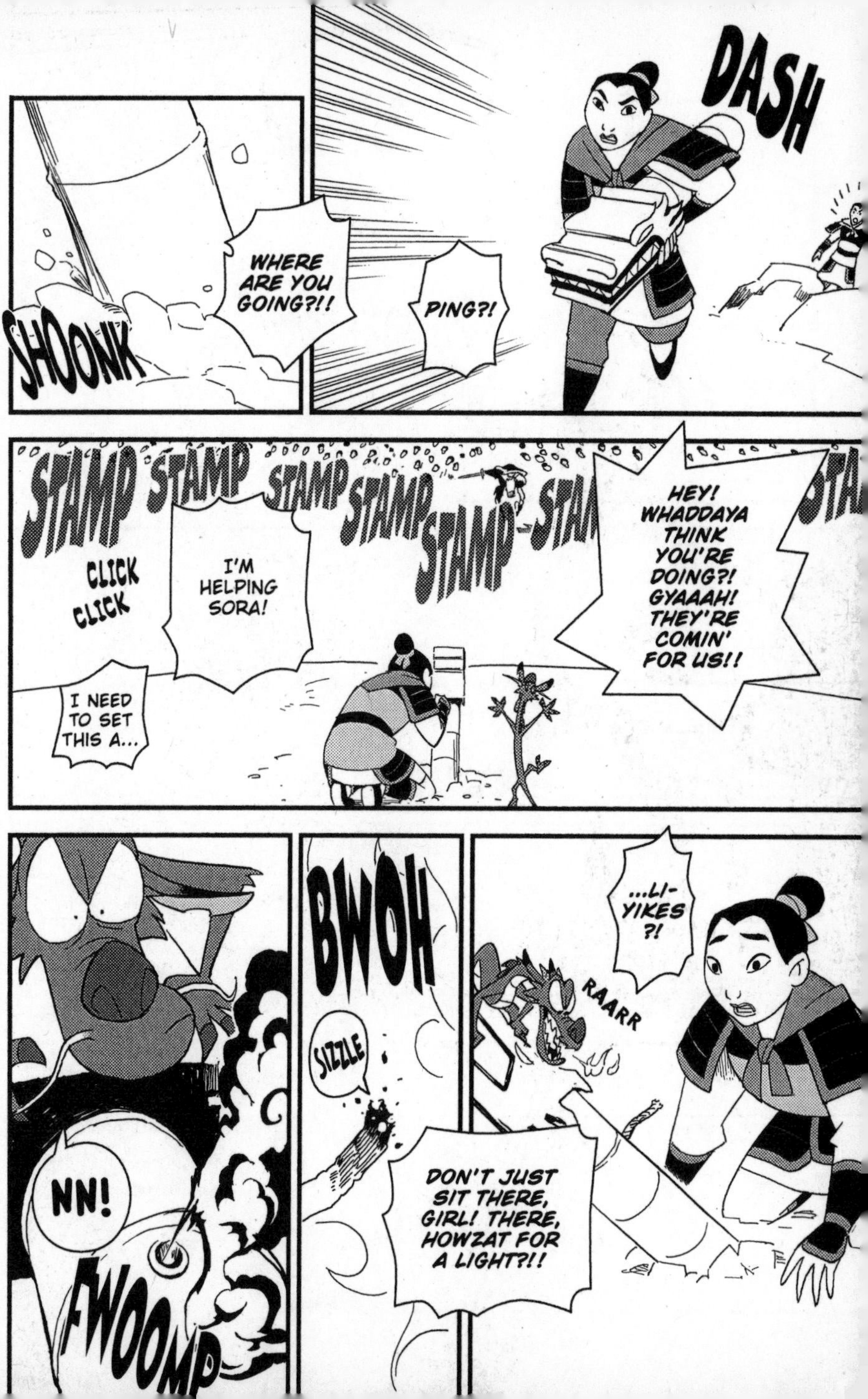
DASH
PING?!
WHERE ARE YOU GOING?!!
SHOONK
STAMP STAMP STAMP STAMP STAMP STAMP
HEY! WHADDAYA THINK YOU'RE DOING?! GYAAAH! THEY'RE COMIN' FOR US!!
I'M HELPING SORA!
CLICK CLICK
I NEED TO SET THIS A...
...LI-YIKES?!
RAARR
DON'T JUST SIT THERE, GIRL! THERE, HOWZAT FOR A LIGHT?!!
BWOH
SIZZLE
NN!
FWOOMP

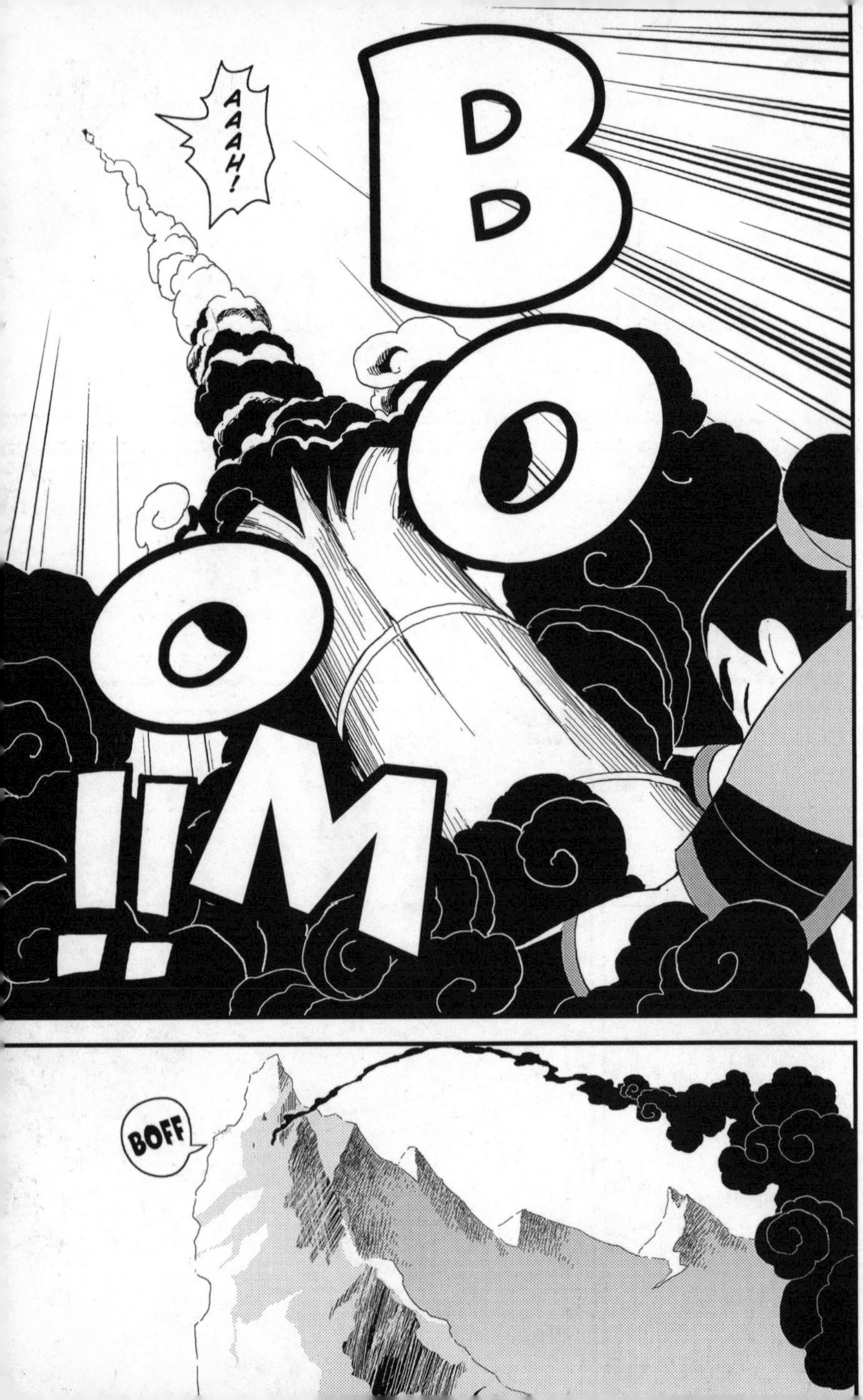
BOOM!!
AAAAH!
BOFF

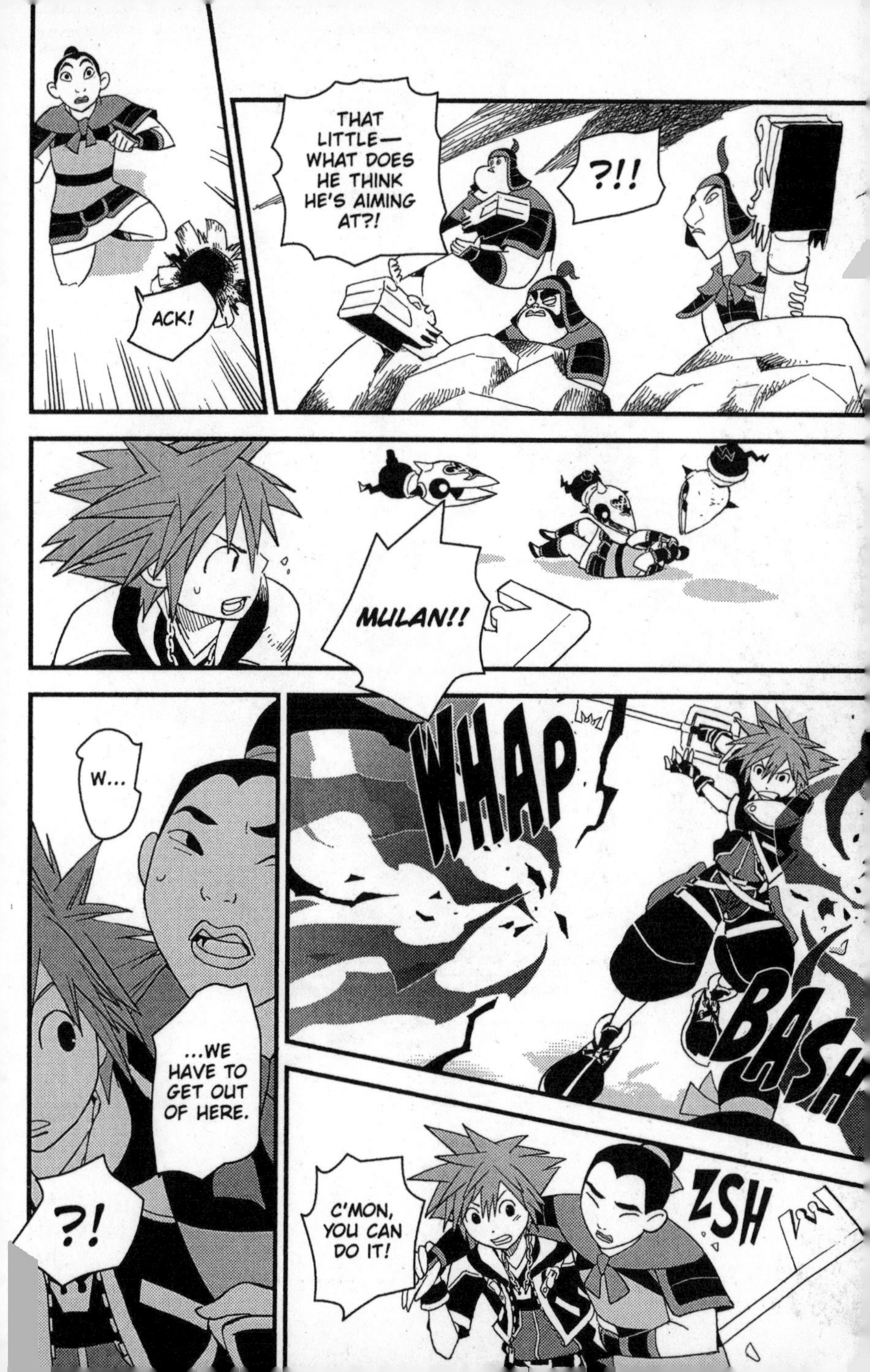
THAT LITTLE— WHAT DOES HE THINK HE'S AIMING AT?!
?!!
ACK!
MULAN!!
WHAP
BASH
ZSH
C'MON, YOU CAN DO IT!
W...
...WE HAVE TO GET OUT OF HERE.
?!

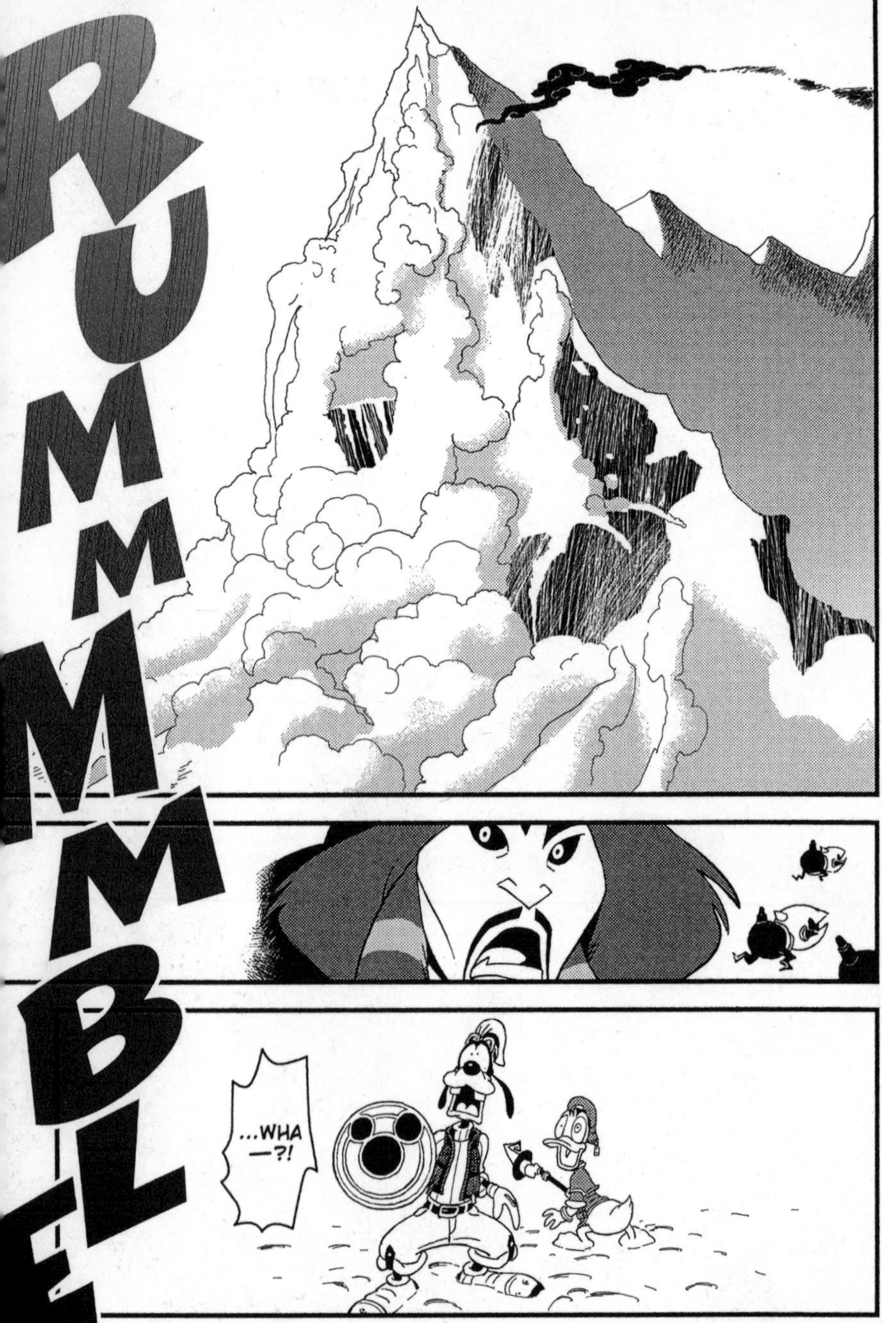
RUMMMMMMBLE
...WHA—?!

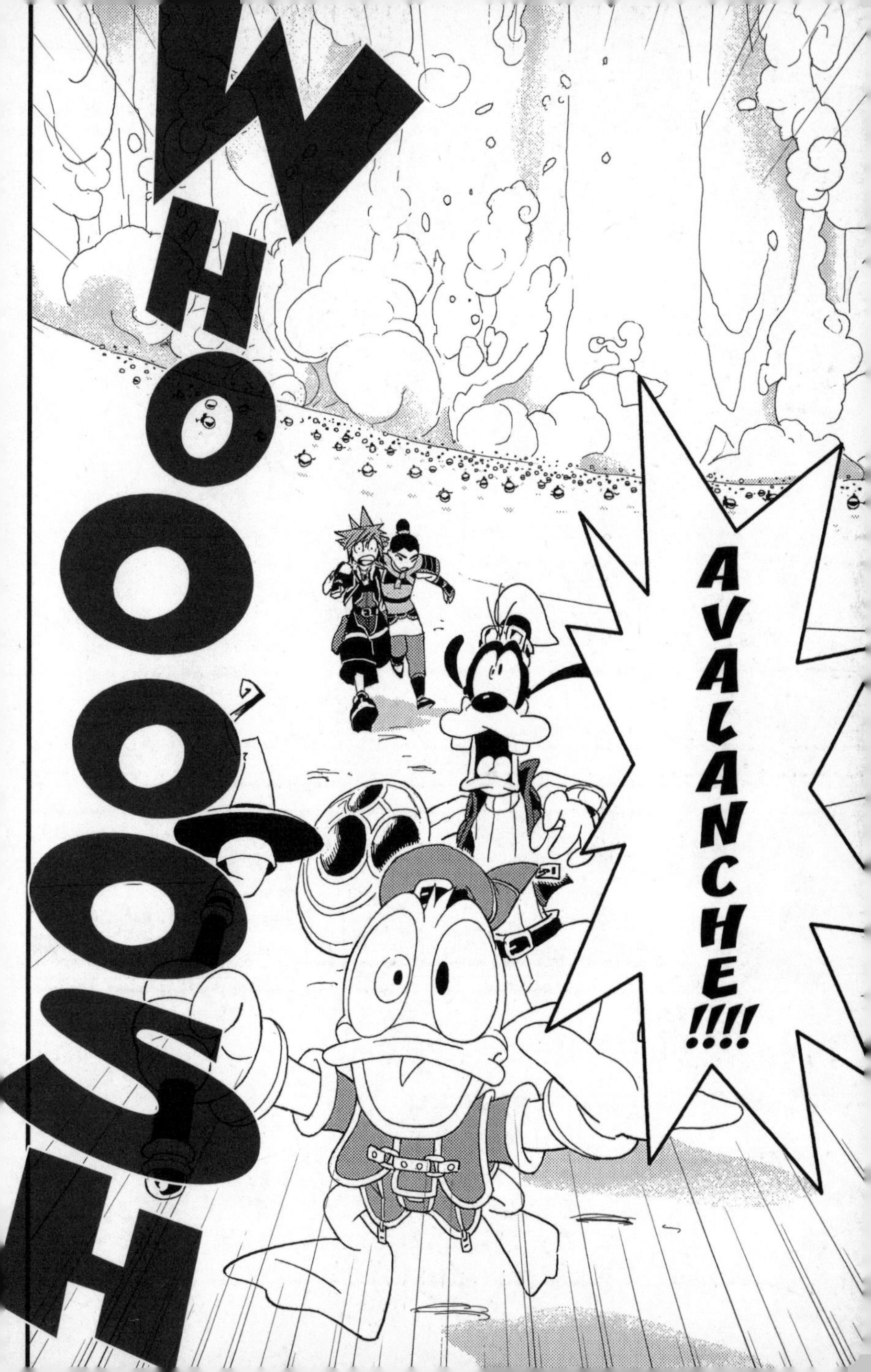
AVALANCHE!!!!
WHOOOOSH

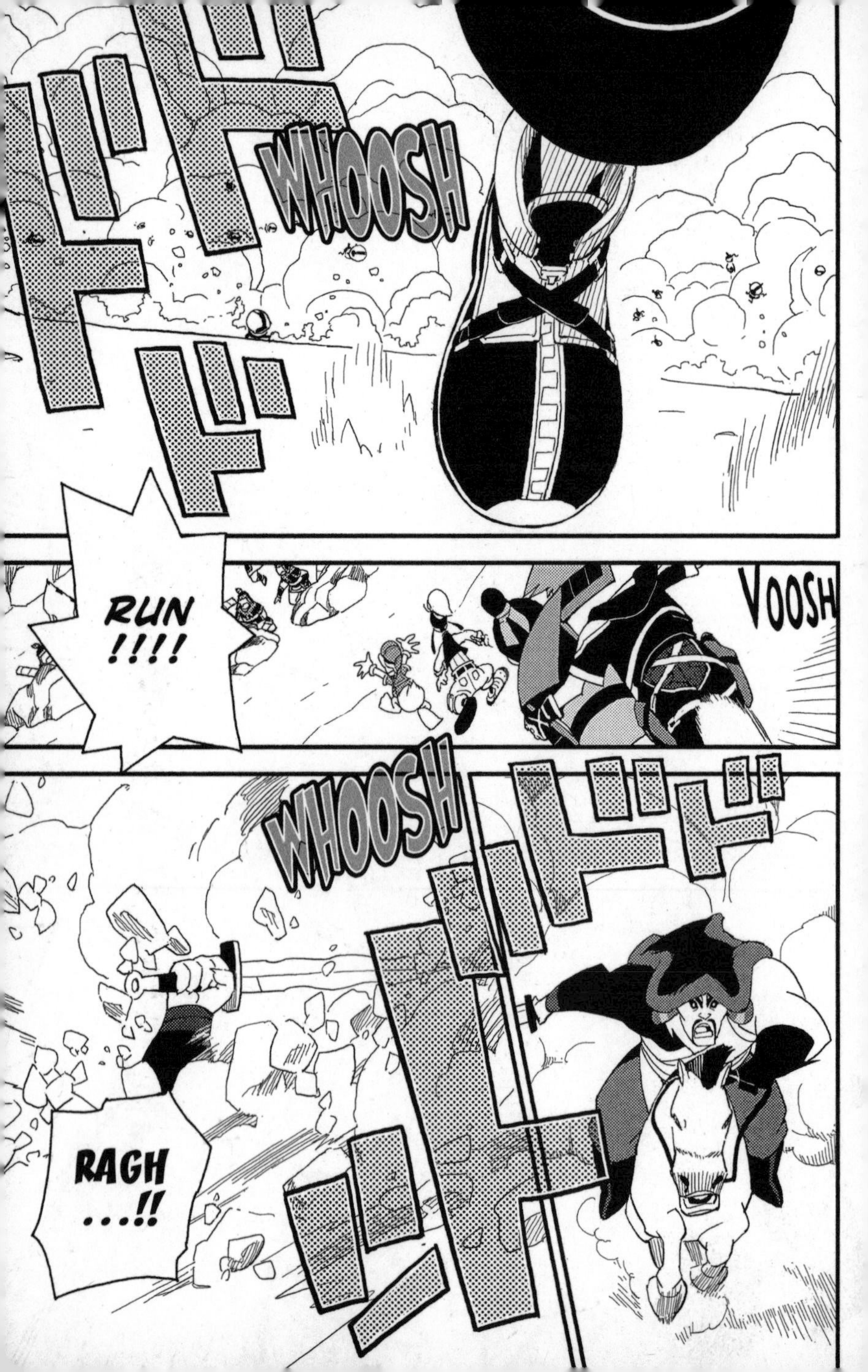
WHOOSH
VOOSH
RUN !!!!
WHOOSH
RAGH ...!!

Chapter 21: Beneath the Snow

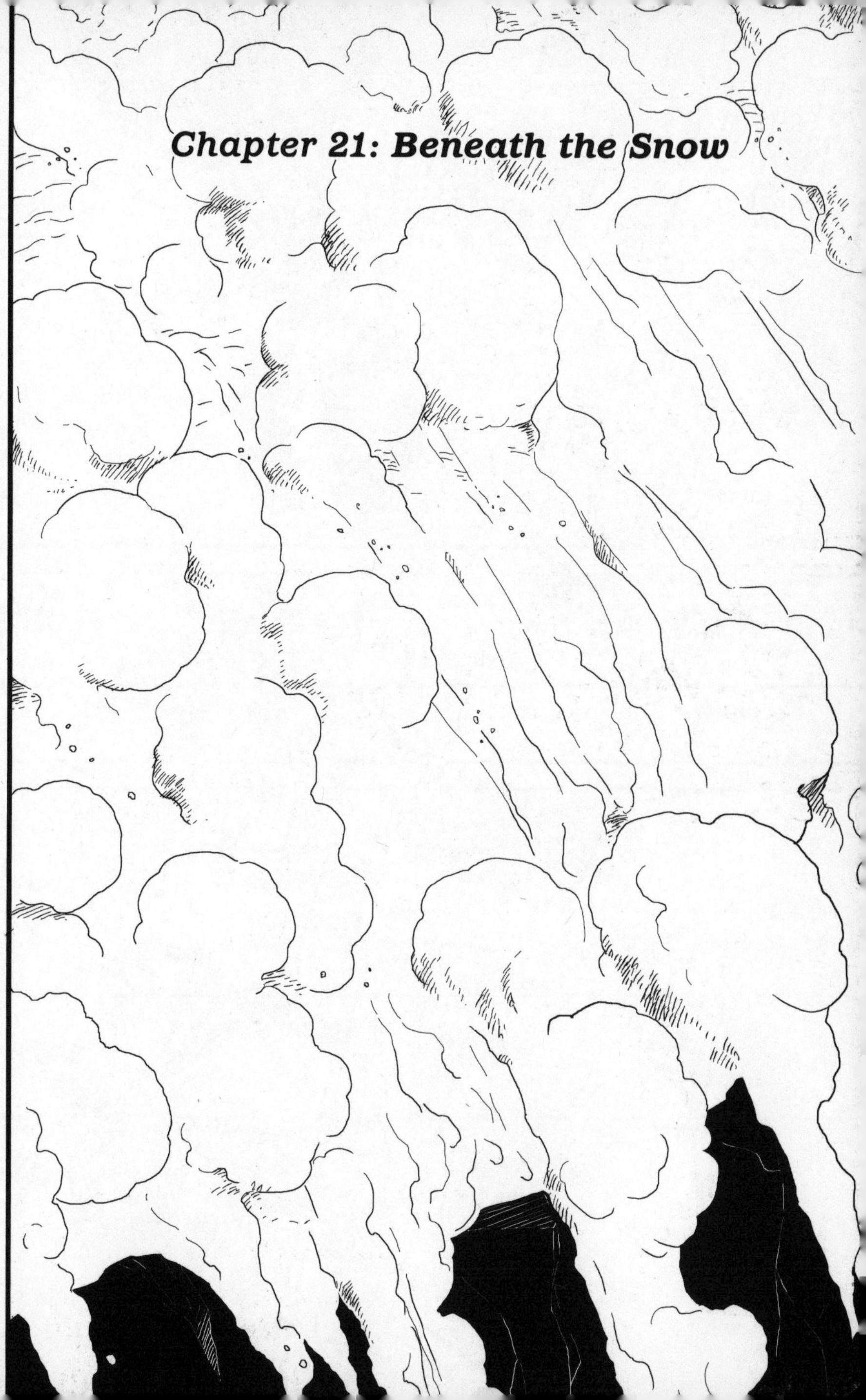

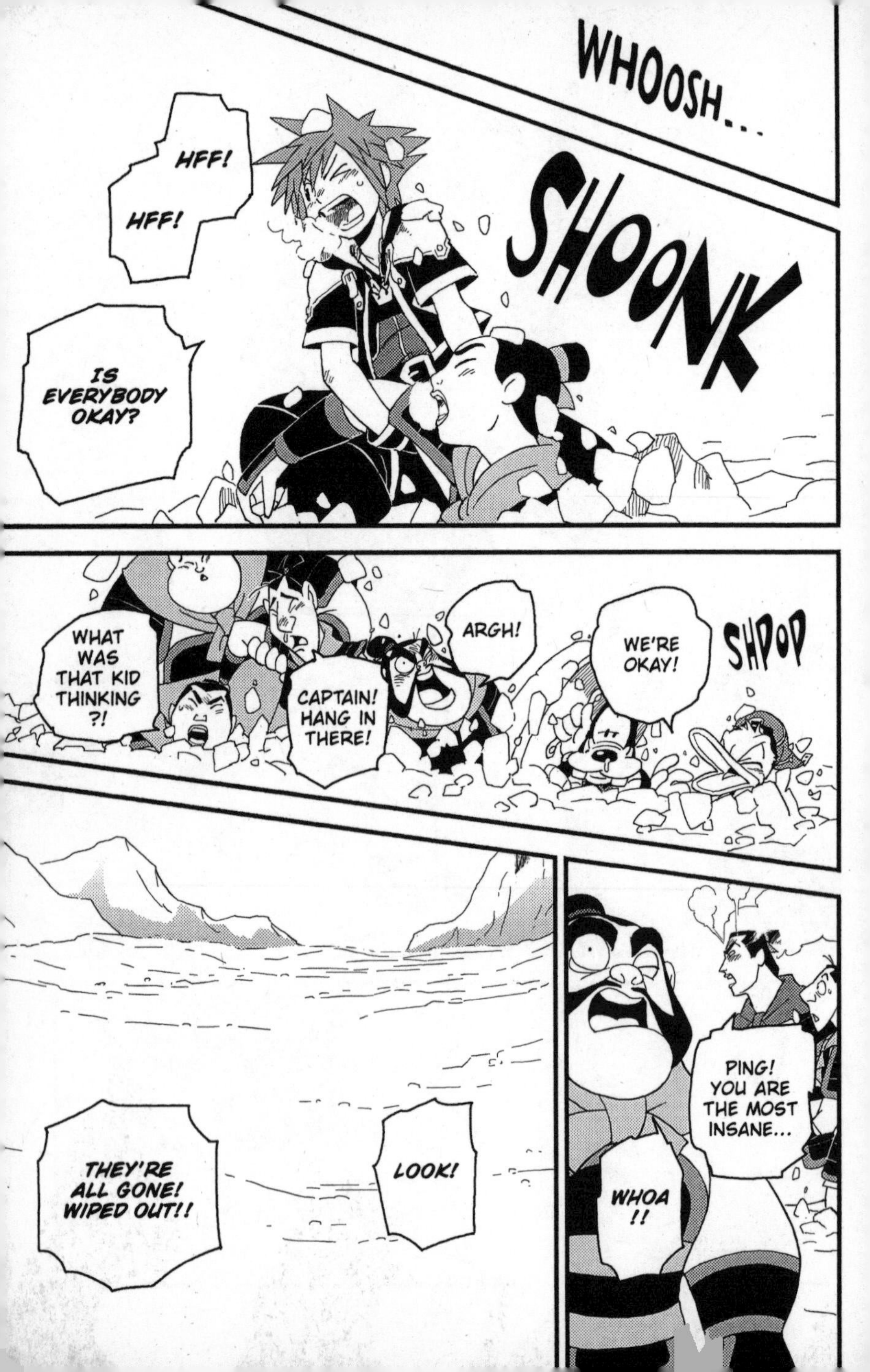
WHOOSH...
SHOONK
HFF! HFF!
IS EVERYBODY OKAY?
SHPOP
WE'RE OKAY!
ARGH!
CAPTAIN! HANG IN THERE!
WHAT WAS THAT KID THINKING?!
PING! YOU ARE THE MOST INSANE...
WHOA!!
LOOK!
THEY'RE ALL GONE! WIPED OUT!!

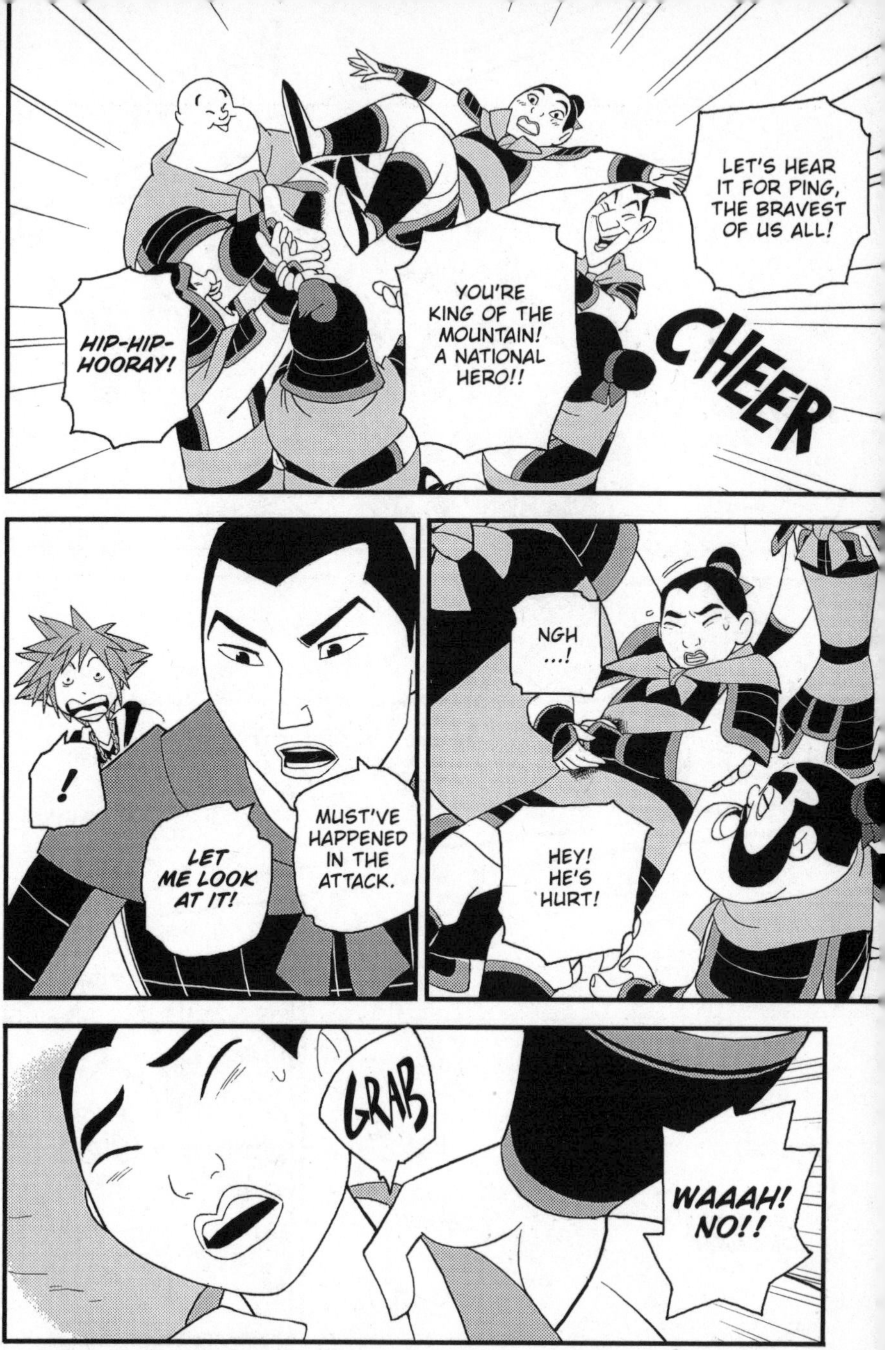
LET'S HEAR IT FOR PING, THE BRAVEST OF US ALL!
CHEER
YOU'RE KING OF THE MOUNTAIN! A NATIONAL HERO!!
HIP-HIP-HOORAY!
NGH ...!
HEY! HE'S HURT!
MUST'VE HAPPENED IN THE ATTACK.
LET ME LOOK AT IT!
!
GRAB
WAAAH! NO!!

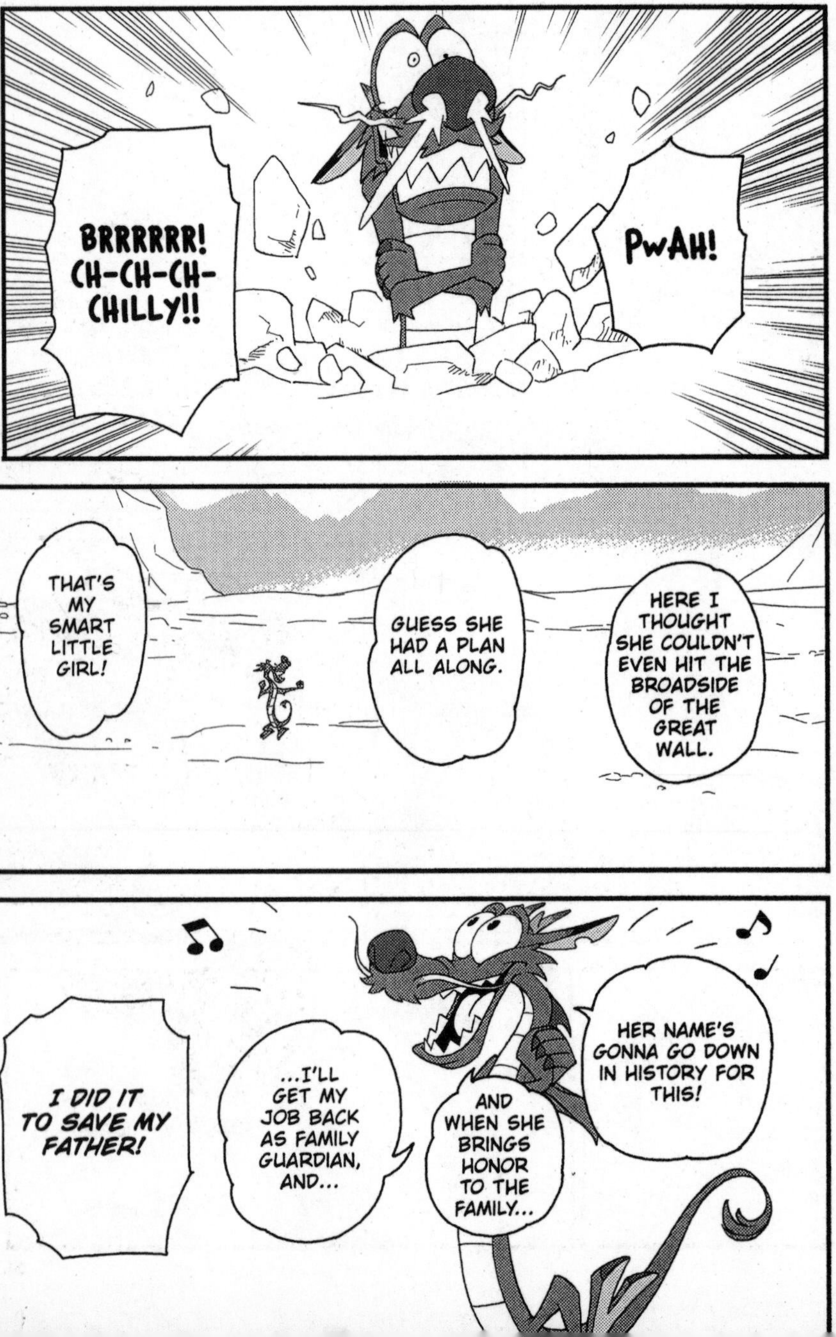
PwAH!
BRRRRRR! CH-CH-CH-CHILLY!!
HERE I THOUGHT SHE COULDN'T EVEN HIT THE BROADSIDE OF THE GREAT WALL.
GUESS SHE HAD A PLAN ALL ALONG.
THAT'S MY SMART LITTLE GIRL!
HER NAME'S GONNA GO DOWN IN HISTORY FOR THIS!
AND WHEN SHE BRINGS HONOR TO THE FAMILY...
...I'LL GET MY JOB BACK AS FAMILY GUARDIAN, AND...
I DID IT TO SAVE MY FATHER!

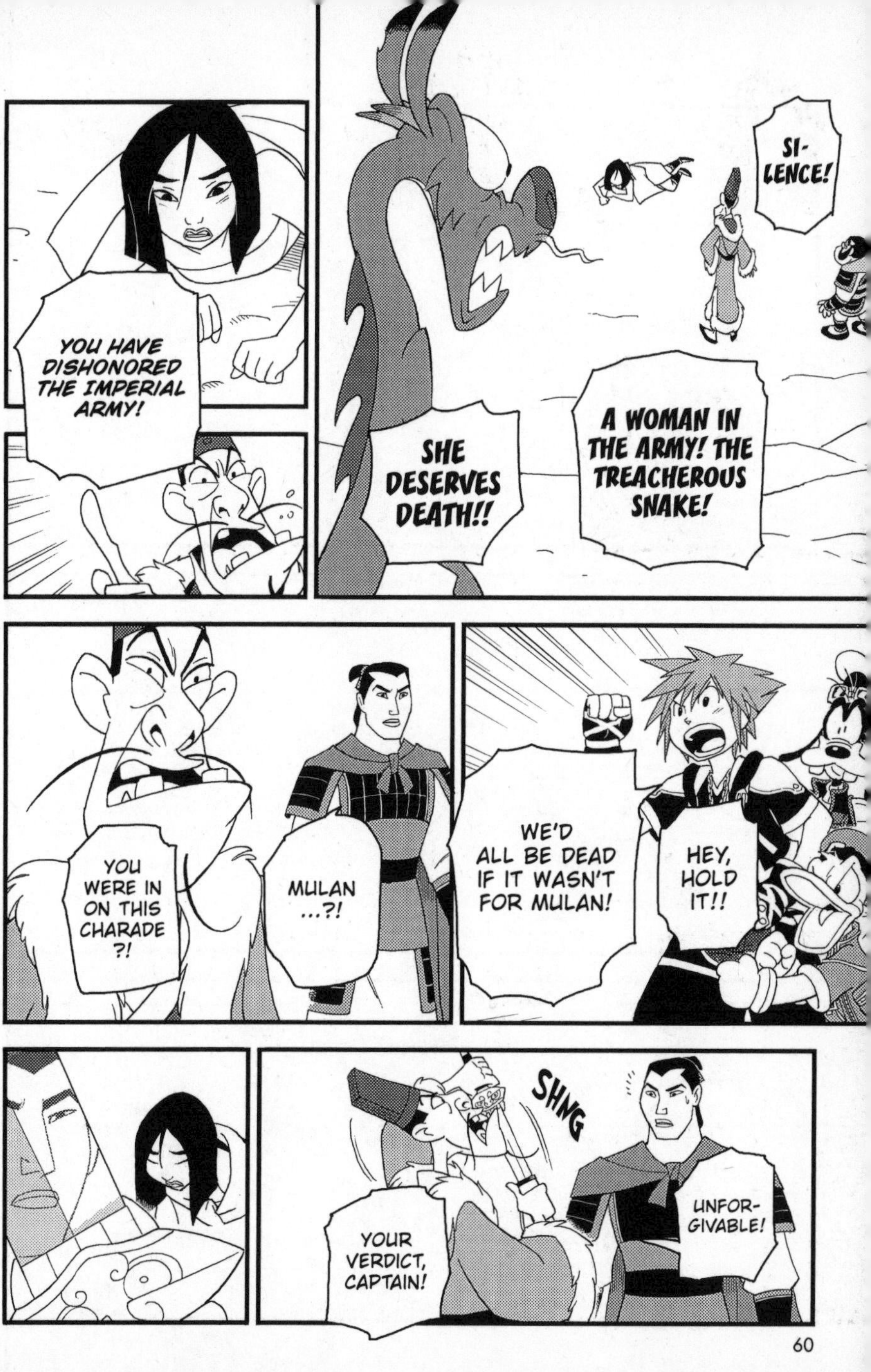
SI-LENCE!
A WOMAN IN THE ARMY! THE TREACHEROUS SNAKE!
SHE DESERVES DEATH!!
YOU HAVE DISHONORED THE IMPERIAL ARMY!
HEY, HOLD IT!!
WE'D ALL BE DEAD IF IT WASN'T FOR MULAN!
MULAN ...?!
YOU WERE IN ON THIS CHARADE ?!
SHNG
UNFOR-GIVABLE!
YOUR VERDICT, CAPTAIN!

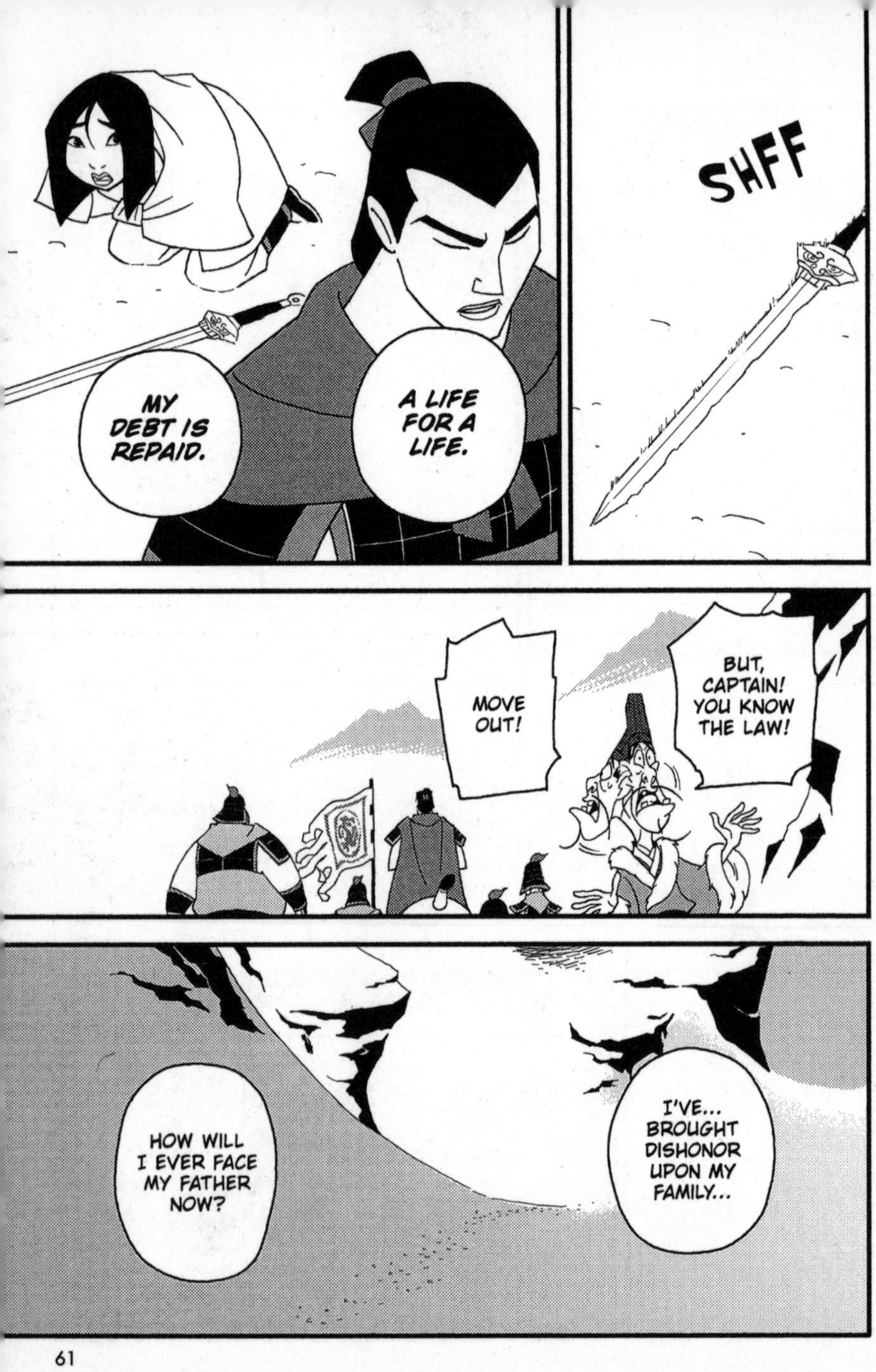
SHFF
A LIFE FOR A LIFE.
MY DEBT IS REPAID.
BUT, CAPTAIN! YOU KNOW THE LAW!
MOVE OUT!
I'VE... BROUGHT DISHONOR UPON MY FAMILY...
HOW WILL I EVER FACE MY FATHER NOW?

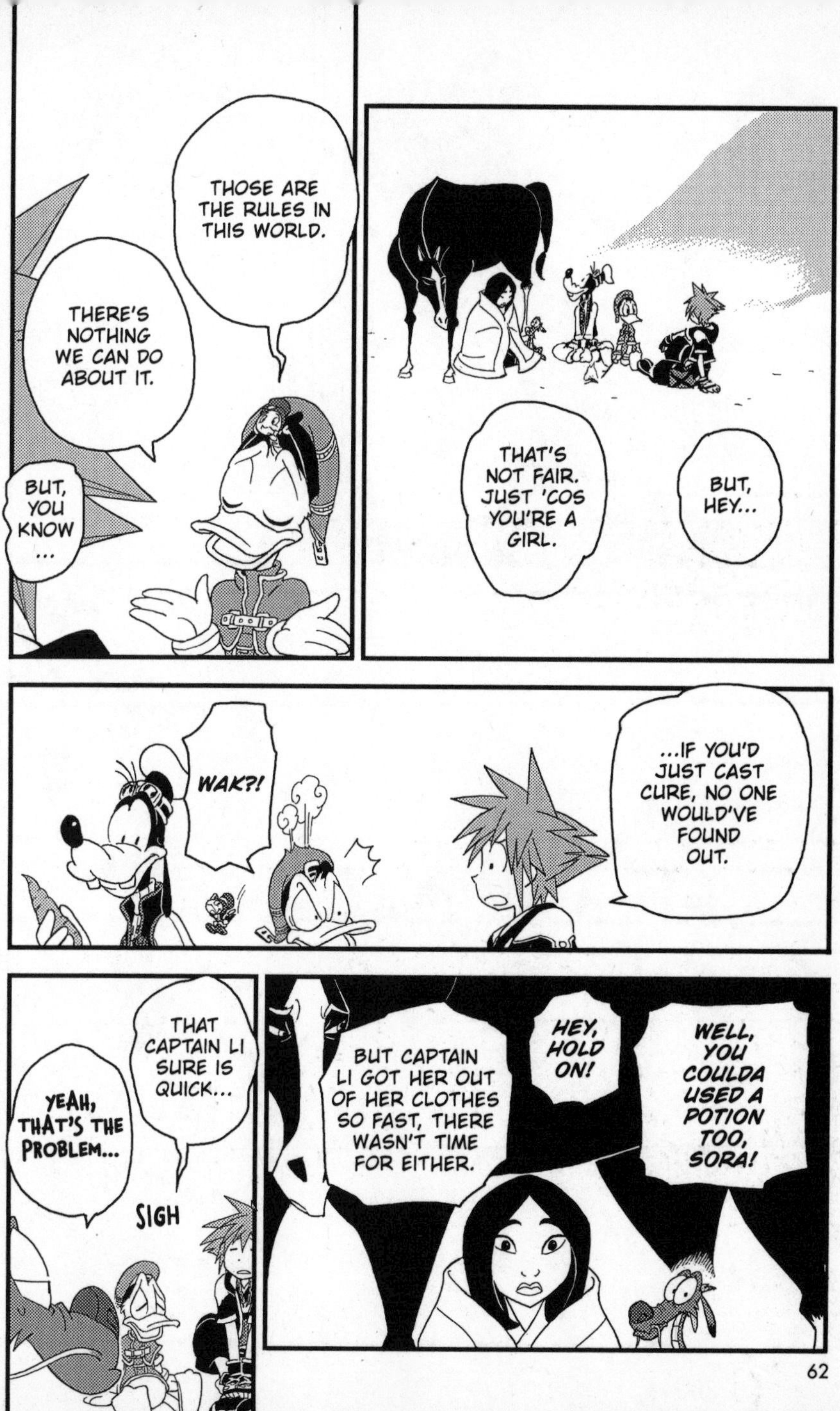
THAT'S NOT FAIR. JUST 'COS YOU'RE A GIRL.
BUT, HEY...
THOSE ARE THE RULES IN THIS WORLD.
THERE'S NOTHING WE CAN DO ABOUT IT.
BUT, YOU KNOW ...
...IF YOU'D JUST CAST CURE, NO ONE WOULD'VE FOUND OUT.
WAK?!
WELL, YOU COULDA USED A POTION TOO, SORA!
HEY, HOLD ON!
BUT CAPTAIN LI GOT HER OUT OF HER CLOTHES SO FAST, THERE WASN'T TIME FOR EITHER.
THAT CAPTAIN LI SURE IS QUICK...
YEAH, THAT'S THE PROBLEM...
SIGH

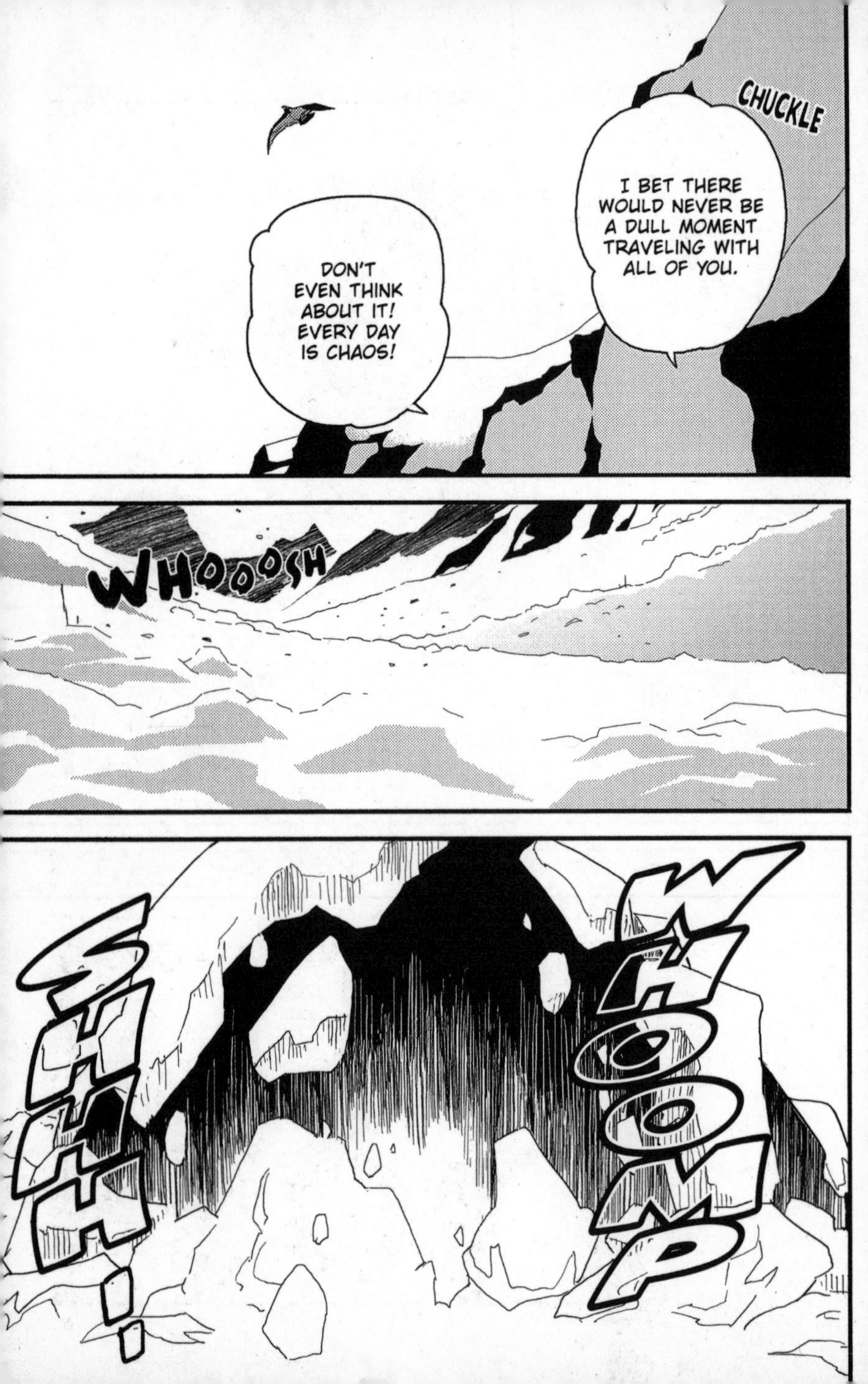
CHUCKLE
I BET THERE WOULD NEVER BE A DULL MOMENT TRAVELING WITH ALL OF YOU.
DON'T EVEN THINK ABOUT IT! EVERY DAY IS CHAOS!
WHOOOSH
WHOOMP
SHHH..

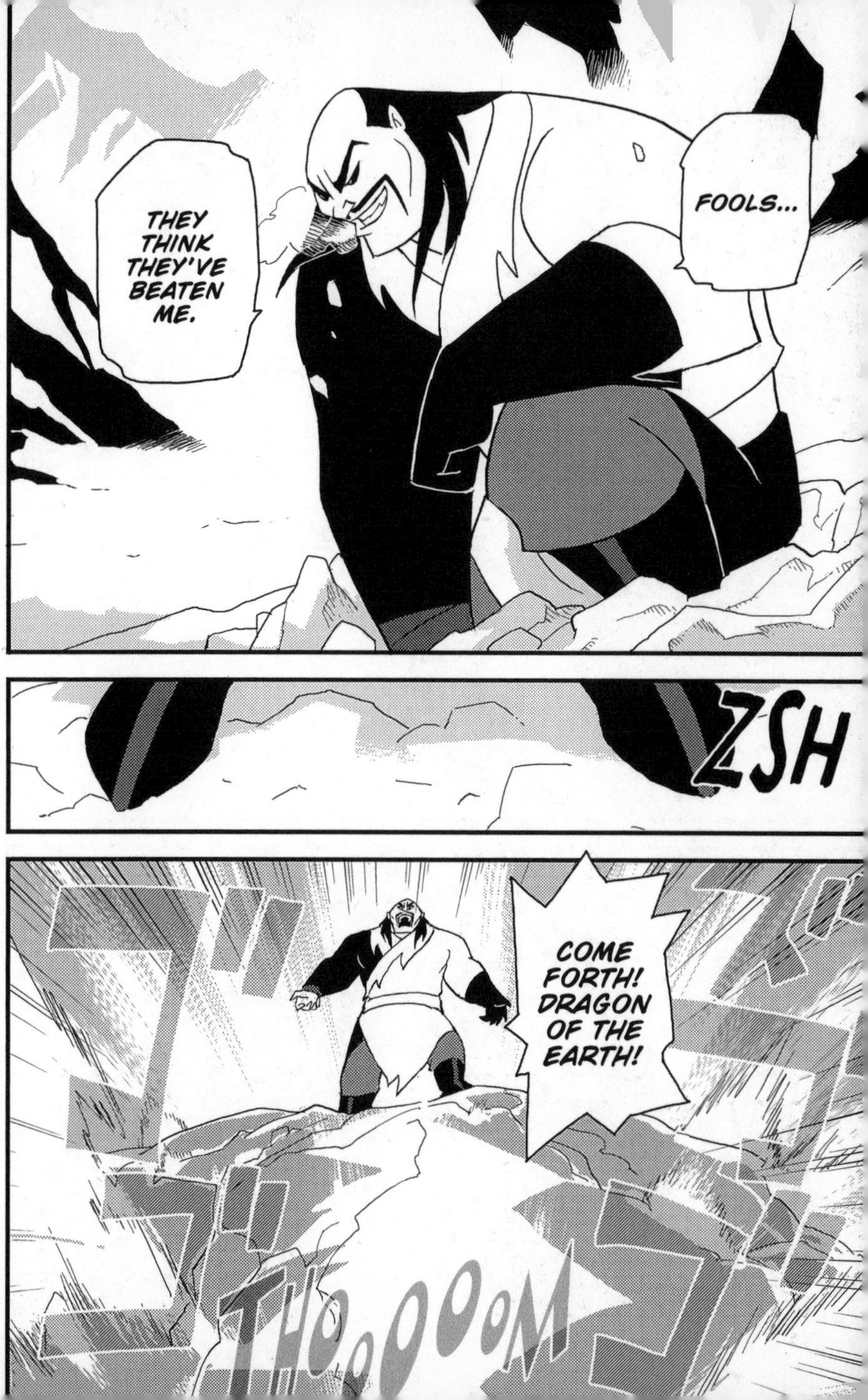
FOOLS...
THEY THINK THEY'VE BEATEN ME.
ZSH
COME FORTH! DRAGON OF THE EARTH!
THOOOOOM

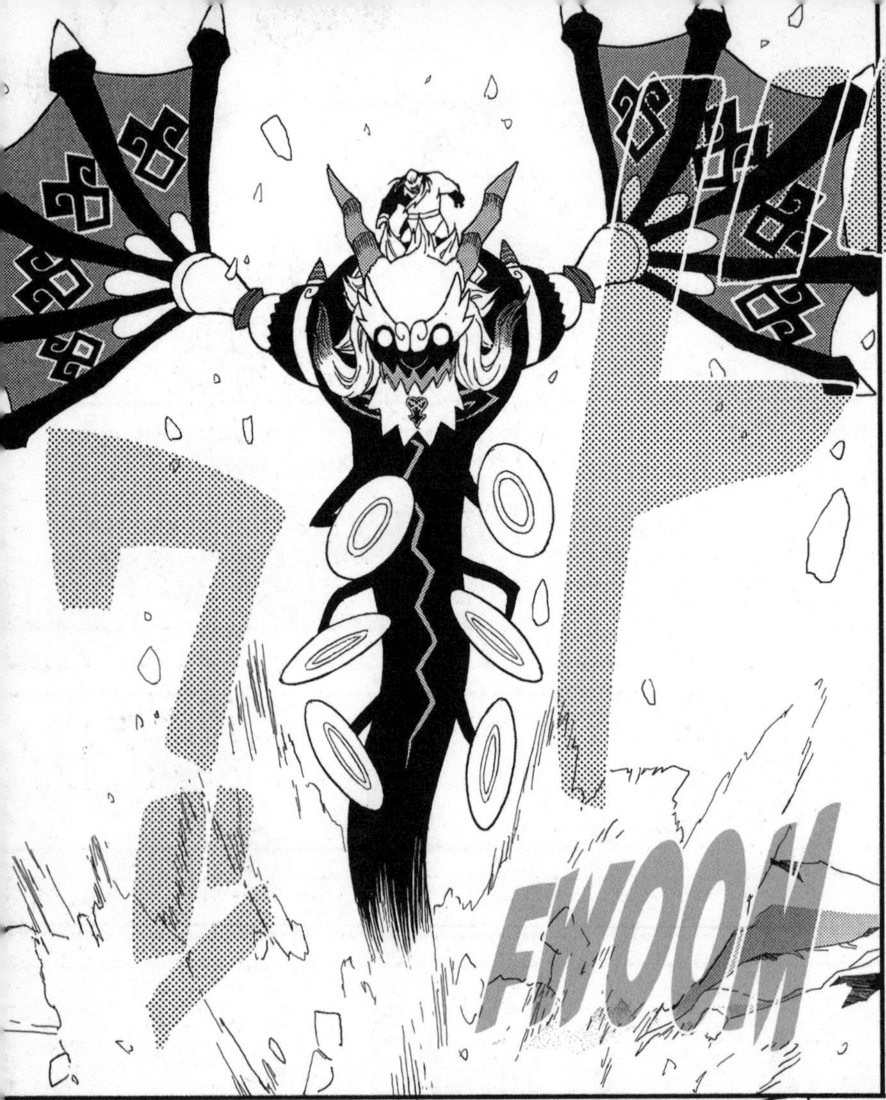
FWOOM

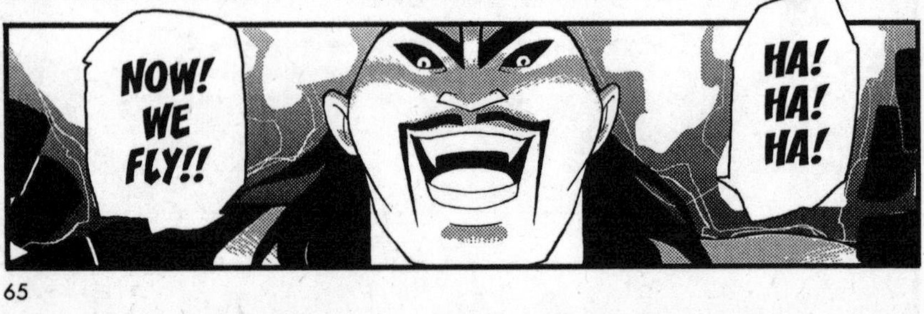
HA! HA! HA!
NOW! WE FLY!!

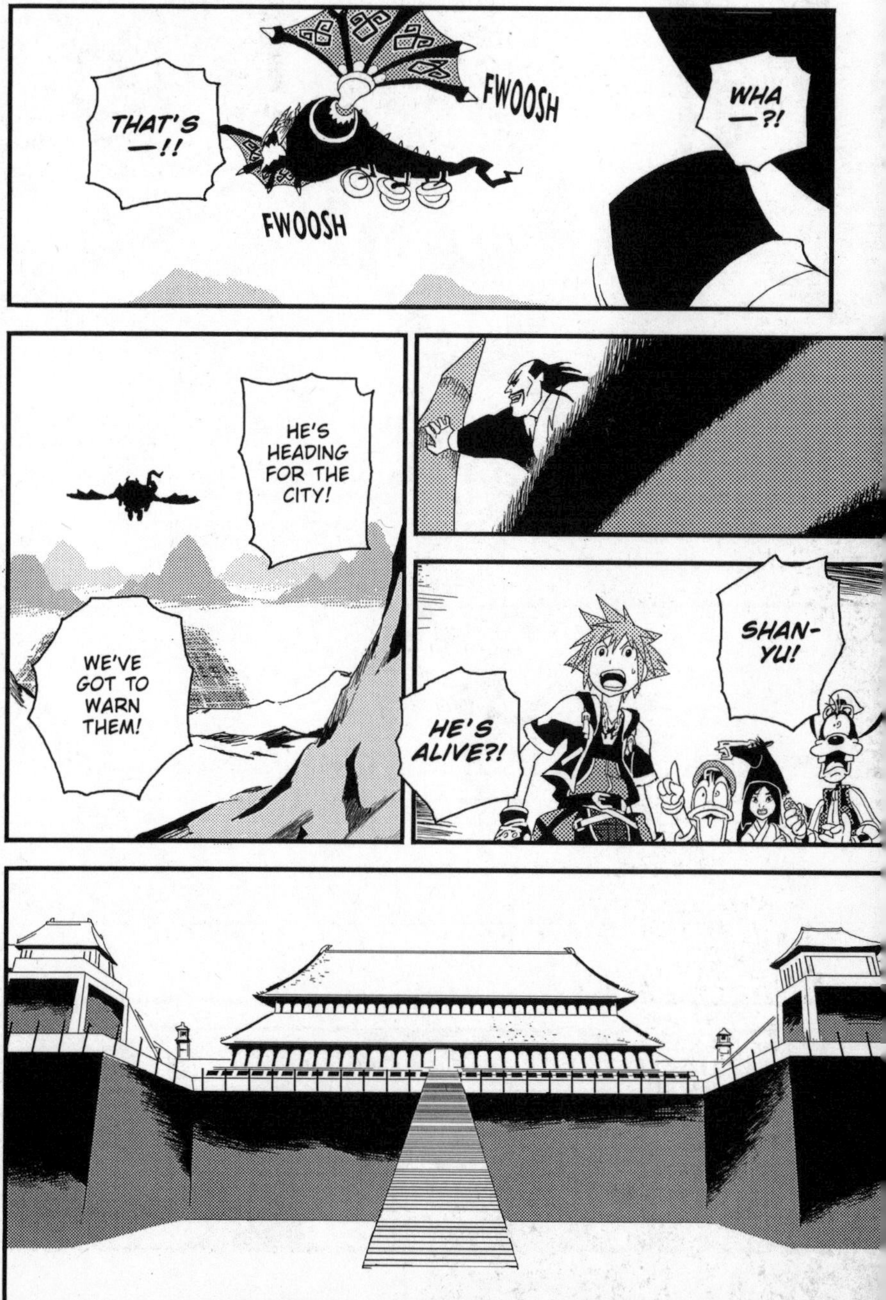
WHA—?!
FWOOSH
THAT'S—!!
FWOOSH
SHAN-YU!
HE'S ALIVE?!
HE'S HEADING FOR THE CITY!
WE'VE GOT TO WARN THEM!

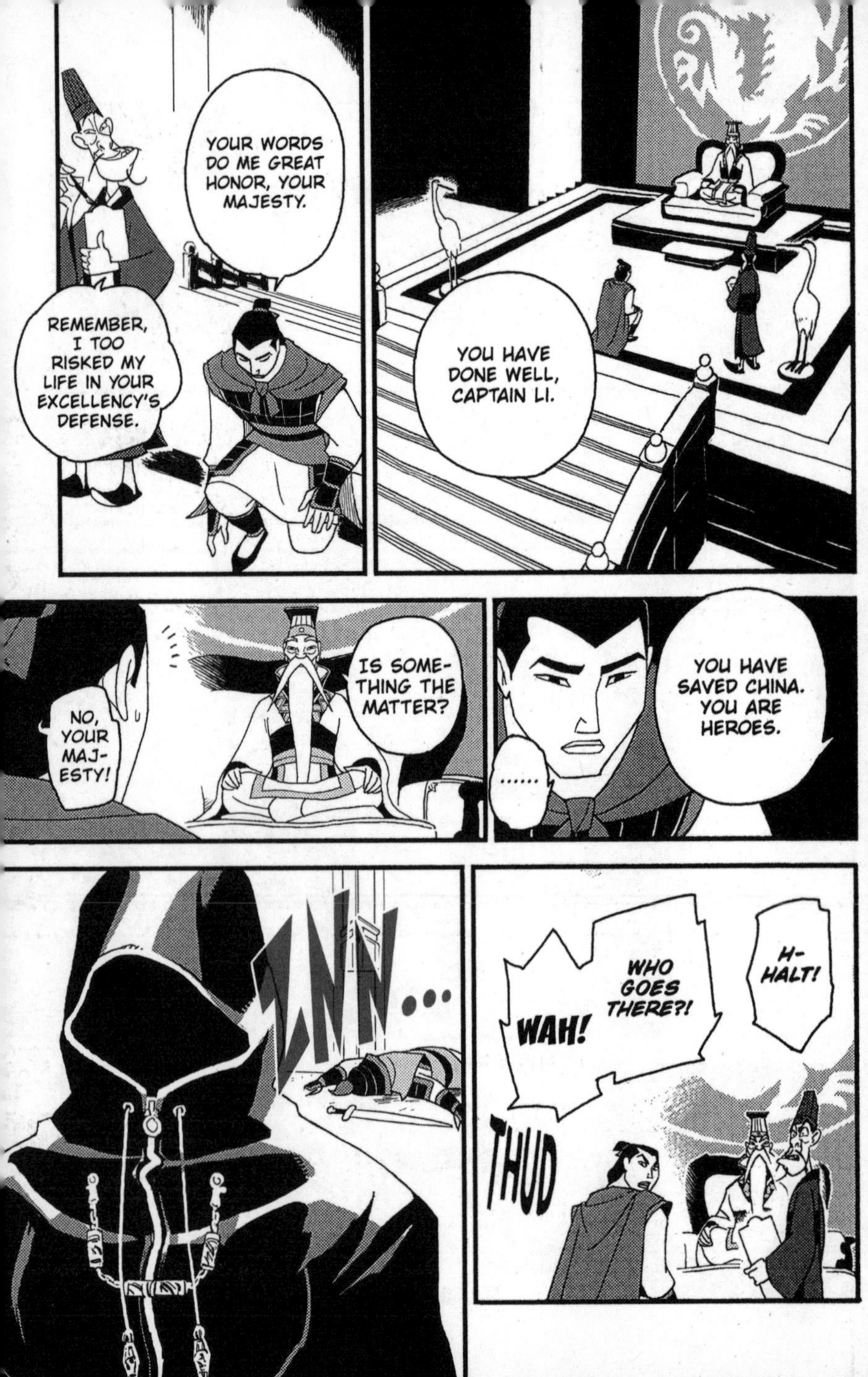
YOU HAVE DONE WELL, CAPTAIN LI.
YOUR WORDS DO ME GREAT HONOR, YOUR MAJESTY.
REMEMBER, I TOO RISKED MY LIFE IN YOUR EXCELLENCY'S DEFENSE.
YOU HAVE SAVED CHINA. YOU ARE HEROES.
......
IS SOME-THING THE MATTER?
NO, YOUR MAJ-ESTY!
H-HALT!
WHO GOES THERE?!
WAH!
THUD
ZNN...

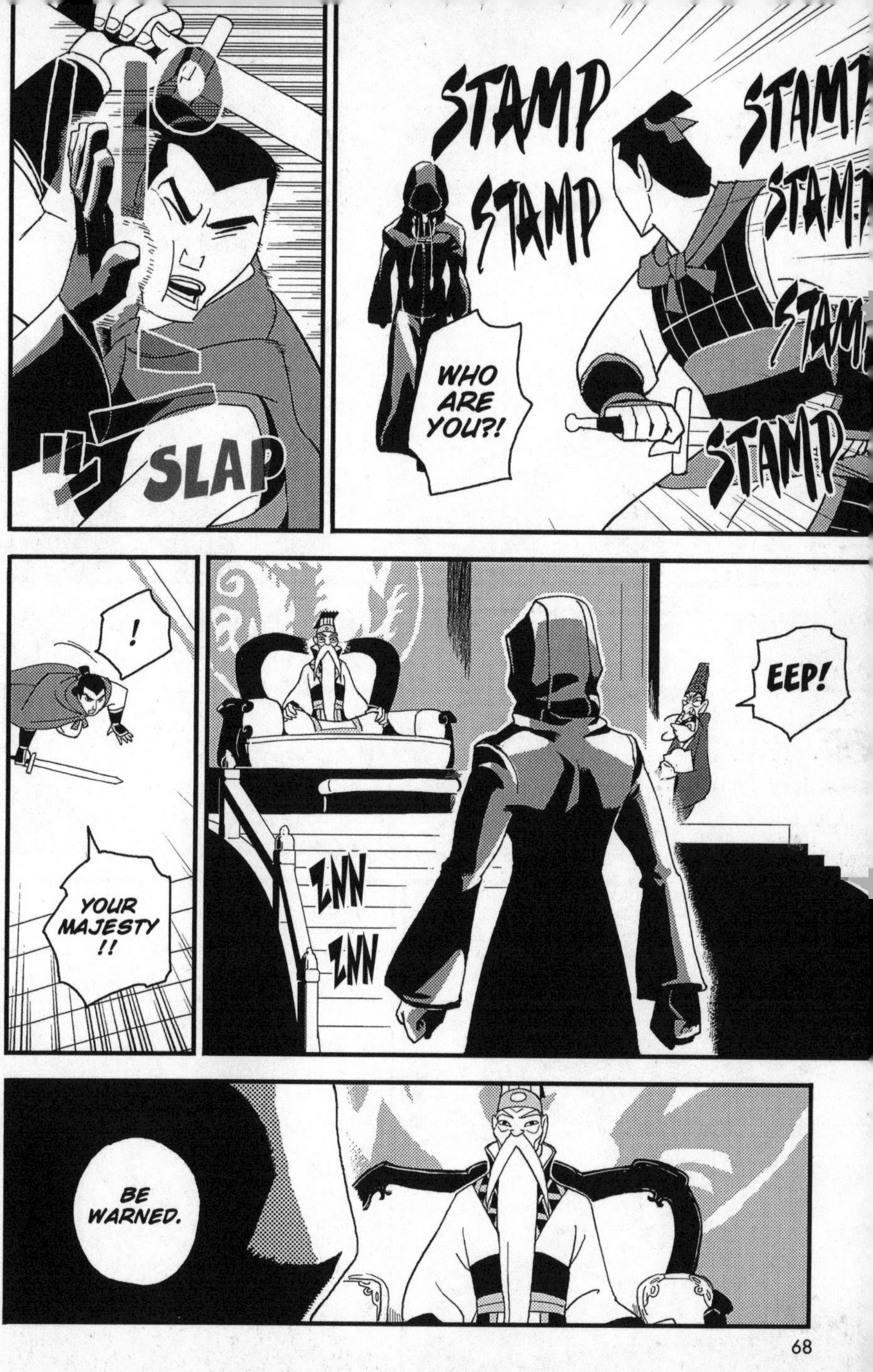
STAMP
STAMP
STAMP
STAMP
STAMP
STAMP
WHO ARE YOU?!
SLAP
EEP!
ZNN
ZNN
!
YOUR MAJESTY !!
BE WARNED.

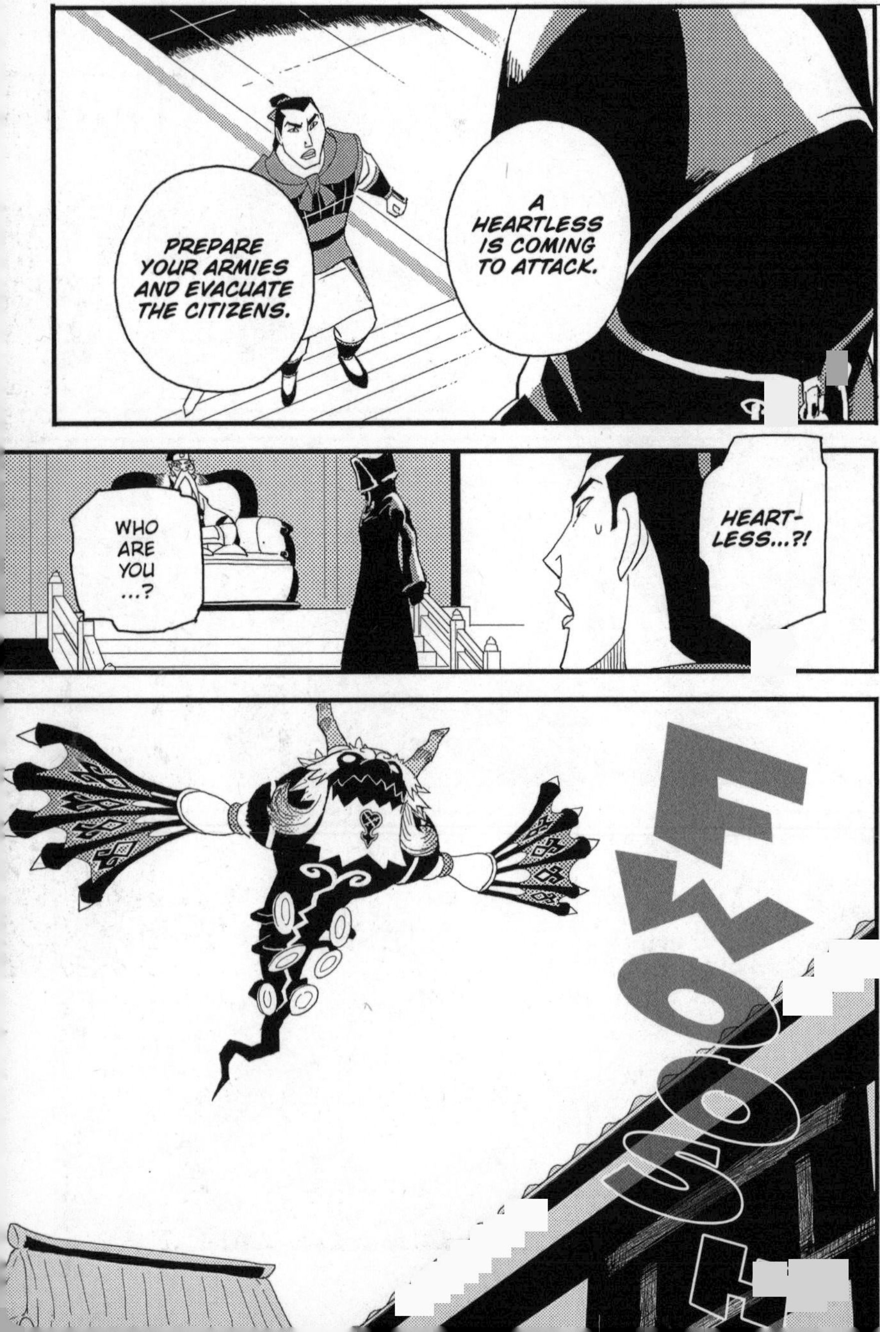
A HEARTLESS IS COMING TO ATTACK.
PREPARE YOUR ARMIES AND EVACUATE THE CITIZENS.
HEART-LESS...?!
WHO ARE YOU ...?

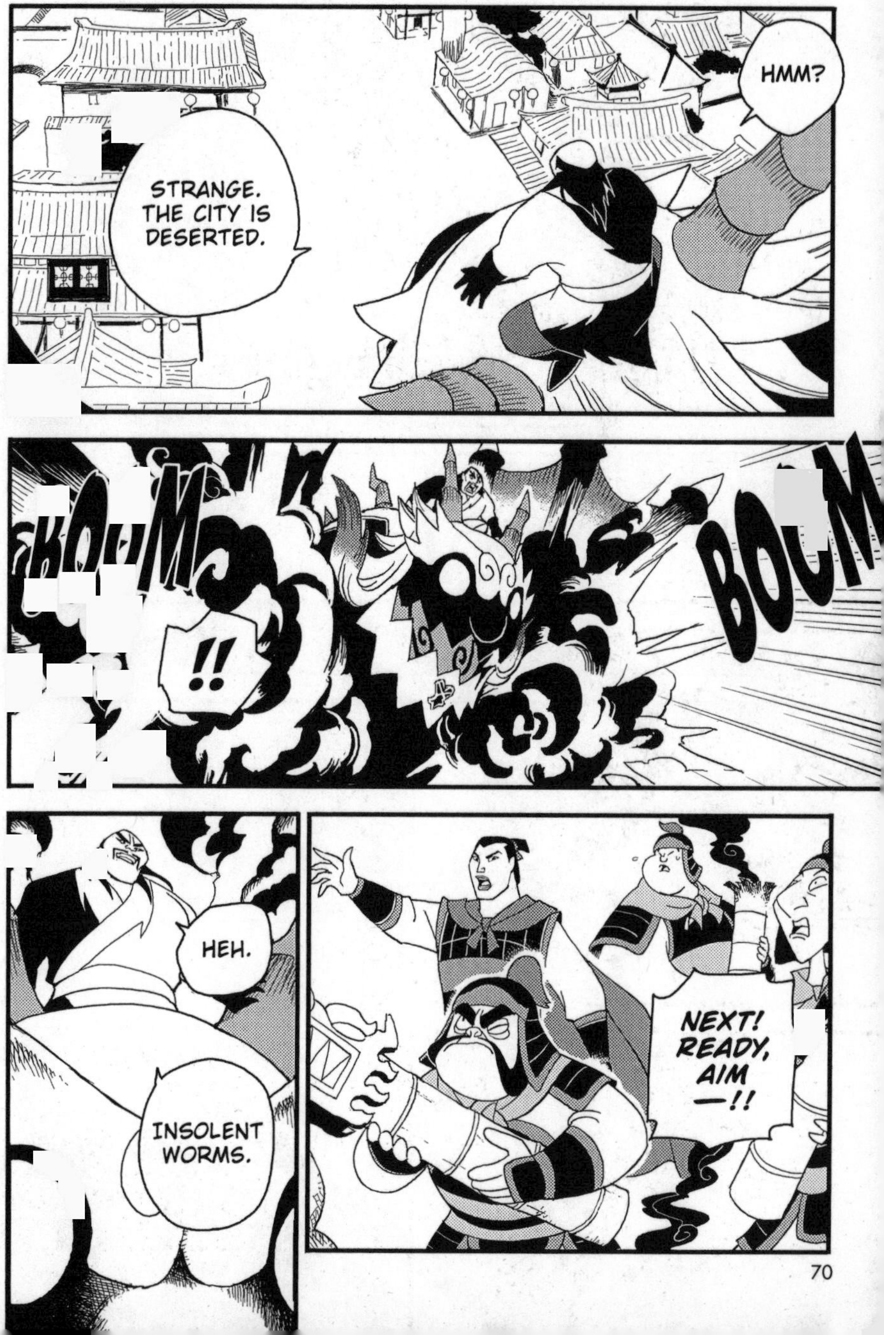
HMM?
STRANGE. THE CITY IS DESERTED.
BOOM
!!
BOOM
NEXT! READY, AIM—!!
HEH.
INSOLENT WORMS.

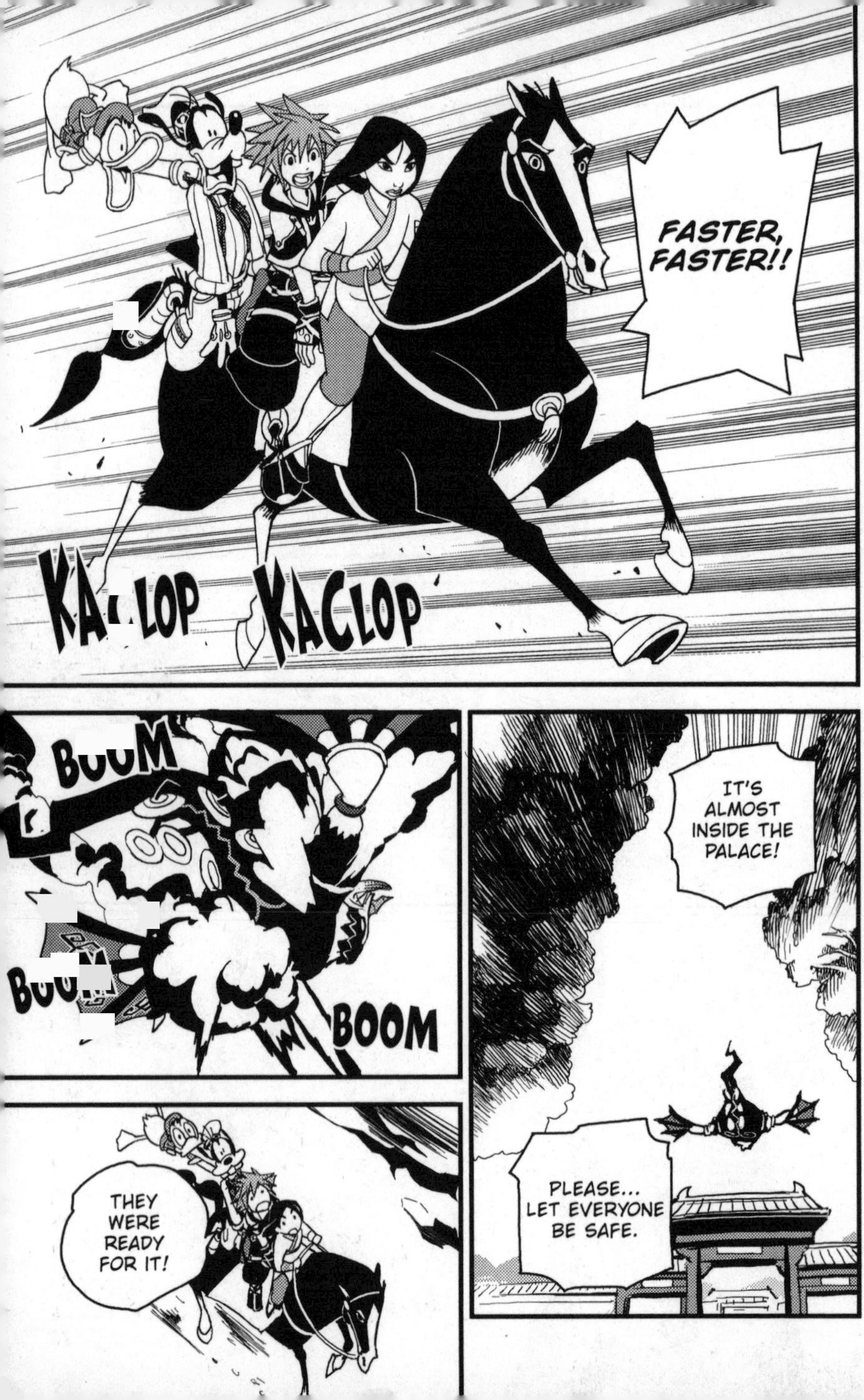
FASTER, FASTER!!
KACLOP
IT'S ALMOST INSIDE THE PALACE!
PLEASE... LET EVERYONE BE SAFE.
BOOM
BOOM
THEY WERE READY FOR IT!

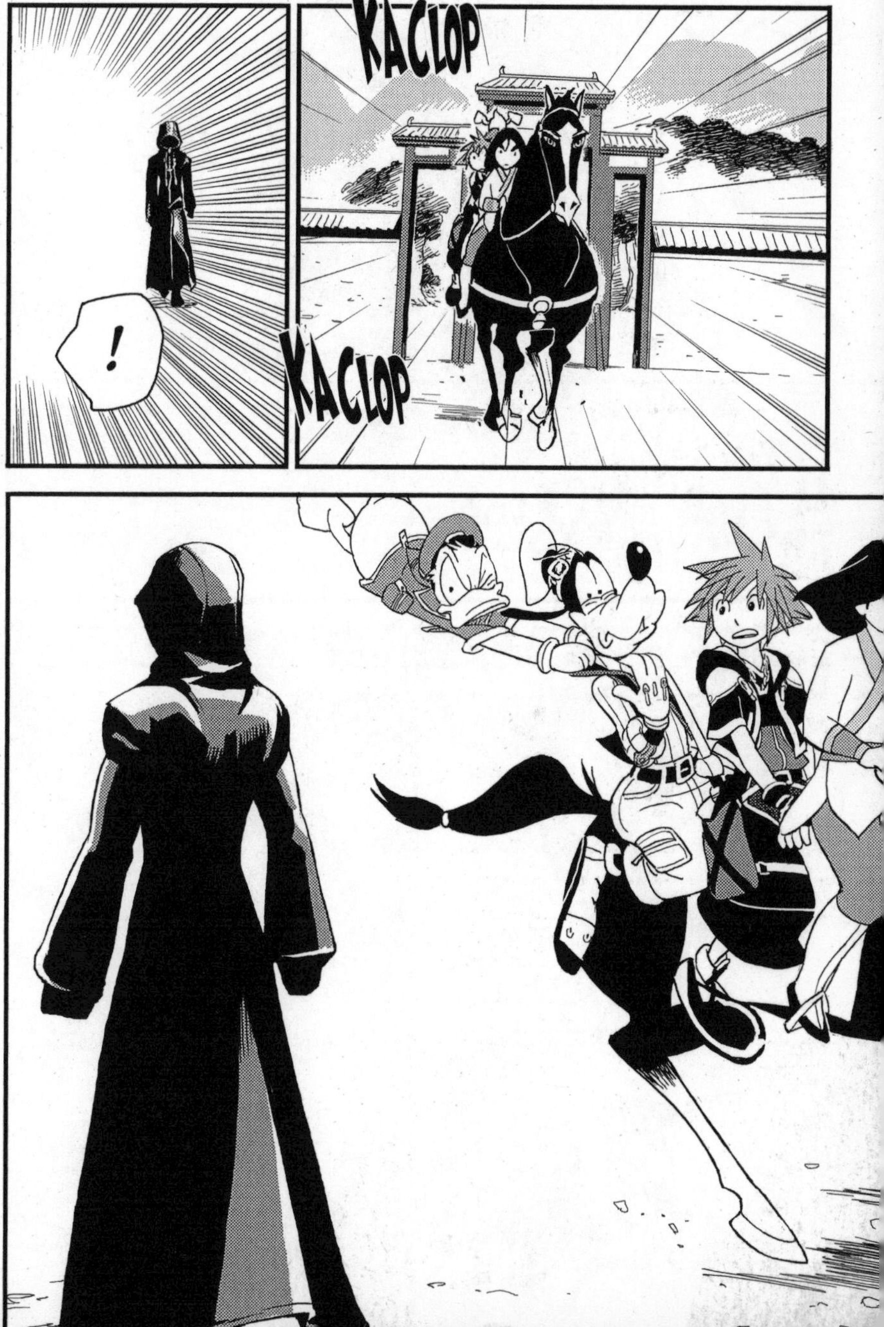
KACLOP
KACLOP
!

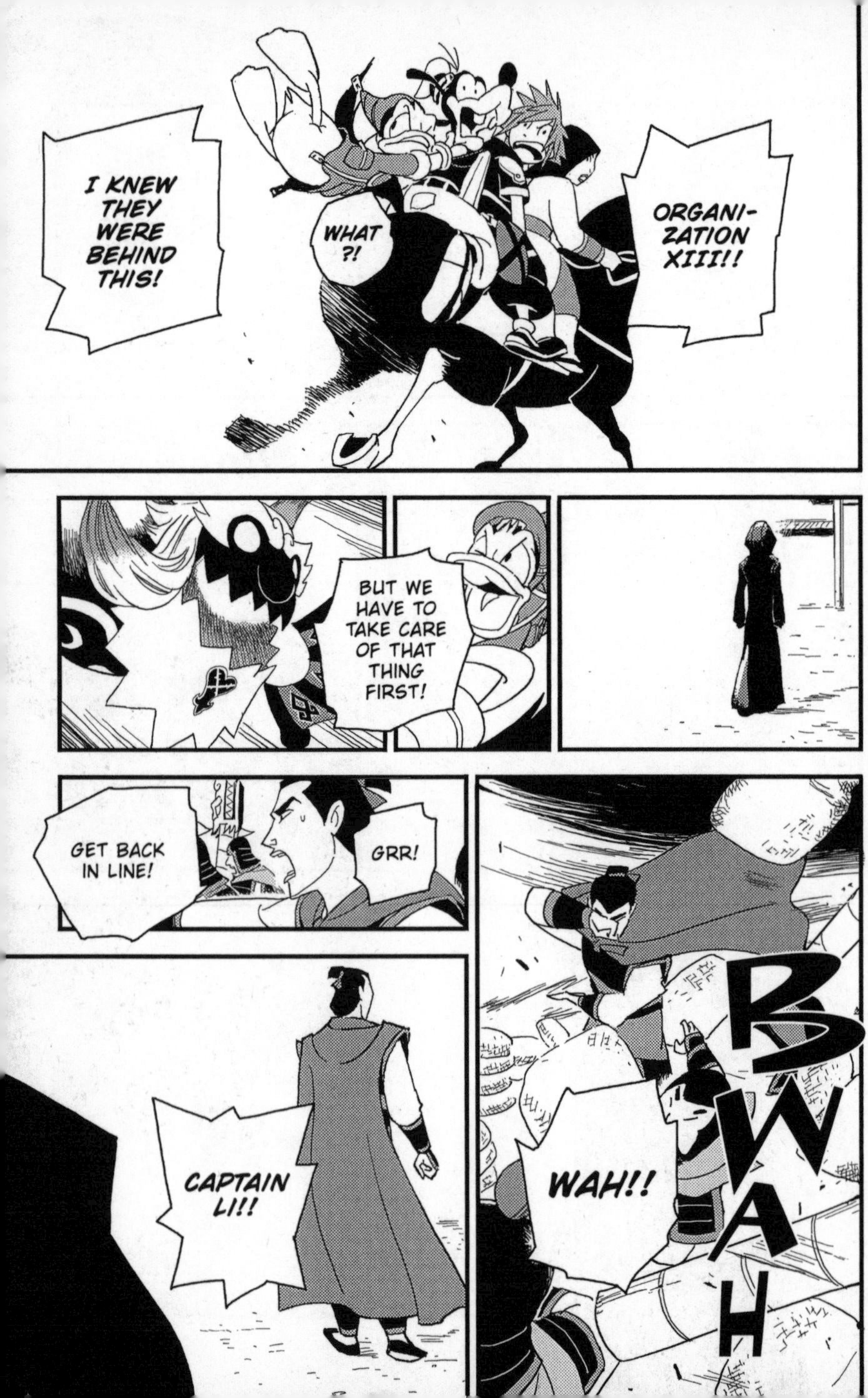
ORGANI-ZATION XIII!!
WHAT?!
I KNEW THEY WERE BEHIND THIS!
BUT WE HAVE TO TAKE CARE OF THAT THING FIRST!
BWAH
WAH!!
GRR!
GET BACK IN LINE!
CAPTAIN LI!!

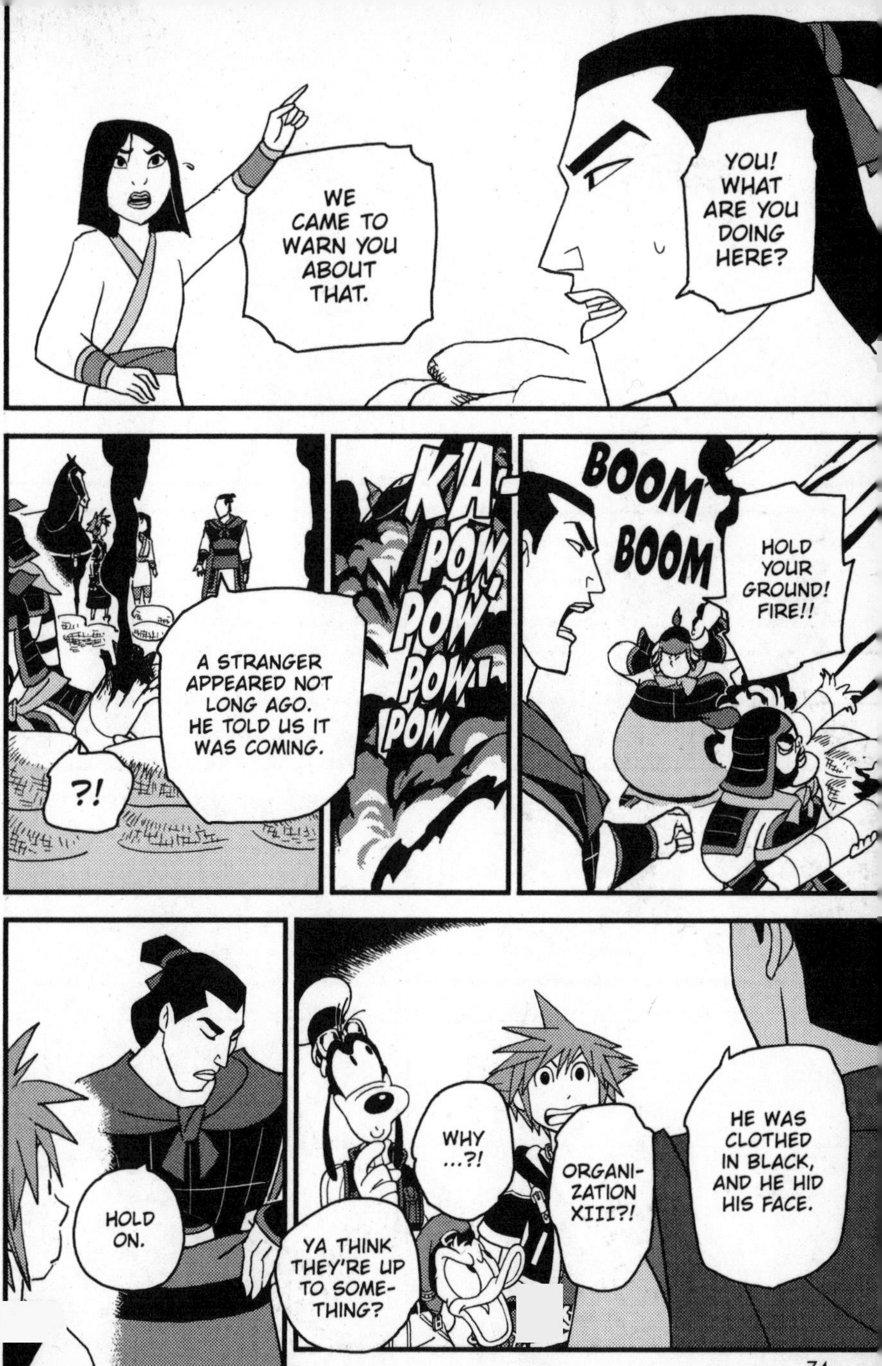
YOU! WHAT ARE YOU DOING HERE?
WE CAME TO WARN YOU ABOUT THAT.
BOOM BOOM
HOLD YOUR GROUND! FIRE!!
KA-POW, POW, POW, POW
A STRANGER APPEARED NOT LONG AGO. HE TOLD US IT WAS COMING.
?!
HE WAS CLOTHED IN BLACK, AND HE HID HIS FACE.
ORGANIZATION XIII?!
WHY...?!
YA THINK THEY'RE UP TO SOMETHING?
HOLD ON.

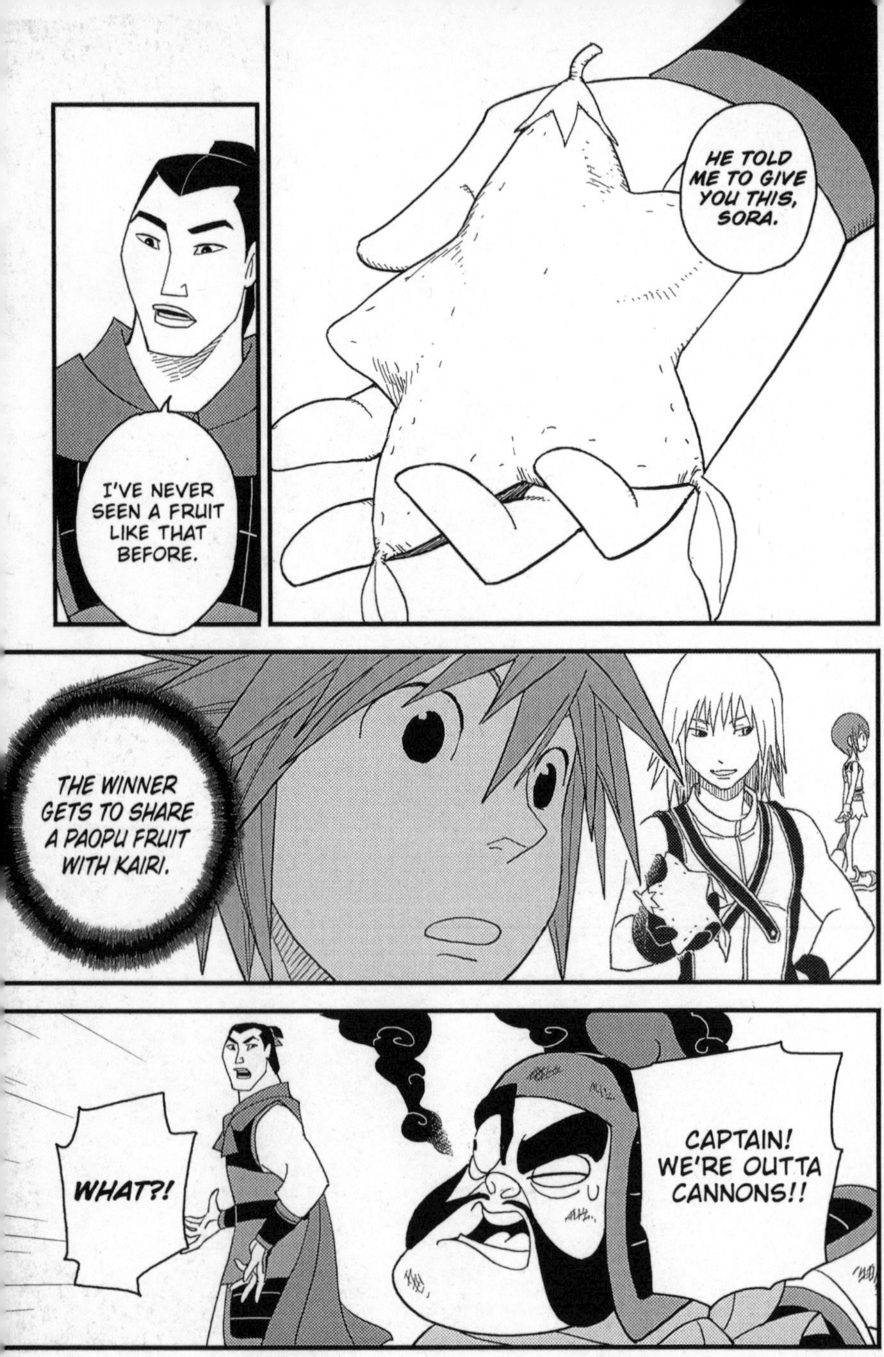
HE TOLD ME TO GIVE YOU THIS, SORA.
I'VE NEVER SEEN A FRUIT LIKE THAT BEFORE.
THE WINNER GETS TO SHARE A PAOPU FRUIT WITH KAIRI.
CAPTAIN! WE'RE OUTTA CANNONS!!
WHAT?!

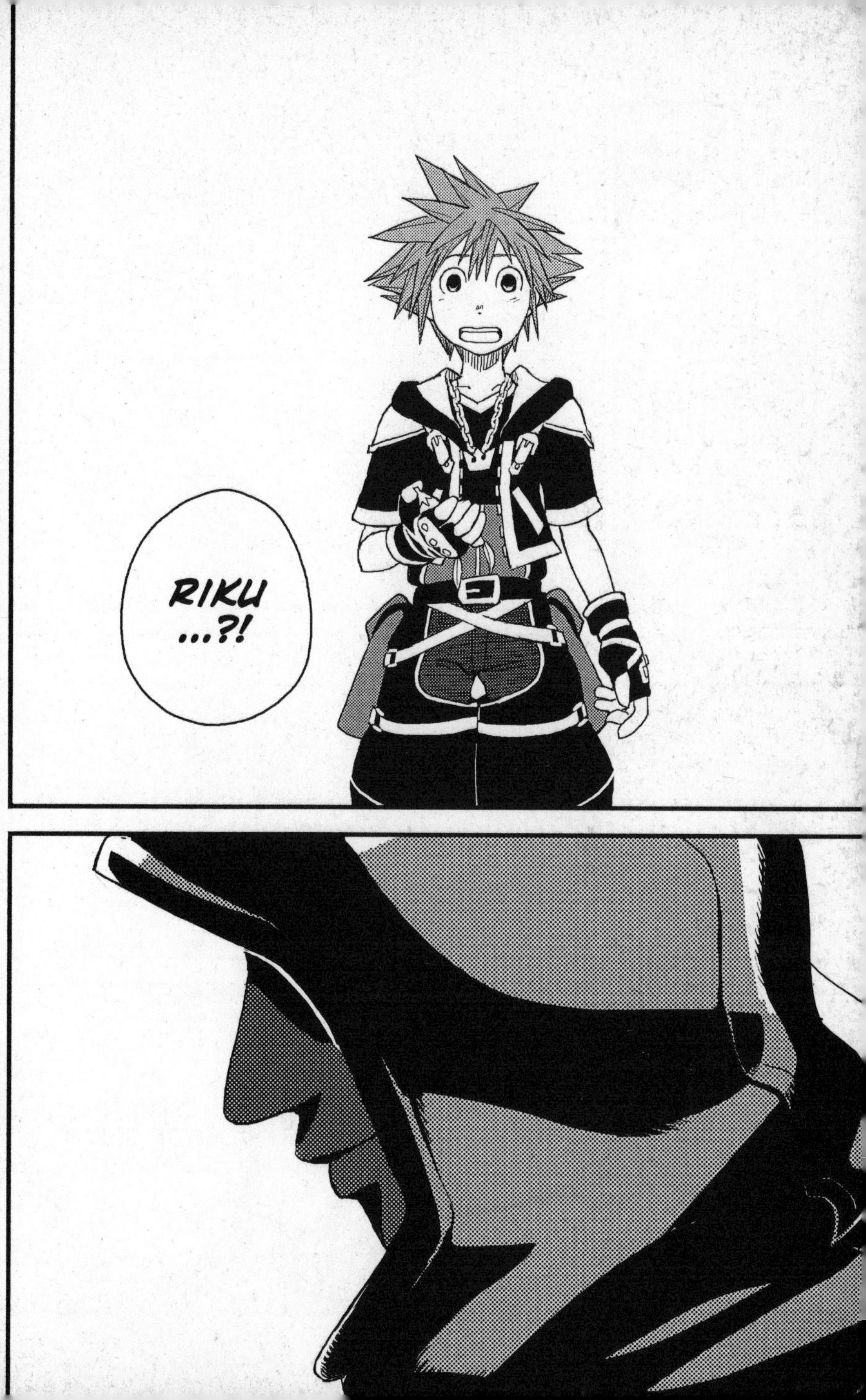
RIKU ...?!

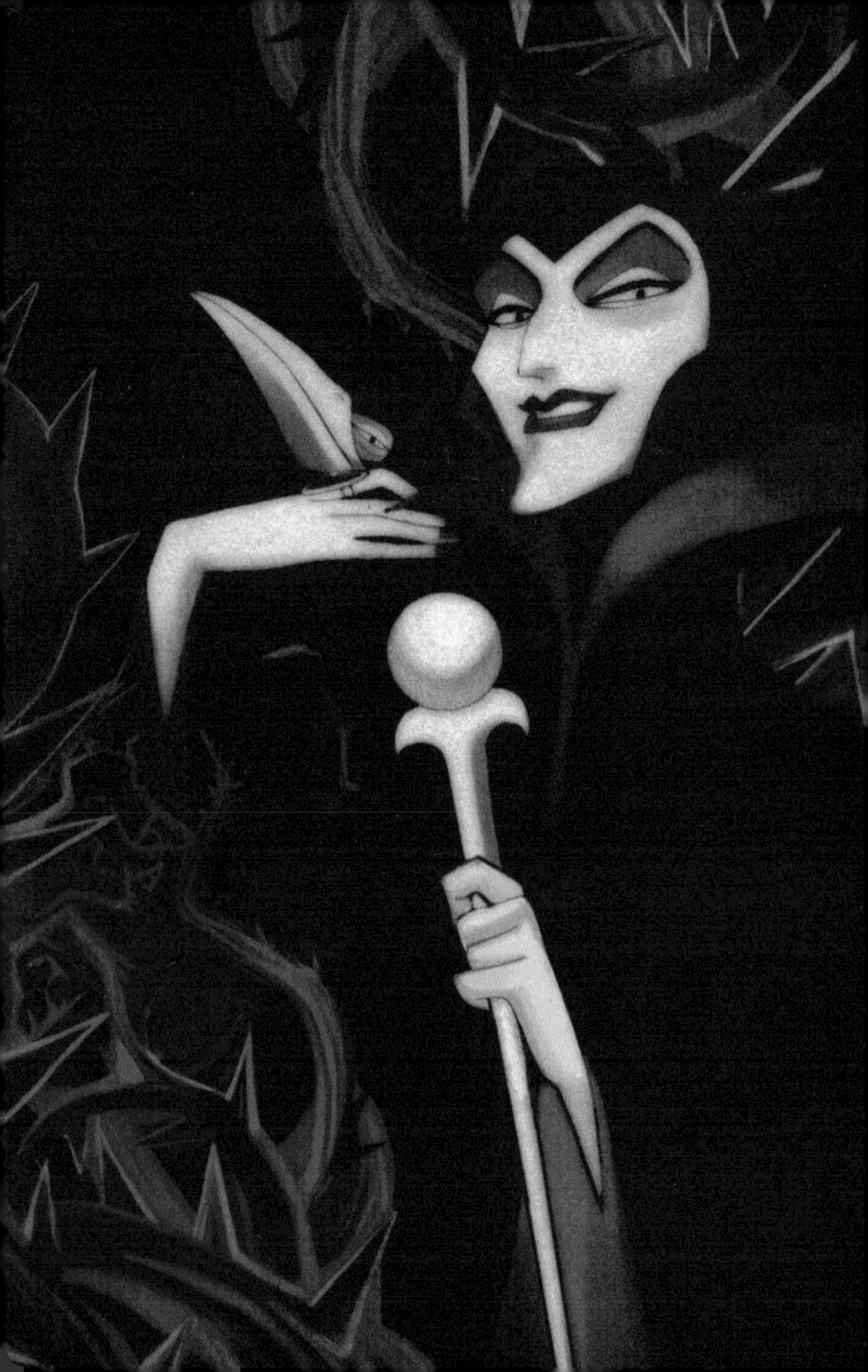

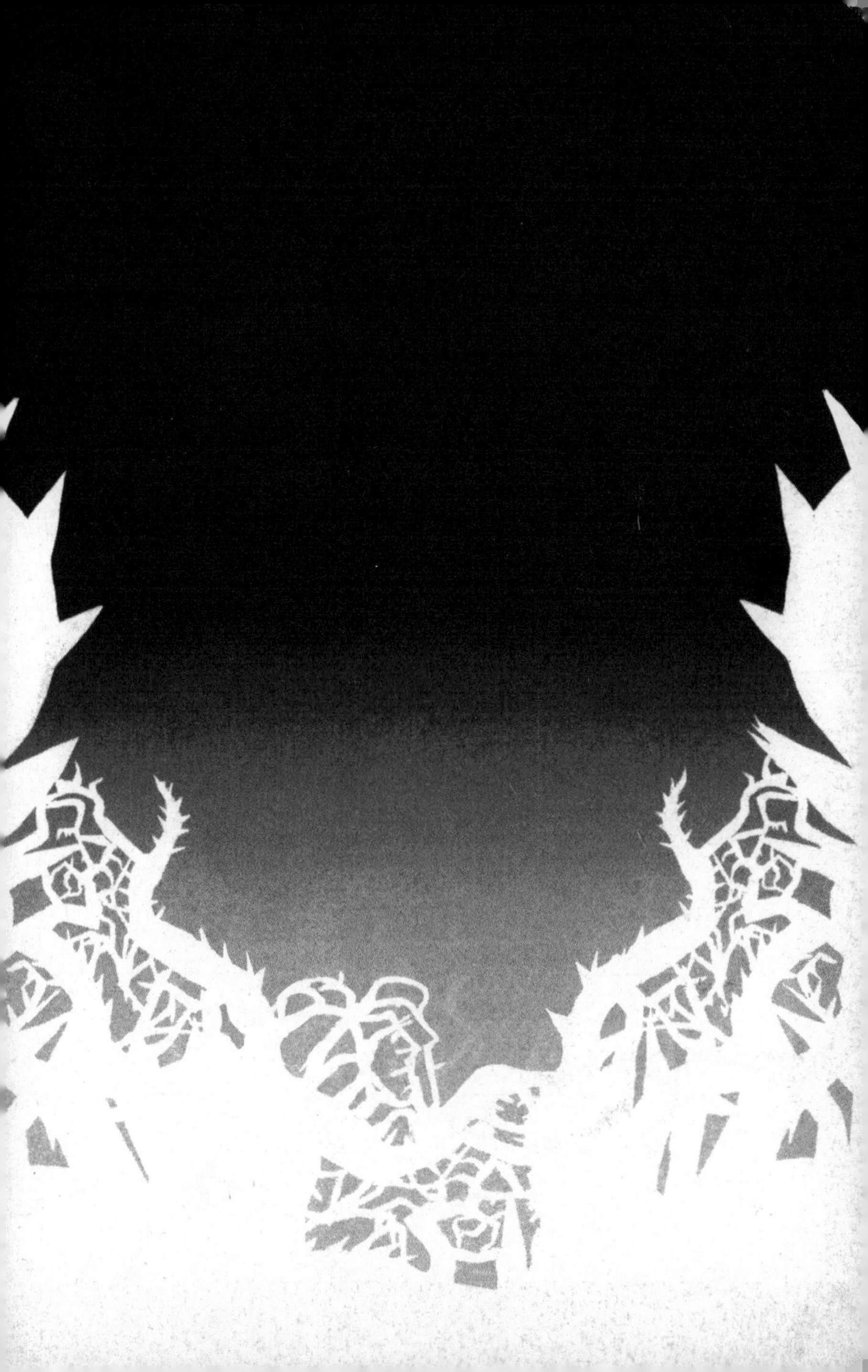

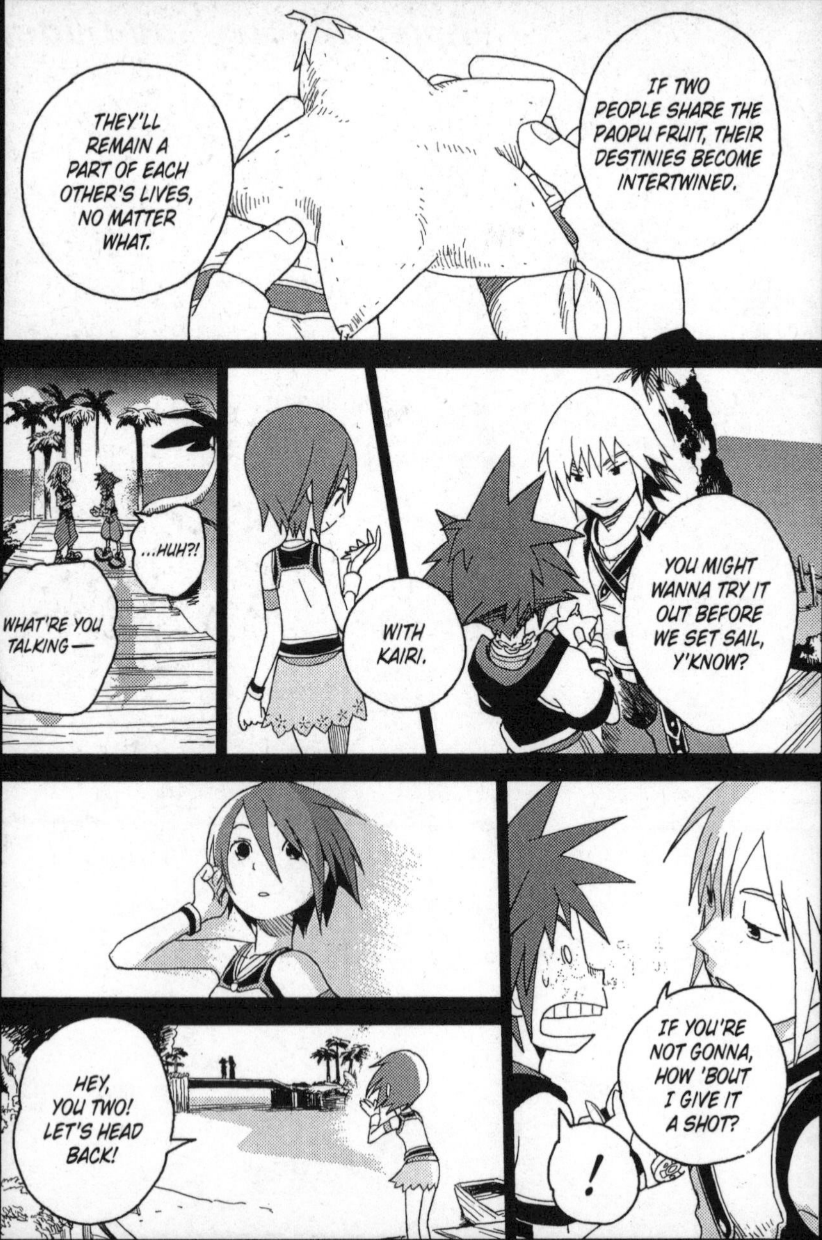
IF TWO PEOPLE SHARE THE PAOPU FRUIT, THEIR DESTINIES BECOME INTERTWINED.
THEY'LL REMAIN A PART OF EACH OTHER'S LIVES, NO MATTER WHAT.
YOU MIGHT WANNA TRY IT OUT BEFORE WE SET SAIL, Y'KNOW?
WITH KAIRI.
...HUH?!
WHAT'RE YOU TALKING—
IF YOU'RE NOT GONNA, HOW 'BOUT I GIVE IT A SHOT?
!
HEY, YOU TWO! LET'S HEAD BACK!

Chapter 22: One Bad Dude

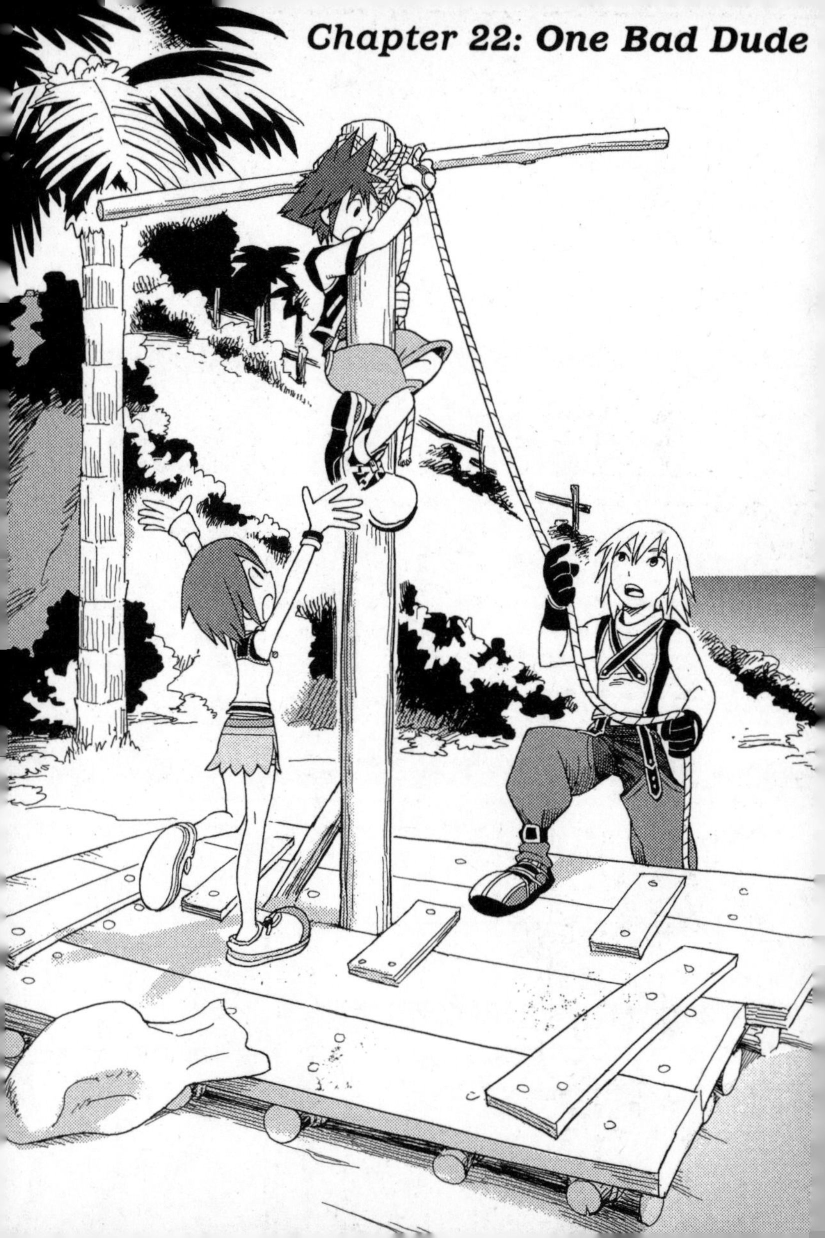

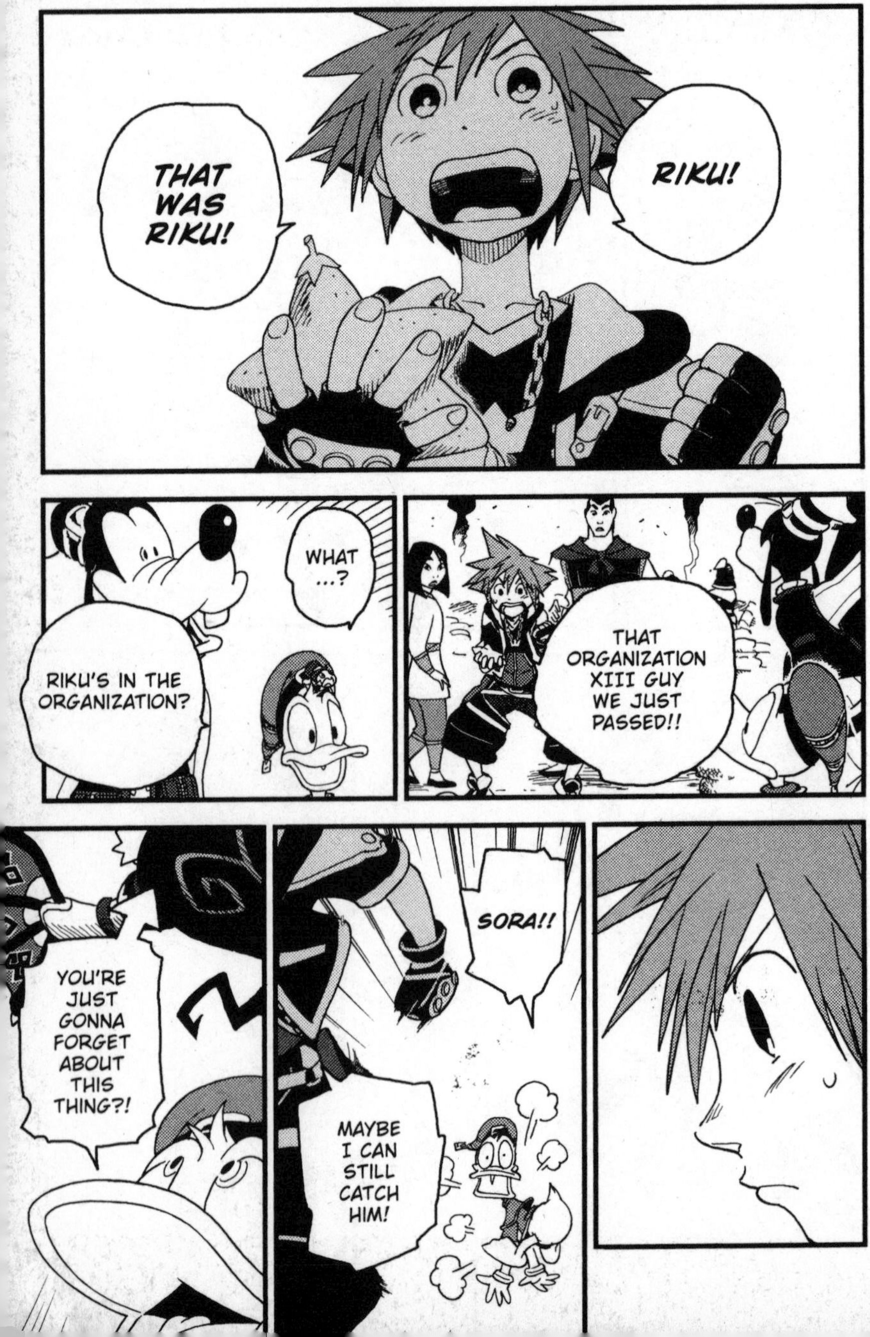
RIKU!
THAT WAS RIKU!
THAT ORGANIZATION XIII GUY WE JUST PASSED!!
WHAT ...?
RIKU'S IN THE ORGANIZATION?
SORA!!
MAYBE I CAN STILL CATCH HIM!
YOU'RE JUST GONNA FORGET ABOUT THIS THING?!

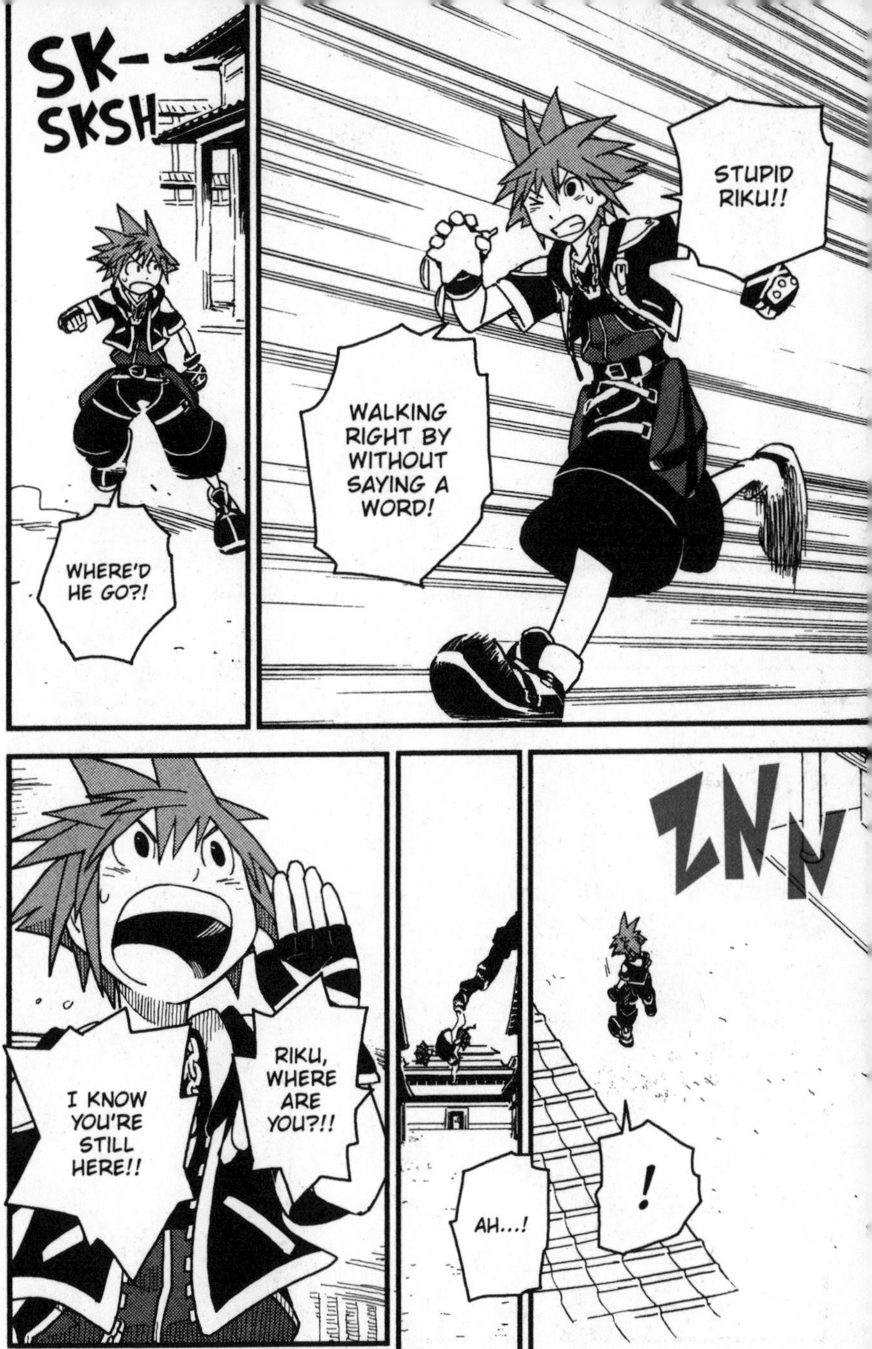
STUPID RIKU!!
WALKING RIGHT BY WITHOUT SAYING A WORD!
SK-SKSH
WHERE'D HE GO?!
ZNN
!
AH...!
RIKU, WHERE ARE YOU?!!
I KNOW YOU'RE STILL HERE!!

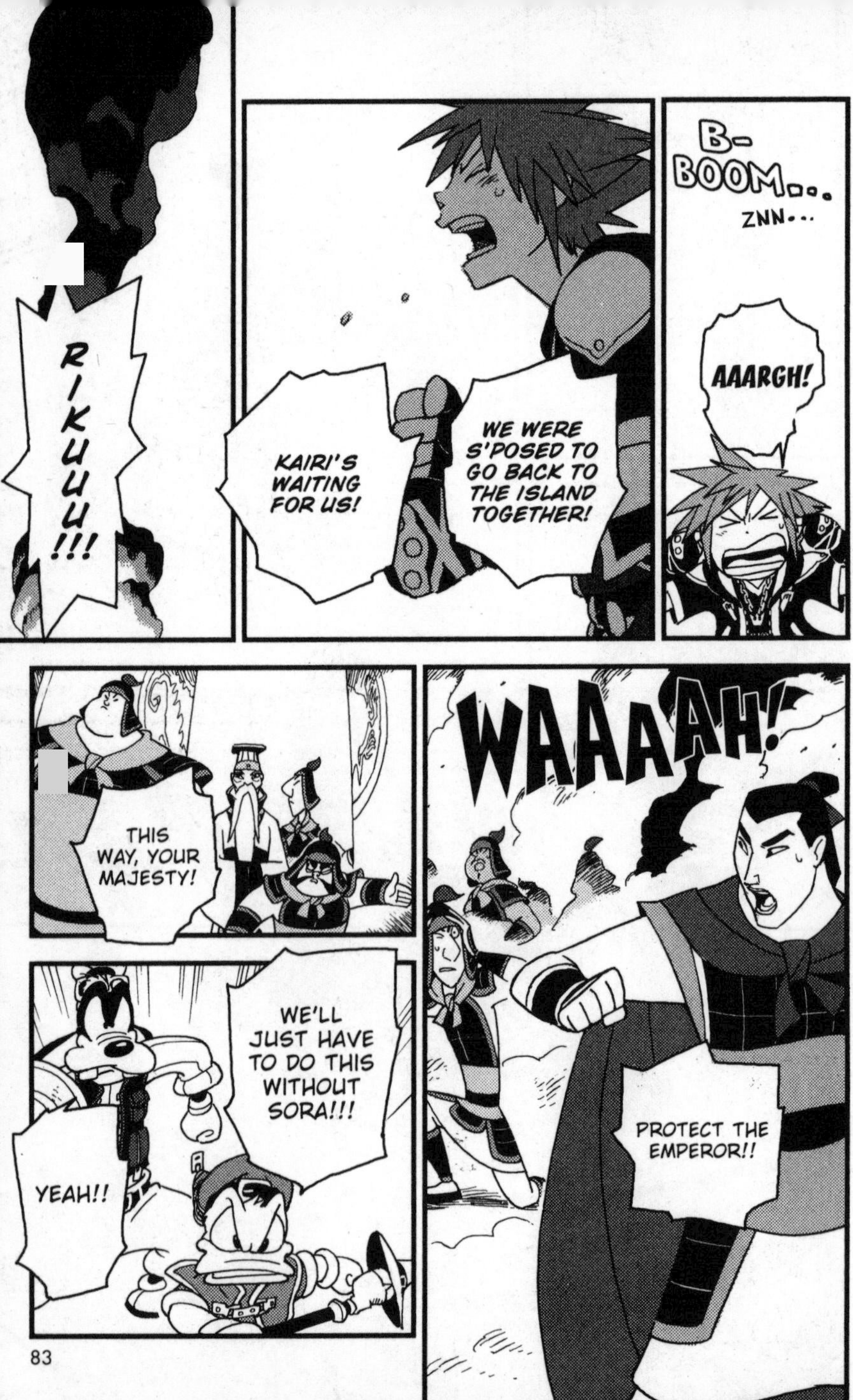

B-BOOM...
ZNN...
AAARGH!
WE WERE S'POSED TO GO BACK TO THE ISLAND TOGETHER!
KAIRI'S WAITING FOR US!
RIKUUU!!!
WAAAAH!
PROTECT THE EMPEROR!!
THIS WAY, YOUR MAJESTY!
WE'LL JUST HAVE TO DO THIS WITHOUT SORA!!!
YEAH!!

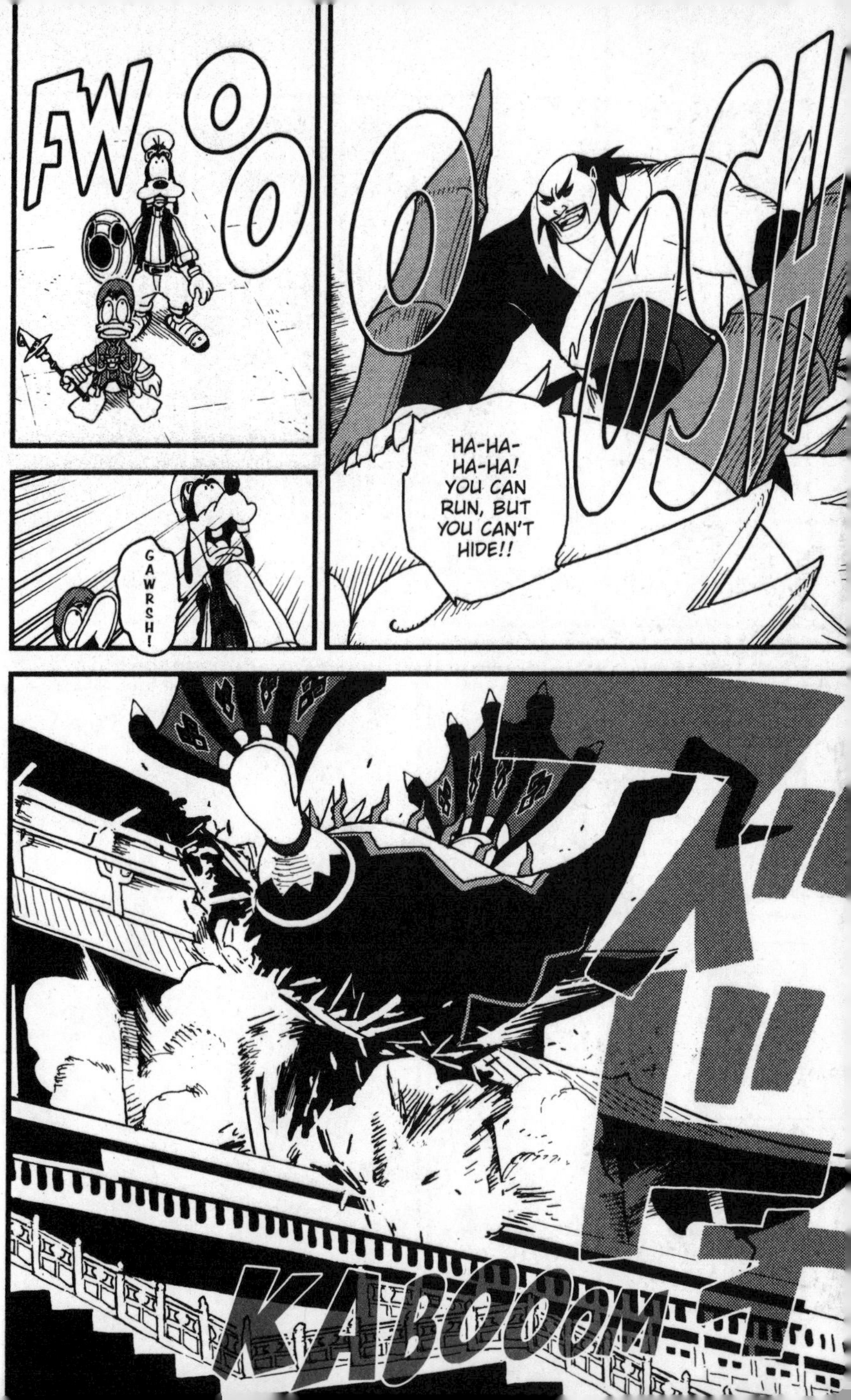
FWOOOSH
HA-HA-HA-HA! YOU CAN RUN, BUT YOU CAN'T HIDE!!
GAWRSH!
KABOOOM

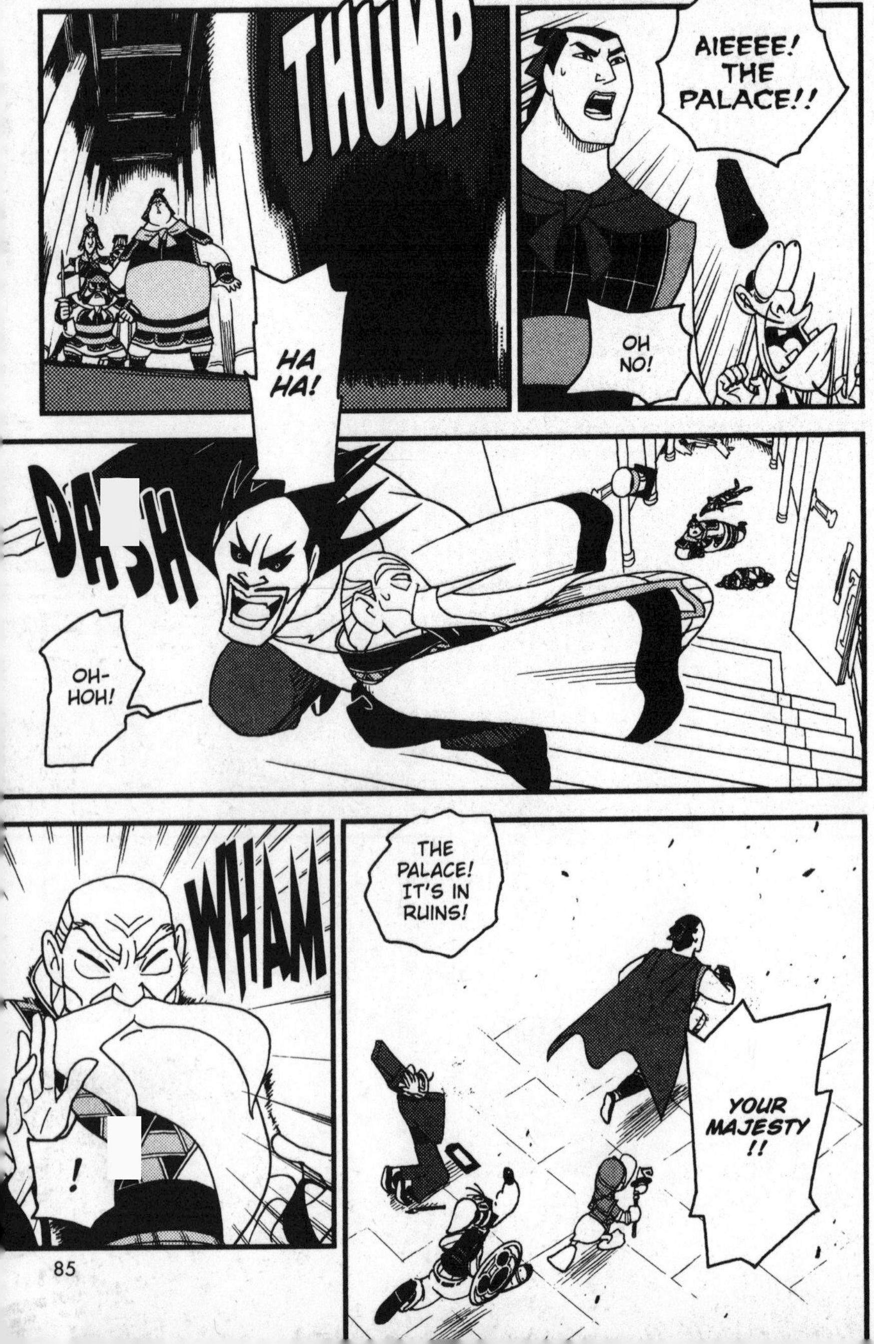
AIEEEE! THE PALACE!!
OH NO!
THUMP
HA HA!
DASH
OH-HOH!
THE PALACE! IT'S IN RUINS!
YOUR MAJESTY !!
WHAM
!

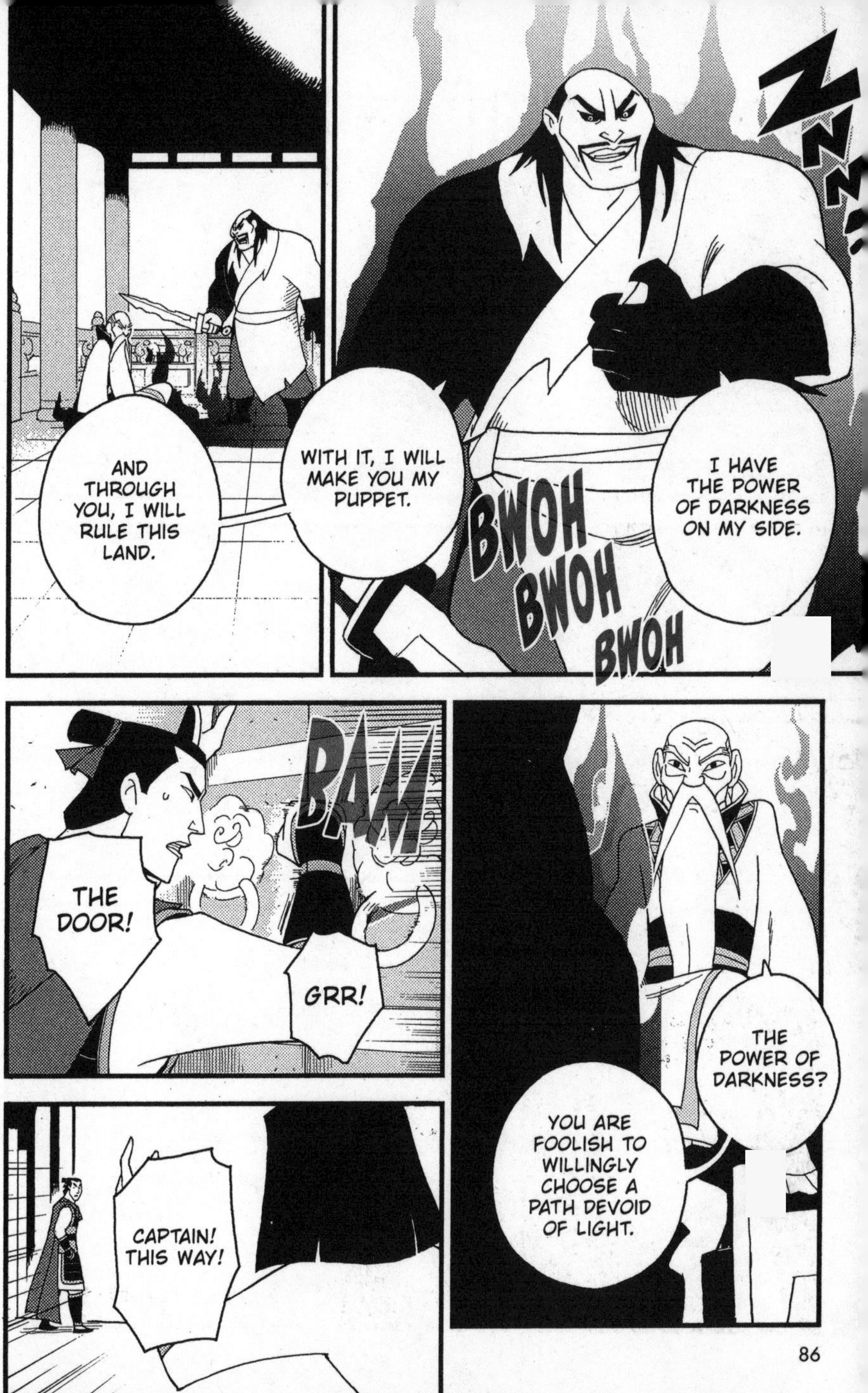
NNN!!
I HAVE THE POWER OF DARKNESS ON MY SIDE.
BWOH BWOH BWOH
WITH IT, I WILL MAKE YOU MY PUPPET.
AND THROUGH YOU, I WILL RULE THIS LAND.
THE POWER OF DARKNESS?
YOU ARE FOOLISH TO WILLINGLY CHOOSE A PATH DEVOID OF LIGHT.
BAM
THE DOOR!
GRR!
CAPTAIN! THIS WAY!

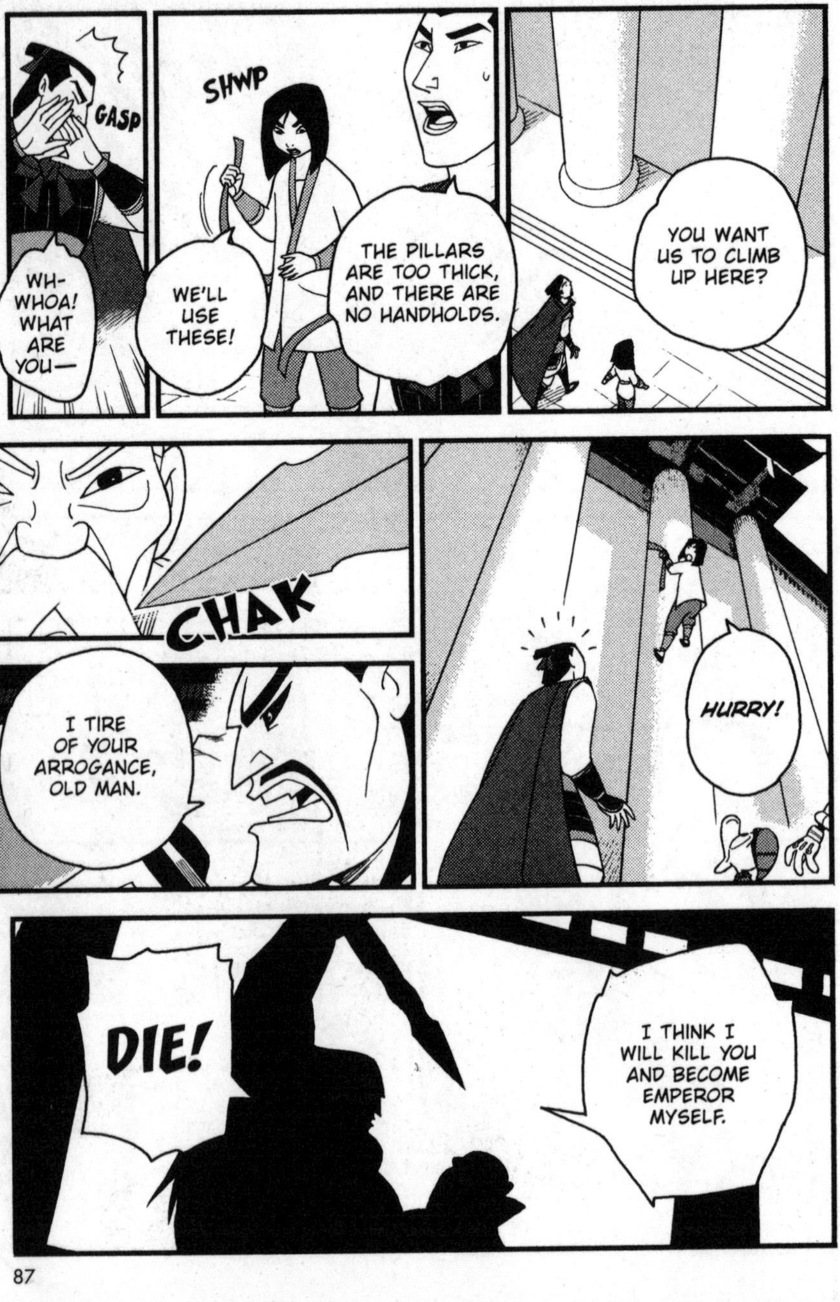
YOU WANT US TO CLIMB UP HERE?
THE PILLARS ARE TOO THICK, AND THERE ARE NO HANDHOLDS.
SHWP
WE'LL USE THESE!
GASP
WH-WHOA! WHAT ARE YOU—
HURRY!
CHAK
I TIRE OF YOUR ARROGANCE, OLD MAN.
I THINK I WILL KILL YOU AND BECOME EMPEROR MYSELF.
DIE!

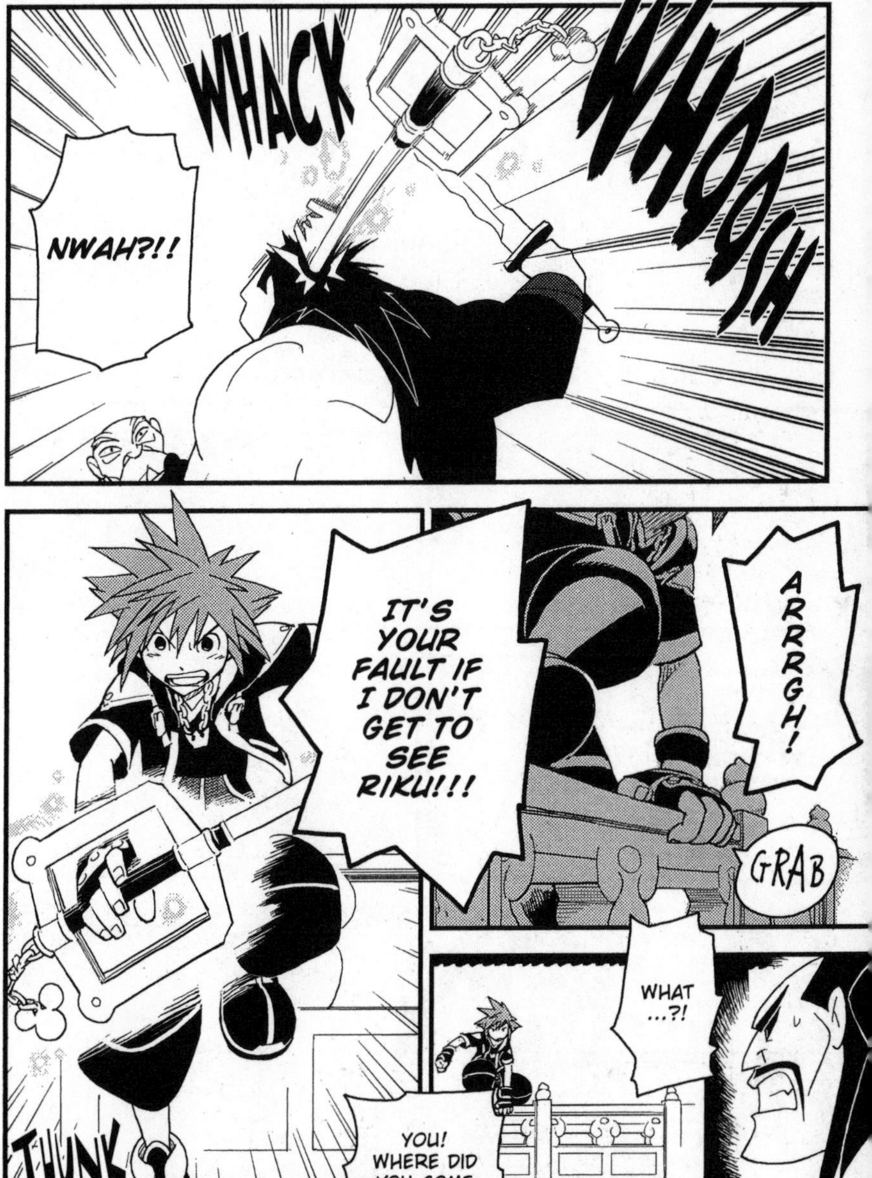
WHOOSH
WHACK
NWAH?!!
ARRRGH!
GRAB
WHAT ...?!
YOU! WHERE DID YOU COME FROM?!
IT'S YOUR FAULT IF I DON'T GET TO SEE RIKU!!!
THUNK

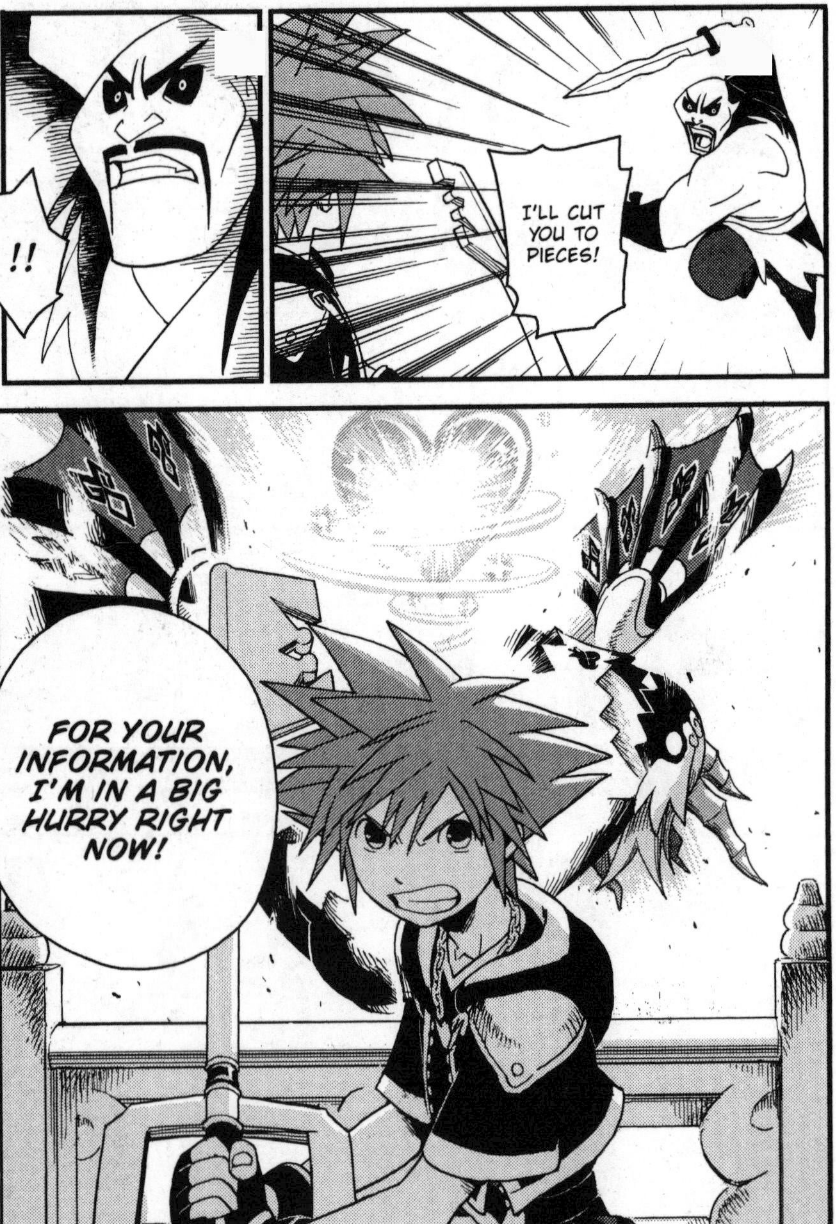
I'LL CUT YOU TO PIECES!
!!
FOR YOUR INFORMATION, I'M IN A BIG HURRY RIGHT NOW!

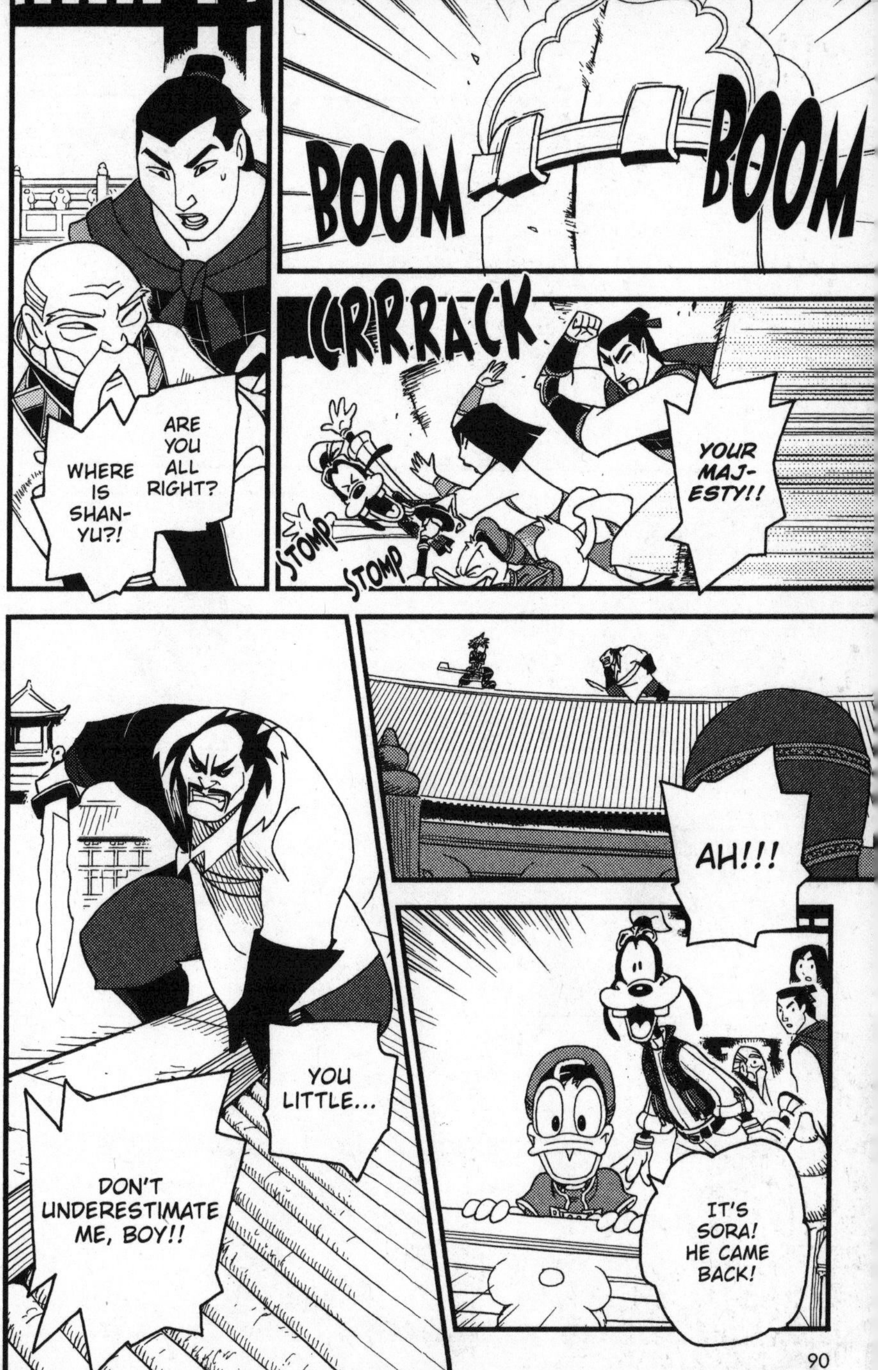
BOOM
BOOM
CRRRACK
YOUR MAJ-ESTY!!
STOMP
STOMP
ARE YOU ALL RIGHT?
WHERE IS SHAN-YU?!
AH!!!
IT'S SORA! HE CAME BACK!
YOU LITTLE...
DON'T UNDERESTIMATE ME, BOY!!

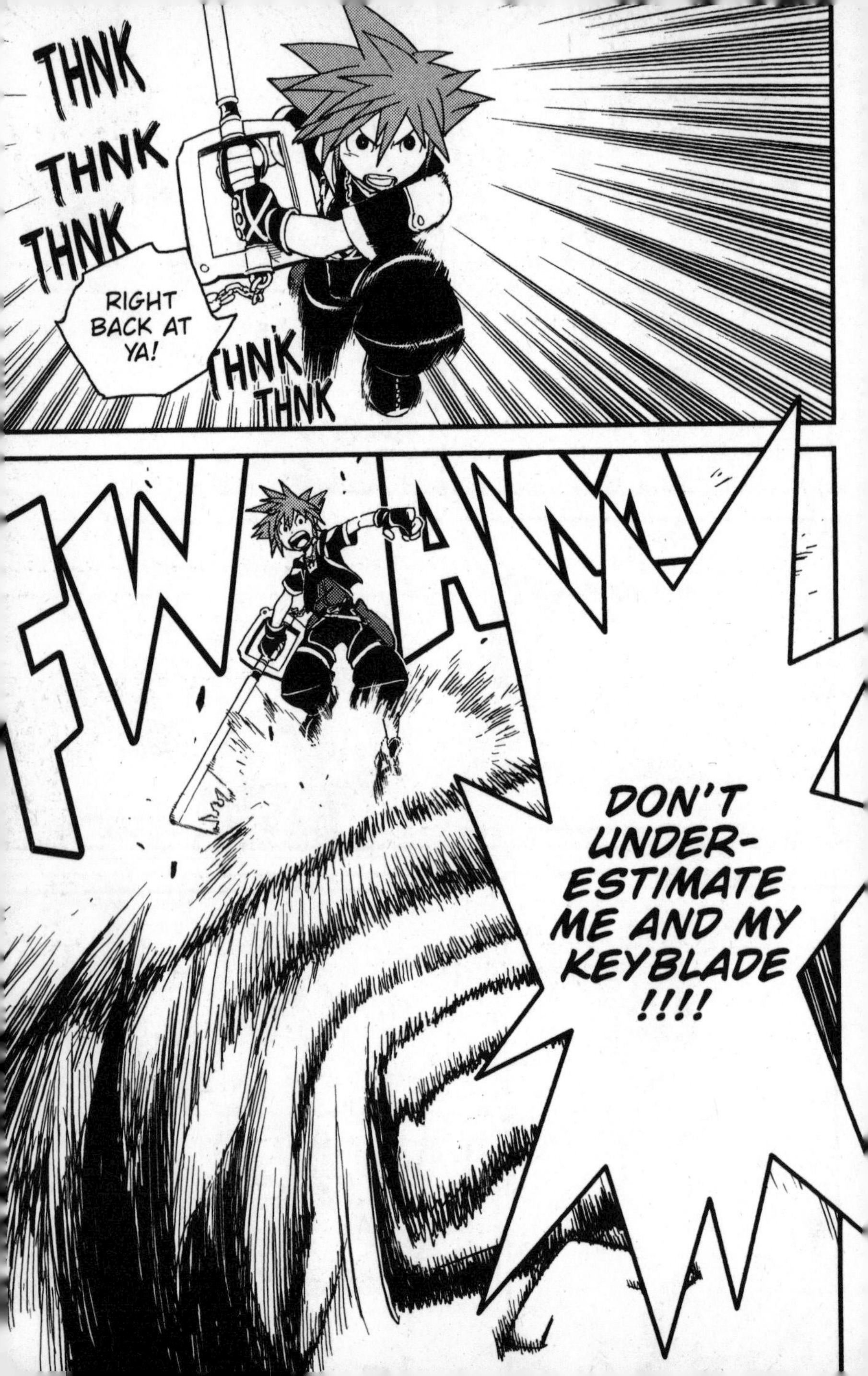
THNK
THNK
THNK
RIGHT BACK AT YA!
THNK
THNK
FWAM
DON'T UNDER-ESTIMATE ME AND MY KEYBLADE !!!!

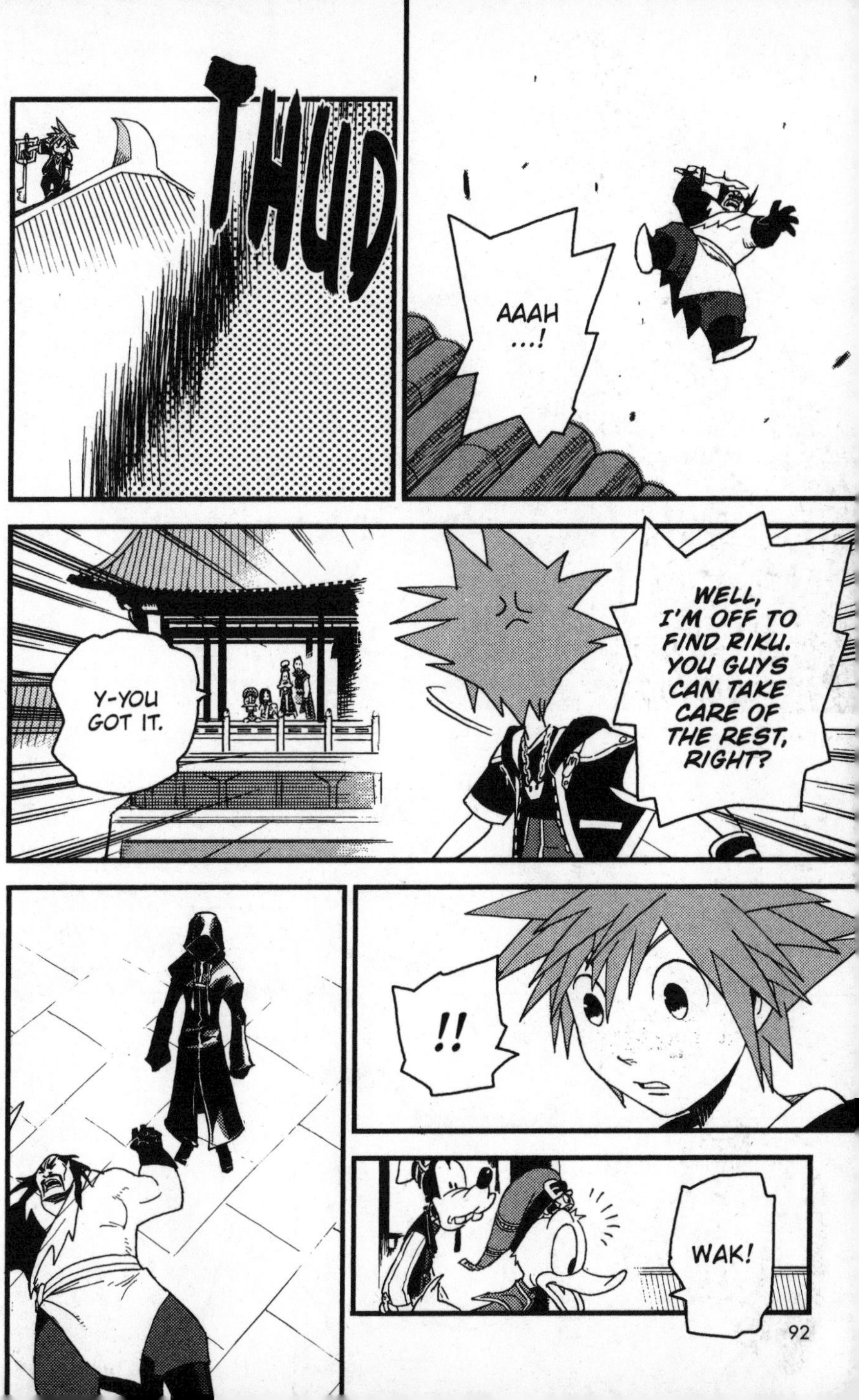
AAAH ...!
THUD
WELL, I'M OFF TO FIND RIKU. YOU GUYS CAN TAKE CARE OF THE REST, RIGHT?
Y-YOU GOT IT.
!!
WAK!

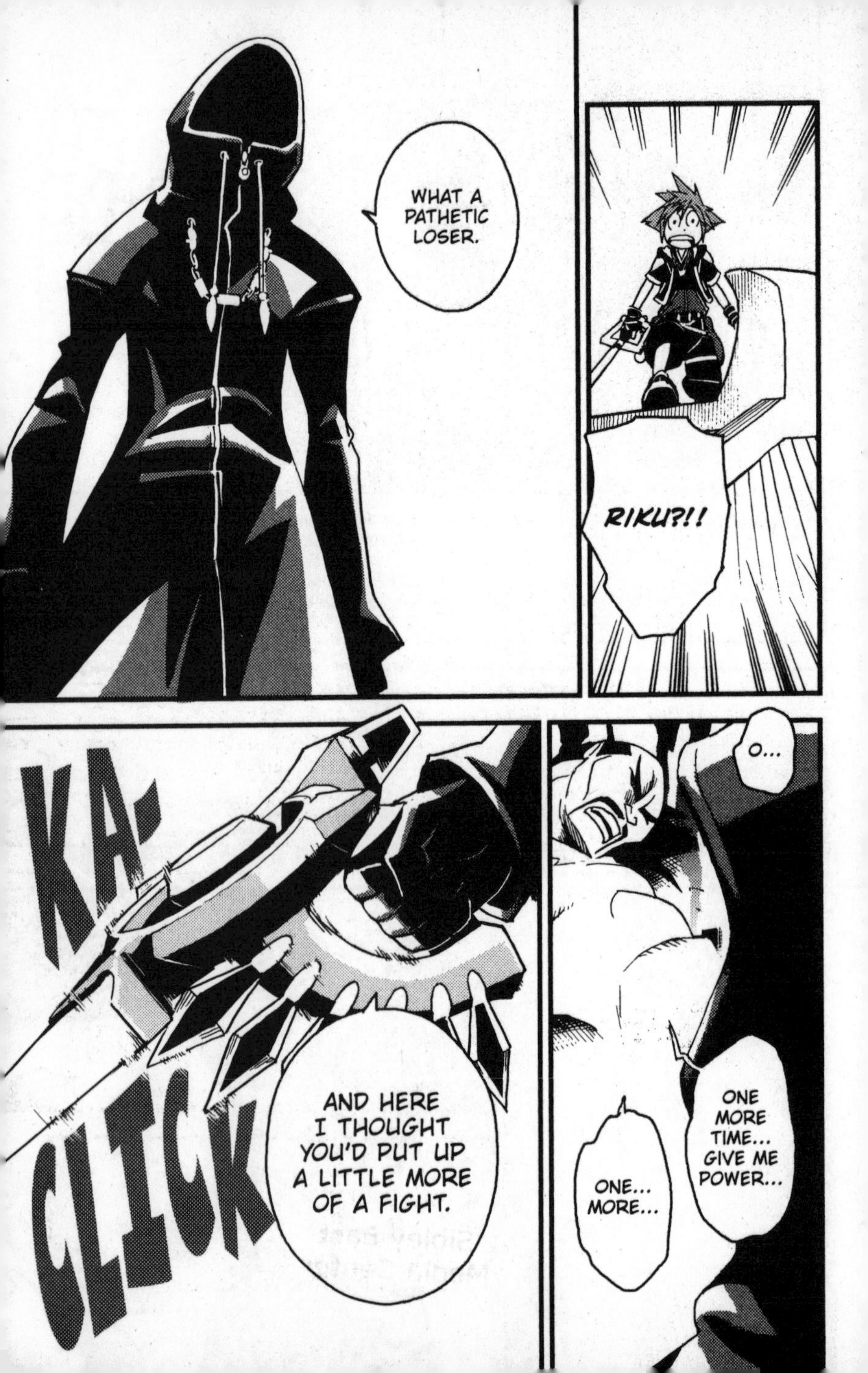
RIKU?!!
WHAT A PATHETIC LOSER.
O...
ONE MORE TIME... GIVE ME POWER...
ONE... MORE...
KA-CLICK
AND HERE I THOUGHT YOU'D PUT UP A LITTLE MORE OF A FIGHT.

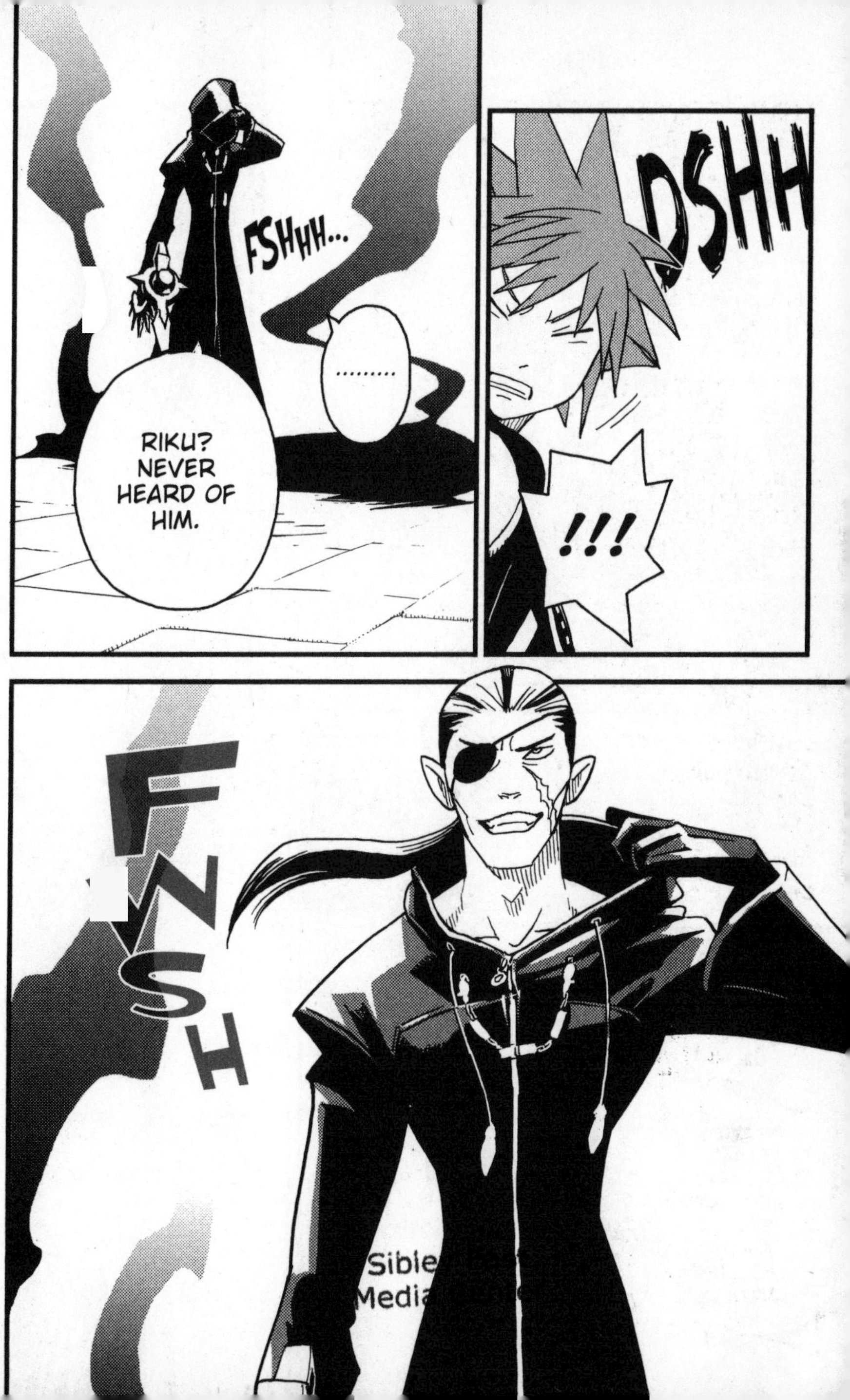
DSHH
!!!
FSHHH...
....
RIKU? NEVER HEARD OF HIM.
FWSH

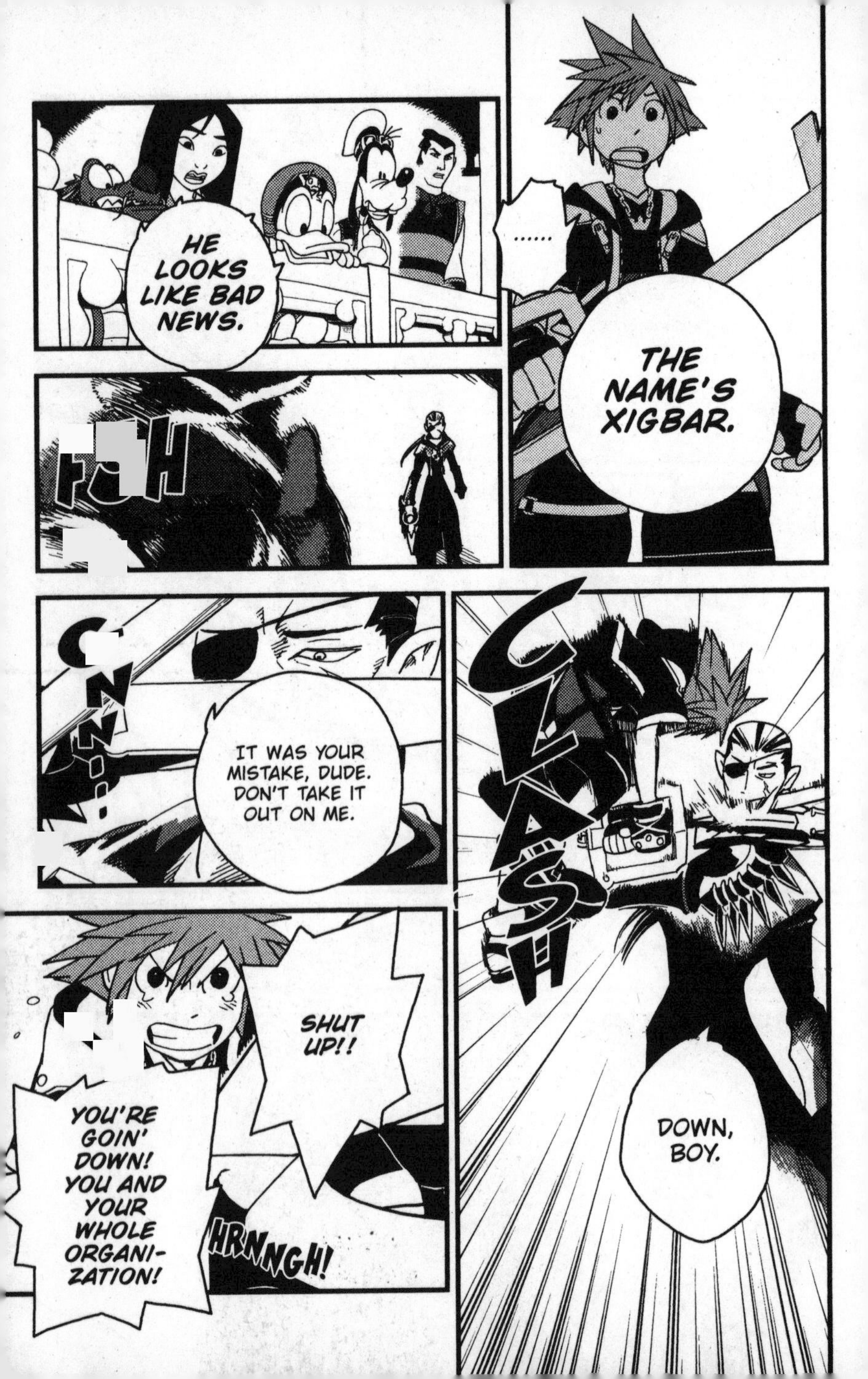
......
THE NAME'S XIGBAR.
HE LOOKS LIKE BAD NEWS.
CLASH
DOWN, BOY.
IT WAS YOUR MISTAKE, DUDE. DON'T TAKE IT OUT ON ME.
SHUT UP!!
YOU'RE GOIN' DOWN! YOU AND YOUR WHOLE ORGANI-ZATION!
HRNNGH!

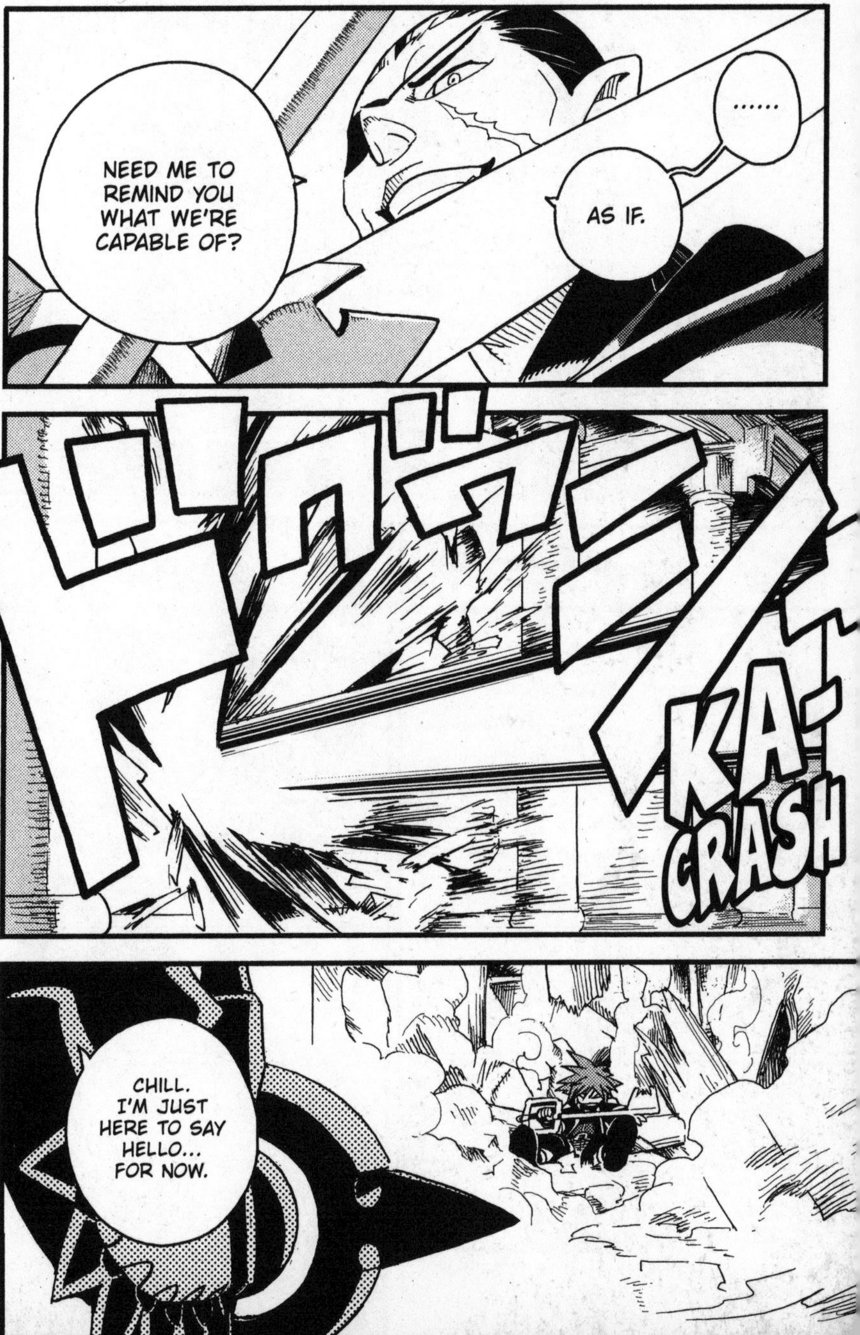
......
AS IF.
NEED ME TO REMIND YOU WHAT WE'RE CAPABLE OF?
ドガァン
KA-CRASH
CHILL. I'M JUST HERE TO SAY HELLO... FOR NOW.

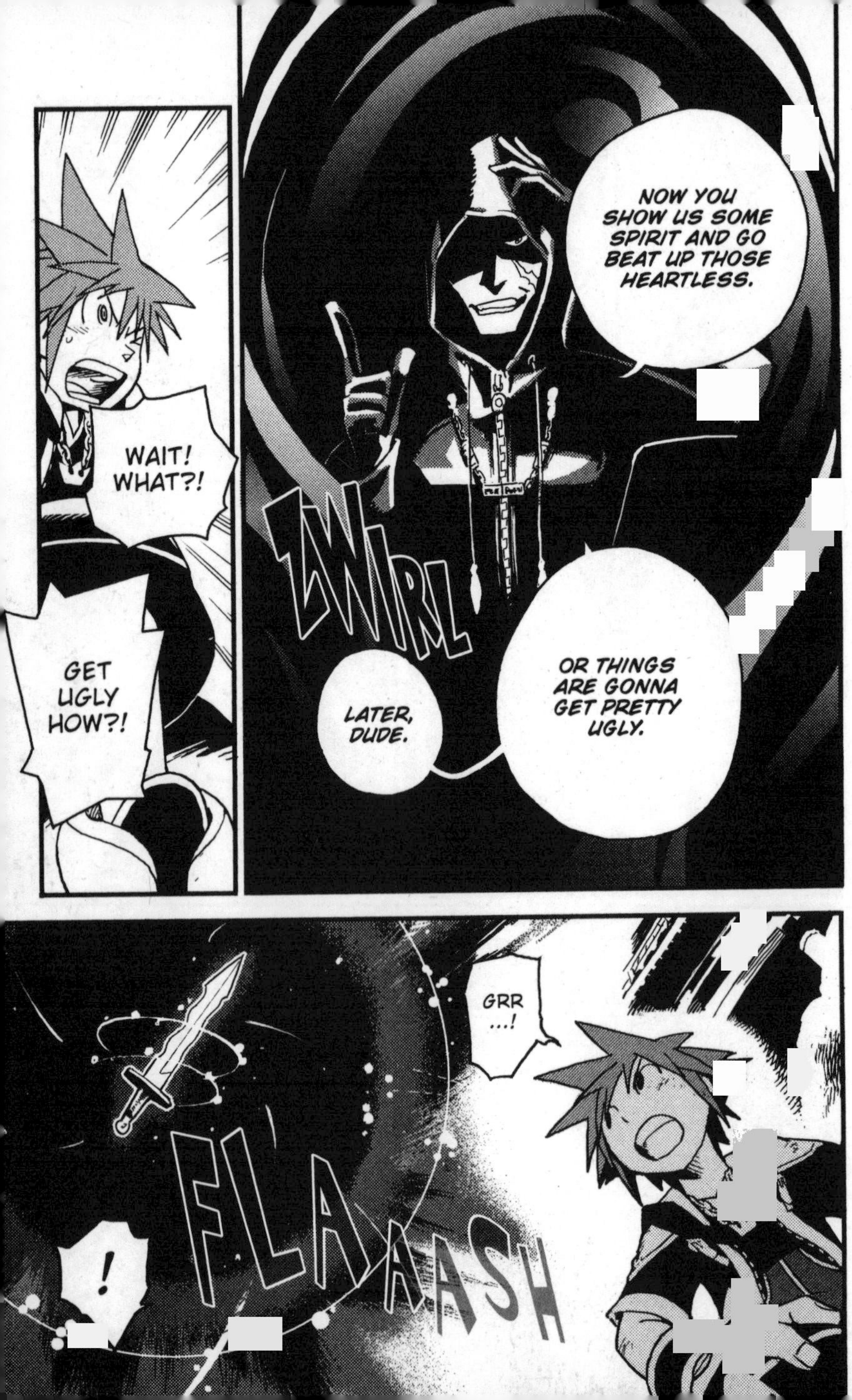
NOW YOU SHOW US SOME SPIRIT AND GO BEAT UP THOSE HEARTLESS.
ZWIRL
OR THINGS ARE GONNA GET PRETTY UGLY.
LATER, DUDE.
WAIT! WHAT?!
GET UGLY HOW?!
GRR ...!
FLAAASH
!

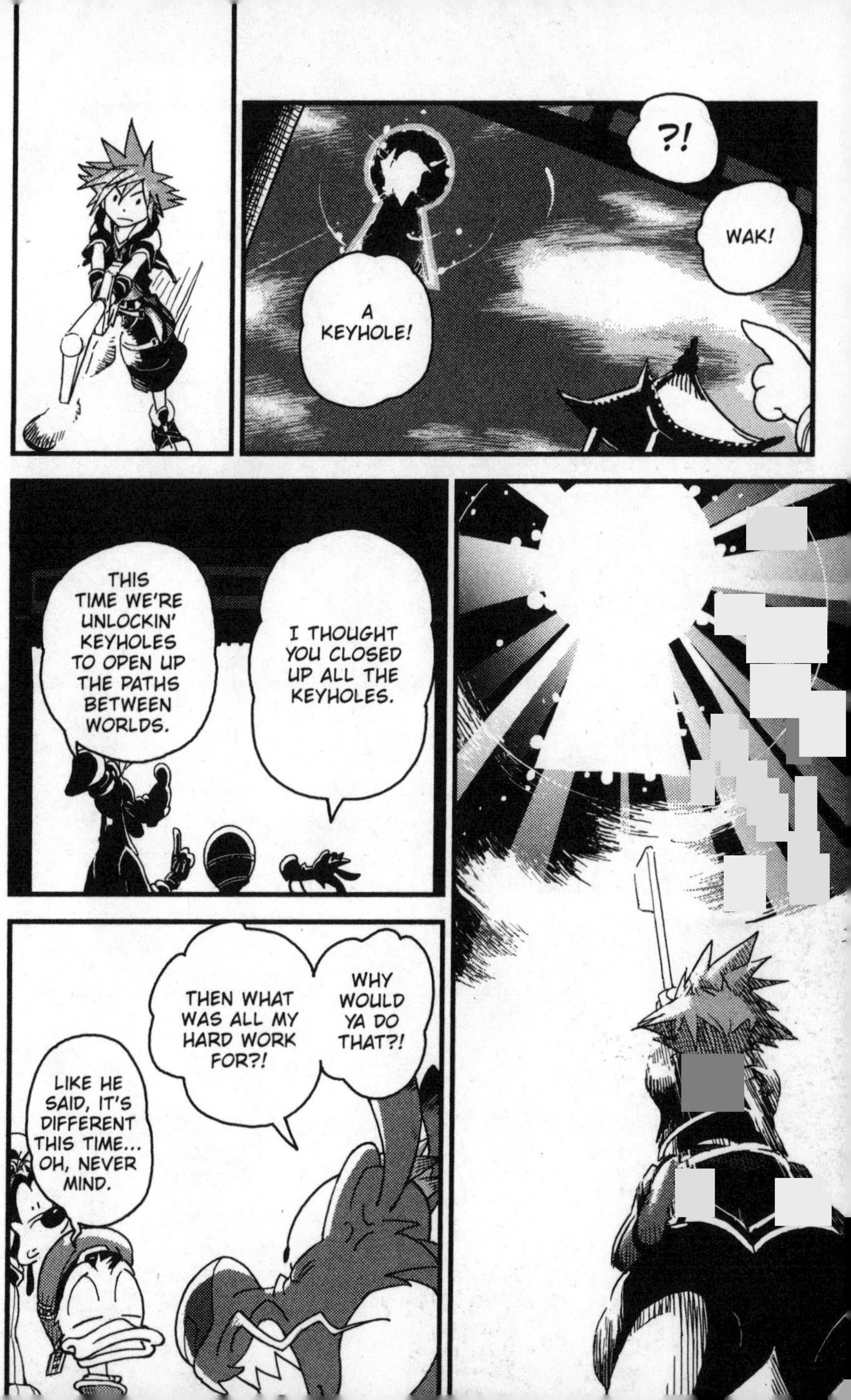
?!
WAK!
A KEYHOLE!
I THOUGHT YOU CLOSED UP ALL THE KEYHOLES.
THIS TIME WE'RE UNLOCKIN' KEYHOLES TO OPEN UP THE PATHS BETWEEN WORLDS.
WHY WOULD YA DO THAT?!
THEN WHAT WAS ALL MY HARD WORK FOR?!
LIKE HE SAID, IT'S DIFFERENT THIS TIME... OH, NEVER MIND.

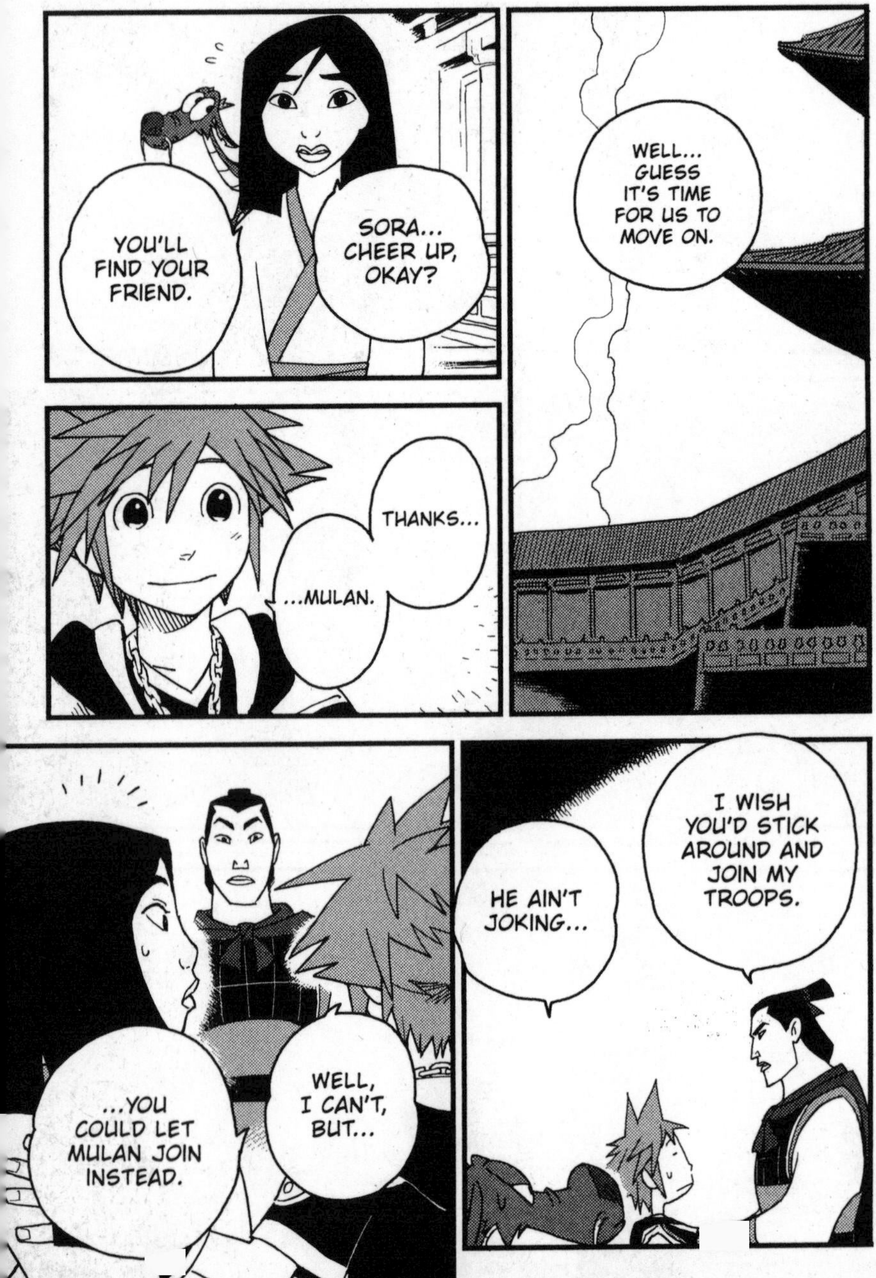
WELL... GUESS IT'S TIME FOR US TO MOVE ON.
SORA... CHEER UP, OKAY?
YOU'LL FIND YOUR FRIEND.
THANKS...
...MULAN.
I WISH YOU'D STICK AROUND AND JOIN MY TROOPS.
HE AIN'T JOKING...
WELL, I CAN'T, BUT...
...YOU COULD LET MULAN JOIN INSTEAD.

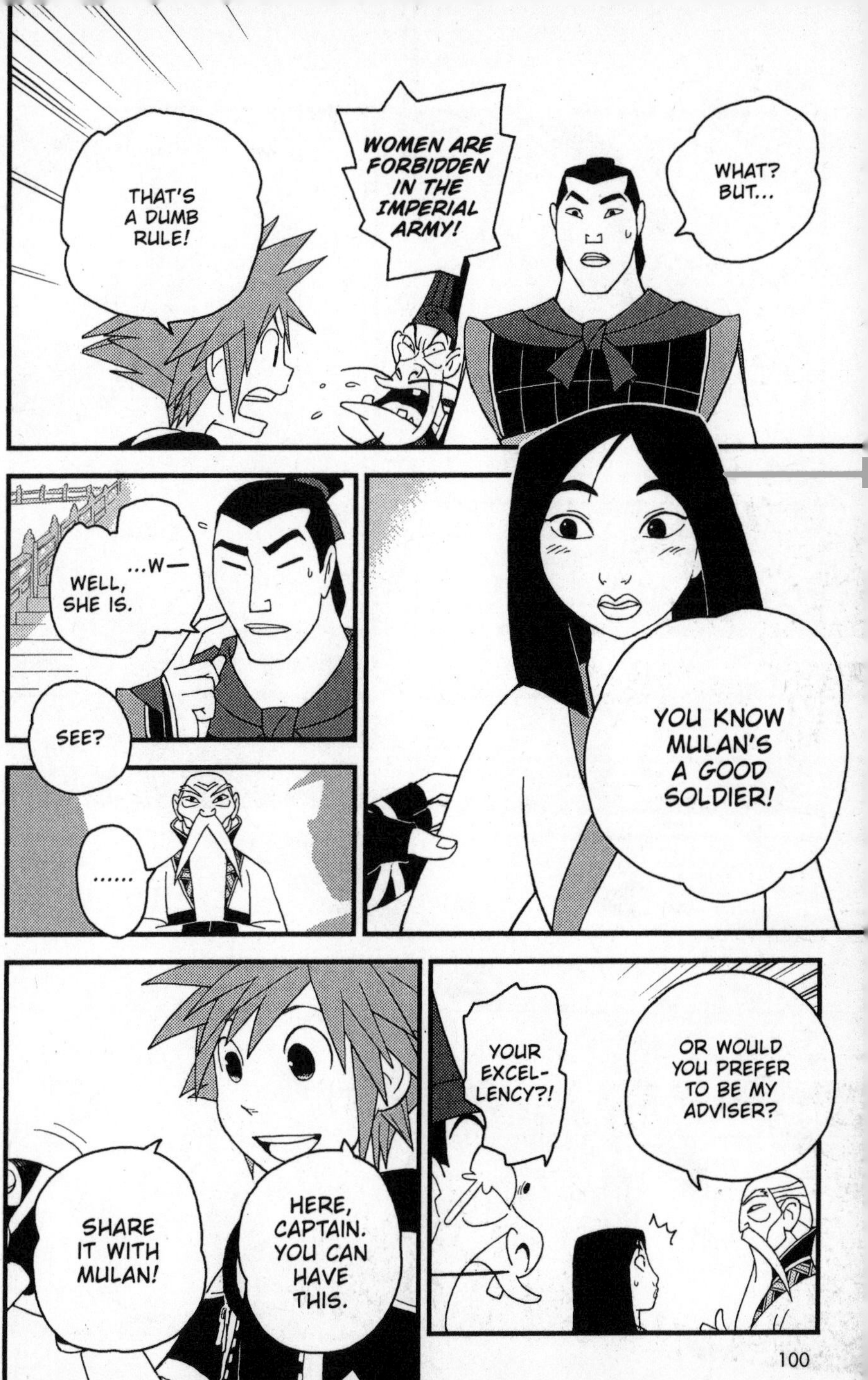
WHAT? BUT...
WOMEN ARE FORBIDDEN IN THE IMPERIAL ARMY!
THAT'S A DUMB RULE!
YOU KNOW MULAN'S A GOOD SOLDIER!
...W—
WELL, SHE IS.
SEE?
......
OR WOULD YOU PREFER TO BE MY ADVISER?
YOUR EXCEL-LENCY?!
HERE, CAPTAIN. YOU CAN HAVE THIS.
SHARE IT WITH MULAN!

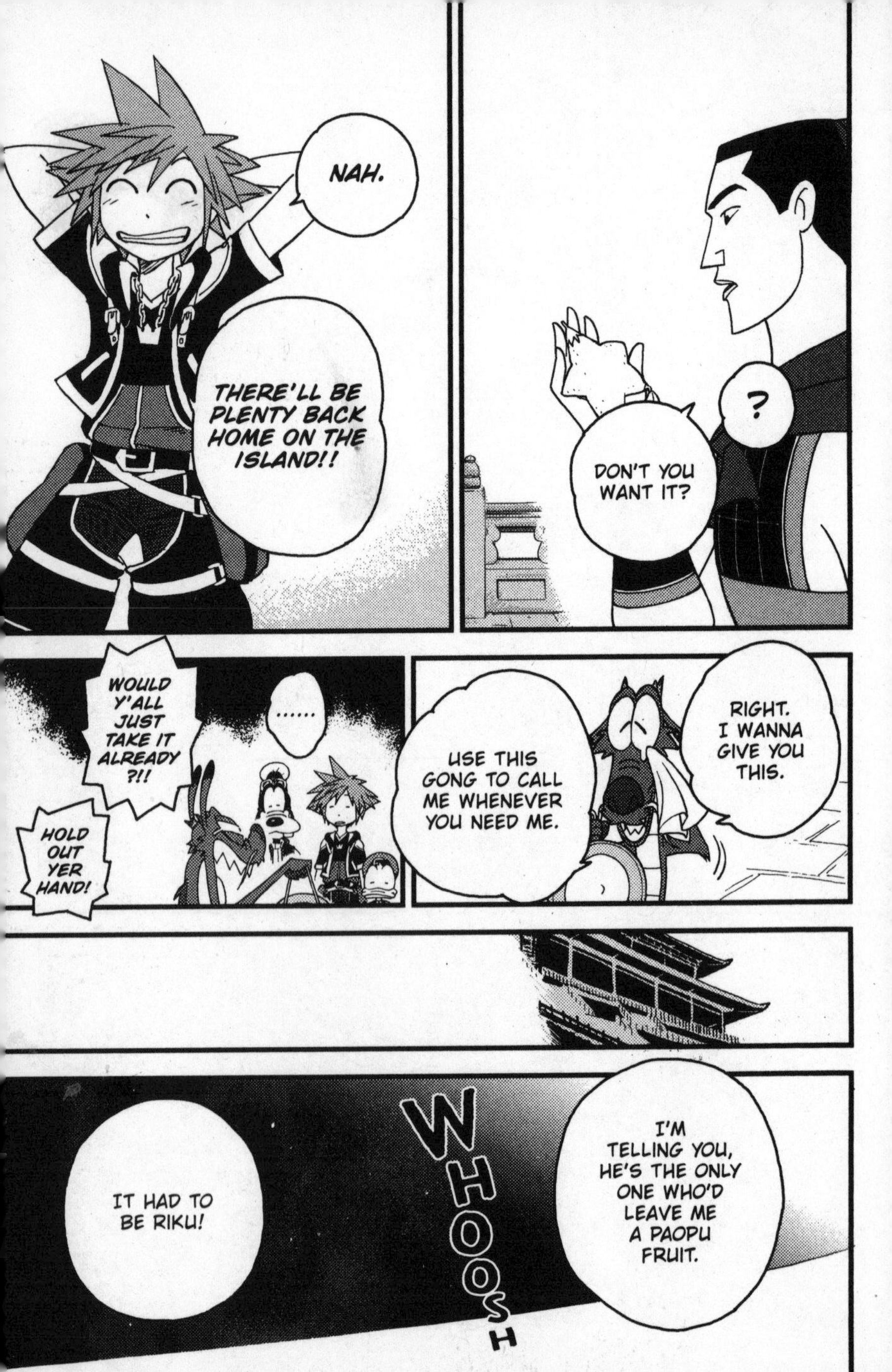
?
DON'T YOU WANT IT?
NAH.
THERE'LL BE PLENTY BACK HOME ON THE ISLAND!!
RIGHT. I WANNA GIVE YOU THIS.
USE THIS GONG TO CALL ME WHENEVER YOU NEED ME.
......
WOULD Y'ALL JUST TAKE IT ALREADY?!!
HOLD OUT YER HAND!
I'M TELLING YOU, HE'S THE ONLY ONE WHO'D LEAVE ME A PAOPU FRUIT.
WHOOSH
IT HAD TO BE RIKU!

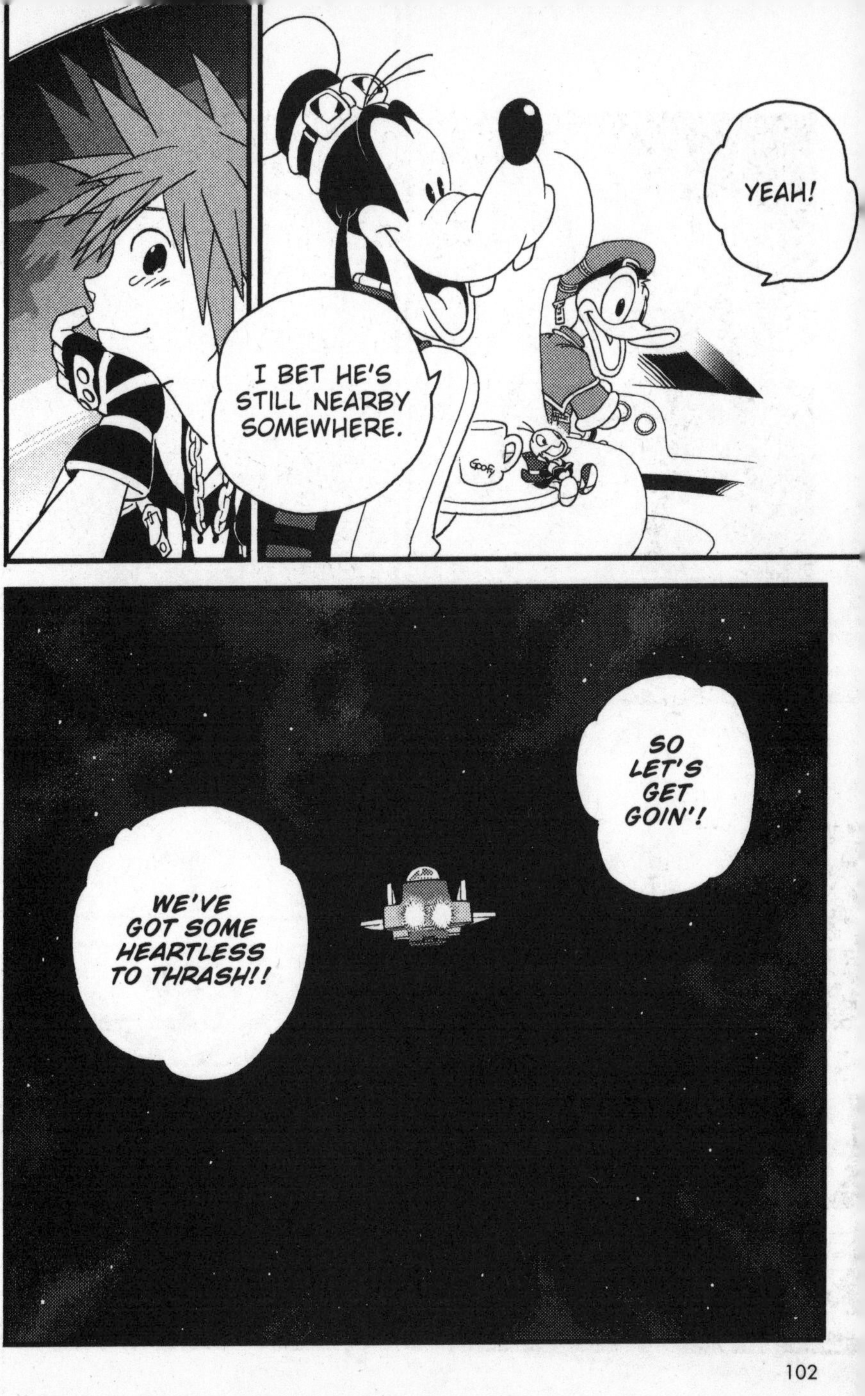
YEAH!
I BET HE'S STILL NEARBY SOMEWHERE.
Goofy
SO LET'S GET GOIN'!
WE'VE GOT SOME HEARTLESS TO THRASH!!

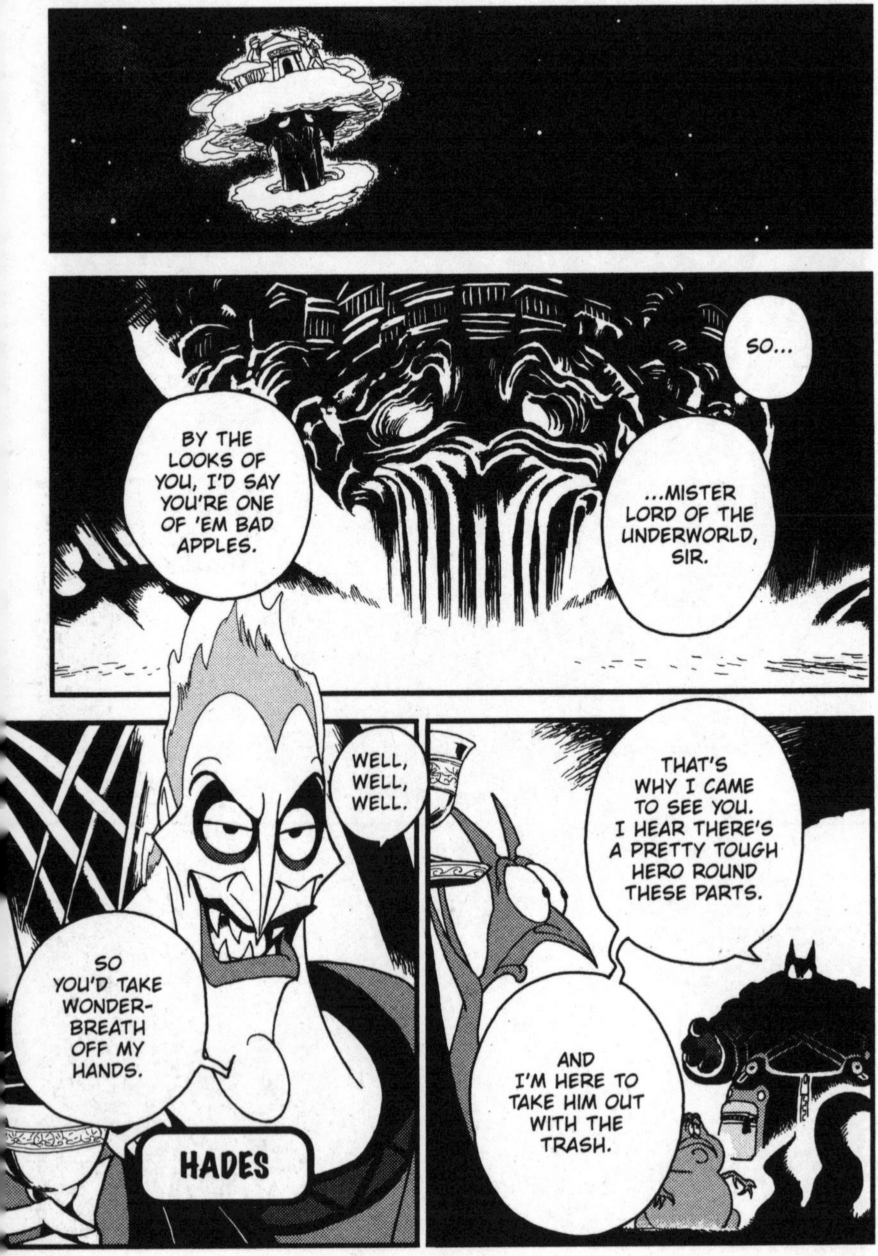
SO...
...MISTER LORD OF THE UNDERWORLD, SIR.
BY THE LOOKS OF YOU, I'D SAY YOU'RE ONE OF 'EM BAD APPLES.
THAT'S WHY I CAME TO SEE YOU. I HEAR THERE'S A PRETTY TOUGH HERO ROUND THESE PARTS.
AND I'M HERE TO TAKE HIM OUT WITH THE TRASH.
WELL, WELL, WELL.
SO YOU'D TAKE WONDER-BREATH OFF MY HANDS.
HADES

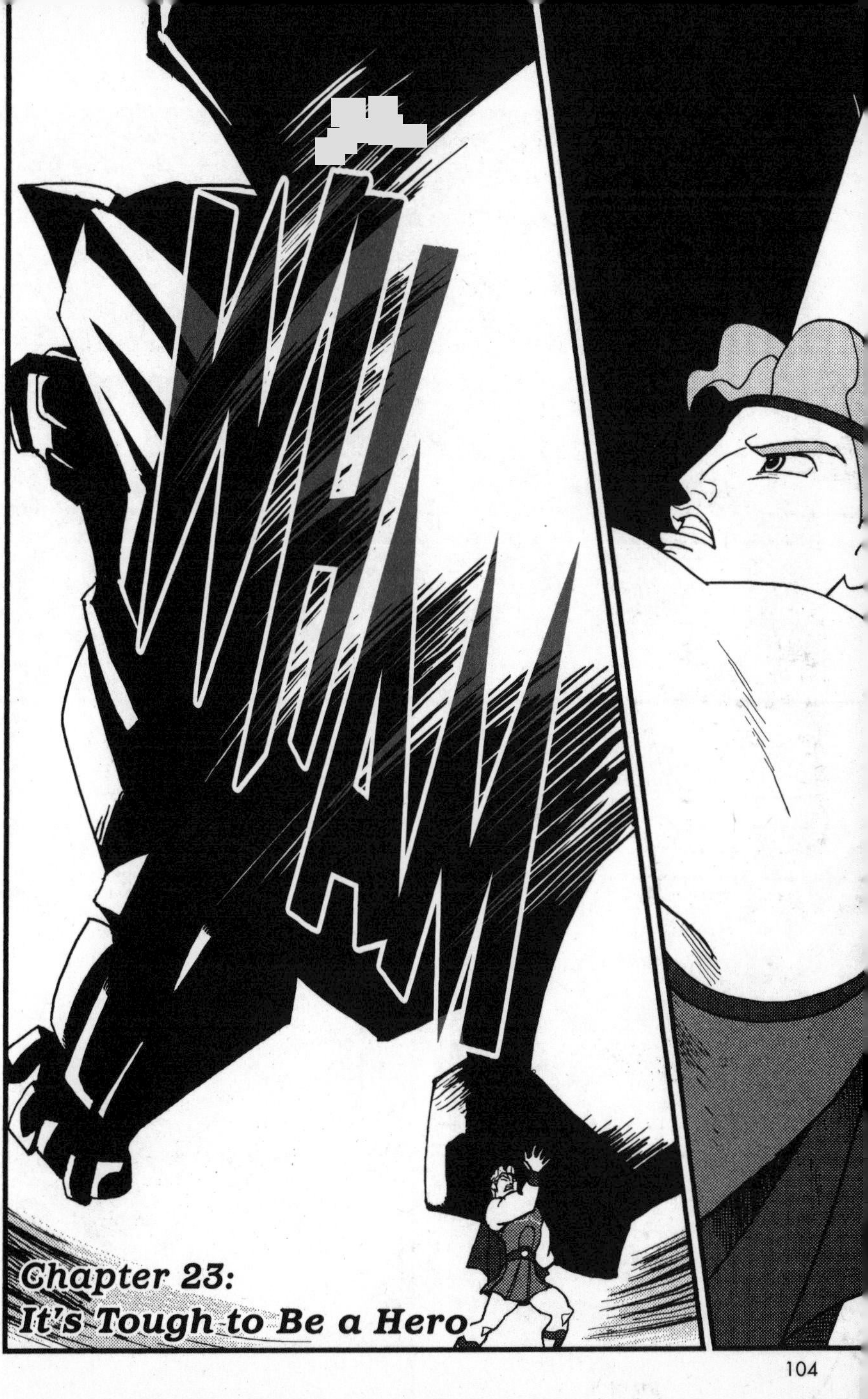

Chapter 23: It's Tough to Be a Hero

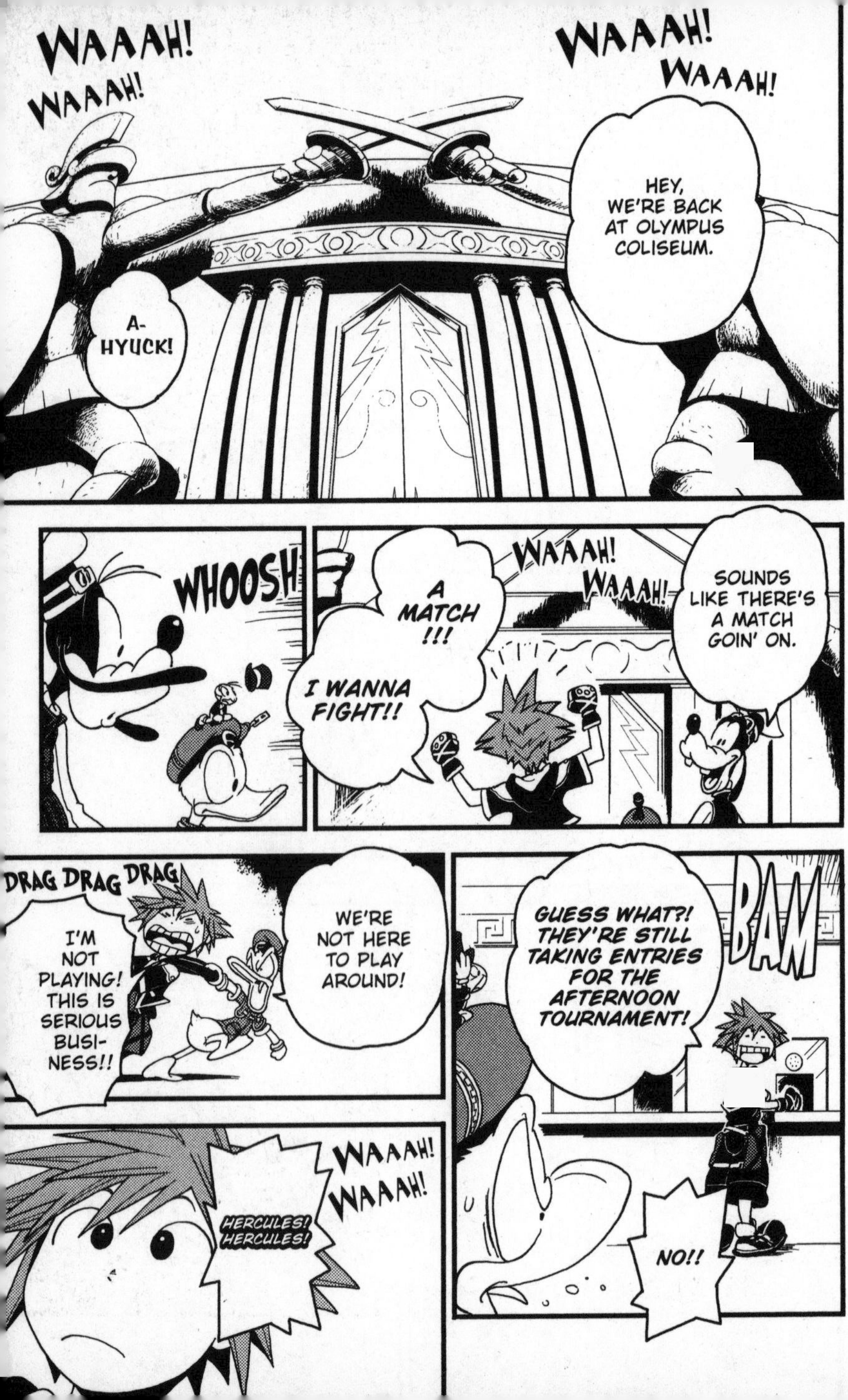
WAAAH!
WAAAH!
HEY, WE'RE BACK AT OLYMPUS COLISEUM.
A-HYUCK!
WAAAH!
WAAAH!
WAAAH!
WAAAH!
SOUNDS LIKE THERE'S A MATCH GOIN' ON.
A MATCH!!!
I WANNA FIGHT!!
WHOOSH
BAM
GUESS WHAT?! THEY'RE STILL TAKING ENTRIES FOR THE AFTERNOON TOURNAMENT!
NO!!
WE'RE NOT HERE TO PLAY AROUND!
DRAG DRAG DRAG
I'M NOT PLAYING! THIS IS SERIOUS BUSI-NESS!!
WAAAH!
WAAAH!
HERCULES! HERCULES!

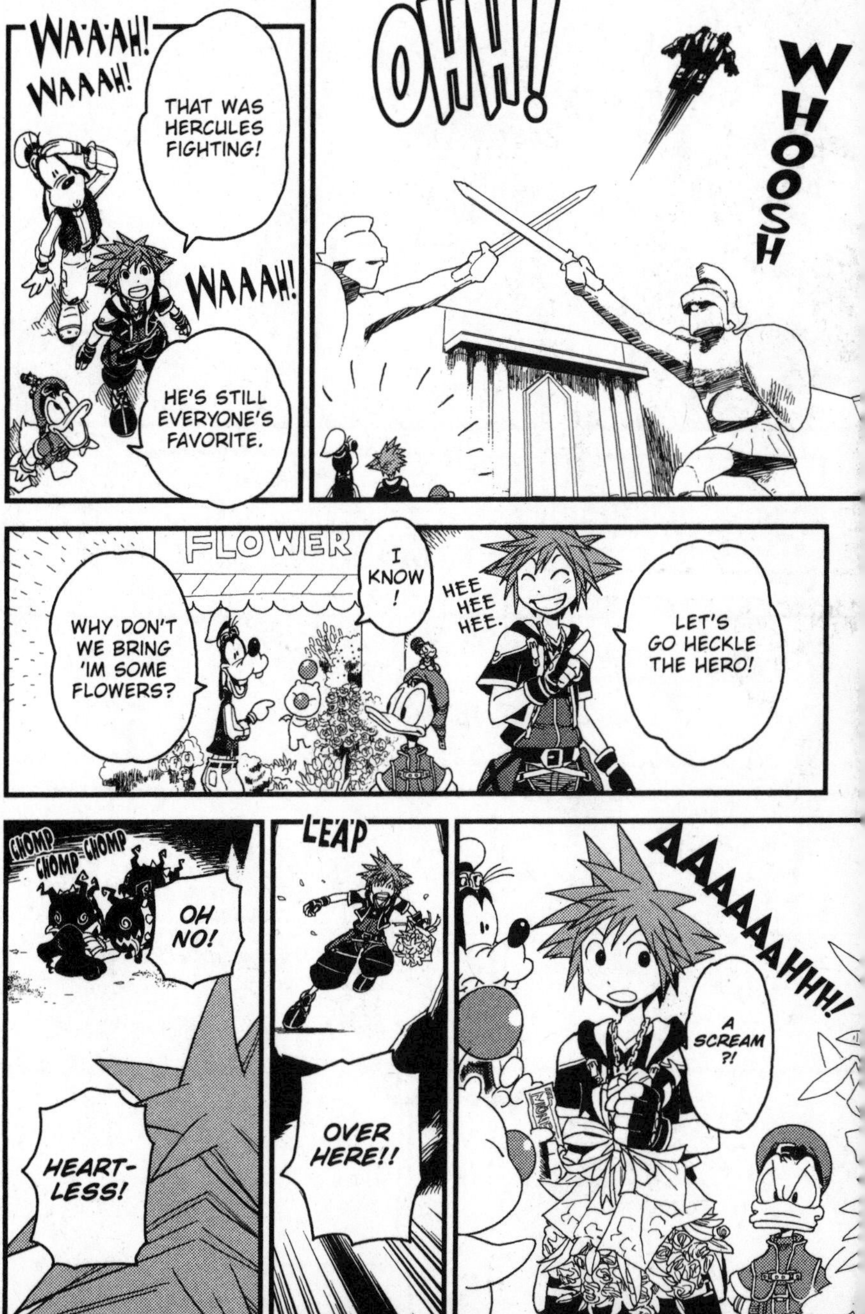
WHOOSH
OHH!
WA-A-AH!
WAAAH!
THAT WAS HERCULES FIGHTING!
WAAAH!
HE'S STILL EVERYONE'S FAVORITE.
LET'S GO HECKLE THE HERO!
HEE HEE HEE.
I KNOW!
FLOWER
WHY DON'T WE BRING 'IM SOME FLOWERS?
AAAAAAHHH!
A SCREAM ?!
LEAP
OVER HERE!!
CHOMP CHOMP CHOMP
OH NO!
HEART-LESS!

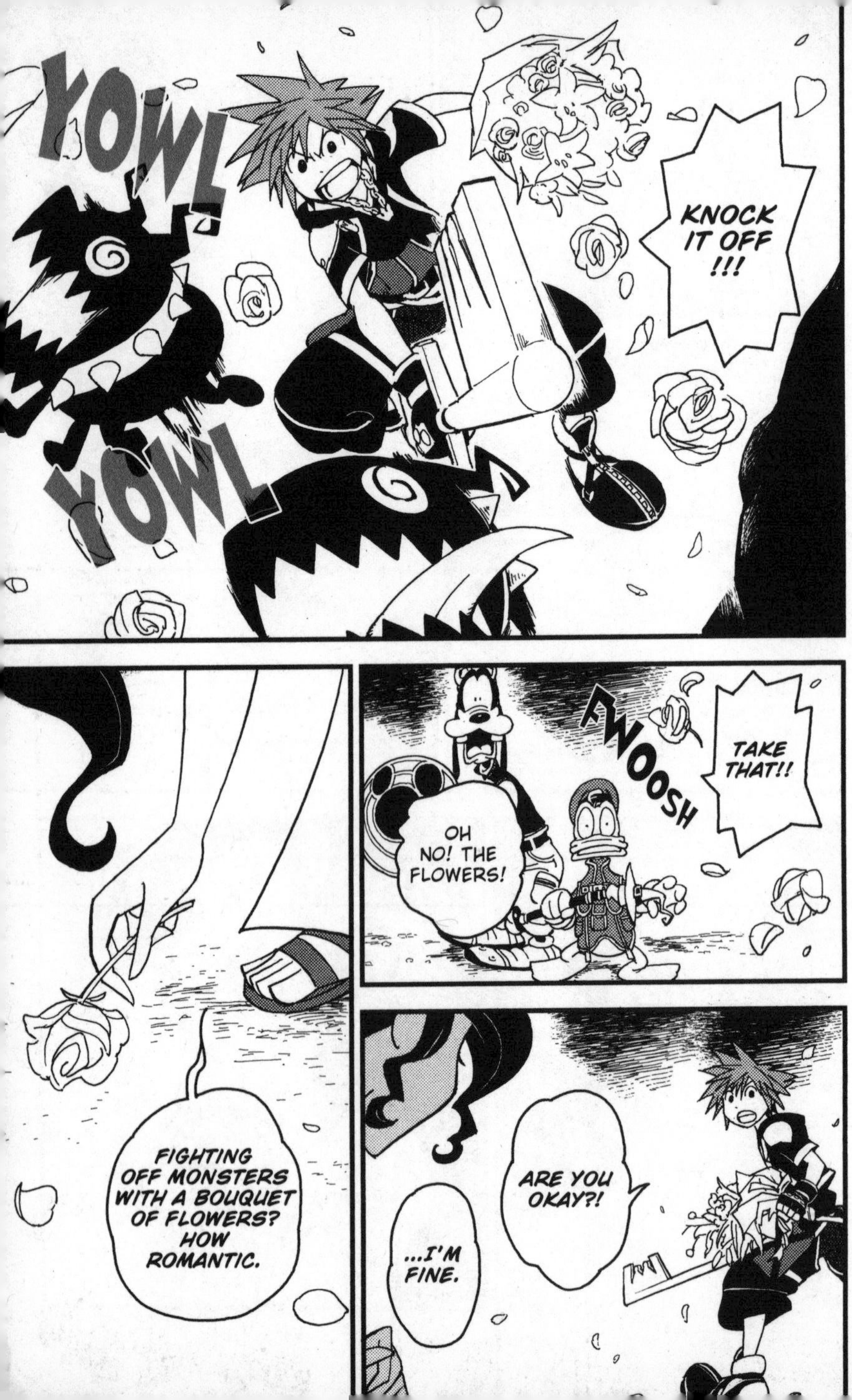
KNOCK IT OFF !!!
YOWL
YOWL
TAKE THAT!!
FWOOSH
OH NO! THE FLOWERS!
ARE YOU OKAY?!
...I'M FINE.
FIGHTING OFF MONSTERS WITH A BOUQUET OF FLOWERS? HOW ROMANTIC.

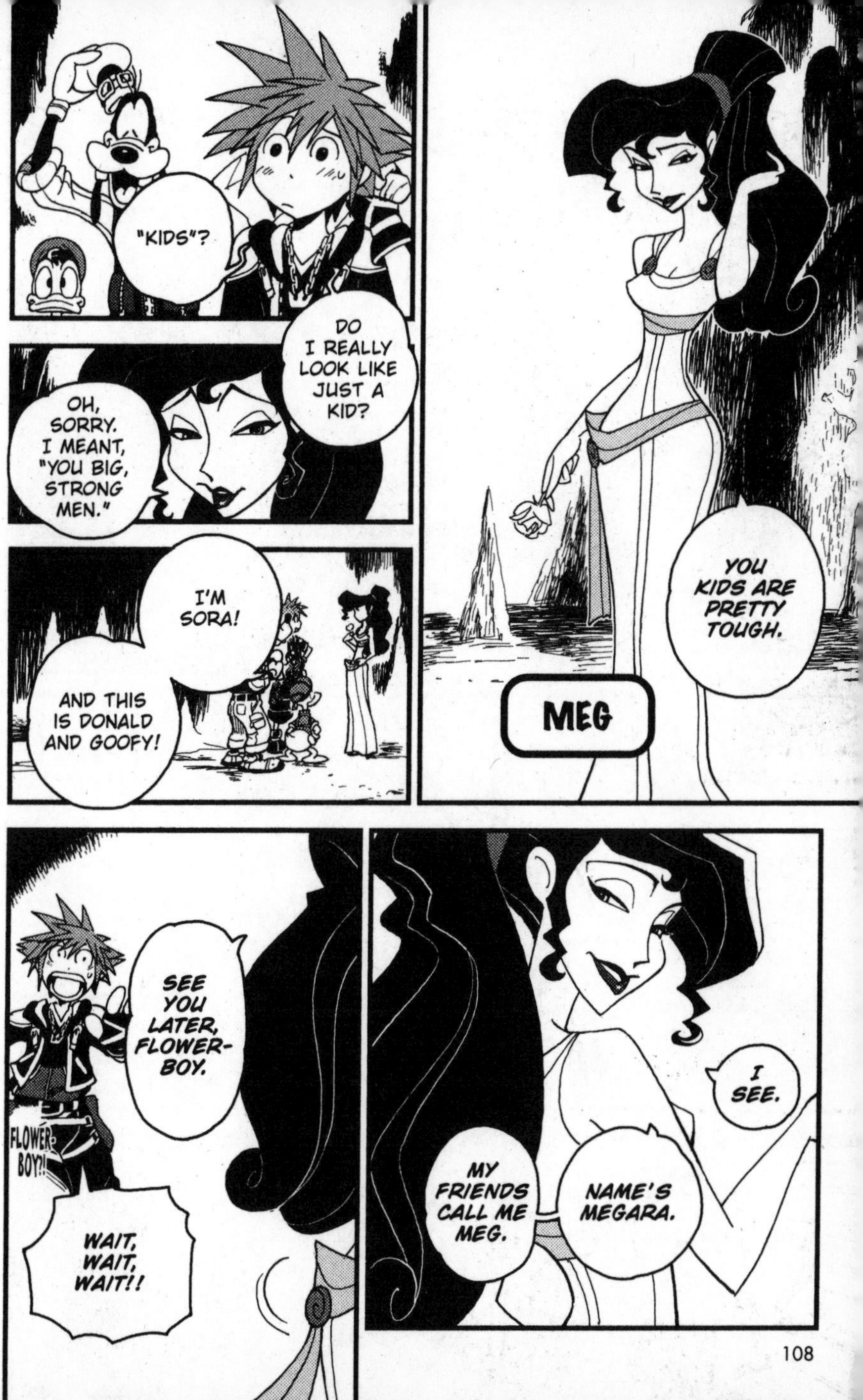
YOU KIDS ARE PRETTY TOUGH.
MEG
"KIDS"?
DO I REALLY LOOK LIKE JUST A KID?
OH, SORRY. I MEANT, "YOU BIG, STRONG MEN."
I'M SORA!
AND THIS IS DONALD AND GOOFY!
I SEE.
NAME'S MEGARA.
MY FRIENDS CALL ME MEG.
SEE YOU LATER, FLOWER-BOY.
FLOWER-BOY?!
WAIT, WAIT, WAIT!!

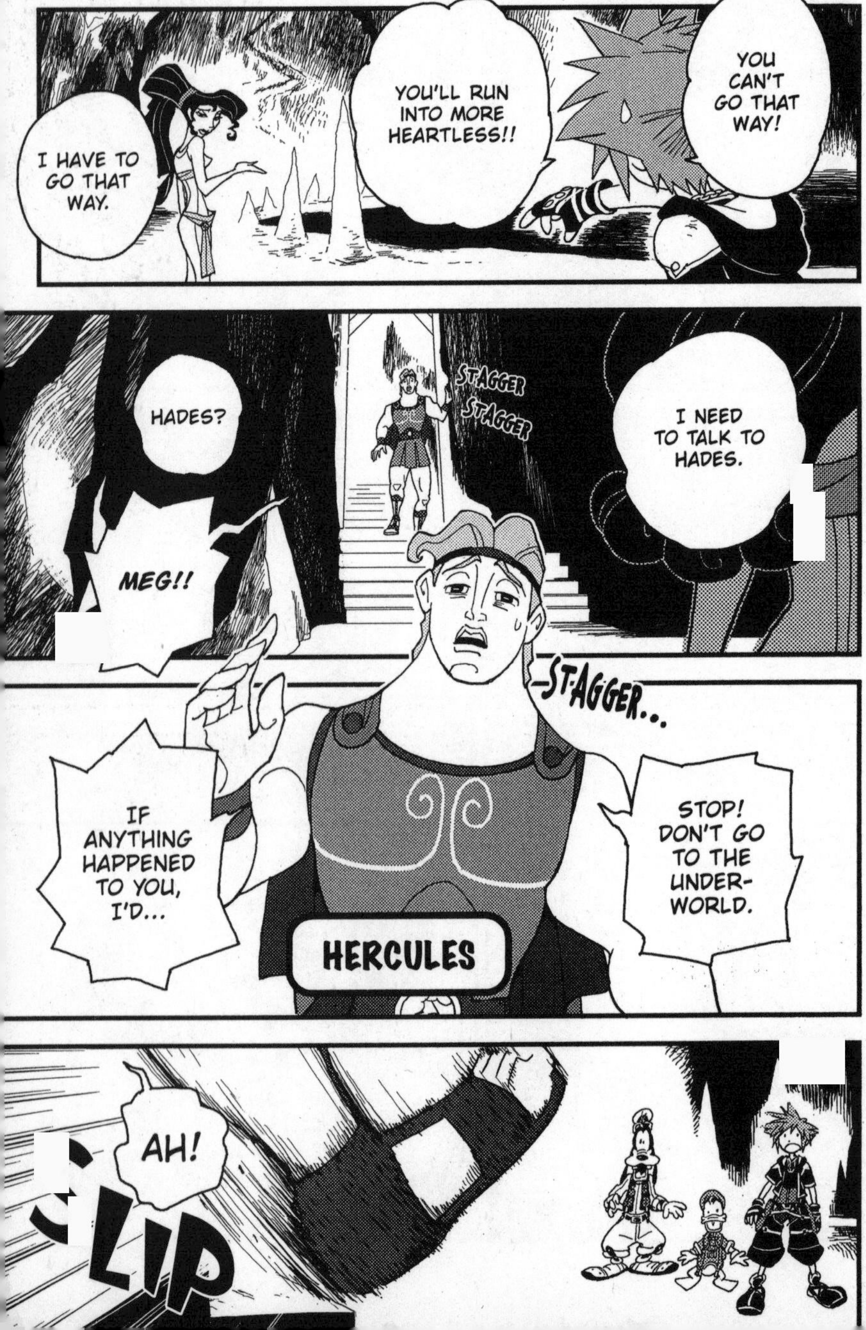
YOU CAN'T GO THAT WAY!
YOU'LL RUN INTO MORE HEARTLESS!!
I HAVE TO GO THAT WAY.
I NEED TO TALK TO HADES.
STAGGER
STAGGER
HADES?
MEG!!
STAGGER...
STOP! DON'T GO TO THE UNDER-WORLD.
HERCULES
IF ANYTHING HAPPENED TO YOU, I'D...
AH!
SLIP

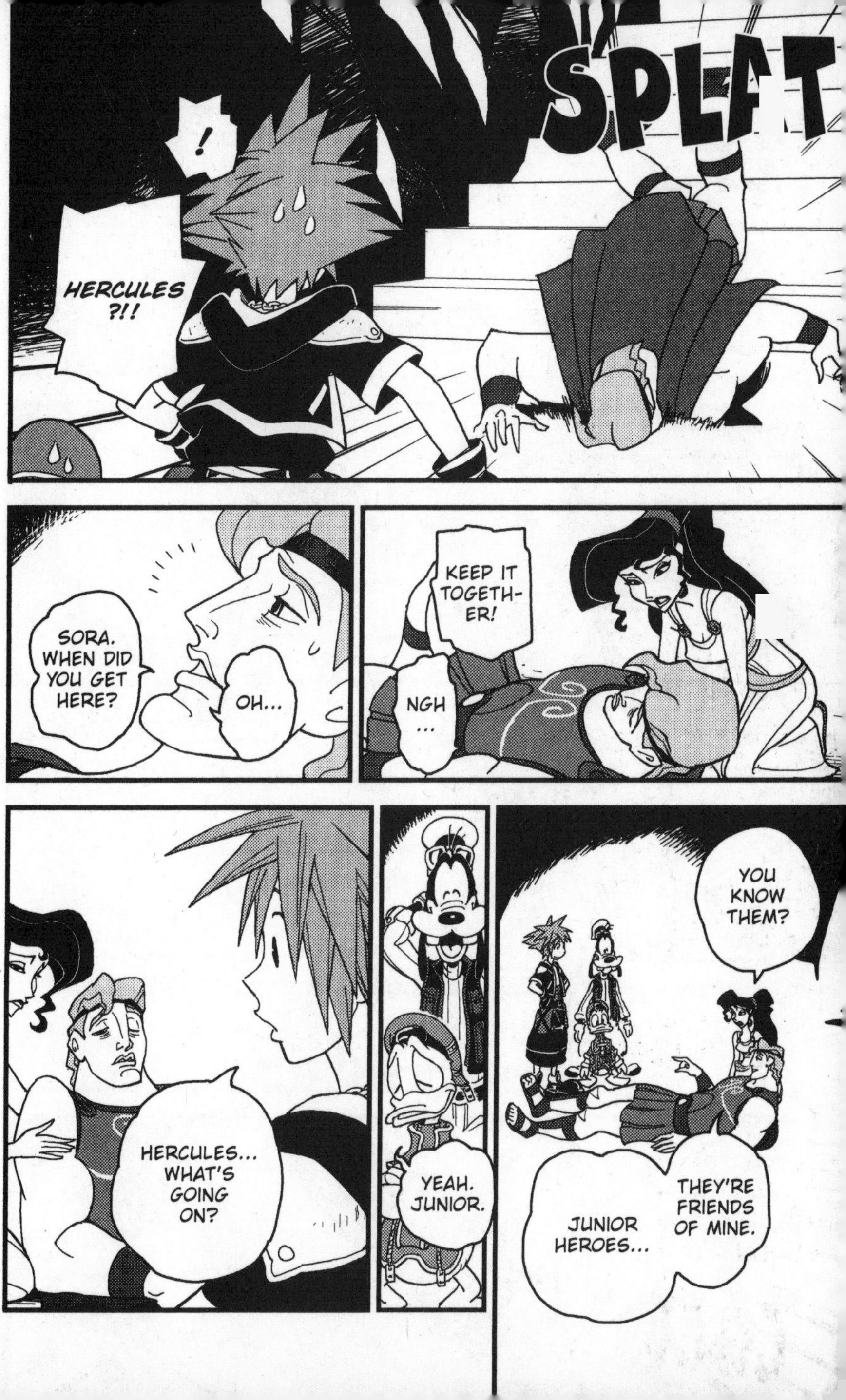
SPLAT
!
HERCULES ?!!
KEEP IT TOGETHER!
NGH...
OH...
SORA. WHEN DID YOU GET HERE?
YOU KNOW THEM?
THEY'RE FRIENDS OF MINE.
JUNIOR HEROES...
YEAH. JUNIOR.
HERCULES... WHAT'S GOING ON?

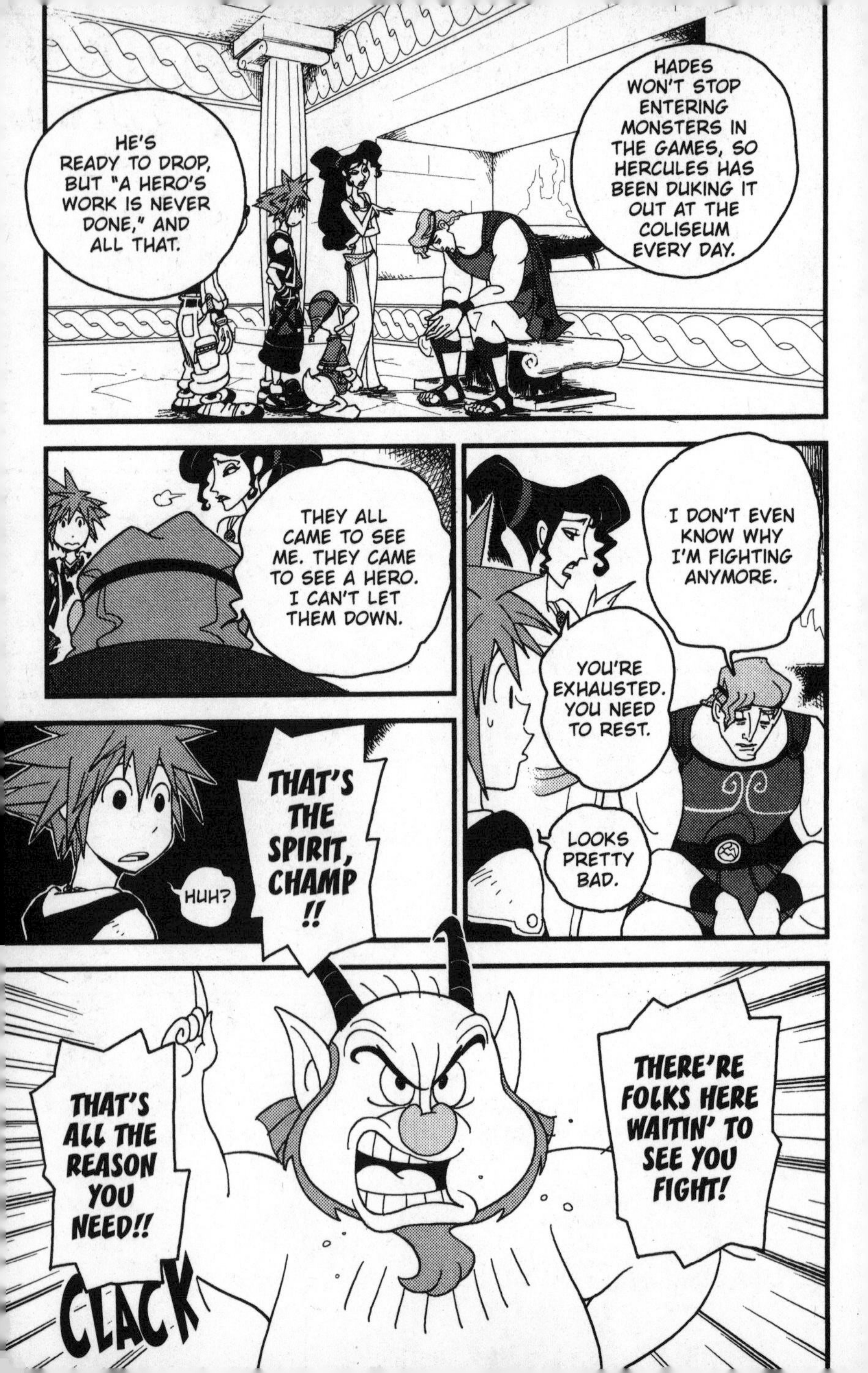
HADES WON'T STOP ENTERING MONSTERS IN THE GAMES, SO HERCULES HAS BEEN DUKING IT OUT AT THE COLISEUM EVERY DAY.
HE'S READY TO DROP, BUT "A HERO'S WORK IS NEVER DONE," AND ALL THAT.
I DON'T EVEN KNOW WHY I'M FIGHTING ANYMORE.
YOU'RE EXHAUSTED. YOU NEED TO REST.
LOOKS PRETTY BAD.
THEY ALL CAME TO SEE ME. THEY CAME TO SEE A HERO. I CAN'T LET THEM DOWN.
THAT'S THE SPIRIT, CHAMP!!
HUH?
THERE'RE FOLKS HERE WAITIN' TO SEE YOU FIGHT!
THAT'S ALL THE REASON YOU NEED!!
CLACK

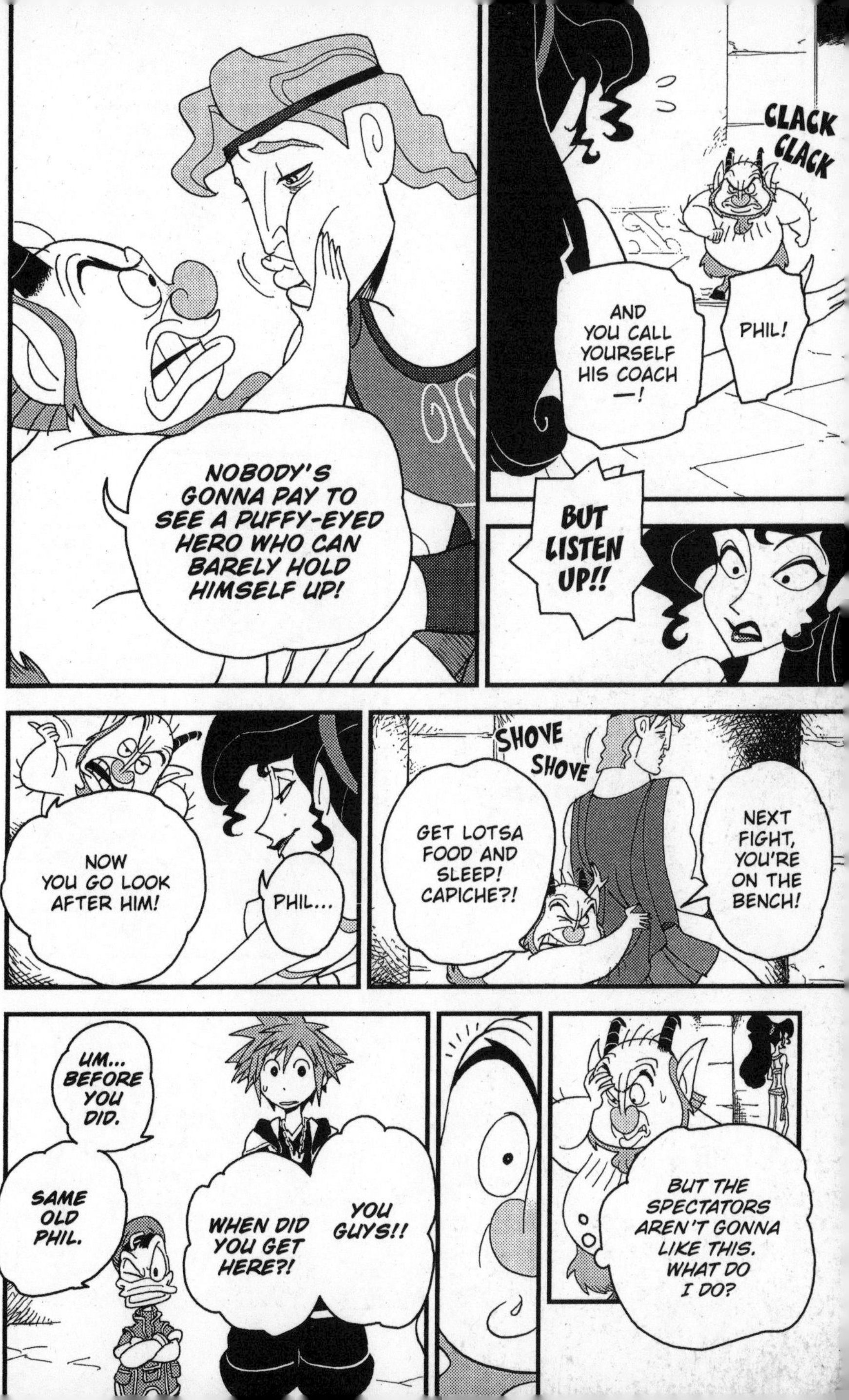
CLACK CLACK
PHIL!
AND YOU CALL YOURSELF HIS COACH —!
BUT LISTEN UP!!
NOBODY'S GONNA PAY TO SEE A PUFFY-EYED HERO WHO CAN BARELY HOLD HIMSELF UP!
SHOVE SHOVE
NEXT FIGHT, YOU'RE ON THE BENCH!
GET LOTSA FOOD AND SLEEP! CAPICHE?!
PHIL...
NOW YOU GO LOOK AFTER HIM!
BUT THE SPECTATORS AREN'T GONNA LIKE THIS. WHAT DO I DO?
YOU GUYS!!
WHEN DID YOU GET HERE?!
UM... BEFORE YOU DID.
SAME OLD PHIL.

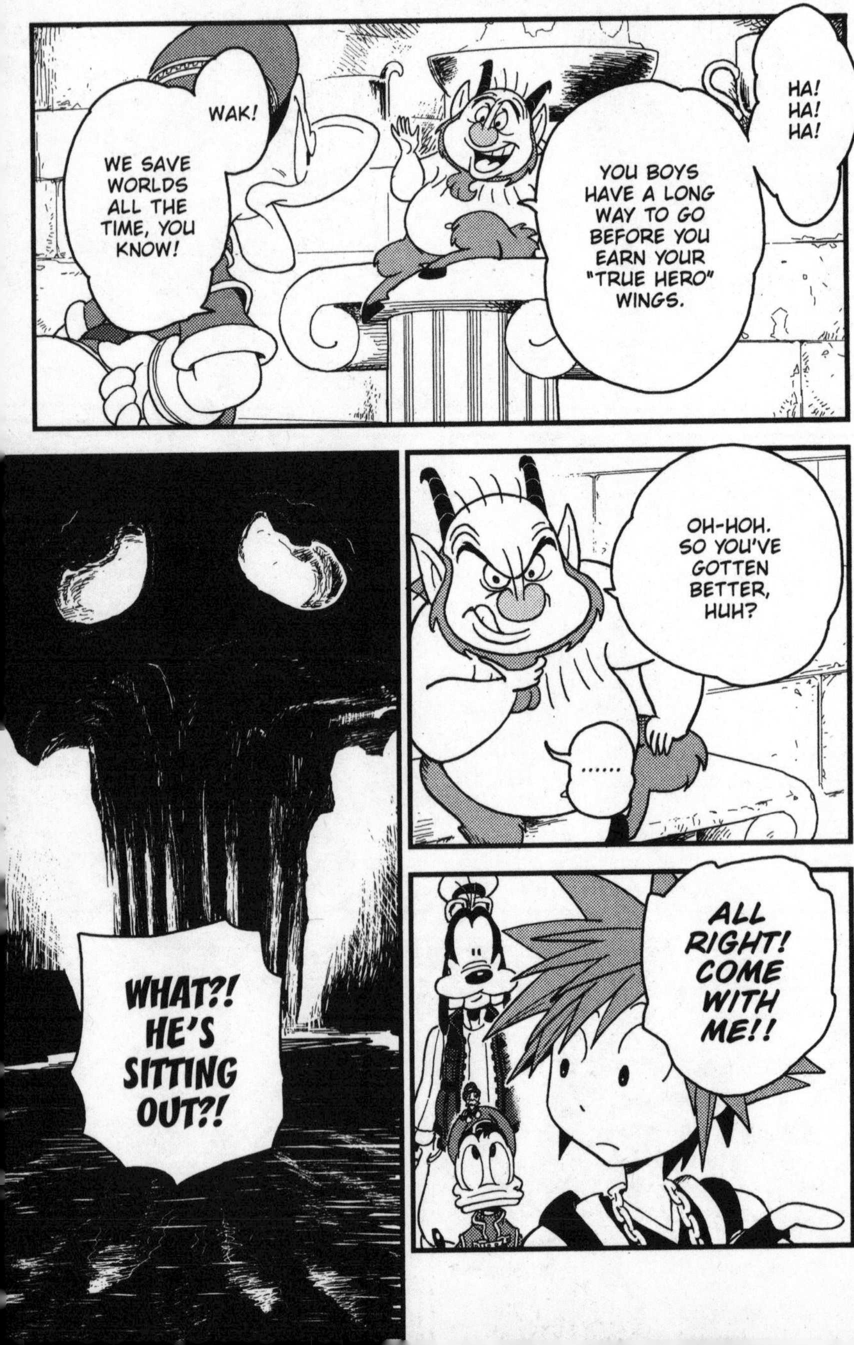
HA! HA! HA!
YOU BOYS HAVE A LONG WAY TO GO BEFORE YOU EARN YOUR "TRUE HERO" WINGS.
WAK!
WE SAVE WORLDS ALL THE TIME, YOU KNOW!
OH-HOH. SO YOU'VE GOTTEN BETTER, HUH?
......
ALL RIGHT! COME WITH ME!!
WHAT?! HE'S SITTING OUT?!

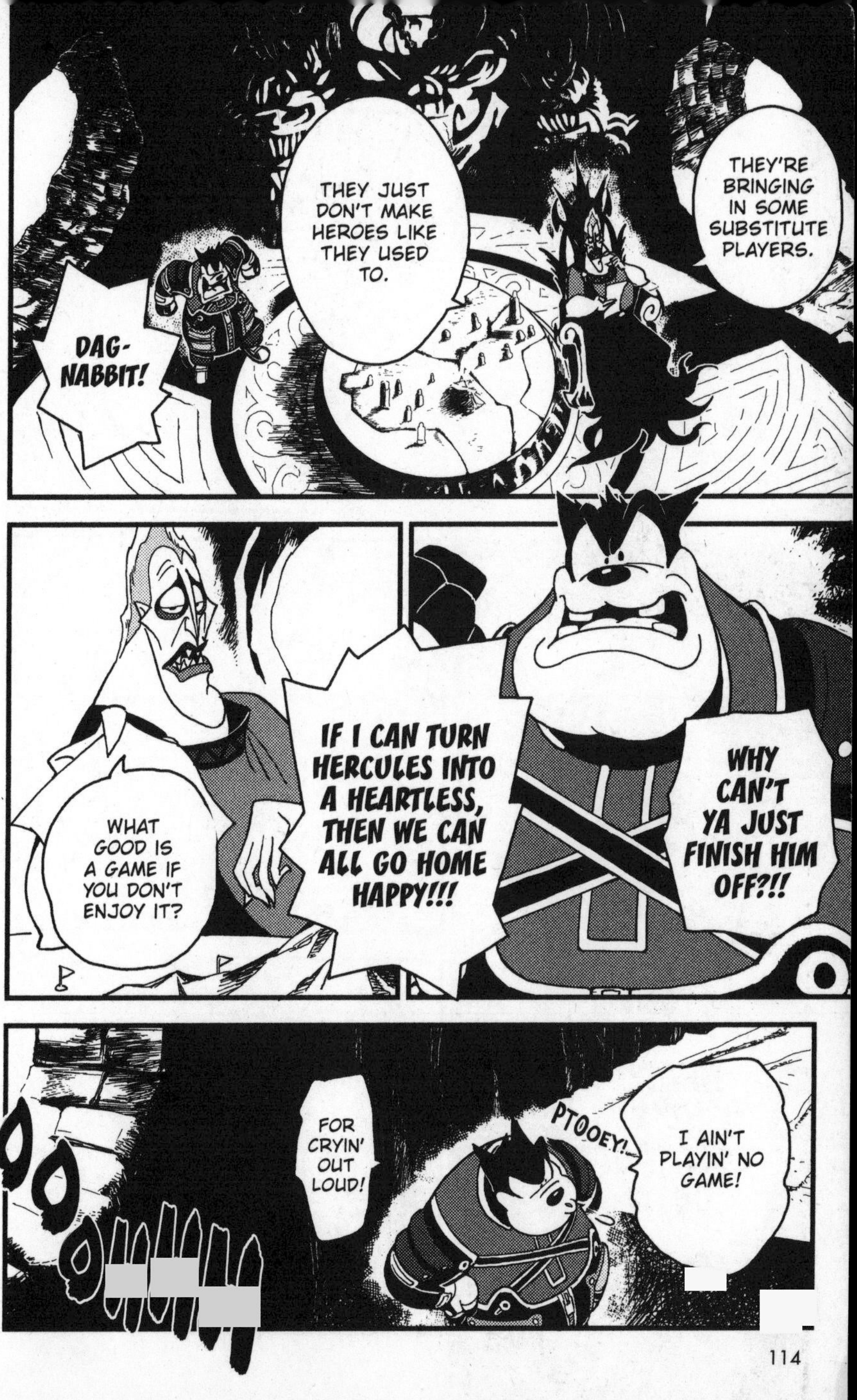
THEY'RE BRINGING IN SOME SUBSTITUTE PLAYERS.
THEY JUST DON'T MAKE HEROES LIKE THEY USED TO.
DAG-NABBIT!
WHY CAN'T YA JUST FINISH HIM OFF?!!
IF I CAN TURN HERCULES INTO A HEARTLESS, THEN WE CAN ALL GO HOME HAPPY!!!
WHAT GOOD IS A GAME IF YOU DON'T ENJOY IT?
I AIN'T PLAYIN' NO GAME!
PTOOEY!
FOR CRYIN' OUT LOUD!

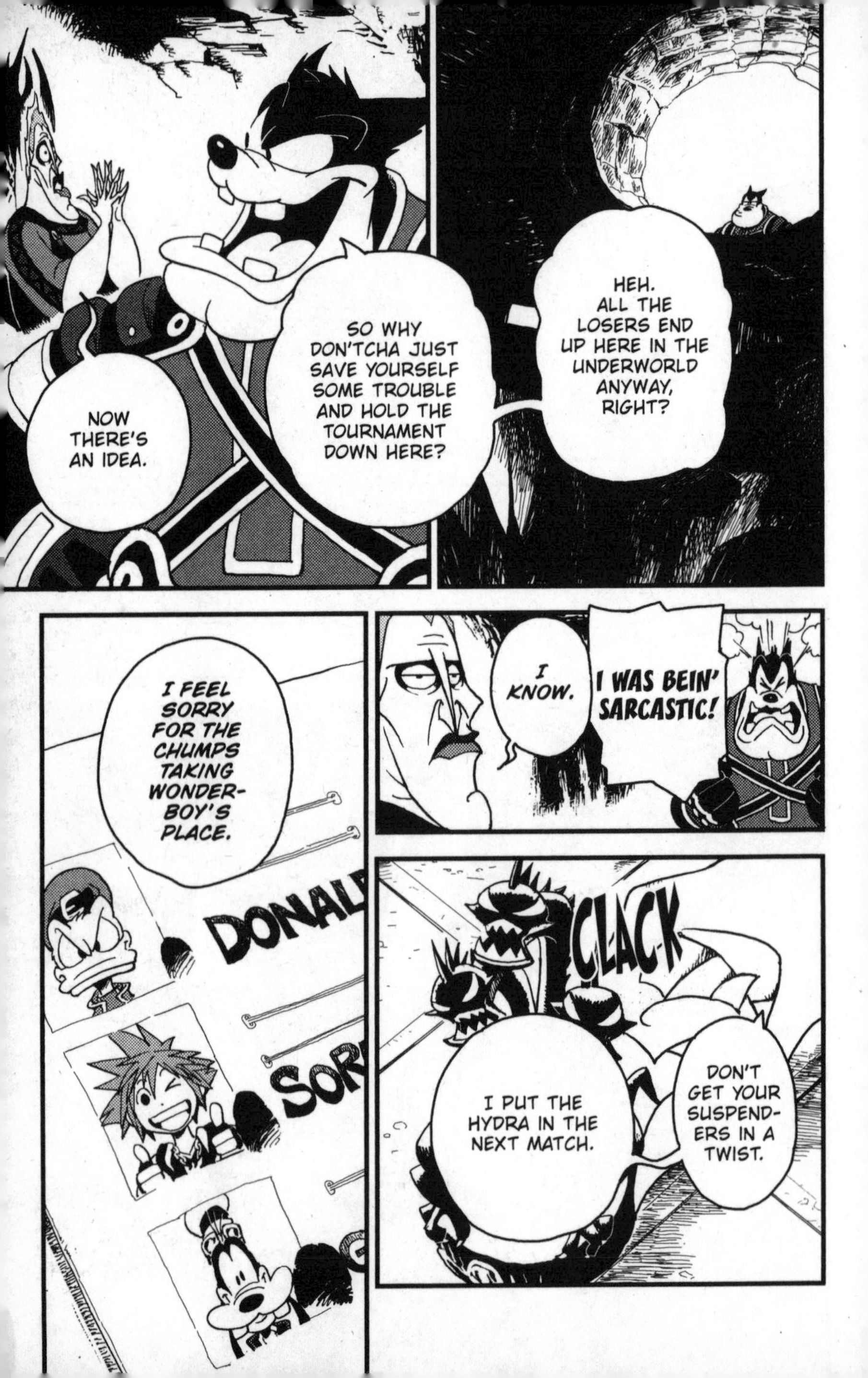
HEH. ALL THE LOSERS END UP HERE IN THE UNDERWORLD ANYWAY, RIGHT?
SO WHY DON'TCHA JUST SAVE YOURSELF SOME TROUBLE AND HOLD THE TOURNAMENT DOWN HERE?
NOW THERE'S AN IDEA.
I WAS BEIN' SARCASTIC!
I KNOW.
CLACK
DON'T GET YOUR SUSPENDERS IN A TWIST.
I PUT THE HYDRA IN THE NEXT MATCH.
I FEEL SORRY FOR THE CHUMPS TAKING WONDER-BOY'S PLACE.
DONAL
SOR

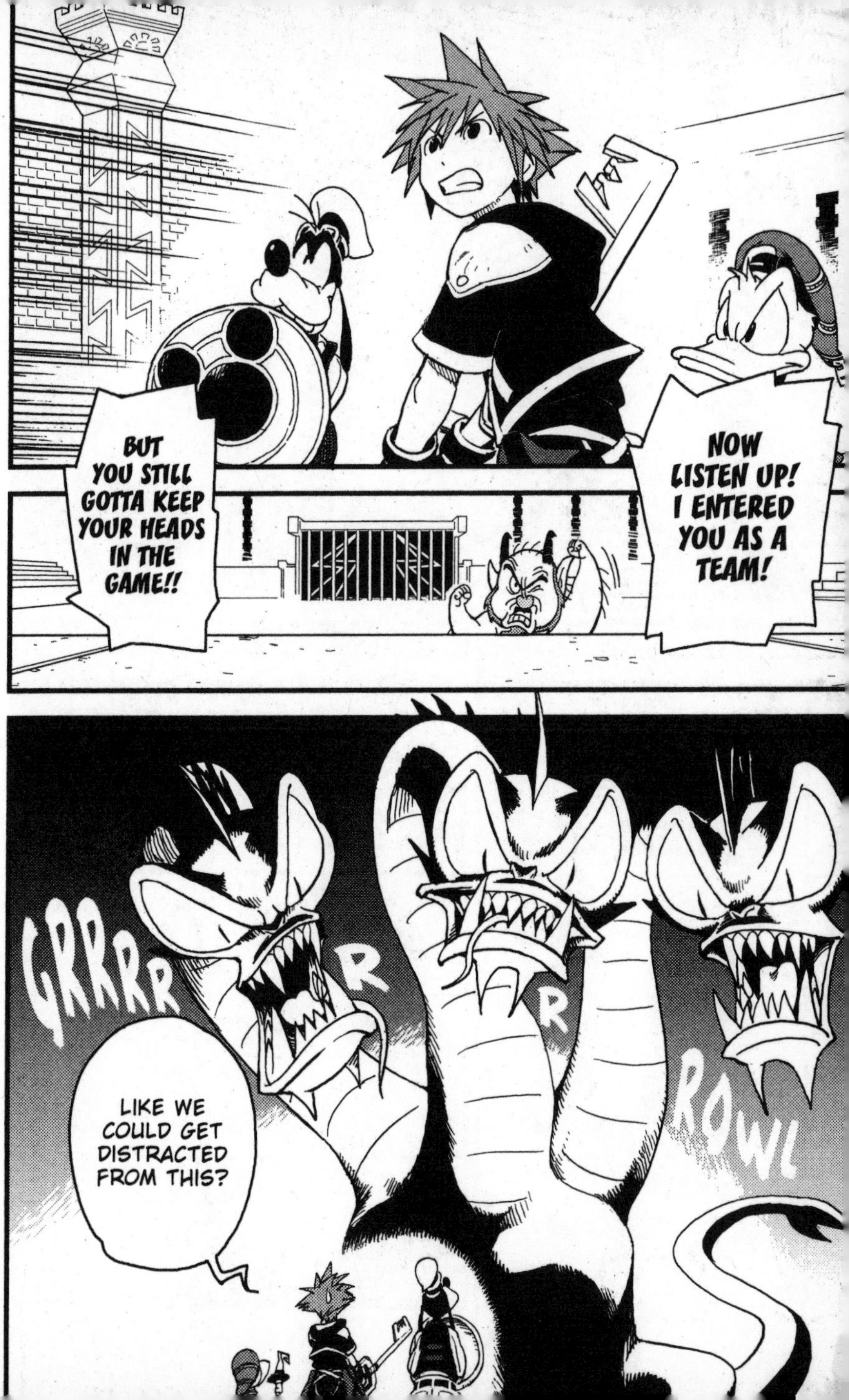
NOW LISTEN UP! I ENTERED YOU AS A TEAM!
BUT YOU STILL GOTTA KEEP YOUR HEADS IN THE GAME!!
GRRRR R R ROWL
LIKE WE COULD GET DISTRACTED FROM THIS?

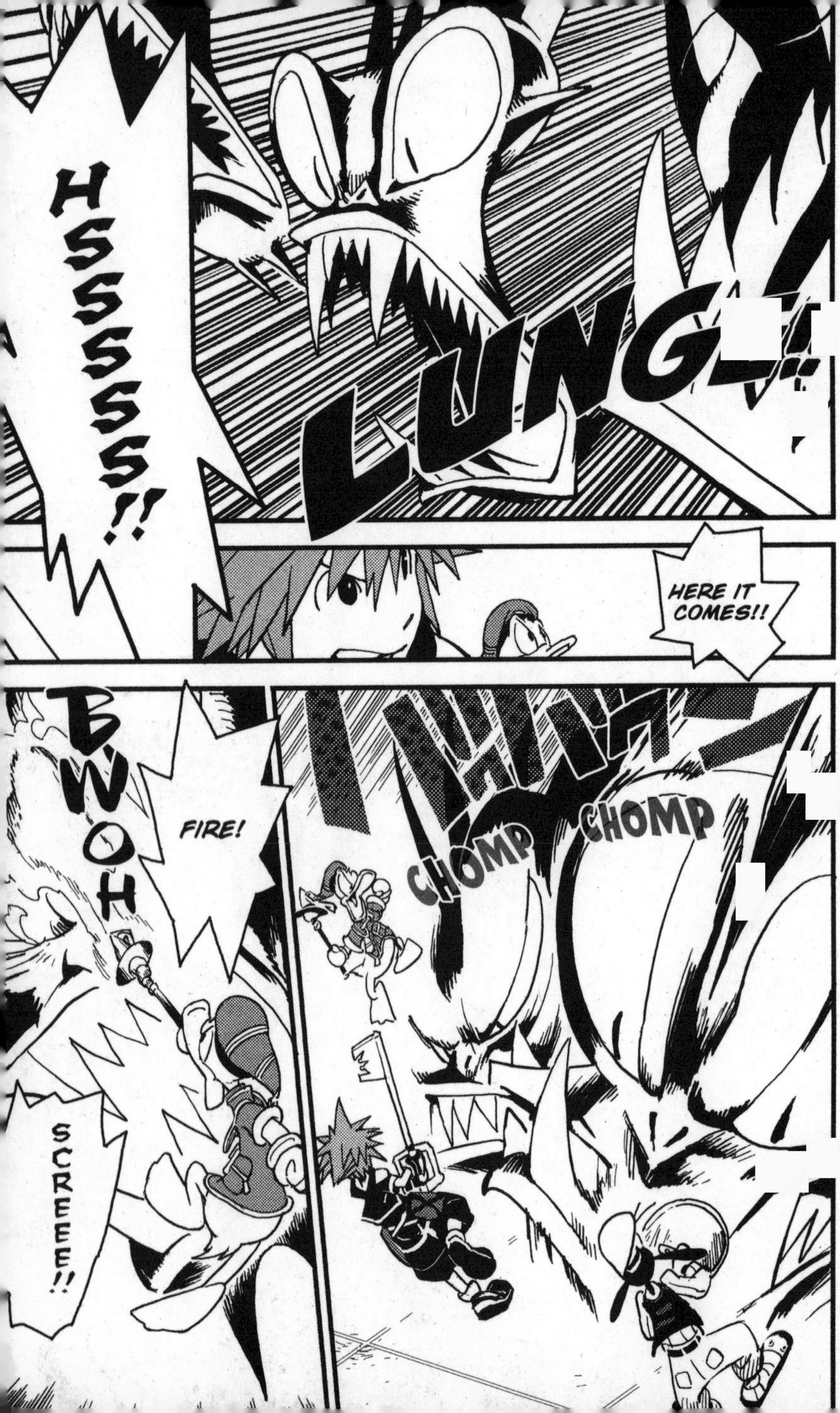
LUNG!!
HSSSSS!!
HERE IT COMES!!
CHOMP CHOMP
BWOH
FIRE!
SCREEE!!

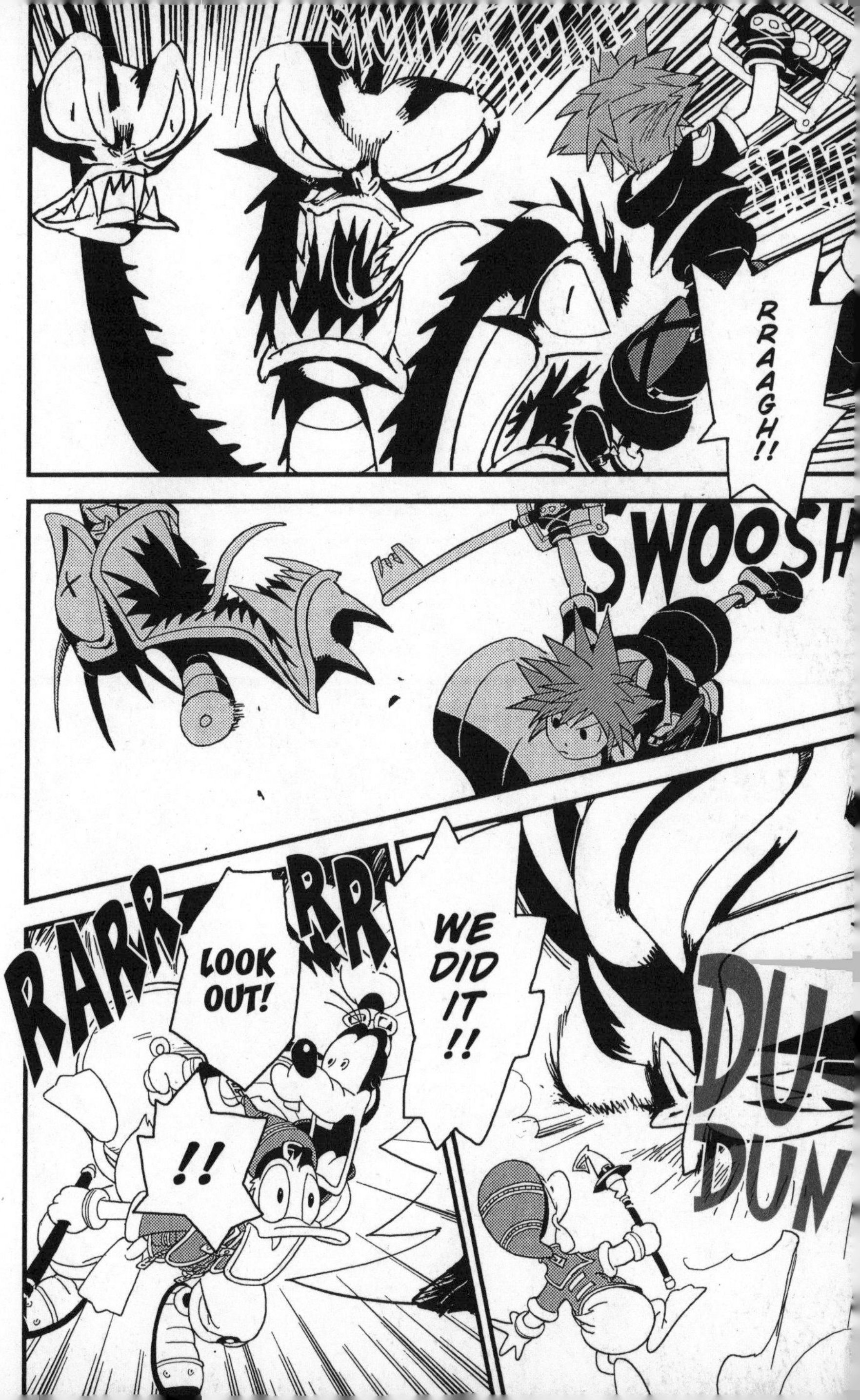
RRAAGH!!
SWOOSH
DU-
DUN
WE DID IT!!
RR
LOOK OUT!
RARR
!!

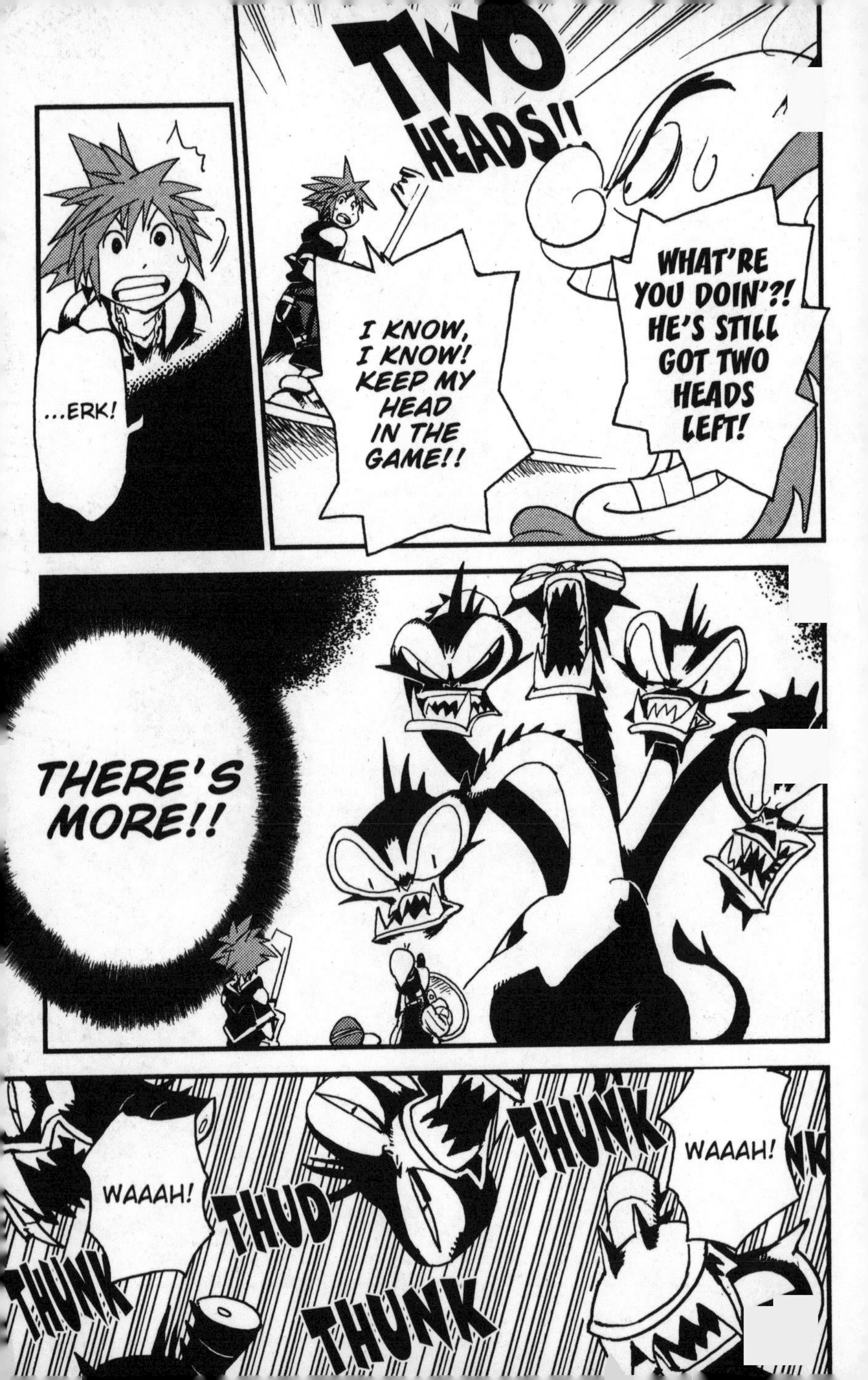
TWO HEADS!!
WHAT'RE YOU DOIN'?! HE'S STILL GOT TWO HEADS LEFT!
I KNOW, I KNOW! KEEP MY HEAD IN THE GAME!!
...ERK!
THERE'S MORE!!
WAAAH!
THUNK
THUD
THUNK
WAAAH!
THUNK

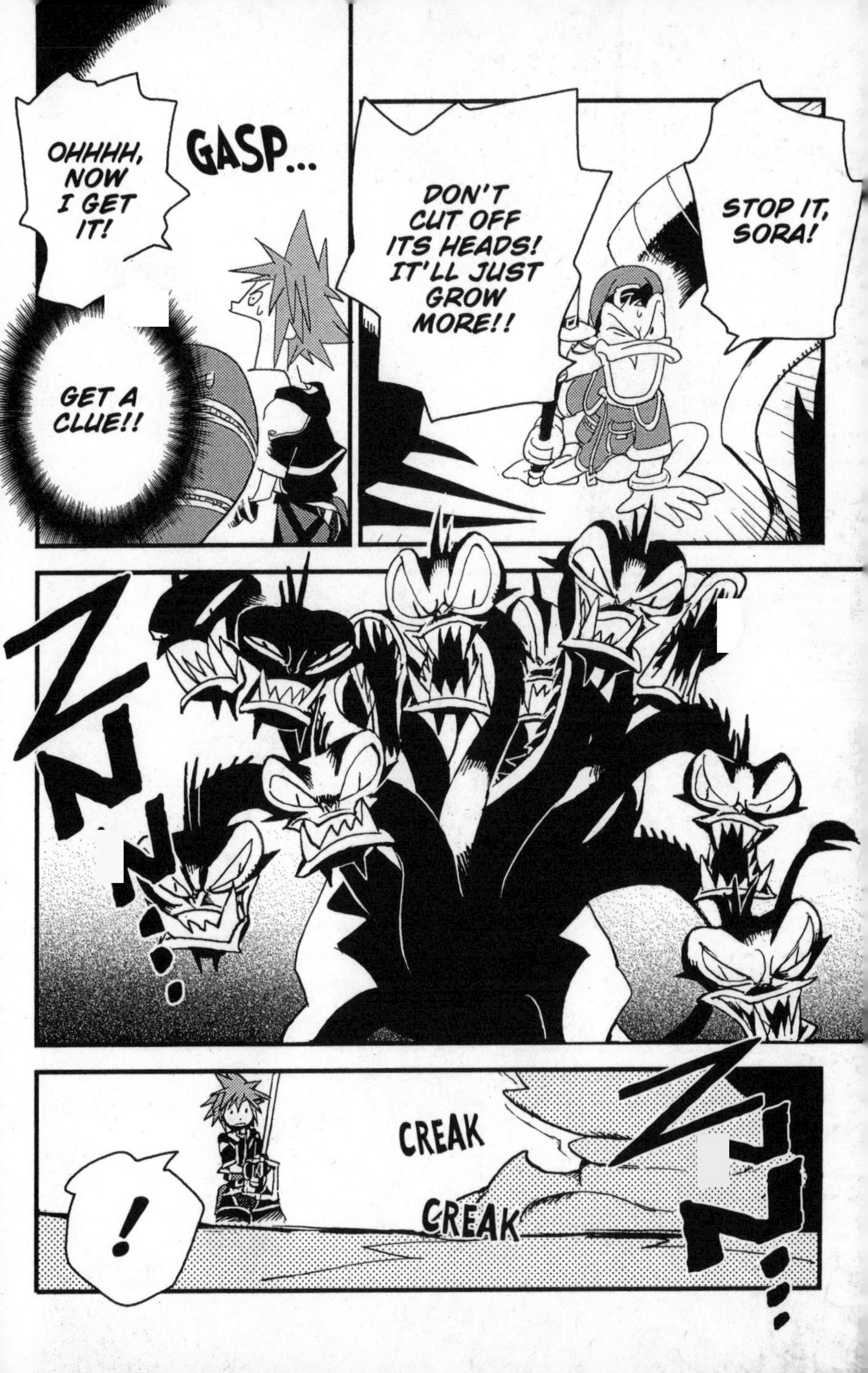
STOP IT, SORA!
DON'T CUT OFF ITS HEADS! IT'LL JUST GROW MORE!!
GASP...
OHHHH, NOW I GET IT!
GET A CLUE!!
CREAK
CREAK
!

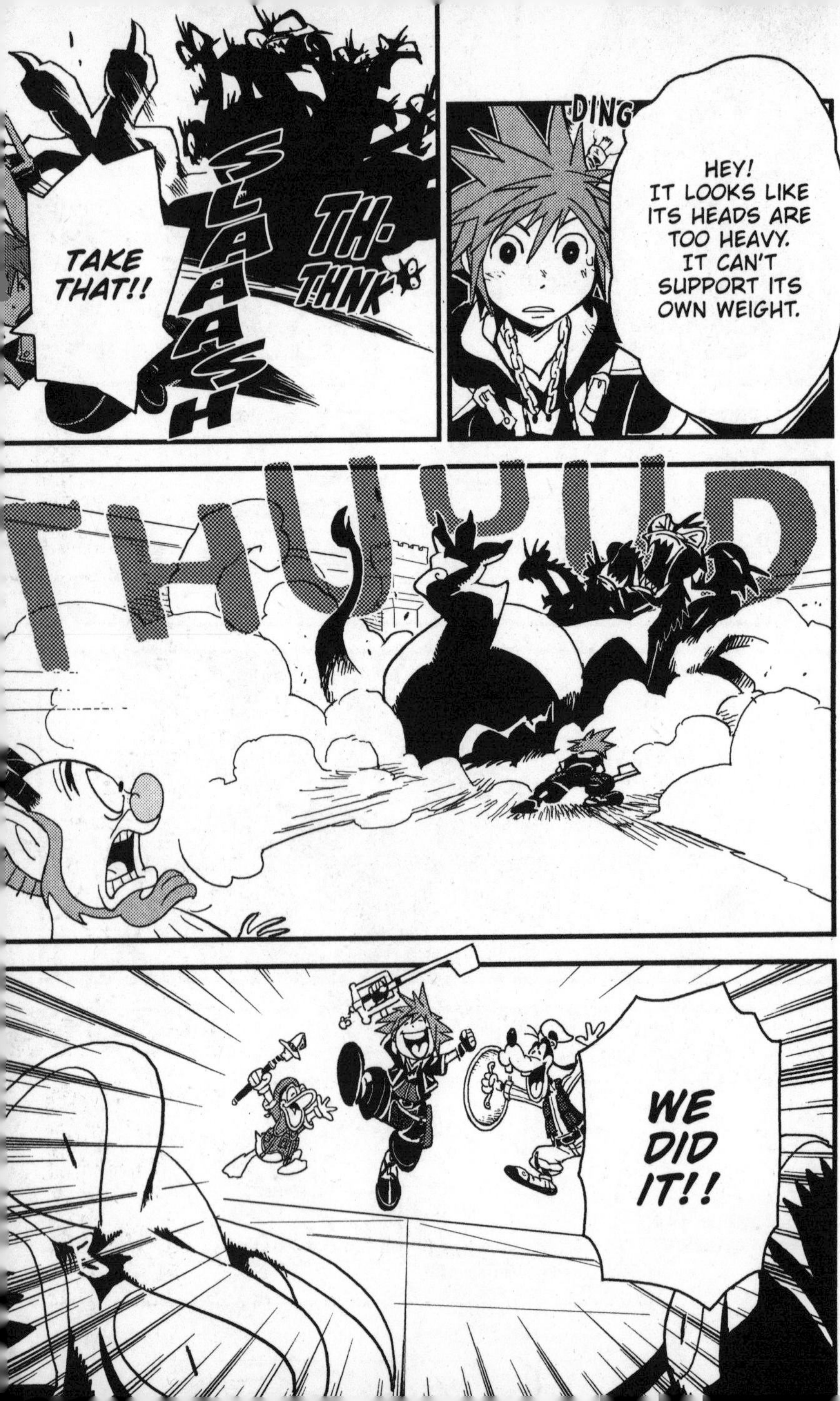
DING
HEY! IT LOOKS LIKE ITS HEADS ARE TOO HEAVY. IT CAN'T SUPPORT ITS OWN WEIGHT.
TAKE THAT!!
SLAAASH
TH-THNK
THUUD
WE DID IT!!

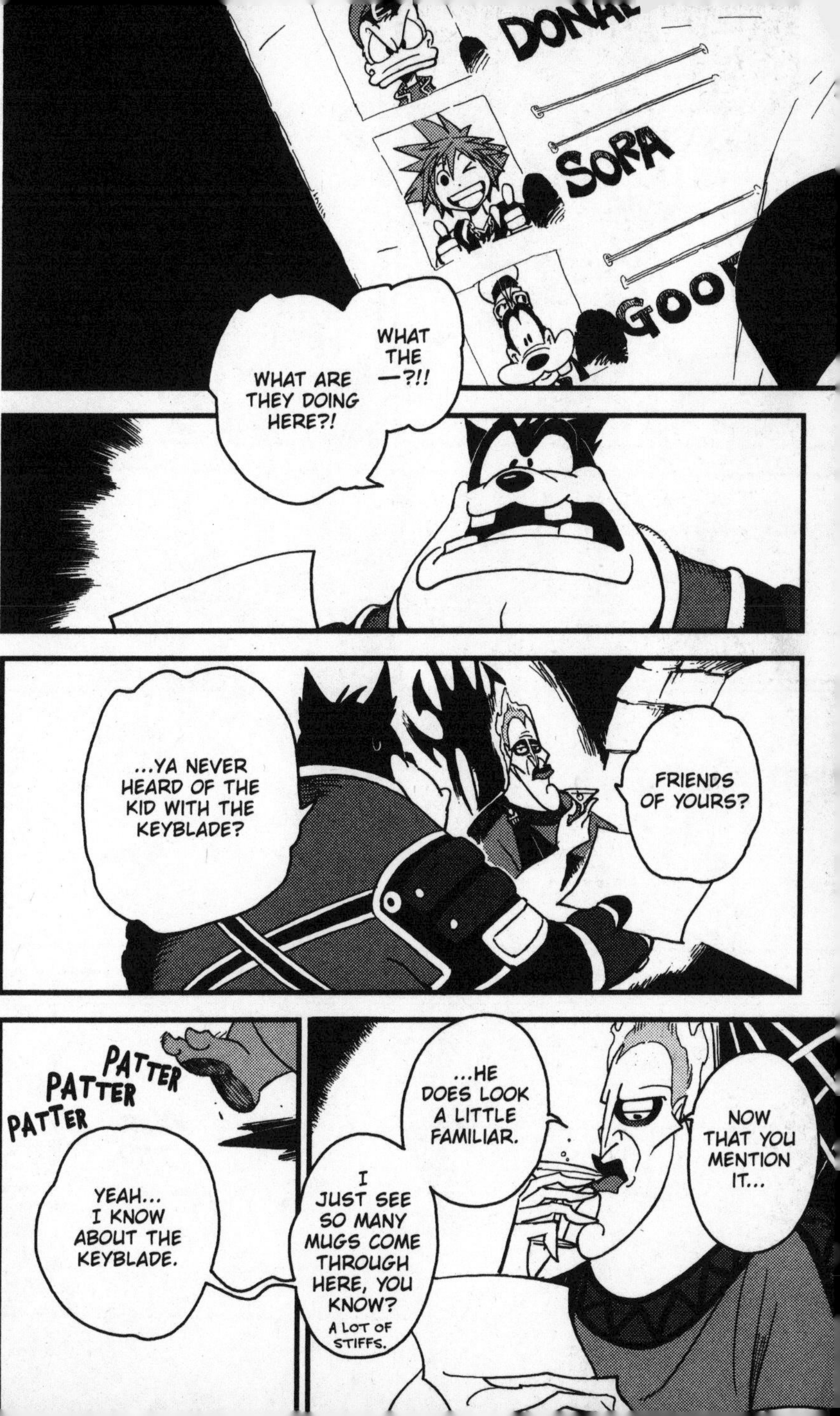
DONAL
SORA
GOOF
WHAT THE —?!!
WHAT ARE THEY DOING HERE?!
FRIENDS OF YOURS?
...YA NEVER HEARD OF THE KID WITH THE KEYBLADE?
NOW THAT YOU MENTION IT...
...HE DOES LOOK A LITTLE FAMILIAR.
I JUST SEE SO MANY MUGS COME THROUGH HERE, YOU KNOW?
A LOT OF STIFFS.
PATTER PATTER PATTER
YEAH... I KNOW ABOUT THE KEYBLADE.

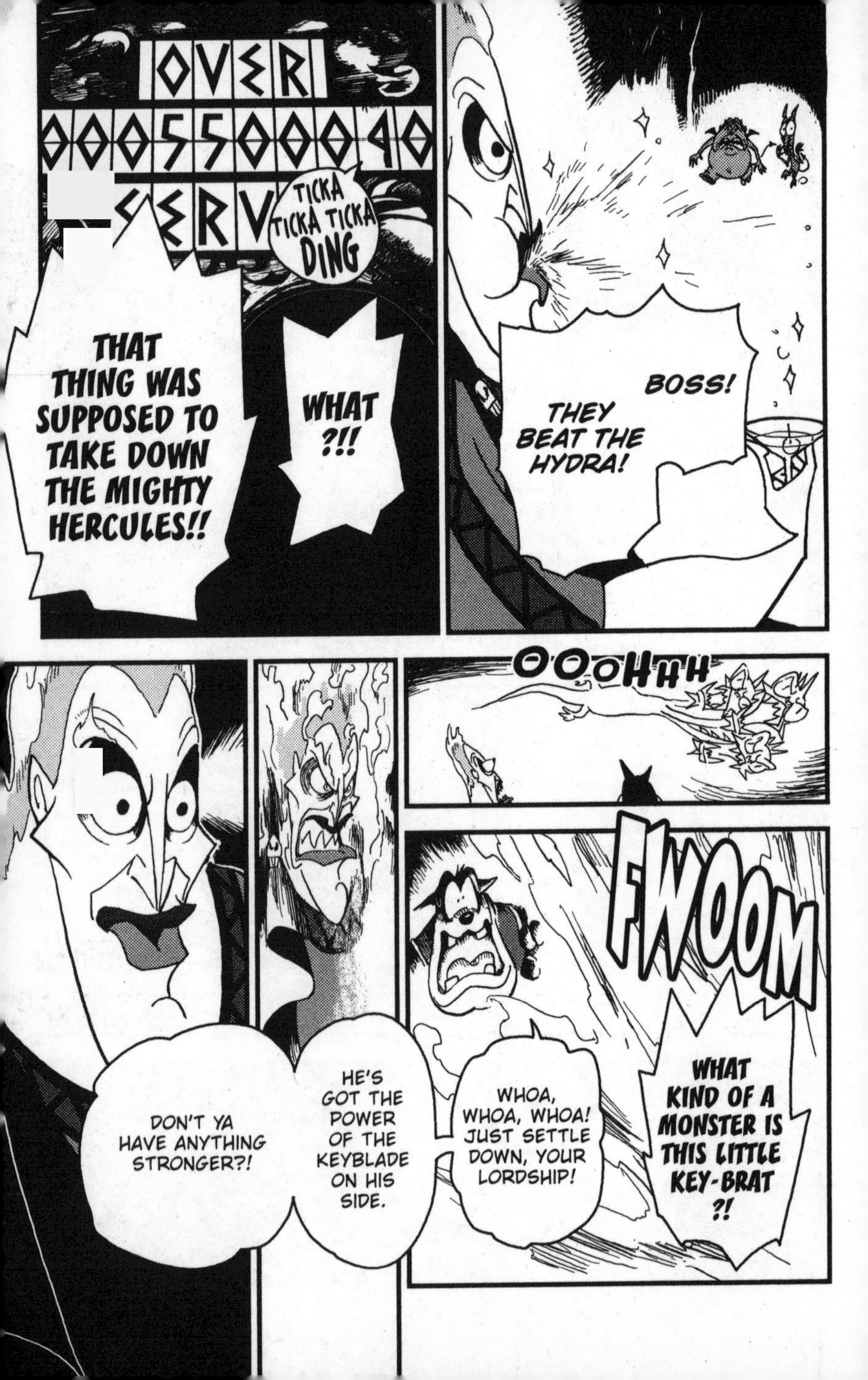
BOSS!
THEY BEAT THE HYDRA!
OVER
0005500040
ERV
TICKA TICKA TICKA DING
WHAT ?!!
THAT THING WAS SUPPOSED TO TAKE DOWN THE MIGHTY HERCULES!!
OOOHHH
FWOOM
WHAT KIND OF A MONSTER IS THIS LITTLE KEY-BRAT ?!
WHOA, WHOA, WHOA! JUST SETTLE DOWN, YOUR LORDSHIP!
HE'S GOT THE POWER OF THE KEYBLADE ON HIS SIDE.
DON'T YA HAVE ANYTHING STRONGER?!

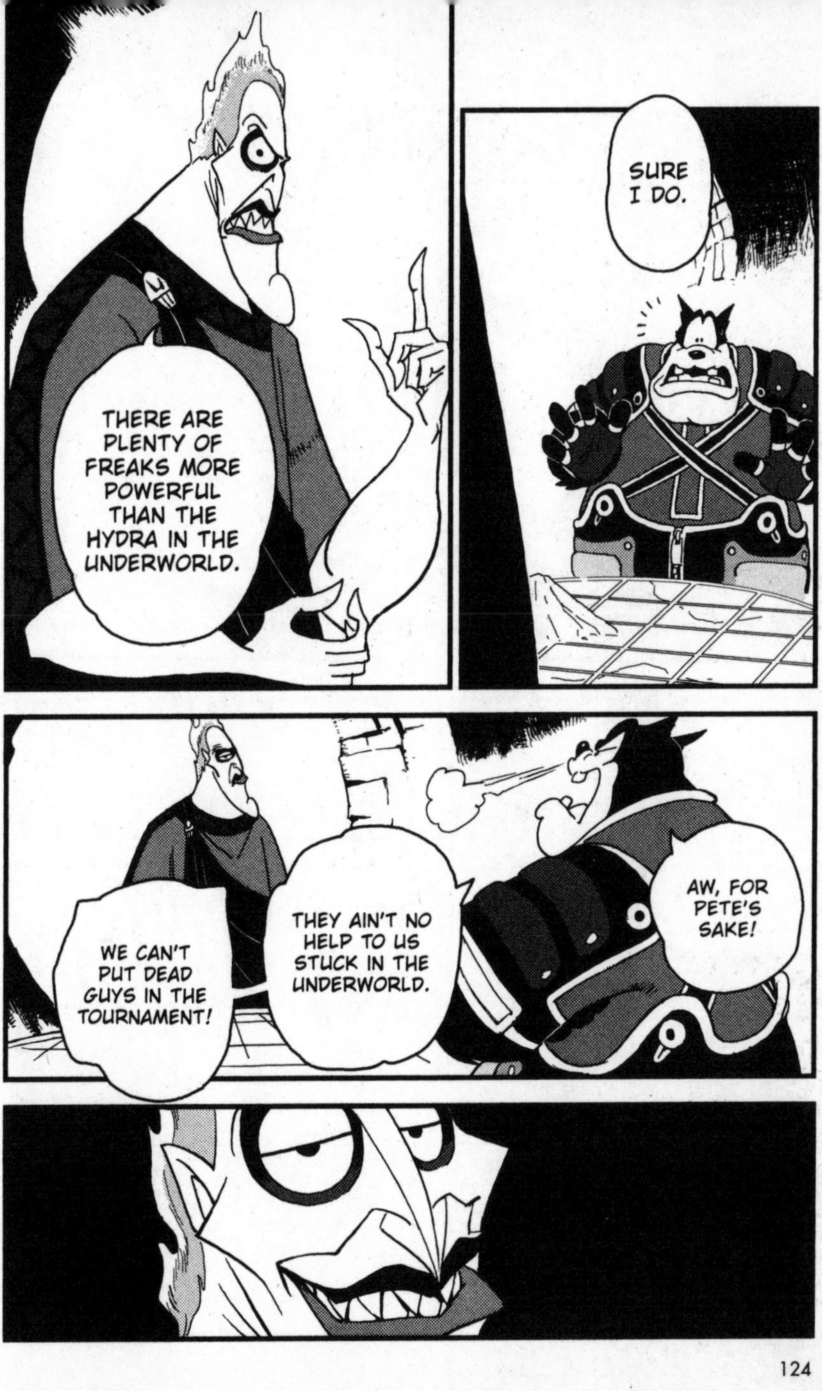
SURE I DO.
THERE ARE PLENTY OF FREAKS MORE POWERFUL THAN THE HYDRA IN THE UNDERWORLD.
AW, FOR PETE'S SAKE!
THEY AIN'T NO HELP TO US STUCK IN THE UNDERWORLD.
WE CAN'T PUT DEAD GUYS IN THE TOURNAMENT!

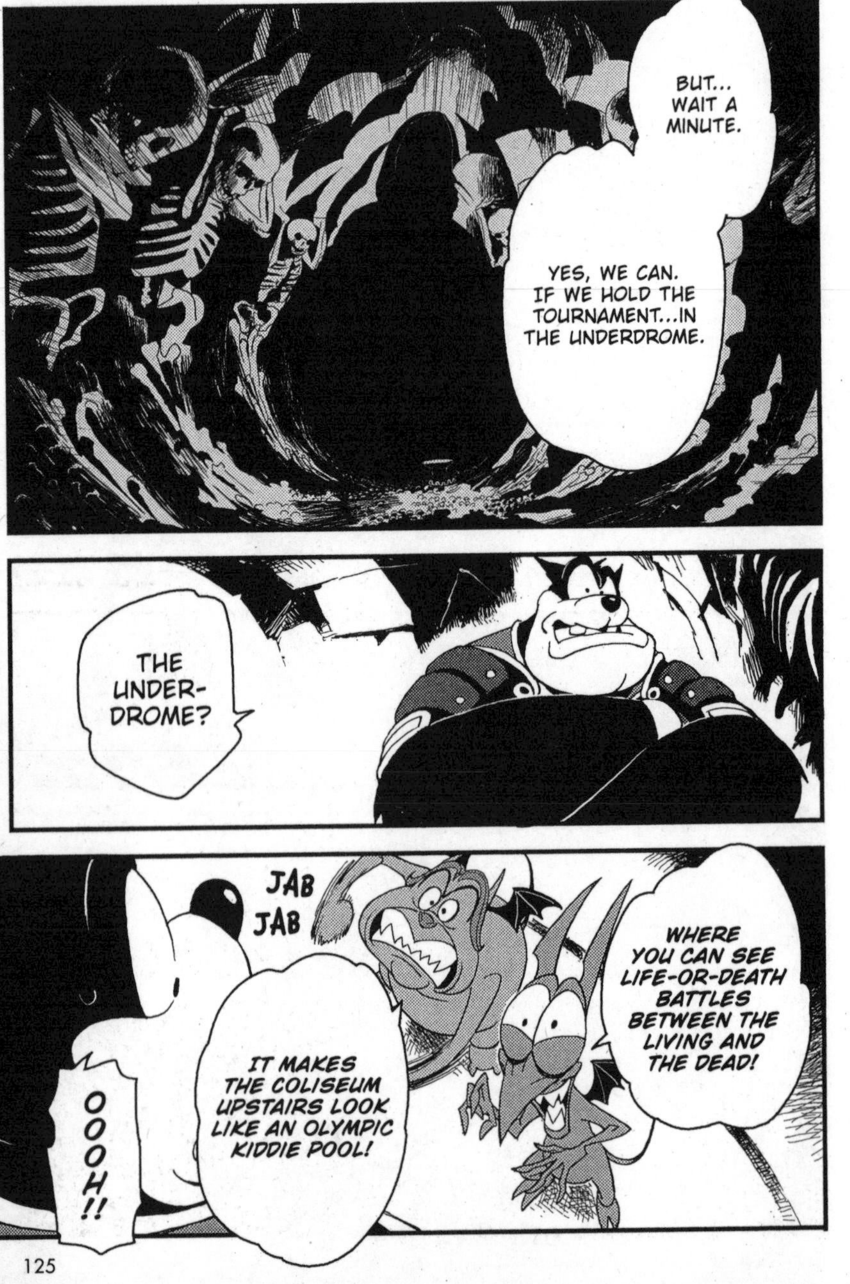
BUT... WAIT A MINUTE.
YES, WE CAN. IF WE HOLD THE TOURNAMENT...IN THE UNDERDROME.
THE UNDER-DROME?
WHERE YOU CAN SEE LIFE-OR-DEATH BATTLES BETWEEN THE LIVING AND THE DEAD!
JAB JAB
IT MAKES THE COLISEUM UPSTAIRS LOOK LIKE AN OLYMPIC KIDDIE POOL!
OOOOH!!

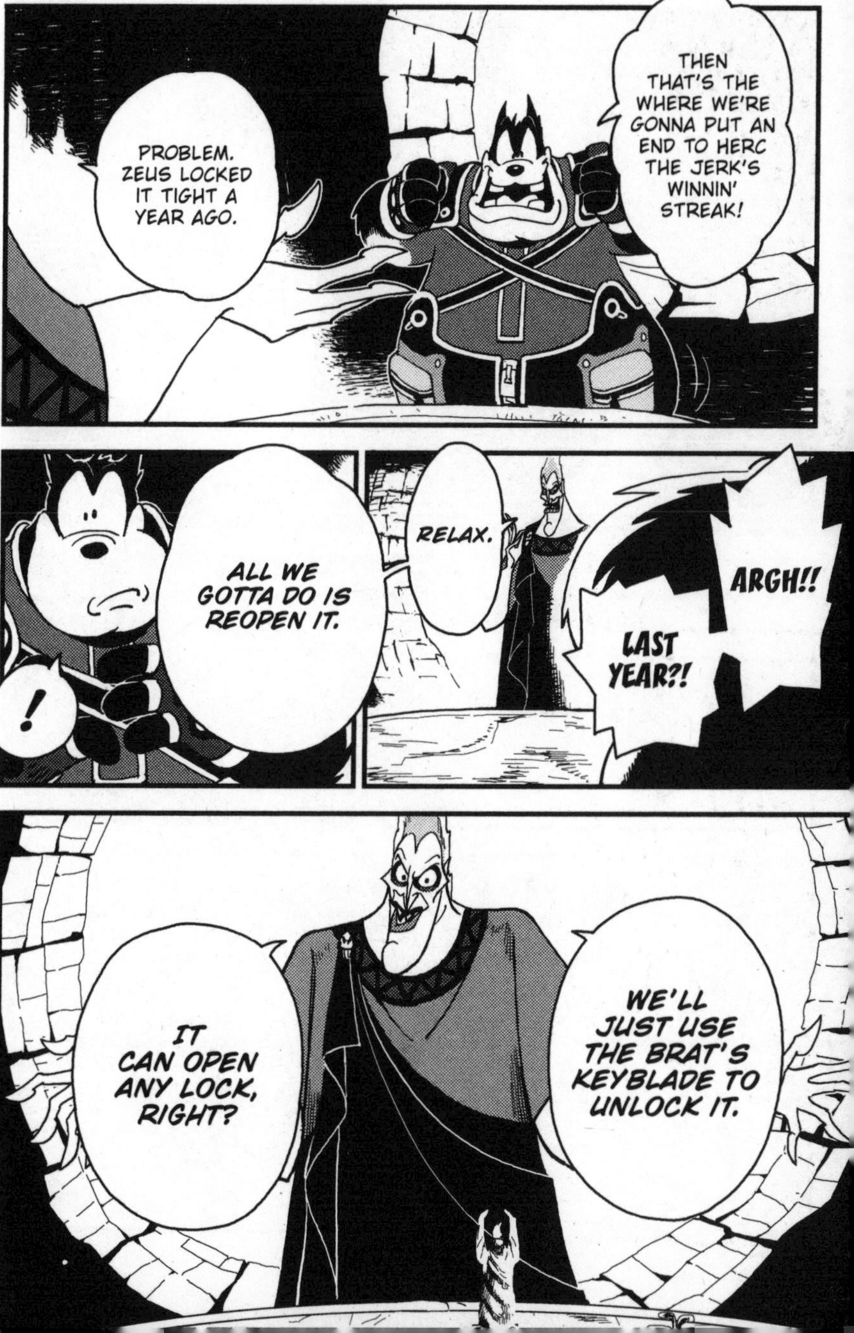
THEN THAT'S THE WHERE WE'RE GONNA PUT AN END TO HERC THE JERK'S WINNIN' STREAK!
PROBLEM. ZEUS LOCKED IT TIGHT A YEAR AGO.
ARGH!!
LAST YEAR?!
RELAX.
ALL WE GOTTA DO IS REOPEN IT.
!
WE'LL JUST USE THE BRAT'S KEYBLADE TO UNLOCK IT.
IT CAN OPEN ANY LOCK, RIGHT?

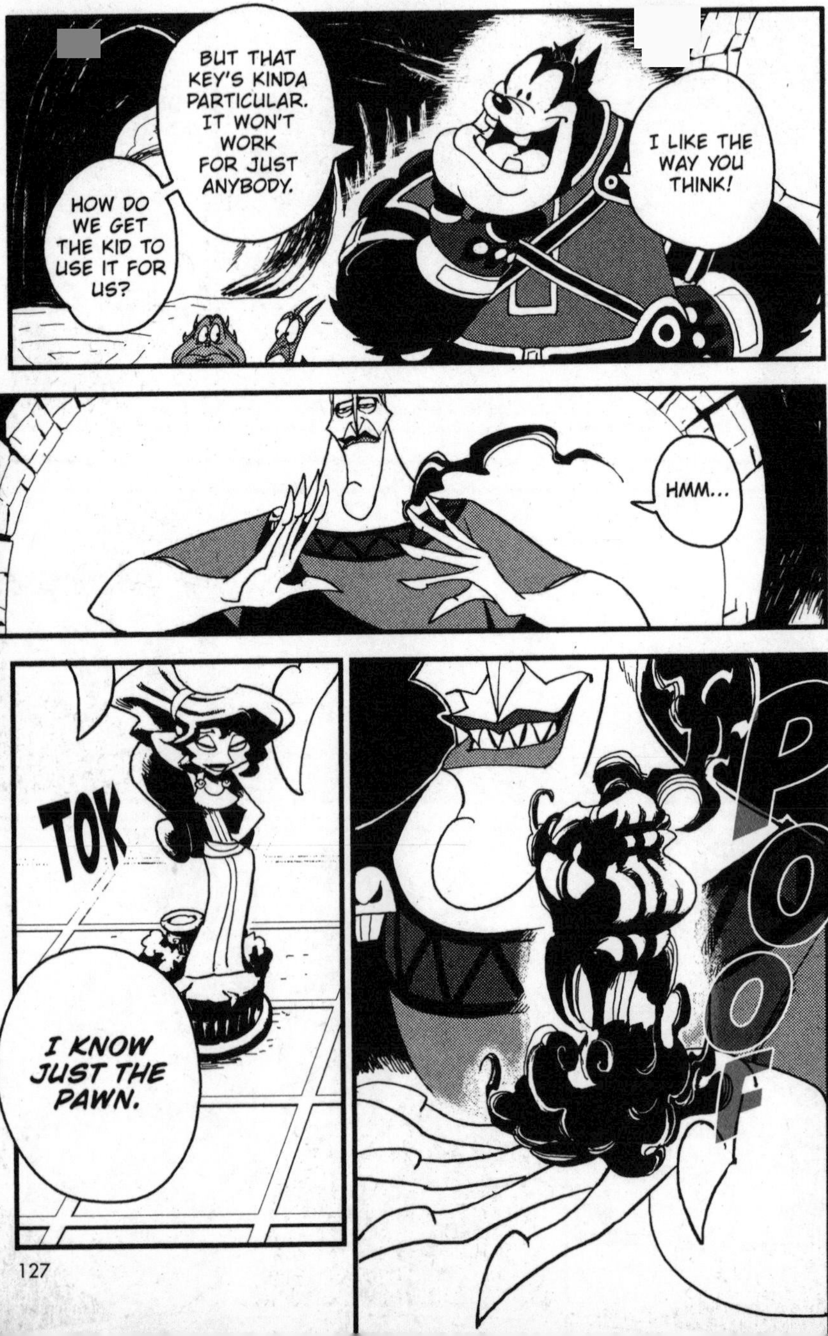
I LIKE THE WAY YOU THINK!
BUT THAT KEY'S KINDA PARTICULAR. IT WON'T WORK FOR JUST ANYBODY.
HOW DO WE GET THE KID TO USE IT FOR US?
HMM...
POOF
TOK
I KNOW JUST THE PAWN.

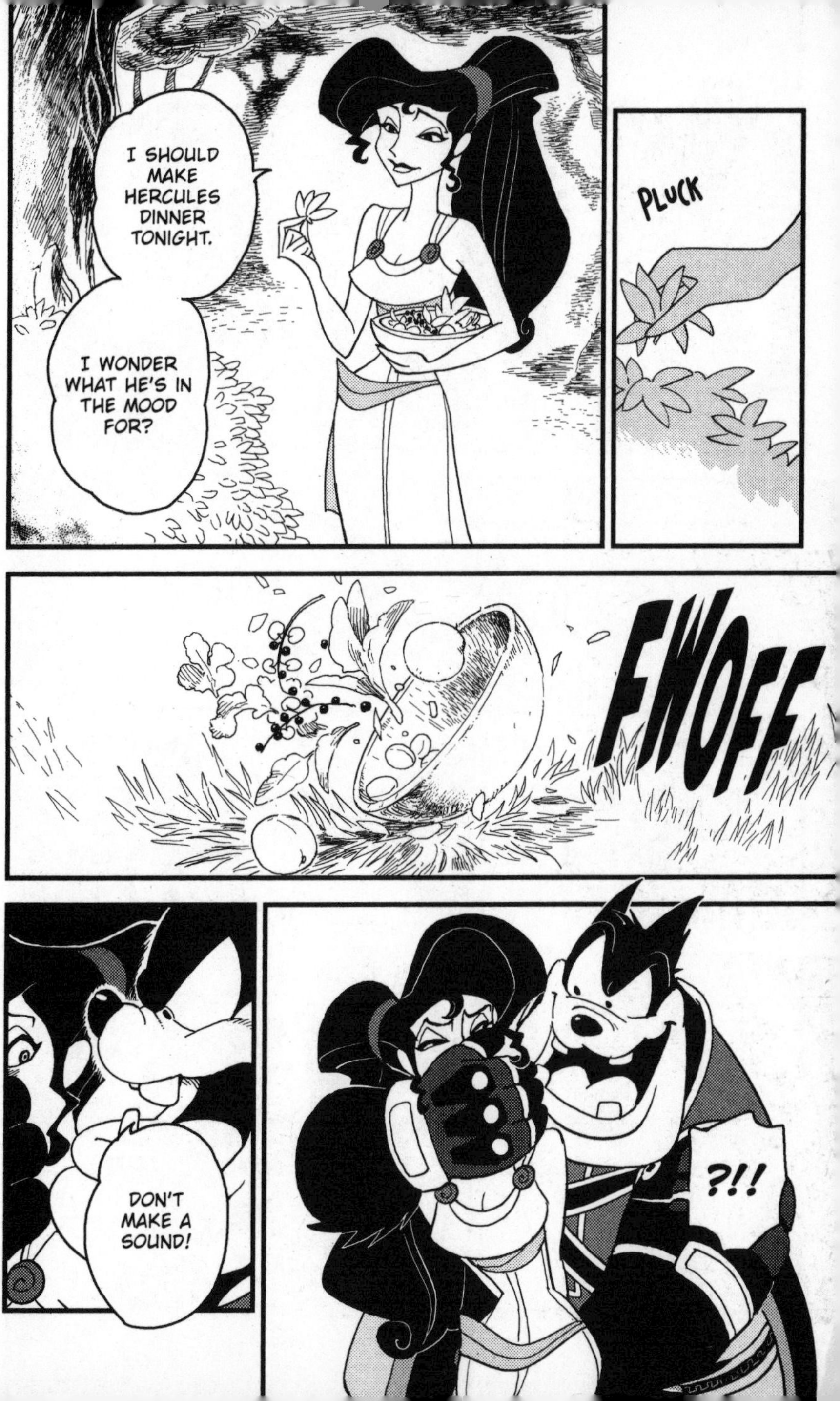
PLUCK
I SHOULD MAKE HERCULES DINNER TONIGHT.
I WONDER WHAT HE'S IN THE MOOD FOR?
FWOFF
?!!
DON'T MAKE A SOUND!

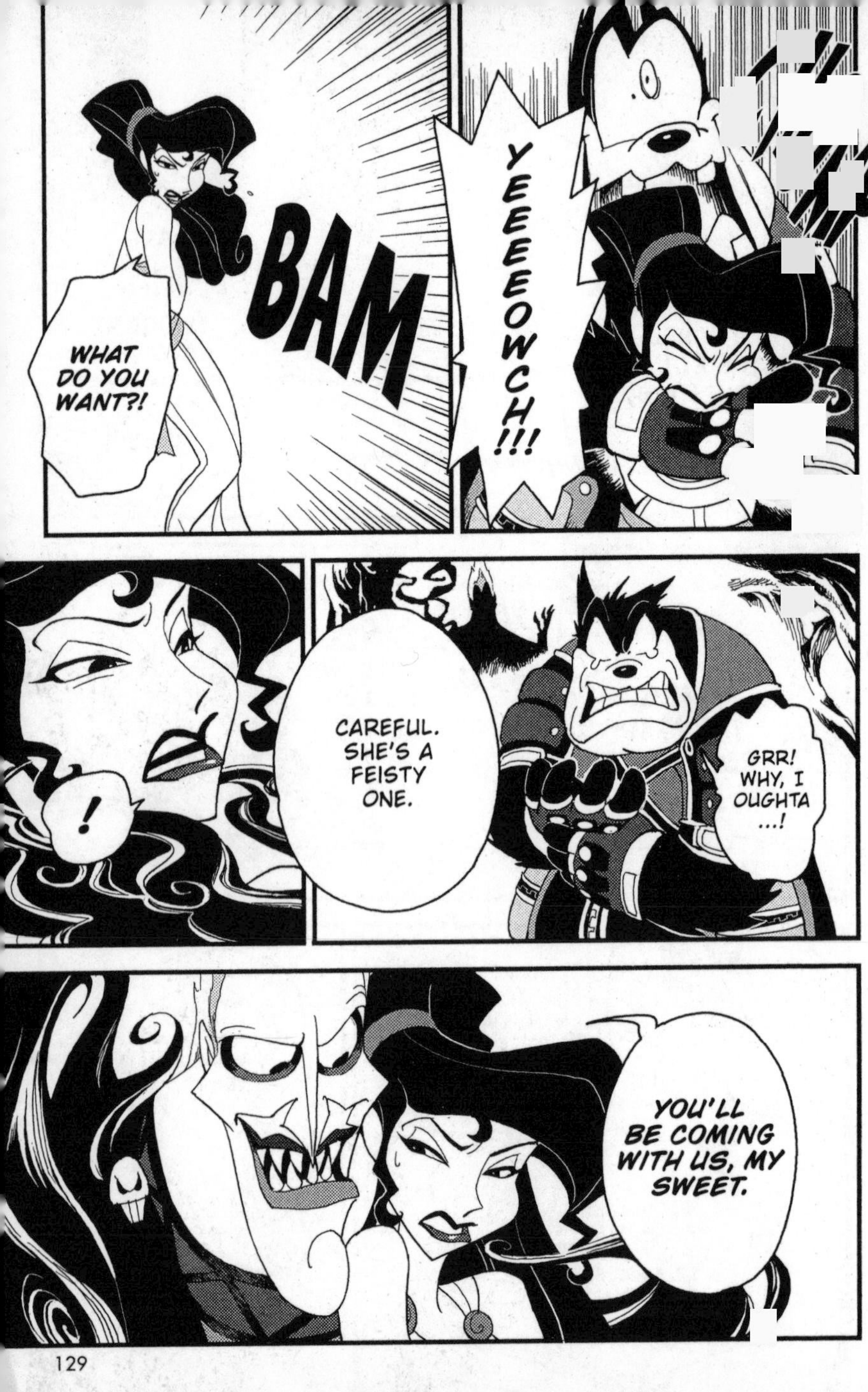
YEEEEOWCH!!!
BAM
WHAT DO YOU WANT?!
CAREFUL. SHE'S A FEISTY ONE.
GRR! WHY, I OUGHTA ...!
!
YOU'LL BE COMING WITH US, MY SWEET.

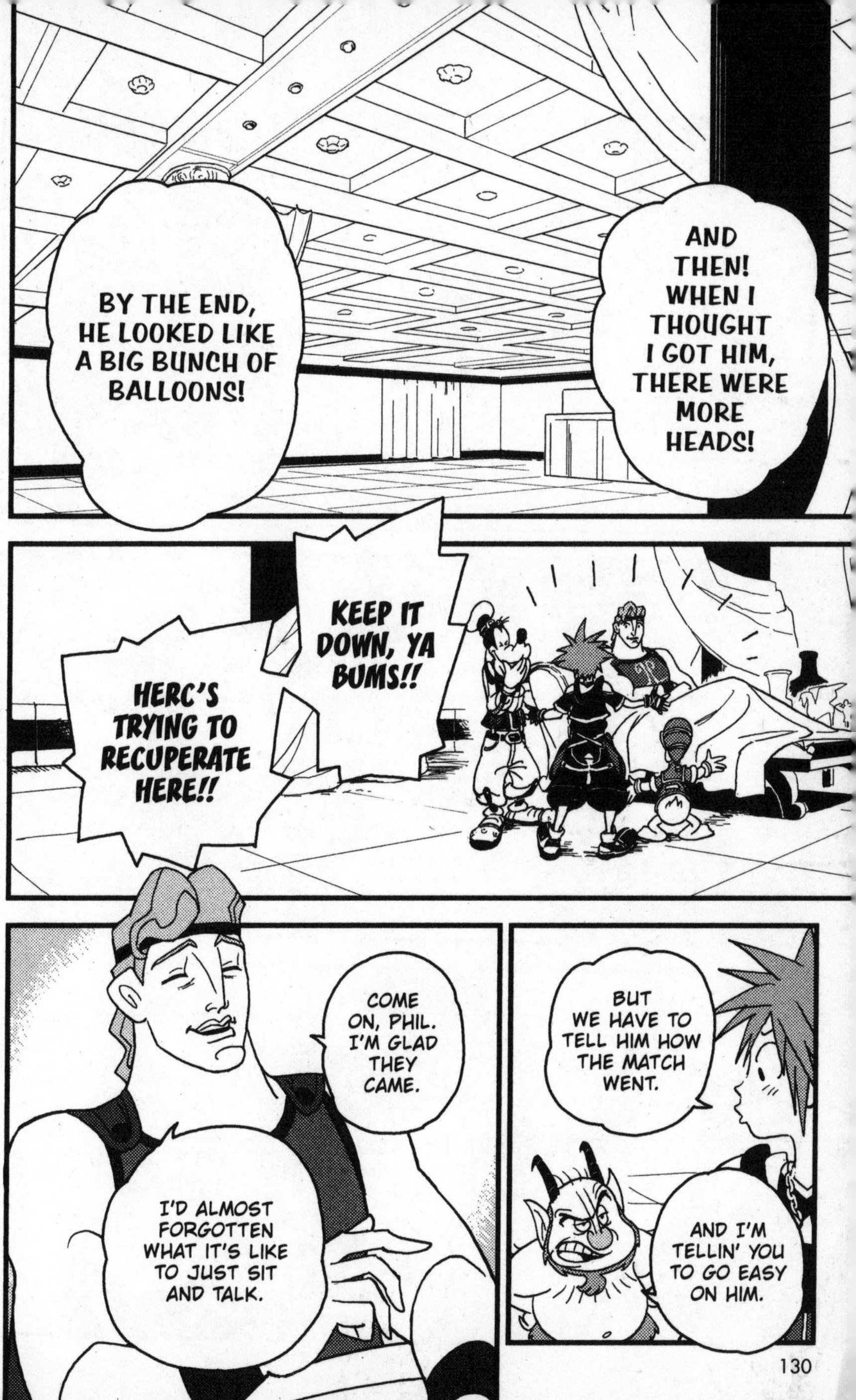
AND THEN! WHEN I THOUGHT I GOT HIM, THERE WERE MORE HEADS!
BY THE END, HE LOOKED LIKE A BIG BUNCH OF BALLOONS!
KEEP IT DOWN, YA BUMS!!
HERC'S TRYING TO RECUPERATE HERE!!
BUT WE HAVE TO TELL HIM HOW THE MATCH WENT.
AND I'M TELLIN' YOU TO GO EASY ON HIM.
COME ON, PHIL. I'M GLAD THEY CAME.
I'D ALMOST FORGOTTEN WHAT IT'S LIKE TO JUST SIT AND TALK.

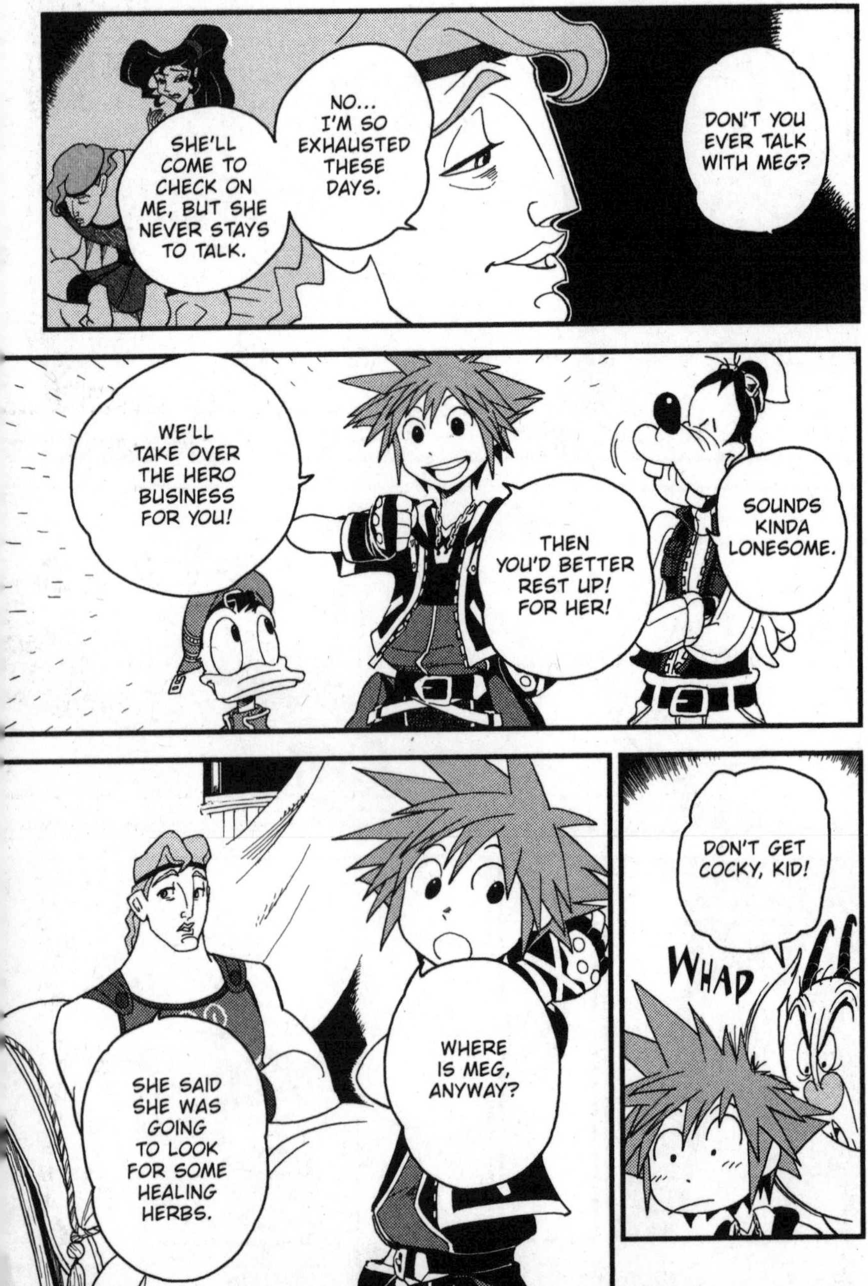
DON'T YOU EVER TALK WITH MEG?
NO... I'M SO EXHAUSTED THESE DAYS.
SHE'LL COME TO CHECK ON ME, BUT SHE NEVER STAYS TO TALK.
SOUNDS KINDA LONESOME.
THEN YOU'D BETTER REST UP! FOR HER!
WE'LL TAKE OVER THE HERO BUSINESS FOR YOU!
DON'T GET COCKY, KID!
WHAP
WHERE IS MEG, ANYWAY?
SHE SAID SHE WAS GOING TO LOOK FOR SOME HEALING HERBS.

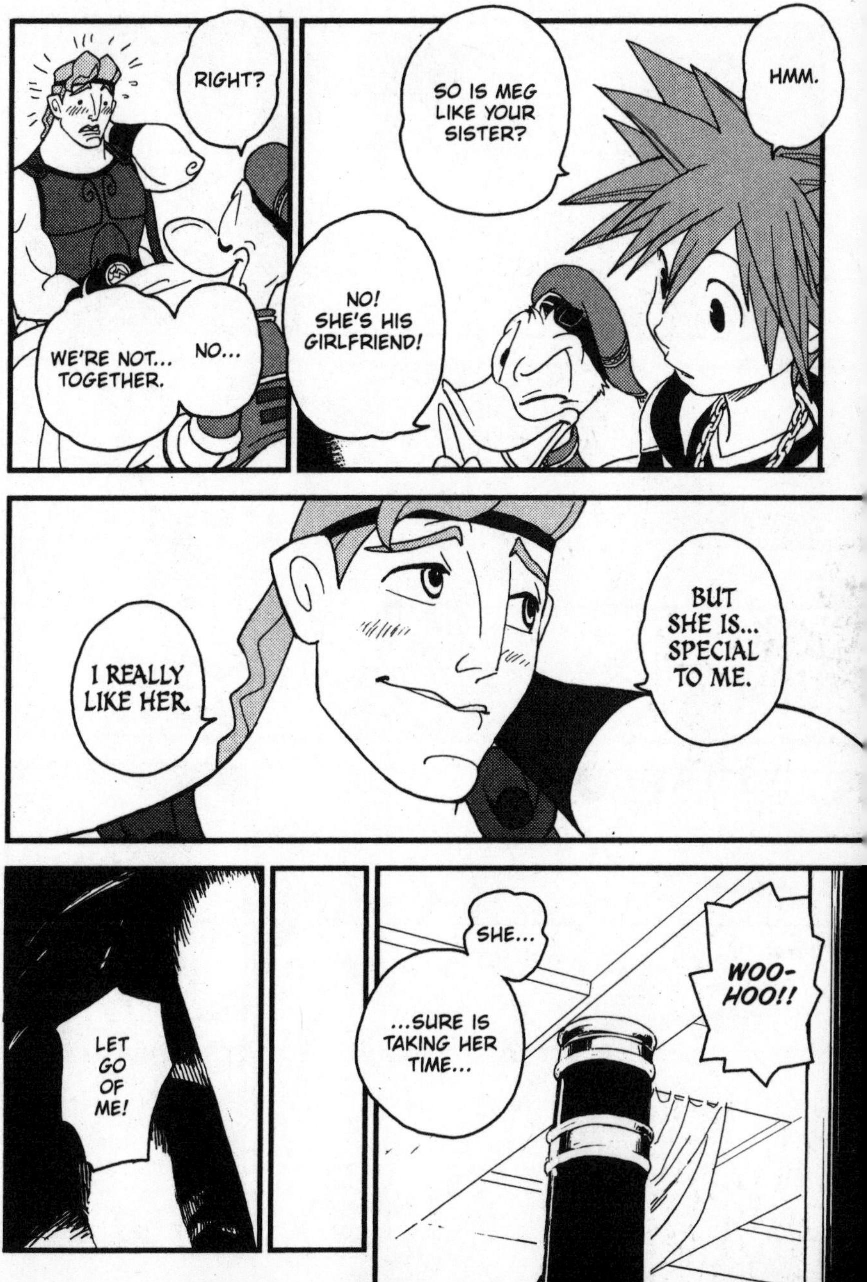
HMM.
SO IS MEG LIKE YOUR SISTER?
NO! SHE'S HIS GIRLFRIEND!
RIGHT?
NO...
WE'RE NOT... TOGETHER.
BUT SHE IS... SPECIAL TO ME.
I REALLY LIKE HER.
SHE...
...SURE IS TAKING HER TIME...
WOO-HOO!!
LET GO OF ME!

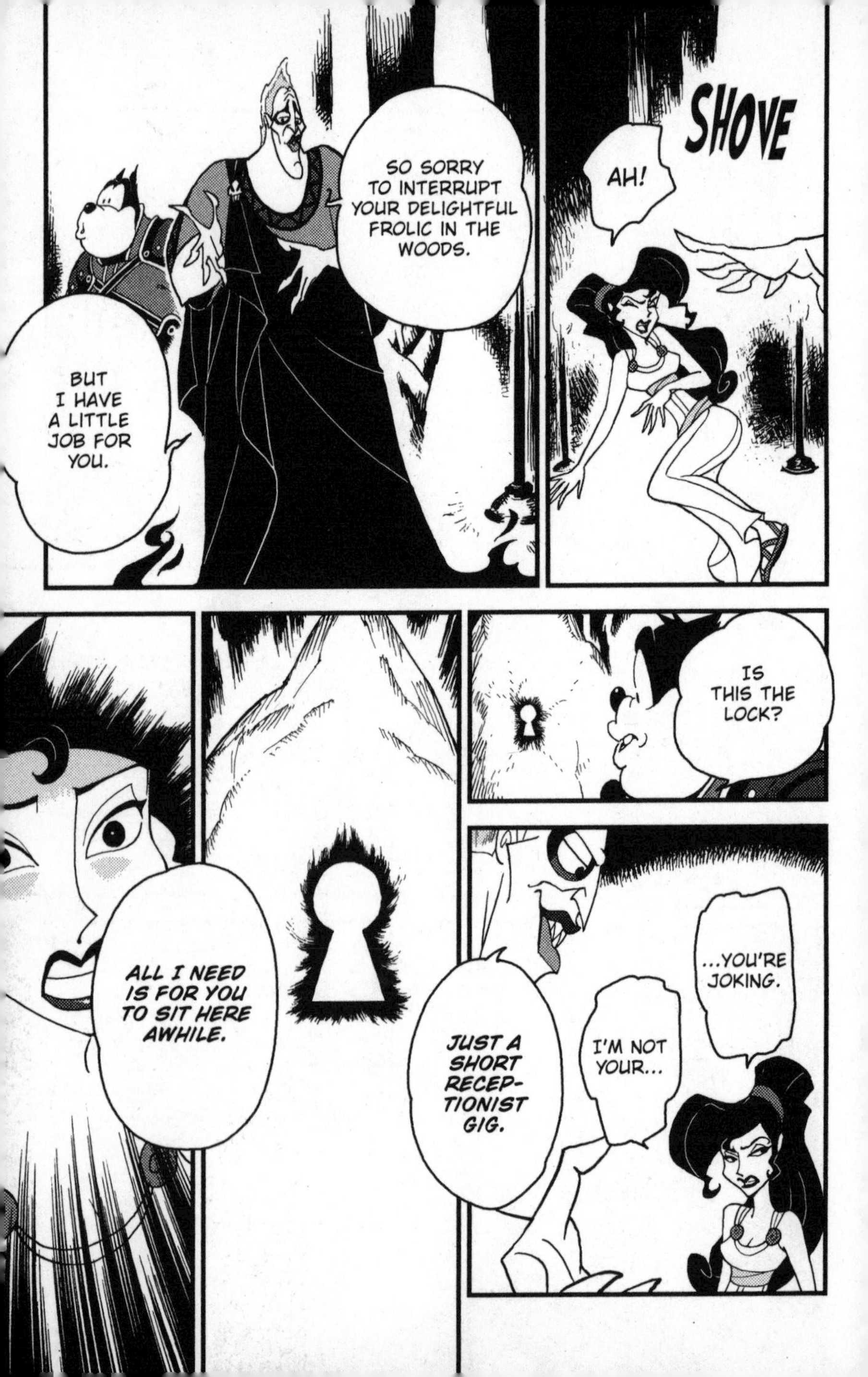
SHOVE
AH!
SO SORRY TO INTERRUPT YOUR DELIGHTFUL FROLIC IN THE WOODS.
BUT I HAVE A LITTLE JOB FOR YOU.
IS THIS THE LOCK?
...YOU'RE JOKING.
I'M NOT YOUR...
JUST A SHORT RECEP-TIONIST GIG.
ALL I NEED IS FOR YOU TO SIT HERE AWHILE.

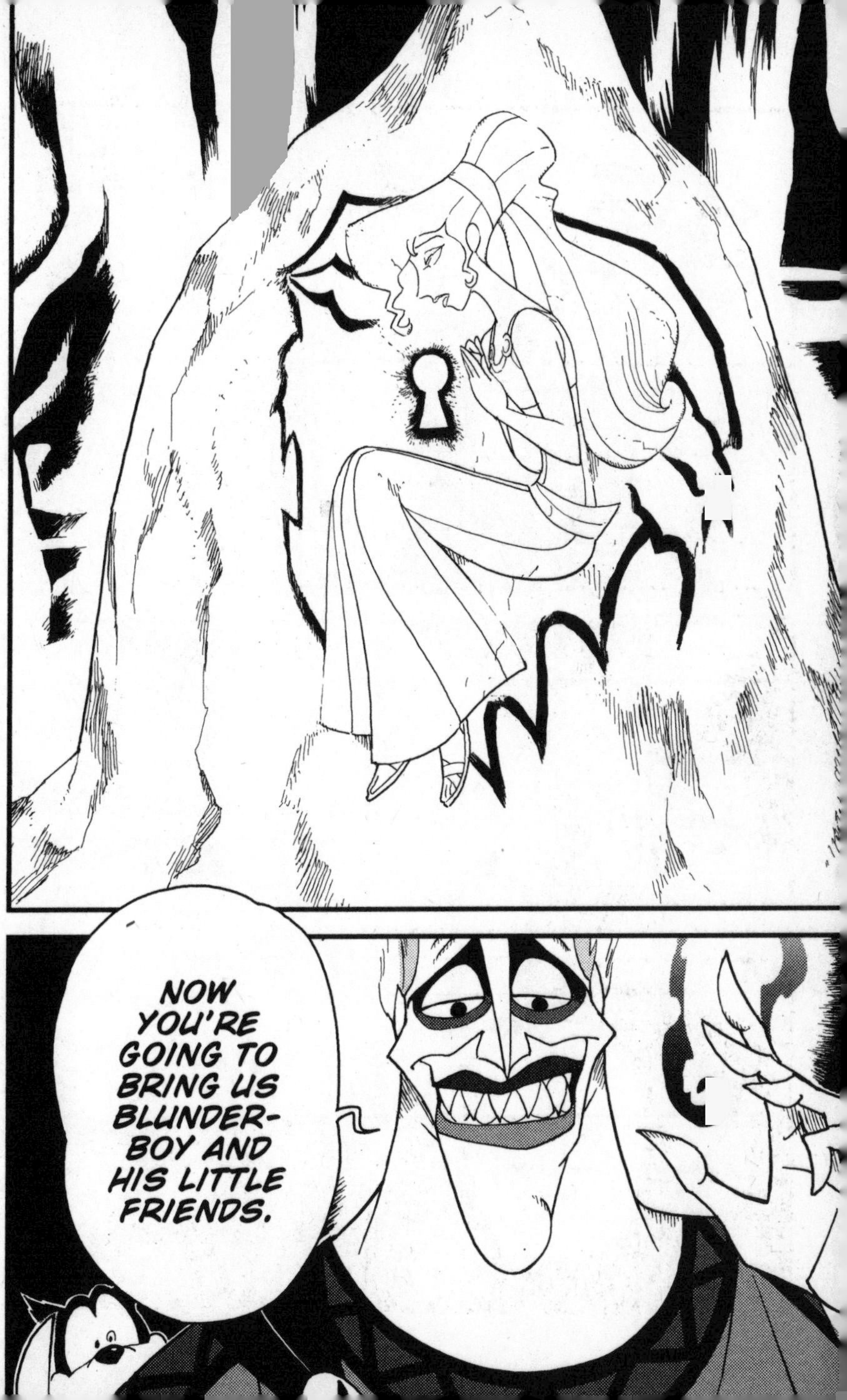
NOW YOU'RE GOING TO BRING US BLUNDER-BOY AND HIS LITTLE FRIENDS.

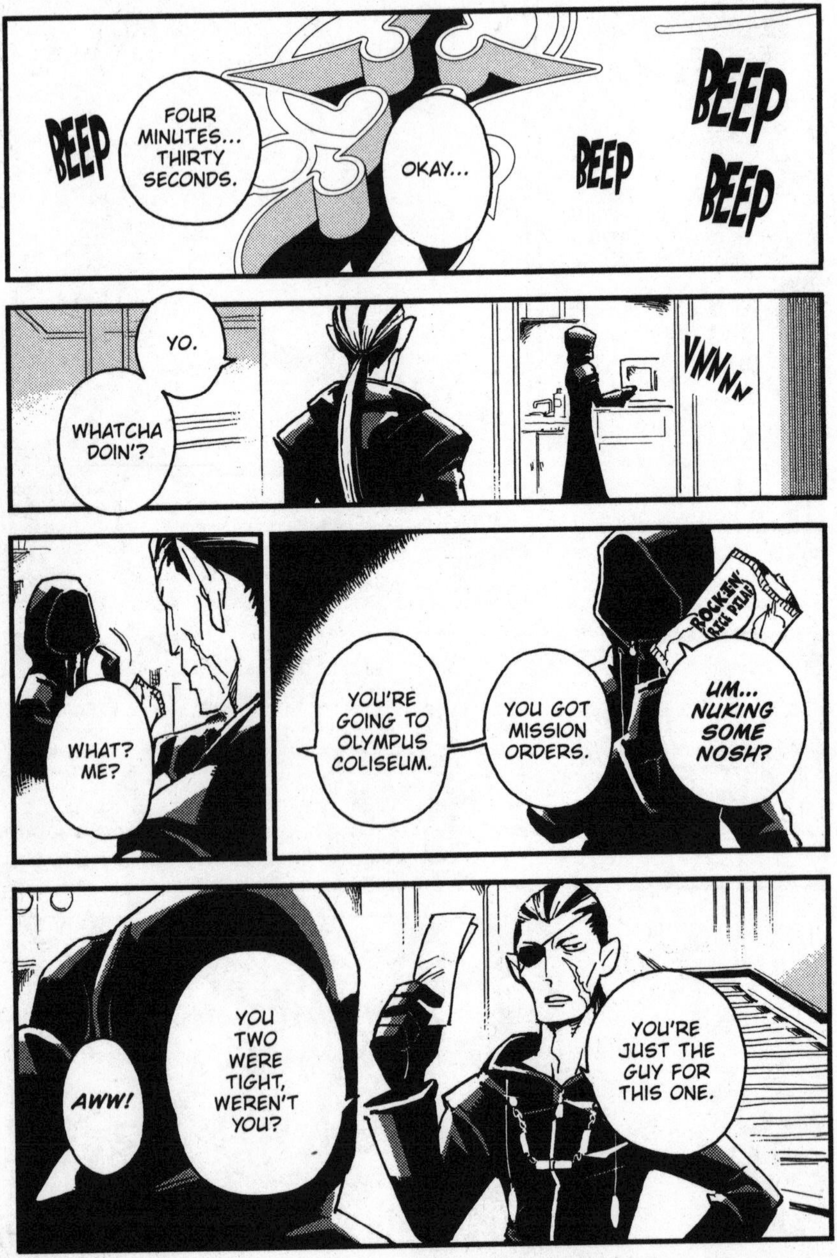
BEEP
BEEP
BEEP
OKAY...
FOUR MINUTES... THIRTY SECONDS.
BEEP
VNNNN
YO.
WHATCHA DOIN'?
ROCKIN' RICE PILAF
UM... NUKING SOME NOSH?
YOU GOT MISSION ORDERS.
YOU'RE GOING TO OLYMPUS COLISEUM.
WHAT? ME?
YOU'RE JUST THE GUY FOR THIS ONE.
YOU TWO WERE TIGHT, WEREN'T YOU?
AWW!

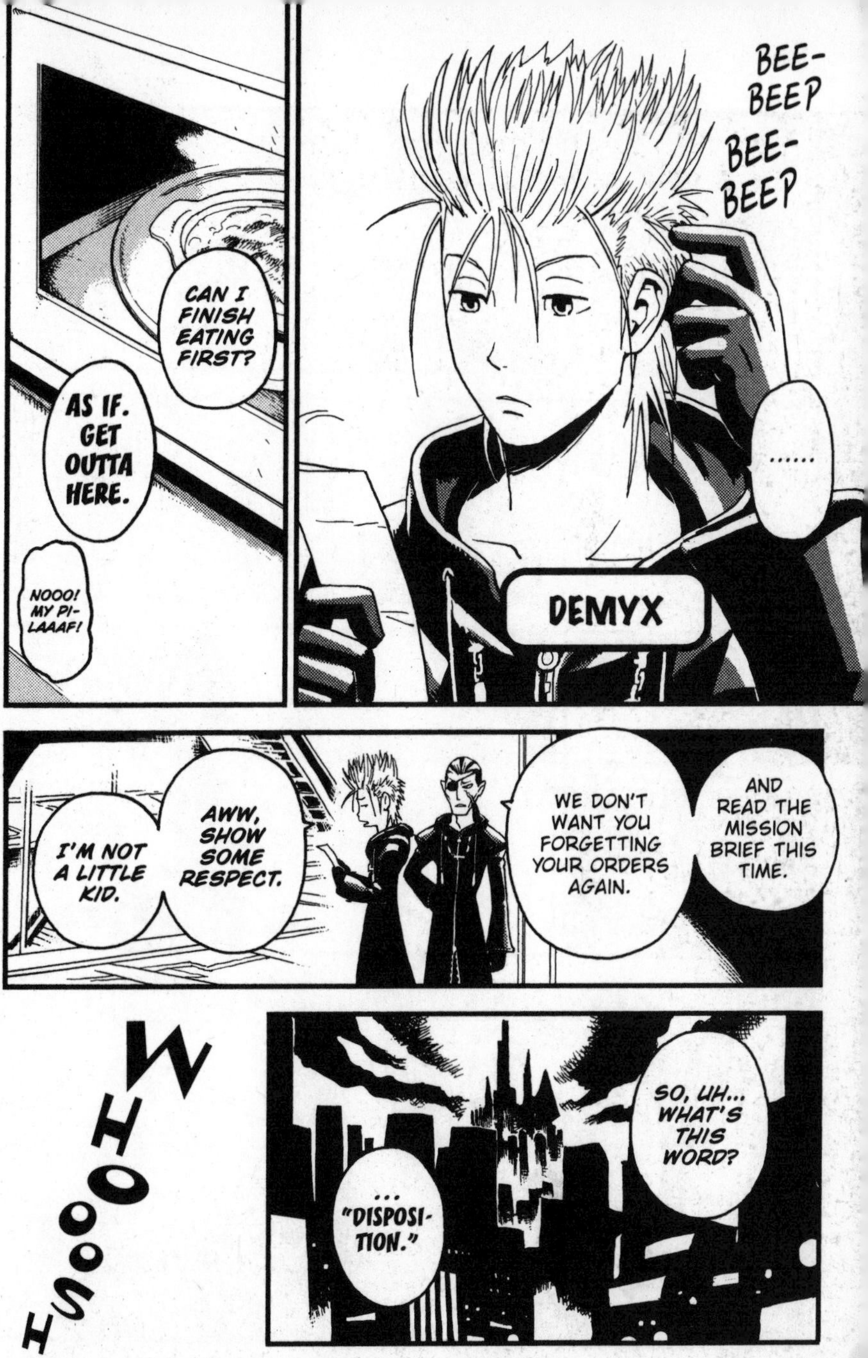
BEE-BEEP
BEE-BEEP
......
DEMYX
CAN I FINISH EATING FIRST?
AS IF. GET OUTTA HERE.
NOOO! MY PI-LAAAF!
AND READ THE MISSION BRIEF THIS TIME.
WE DON'T WANT YOU FORGETTING YOUR ORDERS AGAIN.
AWW, SHOW SOME RESPECT.
I'M NOT A LITTLE KID.
SO, UH... WHAT'S THIS WORD?
... "DISPOSITION."
WHOOOSH

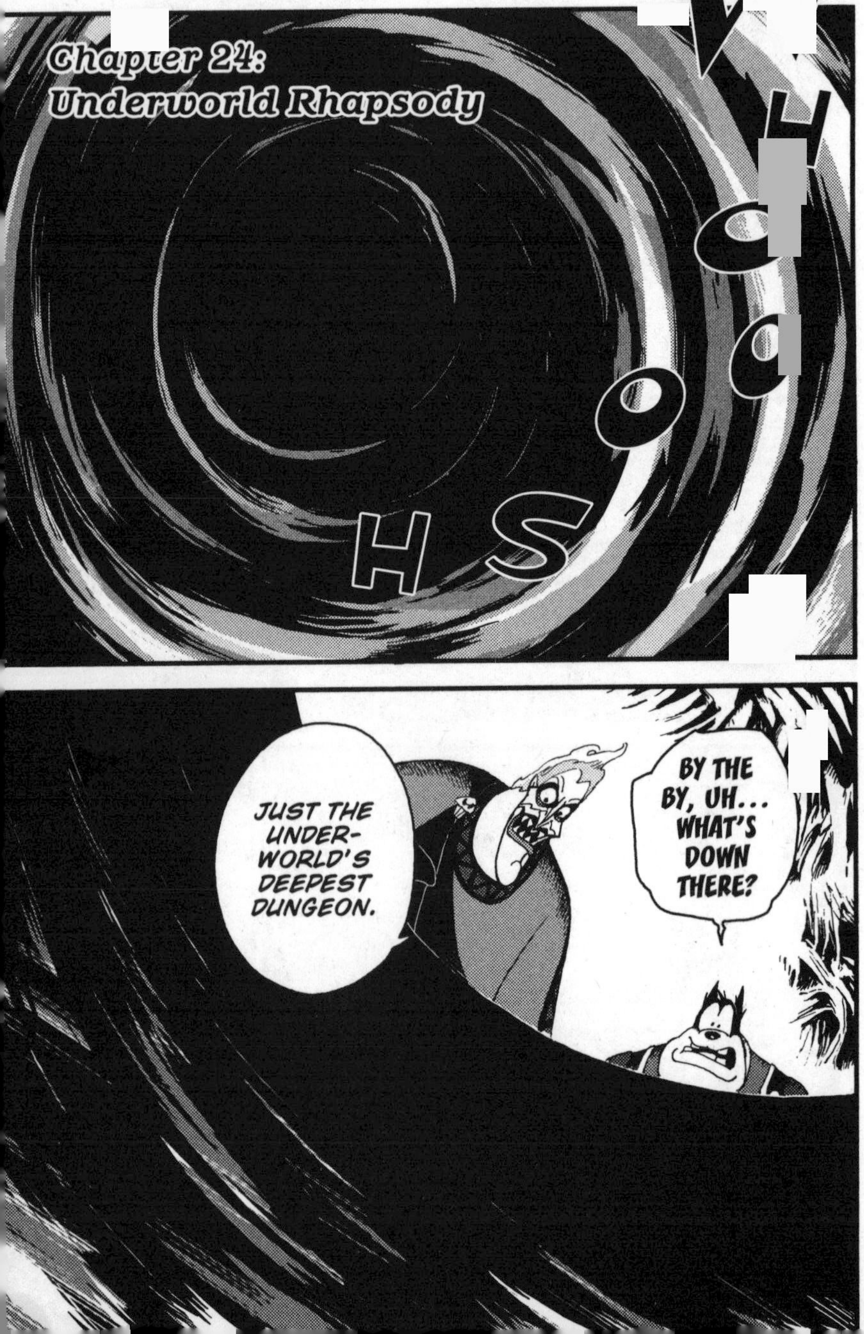
Chapter 24:
Underworld Rhapsody
WHOOOSH
BY THE BY, UH... WHAT'S DOWN THERE?
JUST THE UNDER-WORLD'S DEEPEST DUNGEON.

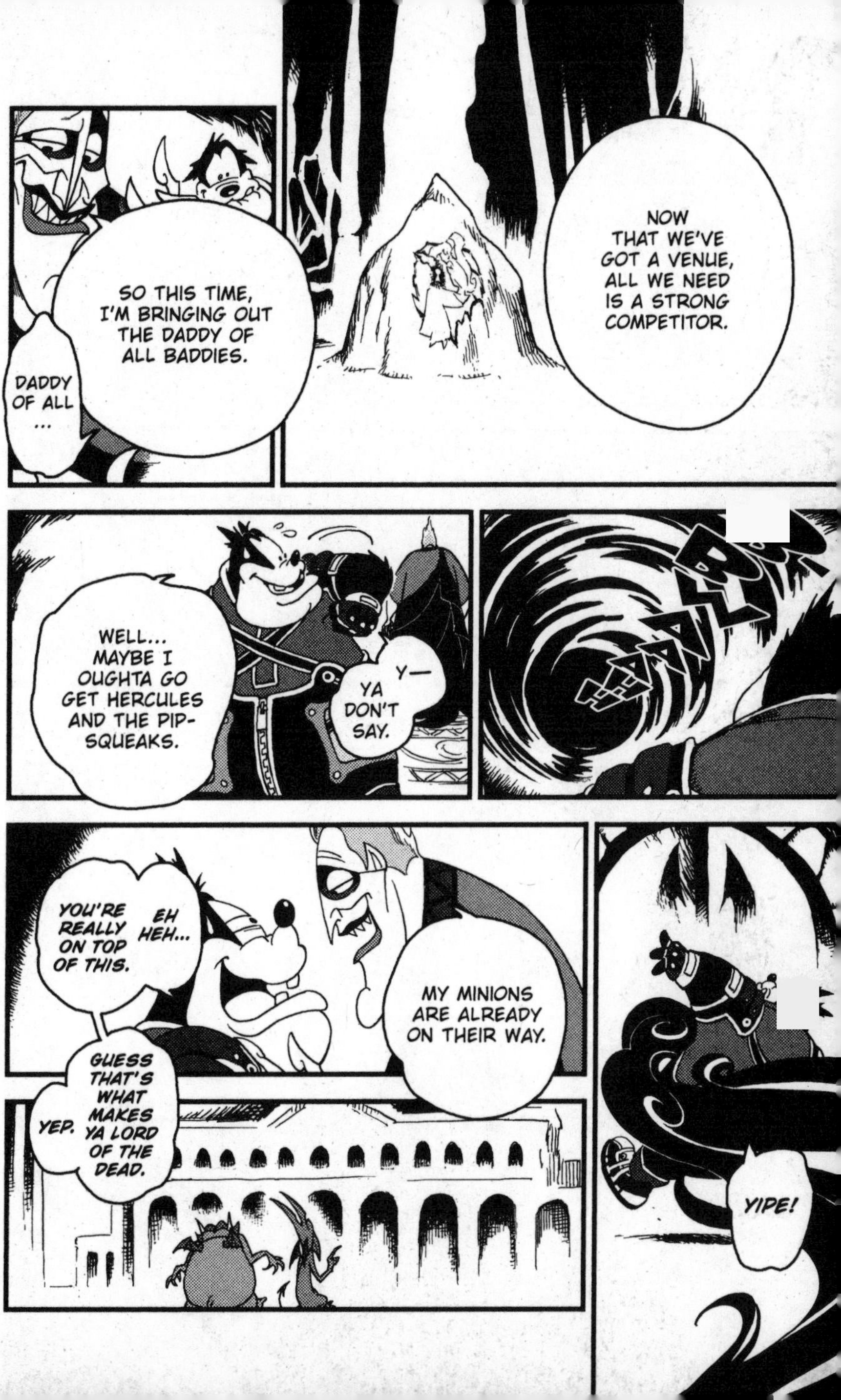
NOW THAT WE'VE GOT A VENUE, ALL WE NEED IS A STRONG COMPETITOR.
SO THIS TIME, I'M BRINGING OUT THE DADDY OF ALL BADDIES.
DADDY OF ALL ...
Y— YA DON'T SAY.
WELL... MAYBE I OUGHTA GO GET HERCULES AND THE PIP-SQUEAKS.
YIPE!
MY MINIONS ARE ALREADY ON THEIR WAY.
EH HEH...
YOU'RE REALLY ON TOP OF THIS.
GUESS THAT'S WHAT MAKES YA LORD OF THE DEAD.
YEP.

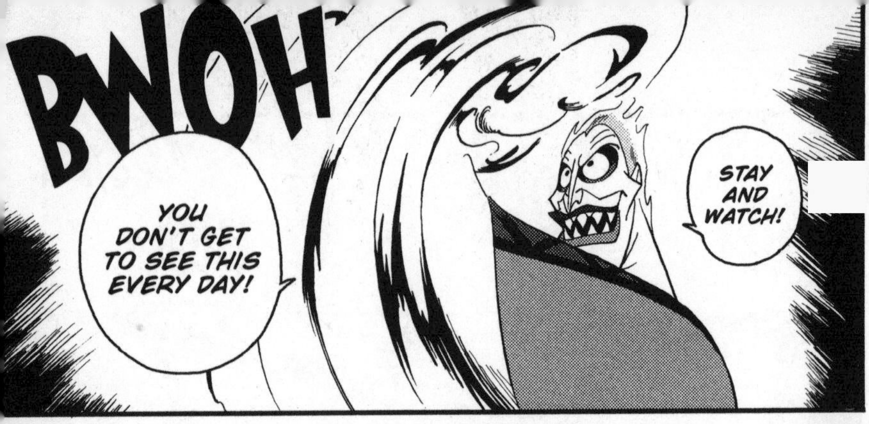
STAY AND WATCH!
YOU DON'T GET TO SEE THIS EVERY DAY!
BWOH
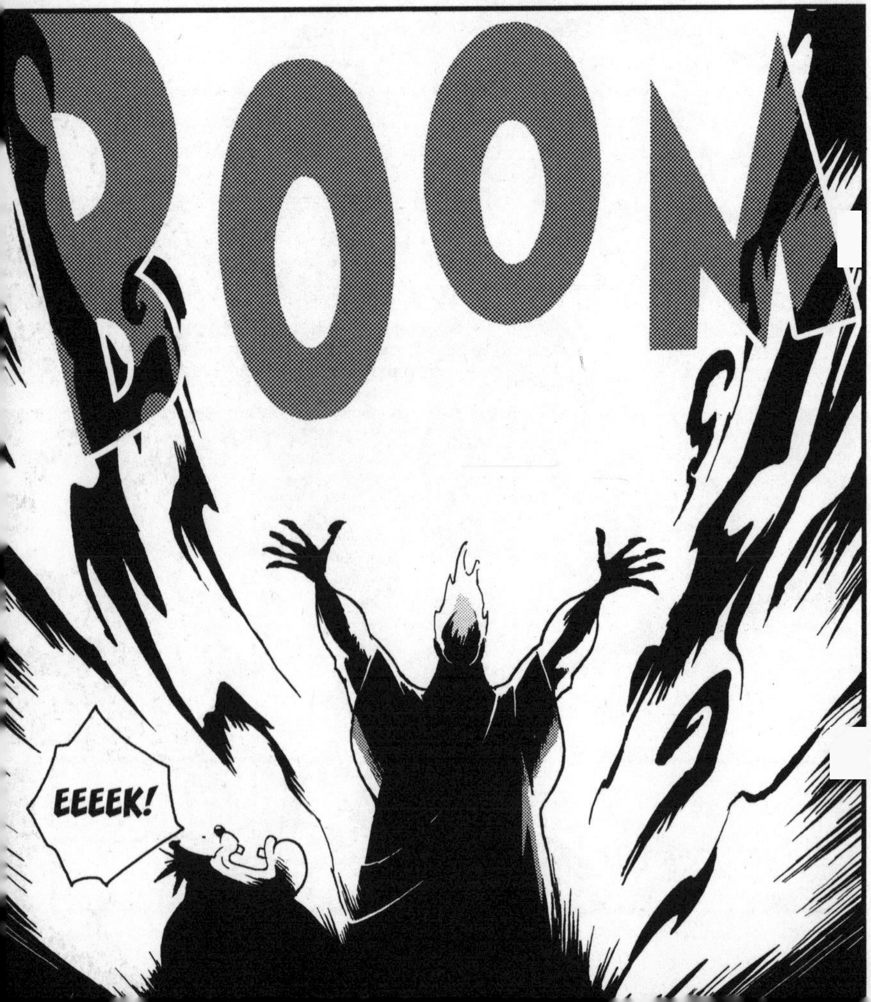
BOOM
EEEEK!

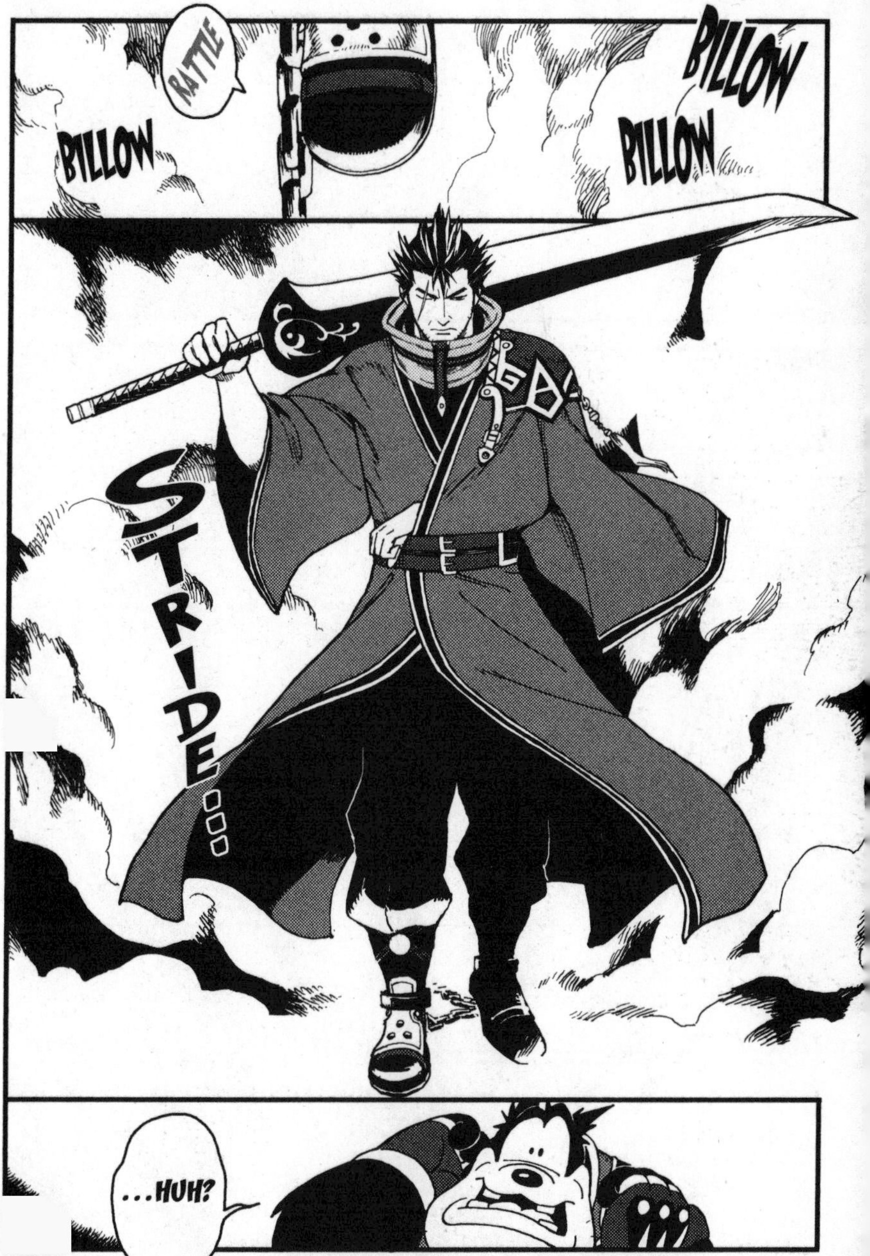
BILLOW
BILLOW
RATTLE
BILLOW
STRIDE...
...HUH?

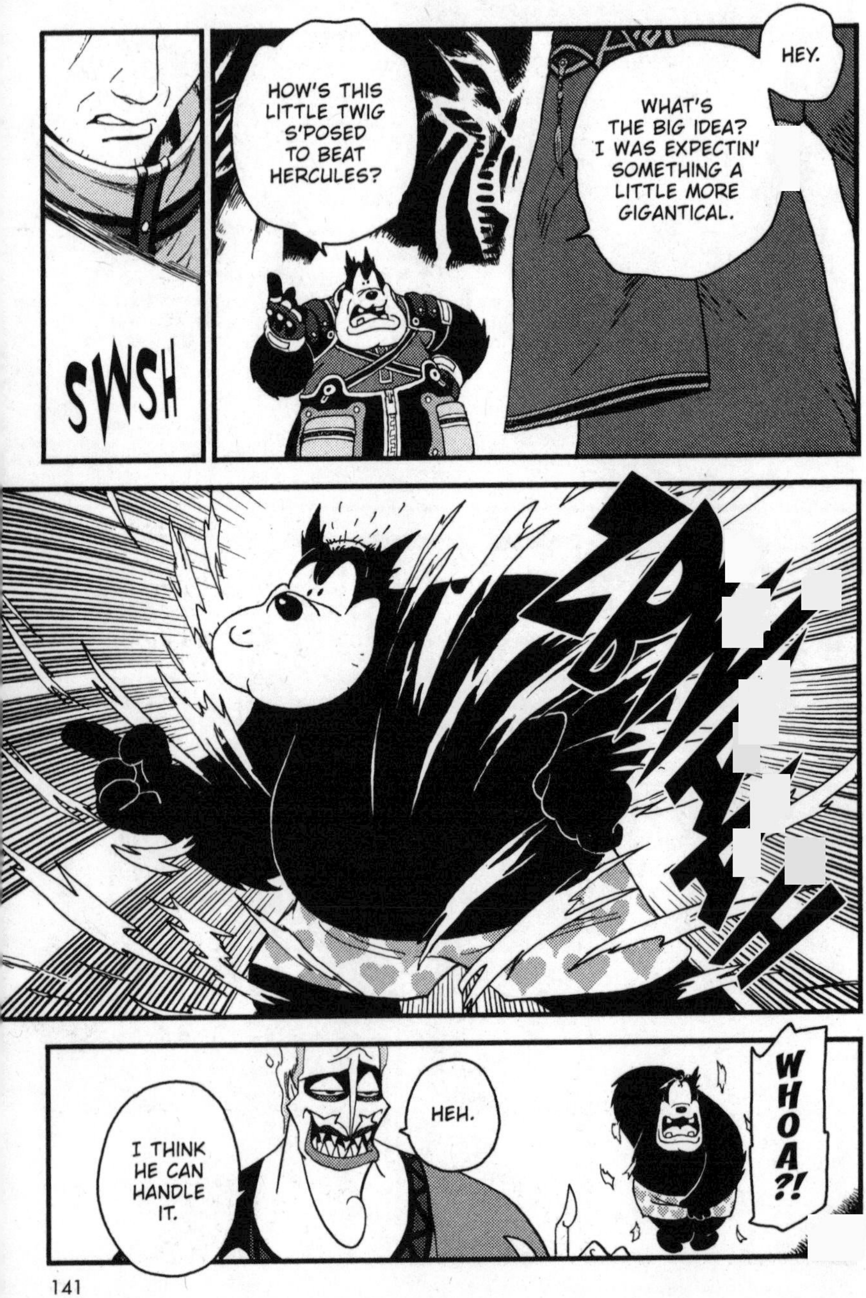
HEY.
WHAT'S THE BIG IDEA? I WAS EXPECTIN' SOMETHING A LITTLE MORE GIGANTICAL.
HOW'S THIS LITTLE TWIG S'POSED TO BEAT HERCULES?
SWSH
WHOA?!
HEH.
I THINK HE CAN HANDLE IT.

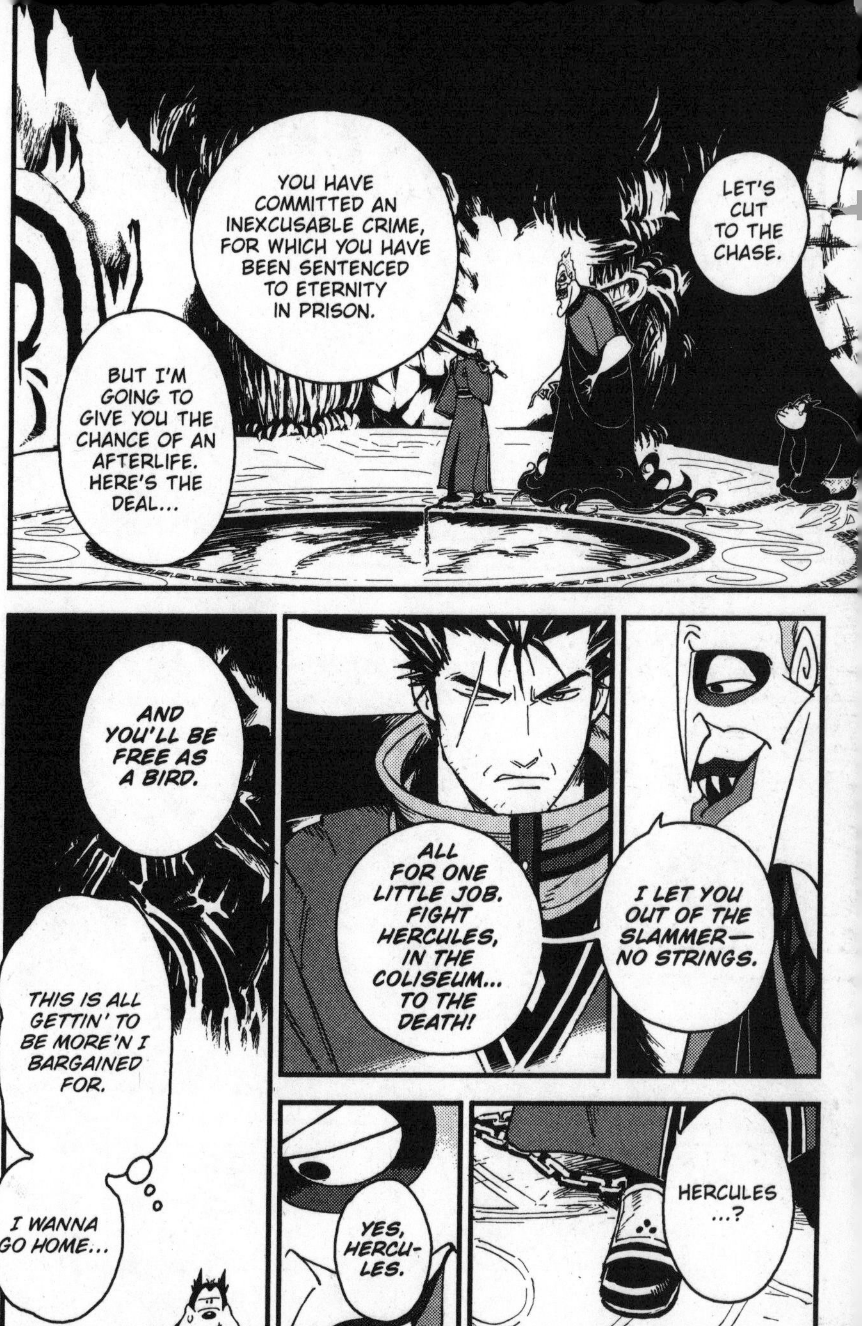
LET'S CUT TO THE CHASE.
YOU HAVE COMMITTED AN INEXCUSABLE CRIME, FOR WHICH YOU HAVE BEEN SENTENCED TO ETERNITY IN PRISON.
BUT I'M GOING TO GIVE YOU THE CHANCE OF AN AFTERLIFE. HERE'S THE DEAL...
I LET YOU OUT OF THE SLAMMER—NO STRINGS.
ALL FOR ONE LITTLE JOB. FIGHT HERCULES, IN THE COLISEUM... TO THE DEATH!
HERCULES ...?
YES, HERCU-LES.
AND YOU'LL BE FREE AS A BIRD.
THIS IS ALL GETTIN' TO BE MORE'N I BARGAINED FOR.
I WANNA GO HOME...

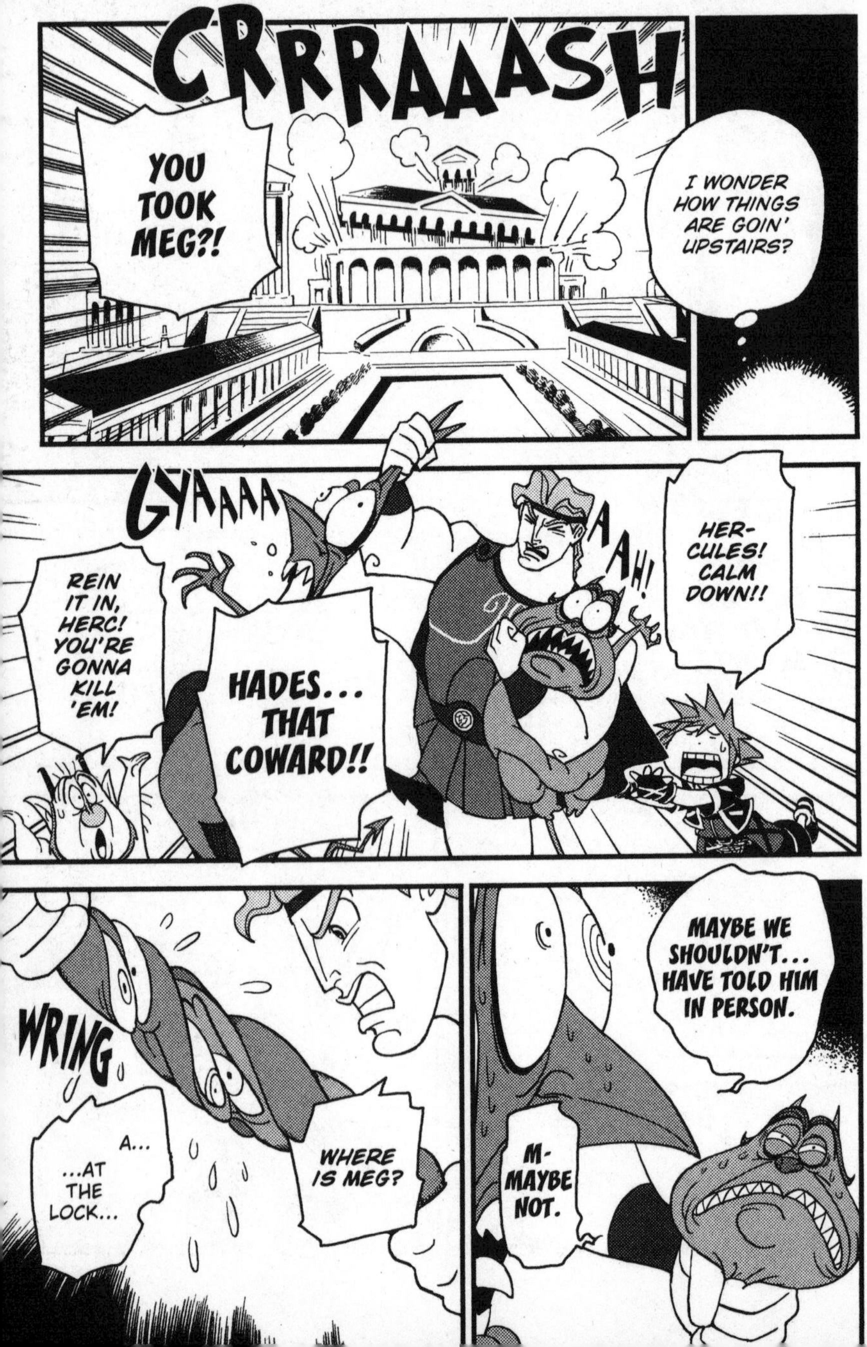
I WONDER HOW THINGS ARE GOIN' UPSTAIRS?
CRRRAAASH
YOU TOOK MEG?!
HER-CULES! CALM DOWN!!
AAH!
GYAAAA
HADES... THAT COWARD!!
REIN IT IN, HERC! YOU'RE GONNA KILL 'EM!
MAYBE WE SHOULDN'T... HAVE TOLD HIM IN PERSON.
M-MAYBE NOT.
WHERE IS MEG?
WRING
A...
...AT THE LOCK...

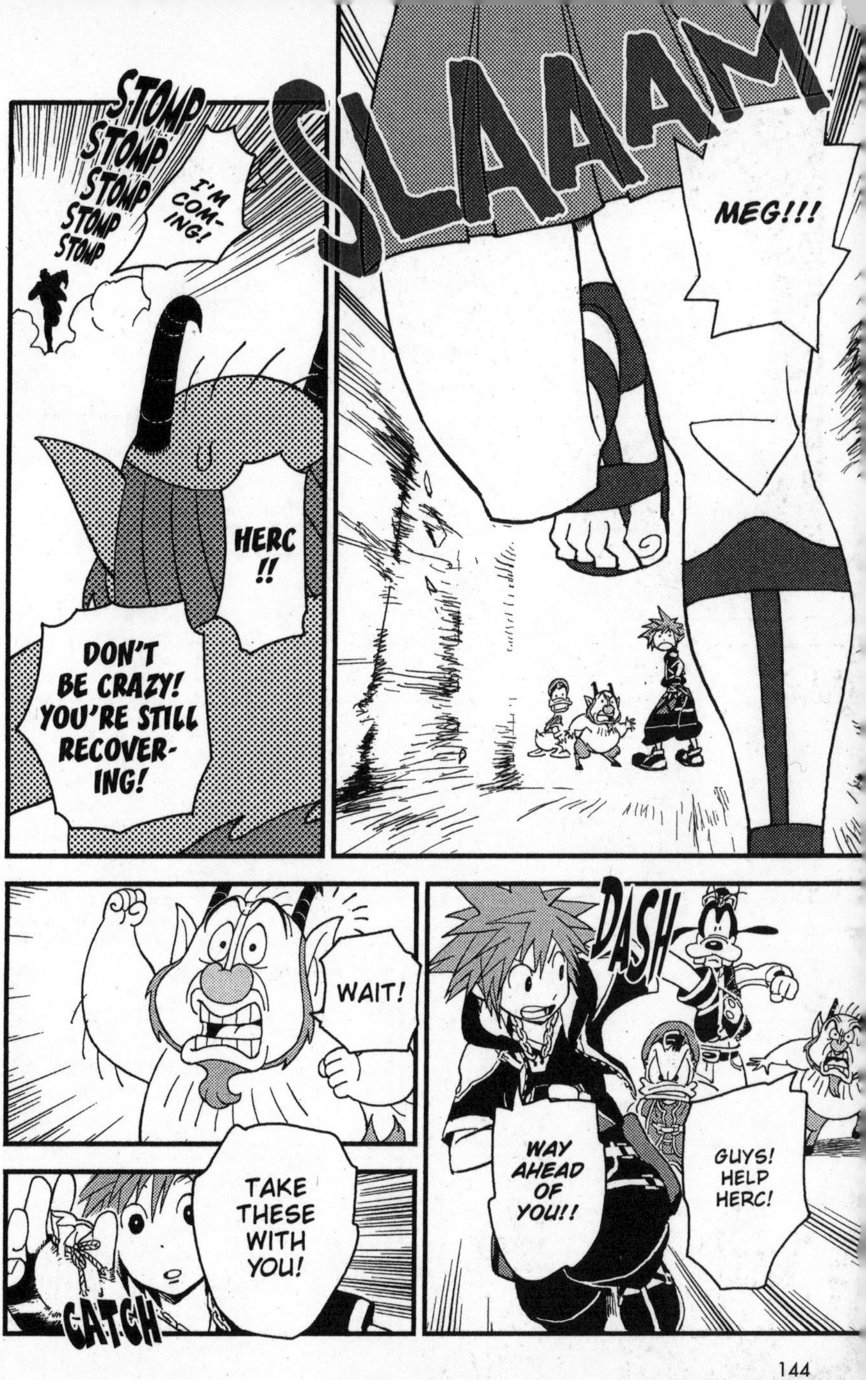
SLAAAM
MEG!!!
STOMP STOMP STOMP STOMP STOMP
I'M COMING!
HERC!!
DON'T BE CRAZY! YOU'RE STILL RECOVERING!
DASH
GUYS! HELP HERC!
WAY AHEAD OF YOU!!
WAIT!
TAKE THESE WITH YOU!
CATCH

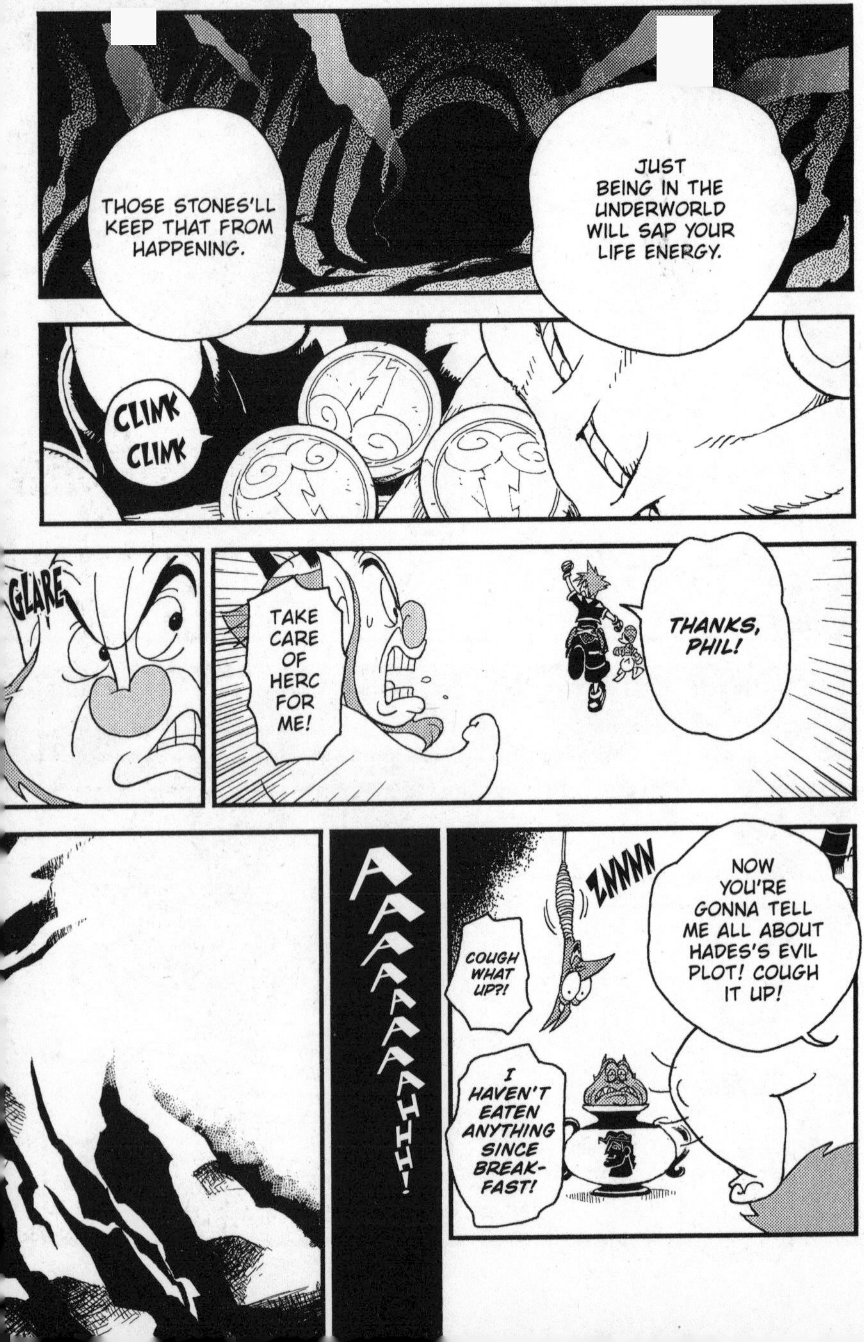
JUST BEING IN THE UNDERWORLD WILL SAP YOUR LIFE ENERGY.
THOSE STONES'LL KEEP THAT FROM HAPPENING.
CLINK CLINK
THANKS, PHIL!
TAKE CARE OF HERC FOR ME!
GLARE
NOW YOU'RE GONNA TELL ME ALL ABOUT HADES'S EVIL PLOT! COUGH IT UP!
ZNNNN
COUGH WHAT UP?!
I HAVEN'T EATEN ANYTHING SINCE BREAK-FAST!
AAAAAAAAHHH!

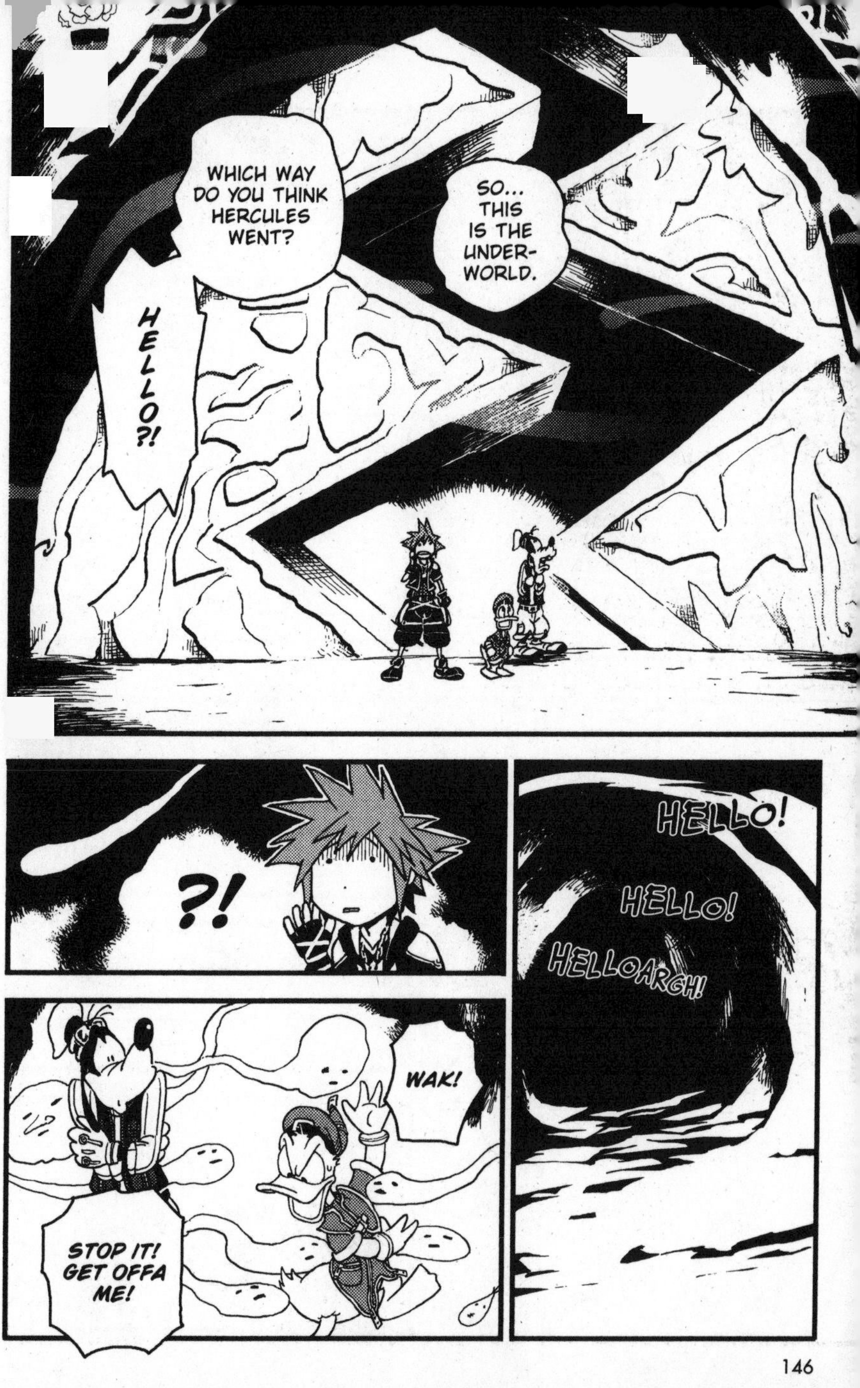
SO... THIS IS THE UNDER-WORLD.
WHICH WAY DO YOU THINK HERCULES WENT?
HELLO?!
HELLO!
HELLO!
HELLOARGH!
?!
WAK!
STOP IT! GET OFFA ME!

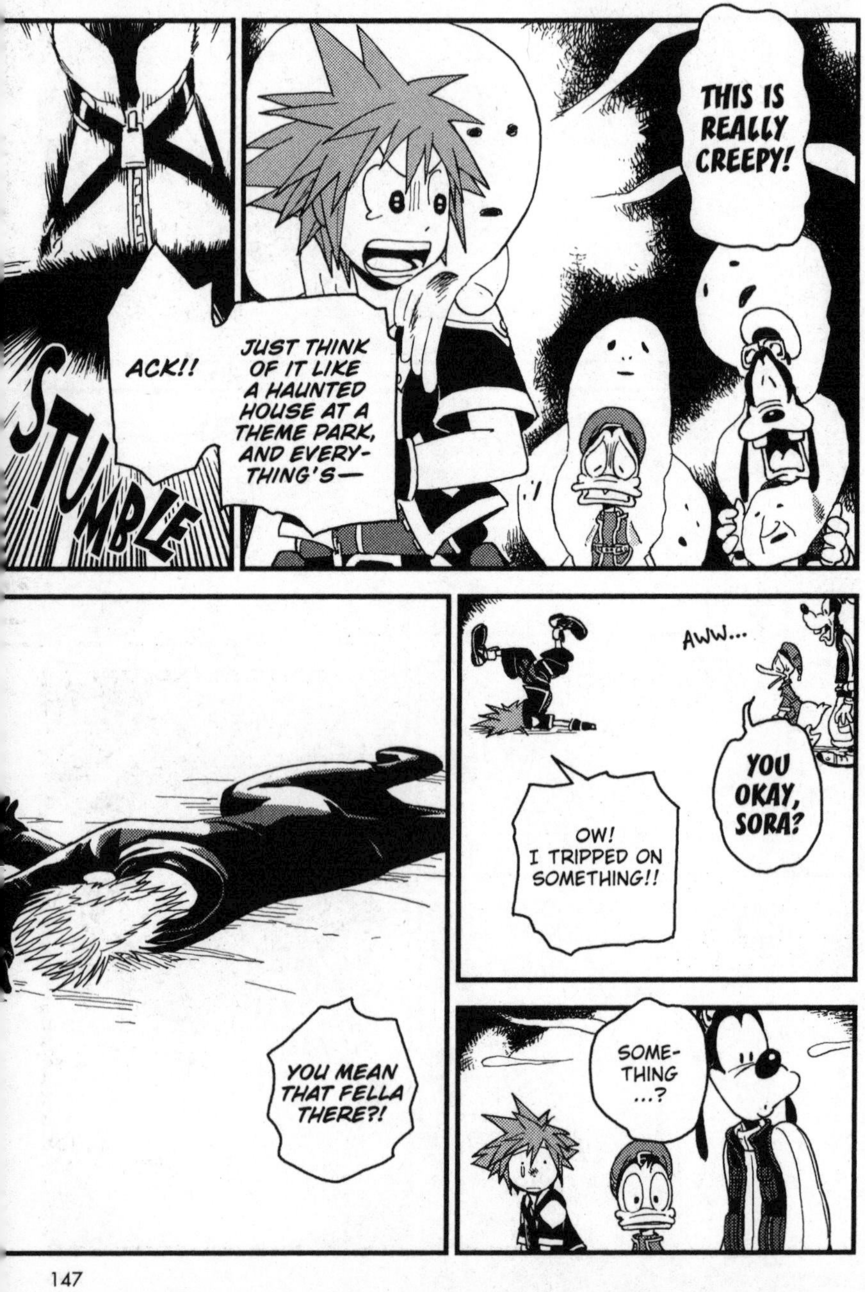
THIS IS REALLY CREEPY!
JUST THINK OF IT LIKE A HAUNTED HOUSE AT A THEME PARK, AND EVERYTHING'S—
ACK!!
STUMBLE
AWW...
YOU OKAY, SORA?
OW! I TRIPPED ON SOMETHING!!
SOME-THING ...?
YOU MEAN THAT FELLA THERE?!

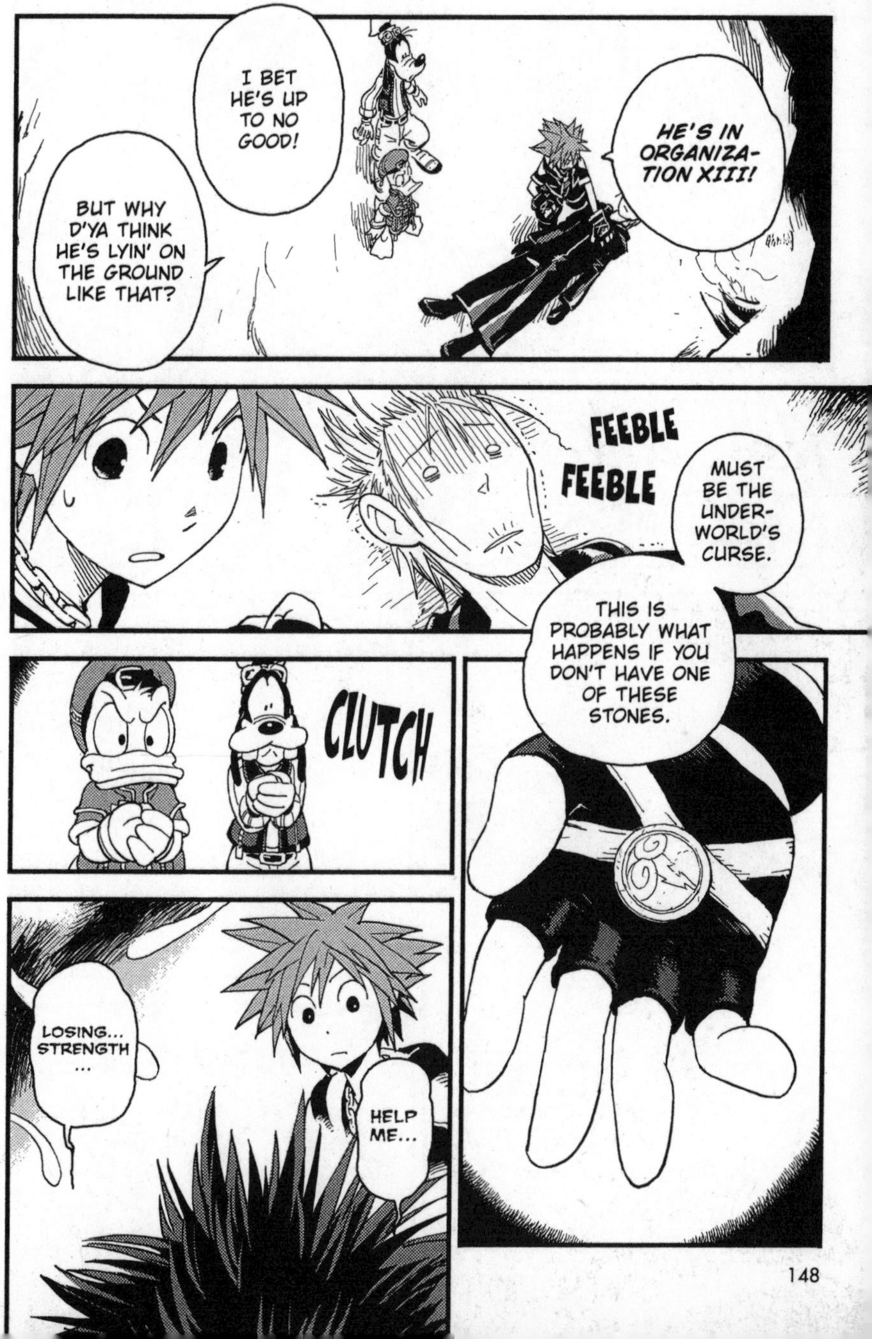
HE'S IN ORGANIZATION XIII!
I BET HE'S UP TO NO GOOD!
BUT WHY D'YA THINK HE'S LYIN' ON THE GROUND LIKE THAT?
FEEBLE
FEEBLE
MUST BE THE UNDERWORLD'S CURSE.
THIS IS PROBABLY WHAT HAPPENS IF YOU DON'T HAVE ONE OF THESE STONES.
CLUTCH
HELP ME...
LOSING... STRENGTH...

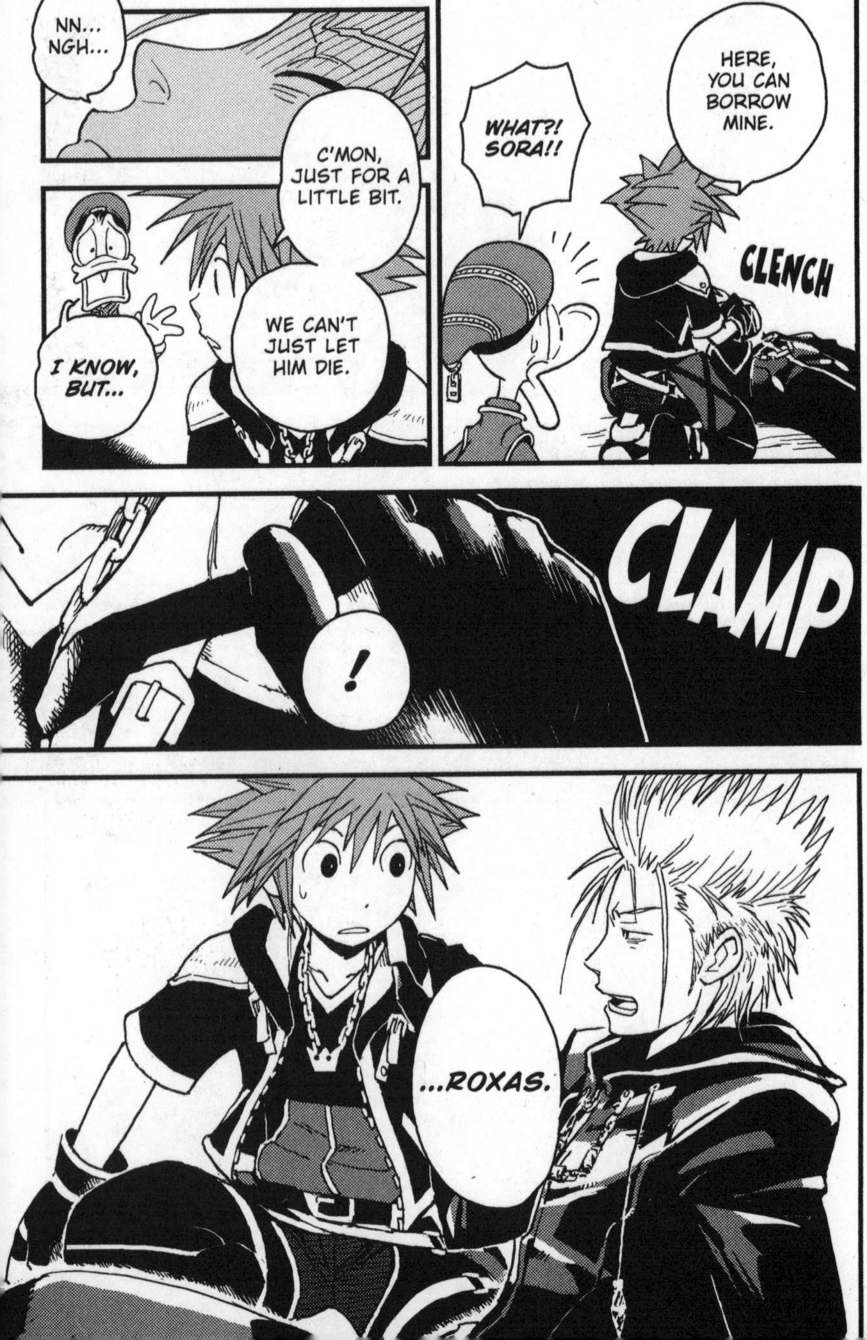
HERE, YOU CAN BORROW MINE.
WHAT?! SORA!!
CLENCH
NN... NGH...
C'MON, JUST FOR A LITTLE BIT.
WE CAN'T JUST LET HIM DIE.
I KNOW, BUT...
CLAMP
!
...ROXAS.

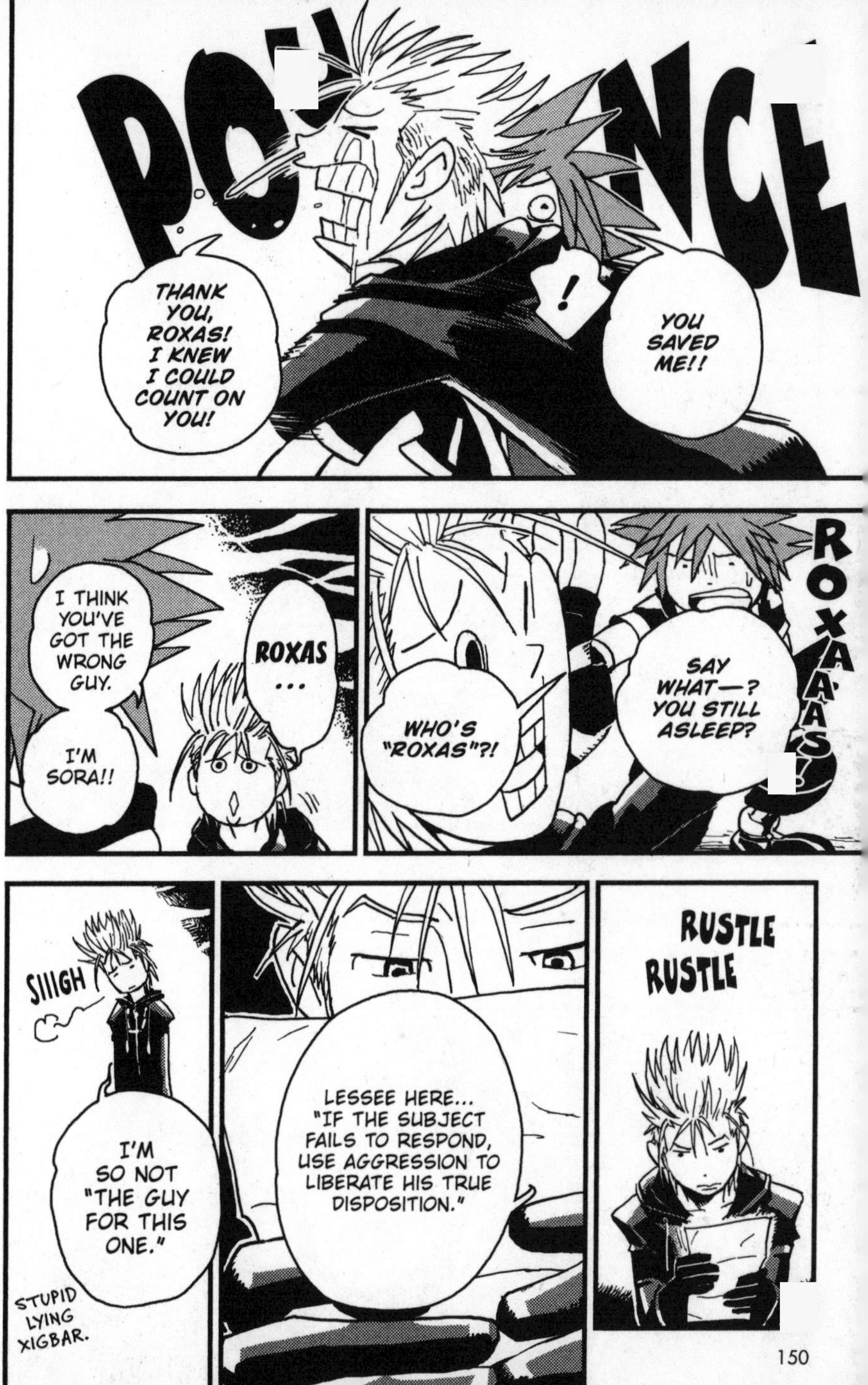

PO
NCE
YOU SAVED ME!!
!
THANK YOU, ROXAS! I KNEW I COULD COUNT ON YOU!
ROXAAAS!
SAY WHAT—? YOU STILL ASLEEP?
WHO'S "ROXAS"?!
I THINK YOU'VE GOT THE WRONG GUY.
I'M SORA!!
ROXAS...
RUSTLE RUSTLE
LESSEE HERE... "IF THE SUBJECT FAILS TO RESPOND, USE AGGRESSION TO LIBERATE HIS TRUE DISPOSITION."
SIIIGH
I'M SO NOT "THE GUY FOR THIS ONE."
STUPID LYING XIGBAR.

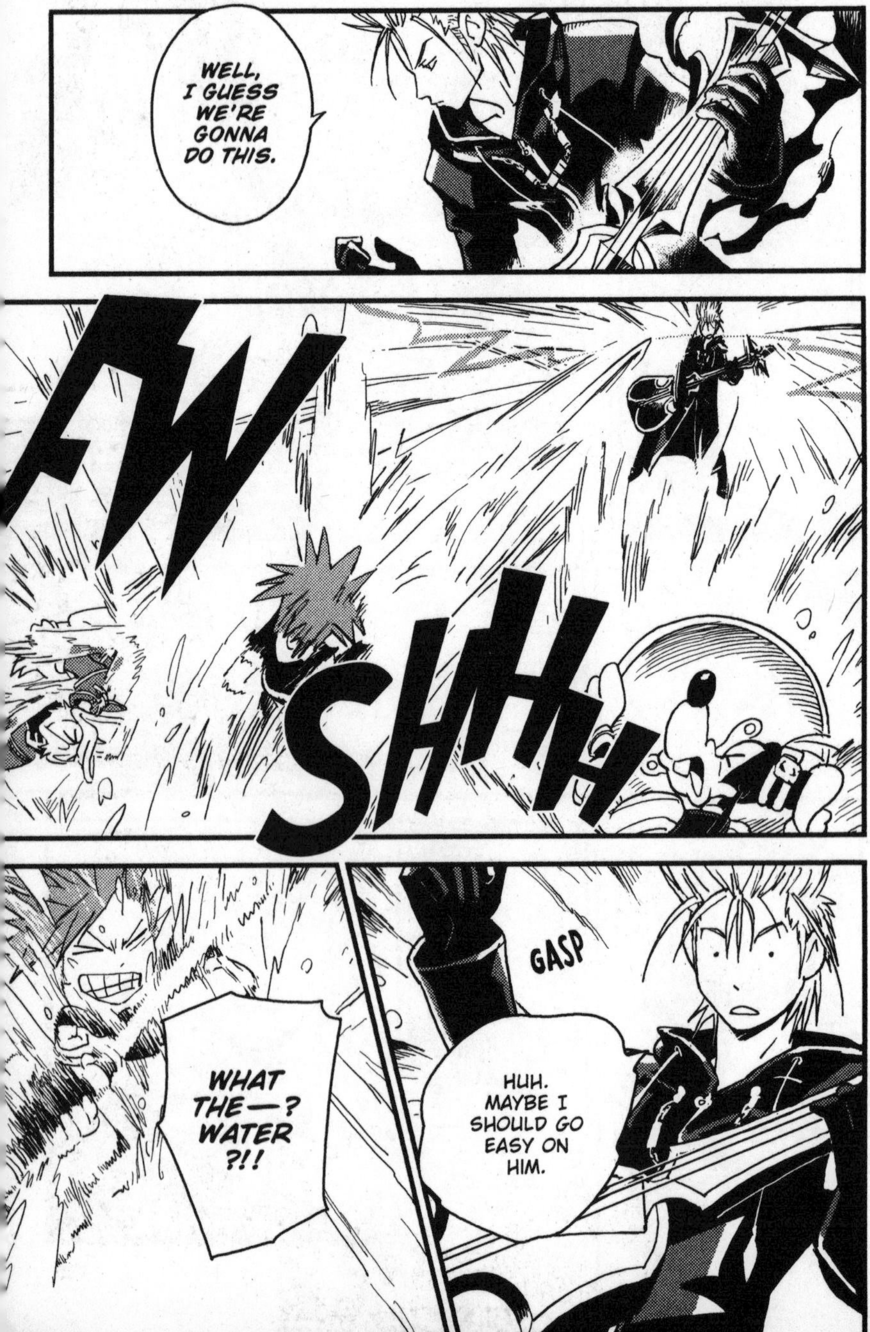
WELL, I GUESS WE'RE GONNA DO THIS.
FWSHHH
GASP
HUH. MAYBE I SHOULD GO EASY ON HIM.
WHAT THE—? WATER ?!!

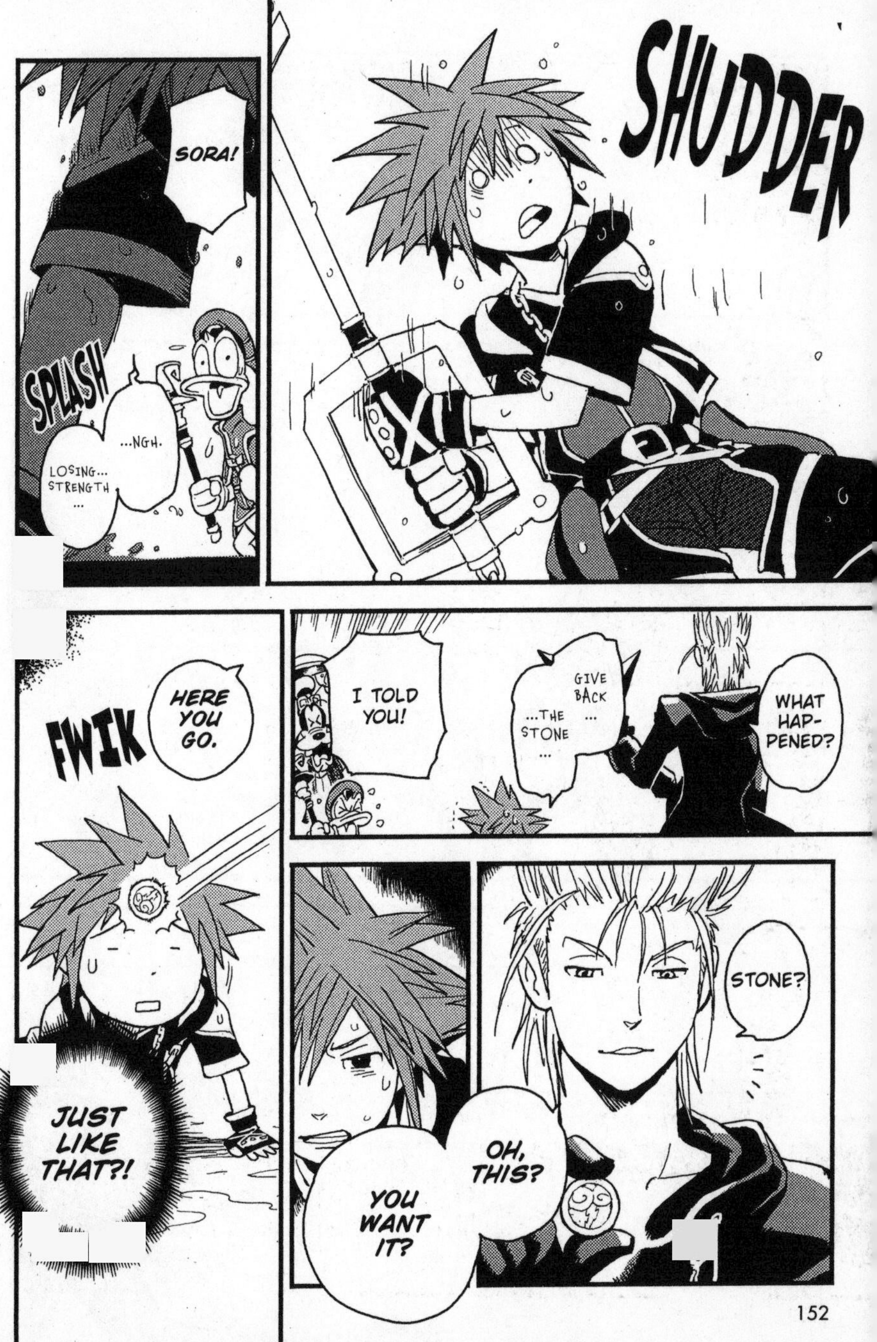
SHUDDER
SORA!
SPLASH
...NGH.
LOSING... STRENGTH ...
WHAT HAP-PENED?
GIVE BACK ... ...THE STONE ...
I TOLD YOU!
STONE?
OH, THIS?
YOU WANT IT?
FWIK
HERE YOU GO.
JUST LIKE THAT?!

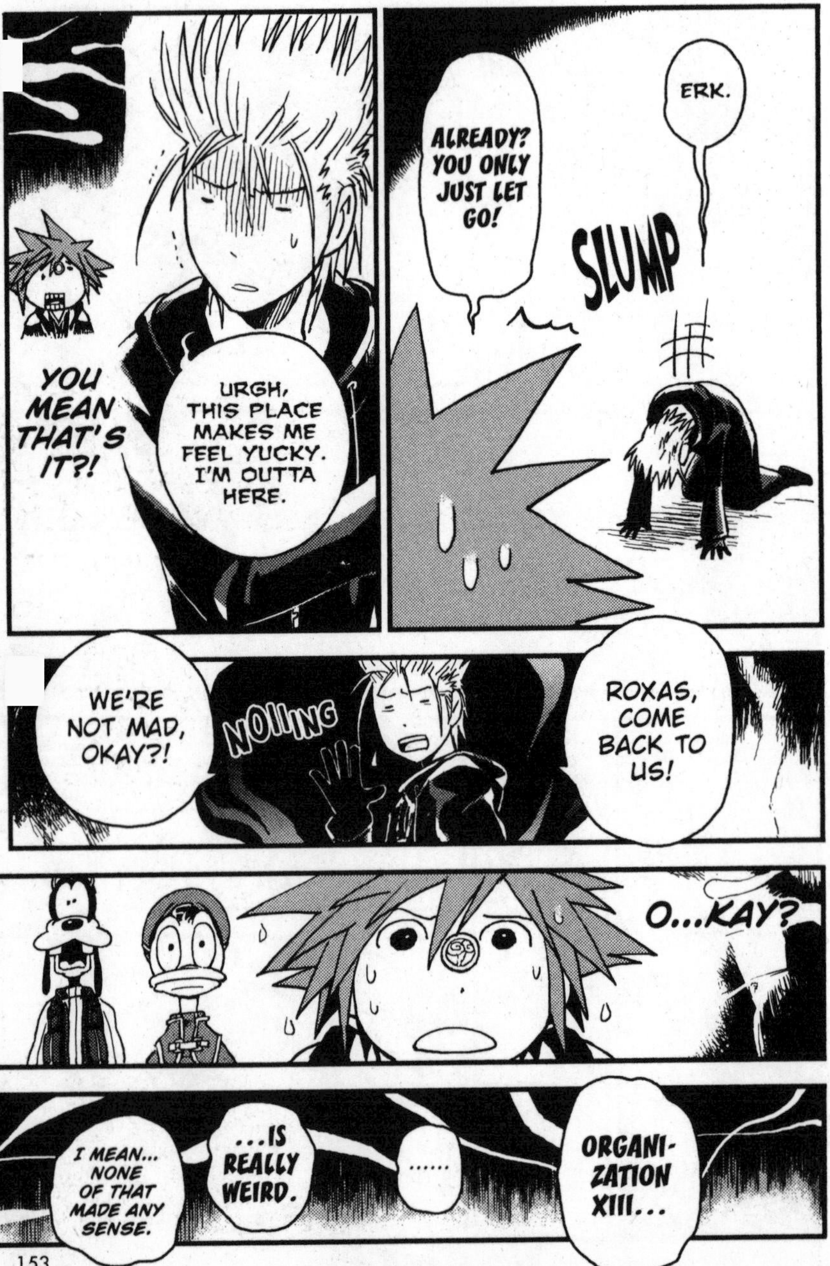

ERK.
ALREADY? YOU ONLY JUST LET GO!
SLUMP
URGH, THIS PLACE MAKES ME FEEL YUCKY. I'M OUTTA HERE.
YOU MEAN THAT'S IT?!
ROXAS, COME BACK TO US!
NOIIING
WE'RE NOT MAD, OKAY?!
O...KAY?
ORGANIZATION XIII...
......
...IS REALLY WEIRD.
I MEAN... NONE OF THAT MADE ANY SENSE.

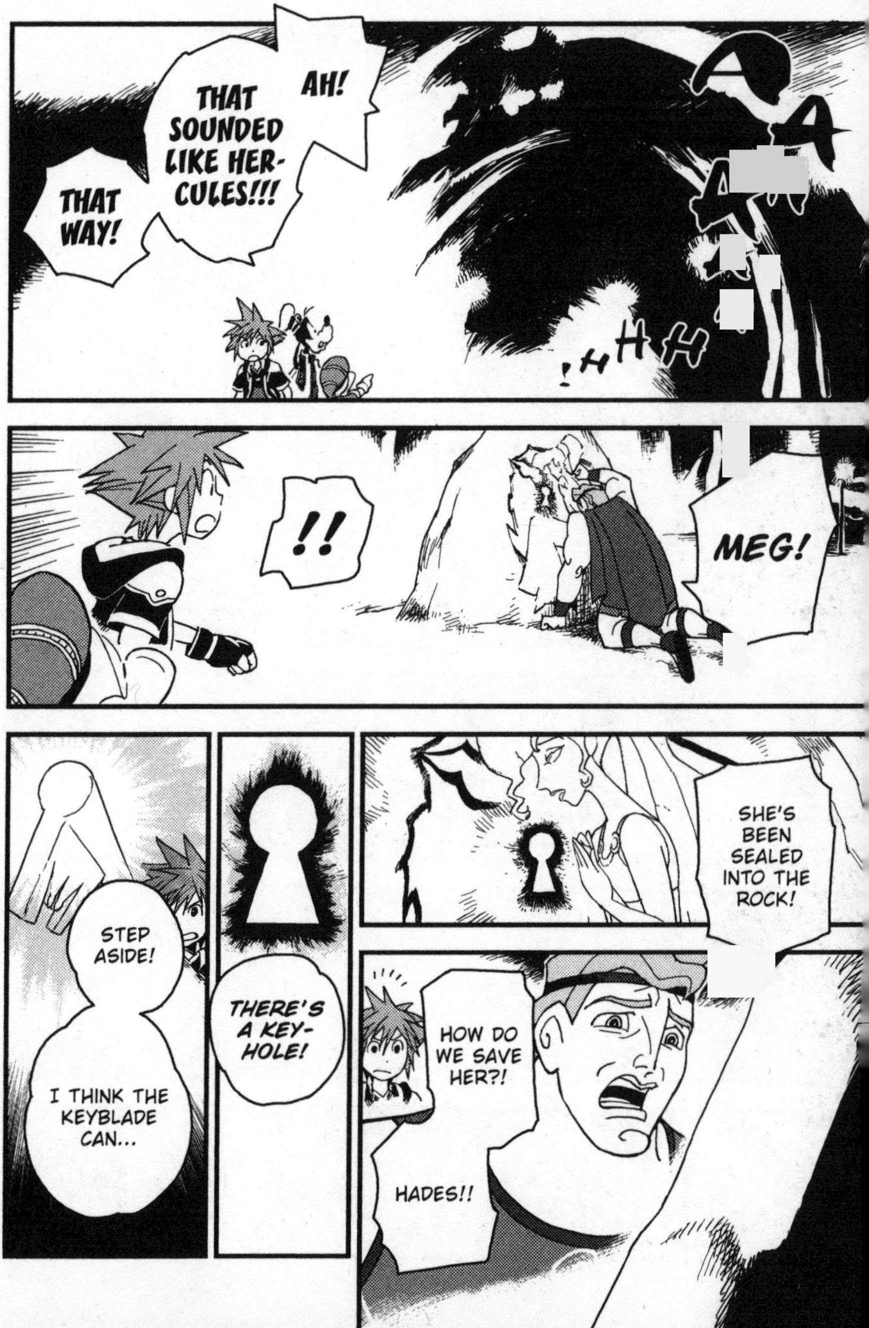
AH!
THAT SOUNDED LIKE HER-CULES!!!
THAT WAY!
MEG!
!!
SHE'S BEEN SEALED INTO THE ROCK!
HOW DO WE SAVE HER?!
HADES!!
THERE'S A KEY-HOLE!
STEP ASIDE!
I THINK THE KEYBLADE CAN...

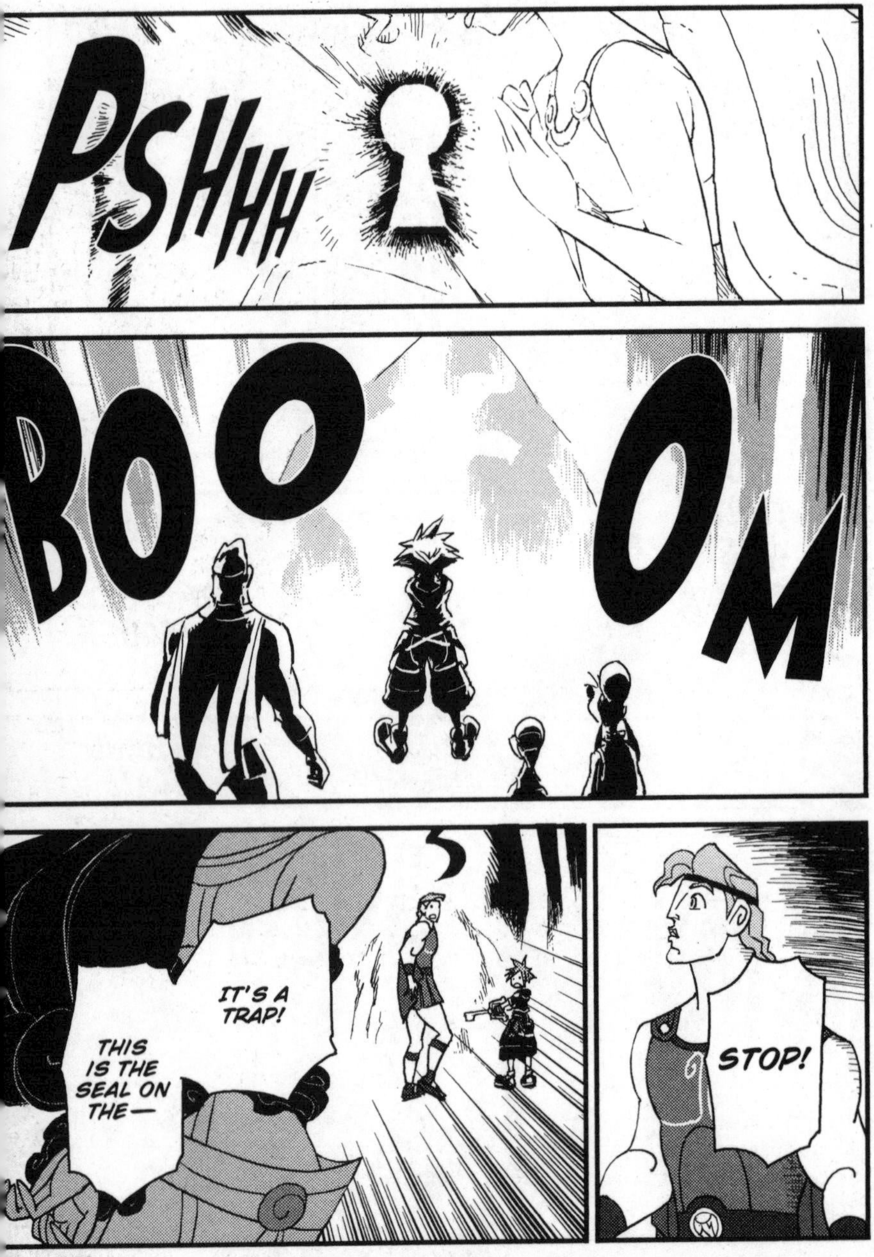
PSHHH
BOOOM
STOP!
IT'S A TRAP!
THIS IS THE SEAL ON THE—

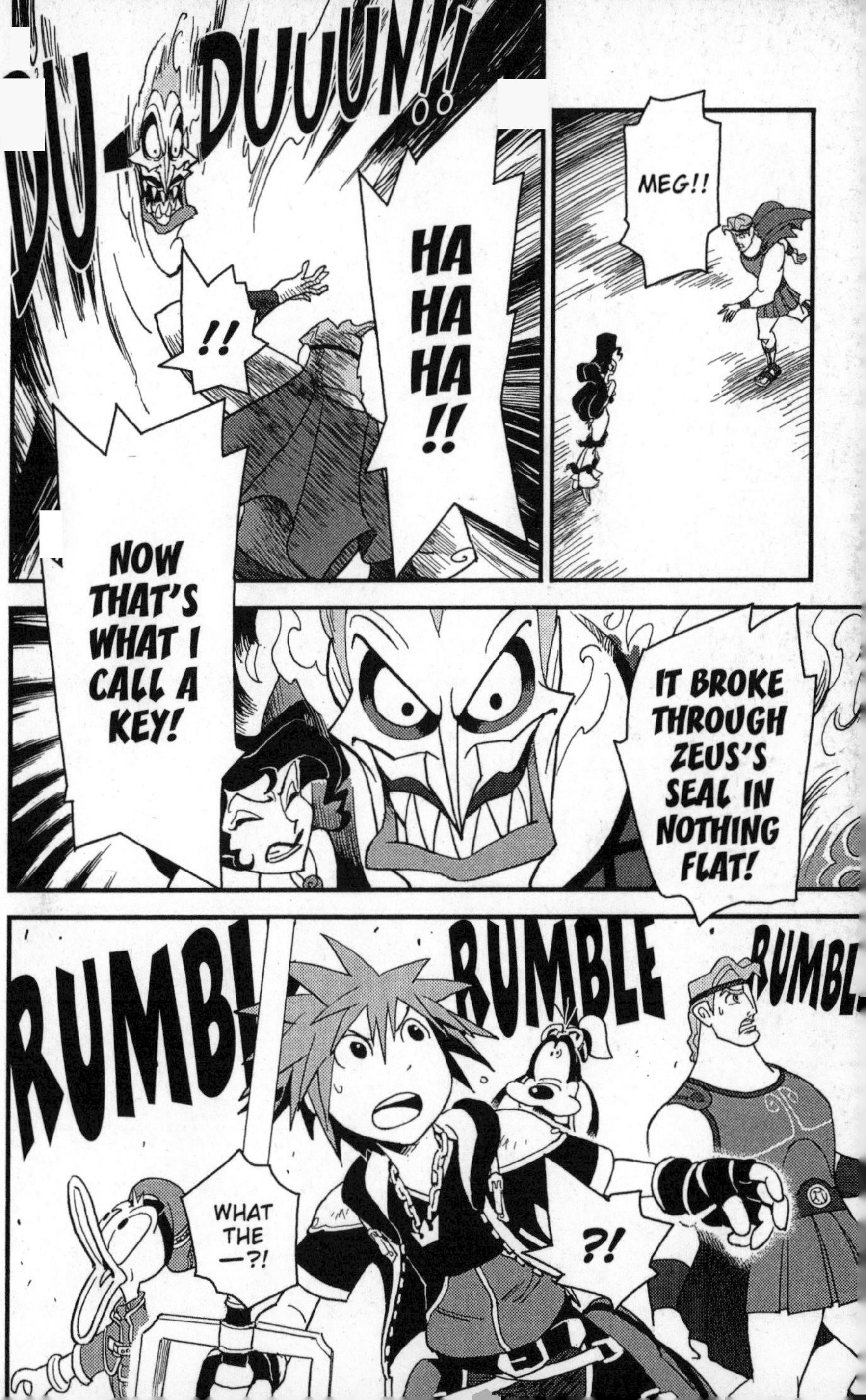
MEG!!
DU-DUUUN!!
HA HA HA !!
!!
IT BROKE THROUGH ZEUS'S SEAL IN NOTHING FLAT!
NOW THAT'S WHAT I CALL A KEY!
RUMBLE
RUMBLE
RUMBL
?!
WHAT THE—?!

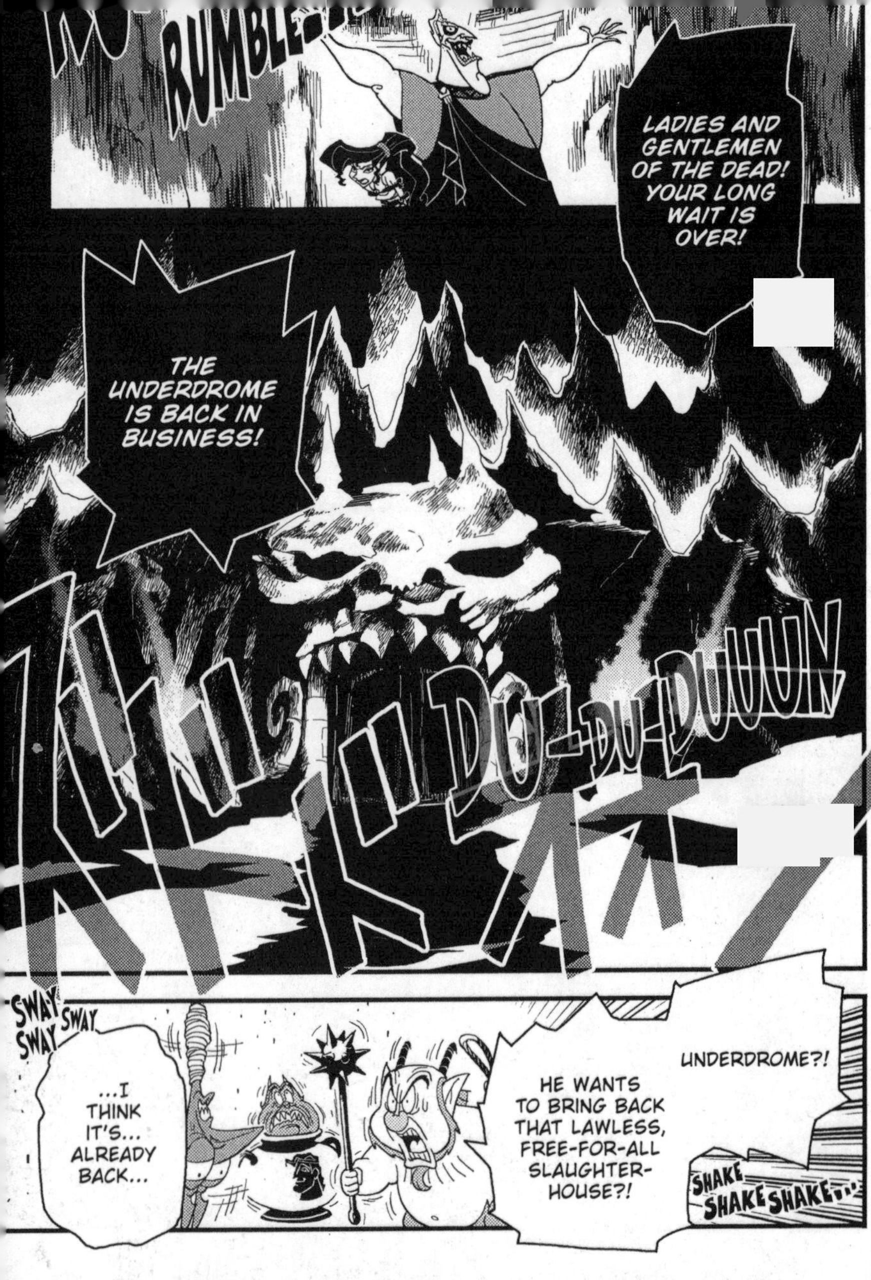
LADIES AND GENTLEMEN OF THE DEAD! YOUR LONG WAIT IS OVER!
RUMBLE...
THE UNDERDROME IS BACK IN BUSINESS!
DU-DU-DUUUN
UNDERDROME?!
SHAKE SHAKE SHAKE...
HE WANTS TO BRING BACK THAT LAWLESS, FREE-FOR-ALL SLAUGHTER-HOUSE?!
...I THINK IT'S... ALREADY BACK...
SWAY SWAY SWAY

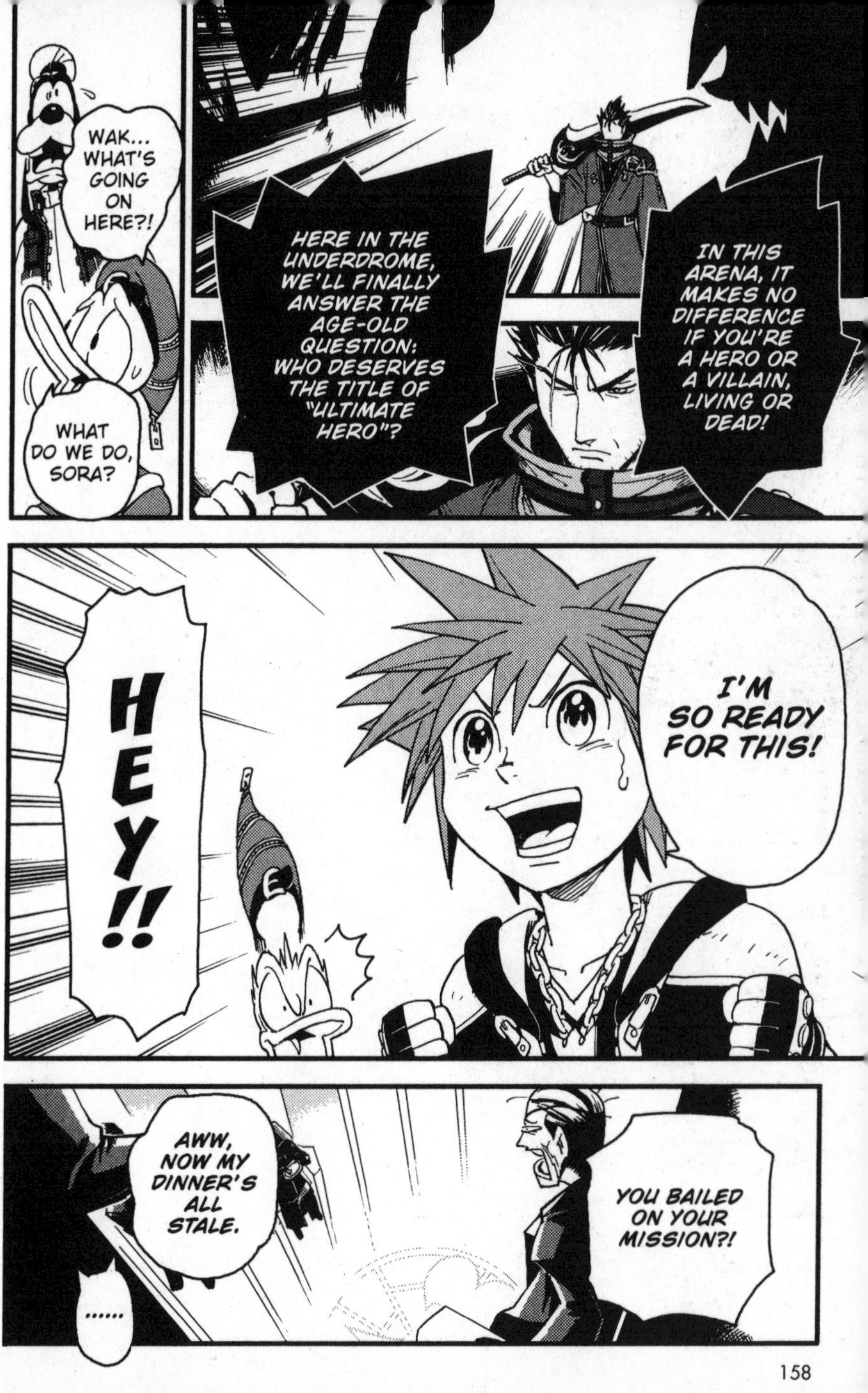
HERE IN THE UNDERDROME, WE'LL FINALLY ANSWER THE AGE-OLD QUESTION: WHO DESERVES THE TITLE OF "ULTIMATE HERO"?
IN THIS ARENA, IT MAKES NO DIFFERENCE IF YOU'RE A HERO OR A VILLAIN, LIVING OR DEAD!
WAK... WHAT'S GOING ON HERE?!
WHAT DO WE DO, SORA?
I'M SO READY FOR THIS!
HEY!!
YOU BAILED ON YOUR MISSION?!
AWW, NOW MY DINNER'S ALL STALE.
......

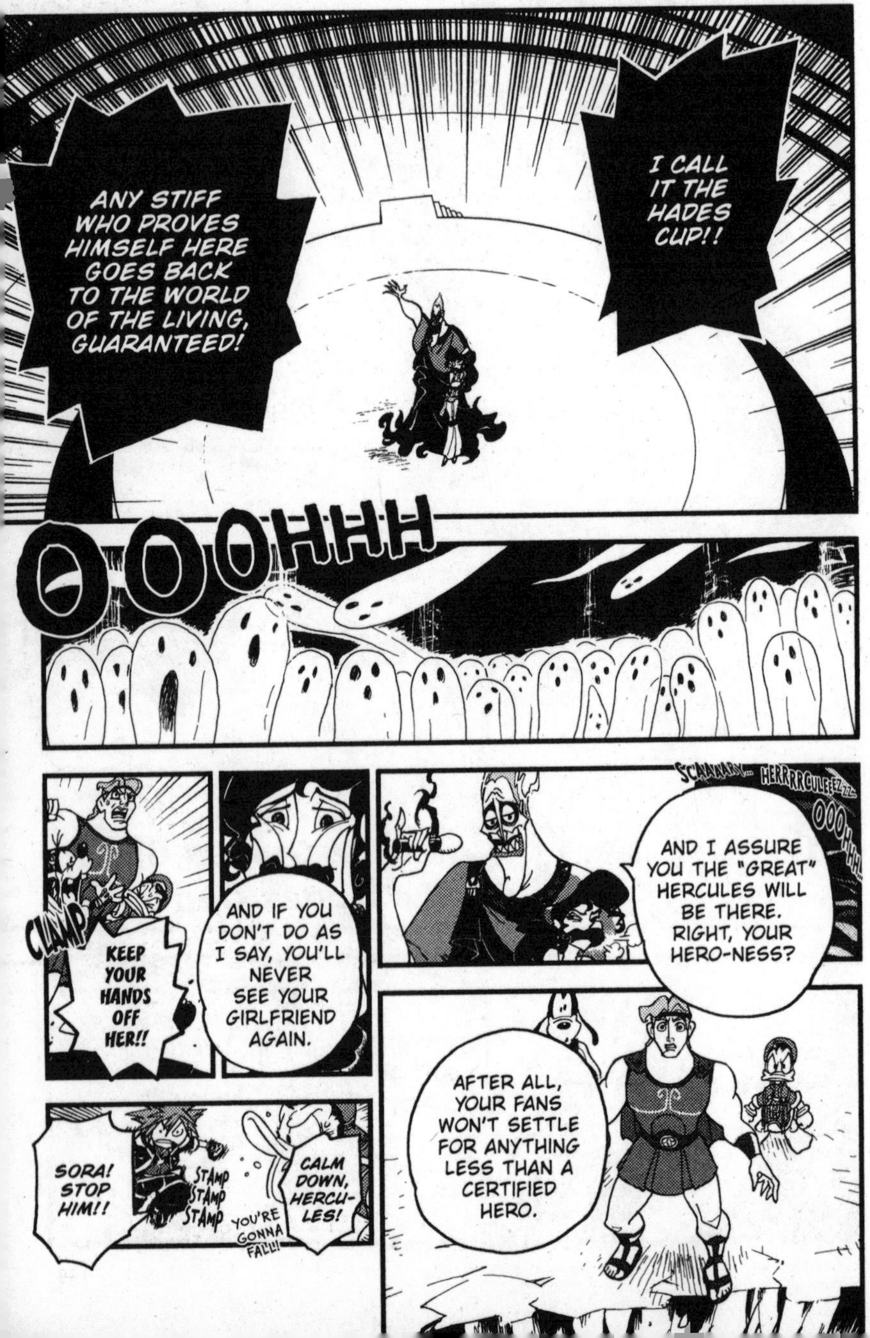
I CALL IT THE HADES CUP!!
ANY STIFF WHO PROVES HIMSELF HERE GOES BACK TO THE WORLD OF THE LIVING, GUARANTEED!
OOOHHH
SCAAAARY... HERRRRCULEEEZZZ... OOOHHH...
AND I ASSURE YOU THE "GREAT" HERCULES WILL BE THERE. RIGHT, YOUR HERO-NESS?
AND IF YOU DON'T DO AS I SAY, YOU'LL NEVER SEE YOUR GIRLFRIEND AGAIN.
CLAMP
KEEP YOUR HANDS OFF HER!!
AFTER ALL, YOUR FANS WON'T SETTLE FOR ANYTHING LESS THAN A CERTIFIED HERO.
CALM DOWN, HERCU-LES!
YOU'RE GONNA FALL!!
STAMP STAMP STAMP
SORA! STOP HIM!!

Chapter 25: Let the Games Begin! The Hades Cup

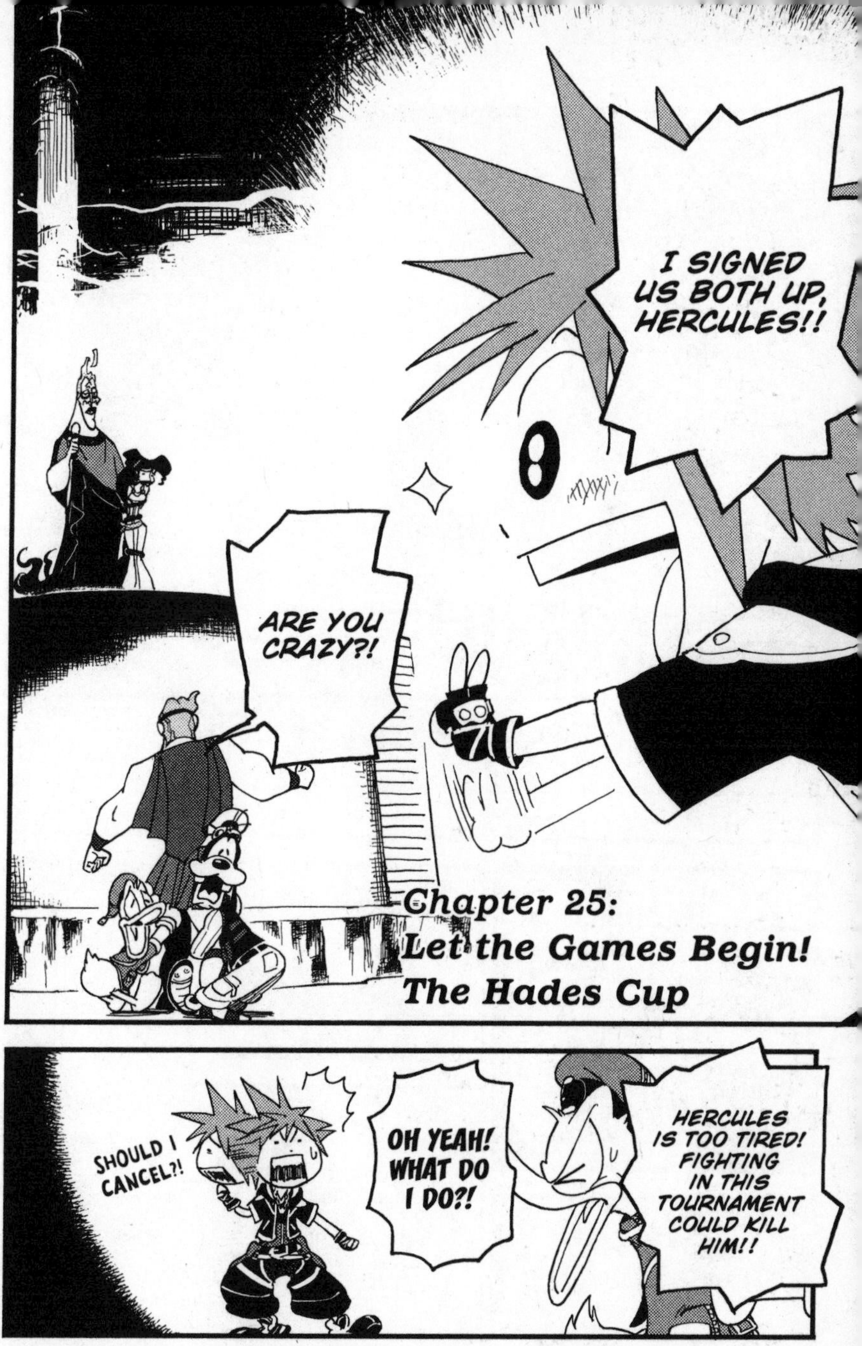
I SIGNED US BOTH UP, HERCULES!!
ARE YOU CRAZY?!
HERCULES IS TOO TIRED! FIGHTING IN THIS TOURNAMENT COULD KILL HIM!!
OH YEAH! WHAT DO I DO?!
SHOULD I CANCEL?!

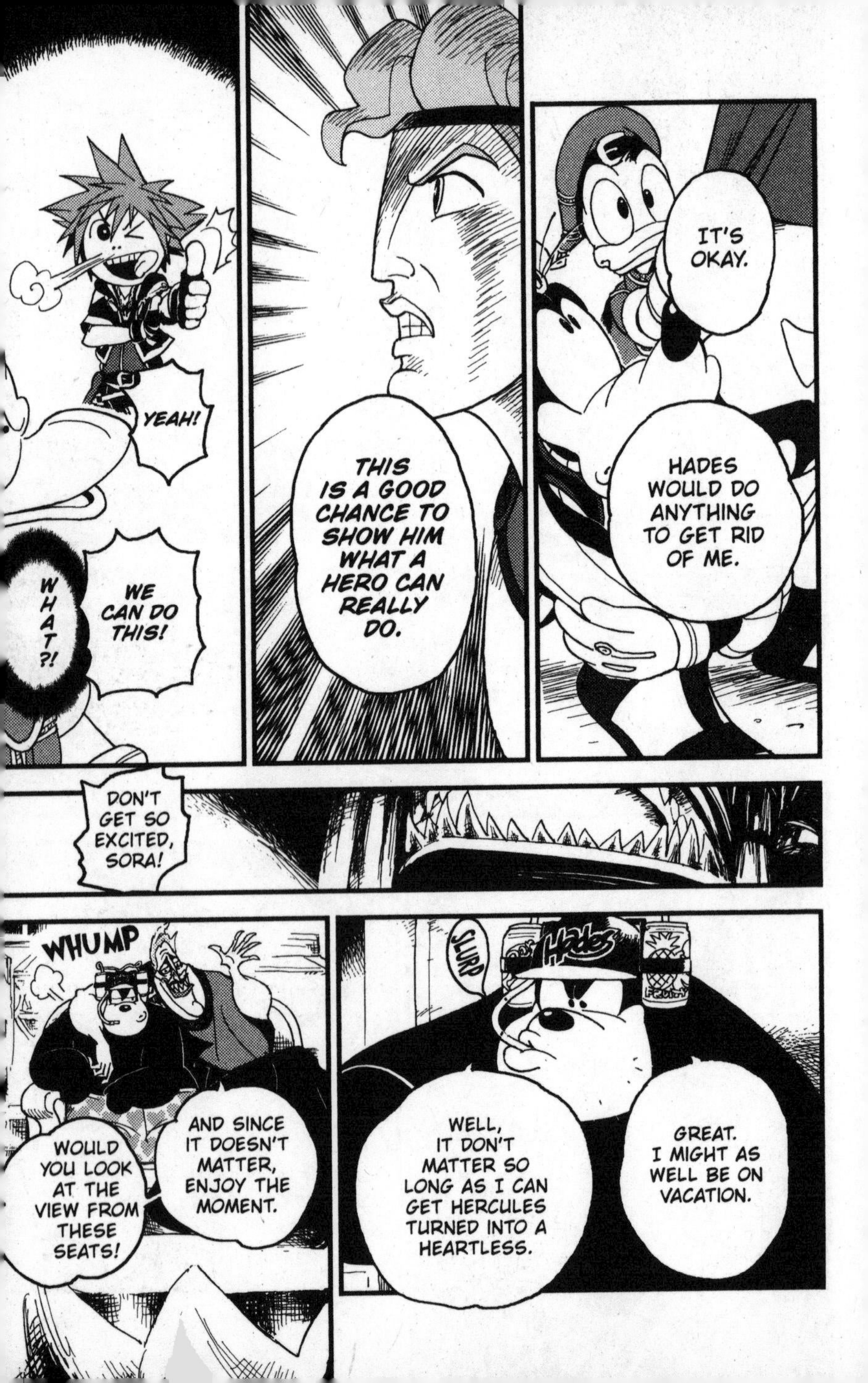
IT'S OKAY.
HADES WOULD DO ANYTHING TO GET RID OF ME.
THIS IS A GOOD CHANCE TO SHOW HIM WHAT A HERO CAN REALLY DO.
YEAH!
WE CAN DO THIS!
WHAT?!
DON'T GET SO EXCITED, SORA!
SLURP
Hades
GREAT. I MIGHT AS WELL BE ON VACATION.
WELL, IT DON'T MATTER SO LONG AS I CAN GET HERCULES TURNED INTO A HEARTLESS.
WHUMP
AND SINCE IT DOESN'T MATTER, ENJOY THE MOMENT.
WOULD YOU LOOK AT THE VIEW FROM THESE SEATS!

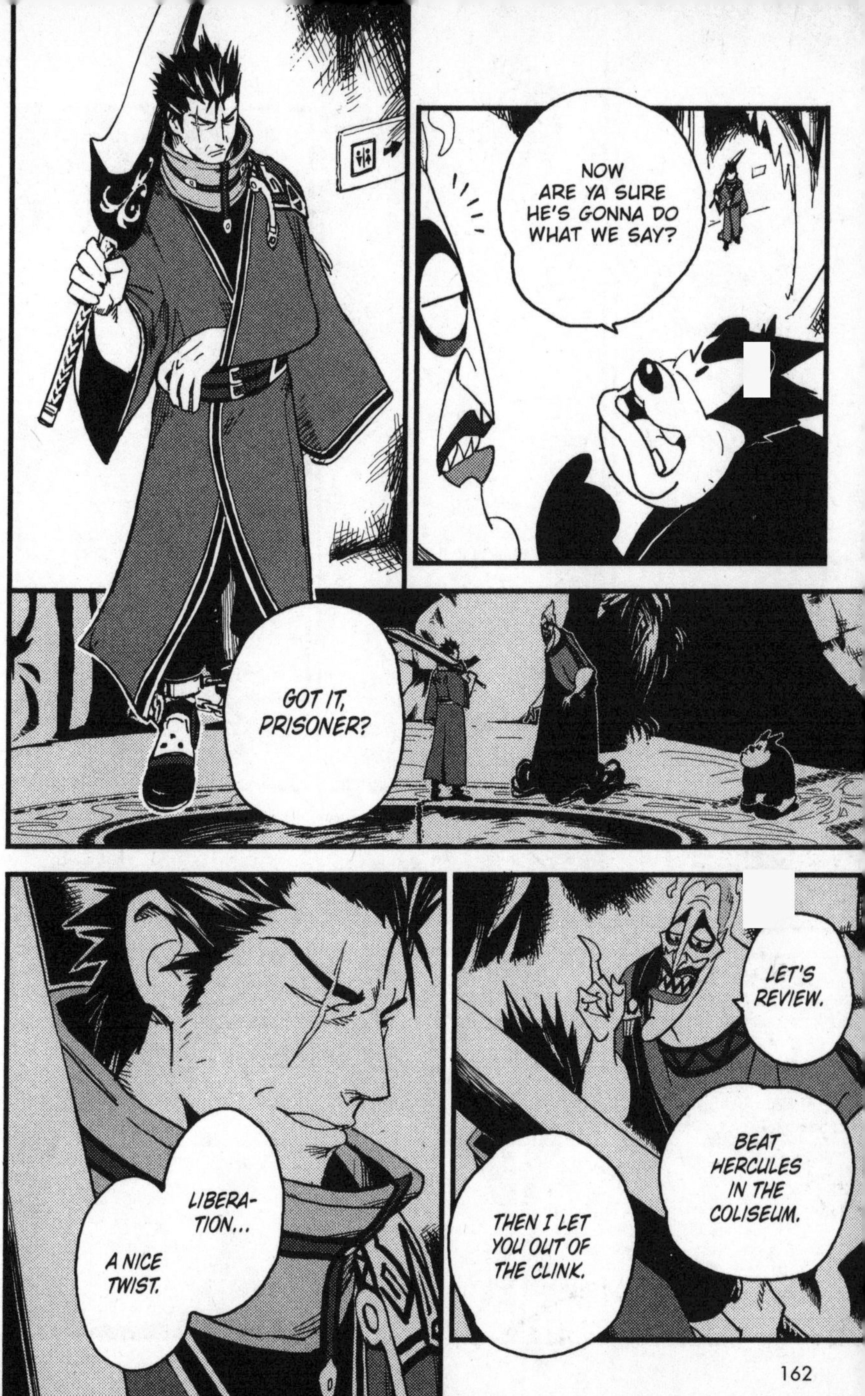
NOW ARE YA SURE HE'S GONNA DO WHAT WE SAY?
GOT IT, PRISONER?
LET'S REVIEW.
BEAT HERCULES IN THE COLISEUM.
THEN I LET YOU OUT OF THE CLINK.
LIBERATION...
A NICE TWIST.

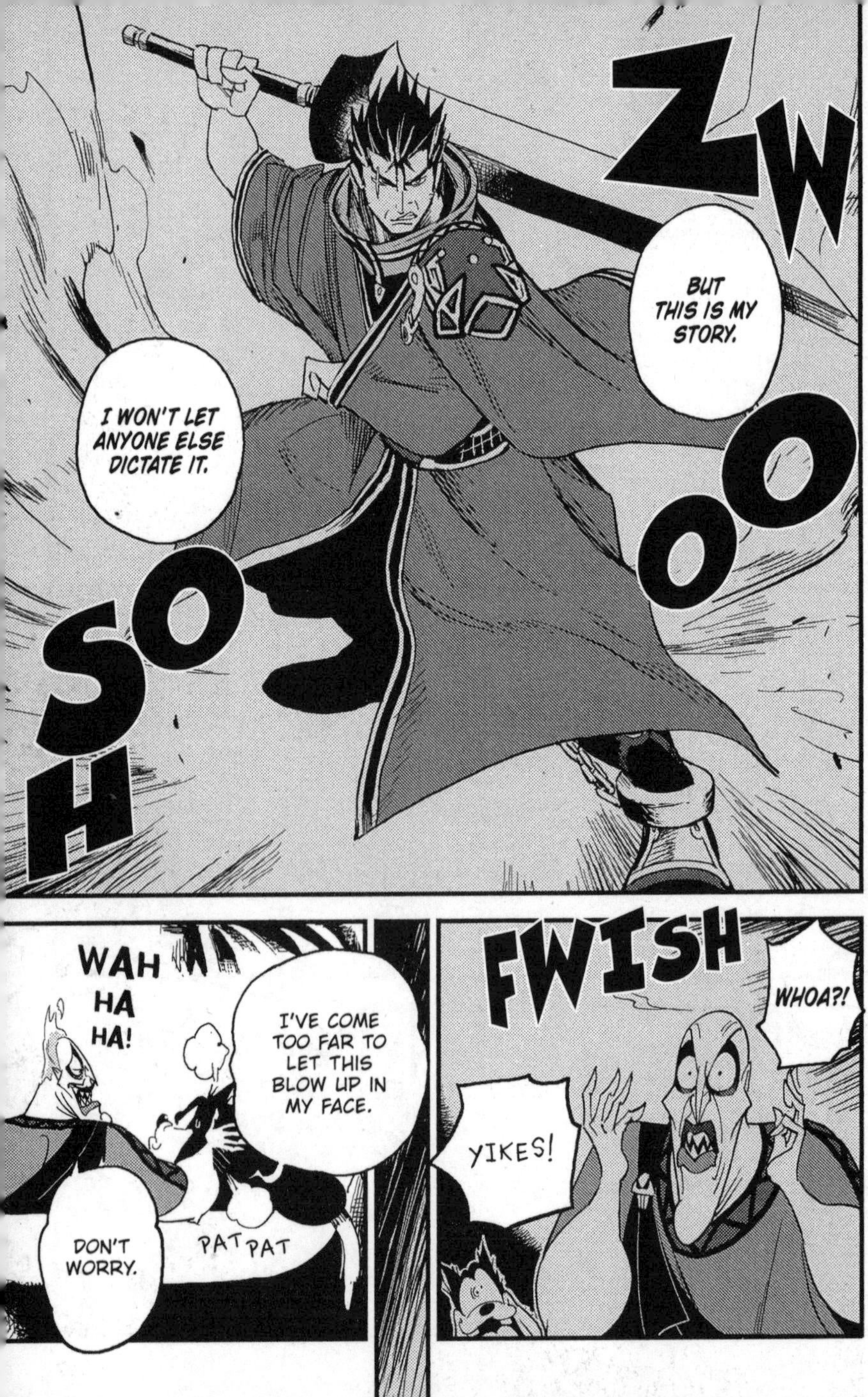
ZWOOOSH
BUT THIS IS MY STORY.
I WON'T LET ANYONE ELSE DICTATE IT.
FWISH
WHOA?!
YIKES!
WAH HA HA!
I'VE COME TOO FAR TO LET THIS BLOW UP IN MY FACE.
DON'T WORRY.
PAT PAT

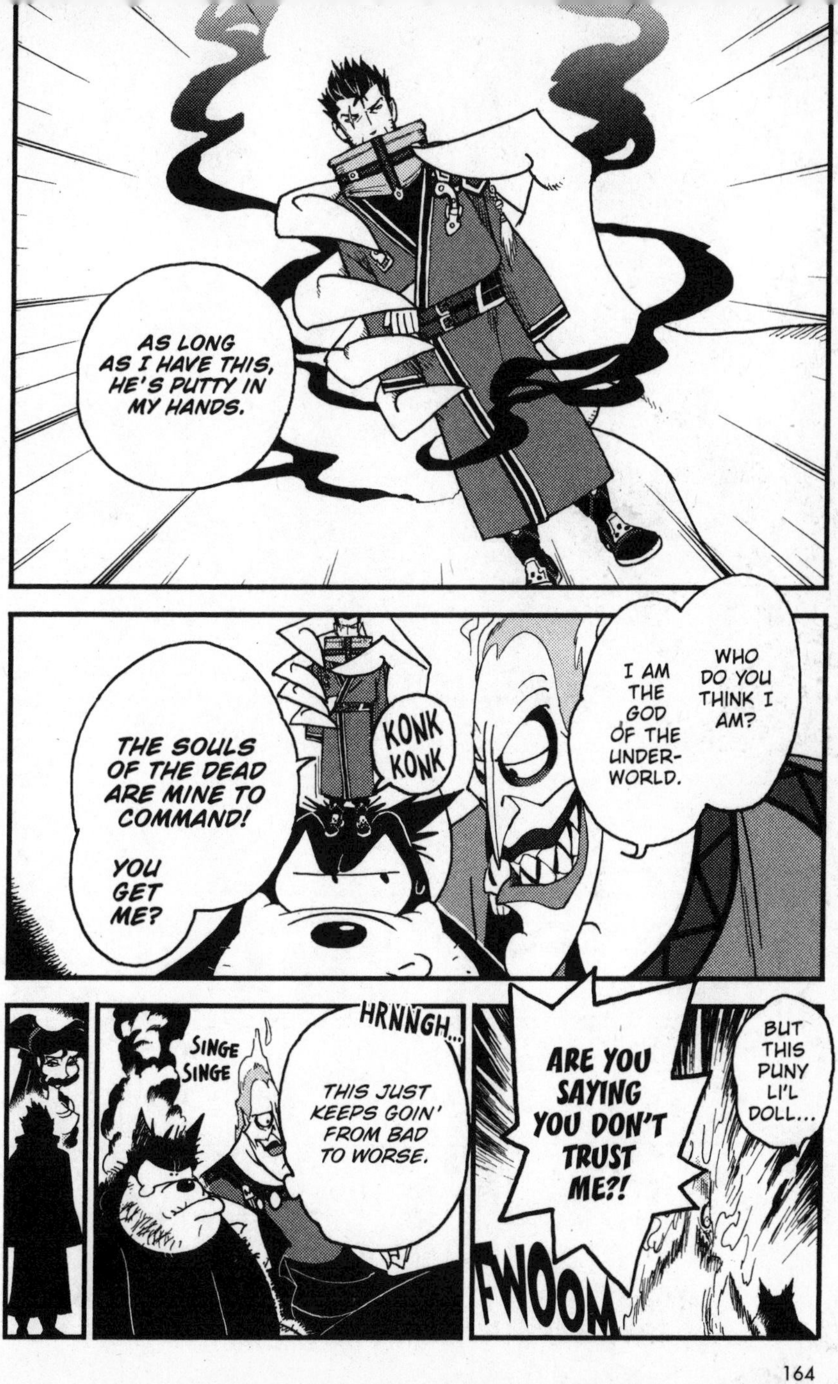
AS LONG AS I HAVE THIS, HE'S PUTTY IN MY HANDS.
WHO DO YOU THINK I AM?
I AM THE GOD OF THE UNDER-WORLD.
KONK KONK
THE SOULS OF THE DEAD ARE MINE TO COMMAND!
YOU GET ME?
BUT THIS PUNY LI'L DOLL...
ARE YOU SAYING YOU DON'T TRUST ME?!
FWOOM
HRNNGH...
SINGE SINGE
THIS JUST KEEPS GOIN' FROM BAD TO WORSE.

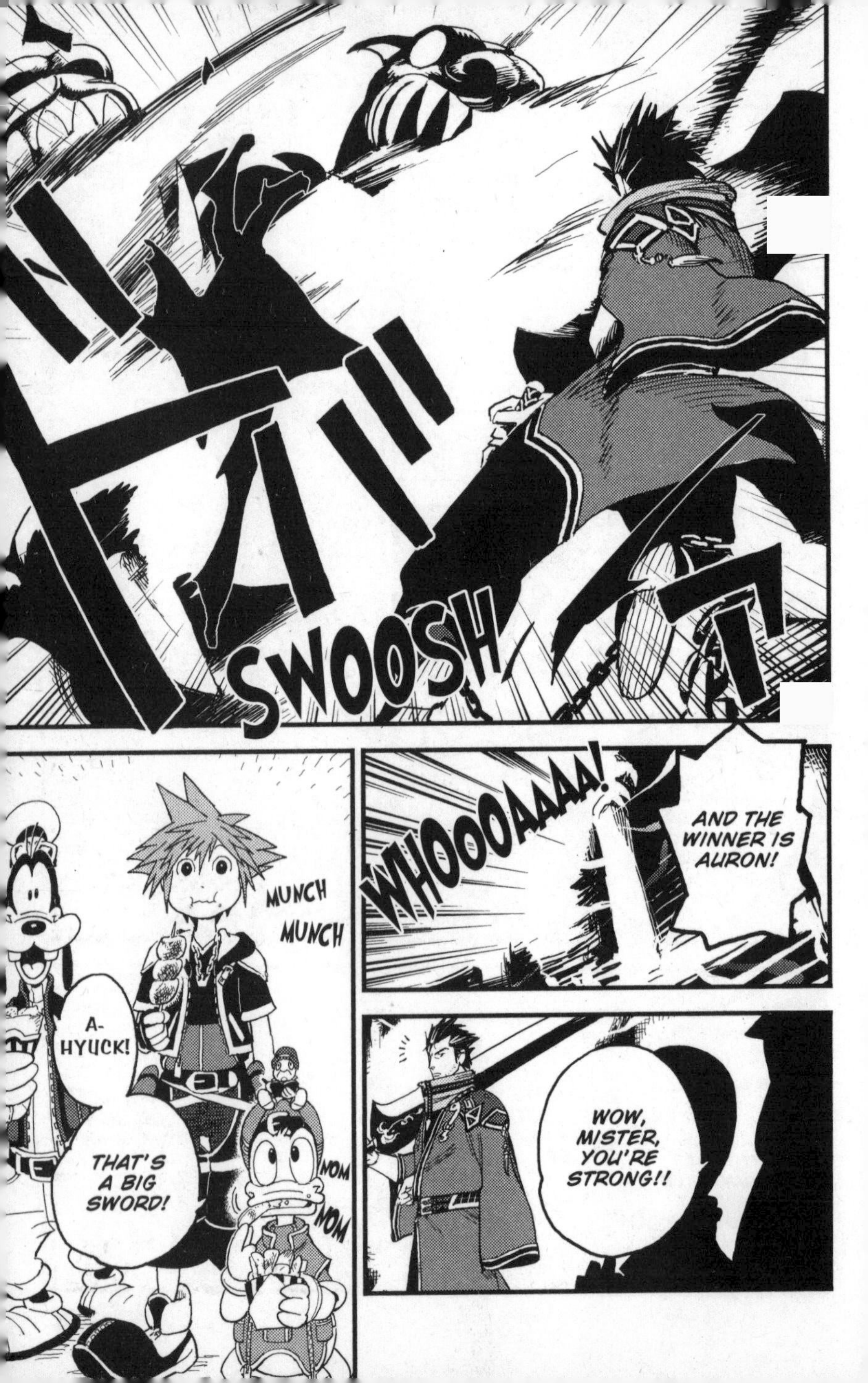
SWOOSH
AND THE WINNER IS AURON!
WHOOOAAAA!
WOW, MISTER, YOU'RE STRONG!!
MUNCH
MUNCH
A-HYUCK!
NOM
NOM
THAT'S A BIG SWORD!

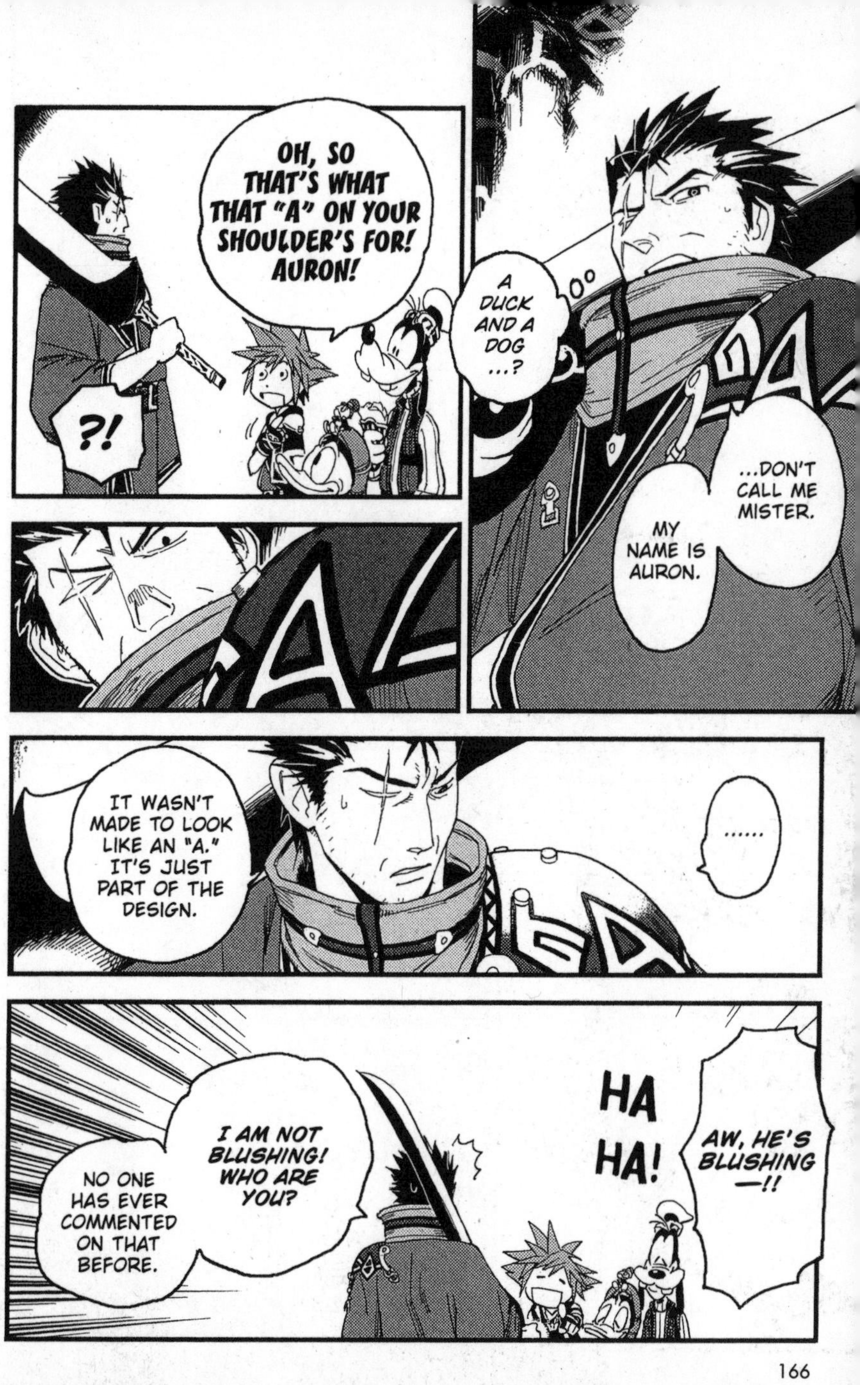
A DUCK AND A DOG ...?
...DON'T CALL ME MISTER.
MY NAME IS AURON.
OH, SO THAT'S WHAT THAT "A" ON YOUR SHOULDER'S FOR! AURON!
?!
......
IT WASN'T MADE TO LOOK LIKE AN "A." IT'S JUST PART OF THE DESIGN.
AW, HE'S BLUSHING—!!
HA HA!
I AM NOT BLUSHING! WHO ARE YOU?
NO ONE HAS EVER COMMENTED ON THAT BEFORE.

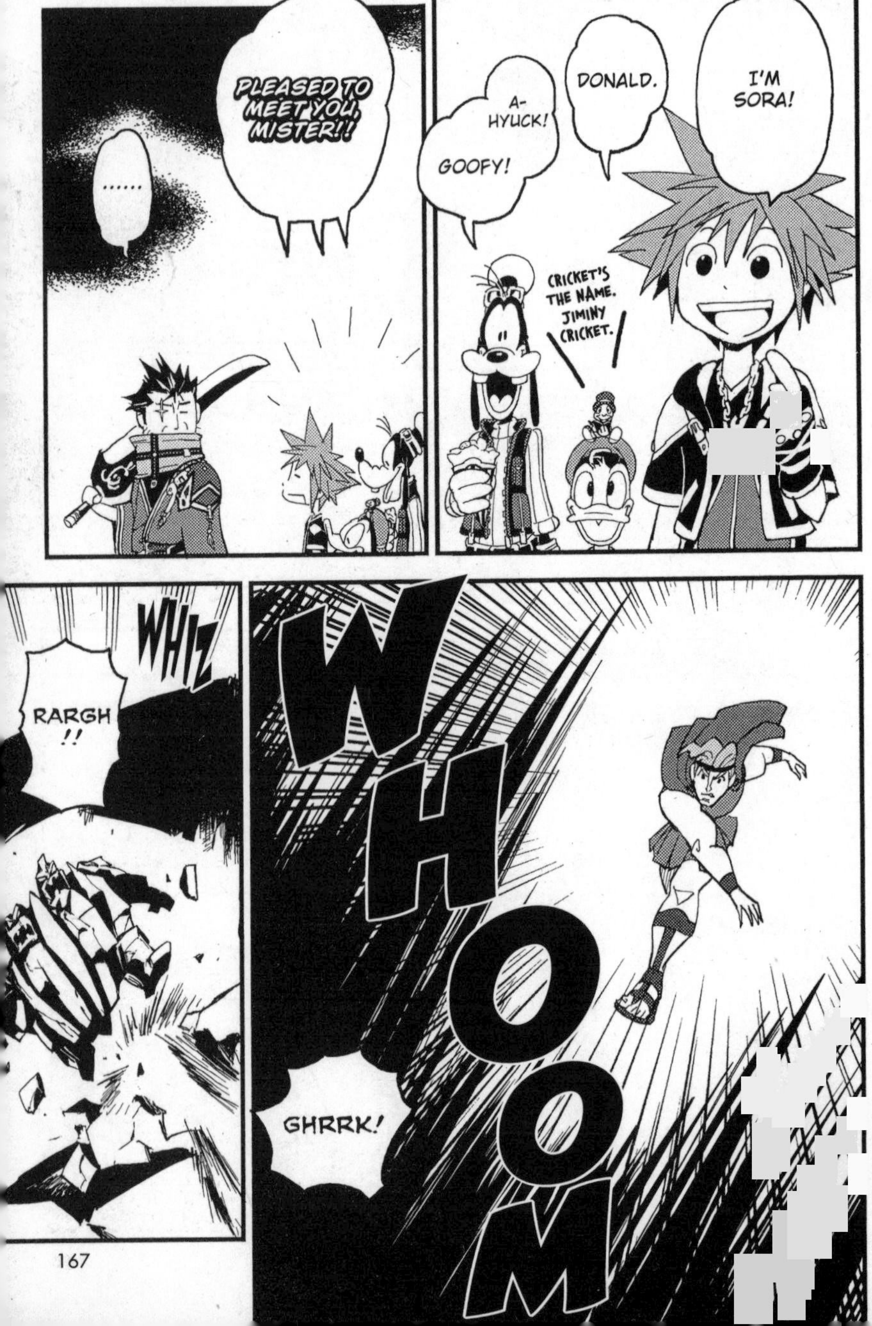
I'M SORA!
DONALD.
A-HYUCK!
GOOFY!
CRICKET'S THE NAME. JIMINY CRICKET.
PLEASED TO MEET YOU, MISTER!!
......
WHOOM
GHRRK!
WHIZ
RARGH !!

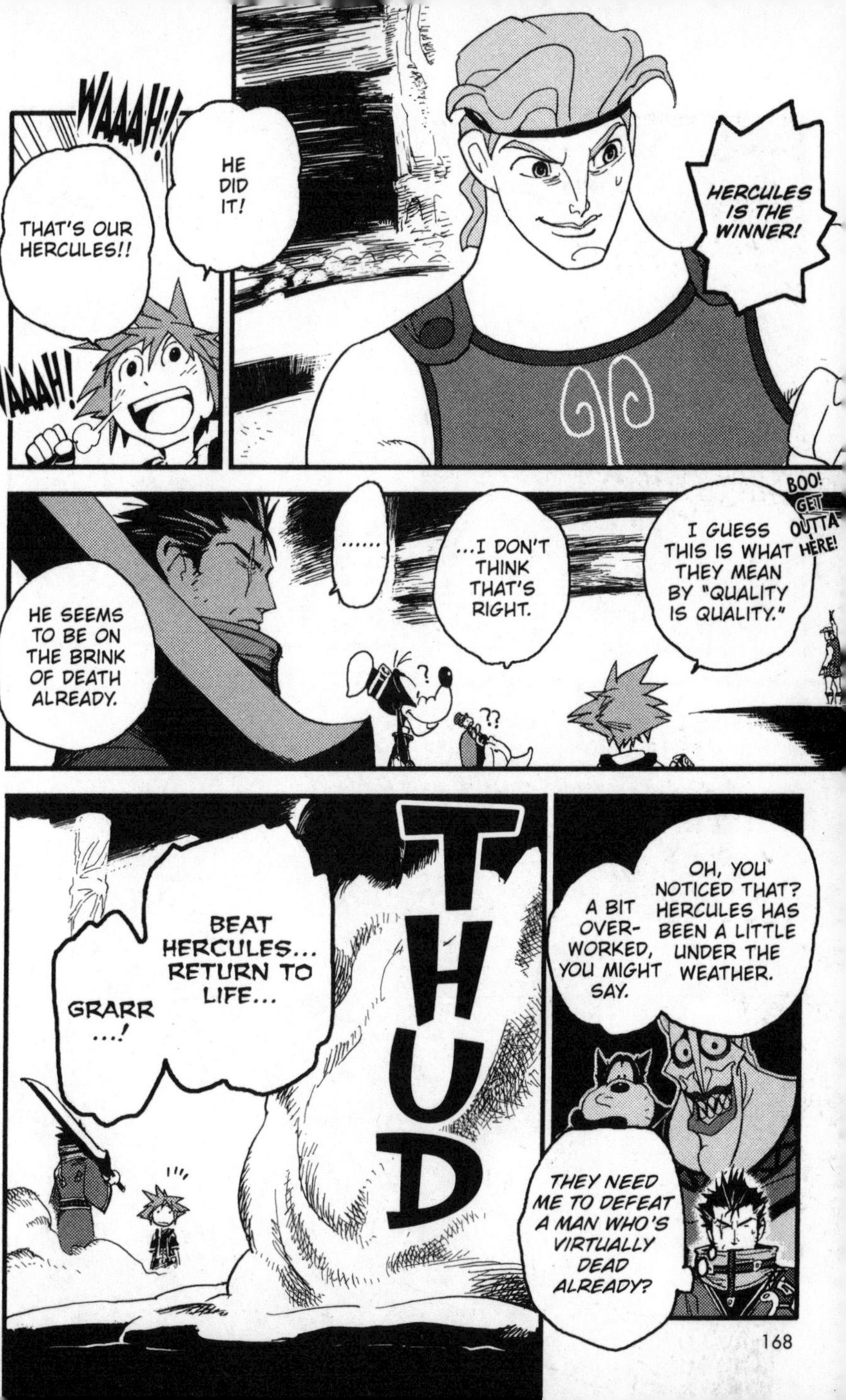
HERCULES IS THE WINNER!
WAAAH!!
HE DID IT!
THAT'S OUR HERCULES!!
WAAAH!
BOO! GET OUTTA HERE!
I GUESS THIS IS WHAT THEY MEAN BY "QUALITY IS QUALITY."
...I DON'T THINK THAT'S RIGHT.
......
HE SEEMS TO BE ON THE BRINK OF DEATH ALREADY.
OH, YOU NOTICED THAT? HERCULES HAS BEEN A LITTLE UNDER THE WEATHER.
A BIT OVER-WORKED, YOU MIGHT SAY.
THEY NEED ME TO DEFEAT A MAN WHO'S VIRTUALLY DEAD ALREADY?
THUD
BEAT HERCULES... RETURN TO LIFE...
GRARR ...!

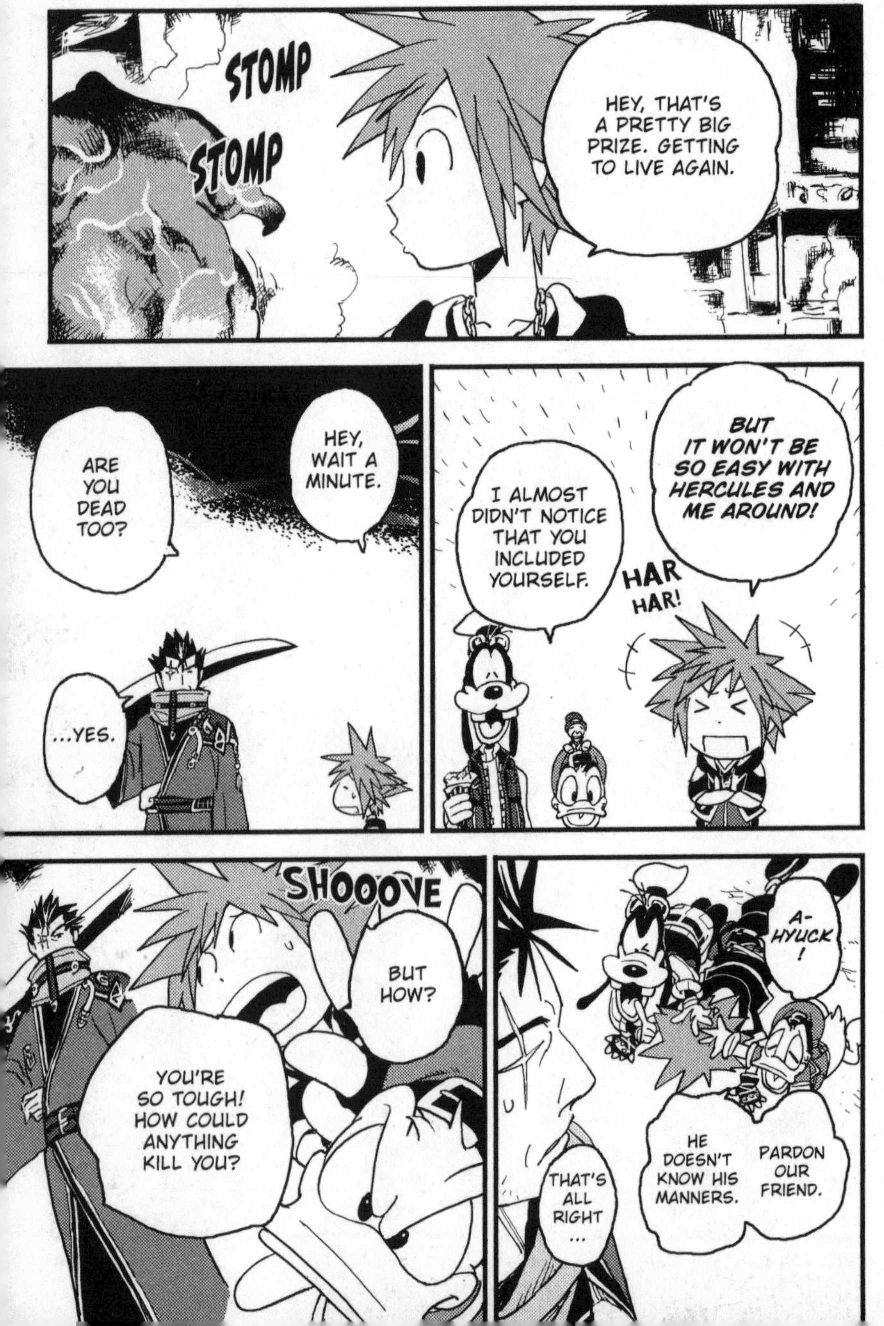
HEY, THAT'S A PRETTY BIG PRIZE. GETTING TO LIVE AGAIN.
STOMP
STOMP
BUT IT WON'T BE SO EASY WITH HERCULES AND ME AROUND!
HAR HAR!
I ALMOST DIDN'T NOTICE THAT YOU INCLUDED YOURSELF.
HEY, WAIT A MINUTE.
ARE YOU DEAD TOO?
...YES.
A-HYUCK!
PARDON OUR FRIEND.
HE DOESN'T KNOW HIS MANNERS.
THAT'S ALL RIGHT...
SHOOOVE
BUT HOW?
YOU'RE SO TOUGH! HOW COULD ANYTHING KILL YOU?

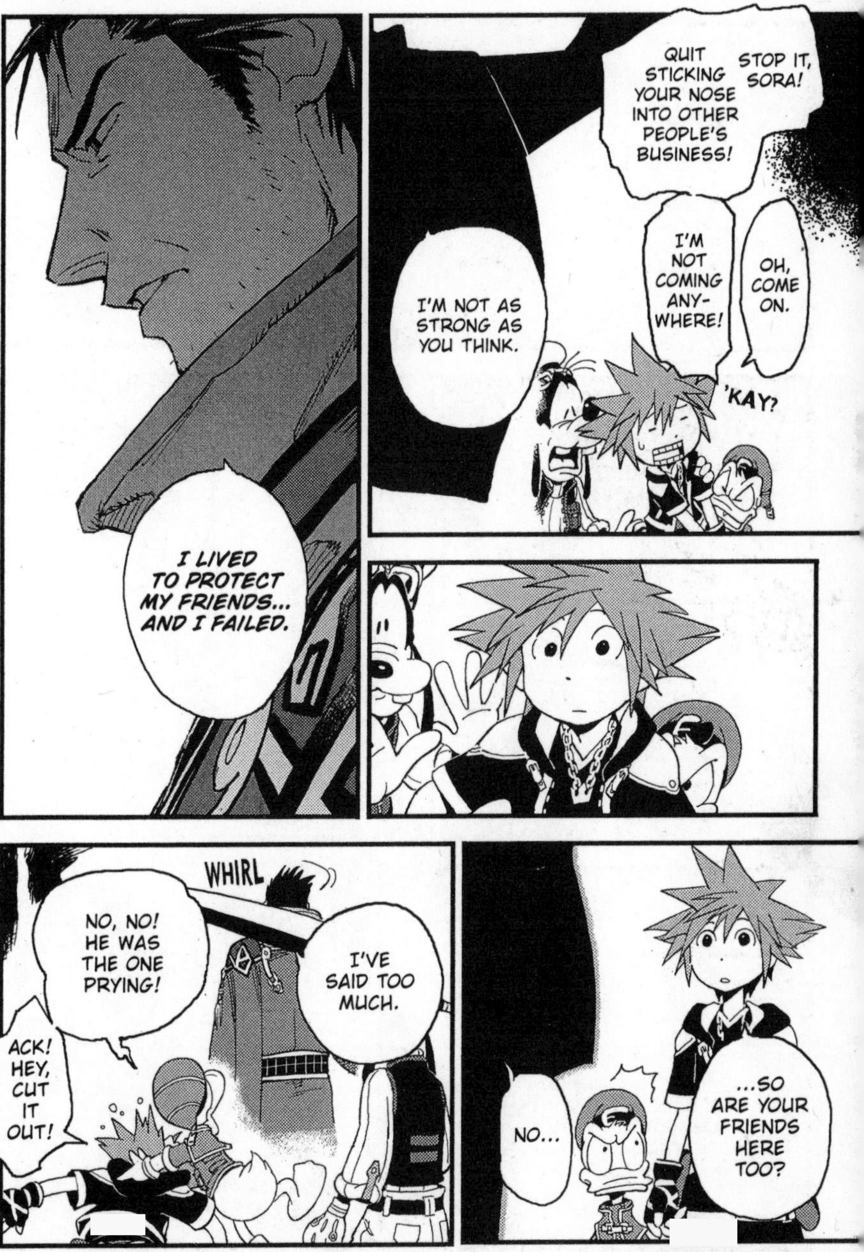
STOP IT, SORA!
QUIT STICKING YOUR NOSE INTO OTHER PEOPLE'S BUSINESS!
OH, COME ON.
'KAY?
I'M NOT COMING ANY-WHERE!
I'M NOT AS STRONG AS YOU THINK.
I LIVED TO PROTECT MY FRIENDS... AND I FAILED.
...SO ARE YOUR FRIENDS HERE TOO?
NO...
WHIRL
I'VE SAID TOO MUCH.
NO, NO! HE WAS THE ONE PRYING!
ACK! HEY, CUT IT OUT!

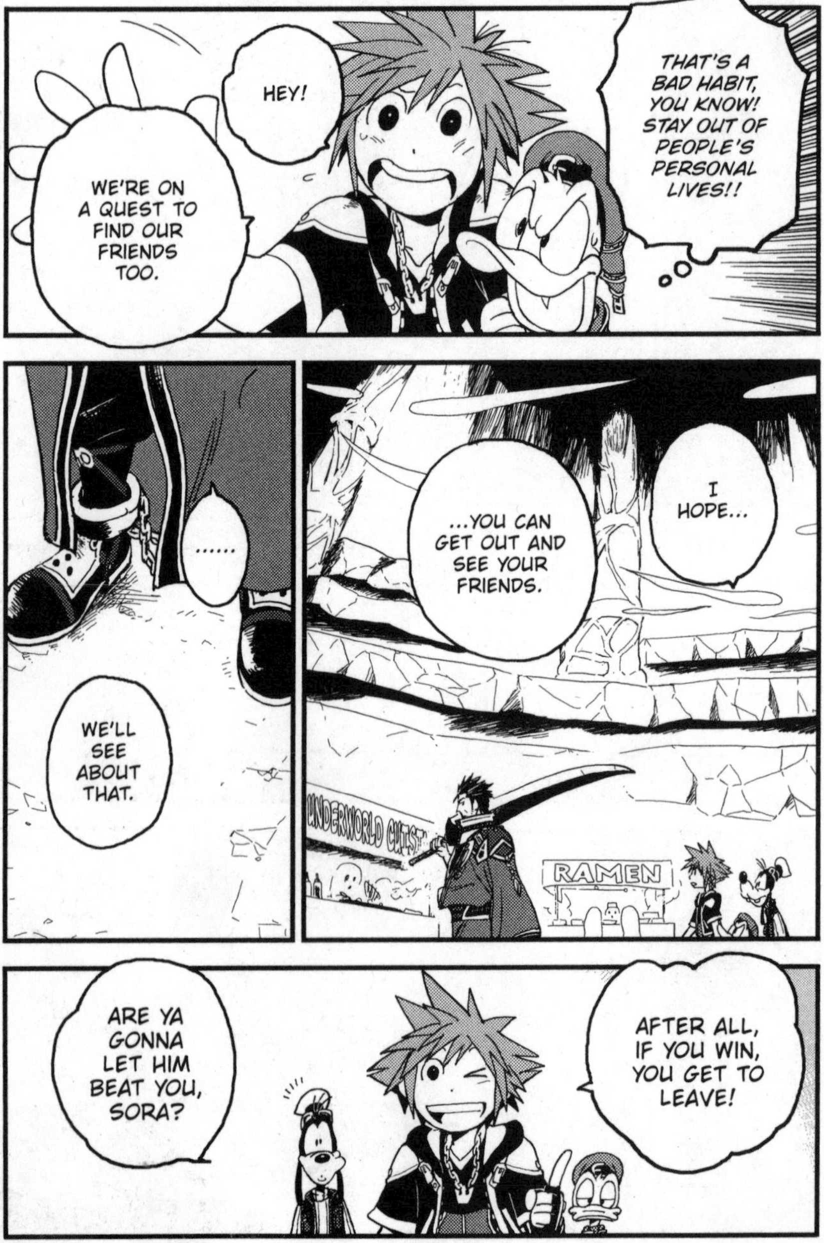
THAT'S A BAD HABIT, YOU KNOW! STAY OUT OF PEOPLE'S PERSONAL LIVES!!
HEY!
WE'RE ON A QUEST TO FIND OUR FRIENDS TOO.
I HOPE...
...YOU CAN GET OUT AND SEE YOUR FRIENDS.
RAMEN
......
WE'LL SEE ABOUT THAT.
AFTER ALL, IF YOU WIN, YOU GET TO LEAVE!
ARE YA GONNA LET HIM BEAT YOU, SORA?

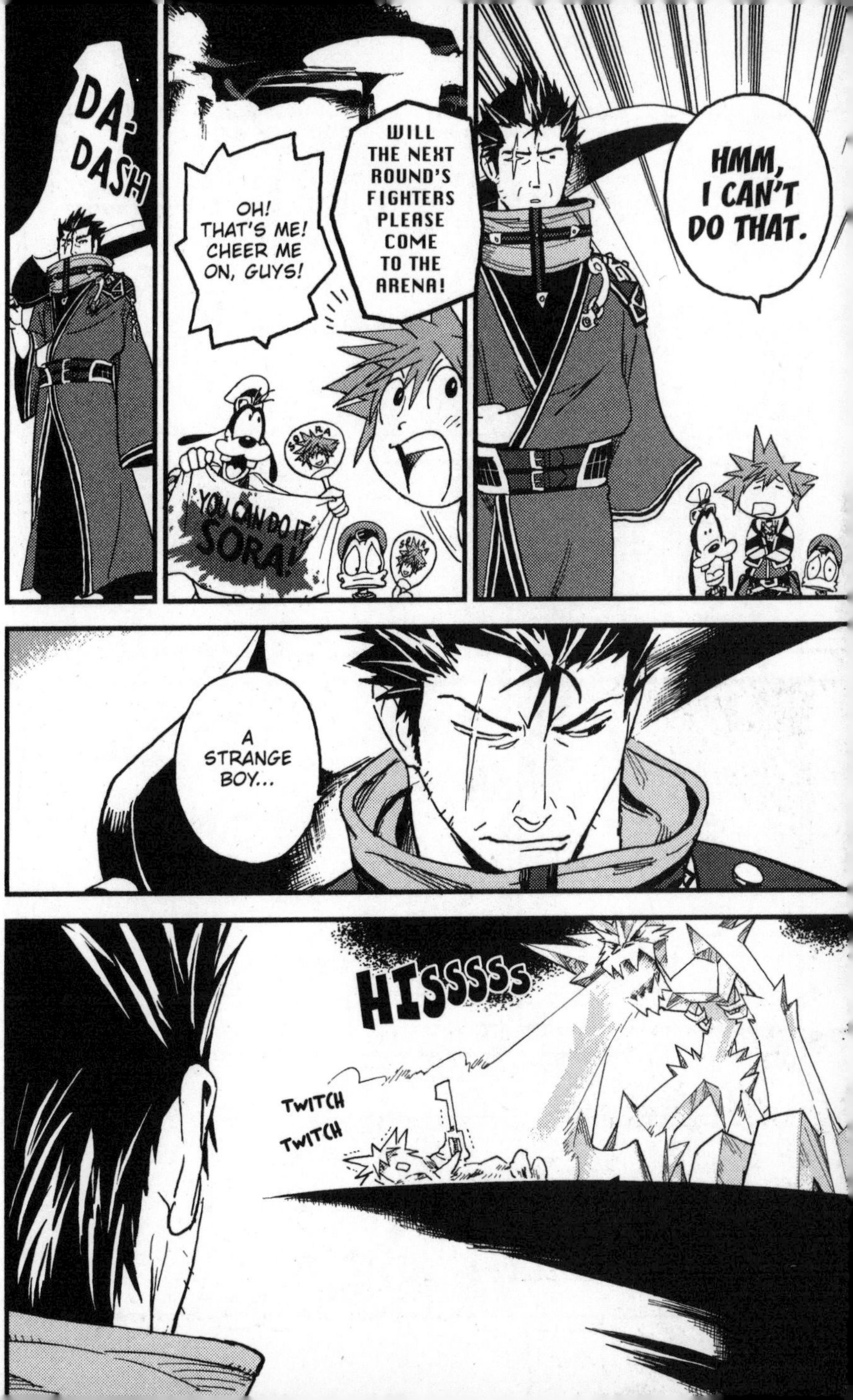
HMM, I CAN'T DO THAT.
WILL THE NEXT ROUND'S FIGHTERS PLEASE COME TO THE ARENA!
OH! THAT'S ME! CHEER ME ON, GUYS!
YOU CAN DO IT SORA!
DA-DASH
A STRANGE BOY...
HISSSSS
TWITCH
TWITCH

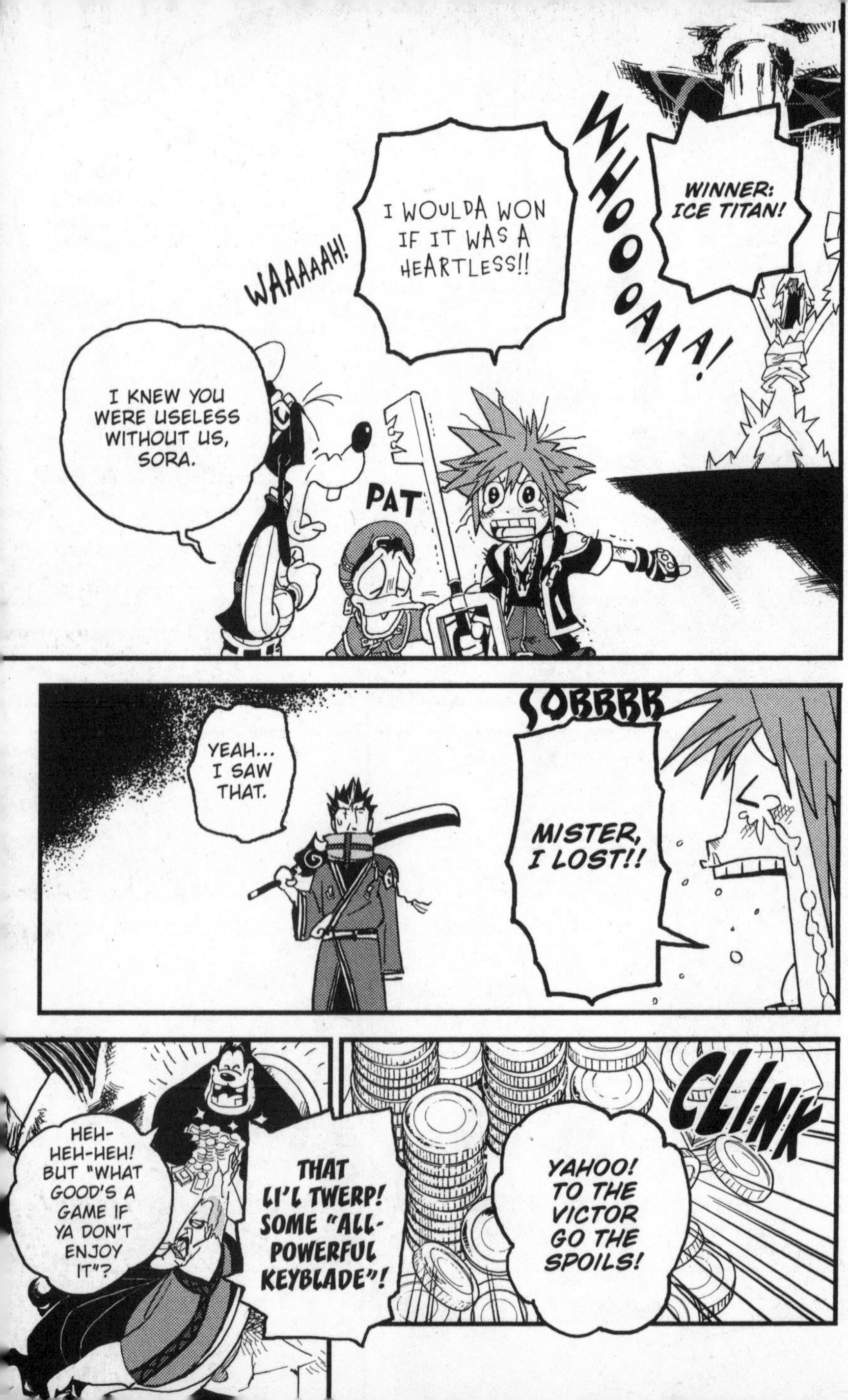
WINNER: ICE TITAN!
WHOOOAAA!
I WOULDA WON IF IT WAS A HEARTLESS!!
WAAAAAH!
I KNEW YOU WERE USELESS WITHOUT US, SORA.
PAT
SOBBBB
MISTER, I LOST!!
YEAH... I SAW THAT.
CLINK
YAHOO! TO THE VICTOR GO THE SPOILS!
THAT LI'L TWERP! SOME "ALL-POWERFUL KEYBLADE"!
HEH-HEH-HEH! BUT "WHAT GOOD'S A GAME IF YA DON'T ENJOY IT"?

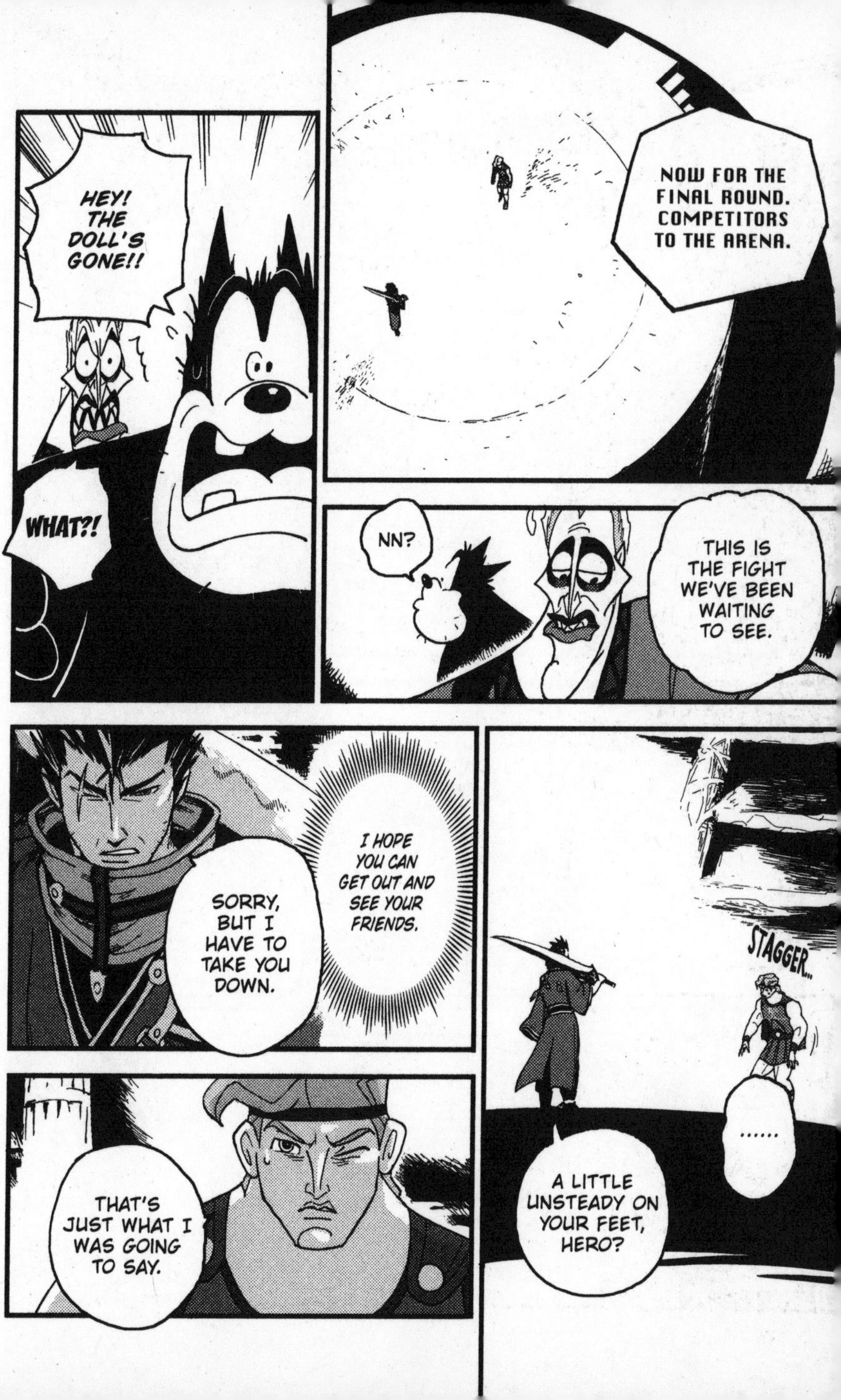
NOW FOR THE FINAL ROUND. COMPETITORS TO THE ARENA.
THIS IS THE FIGHT WE'VE BEEN WAITING TO SEE.
NN?
HEY! THE DOLL'S GONE!!
WHAT?!
STAGGER...
......
A LITTLE UNSTEADY ON YOUR FEET, HERO?
I HOPE YOU CAN GET OUT AND SEE YOUR FRIENDS.
SORRY, BUT I HAVE TO TAKE YOU DOWN.
THAT'S JUST WHAT I WAS GOING TO SAY.

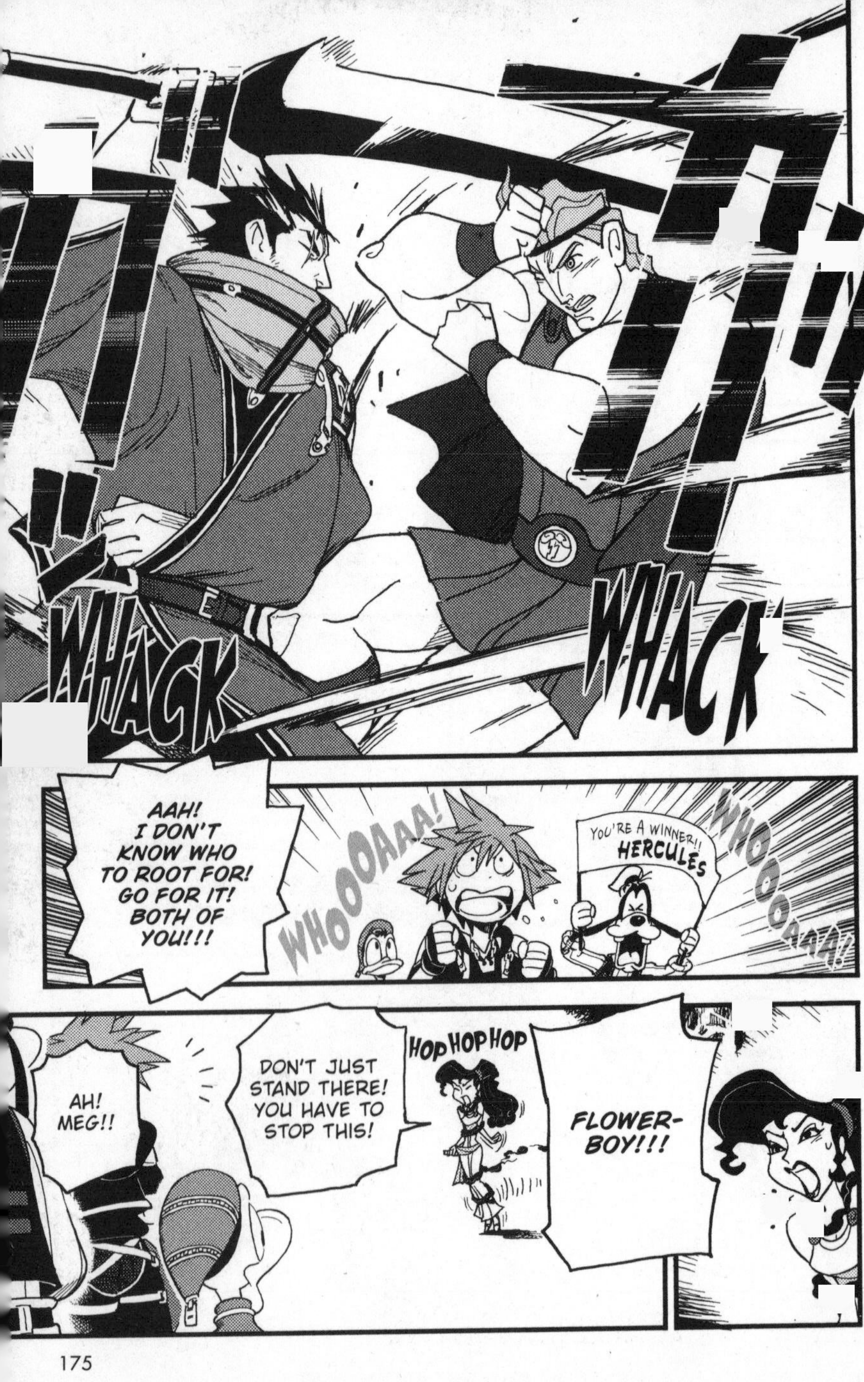
WHACK
WHACK
YOU'RE A WINNER!! HERCULES
WHOOOAAA!?
WHOOOAAA!
AAH! I DON'T KNOW WHO TO ROOT FOR! GO FOR IT! BOTH OF YOU!!!
FLOWER-BOY!!!
HOP HOP HOP
DON'T JUST STAND THERE! YOU HAVE TO STOP THIS!
AH! MEG!!

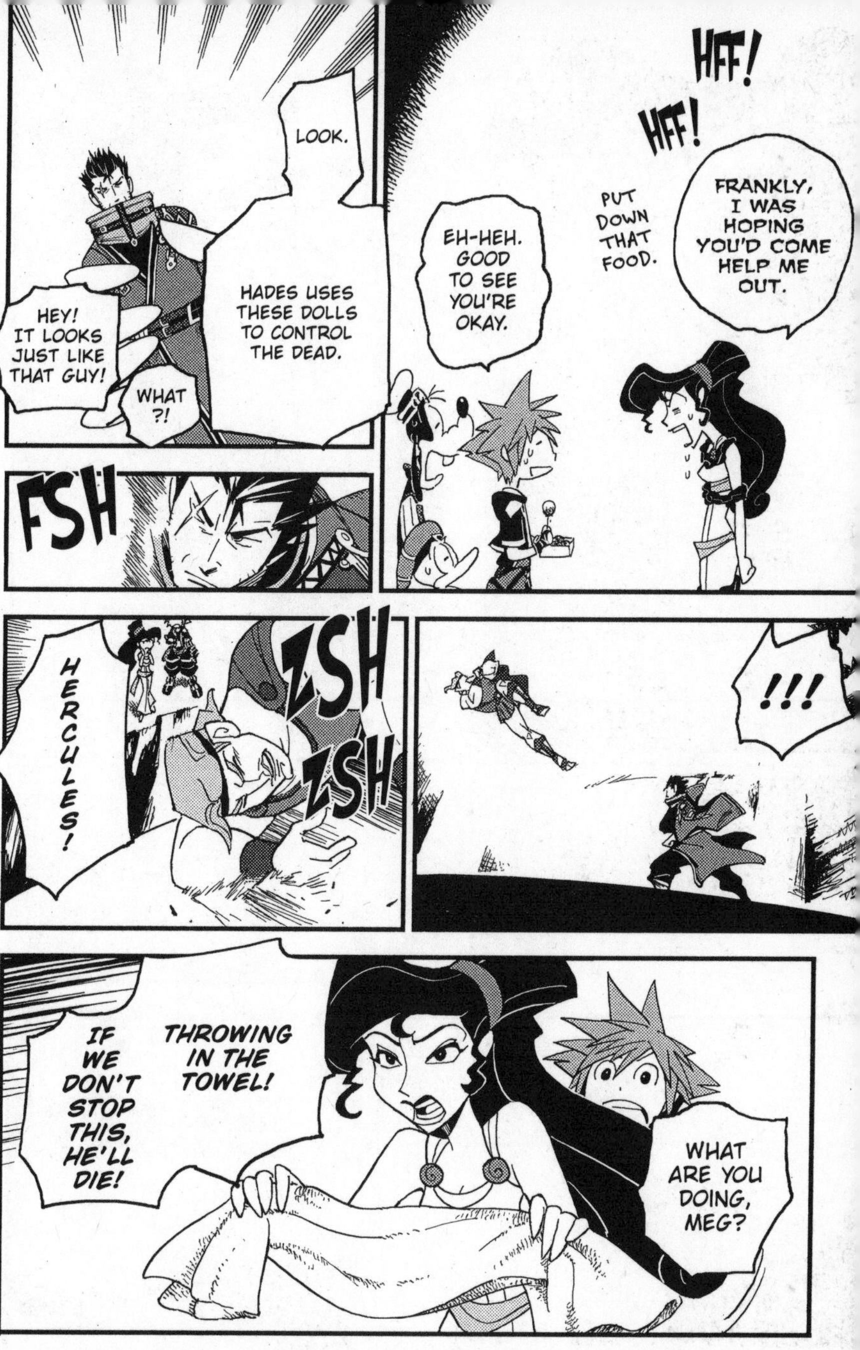
HFF!
HFF!
FRANKLY, I WAS HOPING YOU'D COME HELP ME OUT.
PUT DOWN THAT FOOD.
EH-HEH. GOOD TO SEE YOU'RE OKAY.
LOOK.
HADES USES THESE DOLLS TO CONTROL THE DEAD.
WHAT ?!
HEY! IT LOOKS JUST LIKE THAT GUY!
FSH
!!!
ZSH
ZSH
HERCULES!
WHAT ARE YOU DOING, MEG?
THROWING IN THE TOWEL!
IF WE DON'T STOP THIS, HE'LL DIE!

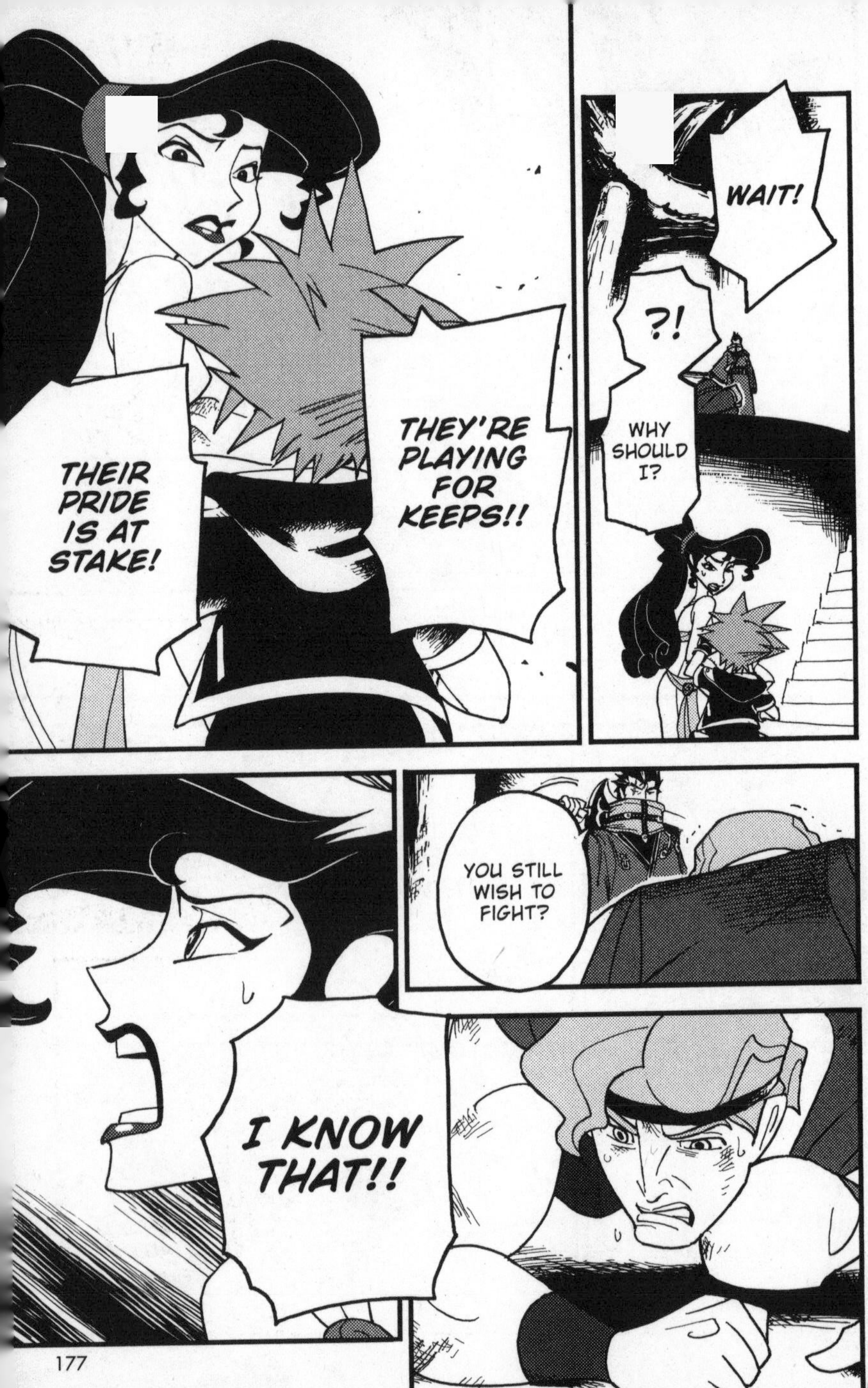
WAIT!
?!
WHY SHOULD I?
THEY'RE PLAYING FOR KEEPS!!
THEIR PRIDE IS AT STAKE!
YOU STILL WISH TO FIGHT?
I KNOW THAT!!

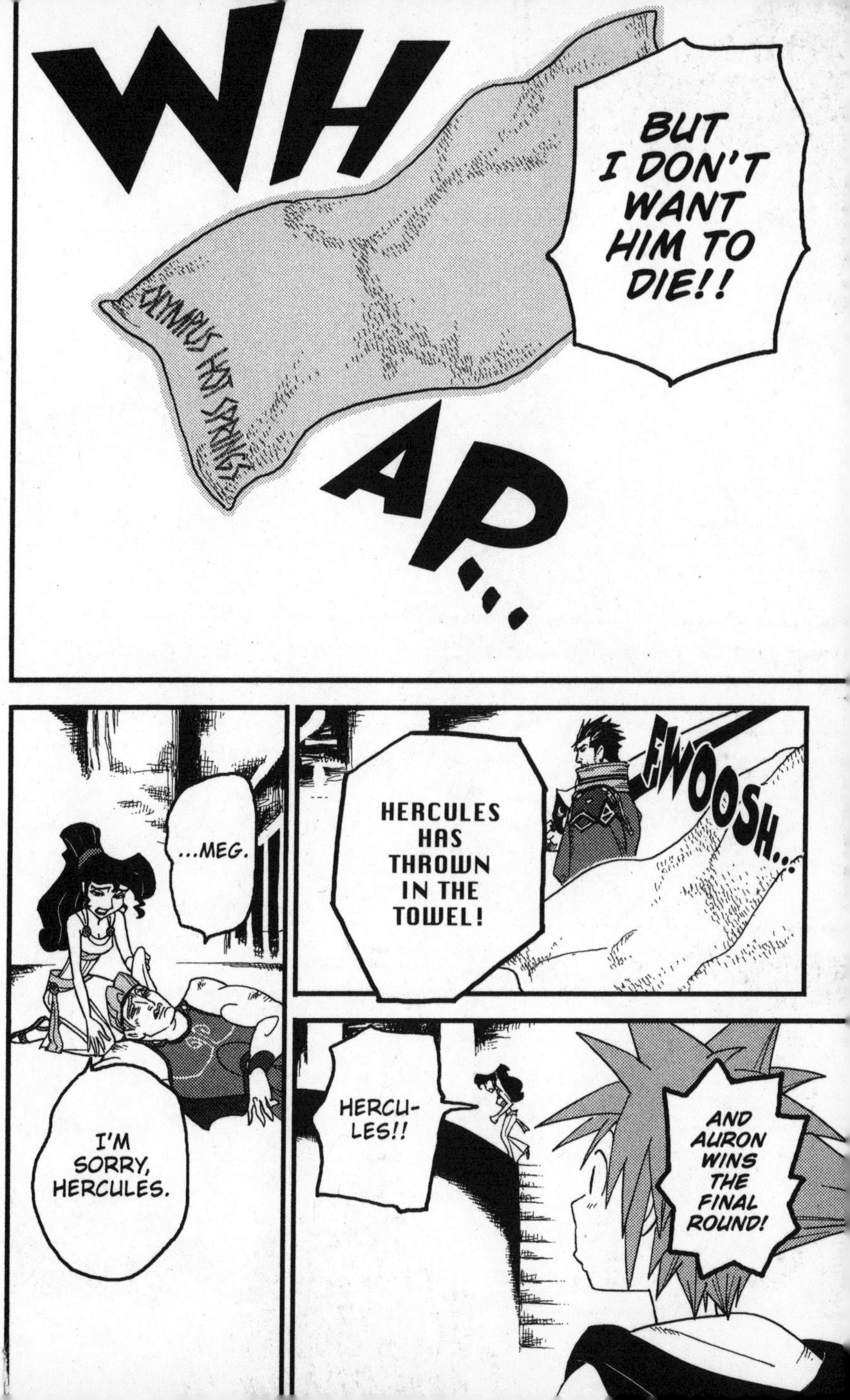
BUT I DON'T WANT HIM TO DIE!!
WH
AP...
OLYMPUS HOT SPRINGS
WOOSH...
HERCULES HAS THROWN IN THE TOWEL!
AND AURON WINS THE FINAL ROUND!
HERCU-LES!!
...MEG.
I'M SORRY, HERCULES.

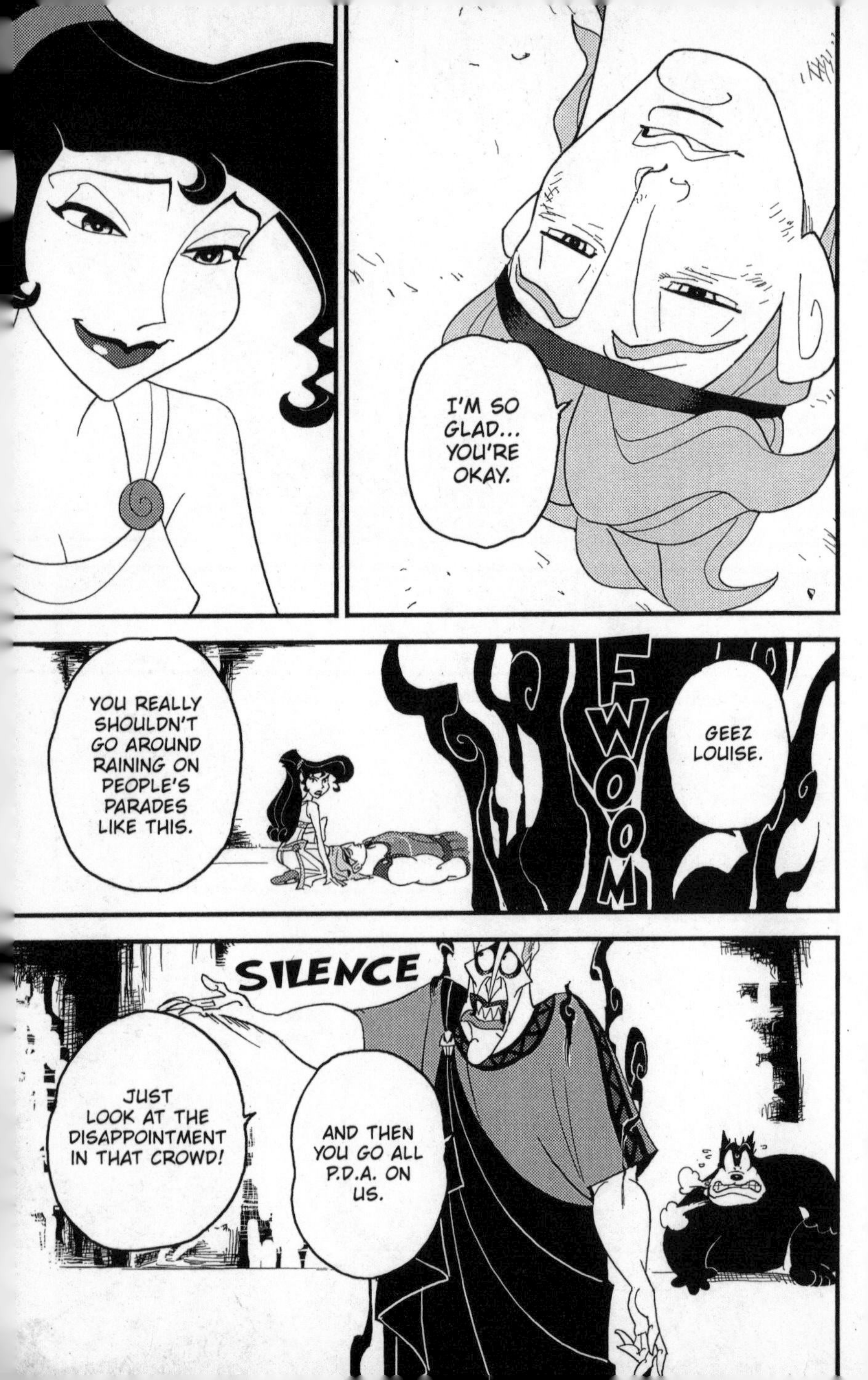
I'M SO GLAD... YOU'RE OKAY.
GEEZ LOUISE.
FWOOM
YOU REALLY SHOULDN'T GO AROUND RAINING ON PEOPLE'S PARADES LIKE THIS.
SILENCE
AND THEN YOU GO ALL P.D.A. ON US.
JUST LOOK AT THE DISAPPOINTMENT IN THAT CROWD!

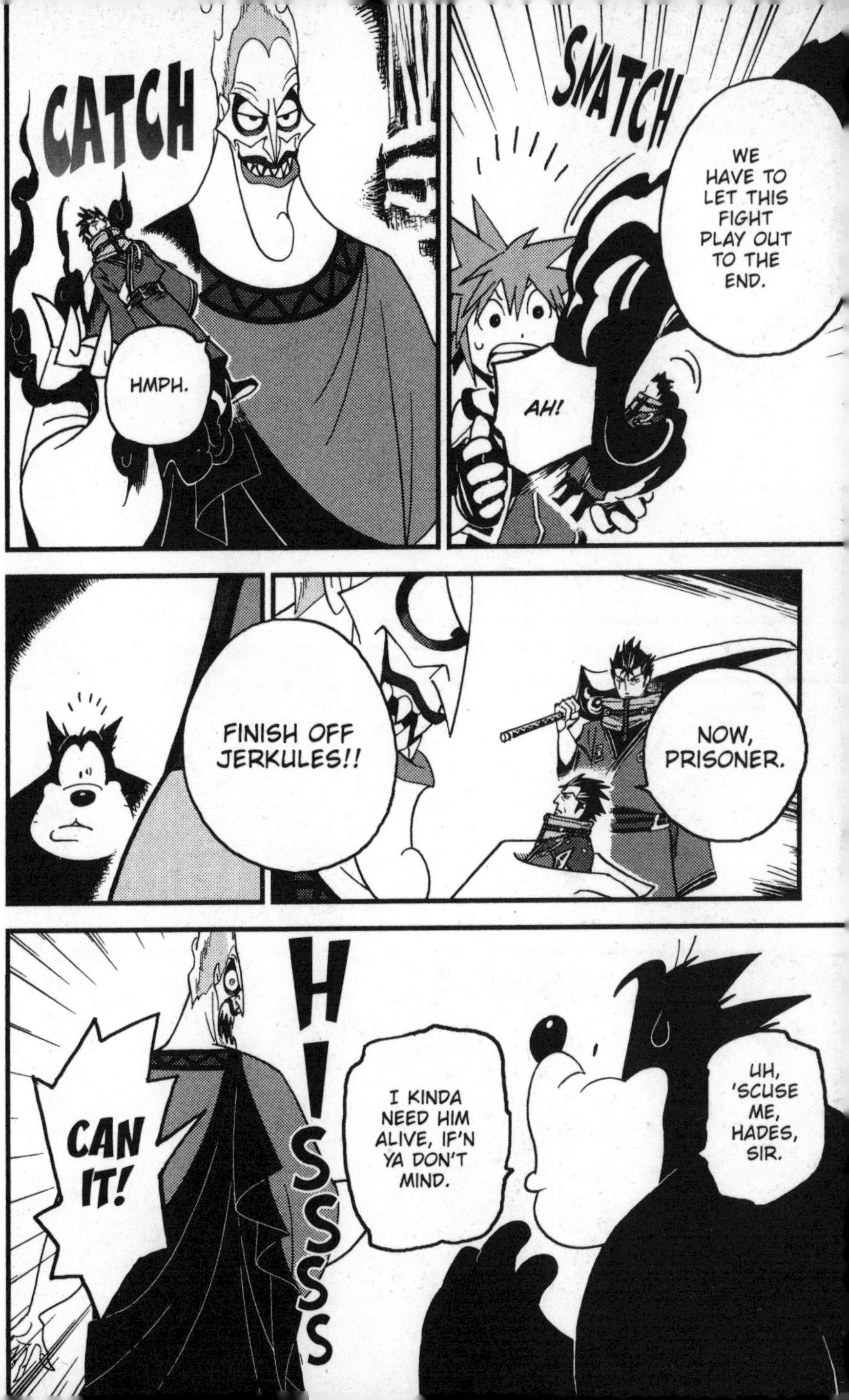
SNATCH
WE HAVE TO LET THIS FIGHT PLAY OUT TO THE END.
AH!
CATCH
HMPH.
NOW, PRISONER.
FINISH OFF JERKULES!!
UH, 'SCUSE ME, HADES, SIR.
I KINDA NEED HIM ALIVE, IF'N YA DON'T MIND.
HISSSS
CAN IT!

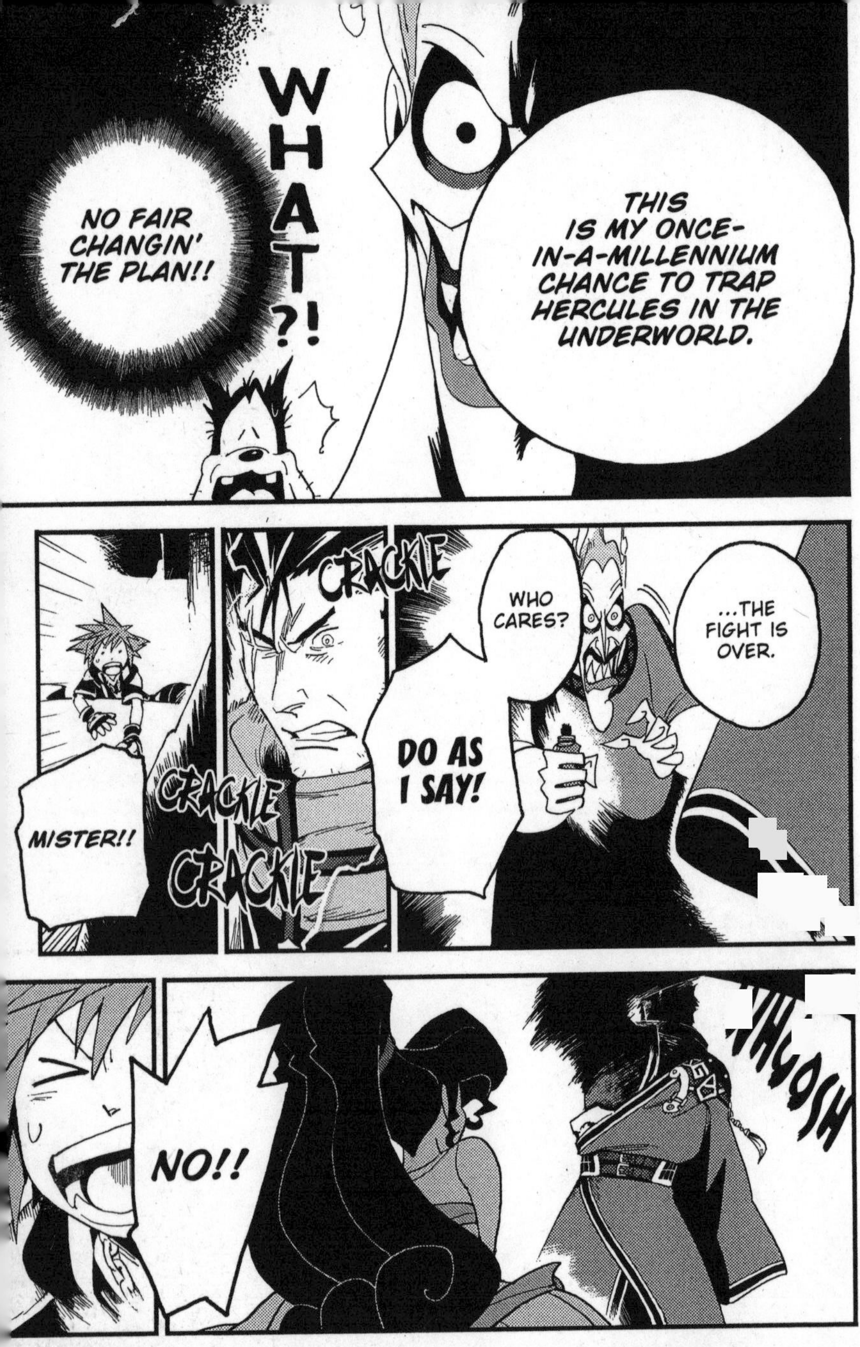
THIS IS MY ONCE-IN-A-MILLENNIUM CHANCE TO TRAP HERCULES IN THE UNDERWORLD.
WHAT?!
NO FAIR CHANGIN' THE PLAN!!
...THE FIGHT IS OVER.
WHO CARES?
DO AS I SAY!
CRACKLE
CRACKLE
CRACKLE
MISTER!!
NO!!

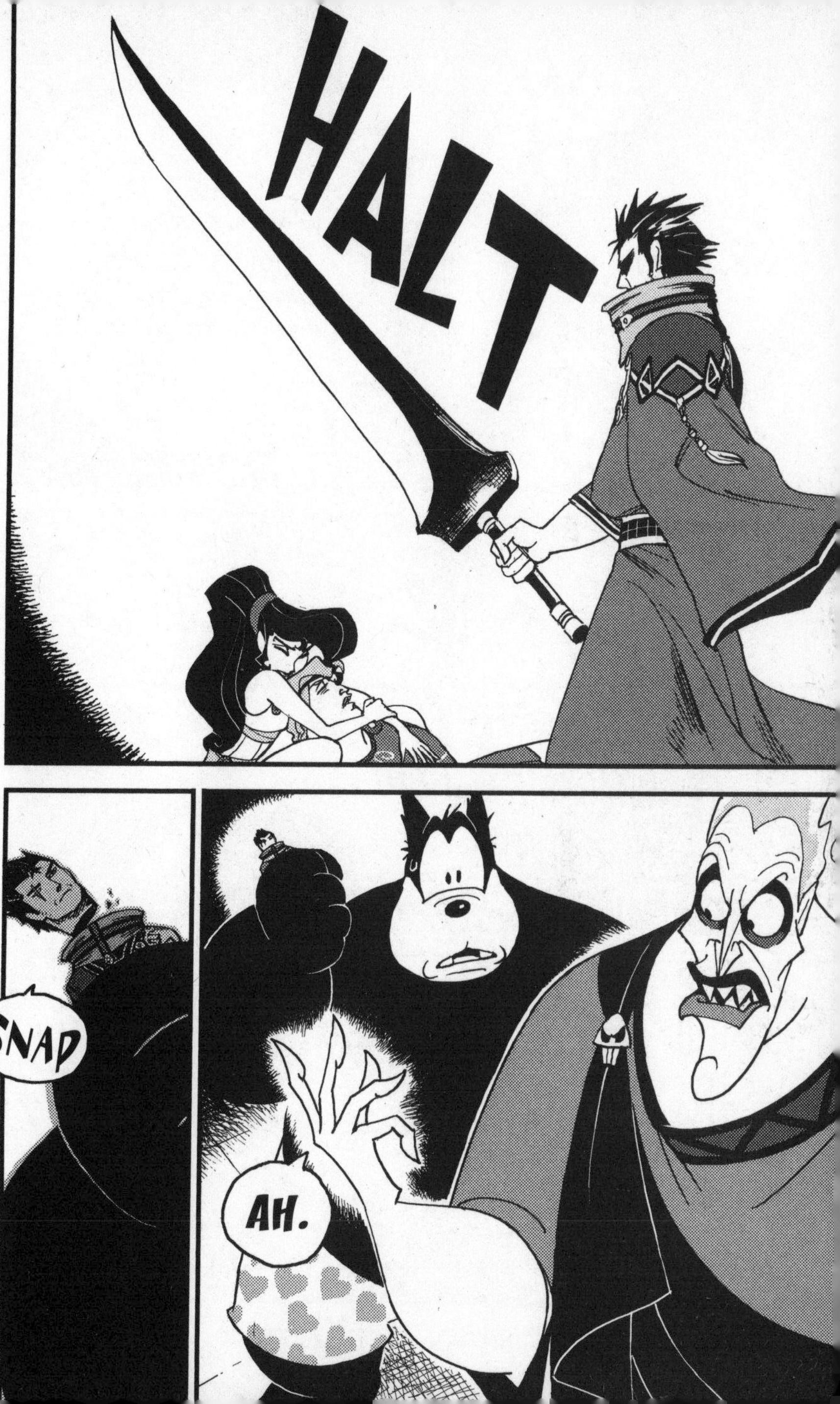
HALT
AH.
SNAP

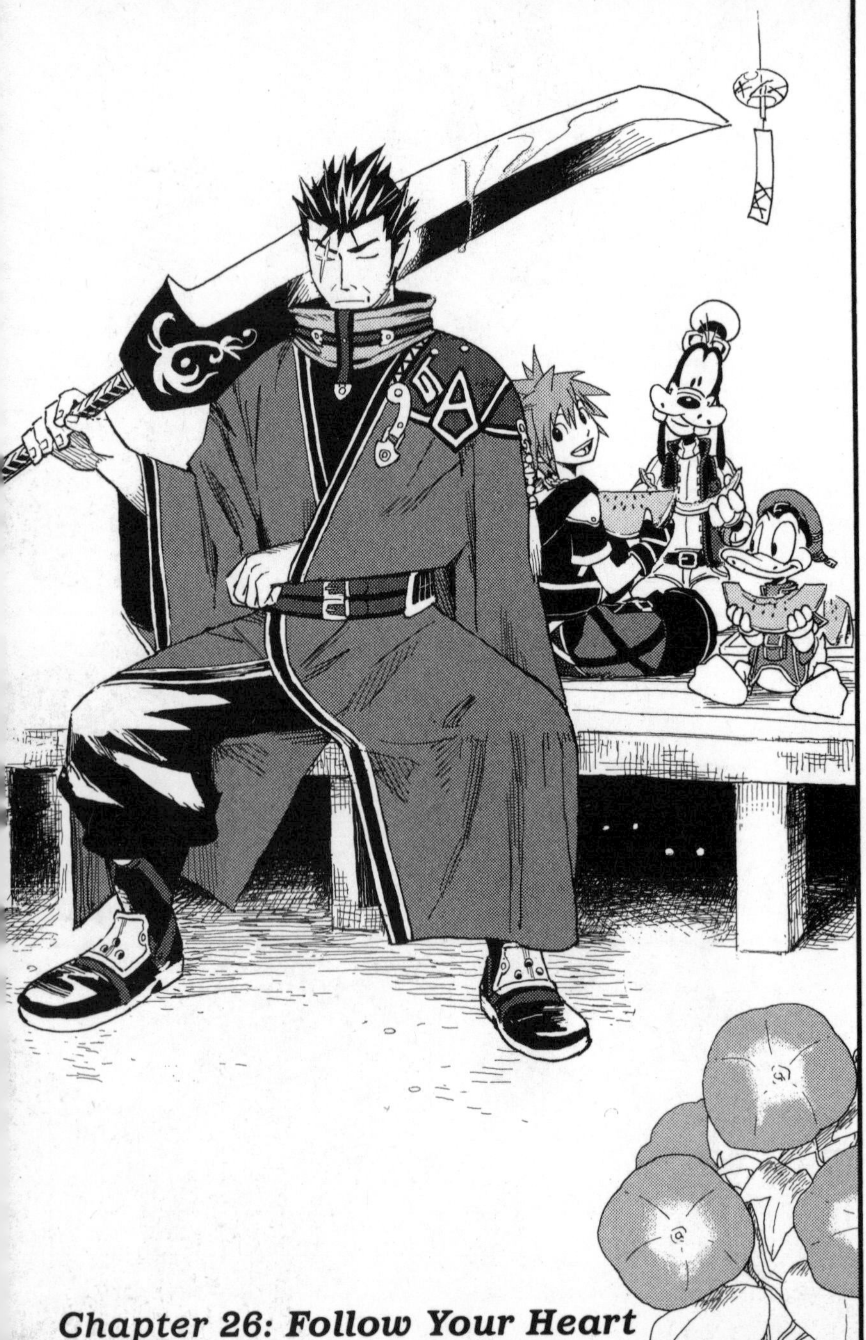

Chapter 26: Follow Your Heart

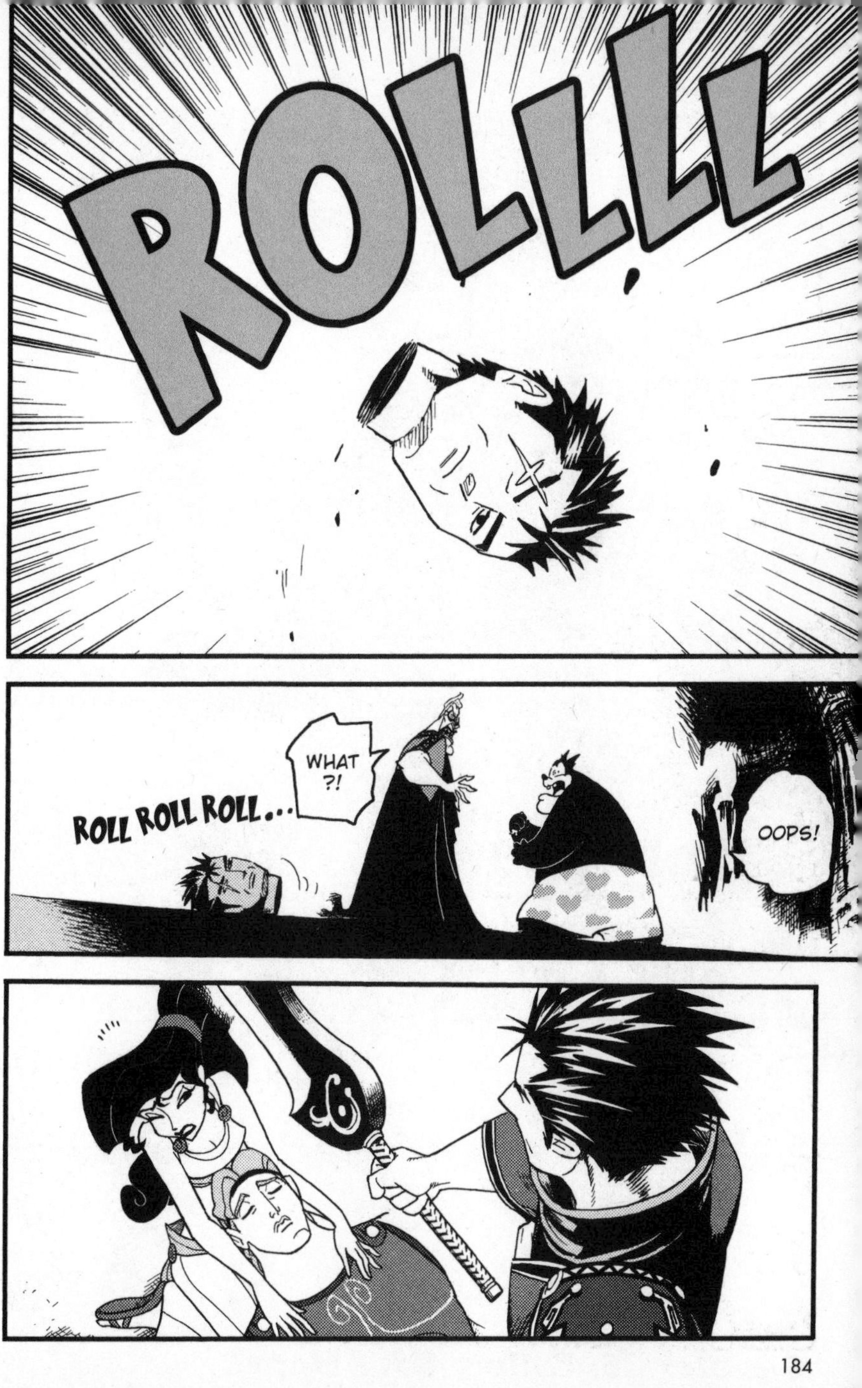
ROLLLL
OOPS!
WHAT ?!
ROLL ROLL ROLL...

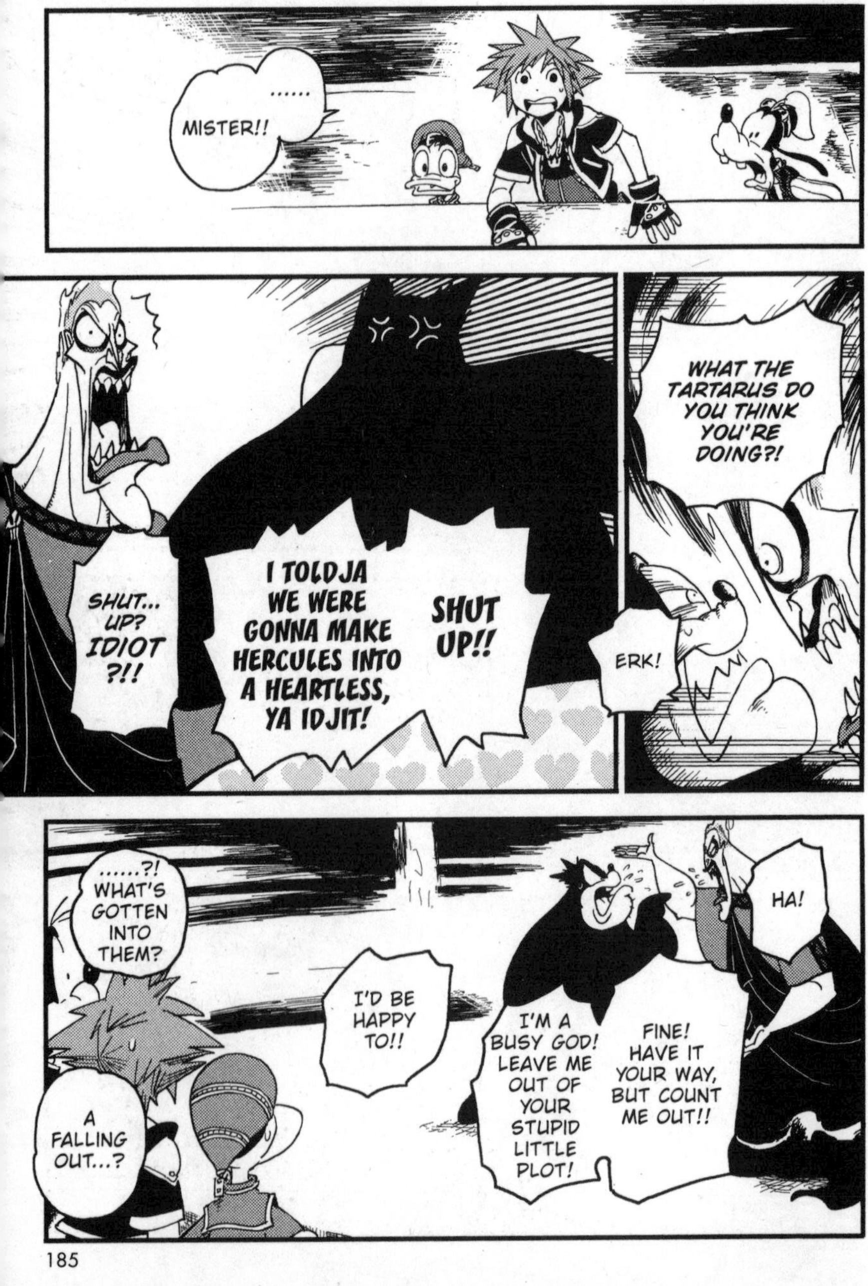

...... MISTER!!
WHAT THE TARTARUS DO YOU THINK YOU'RE DOING?!
ERK!
SHUT UP!!
I TOLDJA WE WERE GONNA MAKE HERCULES INTO A HEARTLESS, YA IDJIT!
SHUT... UP? IDIOT ?!!
HA!
FINE! HAVE IT YOUR WAY, BUT COUNT ME OUT!!
I'M A BUSY GOD! LEAVE ME OUT OF YOUR STUPID LITTLE PLOT!
I'D BE HAPPY TO!!
......?! WHAT'S GOTTEN INTO THEM?
A FALLING OUT...?

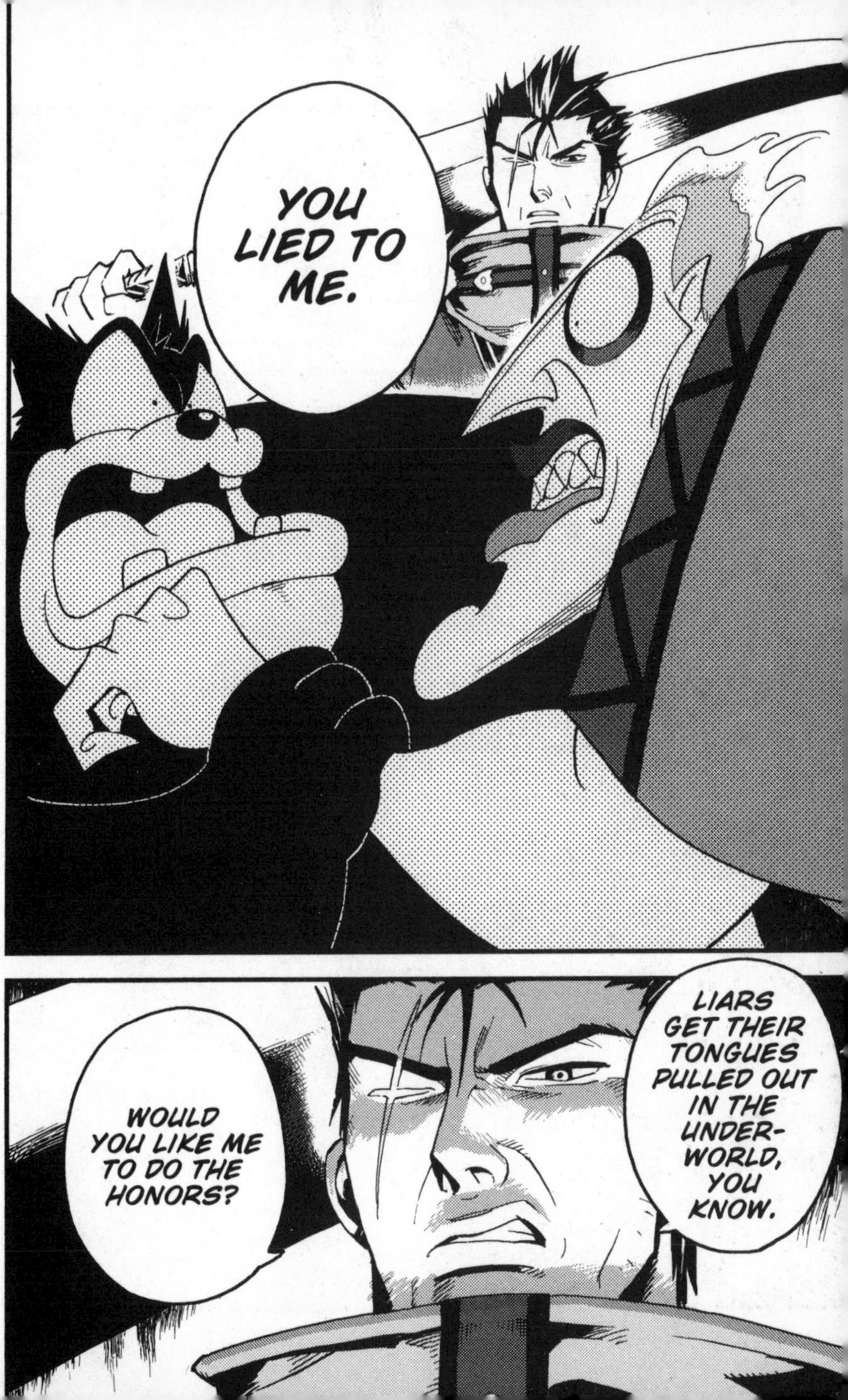
YOU LIED TO ME.
LIARS GET THEIR TONGUES PULLED OUT IN THE UNDER-WORLD, YOU KNOW.
WOULD YOU LIKE ME TO DO THE HONORS?

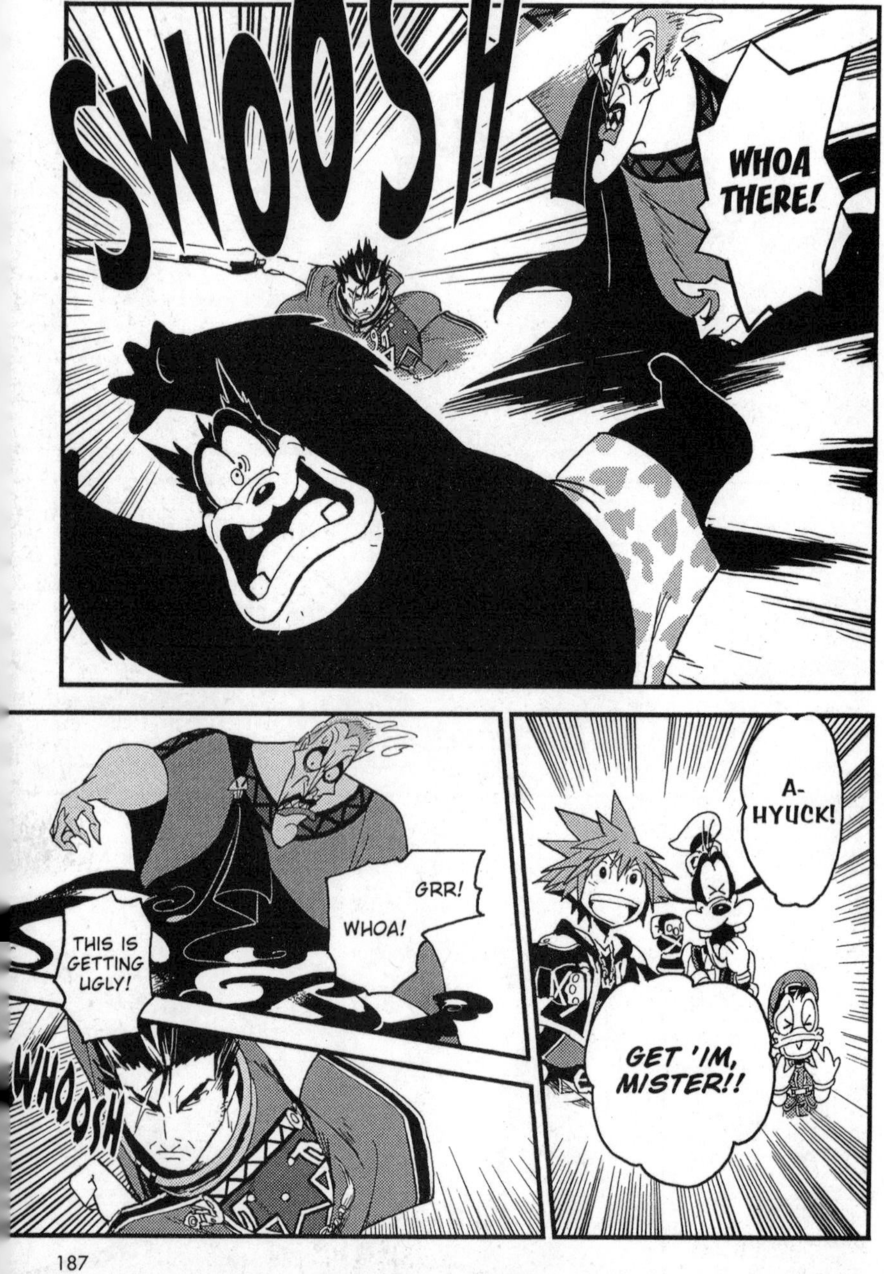
SWOOSH!!
WHOA THERE!
A-HYUCK!
GET 'IM, MISTER!!
GRR!
WHOA!
THIS IS GETTING UGLY!
WHOOSH

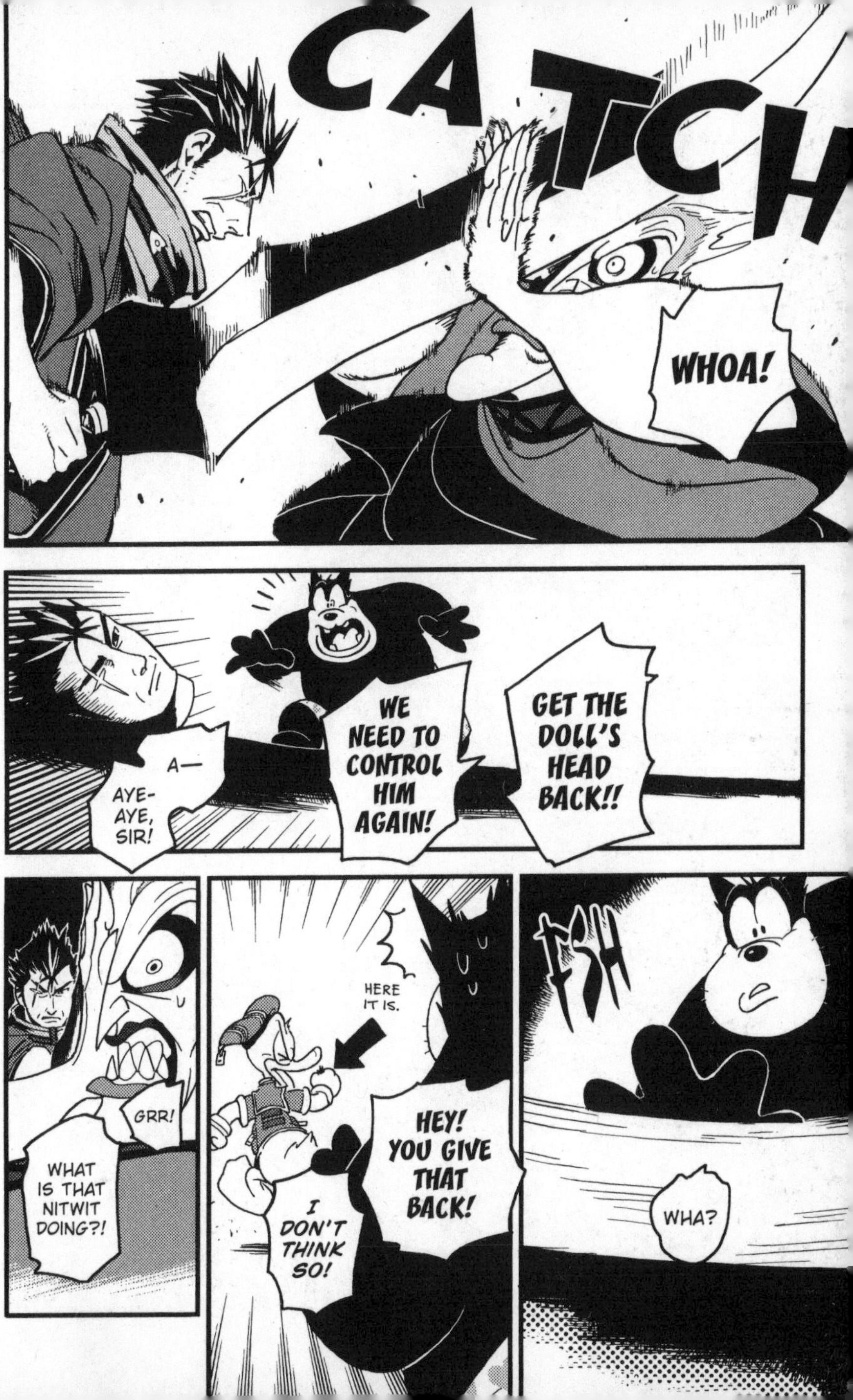
CATCH
WHOA!
GET THE DOLL'S HEAD BACK!!
WE NEED TO CONTROL HIM AGAIN!
A— AYE-AYE, SIR!
FSH
WHA?
HERE IT IS.
HEY! YOU GIVE THAT BACK!
I DON'T THINK SO!
GRR!
WHAT IS THAT NITWIT DOING?!

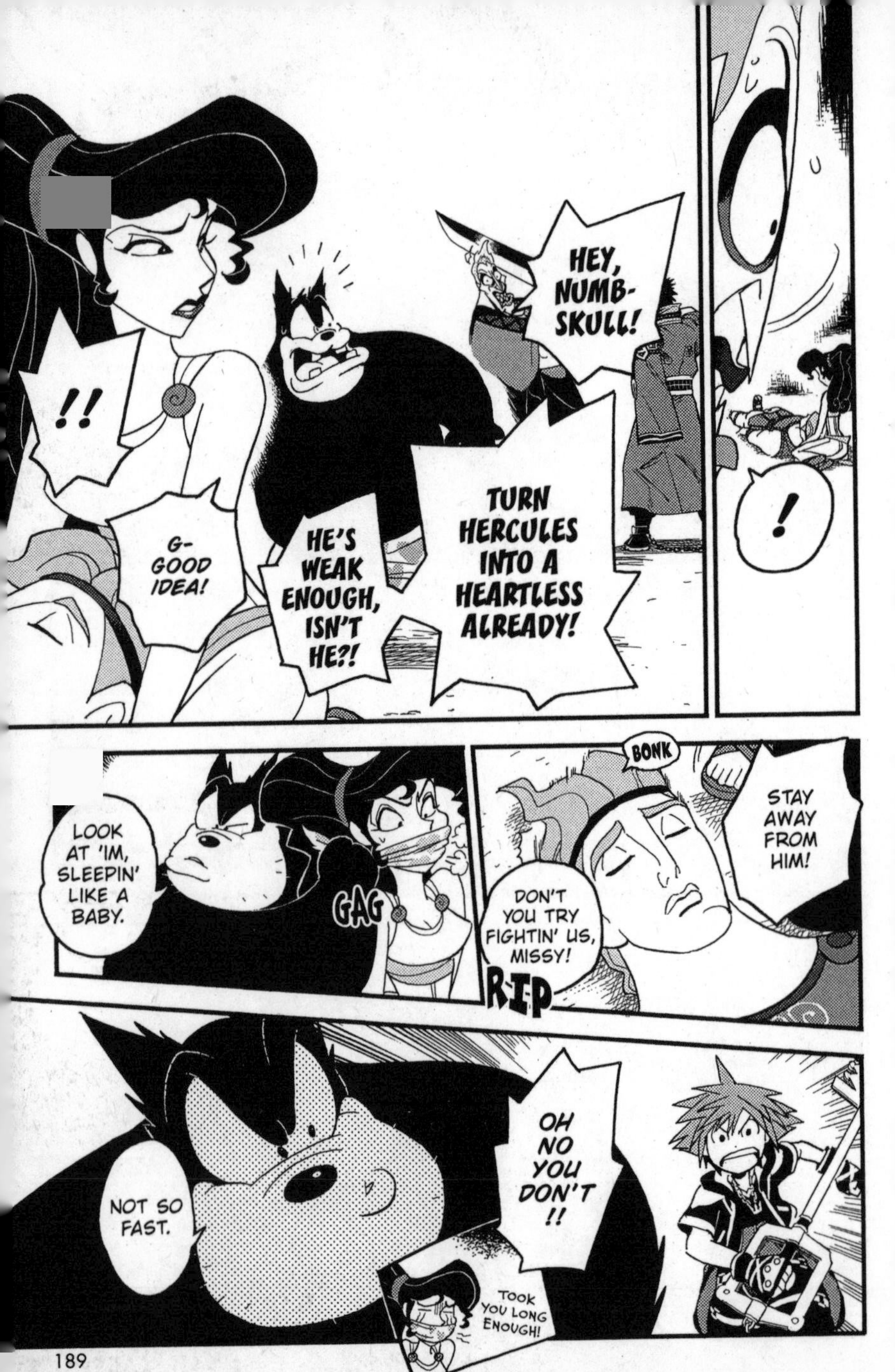
!
HEY, NUMB-SKULL!
TURN HERCULES INTO A HEARTLESS ALREADY!
HE'S WEAK ENOUGH, ISN'T HE?!
!!
G-GOOD IDEA!
BONK
STAY AWAY FROM HIM!
DON'T YOU TRY FIGHTIN' US, MISSY!
RIP
LOOK AT 'IM, SLEEPIN' LIKE A BABY.
GAG
OH NO YOU DON'T!!
NOT SO FAST.
TOOK YOU LONG ENOUGH!

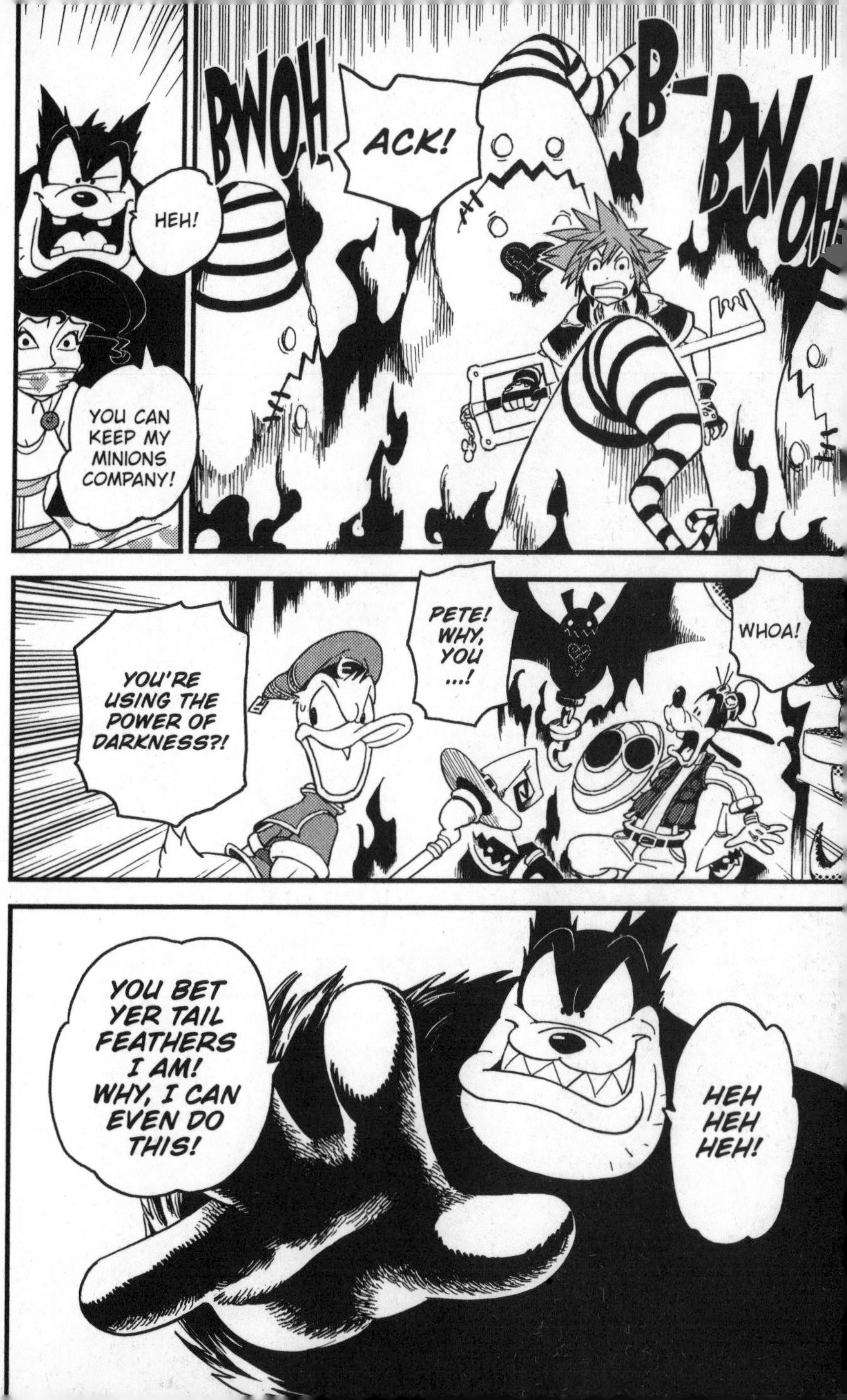
B-BWOH
ACK!
BWOH
HEH!
YOU CAN KEEP MY MINIONS COMPANY!
WHOA!
PETE! WHY, YOU ...!
YOU'RE USING THE POWER OF DARKNESS?!
HEH HEH HEH!
YOU BET YER TAIL FEATHERS I AM! WHY, I CAN EVEN DO THIS!

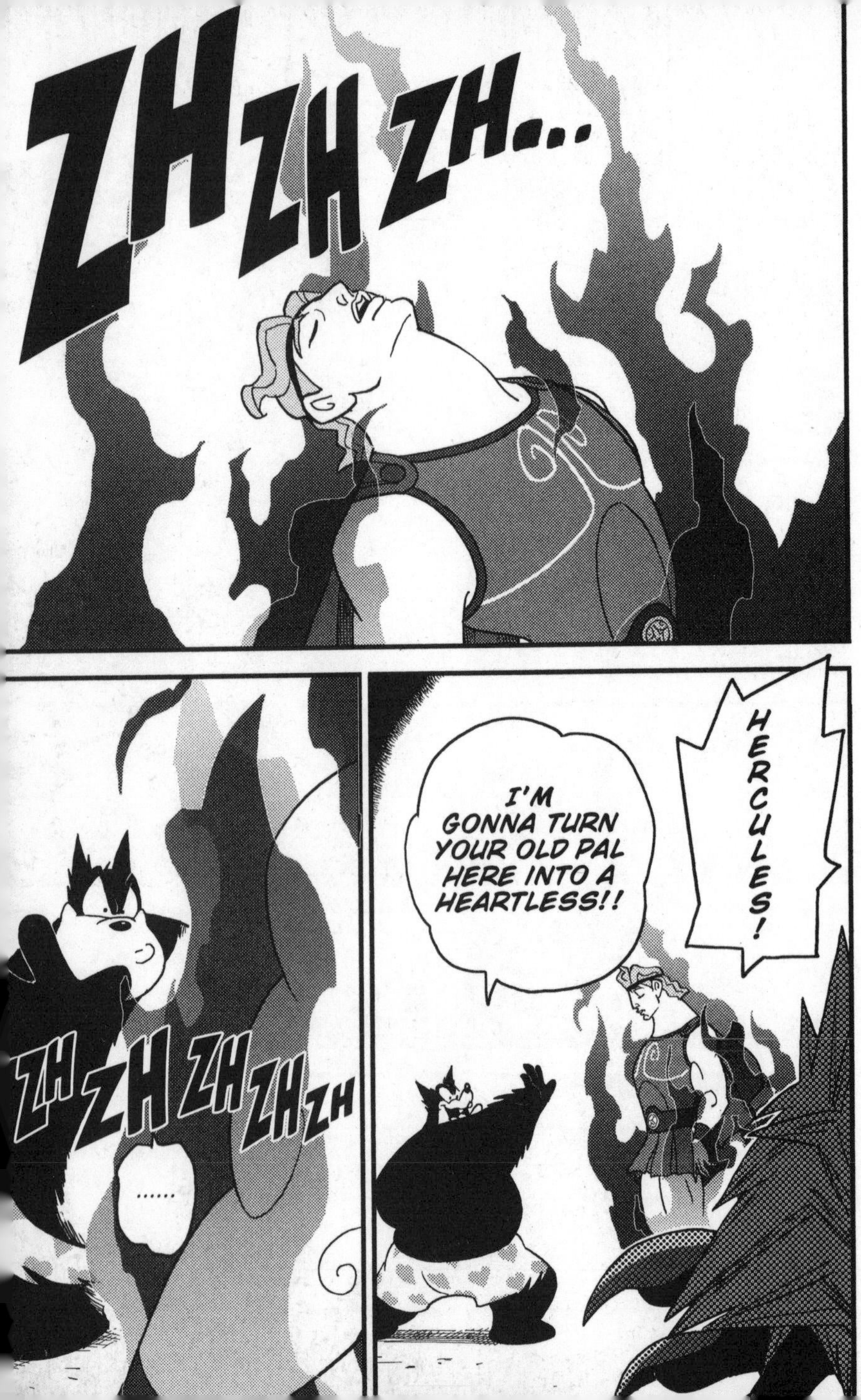
ZHZHZH...
HERCULES!
I'M GONNA TURN YOUR OLD PAL HERE INTO A HEARTLESS!!
ZH ZH ZH ZH ZH
......

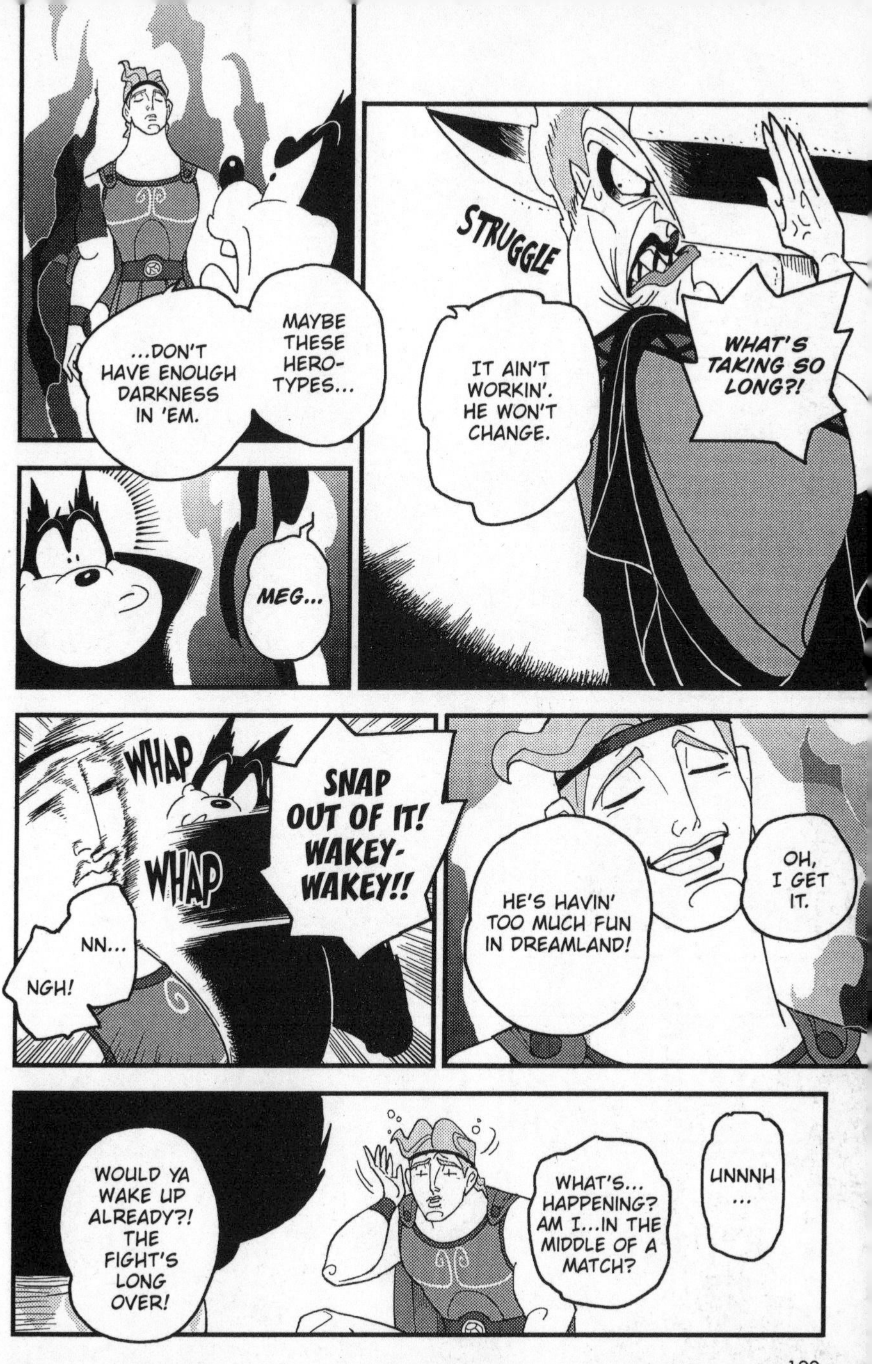
WHAT'S TAKING SO LONG?!
STRUGGLE
IT AIN'T WORKIN'. HE WON'T CHANGE.
MAYBE THESE HERO-TYPES...
...DON'T HAVE ENOUGH DARKNESS IN 'EM.
MEG...
OH, I GET IT.
HE'S HAVIN' TOO MUCH FUN IN DREAMLAND!
SNAP OUT OF IT! WAKEY-WAKEY!!
WHAP
WHAP
NN...
NGH!
UNNNH ...
WHAT'S... HAPPENING? AM I...IN THE MIDDLE OF A MATCH?
WOULD YA WAKE UP ALREADY?! THE FIGHT'S LONG OVER!

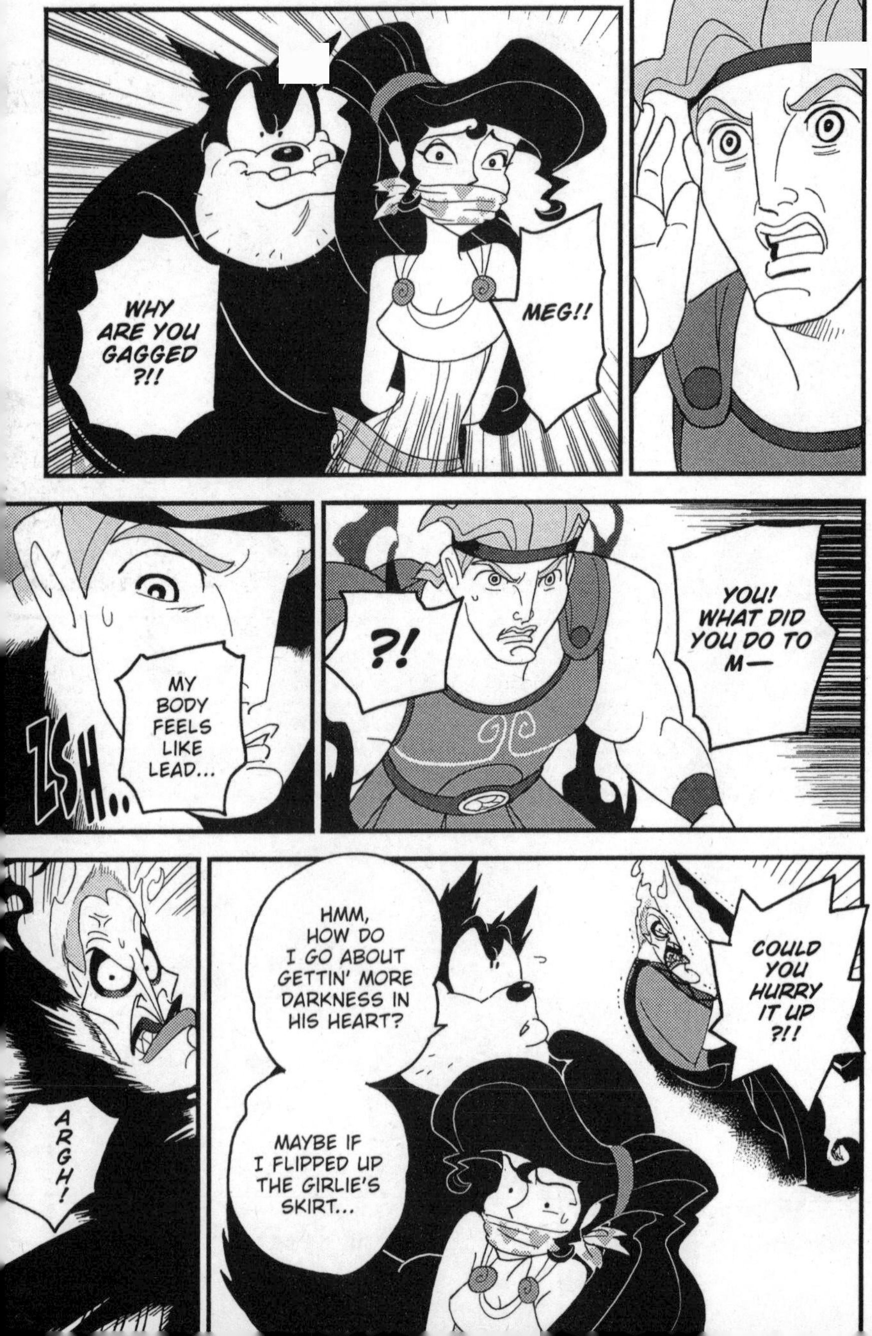
MEG!!
WHY ARE YOU GAGGED ?!!
YOU! WHAT DID YOU DO TO M—
?!
MY BODY FEELS LIKE LEAD...
ZSH..
COULD YOU HURRY IT UP ?!!
HMM, HOW DO I GO ABOUT GETTIN' MORE DARKNESS IN HIS HEART?
MAYBE IF I FLIPPED UP THE GIRLIE'S SKIRT...
ARGH!

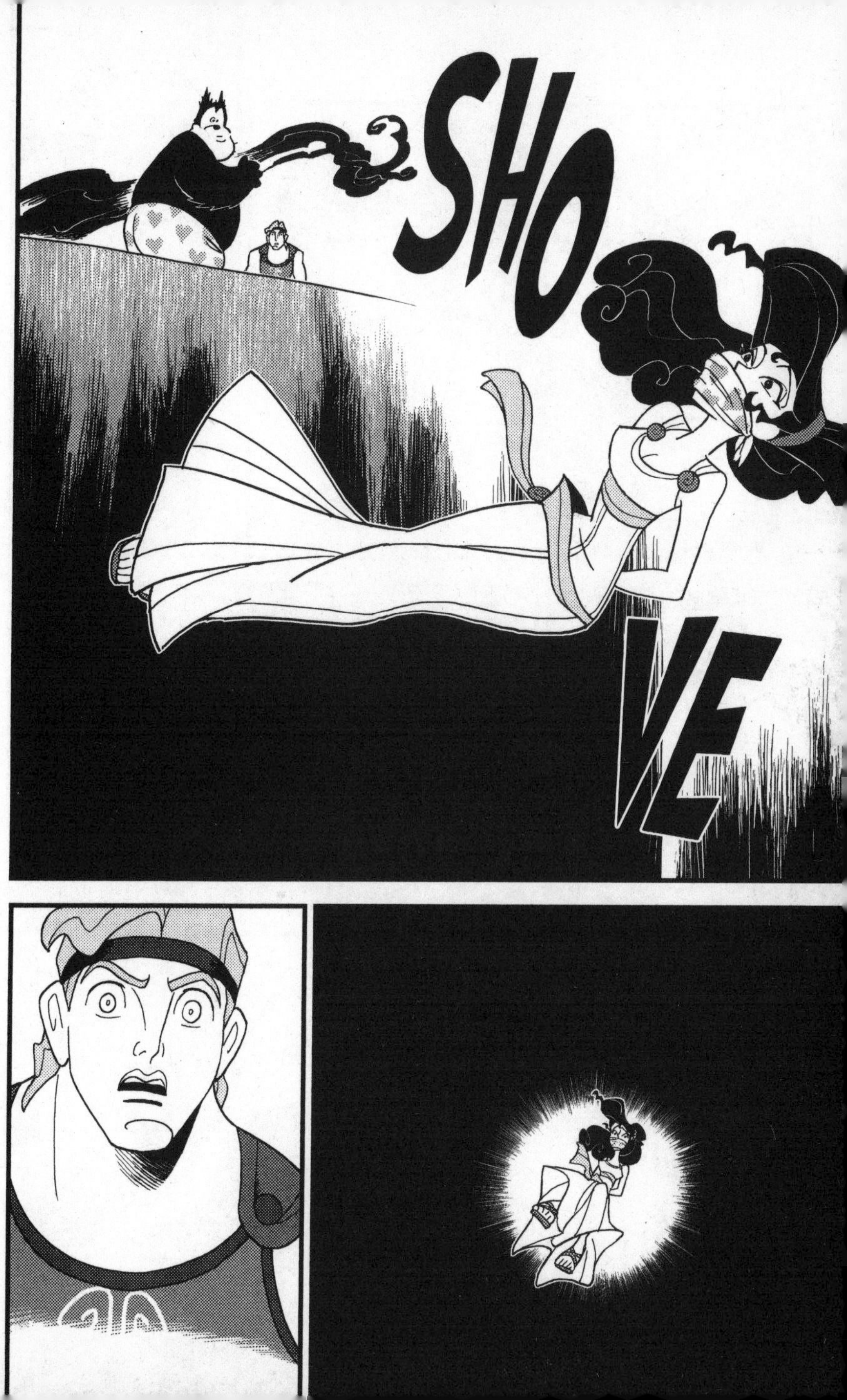
SHOVE

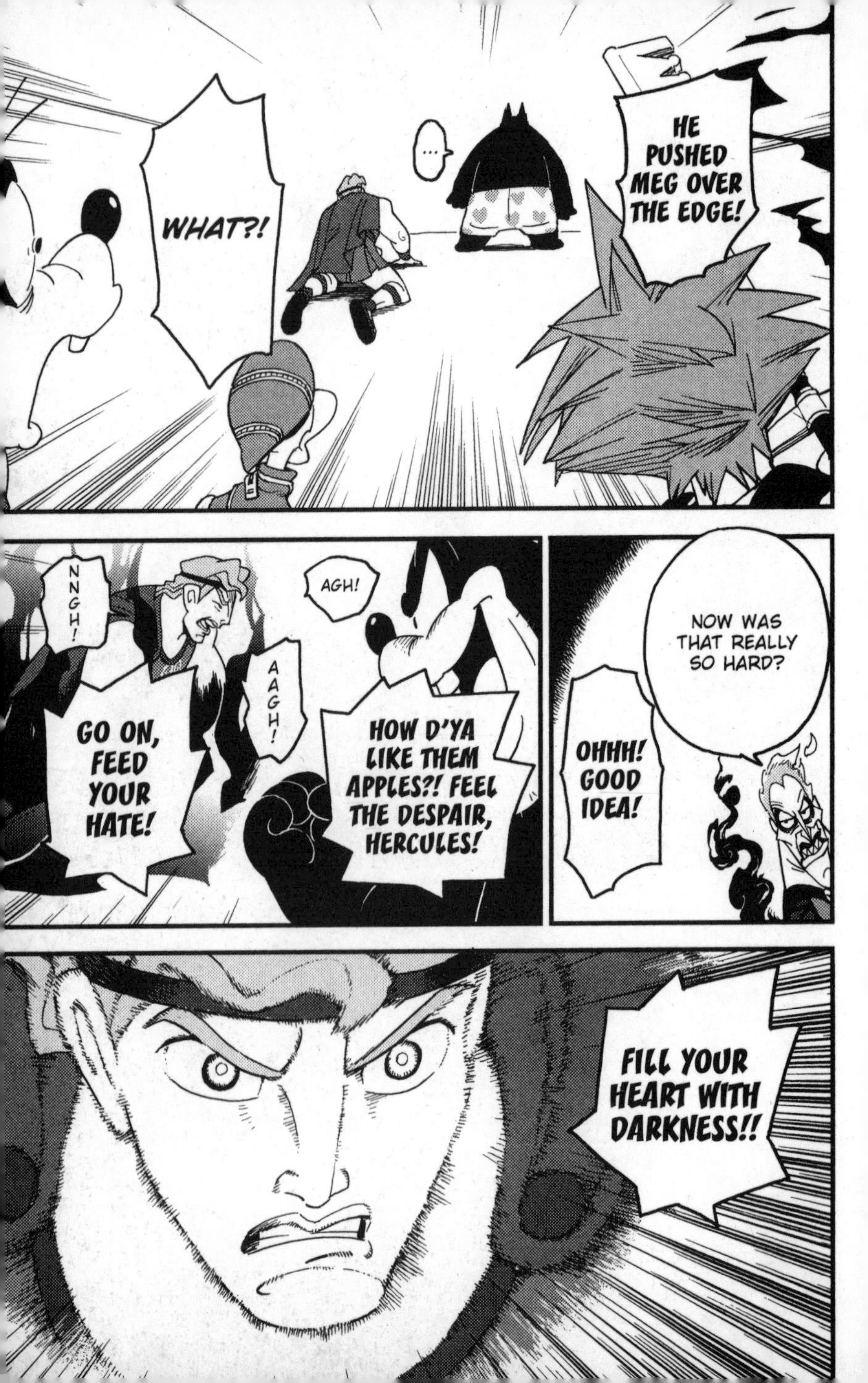
HE PUSHED MEG OVER THE EDGE!
...
WHAT?!
NOW WAS THAT REALLY SO HARD?
OHHH! GOOD IDEA!
AGH!
HOW D'YA LIKE THEM APPLES?! FEEL THE DESPAIR, HERCULES!
AAGH!
NNGH!
GO ON, FEED YOUR HATE!
FILL YOUR HEART WITH DARKNESS!!

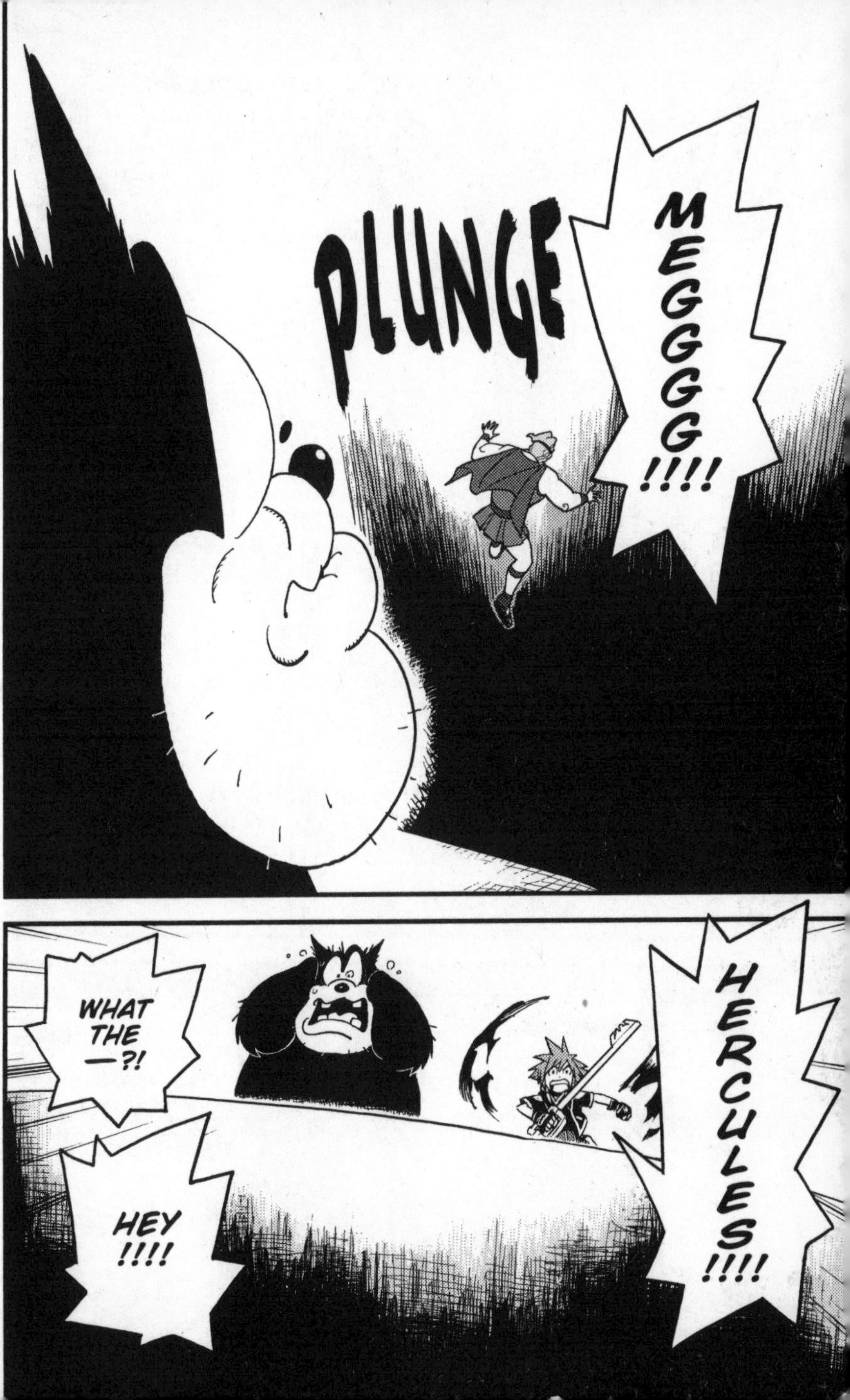
MEGGGG!!!!
PLUNGE
HERCULES!!!!
WHAT THE—?!
HEY!!!!

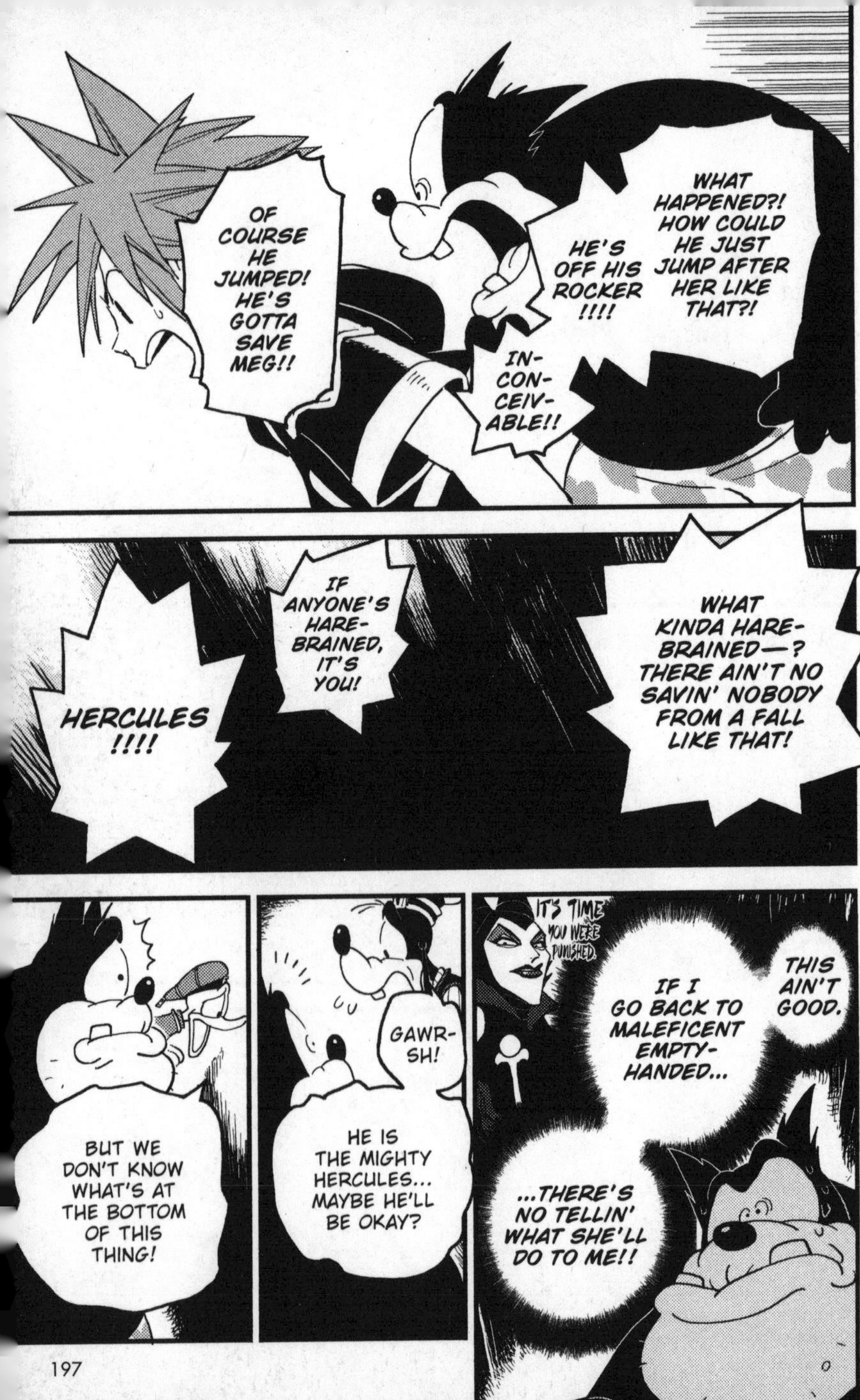

WHAT HAPPENED?! HOW COULD HE JUST JUMP AFTER HER LIKE THAT?!
HE'S OFF HIS ROCKER!!!!
IN-CON-CEIV-ABLE!!
OF COURSE HE JUMPED! HE'S GOTTA SAVE MEG!!
WHAT KINDA HARE-BRAINED—? THERE AIN'T NO SAVIN' NOBODY FROM A FALL LIKE THAT!
IF ANYONE'S HARE-BRAINED, IT'S YOU!
HERCULES!!!!
THIS AIN'T GOOD.
IF I GO BACK TO MALEFICENT EMPTY-HANDED...
IT'S TIME YOU WERE PUNISHED.
...THERE'S NO TELLIN' WHAT SHE'LL DO TO ME!!
GAWR-SH!
HE IS THE MIGHTY HERCULES... MAYBE HE'LL BE OKAY?
BUT WE DON'T KNOW WHAT'S AT THE BOTTOM OF THIS THING!

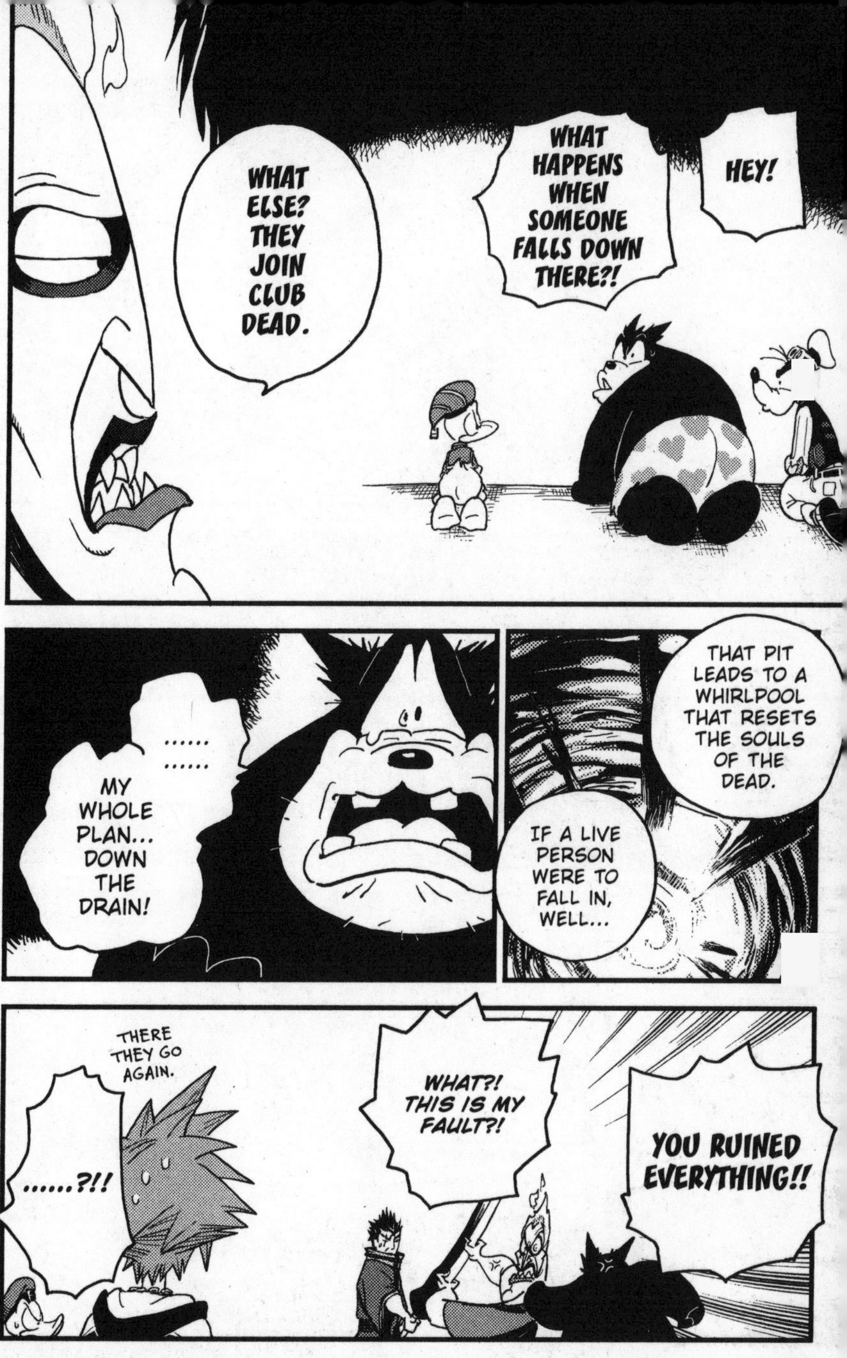
HEY!
WHAT HAPPENS WHEN SOMEONE FALLS DOWN THERE?!
WHAT ELSE? THEY JOIN CLUB DEAD.
THAT PIT LEADS TO A WHIRLPOOL THAT RESETS THE SOULS OF THE DEAD.
IF A LIVE PERSON WERE TO FALL IN, WELL...
....
MY WHOLE PLAN... DOWN THE DRAIN!
YOU RUINED EVERYTHING!!
WHAT?! THIS IS MY FAULT?!
THERE THEY GO AGAIN.
......?!!

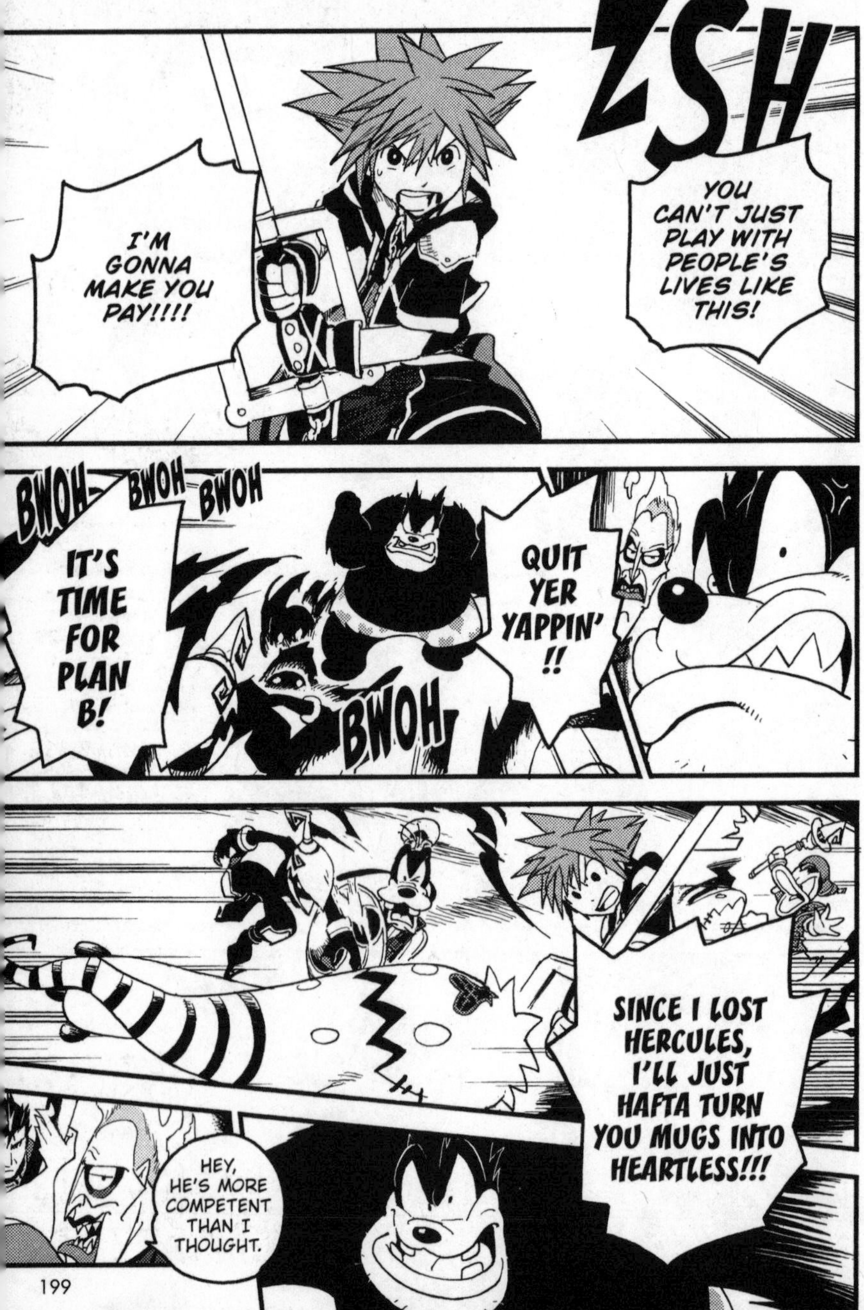
ZSH
YOU CAN'T JUST PLAY WITH PEOPLE'S LIVES LIKE THIS!
I'M GONNA MAKE YOU PAY!!!!
QUIT YER YAPPIN'!!
BWOH
BWOH BWOH BWOH
IT'S TIME FOR PLAN B!
SINCE I LOST HERCULES, I'LL JUST HAFTA TURN YOU MUGS INTO HEARTLESS!!!
HEY, HE'S MORE COMPETENT THAN I THOUGHT.

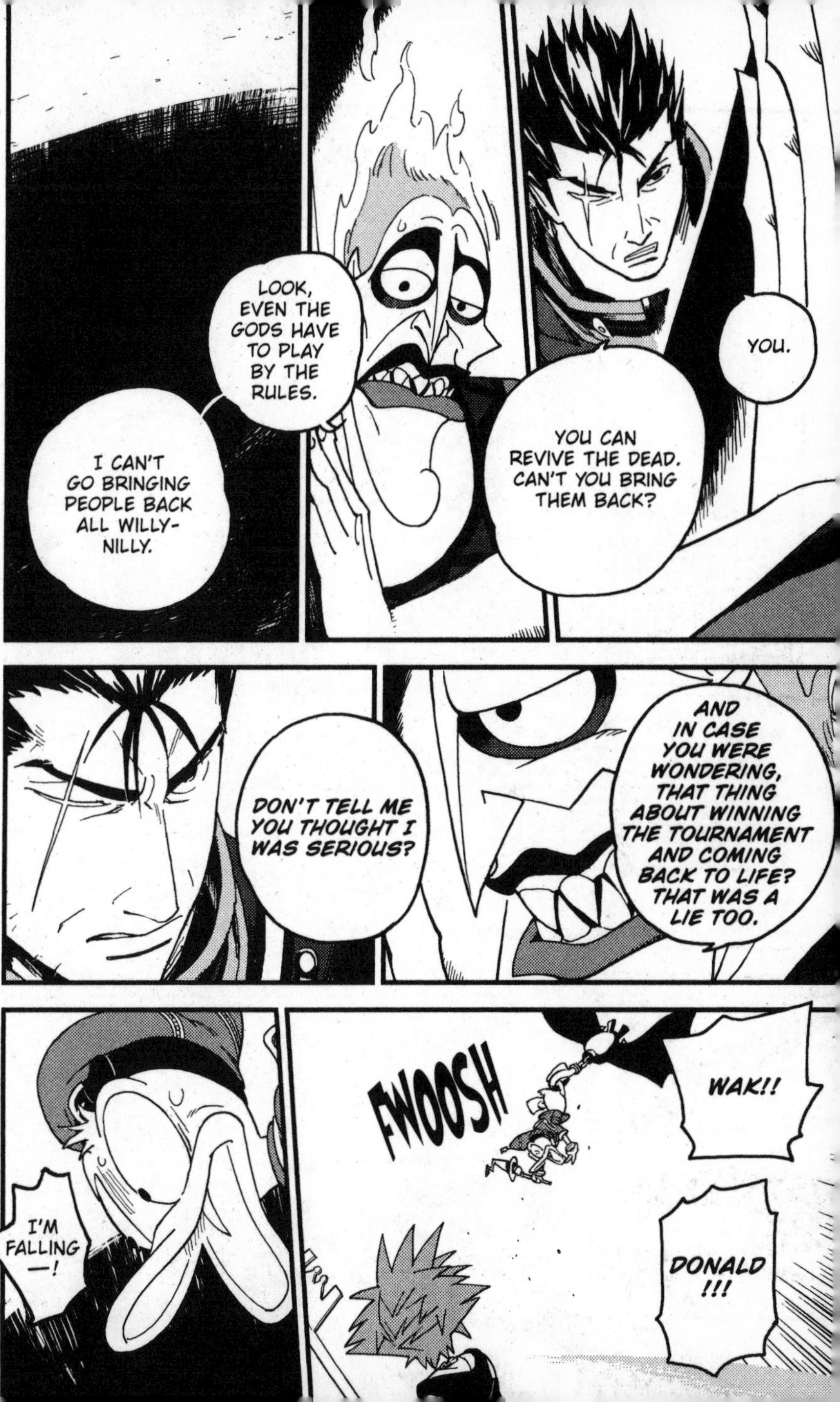
YOU.
YOU CAN REVIVE THE DEAD. CAN'T YOU BRING THEM BACK?
LOOK, EVEN THE GODS HAVE TO PLAY BY THE RULES.
I CAN'T GO BRINGING PEOPLE BACK ALL WILLY-NILLY.
AND IN CASE YOU WERE WONDERING, THAT THING ABOUT WINNING THE TOURNAMENT AND COMING BACK TO LIFE? THAT WAS A LIE TOO.
DON'T TELL ME YOU THOUGHT I WAS SERIOUS?
WAK!!
FWOOSH
DONALD!!!
I'M FALLING—!

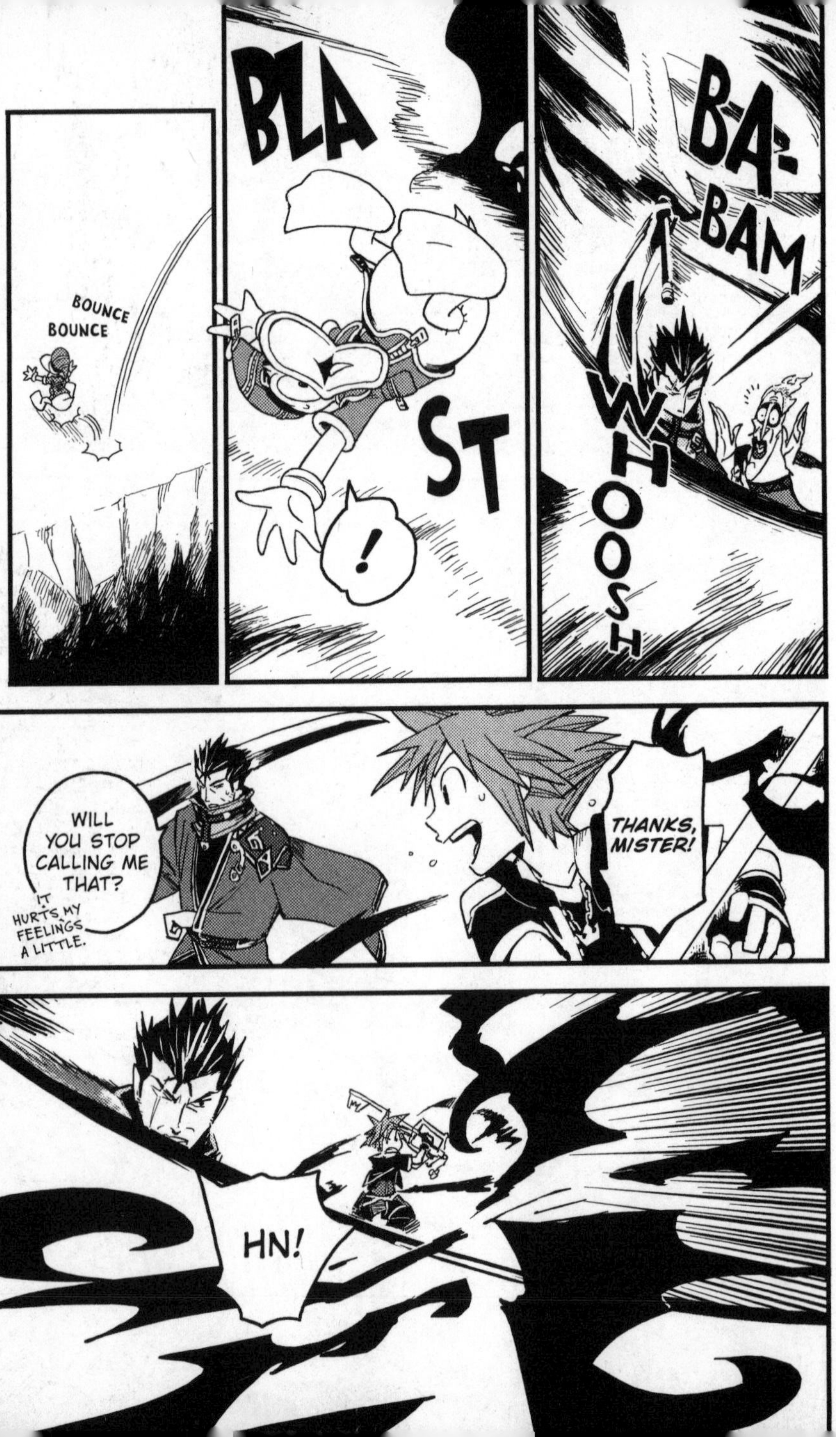

BA-BAM
WHOOSH
BLA
ST
!
BOUNCE
BOUNCE
THANKS, MISTER!
WILL YOU STOP CALLING ME THAT?
IT HURTS MY FEELINGS A LITTLE.
HN!

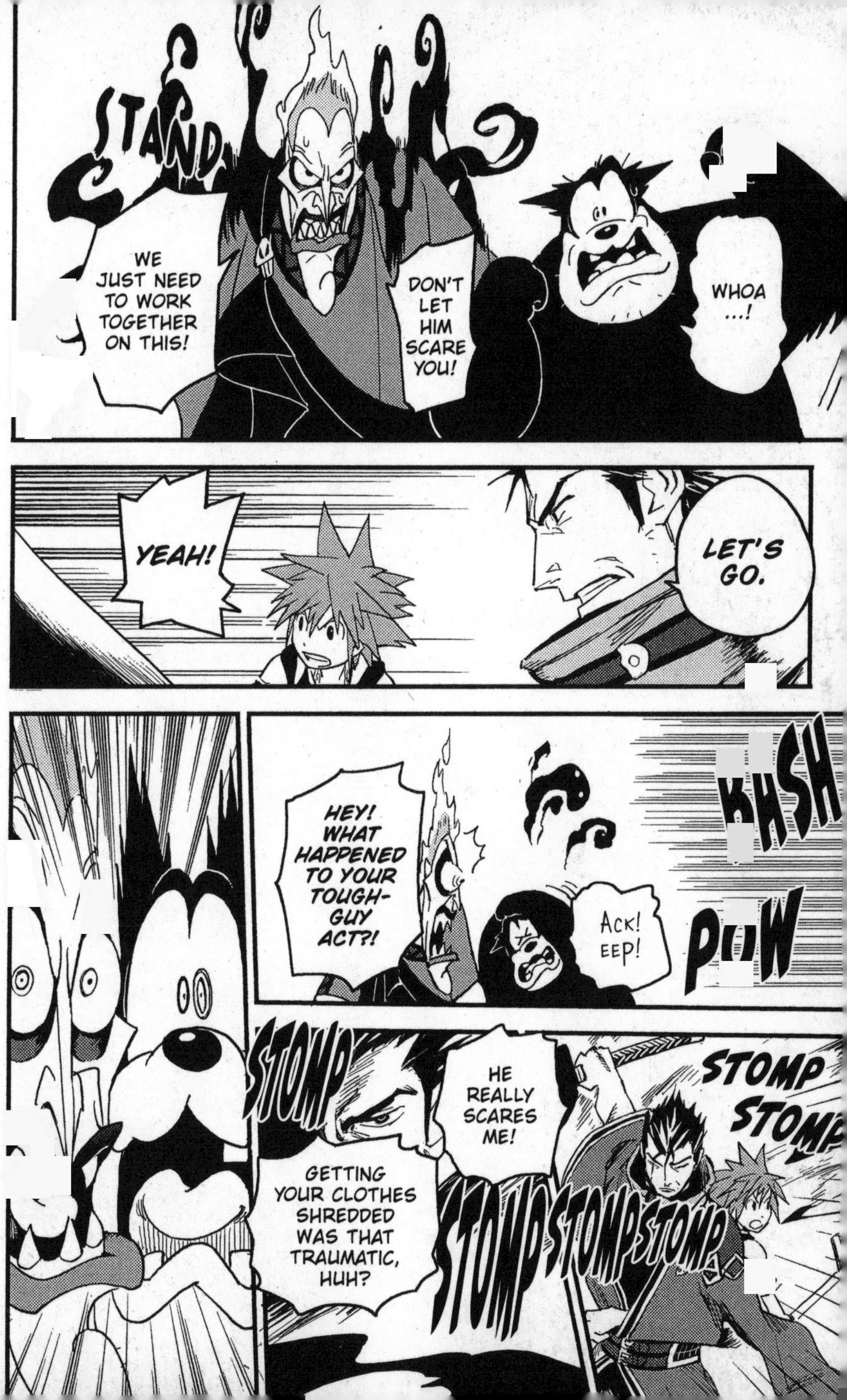
WHOA ...!
DON'T LET HIM SCARE YOU!
STAND
WE JUST NEED TO WORK TOGETHER ON THIS!
LET'S GO.
YEAH!
BASH
POW
ACK! EEP!
HEY! WHAT HAPPENED TO YOUR TOUGH-GUY ACT?!
STOMP
STOMP
HE REALLY SCARES ME!
STOMP
GETTING YOUR CLOTHES SHREDDED WAS THAT TRAUMATIC, HUH?
STOMP STOMP STOMP

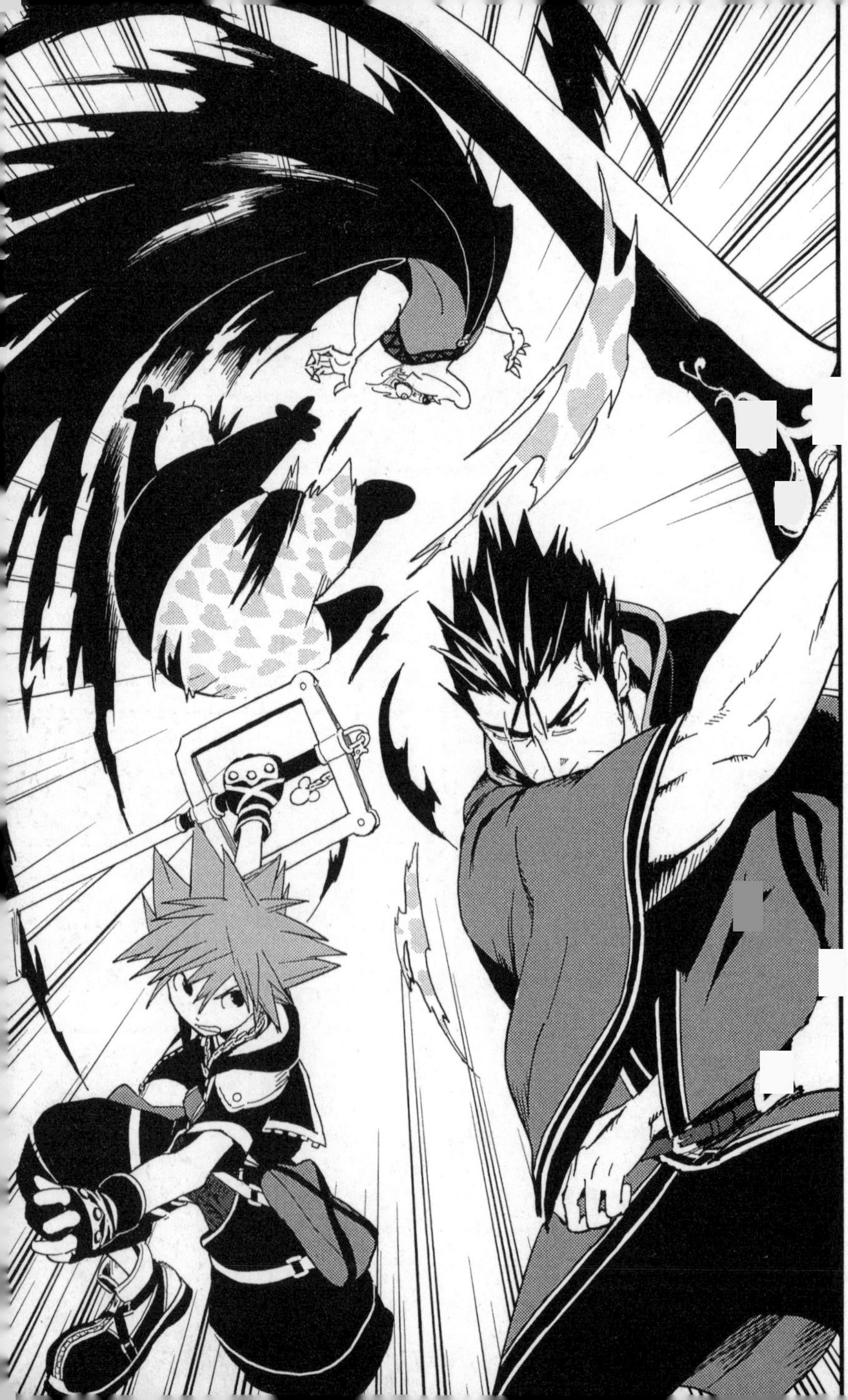

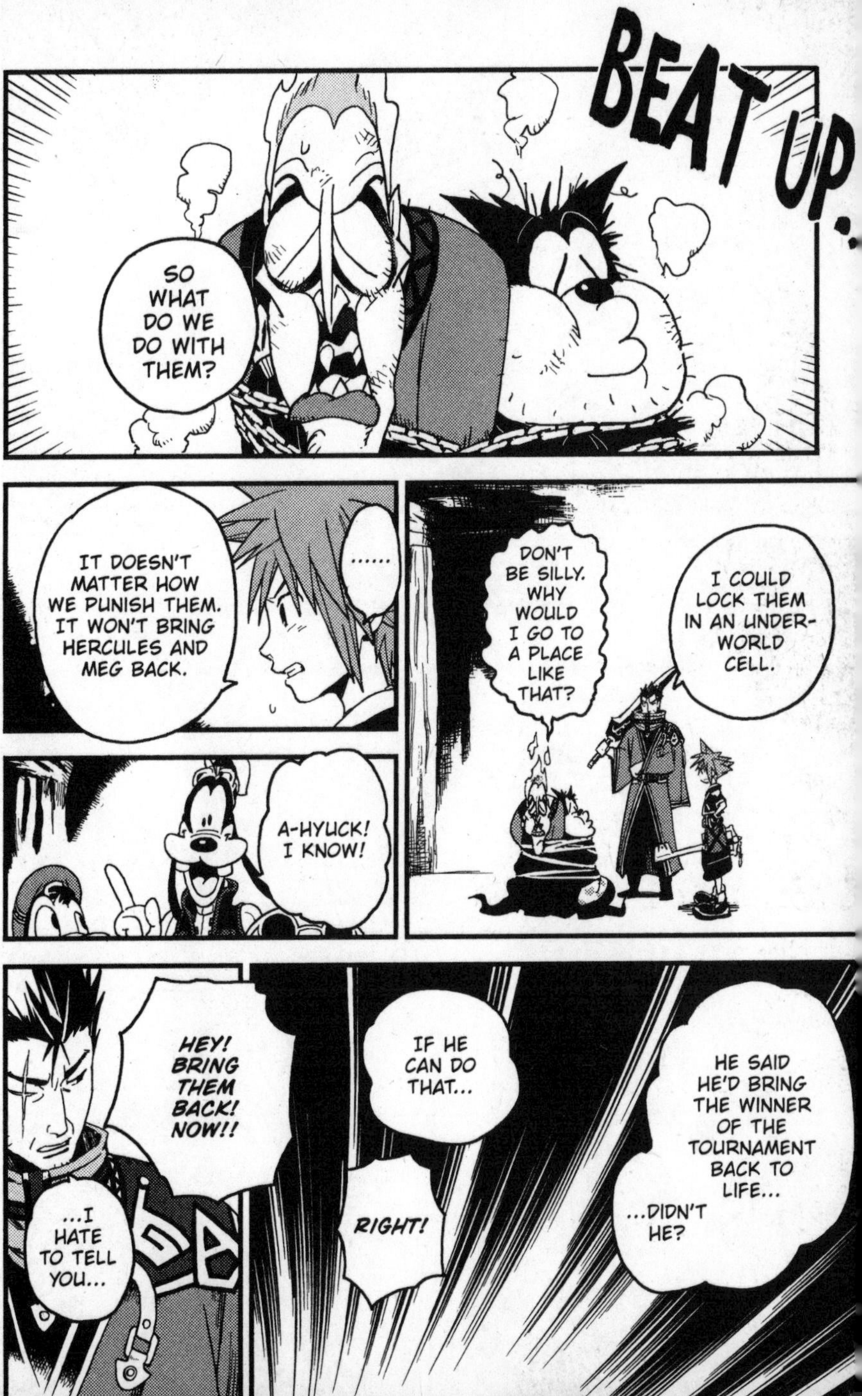
BEAT UP...
SO WHAT DO WE DO WITH THEM?
I COULD LOCK THEM IN AN UNDER-WORLD CELL.
DON'T BE SILLY. WHY WOULD I GO TO A PLACE LIKE THAT?
......
IT DOESN'T MATTER HOW WE PUNISH THEM. IT WON'T BRING HERCULES AND MEG BACK.
A-HYUCK! I KNOW!
HE SAID HE'D BRING THE WINNER OF THE TOURNAMENT BACK TO LIFE...
...DIDN'T HE?
IF HE CAN DO THAT...
RIGHT!
HEY! BRING THEM BACK! NOW!!
...I HATE TO TELL YOU...

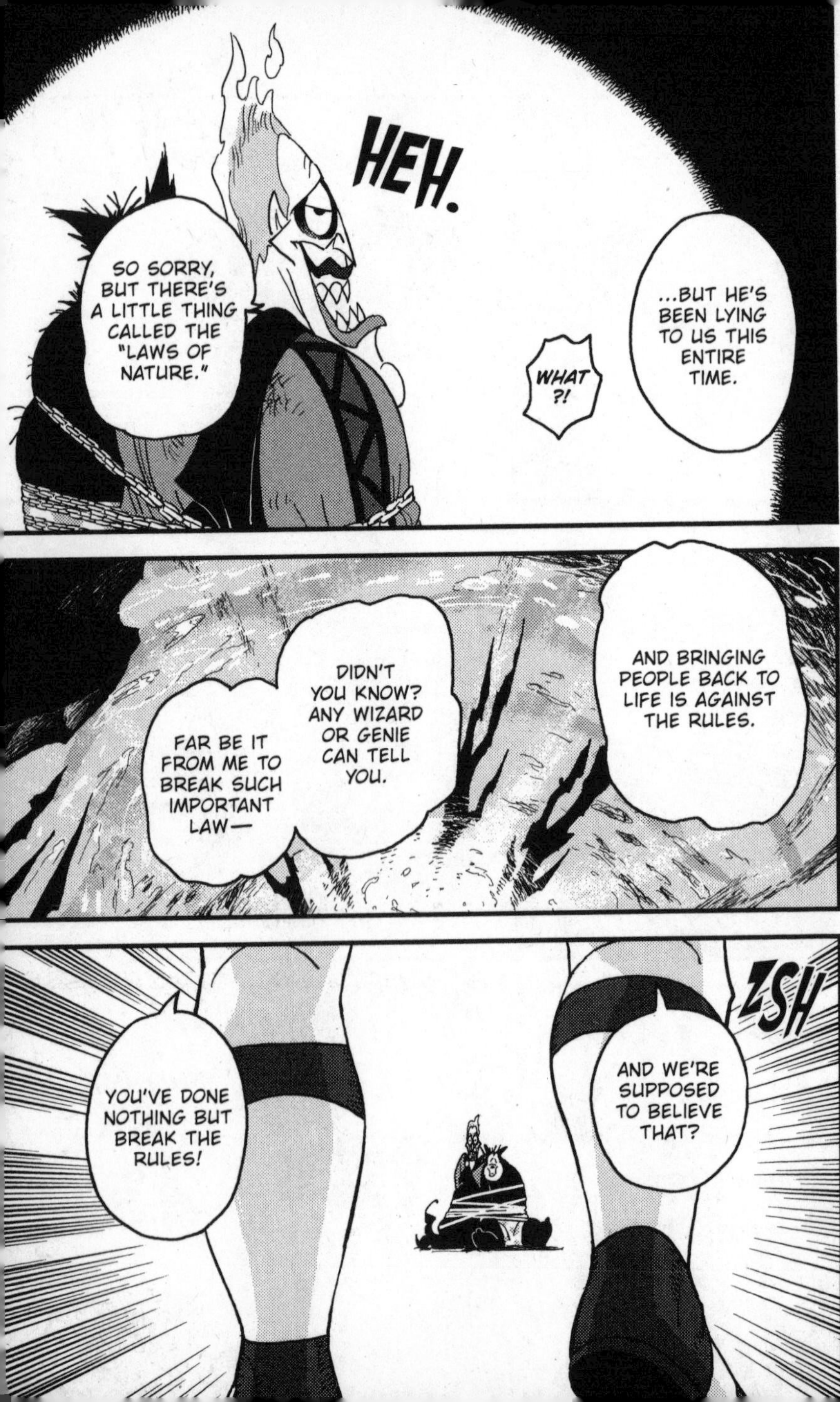
...BUT HE'S BEEN LYING TO US THIS ENTIRE TIME.
WHAT?!
HEH.
SO SORRY, BUT THERE'S A LITTLE THING CALLED THE "LAWS OF NATURE."
AND BRINGING PEOPLE BACK TO LIFE IS AGAINST THE RULES.
DIDN'T YOU KNOW? ANY WIZARD OR GENIE CAN TELL YOU.
FAR BE IT FROM ME TO BREAK SUCH IMPORTANT LAW—
ZSH
AND WE'RE SUPPOSED TO BELIEVE THAT?
YOU'VE DONE NOTHING BUT BREAK THE RULES!

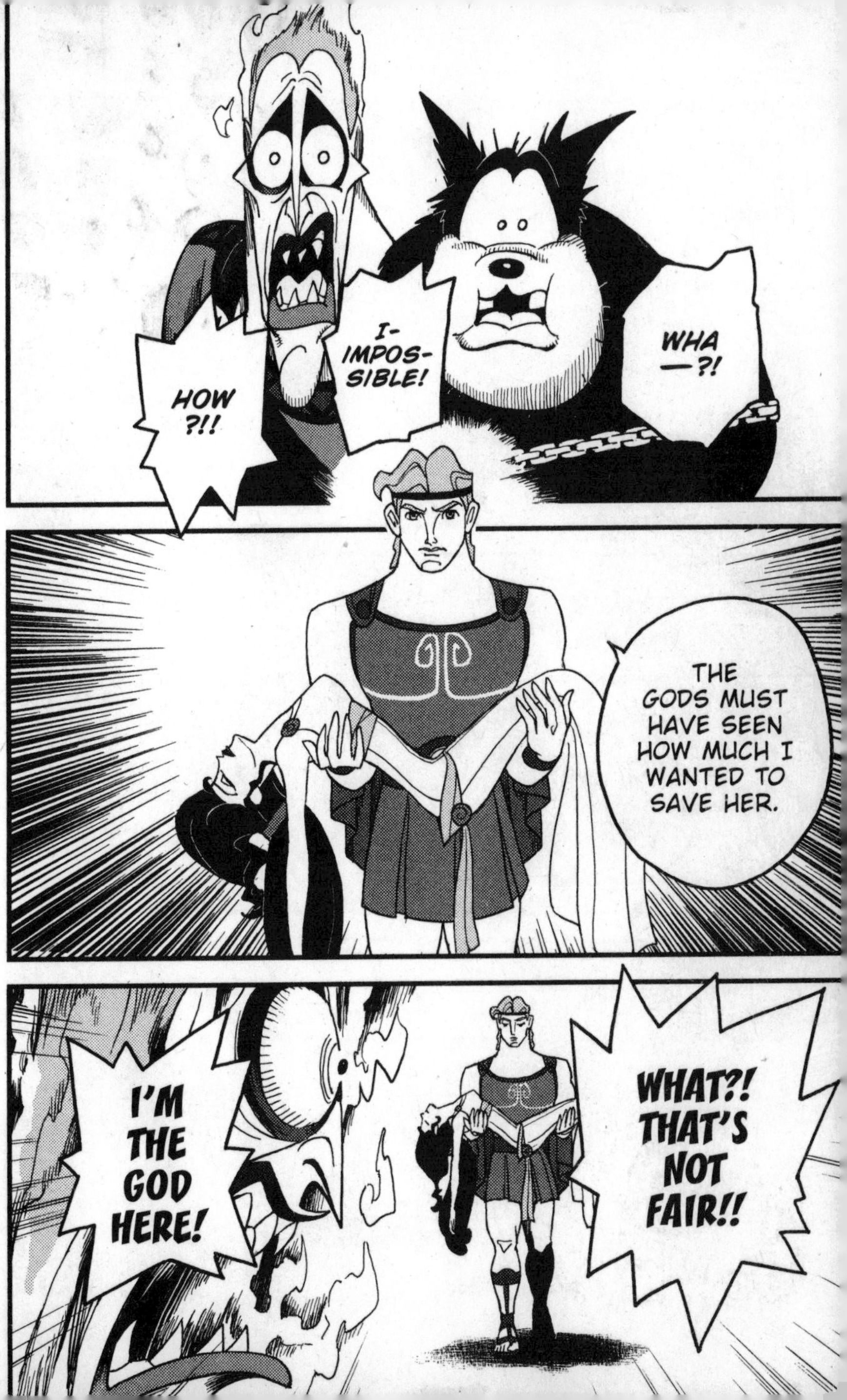
WHA—?!
I-IMPOSSIBLE!
HOW?!!
THE GODS MUST HAVE SEEN HOW MUCH I WANTED TO SAVE HER.
WHAT?! THAT'S NOT FAIR!!
I'M THE GOD HERE!

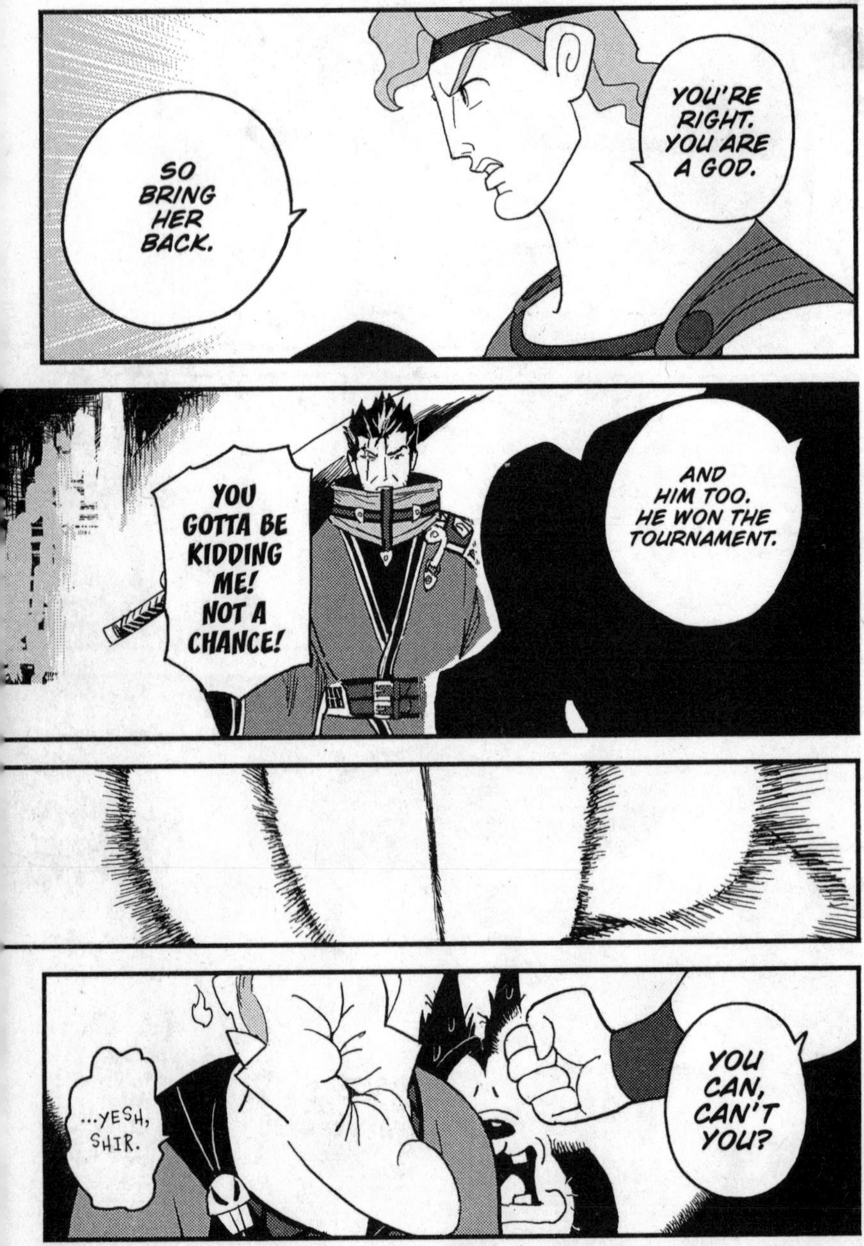
YOU'RE RIGHT. YOU ARE A GOD.
SO BRING HER BACK.
AND HIM TOO. HE WON THE TOURNAMENT.
YOU GOTTA BE KIDDING ME! NOT A CHANCE!
YOU CAN, CAN'T YOU?
...YESH, SHIR.

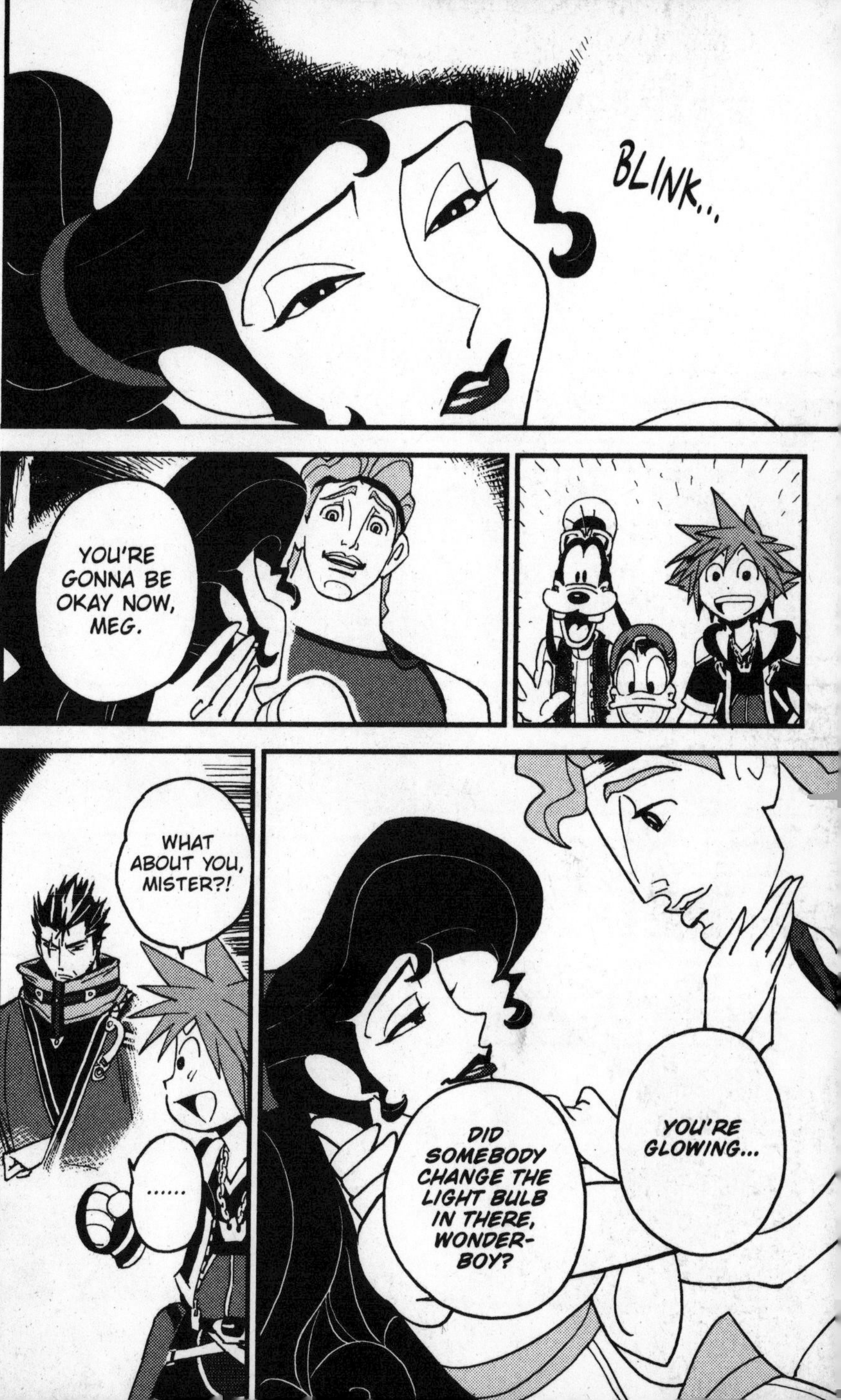
BLINK...
YOU'RE GONNA BE OKAY NOW, MEG.
YOU'RE GLOWING...
DID SOMEBODY CHANGE THE LIGHT BULB IN THERE, WONDER-BOY?
WHAT ABOUT YOU, MISTER?!
......

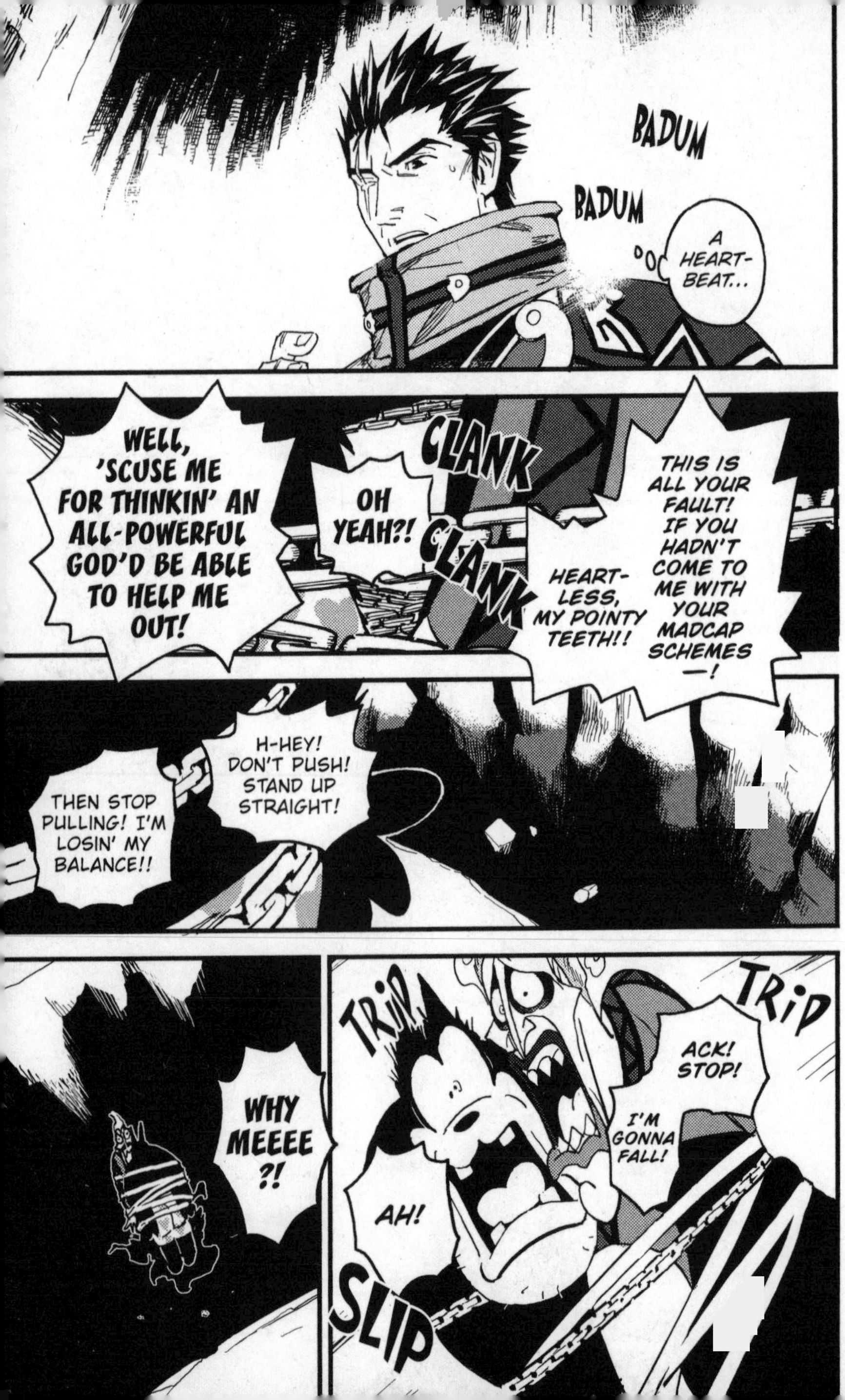
BADUM
BADUM
A HEART-BEAT...
THIS IS ALL YOUR FAULT! IF YOU HADN'T COME TO ME WITH YOUR MADCAP SCHEMES—!
HEART-LESS, MY POINTY TEETH!!
CLANK
CLANK
OH YEAH?!
WELL, 'SCUSE ME FOR THINKIN' AN ALL-POWERFUL GOD'D BE ABLE TO HELP ME OUT!
H-HEY! DON'T PUSH! STAND UP STRAIGHT!
THEN STOP PULLING! I'M LOSIN' MY BALANCE!!
TRIP
TRIP
ACK! STOP!
I'M GONNA FALL!
AH!
SLIP
WHY MEEEE?!

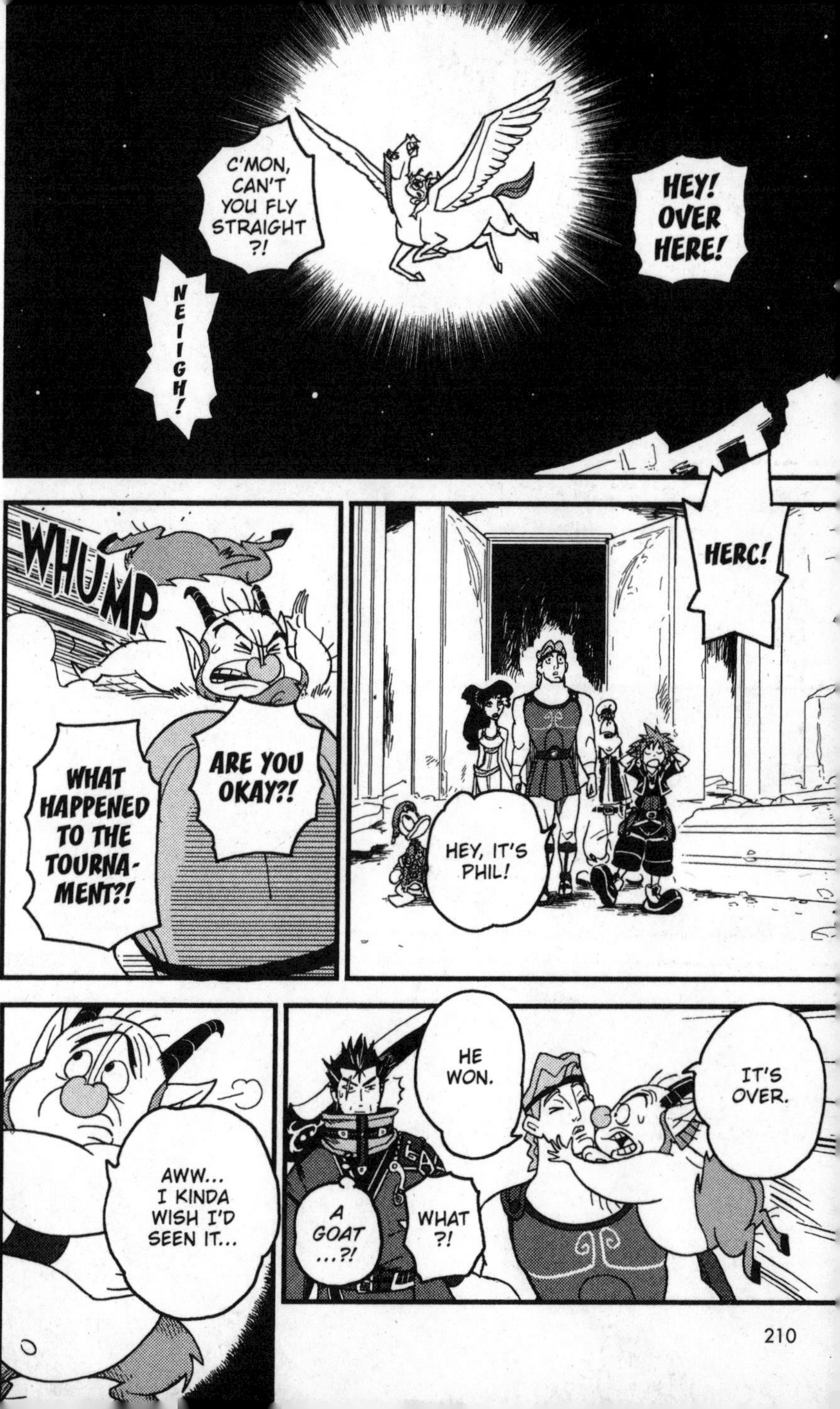
HEY! OVER HERE!
C'MON, CAN'T YOU FLY STRAIGHT ?!
NEIIGH!
HERC!
HEY, IT'S PHIL!
WHUMP
ARE YOU OKAY?!
WHAT HAPPENED TO THE TOURNA-MENT?!
IT'S OVER.
HE WON.
WHAT ?!
A GOAT ...?!
AWW... I KINDA WISH I'D SEEN IT...

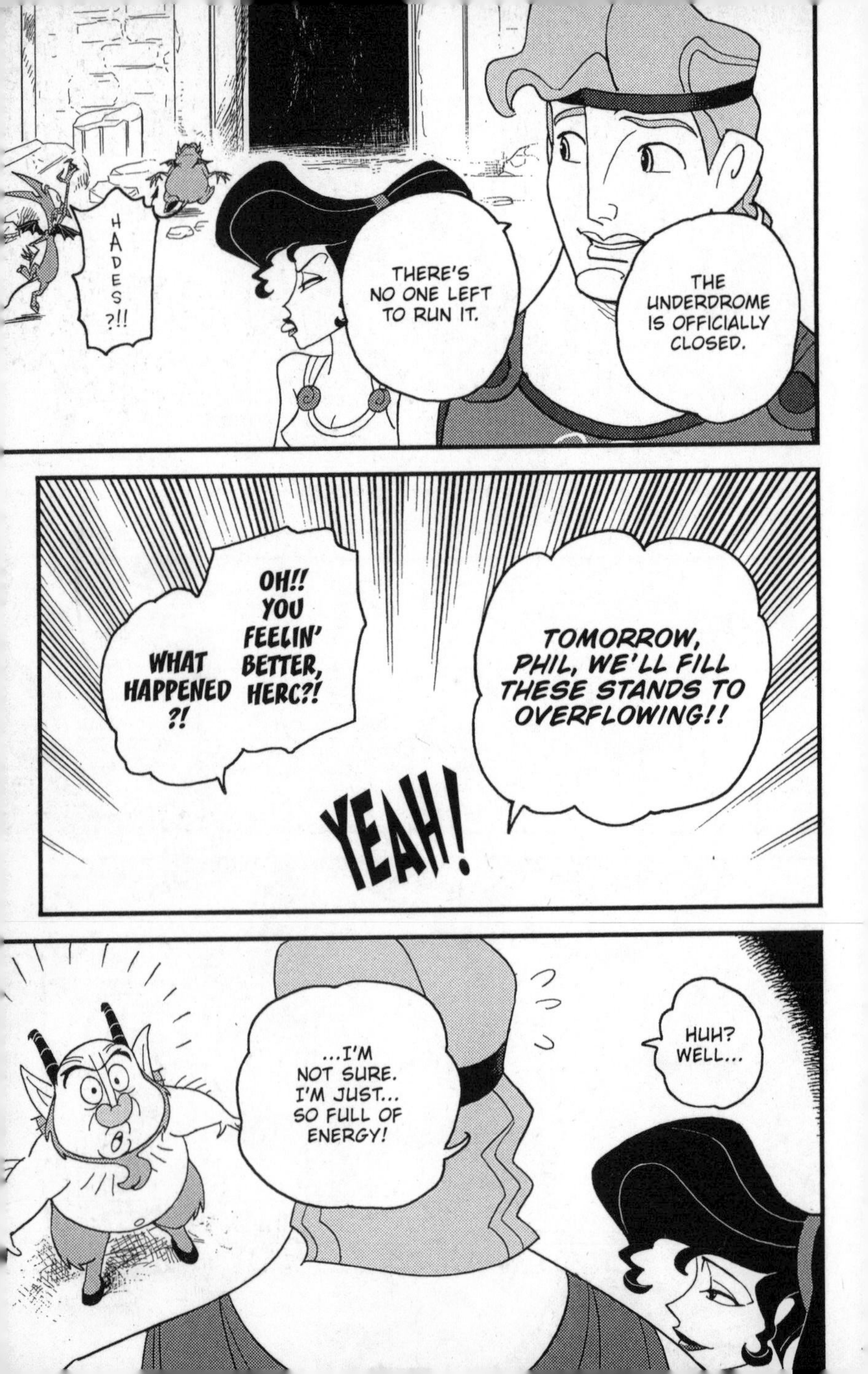
THE UNDERDROME IS OFFICIALLY CLOSED.
THERE'S NO ONE LEFT TO RUN IT.
HADES?!!
TOMORROW, PHIL, WE'LL FILL THESE STANDS TO OVERFLOWING!!
YEAH!
OH!! YOU FEELIN' BETTER, HERC?!
WHAT HAPPENED?!
HUH? WELL...
...I'M NOT SURE. I'M JUST... SO FULL OF ENERGY!

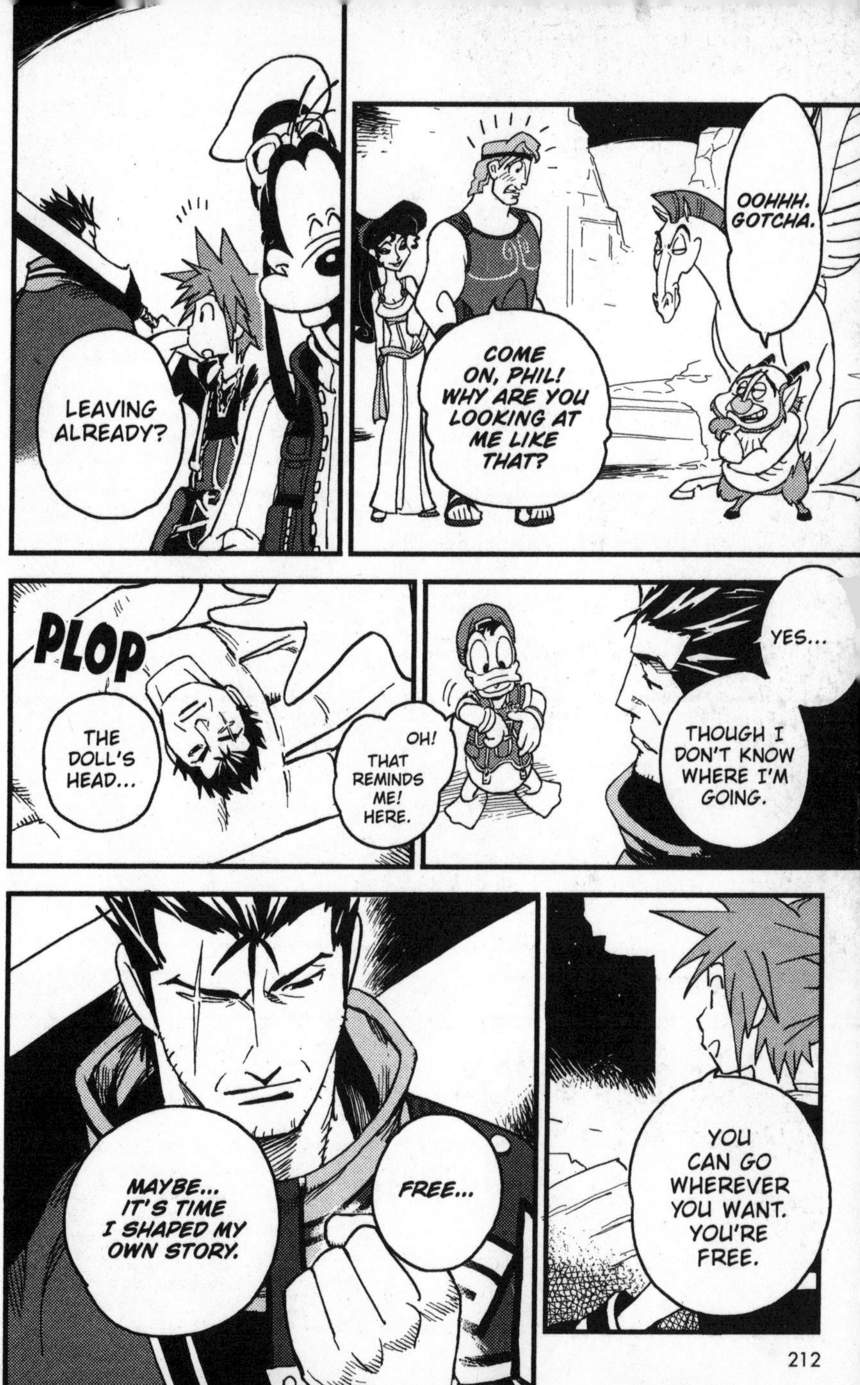
OOHHH. GOTCHA.
COME ON, PHIL! WHY ARE YOU LOOKING AT ME LIKE THAT?
LEAVING ALREADY?
YES...
THOUGH I DON'T KNOW WHERE I'M GOING.
OH! THAT REMINDS ME! HERE.
PLOP
THE DOLL'S HEAD...
YOU CAN GO WHEREVER YOU WANT. YOU'RE FREE.
FREE...
MAYBE... IT'S TIME I SHAPED MY OWN STORY.

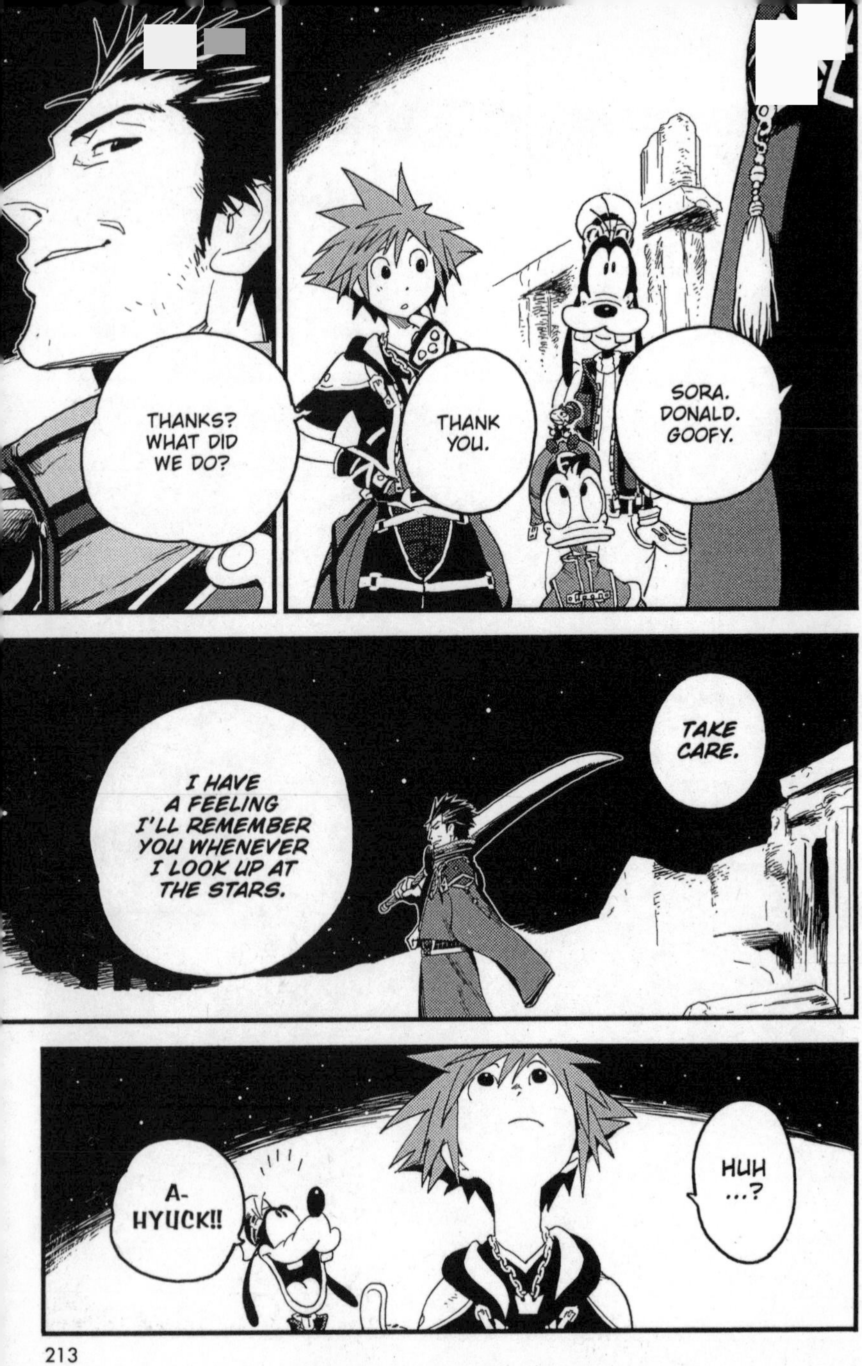
SORA. DONALD. GOOFY.
THANK YOU.
THANKS? WHAT DID WE DO?
TAKE CARE.
I HAVE A FEELING I'LL REMEMBER YOU WHENEVER I LOOK UP AT THE STARS.
HUH ...?
A-HYUCK!!

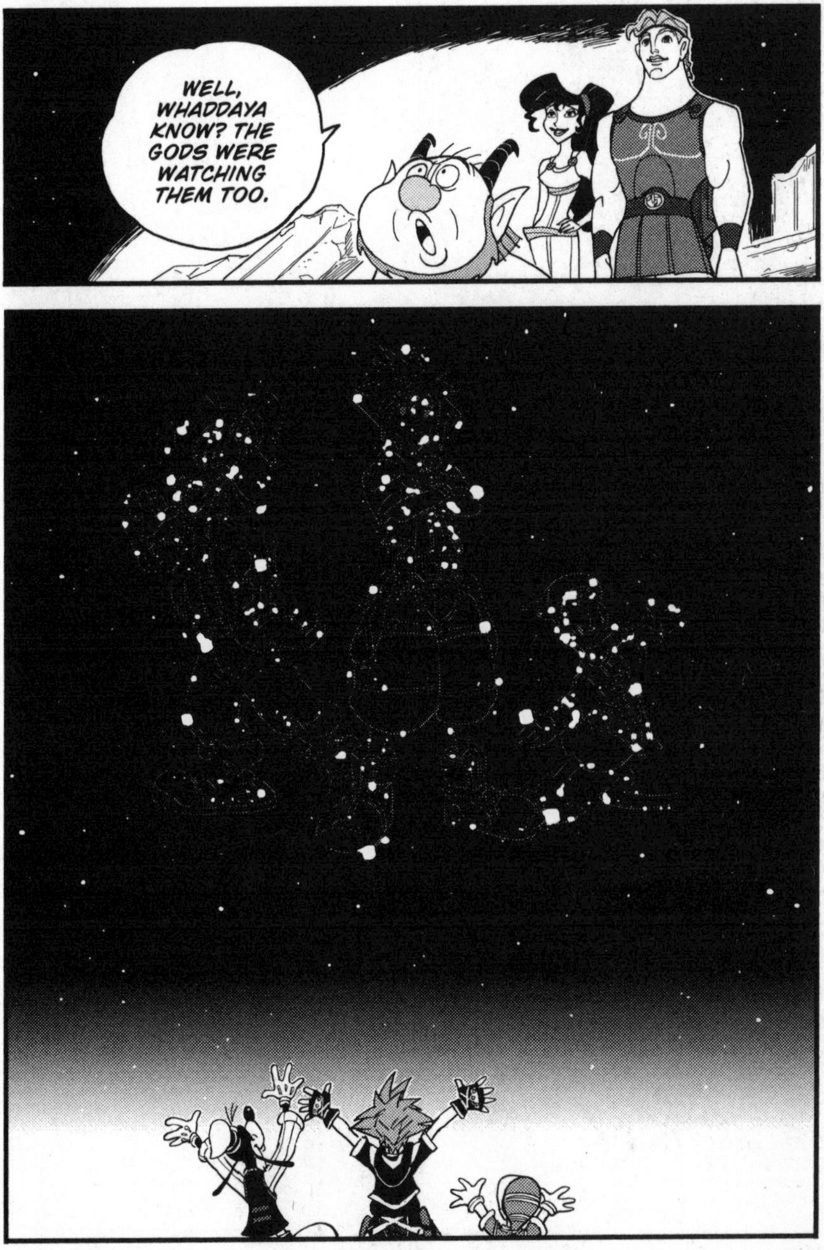
WELL, WHADDAYA KNOW? THE GODS WERE WATCHING THEM TOO.

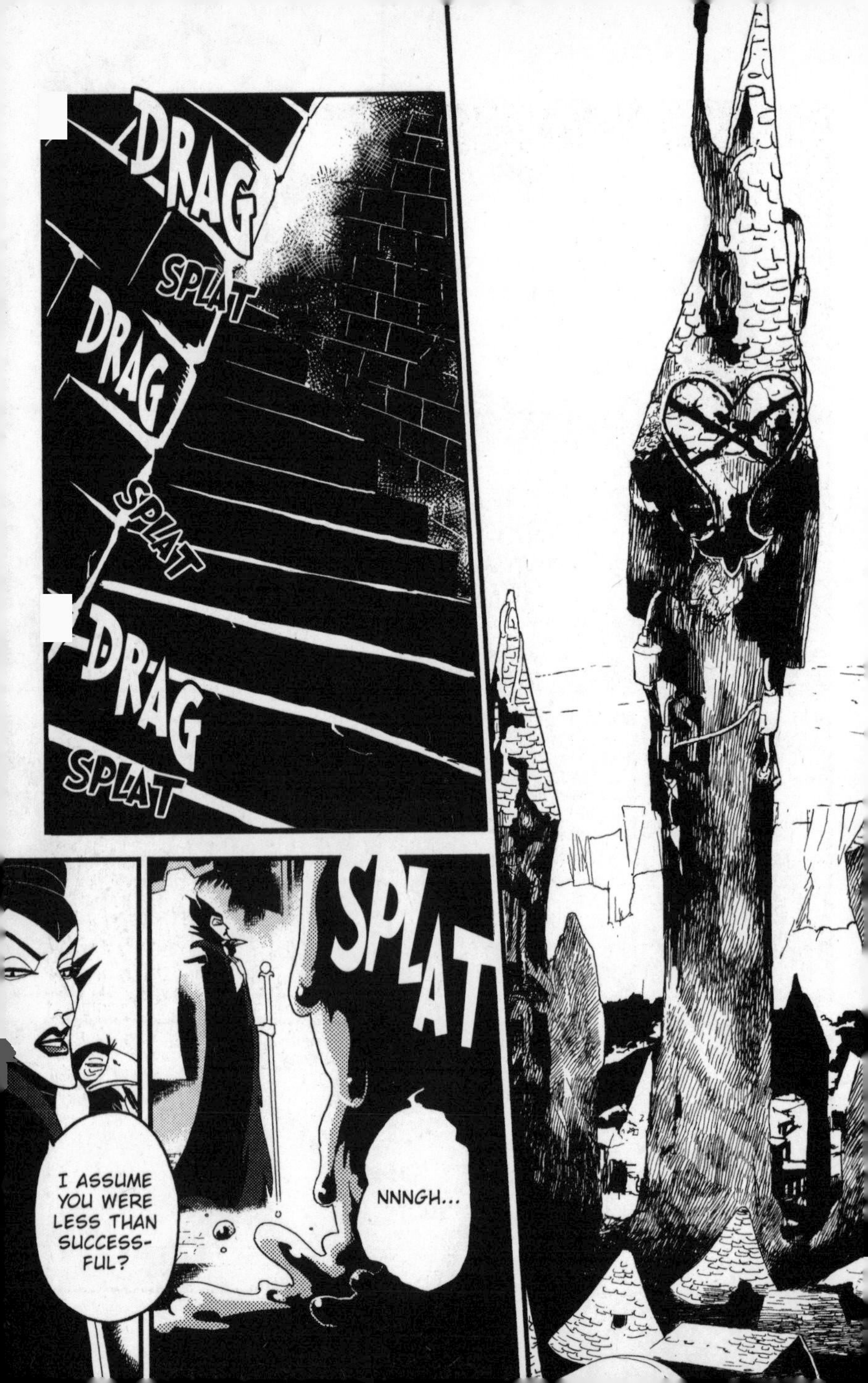
DRAG
SPLAT
DRAG
SPLAT
DRAG
SPLAT
SPLAT
NNNGH...
I ASSUME YOU WERE LESS THAN SUCCESS-FUL?

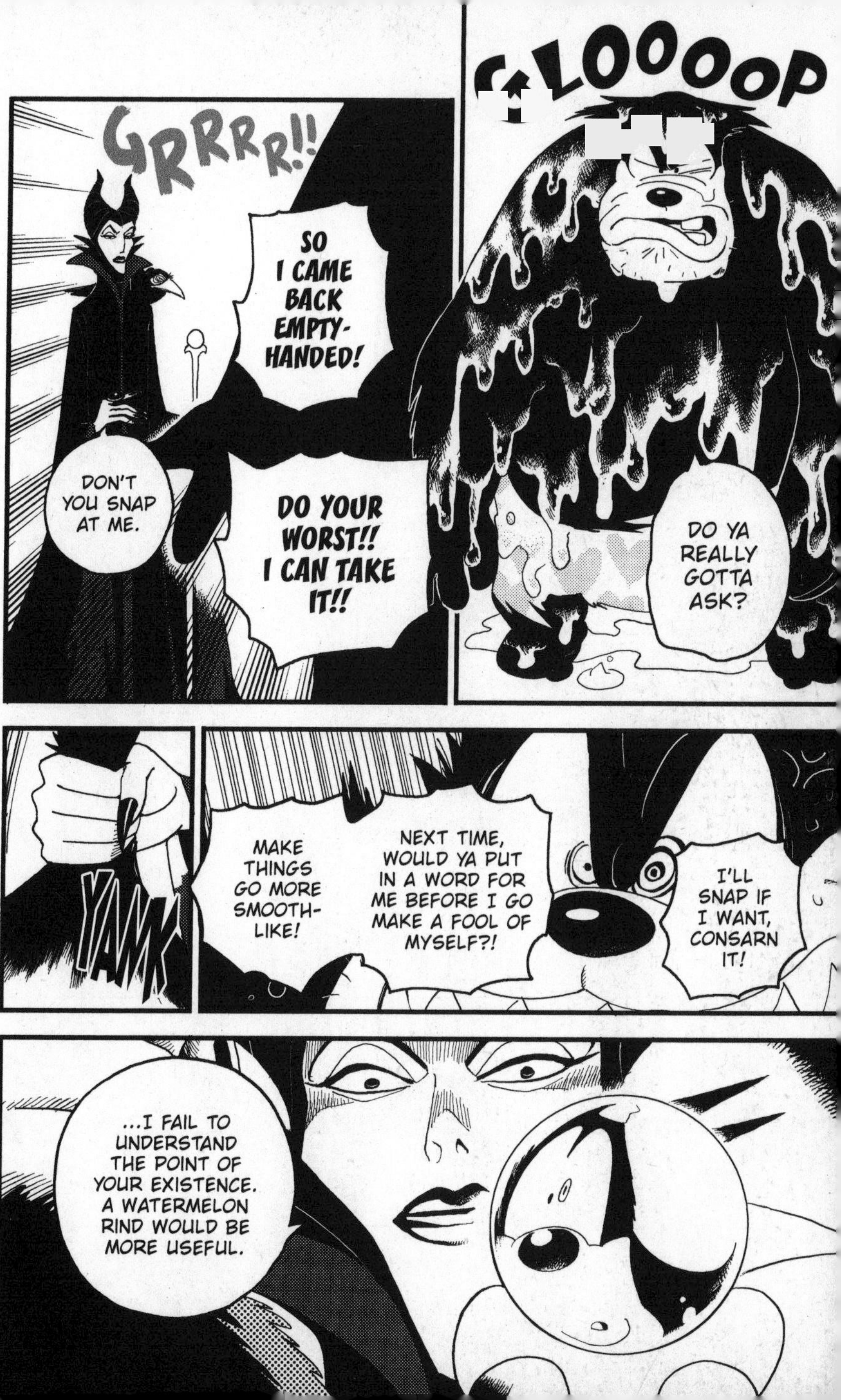

GLOOOOP
DO YA REALLY GOTTA ASK?
GRRRR!!
SO I CAME BACK EMPTY-HANDED!
DO YOUR WORST!! I CAN TAKE IT!!
DON'T YOU SNAP AT ME.
I'LL SNAP IF I WANT, CONSARN IT!
NEXT TIME, WOULD YA PUT IN A WORD FOR ME BEFORE I GO MAKE A FOOL OF MYSELF?!
MAKE THINGS GO MORE SMOOTH-LIKE!
YANK
...I FAIL TO UNDERSTAND THE POINT OF YOUR EXISTENCE. A WATERMELON RIND WOULD BE MORE USEFUL.

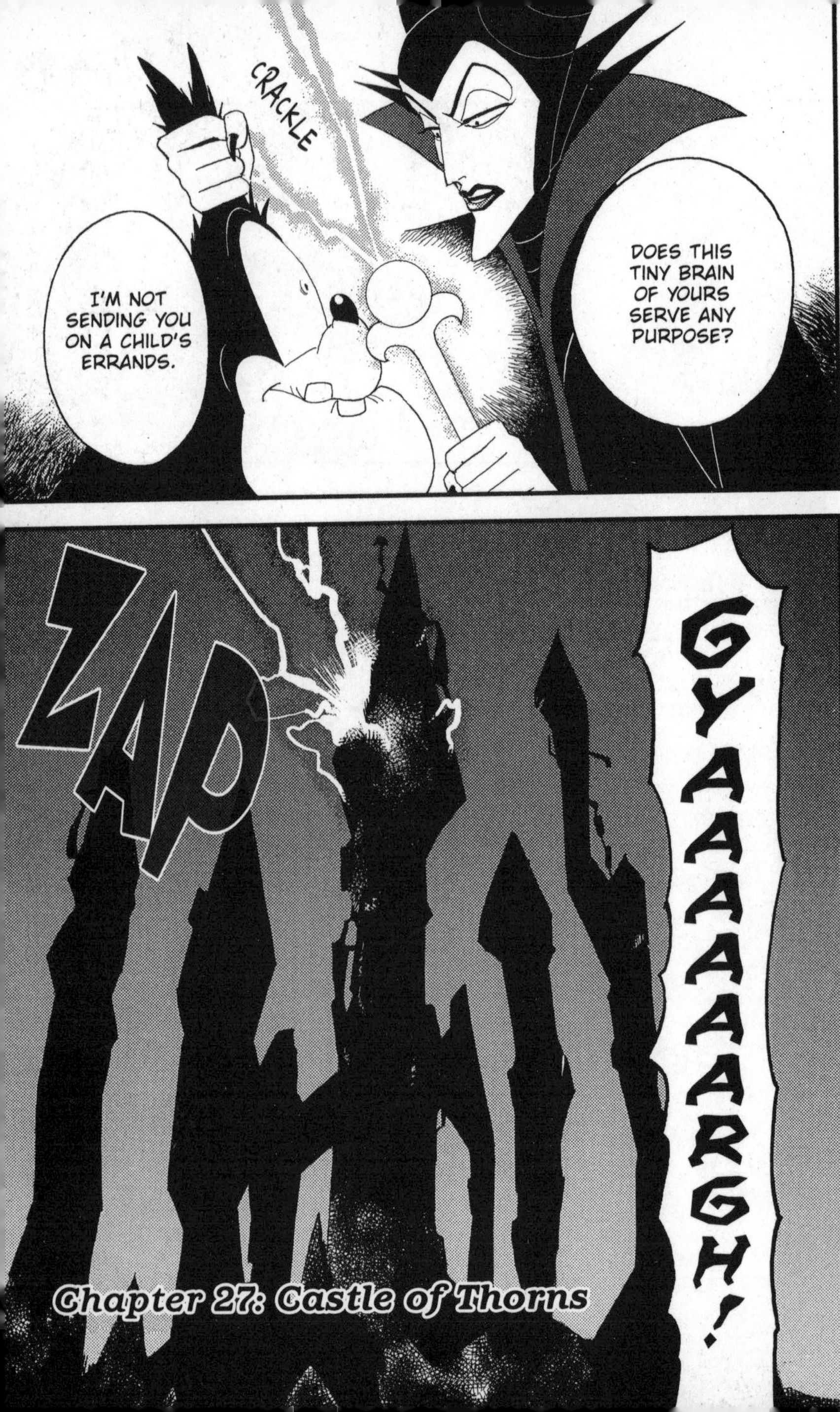
DOES THIS TINY BRAIN OF YOURS SERVE ANY PURPOSE?
CRACKLE
I'M NOT SENDING YOU ON A CHILD'S ERRANDS.
GYAAAARGH!
ZAP

Chapter 27: Castle of Thorns

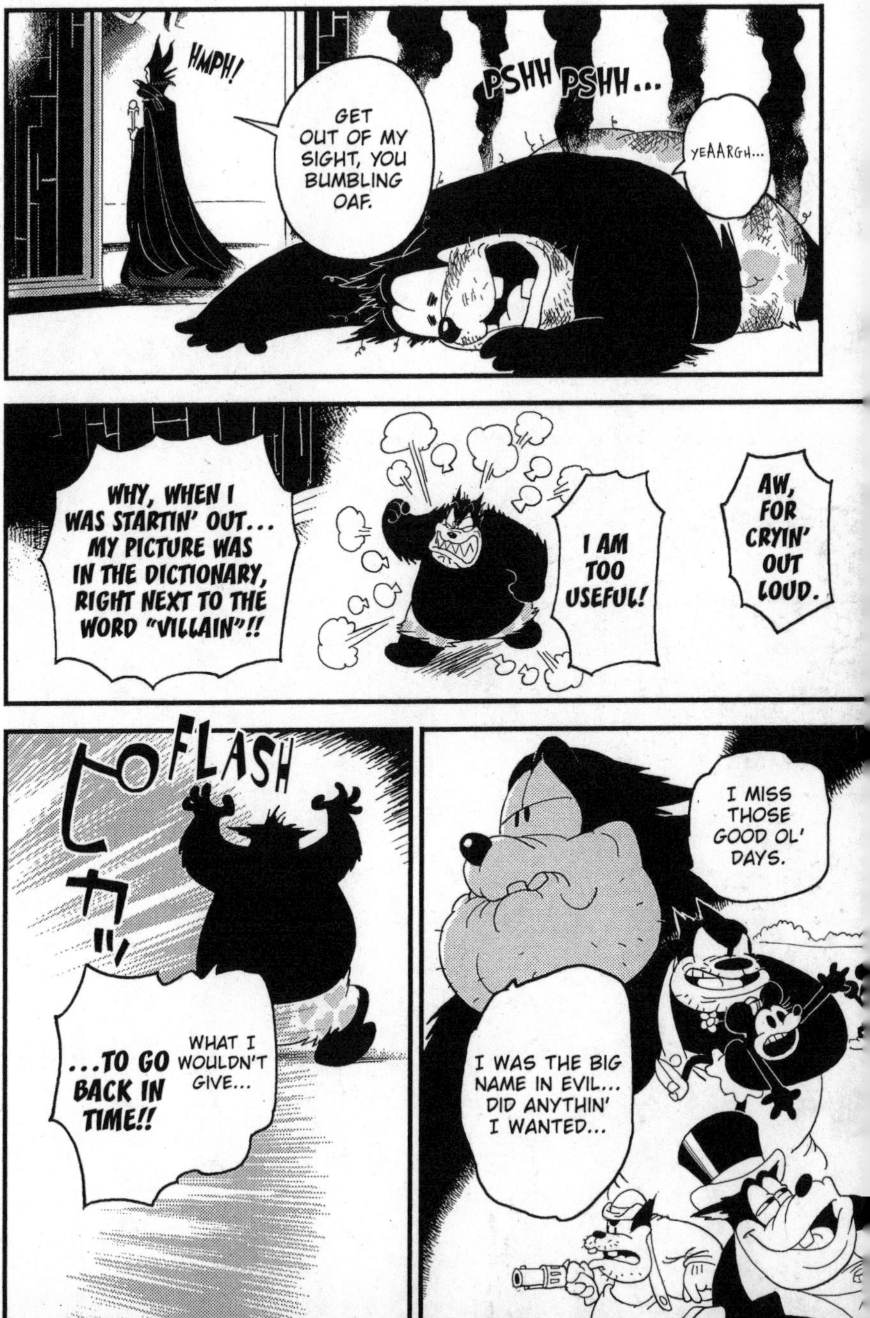
YEAARGH...
PSHH PSHH...
GET OUT OF MY SIGHT, YOU BUMBLING OAF.
HMPH!
AW, FOR CRYIN' OUT LOUD.
I AM TOO USEFUL!
WHY, WHEN I WAS STARTIN' OUT... MY PICTURE WAS IN THE DICTIONARY, RIGHT NEXT TO THE WORD "VILLAIN"!!
I MISS THOSE GOOD OL' DAYS.
I WAS THE BIG NAME IN EVIL... DID ANYTHIN' I WANTED...
FLASH
WHAT I WOULDN'T GIVE...
...TO GO BACK IN TIME!!

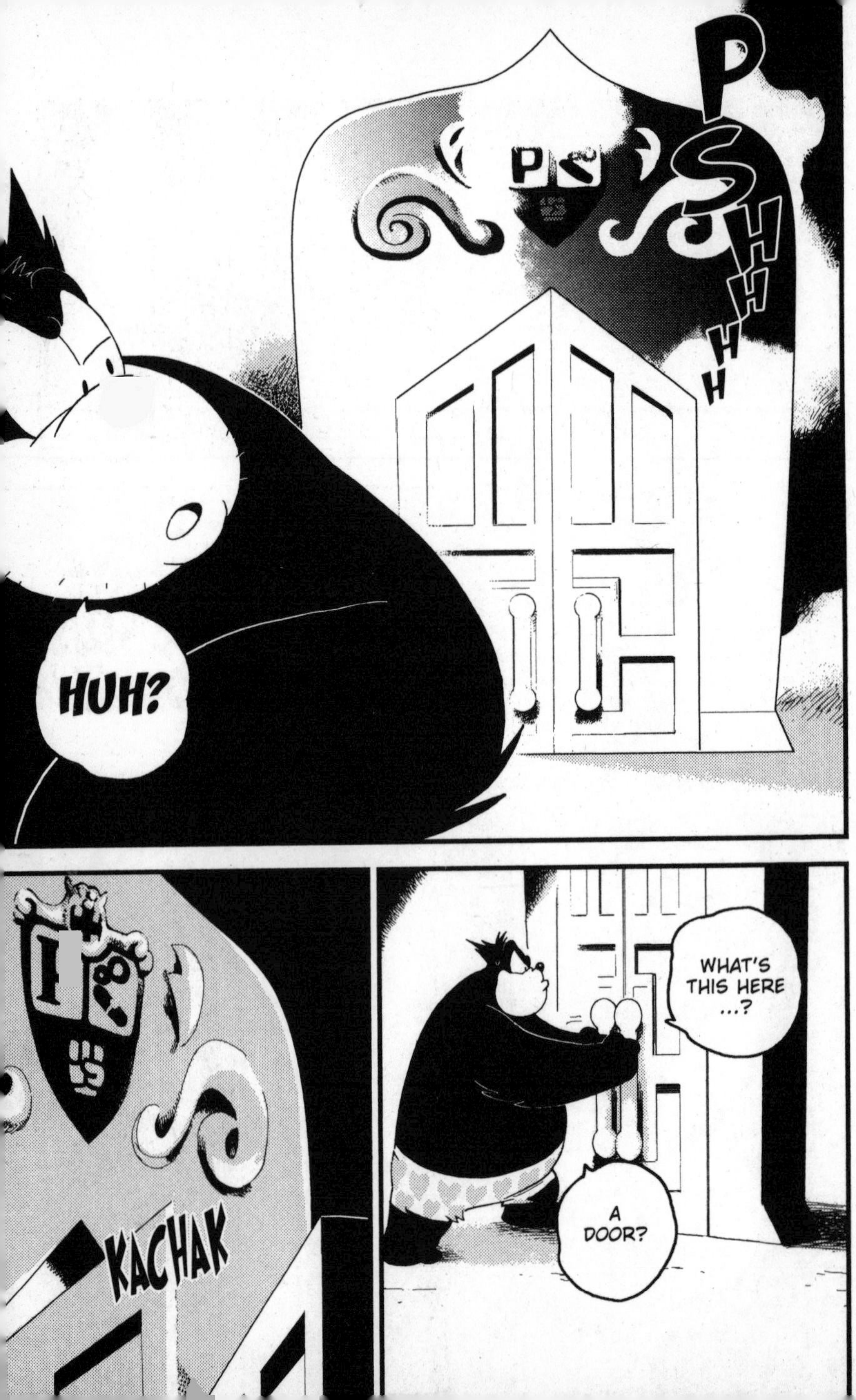
PSHHHHH
HUH?
WHAT'S THIS HERE ...?
A DOOR?
KACHAK

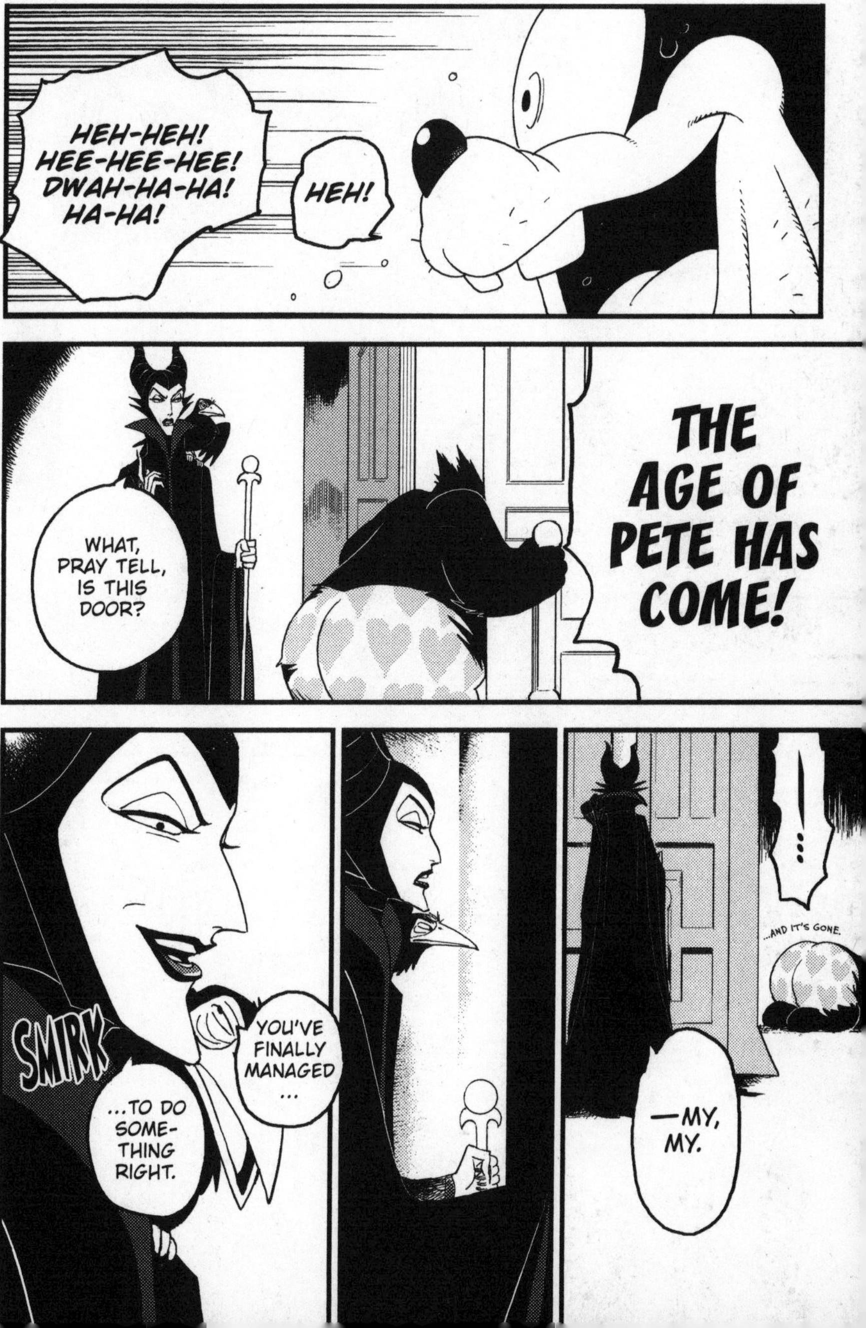
HEH!
HEH-HEH! HEE-HEE-HEE! DWAH-HA-HA! HA-HA!
THE AGE OF PETE HAS COME!
WHAT, PRAY TELL, IS THIS DOOR?
!...
...AND IT'S GONE.
—MY, MY.
YOU'VE FINALLY MANAGED ...
SMIRK
...TO DO SOME-THING RIGHT.

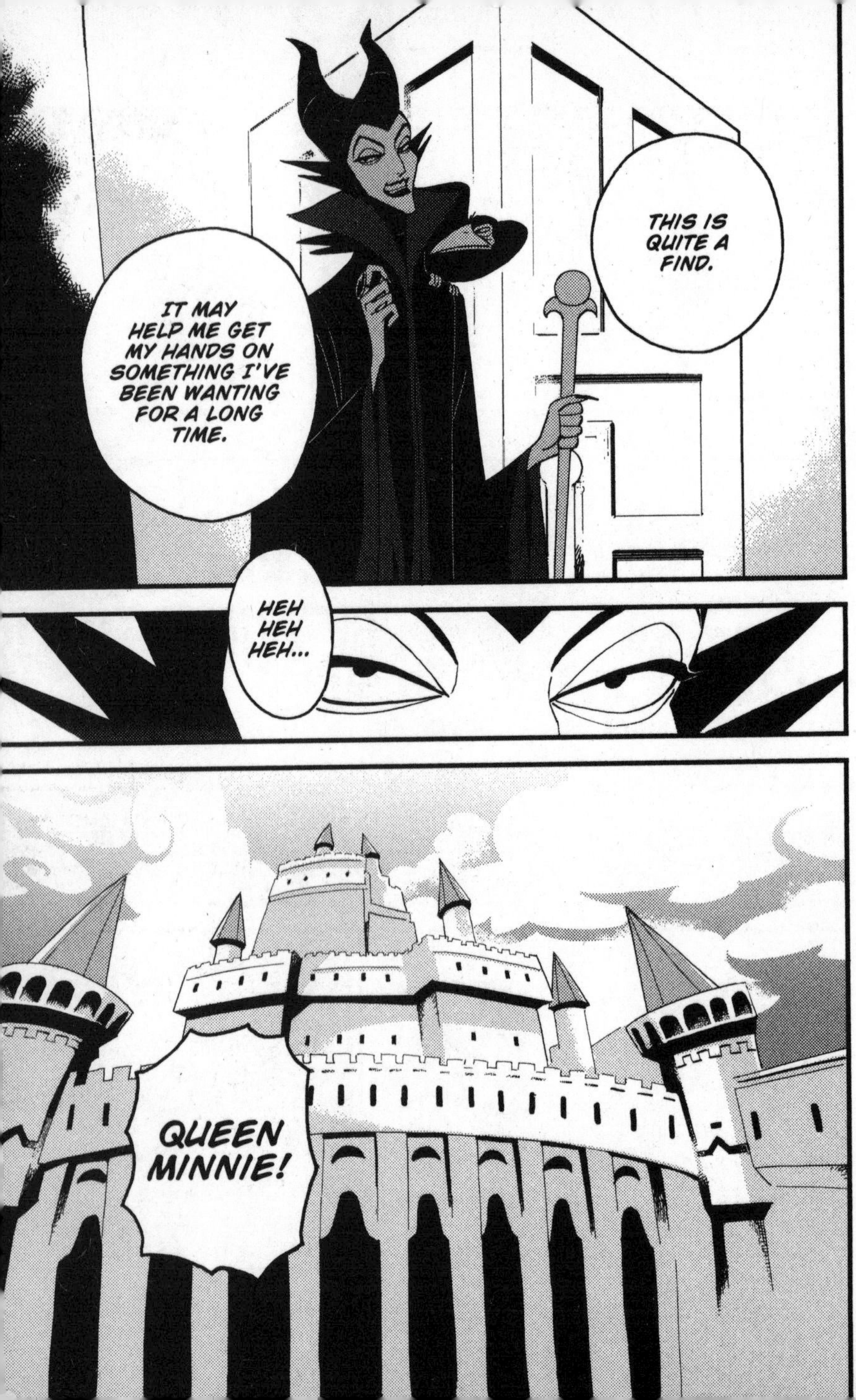
THIS IS QUITE A FIND.
IT MAY HELP ME GET MY HANDS ON SOMETHING I'VE BEEN WANTING FOR A LONG TIME.
HEH HEH HEH...
QUEEN MINNIE!

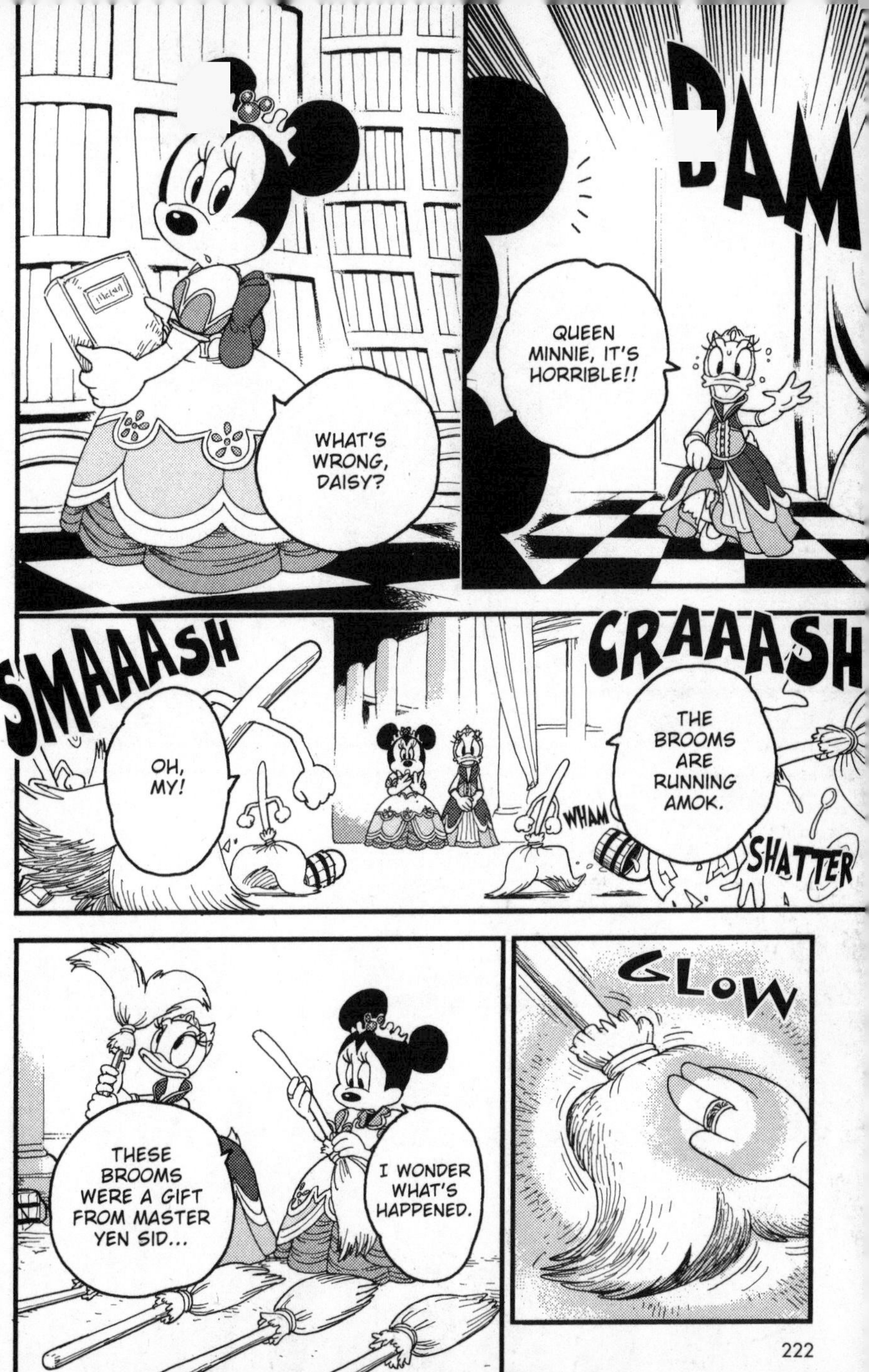
BAM
QUEEN MINNIE, IT'S HORRIBLE!!
WHAT'S WRONG, DAISY?
CRAAASH
THE BROOMS ARE RUNNING AMOK.
SHATTER
WHAM
SMAAASH
OH, MY!
GLOW
I WONDER WHAT'S HAPPENED.
THESE BROOMS WERE A GIFT FROM MASTER YEN SID...

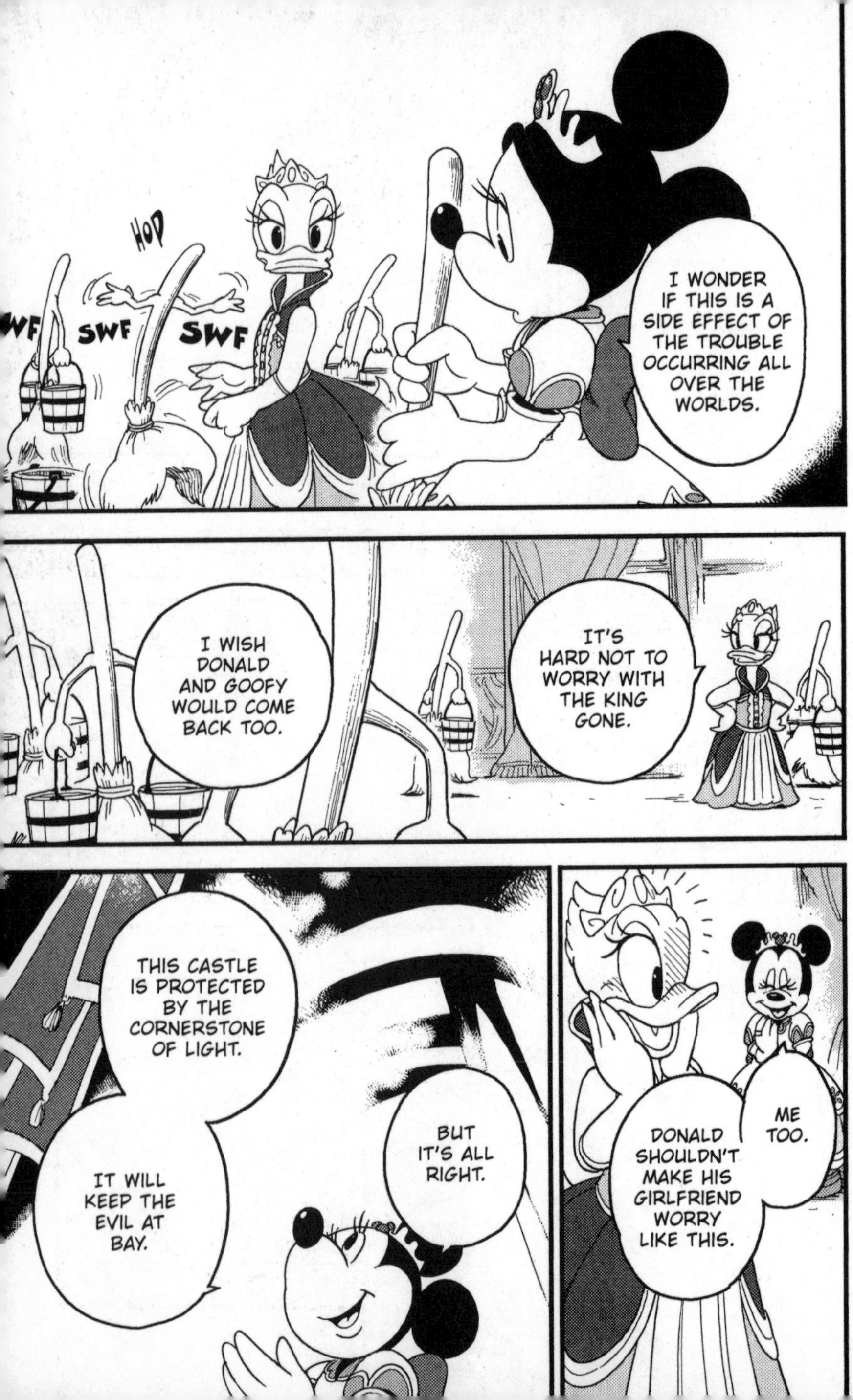
I WONDER IF THIS IS A SIDE EFFECT OF THE TROUBLE OCCURRING ALL OVER THE WORLDS.
HOP
SWF
SWF
WF
IT'S HARD NOT TO WORRY WITH THE KING GONE.
I WISH DONALD AND GOOFY WOULD COME BACK TOO.
ME TOO.
DONALD SHOULDN'T MAKE HIS GIRLFRIEND WORRY LIKE THIS.
THIS CASTLE IS PROTECTED BY THE CORNERSTONE OF LIGHT.
BUT IT'S ALL RIGHT.
IT WILL KEEP THE EVIL AT BAY.

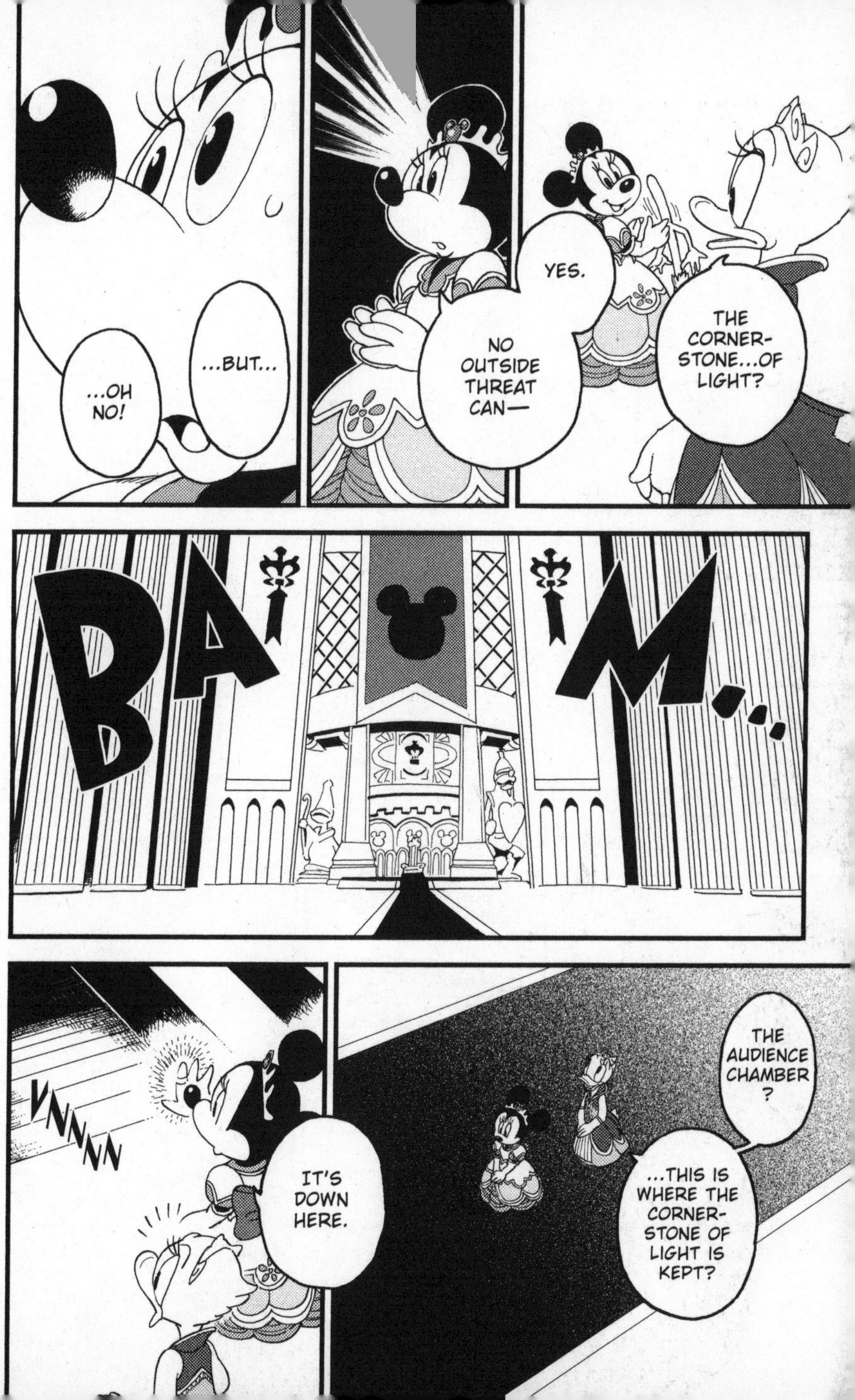
THE CORNER-STONE...OF LIGHT?
YES.
NO OUTSIDE THREAT CAN—
...BUT...
...OH NO!
BAM...
THE AUDIENCE CHAMBER?
...THIS IS WHERE THE CORNER-STONE OF LIGHT IS KEPT?
IT'S DOWN HERE.
VNNNN

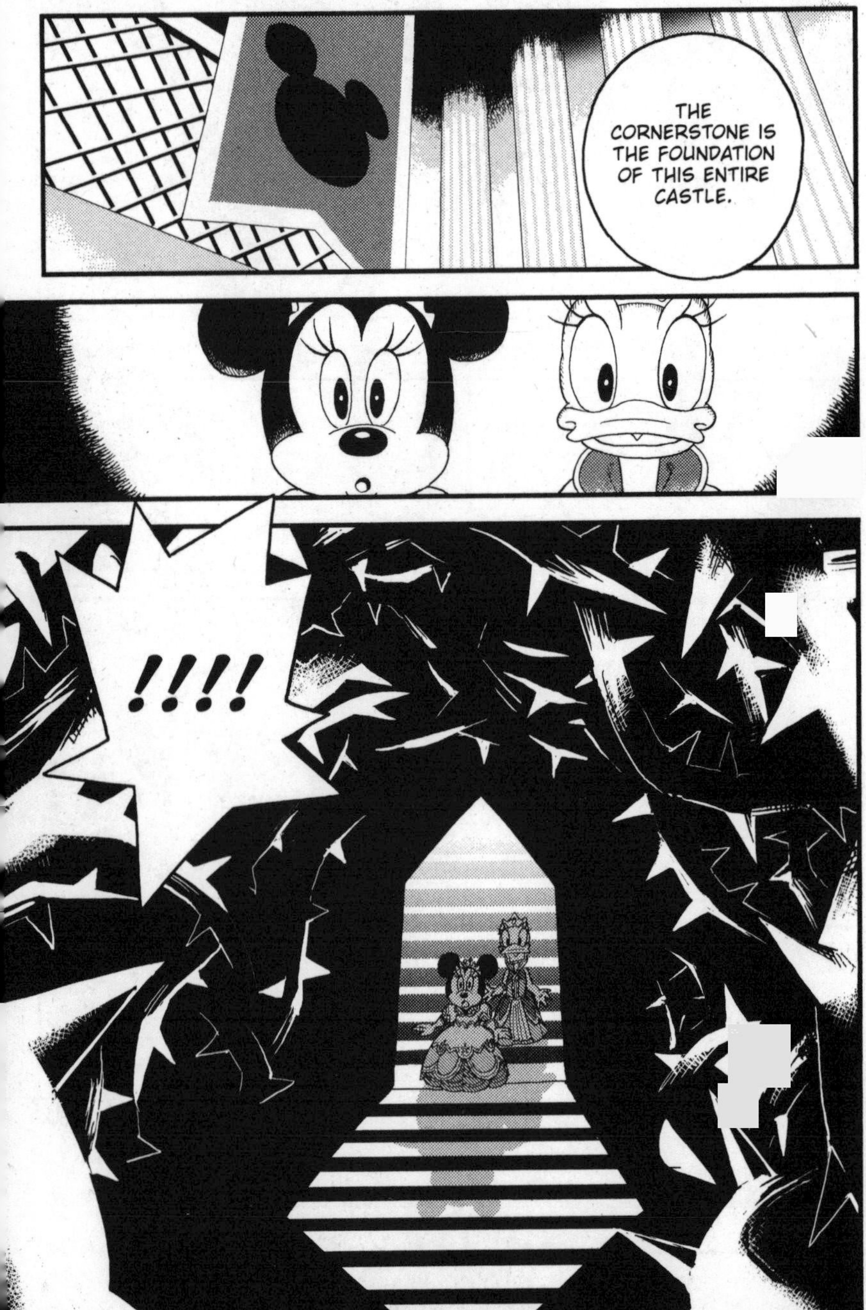
THE CORNERSTONE IS THE FOUNDATION OF THIS ENTIRE CASTLE.
!!!!

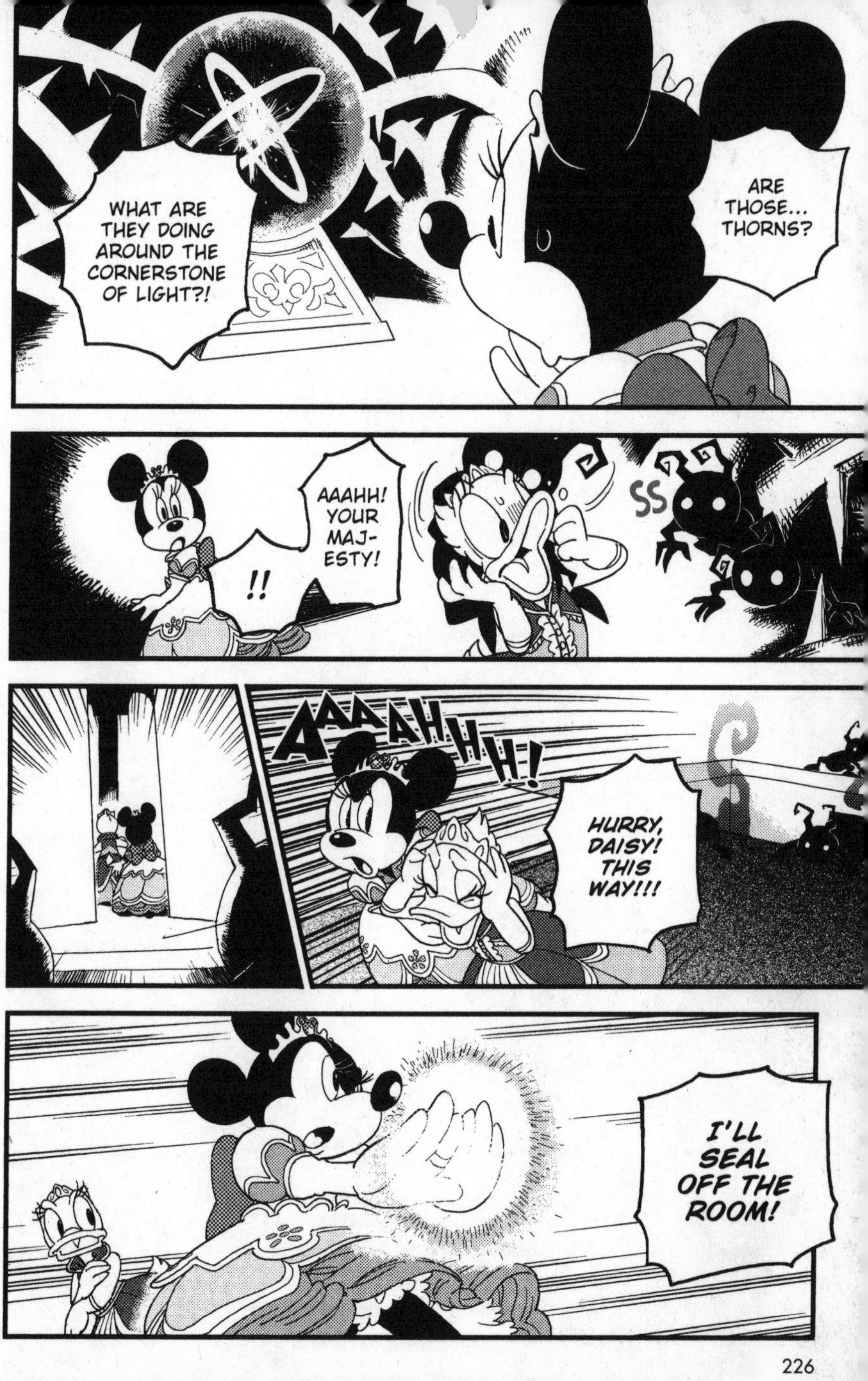
ARE THOSE... THORNS?
WHAT ARE THEY DOING AROUND THE CORNERSTONE OF LIGHT?!
SS
AAAHH! YOUR MAJ-ESTY!
!!
AAAAHHHH!
HURRY, DAISY! THIS WAY!!!
I'LL SEAL OFF THE ROOM!

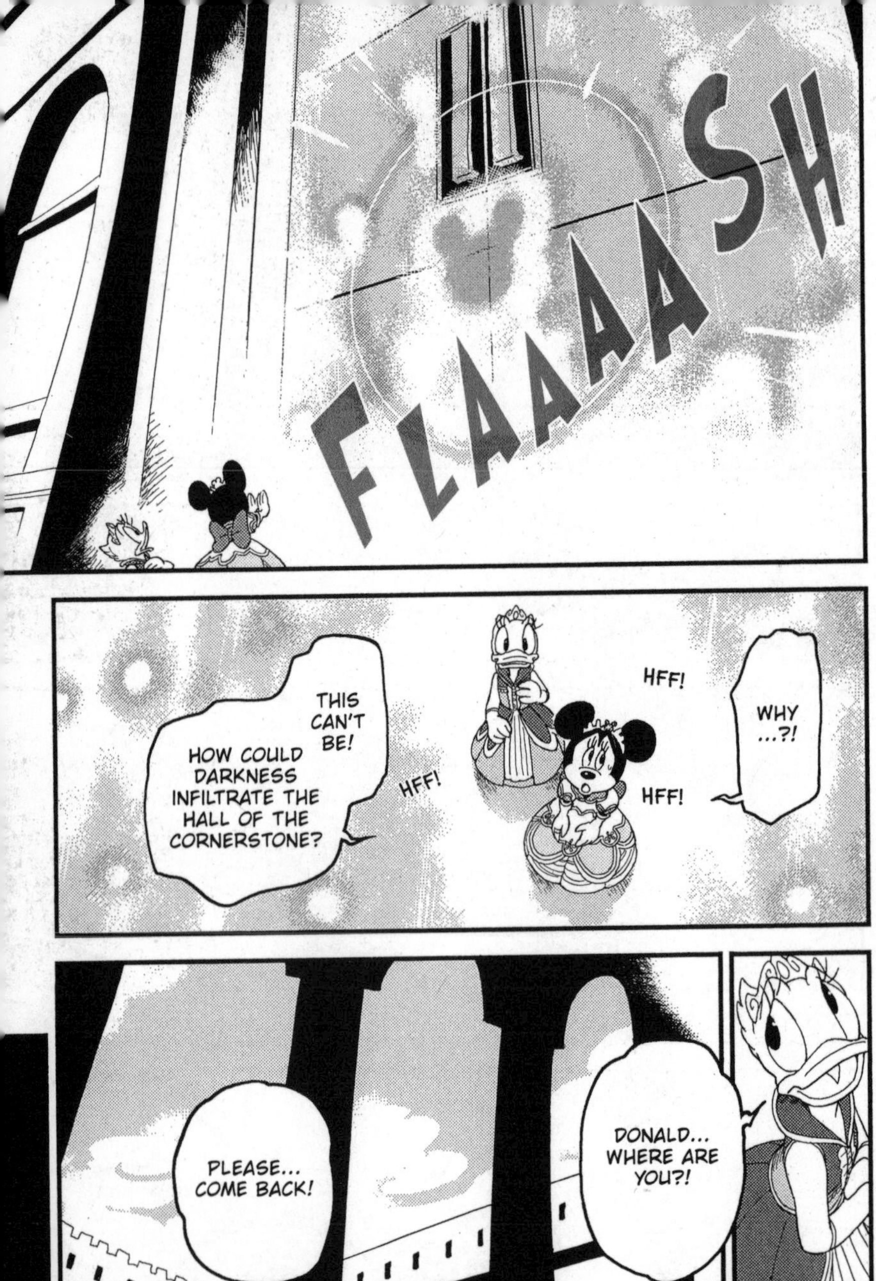
FLAAAASH
WHY ...?!
HFF!
HFF!
HFF!
THIS CAN'T BE!
HOW COULD DARKNESS INFILTRATE THE HALL OF THE CORNERSTONE?
DONALD... WHERE ARE YOU?!
PLEASE... COME BACK!

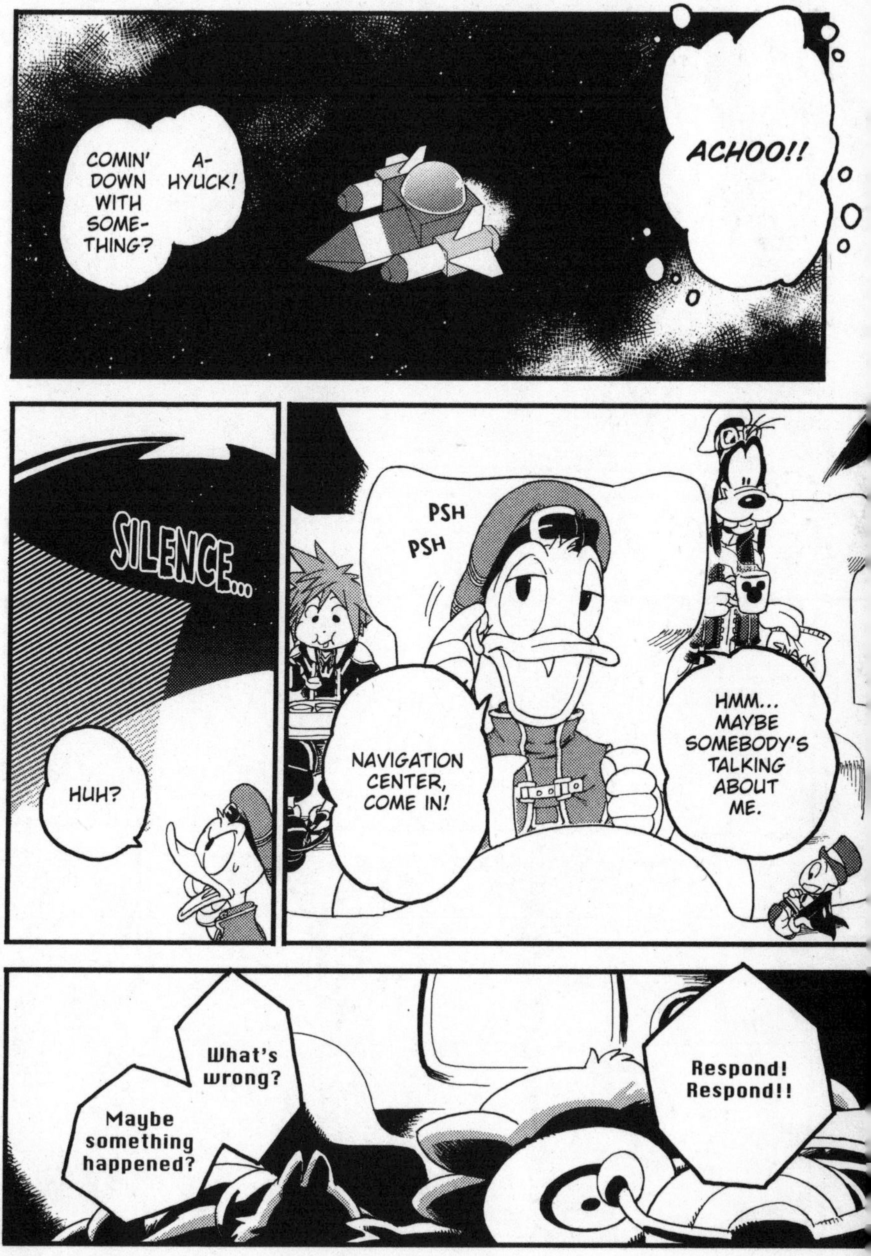
ACHOO!!
COMIN' DOWN WITH SOMETHING? A-HYUCK!
PSH
PSH
HMM... MAYBE SOMEBODY'S TALKING ABOUT ME.
NAVIGATION CENTER, COME IN!
SILENCE...
HUH?
Respond! Respond!!
What's wrong?
Maybe something happened?

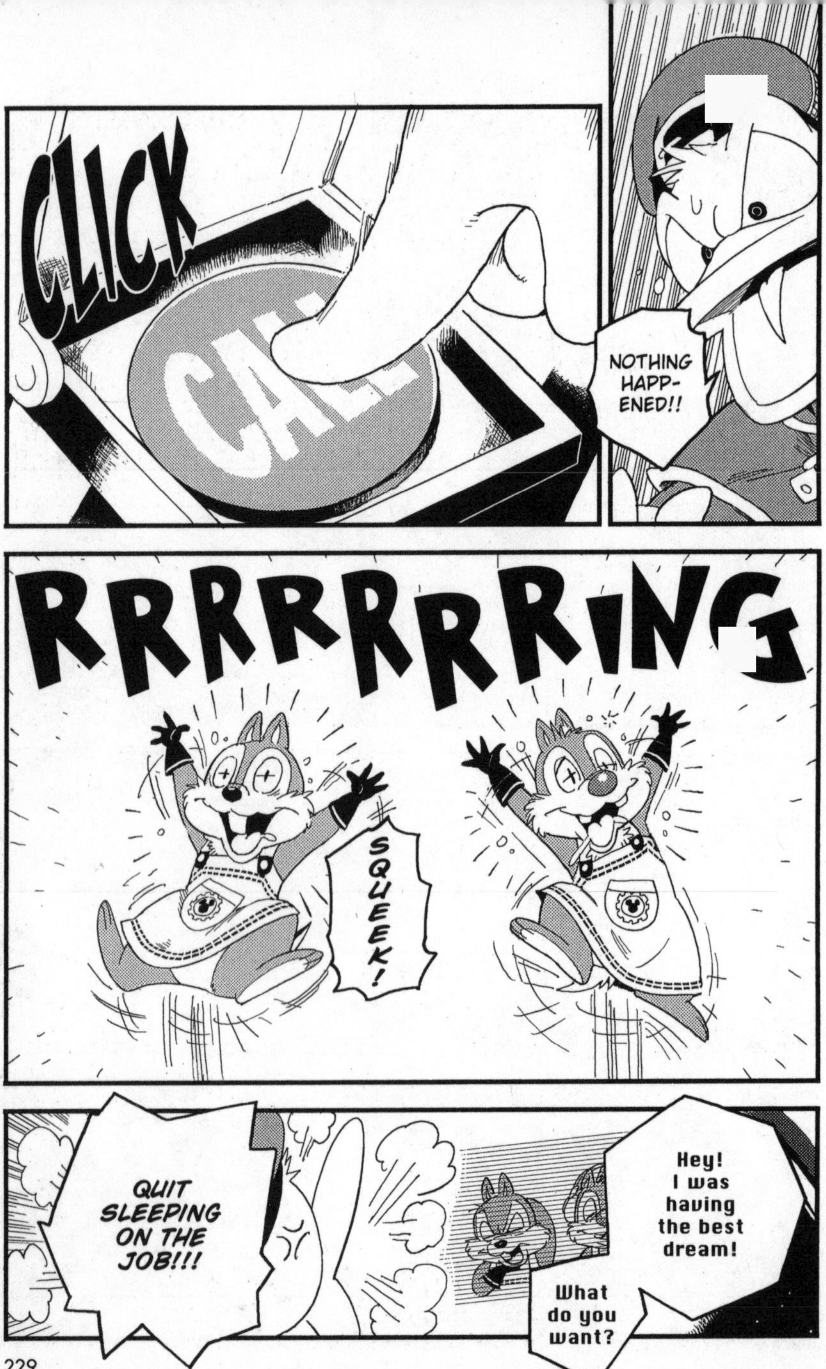
NOTHING HAPP-ENED!!
CLICK
CALL
RRRRRRRING
SQUEEEK!
Hey! I was having the best dream!
What do you want?
QUIT SLEEPING ON THE JOB!!!

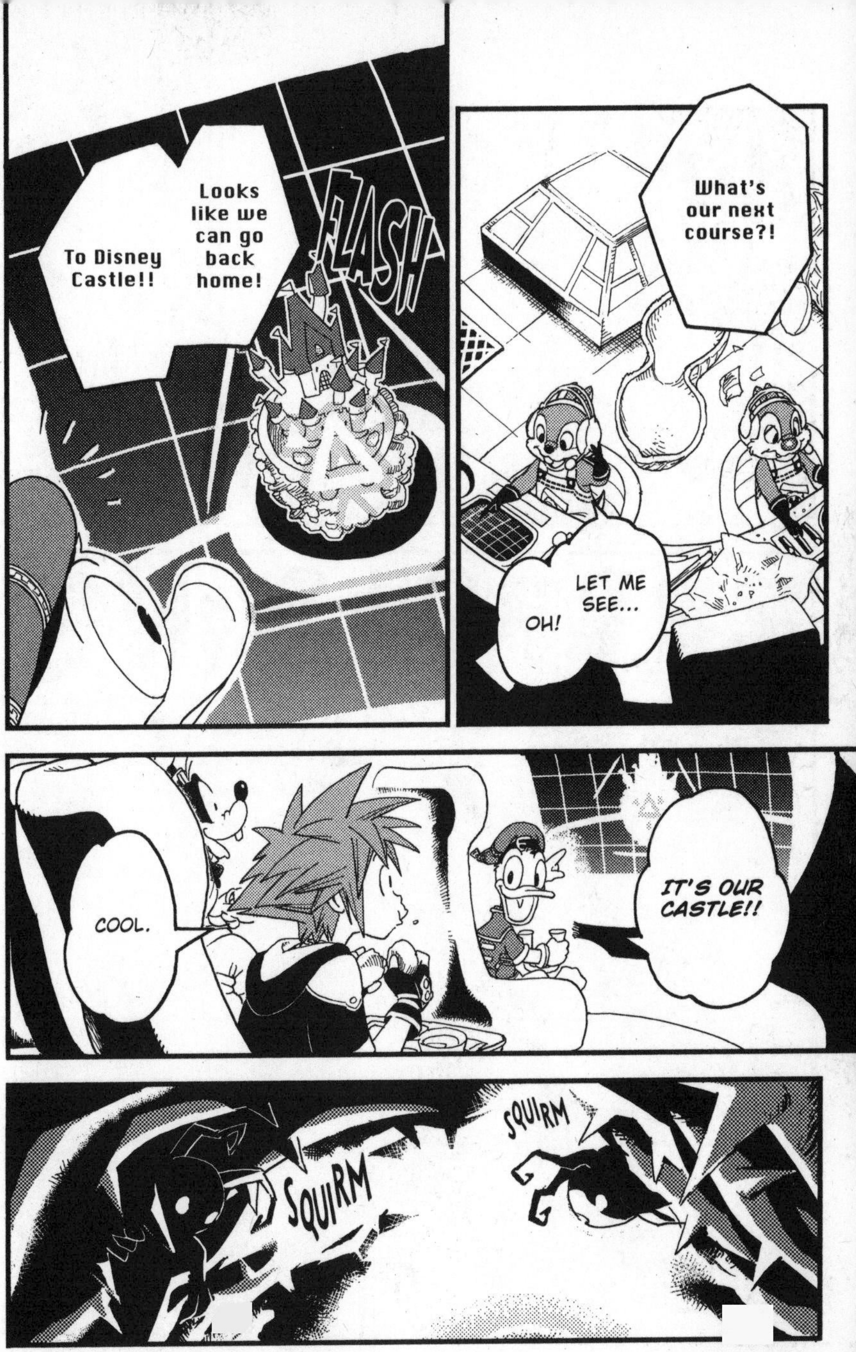
What's our next course?!
LET ME SEE...
OH!
FLASH
Looks like we can go back home!
To Disney Castle!!
IT'S OUR CASTLE!!
COOL.
SQUIRM
SQUIRM

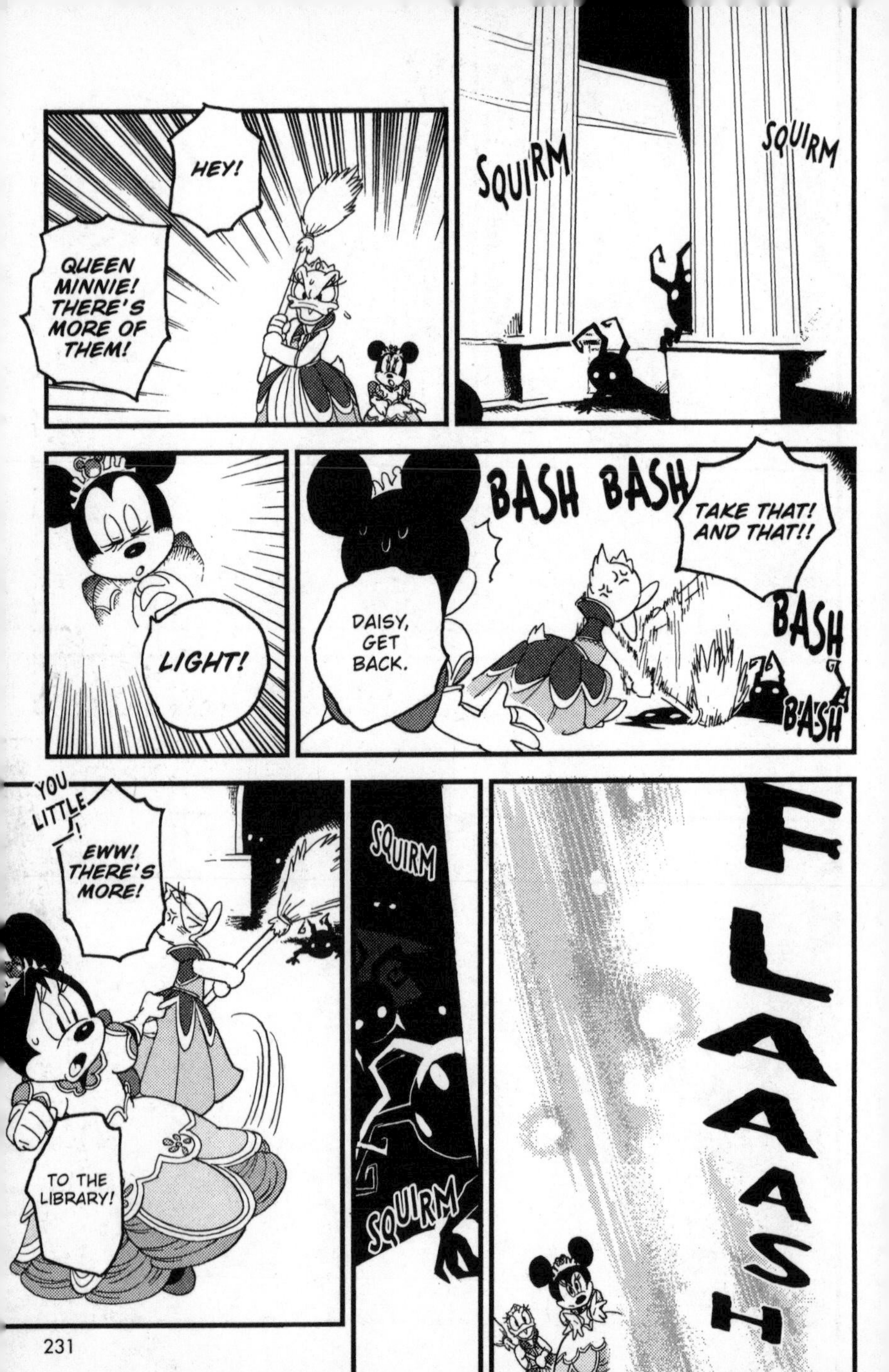
SQUIRM
SQUIRM
HEY!
QUEEN MINNIE! THERE'S MORE OF THEM!
TAKE THAT! AND THAT!!
BASH BASH
DAISY, GET BACK.
BASH
B-A-SH
LIGHT!
FLAAASH
SQUIRM
SQUIRM
YOU LITTLE-!
EWW! THERE'S MORE!
TO THE LIBRARY!

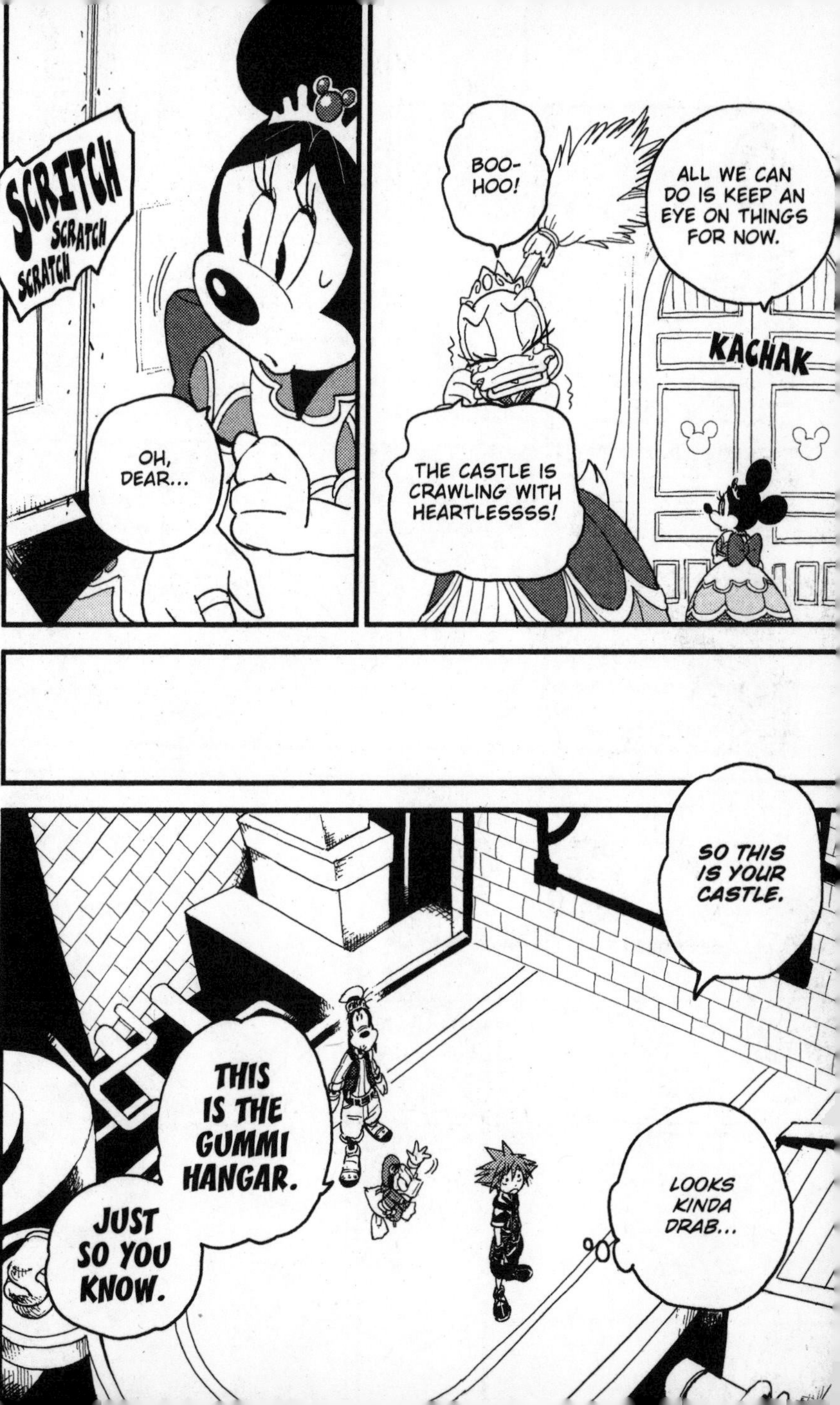
ALL WE CAN DO IS KEEP AN EYE ON THINGS FOR NOW.
BOO-HOO!
KACHAK
THE CASTLE IS CRAWLING WITH HEARTLESSSS!
SCRITCH SCRATCH SCRATCH
OH, DEAR...
SO THIS IS YOUR CASTLE.
LOOKS KINDA DRAB...
THIS IS THE GUMMI HANGAR.
JUST SO YOU KNOW.

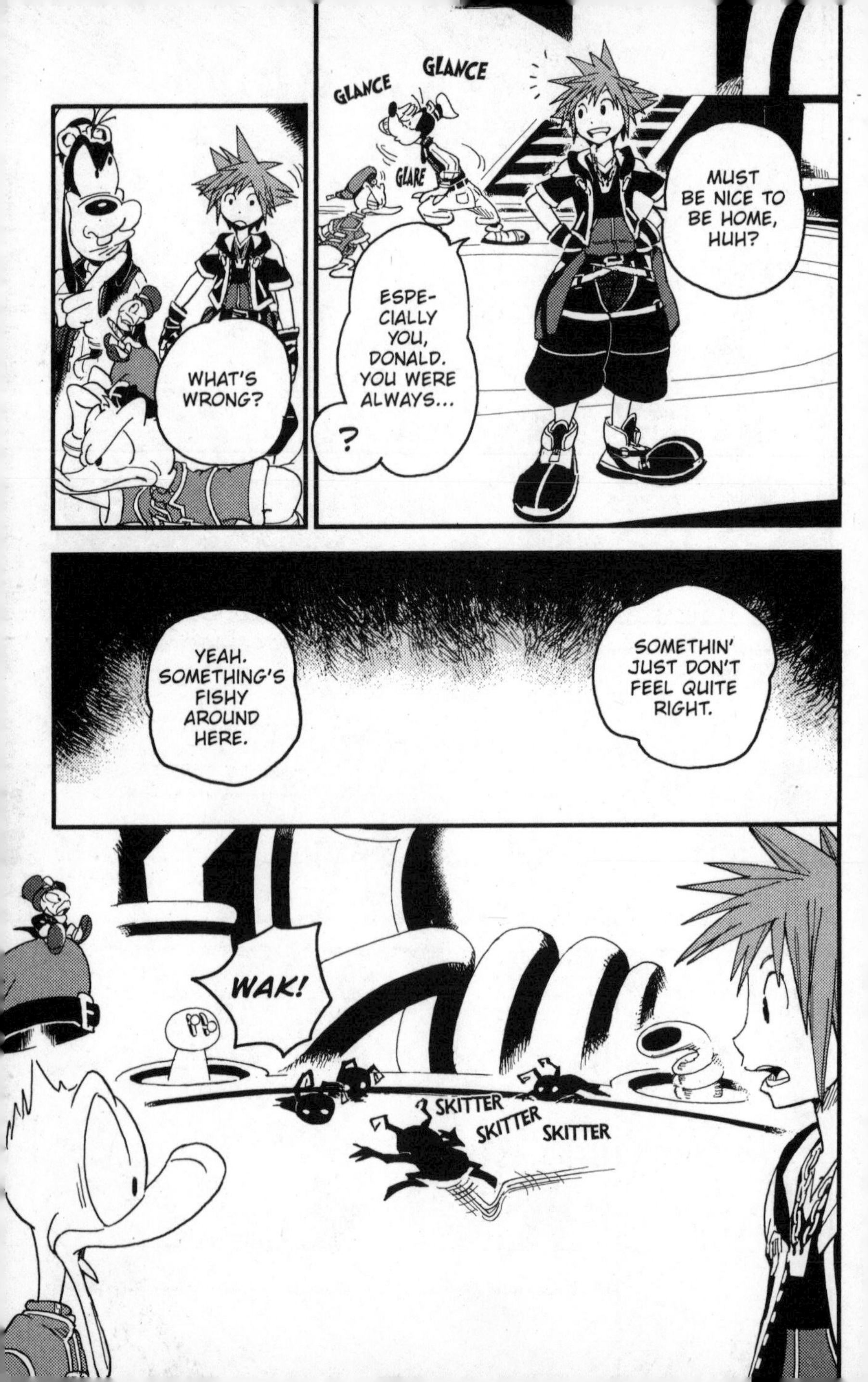
GLANCE
MUST BE NICE TO BE HOME, HUH?
GLANCE
GLARE
ESPE-CIALLY YOU, DONALD. YOU WERE ALWAYS...
?
WHAT'S WRONG?
SOMETHIN' JUST DON'T FEEL QUITE RIGHT.
YEAH. SOMETHING'S FISHY AROUND HERE.
WAK!
SKITTER
SKITTER
SKITTER

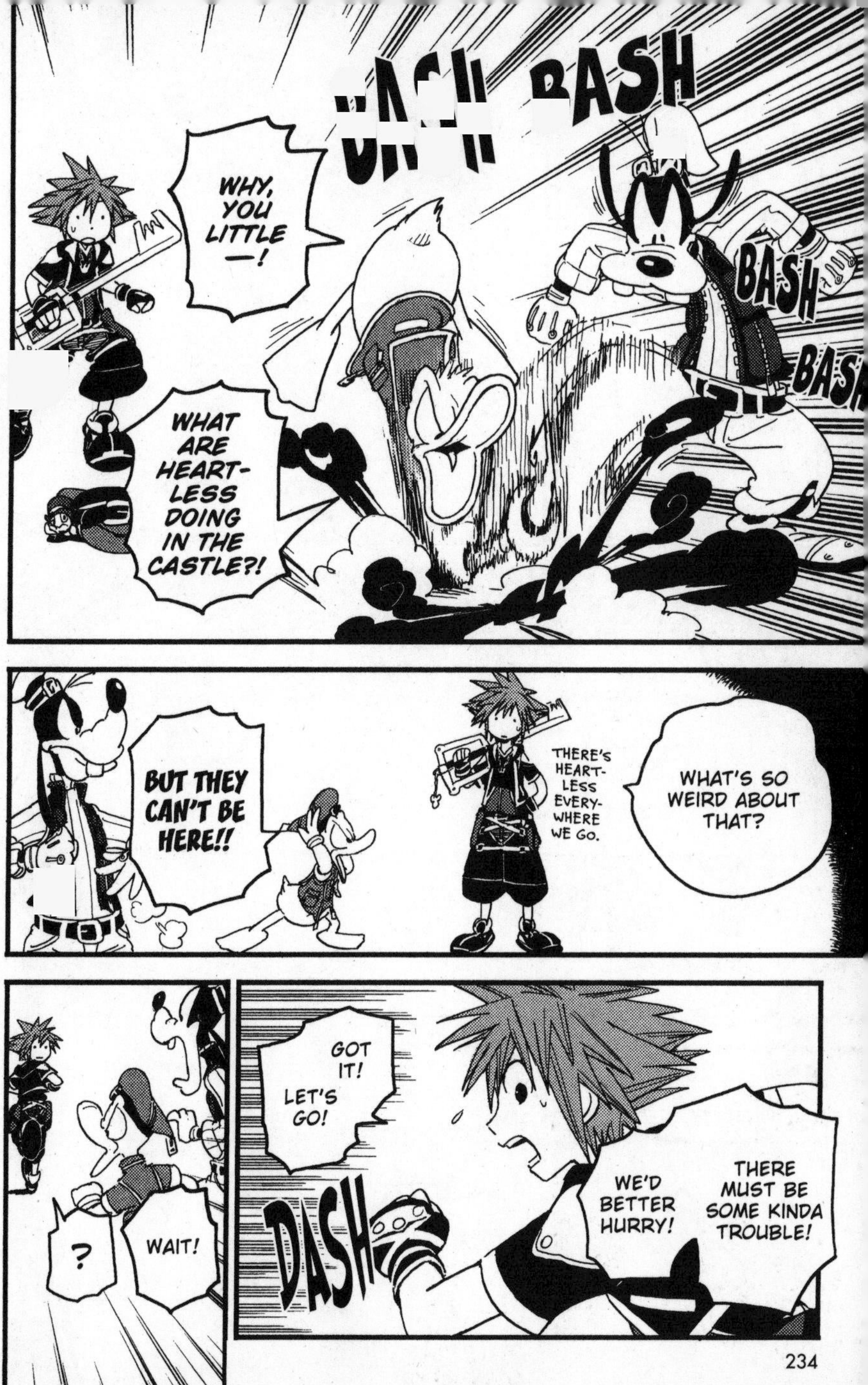
BASH
BASH
BASH
WHY, YOU LITTLE—!
WHAT ARE HEART-LESS DOING IN THE CASTLE?!
WHAT'S SO WEIRD ABOUT THAT?
THERE'S HEART-LESS EVERY-WHERE WE GO.
BUT THEY CAN'T BE HERE!!
THERE MUST BE SOME KINDA TROUBLE!
WE'D BETTER HURRY!
GOT IT!
LET'S GO!
DASH
WAIT!
?

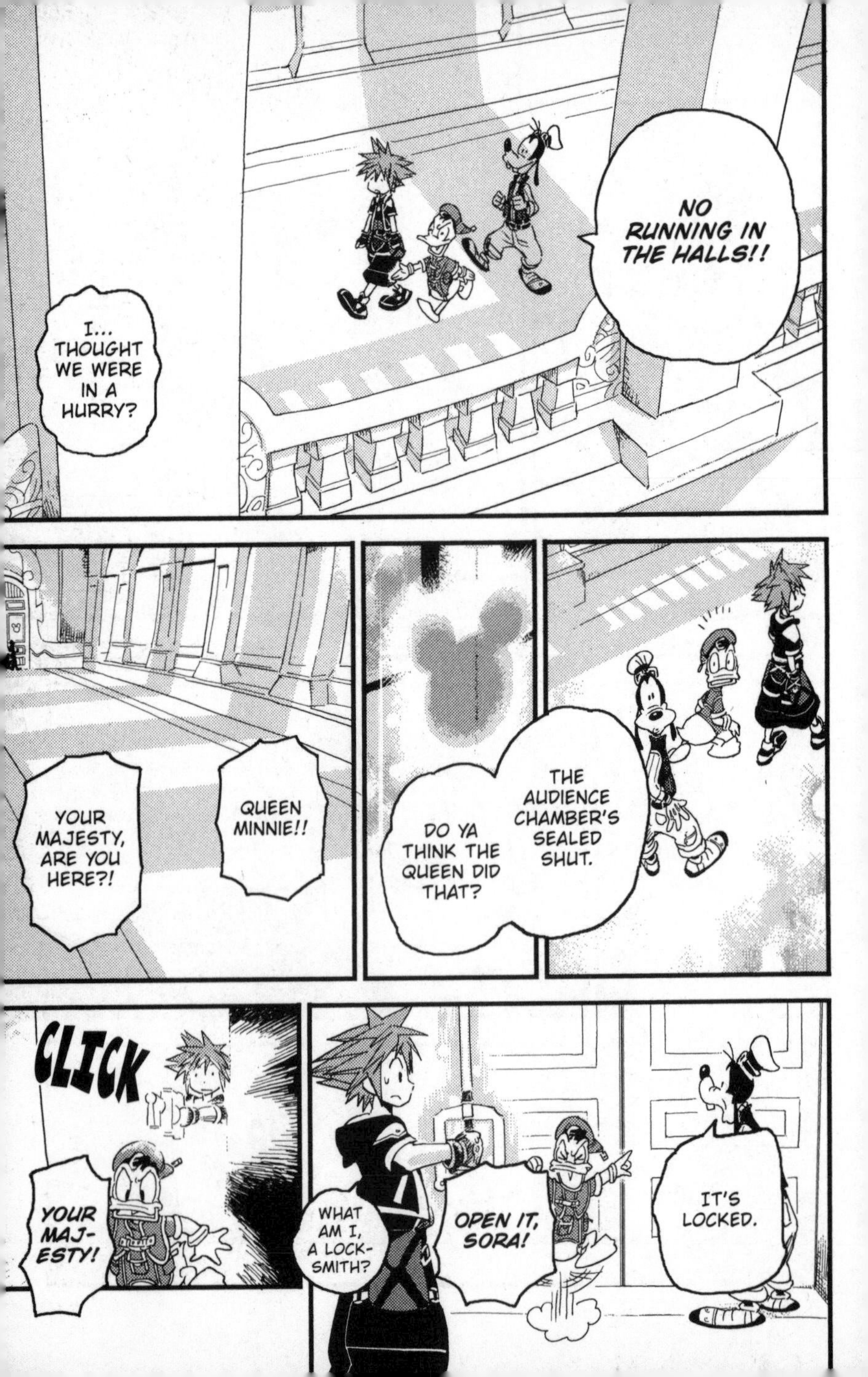
NO RUNNING IN THE HALLS!!
I... THOUGHT WE WERE IN A HURRY?
THE AUDIENCE CHAMBER'S SEALED SHUT.
DO YA THINK THE QUEEN DID THAT?
QUEEN MINNIE!!
YOUR MAJESTY, ARE YOU HERE?!
IT'S LOCKED.
OPEN IT, SORA!
WHAT AM I, A LOCK-SMITH?
CLICK
YOUR MAJ-ESTY!

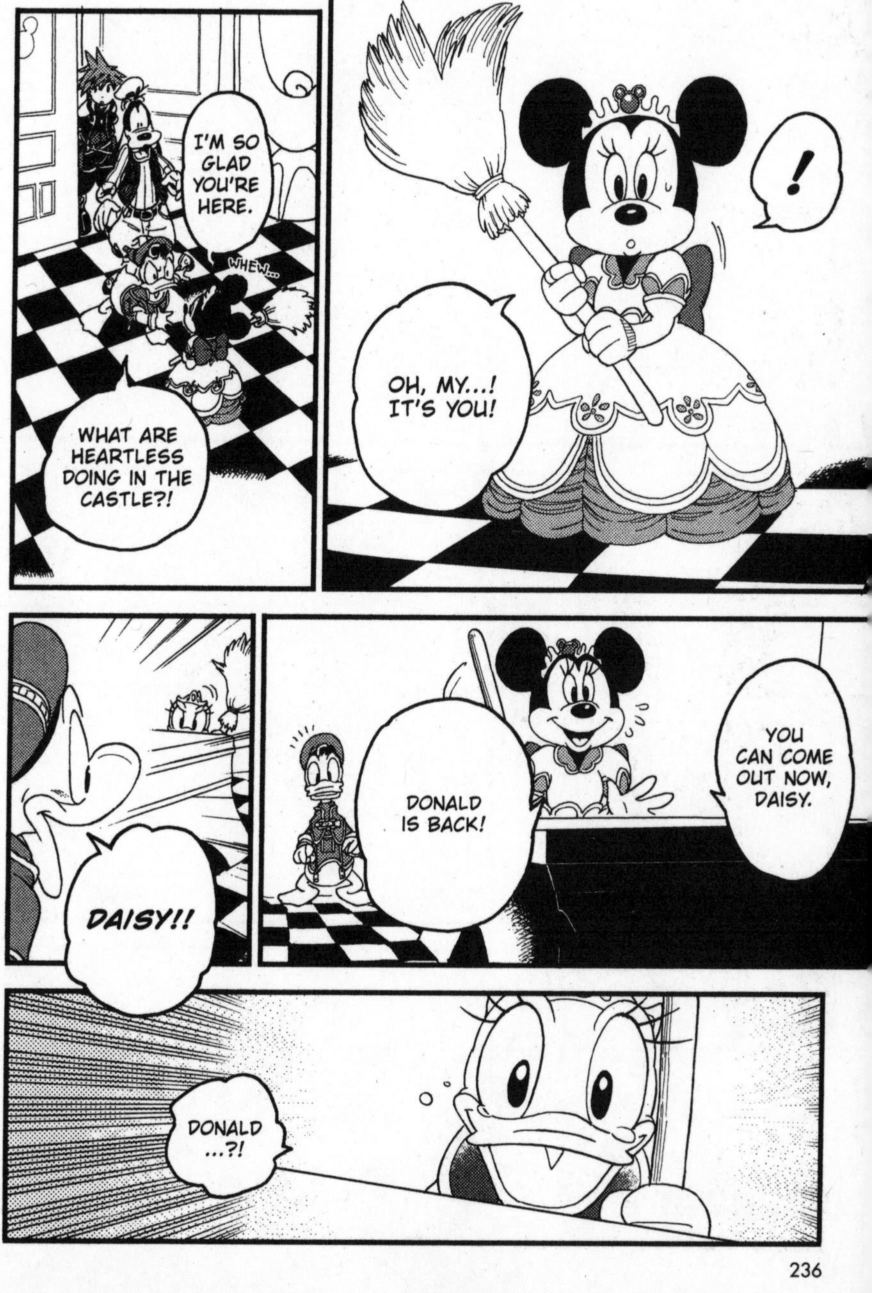
!
OH, MY...! IT'S YOU!
I'M SO GLAD YOU'RE HERE.
WHEW...
WHAT ARE HEARTLESS DOING IN THE CASTLE?!
YOU CAN COME OUT NOW, DAISY.
DONALD IS BACK!
DAISY!!
DONALD ...?!

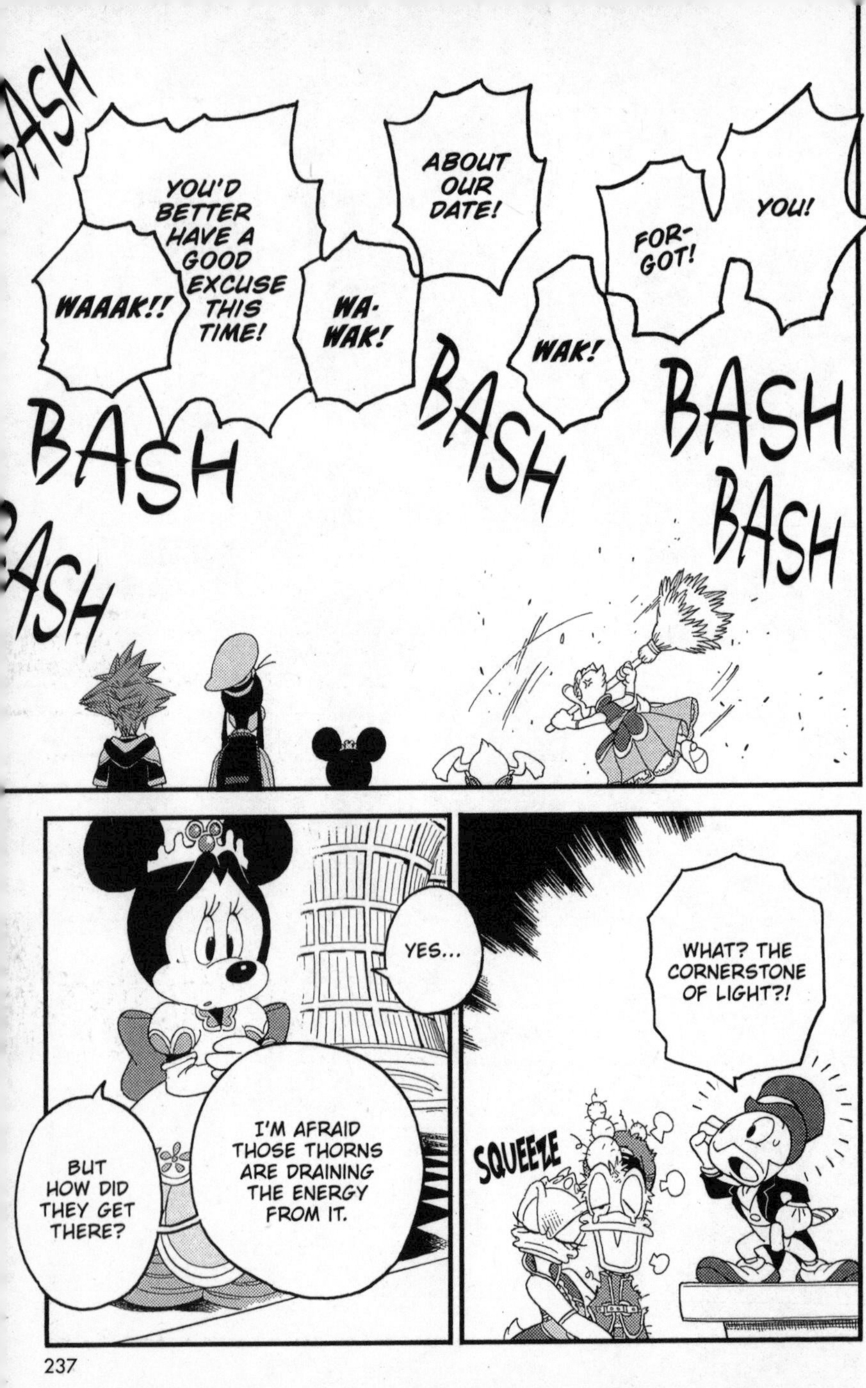
YOU!
FOR-GOT!
BASH
BASH
WAK!
BASH
ABOUT OUR DATE!
WA-WAK!
YOU'D BETTER HAVE A GOOD EXCUSE THIS TIME!
WAAAK!!
BASH
BASH
BASH
WHAT? THE CORNERSTONE OF LIGHT?!
SQUEEZE
YES...
I'M AFRAID THOSE THORNS ARE DRAINING THE ENERGY FROM IT.
BUT HOW DID THEY GET THERE?

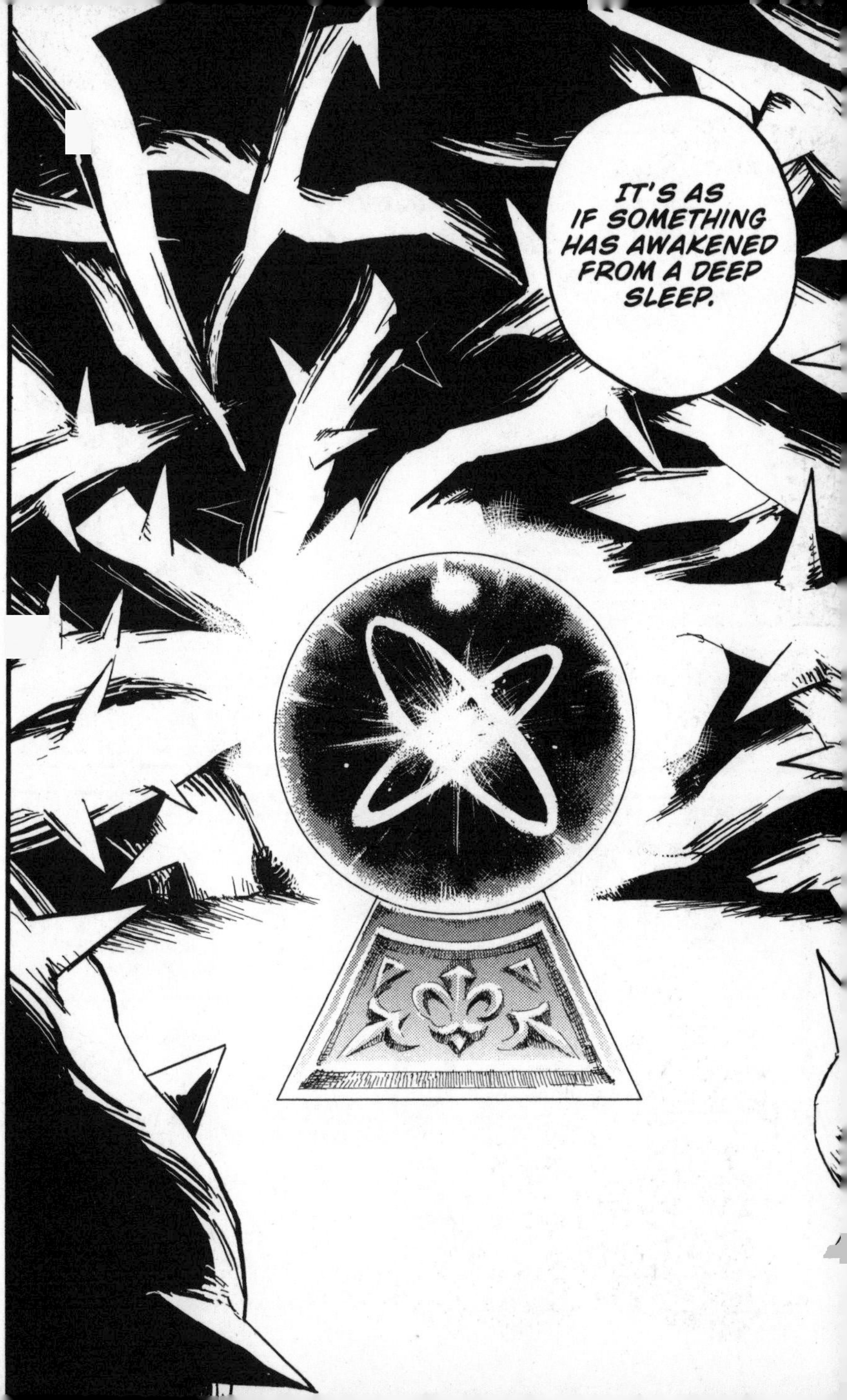
IT'S AS IF SOMETHING HAS AWAKENED FROM A DEEP SLEEP.

Chapter 28: The Castle in Crisis and the Mysterious Door

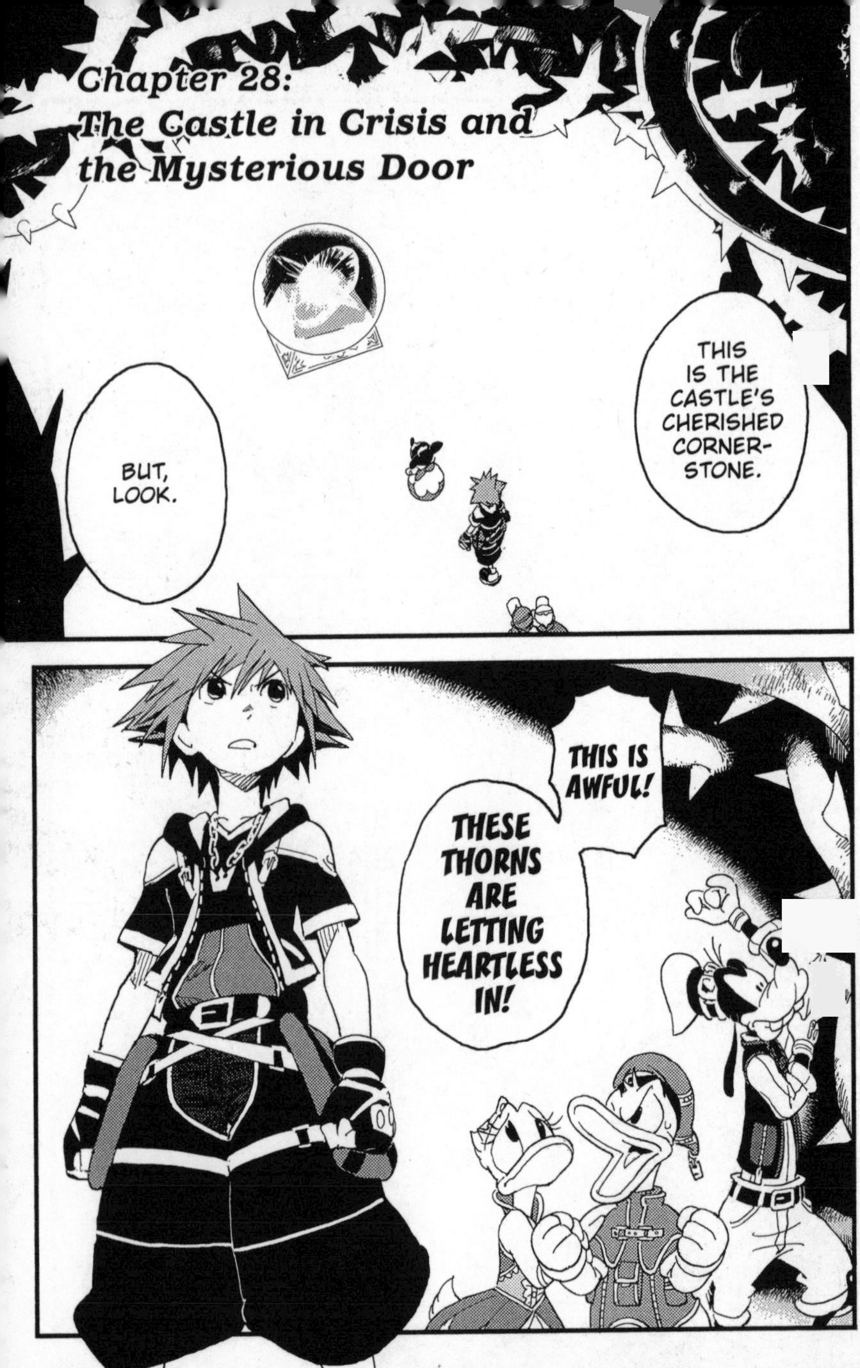
THIS IS THE CASTLE'S CHERISHED CORNER-STONE.
BUT, LOOK.
THIS IS AWFUL!
THESE THORNS ARE LETTING HEARTLESS IN!

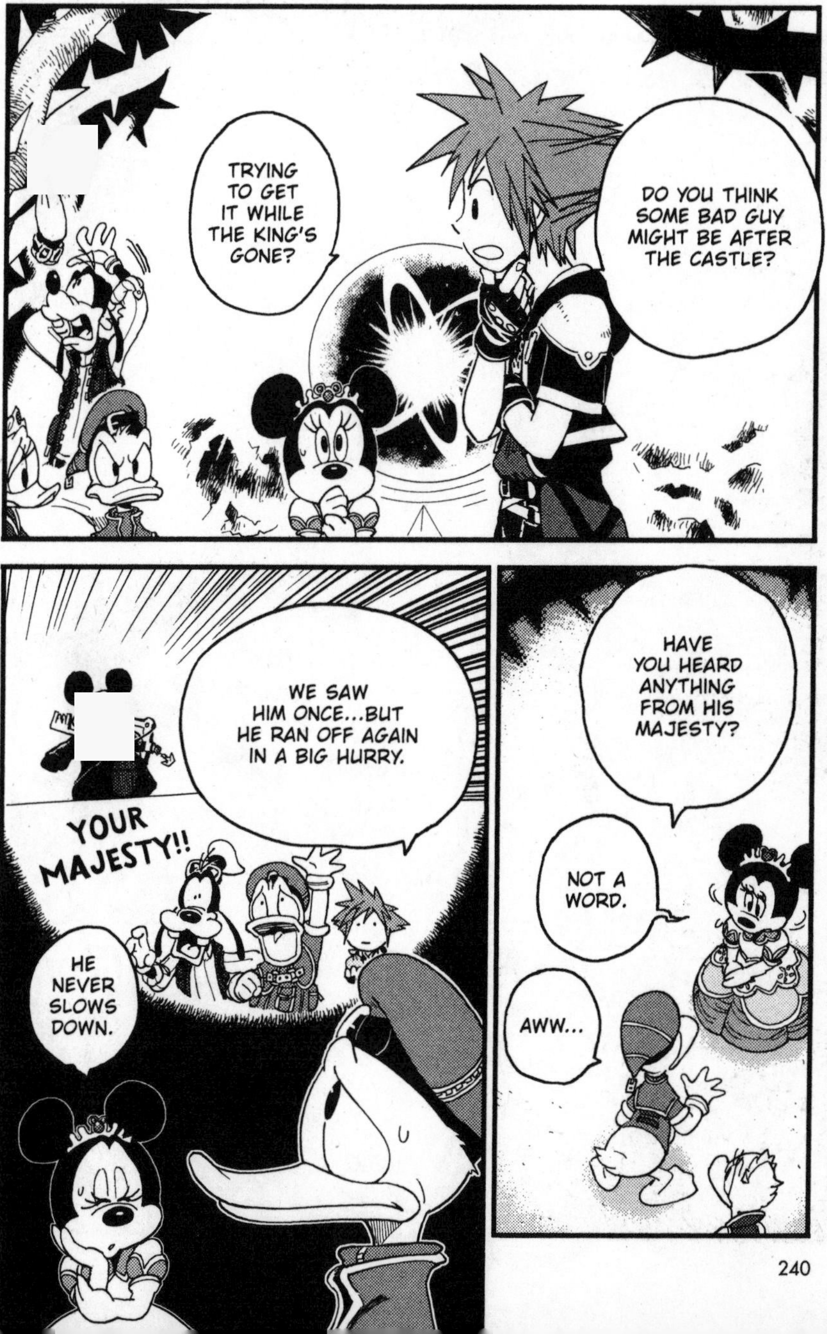
DO YOU THINK SOME BAD GUY MIGHT BE AFTER THE CASTLE?
TRYING TO GET IT WHILE THE KING'S GONE?
HAVE YOU HEARD ANYTHING FROM HIS MAJESTY?
NOT A WORD.
AWW...
WE SAW HIM ONCE...BUT HE RAN OFF AGAIN IN A BIG HURRY.
YOUR MAJESTY!!
HE NEVER SLOWS DOWN.

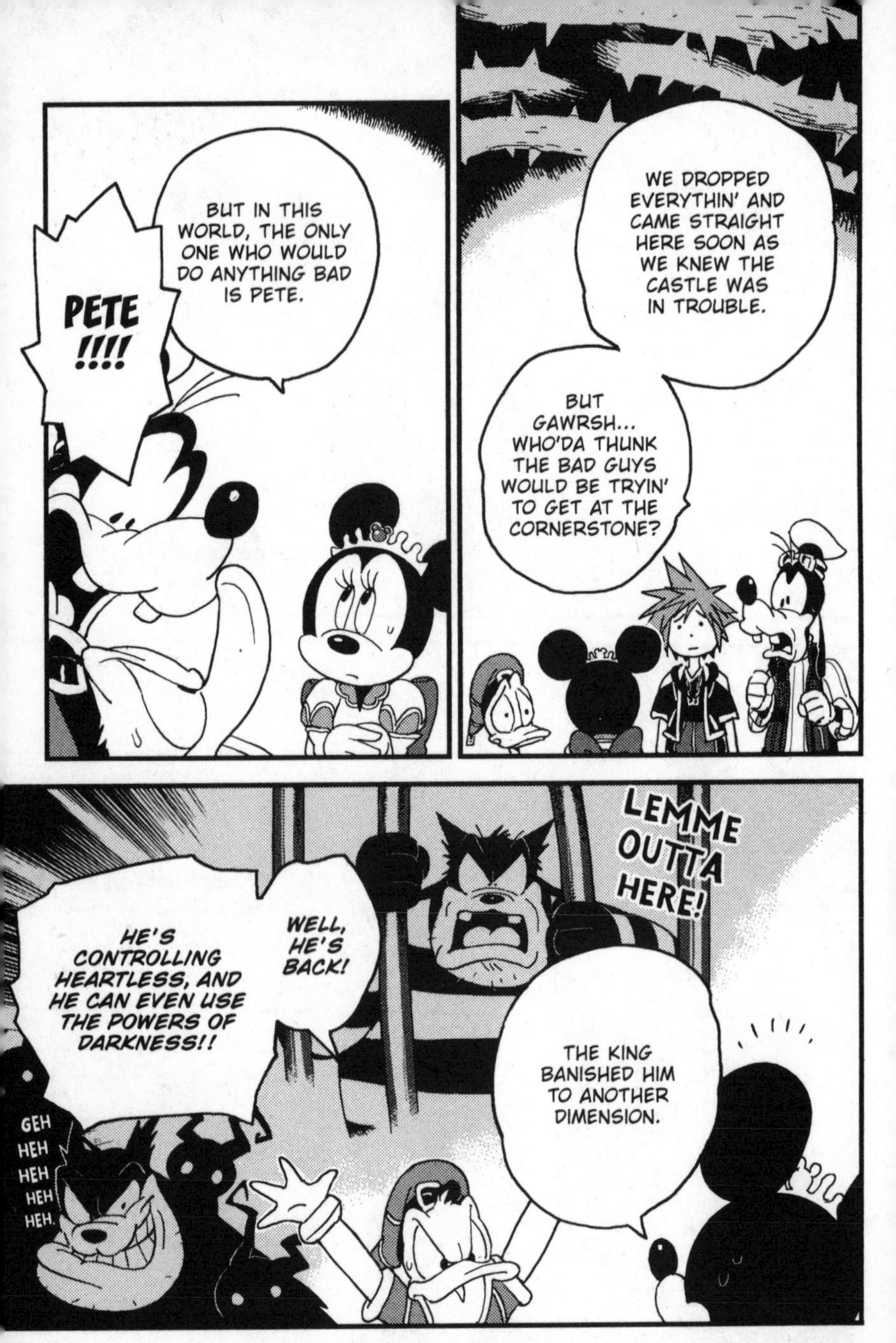
WE DROPPED EVERYTHIN' AND CAME STRAIGHT HERE SOON AS WE KNEW THE CASTLE WAS IN TROUBLE.
BUT GAWRSH... WHO'DA THUNK THE BAD GUYS WOULD BE TRYIN' TO GET AT THE CORNERSTONE?
BUT IN THIS WORLD, THE ONLY ONE WHO WOULD DO ANYTHING BAD IS PETE.
PETE !!!!
LEMME OUTTA HERE!
THE KING BANISHED HIM TO ANOTHER DIMENSION.
WELL, HE'S BACK!
HE'S CONTROLLING HEARTLESS, AND HE CAN EVEN USE THE POWERS OF DARKNESS!!
GEH HEH HEH HEH HEH.

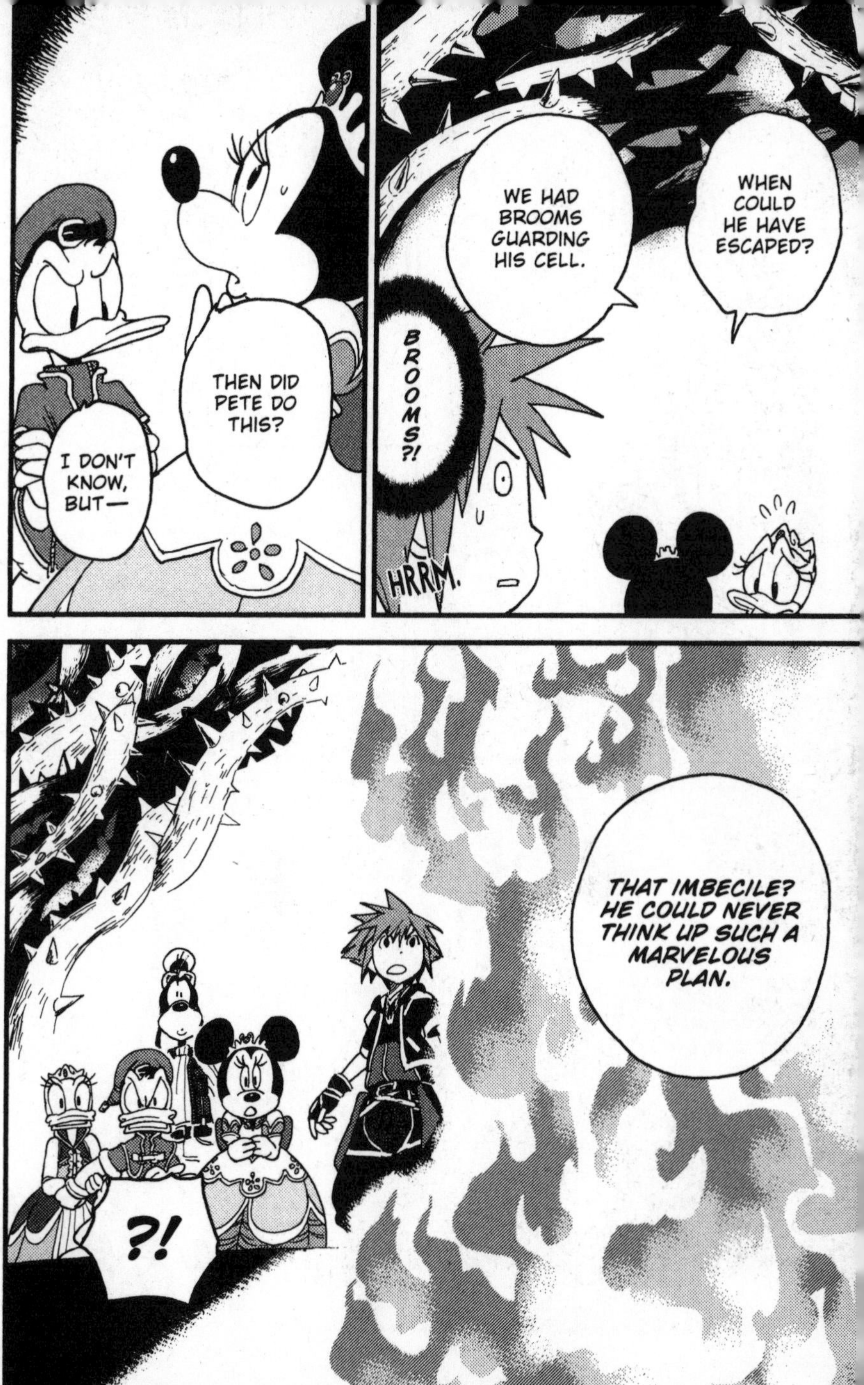
WHEN COULD HE HAVE ESCAPED?
WE HAD BROOMS GUARDING HIS CELL.
BROOMS?!
HRRM.
THEN DID PETE DO THIS?
I DON'T KNOW, BUT—
THAT IMBECILE? HE COULD NEVER THINK UP SUCH A MARVELOUS PLAN.
?!

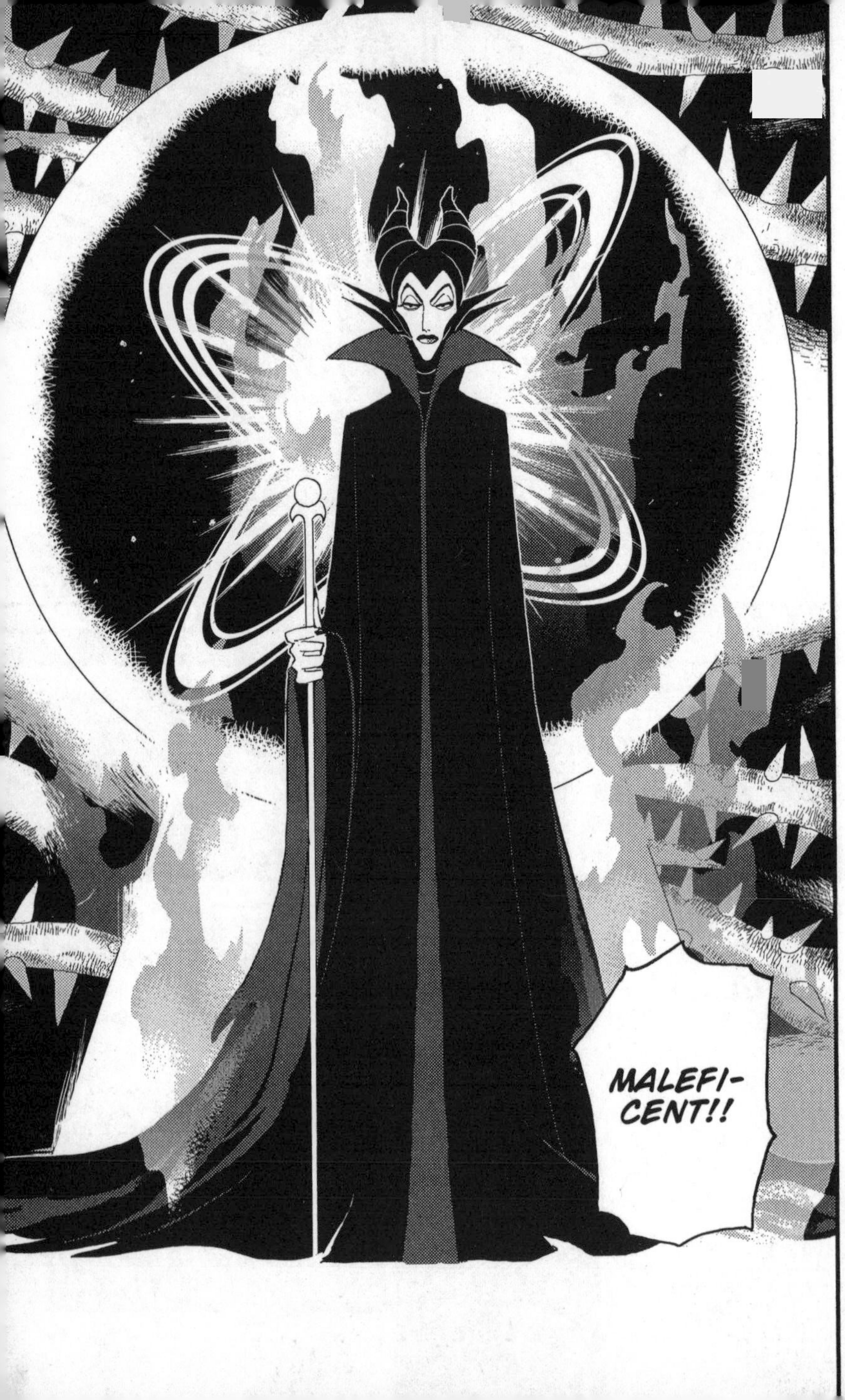
MALEFI-
CENT!!

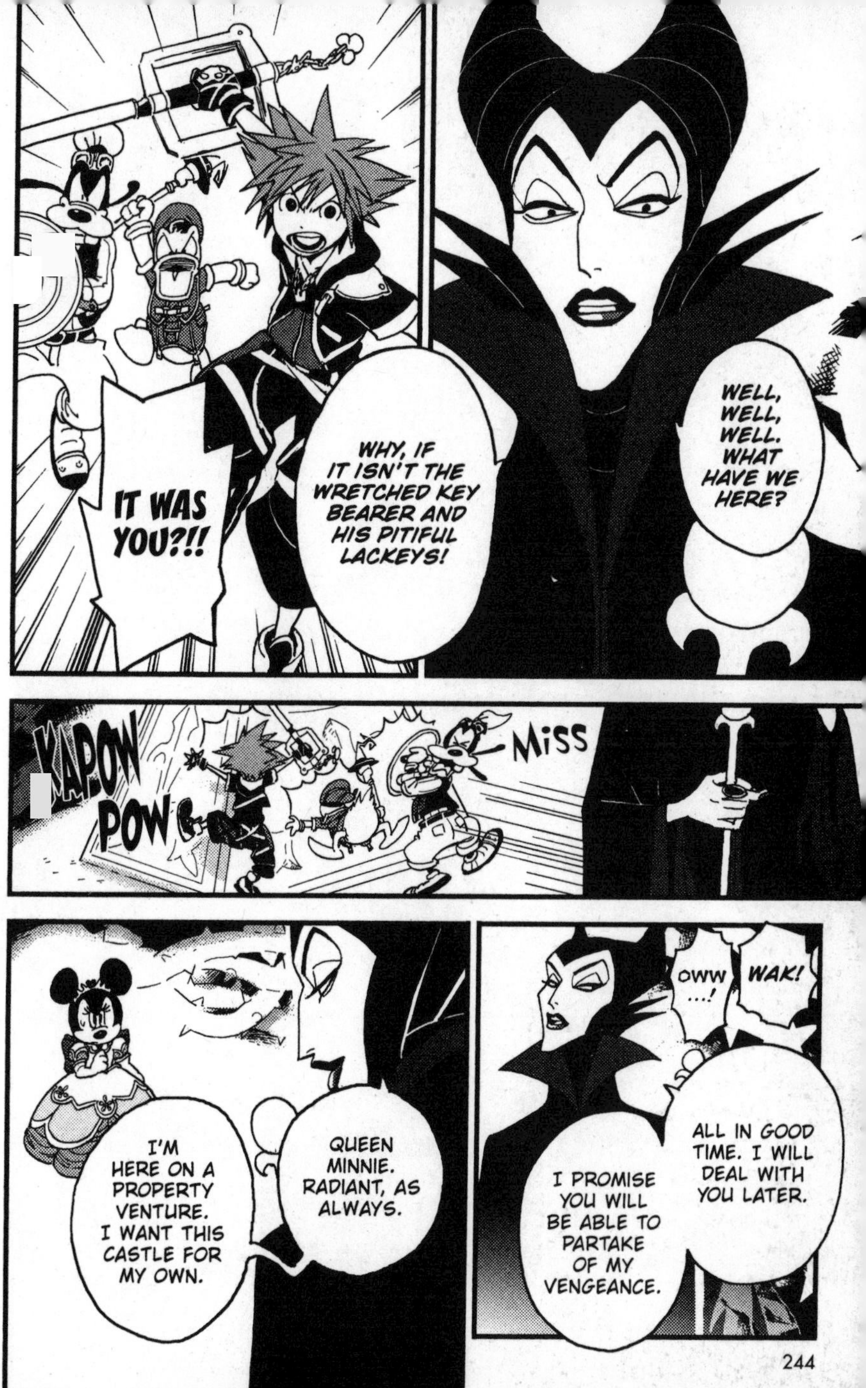
WELL, WELL, WELL. WHAT HAVE WE HERE?
WHY, IF IT ISN'T THE WRETCHED KEY BEARER AND HIS PITIFUL LACKEYS!
IT WAS YOU?!!
MISS
KAPOW
POW
WAK!
OWW ...!
ALL IN GOOD TIME. I WILL DEAL WITH YOU LATER.
I PROMISE YOU WILL BE ABLE TO PARTAKE OF MY VENGEANCE.
QUEEN MINNIE. RADIANT, AS ALWAYS.
I'M HERE ON A PROPERTY VENTURE. I WANT THIS CASTLE FOR MY OWN.

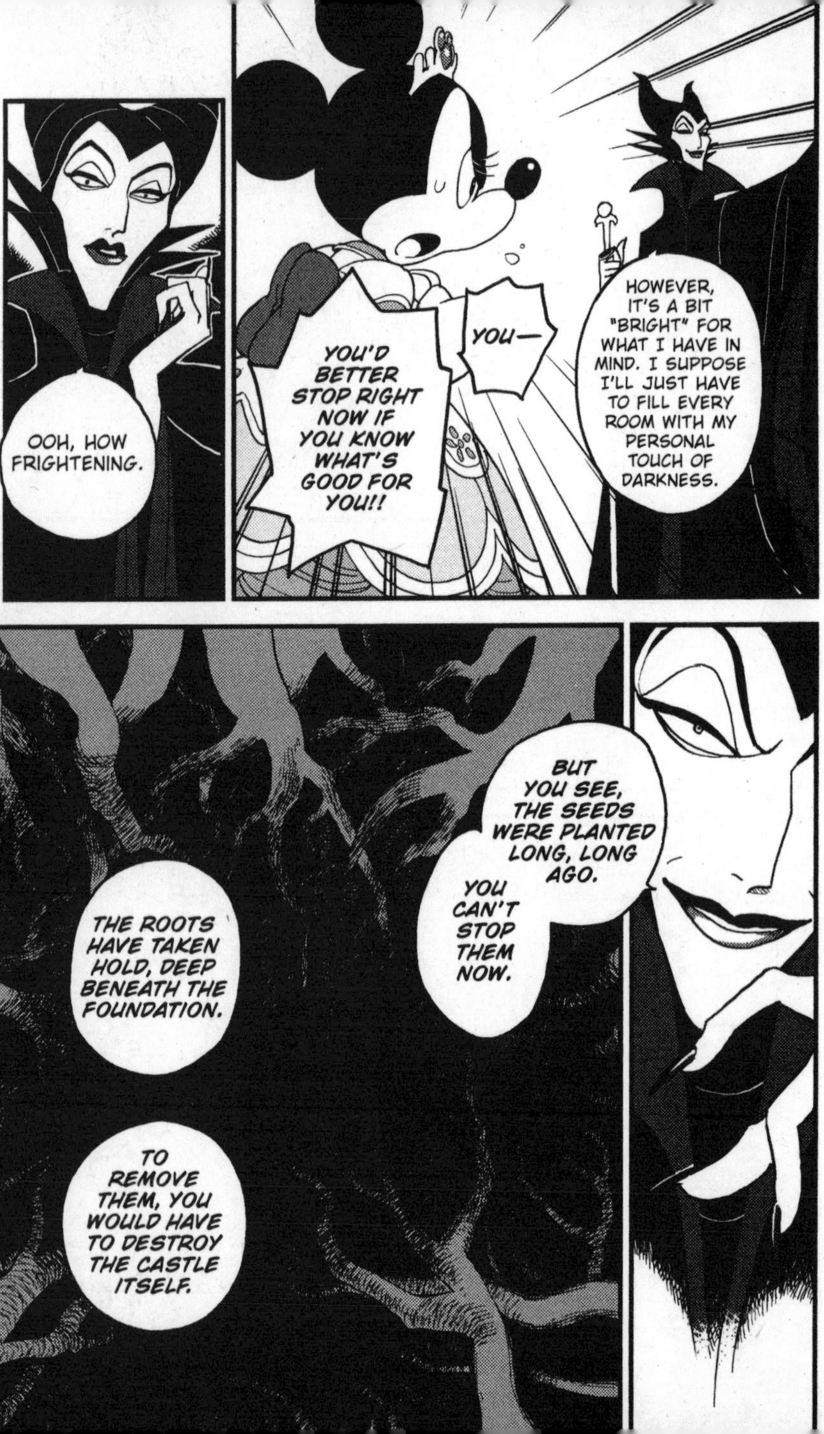
HOWEVER, IT'S A BIT "BRIGHT" FOR WHAT I HAVE IN MIND. I SUPPOSE I'LL JUST HAVE TO FILL EVERY ROOM WITH MY PERSONAL TOUCH OF DARKNESS.
YOU—
YOU'D BETTER STOP RIGHT NOW IF YOU KNOW WHAT'S GOOD FOR YOU!!
OOH, HOW FRIGHTENING.
BUT YOU SEE, THE SEEDS WERE PLANTED LONG, LONG AGO.
YOU CAN'T STOP THEM NOW.
THE ROOTS HAVE TAKEN HOLD, DEEP BENEATH THE FOUNDATION.
TO REMOVE THEM, YOU WOULD HAVE TO DESTROY THE CASTLE ITSELF.

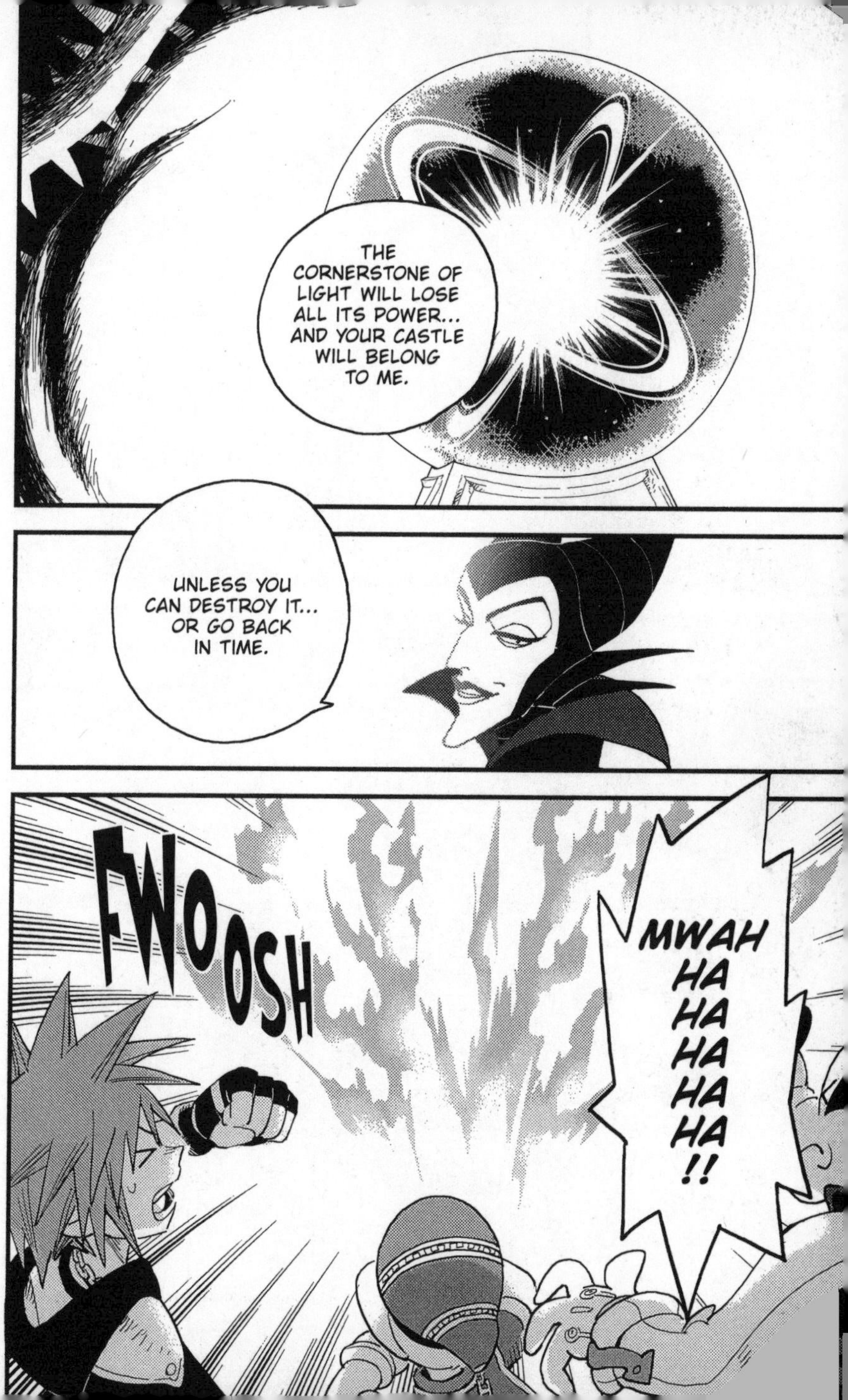
THE CORNERSTONE OF LIGHT WILL LOSE ALL ITS POWER... AND YOUR CASTLE WILL BELONG TO ME.
UNLESS YOU CAN DESTROY IT... OR GO BACK IN TIME.
MWAH HA HA HA HA HA!!
FWOOSH

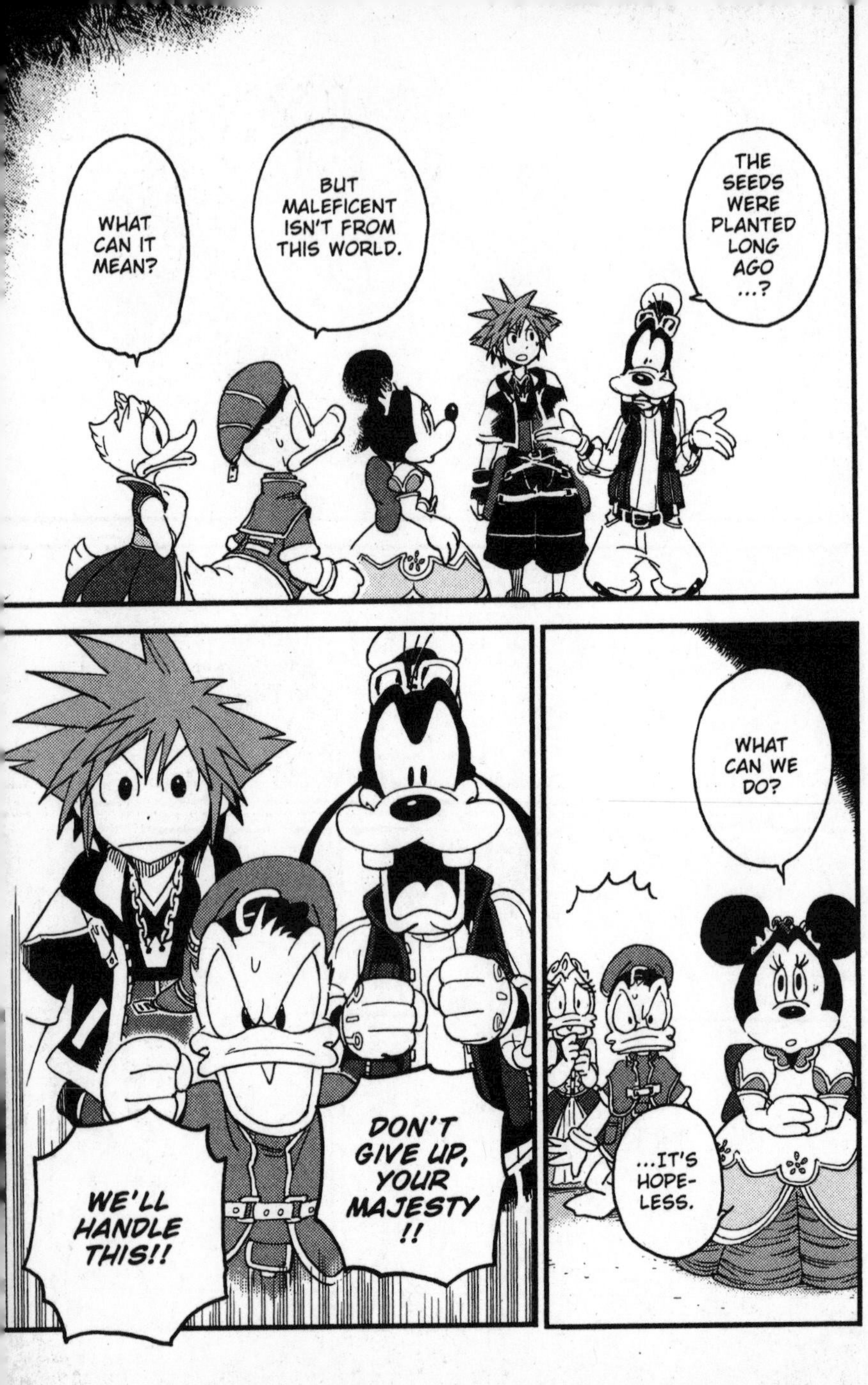
THE SEEDS WERE PLANTED LONG AGO ...?
BUT MALEFICENT ISN'T FROM THIS WORLD.
WHAT CAN IT MEAN?
WHAT CAN WE DO?
...IT'S HOPE-LESS.
DON'T GIVE UP, YOUR MAJESTY !!
WE'LL HANDLE THIS!!

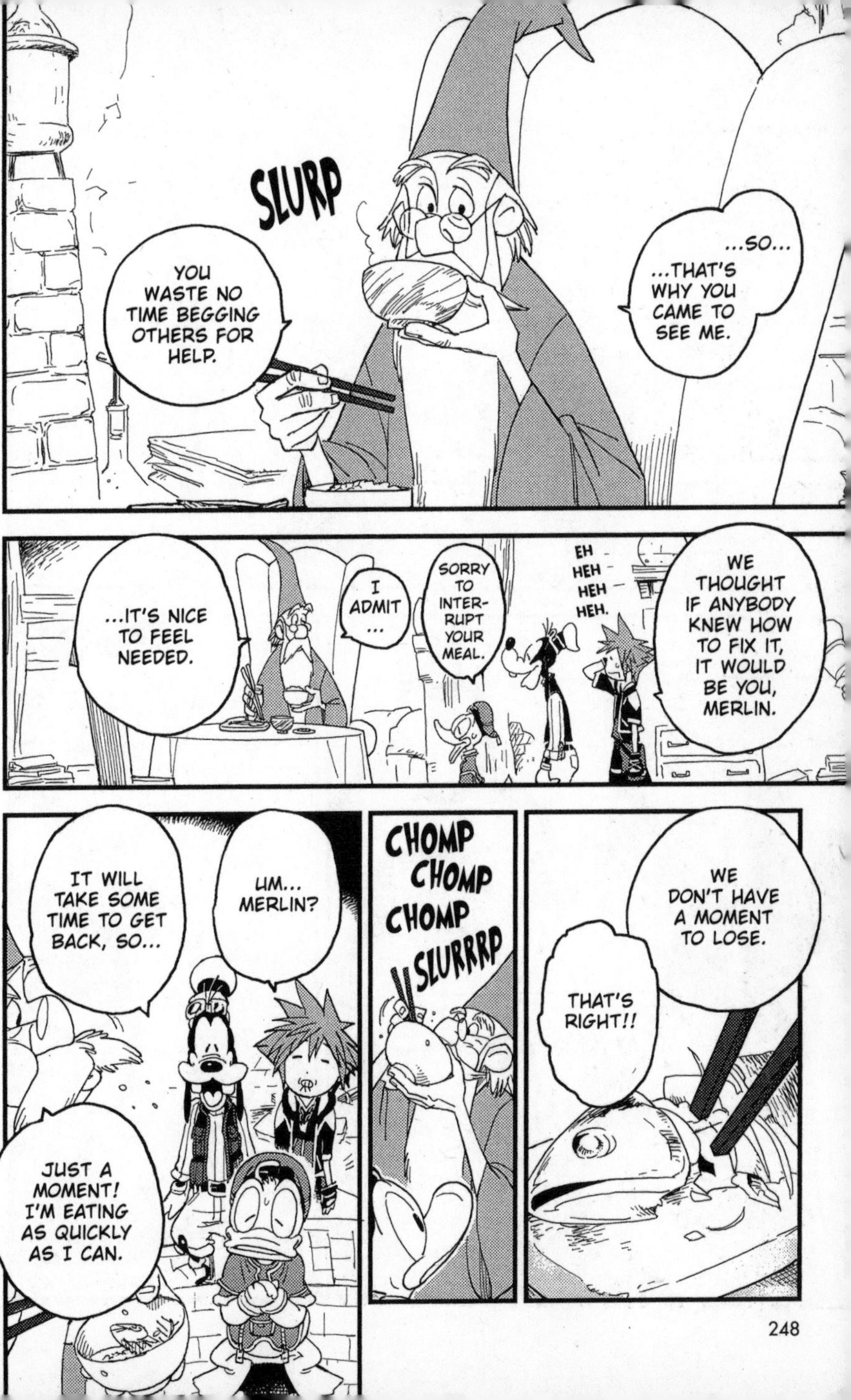
...SO...
...THAT'S WHY YOU CAME TO SEE ME.
SLURP
YOU WASTE NO TIME BEGGING OTHERS FOR HELP.
WE THOUGHT IF ANYBODY KNEW HOW TO FIX IT, IT WOULD BE YOU, MERLIN.
EH HEH HEH HEH.
SORRY TO INTER-RUPT YOUR MEAL.
I ADMIT...
...IT'S NICE TO FEEL NEEDED.
WE DON'T HAVE A MOMENT TO LOSE.
THAT'S RIGHT!!
CHOMP
CHOMP
CHOMP
SLURRRP
UM... MERLIN?
IT WILL TAKE SOME TIME TO GET BACK, SO...
JUST A MOMENT! I'M EATING AS QUICKLY AS I CAN.

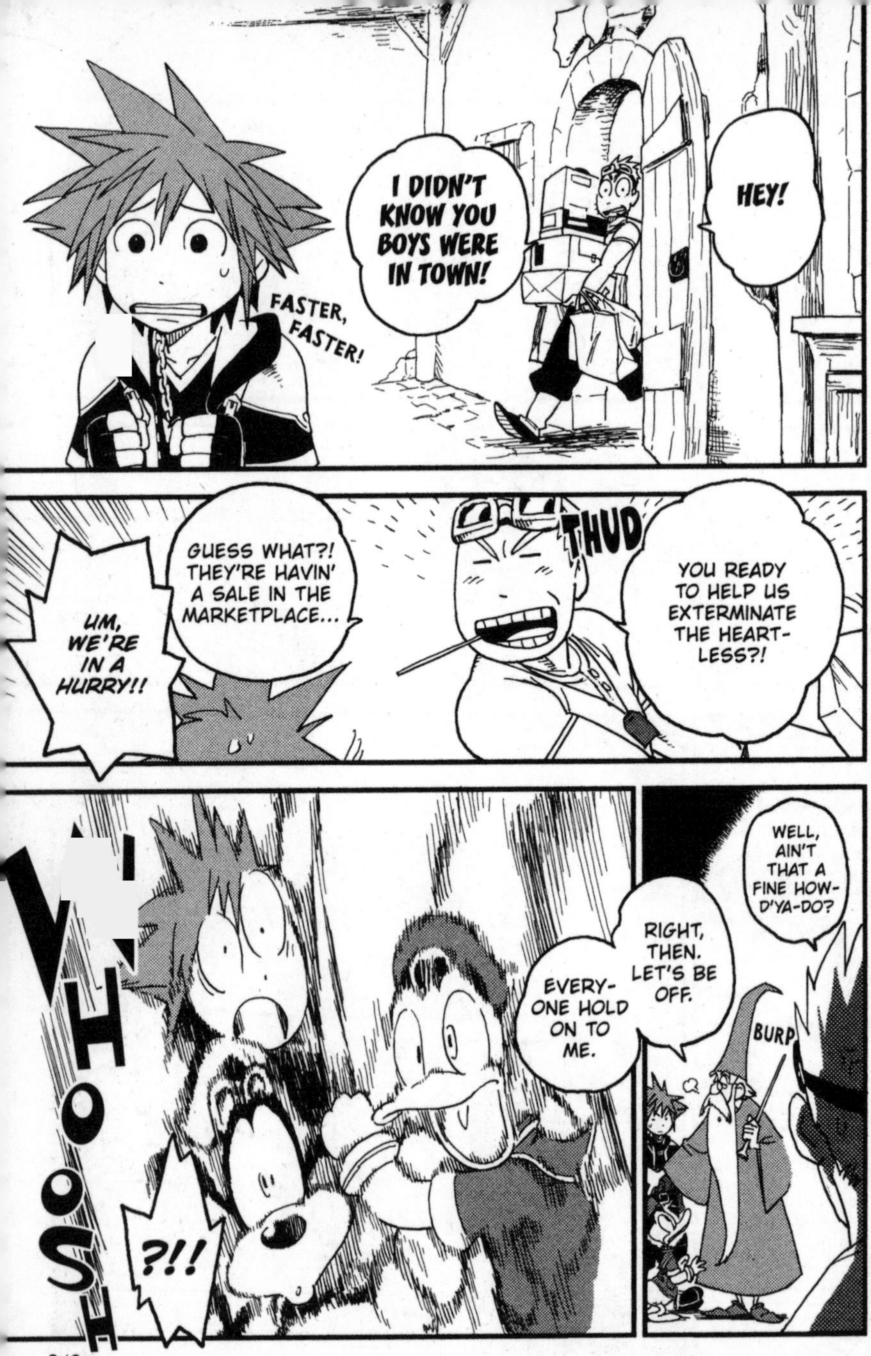
HEY!
I DIDN'T KNOW YOU BOYS WERE IN TOWN!
FASTER, FASTER!
YOU READY TO HELP US EXTERMINATE THE HEART-LESS?!
THUD
GUESS WHAT?! THEY'RE HAVIN' A SALE IN THE MARKETPLACE...
UM, WE'RE IN A HURRY!!
WELL, AIN'T THAT A FINE HOW-D'YA-DO?
RIGHT, THEN. LET'S BE OFF.
EVERY-ONE HOLD ON TO ME.
BURP
?!!
WHOOSH

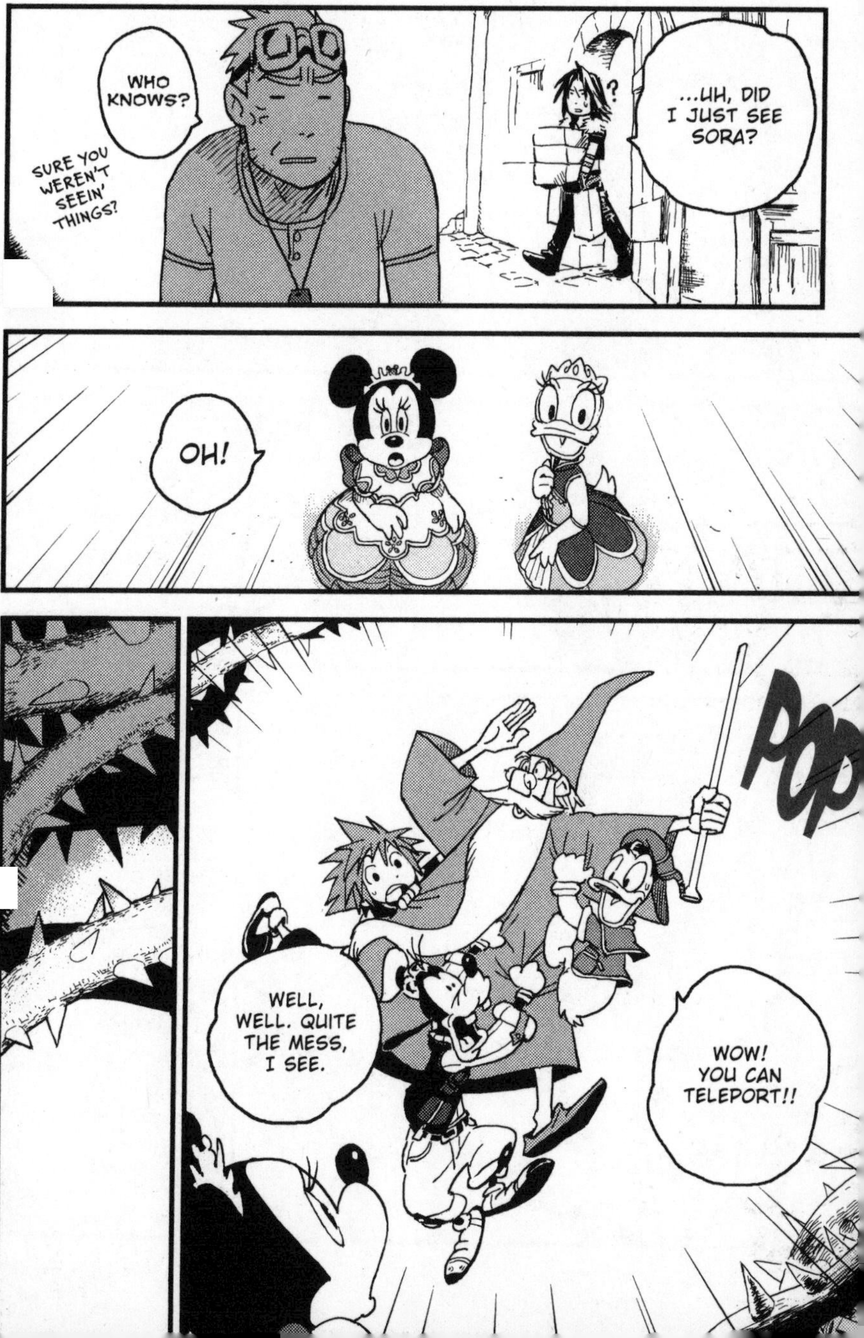
...UH, DID I JUST SEE SORA?
?
WHO KNOWS?
SURE YOU WEREN'T SEEIN' THINGS?
OH!
POP
WELL, WELL. QUITE THE MESS, I SEE.
WOW! YOU CAN TELEPORT!!

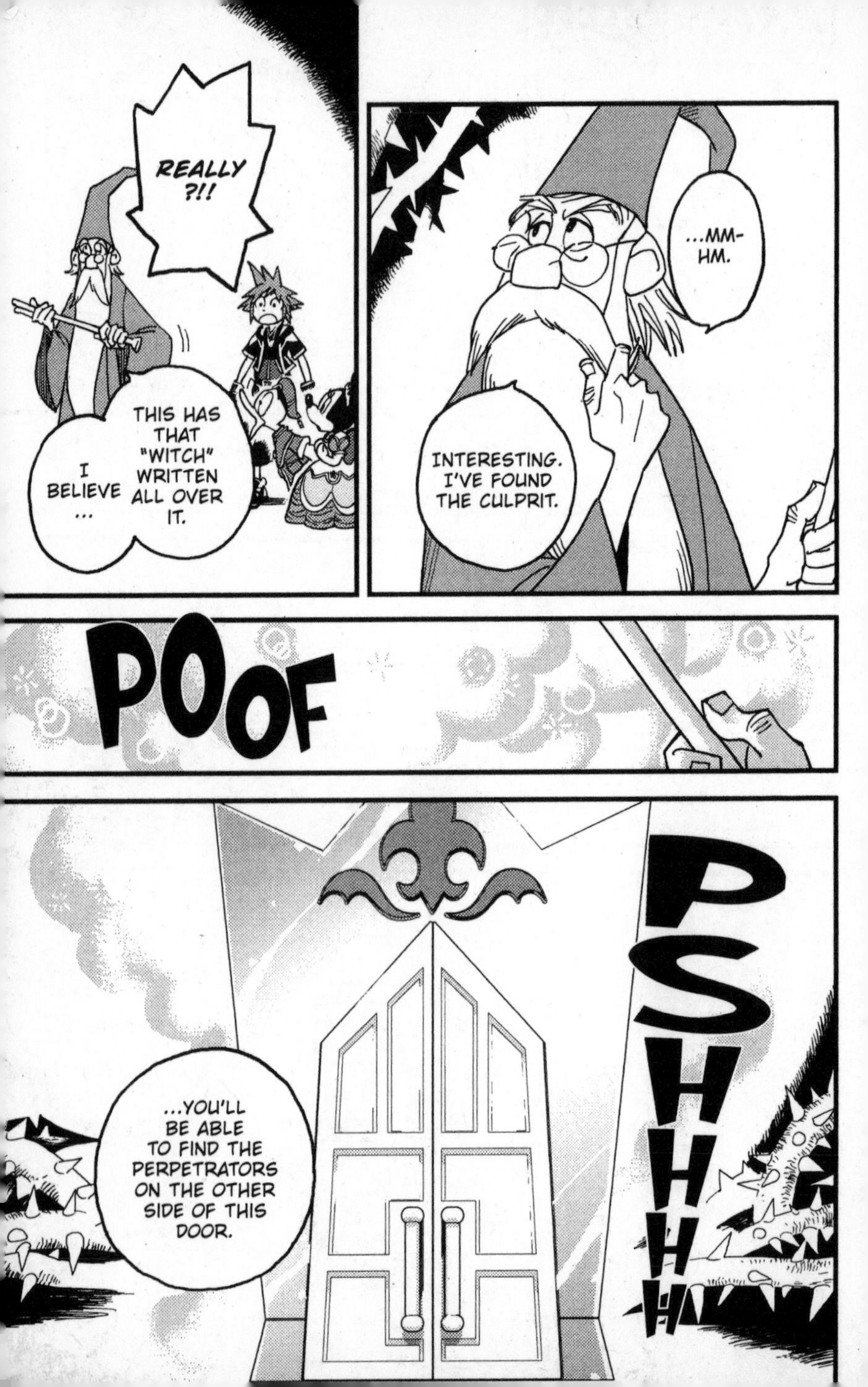
...MM-HM.
INTERESTING. I'VE FOUND THE CULPRIT.
REALLY ?!!
I BELIEVE ... THIS HAS THAT "WITCH" WRITTEN ALL OVER IT.
POOF
PSHHHH
...YOU'LL BE ABLE TO FIND THE PERPETRATORS ON THE OTHER SIDE OF THIS DOOR.

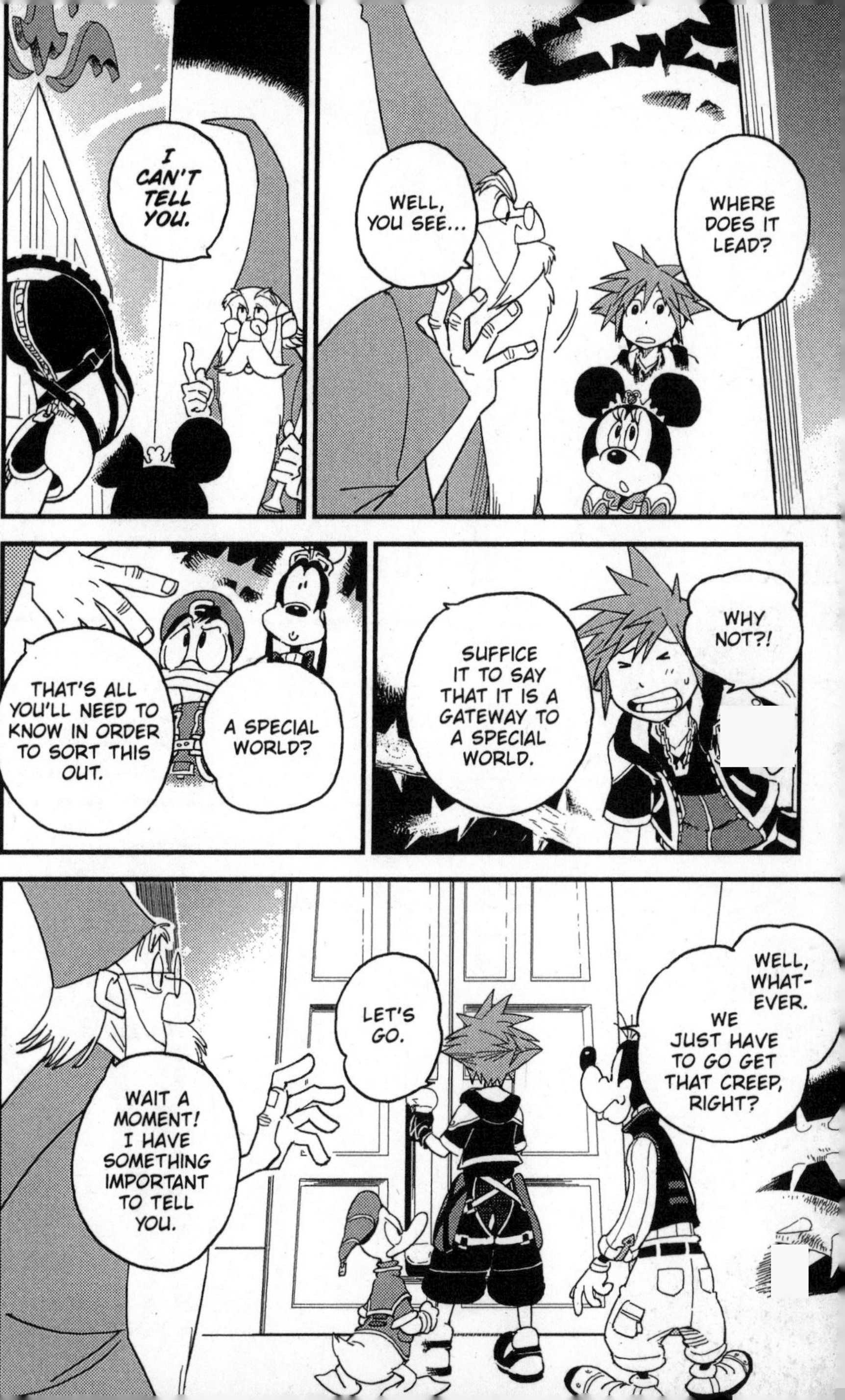
WHERE DOES IT LEAD?
WELL, YOU SEE...
I CAN'T TELL YOU.
WHY NOT?!
SUFFICE IT TO SAY THAT IT IS A GATEWAY TO A SPECIAL WORLD.
A SPECIAL WORLD?
THAT'S ALL YOU'LL NEED TO KNOW IN ORDER TO SORT THIS OUT.
WELL, WHAT-EVER.
WE JUST HAVE TO GO GET THAT CREEP, RIGHT?
LET'S GO.
WAIT A MOMENT! I HAVE SOMETHING IMPORTANT TO TELL YOU.

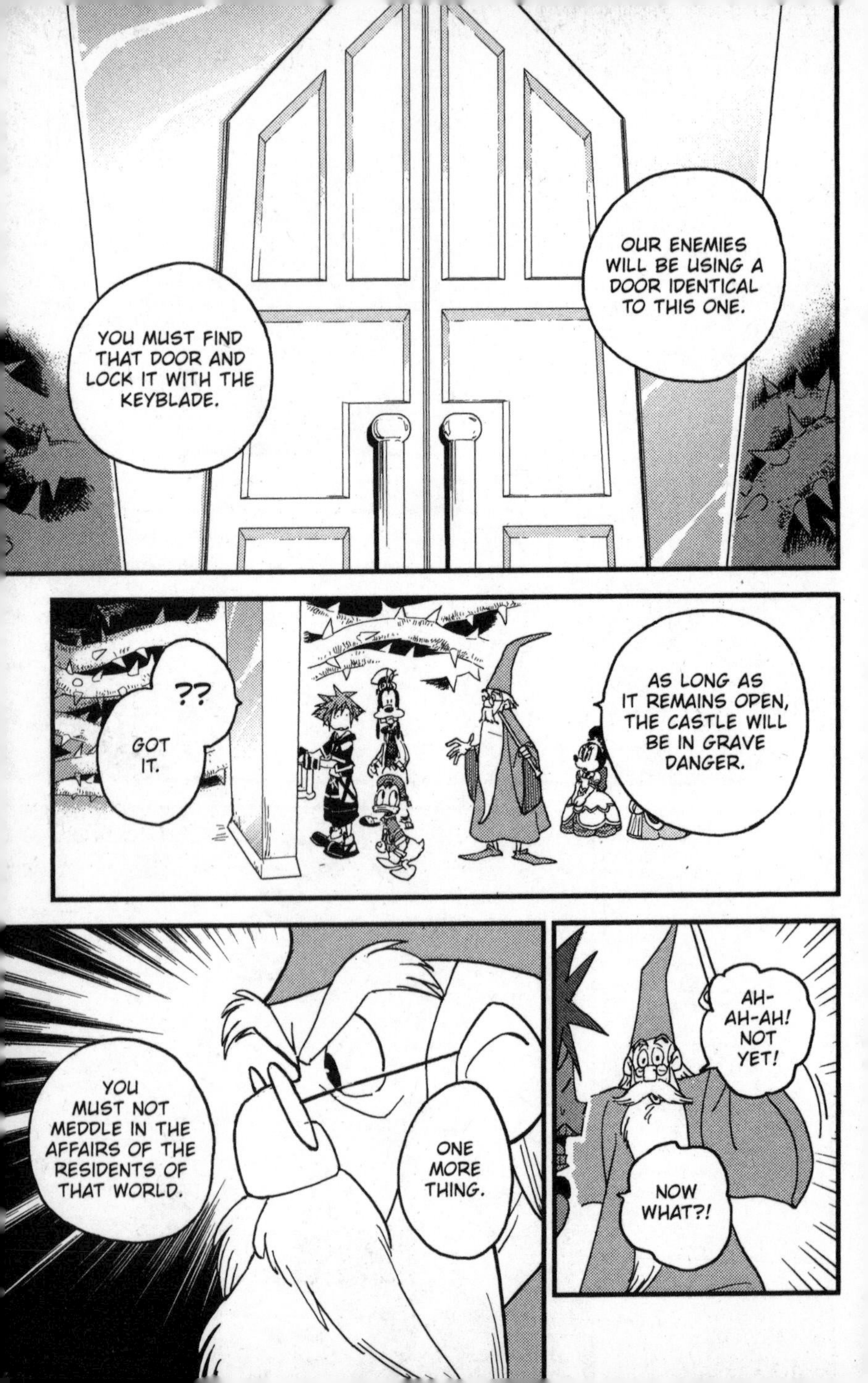
OUR ENEMIES WILL BE USING A DOOR IDENTICAL TO THIS ONE.
YOU MUST FIND THAT DOOR AND LOCK IT WITH THE KEYBLADE.
AS LONG AS IT REMAINS OPEN, THE CASTLE WILL BE IN GRAVE DANGER.
??
GOT IT.
AH-AH-AH! NOT YET!
NOW WHAT?!
ONE MORE THING.
YOU MUST NOT MEDDLE IN THE AFFAIRS OF THE RESIDENTS OF THAT WORLD.

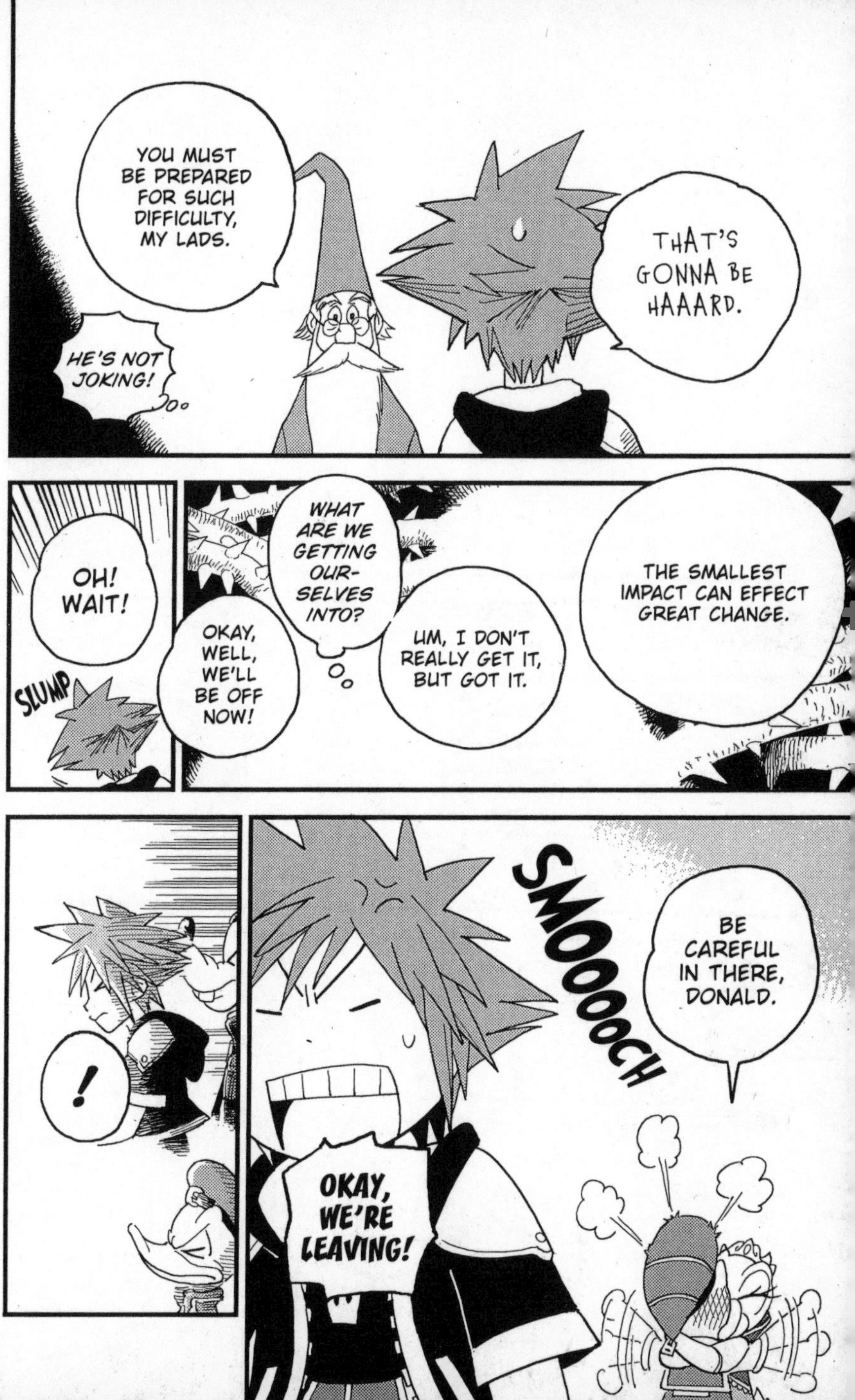
YOU MUST BE PREPARED FOR SUCH DIFFICULTY, MY LADS.
THAT'S GONNA BE HAAARD.
HE'S NOT JOKING!
THE SMALLEST IMPACT CAN EFFECT GREAT CHANGE.
UM, I DON'T REALLY GET IT, BUT GOT IT.
WHAT ARE WE GETTING OUR-SELVES INTO?
OKAY, WELL, WE'LL BE OFF NOW!
OH! WAIT!
SLUMP
BE CAREFUL IN THERE, DONALD.
SMOOOOOCH
OKAY, WE'RE LEAVING!
!

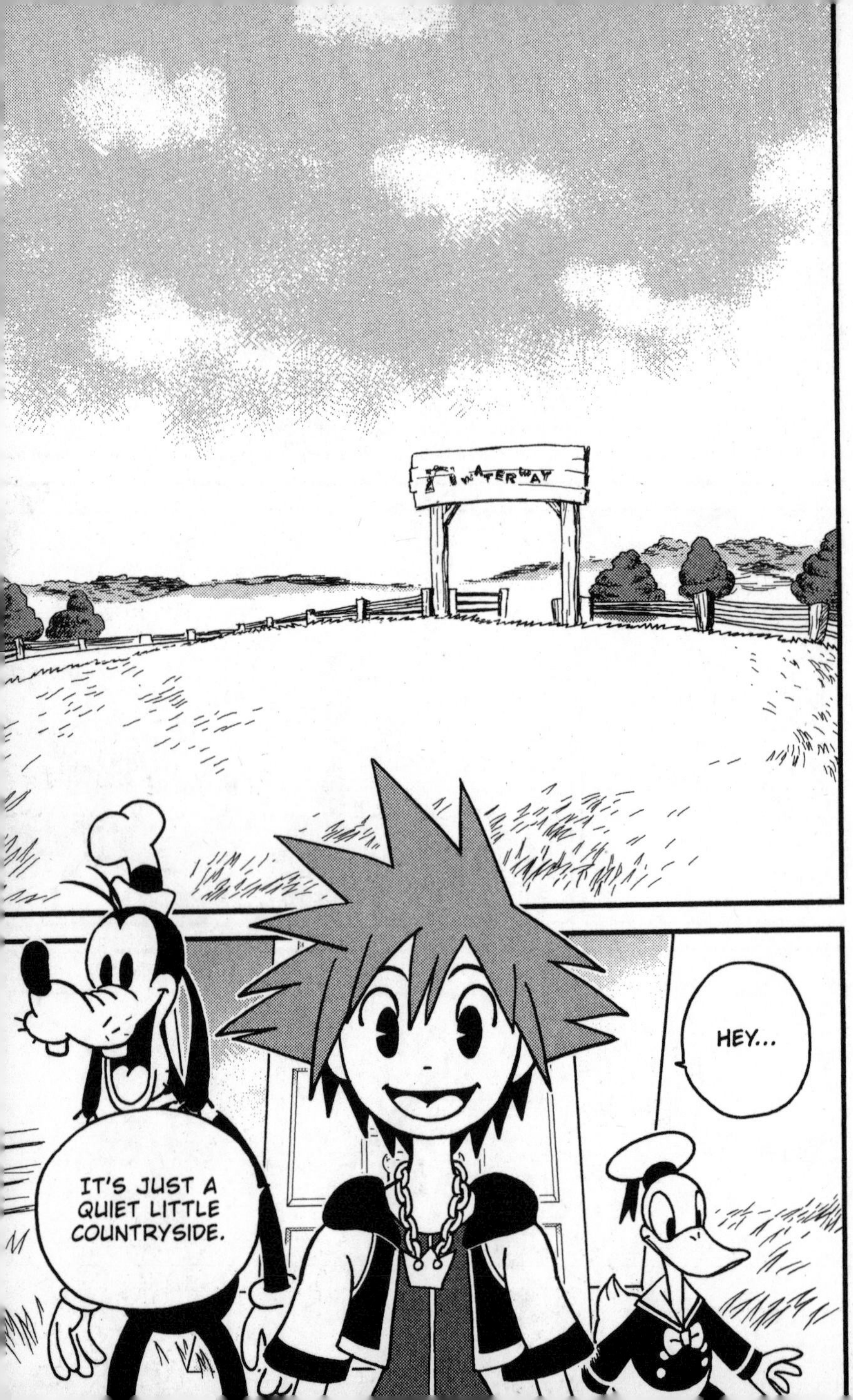
WATERWAY
HEY...
IT'S JUST A QUIET LITTLE COUNTRYSIDE.

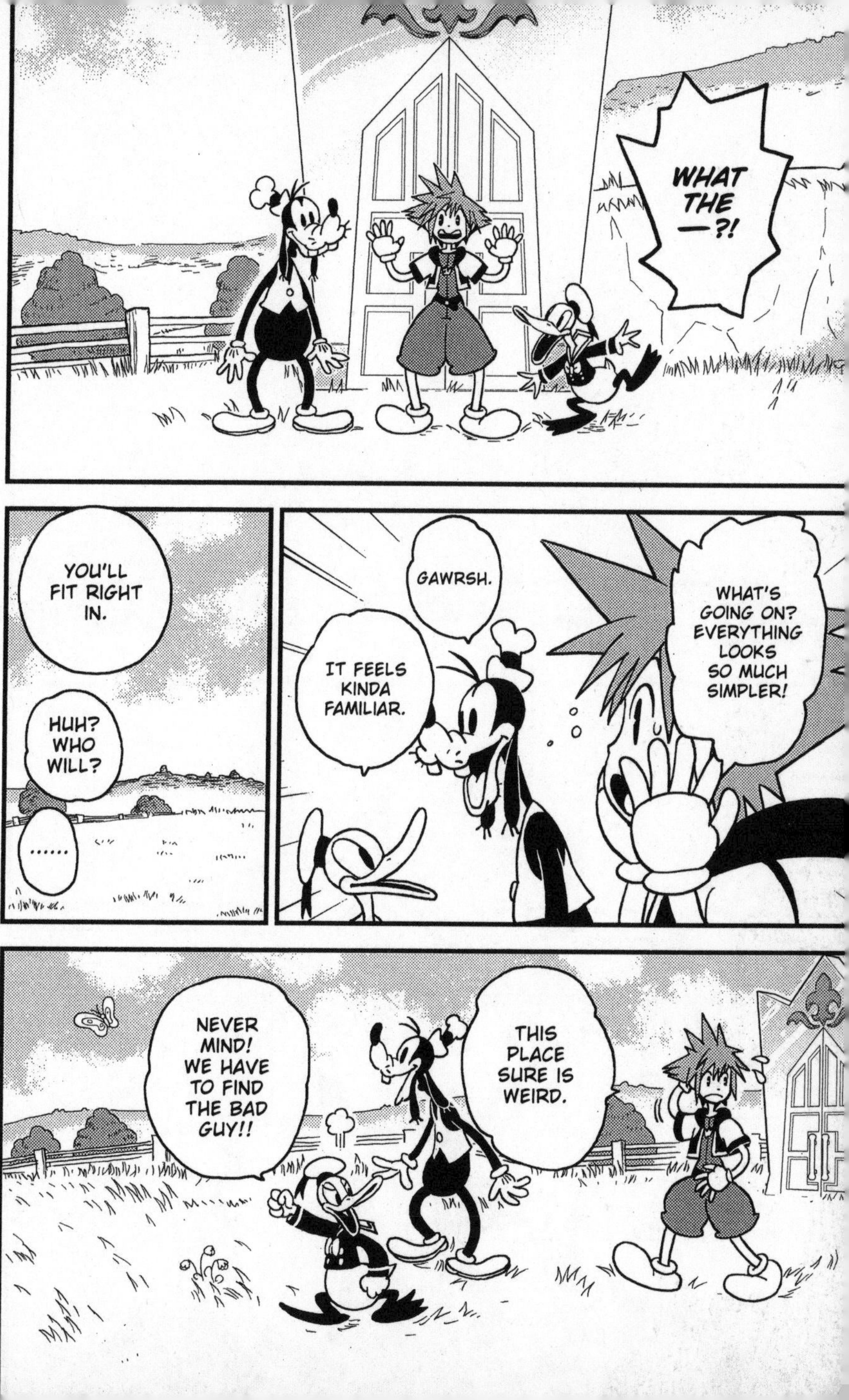
WHAT THE—?!
WHAT'S GOING ON? EVERYTHING LOOKS SO MUCH SIMPLER!
GAWRSH.
IT FEELS KINDA FAMILIAR.
YOU'LL FIT RIGHT IN.
HUH? WHO WILL?
......
THIS PLACE SURE IS WEIRD.
NEVER MIND! WE HAVE TO FIND THE BAD GUY!!

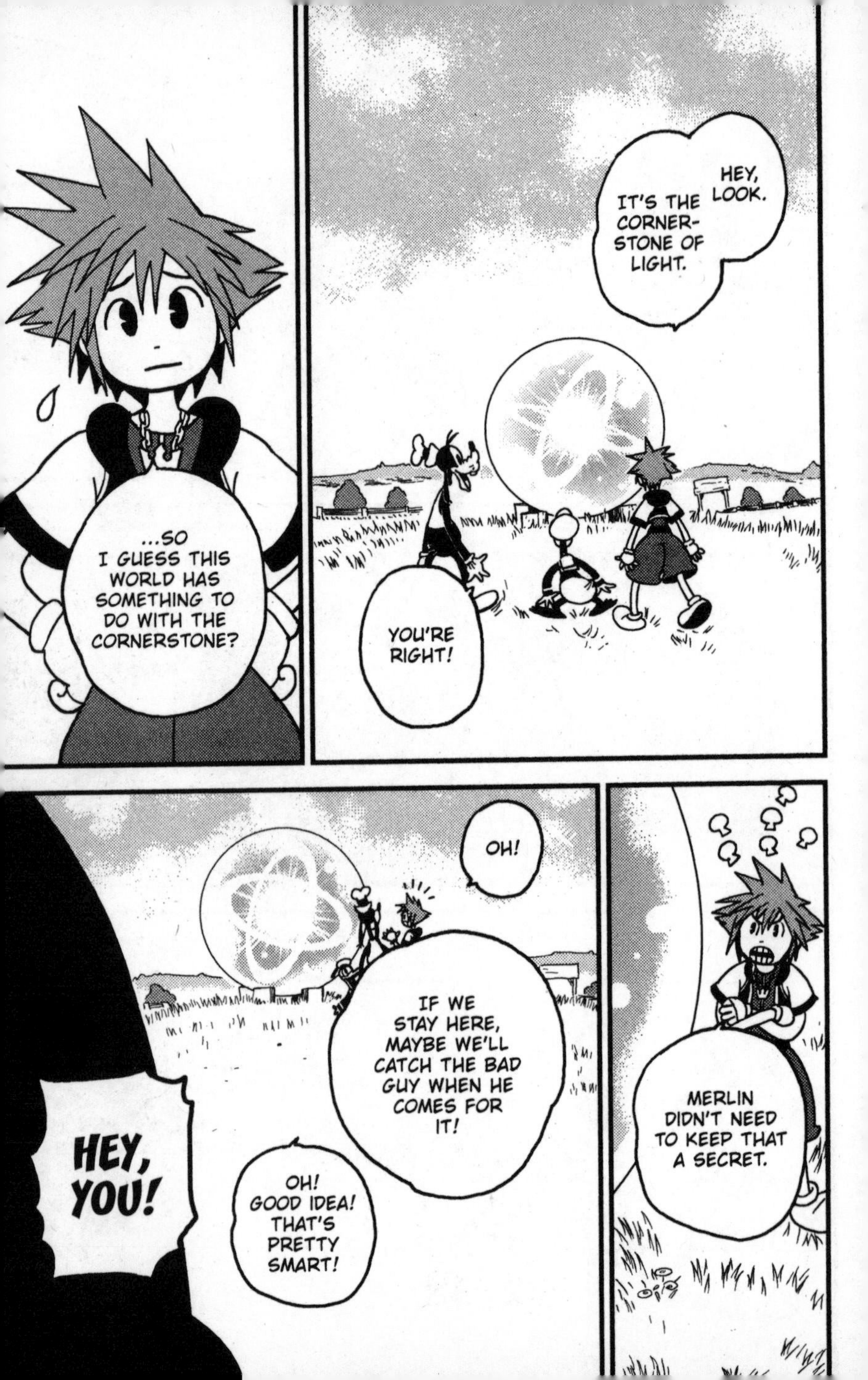
HEY, LOOK. IT'S THE CORNER-STONE OF LIGHT.
YOU'RE RIGHT!
...SO I GUESS THIS WORLD HAS SOMETHING TO DO WITH THE CORNERSTONE?
MERLIN DIDN'T NEED TO KEEP THAT A SECRET.
OH!
IF WE STAY HERE, MAYBE WE'LL CATCH THE BAD GUY WHEN HE COMES FOR IT!
OH! GOOD IDEA! THAT'S PRETTY SMART!
HEY, YOU!

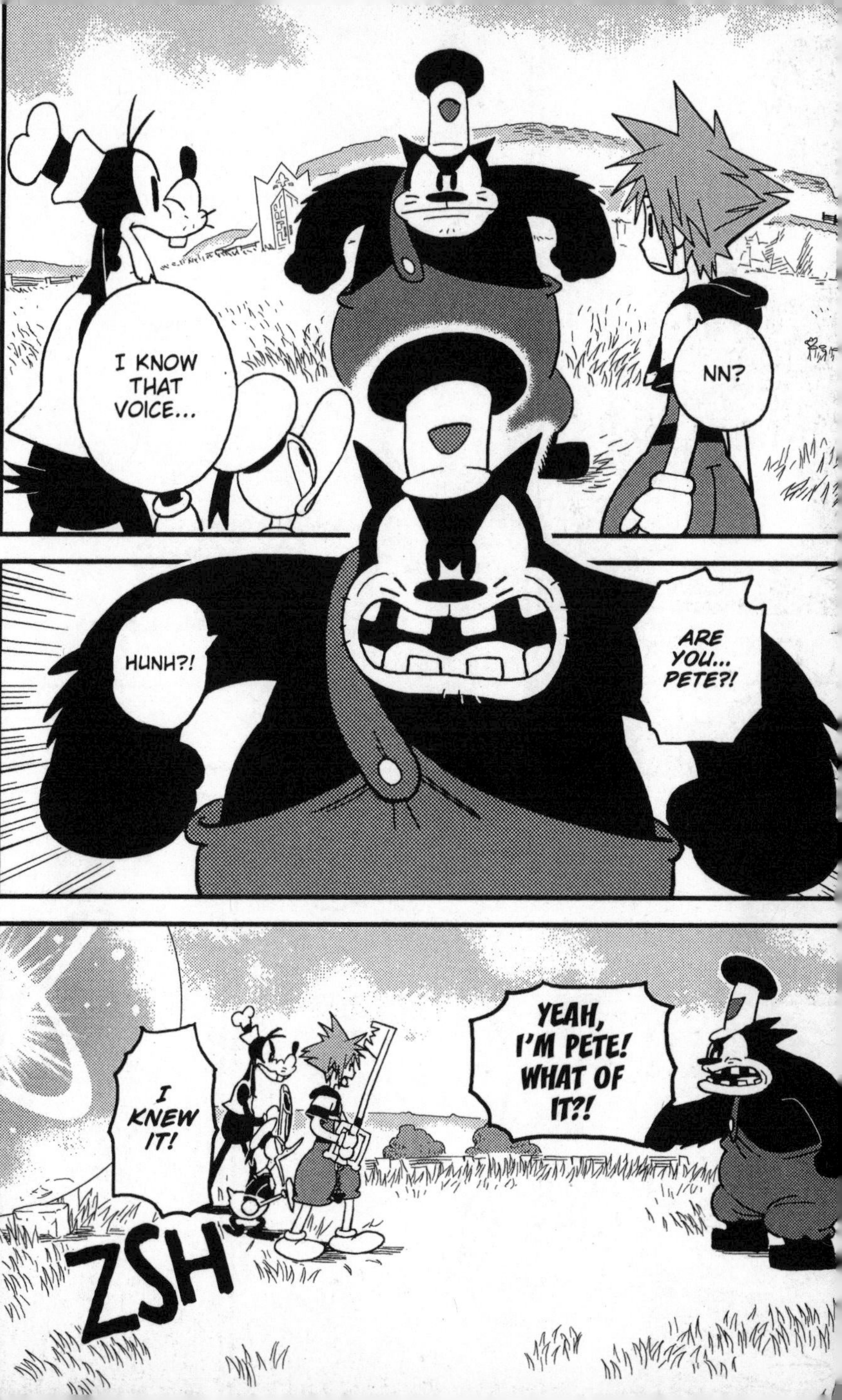
NN?
I KNOW THAT VOICE...
ARE YOU... PETE?!
HUNH?!
YEAH, I'M PETE! WHAT OF IT?!
I KNEW IT!
ZSH

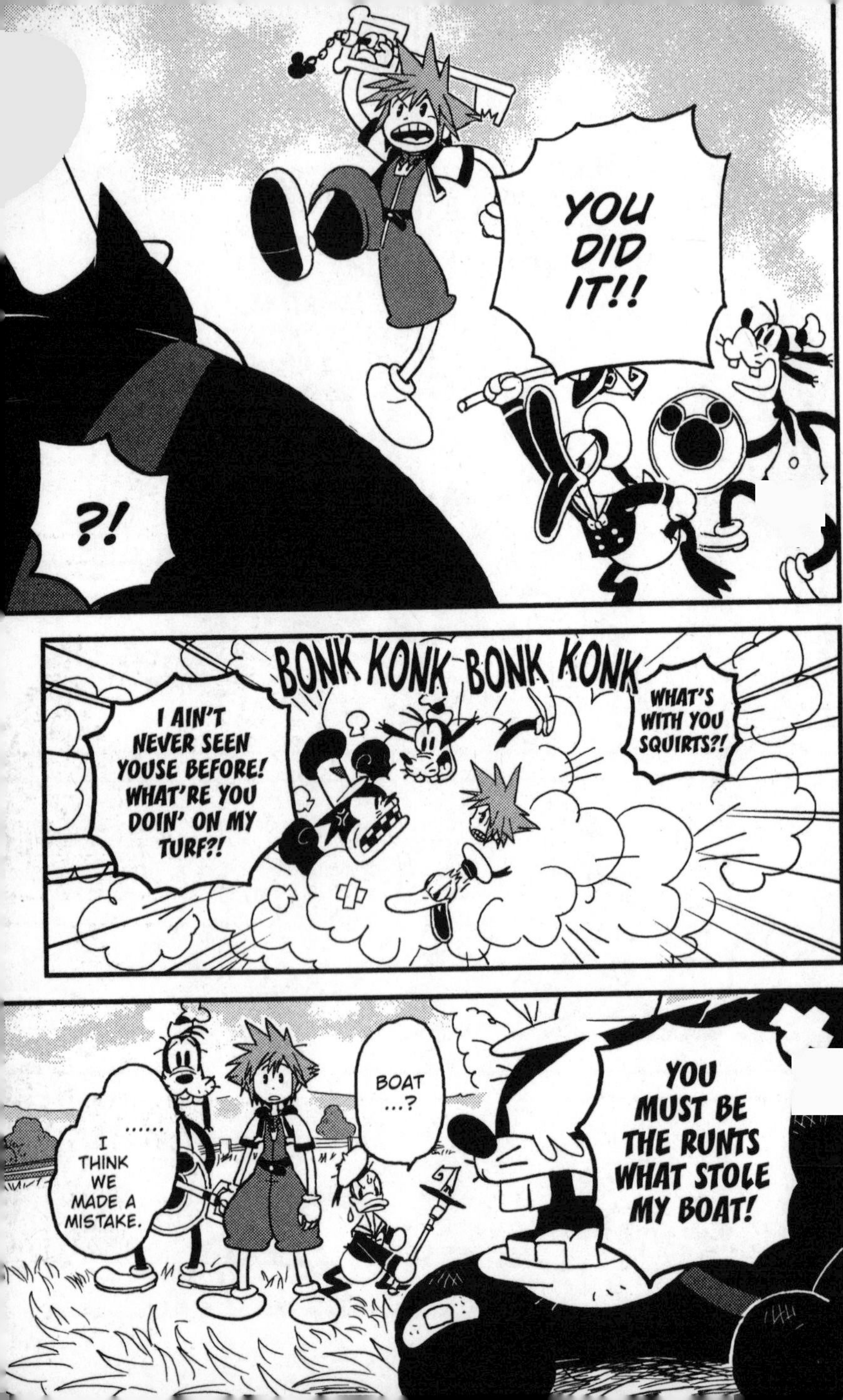
YOU DID IT!!
?!
WHAT'S WITH YOU SQUIRTS?!
BONK KONK BONK KONK
I AIN'T NEVER SEEN YOUSE BEFORE! WHAT'RE YOU DOIN' ON MY TURF?!
YOU MUST BE THE RUNTS WHAT STOLE MY BOAT!
BOAT ...?
......
I THINK WE MADE A MISTAKE.

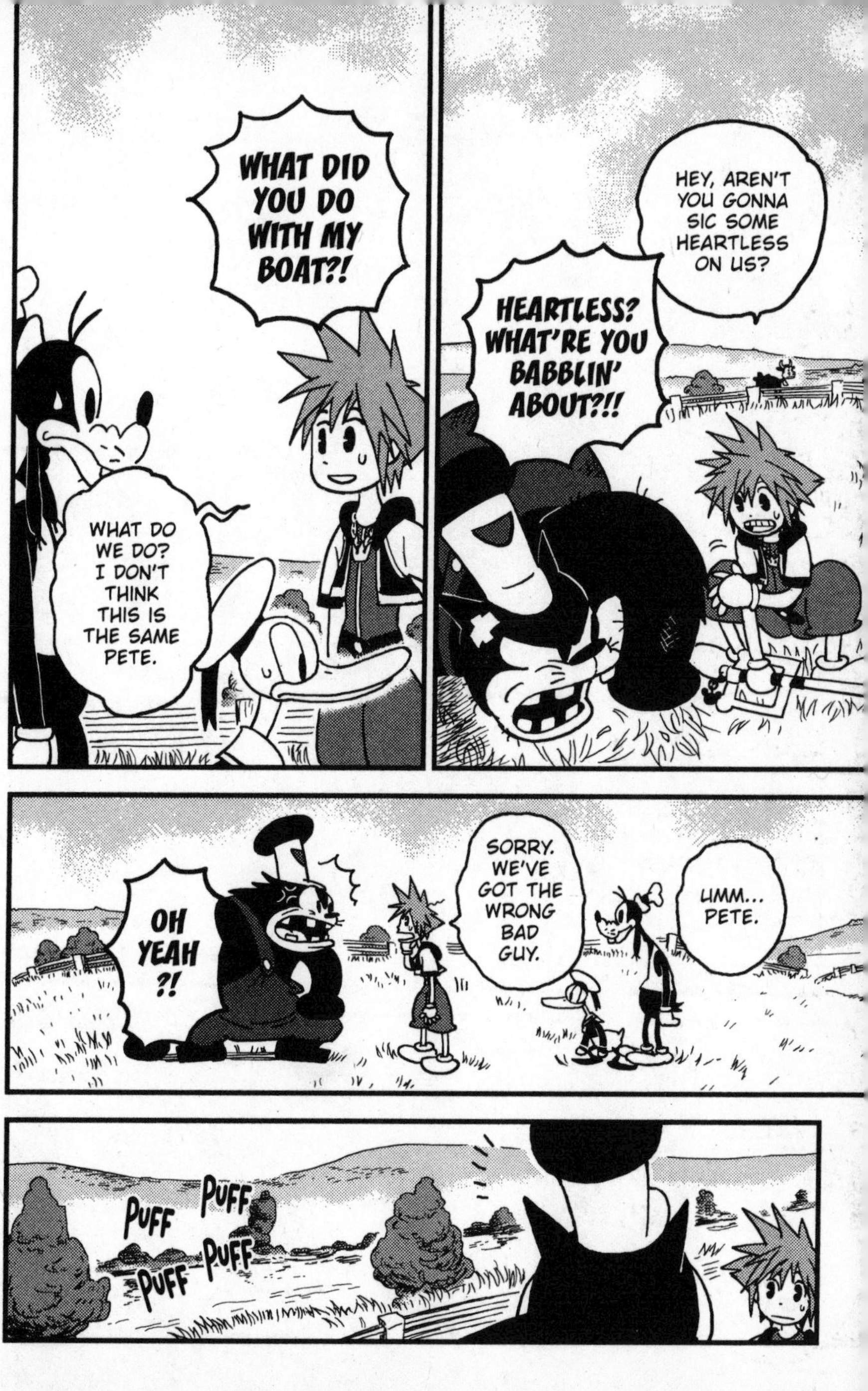
HEY, AREN'T YOU GONNA SIC SOME HEARTLESS ON US?
HEARTLESS? WHAT'RE YOU BABBLIN' ABOUT?!!
WHAT DID YOU DO WITH MY BOAT?!
WHAT DO WE DO? I DON'T THINK THIS IS THE SAME PETE.
UMM... PETE.
SORRY. WE'VE GOT THE WRONG BAD GUY.
OH YEAH ?!
PUFF
PUFF
PUFF
PUFF

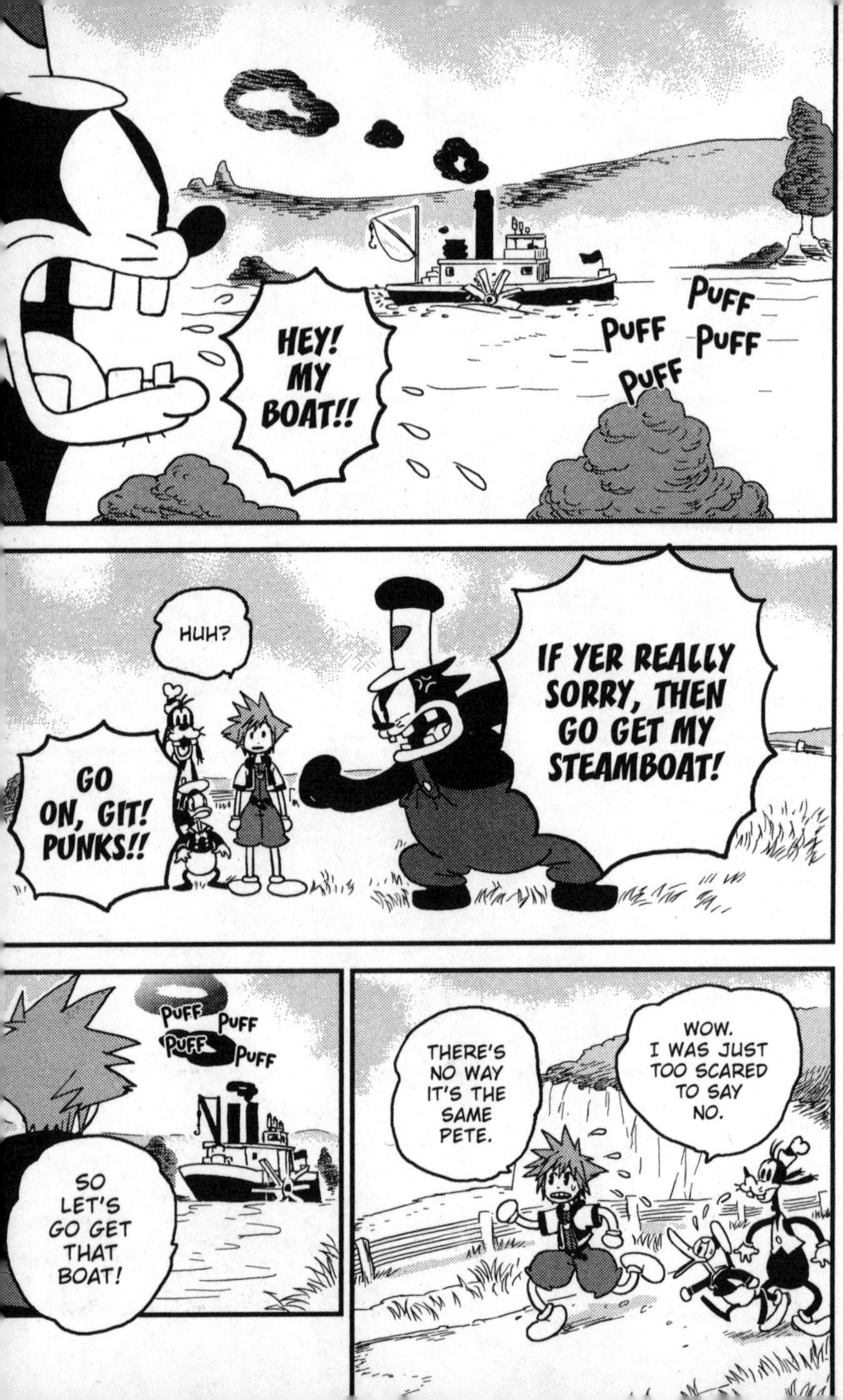
PUFF
PUFF
PUFF
PUFF
HEY! MY BOAT!!
IF YER REALLY SORRY, THEN GO GET MY STEAMBOAT!
HUH?
GO ON, GIT! PUNKS!!
WOW. I WAS JUST TOO SCARED TO SAY NO.
THERE'S NO WAY IT'S THE SAME PETE.
PUFF
PUFF
PUFF
PUFF
SO LET'S GO GET THAT BOAT!

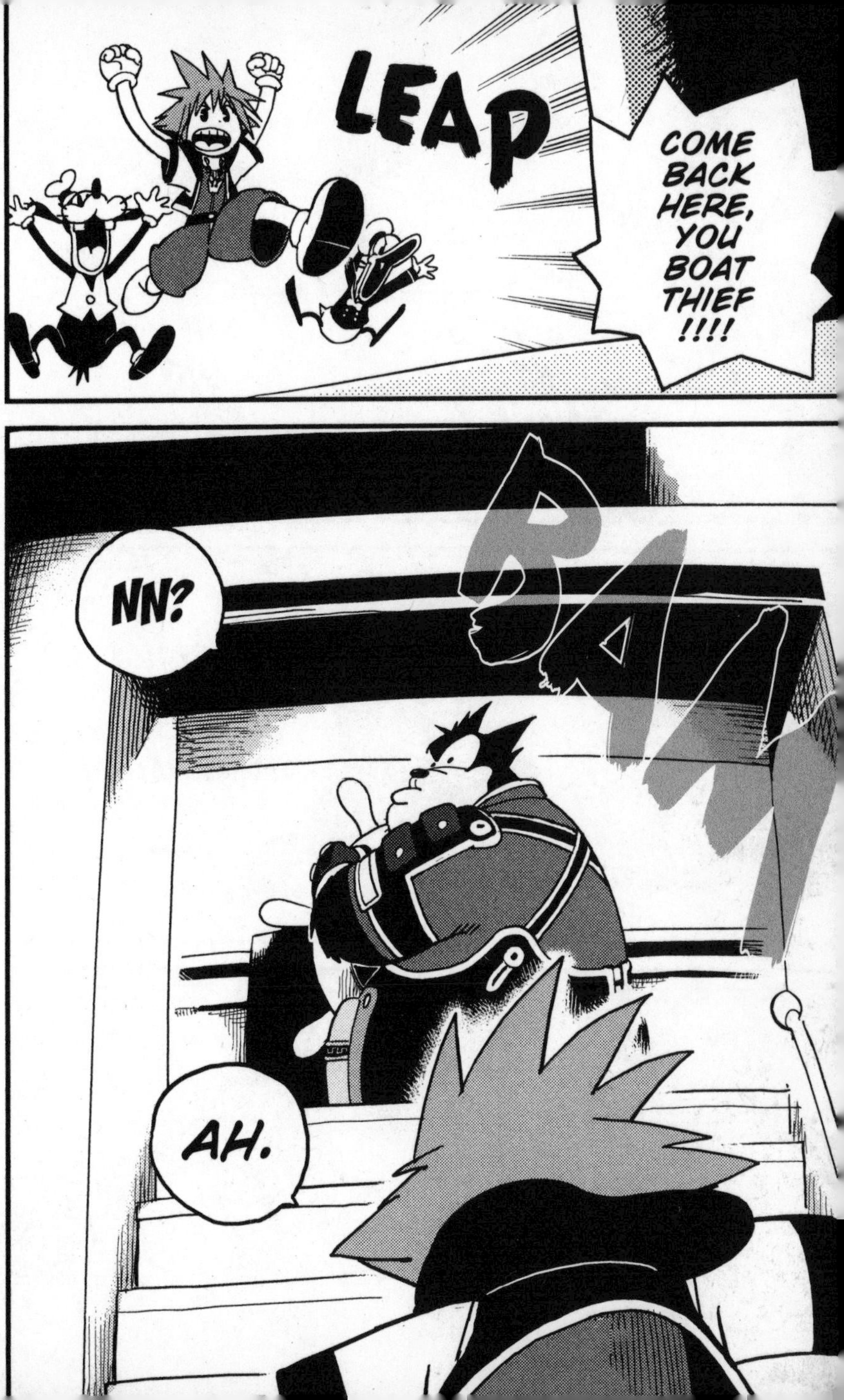
COME BACK HERE, YOU BOAT THIEF!!!!
LEAP
NN?
AH.

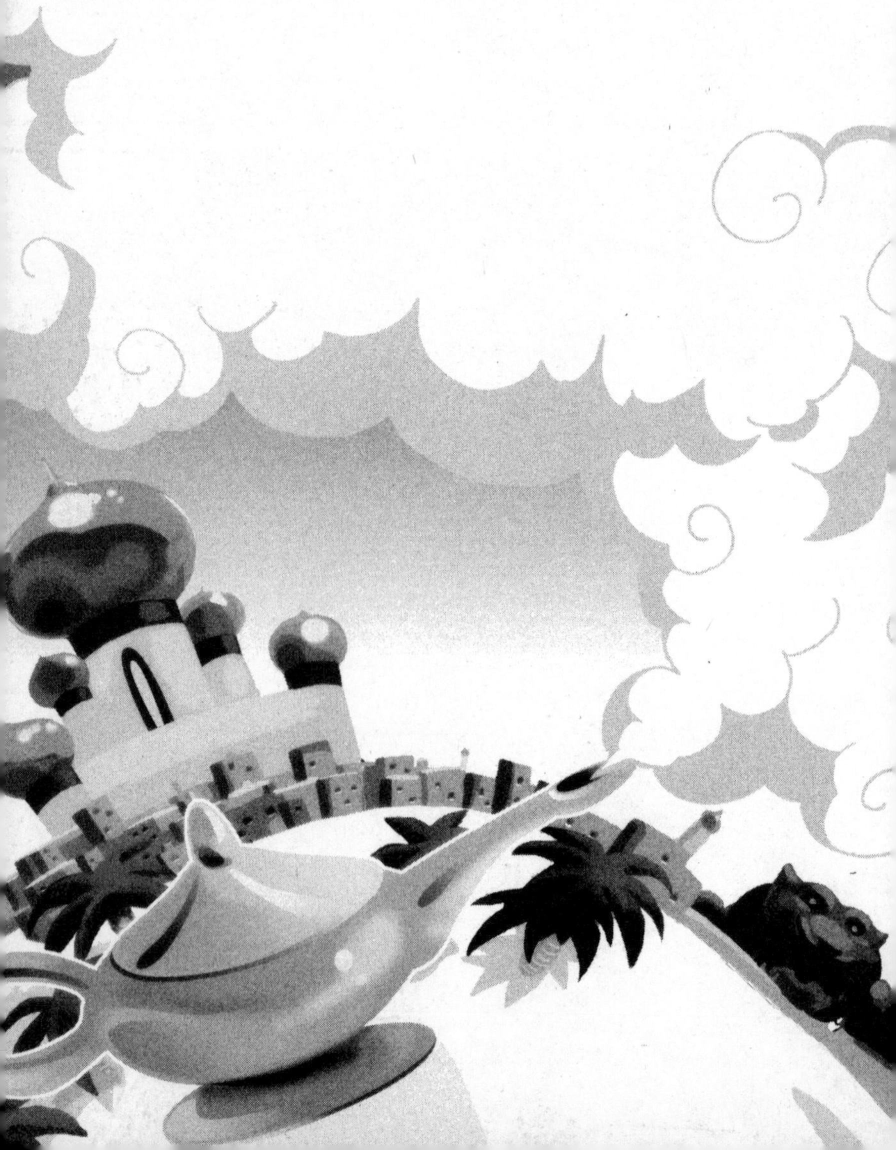

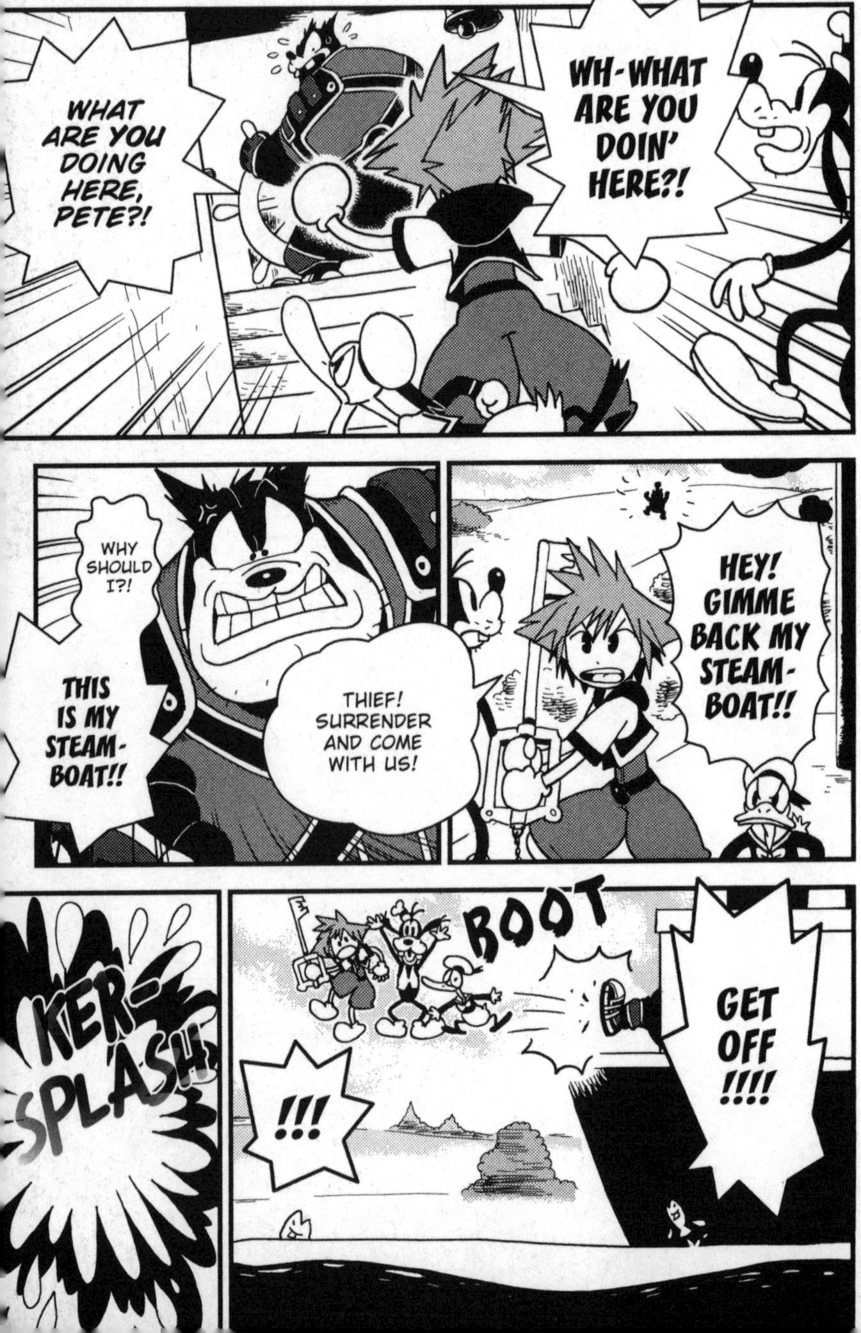
WH-WHAT ARE YOU DOIN' HERE?!
WHAT ARE YOU DOING HERE, PETE?!
HEY! GIMME BACK MY STEAM-BOAT!!
THIEF! SURRENDER AND COME WITH US!
WHY SHOULD I?!
THIS IS MY STEAM-BOAT!!
GET OFF!!!!
BOOT
!!!
KER-SPLASH

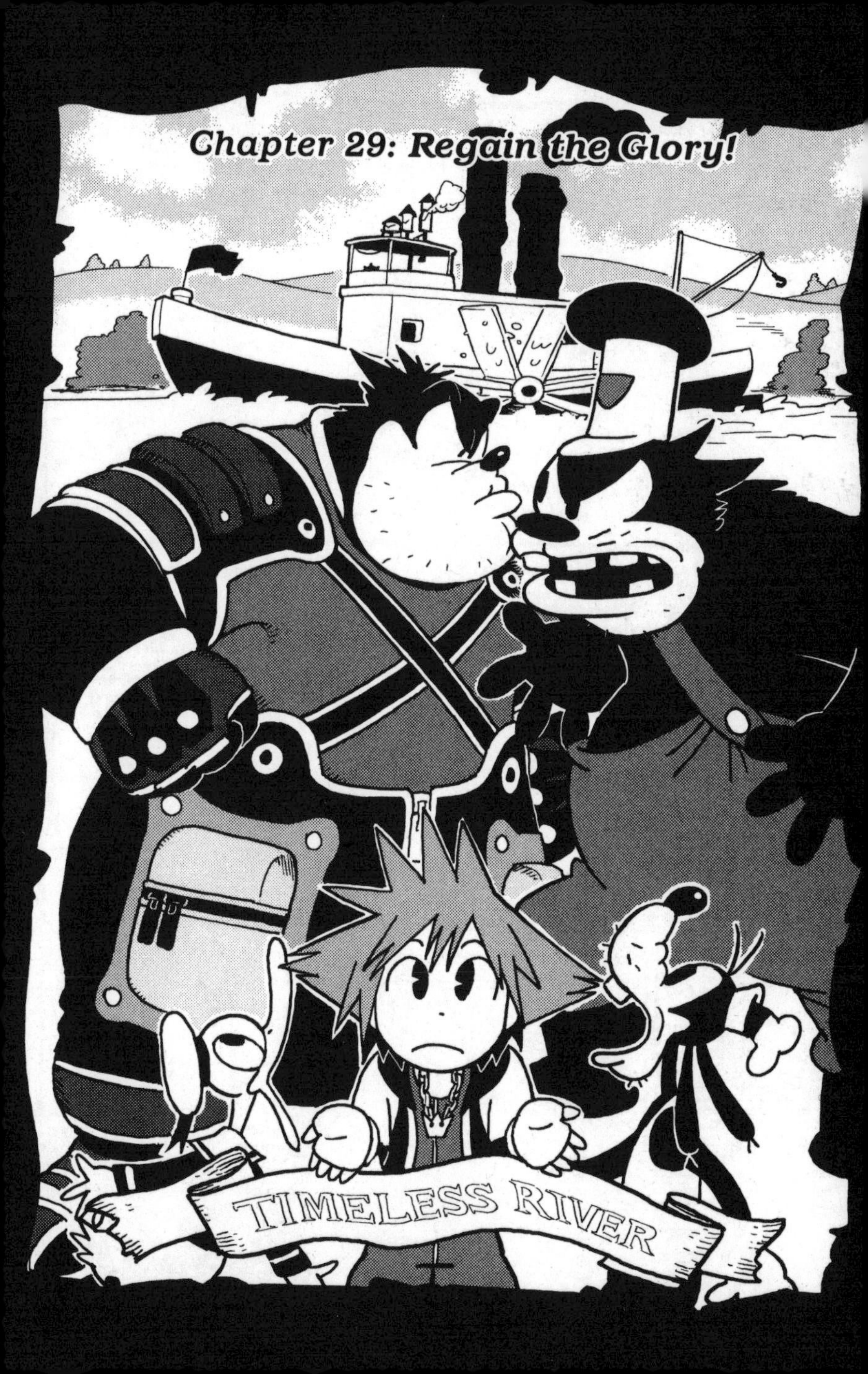
Chapter 29: Regain the Glory!
TIMELESS RIVER

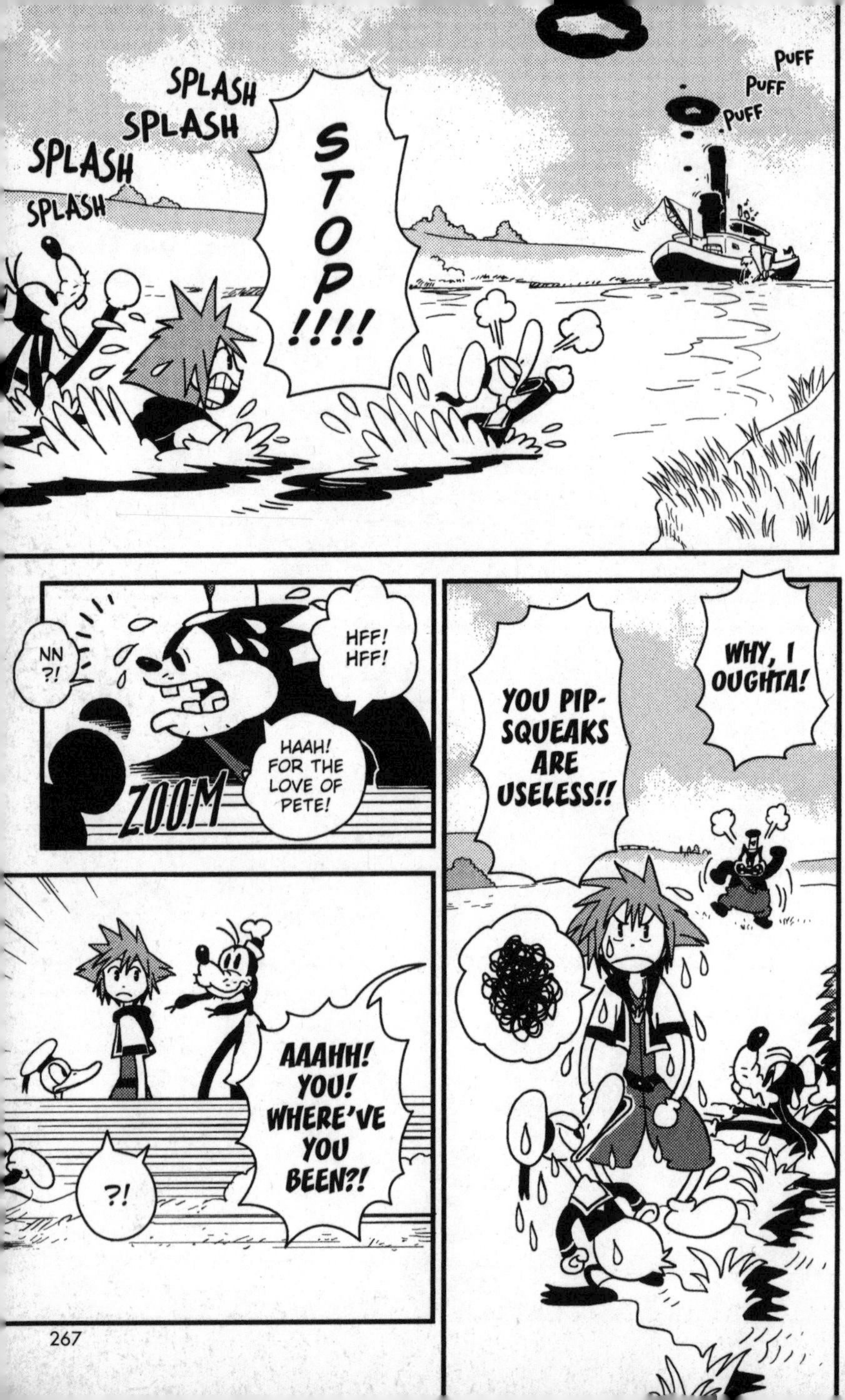
PUFF
PUFF
PUFF
STOP!!!!
SPLASH
SPLASH
SPLASH
SPLASH
WHY, I OUGHTA!
YOU PIP-SQUEAKS ARE USELESS!!
HFF! HFF!
HAAH! FOR THE LOVE OF PETE!
NN ?!
ZOOM
AAAHH! YOU! WHERE'VE YOU BEEN?!
?!

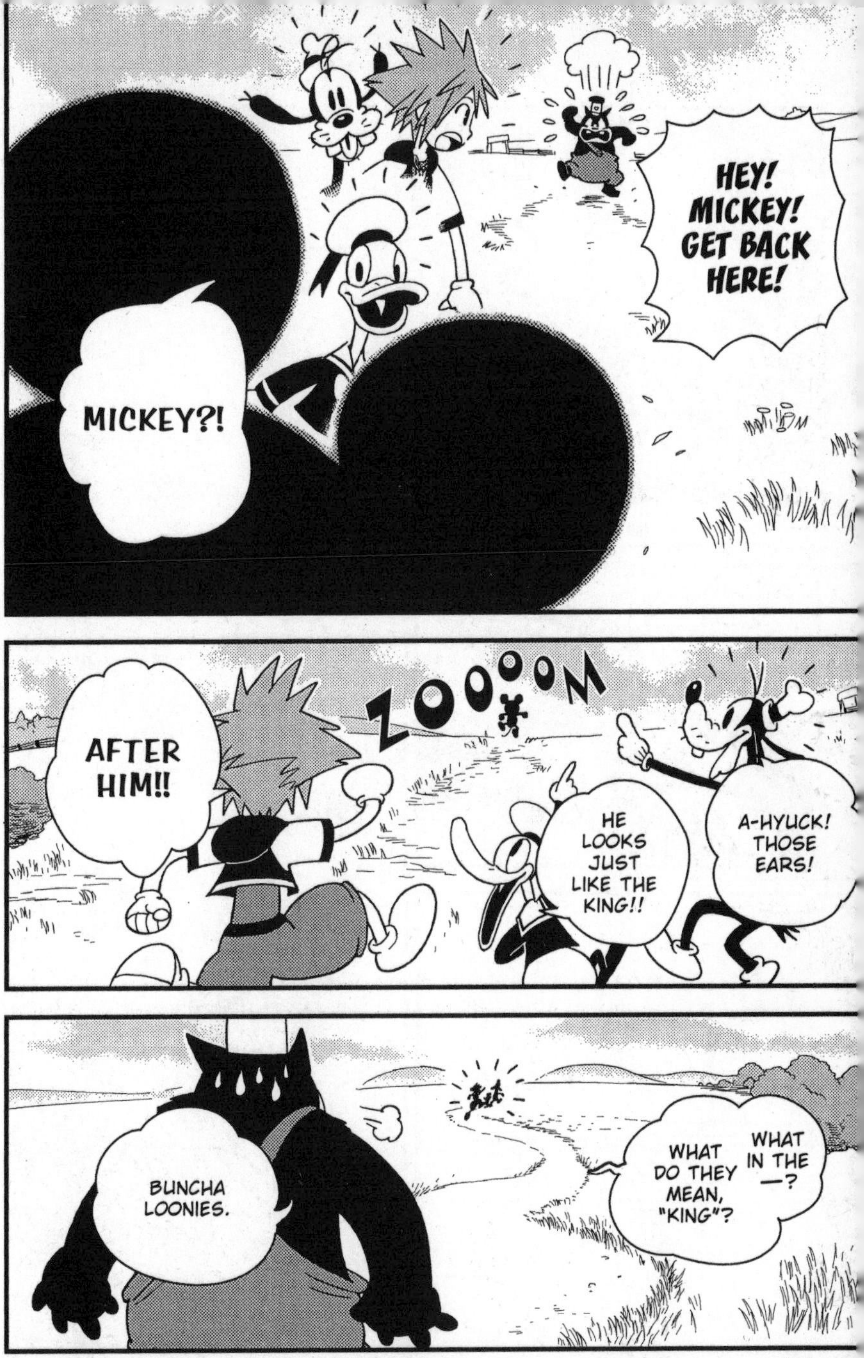
HEY! MICKEY! GET BACK HERE!
MICKEY?!
A-HYUCK! THOSE EARS!
HE LOOKS JUST LIKE THE KING!!
ZOOOOM
AFTER HIM!!
WHAT IN THE—?
WHAT DO THEY MEAN, "KING"?
BUNCHA LOONIES.

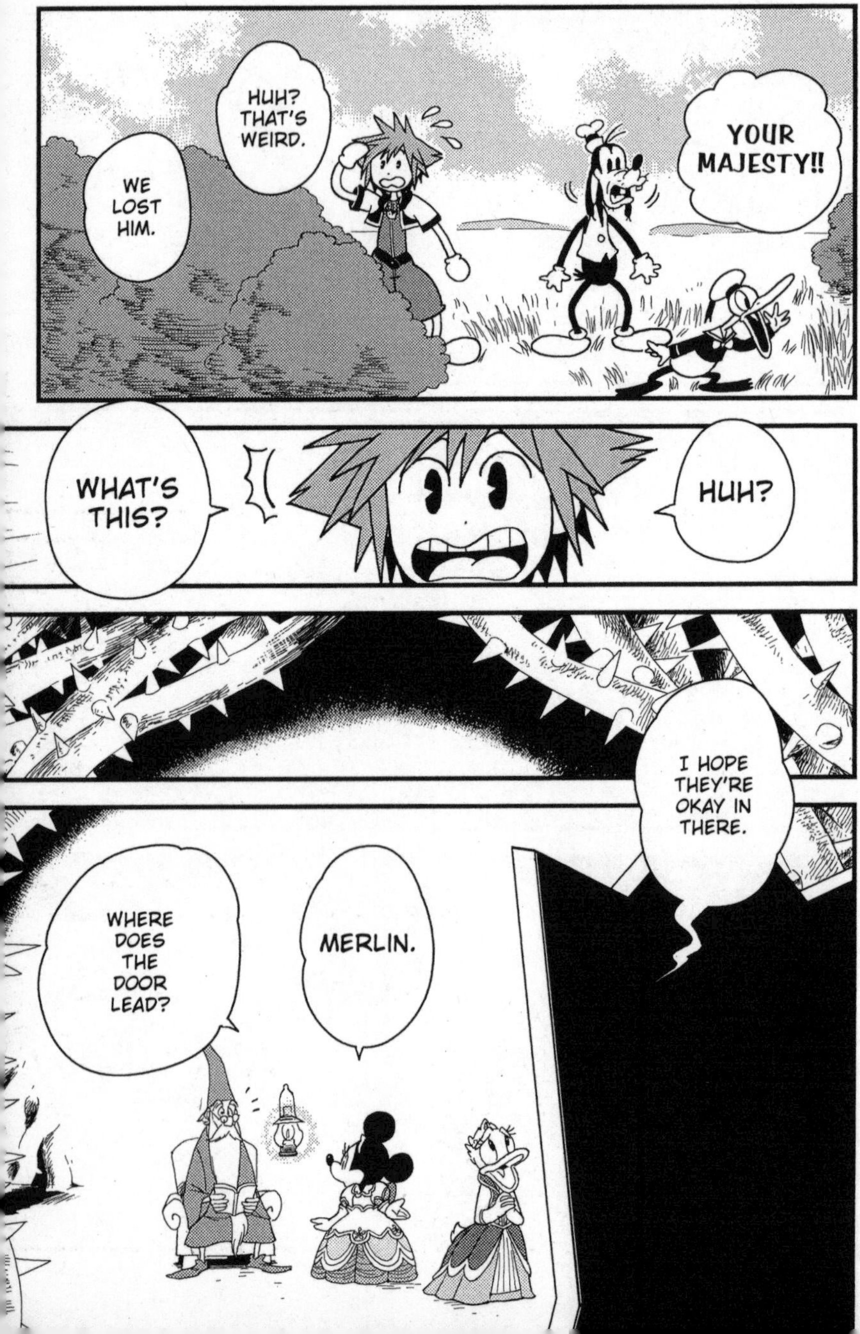
YOUR MAJESTY!!
HUH? THAT'S WEIRD.
WE LOST HIM.
HUH?
WHAT'S THIS?
I HOPE THEY'RE OKAY IN THERE.
MERLIN.
WHERE DOES THE DOOR LEAD?

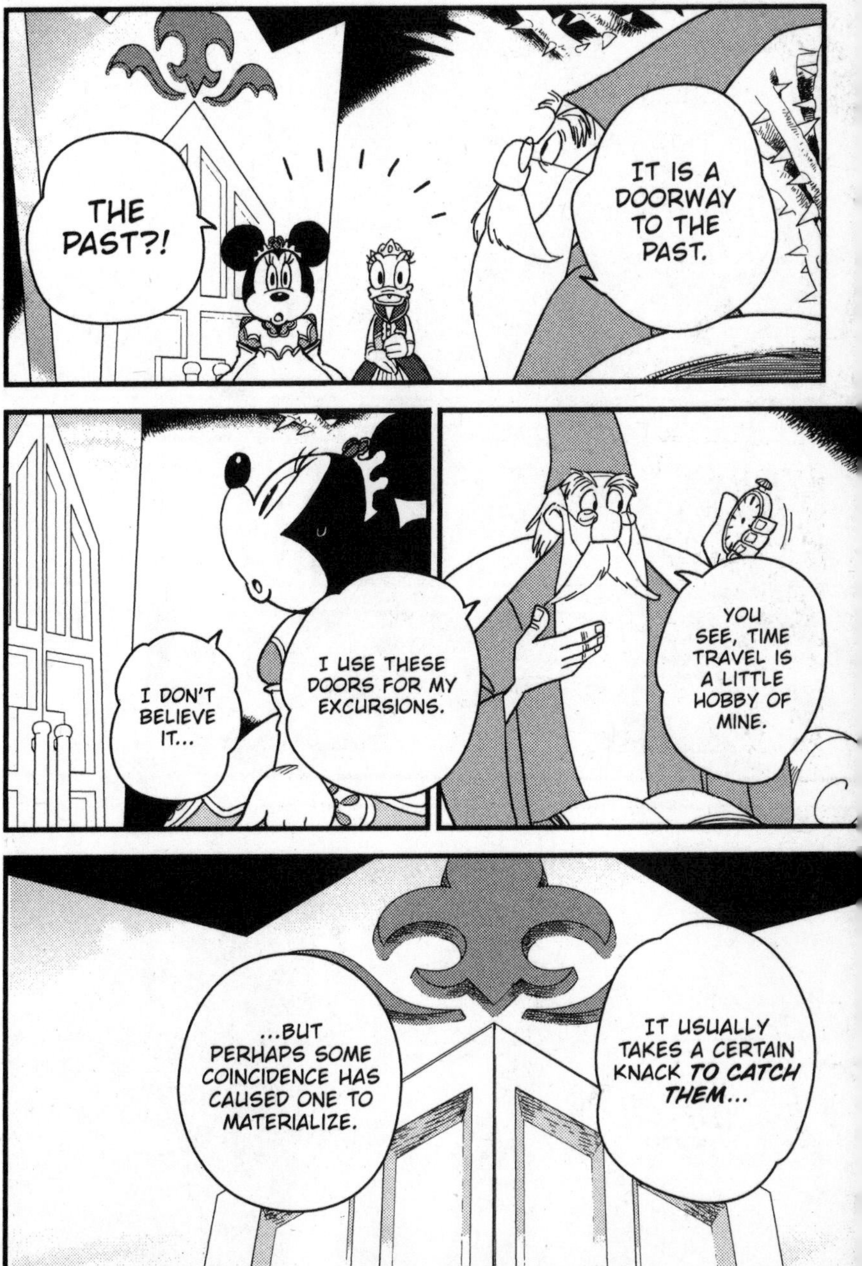
IT IS A DOORWAY TO THE PAST.
THE PAST?!
YOU SEE, TIME TRAVEL IS A LITTLE HOBBY OF MINE.
I USE THESE DOORS FOR MY EXCURSIONS.
I DON'T BELIEVE IT...
IT USUALLY TAKES A CERTAIN KNACK *TO CATCH THEM*...
...BUT PERHAPS SOME COINCIDENCE HAS CAUSED ONE TO MATERIALIZE.

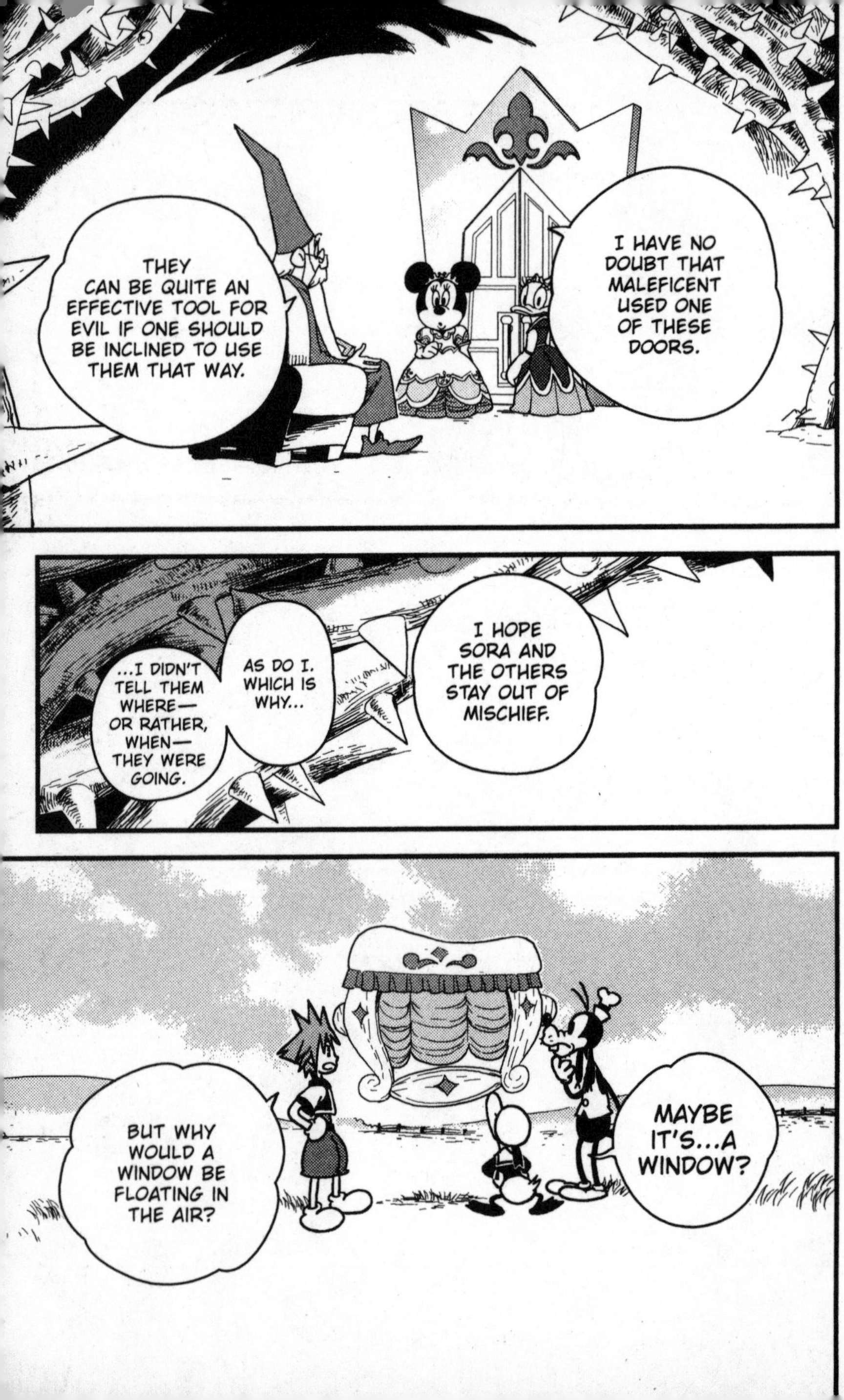
I HAVE NO DOUBT THAT MALEFICENT USED ONE OF THESE DOORS.
THEY CAN BE QUITE AN EFFECTIVE TOOL FOR EVIL IF ONE SHOULD BE INCLINED TO USE THEM THAT WAY.
I HOPE SORA AND THE OTHERS STAY OUT OF MISCHIEF.
AS DO I. WHICH IS WHY...
...I DIDN'T TELL THEM WHERE— OR RATHER, WHEN— THEY WERE GOING.
MAYBE IT'S...A WINDOW?
BUT WHY WOULD A WINDOW BE FLOATING IN THE AIR?

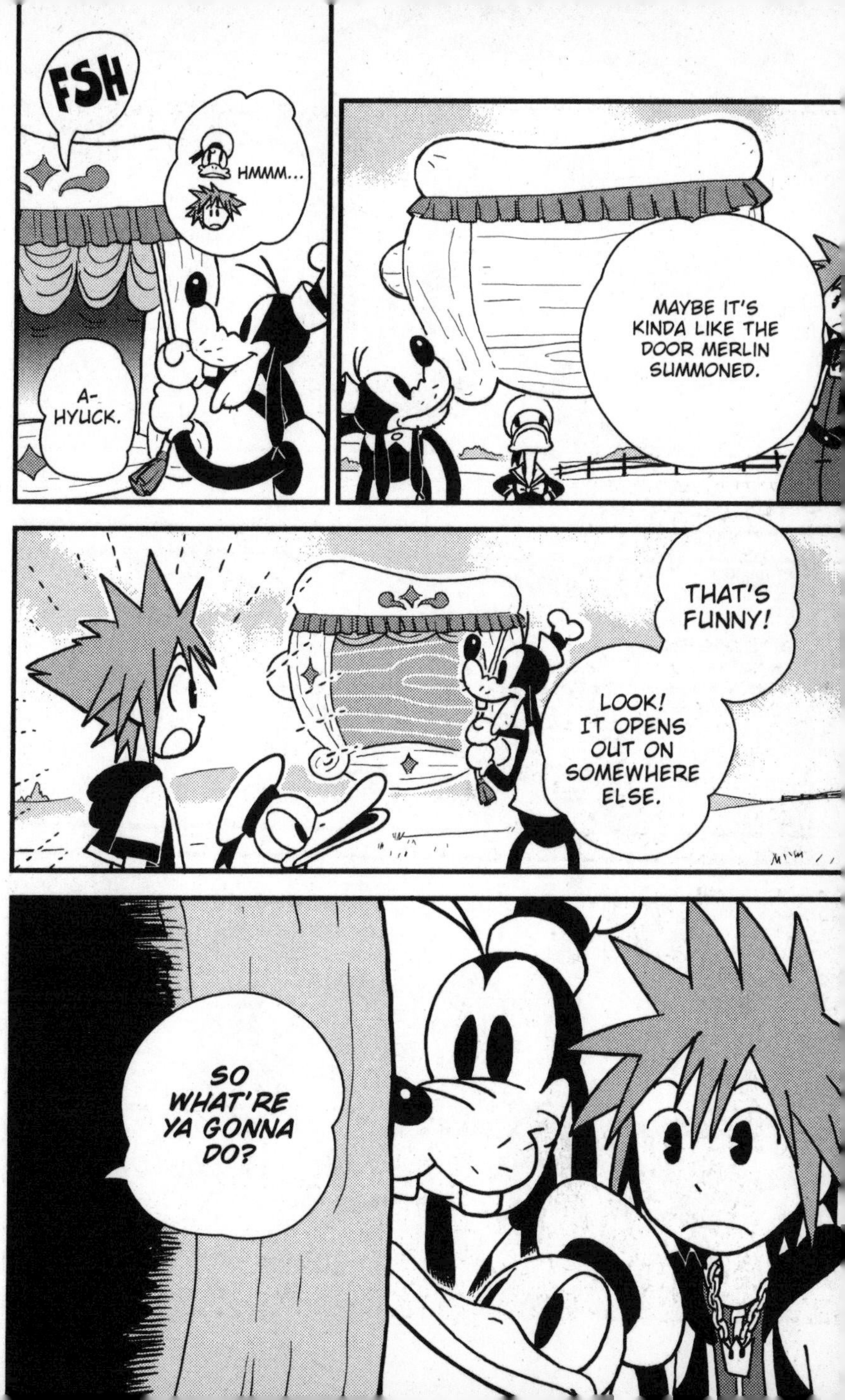
MAYBE IT'S KINDA LIKE THE DOOR MERLIN SUMMONED.
FSH
HMMM...
A-HYUCK.
THAT'S FUNNY!
LOOK! IT OPENS OUT ON SOMEWHERE ELSE.
SO WHAT'RE YA GONNA DO?

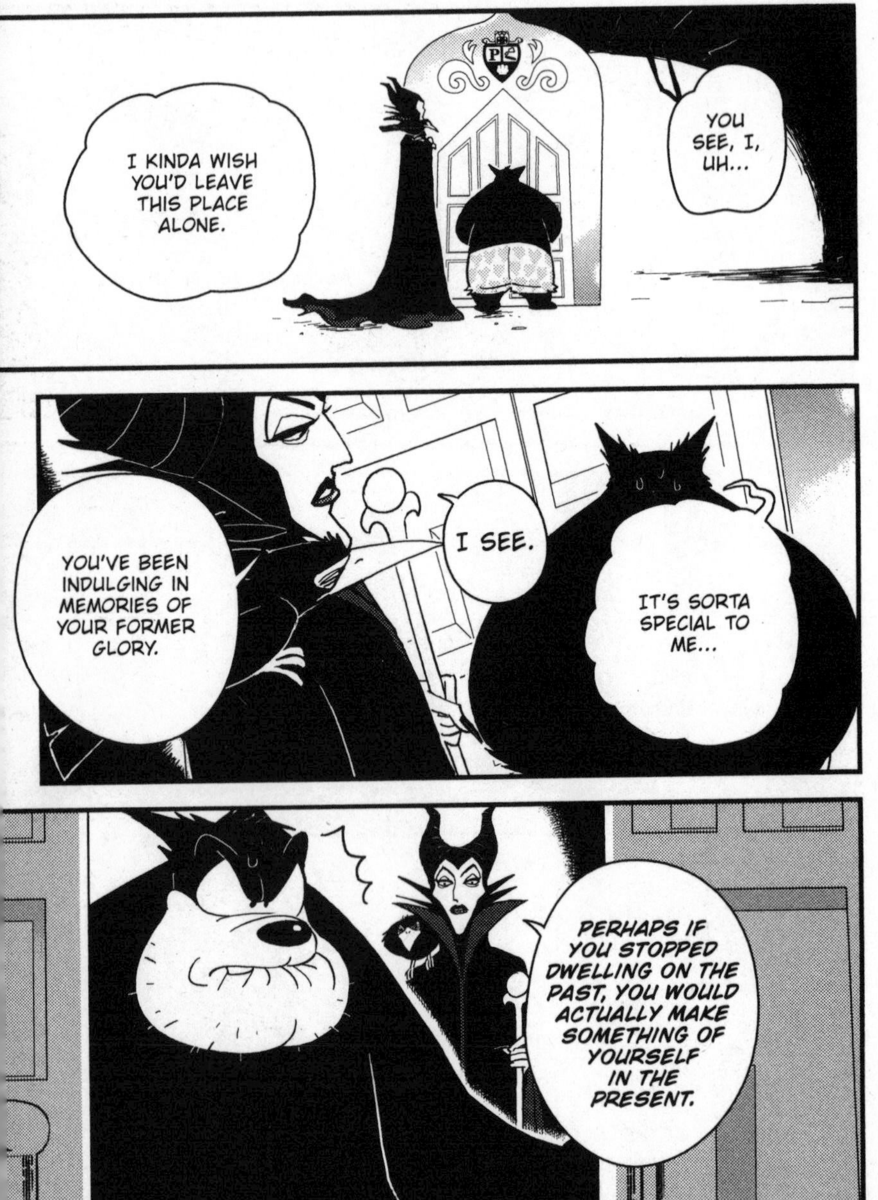
YOU SEE, I, UH...
I KINDA WISH YOU'D LEAVE THIS PLACE ALONE.
IT'S SORTA SPECIAL TO ME...
I SEE.
YOU'VE BEEN INDULGING IN MEMORIES OF YOUR FORMER GLORY.
PERHAPS IF YOU STOPPED DWELLING ON THE PAST, YOU WOULD ACTUALLY MAKE SOMETHING OF YOURSELF IN THE PRESENT.

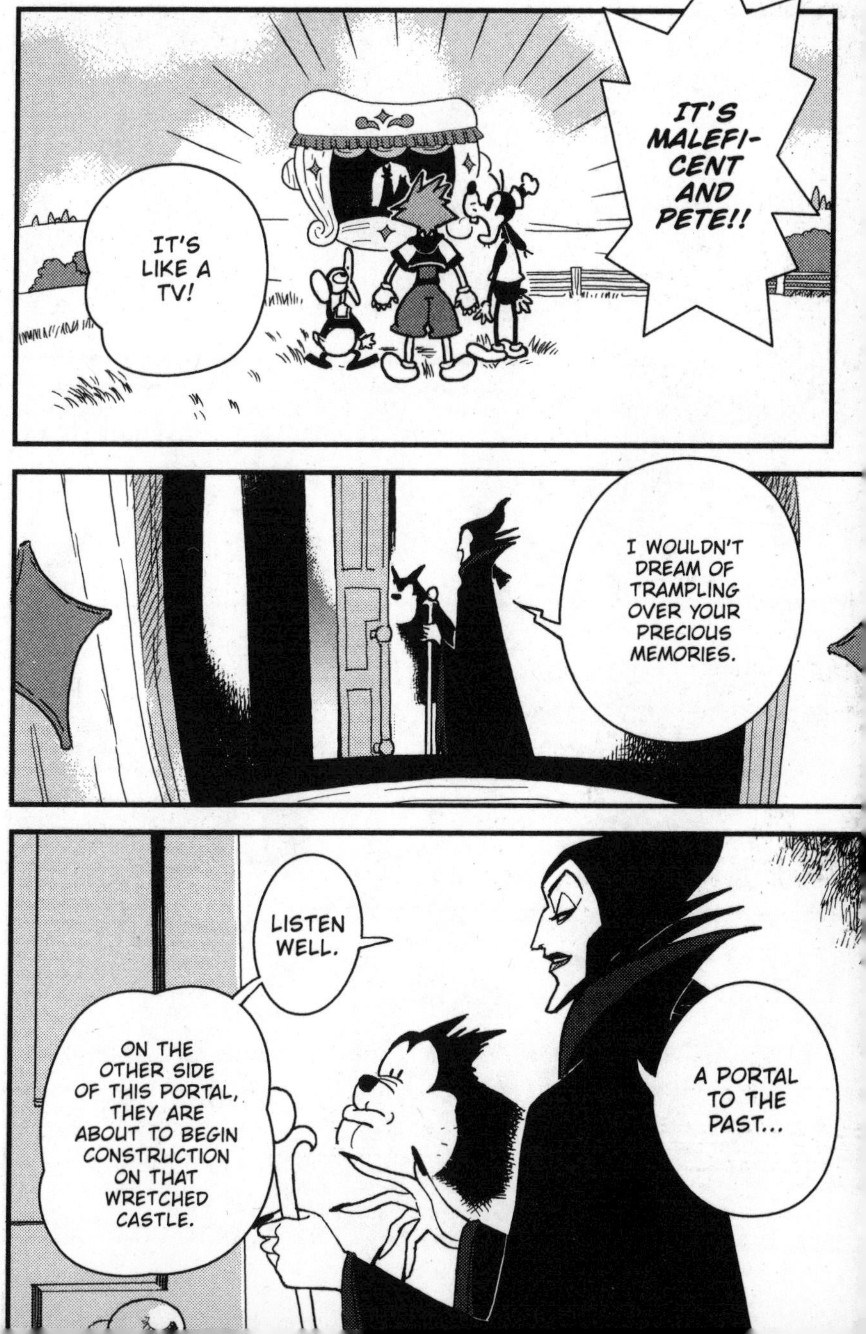
IT'S MALEFI-CENT AND PETE!!
IT'S LIKE A TV!
I WOULDN'T DREAM OF TRAMPLING OVER YOUR PRECIOUS MEMORIES.
A PORTAL TO THE PAST...
LISTEN WELL.
ON THE OTHER SIDE OF THIS PORTAL, THEY ARE ABOUT TO BEGIN CONSTRUCTION ON THAT WRETCHED CASTLE.

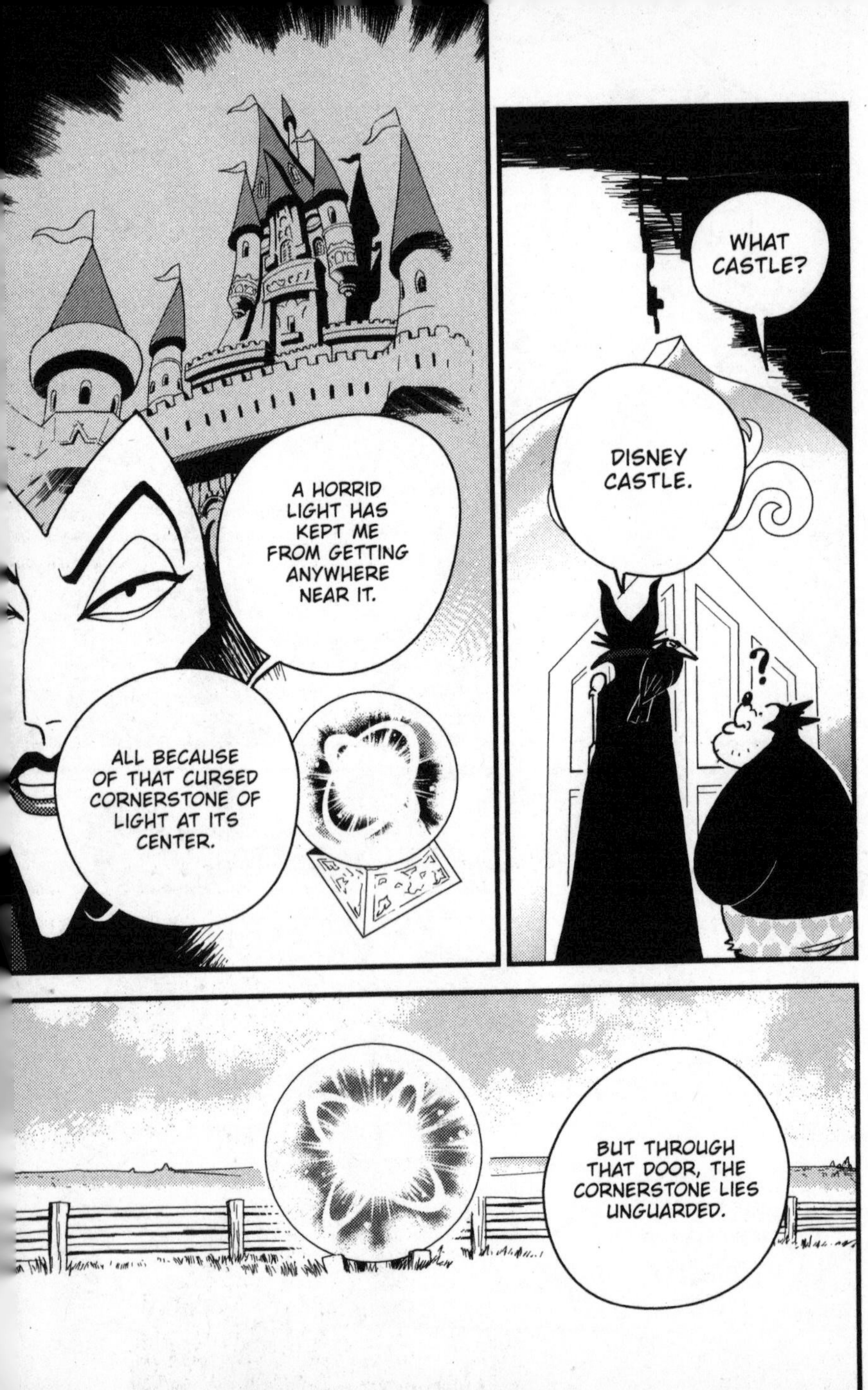
WHAT CASTLE?
DISNEY CASTLE.
A HORRID LIGHT HAS KEPT ME FROM GETTING ANYWHERE NEAR IT.
ALL BECAUSE OF THAT CURSED CORNERSTONE OF LIGHT AT ITS CENTER.
BUT THROUGH THAT DOOR, THE CORNERSTONE LIES UNGUARDED.

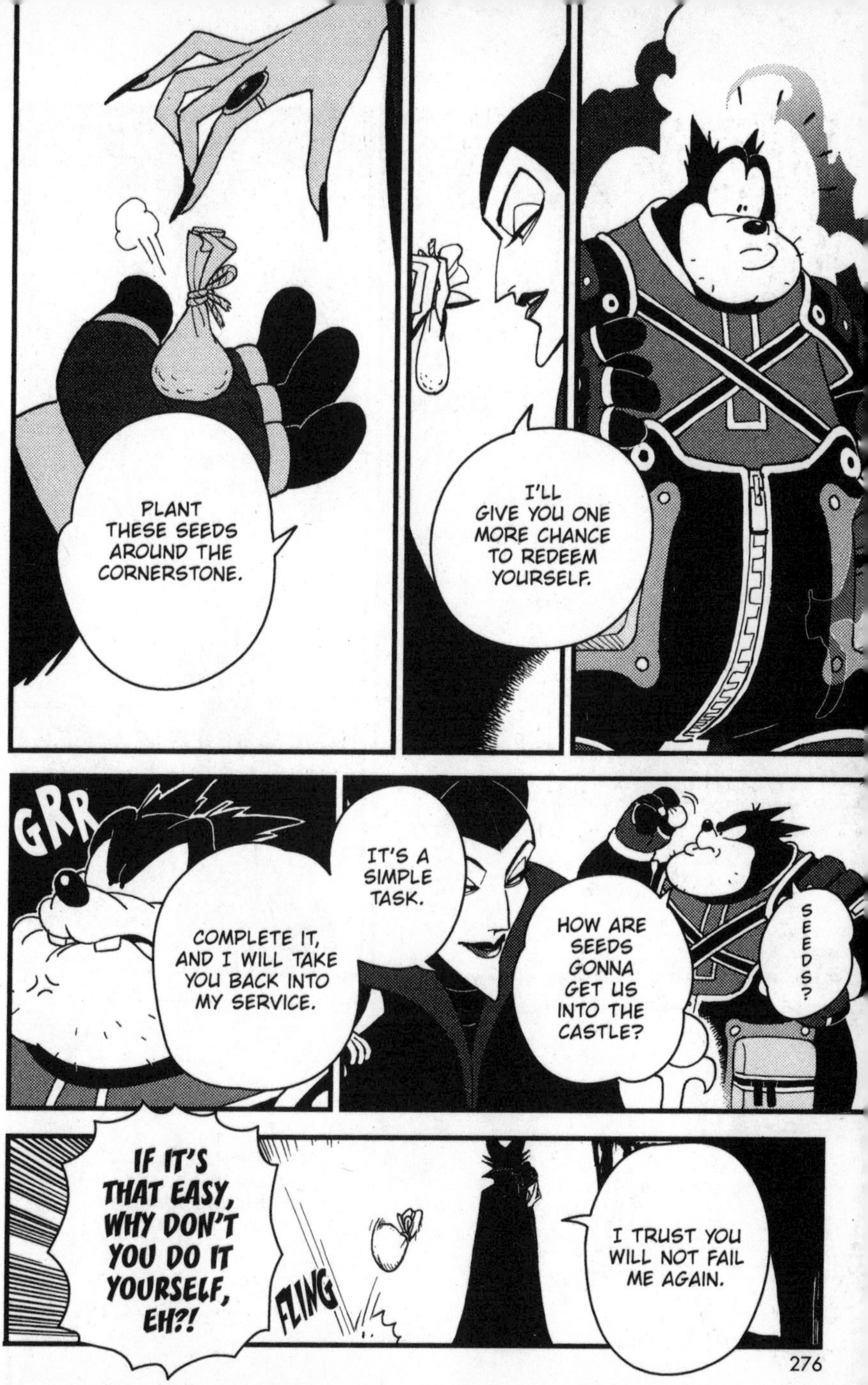
I'LL GIVE YOU ONE MORE CHANCE TO REDEEM YOURSELF.
PLANT THESE SEEDS AROUND THE CORNERSTONE.
SEEDS?
HOW ARE SEEDS GONNA GET US INTO THE CASTLE?
IT'S A SIMPLE TASK.
COMPLETE IT, AND I WILL TAKE YOU BACK INTO MY SERVICE.
GRR
I TRUST YOU WILL NOT FAIL ME AGAIN.
FLING
IF IT'S THAT EASY, WHY DON'T YOU DO IT YOURSELF, EH?!

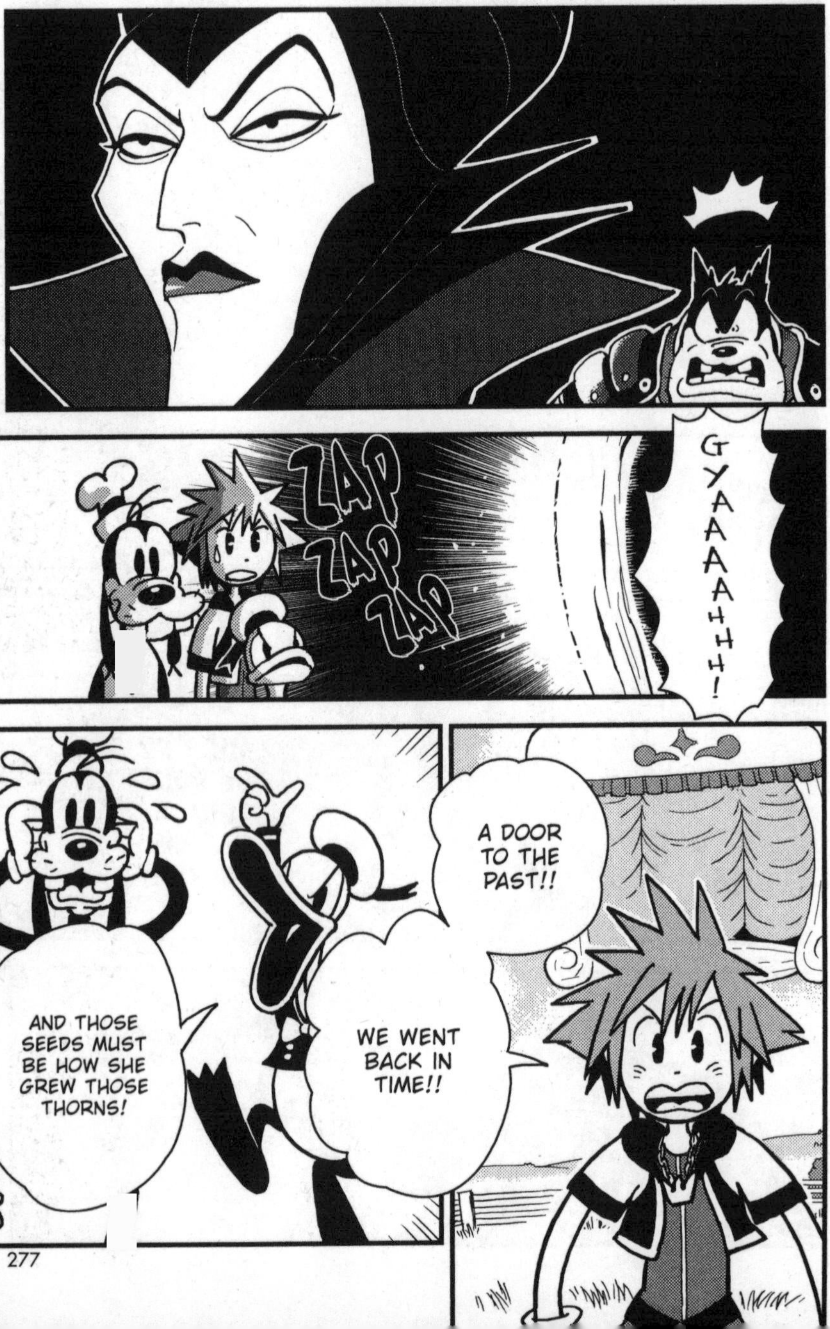
GYAAAAAHHH!
ZAP ZAP ZAP
A DOOR TO THE PAST!!
WE WENT BACK IN TIME!!
AND THOSE SEEDS MUST BE HOW SHE GREW THOSE THORNS!

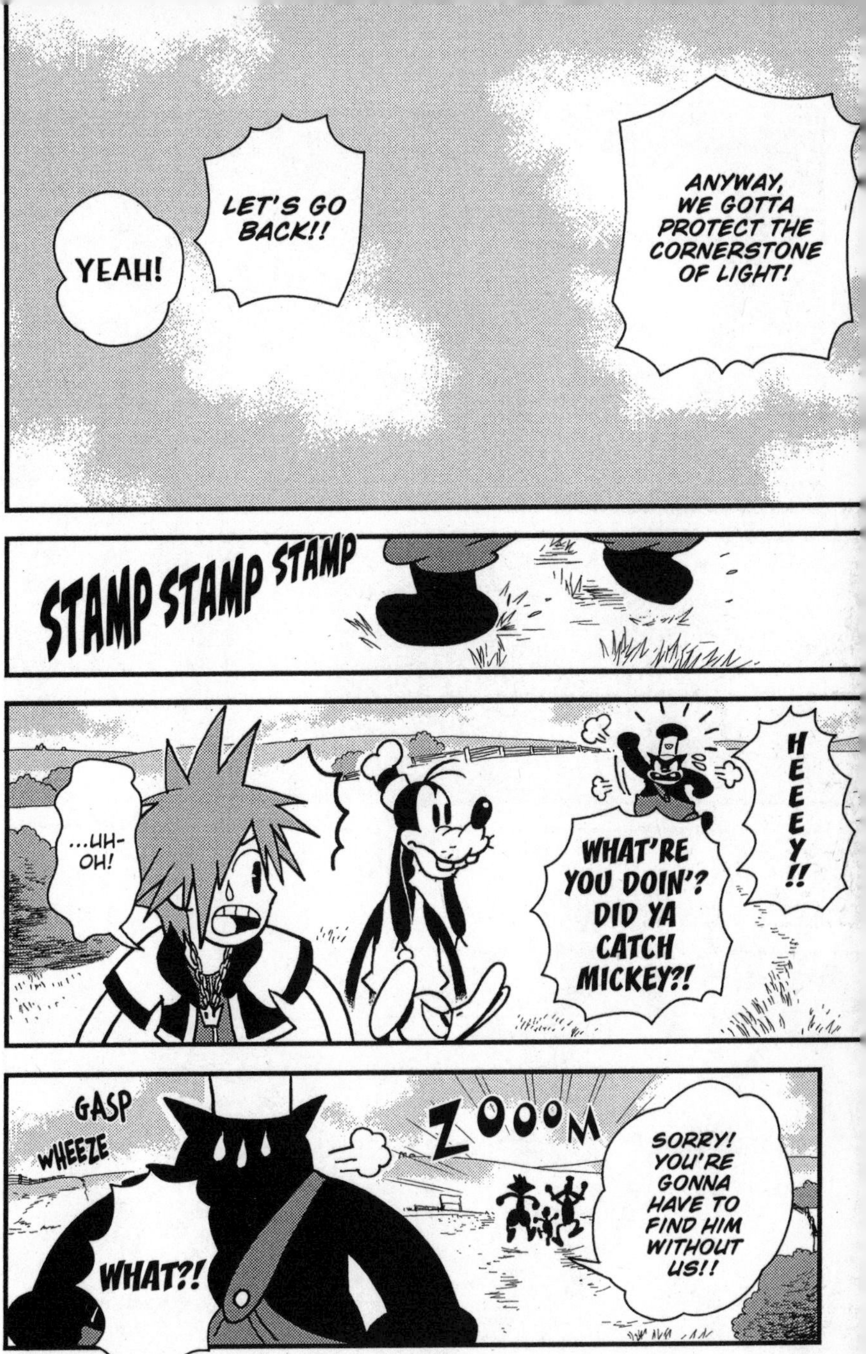
ANYWAY, WE GOTTA PROTECT THE CORNERSTONE OF LIGHT!
LET'S GO BACK!!
YEAH!
STAMP STAMP STAMP
HEEEEY!!
WHAT'RE YOU DOIN'? DID YA CATCH MICKEY?!
...UH-OH!
SORRY! YOU'RE GONNA HAVE TO FIND HIM WITHOUT US!!
ZOOOM
GASP
WHEEZE
WHAT?!

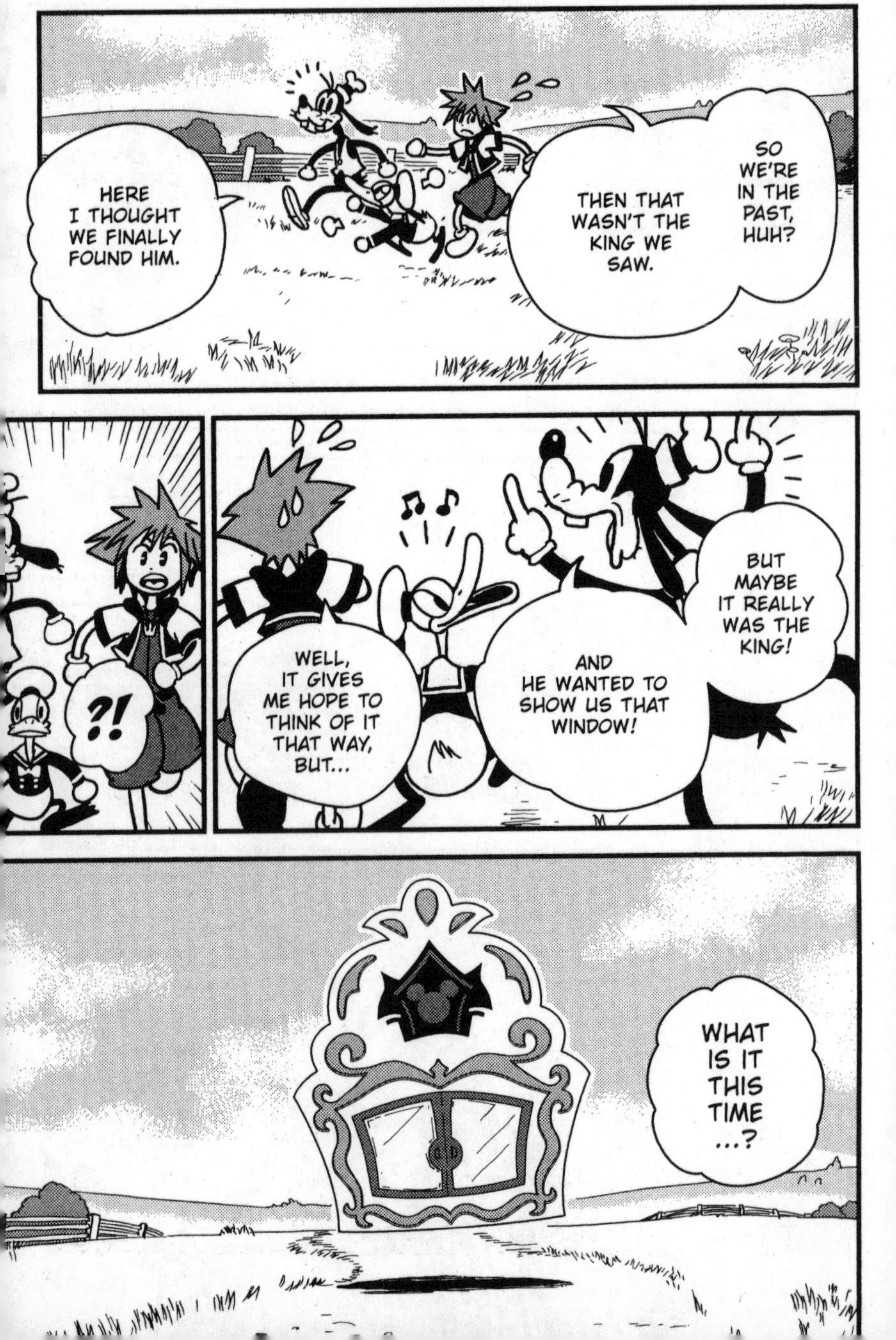
SO WE'RE IN THE PAST, HUH?
THEN THAT WASN'T THE KING WE SAW.
HERE I THOUGHT WE FINALLY FOUND HIM.
BUT MAYBE IT REALLY WAS THE KING!
AND HE WANTED TO SHOW US THAT WINDOW!
WELL, IT GIVES ME HOPE TO THINK OF IT THAT WAY, BUT...
?!
WHAT IS IT THIS TIME ...?

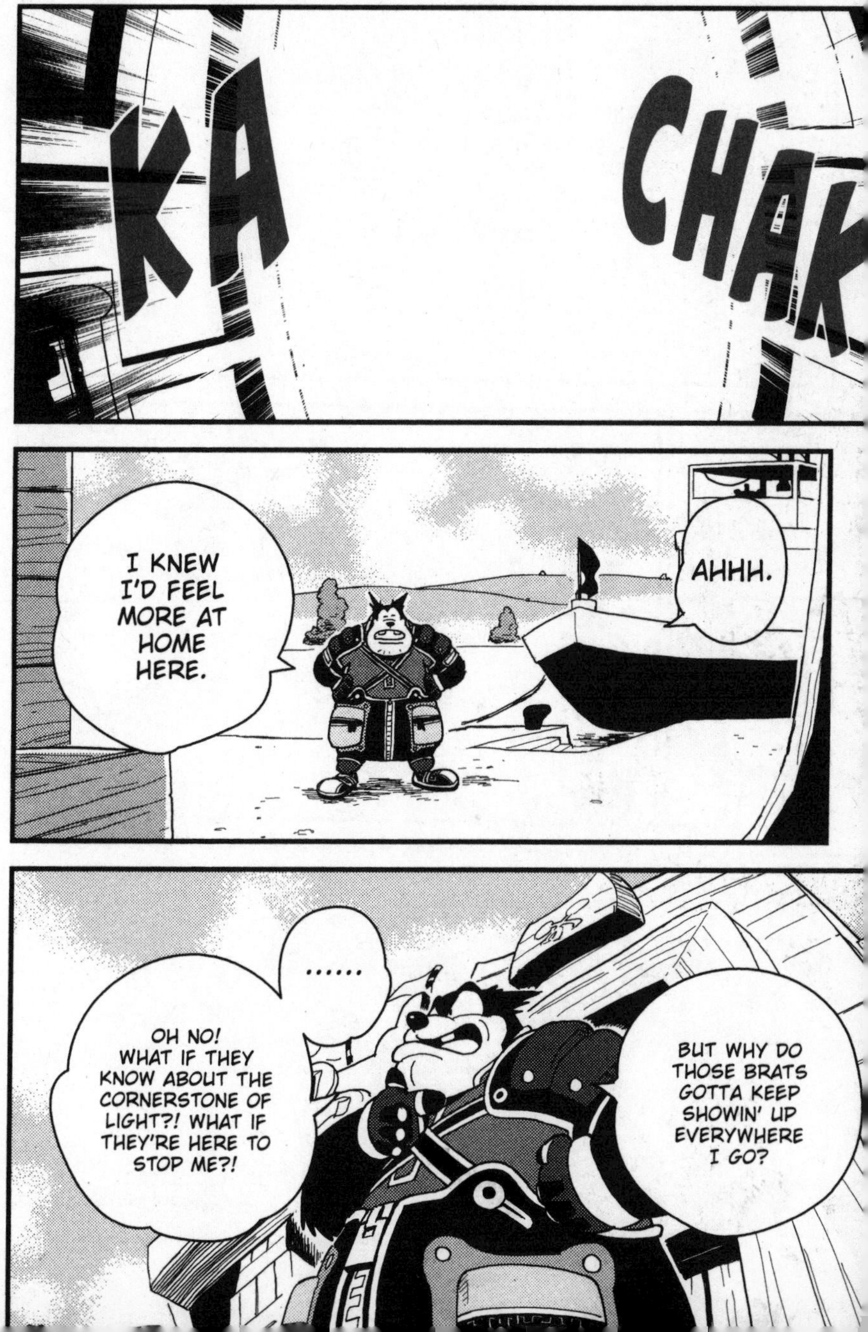
KA
CHAK
AHHH.
I KNEW I'D FEEL MORE AT HOME HERE.
BUT WHY DO THOSE BRATS GOTTA KEEP SHOWIN' UP EVERYWHERE I GO?
......
OH NO! WHAT IF THEY KNOW ABOUT THE CORNERSTONE OF LIGHT?! WHAT IF THEY'RE HERE TO STOP ME?!

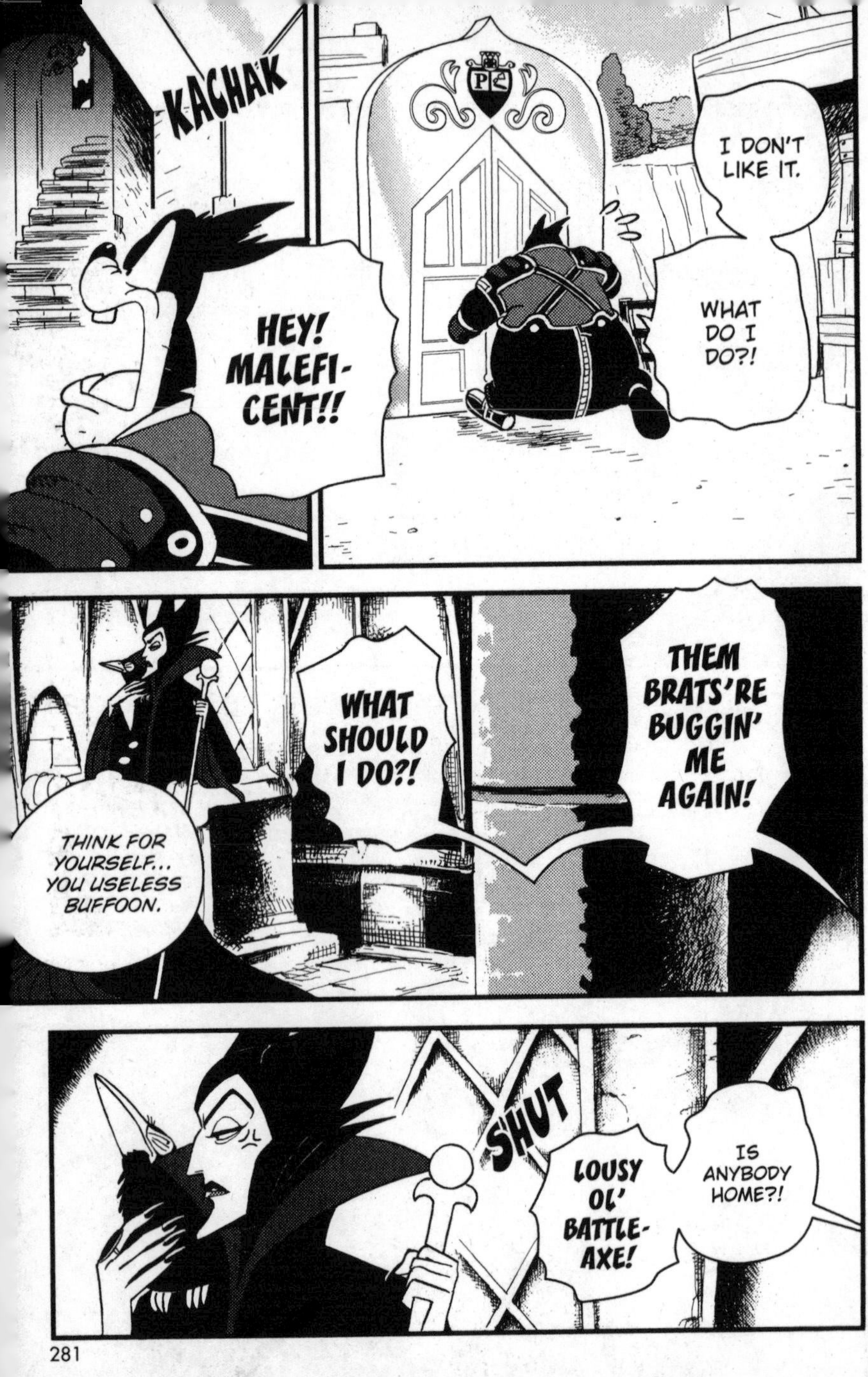
I DON'T LIKE IT.
WHAT DO I DO?!
KACHAK
HEY! MALEFI-CENT!!
THEM BRATS'RE BUGGIN' ME AGAIN!
WHAT SHOULD I DO?!
THINK FOR YOURSELF... YOU USELESS BUFFOON.
IS ANYBODY HOME?!
LOUSY OL' BATTLE-AXE!
SHUT

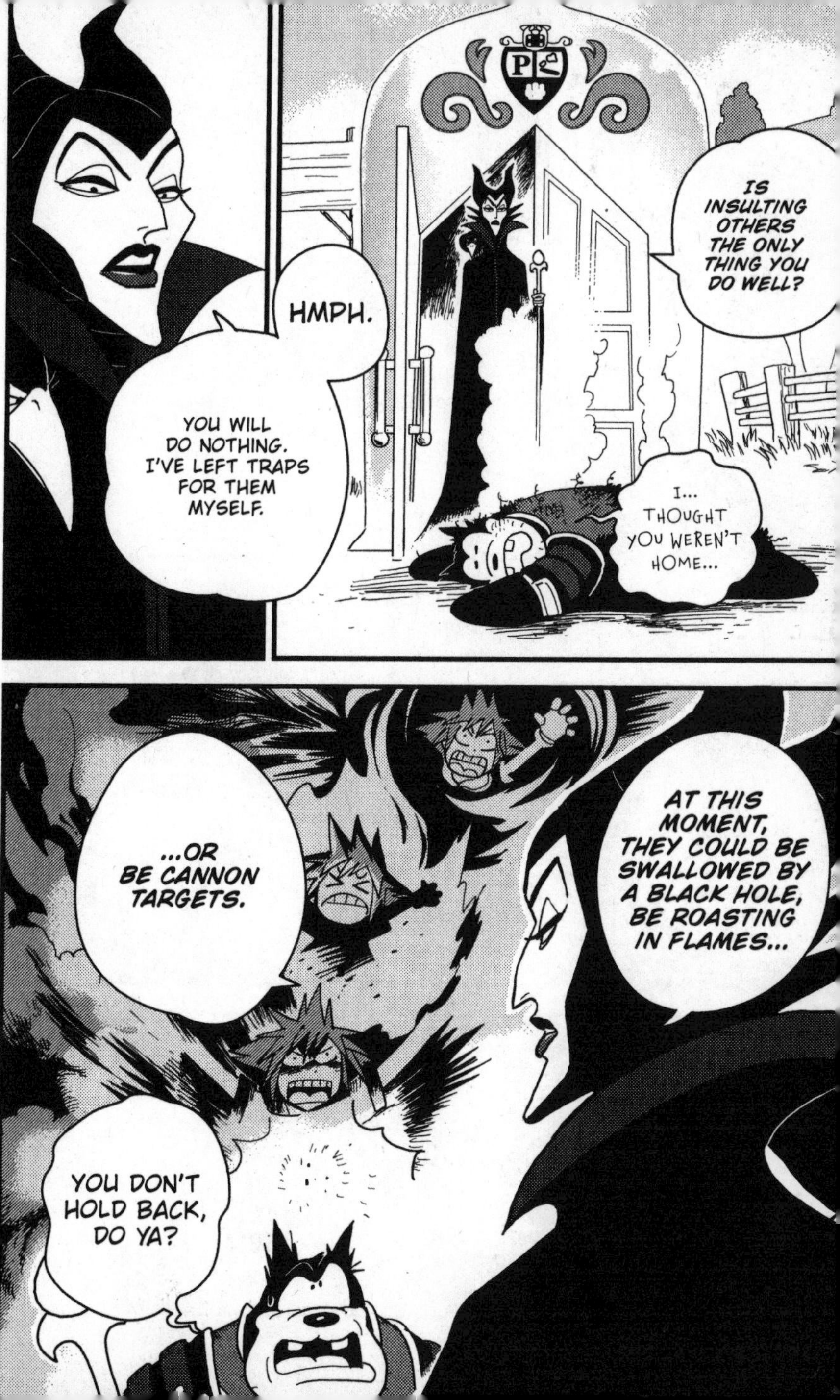
IS INSULTING OTHERS THE ONLY THING YOU DO WELL?
I... THOUGHT YOU WEREN'T HOME...
HMPH.
YOU WILL DO NOTHING. I'VE LEFT TRAPS FOR THEM MYSELF.
AT THIS MOMENT, THEY COULD BE SWALLOWED BY A BLACK HOLE, BE ROASTING IN FLAMES...
...OR BE CANNON TARGETS.
YOU DON'T HOLD BACK, DO YA?

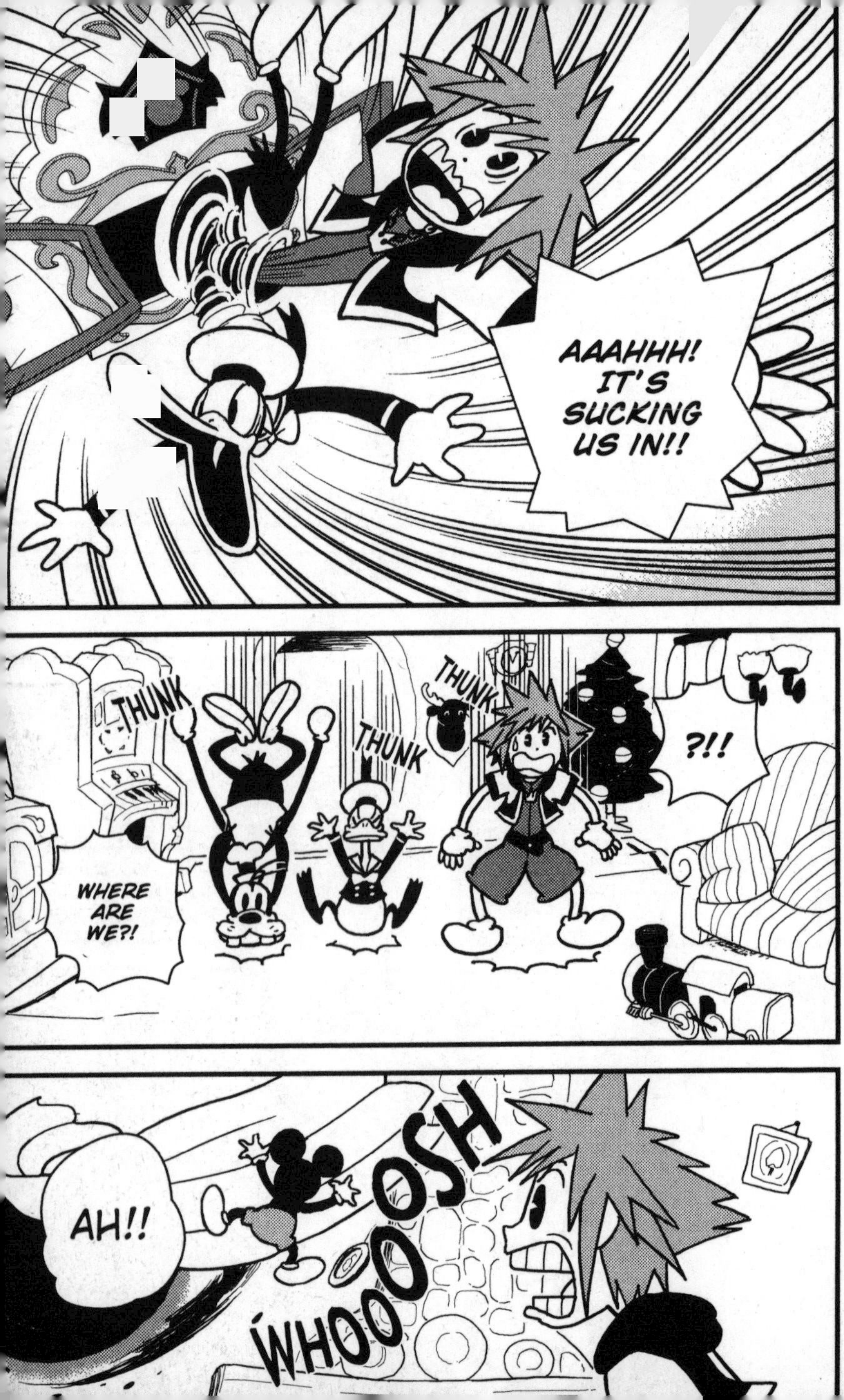
AAAHHH! IT'S SUCKING US IN!!
?!!
THUNK
THUNK
THUNK
WHERE ARE WE?!
WHOOOOSH
AH!!

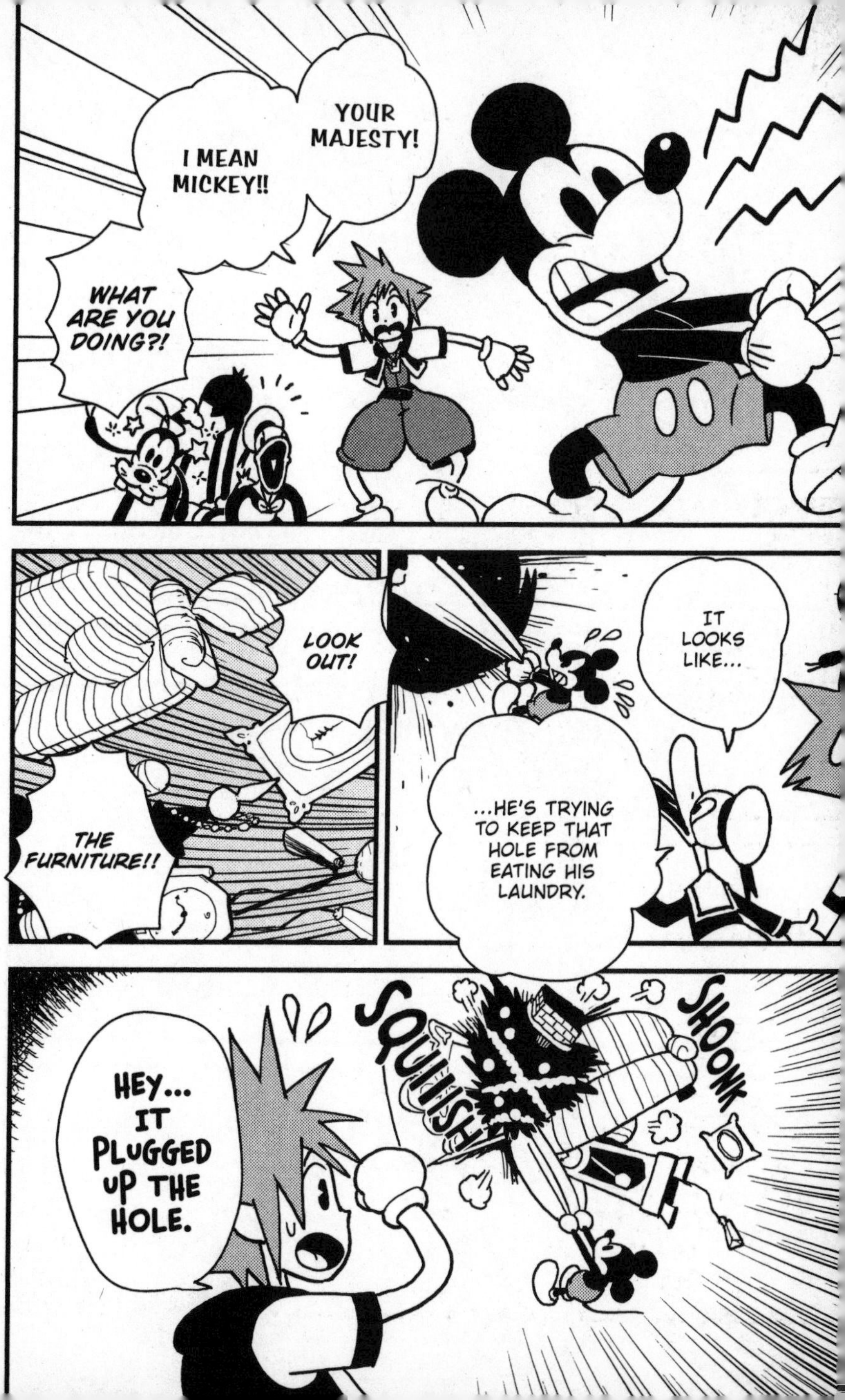
YOUR MAJESTY!
I MEAN MICKEY!!
WHAT ARE YOU DOING?!
IT LOOKS LIKE...
...HE'S TRYING TO KEEP THAT HOLE FROM EATING HIS LAUNDRY.
LOOK OUT!
THE FURNITURE!!
SHOOMK
SQUISH
HEY... IT PLUGGED UP THE HOLE.

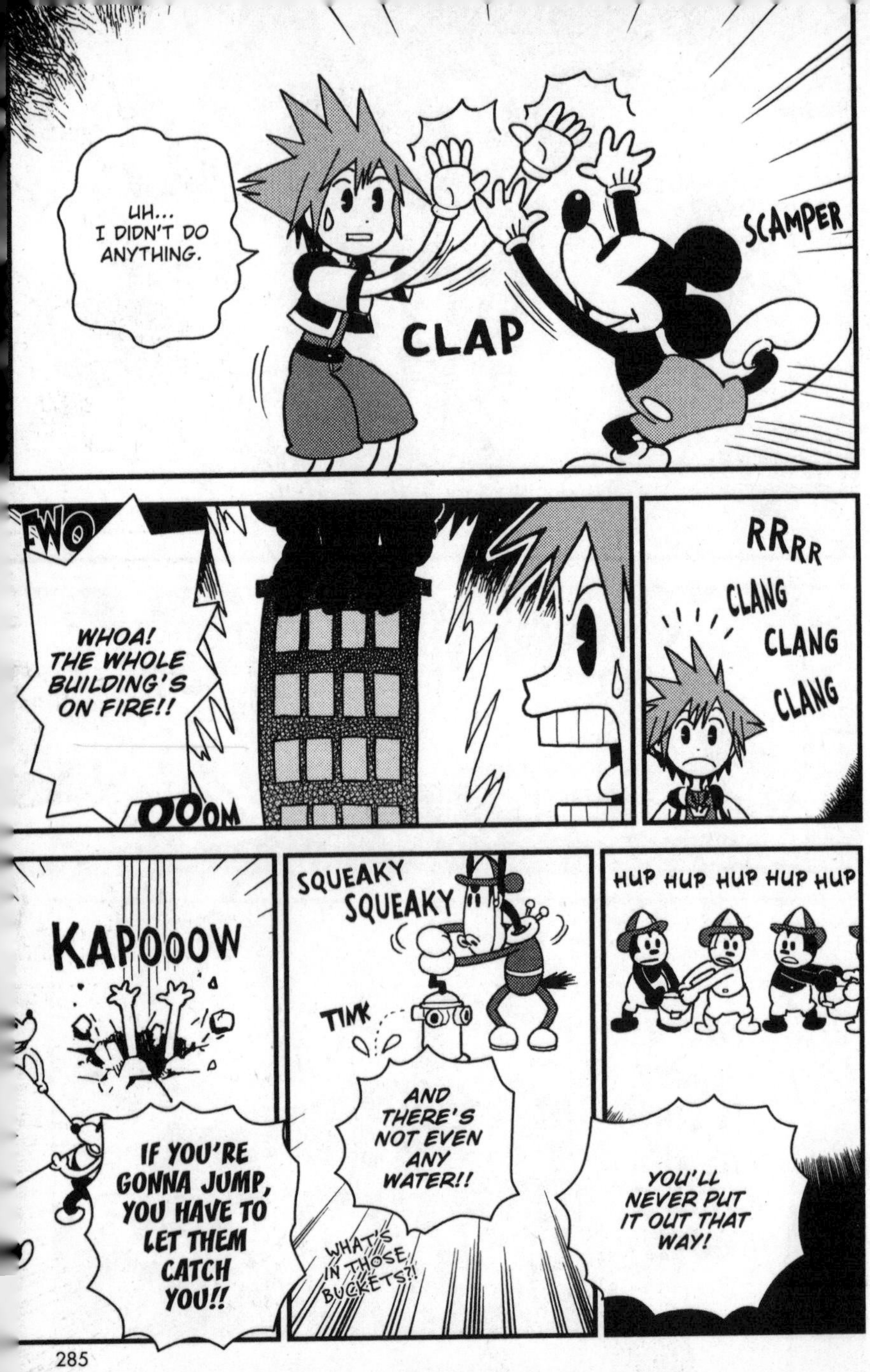
SCAMPER
CLAP
UH... I DIDN'T DO ANYTHING.
RRRR
CLANG
CLANG
CLANG
FWO
WHOA! THE WHOLE BUILDING'S ON FIRE!!
OOOM
HUP HUP HUP HUP HUP
YOU'LL NEVER PUT IT OUT THAT WAY!
SQUEAKY
SQUEAKY
TINK
AND THERE'S NOT EVEN ANY WATER!!
WHAT'S IN THOSE BUCKETS?!
KAPOOOW
IF YOU'RE GONNA JUMP, YOU HAVE TO LET THEM CATCH YOU!!

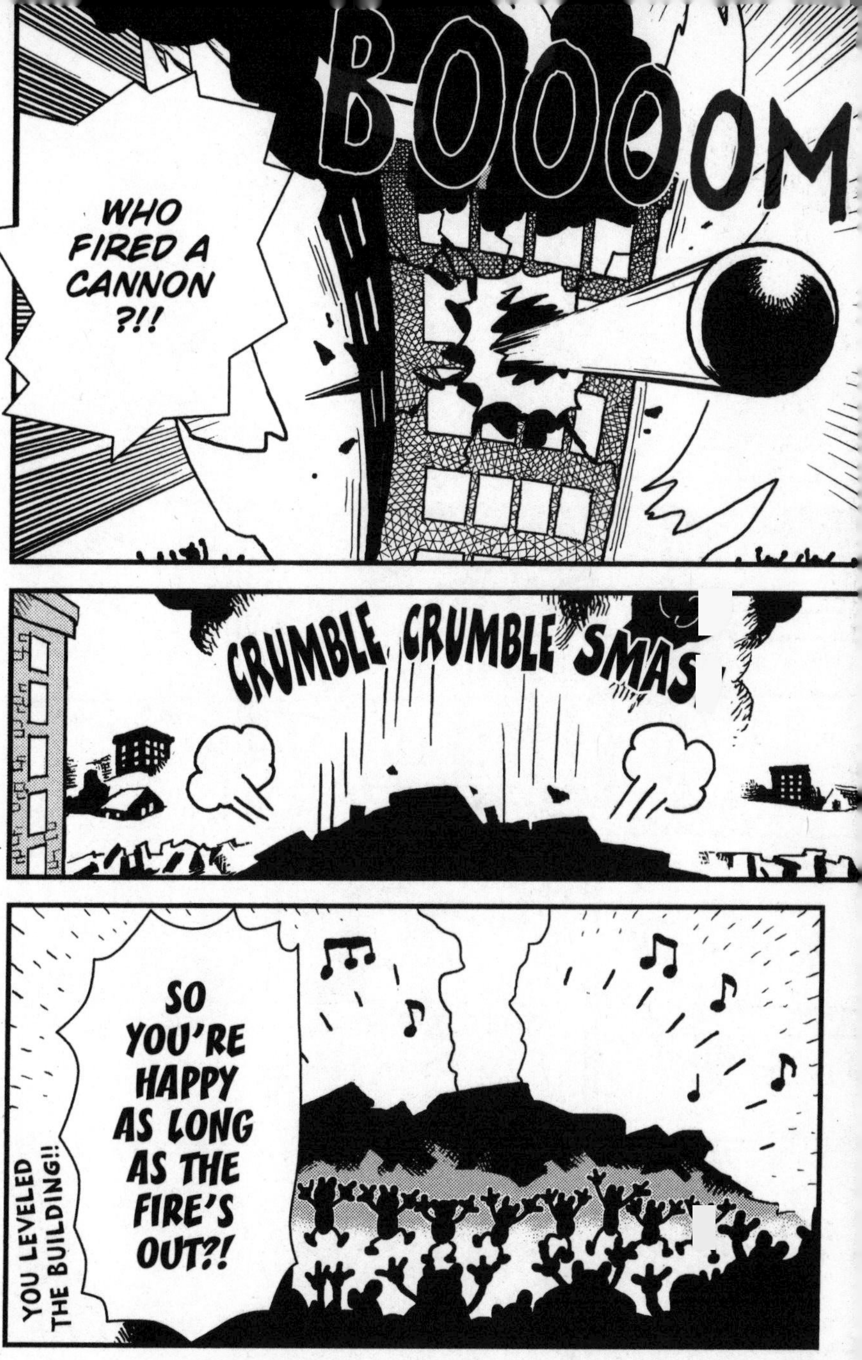
BOOOOM
WHO FIRED A CANNON ?!!
CRUMBLE CRUMBLE SMAS
SO YOU'RE HAPPY AS LONG AS THE FIRE'S OUT?!
YOU LEVELED THE BUILDING!!

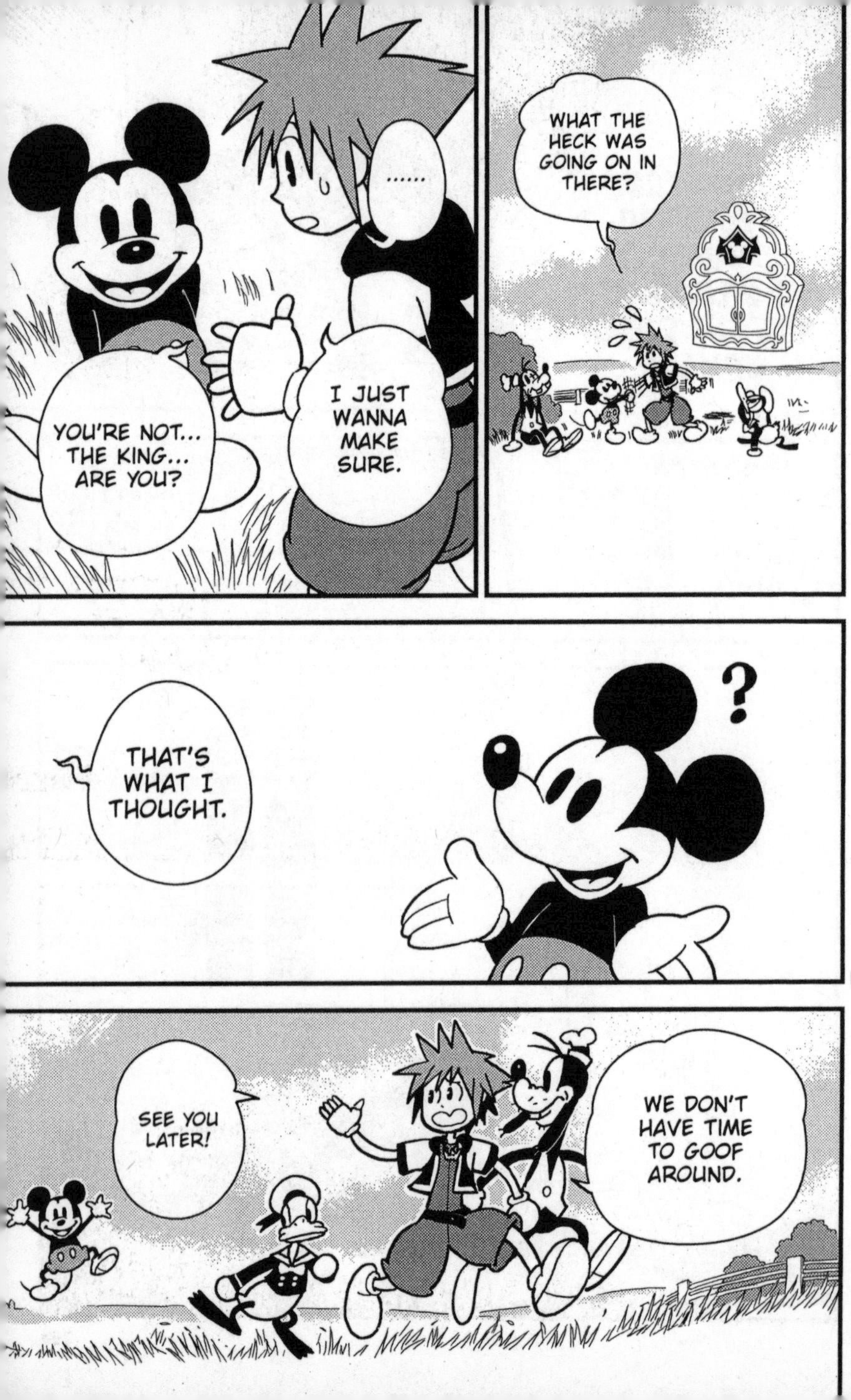
WHAT THE HECK WAS GOING ON IN THERE?
......
I JUST WANNA MAKE SURE.
YOU'RE NOT... THE KING... ARE YOU?
THAT'S WHAT I THOUGHT.
WE DON'T HAVE TIME TO GOOF AROUND.
SEE YOU LATER!

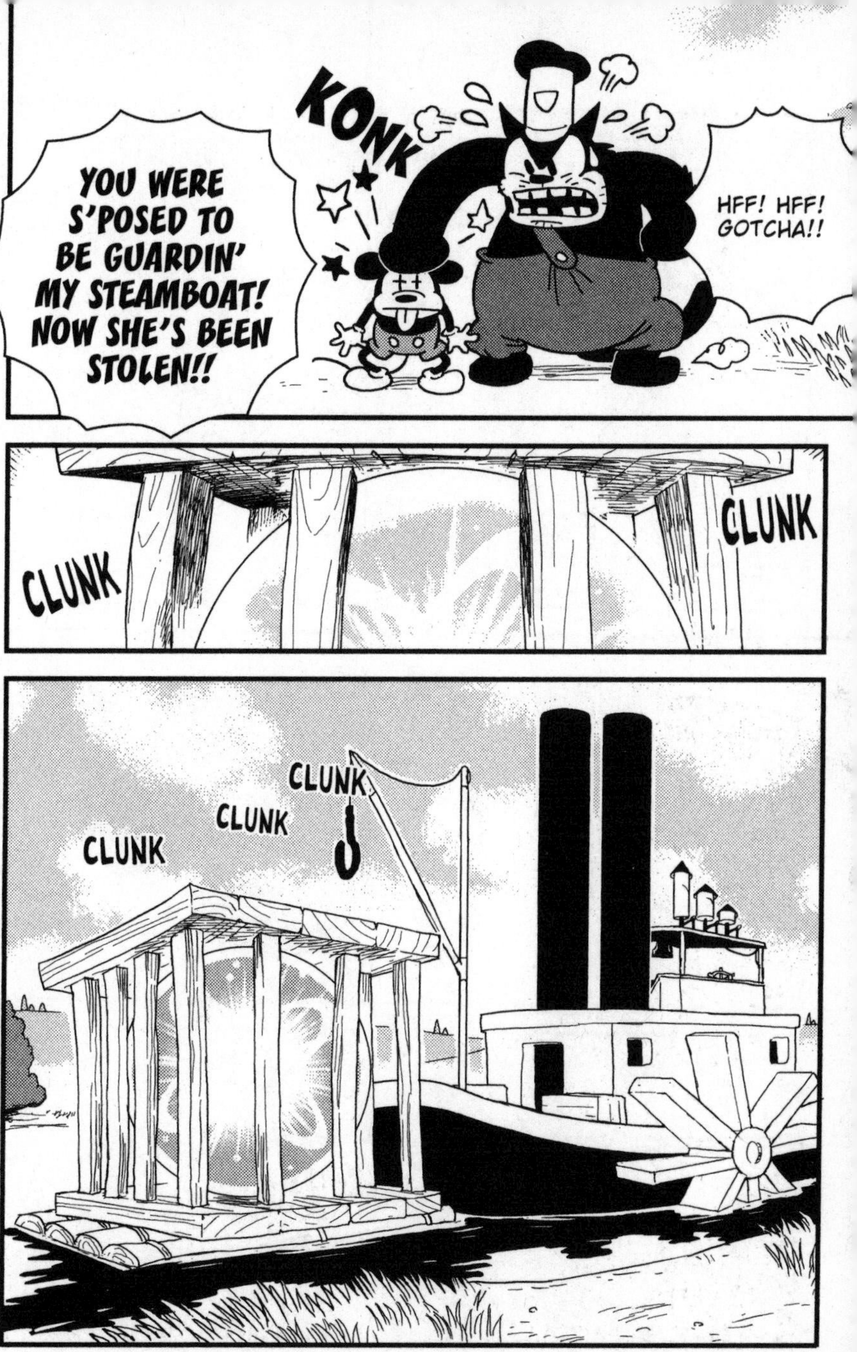
HFF! HFF! GOTCHA!!
KONK
YOU WERE S'POSED TO BE GUARDIN' MY STEAMBOAT! NOW SHE'S BEEN STOLEN!!
CLUNK
CLUNK
CLUNK
CLUNK
CLUNK

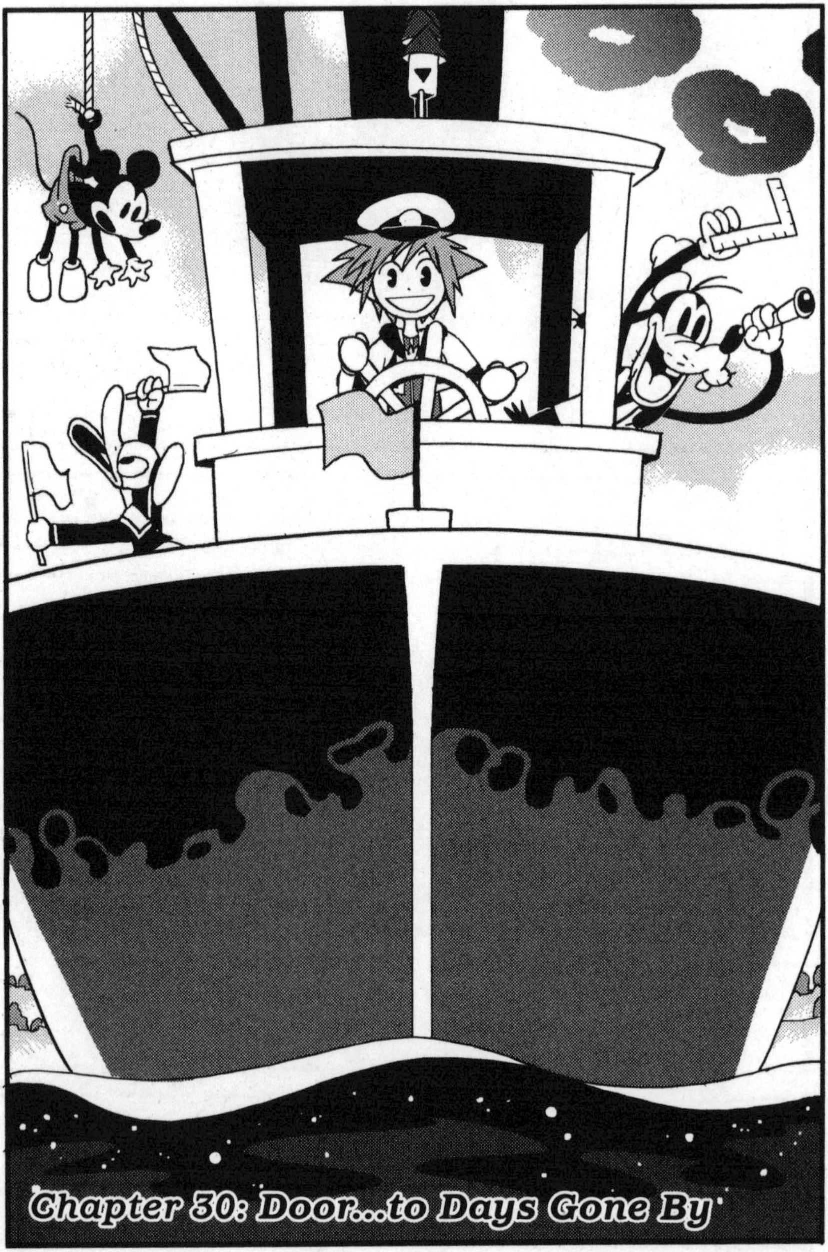
Chapter 30: Door...to Days Gone By

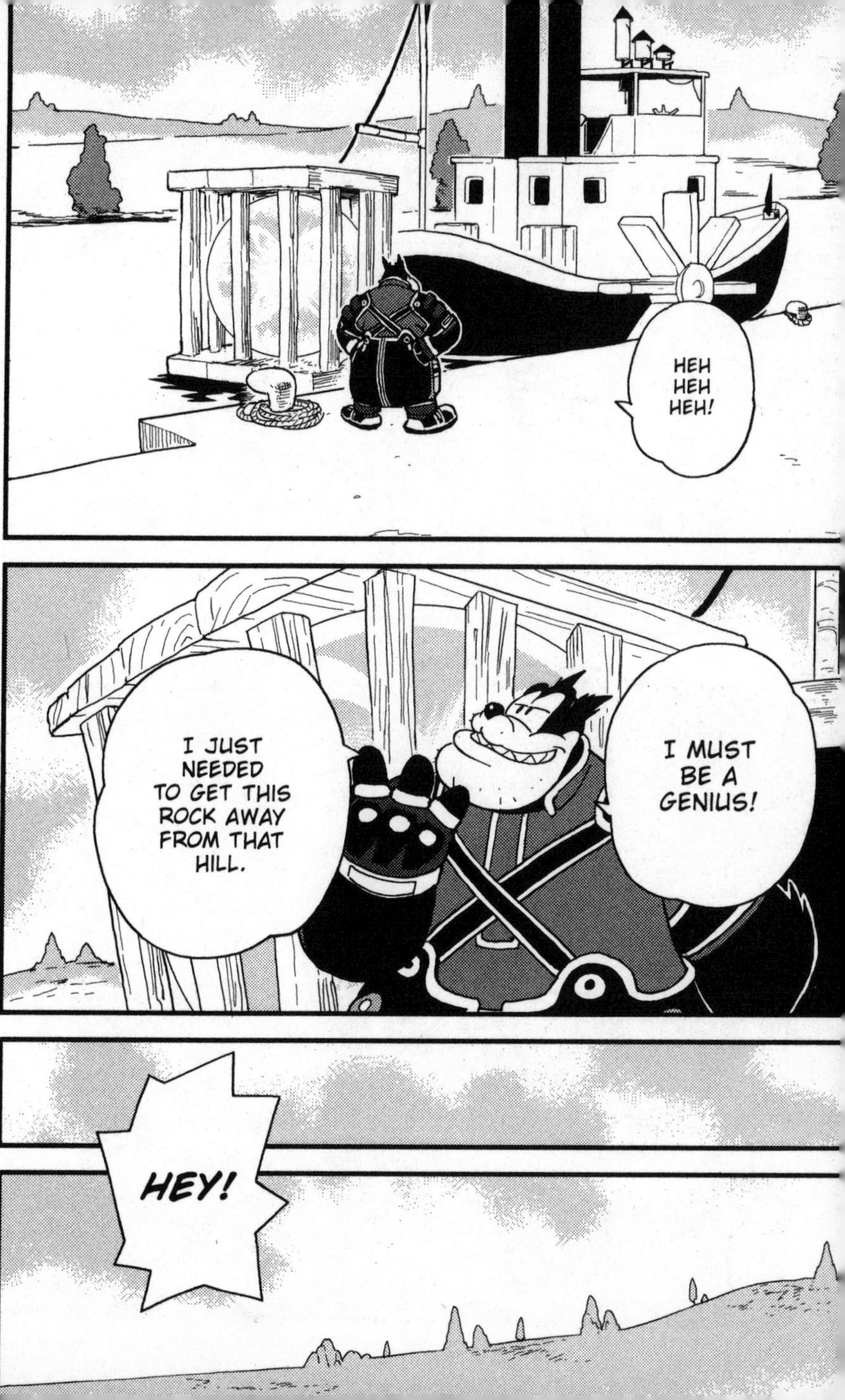
HEH
HEH
HEH!
I MUST BE A GENIUS!
I JUST NEEDED TO GET THIS ROCK AWAY FROM THAT HILL.
HEY!

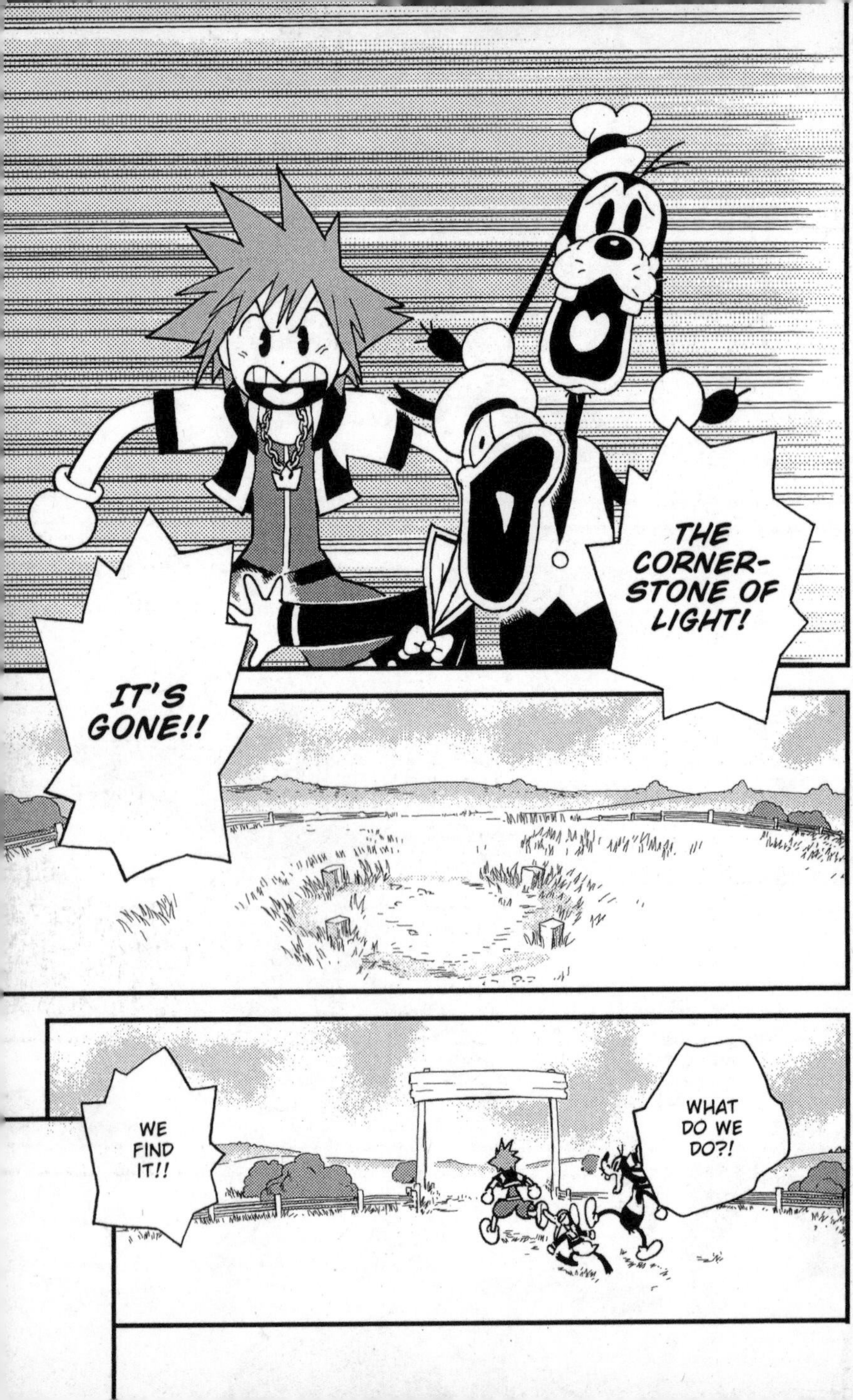
THE CORNER-STONE OF LIGHT!
IT'S GONE!!
WHAT DO WE DO?!
WE FIND IT!!

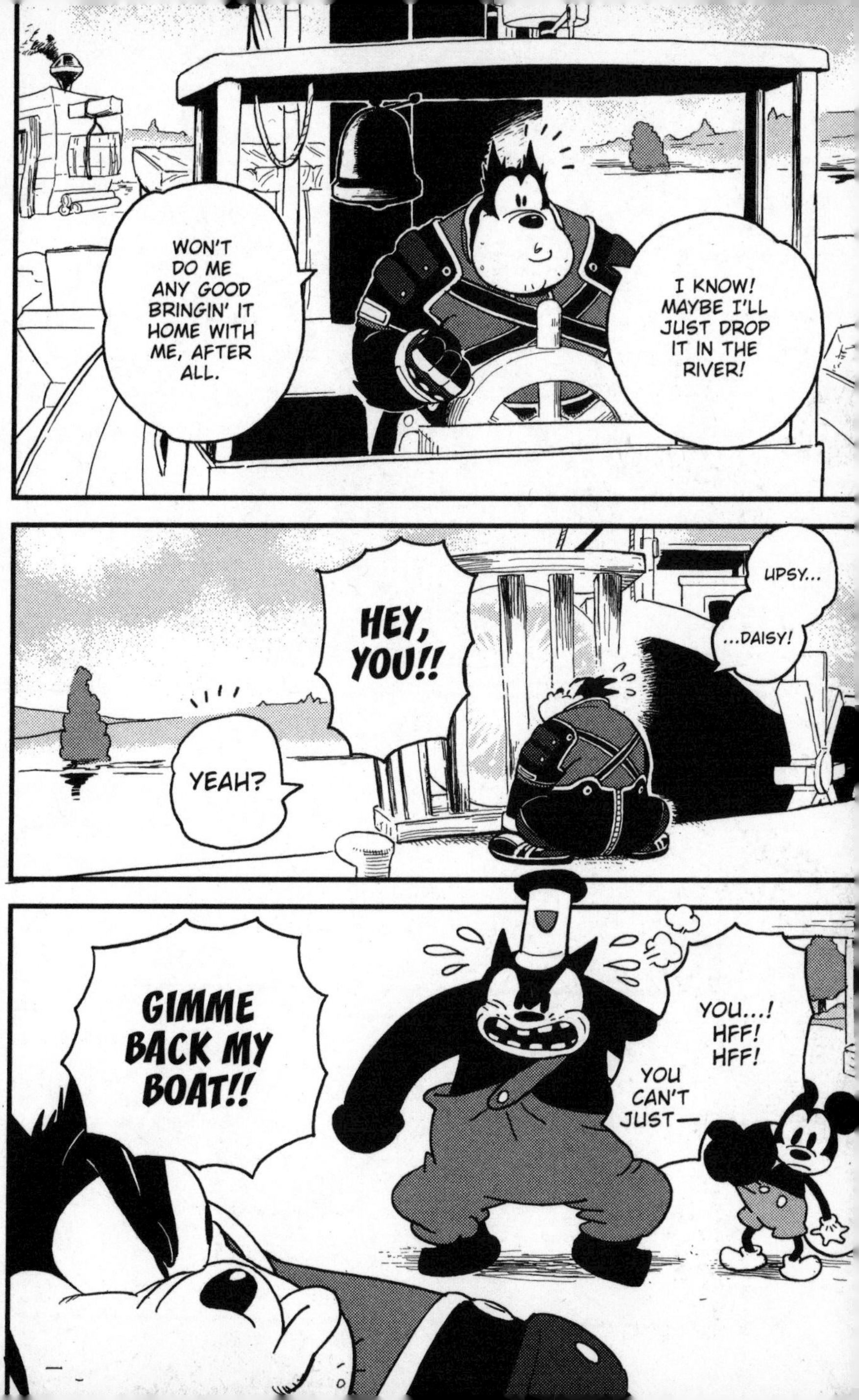
WON'T DO ME ANY GOOD BRINGIN' IT HOME WITH ME, AFTER ALL.
I KNOW! MAYBE I'LL JUST DROP IT IN THE RIVER!
UPSY...
...DAISY!
HEY, YOU!!
YEAH?
YOU...! HFF! HFF!
YOU CAN'T JUST—
GIMME BACK MY BOAT!!

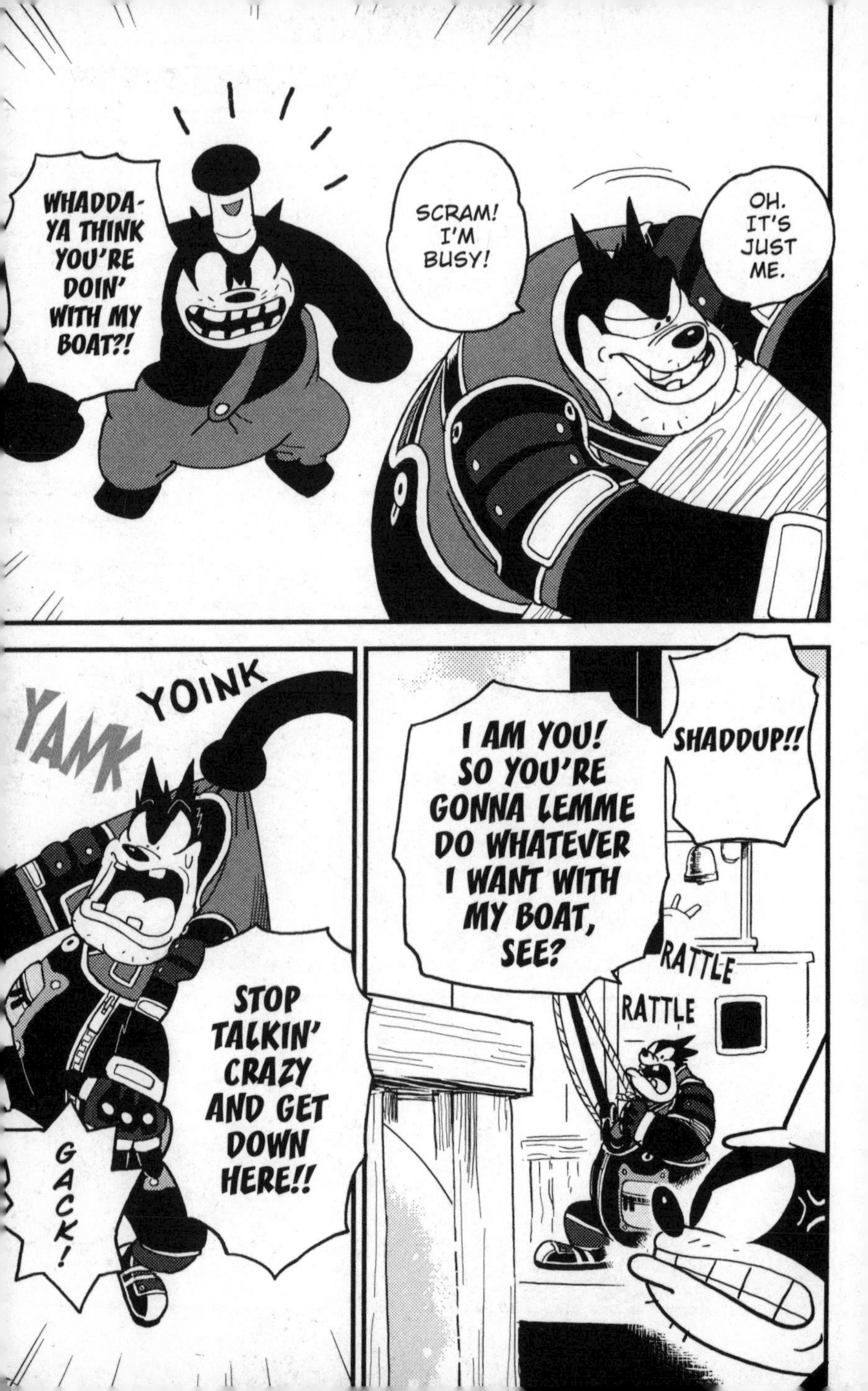
OH. IT'S JUST ME.
SCRAM! I'M BUSY!
WHADDA-YA THINK YOU'RE DOIN' WITH MY BOAT?!
SHADDUP!!
I AM YOU! SO YOU'RE GONNA LEMME DO WHATEVER I WANT WITH MY BOAT, SEE?
RATTLE
RATTLE
YOINK
YANK
STOP TALKIN' CRAZY AND GET DOWN HERE!!
GACK!

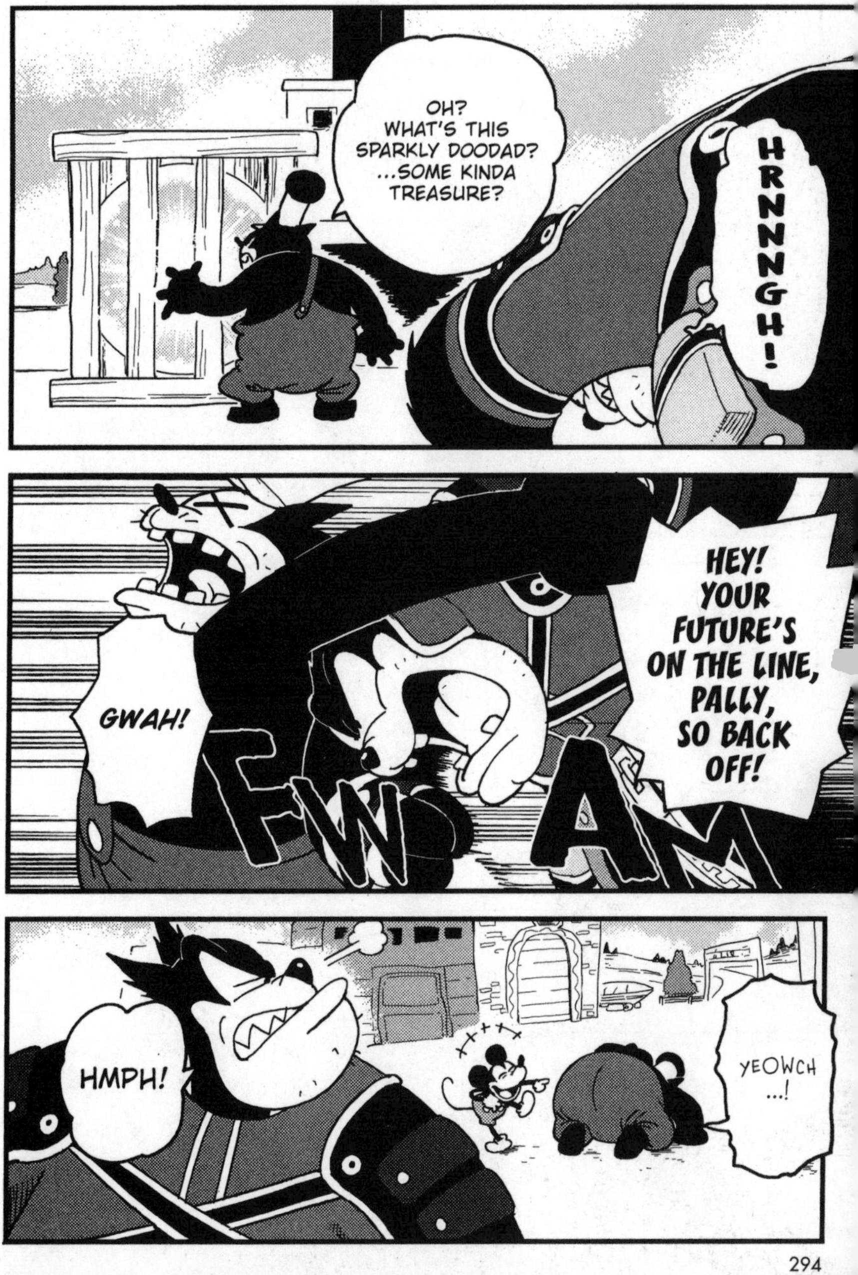
HRNNNGH!
OH? WHAT'S THIS SPARKLY DOODAD? ...SOME KINDA TREASURE?
HEY! YOUR FUTURE'S ON THE LINE, PALLY, SO BACK OFF!
FWAM
GWAH!
YEOWCH ...!
HMPH!

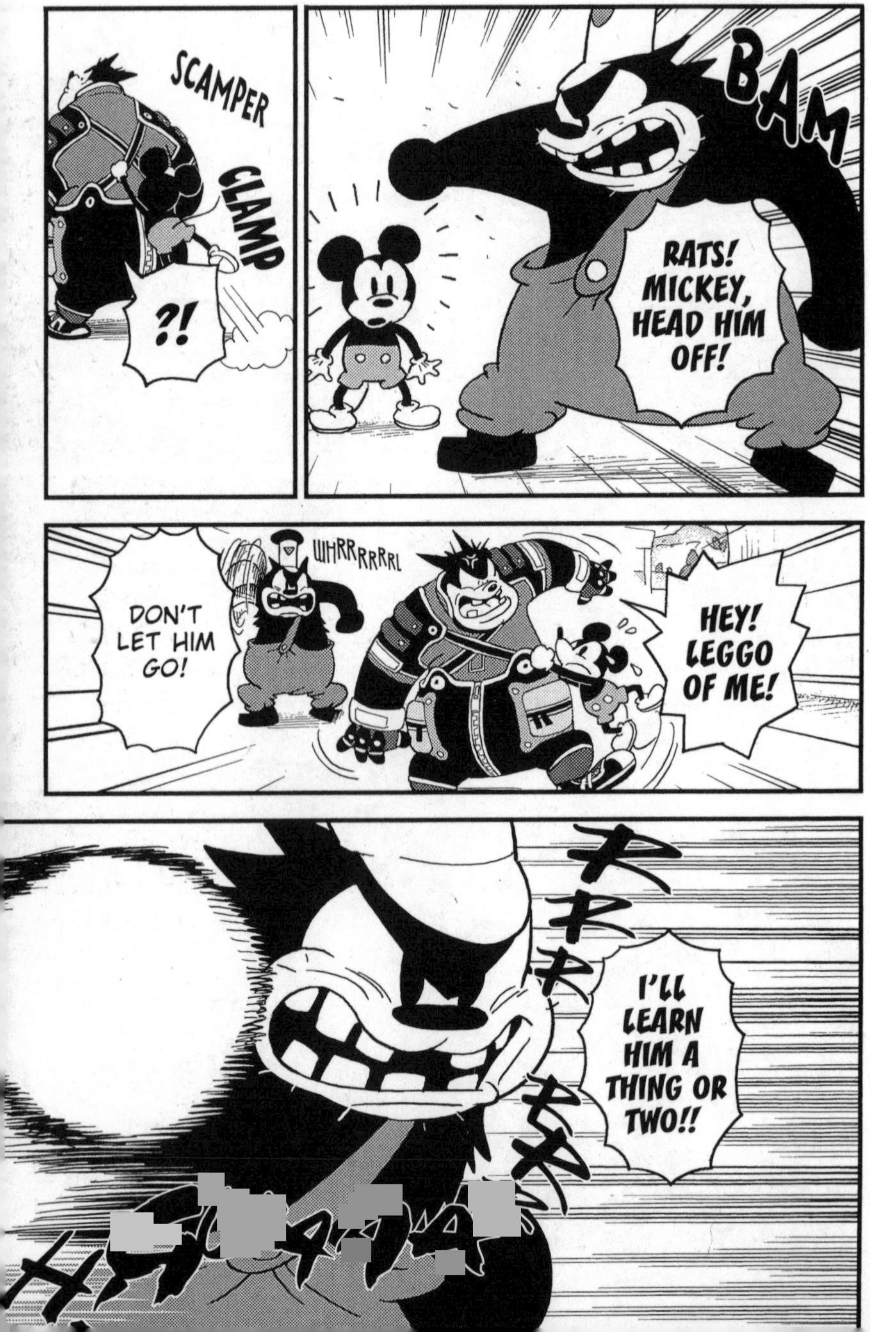
BAM
RATS! MICKEY, HEAD HIM OFF!
SCAMPER
CLAMP
?!
HEY! LEGGO OF ME!
WHRRRRRL
DON'T LET HIM GO!
I'LL LEARN HIM A THING OR TWO!!

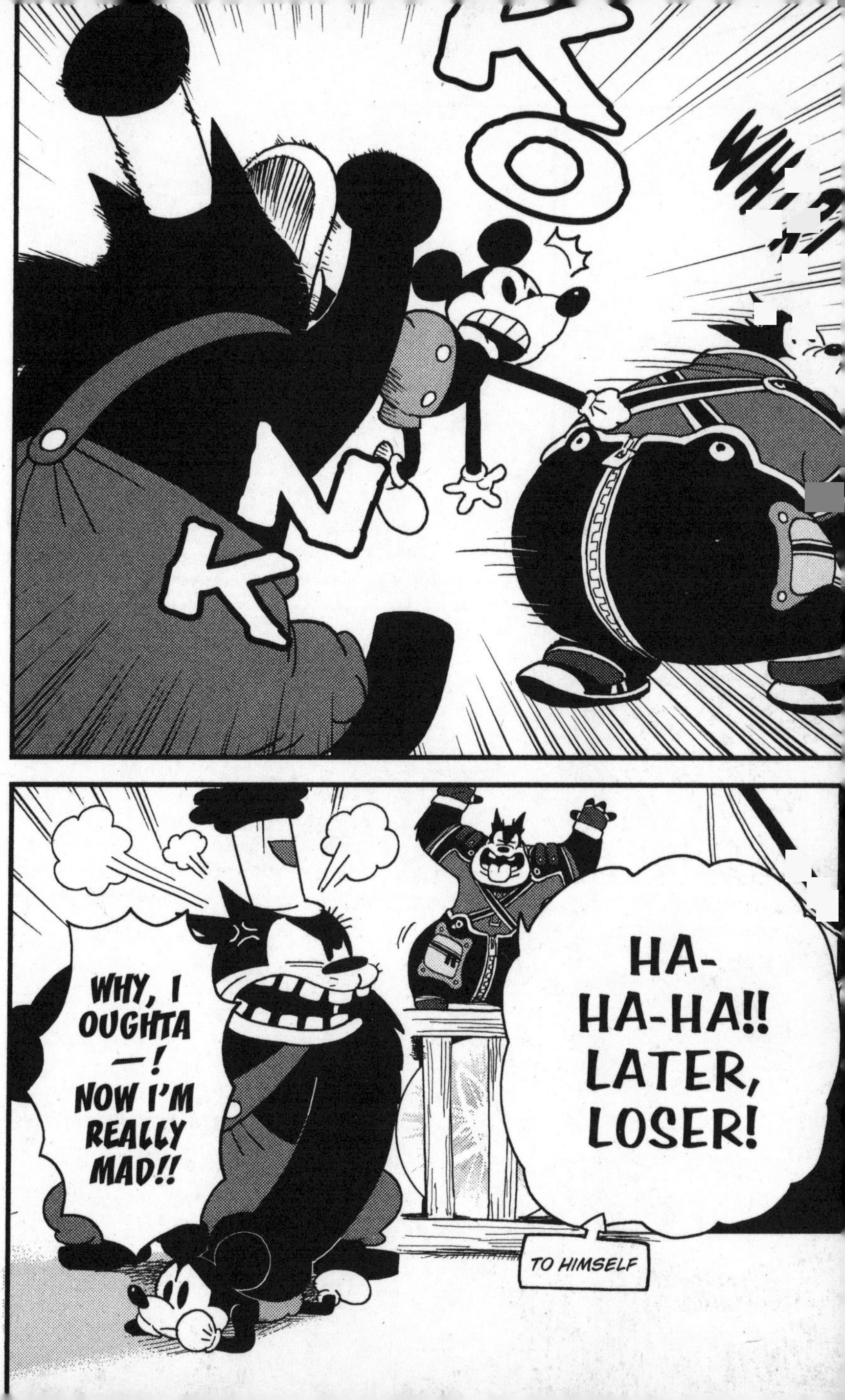
KO
NK
HA-HA-HA!! LATER, LOSER!
TO HIMSELF
WHY, I OUGHTA—! NOW I'M REALLY MAD!!

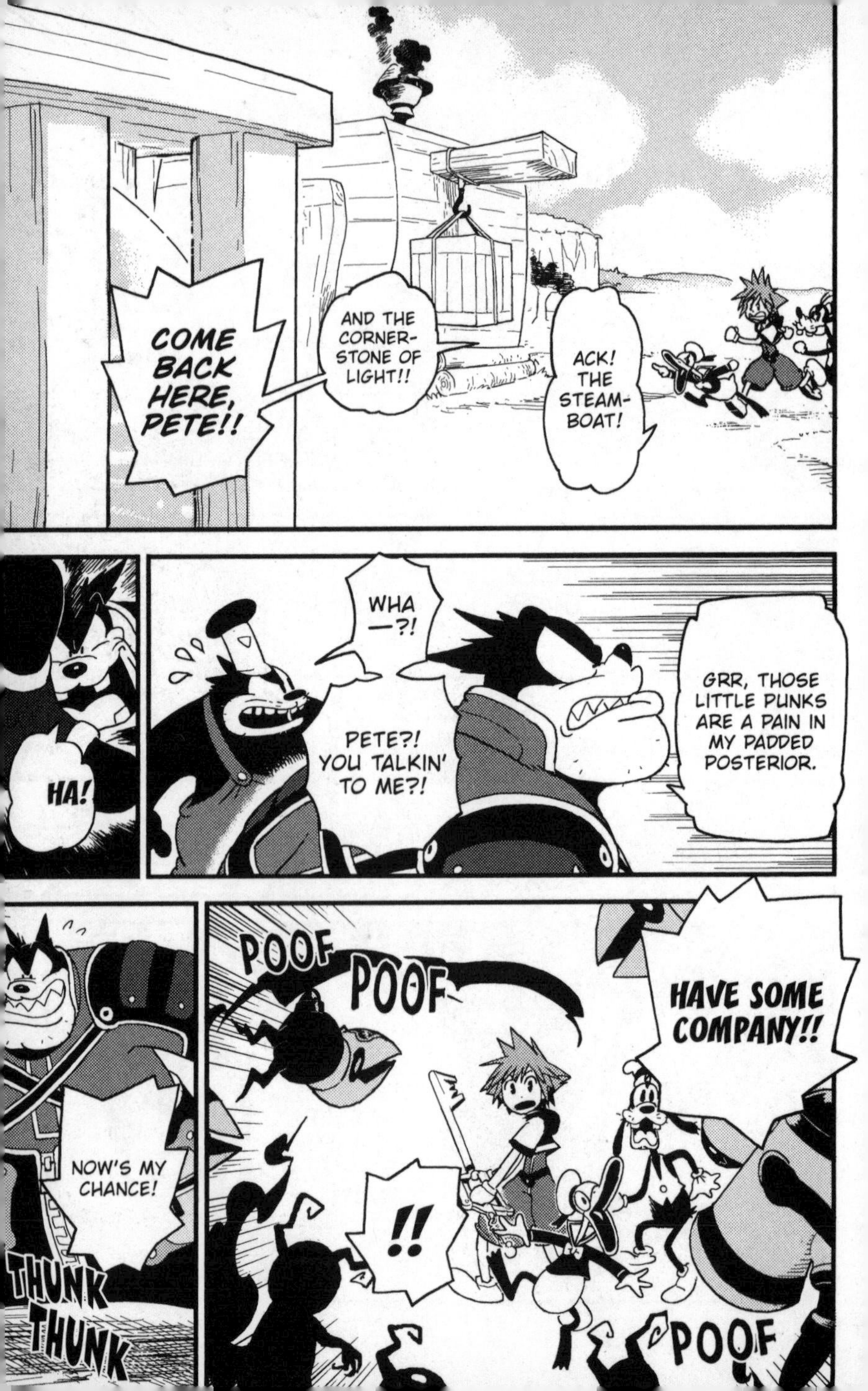
ACK! THE STEAM-BOAT!
AND THE CORNER-STONE OF LIGHT!!
COME BACK HERE, PETE!!
GRR, THOSE LITTLE PUNKS ARE A PAIN IN MY PADDED POSTERIOR.
WHA—?!
PETE?! YOU TALKIN' TO ME?!
HA!
HAVE SOME COMPANY!!
POOF
POOF
!!
POOF
NOW'S MY CHANCE!
THUNK
THUNK

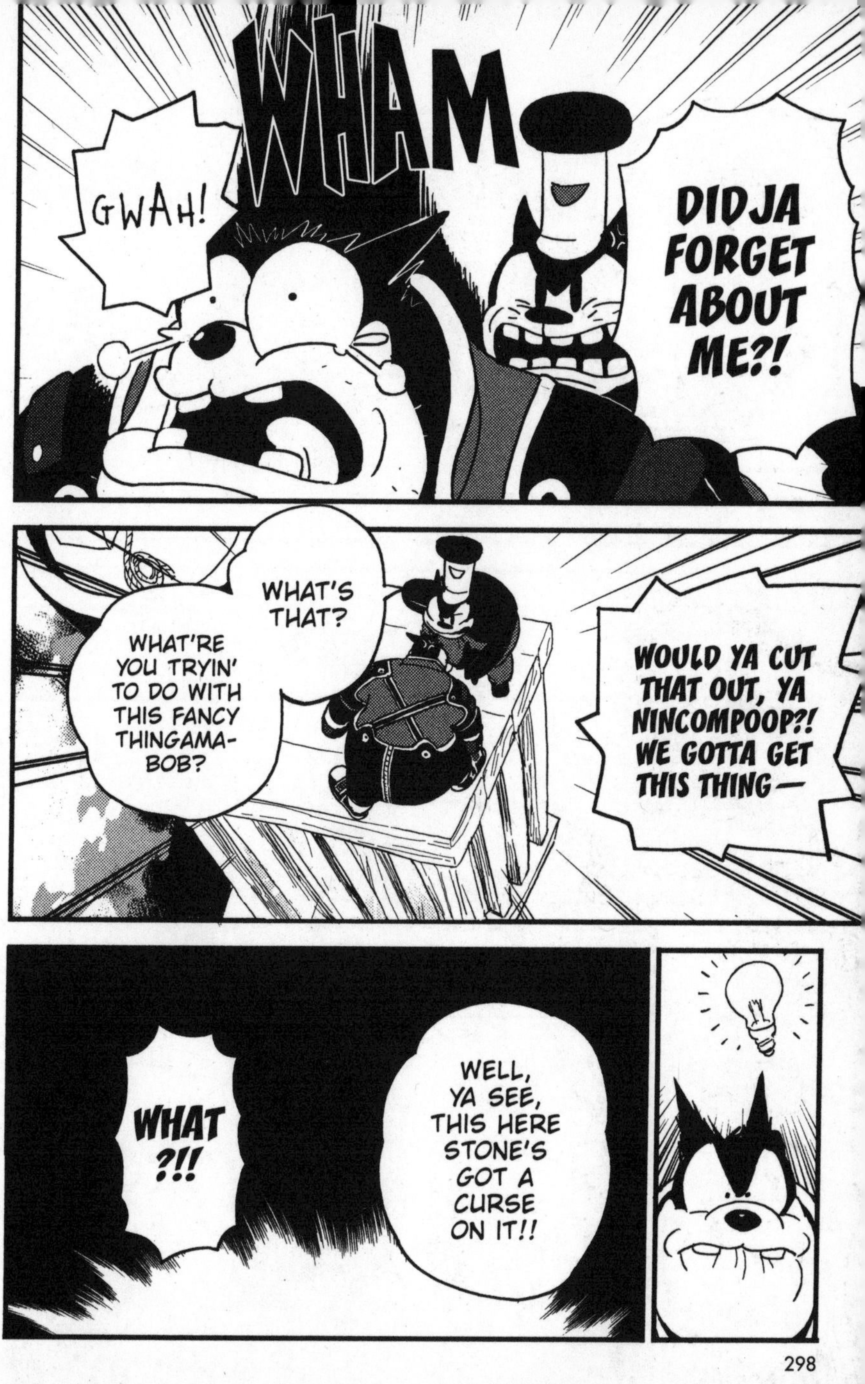
DIDJA FORGET ABOUT ME?!
WHAM
GWAH!
WOULD YA CUT THAT OUT, YA NINCOMPOOP?! WE GOTTA GET THIS THING—
WHAT'S THAT?
WHAT'RE YOU TRYIN' TO DO WITH THIS FANCY THINGAMA-BOB?
WELL, YA SEE, THIS HERE STONE'S GOT A CURSE ON IT!!
WHAT ?!!

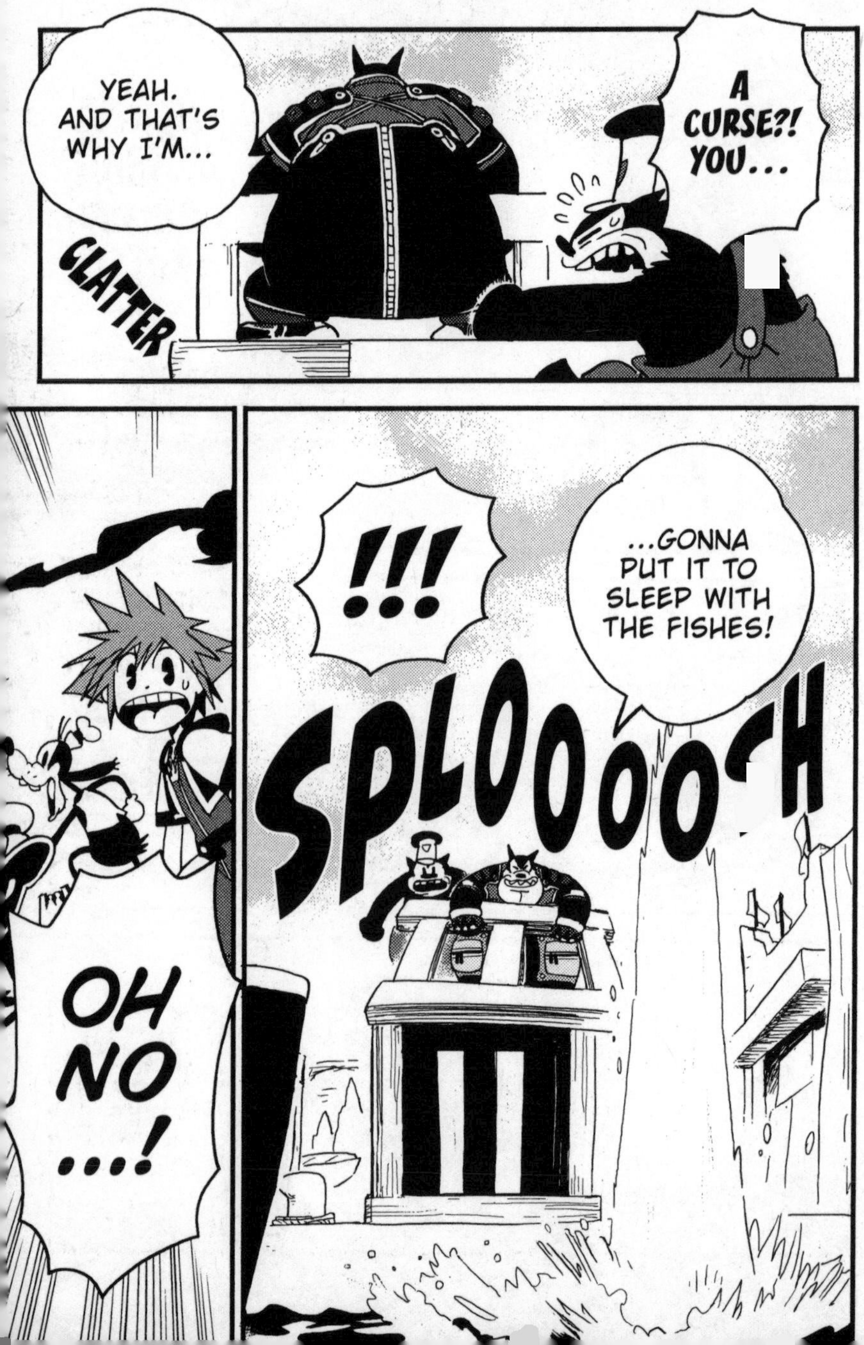
A CURSE?! YOU...
YEAH. AND THAT'S WHY I'M...
CLATTER
...GONNA PUT IT TO SLEEP WITH THE FISHES!
!!!
SPLOOOOO H
OH NO ...!

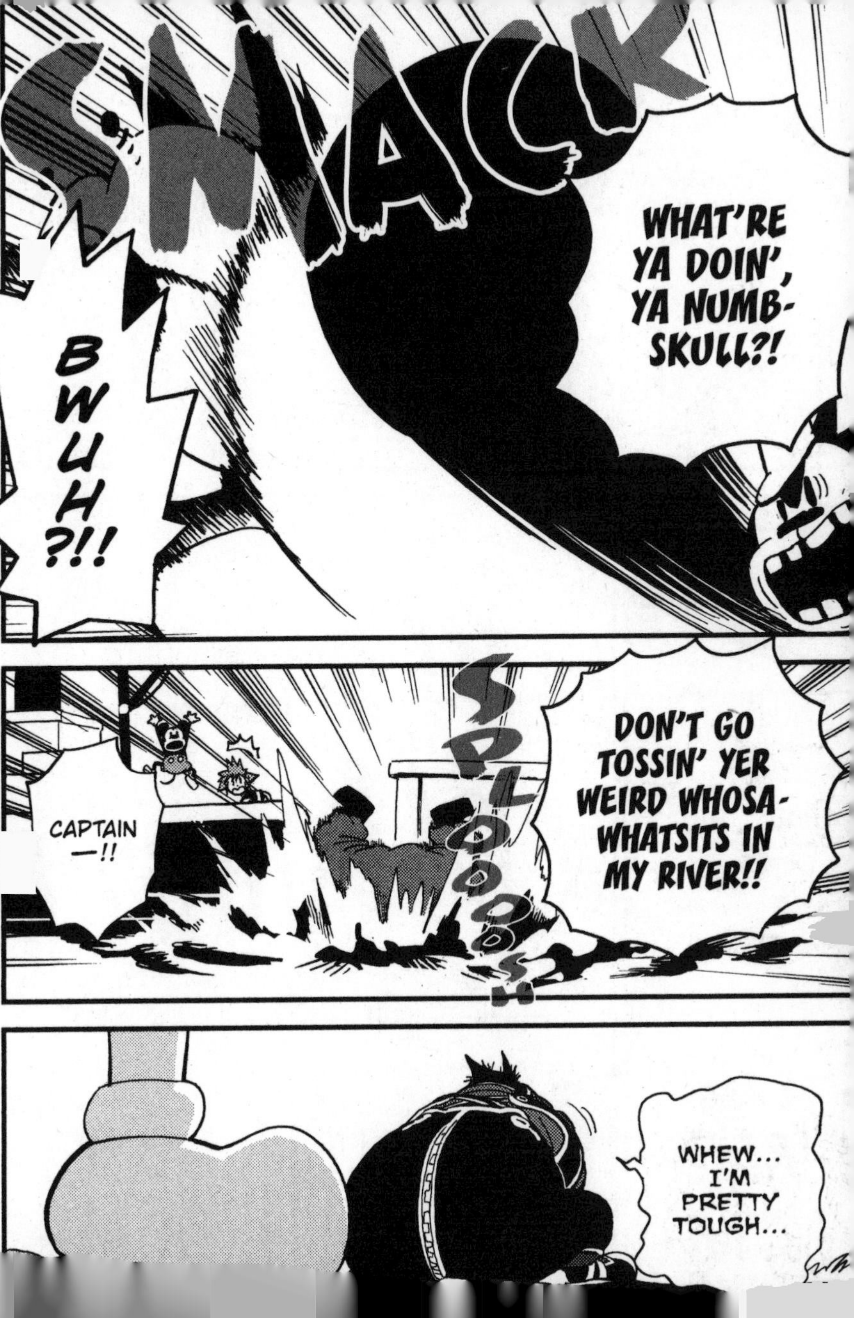
SMACK
WHAT'RE YA DOIN', YA NUMB-SKULL?!
BWUH?!!
DON'T GO TOSSIN' YER WEIRD WHOSA-WHATSITS IN MY RIVER!!
SPLOOOOS!!
CAPTAIN—!!
WHEW… I'M PRETTY TOUGH…

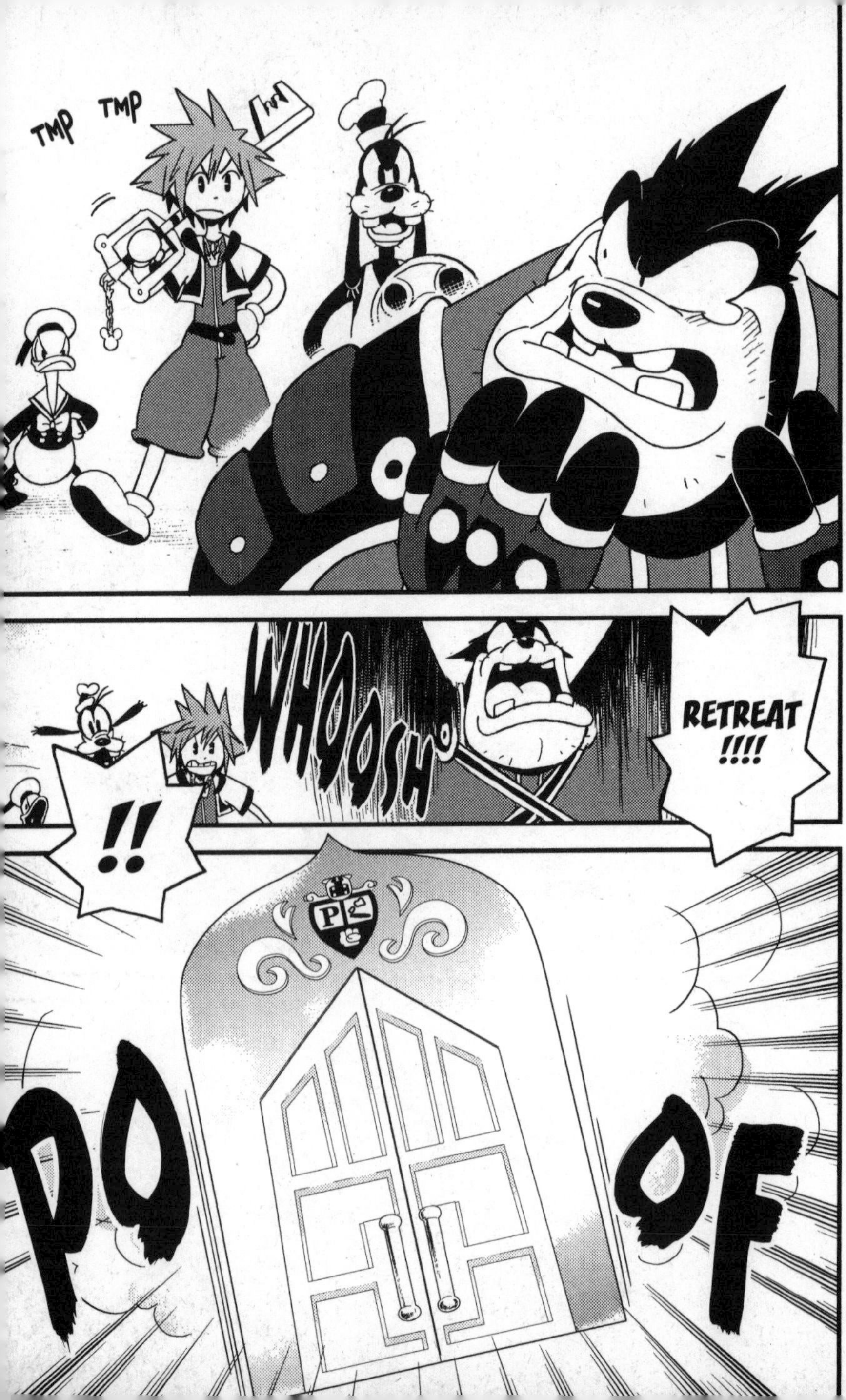
TMP TMP
RETREAT!!!!
WHOOSH
!!
POOF

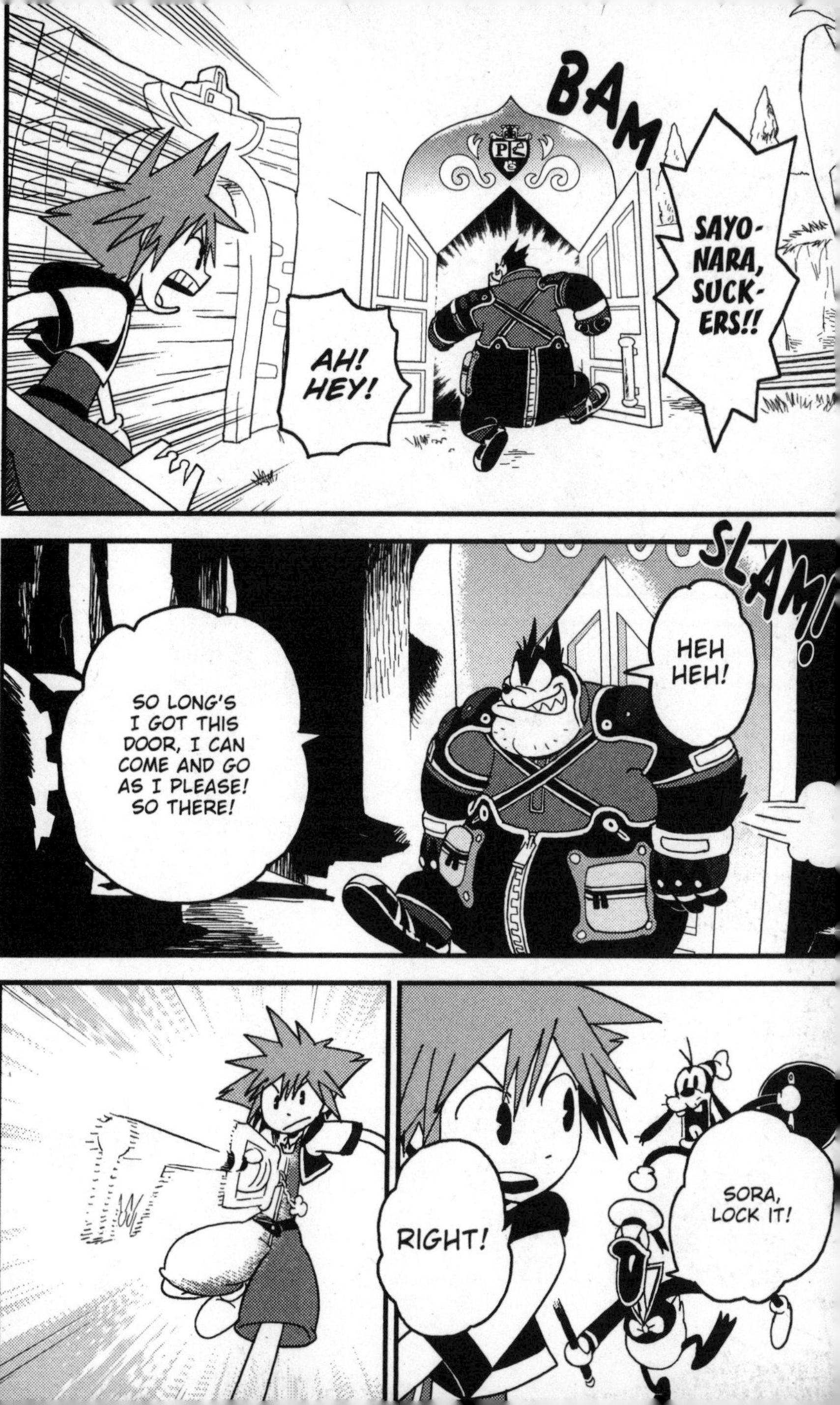
BAM
SAYO-NARA, SUCK-ERS!!
AH! HEY!
SLAM!
HEH HEH!
SO LONG'S I GOT THIS DOOR, I CAN COME AND GO AS I PLEASE! SO THERE!
SORA, LOCK IT!
RIGHT!

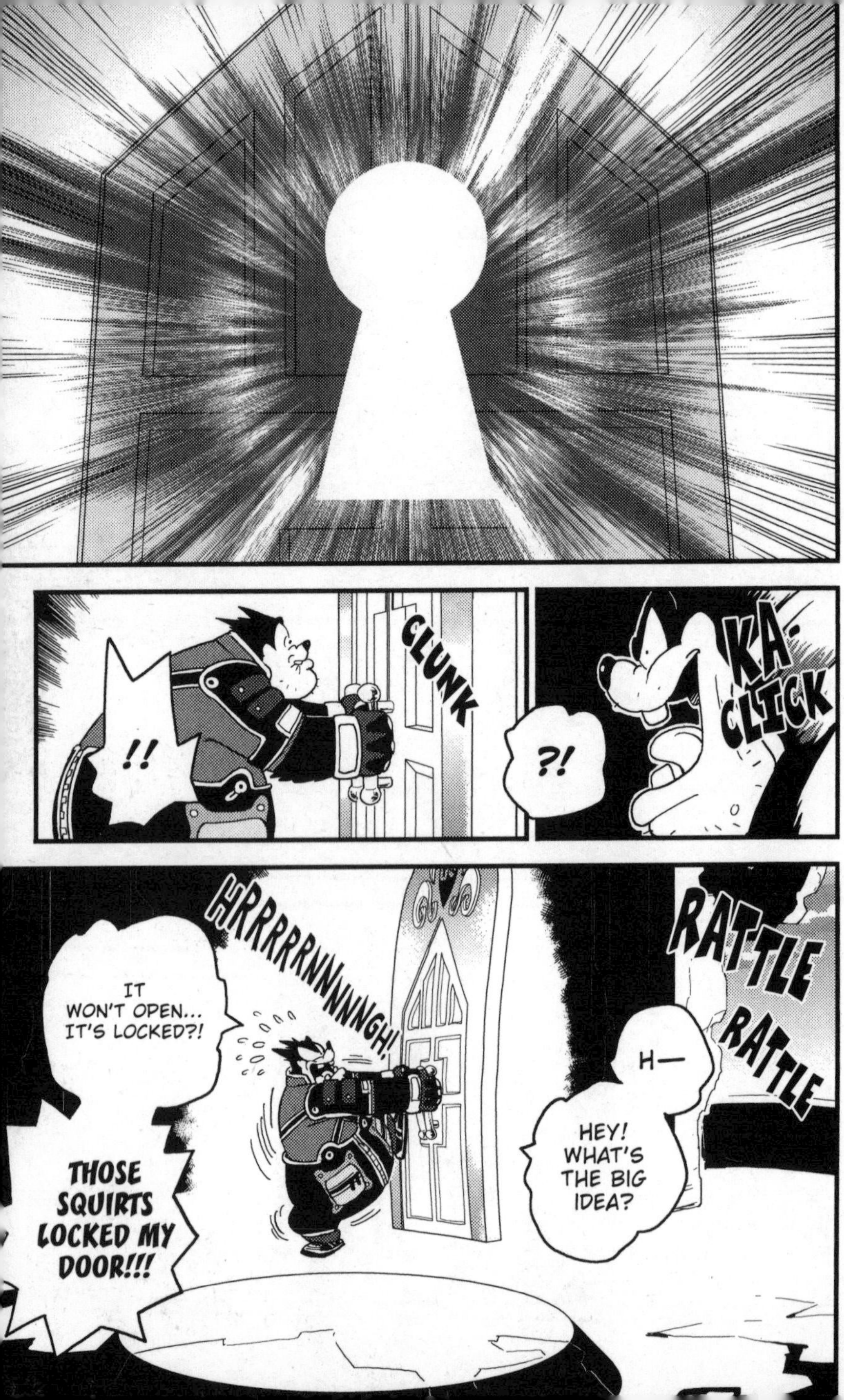
KA-CLICK
?!
CLUNK
!!
RATTLE RATTLE
H—
HEY! WHAT'S THE BIG IDEA?
HRRRRRNNNNNGH!
IT WON'T OPEN... IT'S LOCKED?!
THOSE SQUIRTS LOCKED MY DOOR!!!

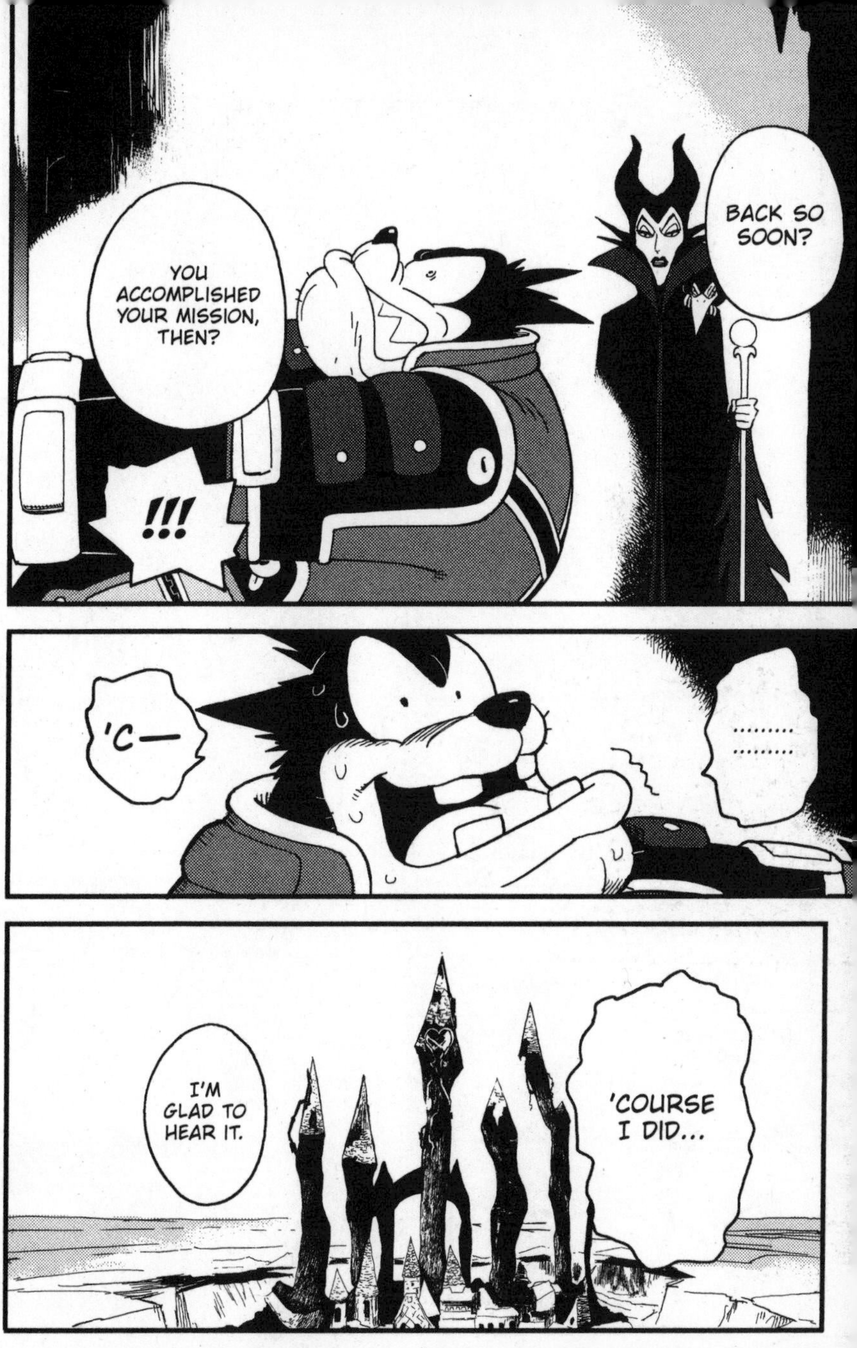
BACK SO SOON?
YOU ACCOMPLISHED YOUR MISSION, THEN?
!!!
....
....
'C—
'COURSE I DID...
I'M GLAD TO HEAR IT.

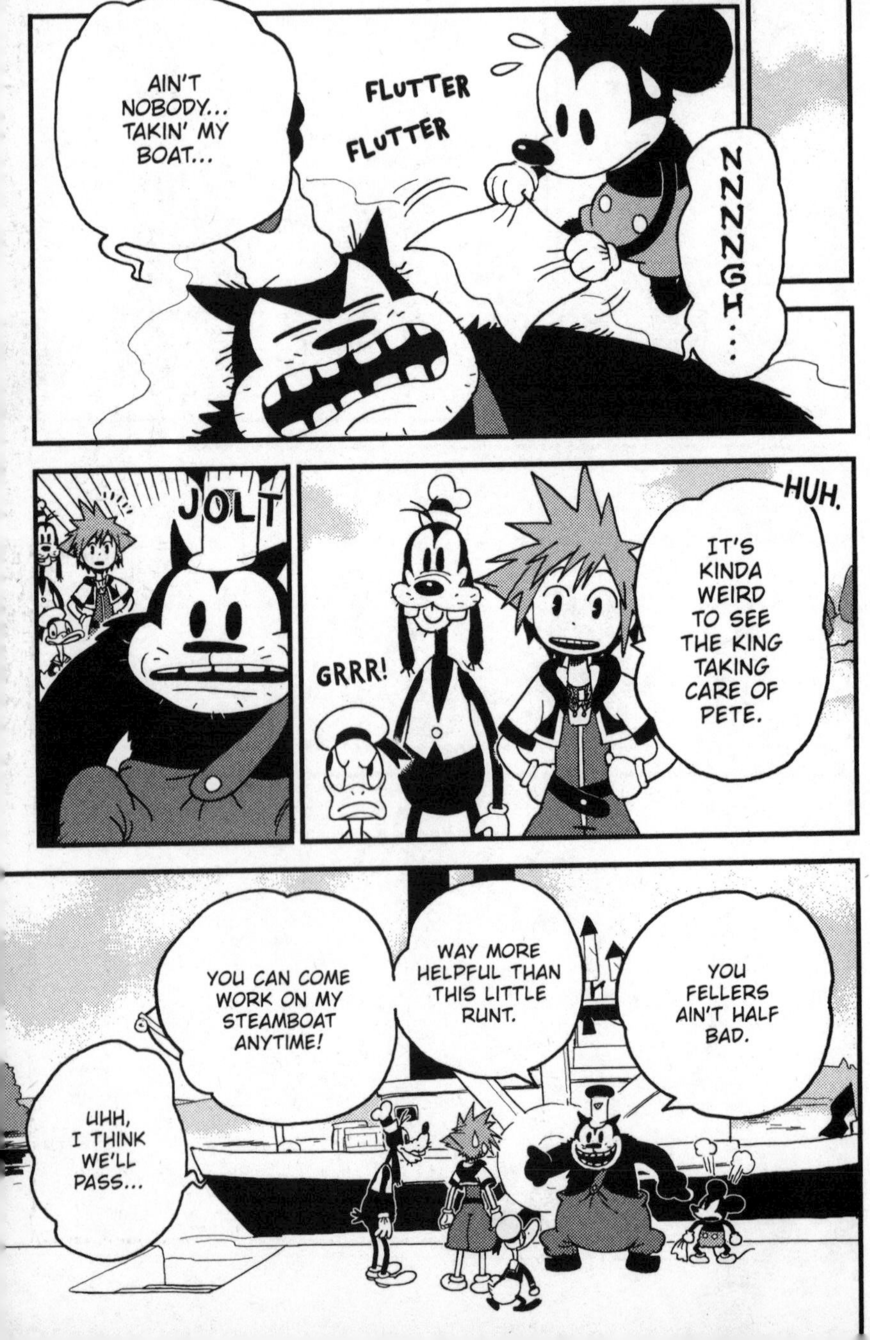
NNNNGH...
FLUTTER
FLUTTER
AIN'T NOBODY... TAKIN' MY BOAT...
HUH.
IT'S KINDA WEIRD TO SEE THE KING TAKING CARE OF PETE.
GRRR!
JOLT
YOU FELLERS AIN'T HALF BAD.
WAY MORE HELPFUL THAN THIS LITTLE RUNT.
YOU CAN COME WORK ON MY STEAMBOAT ANYTIME!
UHH, I THINK WE'LL PASS...

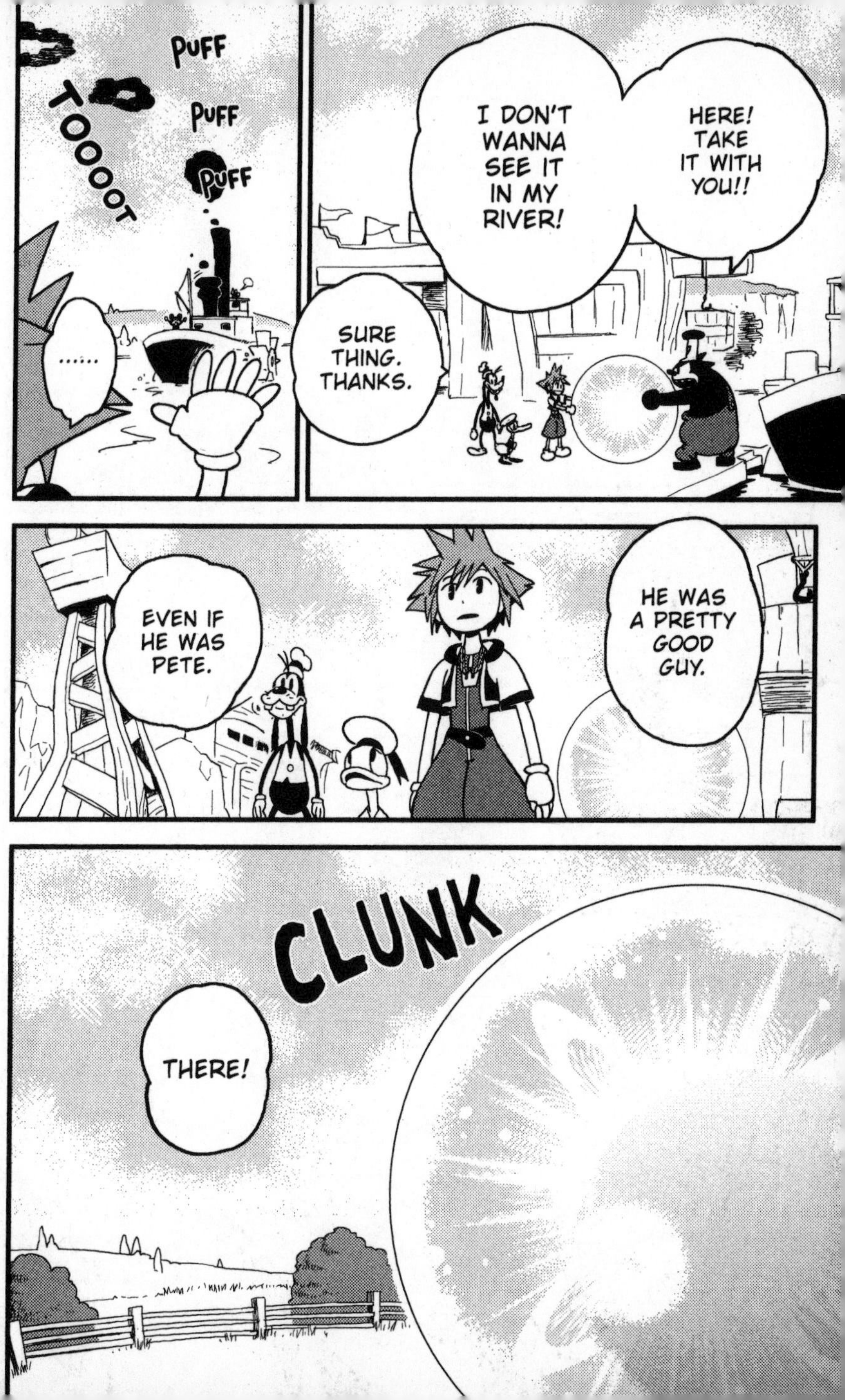
HERE! TAKE IT WITH YOU!!
I DON'T WANNA SEE IT IN MY RIVER!
SURE THING. THANKS.
PUFF
PUFF
PUFF
TOOOOT
......
HE WAS A PRETTY GOOD GUY.
EVEN IF HE WAS PETE.
CLUNK
THERE!

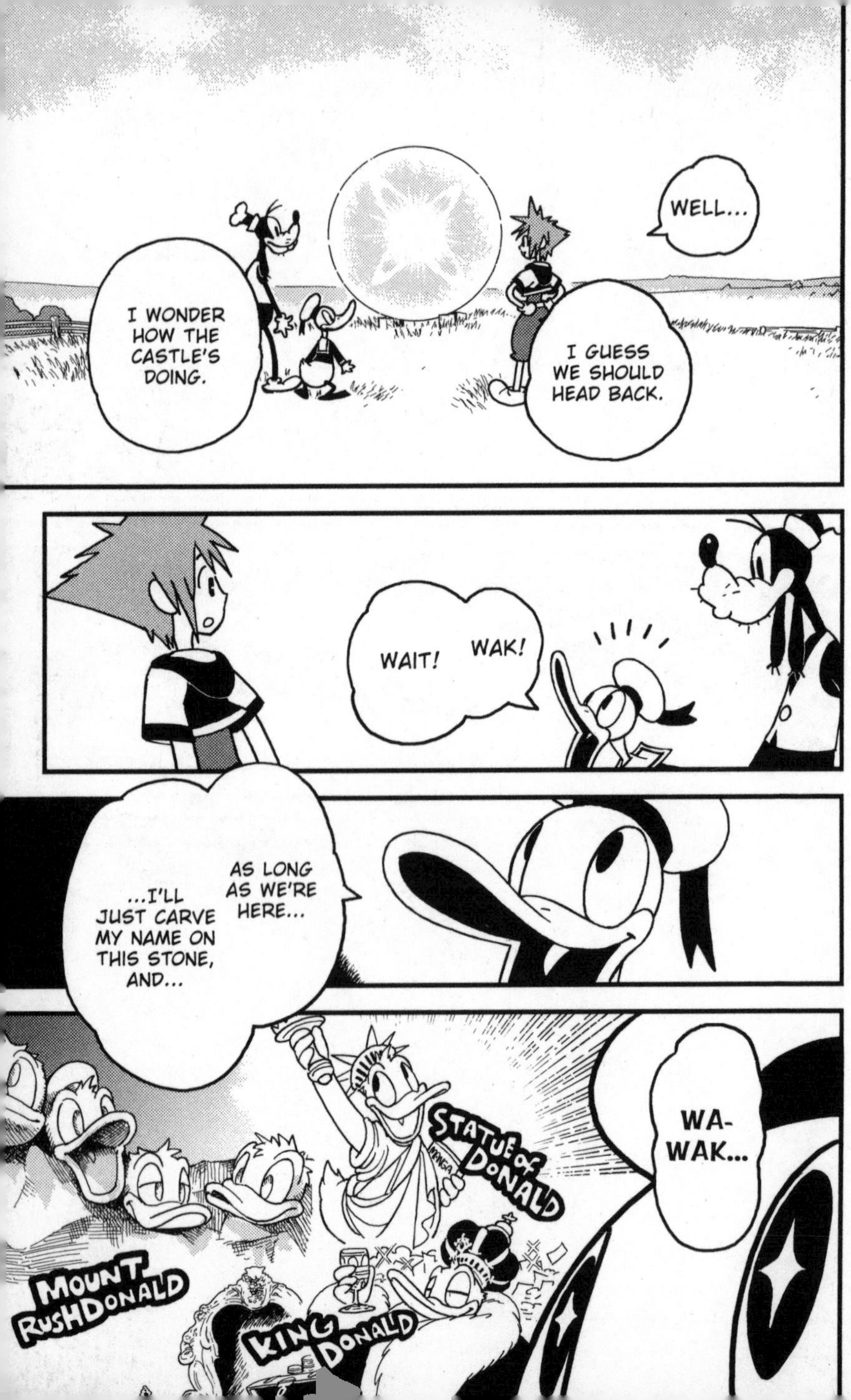
WELL...
I GUESS WE SHOULD HEAD BACK.
I WONDER HOW THE CASTLE'S DOING.
WAIT! WAK!
AS LONG AS WE'RE HERE... ...I'LL JUST CARVE MY NAME ON THIS STONE, AND...
WA-WAK...
STATUE of DONALD
KING DONALD
MOUNT RUSHDONALD

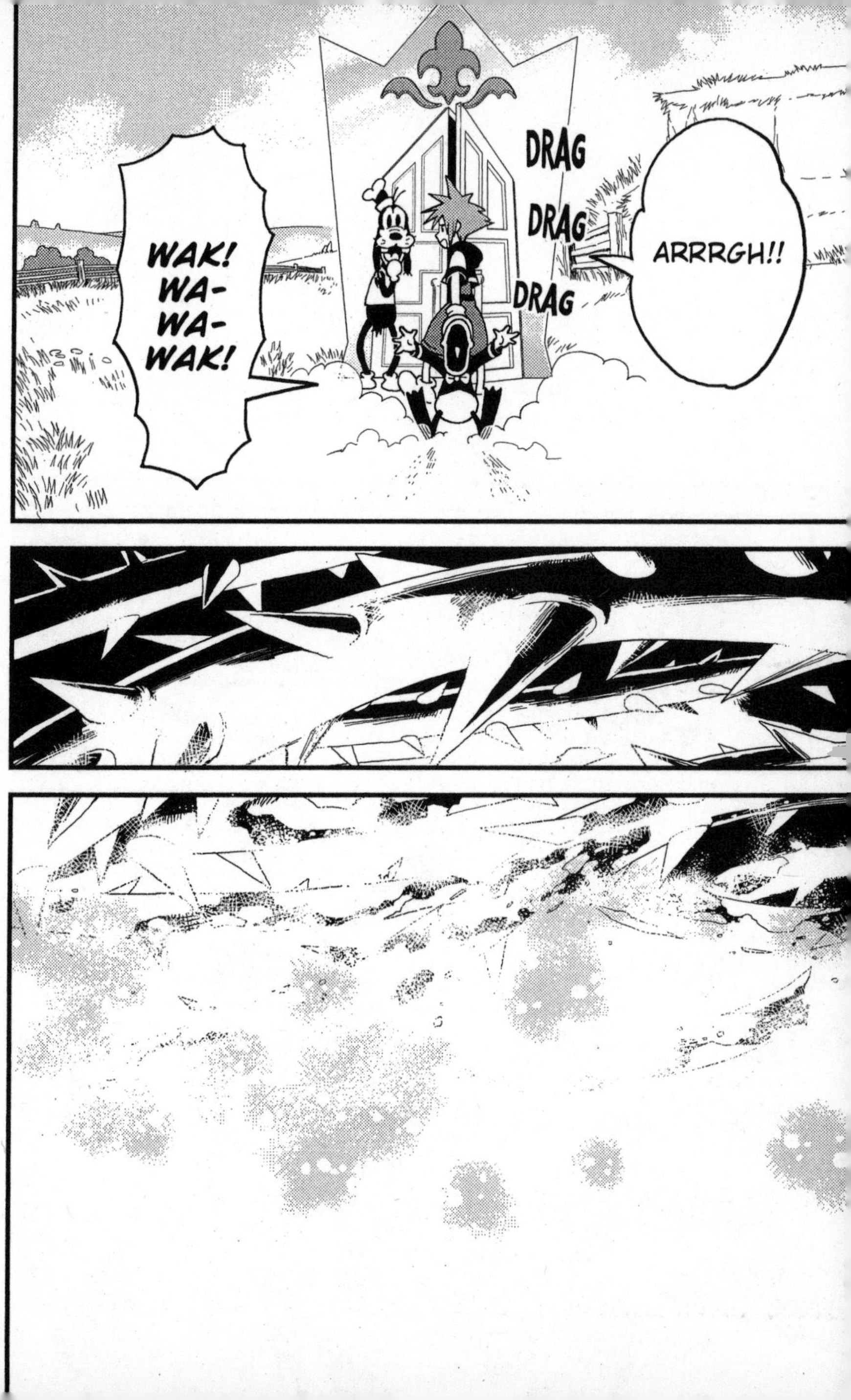
ARRRGH!!
DRAG
DRAG
DRAG
WAK! WA-WA-WAK!

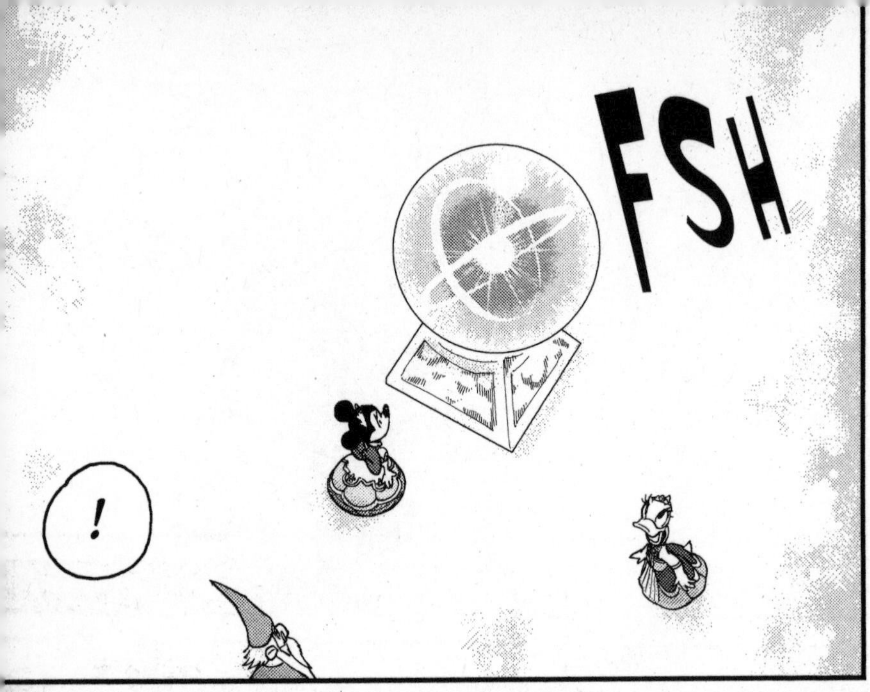
FSH
!
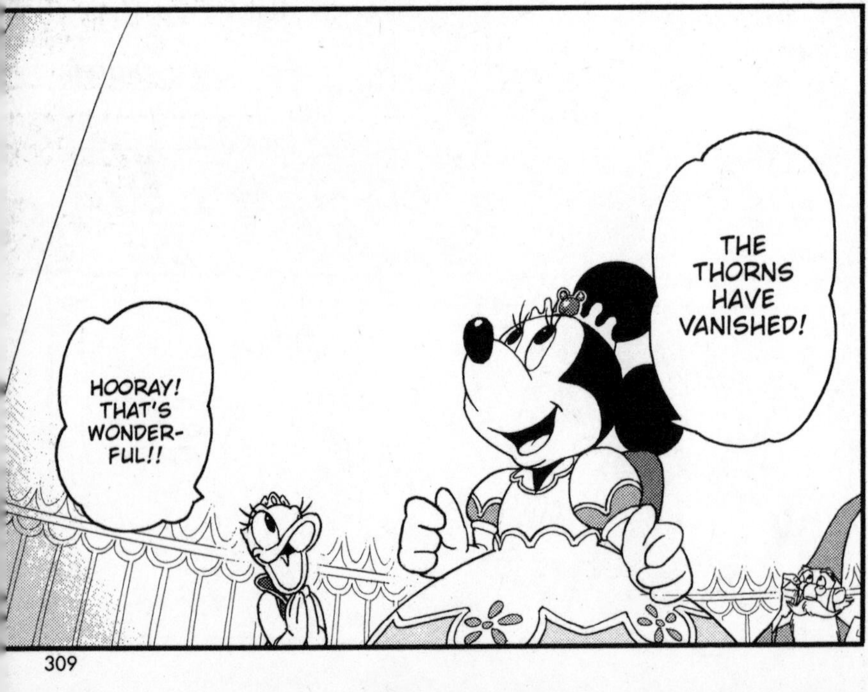
THE THORNS HAVE VANISHED!
HOORAY! THAT'S WONDER-FUL!!

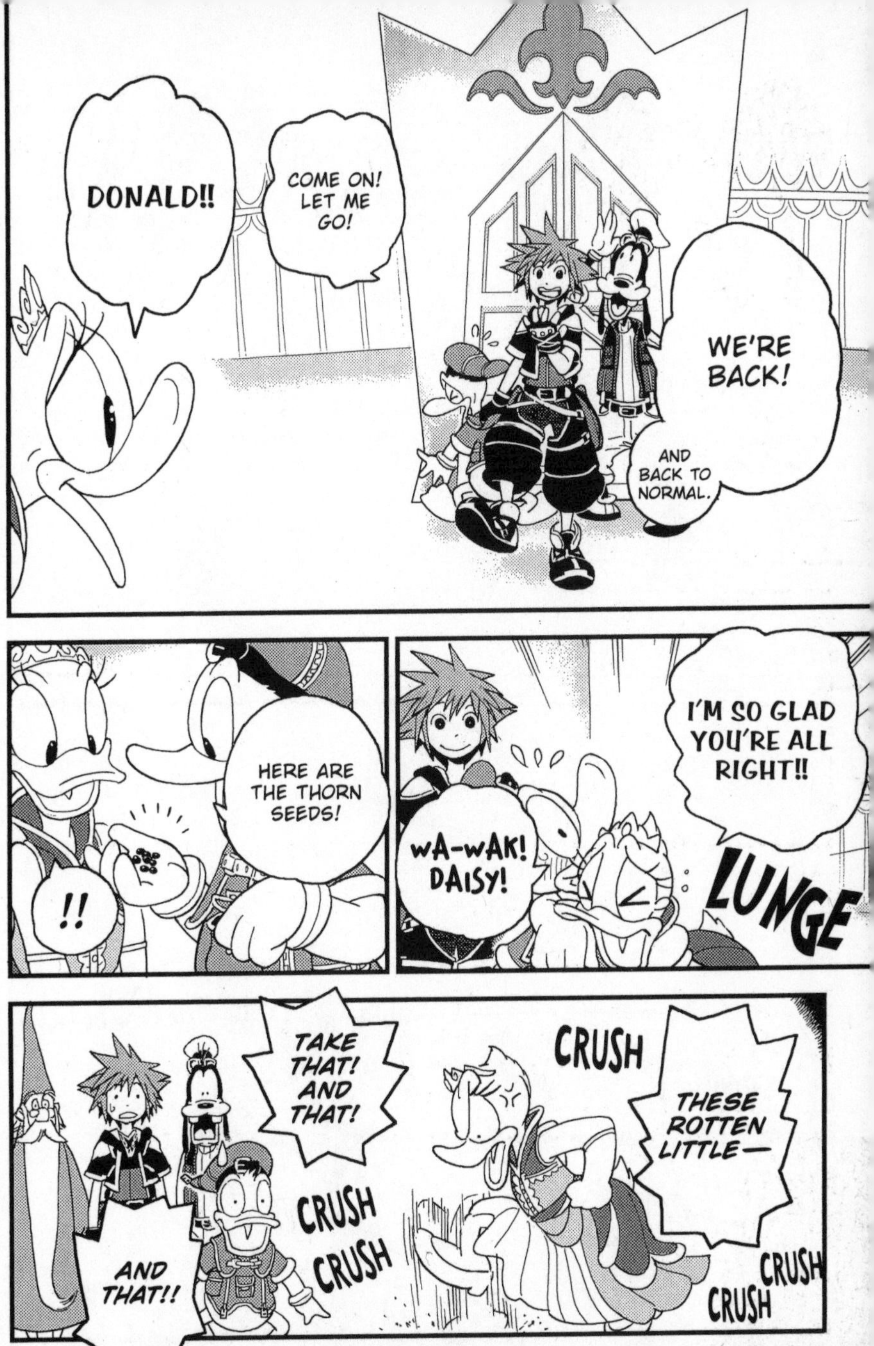
WE'RE BACK!
AND BACK TO NORMAL.
COME ON! LET ME GO!
DONALD!!
I'M SO GLAD YOU'RE ALL RIGHT!!
LUNGE
WA-WAK! DAISY!
HERE ARE THE THORN SEEDS!
!!
THESE ROTTEN LITTLE—
CRUSH
CRUSH
CRUSH
TAKE THAT! AND THAT!
CRUSH
CRUSH
AND THAT!!

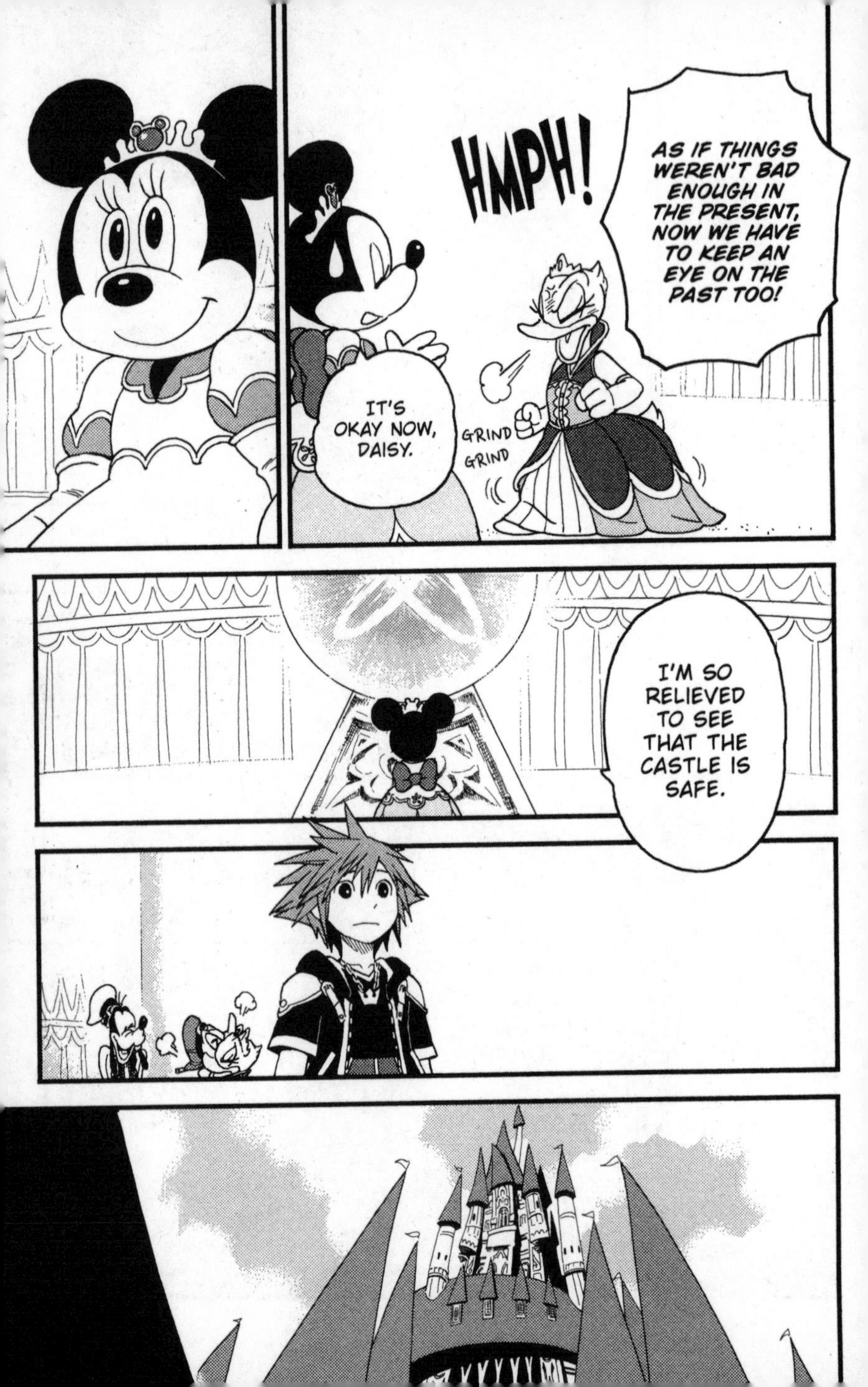
AS IF THINGS WEREN'T BAD ENOUGH IN THE PRESENT, NOW WE HAVE TO KEEP AN EYE ON THE PAST TOO!
HMPH!
GRIND GRIND
IT'S OKAY NOW, DAISY.
I'M SO RELIEVED TO SEE THAT THE CASTLE IS SAFE.

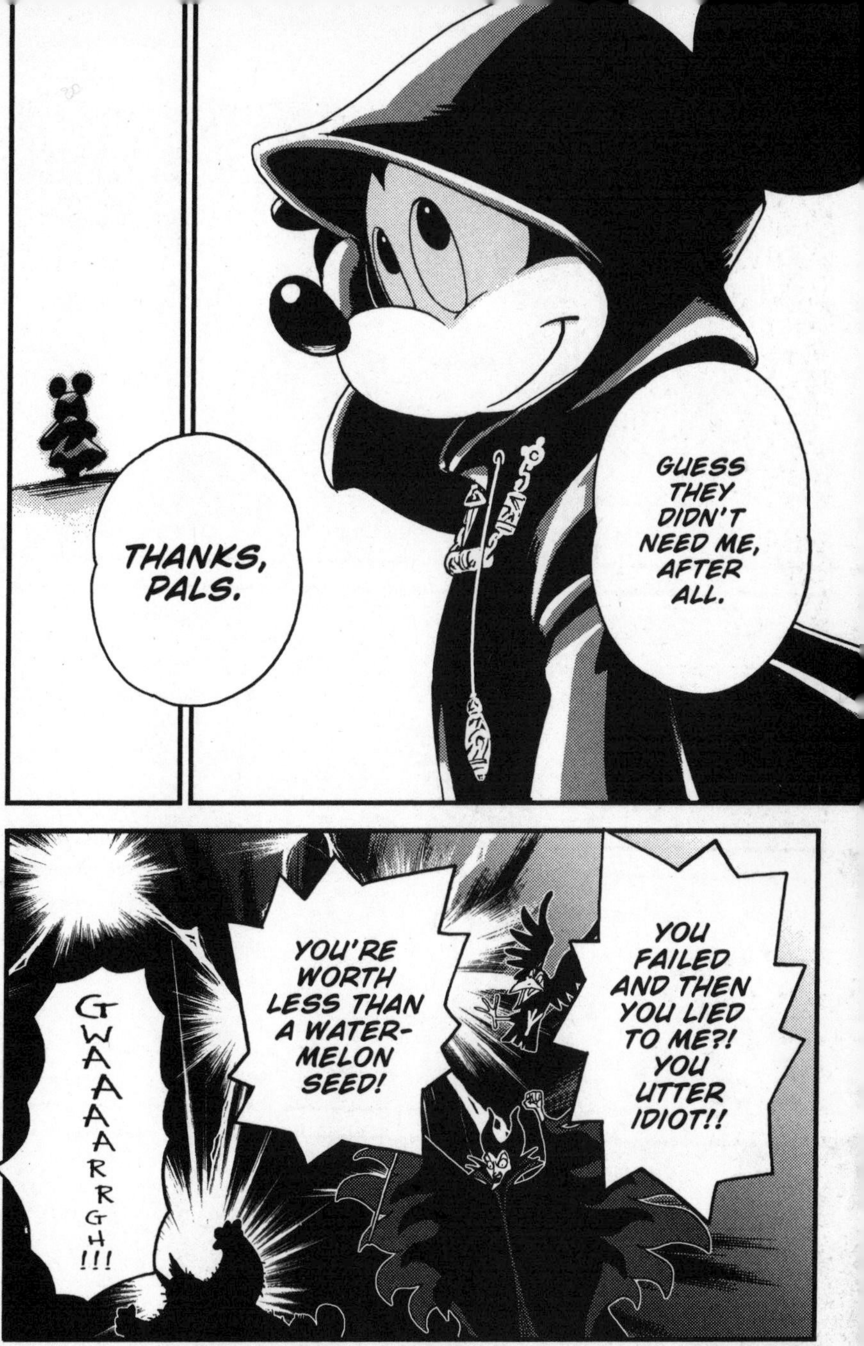
GUESS THEY DIDN'T NEED ME, AFTER ALL.
THANKS, PALS.
YOU FAILED AND THEN YOU LIED TO ME?! YOU UTTER IDIOT!!
YOU'RE WORTH LESS THAN A WATER-MELON SEED!
GWAAAARRGH!!!

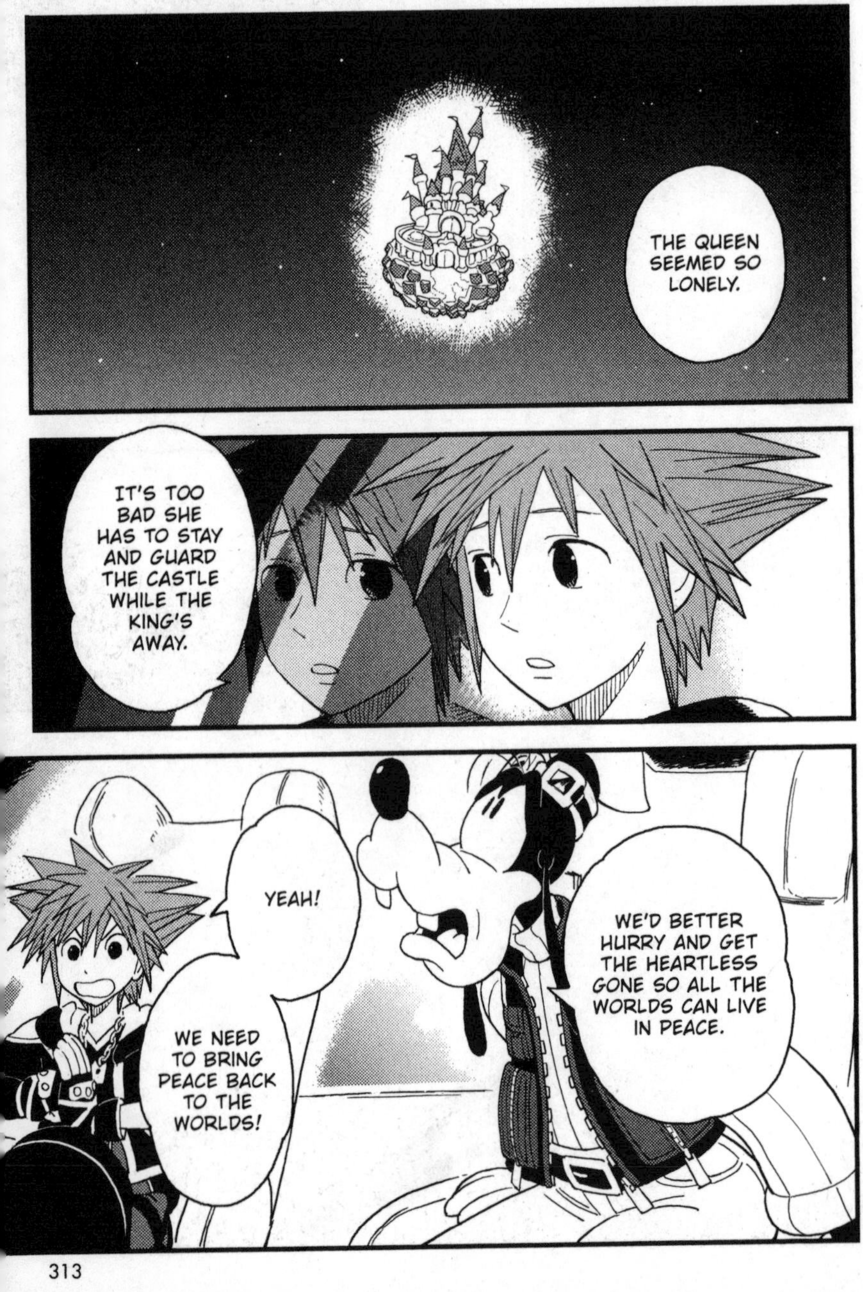
THE QUEEN SEEMED SO LONELY.
IT'S TOO BAD SHE HAS TO STAY AND GUARD THE CASTLE WHILE THE KING'S AWAY.
WE'D BETTER HURRY AND GET THE HEARTLESS GONE SO ALL THE WORLDS CAN LIVE IN PEACE.
YEAH!
WE NEED TO BRING PEACE BACK TO THE WORLDS!

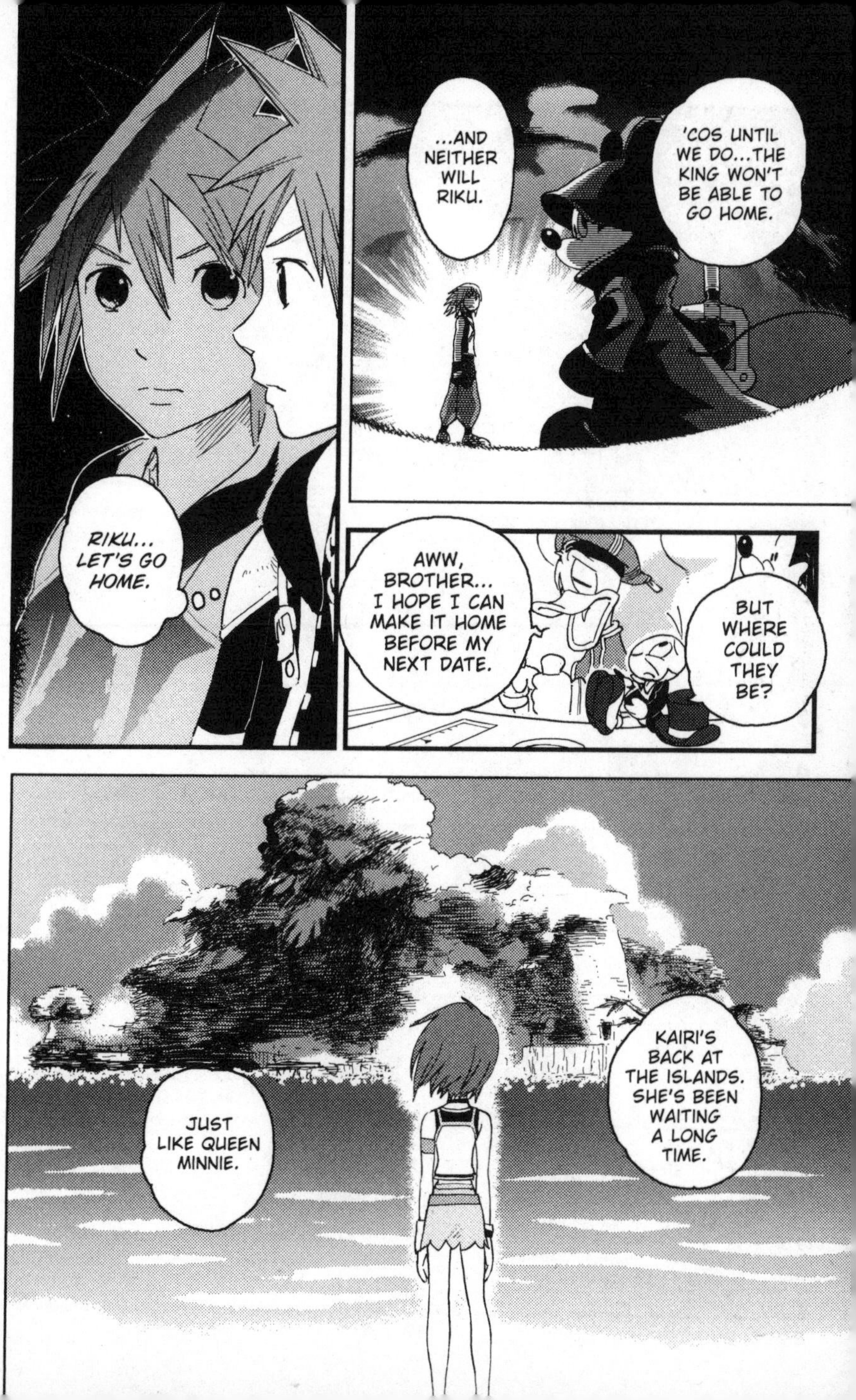
'COS UNTIL WE DO...THE KING WON'T BE ABLE TO GO HOME.
...AND NEITHER WILL RIKU.
BUT WHERE COULD THEY BE?
AWW, BROTHER... I HOPE I CAN MAKE IT HOME BEFORE MY NEXT DATE.
RIKU... LET'S GO HOME.
KAIRI'S BACK AT THE ISLANDS. SHE'S BEEN WAITING A LONG TIME.
JUST LIKE QUEEN MINNIE.

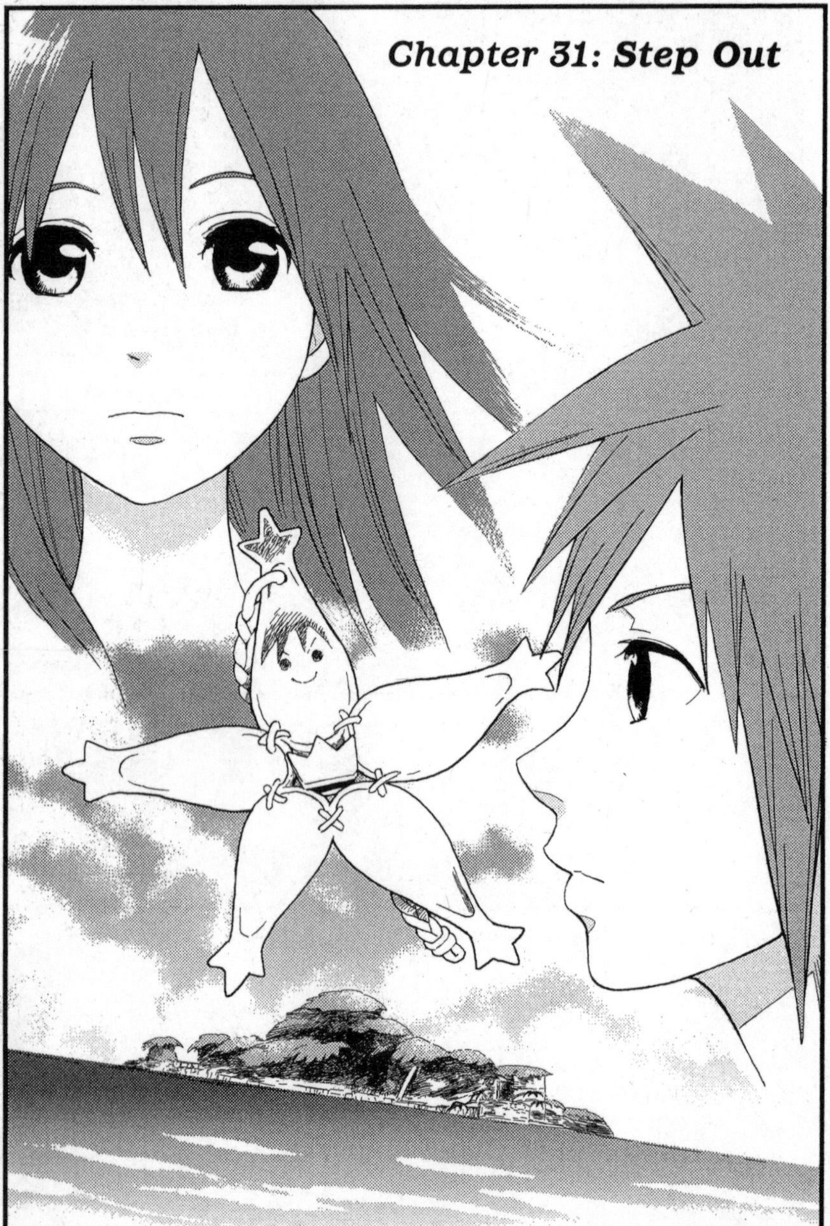
Chapter 31: Step Out

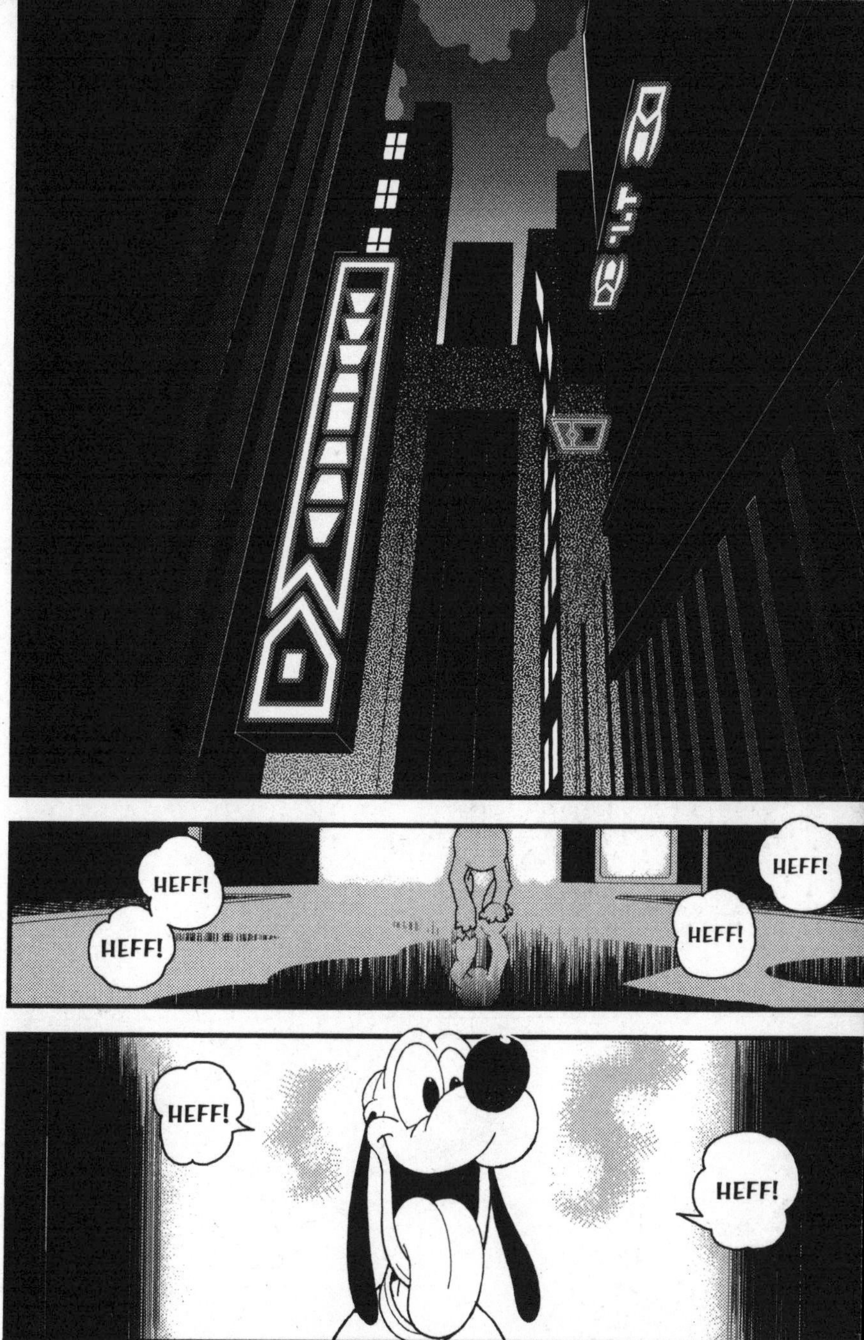
HEFF!
HEFF!
HEFF!
HEFF!
HEFF!
HEFF!

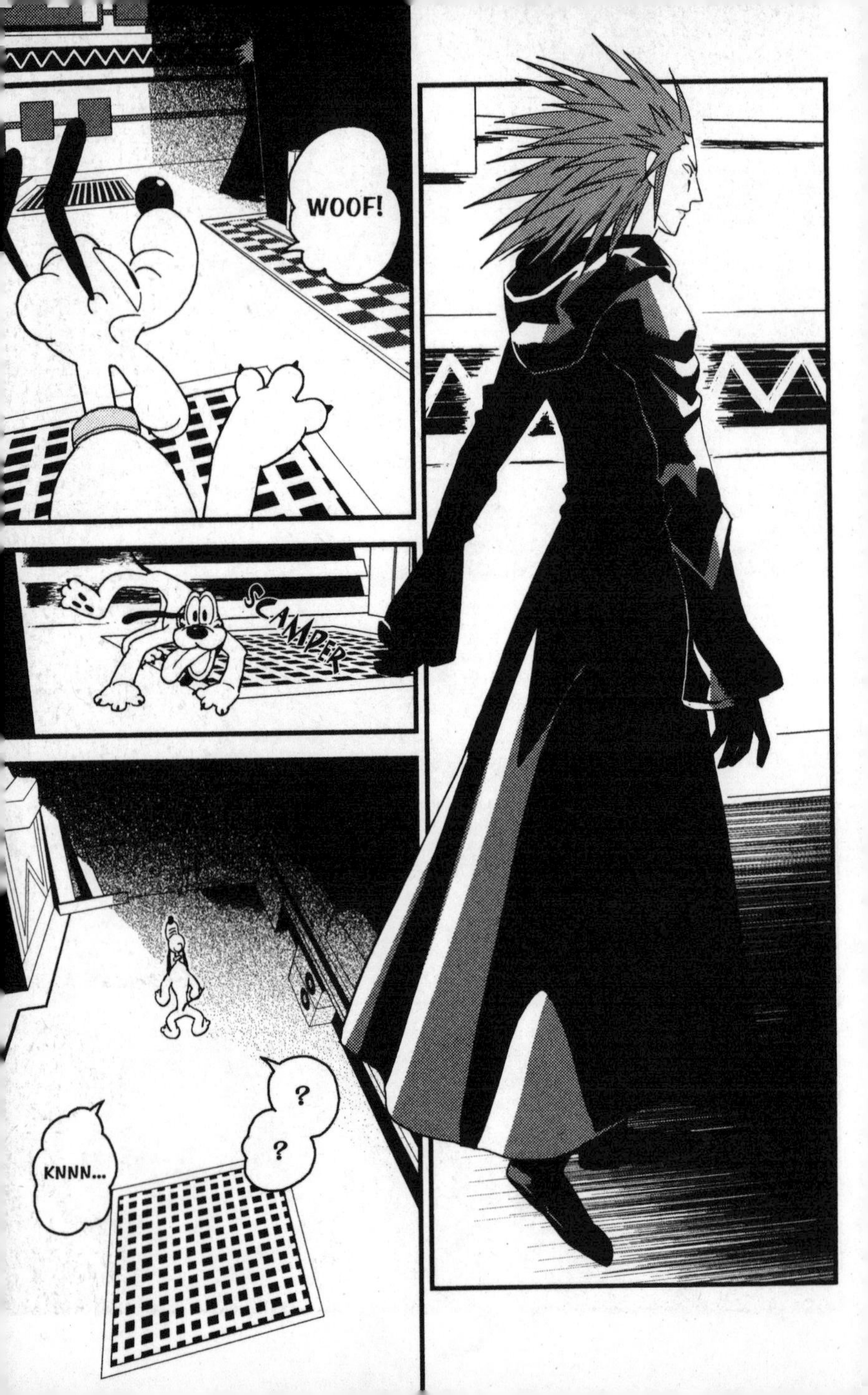
WOOF!
SCAMPER
? ?
KNNN...

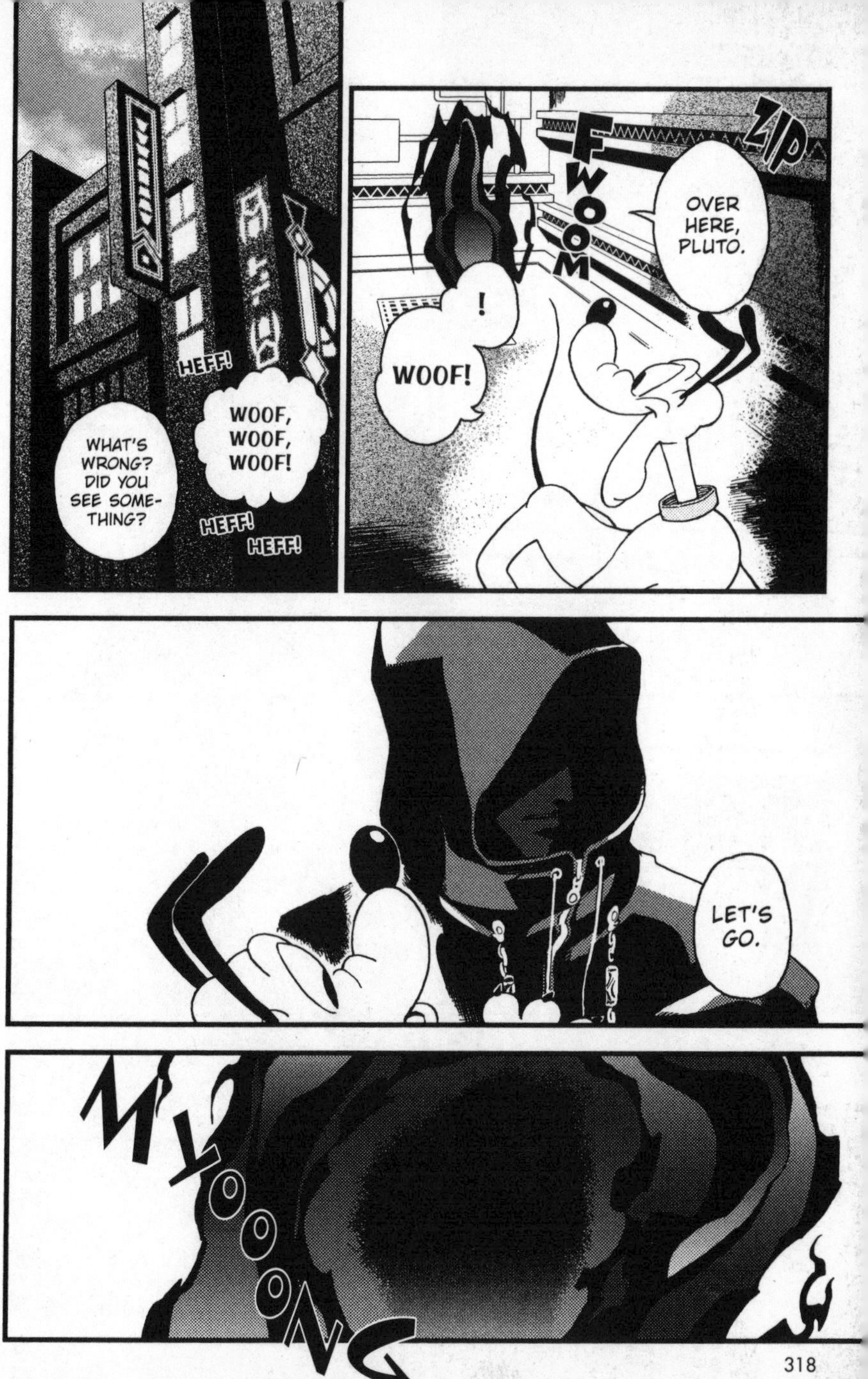
ZIP
FWOOM
OVER HERE, PLUTO.
!
WOOF!
HEFF!
WOOF, WOOF, WOOF!
WHAT'S WRONG? DID YOU SEE SOME-THING?
HEFF!
HEFF!
LET'S GO.
MYOOONG

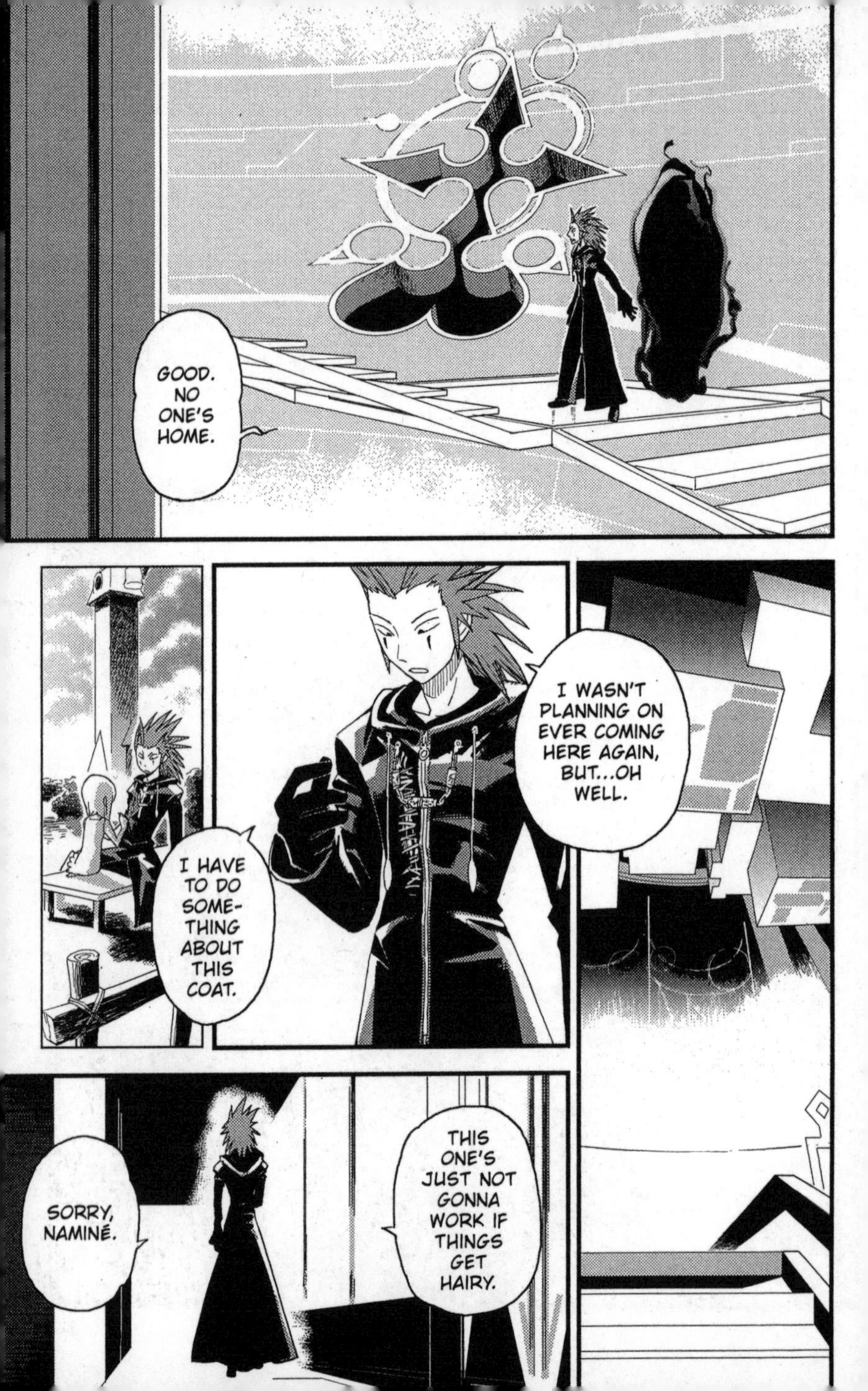
GOOD. NO ONE'S HOME.
I WASN'T PLANNING ON EVER COMING HERE AGAIN, BUT...OH WELL.
I HAVE TO DO SOME-THING ABOUT THIS COAT.
THIS ONE'S JUST NOT GONNA WORK IF THINGS GET HAIRY.
SORRY, NAMINÉ.

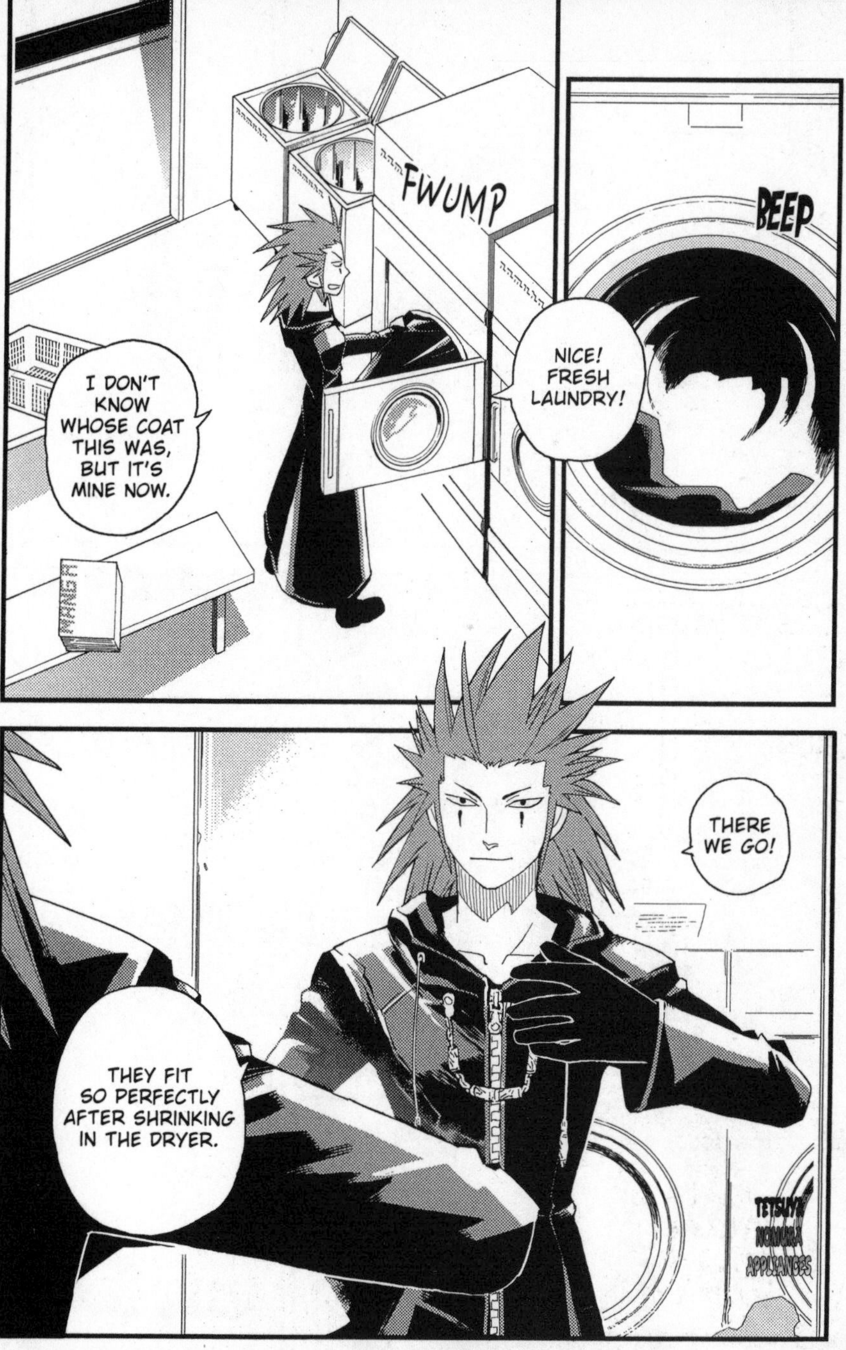
BEEP
FWUMP
NICE! FRESH LAUNDRY!
I DON'T KNOW WHOSE COAT THIS WAS, BUT IT'S MINE NOW.
THERE WE GO!
THEY FIT SO PERFECTLY AFTER SHRINKING IN THE DRYER.
TETSUYA NOMURA APPLIANCES

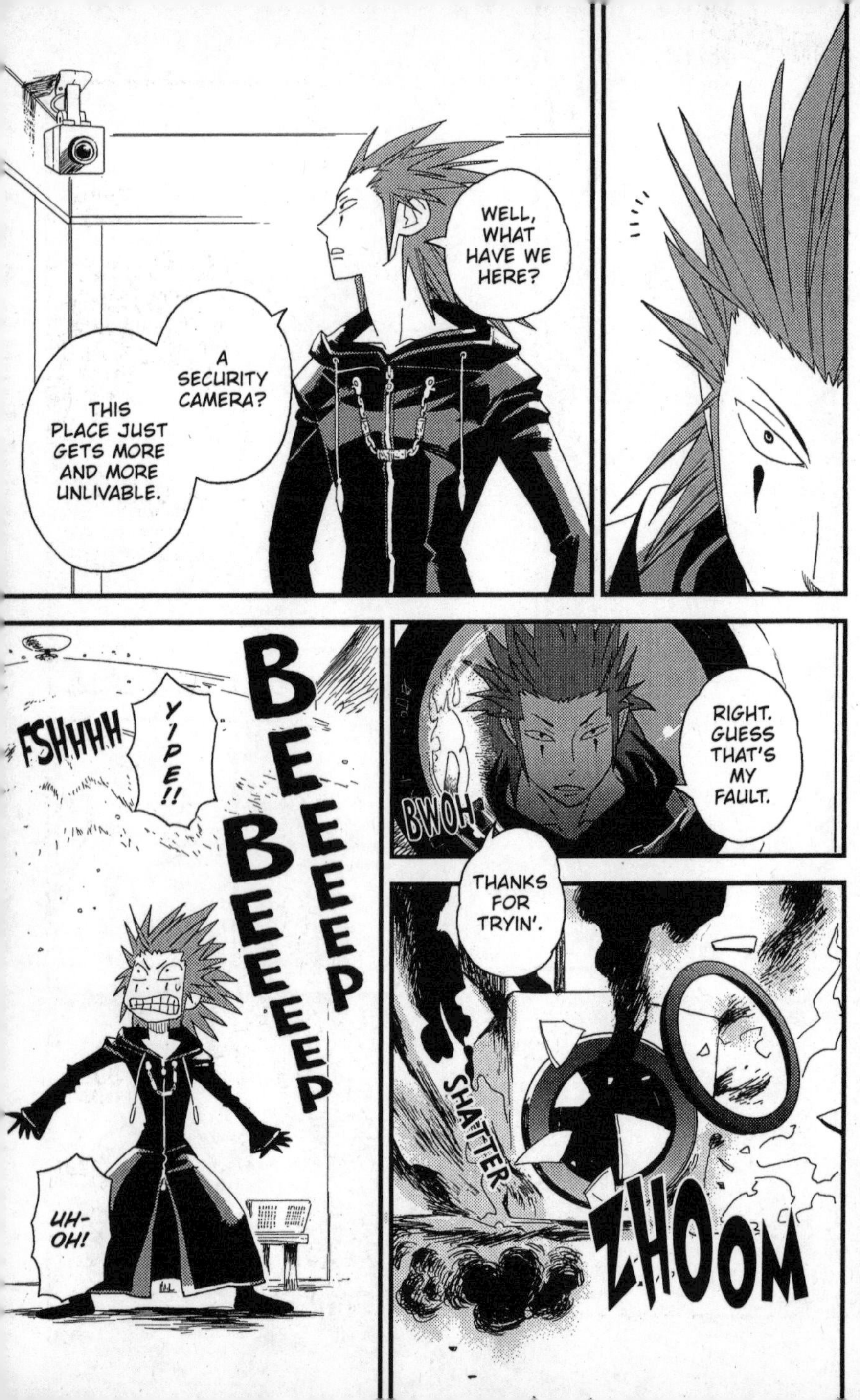
WELL, WHAT HAVE WE HERE?
A SECURITY CAMERA?
THIS PLACE JUST GETS MORE AND MORE UNLIVABLE.
RIGHT. GUESS THAT'S MY FAULT.
BWOH
THANKS FOR TRYIN'.
SHATTER
ZHOOM
BEEEEP
BEEEEEP
YIPE!!
FSHHHH
UH-OH!

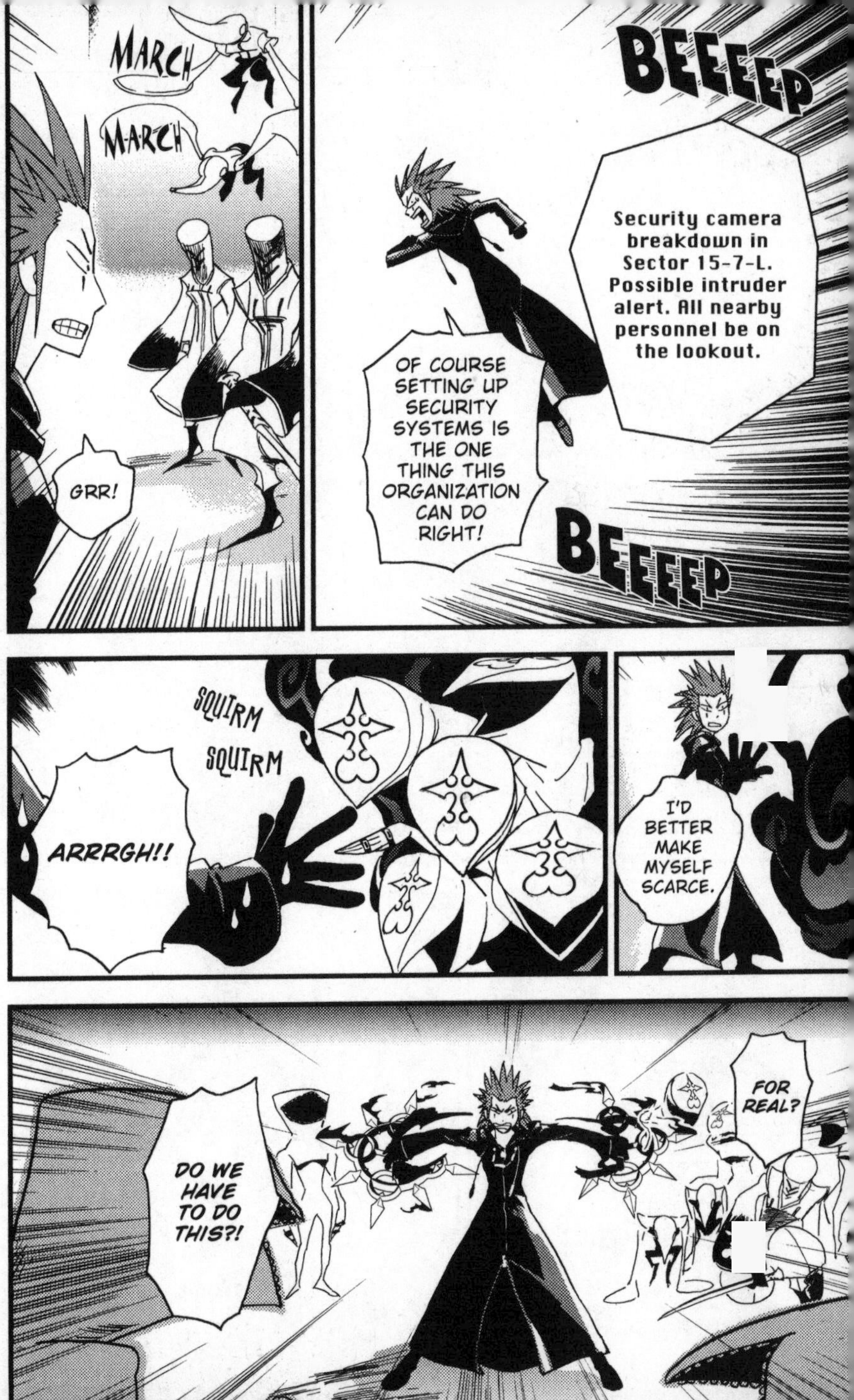
BEEEEP
Security camera breakdown in Sector 15-7-L. Possible intruder alert. All nearby personnel be on the lookout.
OF COURSE SETTING UP SECURITY SYSTEMS IS THE ONE THING THIS ORGANIZATION CAN DO RIGHT!
BEEEEP
MARCH
MARCH
GRR!
I'D BETTER MAKE MYSELF SCARCE.
SQUIRM
SQUIRM
ARRRGH!!
FOR REAL?
DO WE HAVE TO DO THIS?!

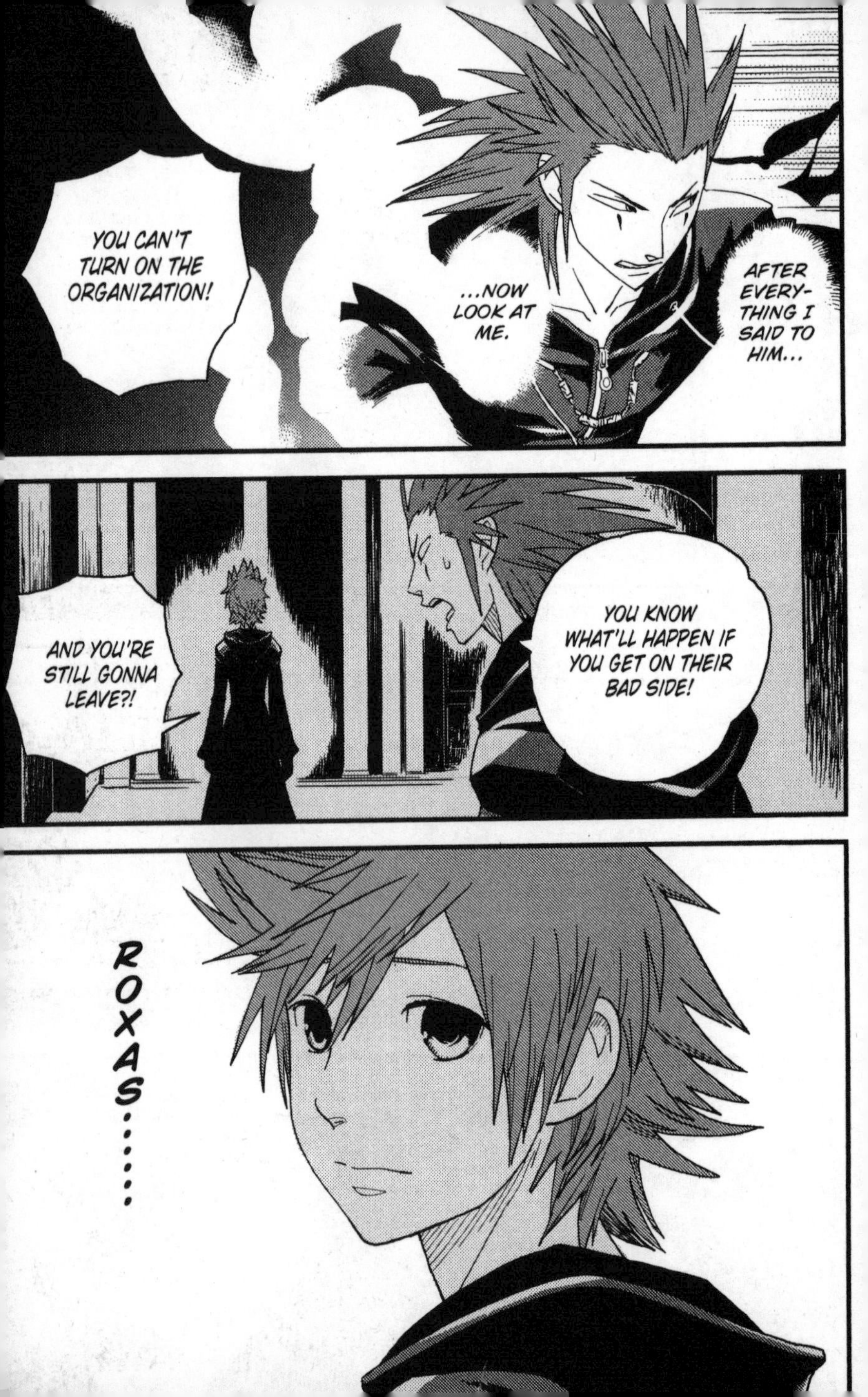
AFTER EVERYTHING I SAID TO HIM...
...NOW LOOK AT ME.
YOU CAN'T TURN ON THE ORGANIZATION!
YOU KNOW WHAT'LL HAPPEN IF YOU GET ON THEIR BAD SIDE!
AND YOU'RE STILL GONNA LEAVE?!
ROXAS......

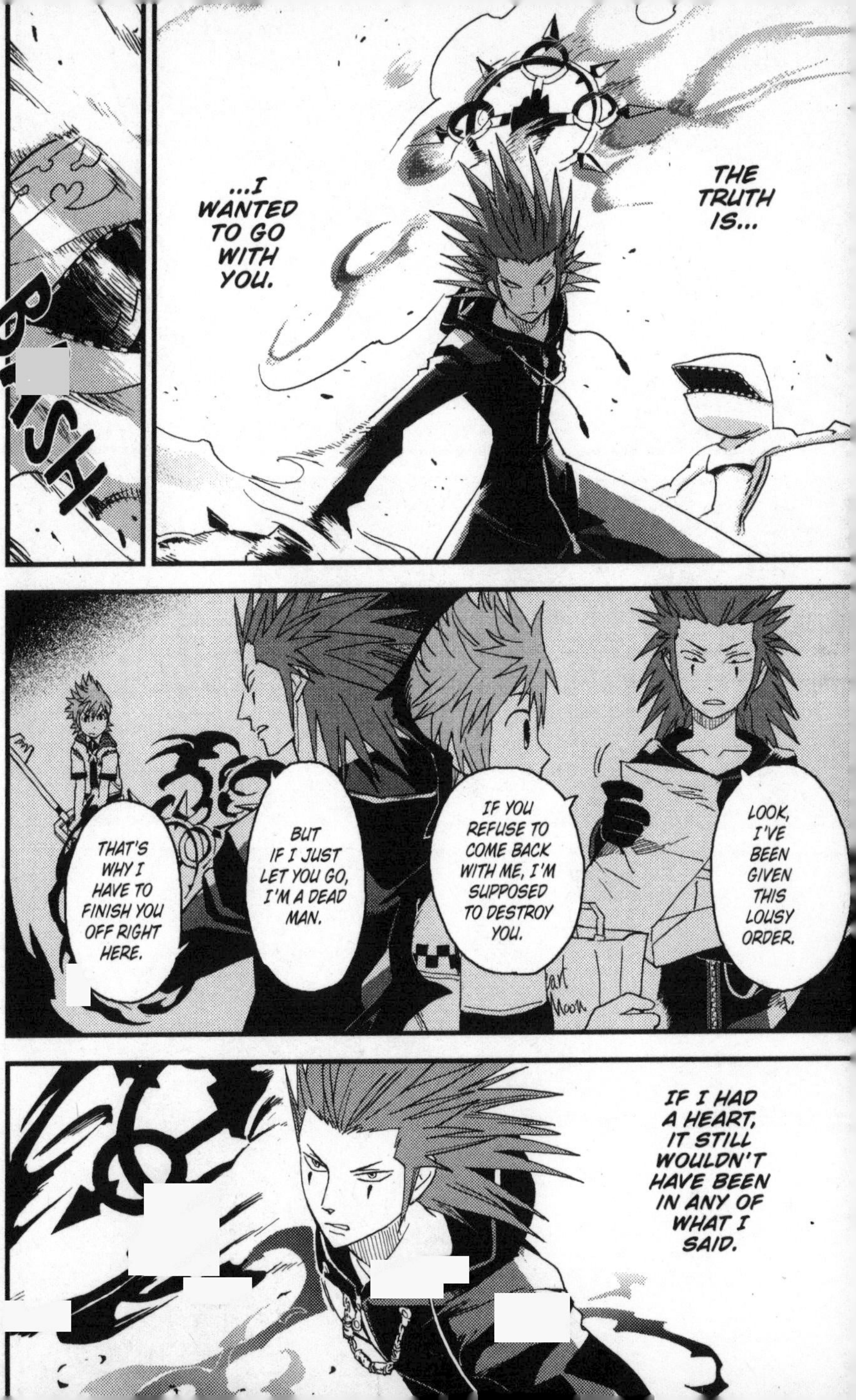
THE TRUTH IS...
...I WANTED TO GO WITH YOU.
LOOK, I'VE BEEN GIVEN THIS LOUSY ORDER.
IF YOU REFUSE TO COME BACK WITH ME, I'M SUPPOSED TO DESTROY YOU.
BUT IF I JUST LET YOU GO, I'M A DEAD MAN.
THAT'S WHY I HAVE TO FINISH YOU OFF RIGHT HERE.
IF I HAD A HEART, IT STILL WOULDN'T HAVE BEEN IN ANY OF WHAT I SAID.

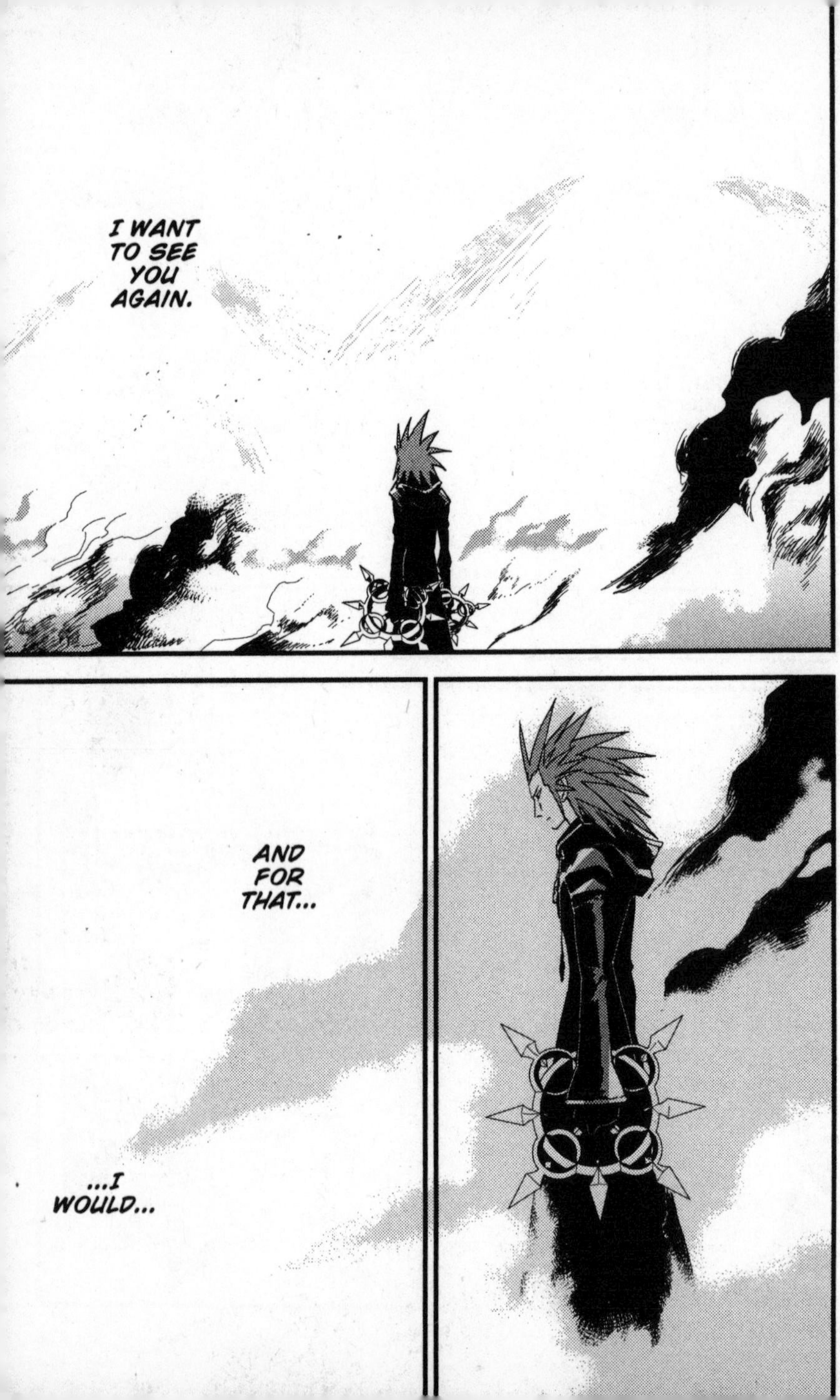
I WANT TO SEE YOU AGAIN.
AND FOR THAT...
...I WOULD...

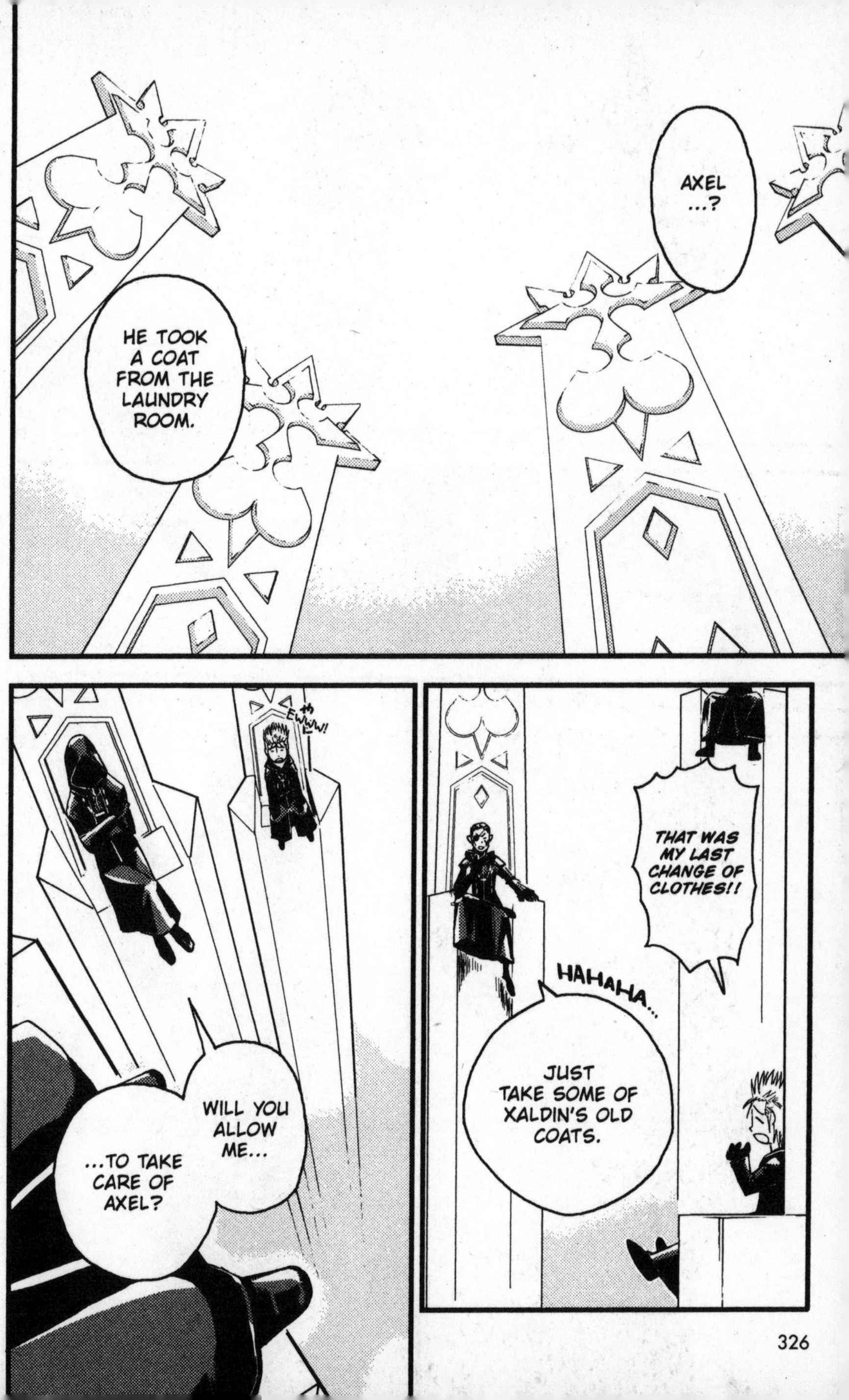

AXEL ...?
HE TOOK A COAT FROM THE LAUNDRY ROOM.
THAT WAS MY LAST CHANGE OF CLOTHES!!
HAHAHA...
JUST TAKE SOME OF XALDIN'S OLD COATS.
EWWW!
WILL YOU ALLOW ME...
...TO TAKE CARE OF AXEL?

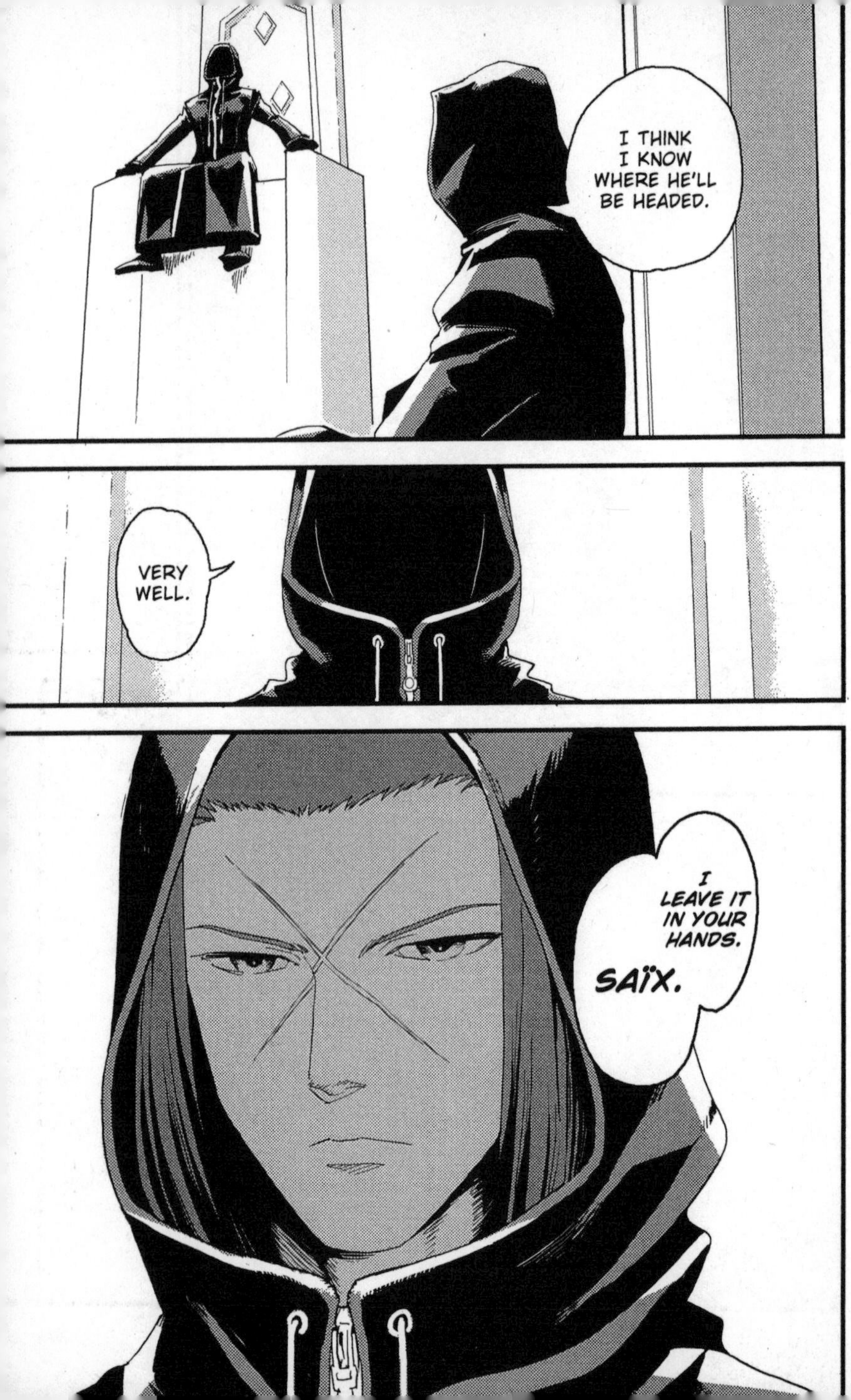
I THINK I KNOW WHERE HE'LL BE HEADED.
VERY WELL.
I LEAVE IT IN YOUR HANDS.
SAÏX.

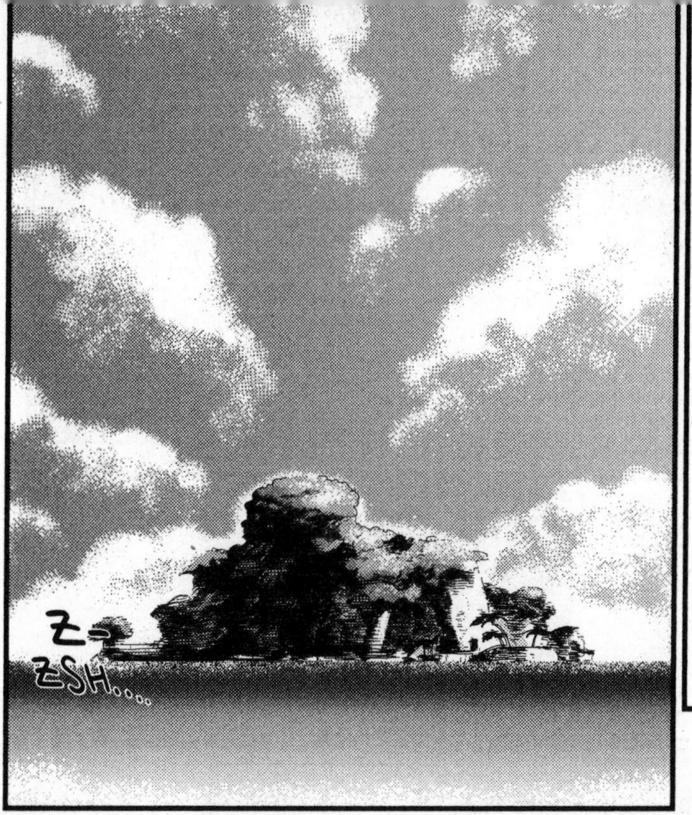
Z-
ZSH....
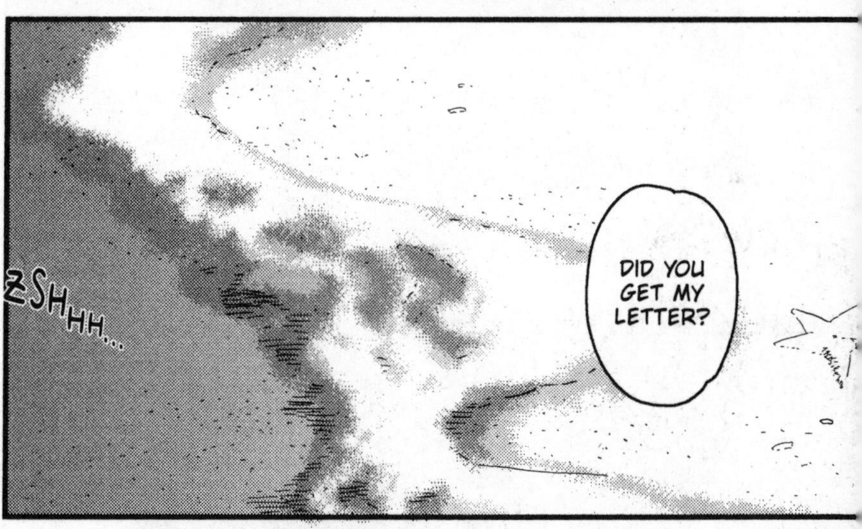
DID YOU GET MY LETTER?
ZSHHH...

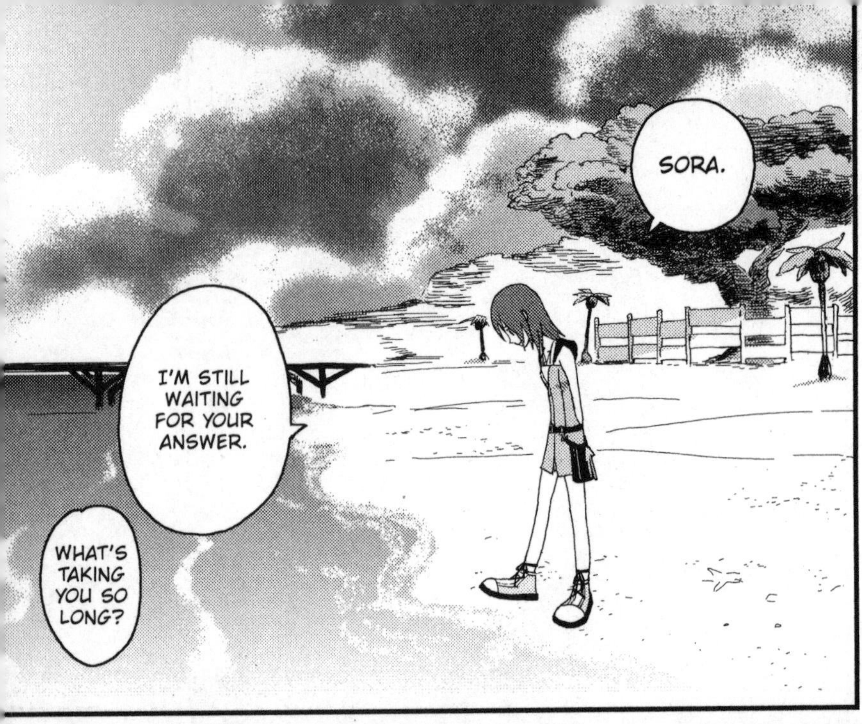
SORA.
I'M STILL WAITING FOR YOUR ANSWER.
WHAT'S TAKING YOU SO LONG?

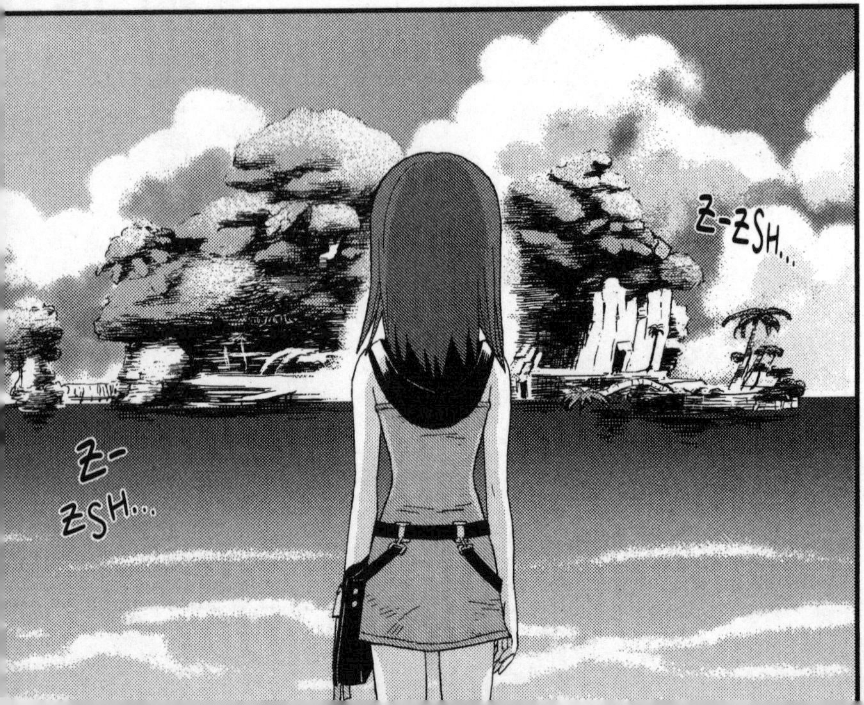
Z-ZSH...
Z-ZSH...

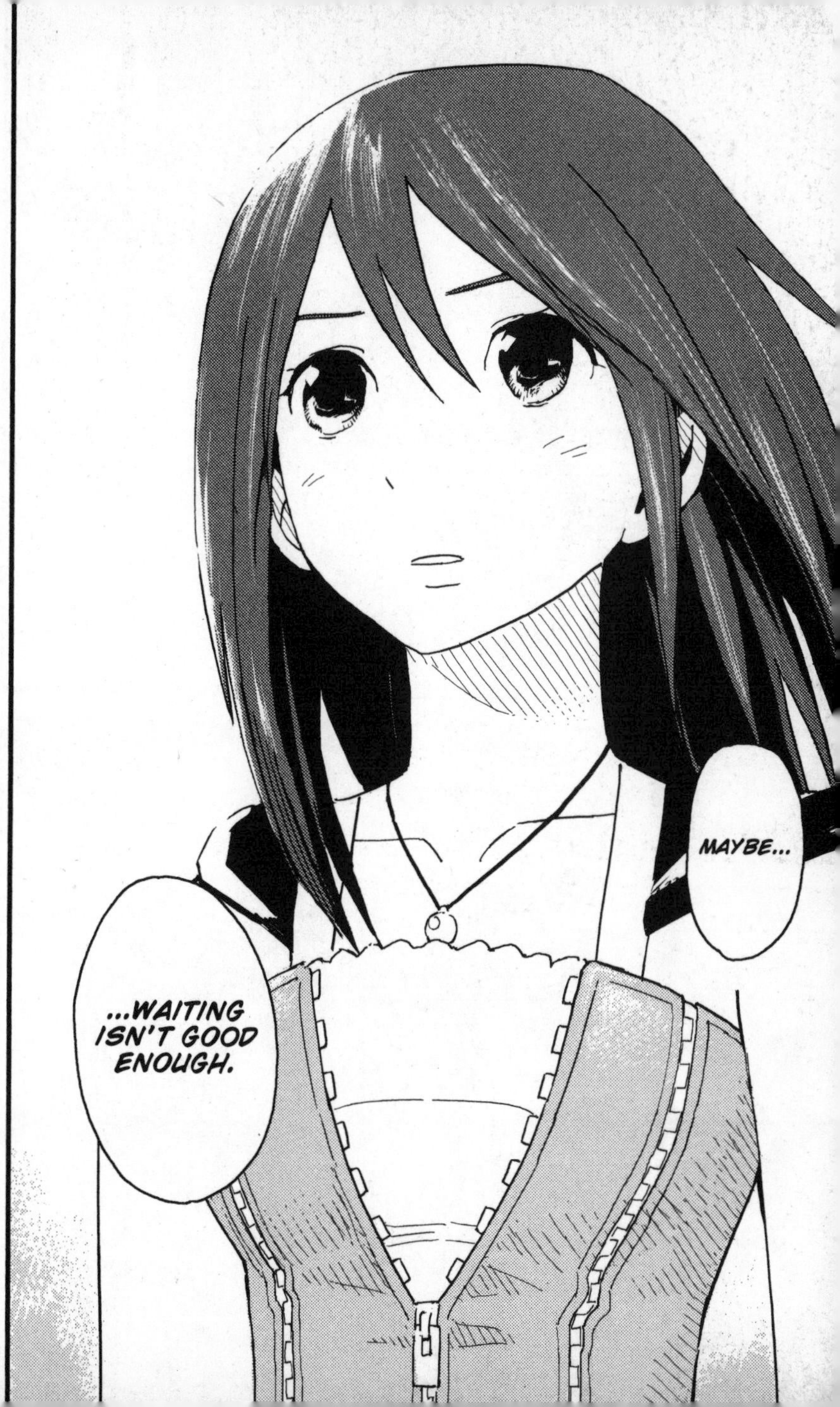
MAYBE...
...WAITING ISN'T GOOD ENOUGH.

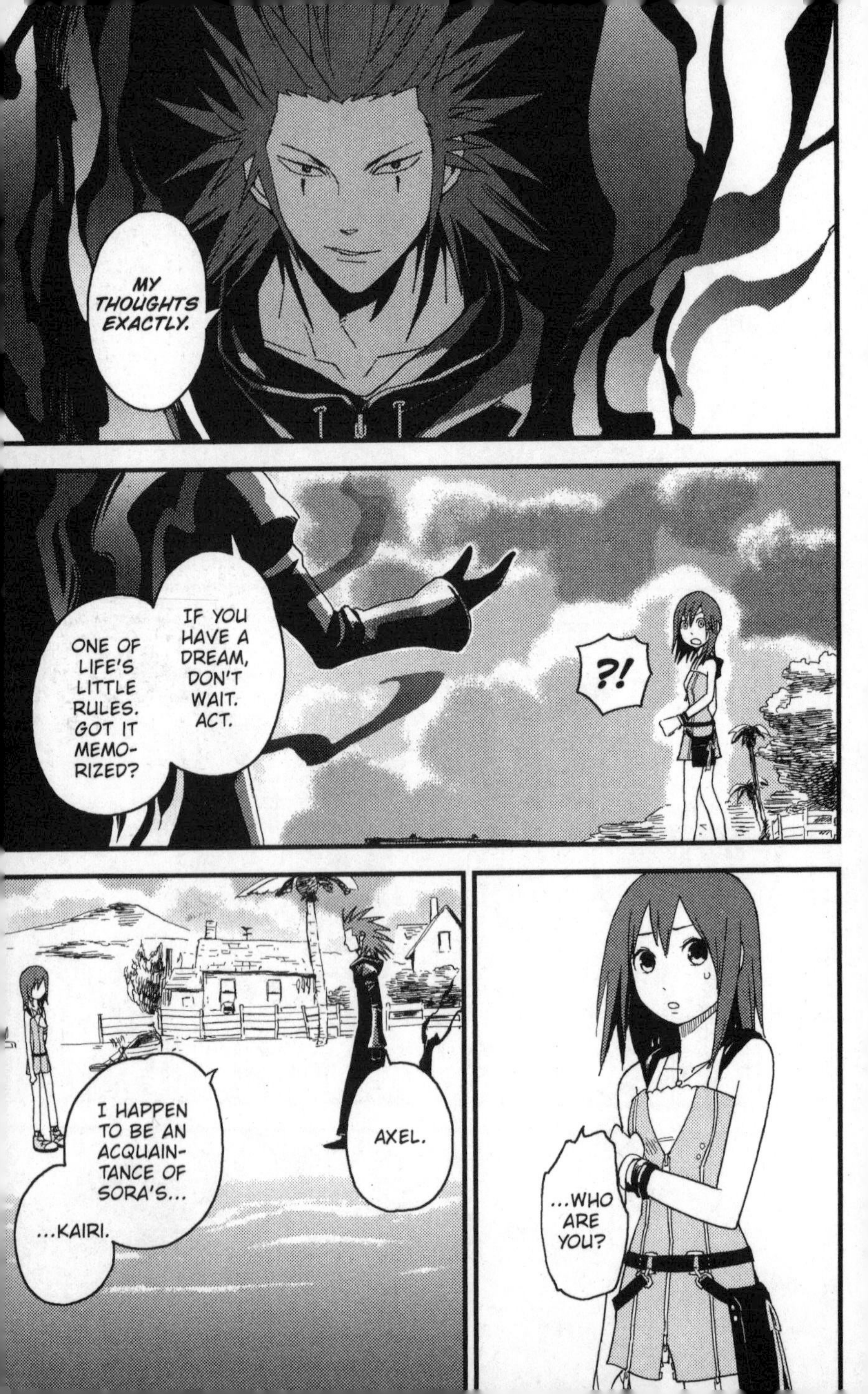
MY THOUGHTS EXACTLY.
?!
IF YOU HAVE A DREAM, DON'T WAIT. ACT.
ONE OF LIFE'S LITTLE RULES. GOT IT MEMO-RIZED?
...WHO ARE YOU?
AXEL.
I HAPPEN TO BE AN ACQUAIN-TANCE OF SORA'S...
...KAIRI.

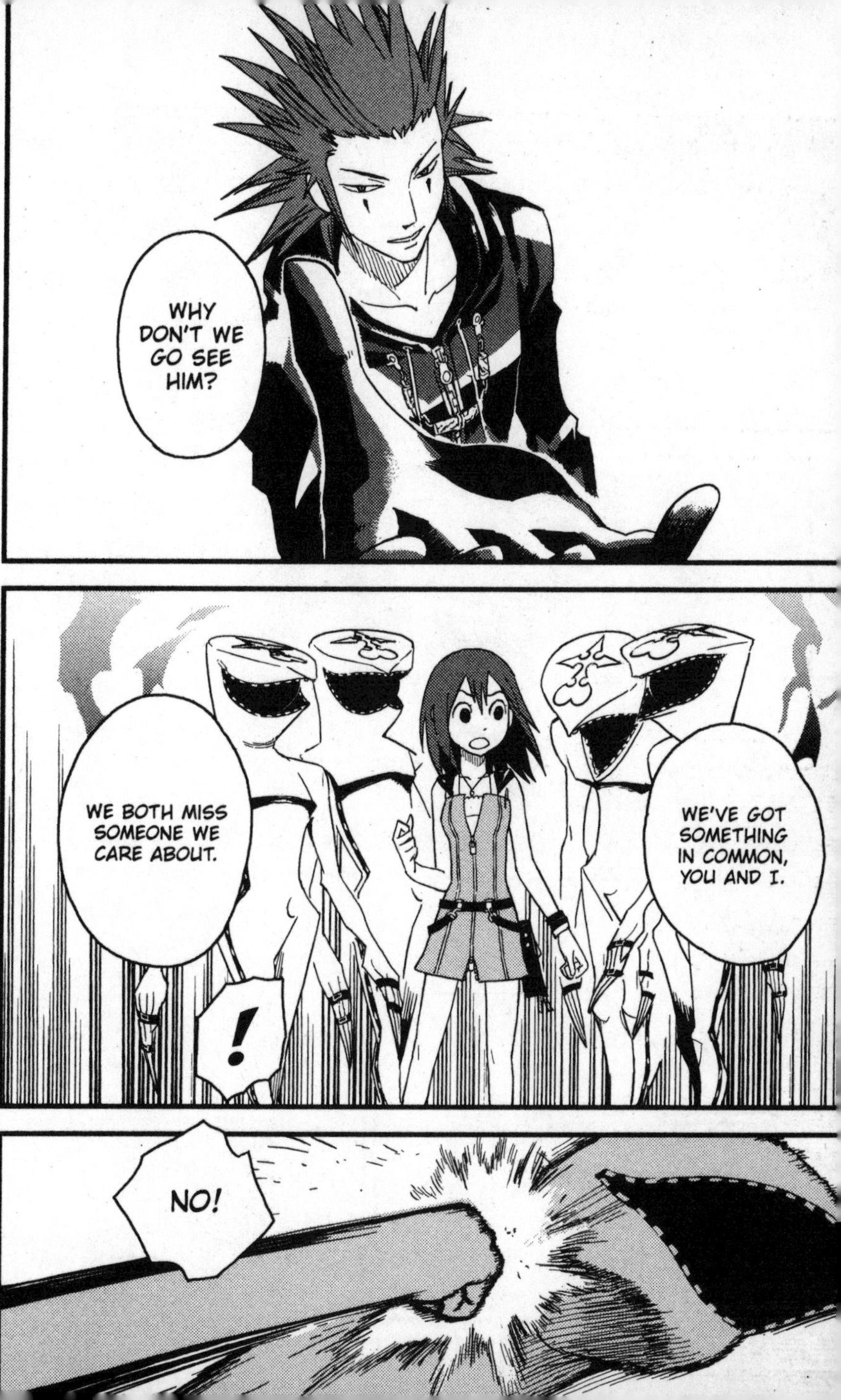
WHY DON'T WE GO SEE HIM?
WE'VE GOT SOMETHING IN COMMON, YOU AND I.
WE BOTH MISS SOMEONE WE CARE ABOUT.
!
NO!

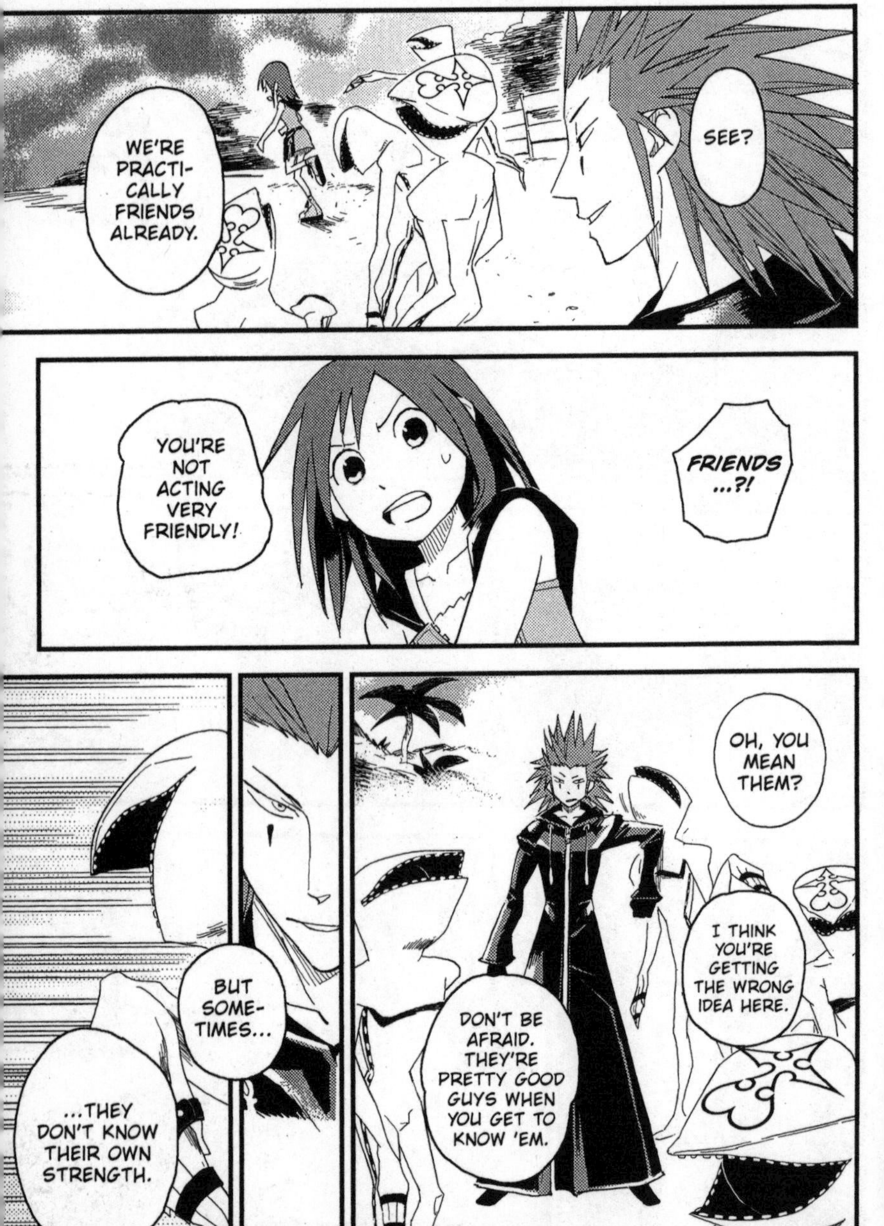
SEE?
WE'RE PRACTI-CALLY FRIENDS ALREADY.
FRIENDS ...?!
YOU'RE NOT ACTING VERY FRIENDLY!
OH, YOU MEAN THEM?
I THINK YOU'RE GETTING THE WRONG IDEA HERE.
DON'T BE AFRAID. THEY'RE PRETTY GOOD GUYS WHEN YOU GET TO KNOW 'EM.
BUT SOME-TIMES...
...THEY DON'T KNOW THEIR OWN STRENGTH.

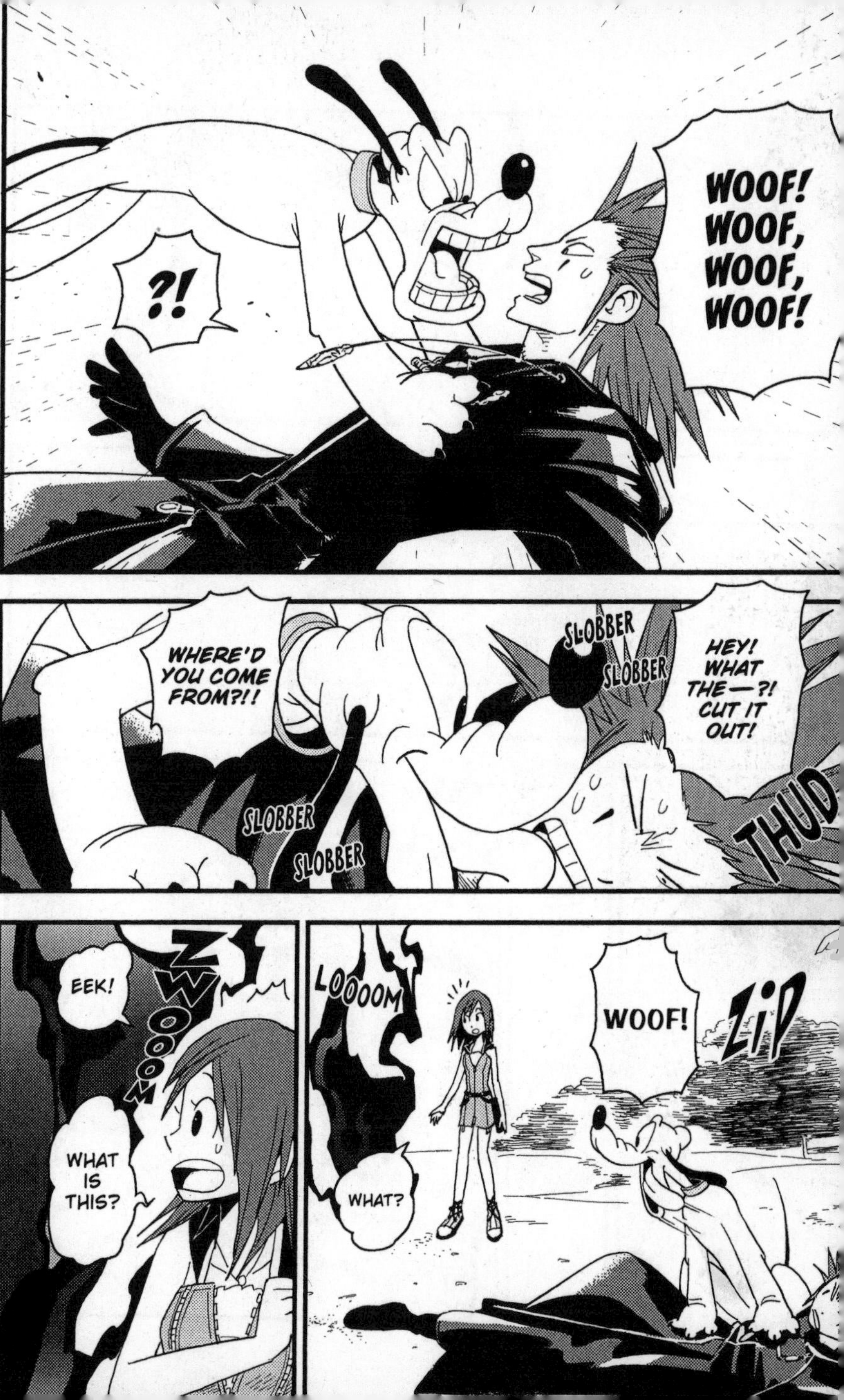
WOOF! WOOF, WOOF, WOOF!
?!
HEY! WHAT THE—?! CUT IT OUT!
THUD
SLOBBER SLOBBER
WHERE'D YOU COME FROM?!!
SLOBBER SLOBBER
ZIP
WOOF!
LOOOOM
WHAT?
ZWOOOOM
EEK!
WHAT IS THIS?

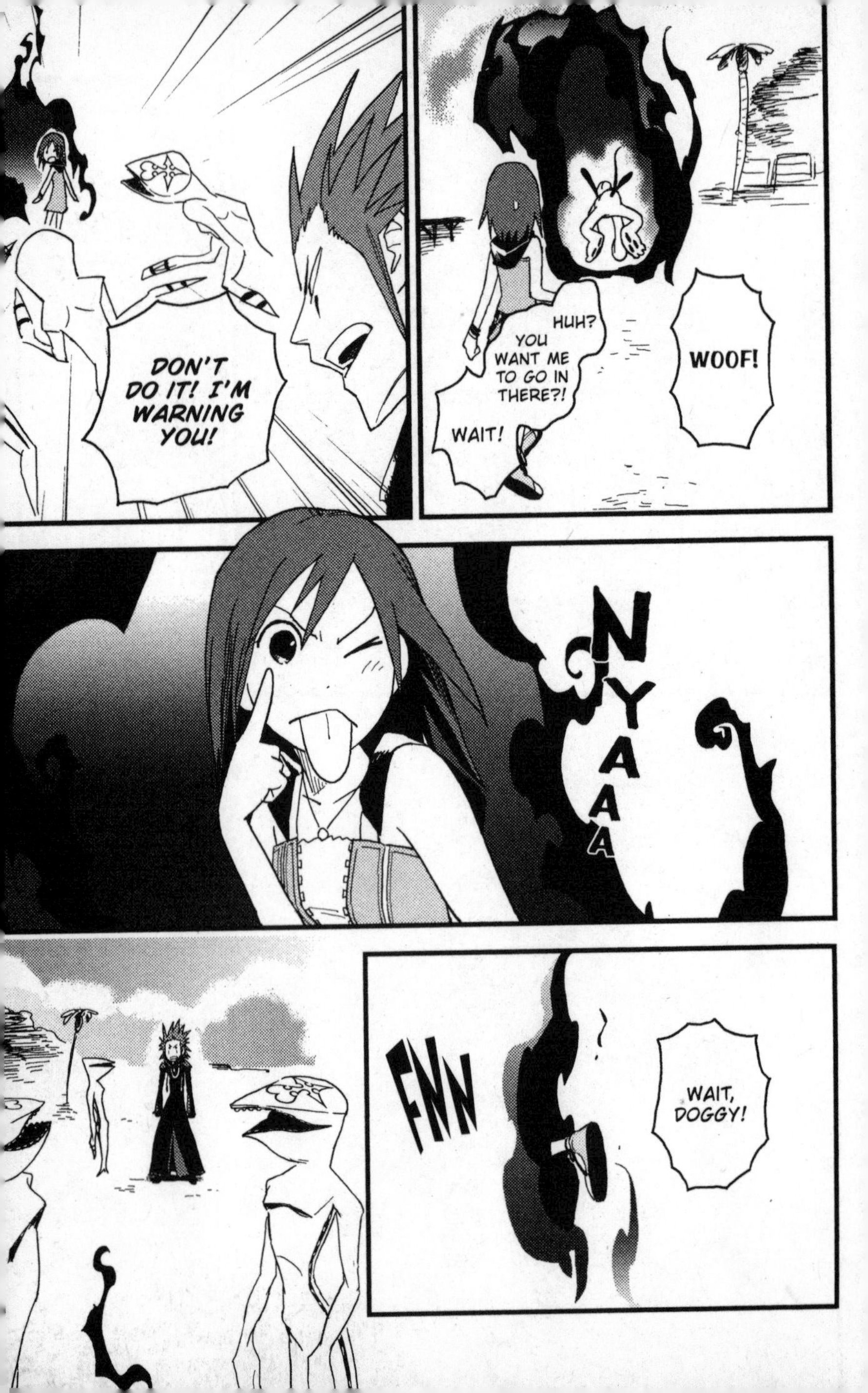
WOOF!
HUH? YOU WANT ME TO GO IN THERE?! WAIT!
DON'T DO IT! I'M WARNING YOU!
NYAAAA
WAIT, DOGGY!
FNN

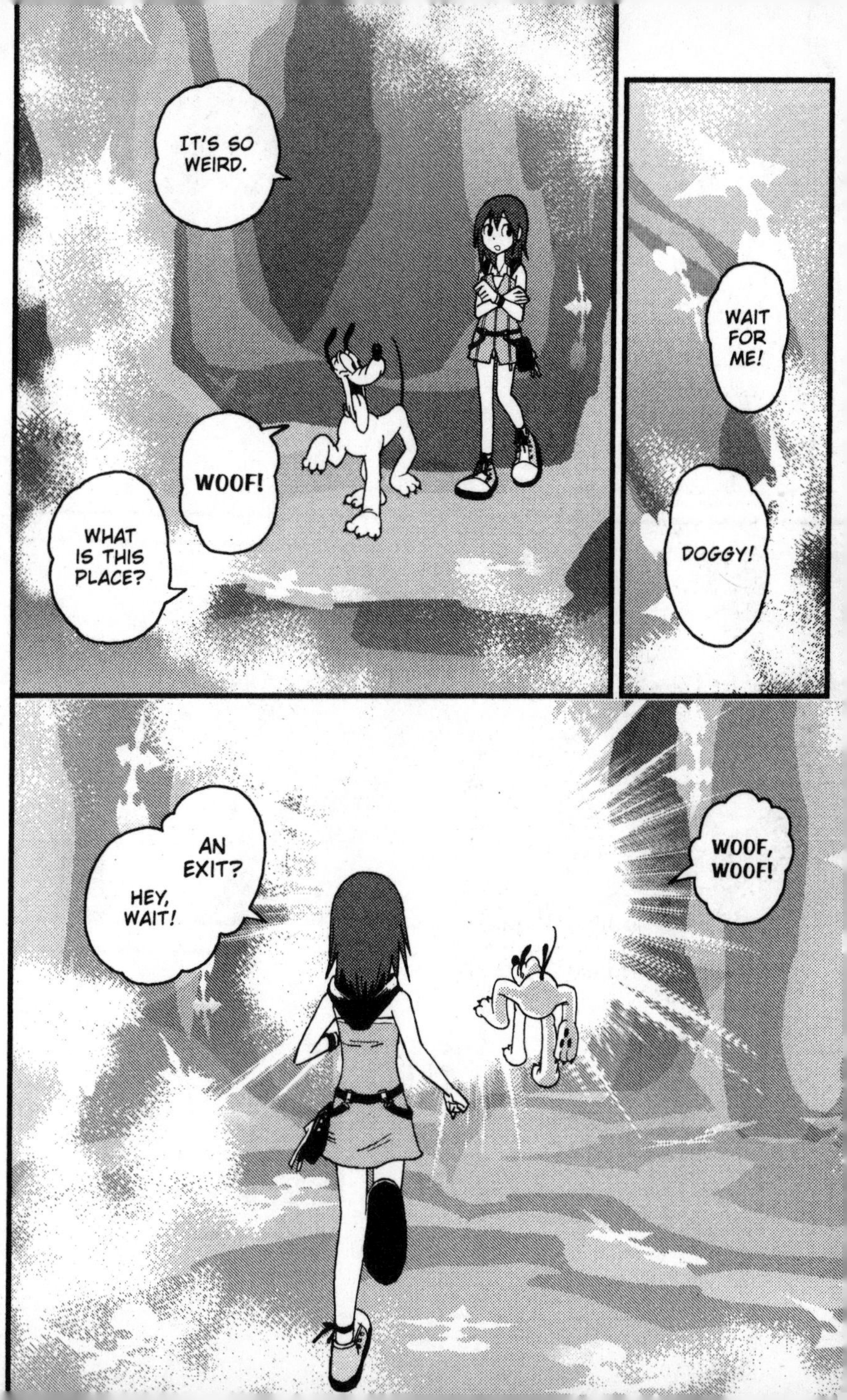
WAIT FOR ME!
DOGGY!
IT'S SO WEIRD.
WOOF!
WHAT IS THIS PLACE?
WOOF, WOOF!
AN EXIT?
HEY, WAIT!

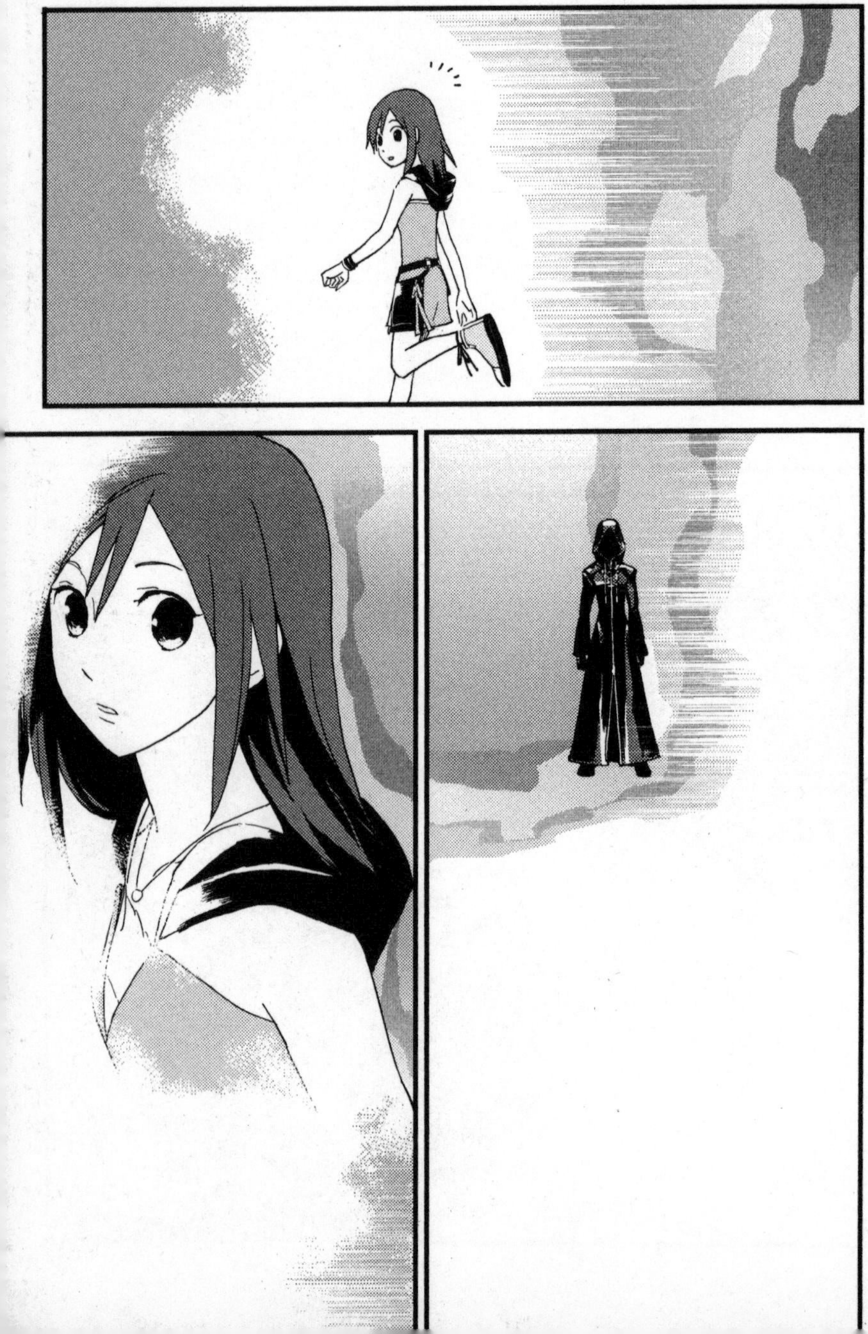

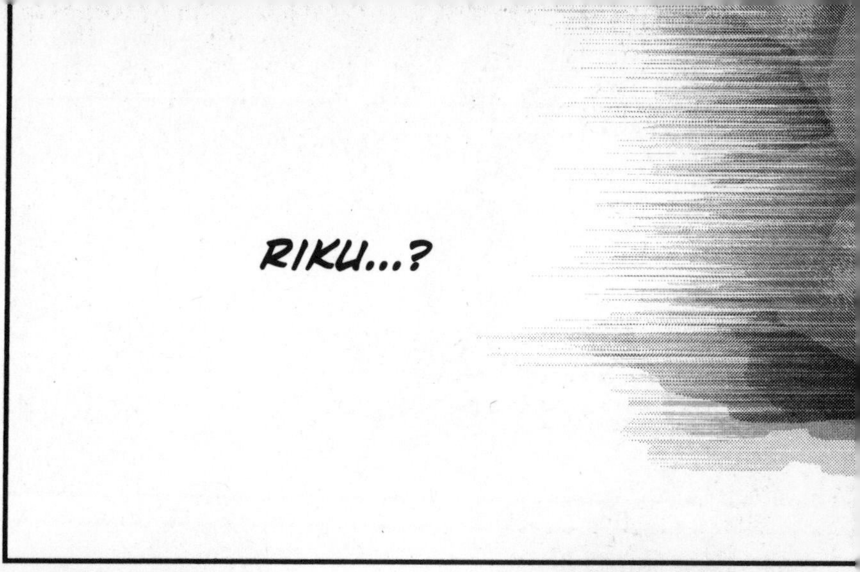
RIKU...?
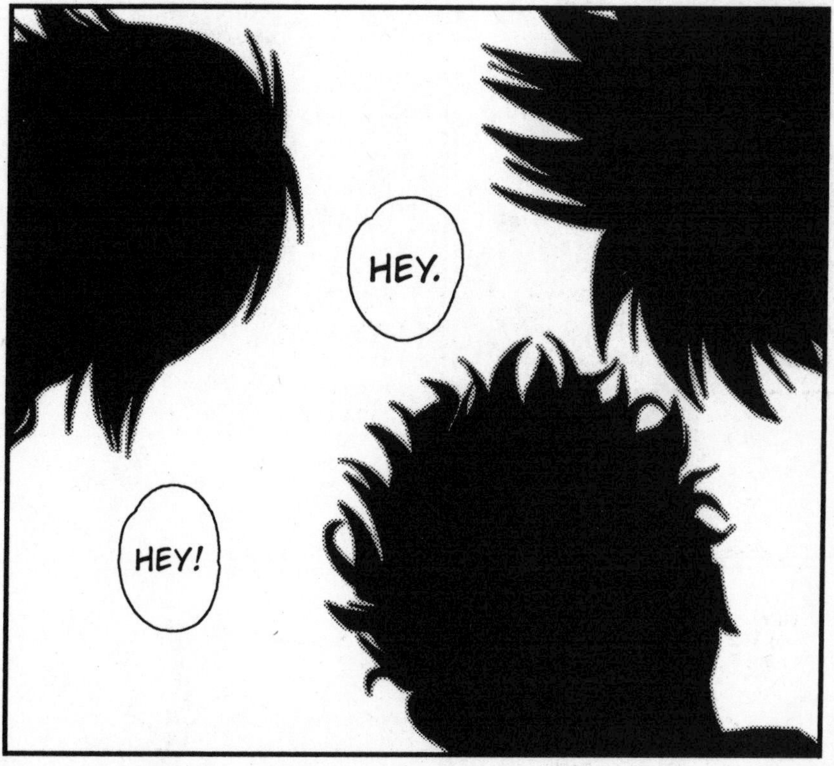
HEY.
HEY!

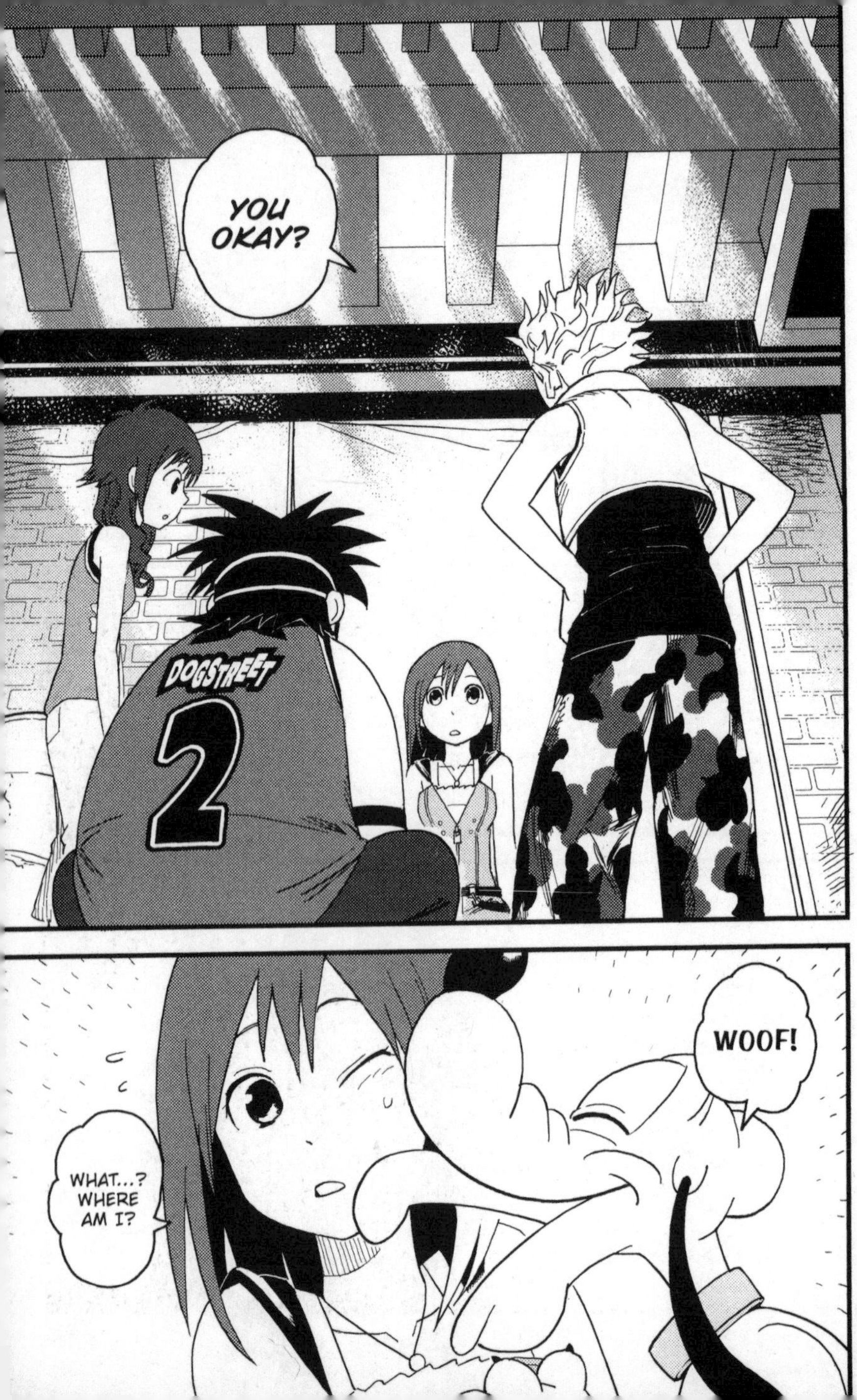
YOU OKAY?
DOGSTREET 2
WOOF!
WHAT...? WHERE AM I?

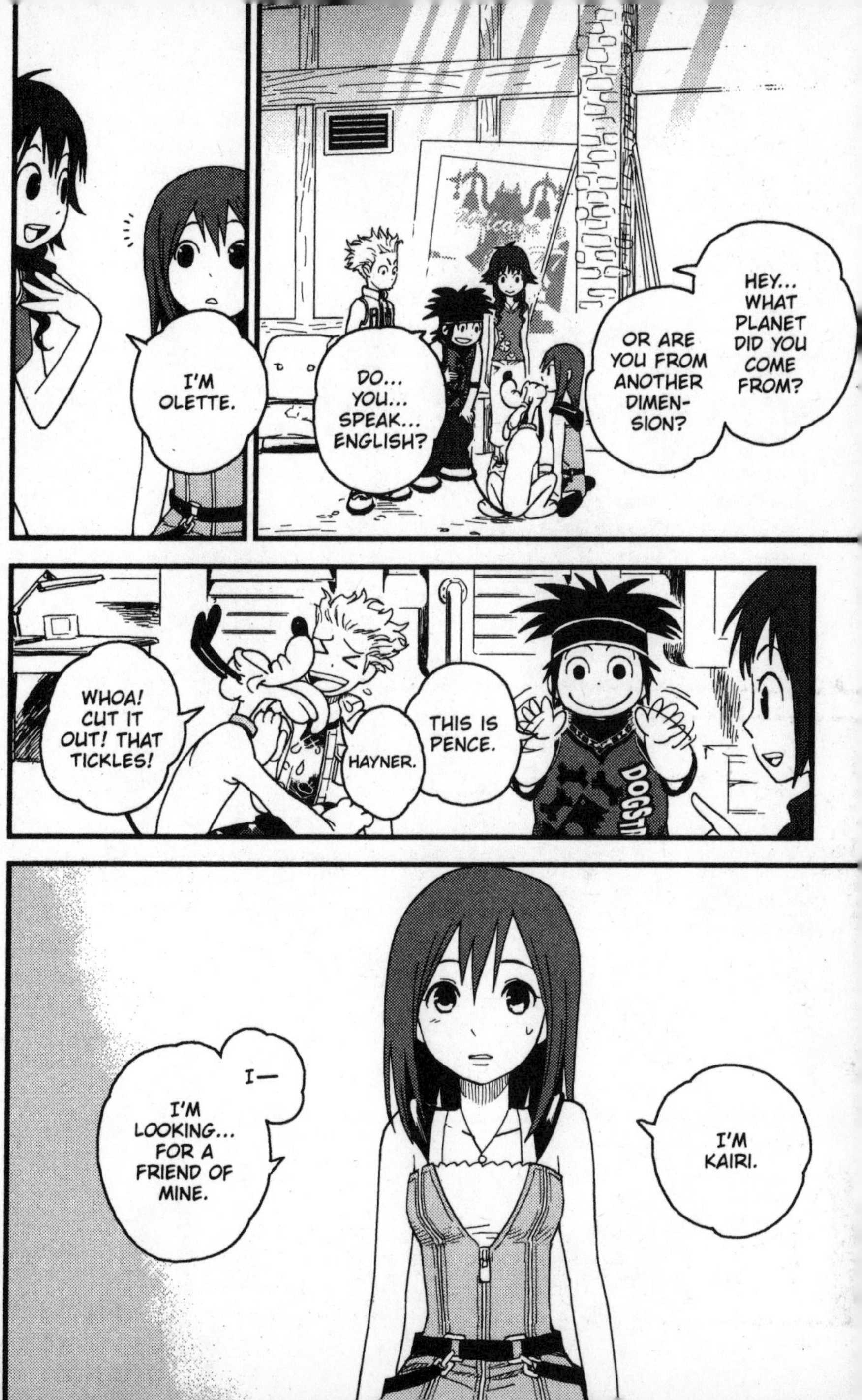
HEY... WHAT PLANET DID YOU COME FROM?
OR ARE YOU FROM ANOTHER DIMEN-SION?
DO... YOU... SPEAK... ENGLISH?
I'M OLETTE.
THIS IS PENCE.
HAYNER.
WHOA! CUT IT OUT! THAT TICKLES!
I'M KAIRI.
I—
I'M LOOKING... FOR A FRIEND OF MINE.

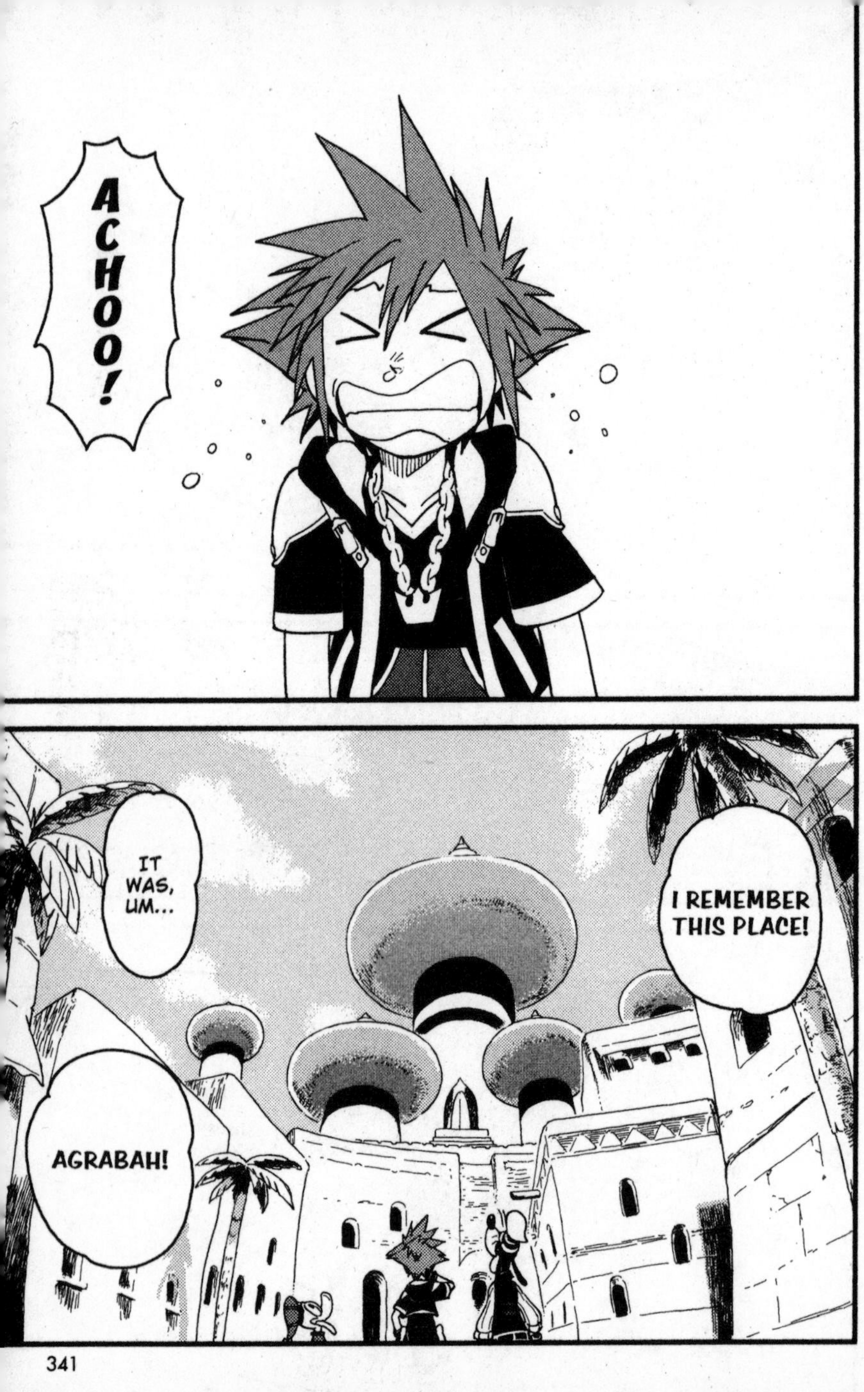
ACHOO!
I REMEMBER THIS PLACE!
IT WAS, UM...
AGRABAH!

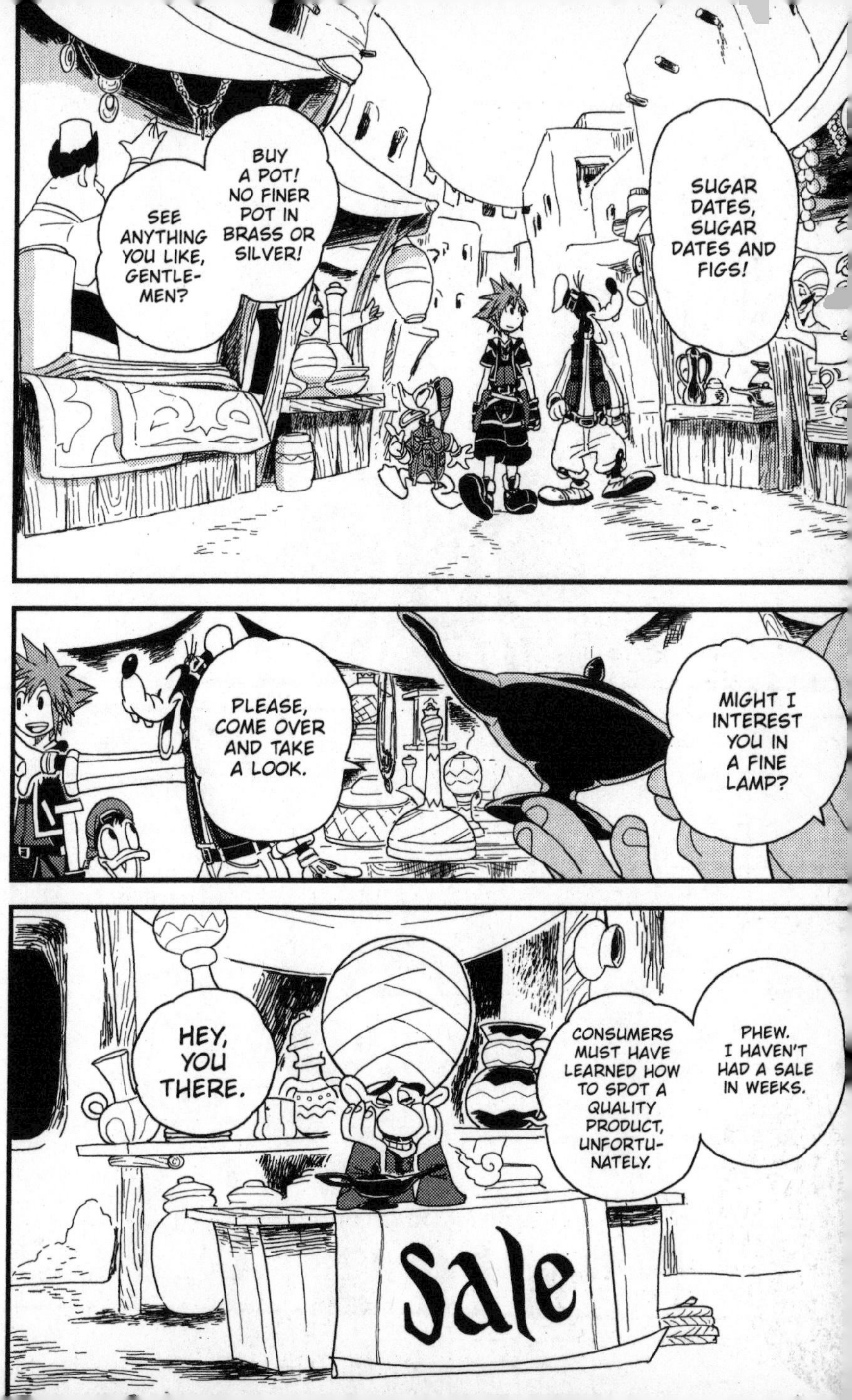

SUGAR DATES, SUGAR DATES AND FIGS!
BUY A POT! NO FINER POT IN BRASS OR SILVER!
SEE ANYTHING YOU LIKE, GENTLE-MEN?
MIGHT I INTEREST YOU IN A FINE LAMP?
PLEASE, COME OVER AND TAKE A LOOK.
PHEW. I HAVEN'T HAD A SALE IN WEEKS.
CONSUMERS MUST HAVE LEARNED HOW TO SPOT A QUALITY PRODUCT, UNFORTU-NATELY.
HEY, YOU THERE.
Sale

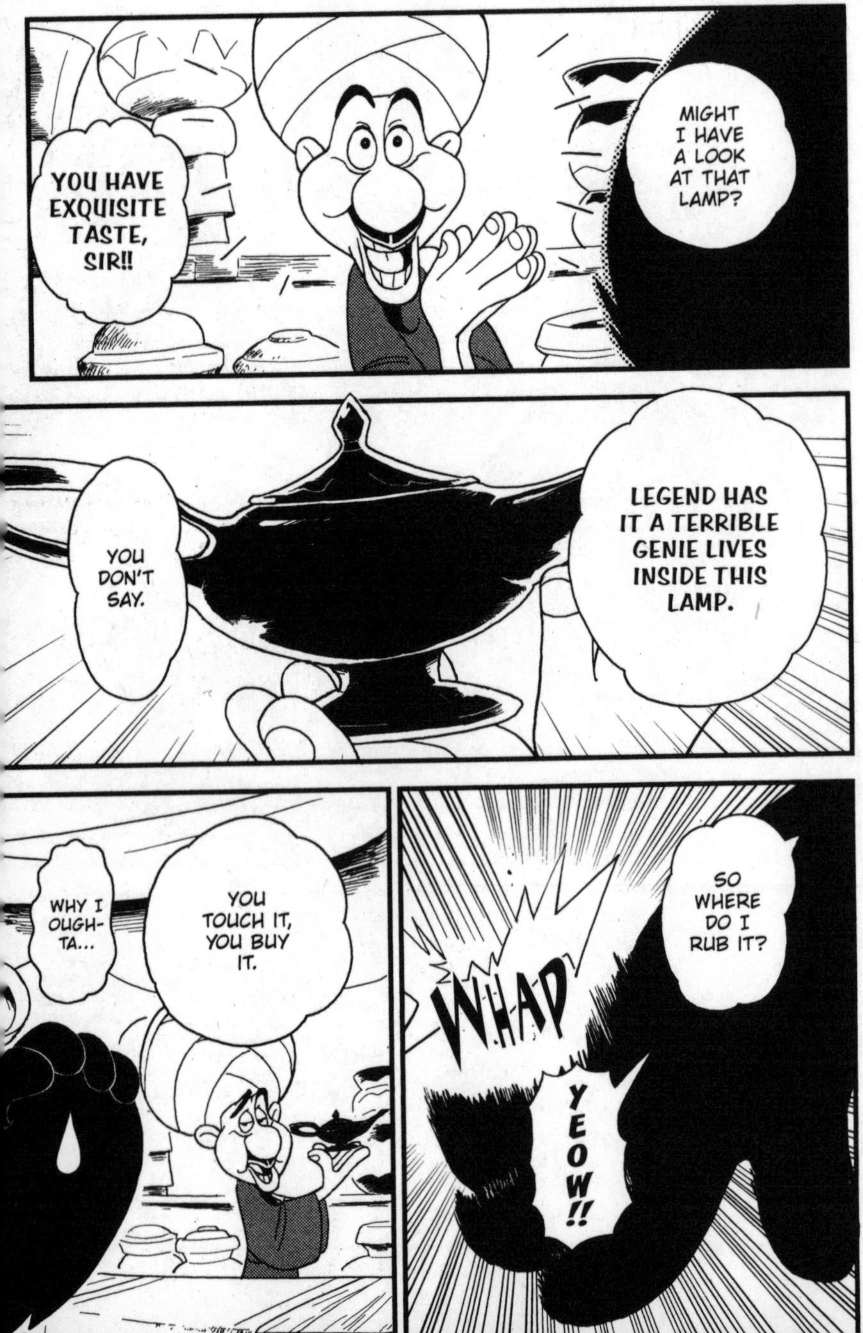
MIGHT I HAVE A LOOK AT THAT LAMP?
YOU HAVE EXQUISITE TASTE, SIR!!
LEGEND HAS IT A TERRIBLE GENIE LIVES INSIDE THIS LAMP.
YOU DON'T SAY.
SO WHERE DO I RUB IT?
WHAP
YEOW!!
YOU TOUCH IT, YOU BUY IT.
WHY I OUGH-TA...

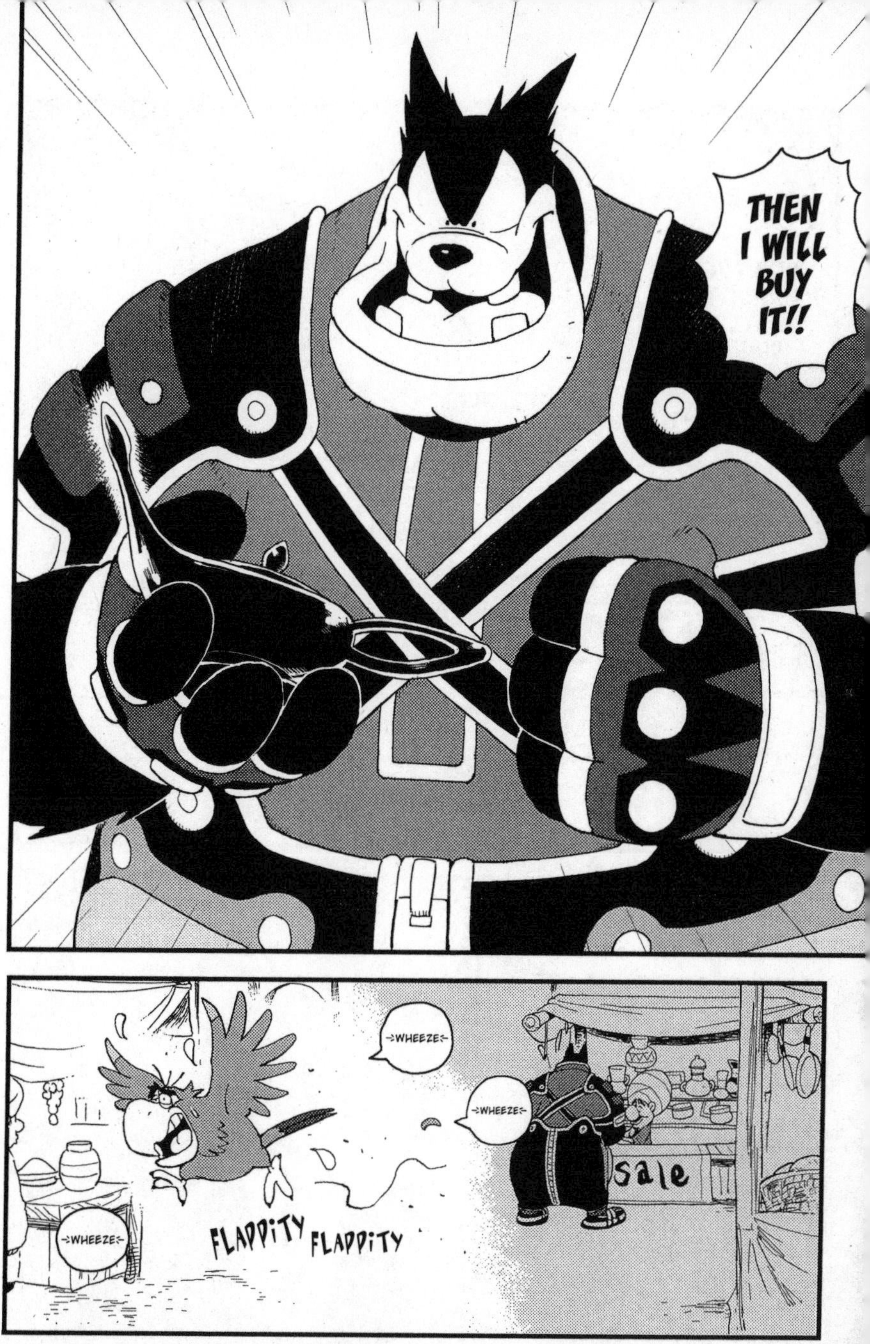
THEN I WILL BUY IT!!
WHEEZE
WHEEZE
sale
WHEEZE
FLAPPDITY FLAPPDITY

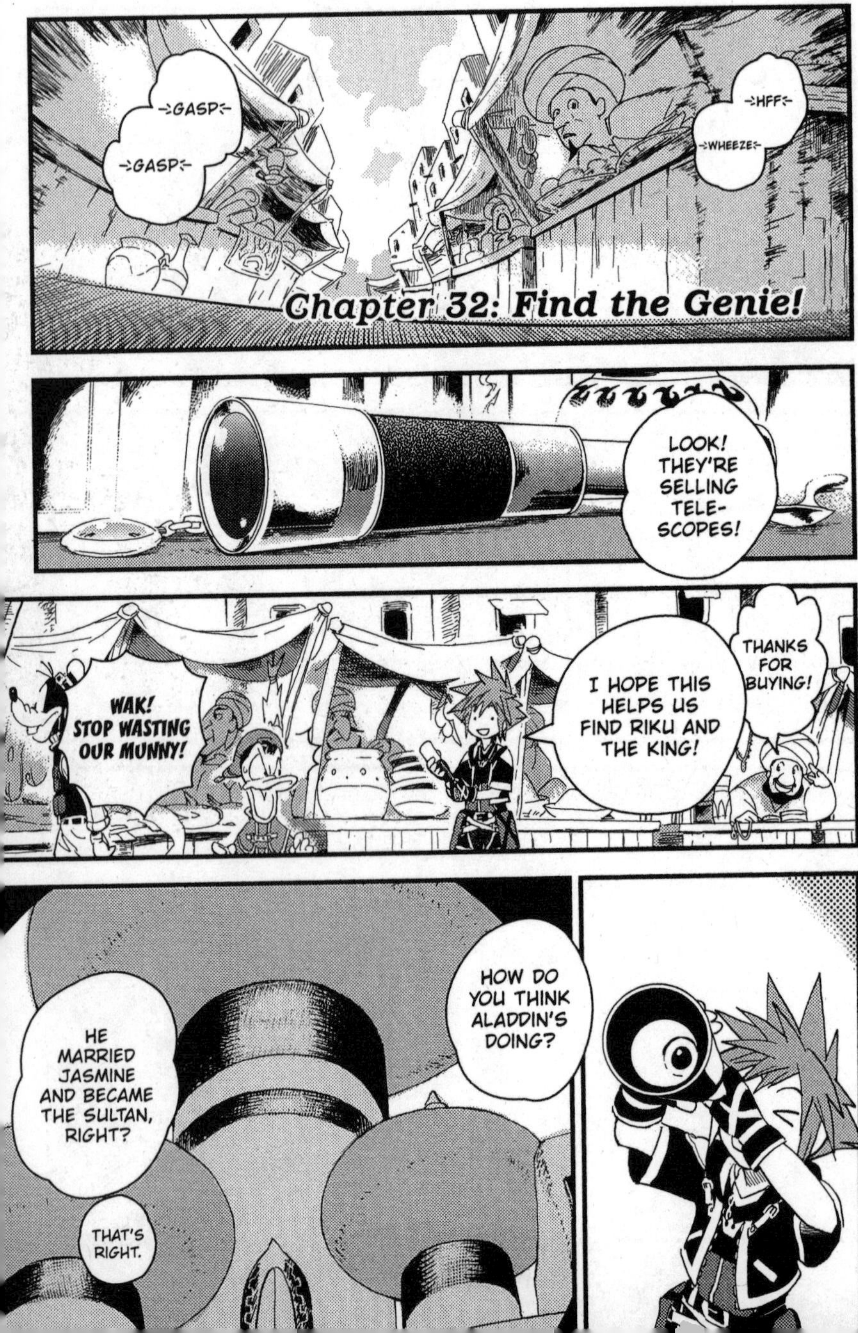

Chapter 32: Find the Genie!
⊰HFF⊱
⊰WHEEZE⊱
⊰GASP⊱
⊰GASP⊱
LOOK! THEY'RE SELLING TELE-SCOPES!
THANKS FOR BUYING!
I HOPE THIS HELPS US FIND RIKU AND THE KING!
WAK! STOP WASTING OUR MUNNY!
HOW DO YOU THINK ALADDIN'S DOING?
HE MARRIED JASMINE AND BECAME THE SULTAN, RIGHT?
THAT'S RIGHT.

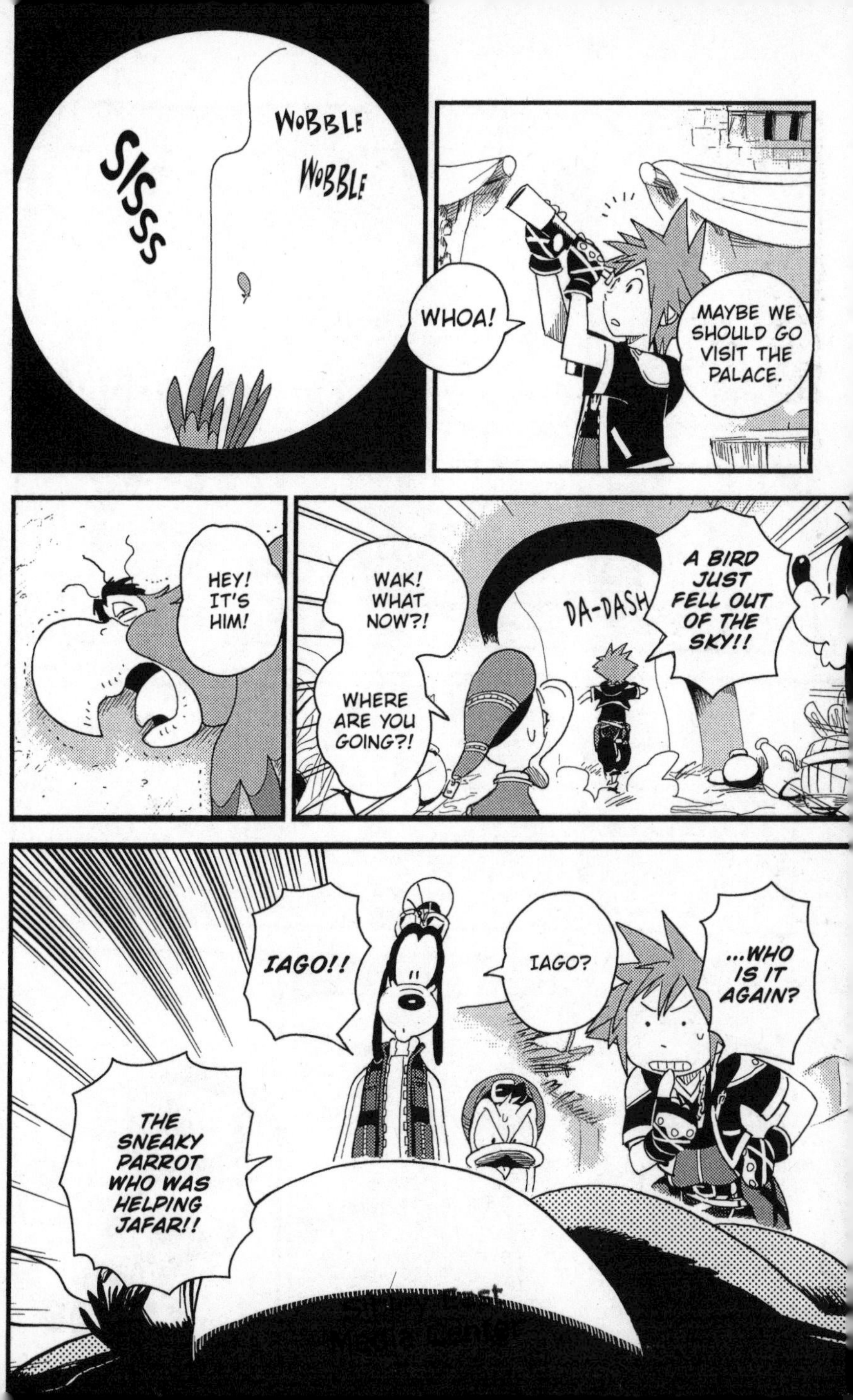
MAYBE WE SHOULD GO VISIT THE PALACE.
WHOA!
WOBBLE
WOBBLE
SISSS
A BIRD JUST FELL OUT OF THE SKY!!
DA-DASH
WAK! WHAT NOW?!
WHERE ARE YOU GOING?!
HEY! IT'S HIM!
...WHO IS IT AGAIN?
IAGO?
IAGO!!
THE SNEAKY PARROT WHO WAS HELPING JAFAR!!

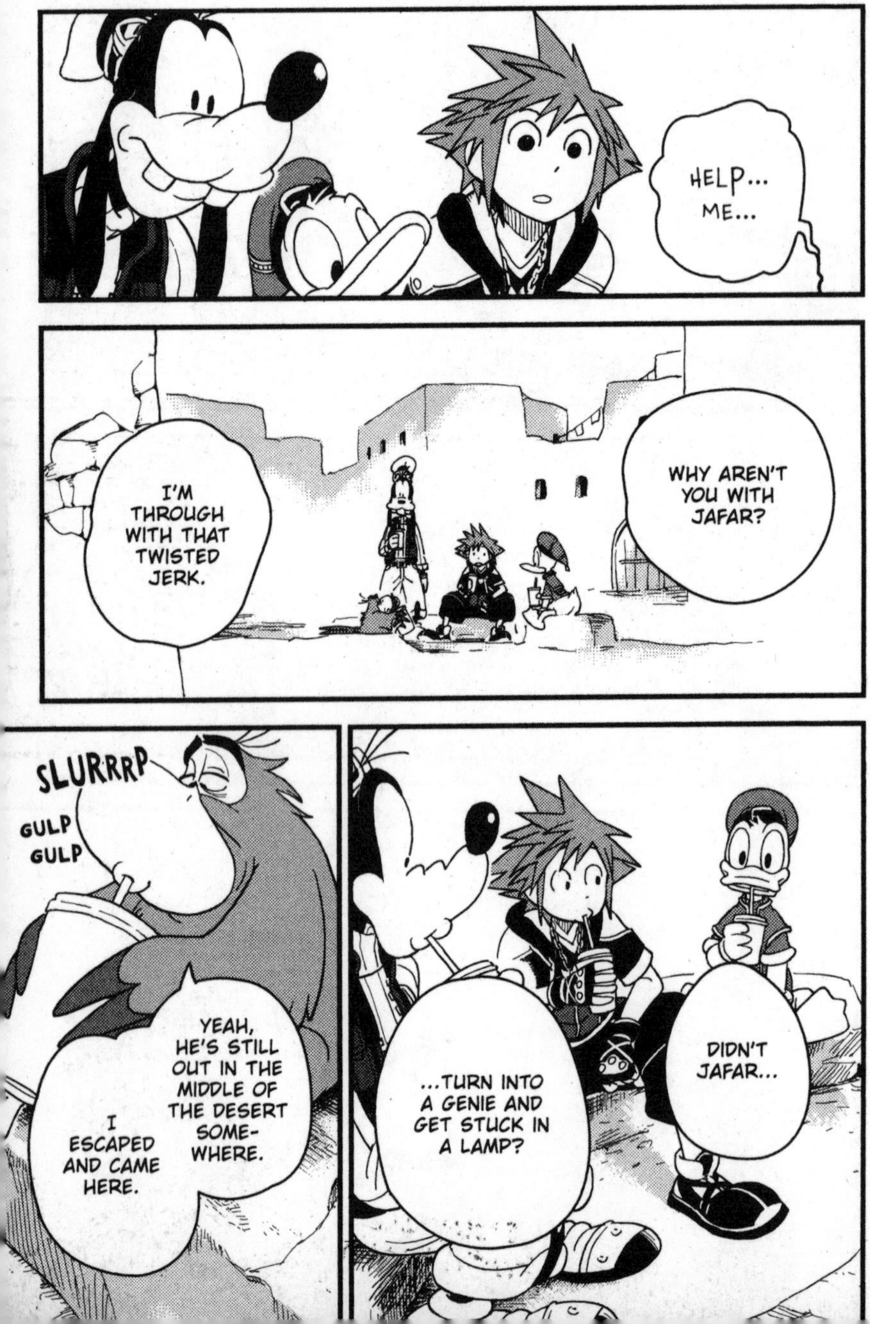
HELP... ME...
WHY AREN'T YOU WITH JAFAR?
I'M THROUGH WITH THAT TWISTED JERK.
DIDN'T JAFAR...
...TURN INTO A GENIE AND GET STUCK IN A LAMP?
SLURRRP
GULP GULP
YEAH, HE'S STILL OUT IN THE MIDDLE OF THE DESERT SOME-WHERE.
I ESCAPED AND CAME HERE.

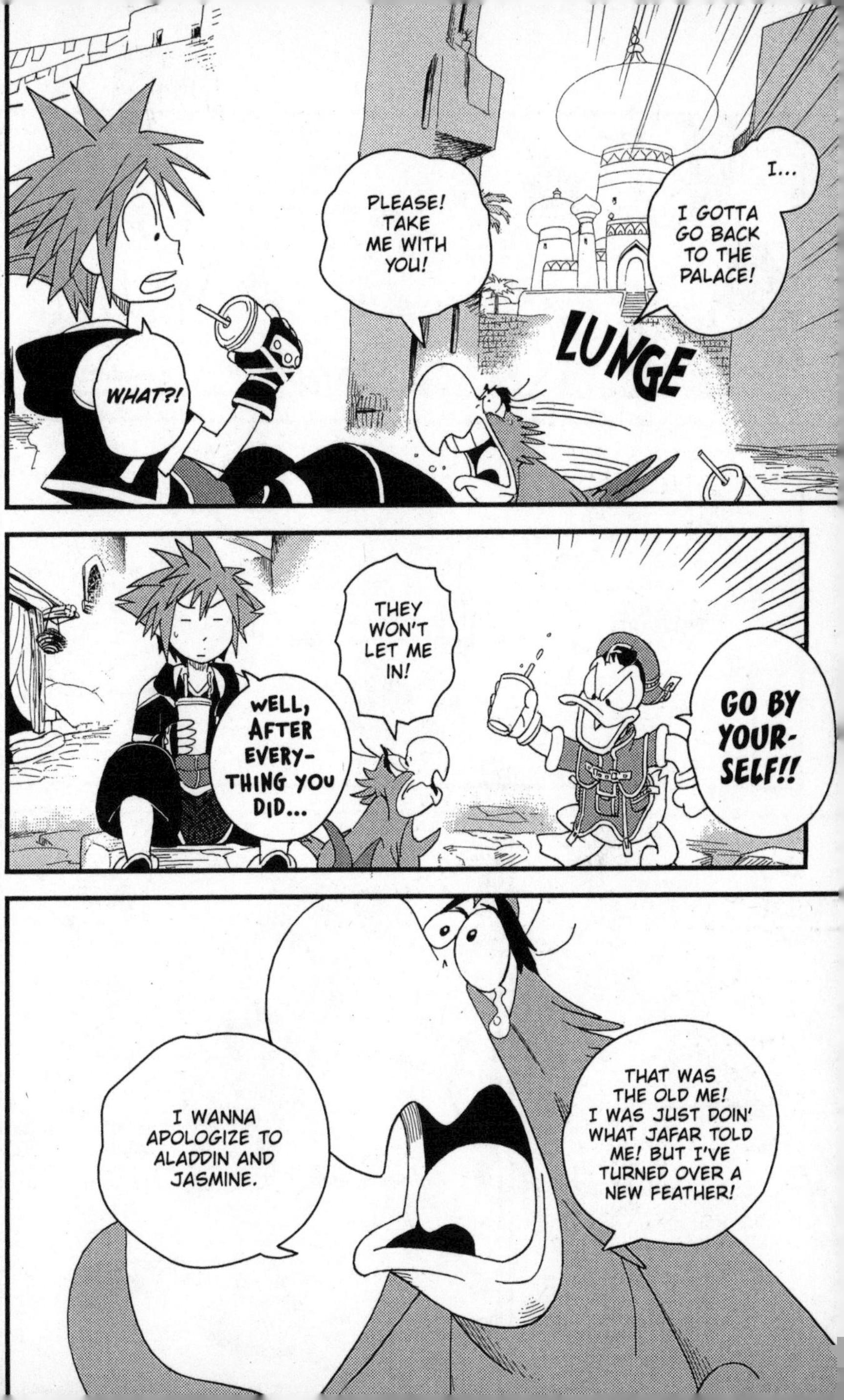
I...
I GOTTA GO BACK TO THE PALACE!
LUNGE
PLEASE! TAKE ME WITH YOU!
WHAT?!
GO BY YOURSELF!!
THEY WON'T LET ME IN!
WELL, AFTER EVERYTHING YOU DID...
THAT WAS THE OLD ME! I WAS JUST DOIN' WHAT JAFAR TOLD ME! BUT I'VE TURNED OVER A NEW FEATHER!
I WANNA APOLOGIZE TO ALADDIN AND JASMINE.

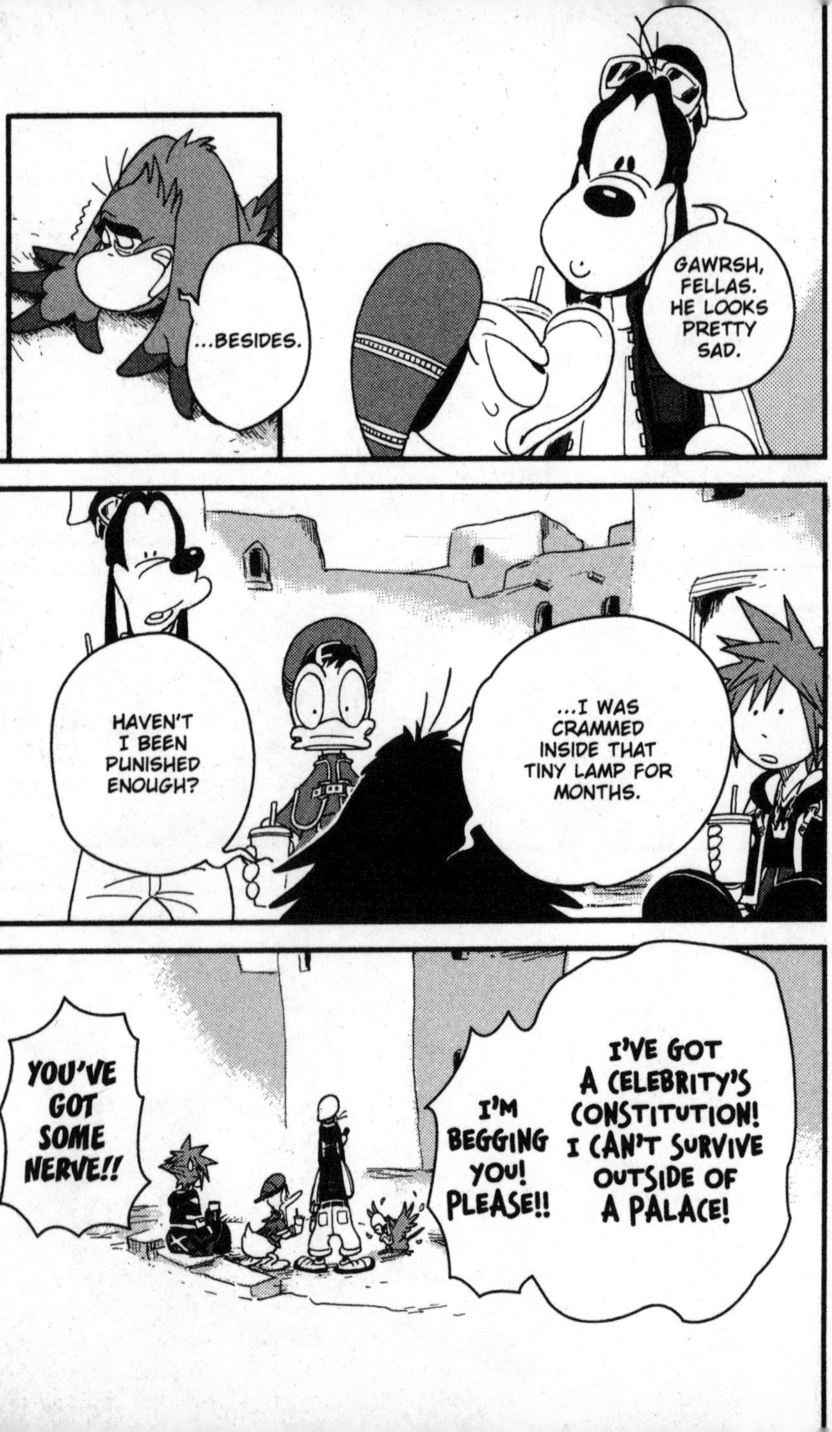
GAWRSH, FELLAS. HE LOOKS PRETTY SAD.
...BESIDES.
...I WAS CRAMMED INSIDE THAT TINY LAMP FOR MONTHS.
HAVEN'T I BEEN PUNISHED ENOUGH?
I'VE GOT A CELEBRITY'S CONSTITUTION! I CAN'T SURVIVE OUTSIDE OF A PALACE!
I'M BEGGING YOU! PLEASE!!
YOU'VE GOT SOME NERVE!!

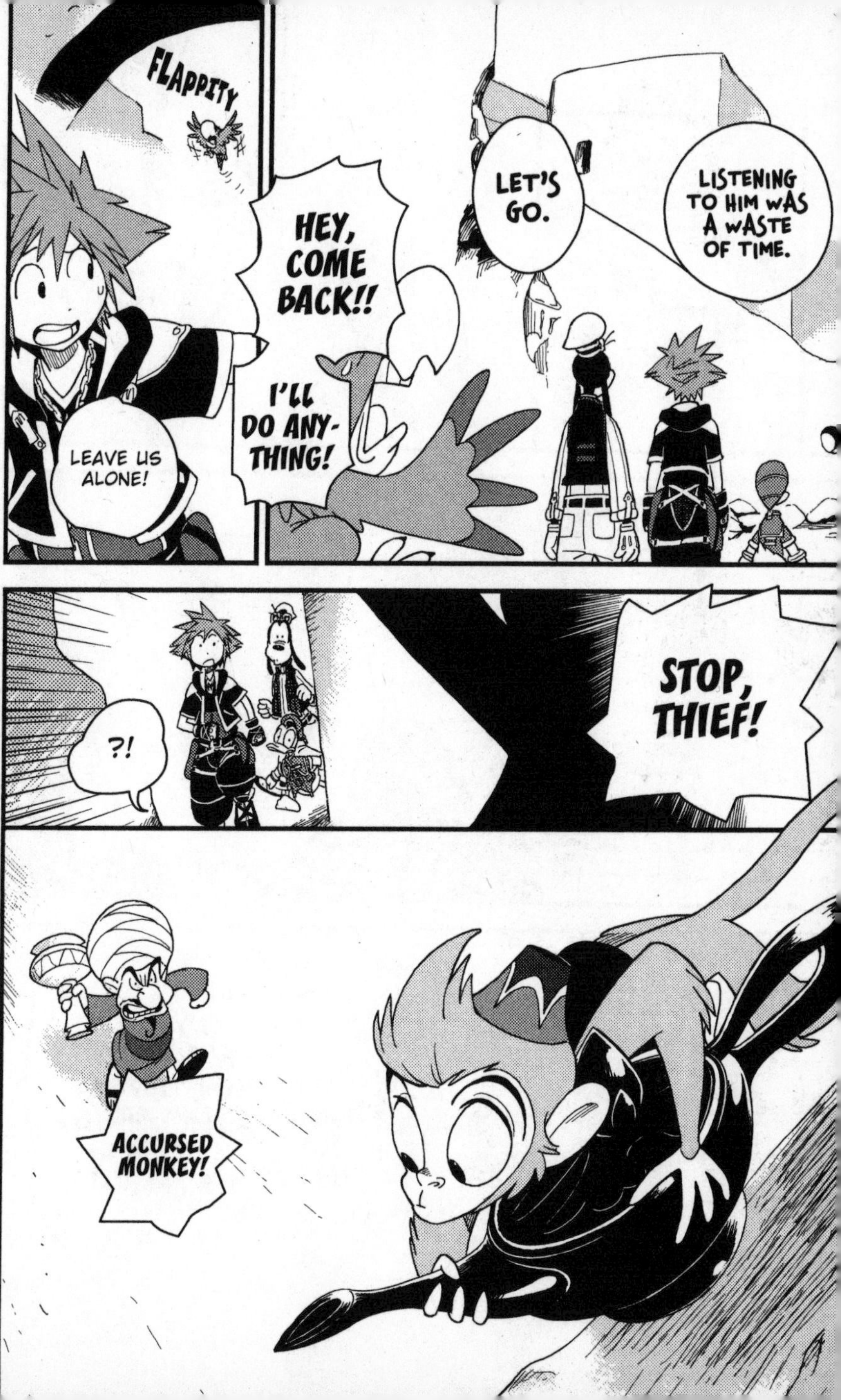
LISTENING TO HIM WAS A WASTE OF TIME.
LET'S GO.
HEY, COME BACK!!
I'LL DO ANY-THING!
FLAPPITY
LEAVE US ALONE!
STOP, THIEF!
?!
ACCURSED MONKEY!

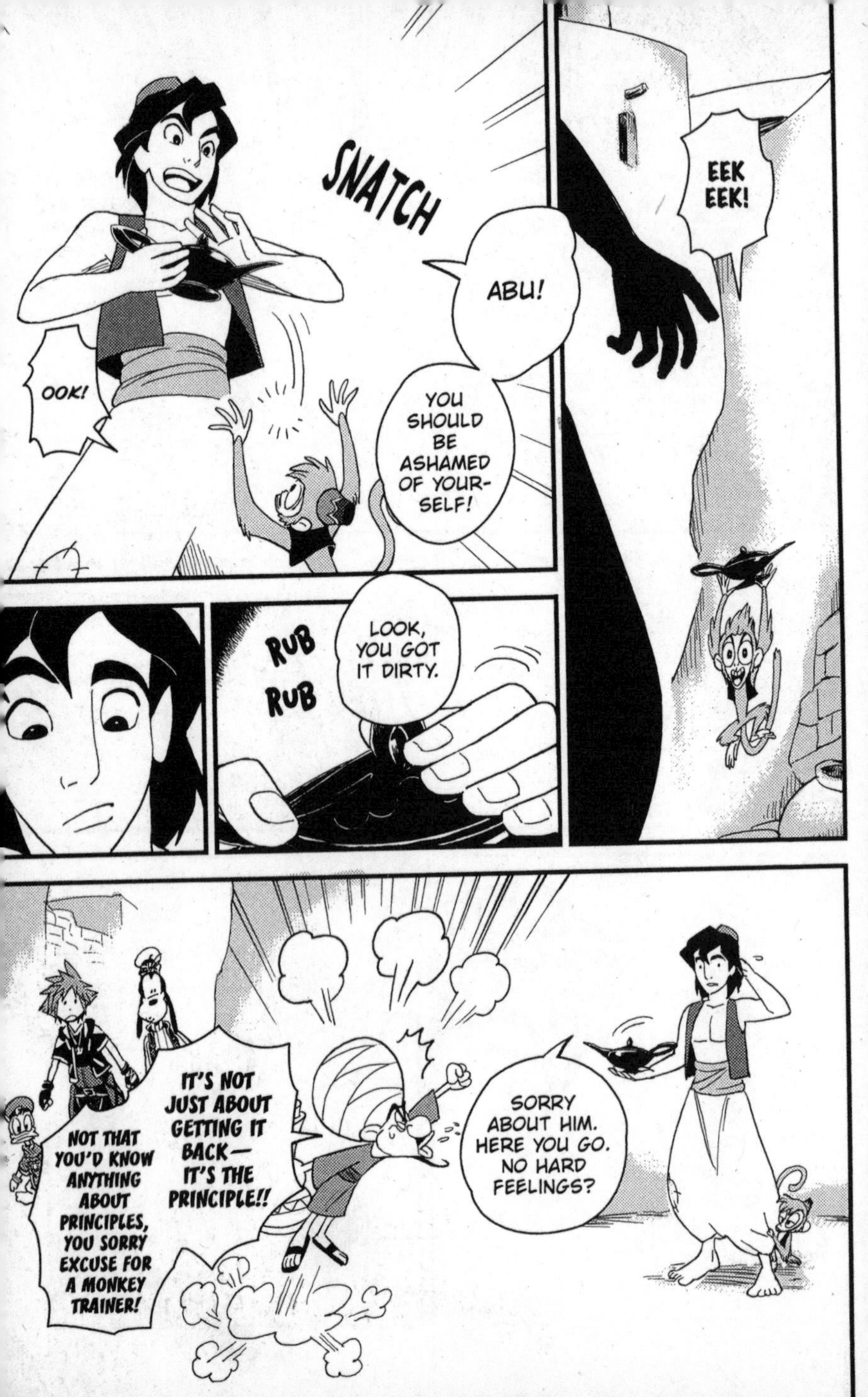
EEK EEK!
SNATCH
ABU!
YOU SHOULD BE ASHAMED OF YOURSELF!
OOK!
LOOK, YOU GOT IT DIRTY.
RUB RUB
SORRY ABOUT HIM. HERE YOU GO. NO HARD FEELINGS?
IT'S NOT JUST ABOUT GETTING IT BACK— IT'S THE PRINCIPLE!!
NOT THAT YOU'D KNOW ANYTHING ABOUT PRINCIPLES, YOU SORRY EXCUSE FOR A MONKEY TRAINER!

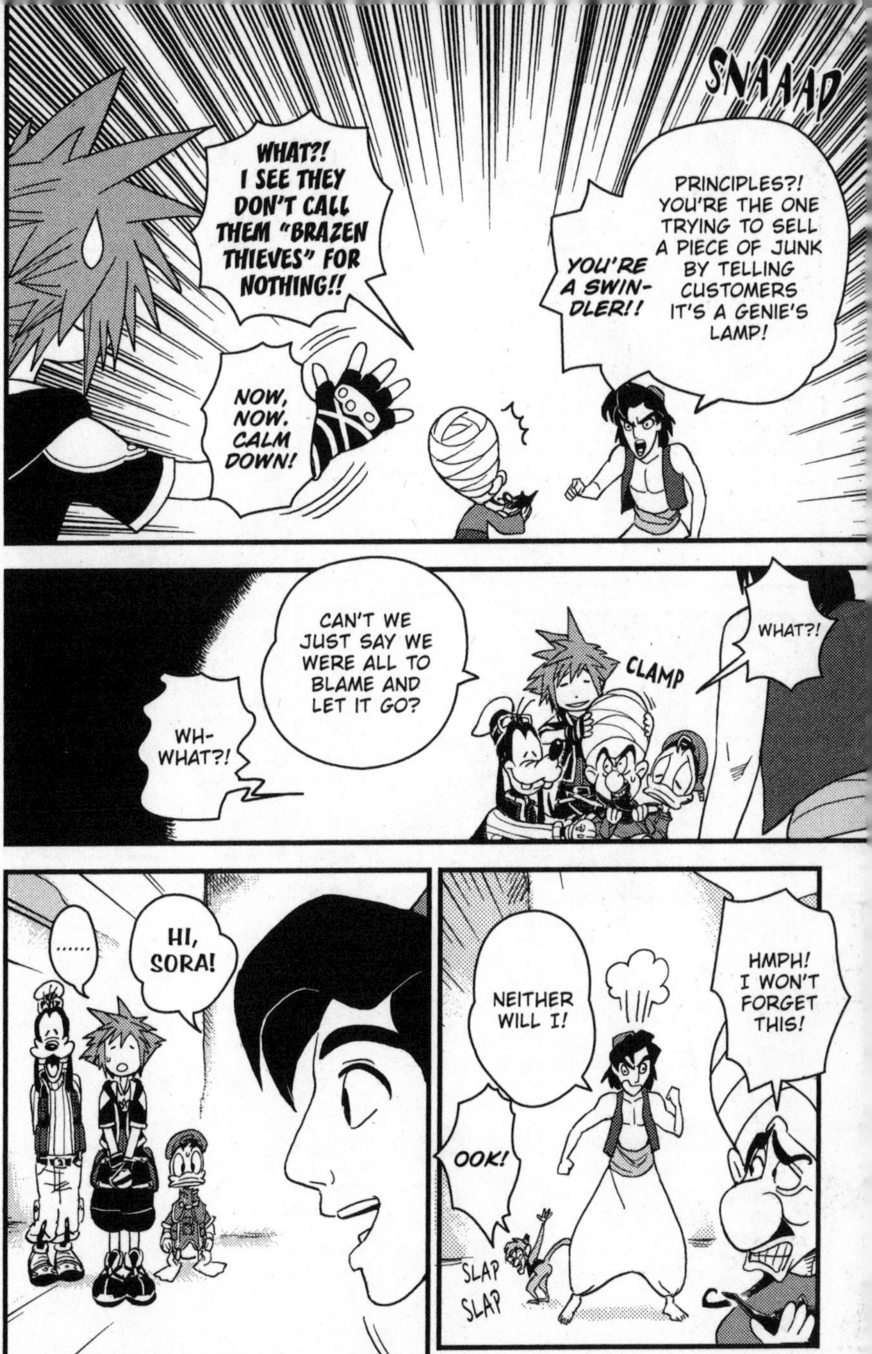
SNAAAP
PRINCIPLES?! YOU'RE THE ONE TRYING TO SELL A PIECE OF JUNK BY TELLING CUSTOMERS IT'S A GENIE'S LAMP!
YOU'RE A SWIN-DLER!!
WHAT?! I SEE THEY DON'T CALL THEM "BRAZEN THIEVES" FOR NOTHING!!
NOW, NOW. CALM DOWN!
WHAT?!
CLAMP
CAN'T WE JUST SAY WE WERE ALL TO BLAME AND LET IT GO?
WH-WHAT?!
HMPH! I WON'T FORGET THIS!
NEITHER WILL I!
OOK!
SLAP SLAP
HI, SORA!
......

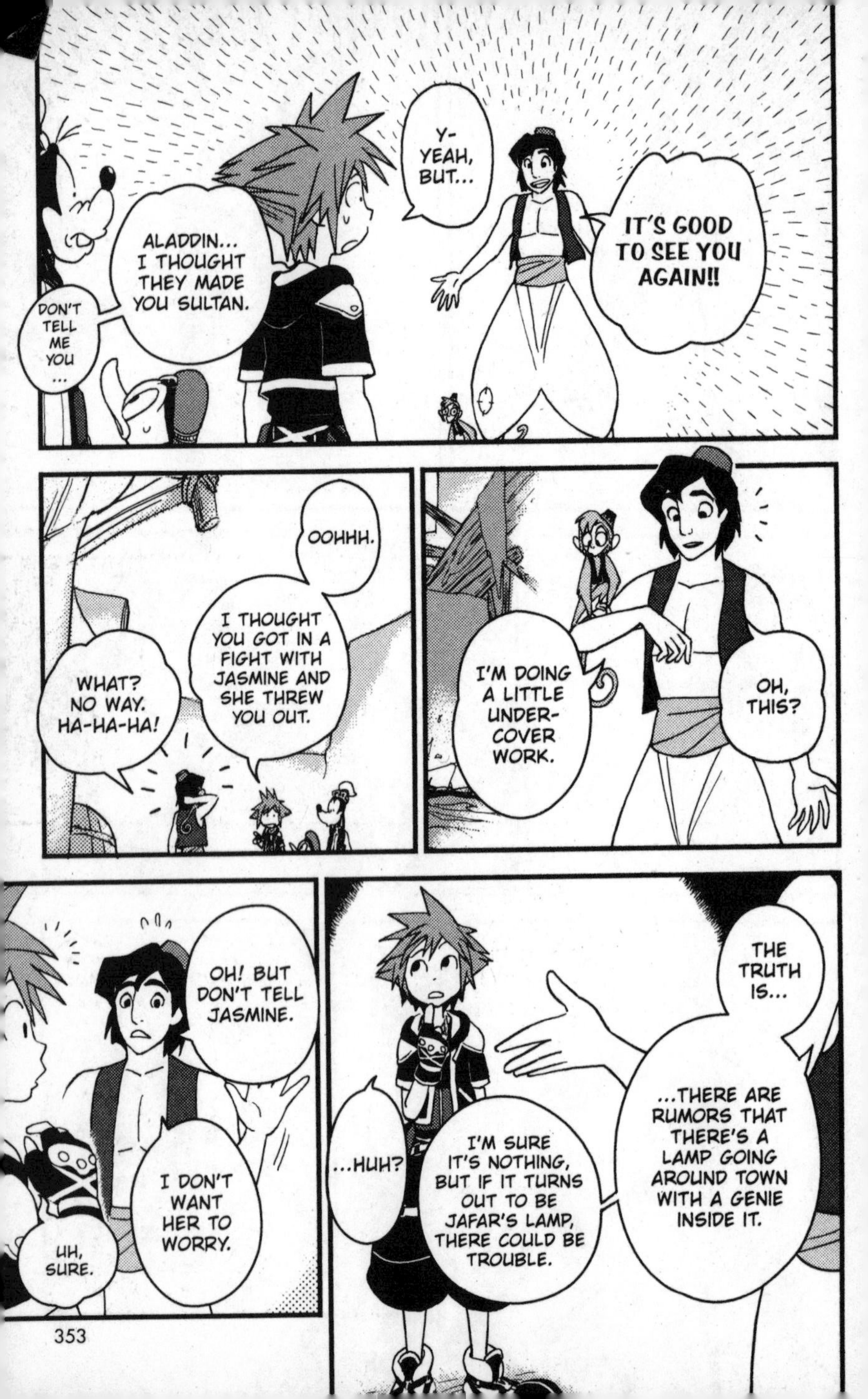
IT'S GOOD TO SEE YOU AGAIN!!
Y-YEAH, BUT...
ALADDIN... I THOUGHT THEY MADE YOU SULTAN.
DON'T TELL ME YOU ...
OH, THIS?
I'M DOING A LITTLE UNDER-COVER WORK.
OOHHH.
I THOUGHT YOU GOT IN A FIGHT WITH JASMINE AND SHE THREW YOU OUT.
WHAT? NO WAY. HA-HA-HA!
THE TRUTH IS...
...THERE ARE RUMORS THAT THERE'S A LAMP GOING AROUND TOWN WITH A GENIE INSIDE IT.
I'M SURE IT'S NOTHING, BUT IF IT TURNS OUT TO BE JAFAR'S LAMP, THERE COULD BE TROUBLE.
...HUH?
OH! BUT DON'T TELL JASMINE.
I DON'T WANT HER TO WORRY.
UH, SURE.

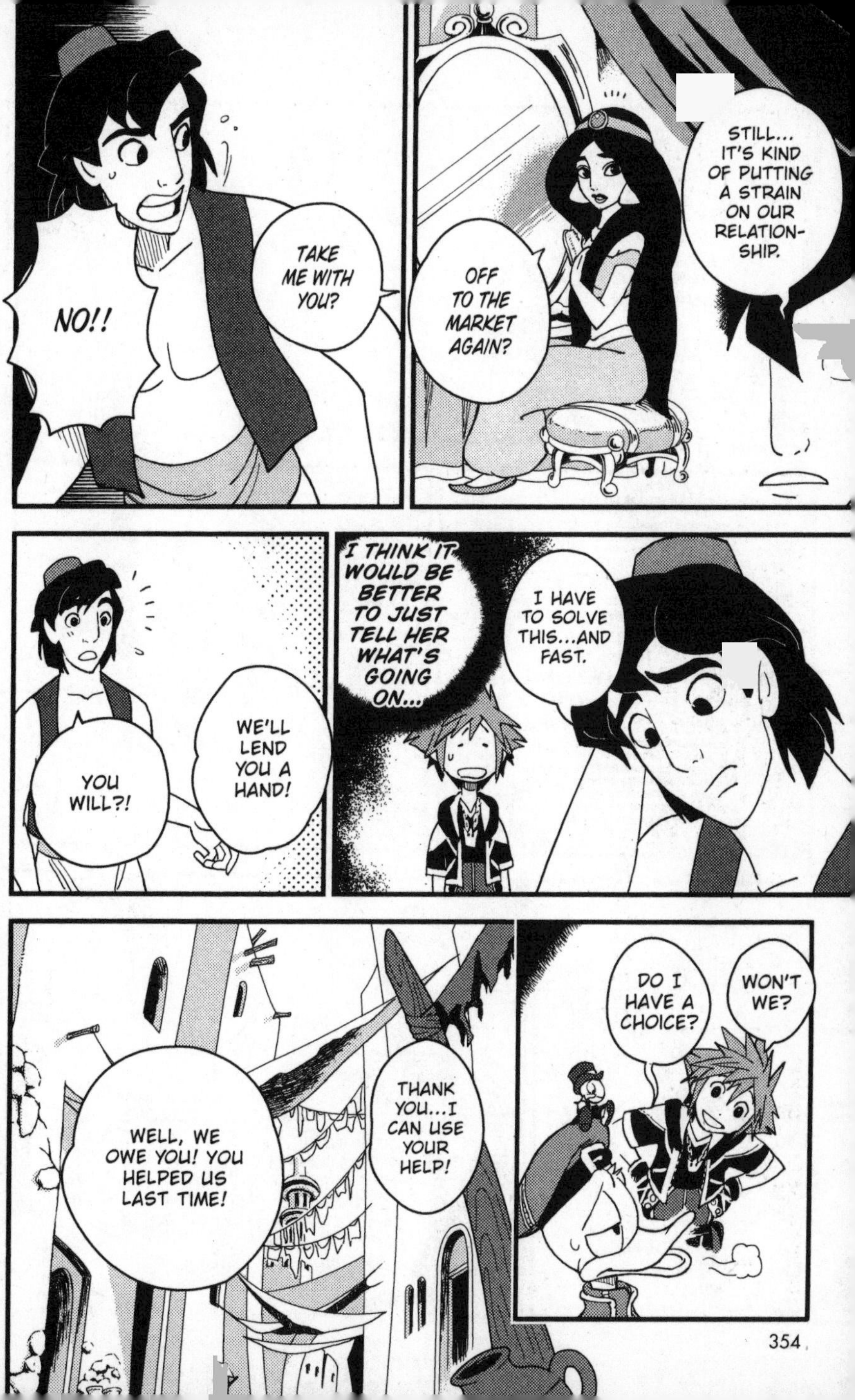
STILL... IT'S KIND OF PUTTING A STRAIN ON OUR RELATION-SHIP.
OFF TO THE MARKET AGAIN?
TAKE ME WITH YOU?
NO!!
I HAVE TO SOLVE THIS...AND FAST.
I THINK IT WOULD BE BETTER TO JUST TELL HER WHAT'S GOING ON...
WE'LL LEND YOU A HAND!
YOU WILL?!
WON'T WE?
DO I HAVE A CHOICE?
THANK YOU...I CAN USE YOUR HELP!
WELL, WE OWE YOU! YOU HELPED US LAST TIME!

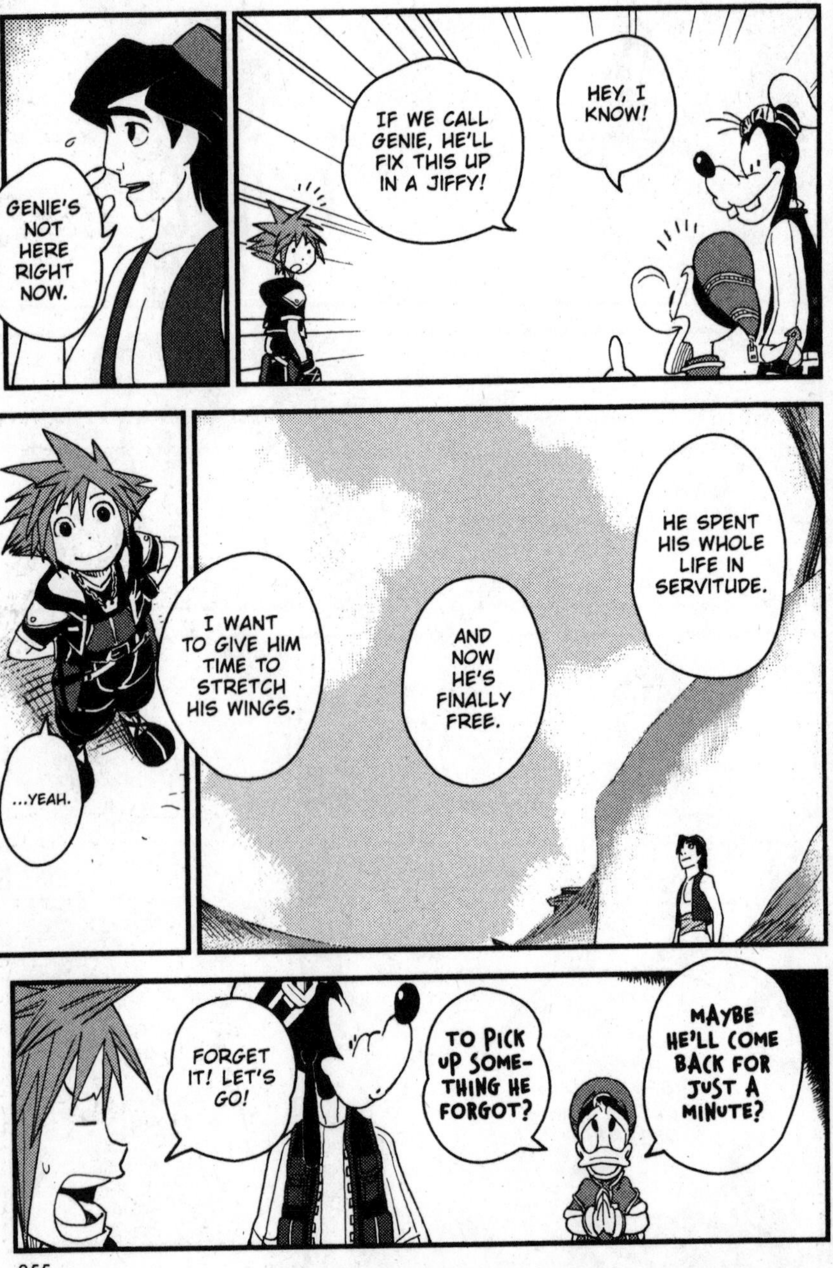
HEY, I KNOW!
IF WE CALL GENIE, HE'LL FIX THIS UP IN A JIFFY!
GENIE'S NOT HERE RIGHT NOW.
HE SPENT HIS WHOLE LIFE IN SERVITUDE.
AND NOW HE'S FINALLY FREE.
I WANT TO GIVE HIM TIME TO STRETCH HIS WINGS.
...YEAH.
MAYBE HE'LL COME BACK FOR JUST A MINUTE?
TO PICK UP SOME-THING HE FORGOT?
FORGET IT! LET'S GO!

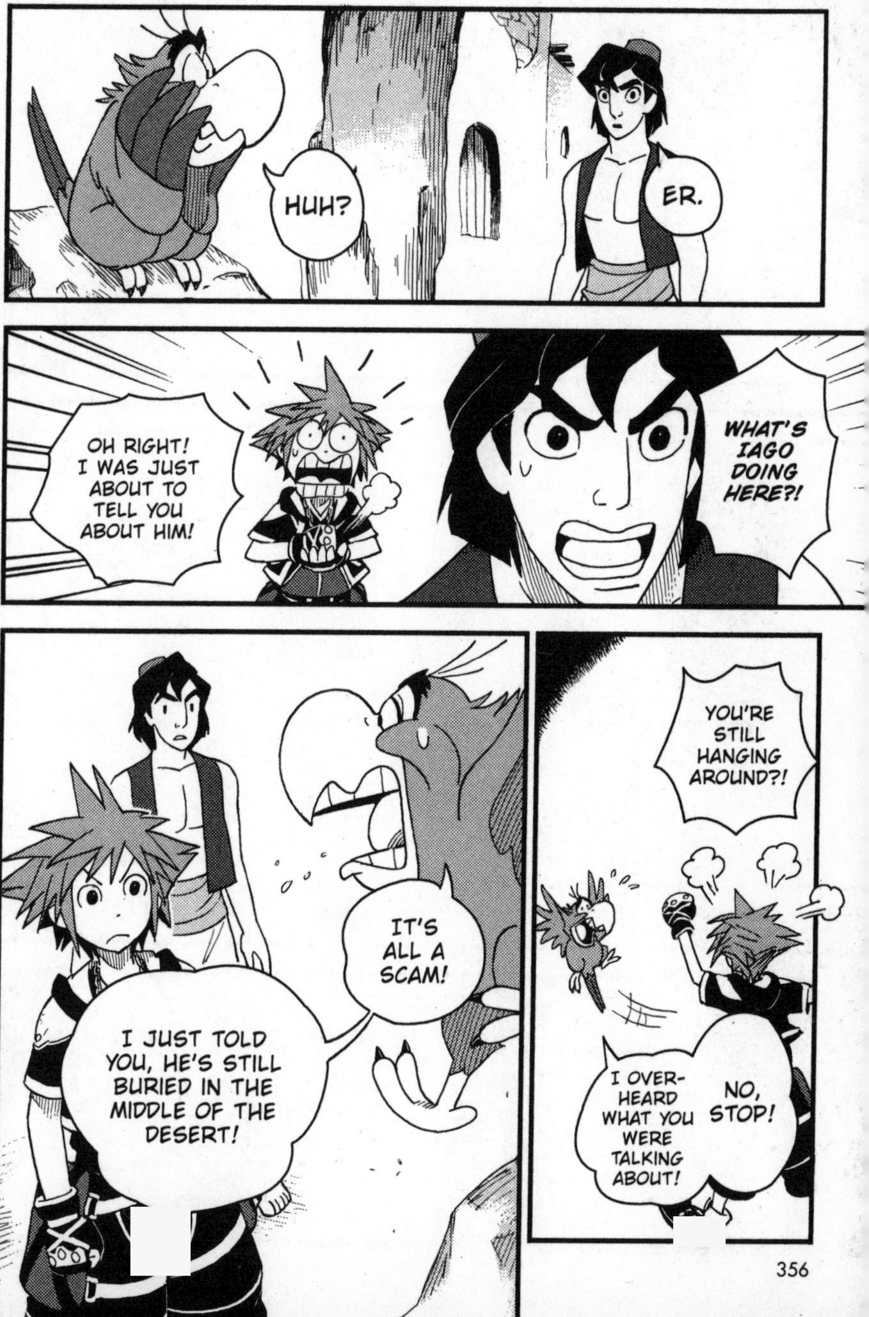
HUH?
ER.
OH RIGHT! I WAS JUST ABOUT TO TELL YOU ABOUT HIM!
WHAT'S IAGO DOING HERE?!
I JUST TOLD YOU, HE'S STILL BURIED IN THE MIDDLE OF THE DESERT!
IT'S ALL A SCAM!
YOU'RE STILL HANGING AROUND?!
NO, STOP!
I OVER-HEARD WHAT YOU WERE TALKING ABOUT!

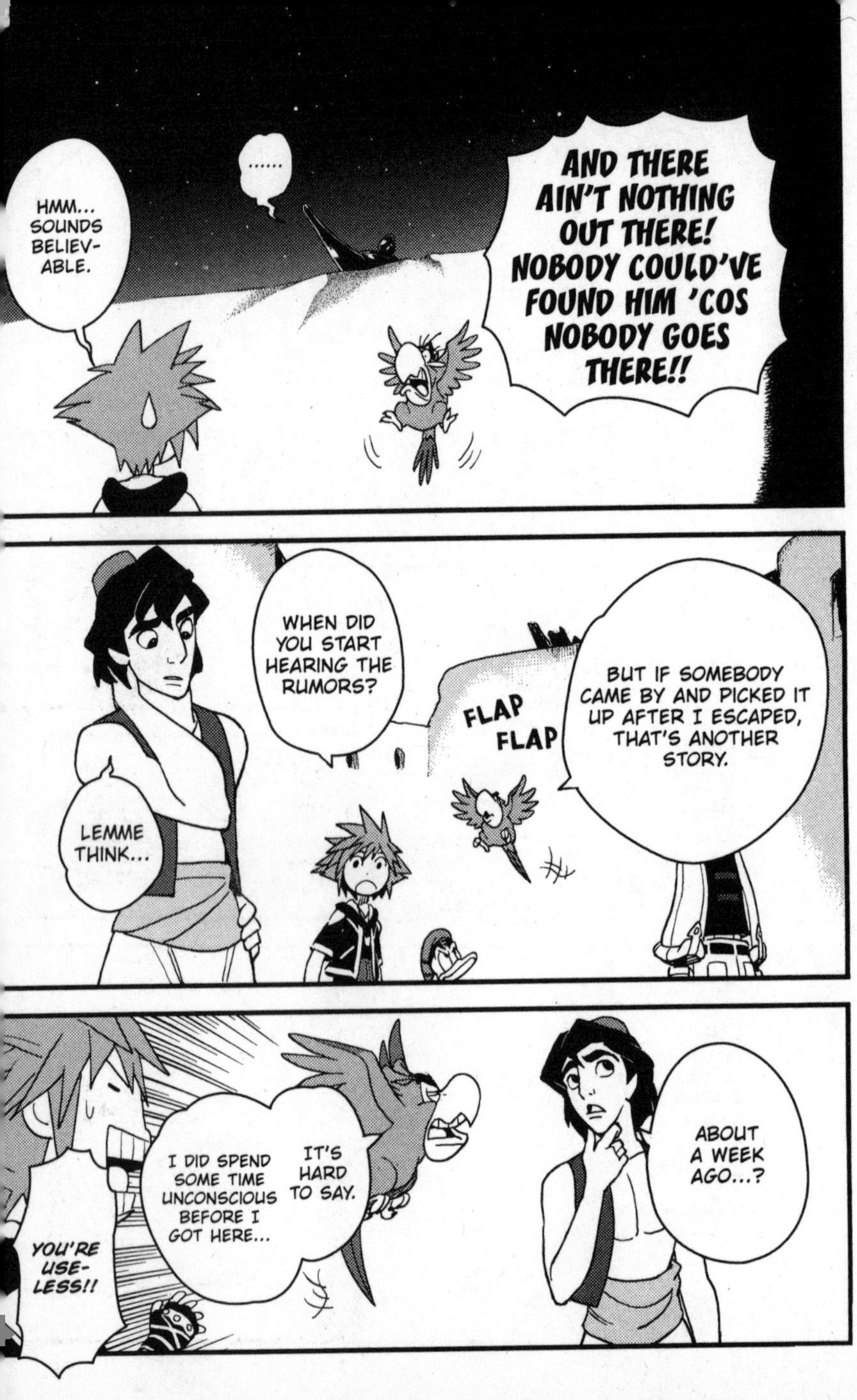
AND THERE AIN'T NOTHING OUT THERE! NOBODY COULD'VE FOUND HIM 'COS NOBODY GOES THERE!!
......
HMM... SOUNDS BELIEV-ABLE.
BUT IF SOMEBODY CAME BY AND PICKED IT UP AFTER I ESCAPED, THAT'S ANOTHER STORY.
FLAP FLAP
WHEN DID YOU START HEARING THE RUMORS?
LEMME THINK...
ABOUT A WEEK AGO...?
IT'S HARD TO SAY.
I DID SPEND SOME TIME UNCONSCIOUS BEFORE I GOT HERE...
YOU'RE USE-LESS!!

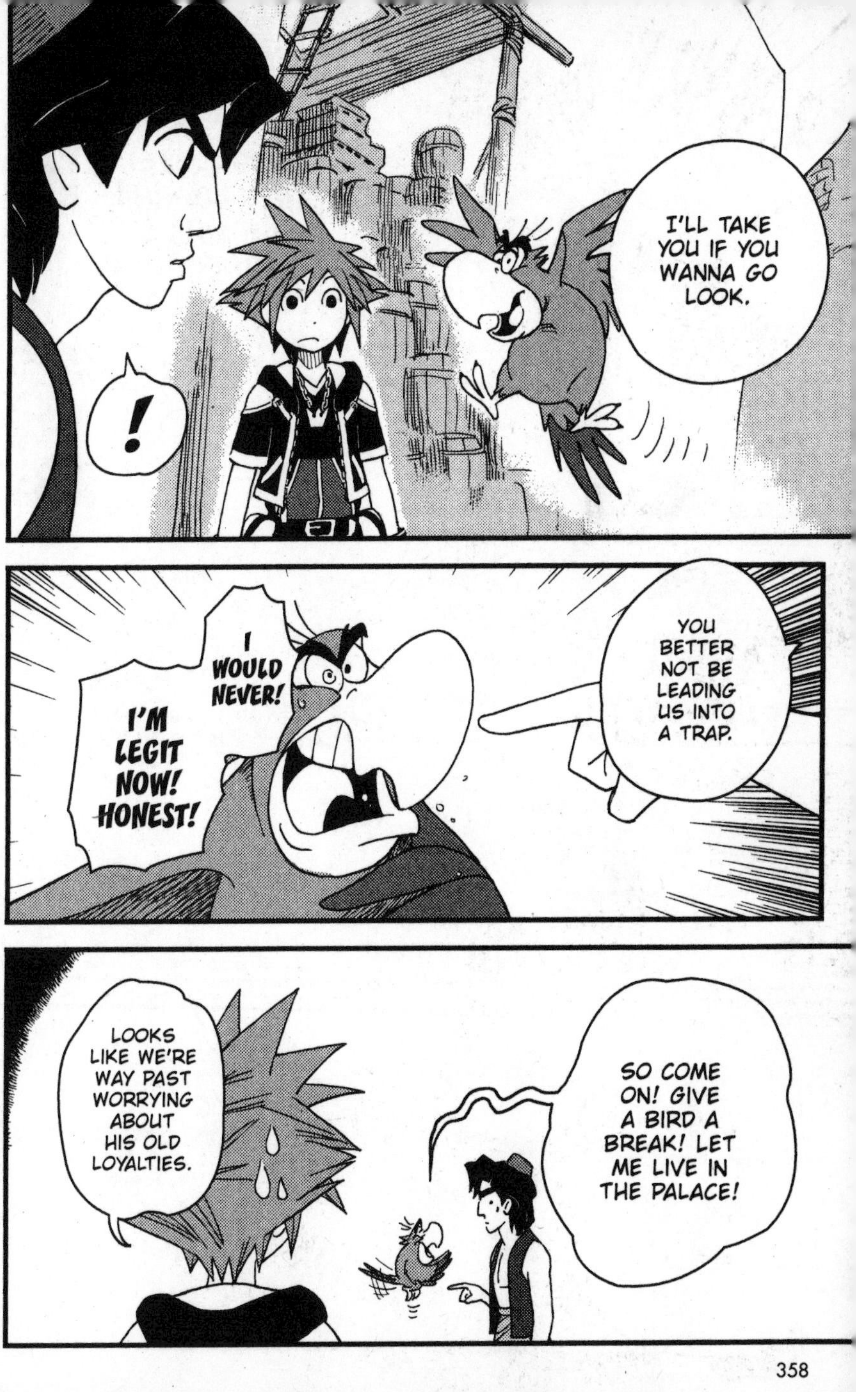
I'LL TAKE YOU IF YOU WANNA GO LOOK.
!
YOU BETTER NOT BE LEADING US INTO A TRAP.
I WOULD NEVER!
I'M LEGIT NOW! HONEST!
SO COME ON! GIVE A BIRD A BREAK! LET ME LIVE IN THE PALACE!
LOOKS LIKE WE'RE WAY PAST WORRYING ABOUT HIS OLD LOYALTIES.

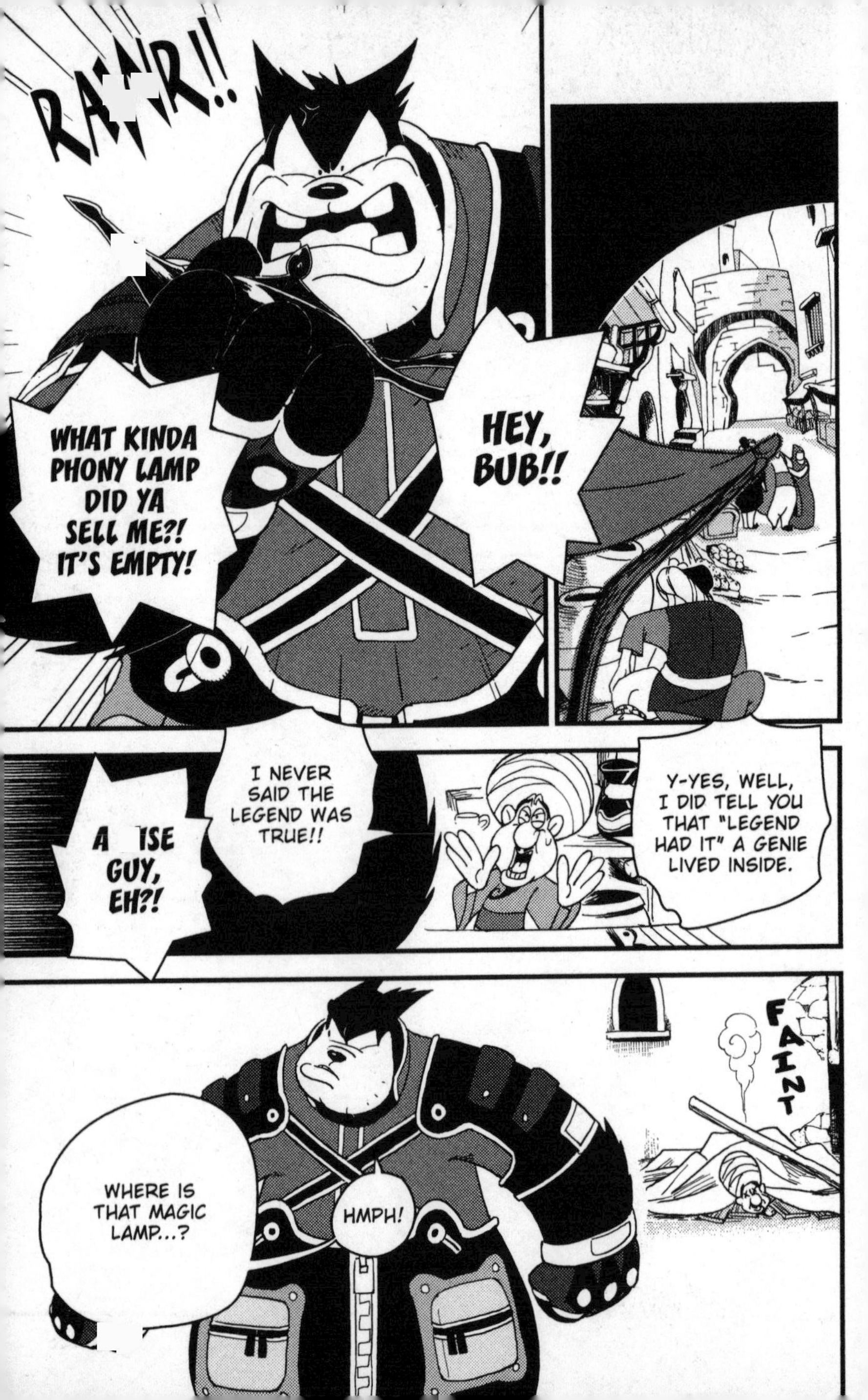
HEY, BUB!!
RA R!!
WHAT KINDA PHONY LAMP DID YA SELL ME?! IT'S EMPTY!
Y-YES, WELL, I DID TELL YOU THAT "LEGEND HAD IT" A GENIE LIVED INSIDE.
I NEVER SAID THE LEGEND WAS TRUE!!
A ISE GUY, EH?!
FAINT
HMPH!
WHERE IS THAT MAGIC LAMP...?

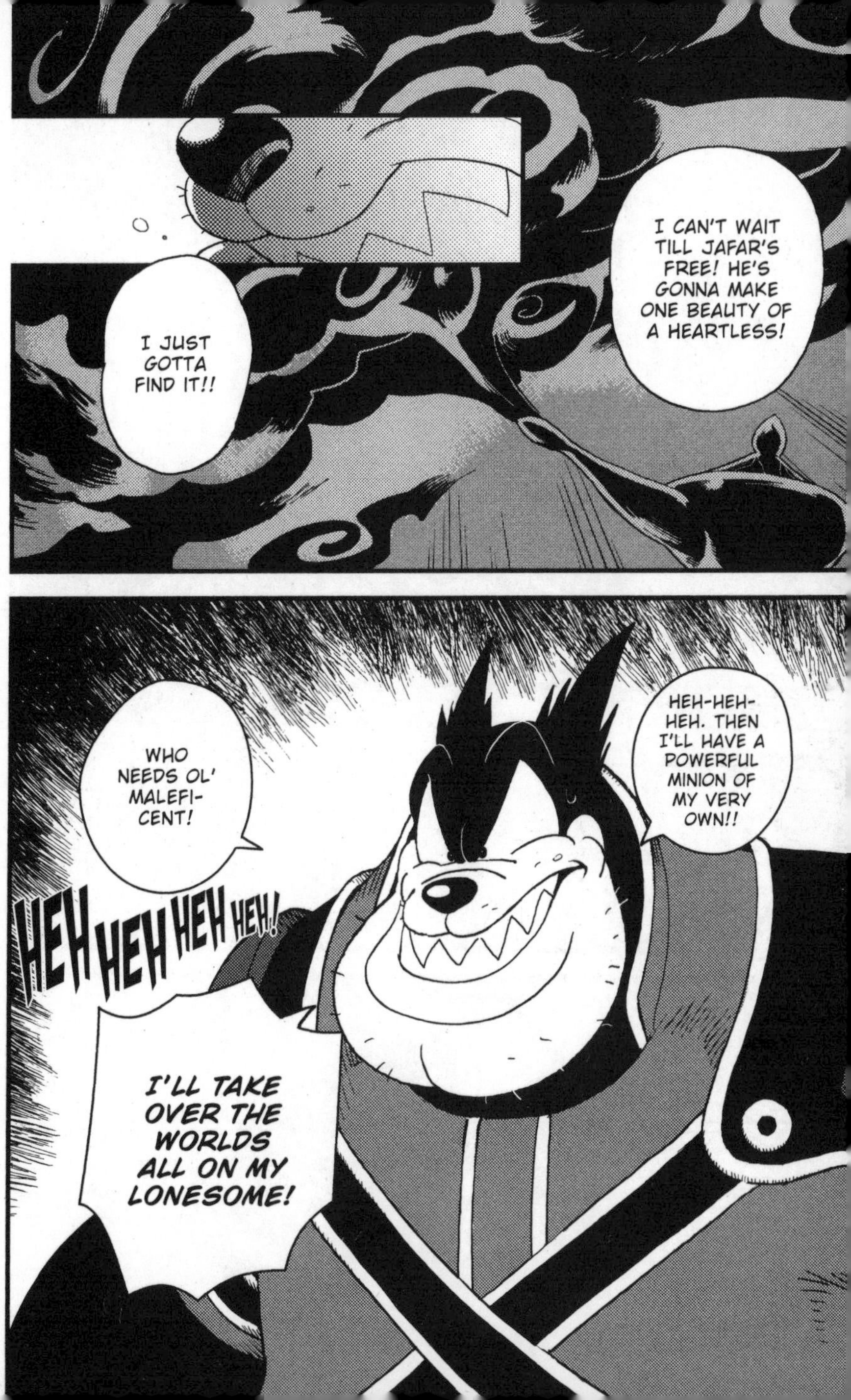
I CAN'T WAIT TILL JAFAR'S FREE! HE'S GONNA MAKE ONE BEAUTY OF A HEARTLESS!
I JUST GOTTA FIND IT!!
HEH-HEH-HEH. THEN I'LL HAVE A POWERFUL MINION OF MY VERY OWN!!
WHO NEEDS OL' MALEFI-CENT!
HEH HEH HEH HEH!
I'LL TAKE OVER THE WORLDS ALL ON MY LONESOME!

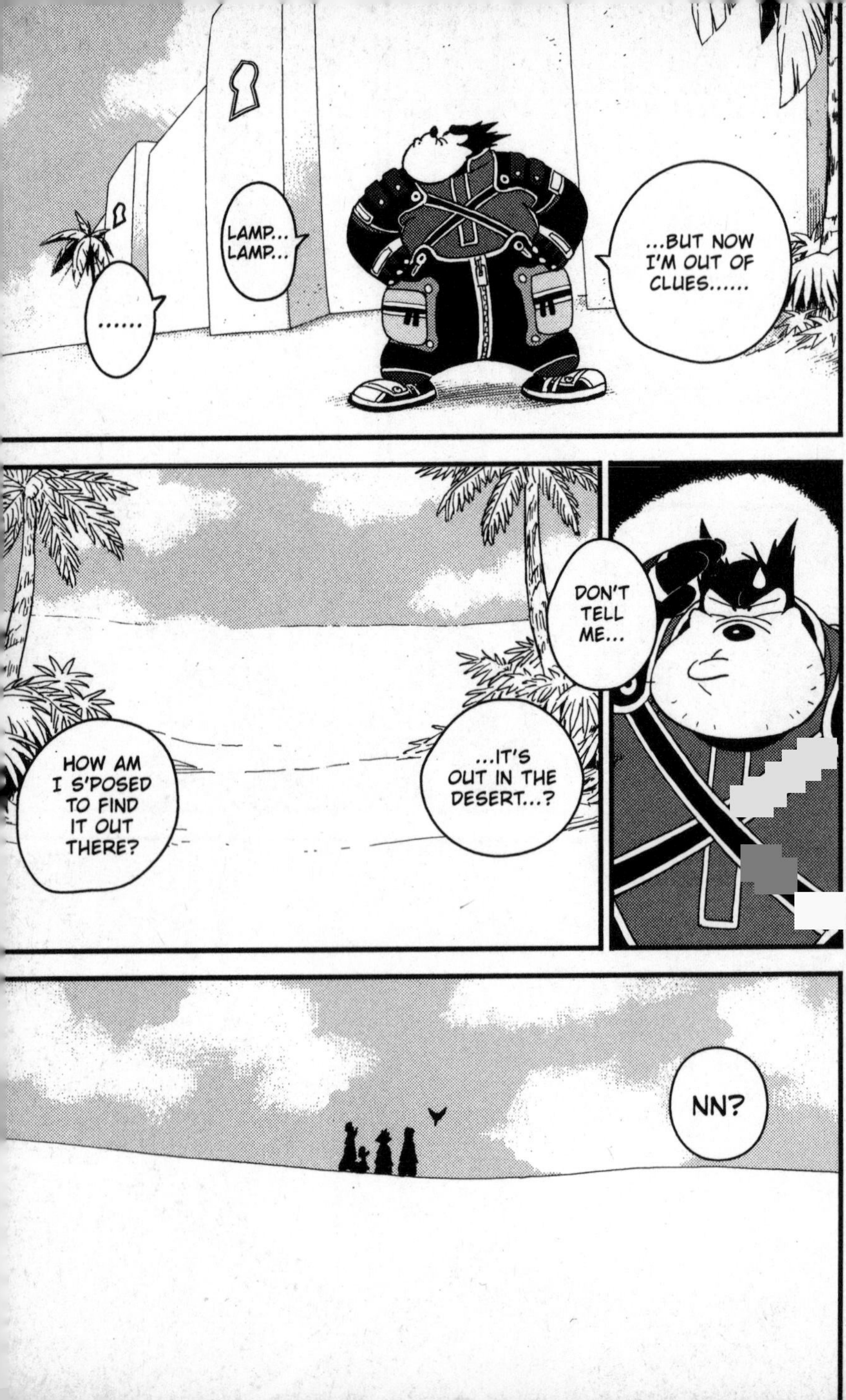
...BUT NOW I'M OUT OF CLUES......
LAMP... LAMP...
......
DON'T TELL ME...
...IT'S OUT IN THE DESERT...?
HOW AM I S'POSED TO FIND IT OUT THERE?
NN?

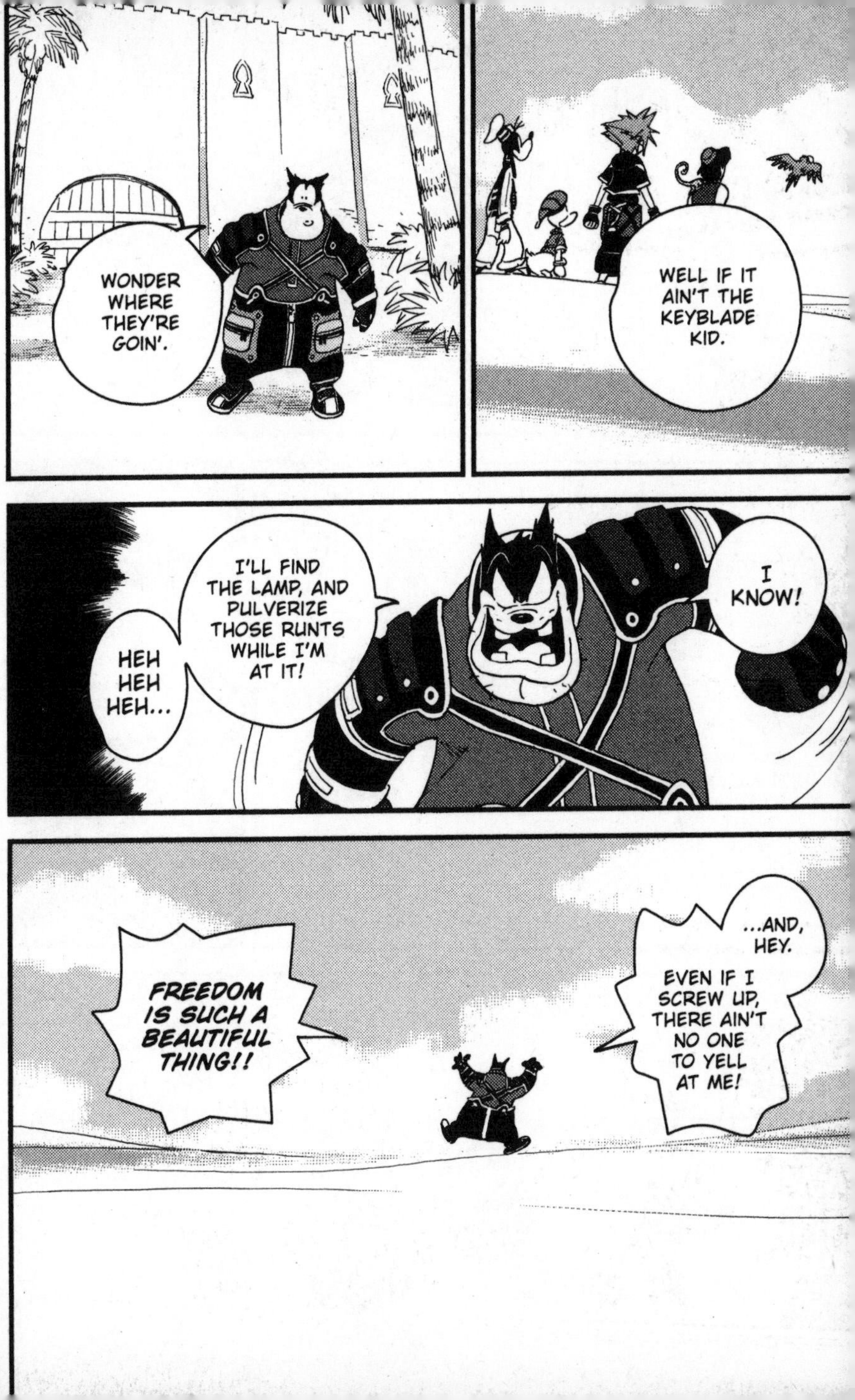
WELL IF IT AIN'T THE KEYBLADE KID.
WONDER WHERE THEY'RE GOIN'.
I KNOW!
I'LL FIND THE LAMP, AND PULVERIZE THOSE RUNTS WHILE I'M AT IT!
HEH HEH HEH...
...AND, HEY.
EVEN IF I SCREW UP, THERE AIN'T NO ONE TO YELL AT ME!
FREEDOM IS SUCH A BEAUTIFUL THING!!

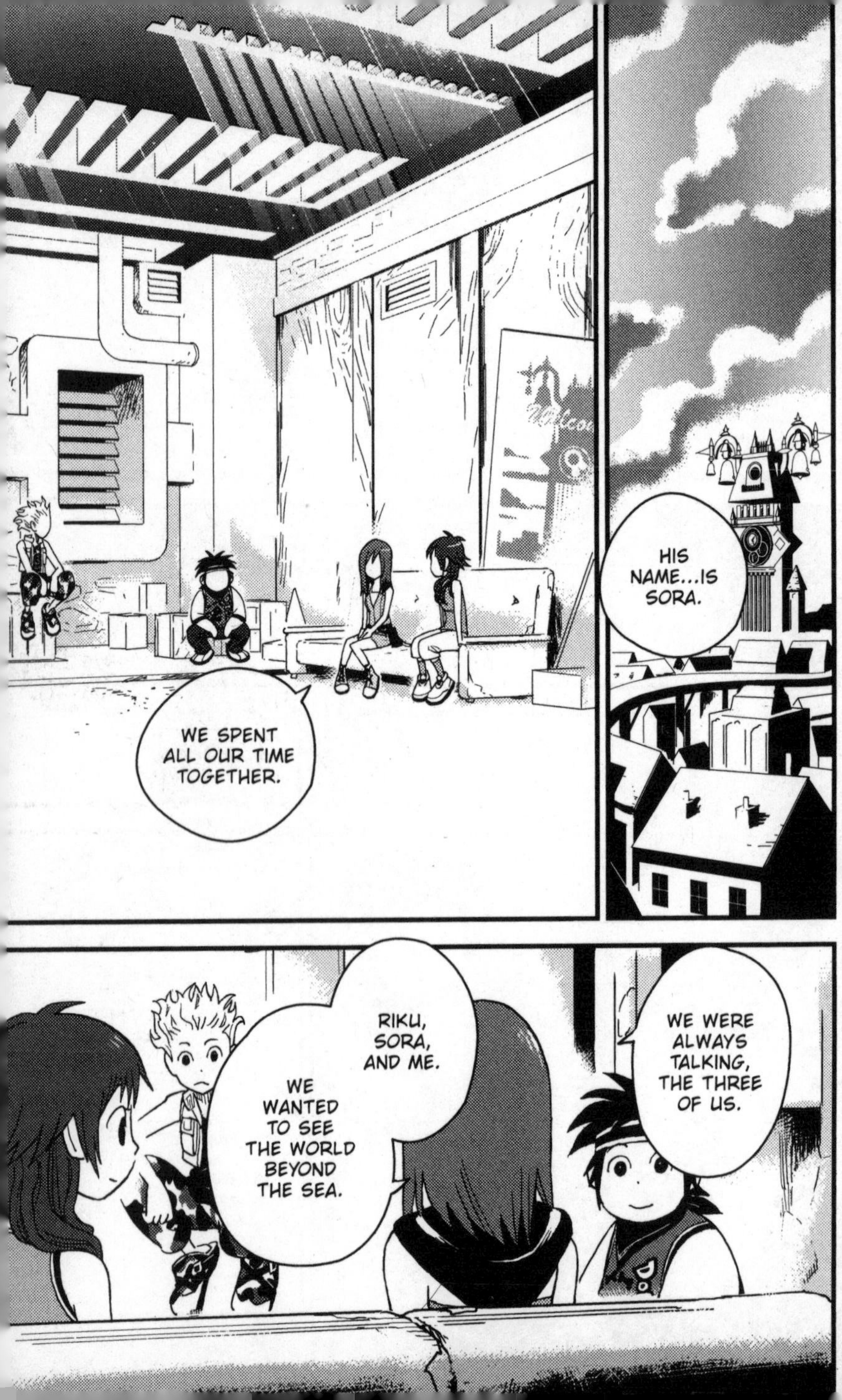
HIS NAME...IS SORA.
WE SPENT ALL OUR TIME TOGETHER.
WE WERE ALWAYS TALKING, THE THREE OF US.
RIKU, SORA, AND ME.
WE WANTED TO SEE THE WORLD BEYOND THE SEA.

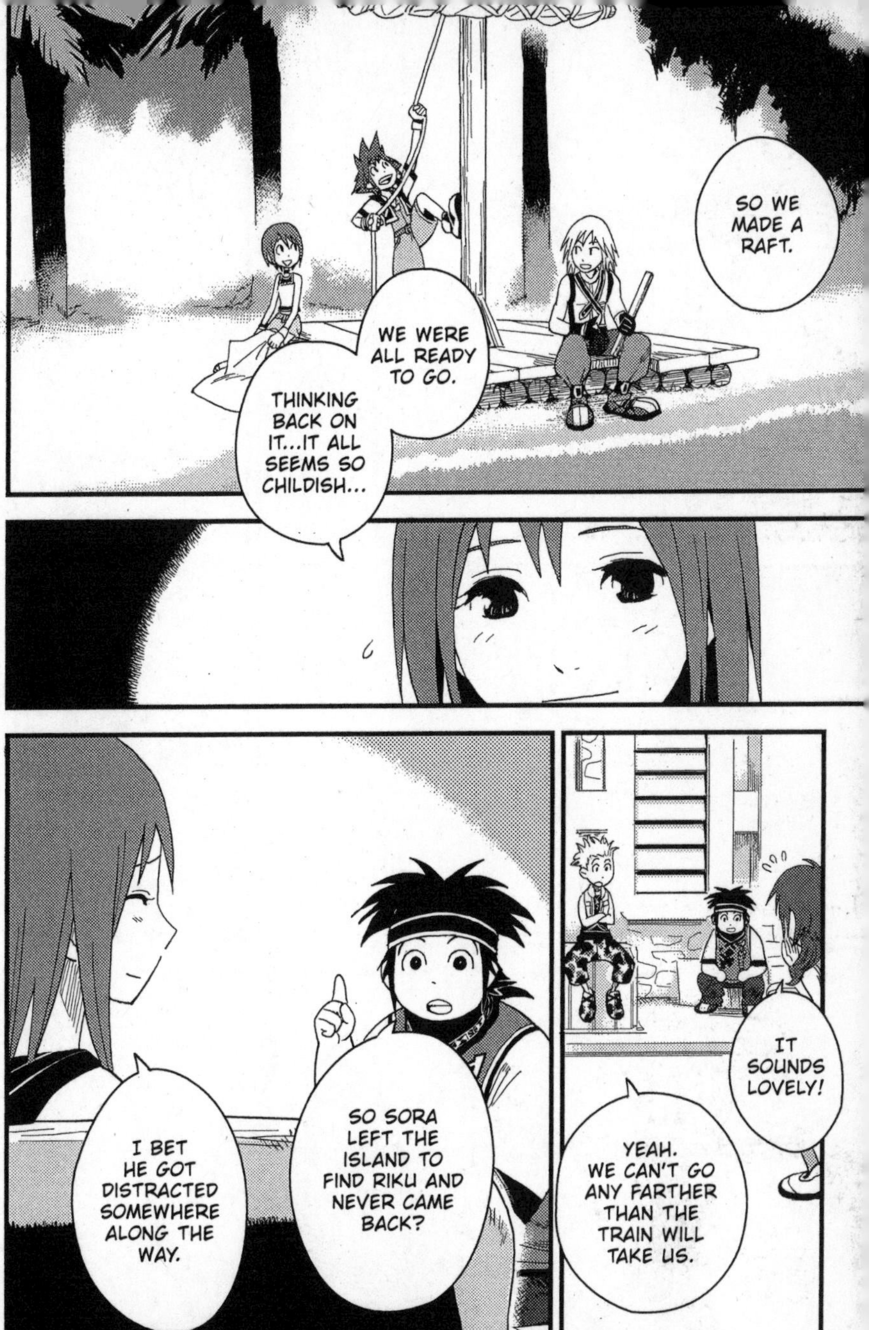
SO WE MADE A RAFT.
WE WERE ALL READY TO GO.
THINKING BACK ON IT...IT ALL SEEMS SO CHILDISH...
IT SOUNDS LOVELY!
YEAH. WE CAN'T GO ANY FARTHER THAN THE TRAIN WILL TAKE US.
SO SORA LEFT THE ISLAND TO FIND RIKU AND NEVER CAME BACK?
I BET HE GOT DISTRACTED SOMEWHERE ALONG THE WAY.

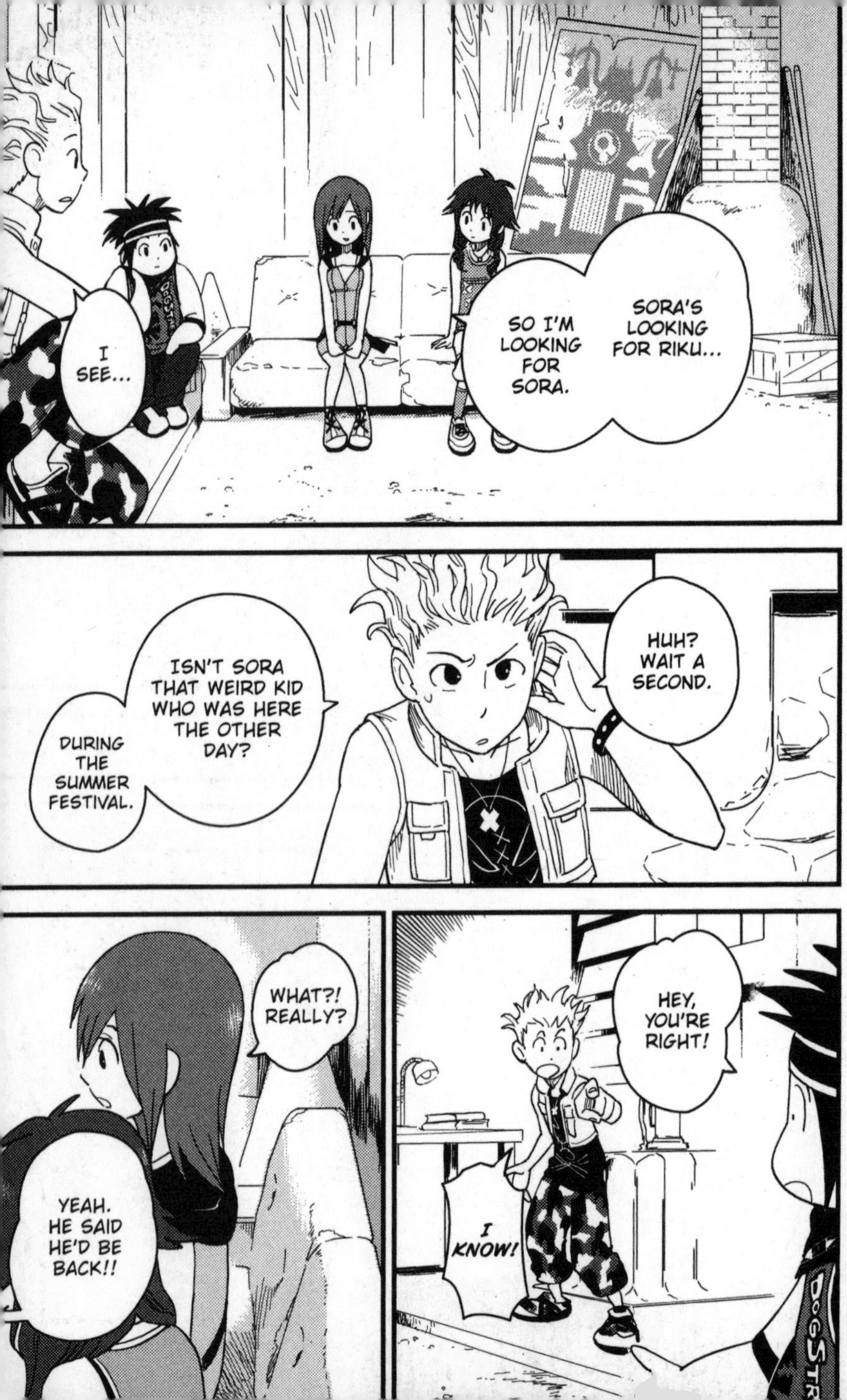
SORA'S LOOKING FOR RIKU...
SO I'M LOOKING FOR SORA.
I SEE...
HUH? WAIT A SECOND.
ISN'T SORA THAT WEIRD KID WHO WAS HERE THE OTHER DAY?
DURING THE SUMMER FESTIVAL.
HEY, YOU'RE RIGHT!
I KNOW!
WHAT?! REALLY?
YEAH. HE SAID HE'D BE BACK!!

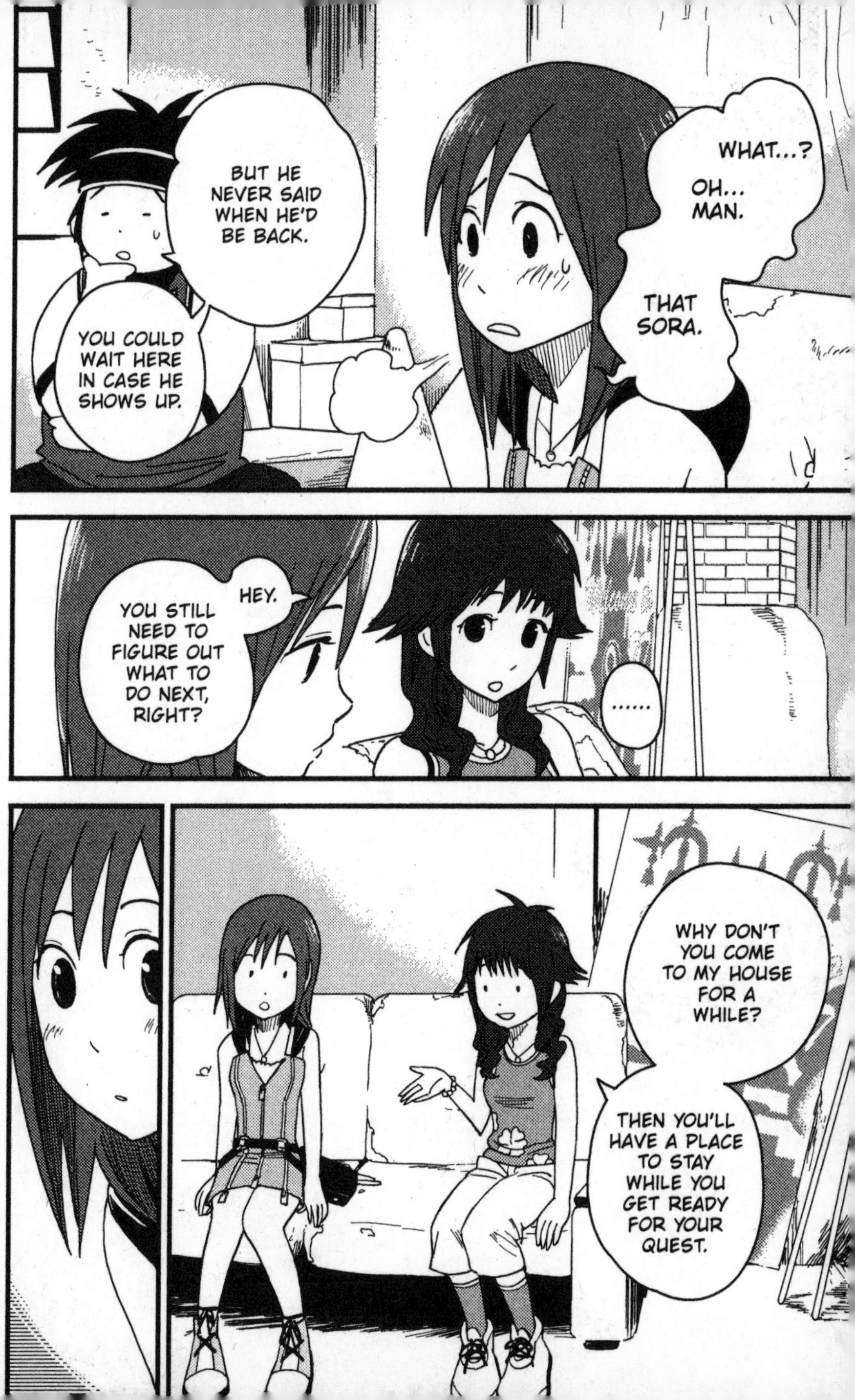
WHAT...?
OH... MAN.
THAT SORA.
BUT HE NEVER SAID WHEN HE'D BE BACK.
YOU COULD WAIT HERE IN CASE HE SHOWS UP.
HEY.
YOU STILL NEED TO FIGURE OUT WHAT TO DO NEXT, RIGHT?
......
WHY DON'T YOU COME TO MY HOUSE FOR A WHILE?
THEN YOU'LL HAVE A PLACE TO STAY WHILE YOU GET READY FOR YOUR QUEST.

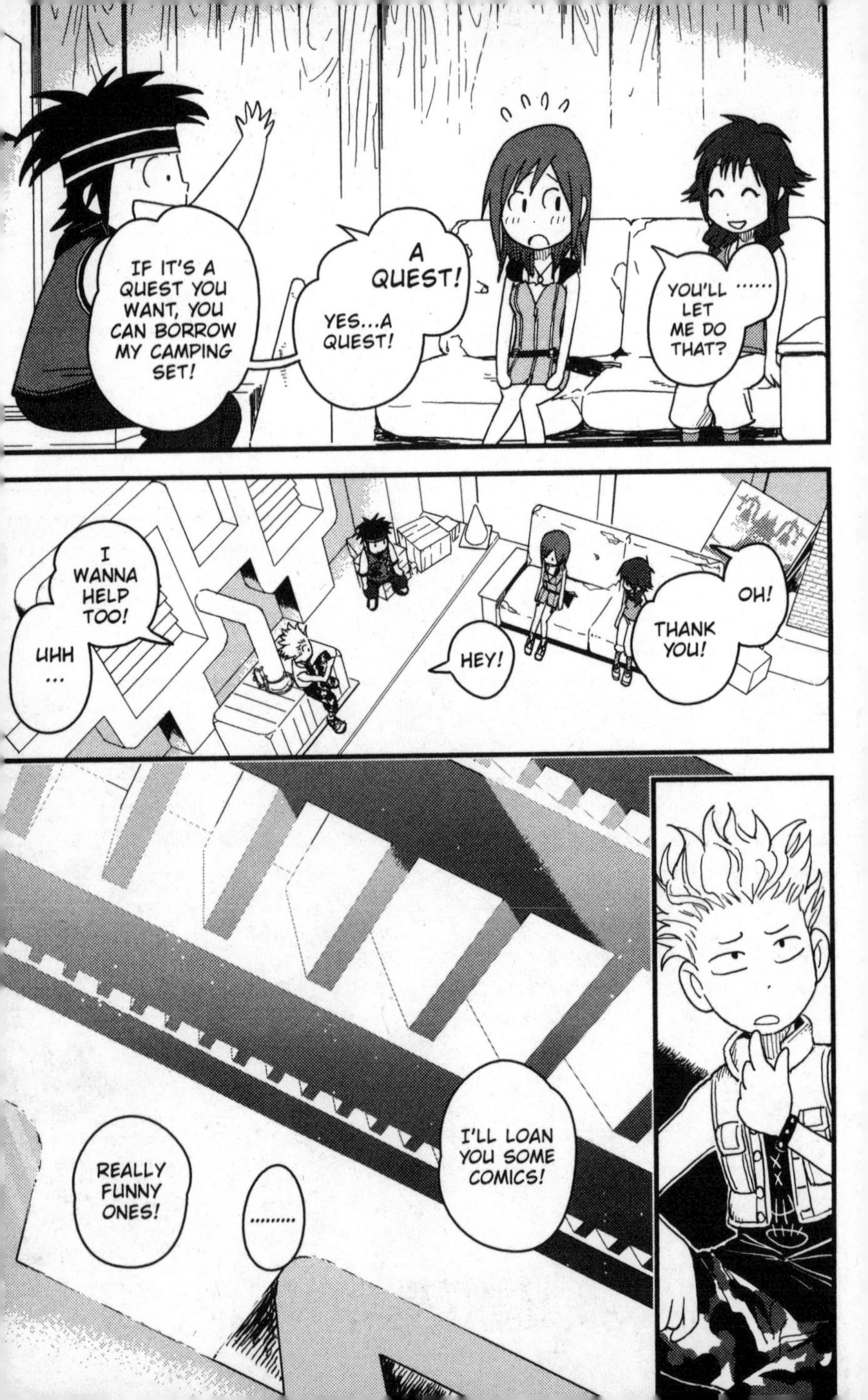
......
YOU'LL LET ME DO THAT?
A QUEST!
YES...A QUEST!
IF IT'S A QUEST YOU WANT, YOU CAN BORROW MY CAMPING SET!
OH!
THANK YOU!
HEY!
I WANNA HELP TOO!
UHH...
I'LL LOAN YOU SOME COMICS!
....
REALLY FUNNY ONES!

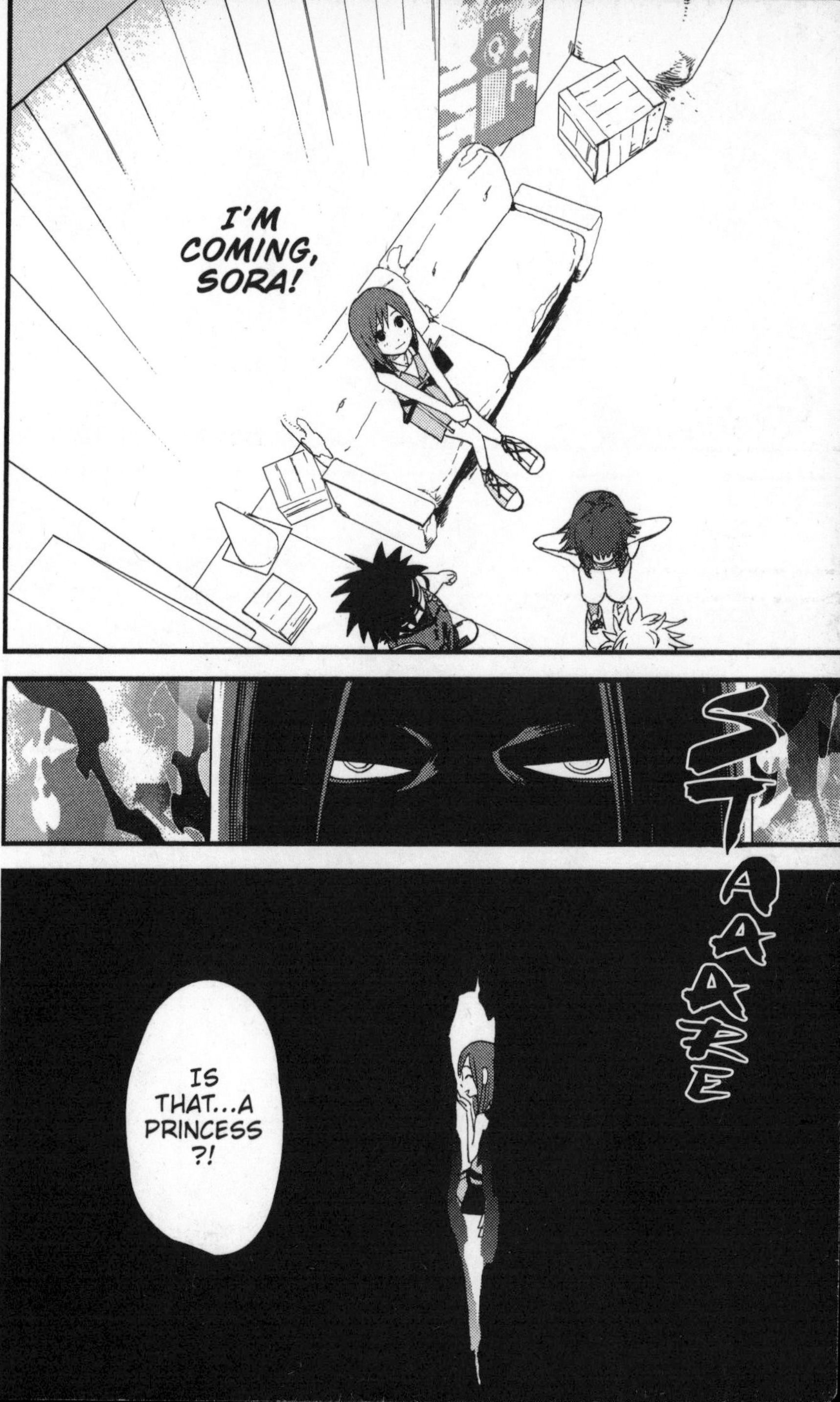
I'M COMING, SORA!
STAAAARE
IS THAT...A PRINCESS ?!

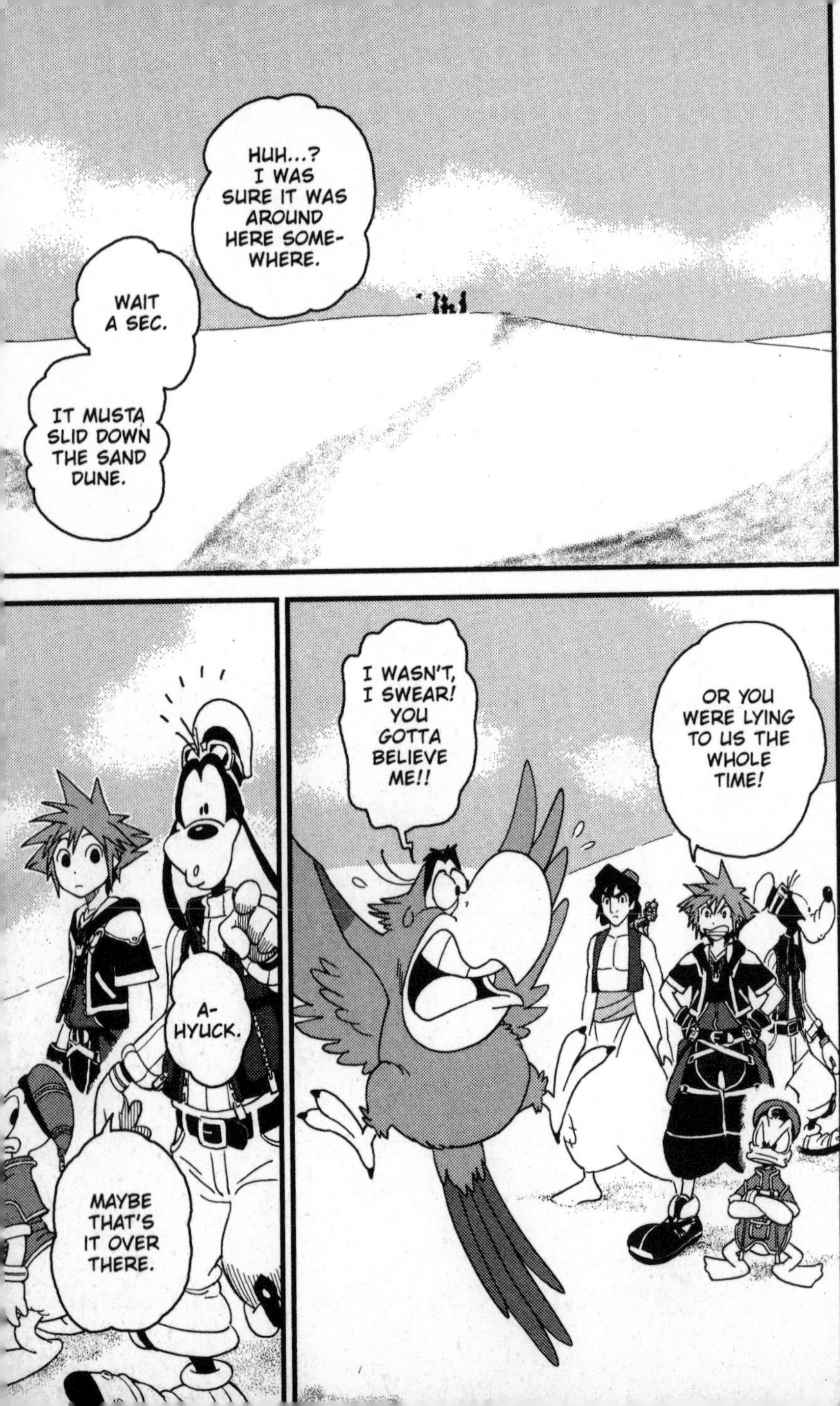
HUH...? I WAS SURE IT WAS AROUND HERE SOMEWHERE.
WAIT A SEC.
IT MUSTA SLID DOWN THE SAND DUNE.
OR YOU WERE LYING TO US THE WHOLE TIME!
I WASN'T, I SWEAR! YOU GOTTA BELIEVE ME!!
A-HYUCK.
MAYBE THAT'S IT OVER THERE.

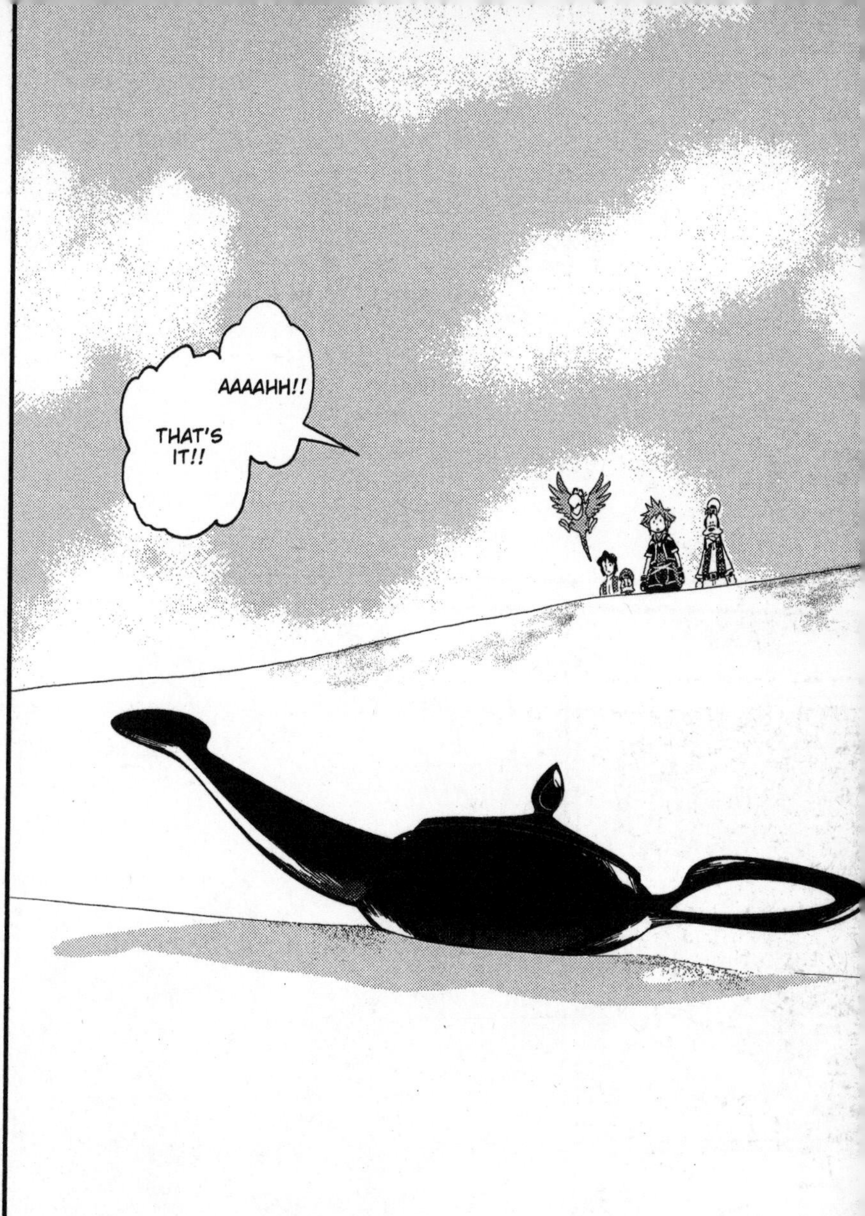
AAAAHH!!
THAT'S IT!!

Chapter 33: Battle for the Lamp

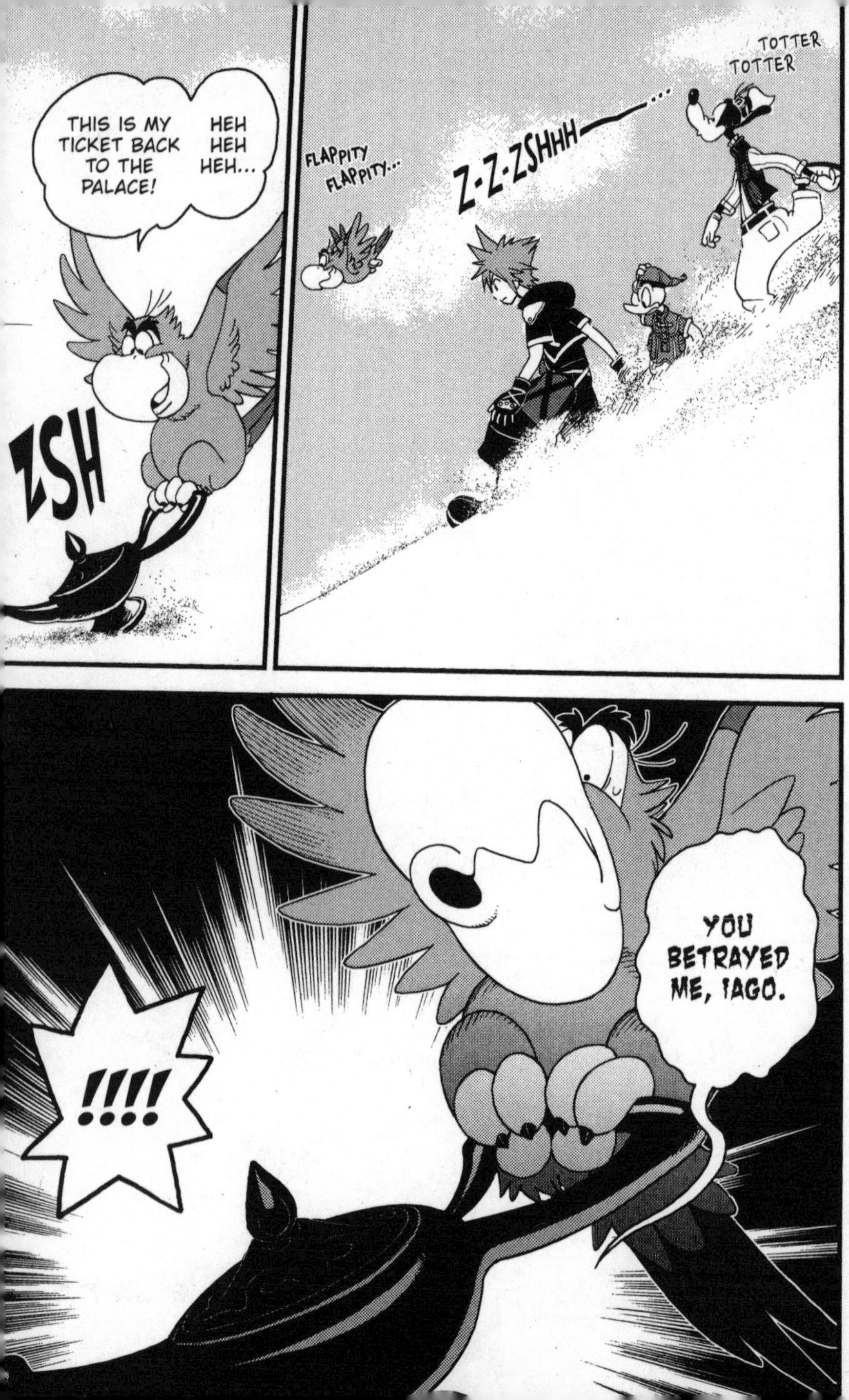
TOTTER TOTTER
Z-Z-ZSHHH
FLAPPITY FLAPPITY...
HEH HEH HEH...
THIS IS MY TICKET BACK TO THE PALACE!
ZSH
YOU BETRAYED ME, IAGO.
!!!!

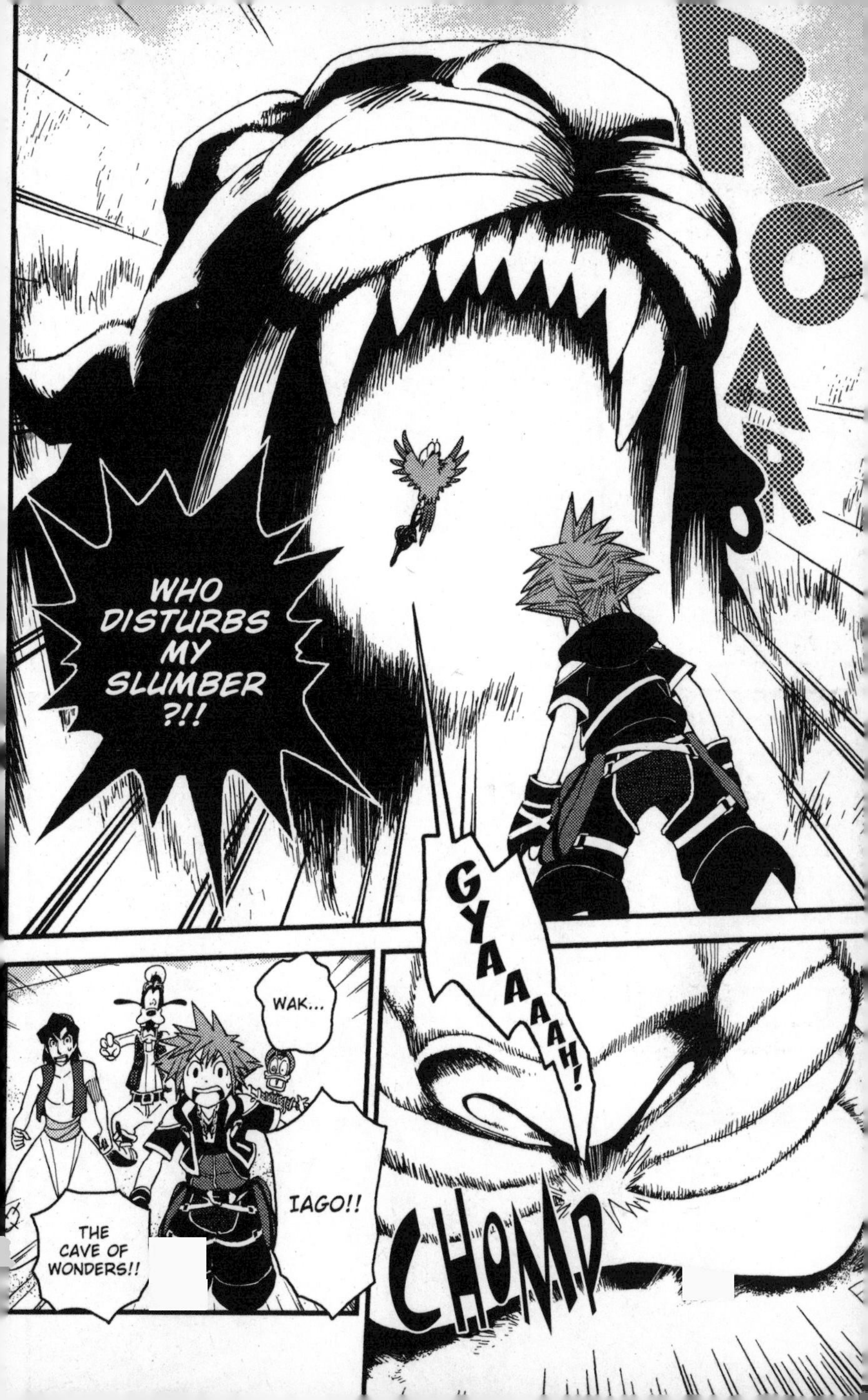
ROAR
WHO DISTURBS MY SLUMBER?!!
GYAAAAAH!
CHOMP
WAK...
IAGO!!
THE CAVE OF WONDERS!!

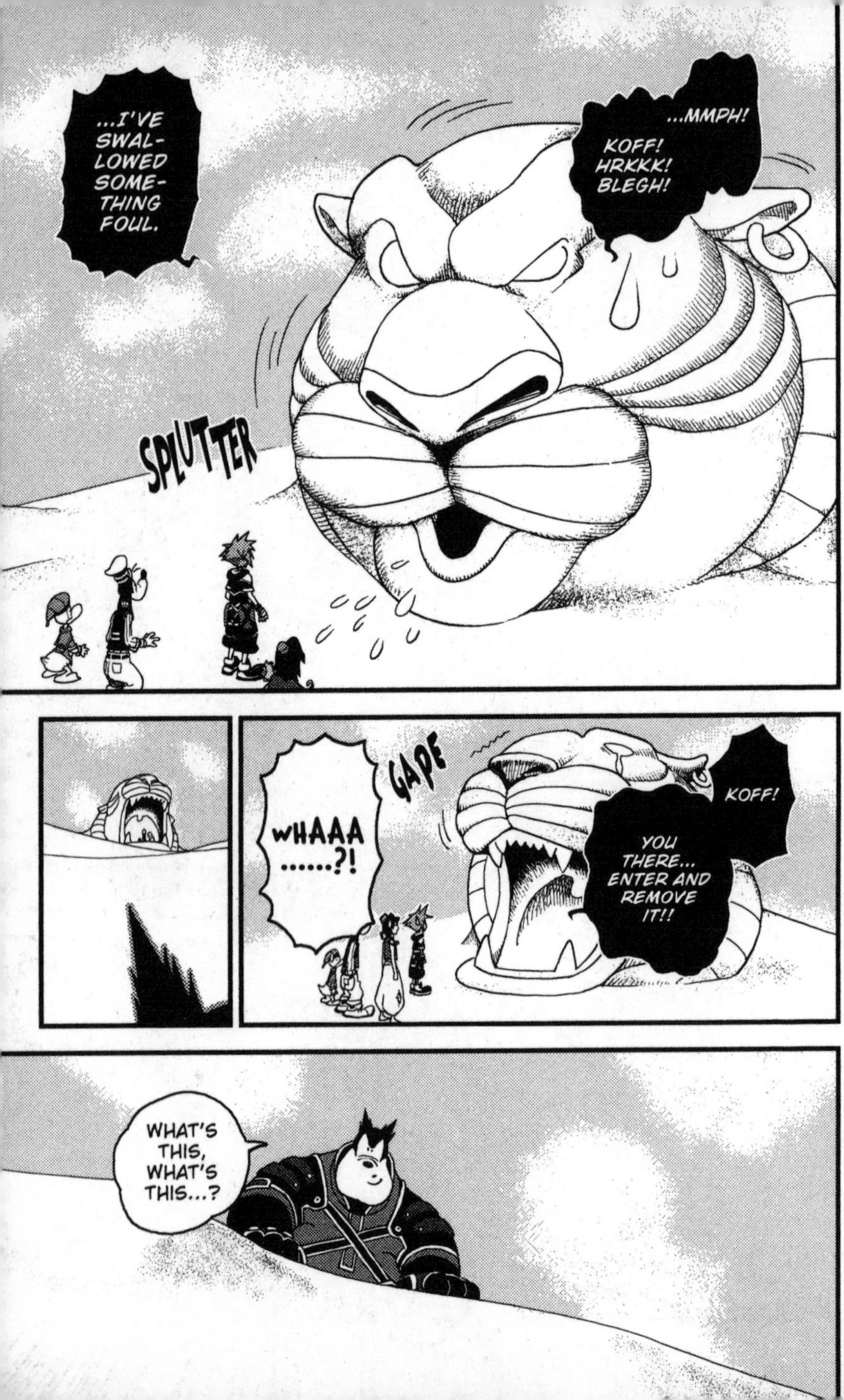
...MMPH! KOFF! HRKKK! BLEGH!
...I'VE SWAL-LOWED SOME-THING FOUL.
SPLUTTER
KOFF!
YOU THERE... ENTER AND REMOVE IT!!
GAPE
WHAAA ......?!
WHAT'S THIS, WHAT'S THIS...?

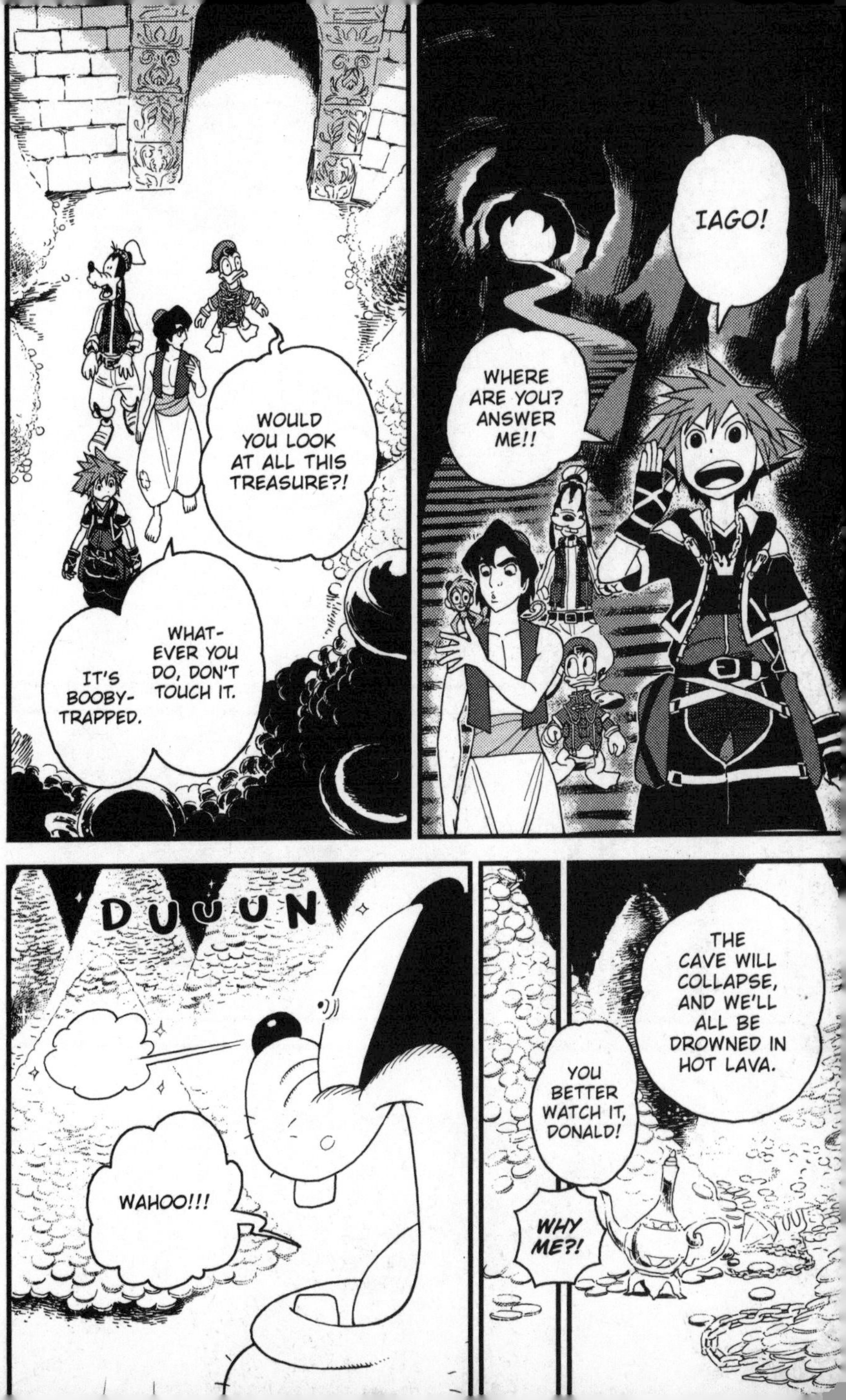
IAGO!
WHERE ARE YOU? ANSWER ME!!
WOULD YOU LOOK AT ALL THIS TREASURE?!
WHAT-EVER YOU DO, DON'T TOUCH IT.
IT'S BOOBY-TRAPPED.
THE CAVE WILL COLLAPSE, AND WE'LL ALL BE DROWNED IN HOT LAVA.
YOU BETTER WATCH IT, DONALD!
WHY ME?!
DUUUN
WAHOO!!!

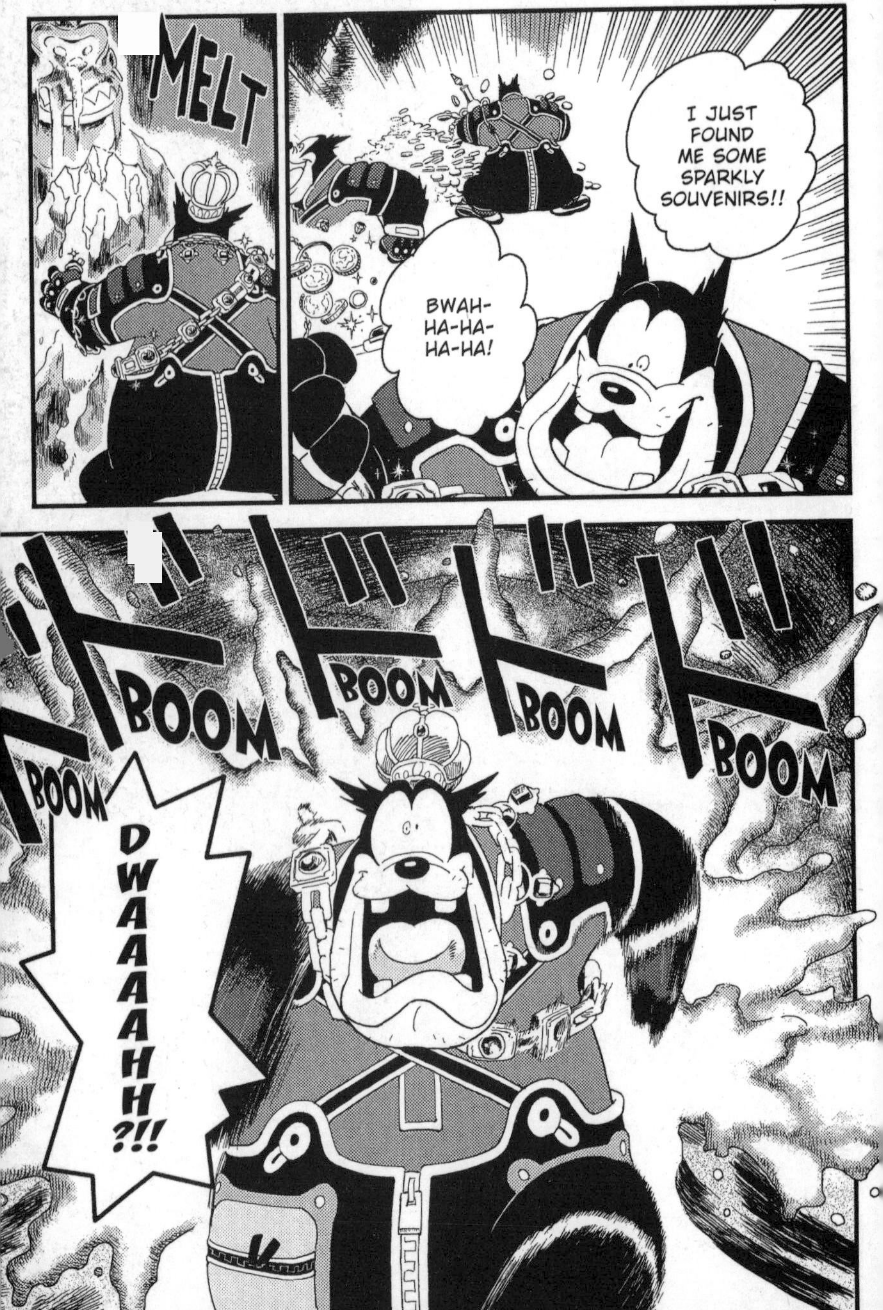
I JUST FOUND ME SOME SPARKLY SOUVENIRS!!
BWAH-HA-HA-HA-HA!
MELT
BOOM
BOOM
BOOM
BOOM
BOOM
DWAAAAAAHH?!!

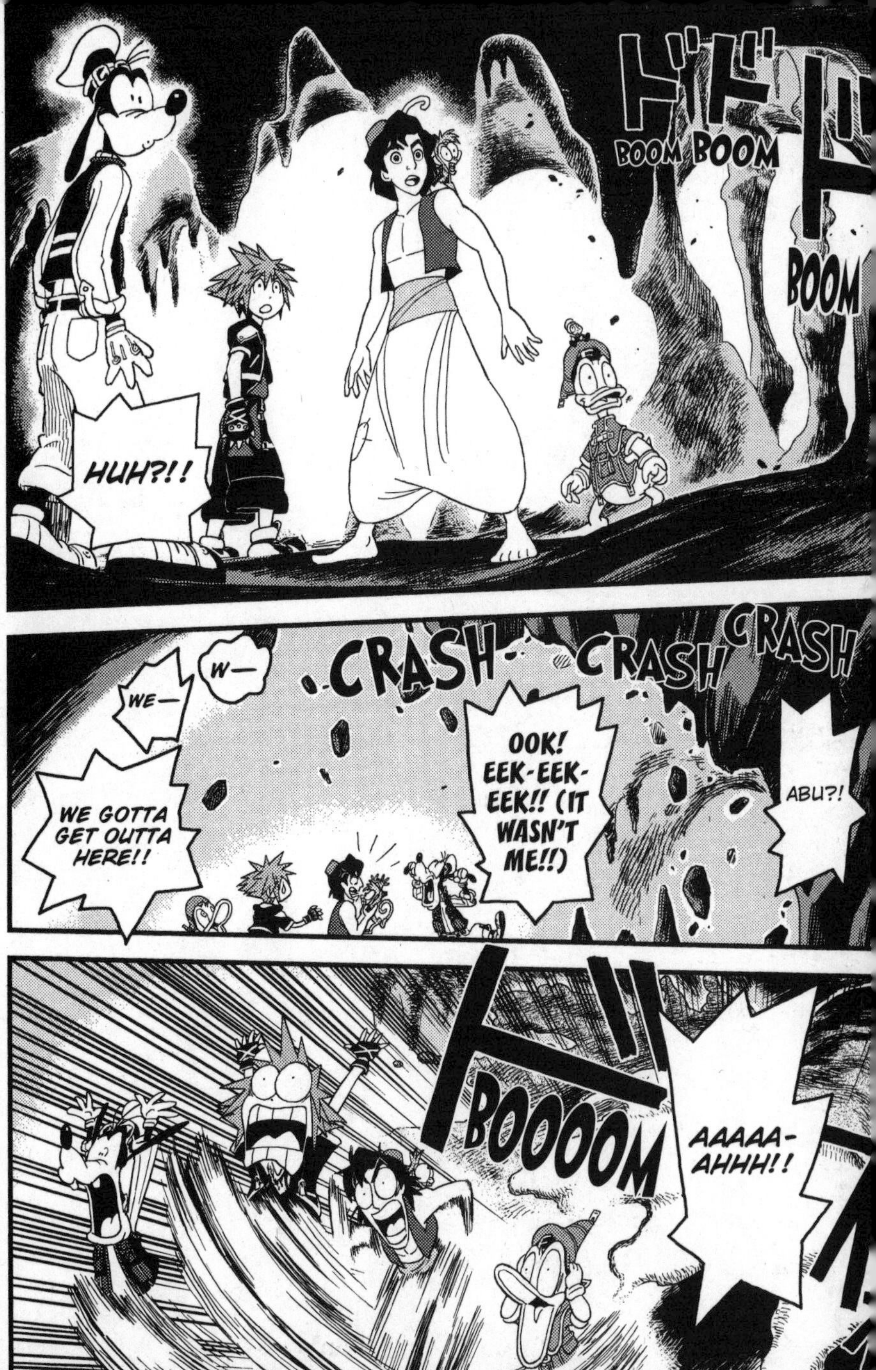
BOOM BOOM
BOOM
HUH?!!
CRASH
CRASH
CRASH
ABU?!
OOK! EEK-EEK-EEK!! (IT WASN'T ME!!)
W—
WE—
WE GOTTA GET OUTTA HERE!!
BOOOOM
AAAAA-AHHH!!

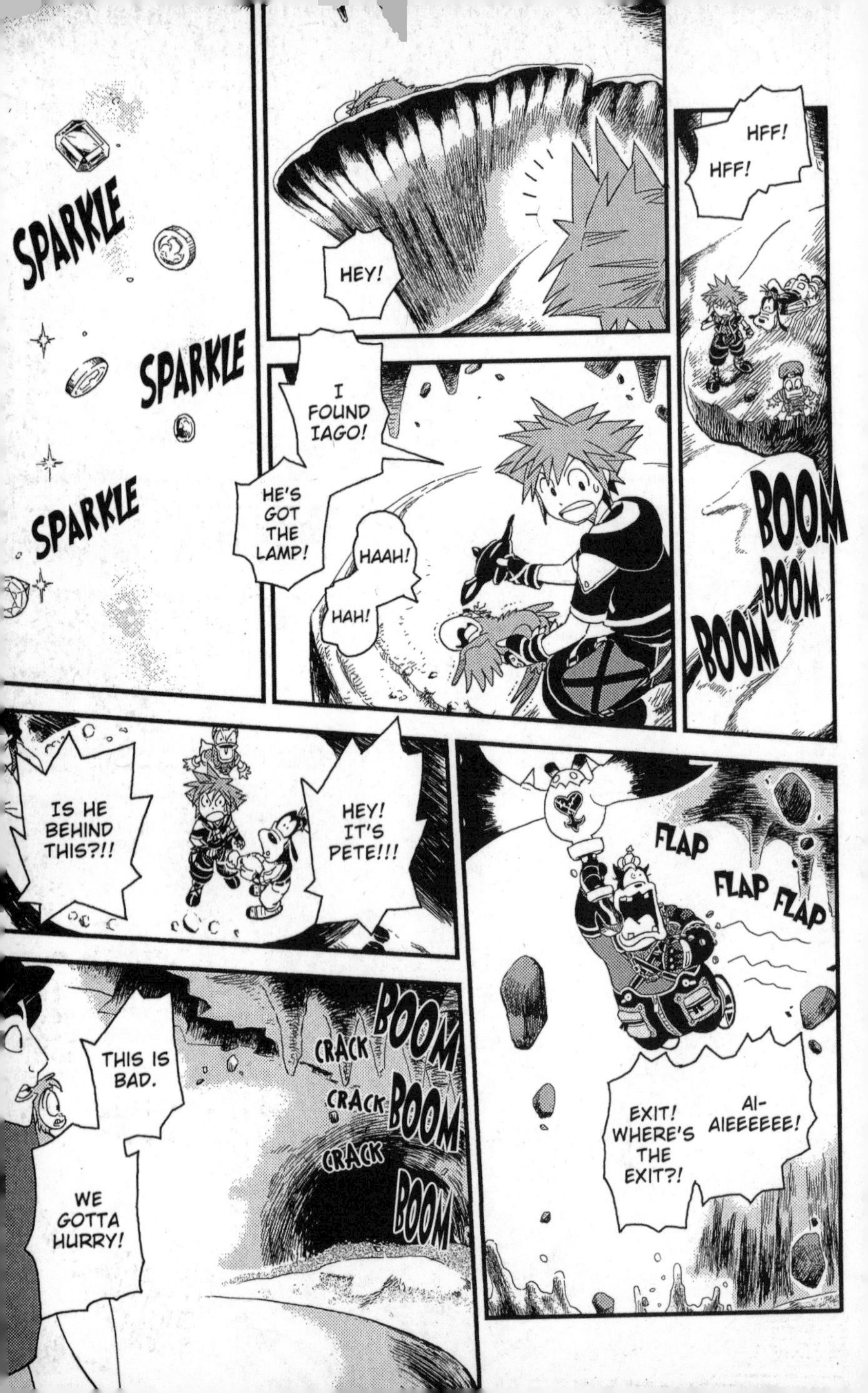
HFF!
HFF!
BOOM
BOOM
BOOM
HEY!
I FOUND IAGO!
HE'S GOT THE LAMP!
HAAH!
HAH!
SPARKLE
SPARKLE
SPARKLE
FLAP
FLAP
FLAP
AI-AIEEEEEE!
EXIT! WHERE'S THE EXIT?!
HEY! IT'S PETE!!!
IS HE BEHIND THIS?!!
BOOM
CRACK
BOOM
CRACK
CRACK
BOOM
THIS IS BAD.
WE GOTTA HURRY!

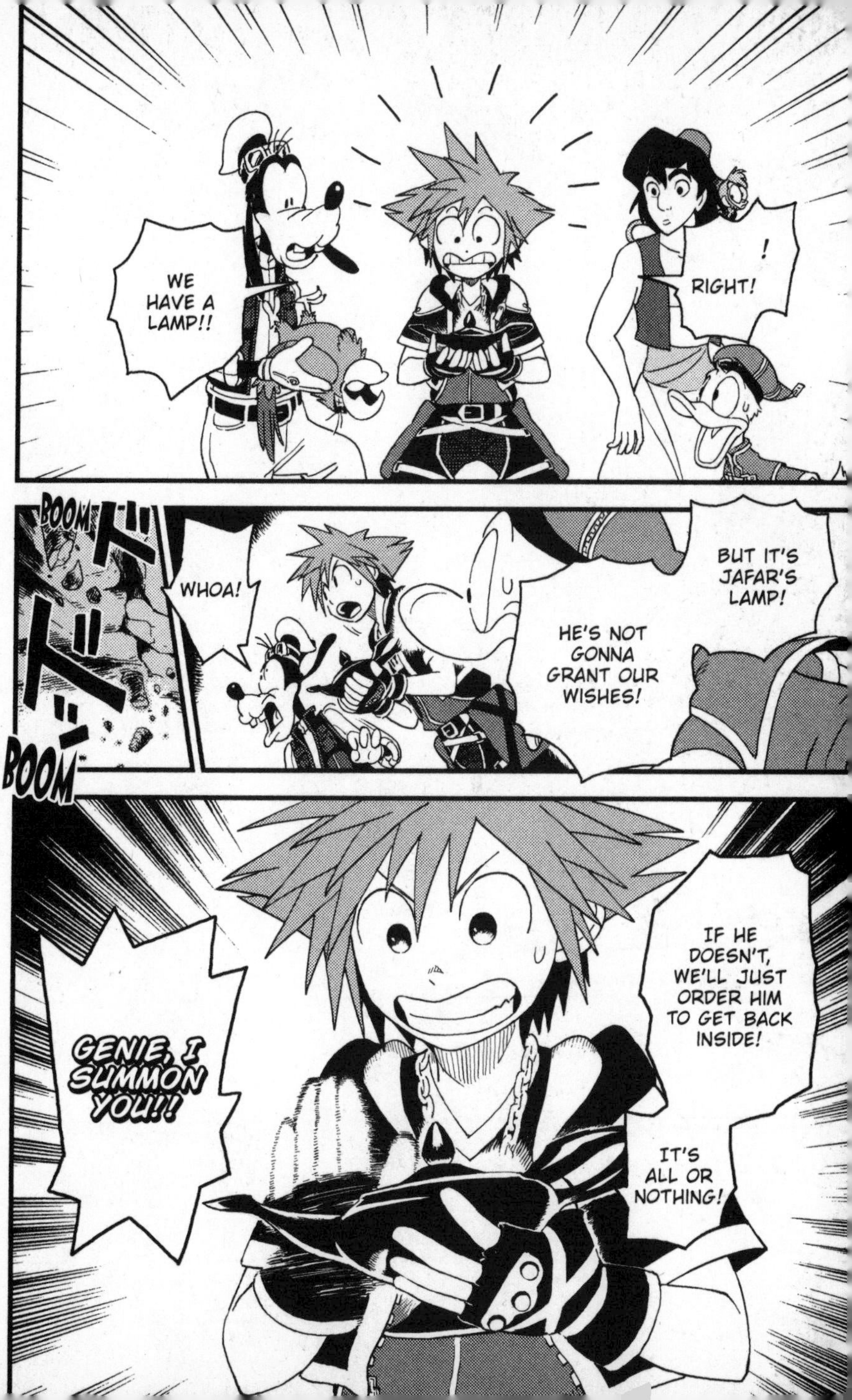
!
RIGHT!
WE HAVE A LAMP!!
BUT IT'S JAFAR'S LAMP!
HE'S NOT GONNA GRANT OUR WISHES!
WHOA!
BOOM
BOOM
IF HE DOESN'T, WE'LL JUST ORDER HIM TO GET BACK INSIDE!
IT'S ALL OR NOTHING!
GENIE, I SUMMON YOU!!

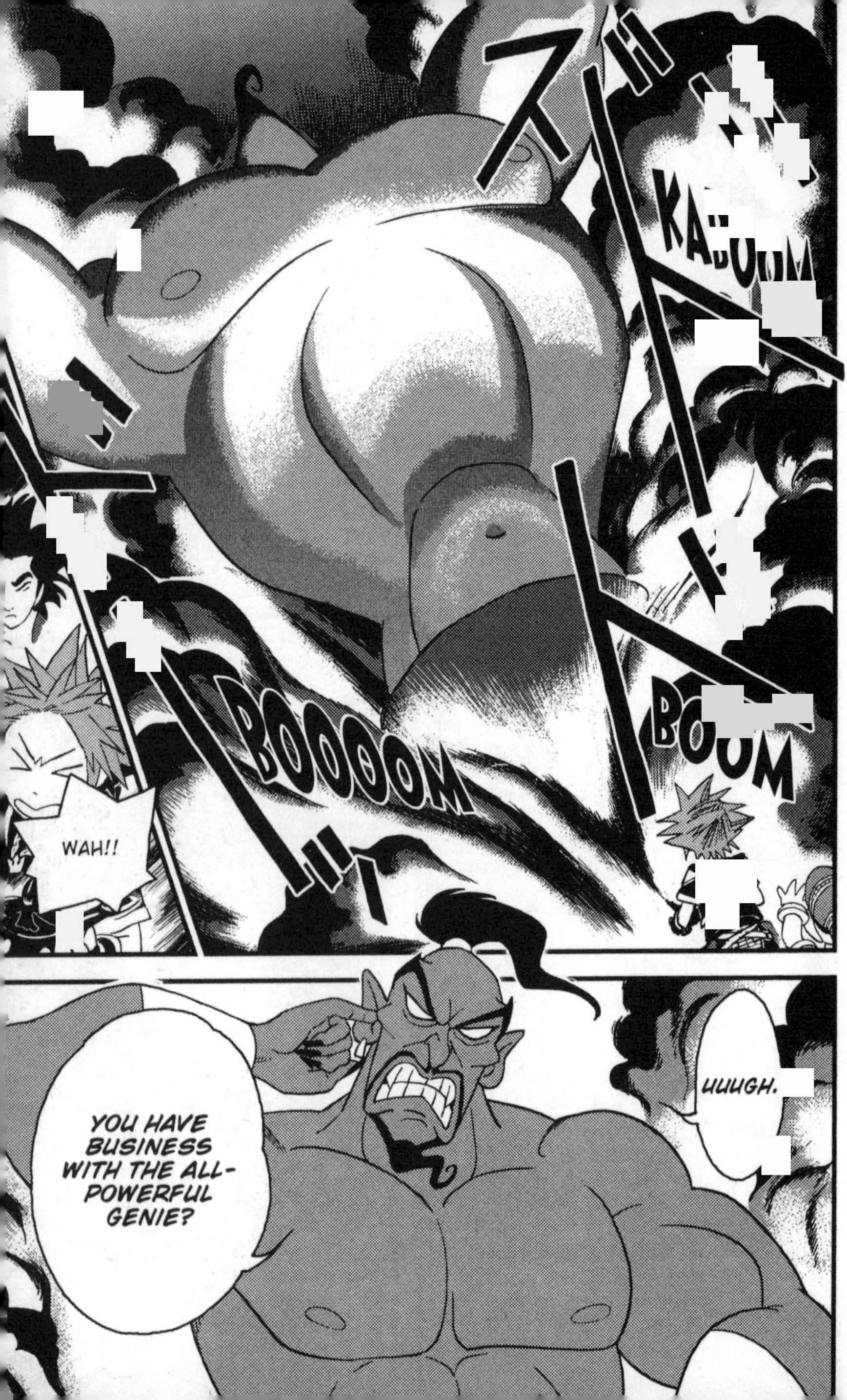

KABOOM
BOOM
BOOOOM
WAH!!
UUUGH.
YOU HAVE BUSINESS WITH THE ALL-POWERFUL GENIE?

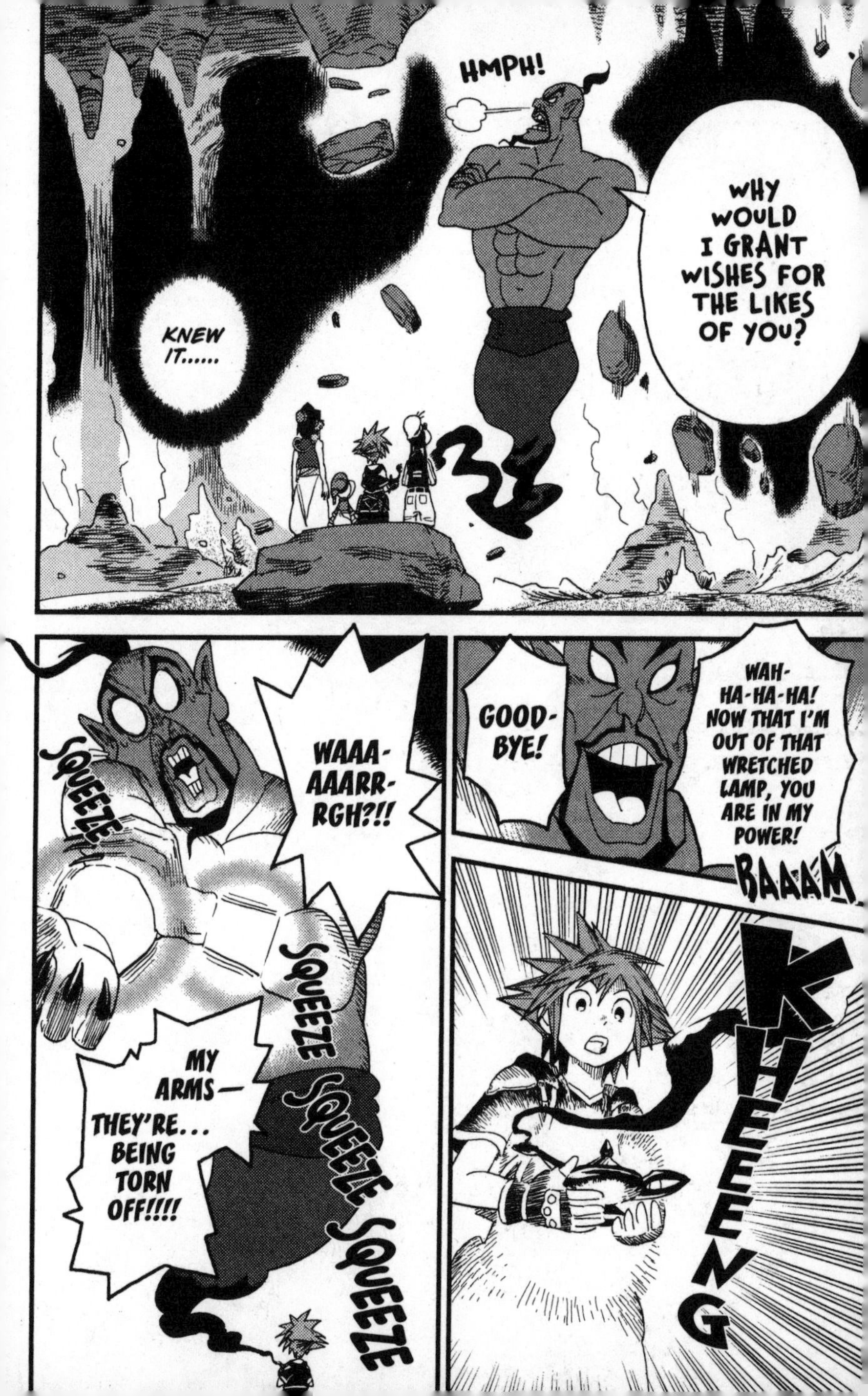
HMPH!
WHY WOULD I GRANT WISHES FOR THE LIKES OF YOU?
KNEW IT......
WAH-HA-HA-HA! NOW THAT I'M OUT OF THAT WRETCHED LAMP, YOU ARE IN MY POWER!
GOOD-BYE!
BAAAM
KHEEEENG
WAAA-AAARR-RGH?!!
SQUEEZE
SQUEEZE
SQUEEZE
SQUEEZE
SQUEEZE
MY ARMS—THEY'RE... BEING TORN OFF!!!!

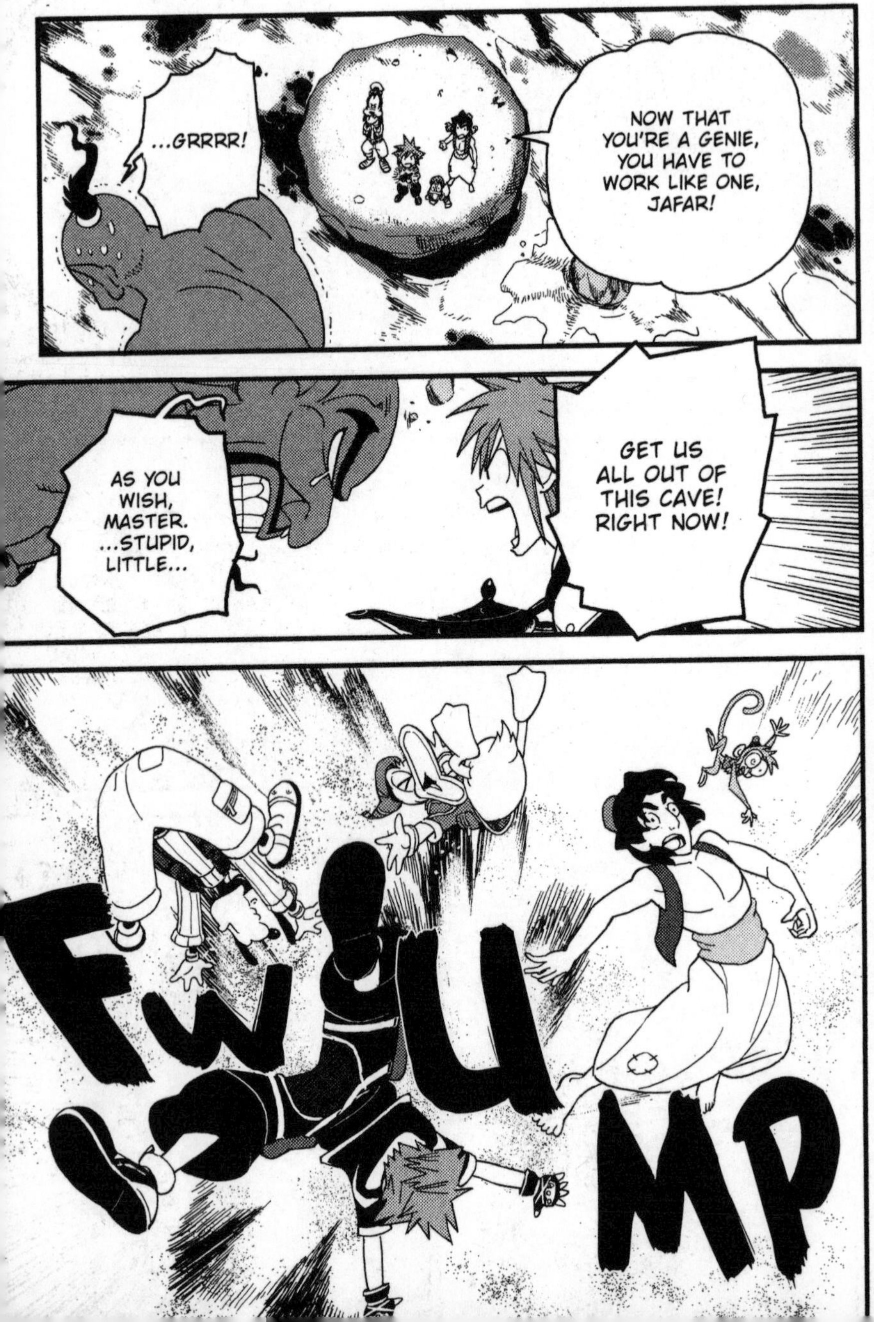
...GRRRR!
NOW THAT YOU'RE A GENIE, YOU HAVE TO WORK LIKE ONE, JAFAR!
GET US ALL OUT OF THIS CAVE! RIGHT NOW!
AS YOU WISH, MASTER. ...STUPID, LITTLE...
FWUMP

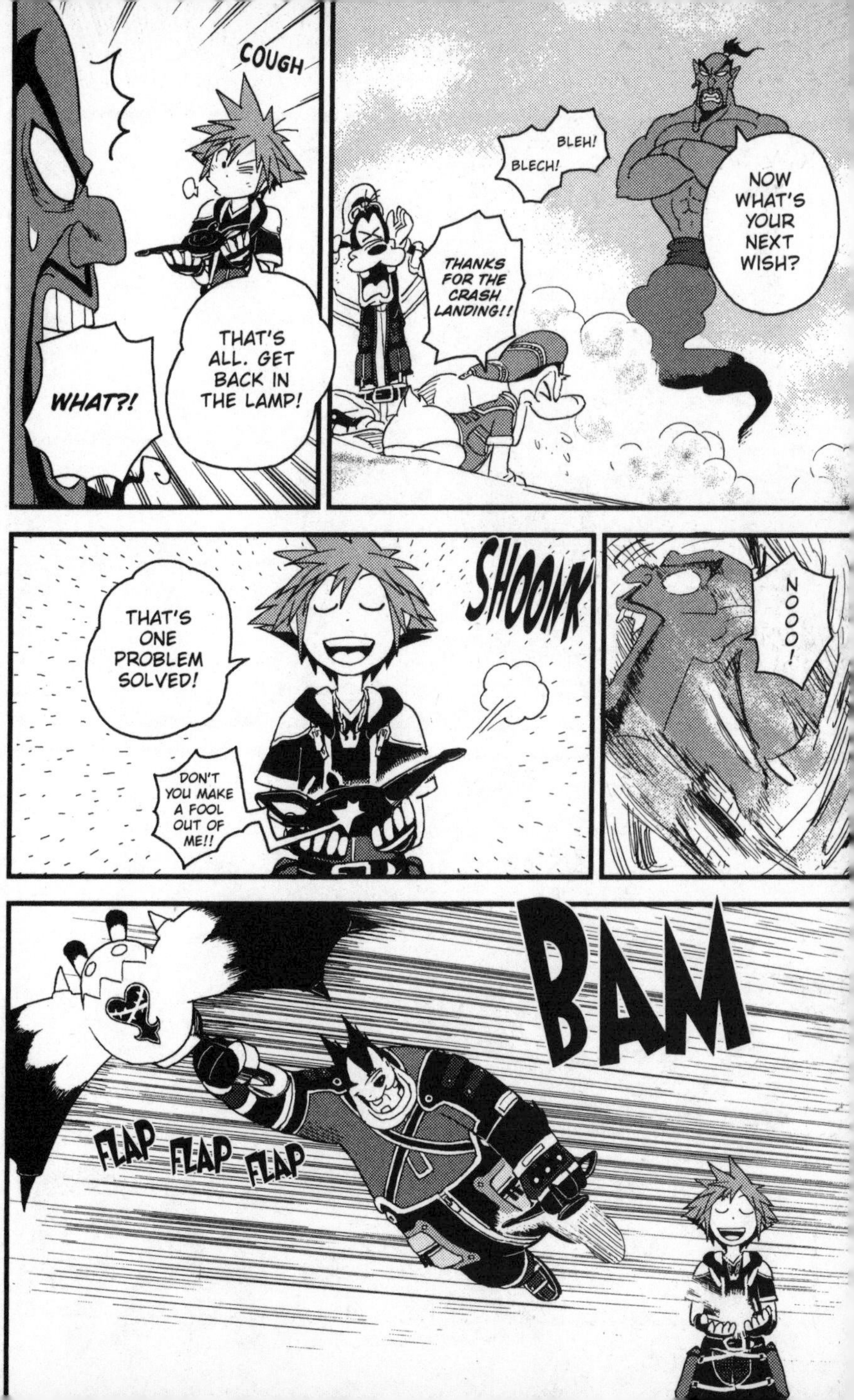
NOW WHAT'S YOUR NEXT WISH?
BLEH!
BLECH!
THANKS FOR THE CRASH LANDING!!
COUGH
THAT'S ALL. GET BACK IN THE LAMP!
WHAT?!
NOOOO!
SHOOMK
THAT'S ONE PROBLEM SOLVED!
DON'T YOU MAKE A FOOL OUT OF ME!!
BAM
FLAP FLAP FLAP

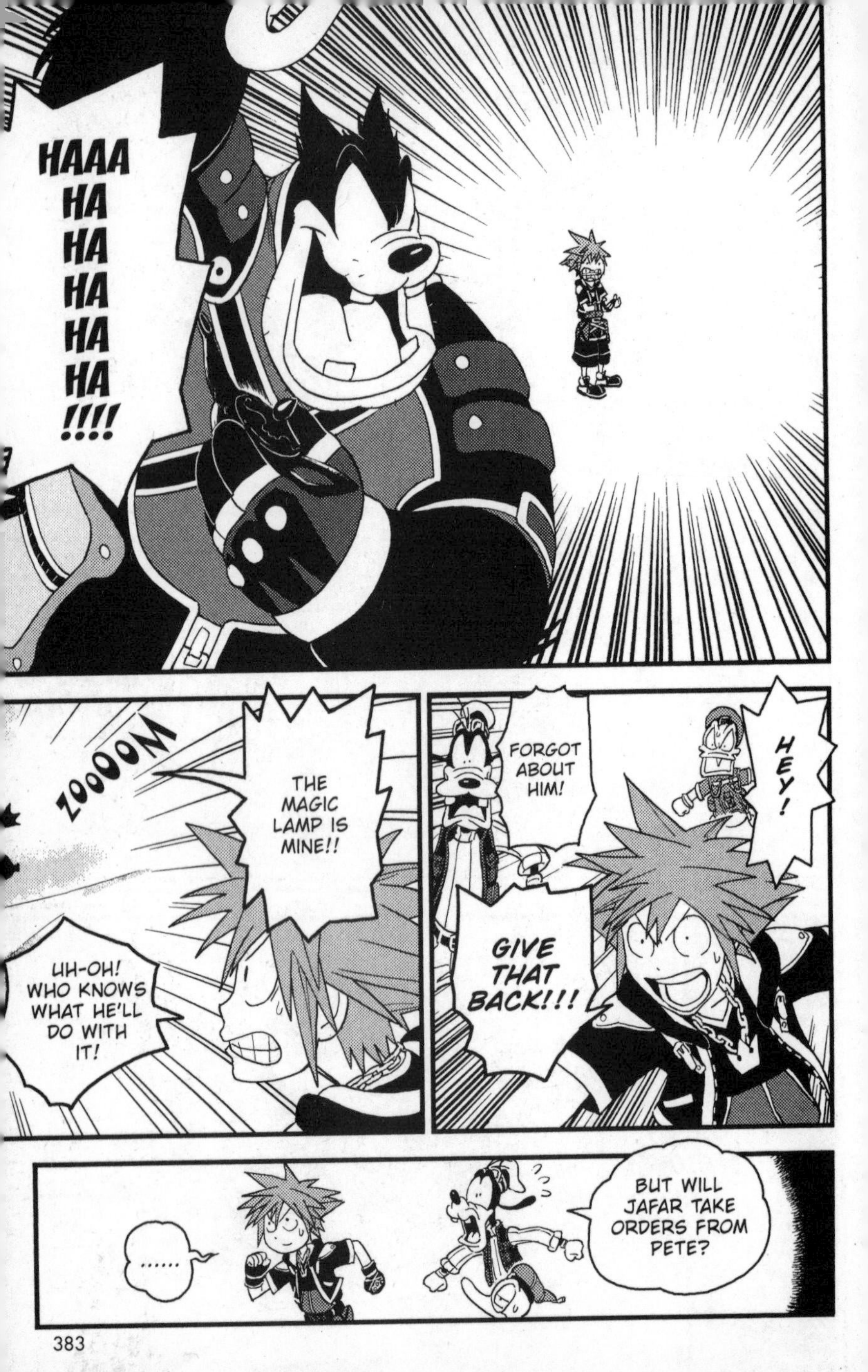
HAAAA HA HA HA HA HA !!!!
HEY!
FORGOT ABOUT HIM!
GIVE THAT BACK!!!
THE MAGIC LAMP IS MINE!!
ZOOOOM
UH-OH! WHO KNOWS WHAT HE'LL DO WITH IT!
BUT WILL JAFAR TAKE ORDERS FROM PETE?
......

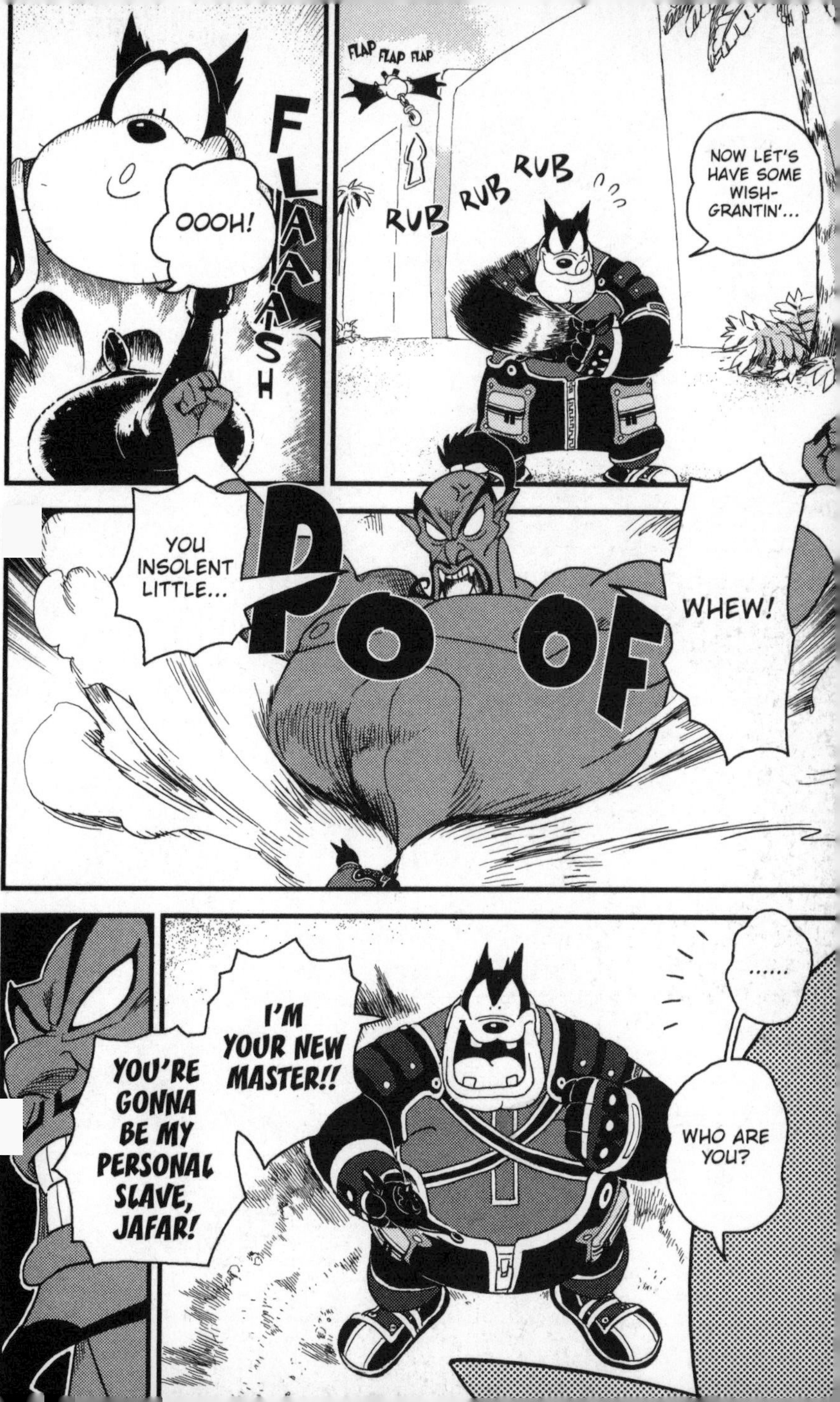
FLAP FLAP FLAP
RUB RUB RUB
NOW LET'S HAVE SOME WISH-GRANTIN'...
OOOH!
FLAAAASH
WHEW!
POOF
YOU INSOLENT LITTLE...
......
WHO ARE YOU?
I'M YOUR NEW MASTER!!
YOU'RE GONNA BE MY PERSONAL SLAVE, JAFAR!

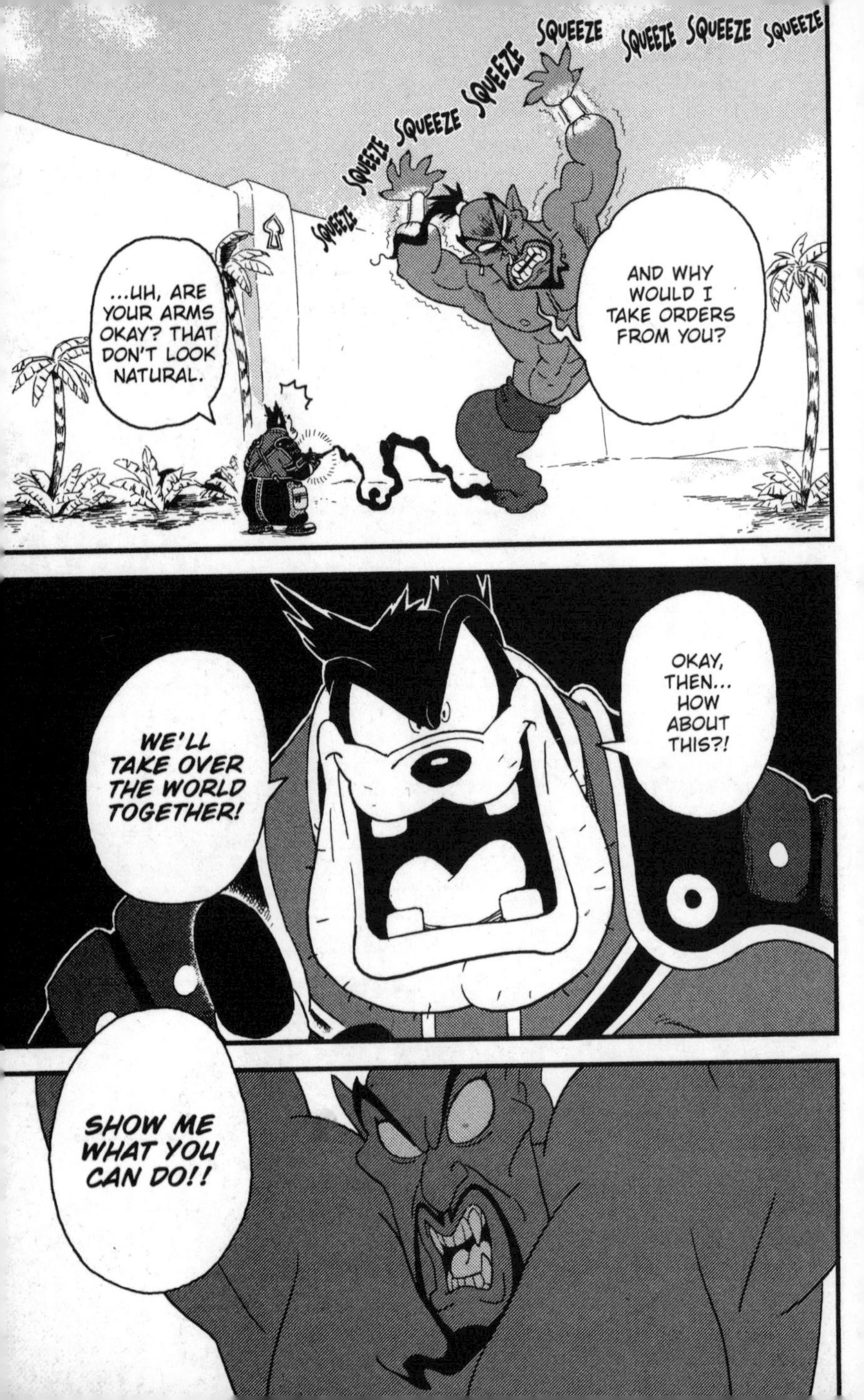
SQUEEZE SQUEEZE SQUEEZE SQUEEZE SQUEEZE SQUEEZE SQUEEZE SQUEEZE
AND WHY WOULD I TAKE ORDERS FROM YOU?
...UH, ARE YOUR ARMS OKAY? THAT DON'T LOOK NATURAL.
OKAY, THEN... HOW ABOUT THIS?!
WE'LL TAKE OVER THE WORLD TOGETHER!
SHOW ME WHAT YOU CAN DO!!

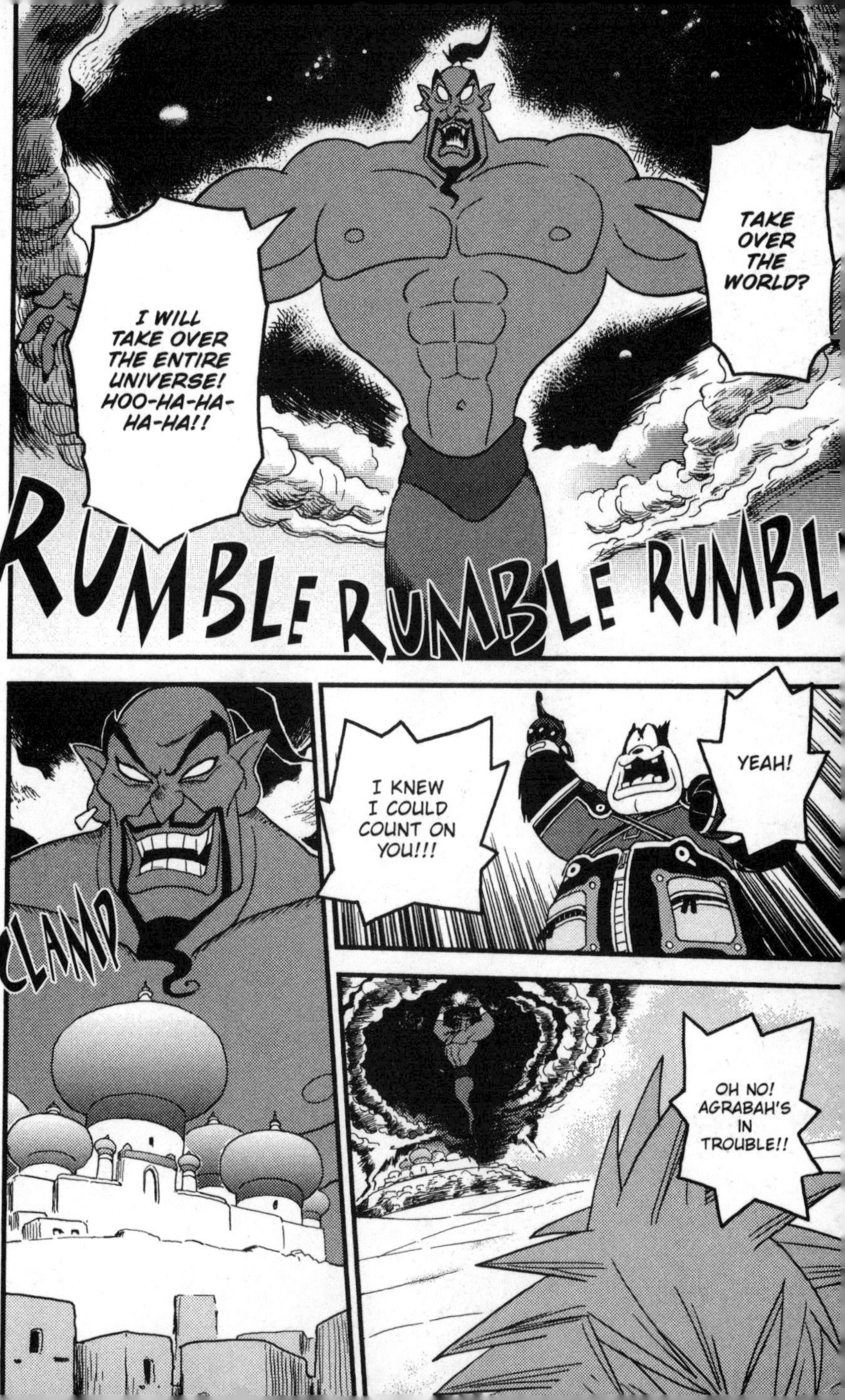
TAKE OVER THE WORLD?
I WILL TAKE OVER THE ENTIRE UNIVERSE! HOO-HA-HA-HA-HA!!
RUMBLE RUMBLE RUMBL
YEAH!
I KNEW I COULD COUNT ON YOU!!!
OH NO! AGRABAH'S IN TROUBLE!!
CLAMP

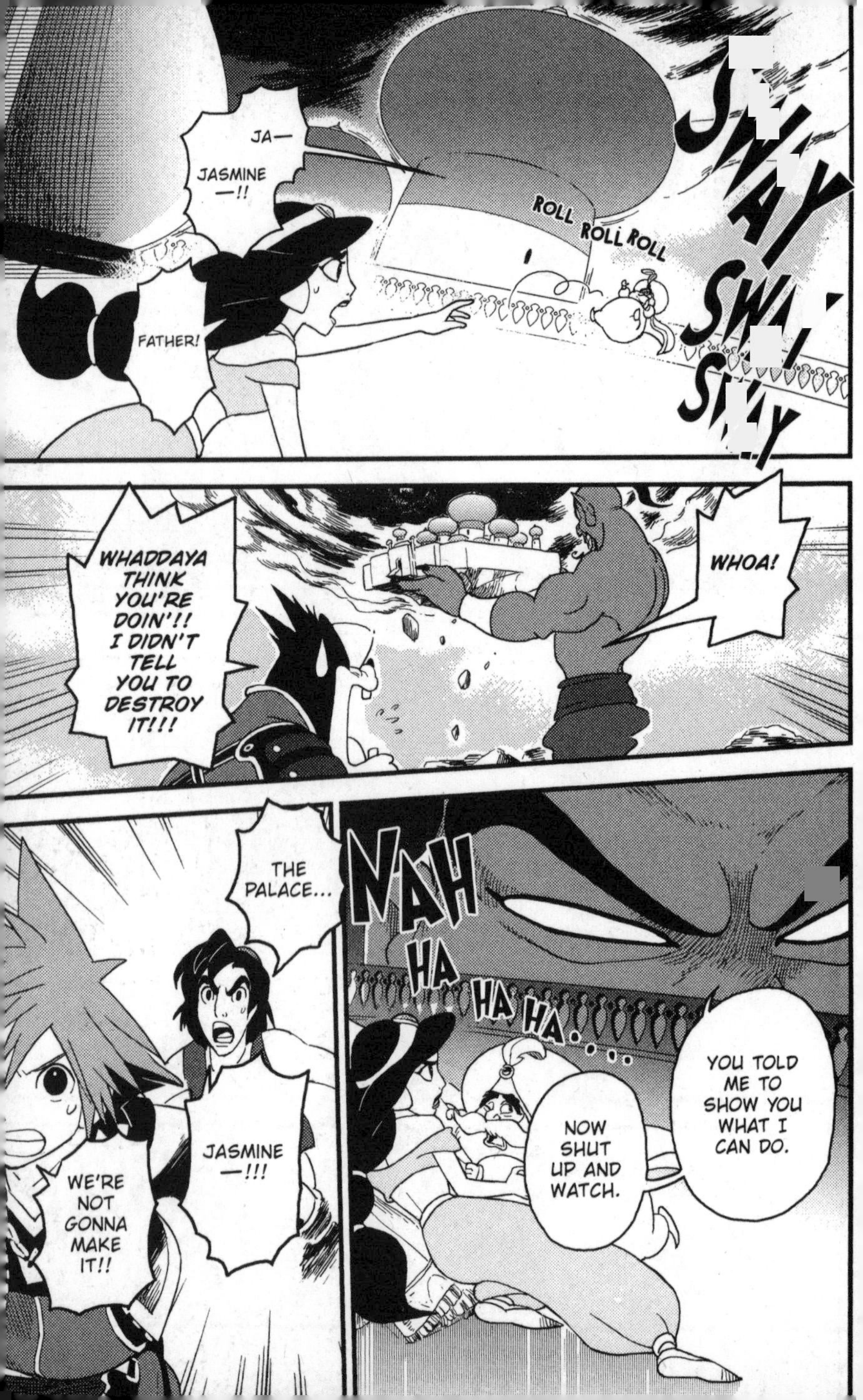
SWAY SWAY SWAY
ROLL ROLL ROLL
JA— JASMINE—!!
FATHER!
WHOA!
WHADDAYA THINK YOU'RE DOIN'!! I DIDN'T TELL YOU TO DESTROY IT!!!
NAH HA HA HA...
YOU TOLD ME TO SHOW YOU WHAT I CAN DO.
NOW SHUT UP AND WATCH.
THE PALACE...
JASMINE—!!!
WE'RE NOT GONNA MAKE IT!!

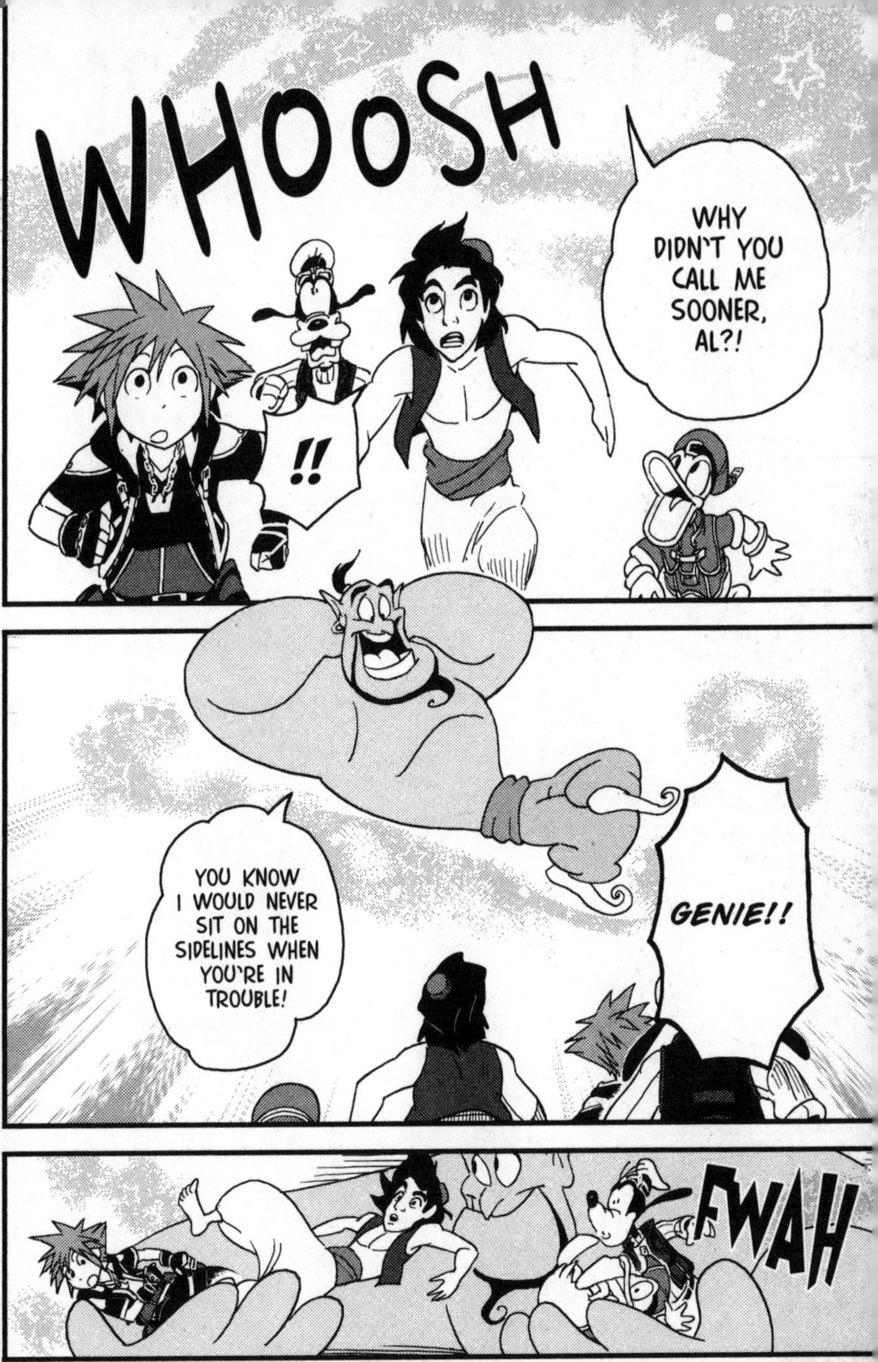
WHY DIDN'T YOU CALL ME SOONER, AL?!
WHOOSH
!!
GENIE!!
YOU KNOW I WOULD NEVER SIT ON THE SIDELINES WHEN YOU'RE IN TROUBLE!
FWAH

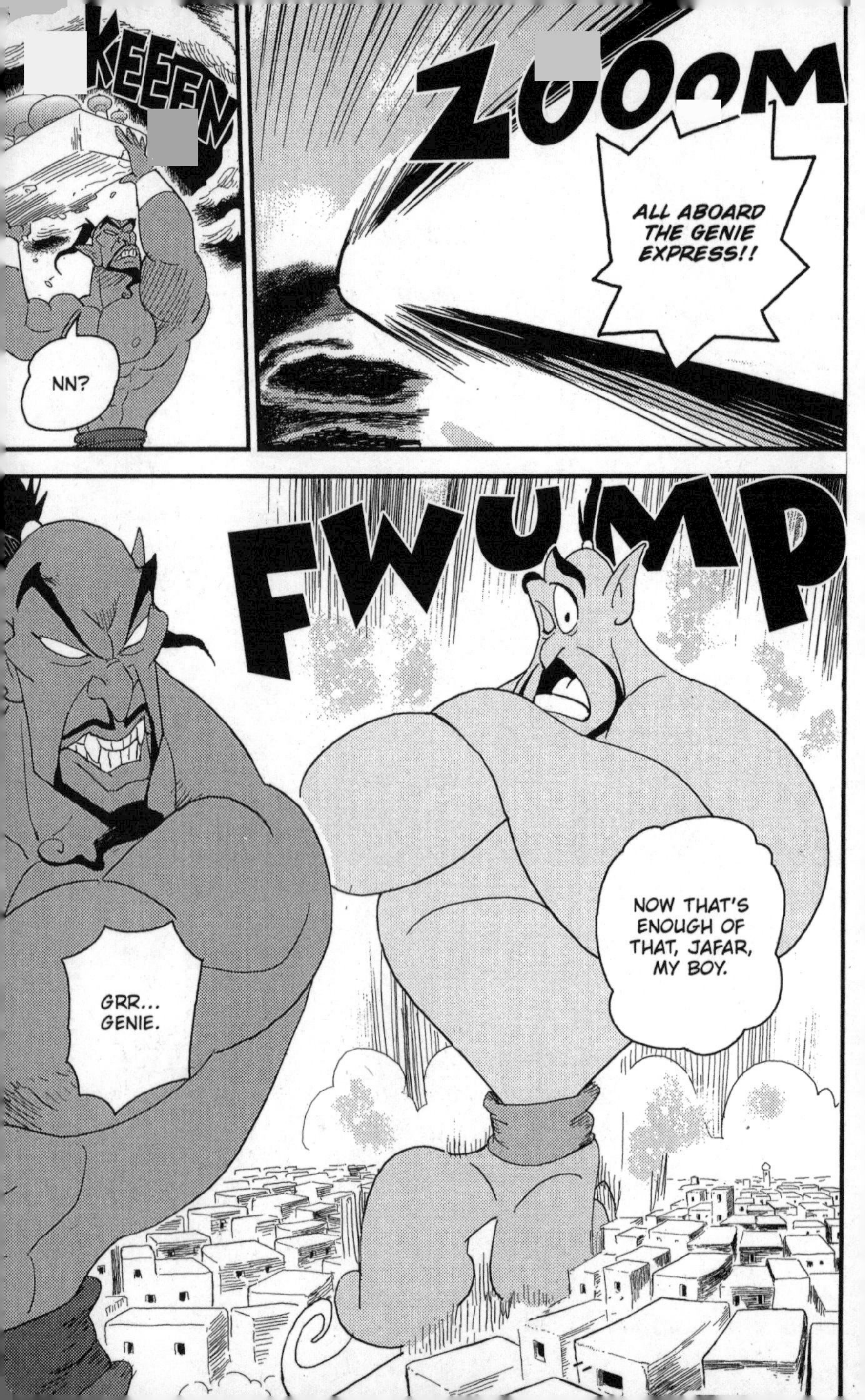
ZOOOM
ALL ABOARD THE GENIE EXPRESS!!
KEEEN
NN?
FWUMP
NOW THAT'S ENOUGH OF THAT, JAFAR, MY BOY.
GRR... GENIE.

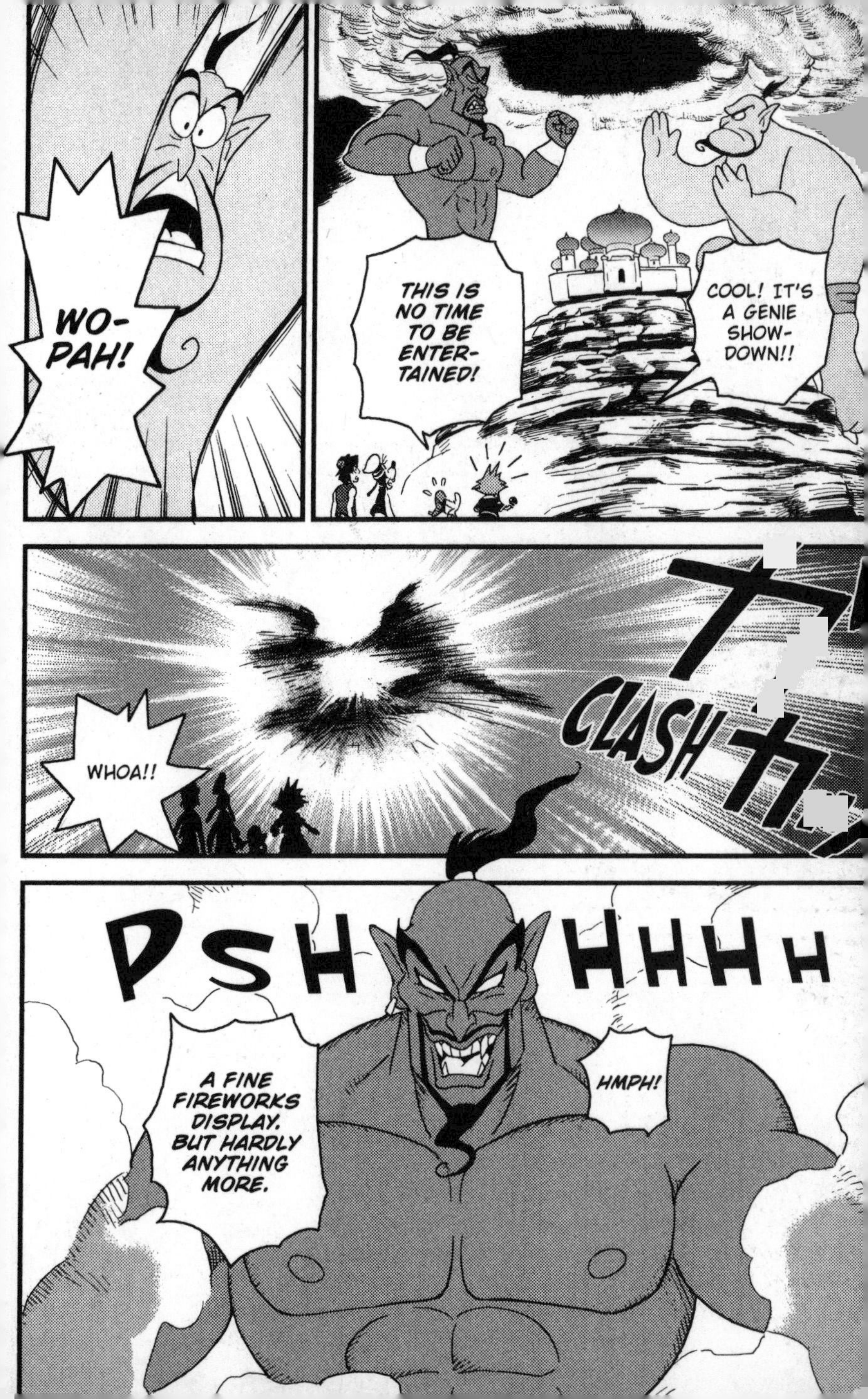
COOL! IT'S A GENIE SHOW-DOWN!!
THIS IS NO TIME TO BE ENTER-TAINED!
WO-PAH!
CLASH
WHOA!!
PSHHHHHH
HMPH!
A FINE FIREWORKS DISPLAY. BUT HARDLY ANYTHING MORE.

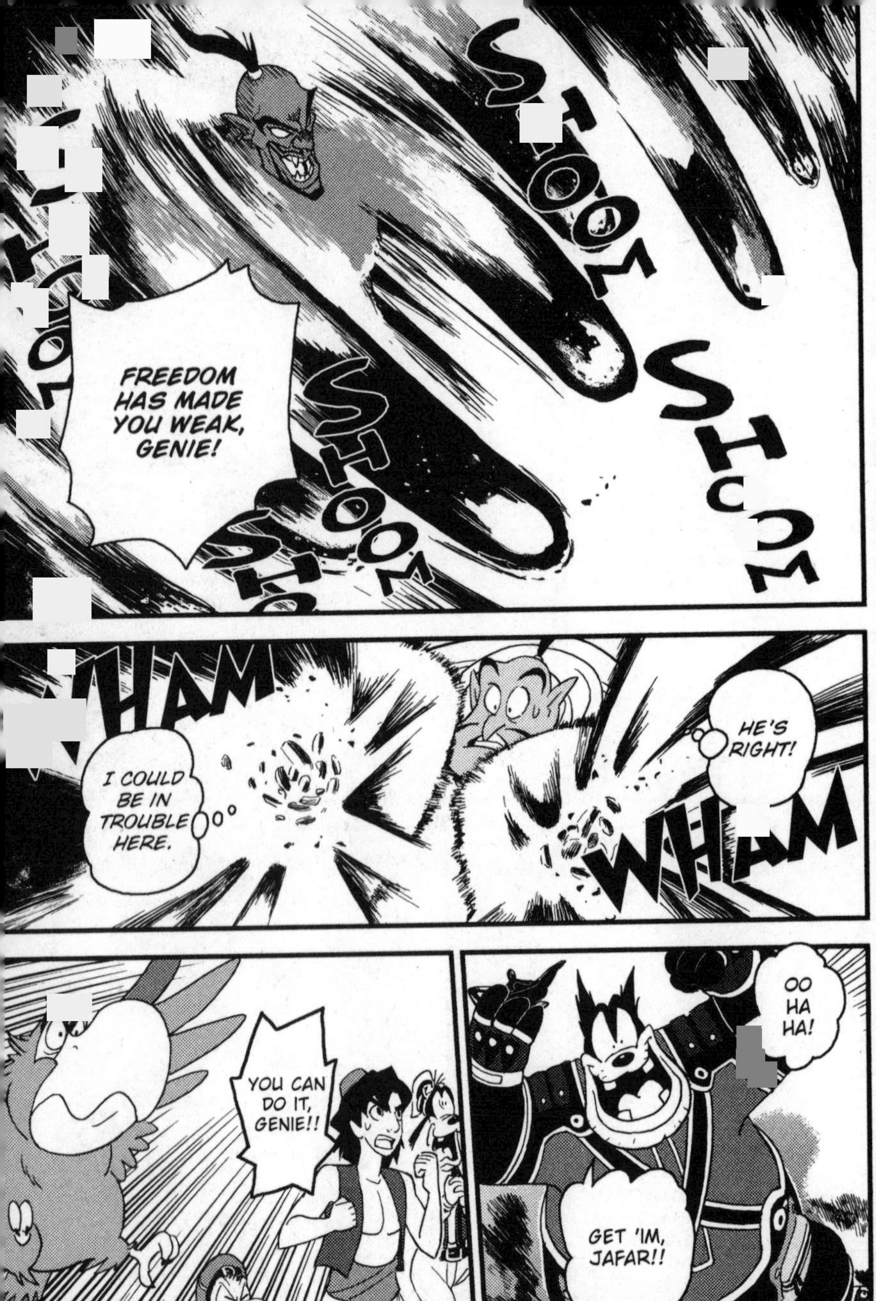
SHOOM
SHOOM
FREEDOM HAS MADE YOU WEAK, GENIE!
SHOOM
HE'S RIGHT!
WHAM
I COULD BE IN TROUBLE HERE.
WHAM
OO HA HA!
GET 'IM, JAFAR!!
YOU CAN DO IT, GENIE!!

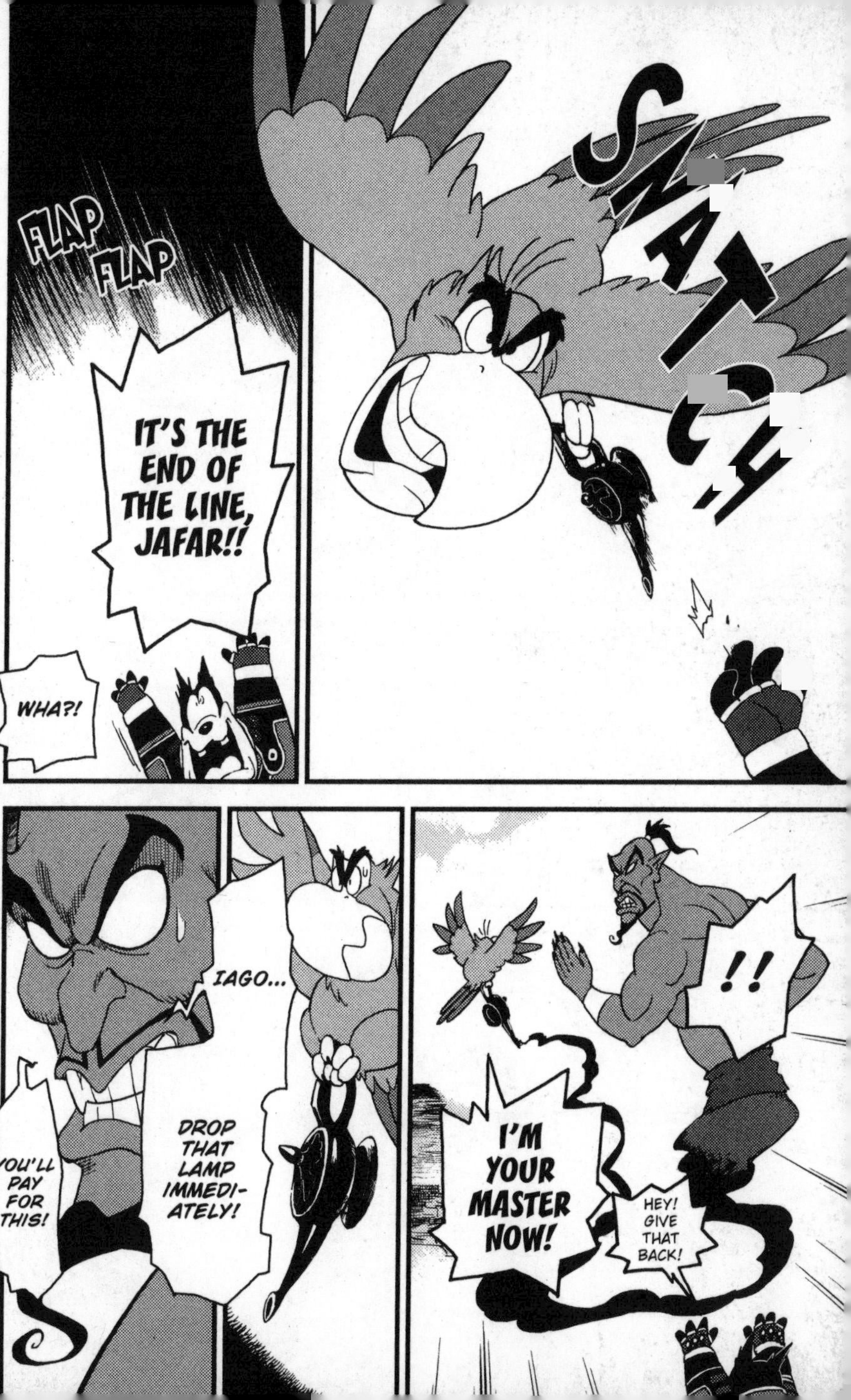

SNATCH
FLAP FLAP
IT'S THE END OF THE LINE, JAFAR!!
WHA?!
!!
I'M YOUR MASTER NOW!
HEY! GIVE THAT BACK!
IAGO...
DROP THAT LAMP IMMEDI-ATELY!
YOU'LL PAY FOR THIS!

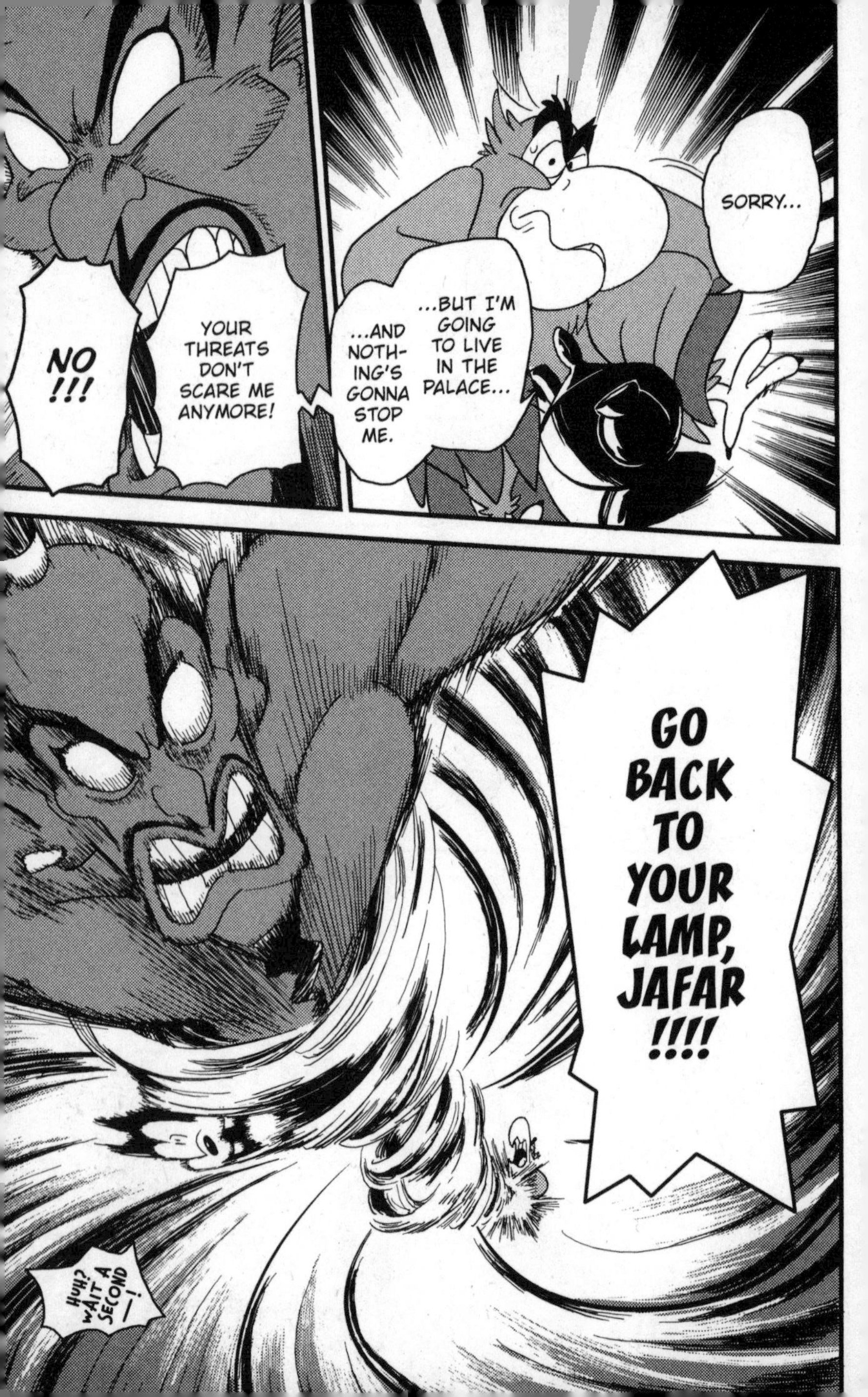
SORRY...
...BUT I'M GOING TO LIVE IN THE PALACE...
...AND NOTHING'S GONNA STOP ME.
YOUR THREATS DON'T SCARE ME ANYMORE!
NO !!!
GO BACK TO YOUR LAMP, JAFAR !!!!
HUH? WAIT A SECOND —!

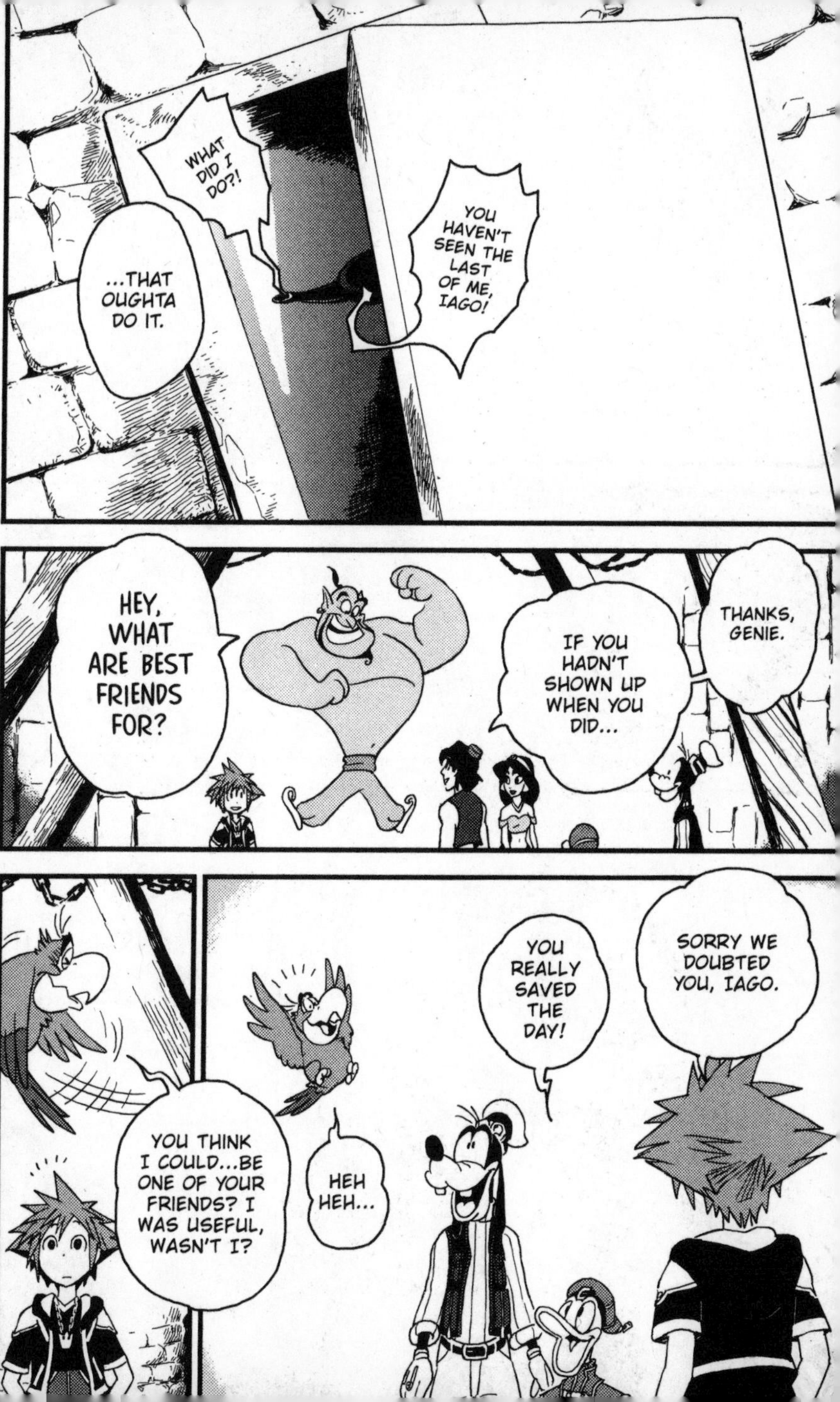
YOU HAVEN'T SEEN THE LAST OF ME, IAGO!
WHAT DID I DO?!
...THAT OUGHTA DO IT.
THANKS, GENIE.
IF YOU HADN'T SHOWN UP WHEN YOU DID...
HEY, WHAT ARE BEST FRIENDS FOR?
SORRY WE DOUBTED YOU, IAGO.
YOU REALLY SAVED THE DAY!
HEH HEH...
YOU THINK I COULD...BE ONE OF YOUR FRIENDS? I WAS USEFUL, WASN'T I?

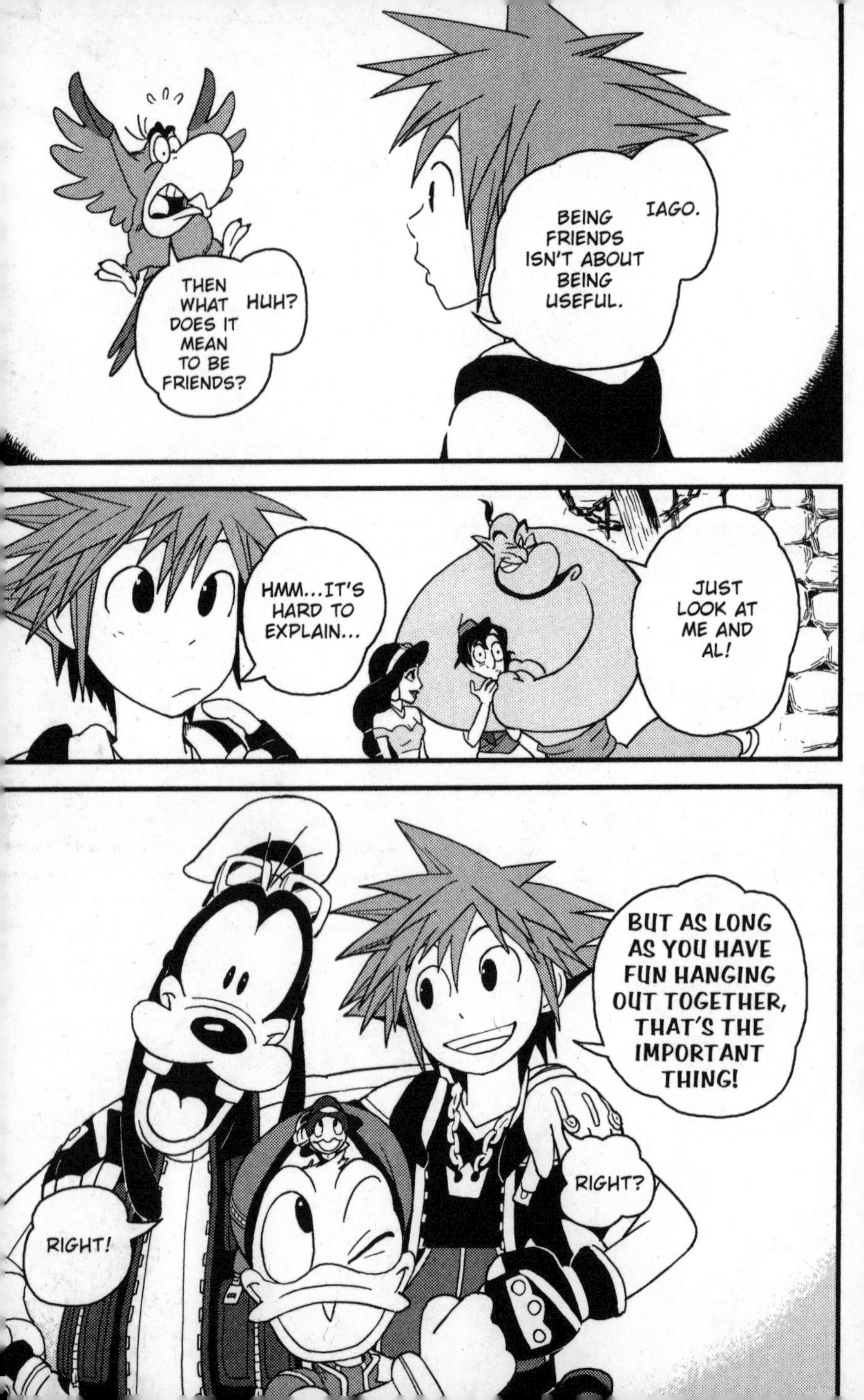
IAGO.
BEING FRIENDS ISN'T ABOUT BEING USEFUL.
HUH?
THEN WHAT DOES IT MEAN TO BE FRIENDS?
JUST LOOK AT ME AND AL!
HMM...IT'S HARD TO EXPLAIN...
BUT AS LONG AS YOU HAVE FUN HANGING OUT TOGETHER, THAT'S THE IMPORTANT THING!
RIGHT?
RIGHT!

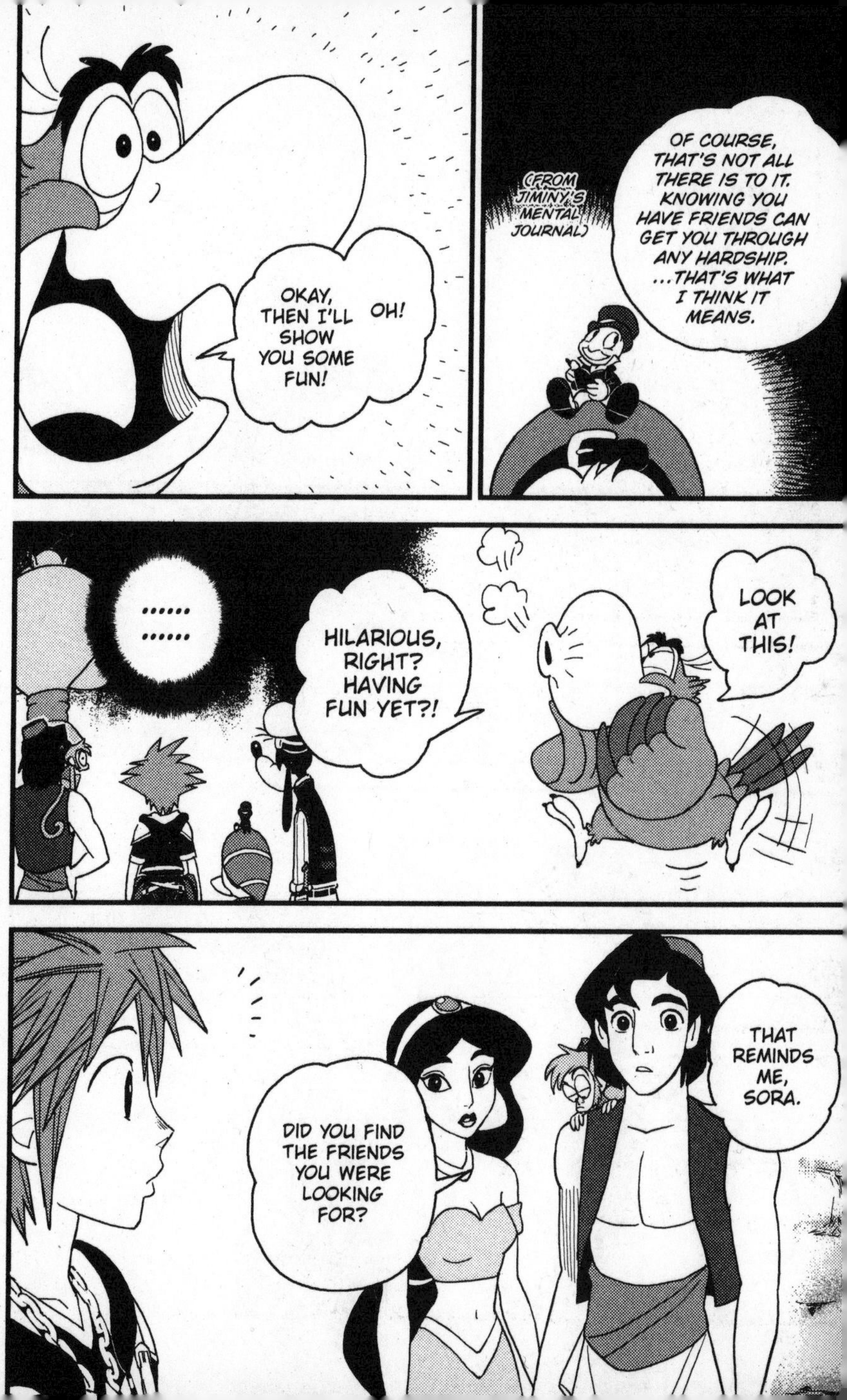
OF COURSE, THAT'S NOT ALL THERE IS TO IT. KNOWING YOU HAVE FRIENDS CAN GET YOU THROUGH ANY HARDSHIP. ...THAT'S WHAT I THINK IT MEANS.
(FROM JIMINY'S MENTAL JOURNAL)
OH!
OKAY, THEN I'LL SHOW YOU SOME FUN!
LOOK AT THIS!
HILARIOUS, RIGHT? HAVING FUN YET?!
....
THAT REMINDS ME, SORA.
DID YOU FIND THE FRIENDS YOU WERE LOOKING FOR?

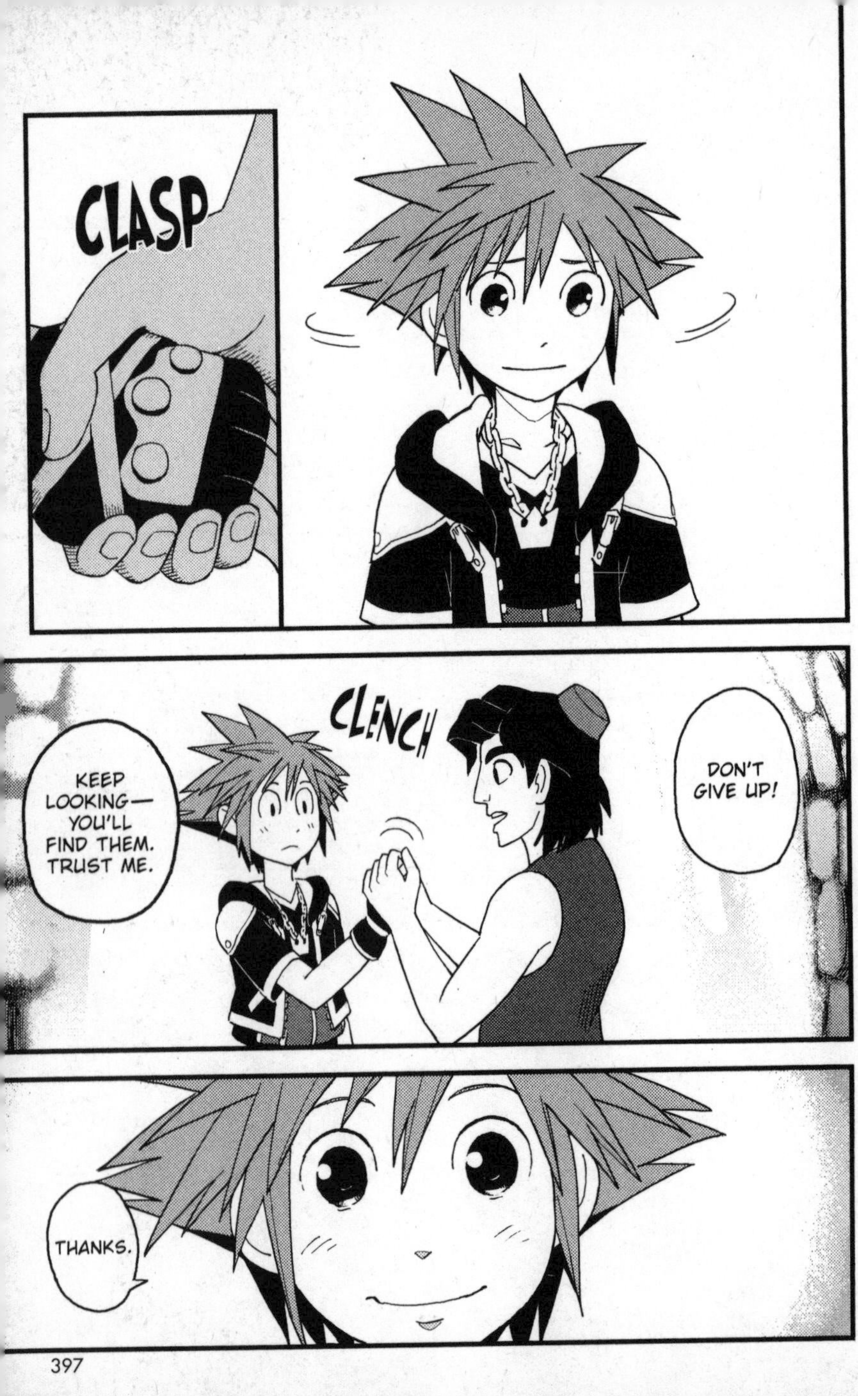
CLASP
DON'T GIVE UP!
CLENCH
KEEP LOOKING—YOU'LL FIND THEM. TRUST ME.
THANKS.

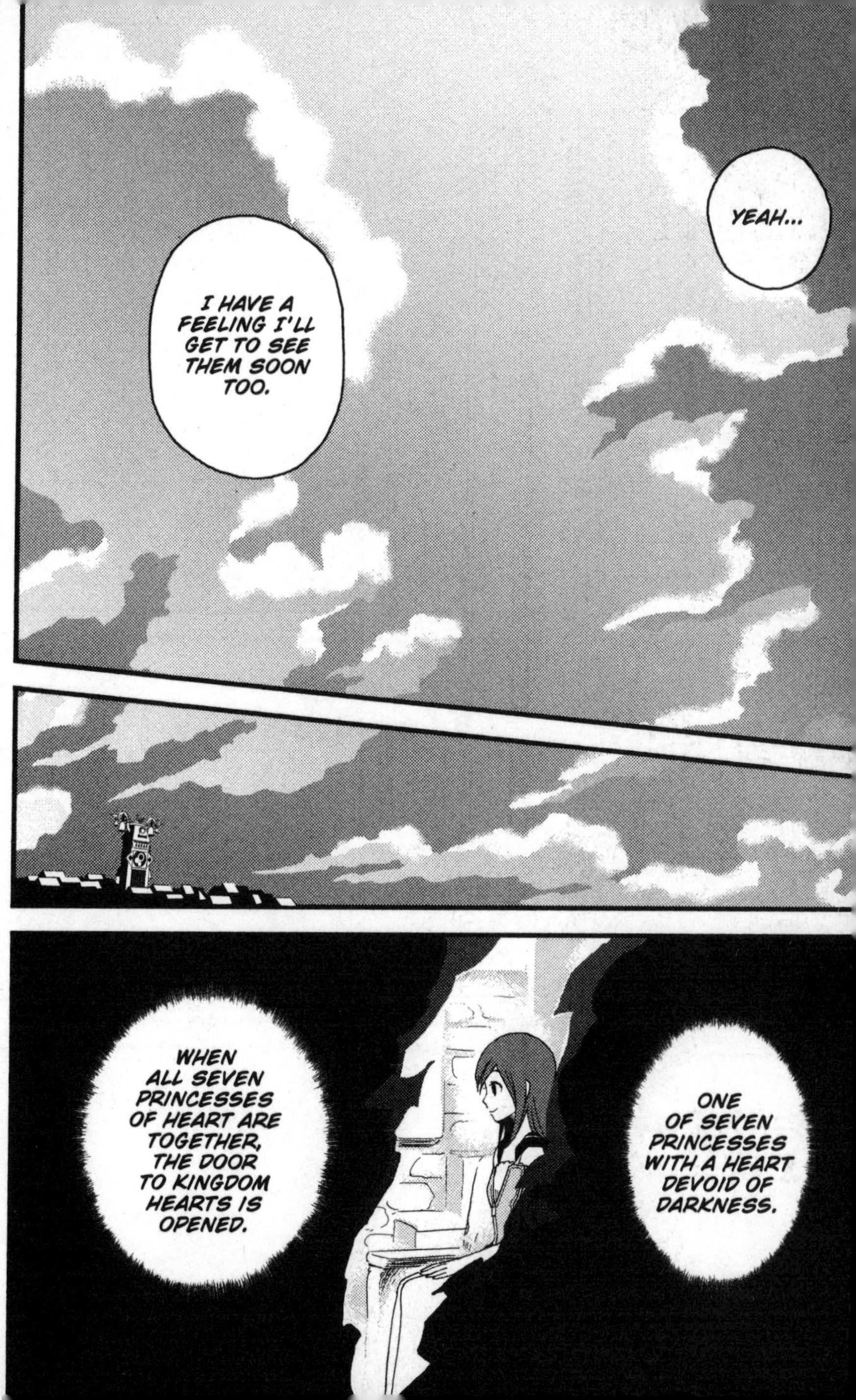
YEAH...
I HAVE A FEELING I'LL GET TO SEE THEM SOON TOO.
ONE OF SEVEN PRINCESSES WITH A HEART DEVOID OF DARKNESS.
WHEN ALL SEVEN PRINCESSES OF HEART ARE TOGETHER, THE DOOR TO KINGDOM HEARTS IS OPENED.

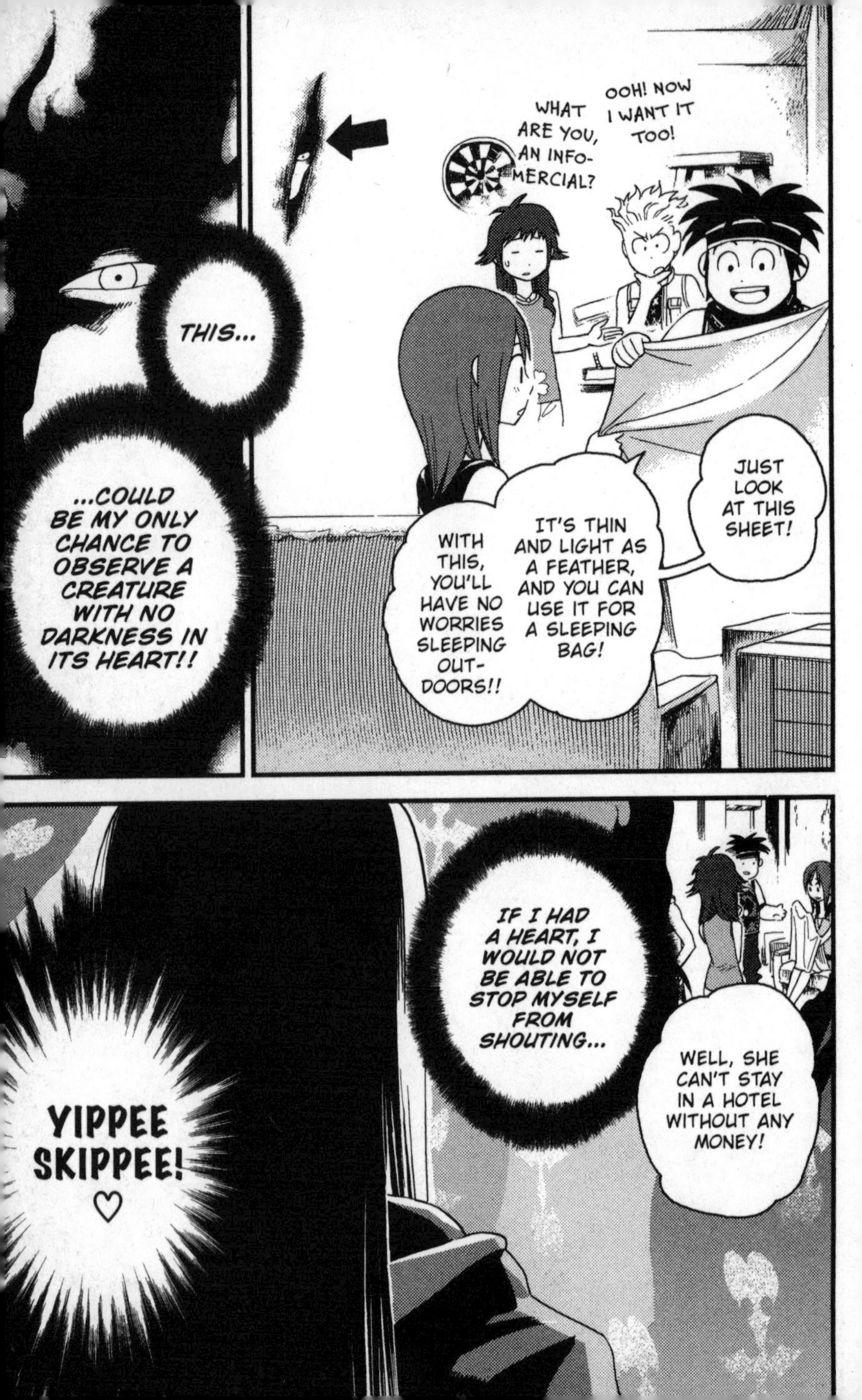
JUST LOOK AT THIS SHEET!
IT'S THIN AND LIGHT AS A FEATHER, AND YOU CAN USE IT FOR A SLEEPING BAG!
WITH THIS, YOU'LL HAVE NO WORRIES SLEEPING OUT-DOORS!!
OOH! NOW I WANT IT TOO!
WHAT ARE YOU, AN INFO-MERCIAL?
THIS...
...COULD BE MY ONLY CHANCE TO OBSERVE A CREATURE WITH NO DARKNESS IN ITS HEART!!
WELL, SHE CAN'T STAY IN A HOTEL WITHOUT ANY MONEY!
IF I HAD A HEART, I WOULD NOT BE ABLE TO STOP MYSELF FROM SHOUTING...
YIPPEE SKIPPEE! ♡

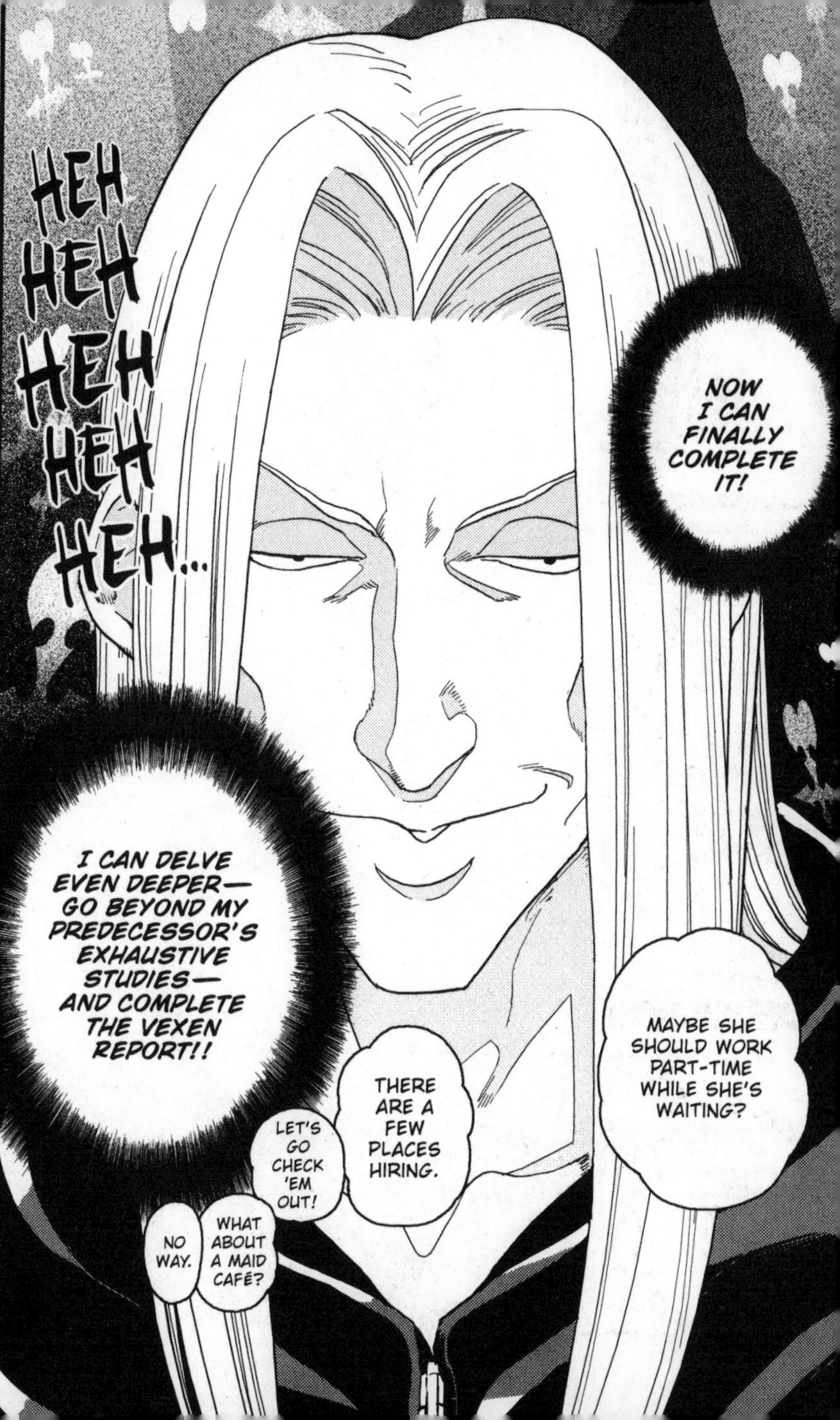
NOW I CAN FINALLY COMPLETE IT!
HEH HEH HEH HEH HEH...
I CAN DELVE EVEN DEEPER— GO BEYOND MY PREDECESSOR'S EXHAUSTIVE STUDIES— AND COMPLETE THE VEXEN REPORT!!
MAYBE SHE SHOULD WORK PART-TIME WHILE SHE'S WAITING?
THERE ARE A FEW PLACES HIRING.
LET'S GO CHECK 'EM OUT!
WHAT ABOUT A MAID CAFÉ?
NO WAY.

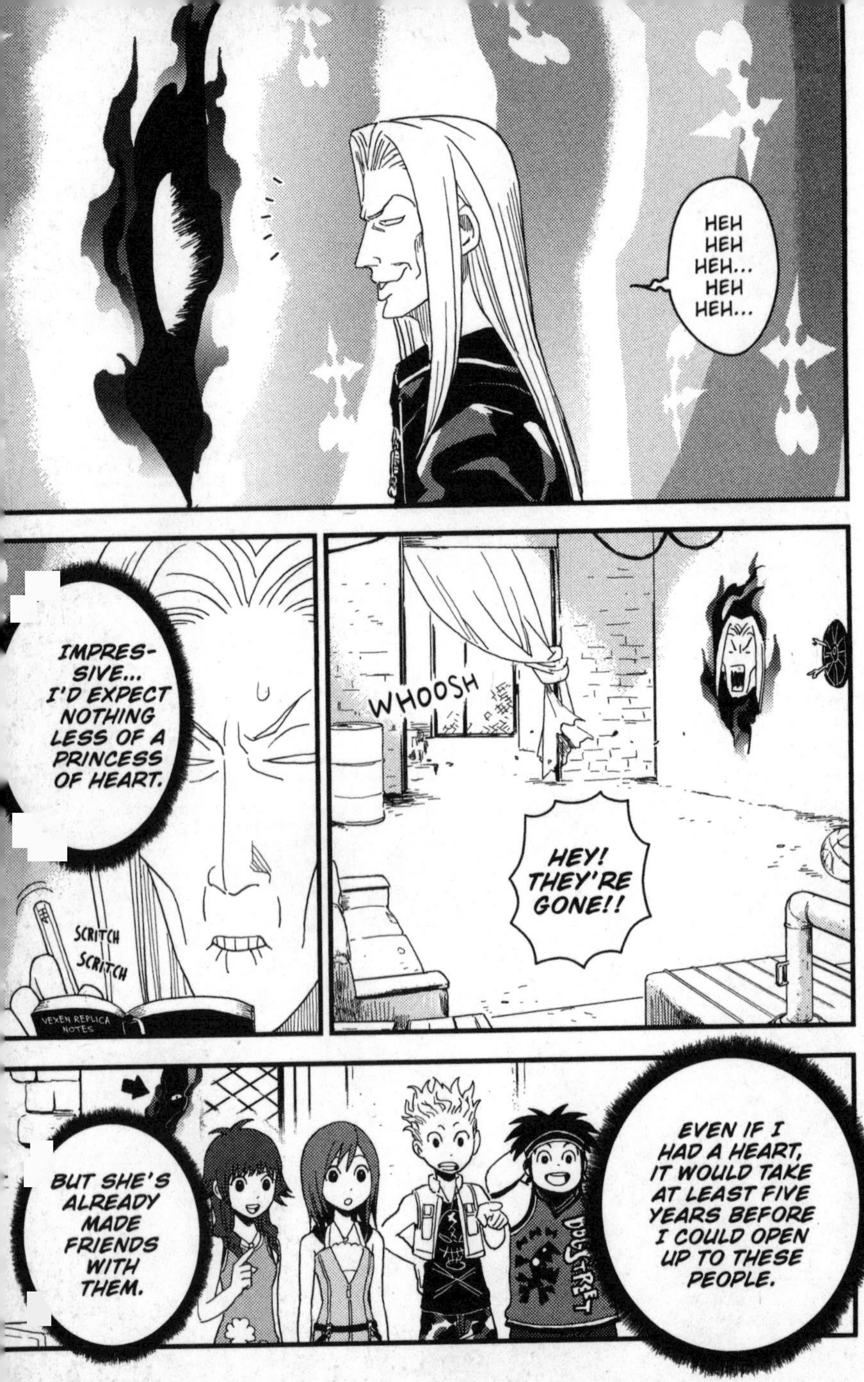
HEH HEH HEH... HEH HEH...
WHOOSH
HEY! THEY'RE GONE!!
IMPRES-SIVE... I'D EXPECT NOTHING LESS OF A PRINCESS OF HEART.
SCRITCH SCRITCH
VEXEN REPLICA NOTES
EVEN IF I HAD A HEART, IT WOULD TAKE AT LEAST FIVE YEARS BEFORE I COULD OPEN UP TO THESE PEOPLE.
BUT SHE'S ALREADY MADE FRIENDS WITH THEM.

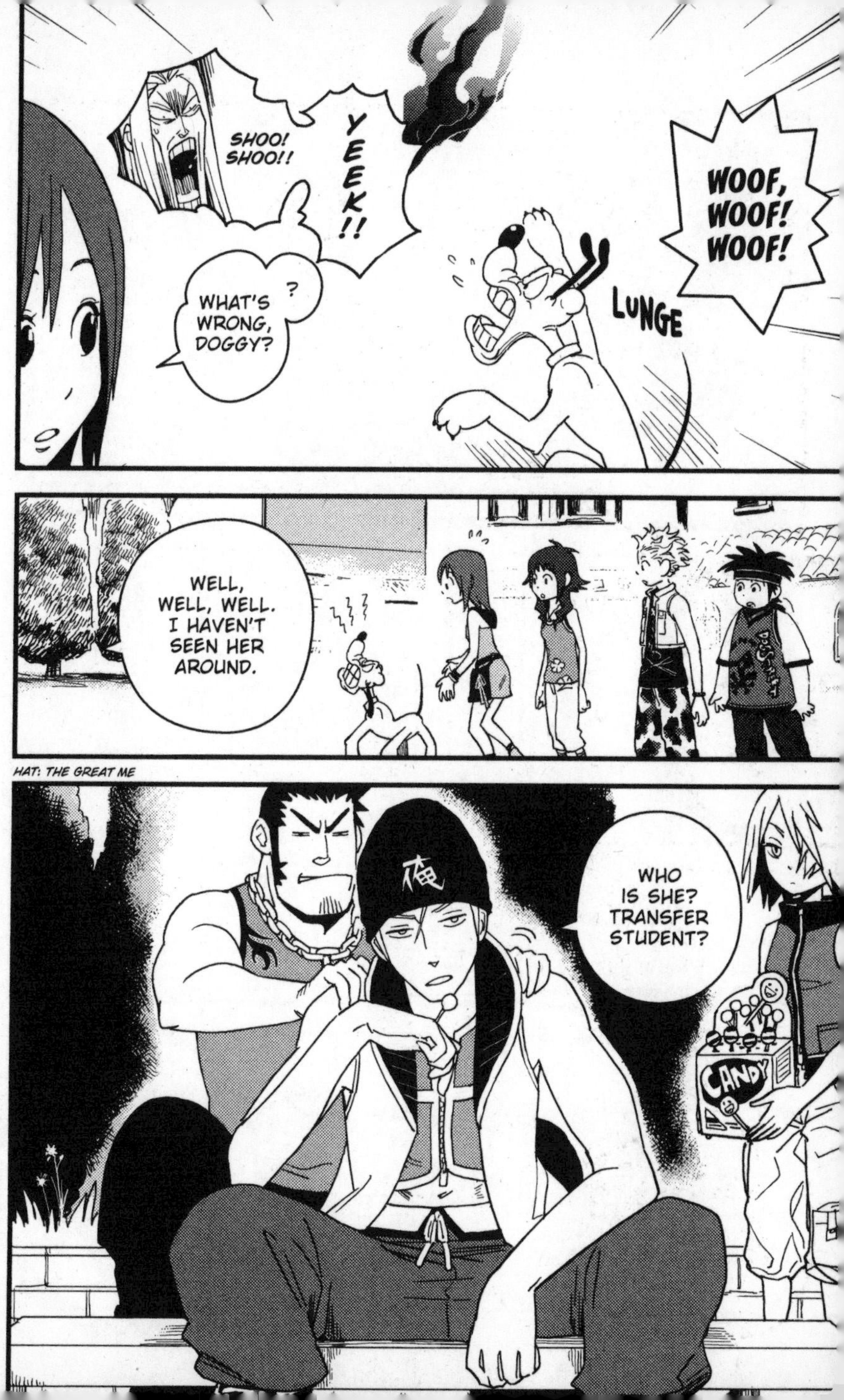
WOOF, WOOF! WOOF!
YEEK!!
SHOO! SHOO!!
LUNGE
?
WHAT'S WRONG, DOGGY?
WELL, WELL, WELL. I HAVEN'T SEEN HER AROUND.
HAT: THE GREAT ME
WHO IS SHE? TRANSFER STUDENT?
CANDY

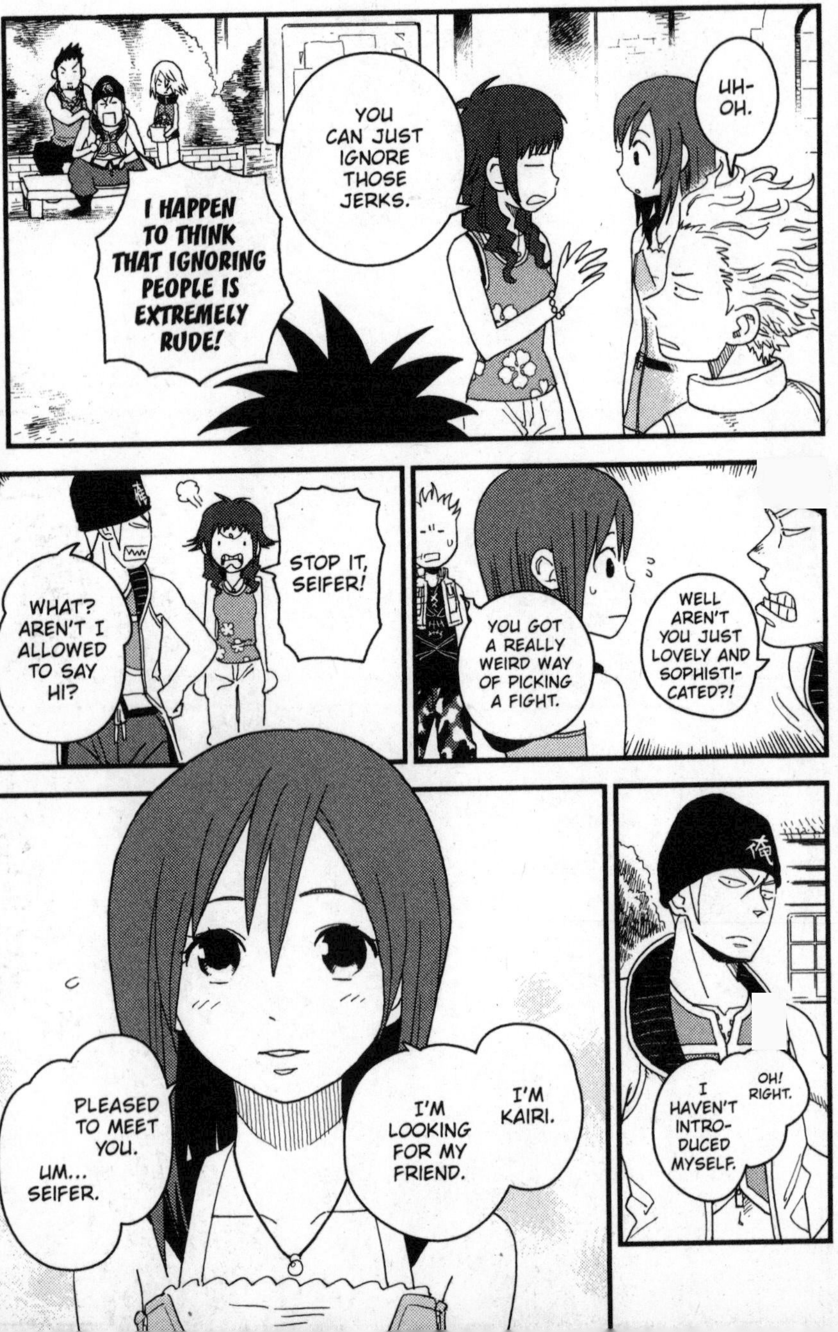
UH-OH.
YOU CAN JUST IGNORE THOSE JERKS.
I HAPPEN TO THINK THAT IGNORING PEOPLE IS EXTREMELY RUDE!
WELL AREN'T YOU JUST LOVELY AND SOPHISTI-CATED?!
YOU GOT A REALLY WEIRD WAY OF PICKING A FIGHT.
STOP IT, SEIFER!
WHAT? AREN'T I ALLOWED TO SAY HI?
OH! RIGHT.
I HAVEN'T INTRO-DUCED MYSELF.
I'M KAIRI.
I'M LOOKING FOR MY FRIEND.
PLEASED TO MEET YOU.
UM... SEIFER.

Chapter 34: Kairi-napped!

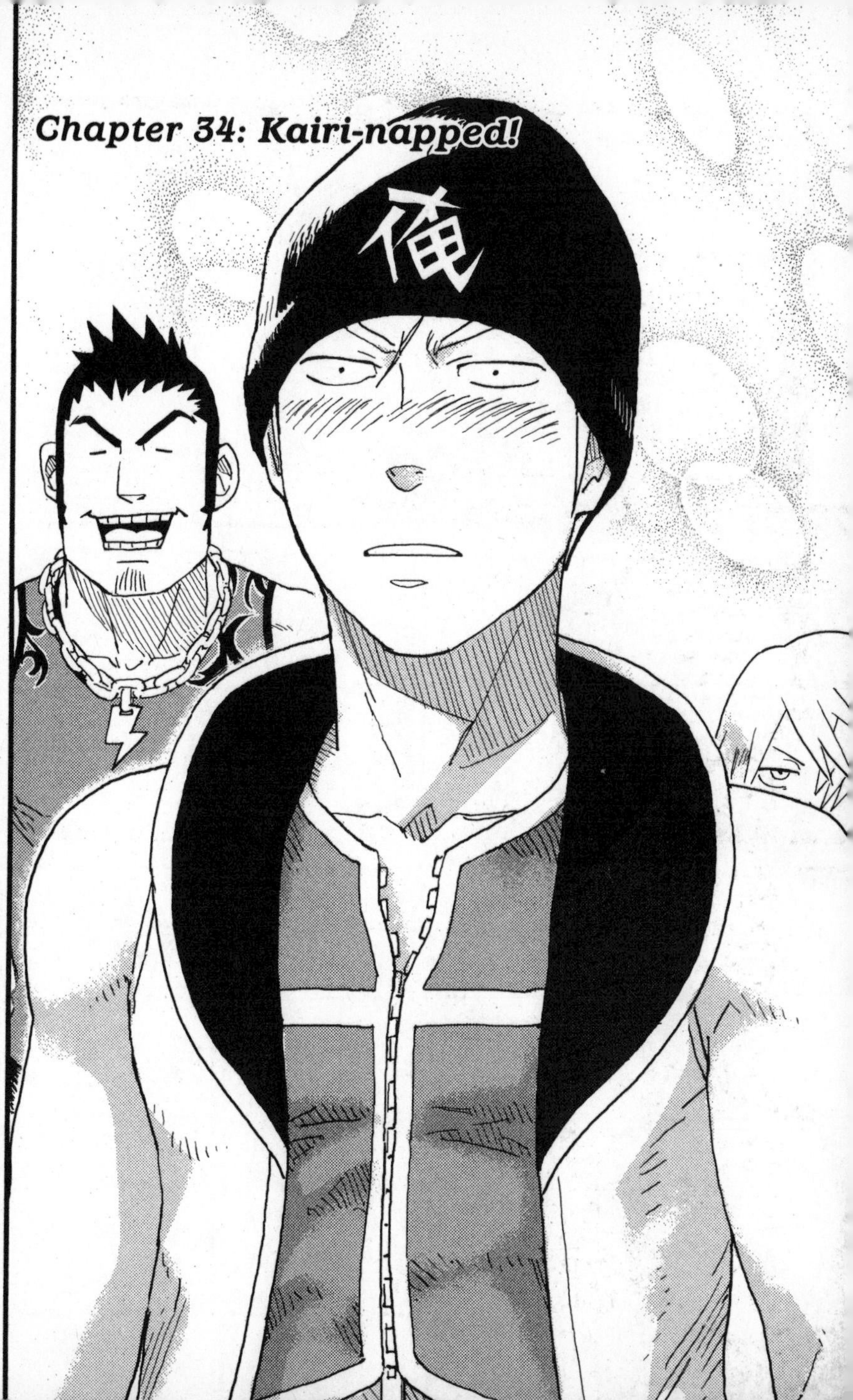
俺

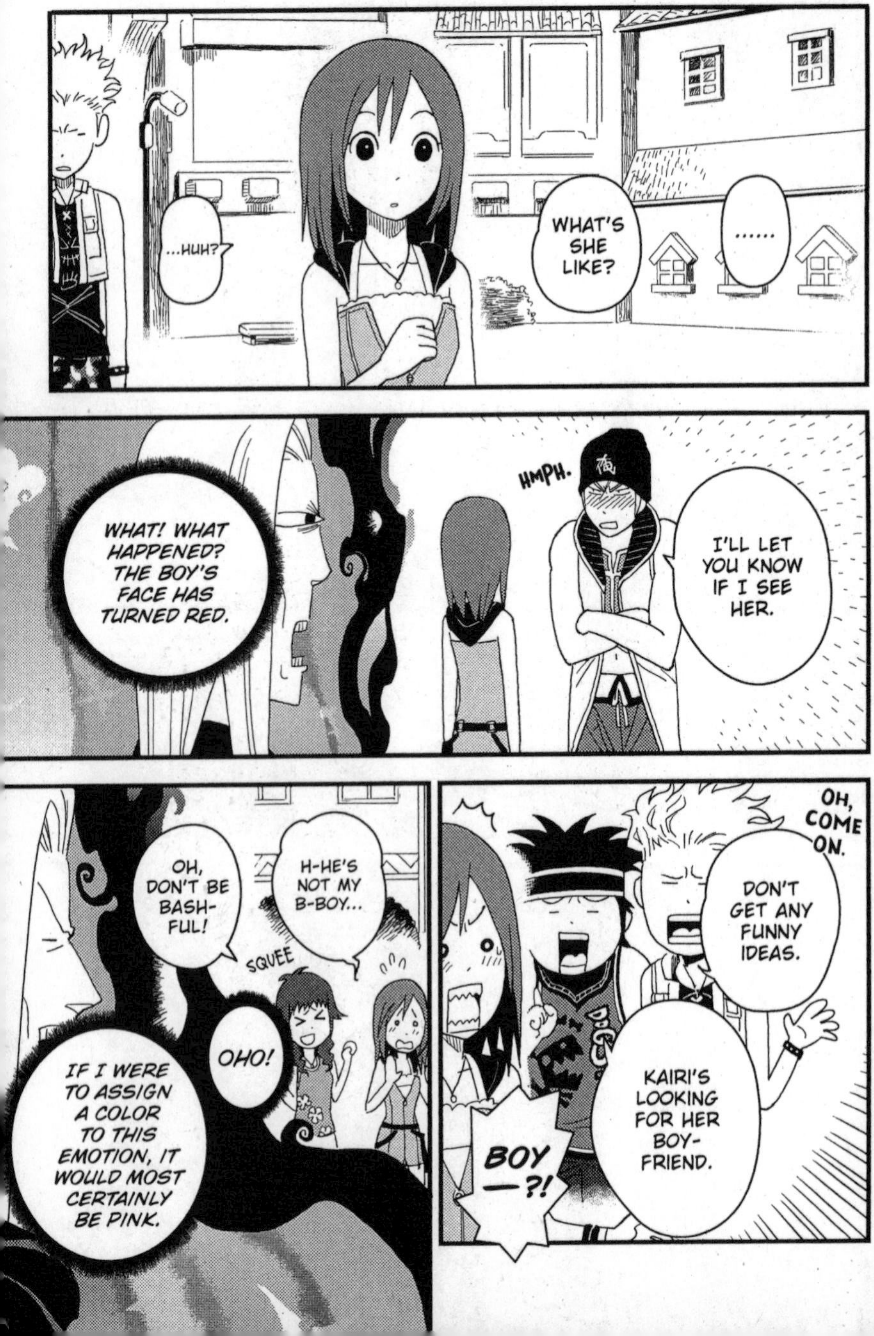
......
WHAT'S SHE LIKE?
...HUH?
HMPH.
I'LL LET YOU KNOW IF I SEE HER.
WHAT! WHAT HAPPENED? THE BOY'S FACE HAS TURNED RED.
OH, COME ON.
DON'T GET ANY FUNNY IDEAS.
KAIRI'S LOOKING FOR HER BOY-FRIEND.
BOY—?!
H-HE'S NOT MY B-BOY...
OH, DON'T BE BASH-FUL!
SQUEE
OHO!
IF I WERE TO ASSIGN A COLOR TO THIS EMOTION, IT WOULD MOST CERTAINLY BE PINK.

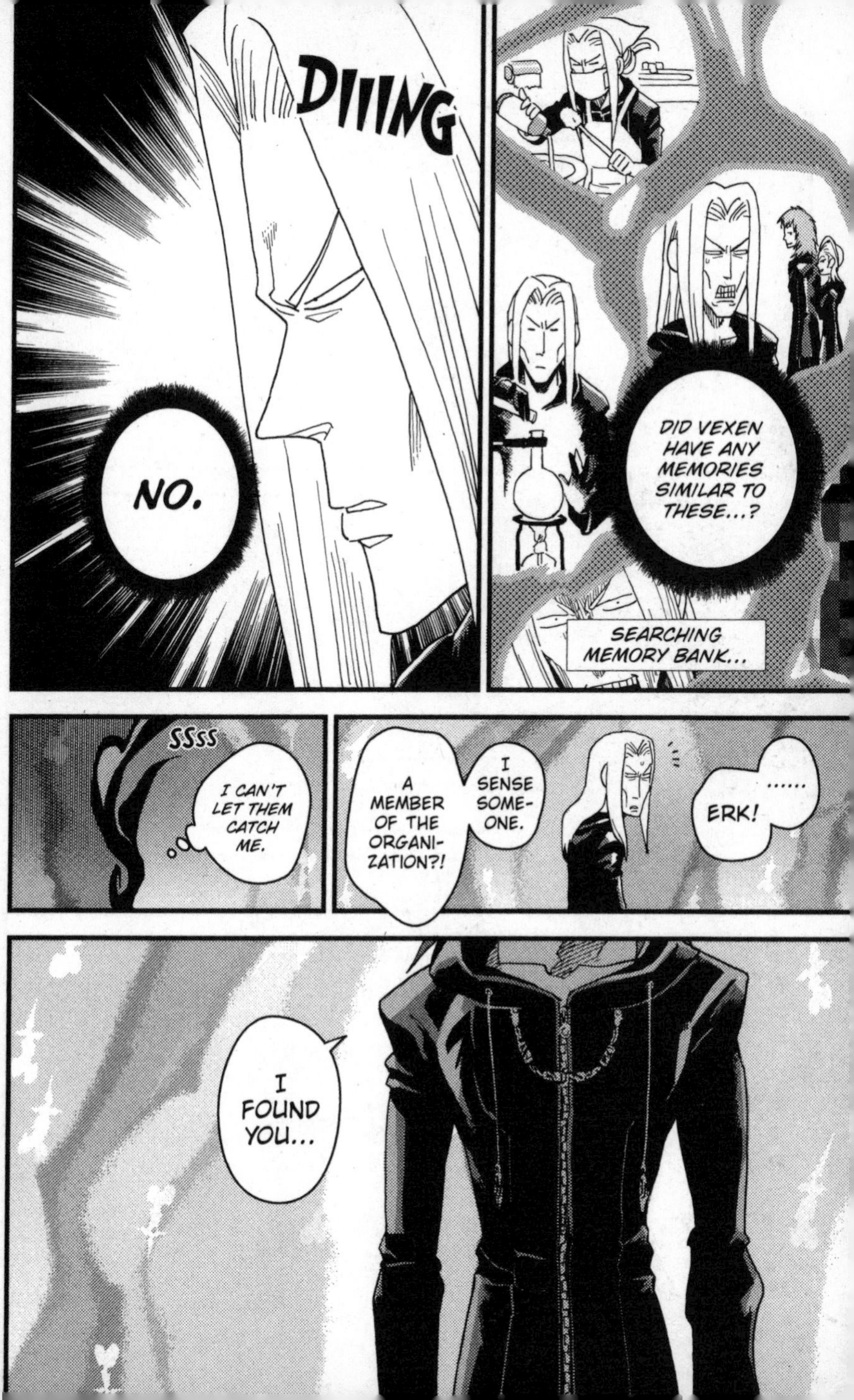
DID VEXEN HAVE ANY MEMORIES SIMILAR TO THESE...?
SEARCHING MEMORY BANK...
DIIING
NO.
......
ERK!
I SENSE SOME-ONE.
A MEMBER OF THE ORGANI-ZATION?!
SSSS
I CAN'T LET THEM CATCH ME.
I FOUND YOU...

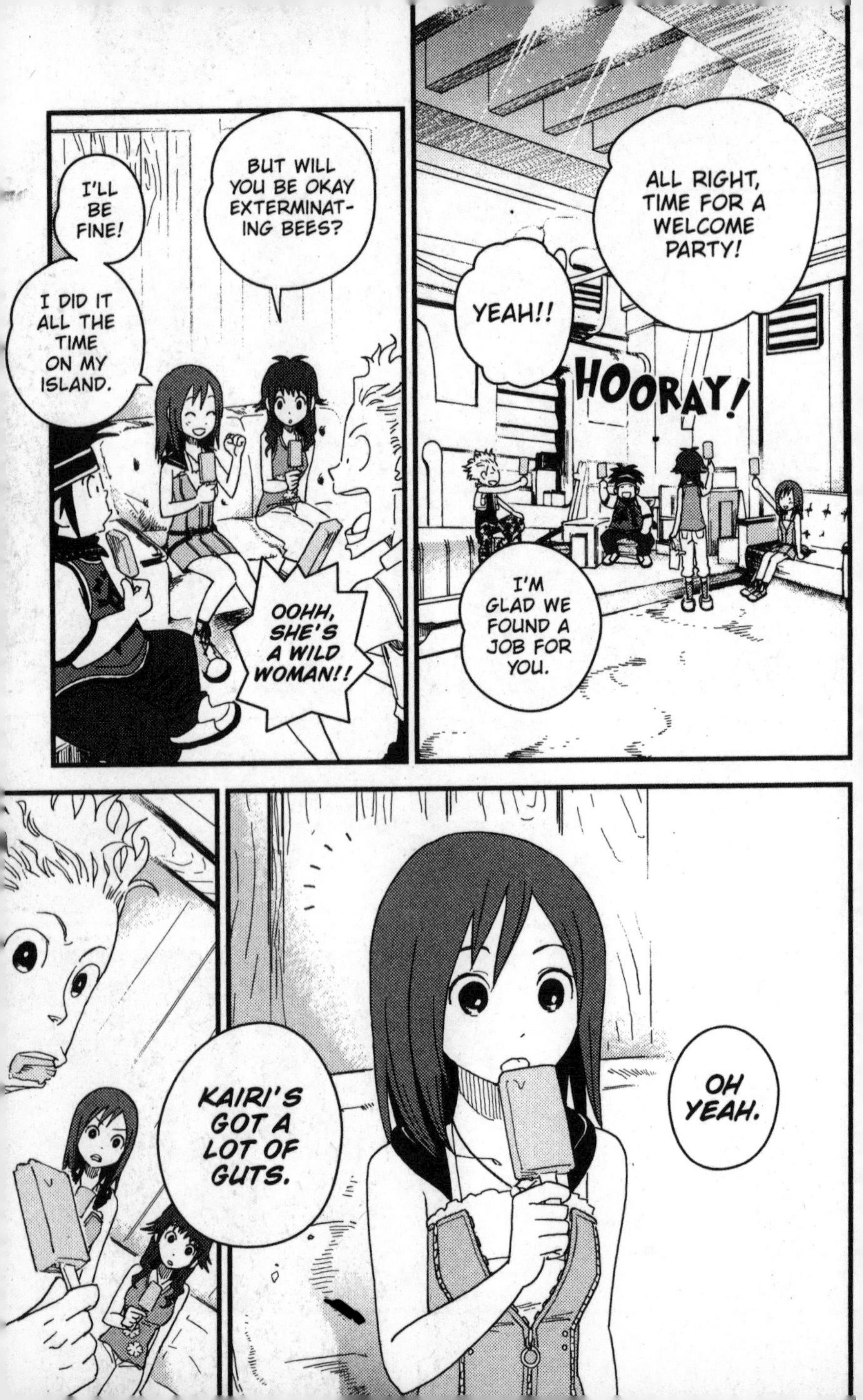
ALL RIGHT, TIME FOR A WELCOME PARTY!
YEAH!!
HOORAY!
I'M GLAD WE FOUND A JOB FOR YOU.
BUT WILL YOU BE OKAY EXTERMINAT-ING BEES?
I'LL BE FINE!
I DID IT ALL THE TIME ON MY ISLAND.
OOHH, SHE'S A WILD WOMAN!!
KAIRI'S GOT A LOT OF GUTS.
OH YEAH.

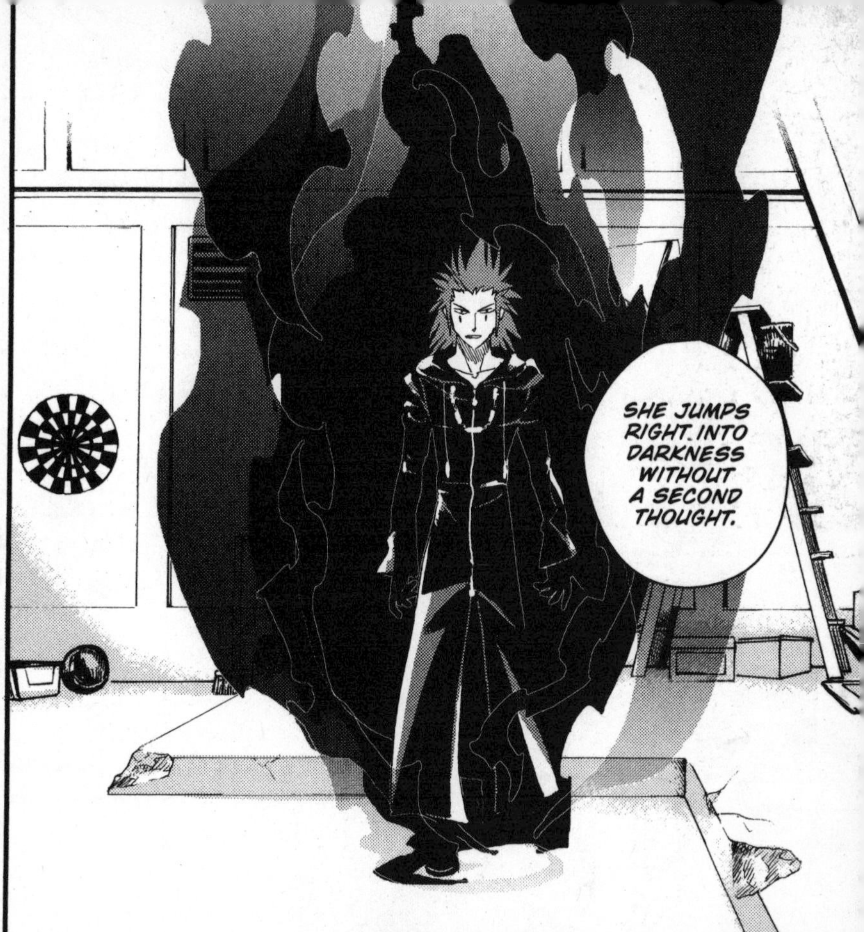
SHE JUMPS RIGHT INTO DARKNESS WITHOUT A SECOND THOUGHT.

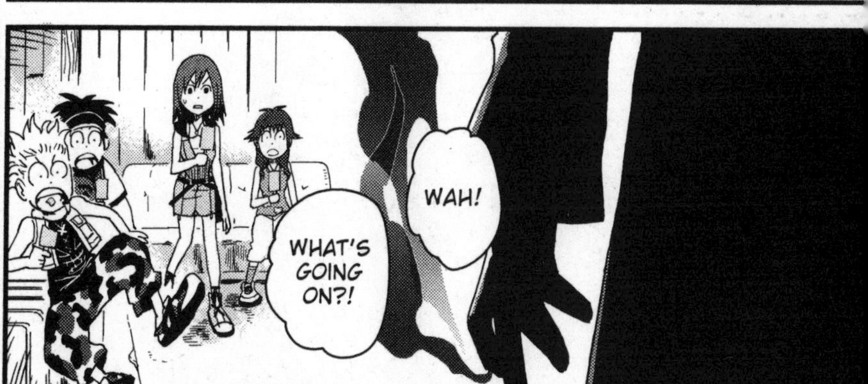
WAH!
WHAT'S GOING ON?!

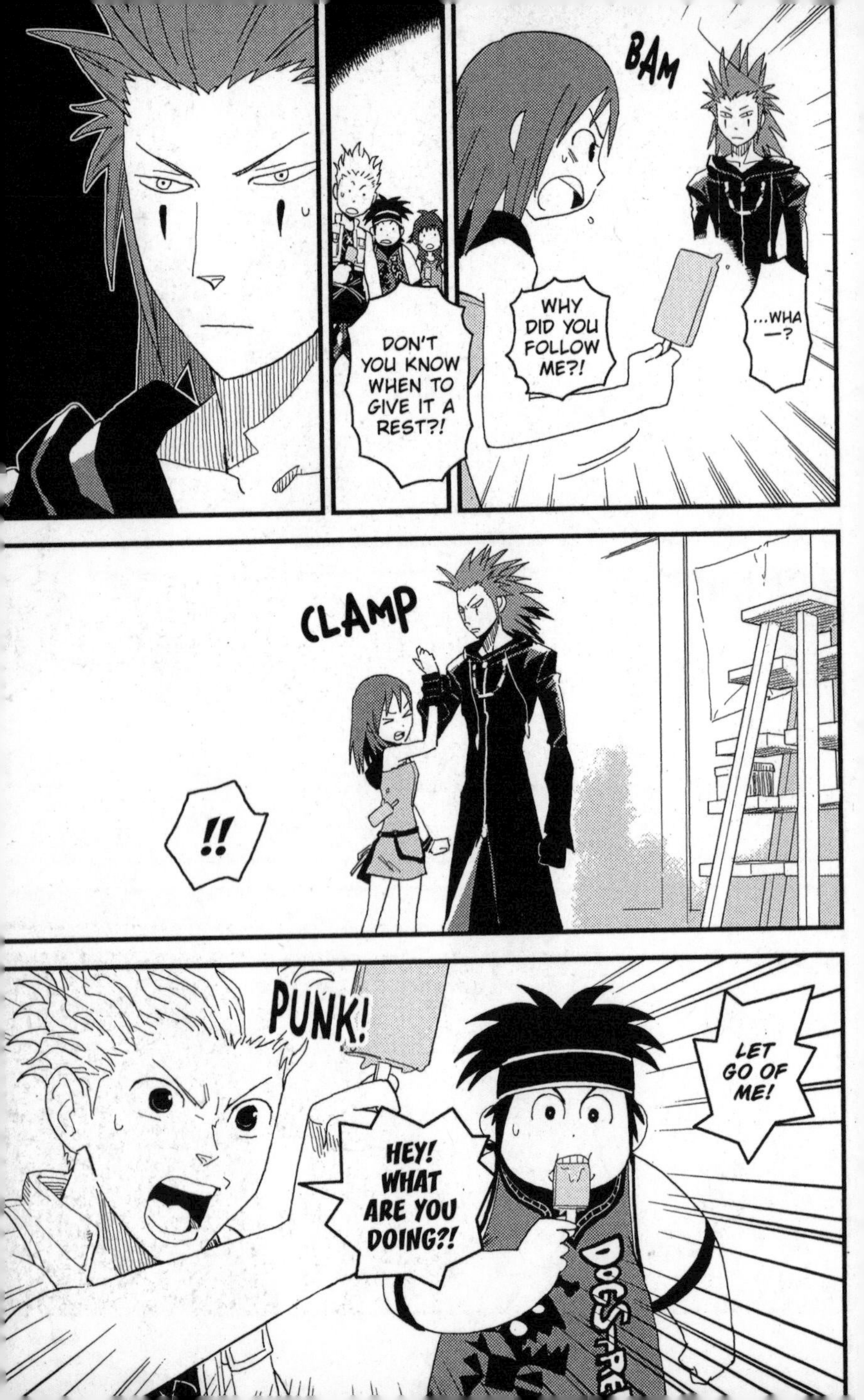
BAM
...WHA—?
WHY DID YOU FOLLOW ME?!
DON'T YOU KNOW WHEN TO GIVE IT A REST?!
CLAMP
!!
LET GO OF ME!
PUNK!
HEY! WHAT ARE YOU DOING?!

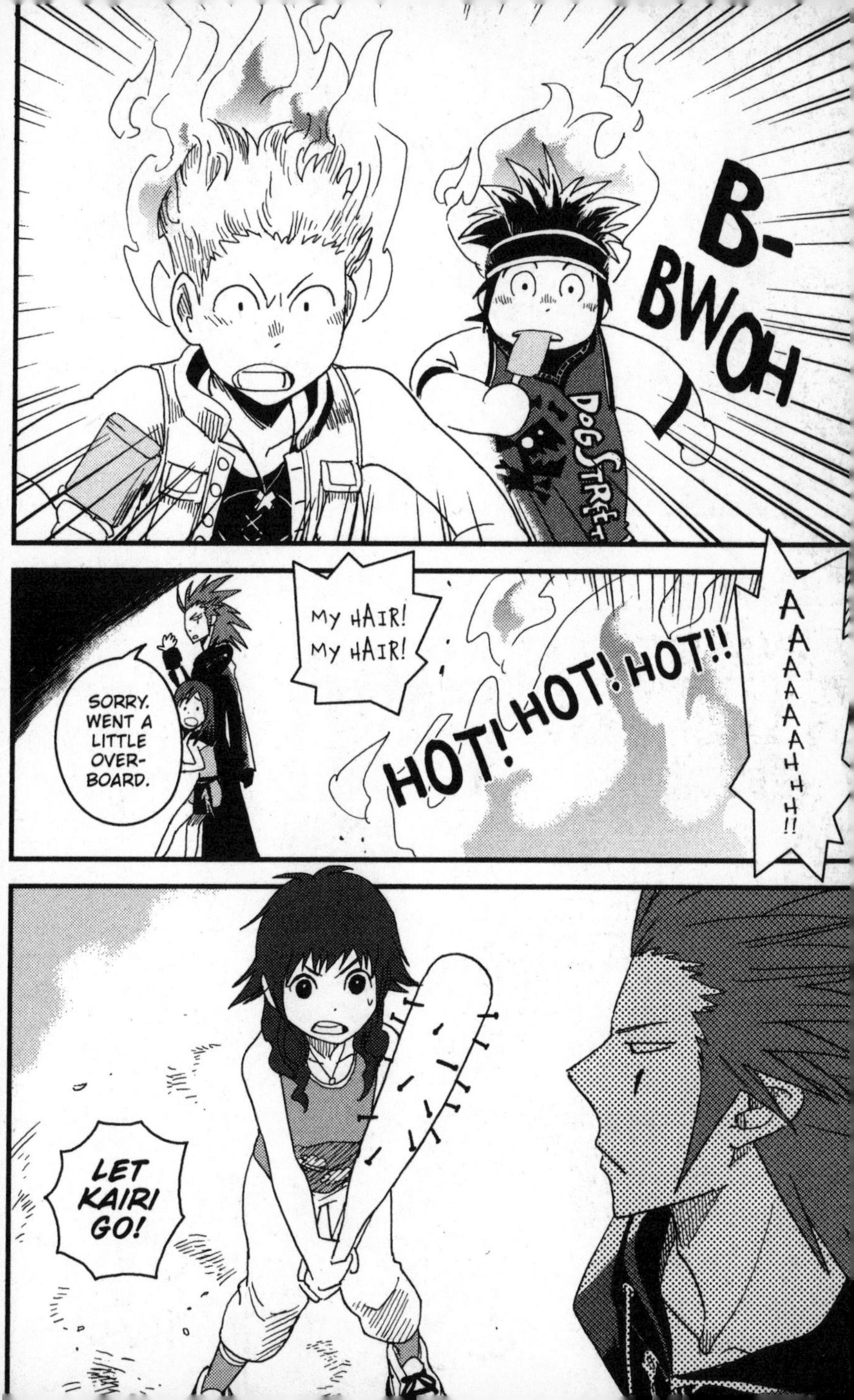
B-BWOH
AAAAAAHHH!!
HOT! HOT! HOT!!
MY HAIR! MY HAIR!
SORRY. WENT A LITTLE OVER-BOARD.
LET KAIRI GO!

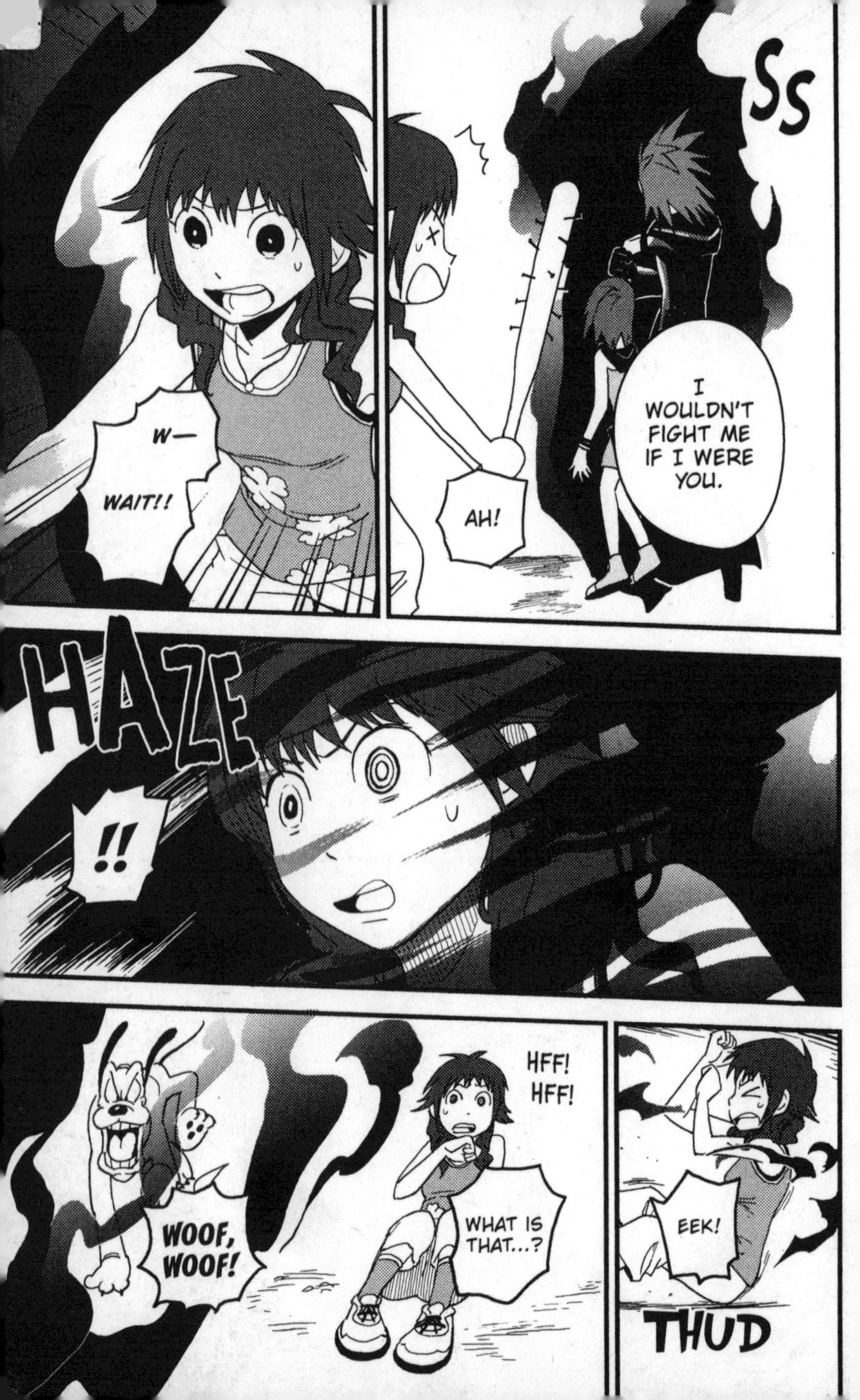
SS
I WOULDN'T FIGHT ME IF I WERE YOU.
AH!
W— WAIT!!
HAZE
!!
EEK!
THUD
HFF! HFF!
WHAT IS THAT...?
WOOF, WOOF!

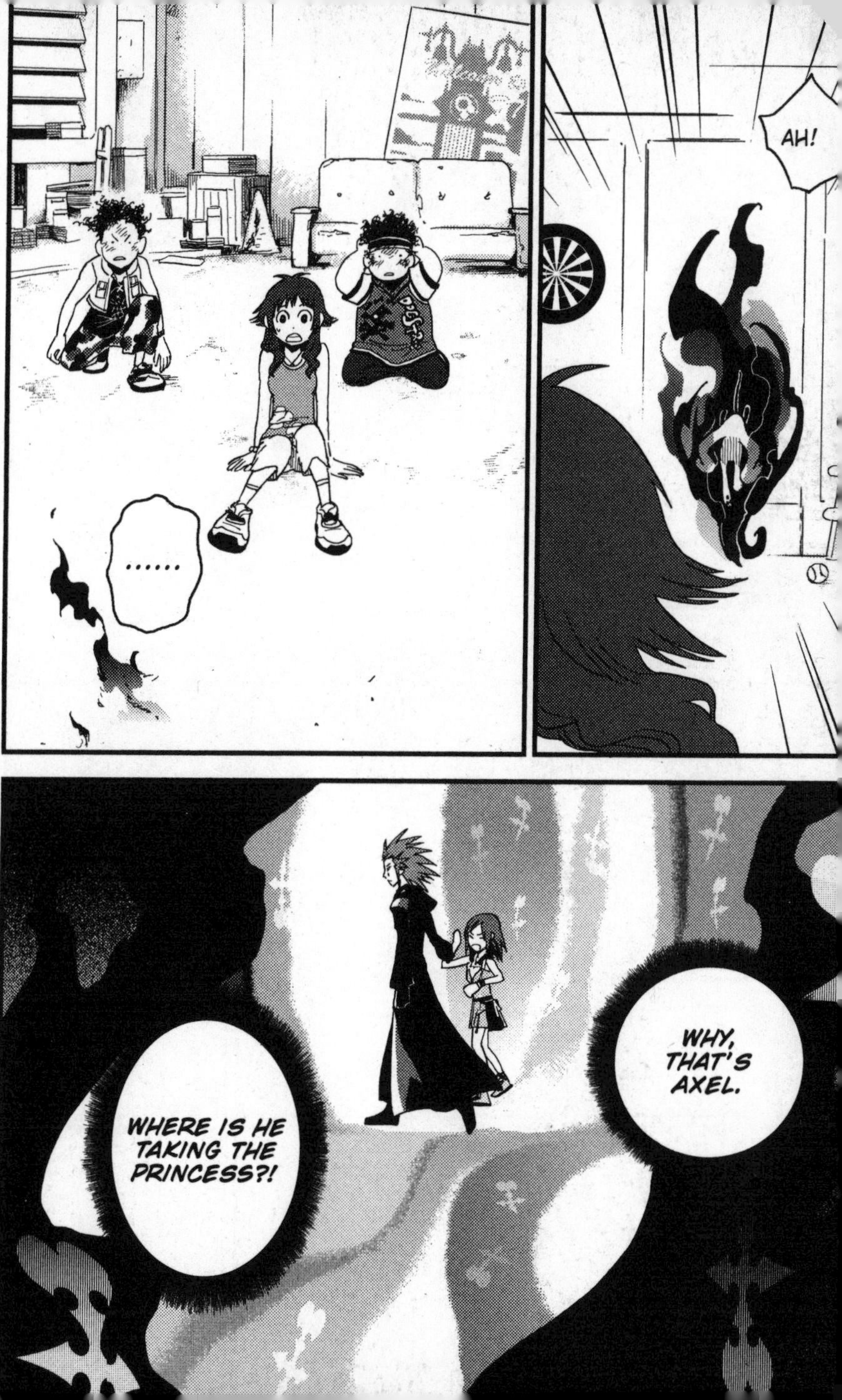
AH!
......
WHY, THAT'S AXEL.
WHERE IS HE TAKING THE PRINCESS?!

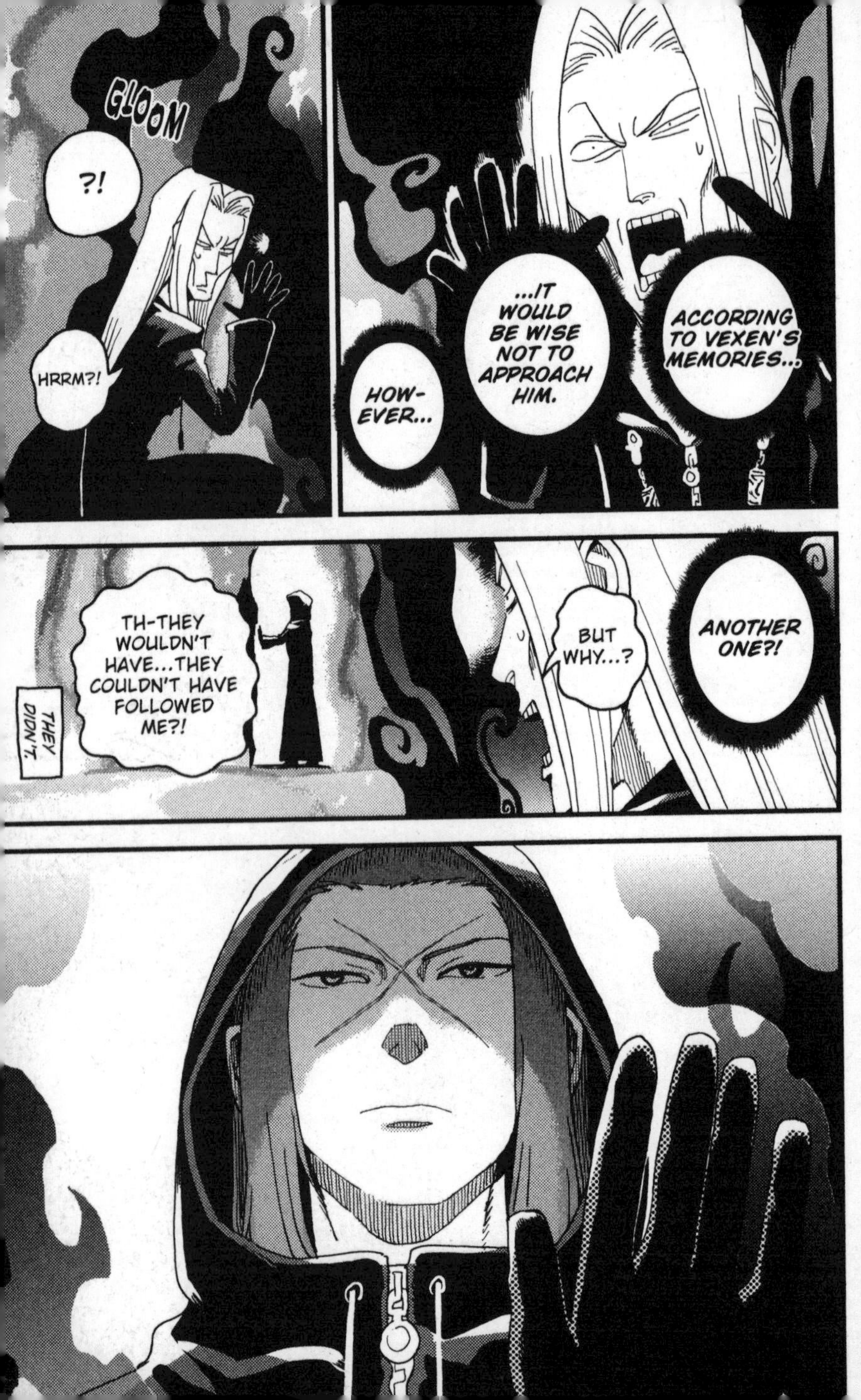
ACCORDING TO VEXEN'S MEMORIES...
...IT WOULD BE WISE NOT TO APPROACH HIM.
HOW-EVER...
GLOOM
?!
HRRM?!
ANOTHER ONE?!
BUT WHY...?
TH-THEY WOULDN'T HAVE...THEY COULDN'T HAVE FOLLOWED ME?!
THEY DIDN'T.

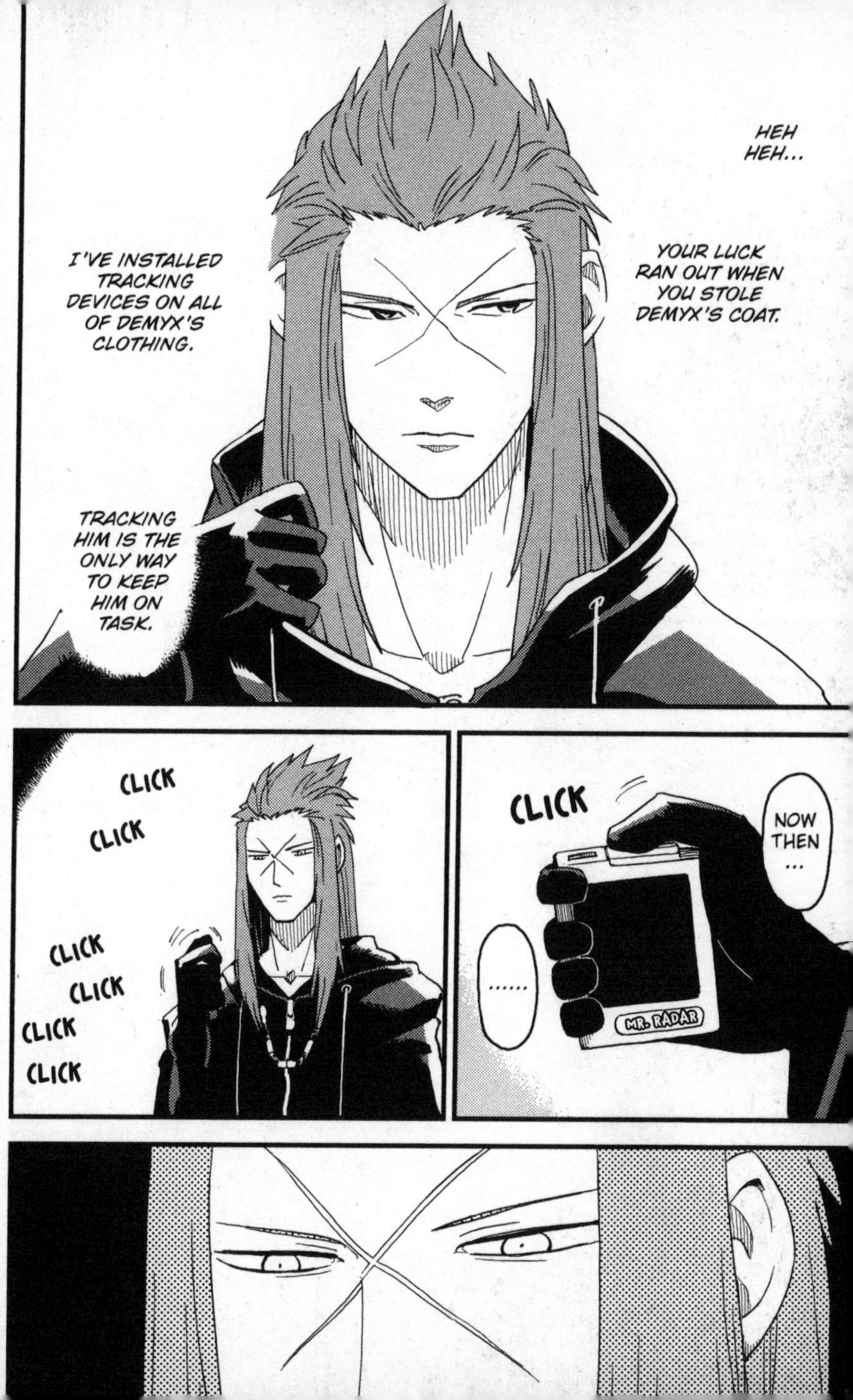
HEH HEH...
YOUR LUCK RAN OUT WHEN YOU STOLE DEMYX'S COAT.
I'VE INSTALLED TRACKING DEVICES ON ALL OF DEMYX'S CLOTHING.
TRACKING HIM IS THE ONLY WAY TO KEEP HIM ON TASK.
NOW THEN ...
CLICK
MR. RADAR
......
CLICK
CLICK
CLICK
CLICK
CLICK
CLICK

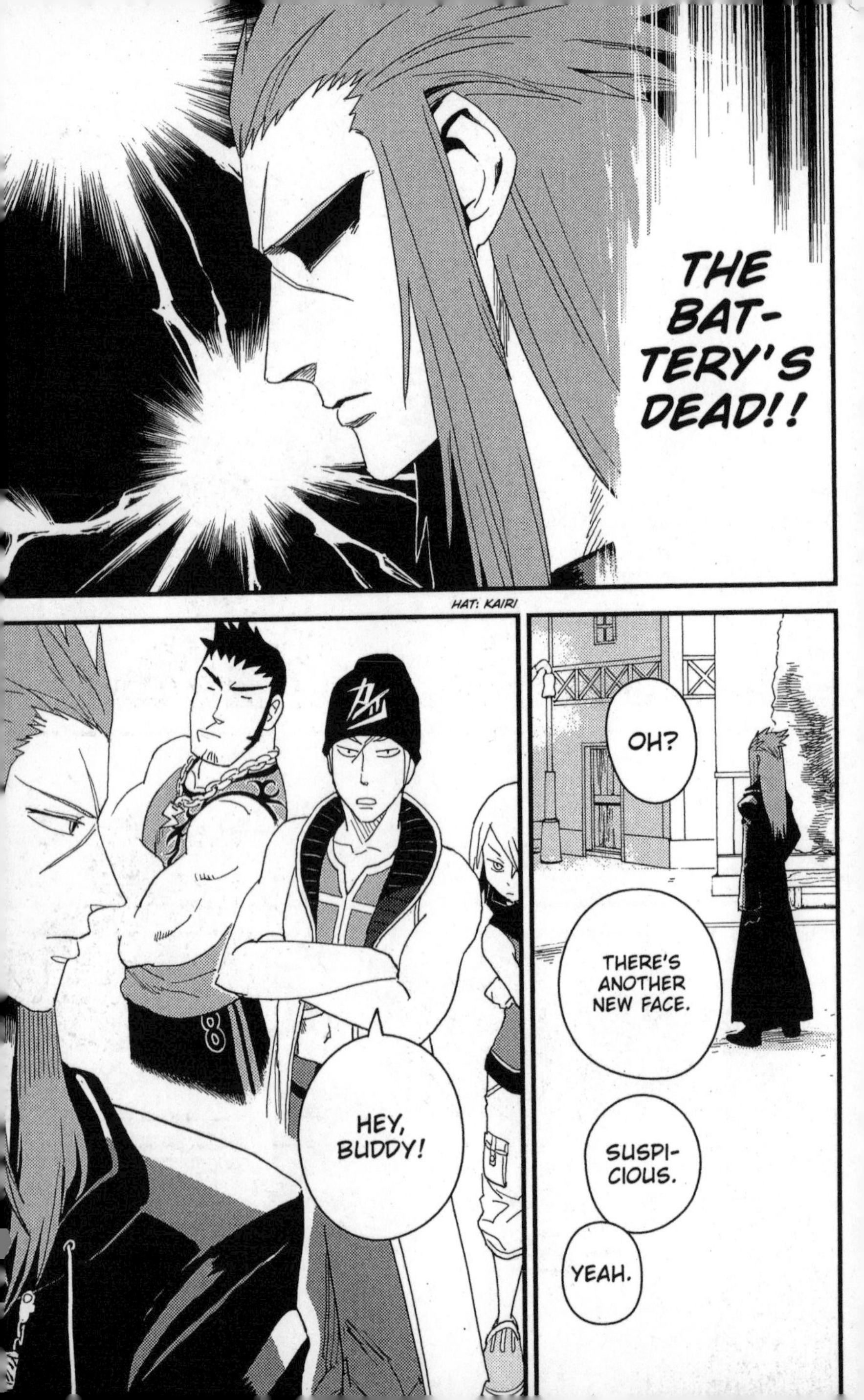
THE BAT-
TERY'S
DEAD!!
HAT: KAIRI
OH?
THERE'S ANOTHER NEW FACE.
SUSPI-
CIOUS.
YEAH.
HEY, BUDDY!

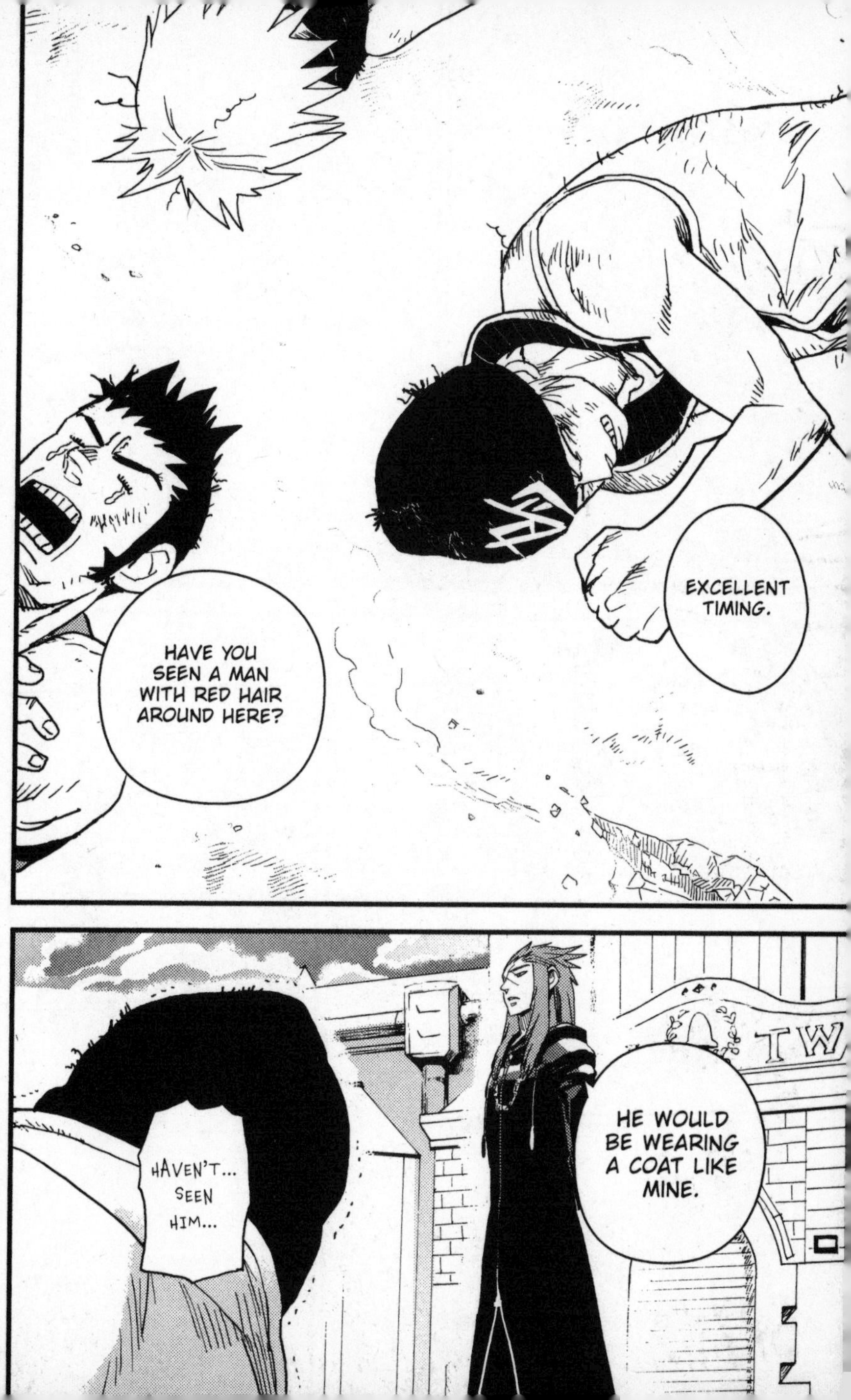
EXCELLENT TIMING.
HAVE YOU SEEN A MAN WITH RED HAIR AROUND HERE?
HE WOULD BE WEARING A COAT LIKE MINE.
HAVEN'T... SEEN HIM...

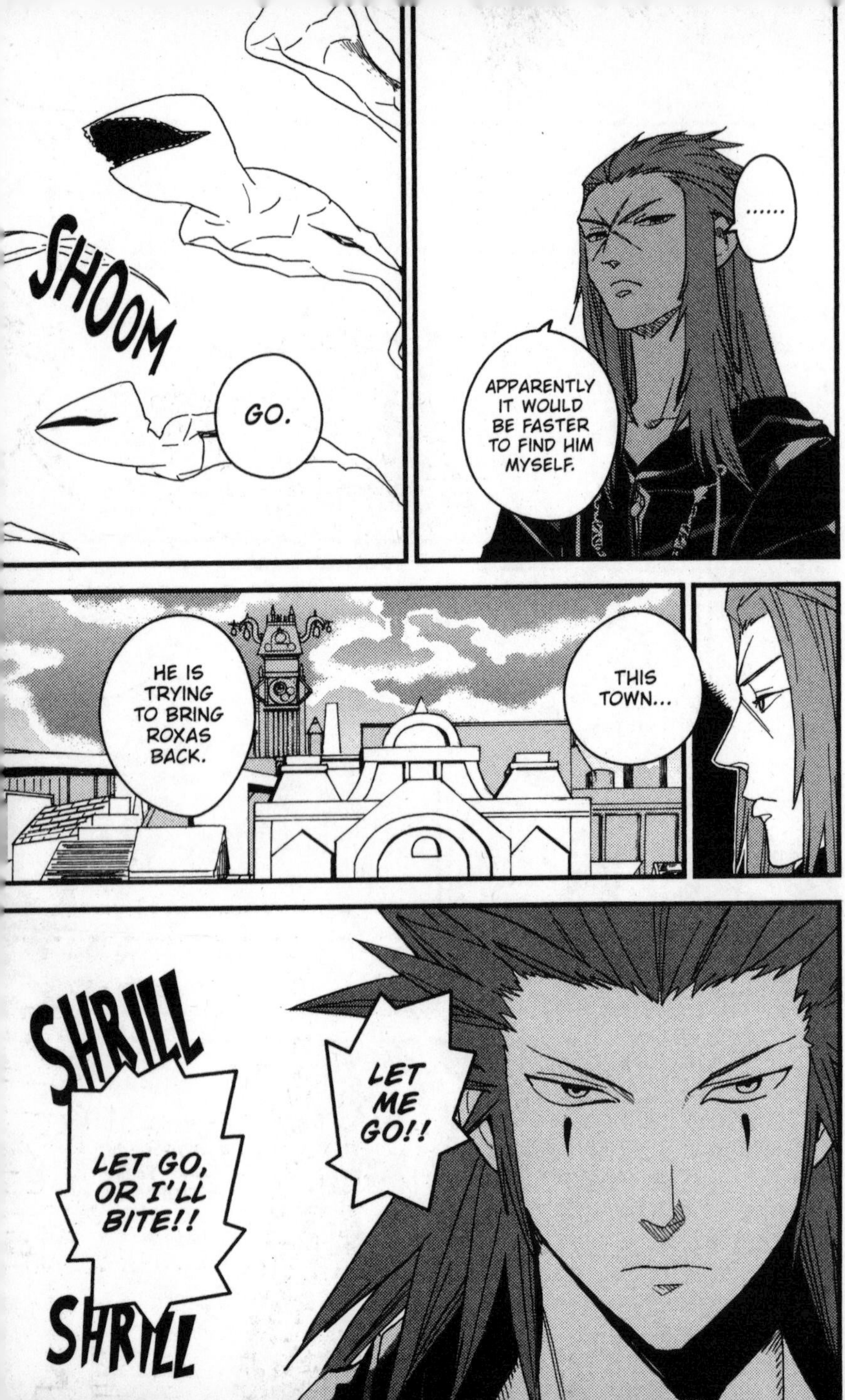
......
APPARENTLY IT WOULD BE FASTER TO FIND HIM MYSELF.
SHOOM
GO.
THIS TOWN...
HE IS TRYING TO BRING ROXAS BACK.
LET ME GO!!
SHRILL
LET GO, OR I'LL BITE!!
SHRILL

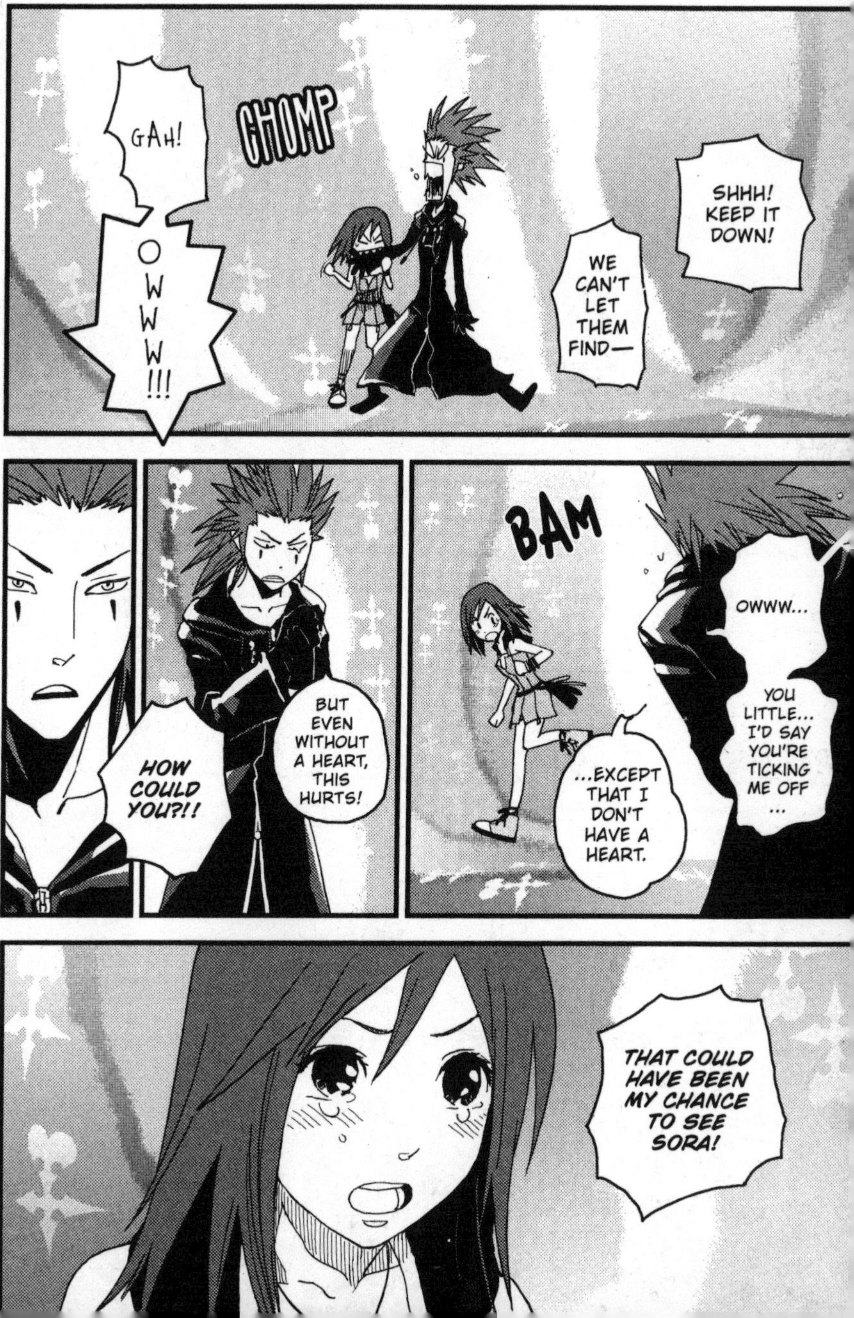
SHHH! KEEP IT DOWN!
WE CAN'T LET THEM FIND—
CHOMP
GAH!
OWWW!!!
OWWW...
YOU LITTLE... I'D SAY YOU'RE TICKING ME OFF...
BAM
...EXCEPT THAT I DON'T HAVE A HEART.
BUT EVEN WITHOUT A HEART, THIS HURTS!
HOW COULD YOU?!!
THAT COULD HAVE BEEN MY CHANCE TO SEE SORA!

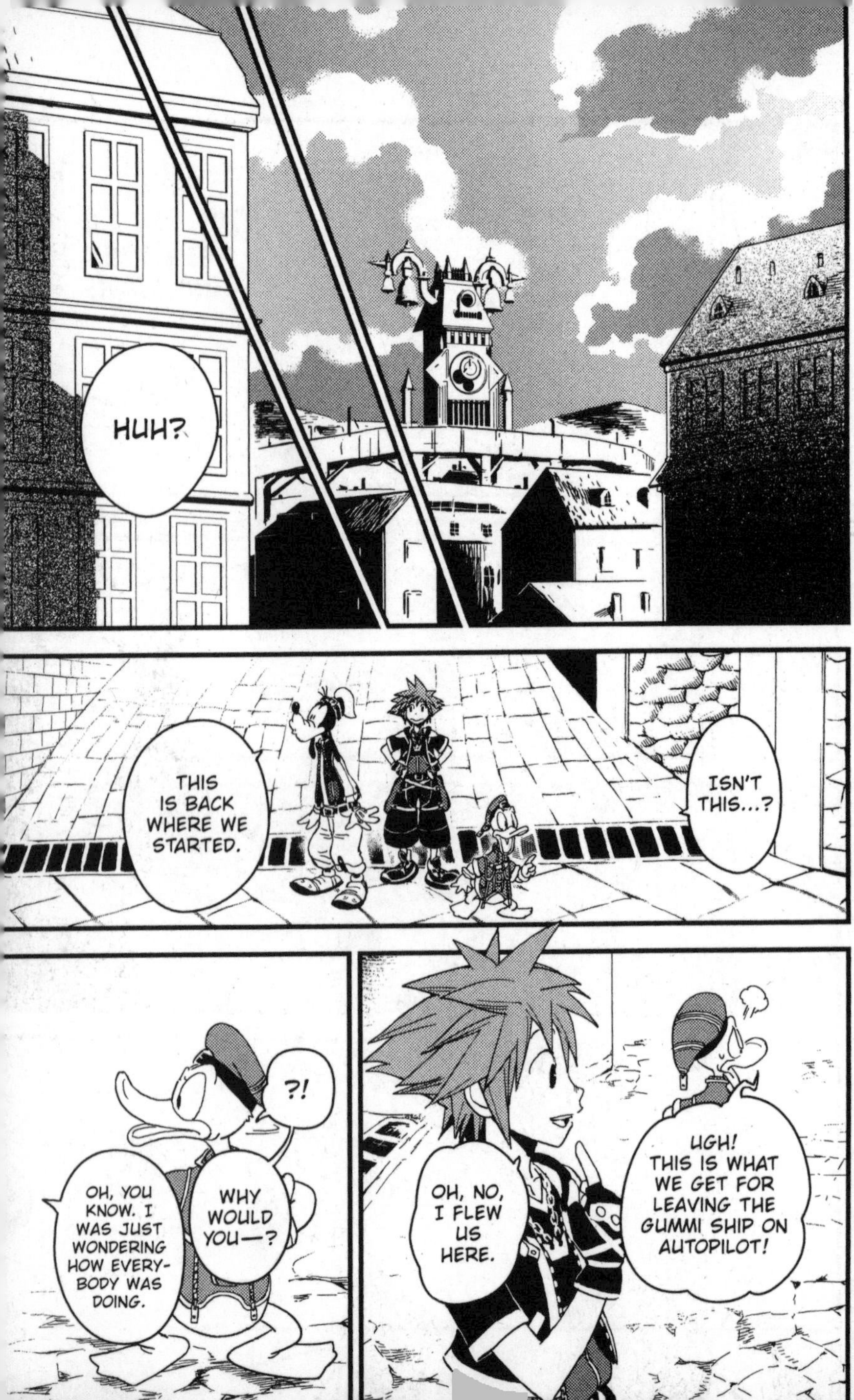
HUH?
ISN'T THIS...?
THIS IS BACK WHERE WE STARTED.
UGH! THIS IS WHAT WE GET FOR LEAVING THE GUMMI SHIP ON AUTOPILOT!
OH, NO, I FLEW US HERE.
?!
WHY WOULD YOU—?
OH, YOU KNOW. I WAS JUST WONDERING HOW EVERY-BODY WAS DOING.

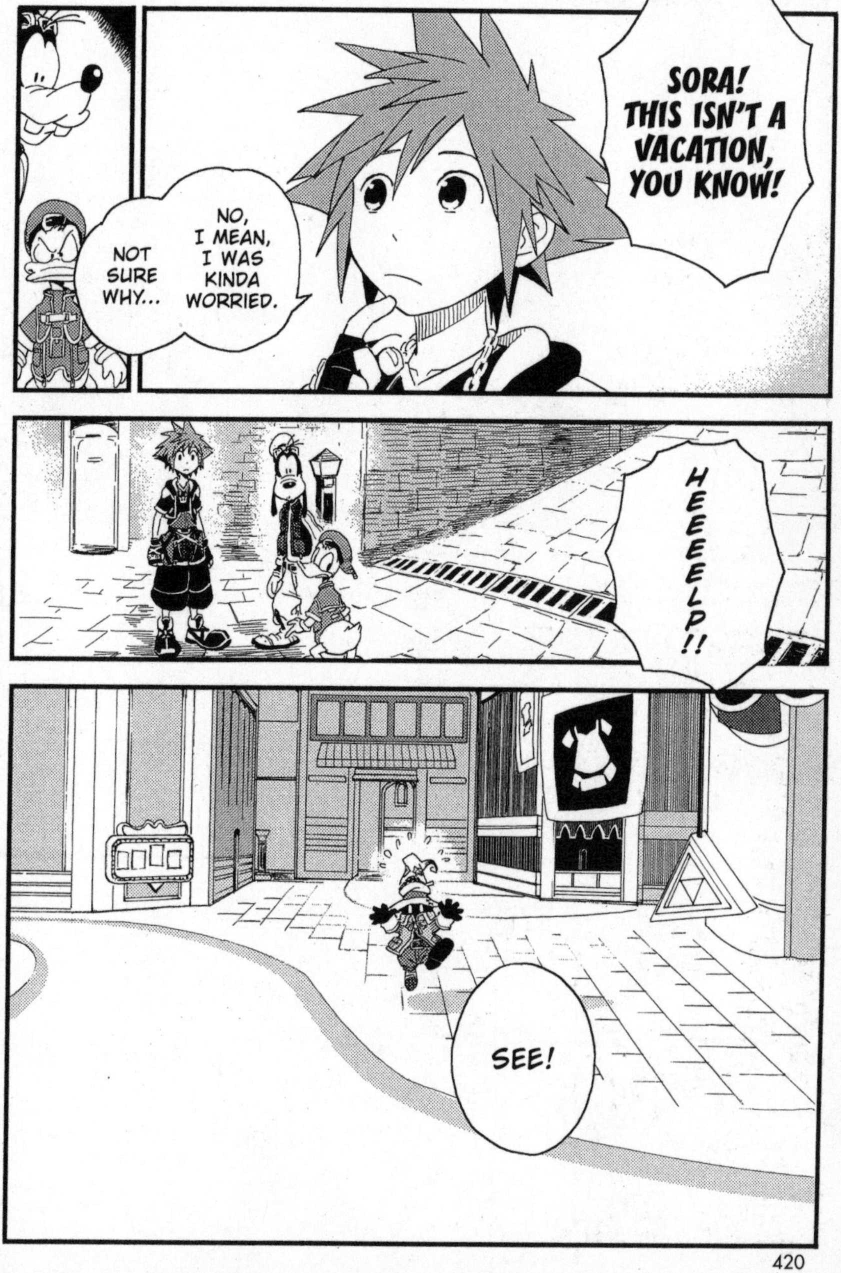
SORA! THIS ISN'T A VACATION, YOU KNOW!
NO, I MEAN, I WAS KINDA WORRIED.
NOT SURE WHY...
HEEEEELP!!
SEE!

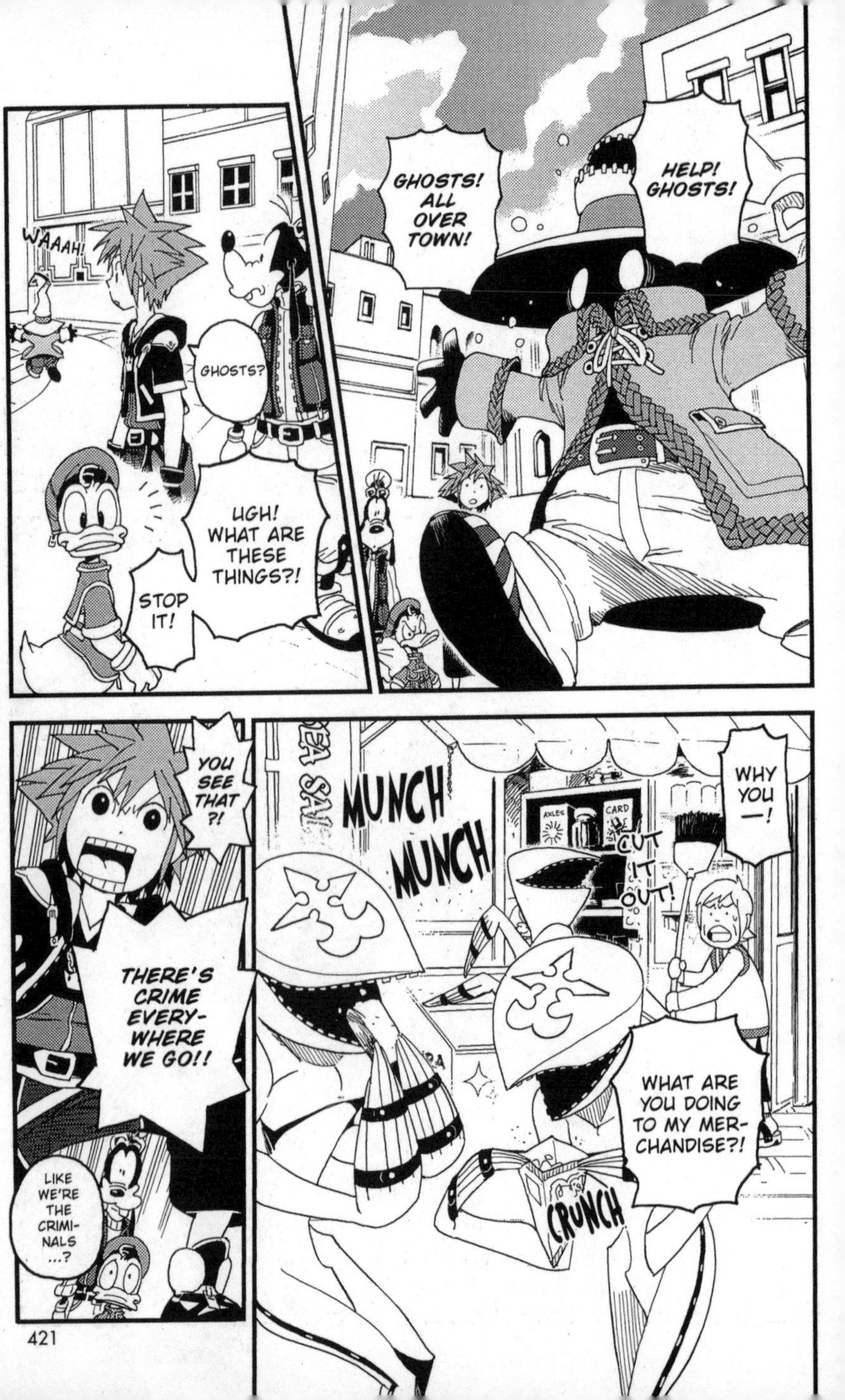
HELP! GHOSTS!
GHOSTS! ALL OVER TOWN!
WAAAH!
GHOSTS?
UGH! WHAT ARE THESE THINGS?!
STOP IT!
WHY YOU—!
MUNCH
MUNCH
AXLES
CARD
CUT IT OUT!
WHAT ARE YOU DOING TO MY MERCHANDISE?!
CRUNCH
YOU SEE THAT?!
THERE'S CRIME EVERYWHERE WE GO!!
LIKE WE'RE THE CRIMINALS...?

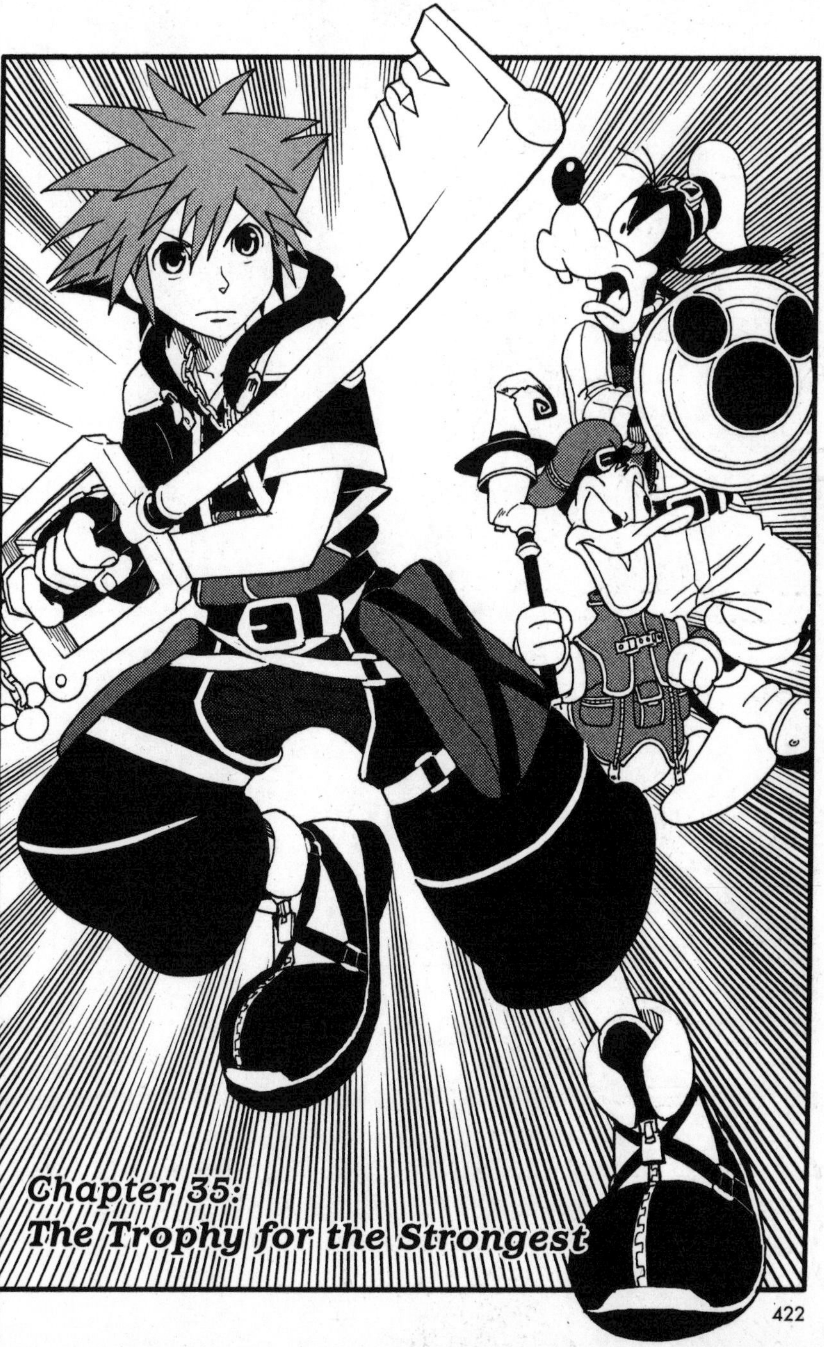
Chapter 35:
The Trophy for the Strongest

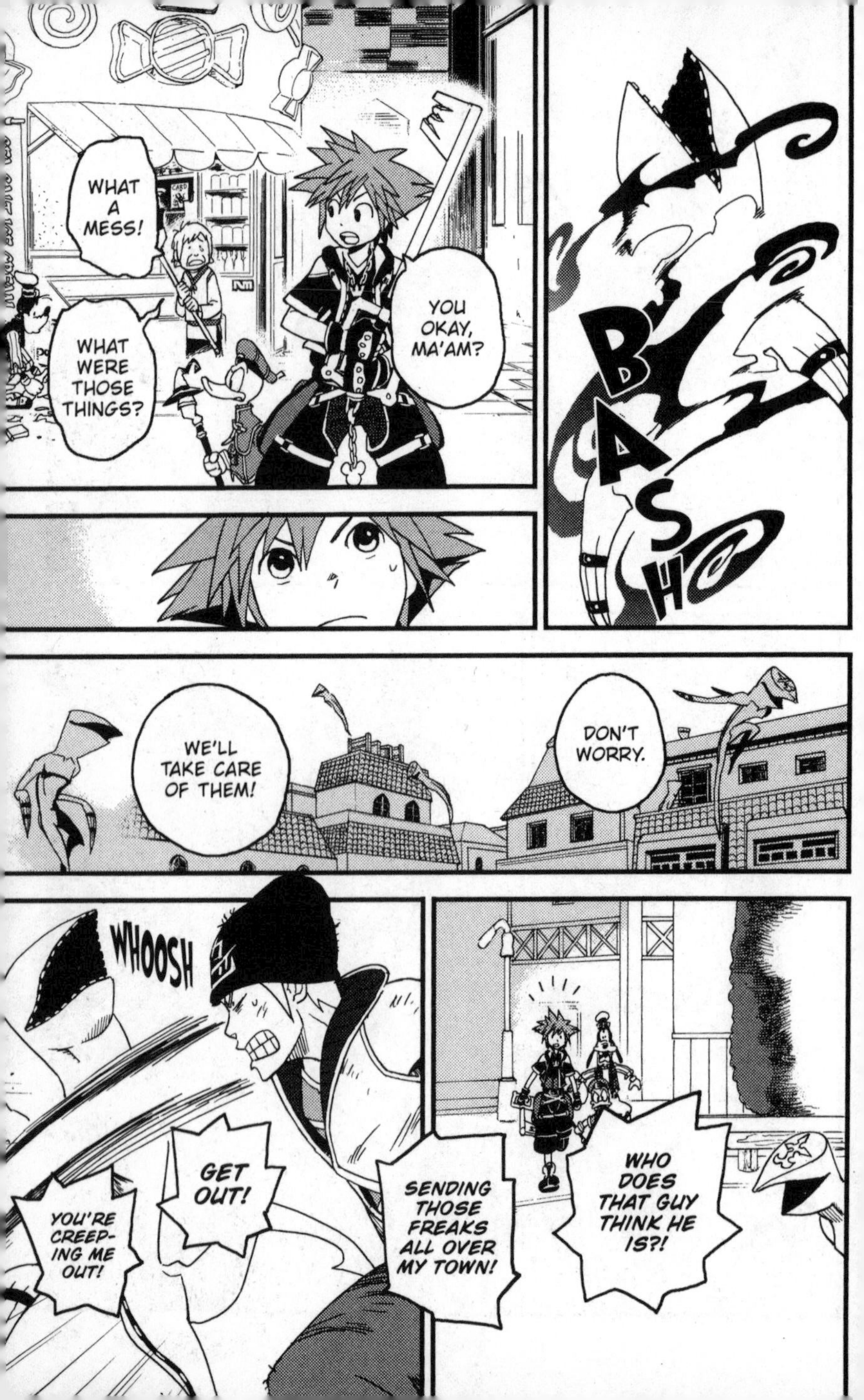
BASH
YOU OKAY, MA'AM?
WHAT A MESS!
WHAT WERE THOSE THINGS?
DON'T WORRY.
WE'LL TAKE CARE OF THEM!
WHO DOES THAT GUY THINK HE IS?!
SENDING THOSE FREAKS ALL OVER MY TOWN!
WHOOSH
GET OUT!
YOU'RE CREEP-ING ME OUT!

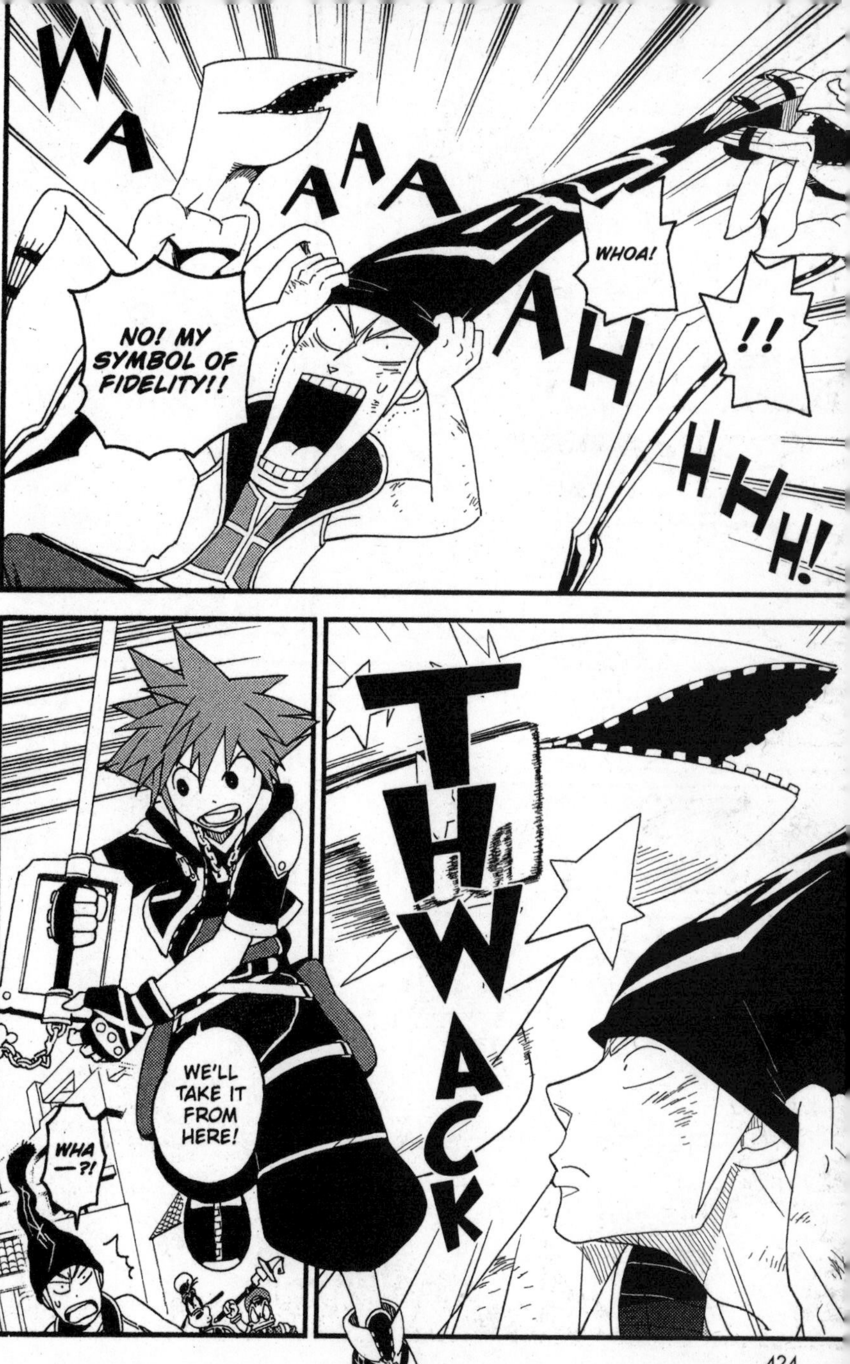
WHOA!
!!
WAAAAAHHHHH!
NO! MY SYMBOL OF FIDELITY!!
THWACK
WE'LL TAKE IT FROM HERE!
WHA—?!

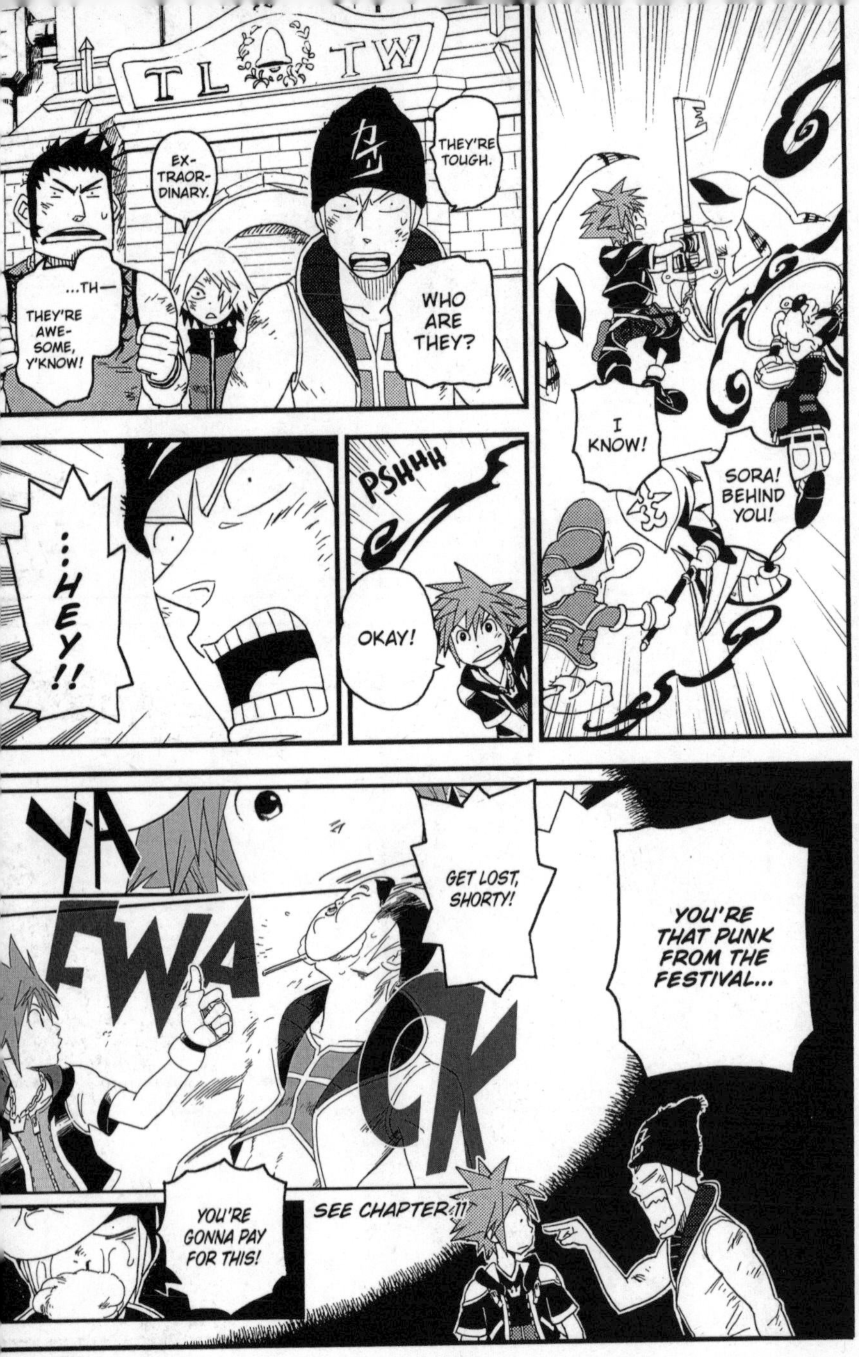
SORA! BEHIND YOU!
I KNOW!
THEY'RE TOUGH.
WHO ARE THEY?
EX-TRAORDINARY.
...TH—
THEY'RE AWESOME, Y'KNOW!
PSHHH
OKAY!
...HEY!!
YOU'RE THAT PUNK FROM THE FESTIVAL...
SEE CHAPTER 11
GET LOST, SHORTY!
YA
FWACK
YOU'RE GONNA PAY FOR THIS!

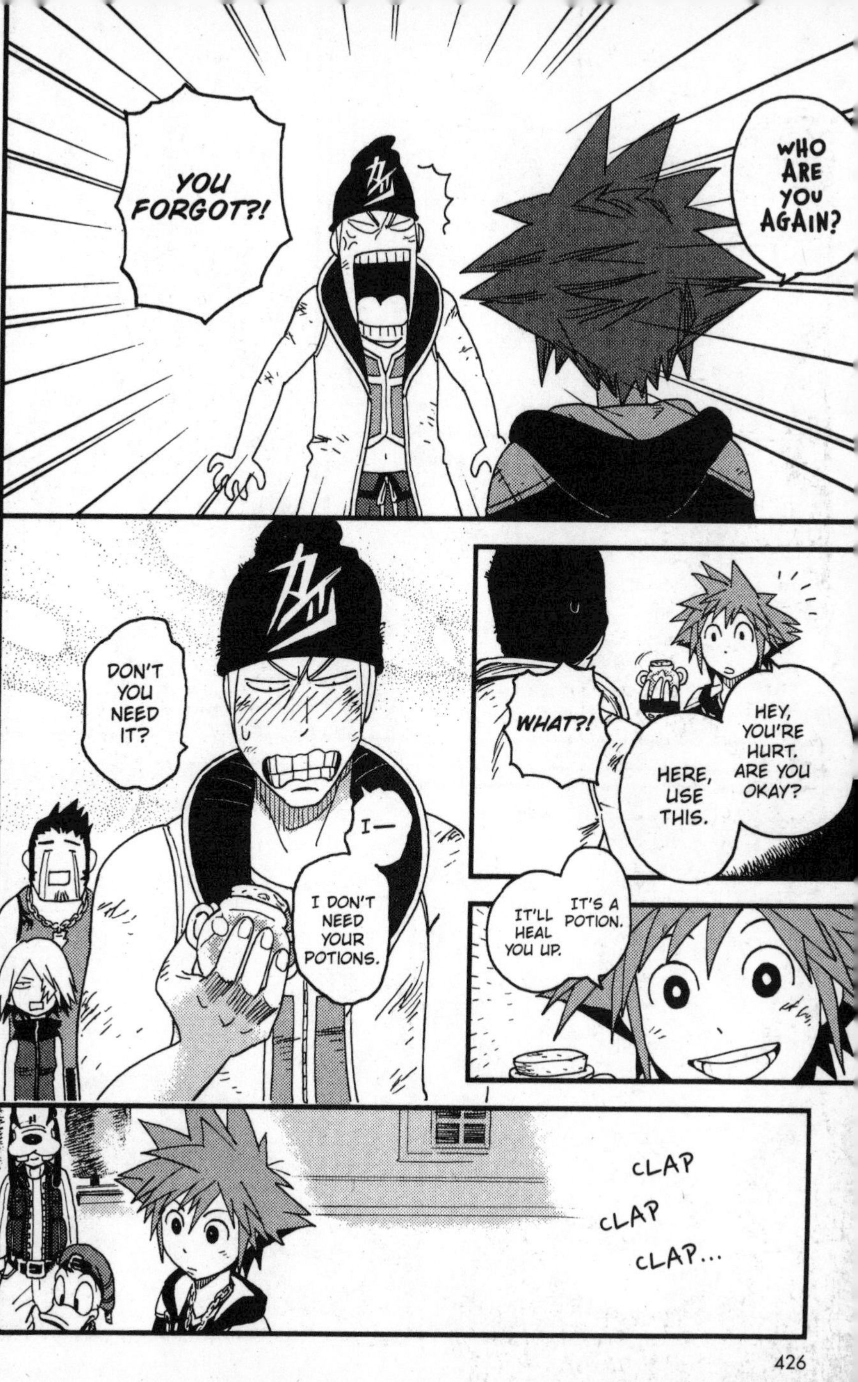
WHO ARE YOU AGAIN?
YOU FORGOT?!
HEY, YOU'RE HURT. ARE YOU OKAY?
HERE, USE THIS.
WHAT?!
IT'S A POTION.
IT'LL HEAL YOU UP.
DON'T YOU NEED IT?
I—
I DON'T NEED YOUR POTIONS.
CLAP
CLAP
CLAP...

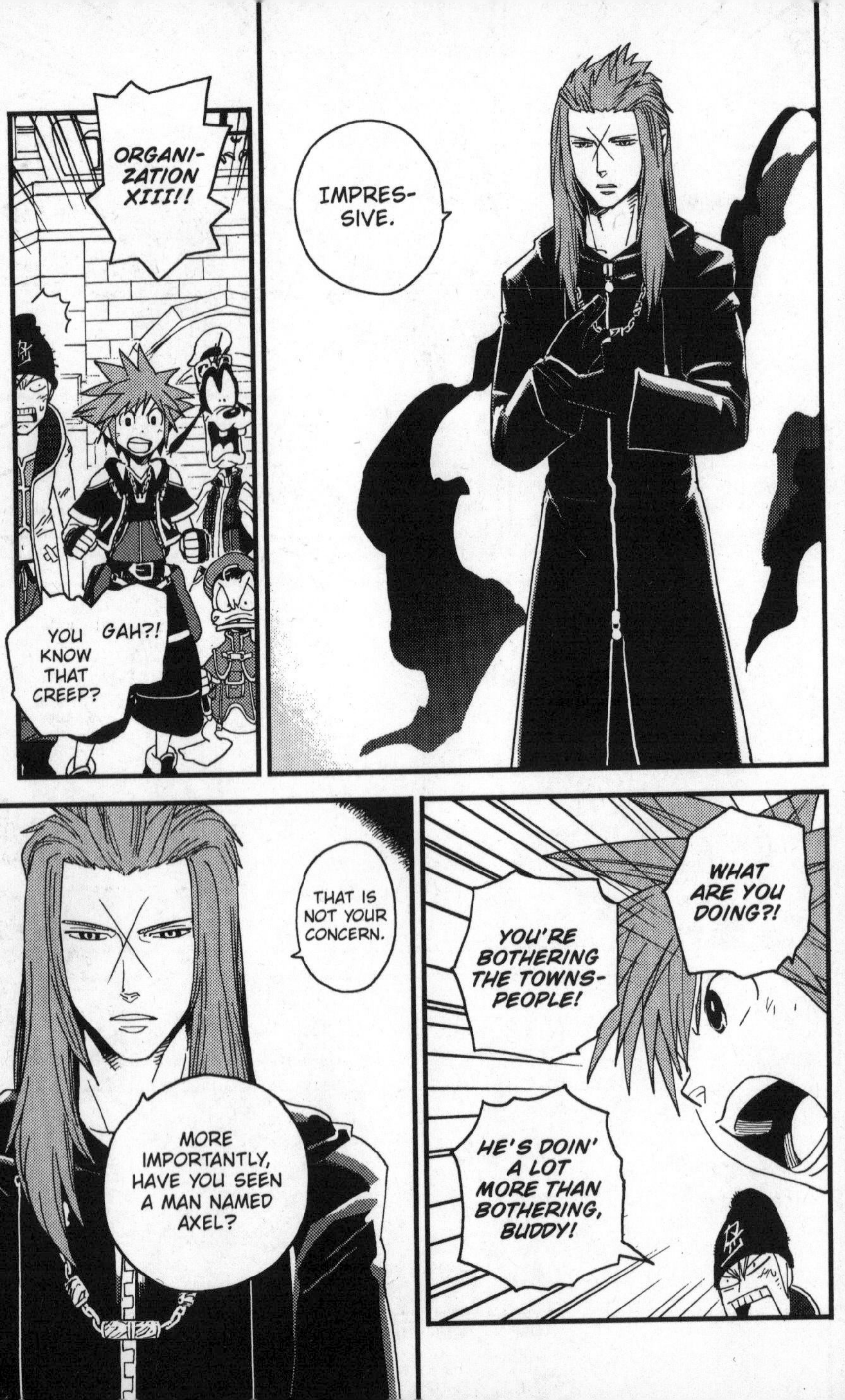
IMPRES-SIVE.
ORGANI-ZATION XIII!!
GAH?!
YOU KNOW THAT CREEP?
WHAT ARE YOU DOING?!
YOU'RE BOTHERING THE TOWNS-PEOPLE!
HE'S DOIN' A LOT MORE THAN BOTHERING, BUDDY!
THAT IS NOT YOUR CONCERN.
MORE IMPORTANTLY, HAVE YOU SEEN A MAN NAMED AXEL?

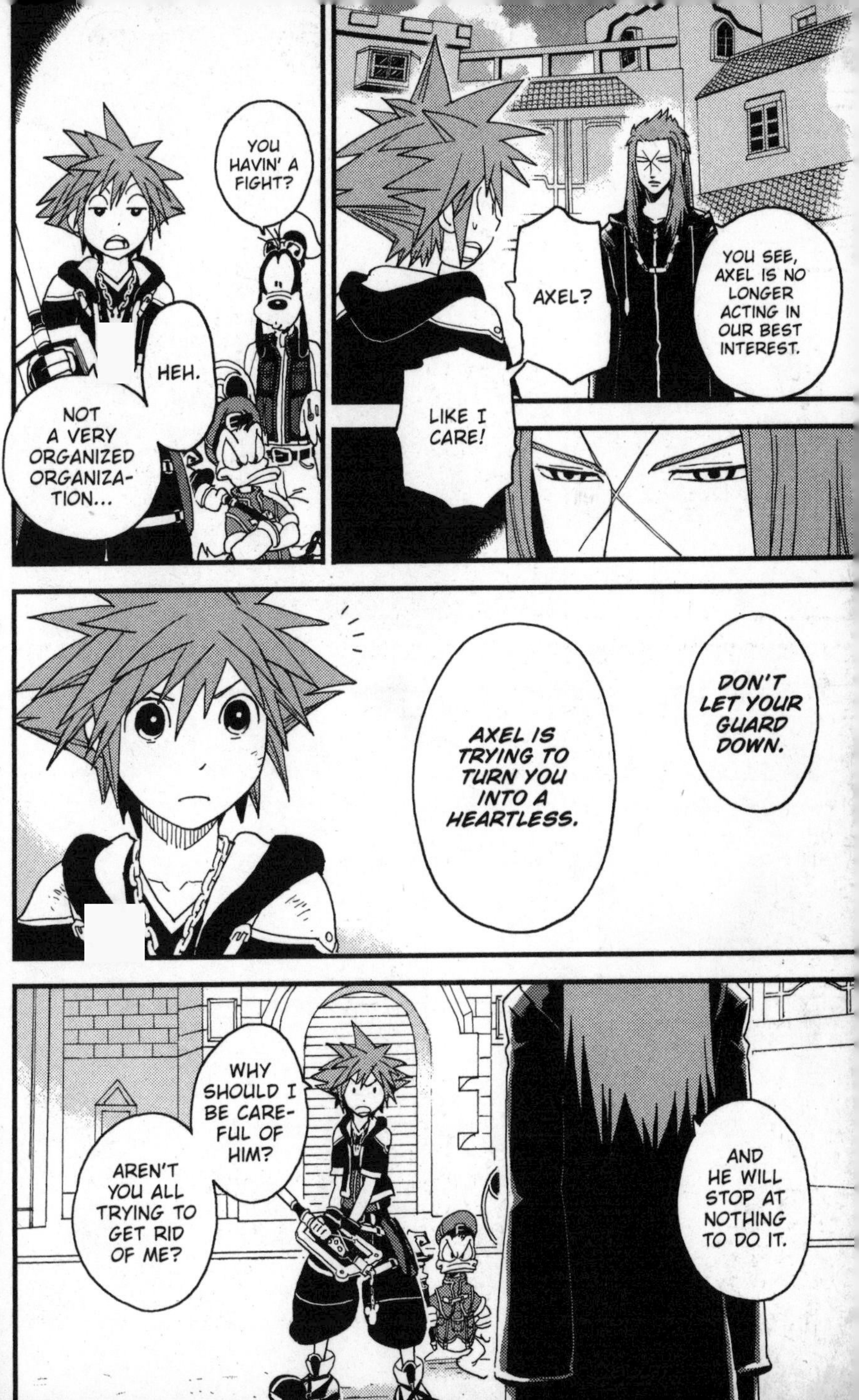
YOU SEE, AXEL IS NO LONGER ACTING IN OUR BEST INTEREST.
AXEL?
LIKE I CARE!
YOU HAVIN' A FIGHT?
HEH.
NOT A VERY ORGANIZED ORGANIZA-TION...
DON'T LET YOUR GUARD DOWN.
AXEL IS TRYING TO TURN YOU INTO A HEARTLESS.
AND HE WILL STOP AT NOTHING TO DO IT.
WHY SHOULD I BE CARE-FUL OF HIM?
AREN'T YOU ALL TRYING TO GET RID OF ME?

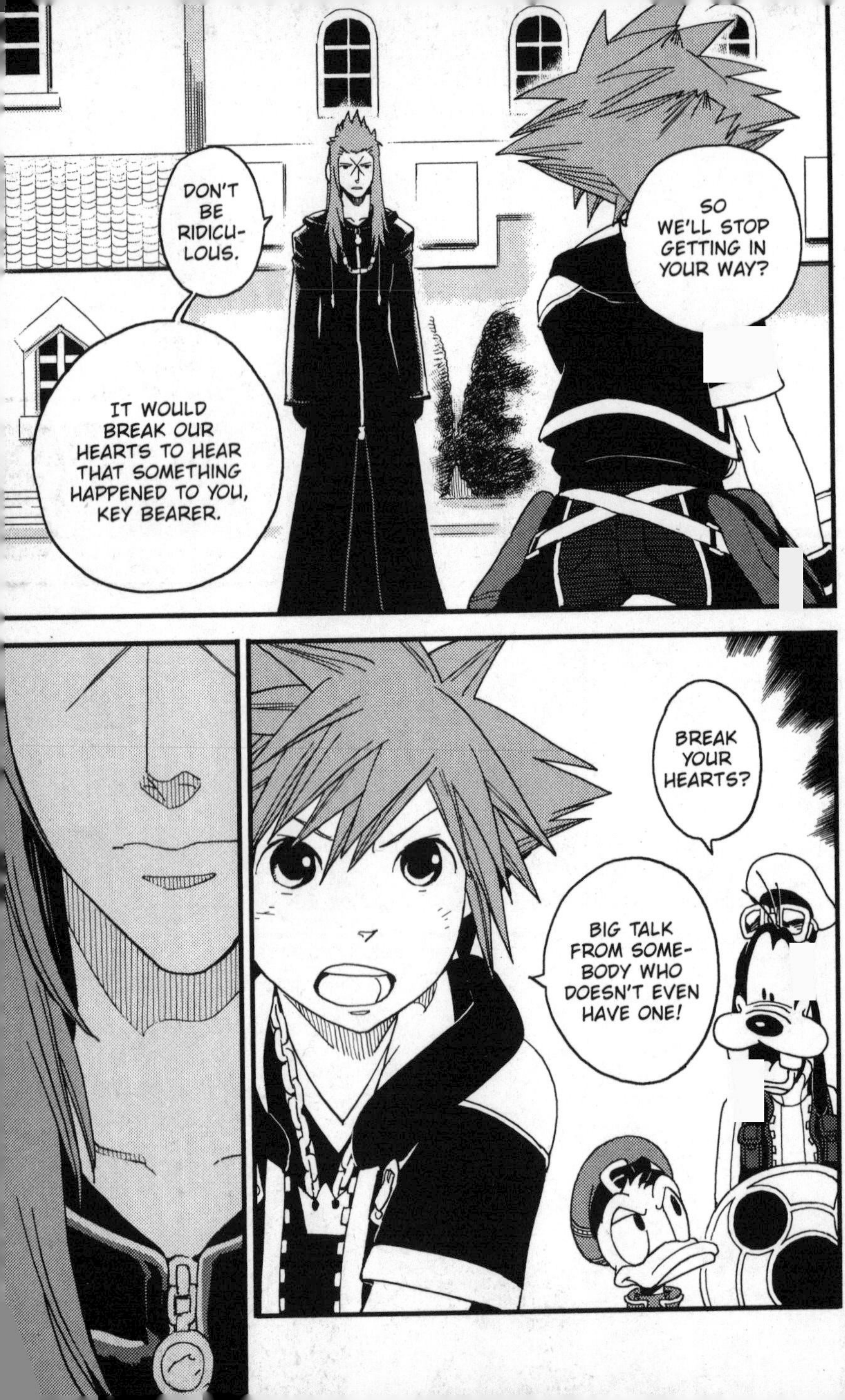
SO WE'LL STOP GETTING IN YOUR WAY?
DON'T BE RIDICU-LOUS.
IT WOULD BREAK OUR HEARTS TO HEAR THAT SOMETHING HAPPENED TO YOU, KEY BEARER.
BREAK YOUR HEARTS?
BIG TALK FROM SOME-BODY WHO DOESN'T EVEN HAVE ONE!

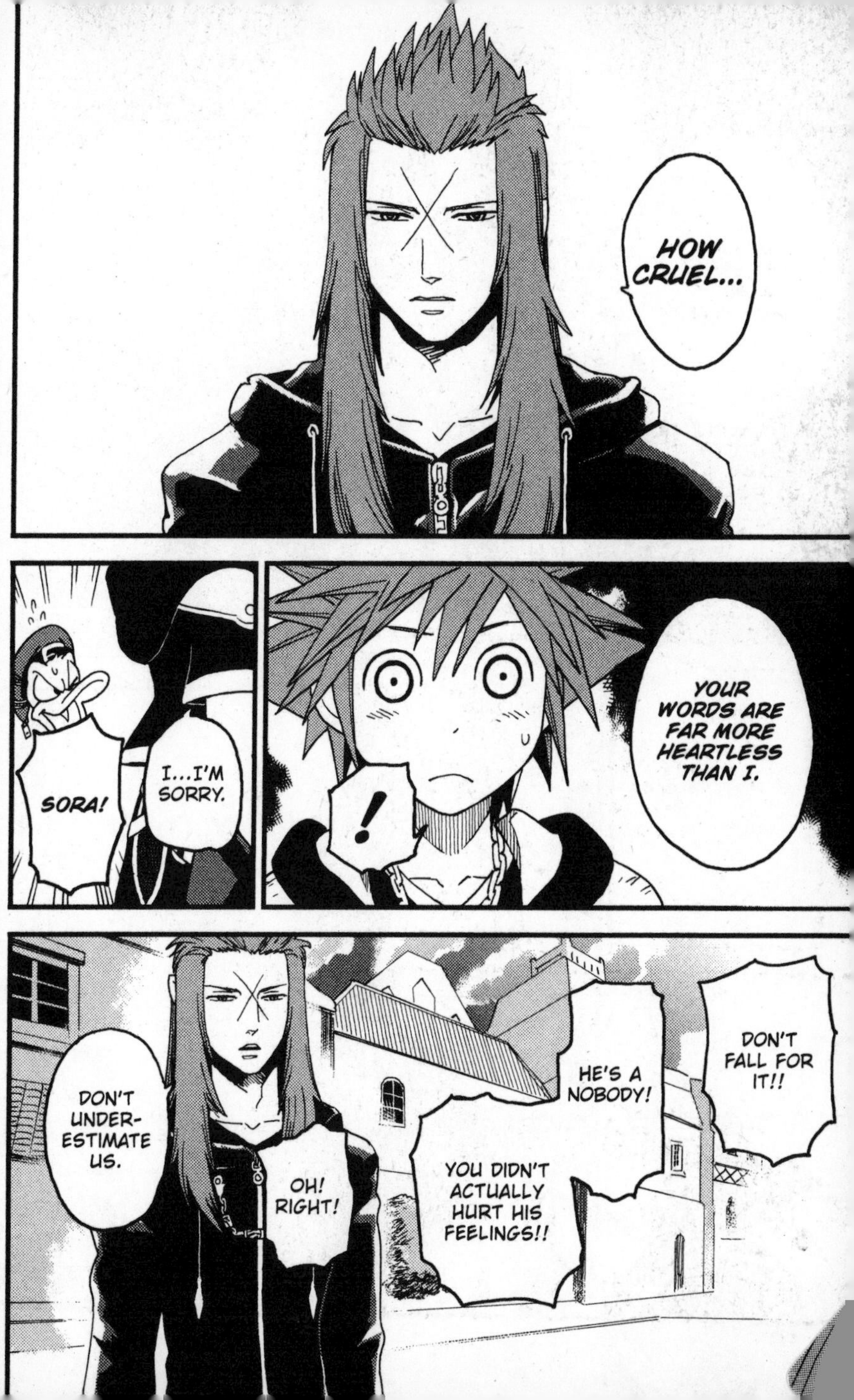
HOW CRUEL...
YOUR WORDS ARE FAR MORE HEARTLESS THAN I.
!
I...I'M SORRY.
SORA!
DON'T FALL FOR IT!!
HE'S A NOBODY!
YOU DIDN'T ACTUALLY HURT HIS FEELINGS!!
OH! RIGHT!
DON'T UNDER-ESTIMATE US.

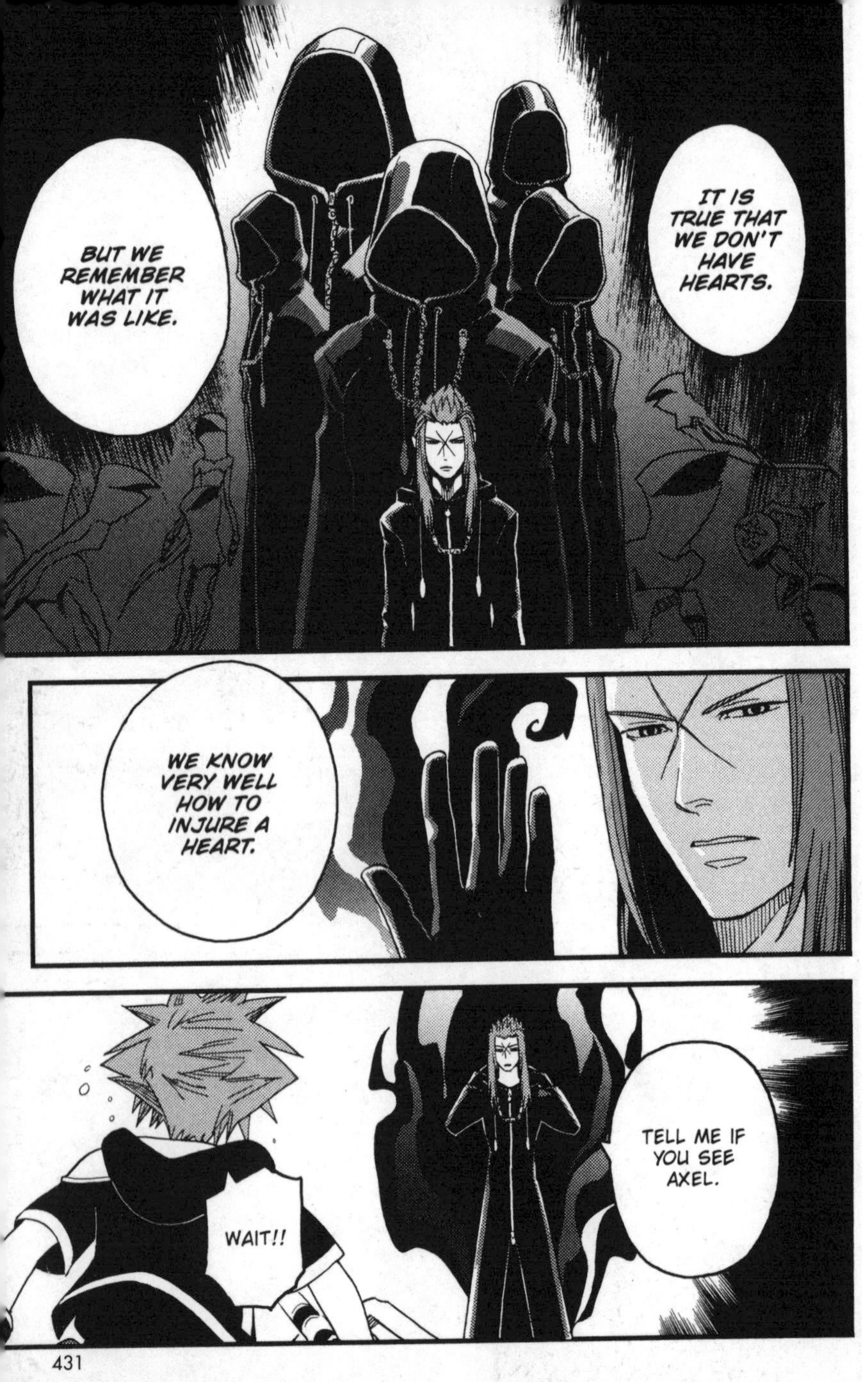
IT IS TRUE THAT WE DON'T HAVE HEARTS.
BUT WE REMEMBER WHAT IT WAS LIKE.
WE KNOW VERY WELL HOW TO INJURE A HEART.
TELL ME IF YOU SEE AXEL.
WAIT!!

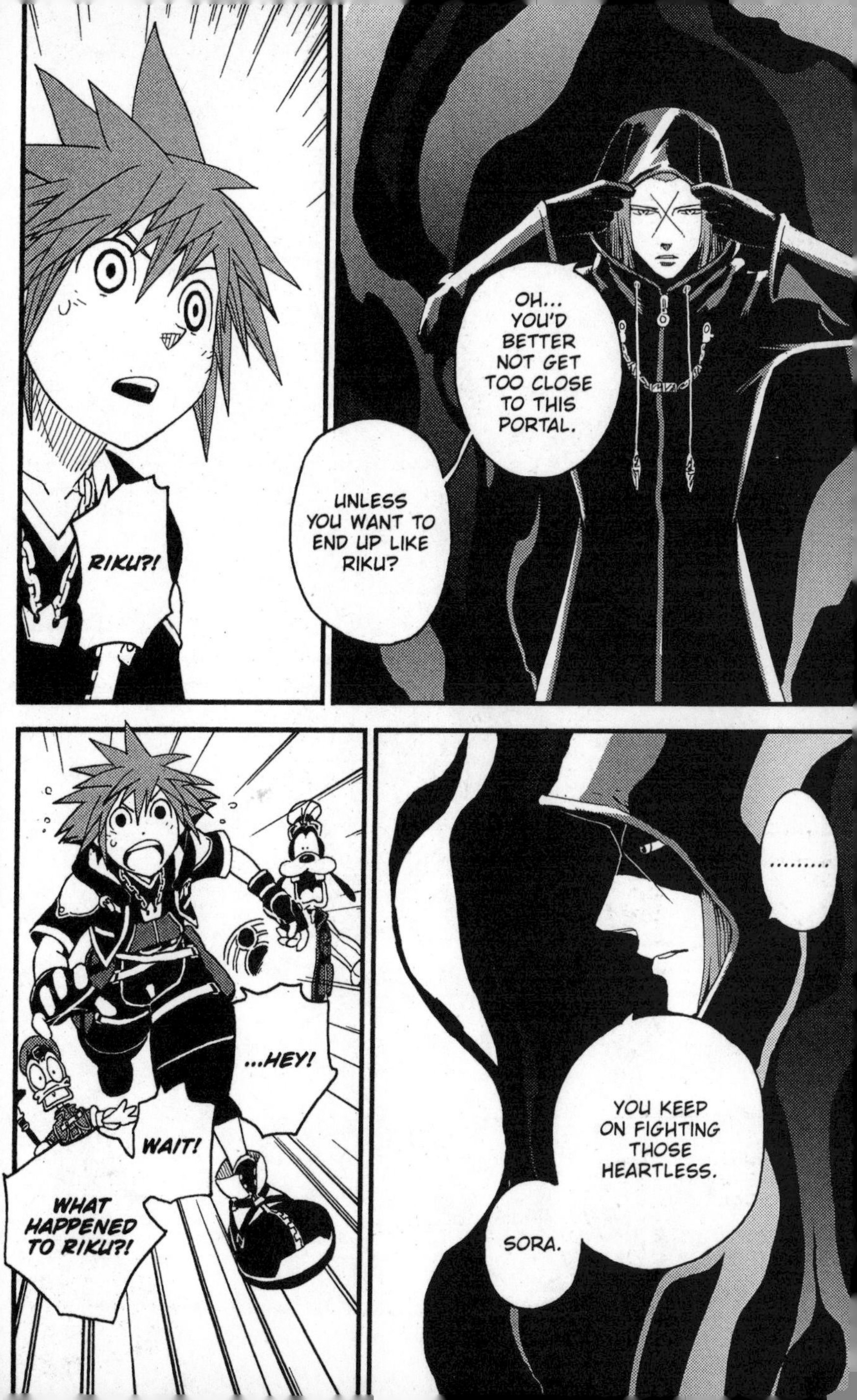
OH... YOU'D BETTER NOT GET TOO CLOSE TO THIS PORTAL.
UNLESS YOU WANT TO END UP LIKE RIKU?
RIKU?!
....
YOU KEEP ON FIGHTING THOSE HEARTLESS.
SORA.
...HEY!
WAIT!
WHAT HAPPENED TO RIKU?!

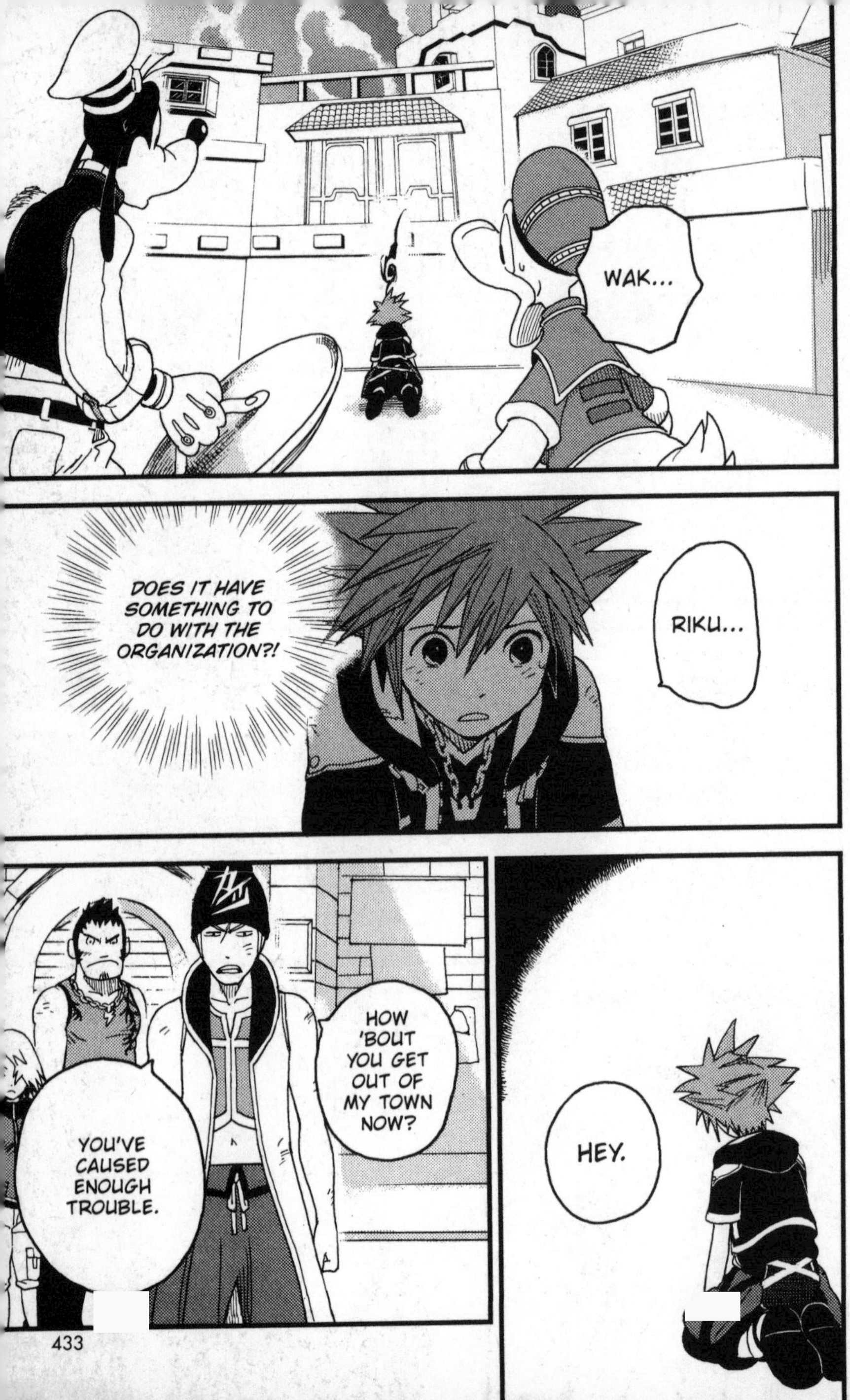
WAK...
RIKU...
DOES IT HAVE SOMETHING TO DO WITH THE ORGANIZATION?!
HEY.
HOW 'BOUT YOU GET OUT OF MY TOWN NOW?
YOU'VE CAUSED ENOUGH TROUBLE.

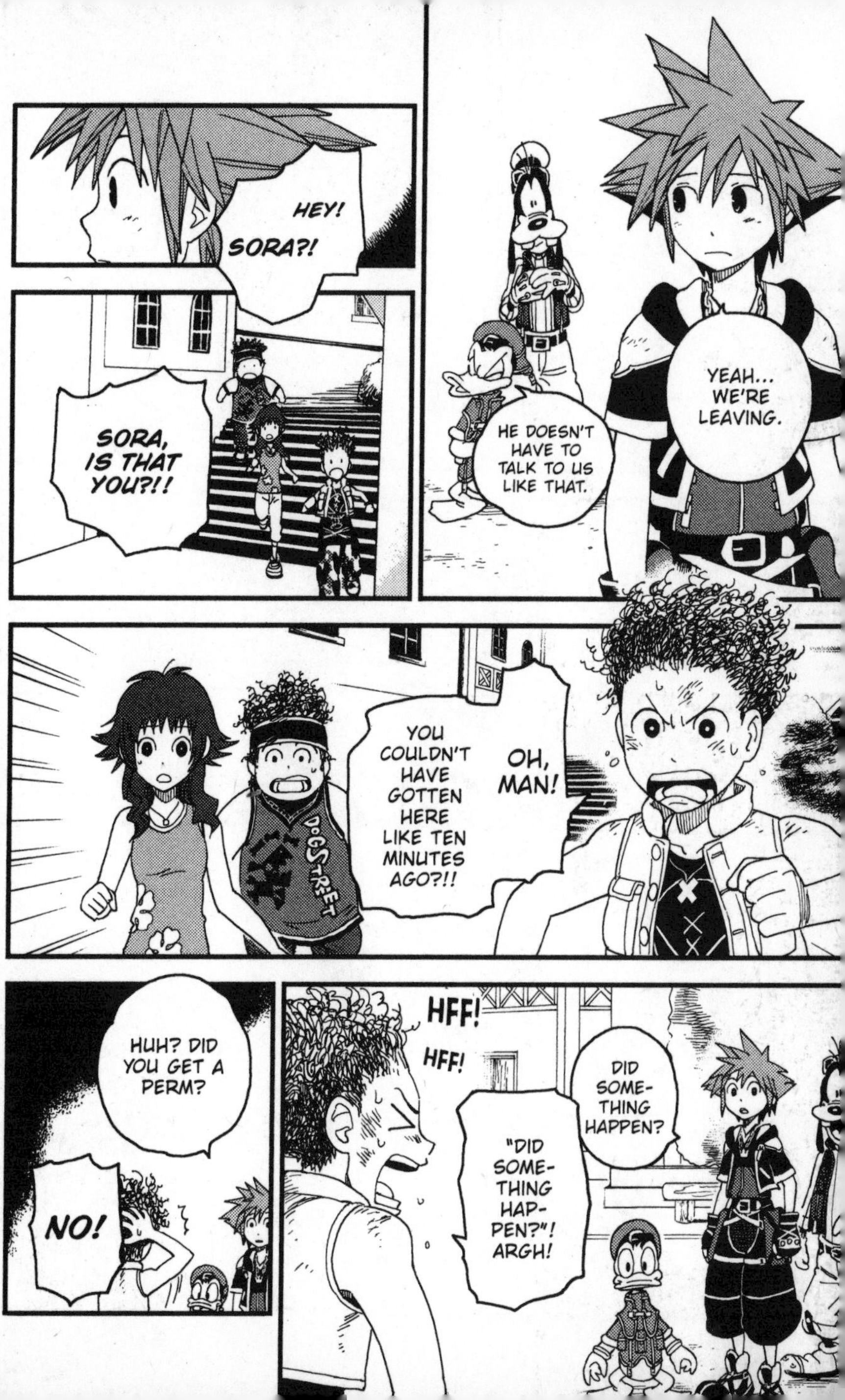
YEAH... WE'RE LEAVING.
HE DOESN'T HAVE TO TALK TO US LIKE THAT.
HEY! SORA?!
SORA, IS THAT YOU?!!
OH, MAN!
YOU COULDN'T HAVE GOTTEN HERE LIKE TEN MINUTES AGO?!!
HFF! HFF!
DID SOMETHING HAPPEN?
"DID SOMETHING HAPPEN?"! ARGH!
HUH? DID YOU GET A PERM?
NO!

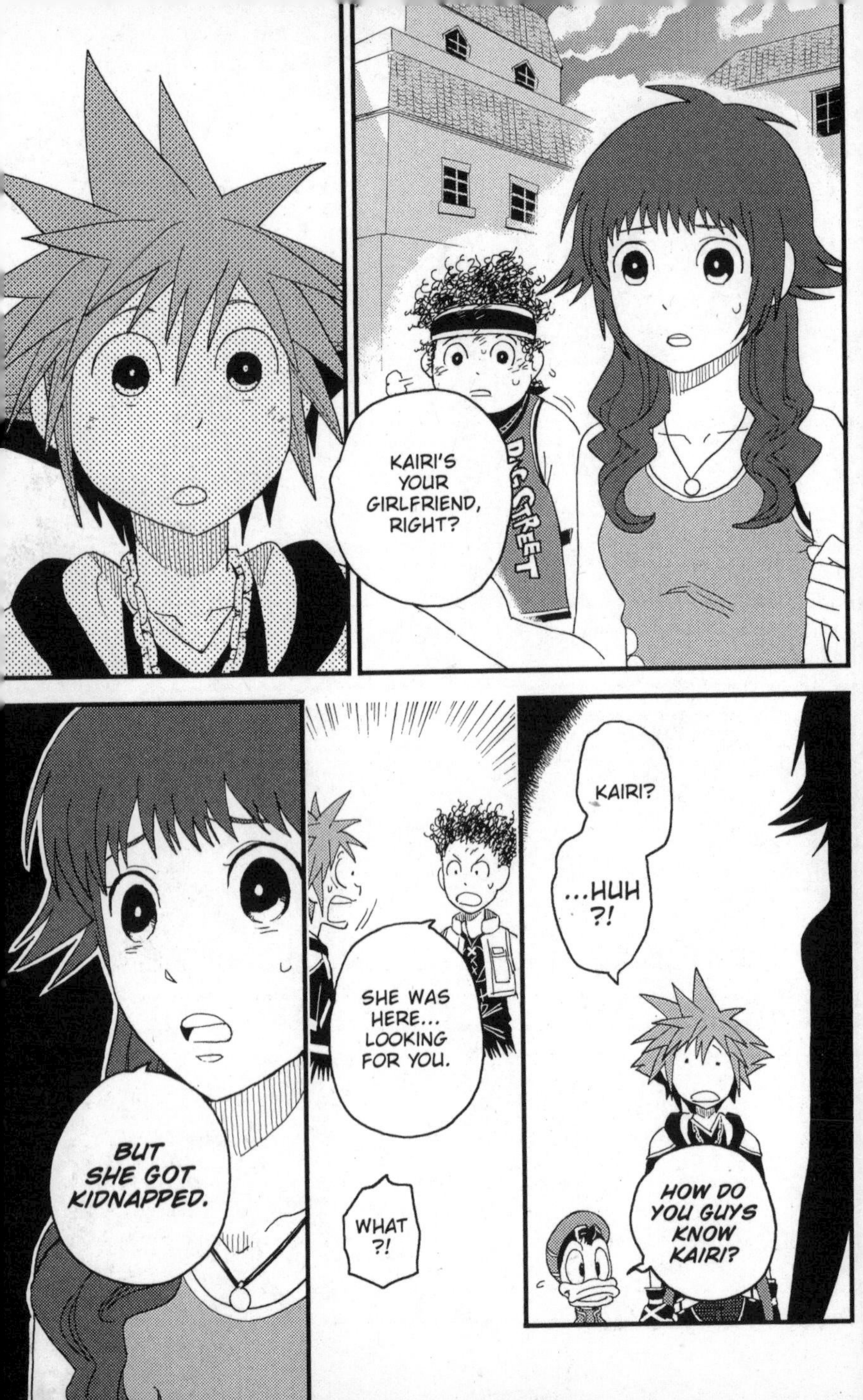
KAIRI'S YOUR GIRLFRIEND, RIGHT?
KAIRI?
...HUH ?!
HOW DO YOU GUYS KNOW KAIRI?
SHE WAS HERE... LOOKING FOR YOU.
WHAT ?!
BUT SHE GOT KIDNAPPED.

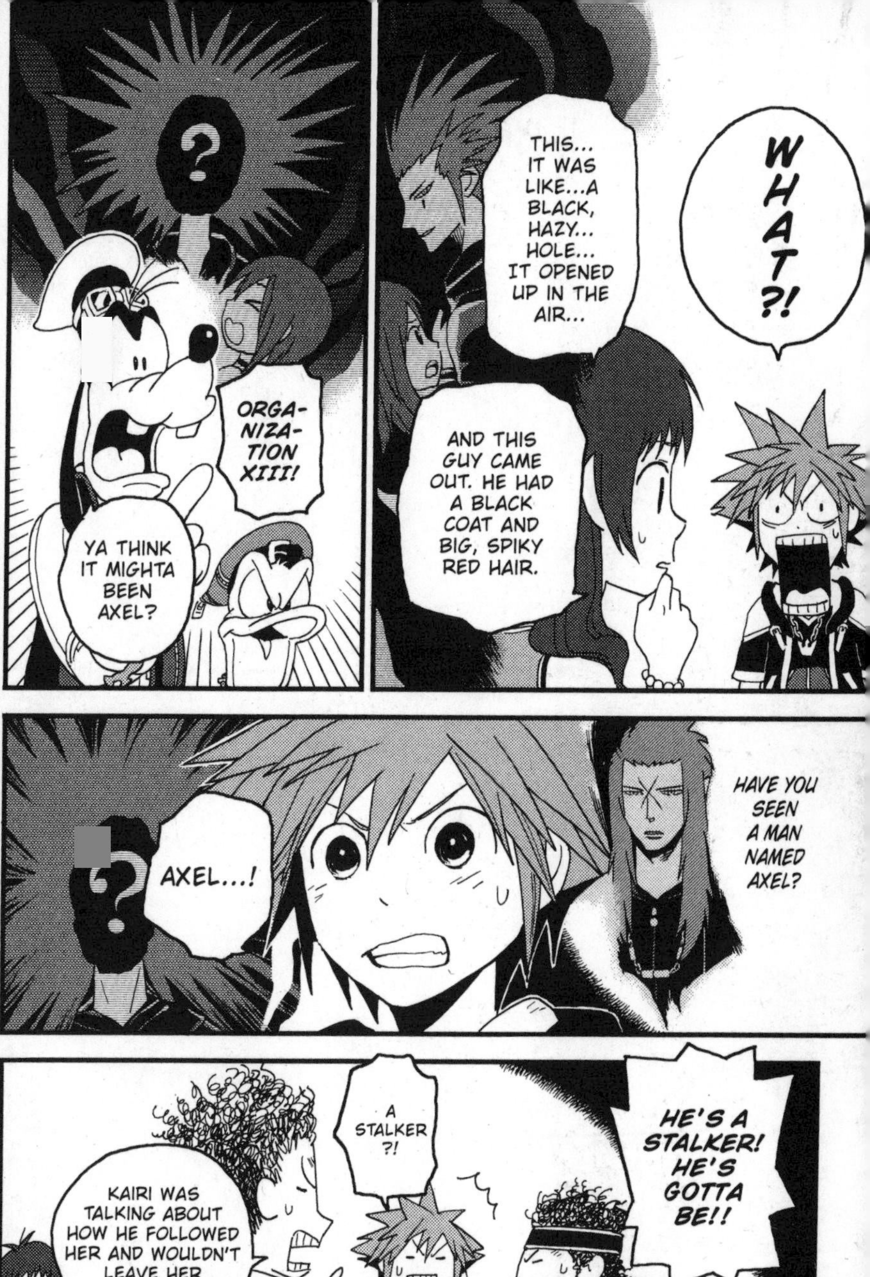
WHAT?!
THIS... IT WAS LIKE...A BLACK, HAZY... HOLE... IT OPENED UP IN THE AIR...
AND THIS GUY CAME OUT. HE HAD A BLACK COAT AND BIG, SPIKY RED HAIR.
ORGA-NIZA-TION XIII!
YA THINK IT MIGHTA BEEN AXEL?
HAVE YOU SEEN A MAN NAMED AXEL?
AXEL...!
HE'S A STALKER! HE'S GOTTA BE!!
A STALKER?!
KAIRI WAS TALKING ABOUT HOW HE FOLLOWED HER AND WOULDN'T LEAVE HER ALONE...

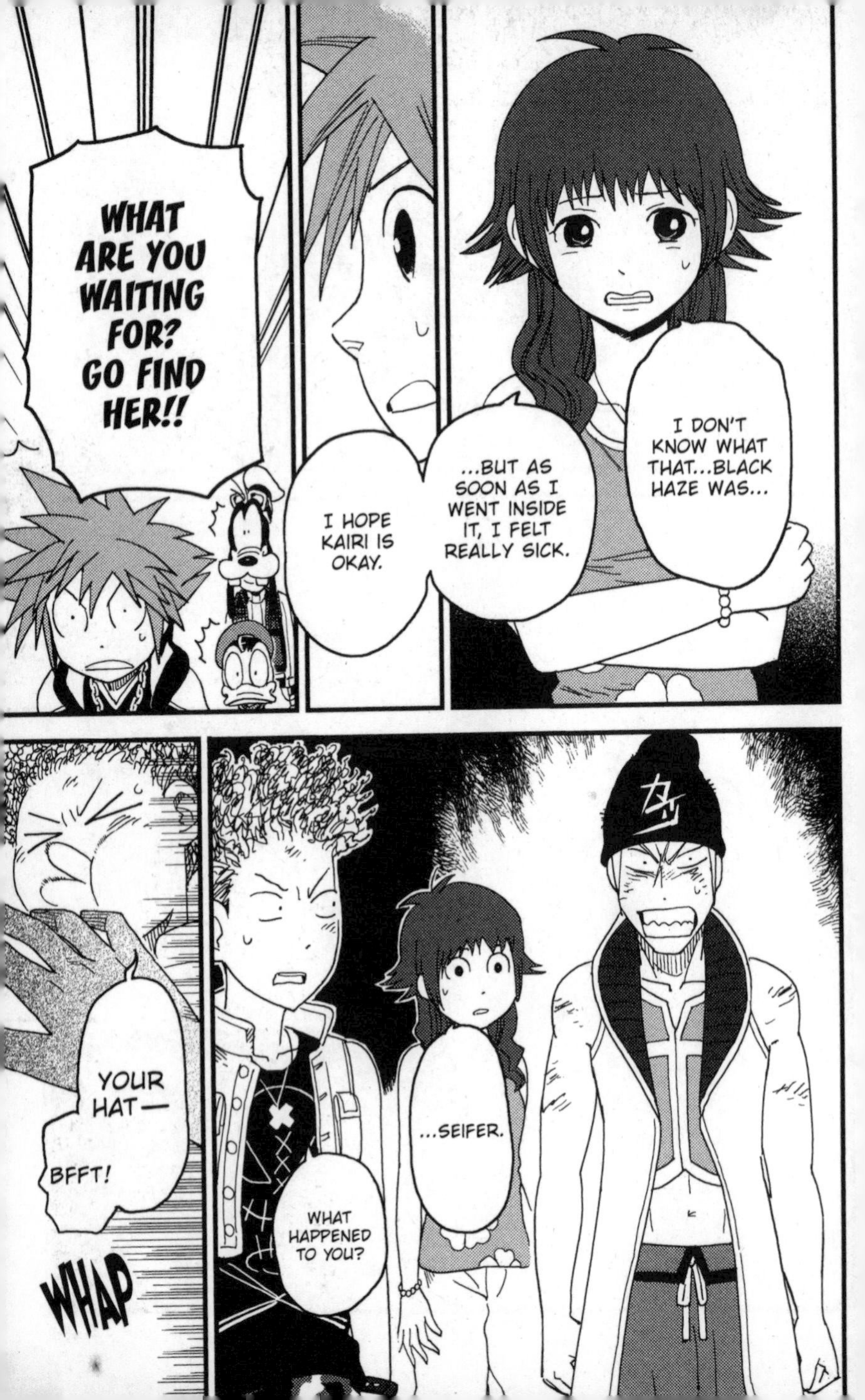
I DON'T KNOW WHAT THAT...BLACK HAZE WAS...
...BUT AS SOON AS I WENT INSIDE IT, I FELT REALLY SICK.
I HOPE KAIRI IS OKAY.
WHAT ARE YOU WAITING FOR? GO FIND HER!!
...SEIFER.
WHAT HAPPENED TO YOU?
YOUR HAT—
BFFT!
WHAP

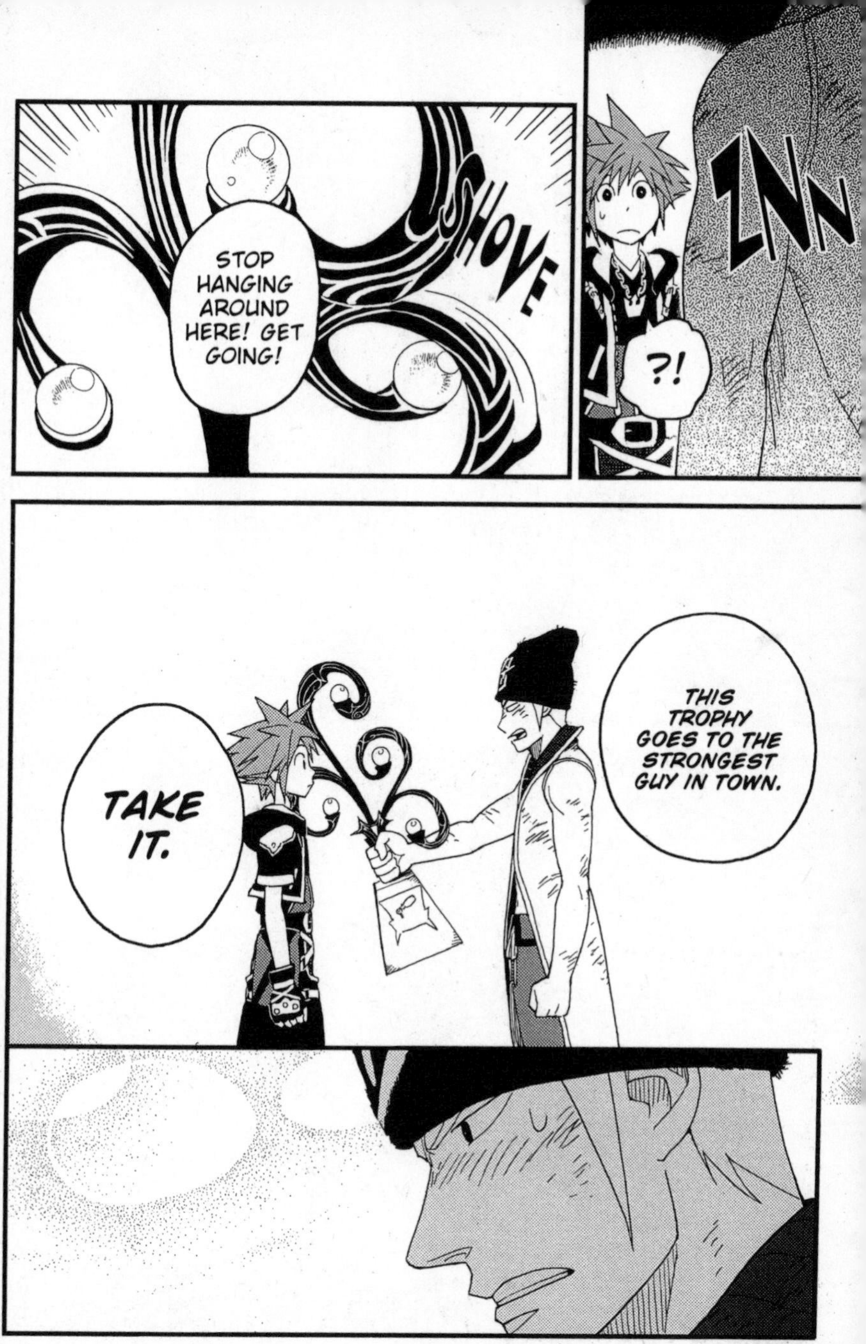
ZNN
?!
SHOVE
STOP HANGING AROUND HERE! GET GOING!
THIS TROPHY GOES TO THE STRONGEST GUY IN TOWN.
TAKE IT.

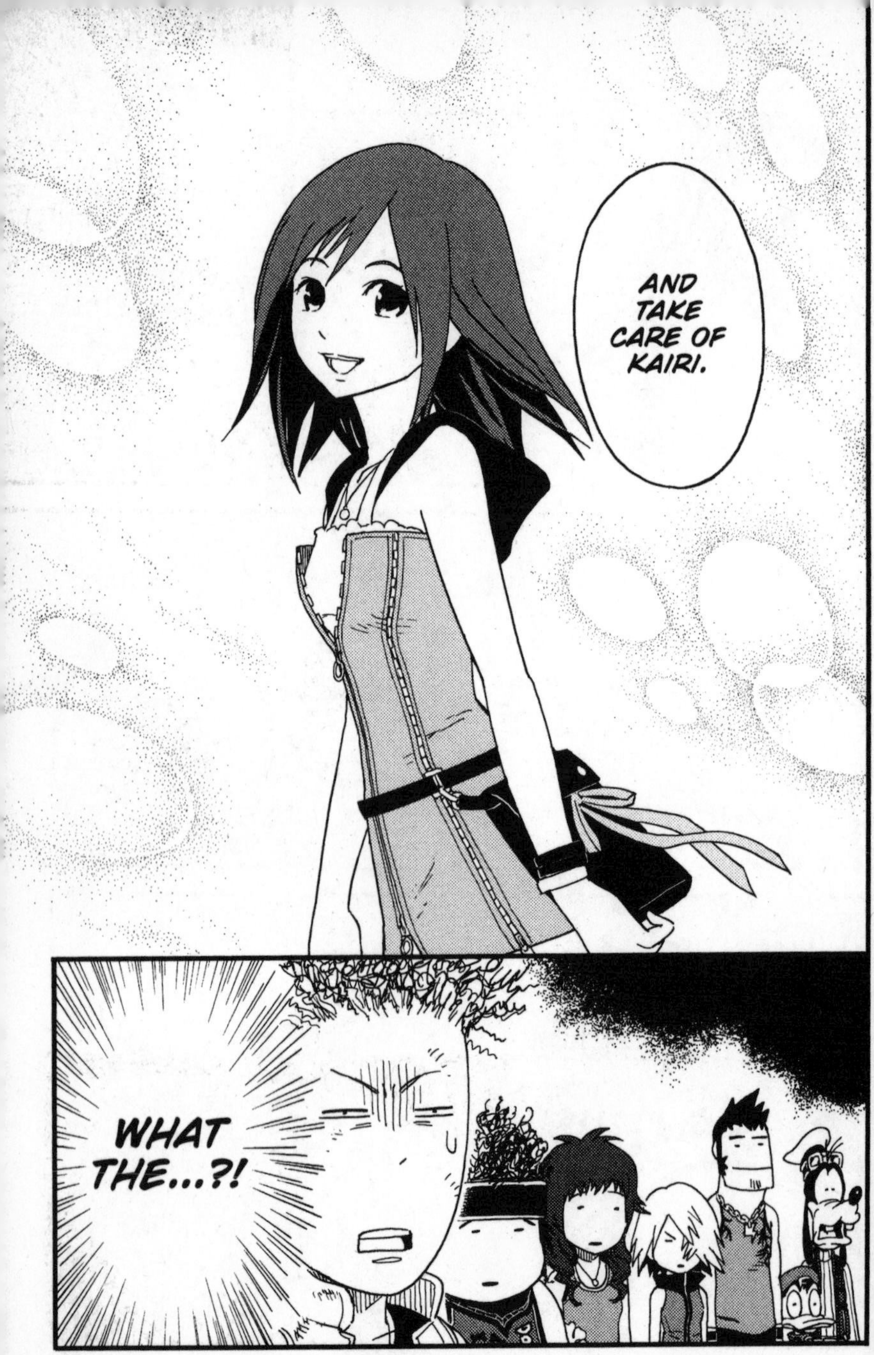
AND TAKE CARE OF KAIRI.
WHAT THE...?!

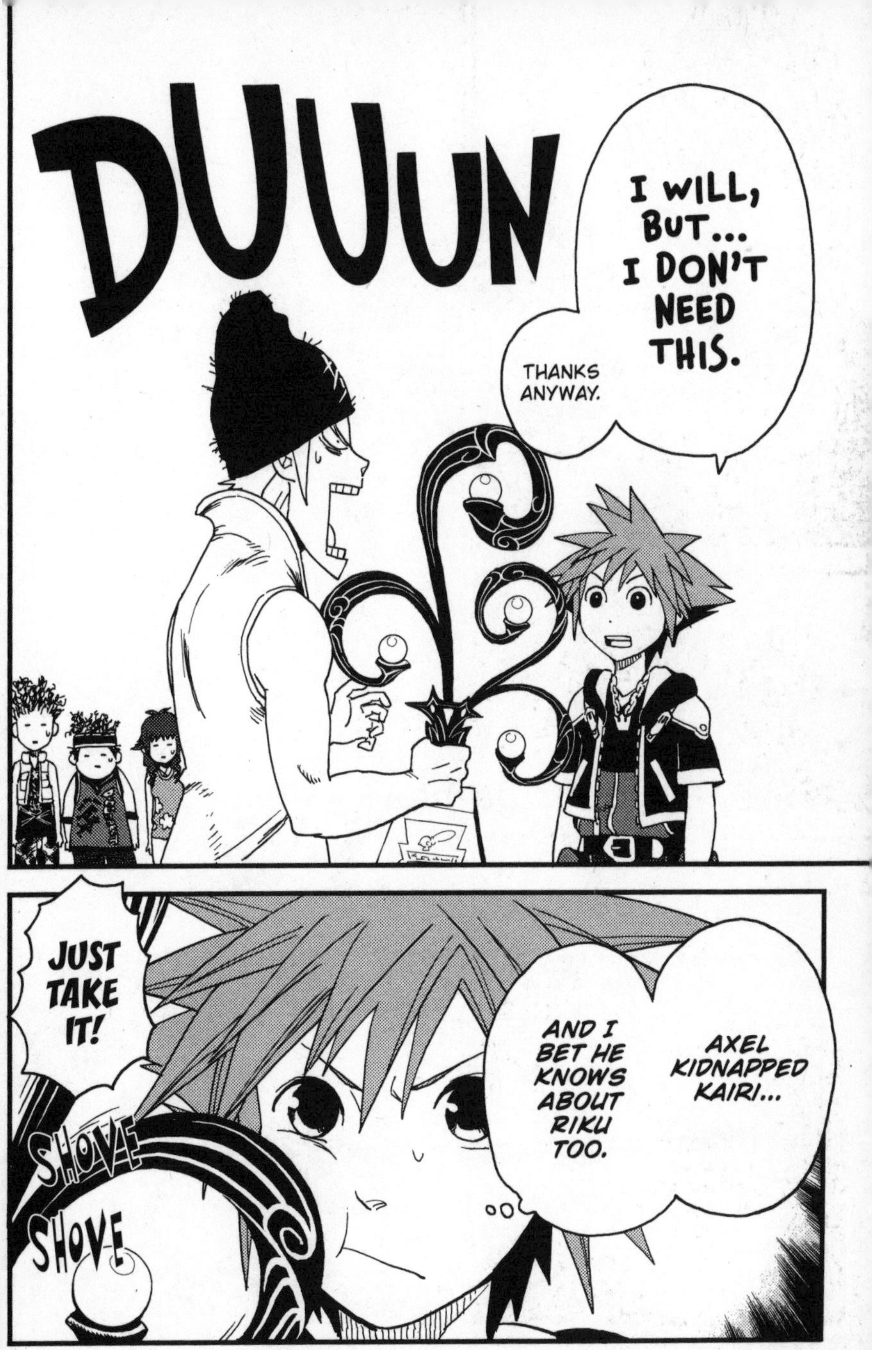
I WILL, BUT... I DON'T NEED THIS.
THANKS ANYWAY.
DUUUN
AXEL KIDNAPPED KAIRI...
AND I BET HE KNOWS ABOUT RIKU TOO.
JUST TAKE IT!
SHOVE
SHOVE

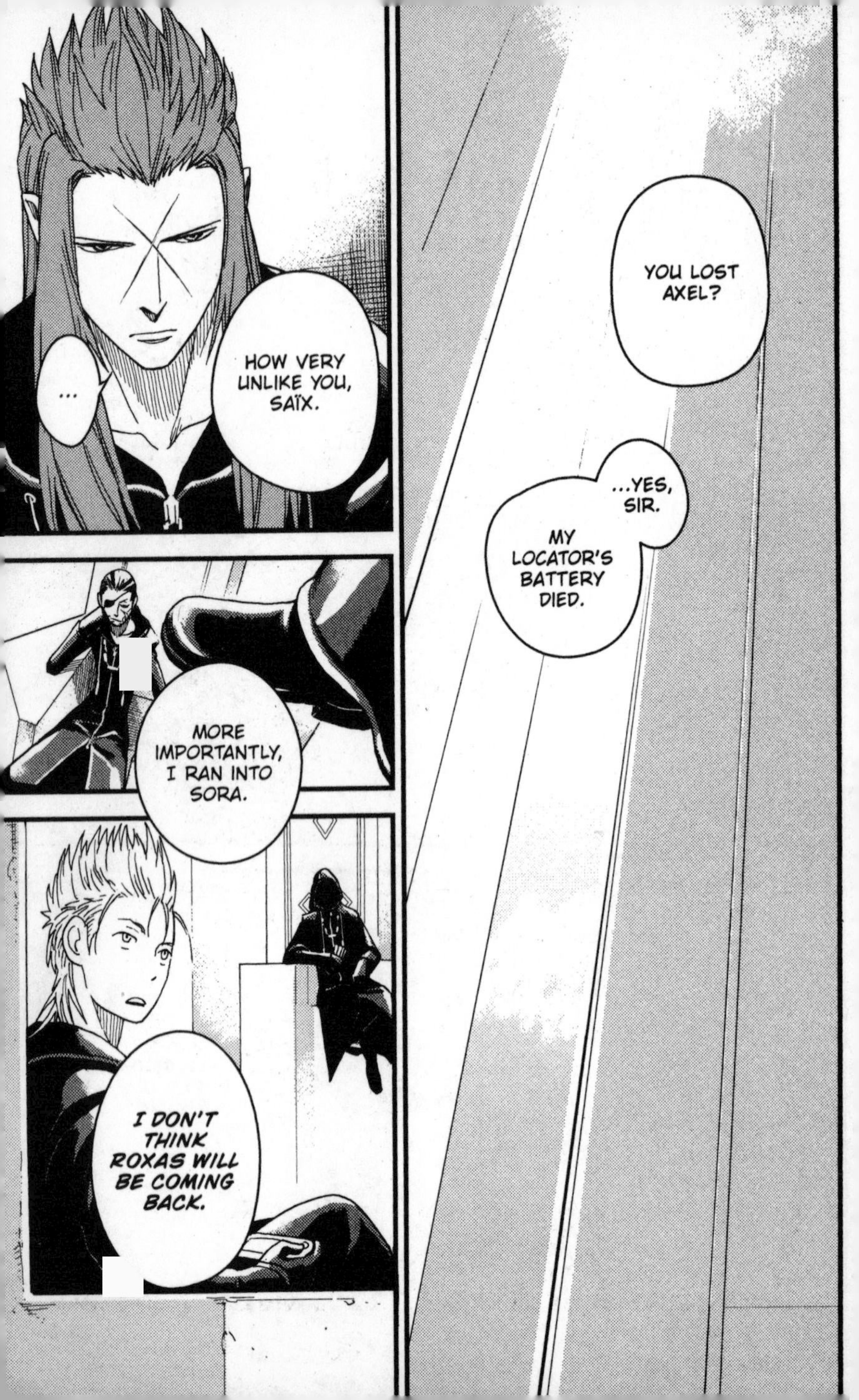
YOU LOST AXEL?
...YES, SIR.
MY LOCATOR'S BATTERY DIED.
HOW VERY UNLIKE YOU, SAÏX.
...
MORE IMPORTANTLY, I RAN INTO SORA.
I DON'T THINK ROXAS WILL BE COMING BACK.

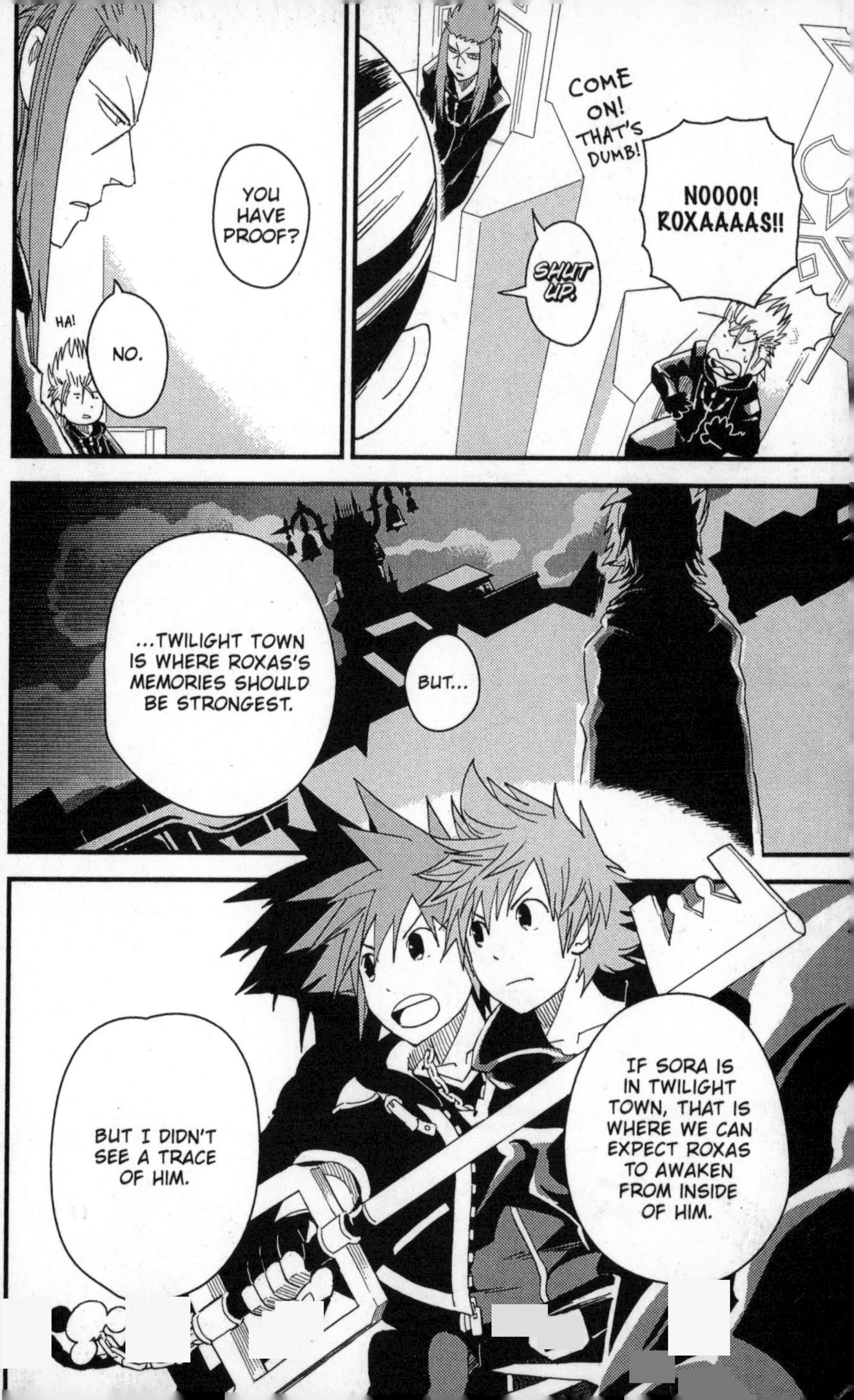
NOOOO! ROXAAAAS!!
COME ON! THAT'S DUMB!
SHUT UP.
YOU HAVE PROOF?
NO.
HA!
...TWILIGHT TOWN IS WHERE ROXAS'S MEMORIES SHOULD BE STRONGEST.
BUT...
IF SORA IS IN TWILIGHT TOWN, THAT IS WHERE WE CAN EXPECT ROXAS TO AWAKEN FROM INSIDE OF HIM.
BUT I DIDN'T SEE A TRACE OF HIM.

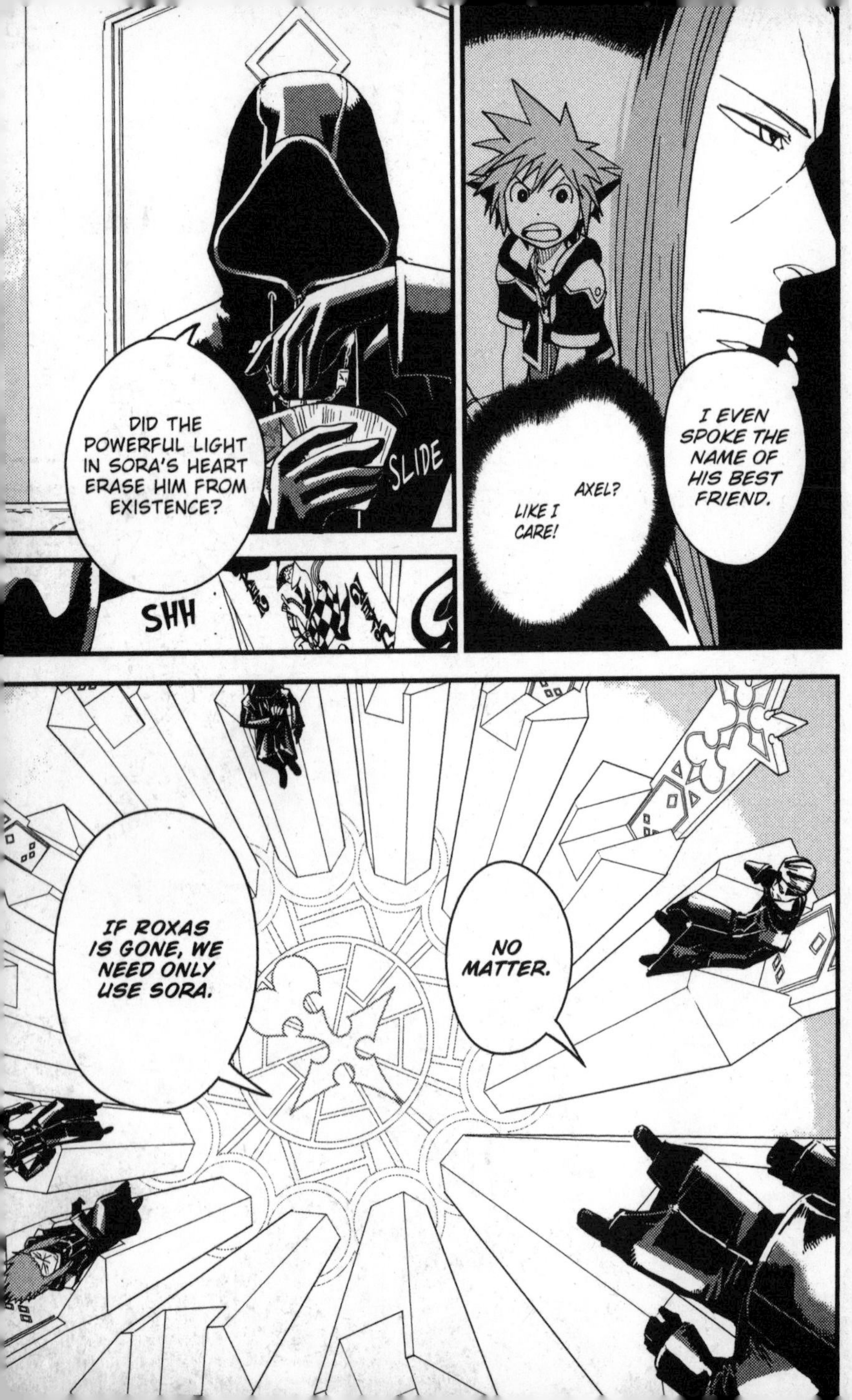
I EVEN SPOKE THE NAME OF HIS BEST FRIEND.
AXEL? LIKE I CARE!
DID THE POWERFUL LIGHT IN SORA'S HEART ERASE HIM FROM EXISTENCE?
SLIDE
SHH
NO MATTER.
IF ROXAS IS GONE, WE NEED ONLY USE SORA.

Chapter 36: Traces of a Friend

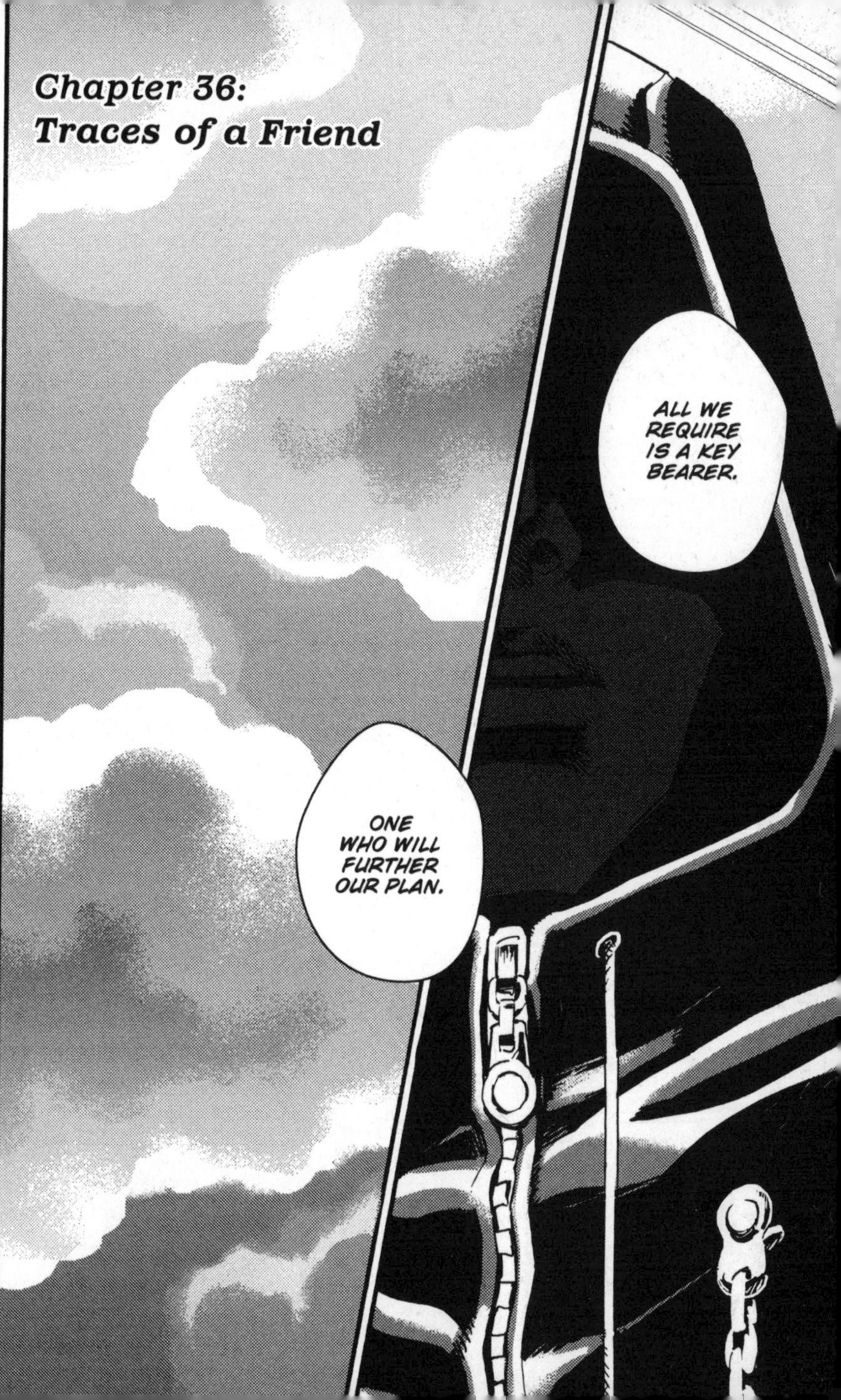
ALL WE REQUIRE IS A KEY BEARER.
ONE WHO WILL FURTHER OUR PLAN.

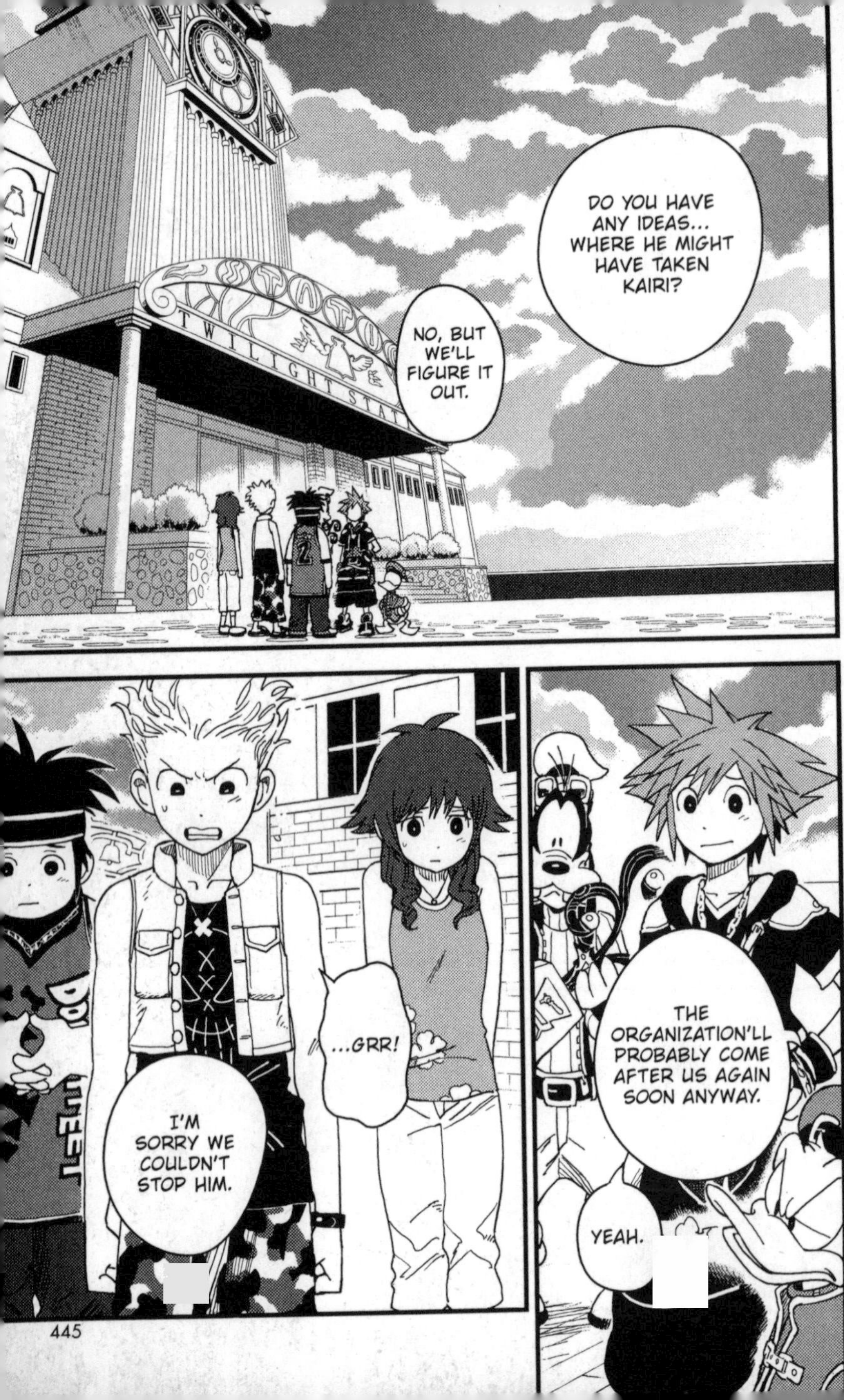
TWILIGHT STATION
DO YOU HAVE ANY IDEAS... WHERE HE MIGHT HAVE TAKEN KAIRI?
NO, BUT WE'LL FIGURE IT OUT.
THE ORGANIZATION'LL PROBABLY COME AFTER US AGAIN SOON ANYWAY.
YEAH.
...GRR!
I'M SORRY WE COULDN'T STOP HIM.

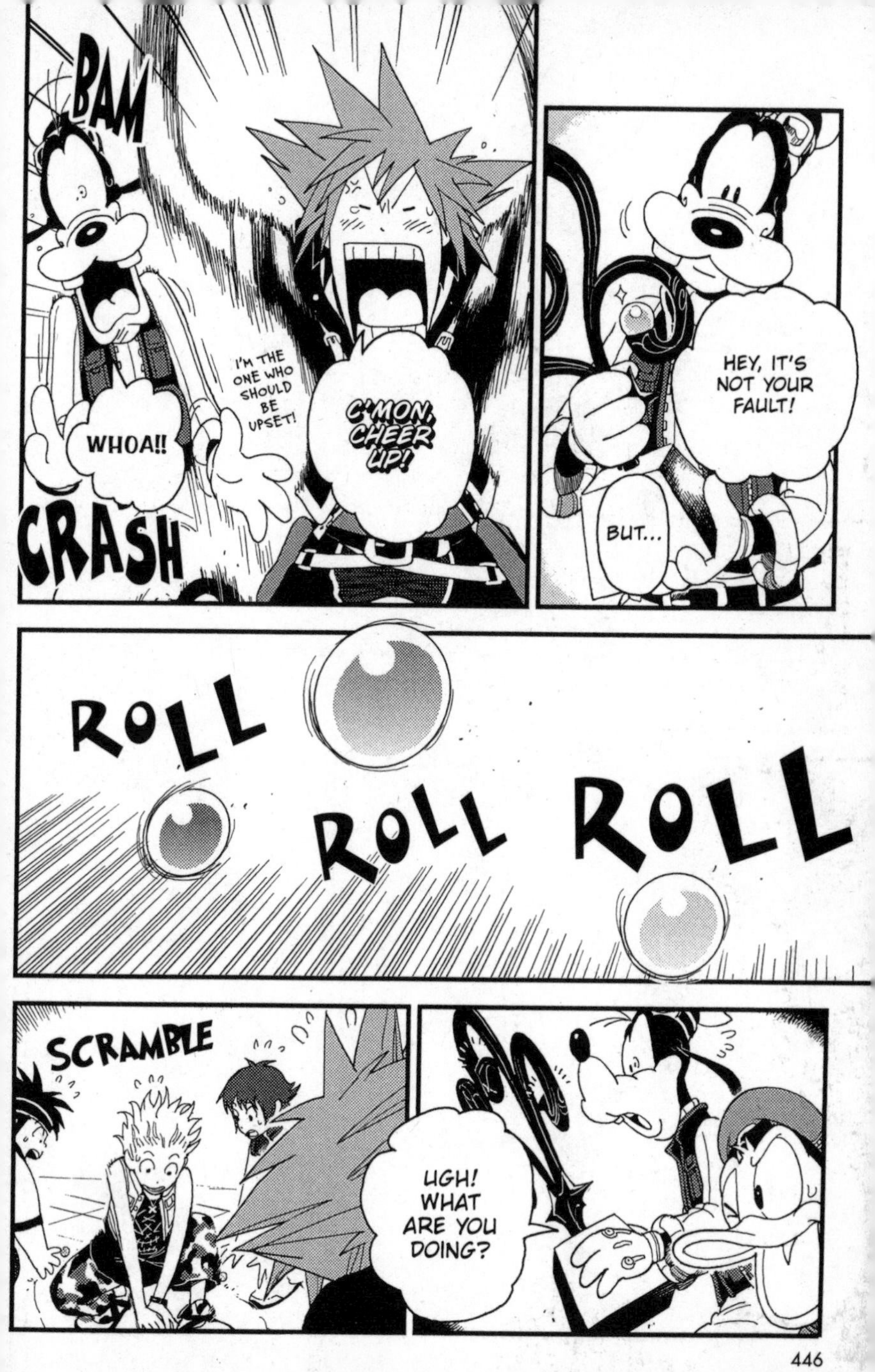
HEY, IT'S NOT YOUR FAULT!
BUT...
C'MON, CHEER UP!
I'M THE ONE WHO SHOULD BE UPSET!
BAM
WHOA!!
CRASH
ROLL
ROLL
ROLL
UGH! WHAT ARE YOU DOING?
SCRAMBLE

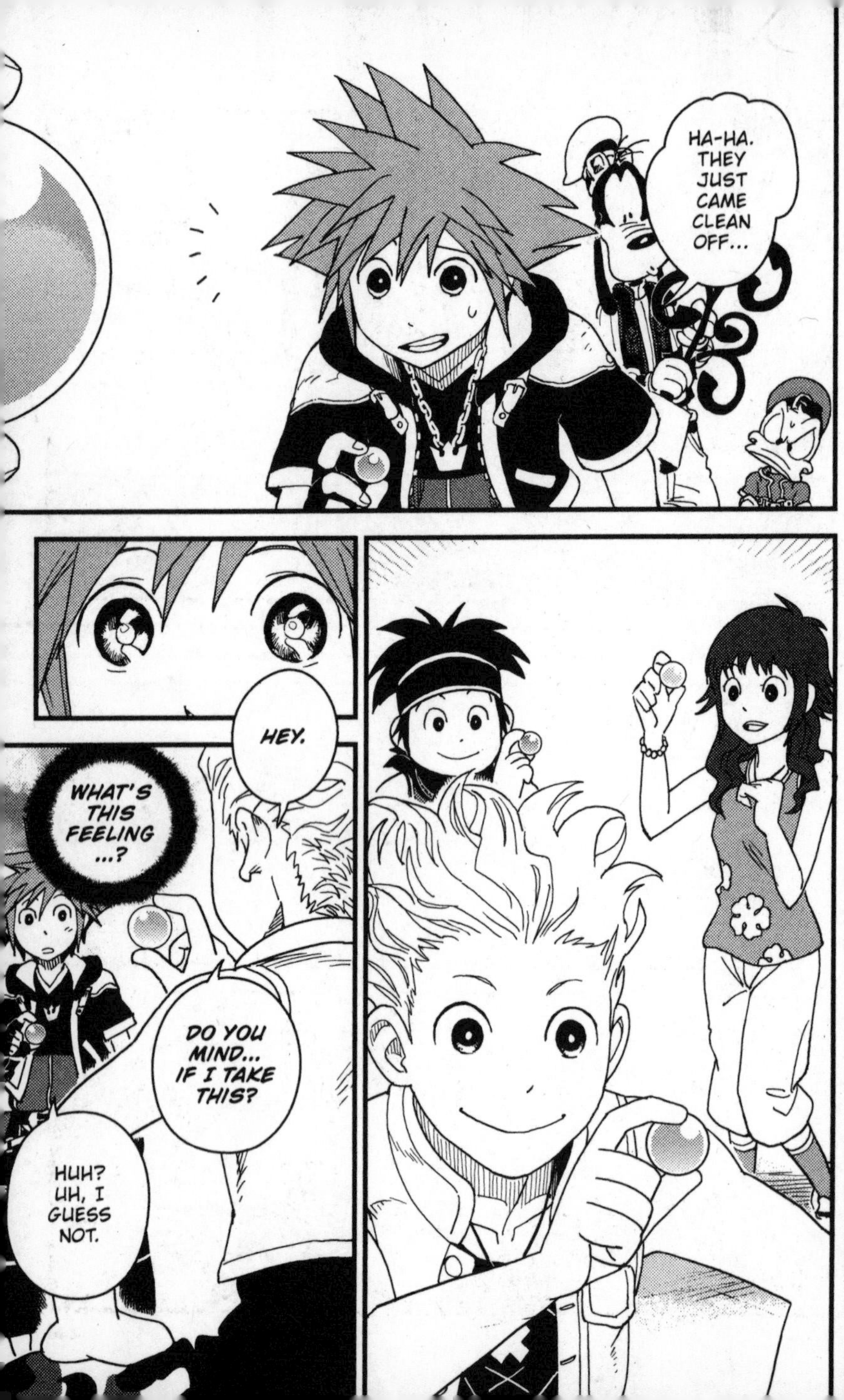
HA-HA. THEY JUST CAME CLEAN OFF...
HEY.
WHAT'S THIS FEELING ...?
DO YOU MIND... IF I TAKE THIS?
HUH? UH, I GUESS NOT.

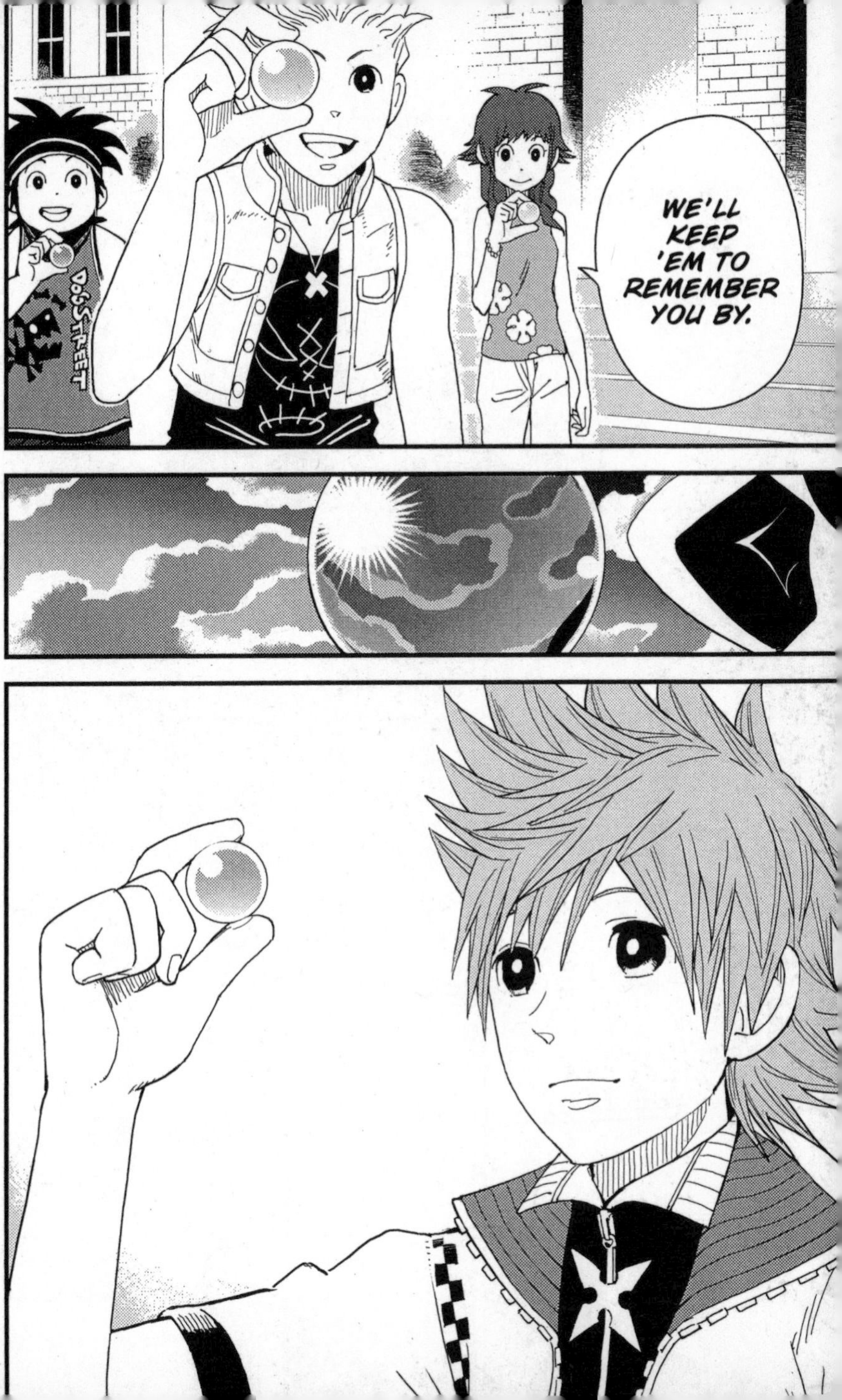
WE'LL KEEP 'EM TO REMEMBER YOU BY.
DOGSTREET

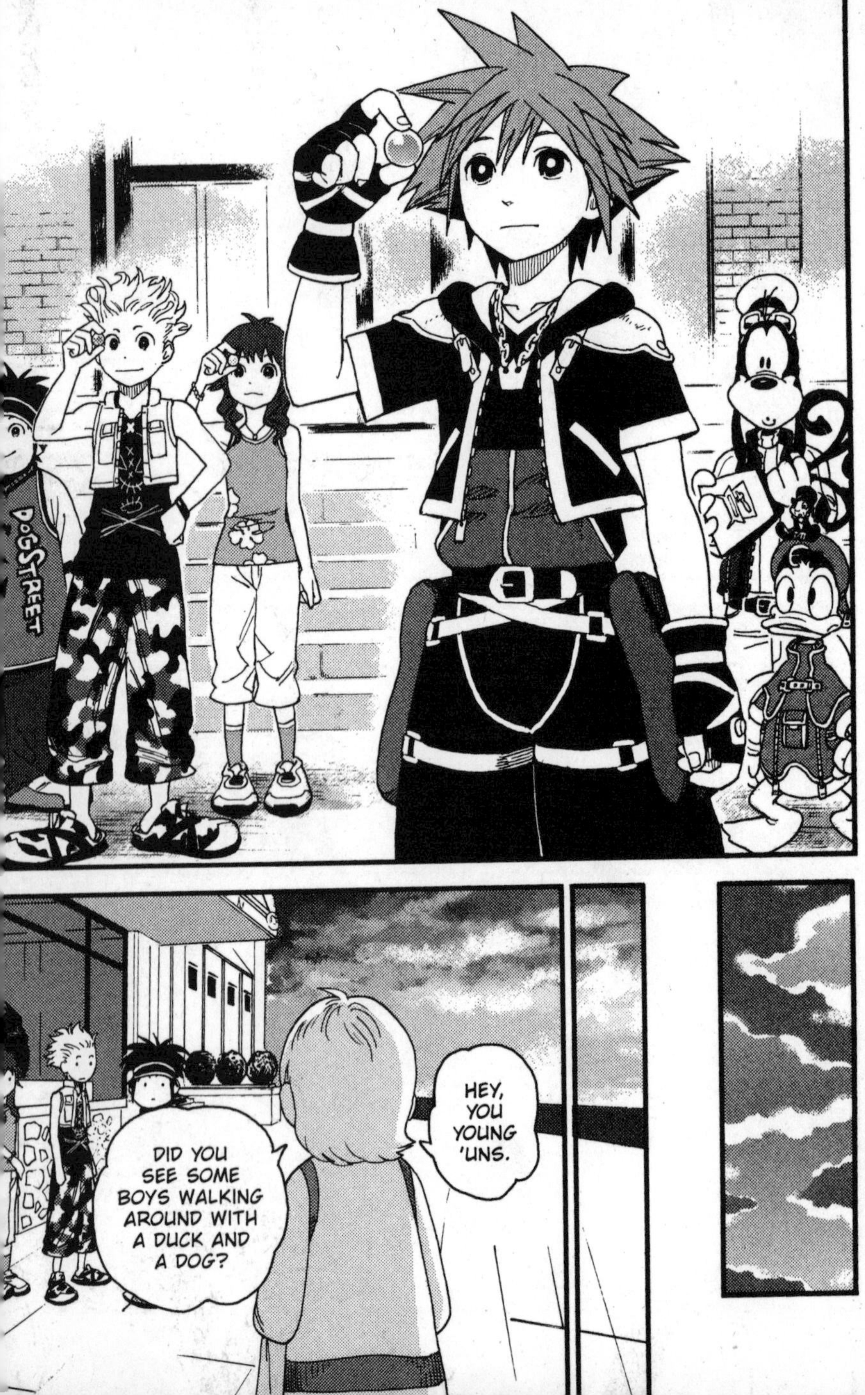
DOGSTREET
HEY, YOU YOUNG 'UNS.
DID YOU SEE SOME BOYS WALKING AROUND WITH A DUCK AND A DOG?

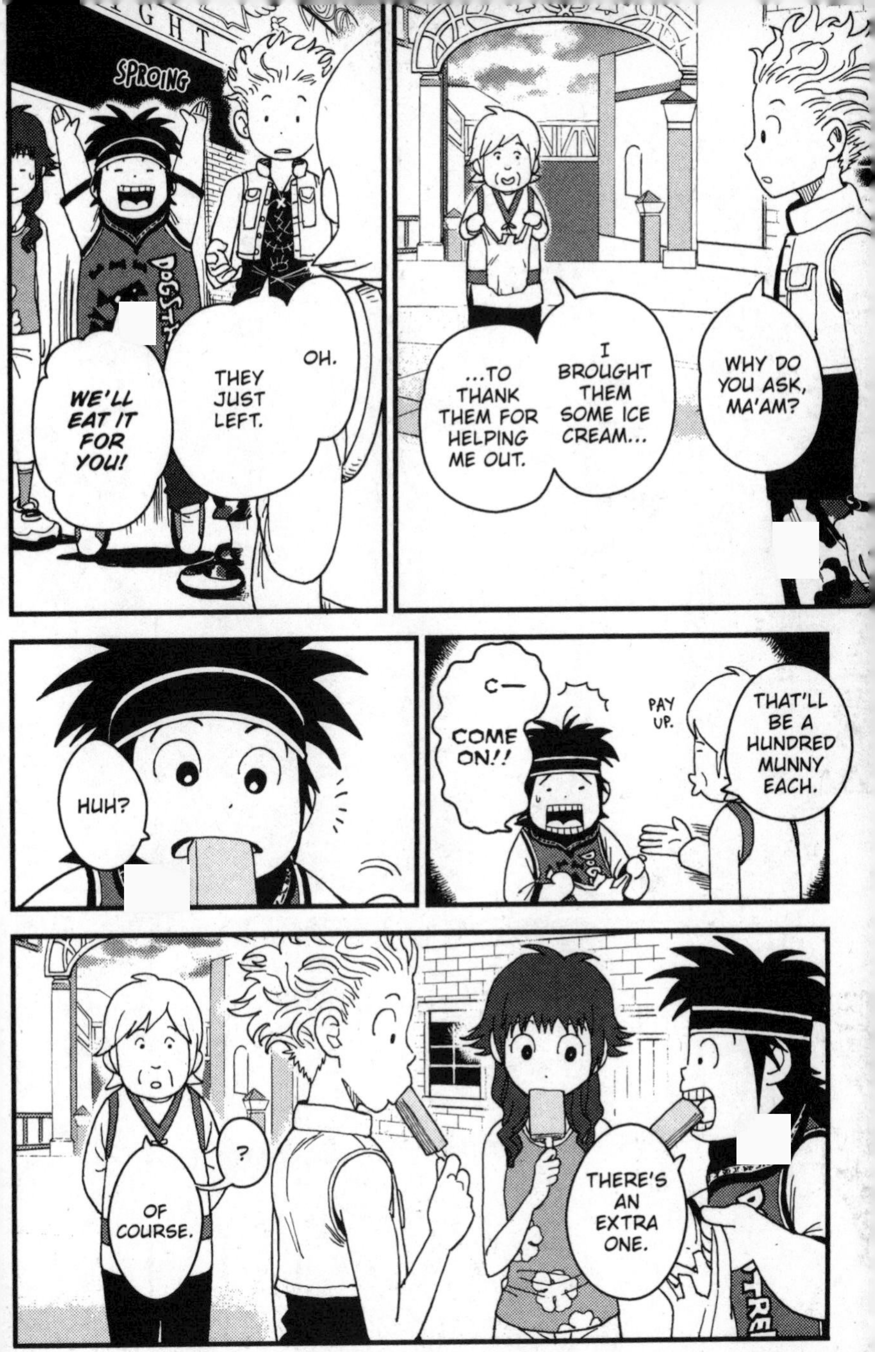
WHY DO YOU ASK, MA'AM?
I BROUGHT THEM SOME ICE CREAM...
...TO THANK THEM FOR HELPING ME OUT.
SPROING
OH.
THEY JUST LEFT.
WE'LL EAT IT FOR YOU!
THAT'LL BE A HUNDRED MUNNY EACH.
PAY UP.
C—
COME ON!!
HUH?
THERE'S AN EXTRA ONE.
?
OF COURSE.

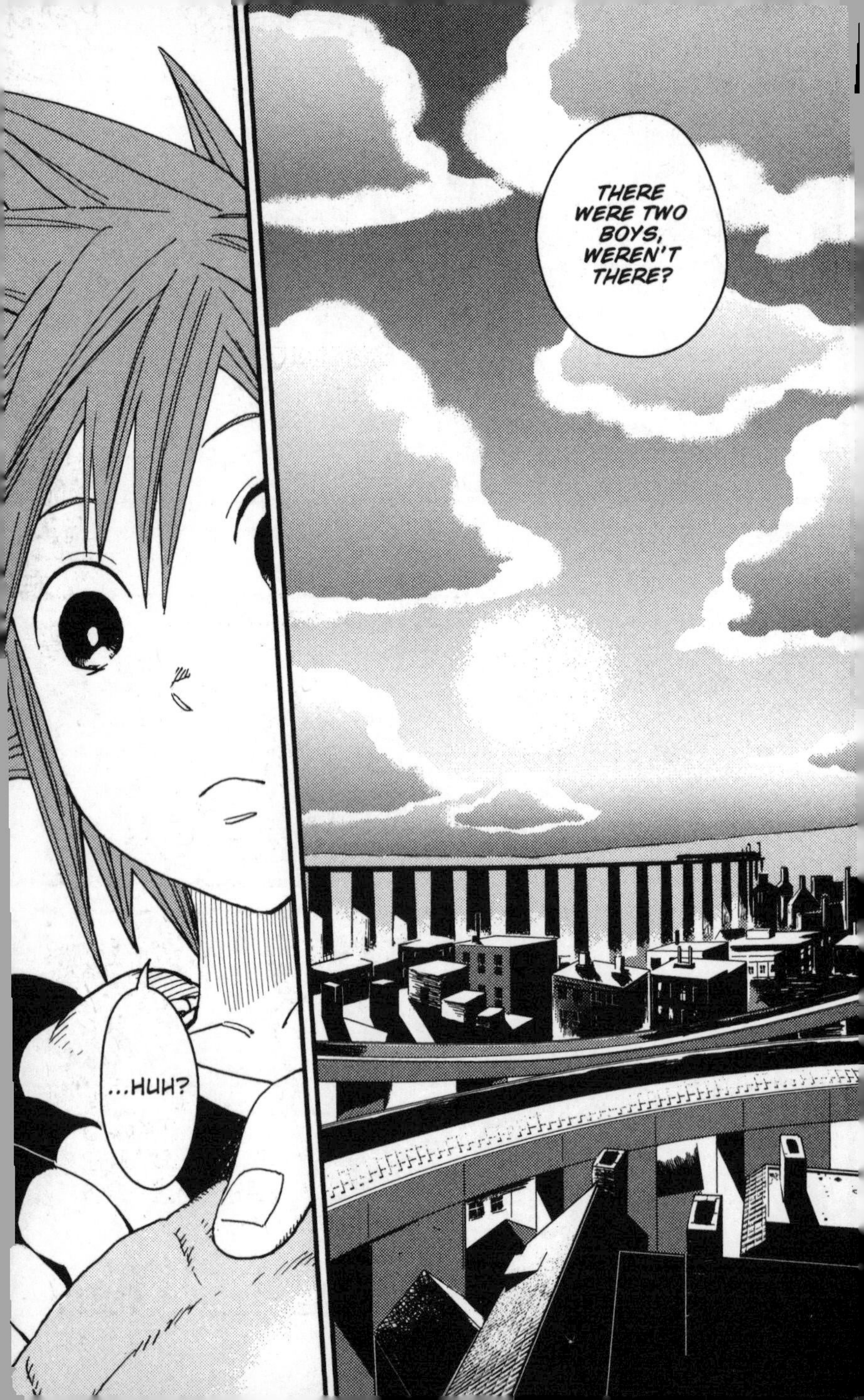
THERE WERE TWO BOYS, WEREN'T THERE?
...HUH?

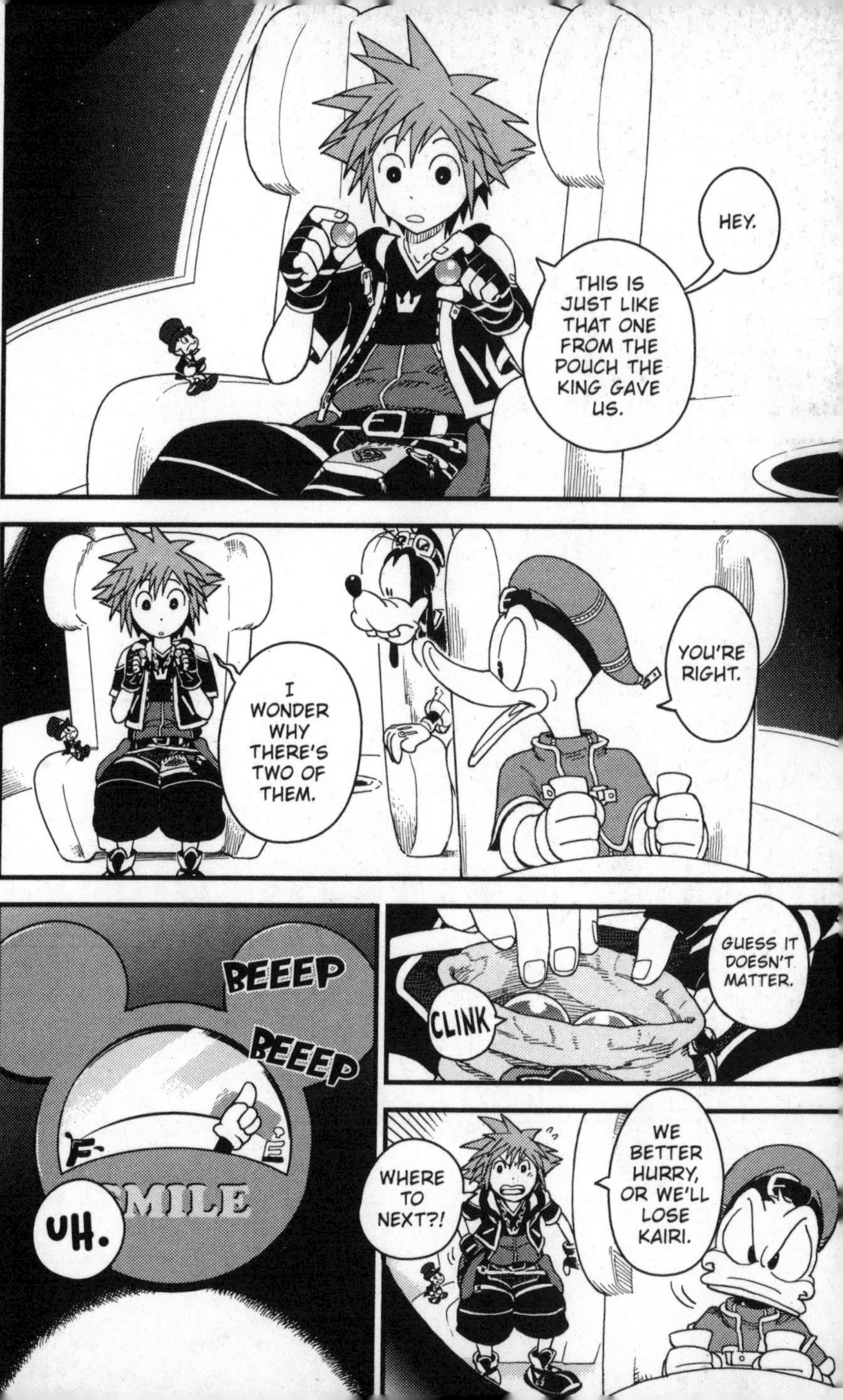
HEY.
THIS IS JUST LIKE THAT ONE FROM THE POUCH THE KING GAVE US.
YOU'RE RIGHT.
I WONDER WHY THERE'S TWO OF THEM.
GUESS IT DOESN'T MATTER.
CLINK
WE BETTER HURRY, OR WE'LL LOSE KAIRI.
WHERE TO NEXT?!
BEEEP
BEEEP
F
E
MILE
UH.

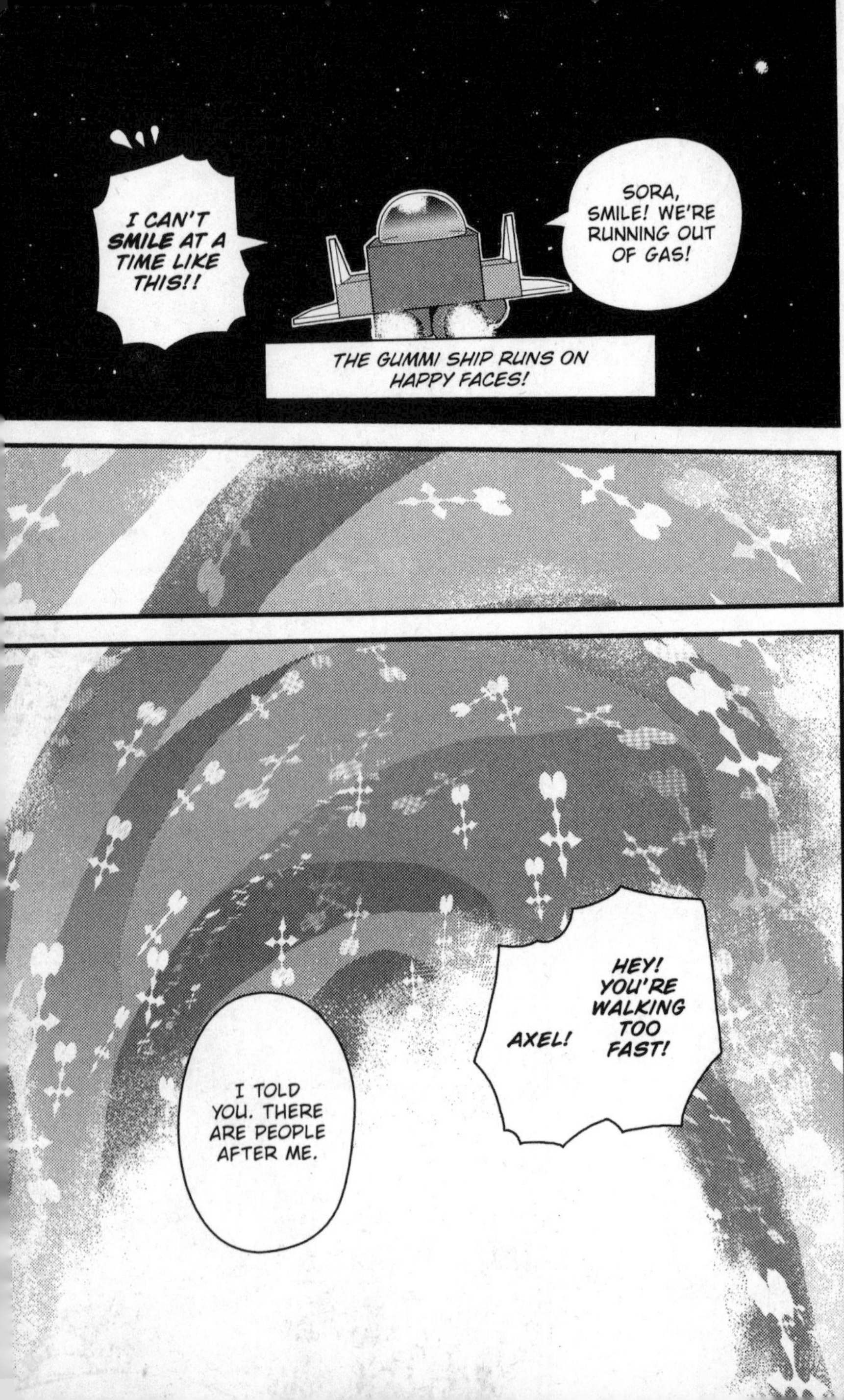
SORA, SMILE! WE'RE RUNNING OUT OF GAS!
I CAN'T SMILE AT A TIME LIKE THIS!!
THE GUMMI SHIP RUNS ON HAPPY FACES!
HEY! YOU'RE WALKING TOO FAST! AXEL!
I TOLD YOU. THERE ARE PEOPLE AFTER ME.

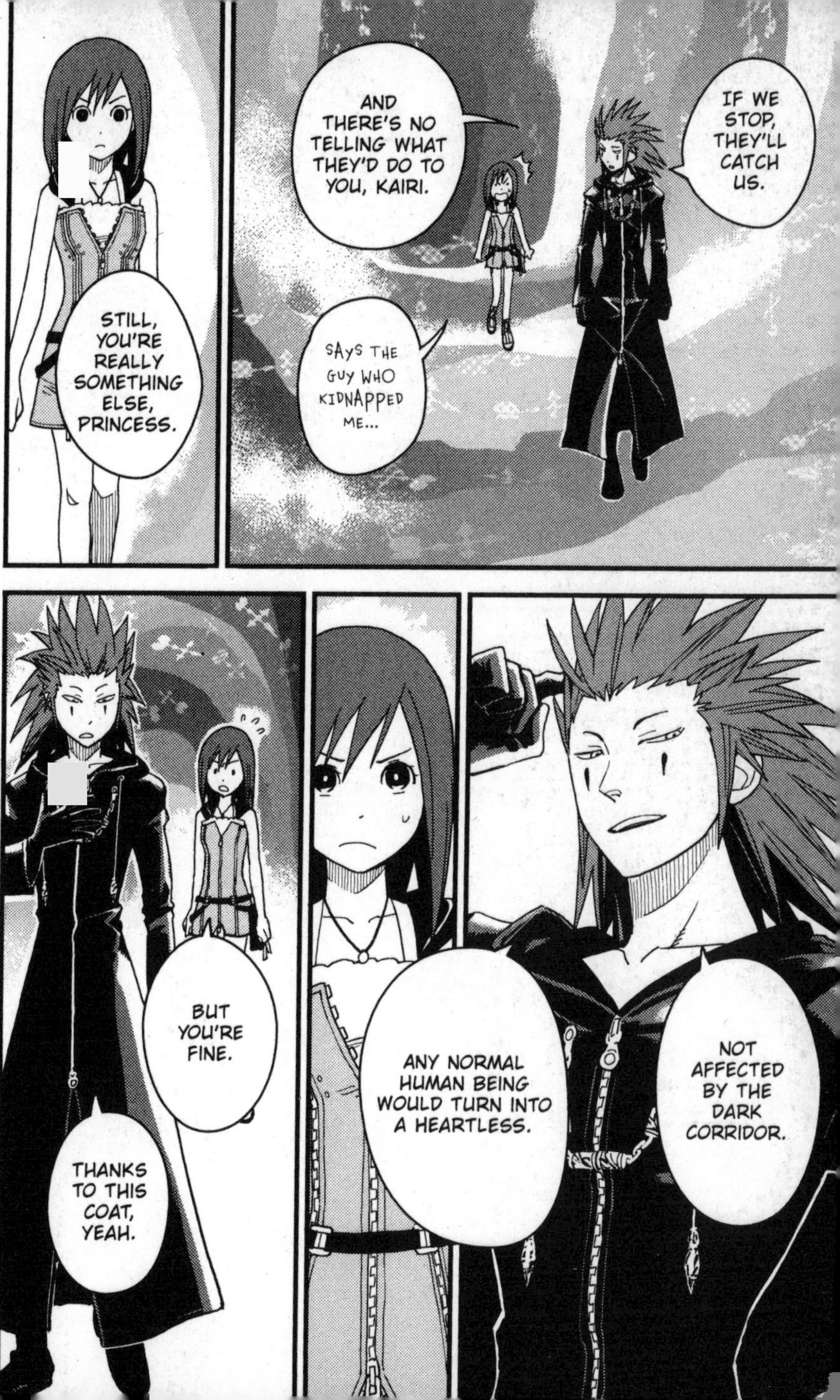
IF WE STOP, THEY'LL CATCH US.
AND THERE'S NO TELLING WHAT THEY'D DO TO YOU, KAIRI.
SAYS THE GUY WHO KIDNAPPED ME...
STILL, YOU'RE REALLY SOMETHING ELSE, PRINCESS.
NOT AFFECTED BY THE DARK CORRIDOR.
ANY NORMAL HUMAN BEING WOULD TURN INTO A HEARTLESS.
BUT YOU'RE FINE.
THANKS TO THIS COAT, YEAH.

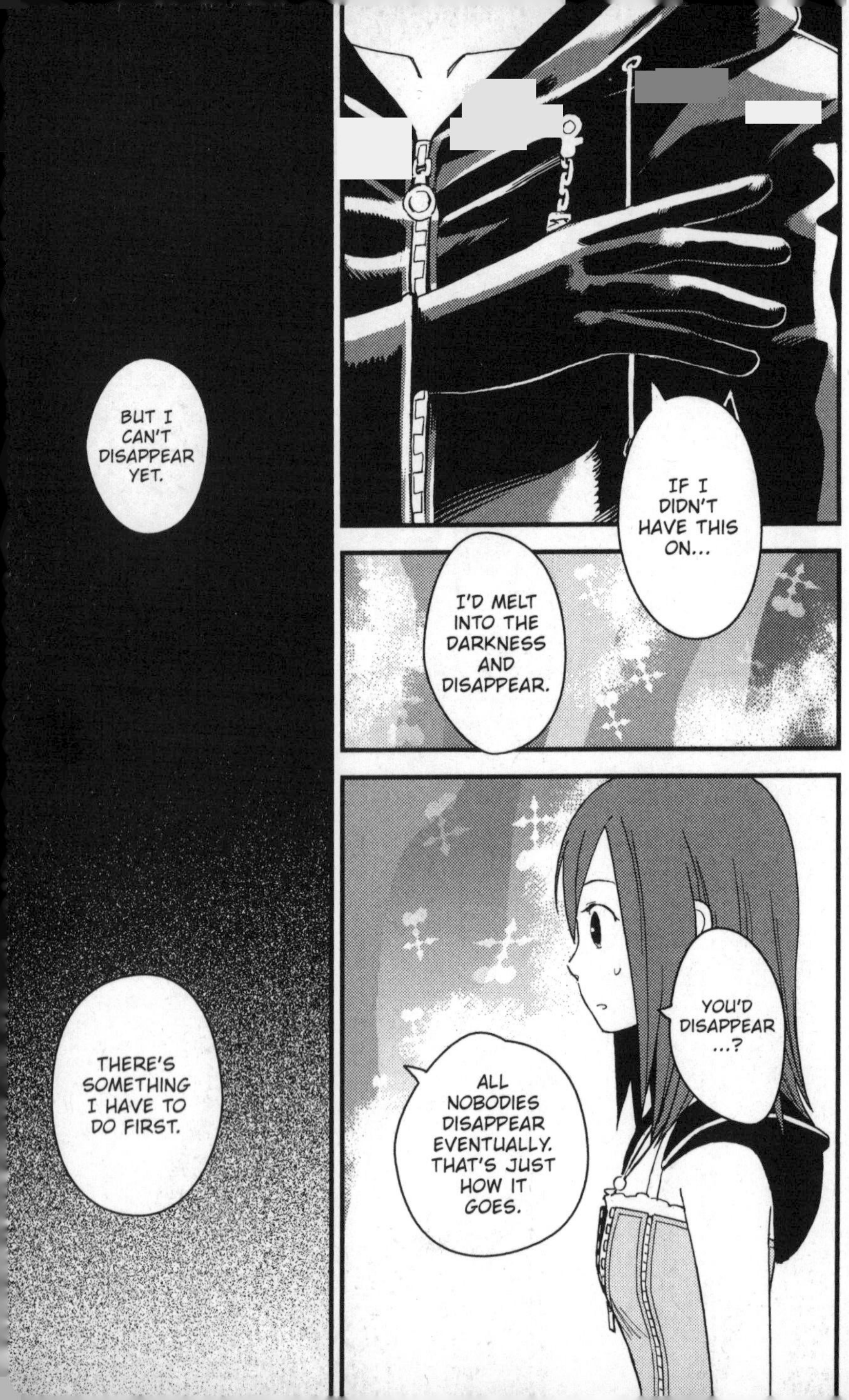
IF I DIDN'T HAVE THIS ON...
I'D MELT INTO THE DARKNESS AND DISAPPEAR.
YOU'D DISAPPEAR ...?
ALL NOBODIES DISAPPEAR EVENTUALLY. THAT'S JUST HOW IT GOES.
BUT I CAN'T DISAPPEAR YET.
THERE'S SOMETHING I HAVE TO DO FIRST.

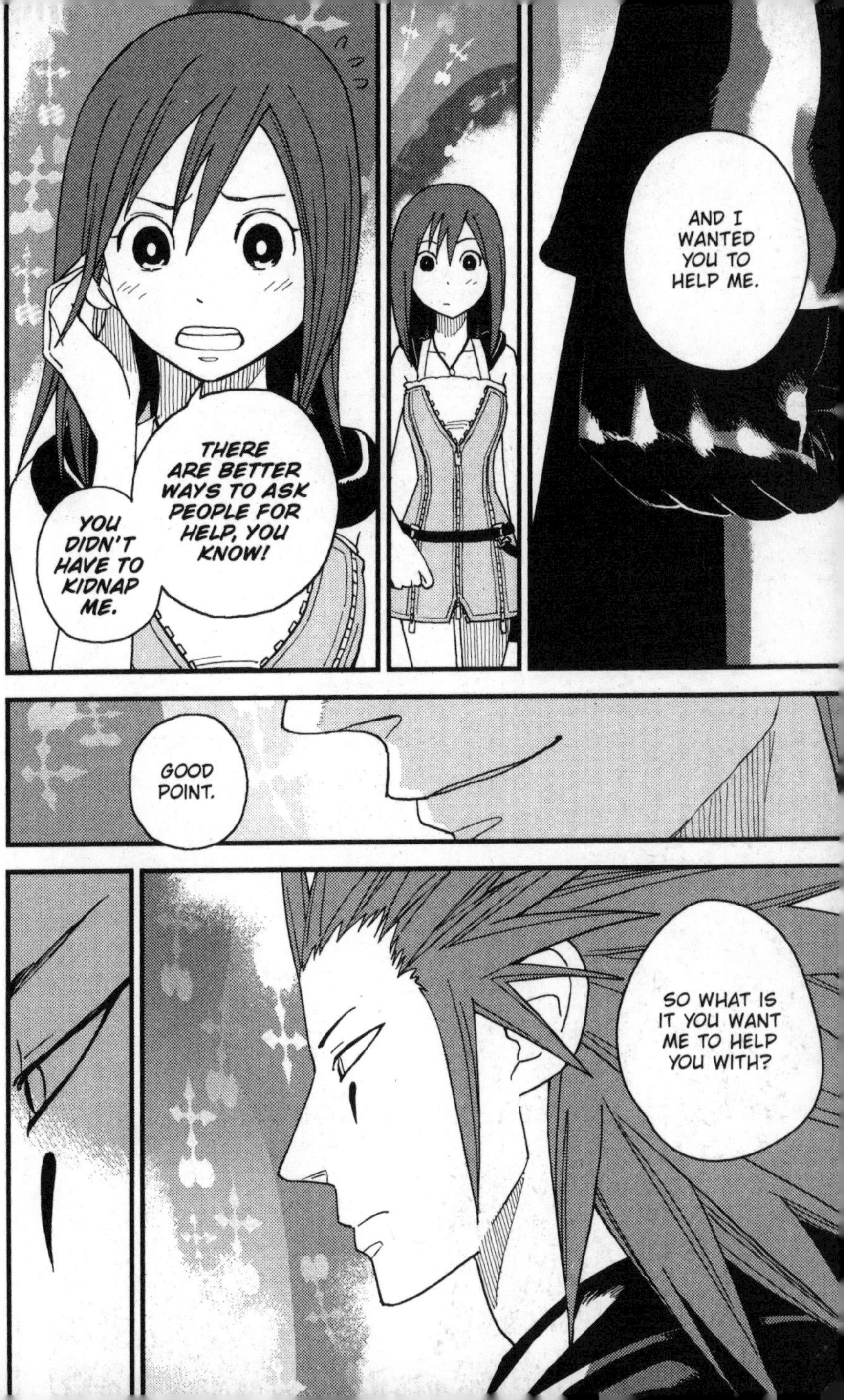
AND I WANTED YOU TO HELP ME.
THERE ARE BETTER WAYS TO ASK PEOPLE FOR HELP, YOU KNOW!
YOU DIDN'T HAVE TO KIDNAP ME.
GOOD POINT.
SO WHAT IS IT YOU WANT ME TO HELP YOU WITH?

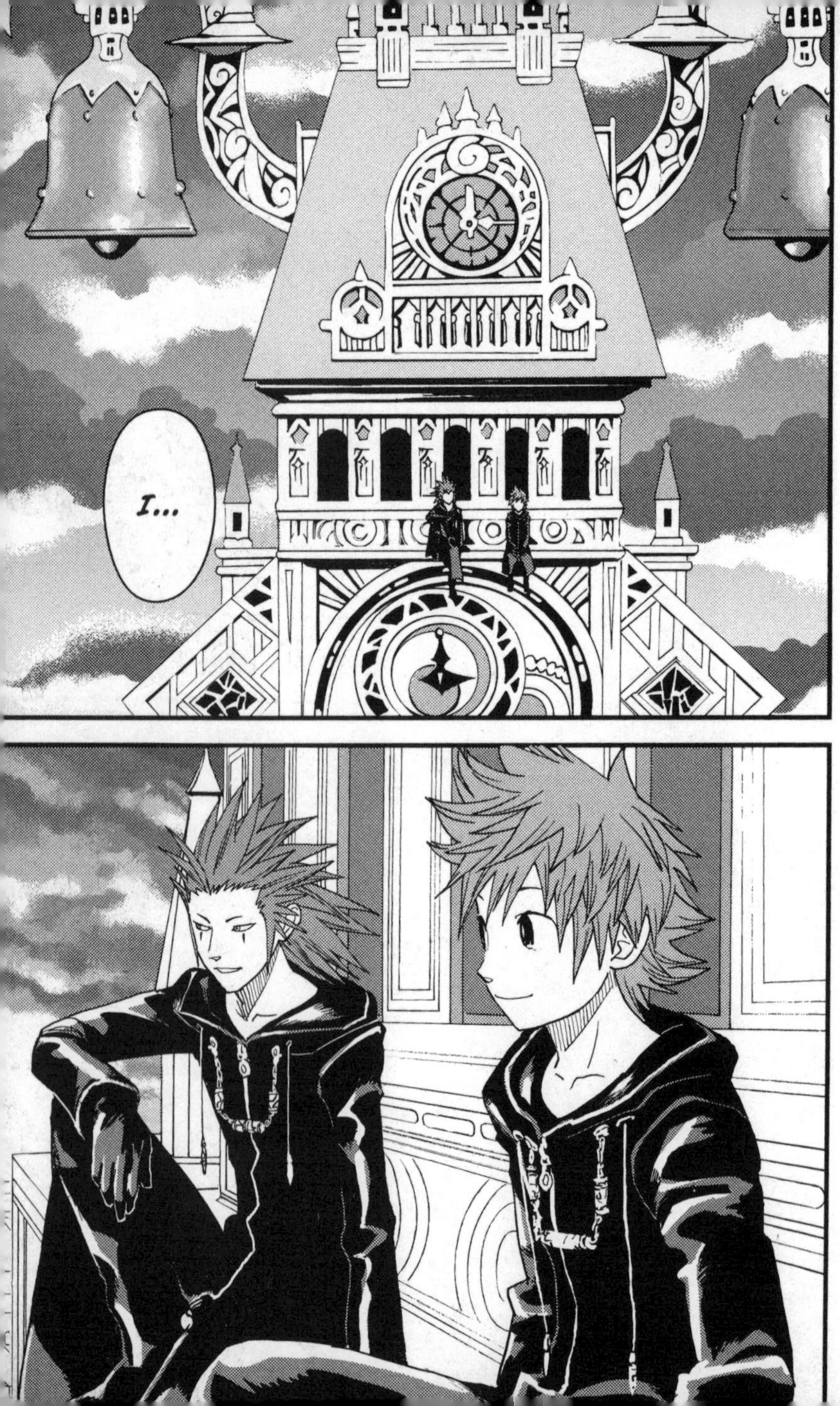
I...

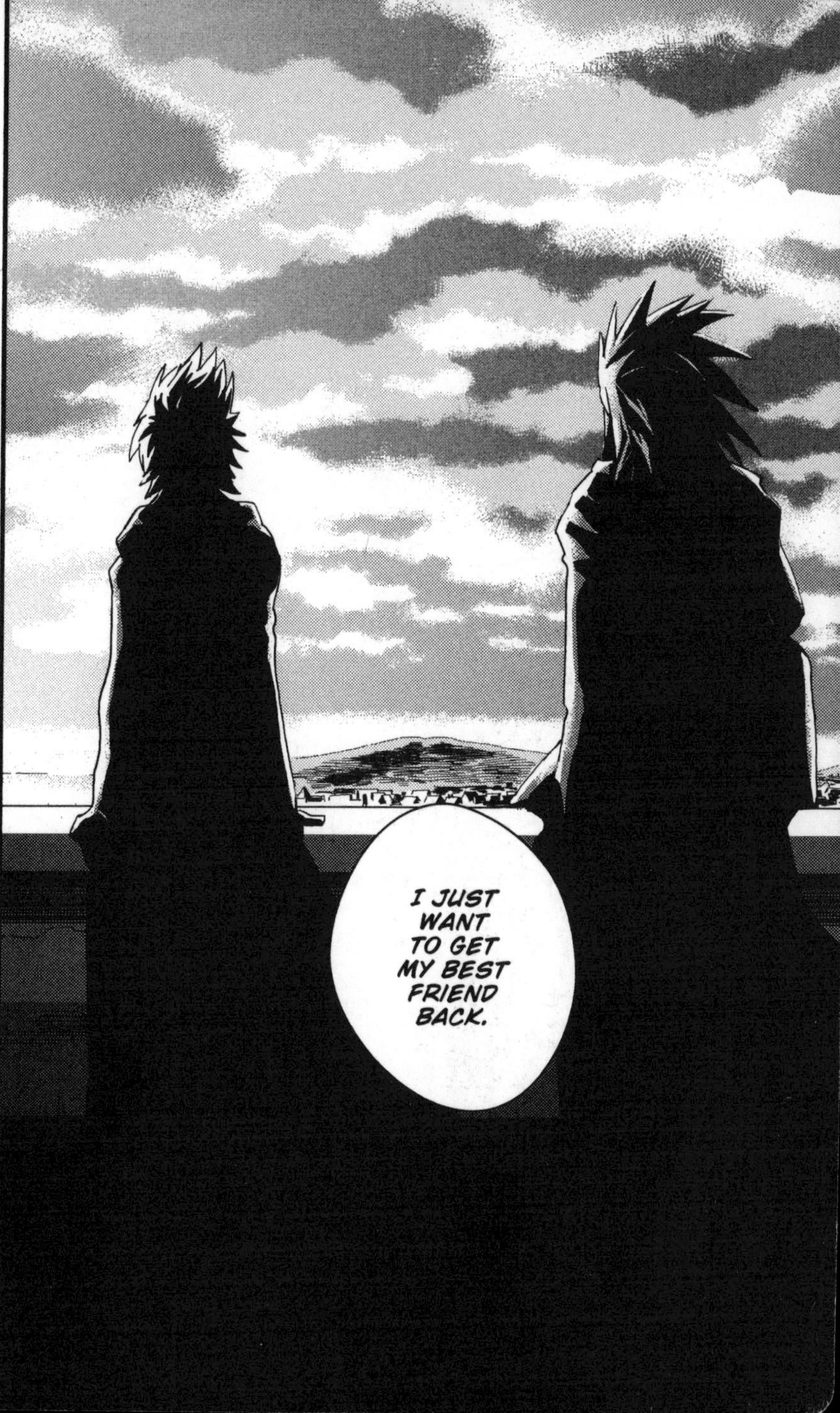
I JUST WANT TO GET MY BEST FRIEND BACK.

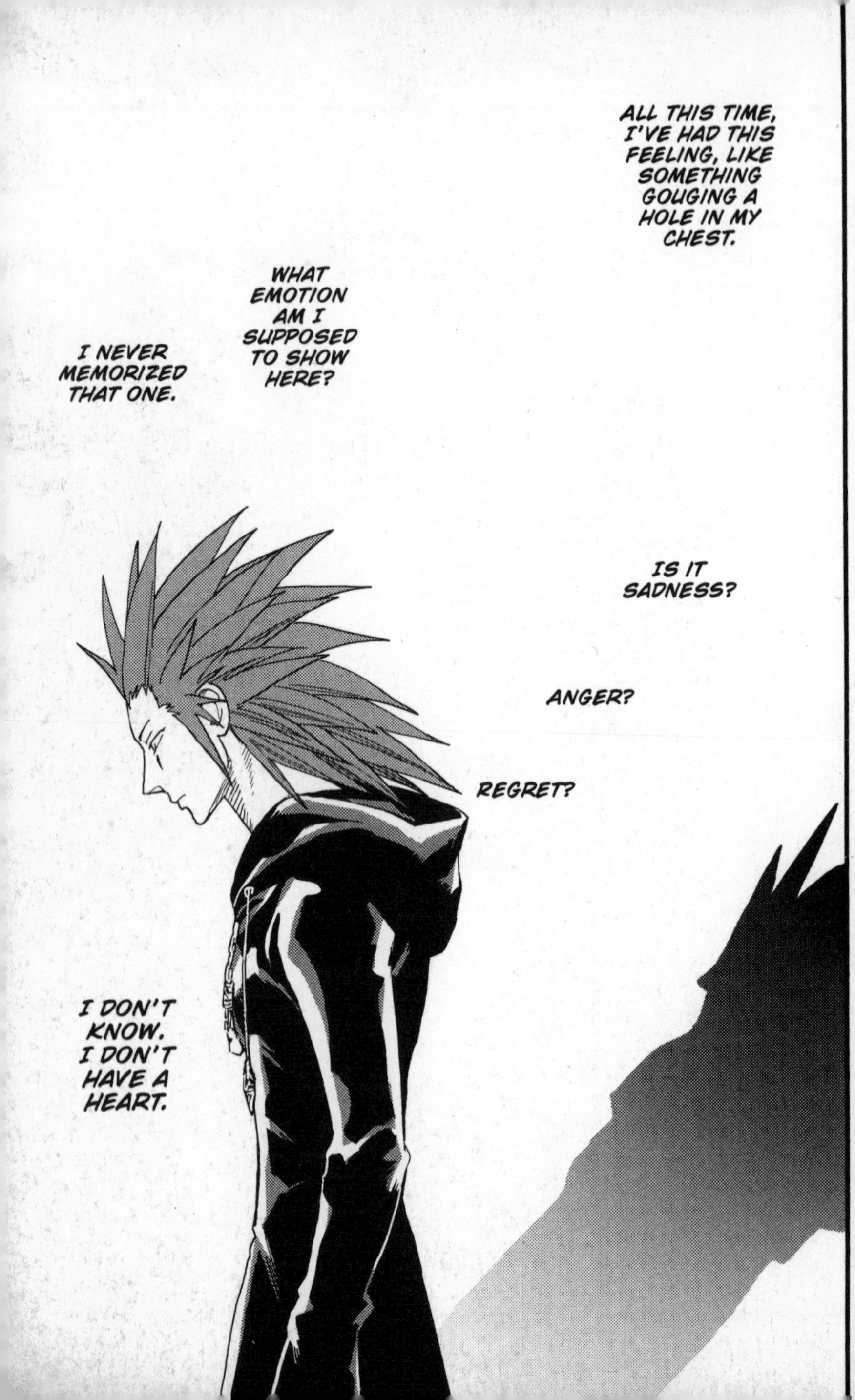
ALL THIS TIME, I'VE HAD THIS FEELING, LIKE SOMETHING GOUGING A HOLE IN MY CHEST.
WHAT EMOTION AM I SUPPOSED TO SHOW HERE?
I NEVER MEMORIZED THAT ONE.
IS IT SADNESS?
ANGER?
REGRET?
I DON'T KNOW. I DON'T HAVE A HEART.

Chapter 37: Plastic Friend

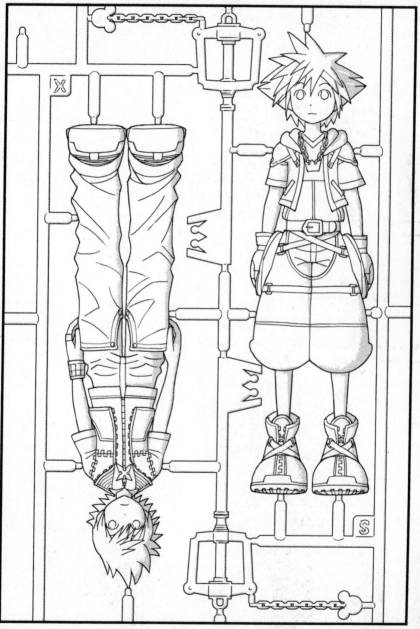

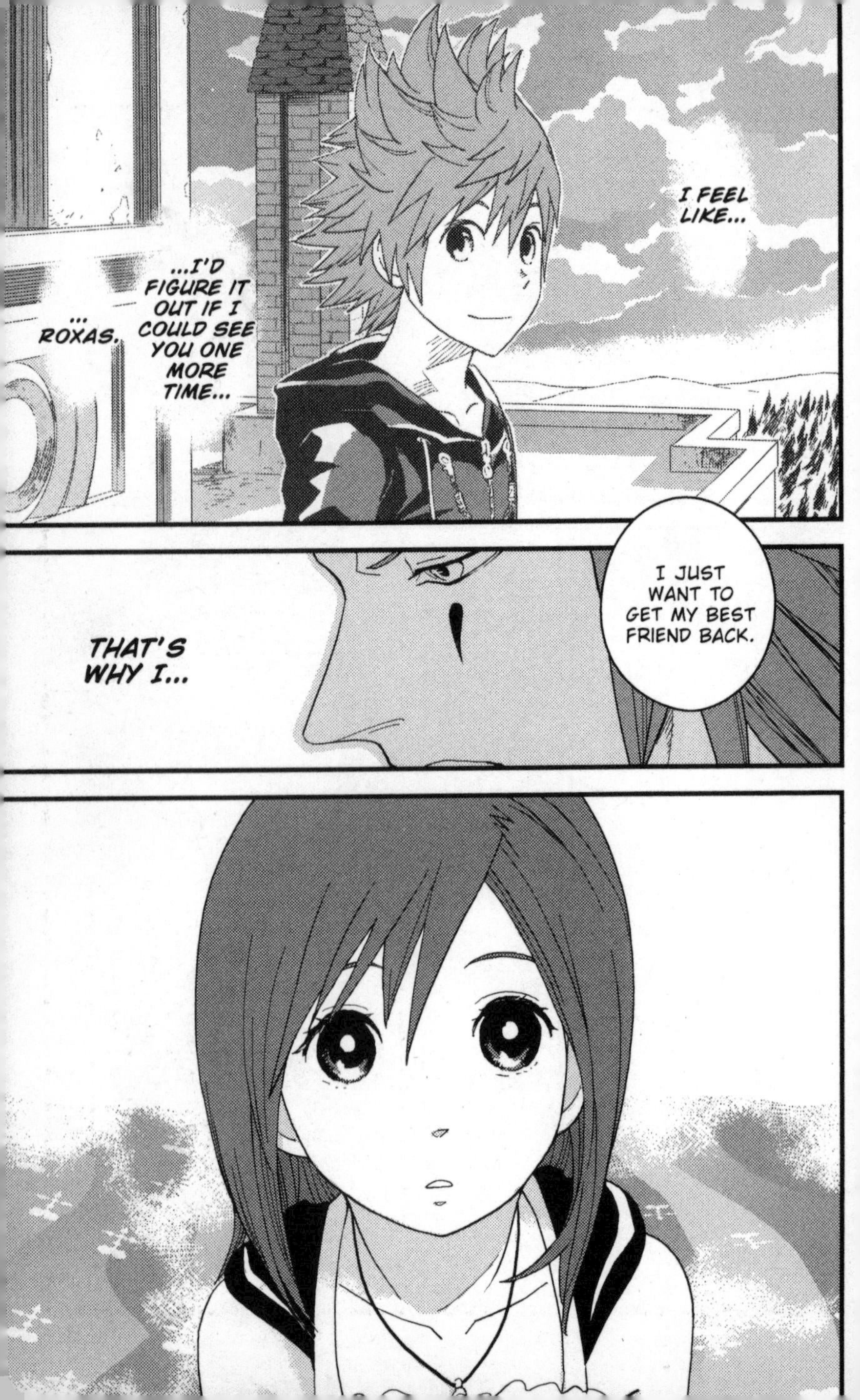
I FEEL LIKE...
...I'D FIGURE IT OUT IF I COULD SEE YOU ONE MORE TIME...
... ROXAS.
I JUST WANT TO GET MY BEST FRIEND BACK.
THAT'S WHY I...

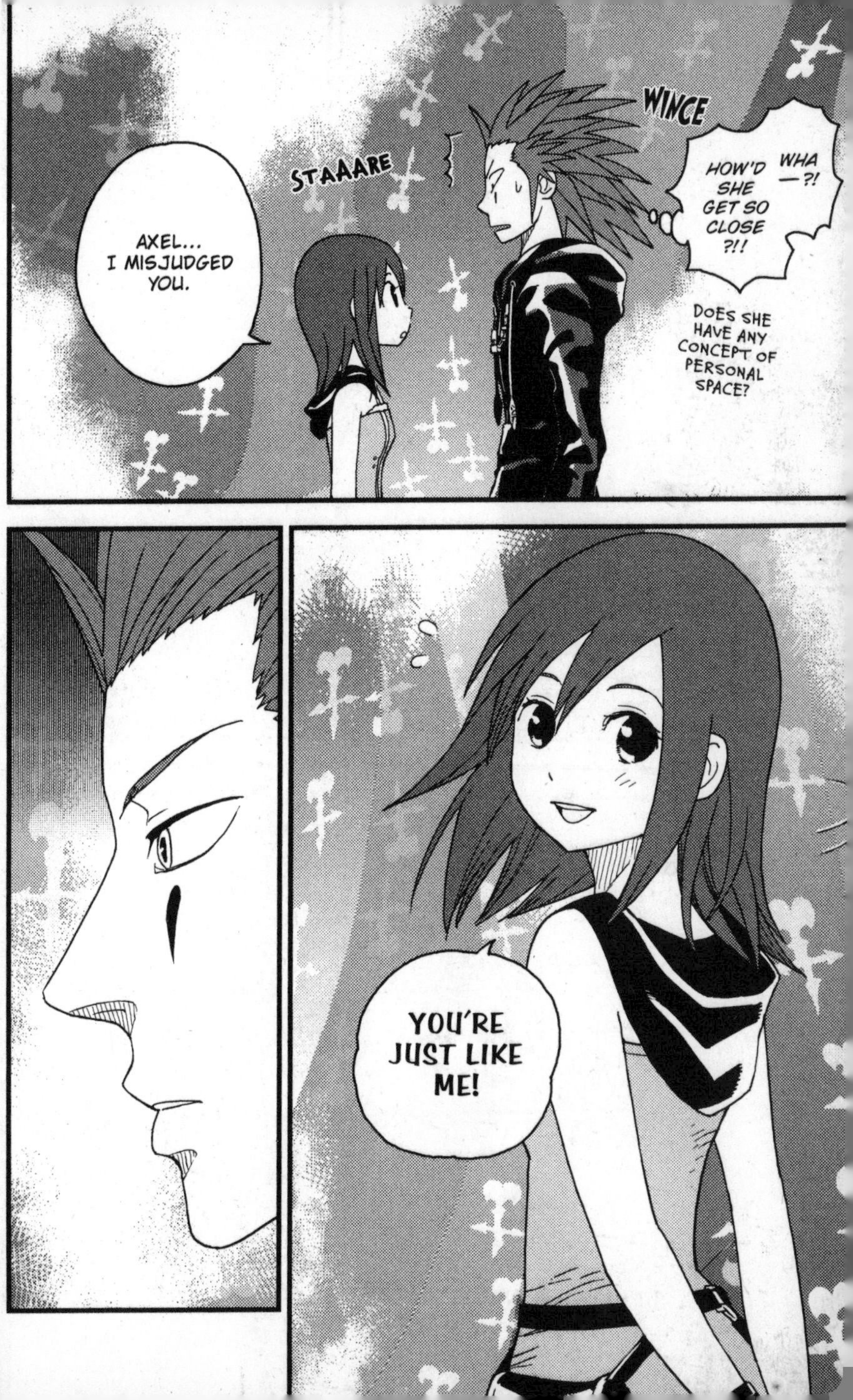
WINCE
WHA—?!
HOW'D SHE GET SO CLOSE ?!!
DOES SHE HAVE ANY CONCEPT OF PERSONAL SPACE?
STAAARE
AXEL... I MISJUDGED YOU.
YOU'RE JUST LIKE ME!

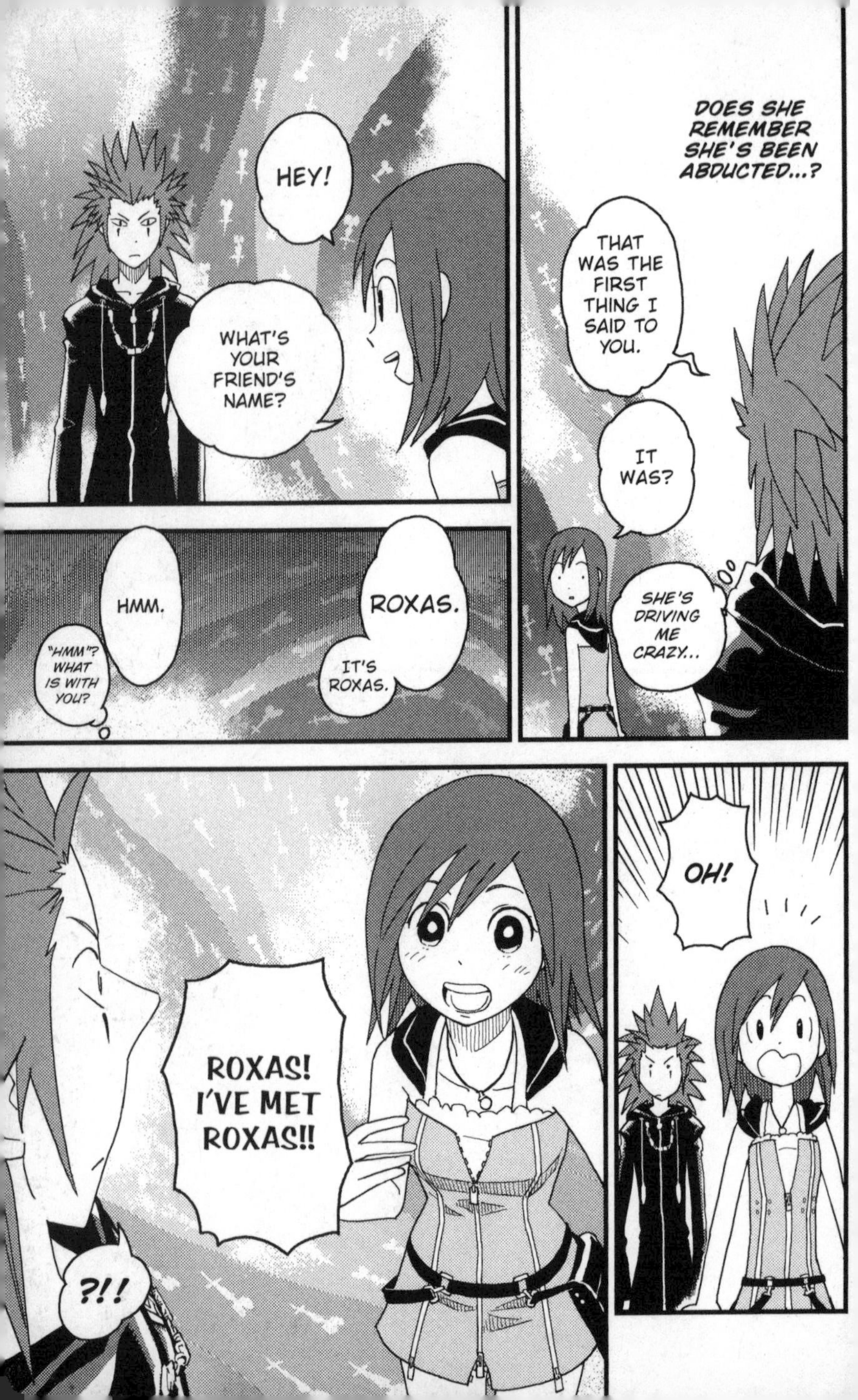
DOES SHE REMEMBER SHE'S BEEN ABDUCTED...?
THAT WAS THE FIRST THING I SAID TO YOU.
IT WAS?
SHE'S DRIVING ME CRAZY...
HEY!
WHAT'S YOUR FRIEND'S NAME?
ROXAS.
IT'S ROXAS.
HMM.
"HMM"? WHAT IS WITH YOU?
OH!
ROXAS! I'VE MET ROXAS!!
?!!

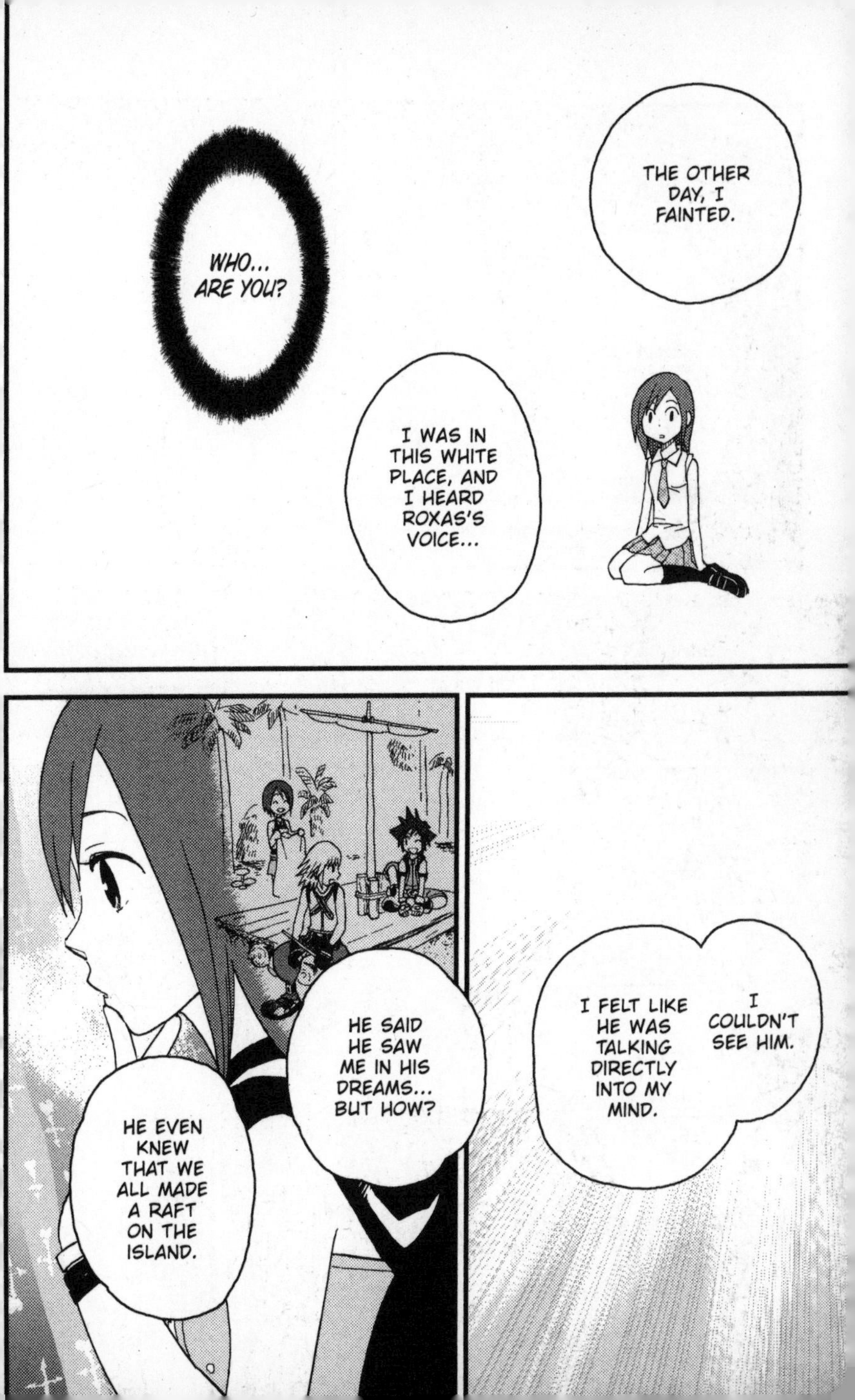
THE OTHER DAY, I FAINTED.
I WAS IN THIS WHITE PLACE, AND I HEARD ROXAS'S VOICE...
WHO... ARE YOU?
I COULDN'T SEE HIM.
I FELT LIKE HE WAS TALKING DIRECTLY INTO MY MIND.
HE SAID HE SAW ME IN HIS DREAMS... BUT HOW?
HE EVEN KNEW THAT WE ALL MADE A RAFT ON THE ISLAND.

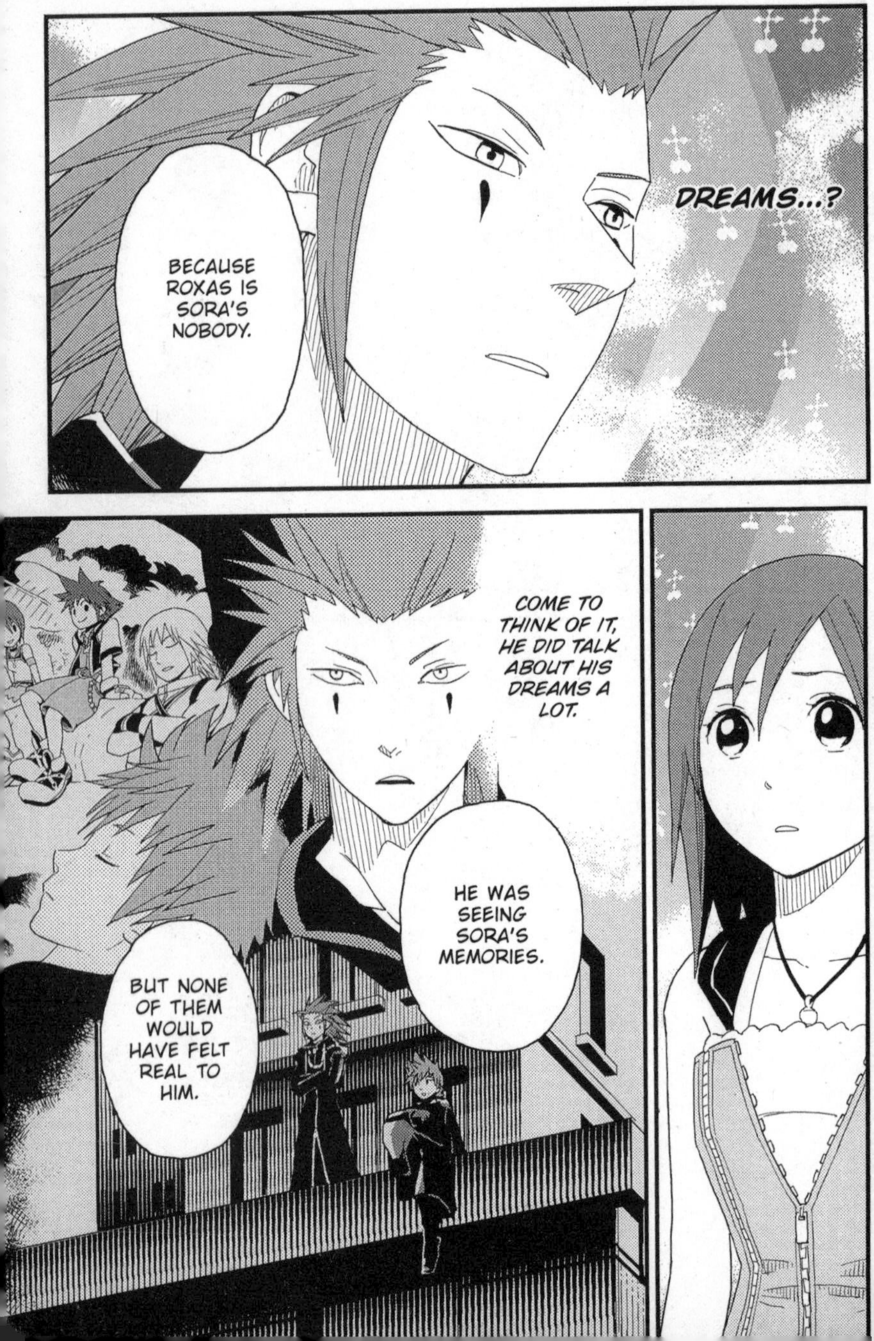
DREAMS...?
BECAUSE ROXAS IS SORA'S NOBODY.
COME TO THINK OF IT, HE DID TALK ABOUT HIS DREAMS A LOT.
HE WAS SEEING SORA'S MEMORIES.
BUT NONE OF THEM WOULD HAVE FELT REAL TO HIM.

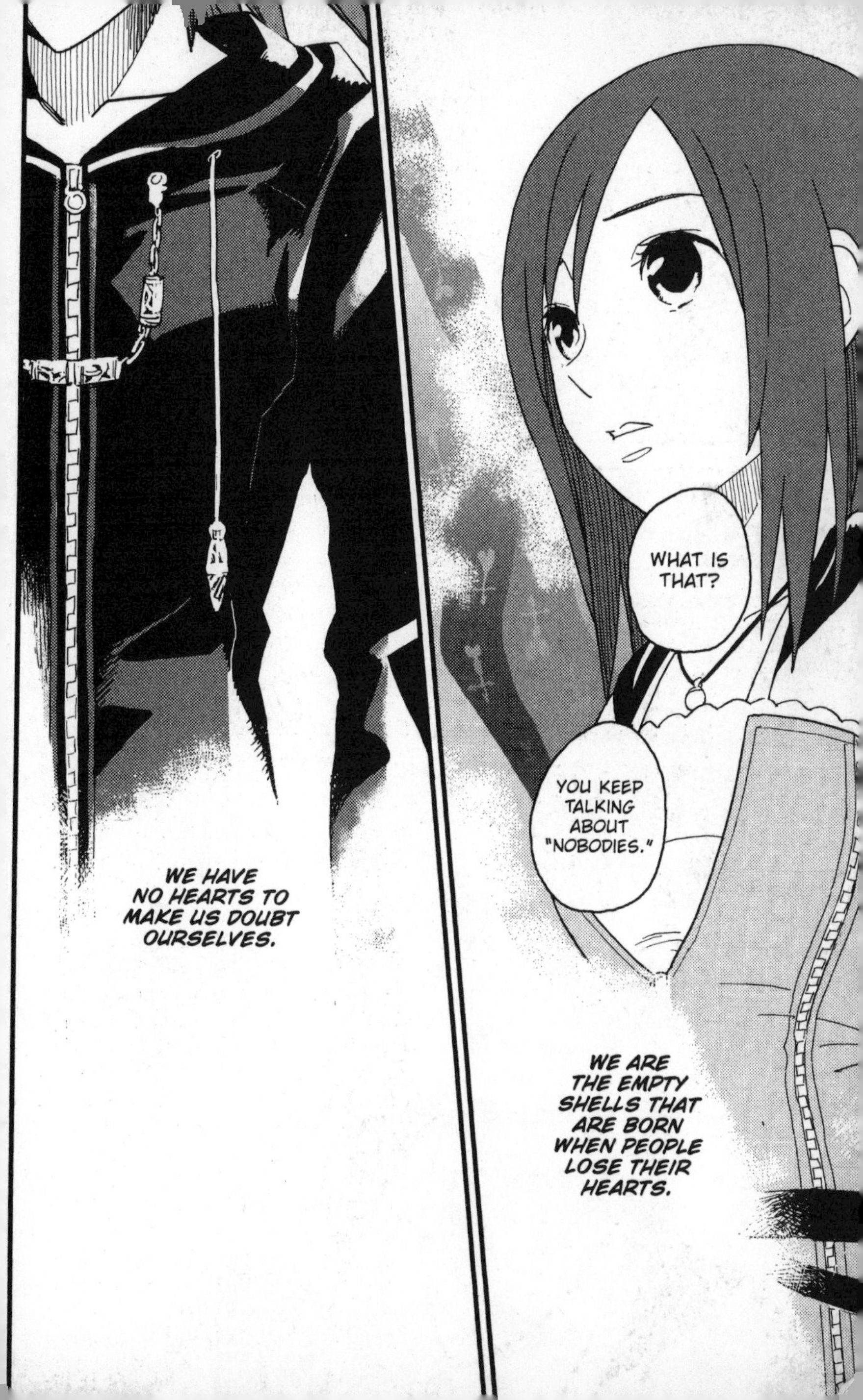
WHAT IS THAT?
YOU KEEP TALKING ABOUT "NOBODIES."
WE ARE THE EMPTY SHELLS THAT ARE BORN WHEN PEOPLE LOSE THEIR HEARTS.
WE HAVE NO HEARTS TO MAKE US DOUBT OURSELVES.

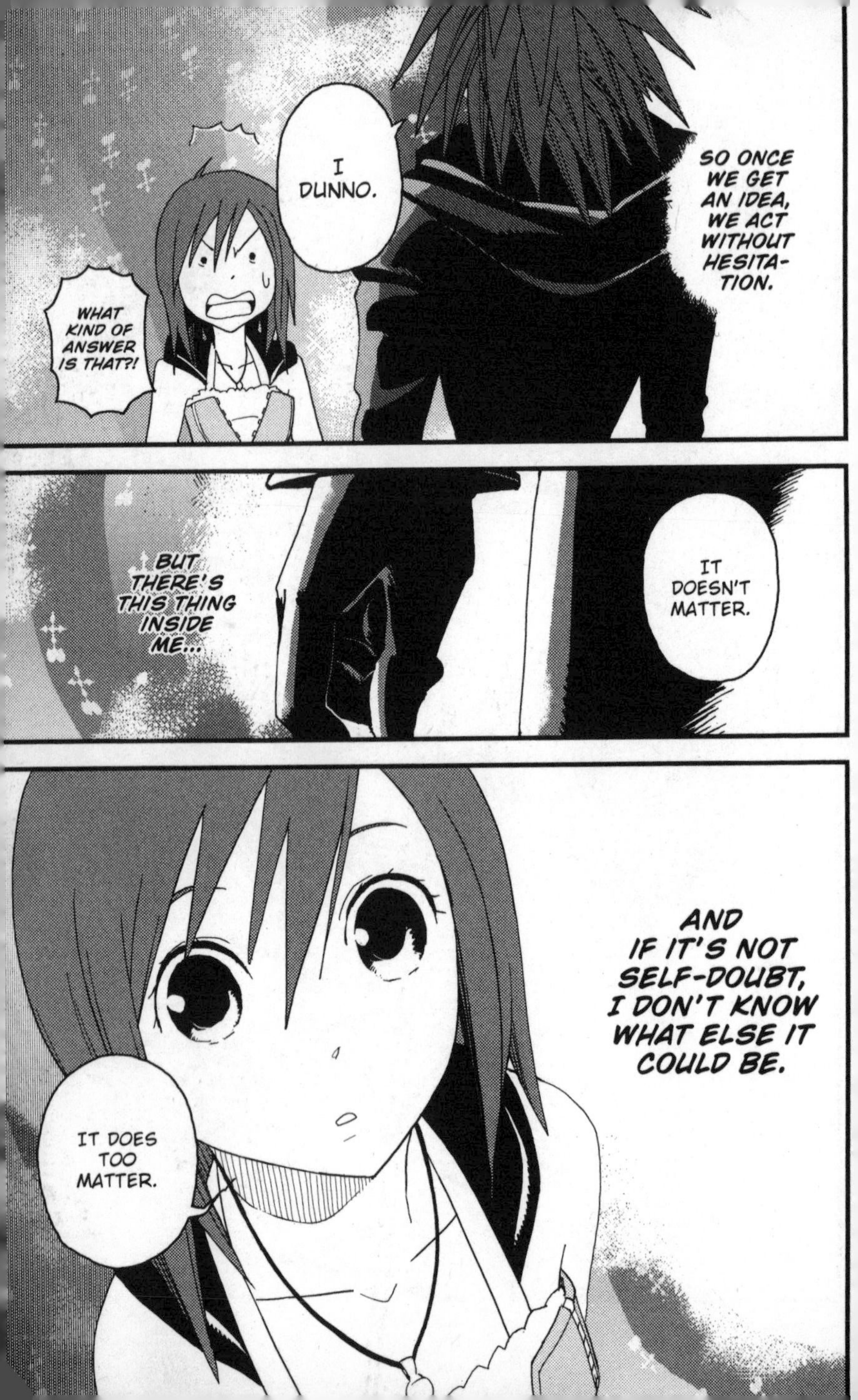
SO ONCE WE GET AN IDEA, WE ACT WITHOUT HESITATION.
I DUNNO.
WHAT KIND OF ANSWER IS THAT?!
IT DOESN'T MATTER.
BUT THERE'S THIS THING INSIDE ME...
AND IF IT'S NOT SELF-DOUBT, I DON'T KNOW WHAT ELSE IT COULD BE.
IT DOES TOO MATTER.

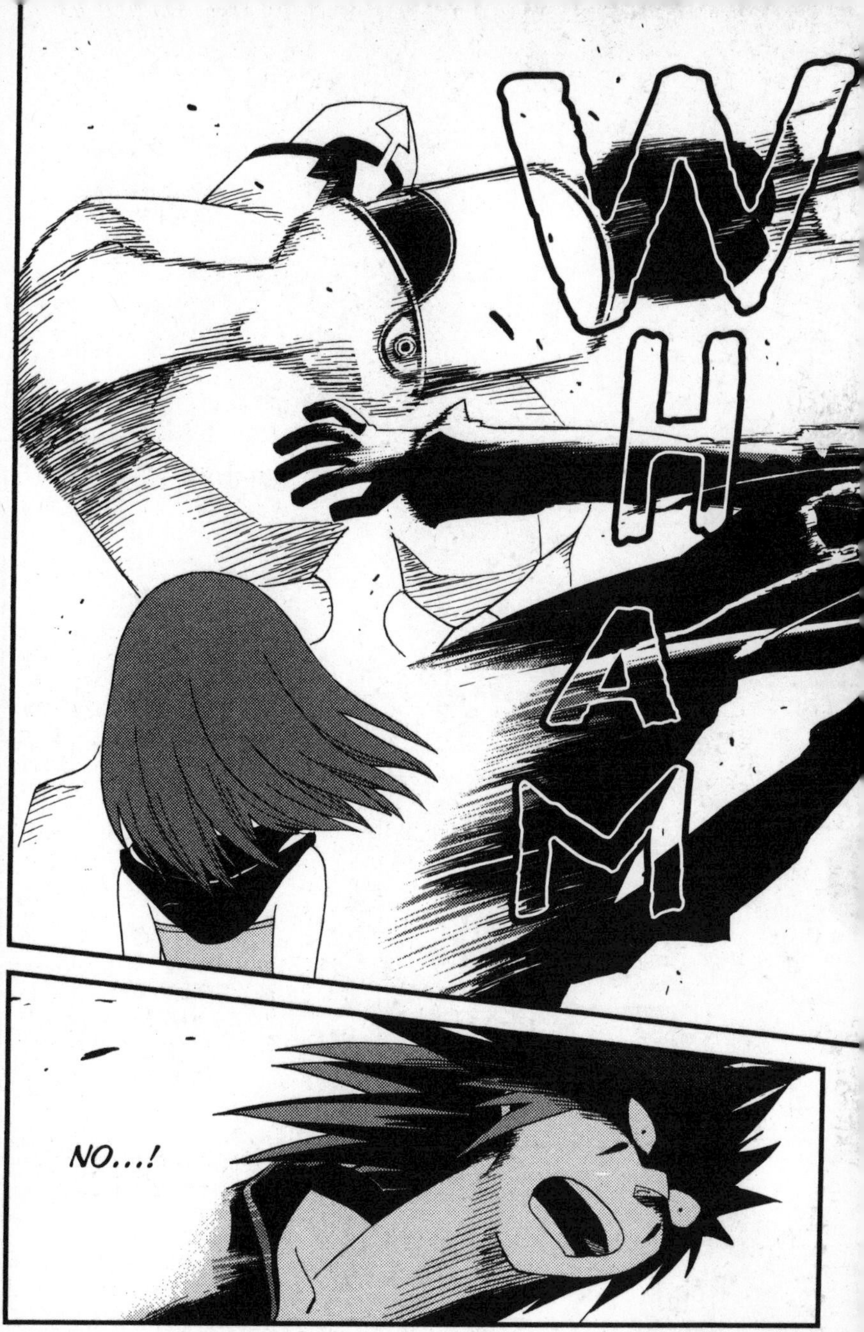
WHAM
NO...!

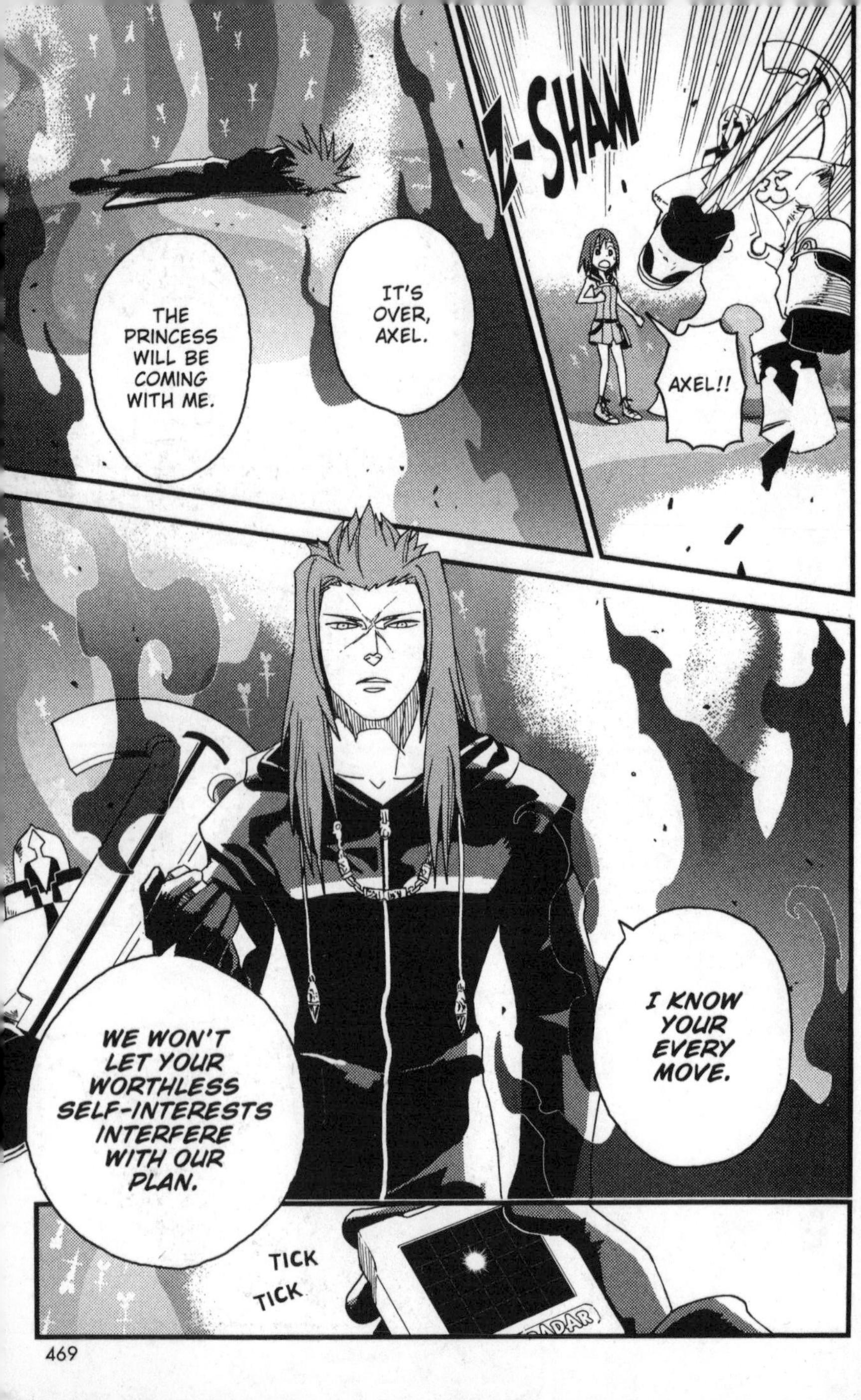
Z-SHAM
AXEL!!
IT'S OVER, AXEL.
THE PRINCESS WILL BE COMING WITH ME.
I KNOW YOUR EVERY MOVE.
WE WON'T LET YOUR WORTHLESS SELF-INTERESTS INTERFERE WITH OUR PLAN.
TICK
TICK
RADAR

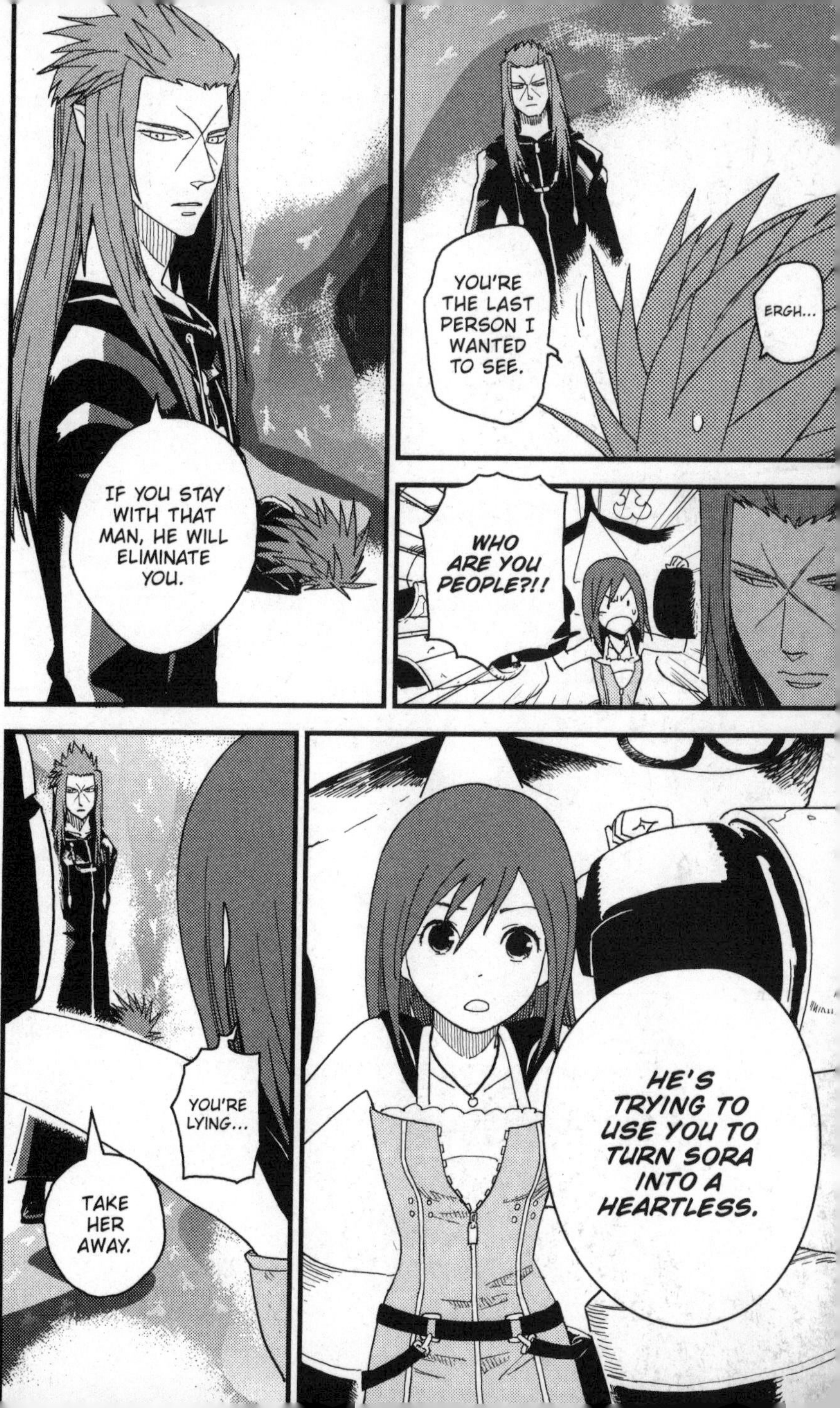
ERGH...
YOU'RE THE LAST PERSON I WANTED TO SEE.
WHO ARE YOU PEOPLE?!!
IF YOU STAY WITH THAT MAN, HE WILL ELIMINATE YOU.
HE'S TRYING TO USE YOU TO TURN SORA INTO A HEARTLESS.
YOU'RE LYING...
TAKE HER AWAY.

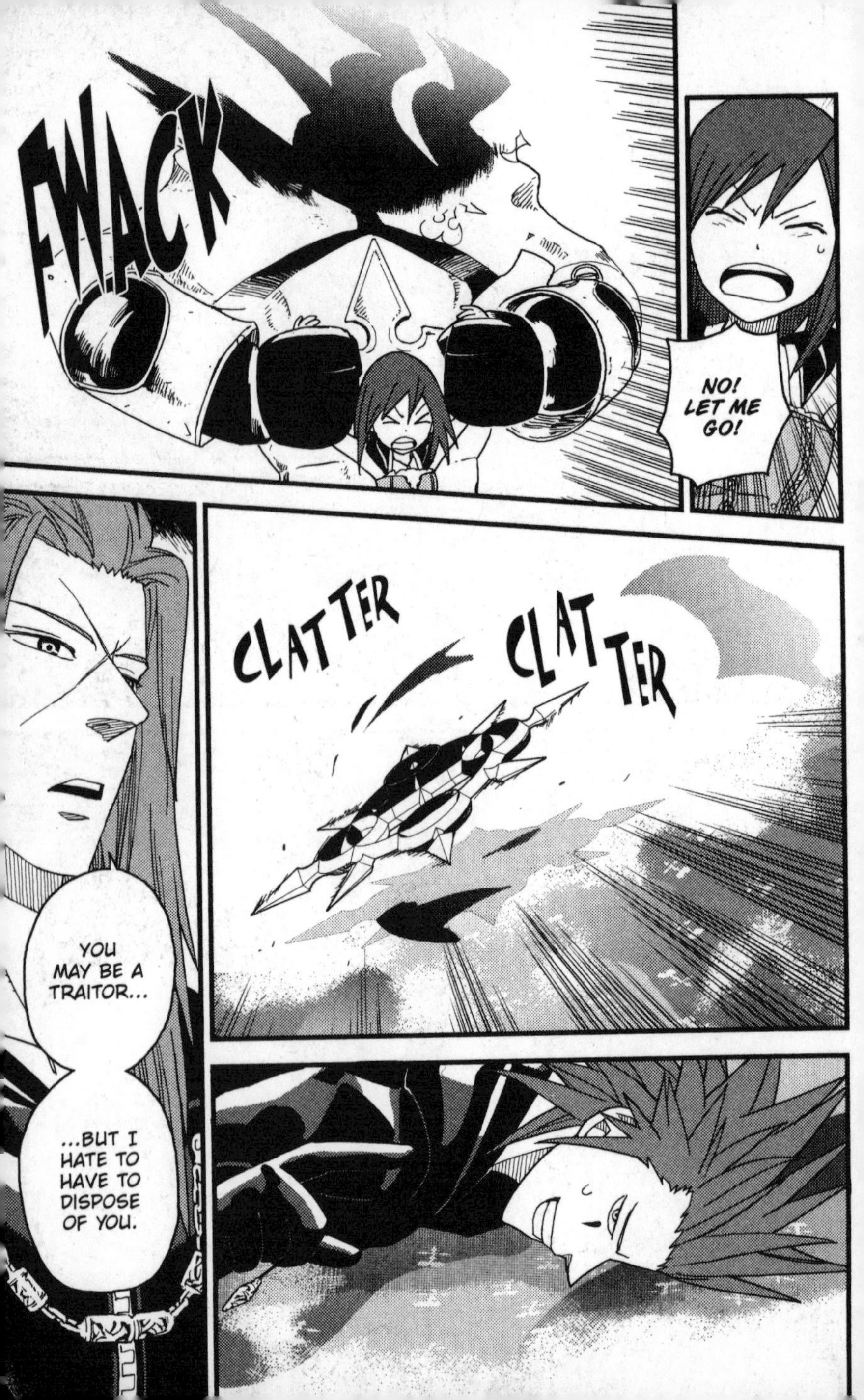
NO! LET ME GO!
FWACK
CLATTER
CLATTER
YOU MAY BE A TRAITOR...
...BUT I HATE TO HAVE TO DISPOSE OF YOU.

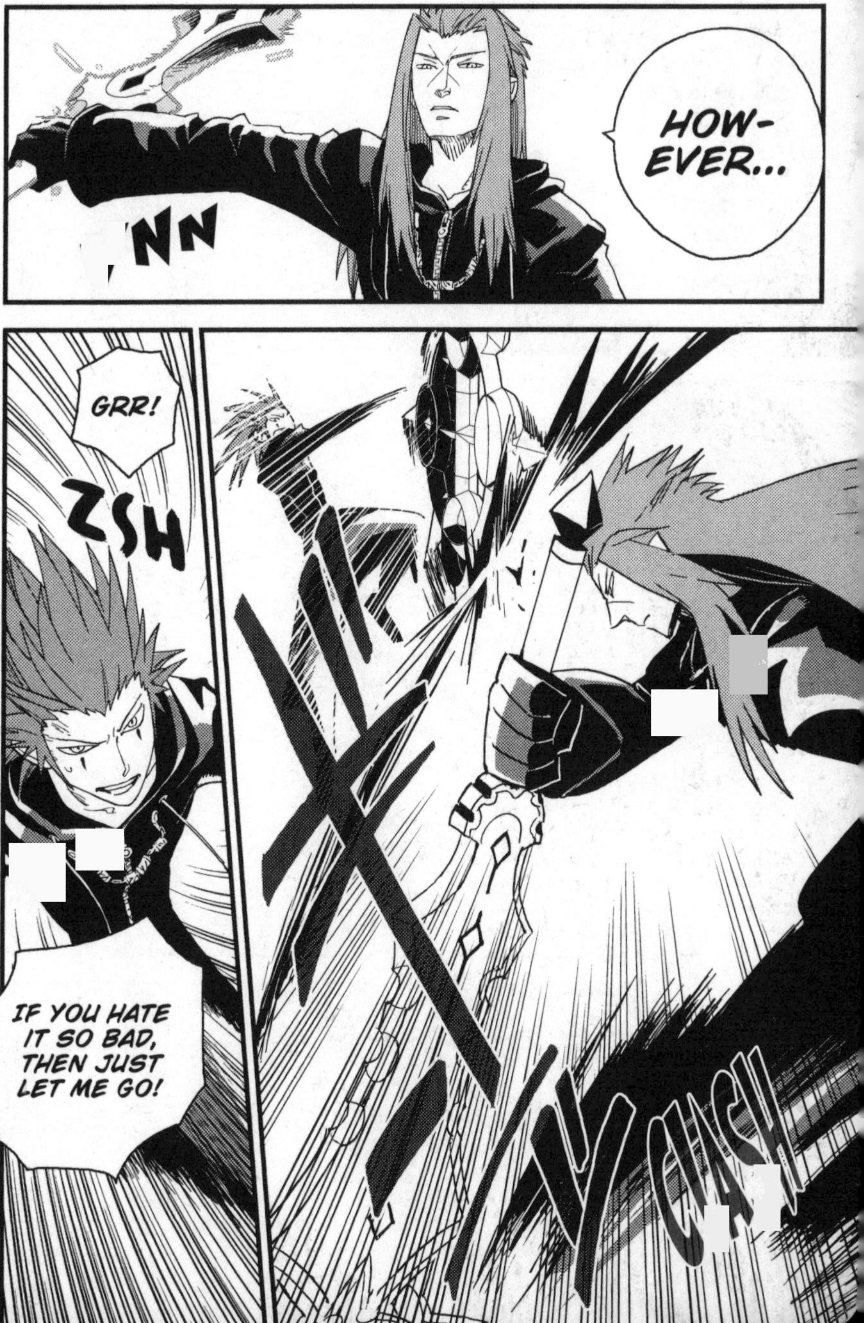
HOW-EVER...
CLASH
GRR!
ZSH
IF YOU HATE IT SO BAD, THEN JUST LET ME GO!

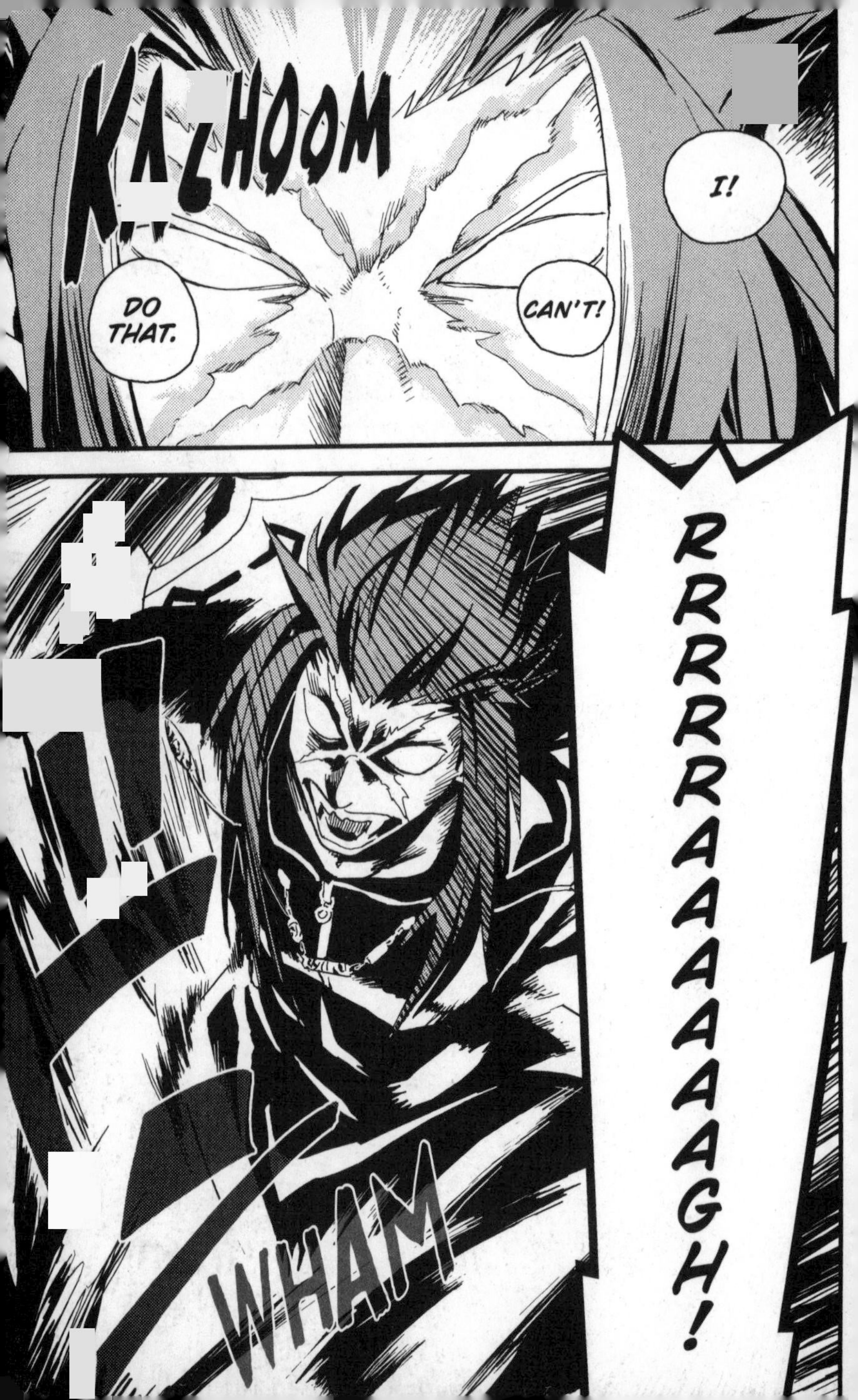
KA ZHOOM
I!
CAN'T!
DO THAT.
RRRRRAAAAAAGH!
WHAM

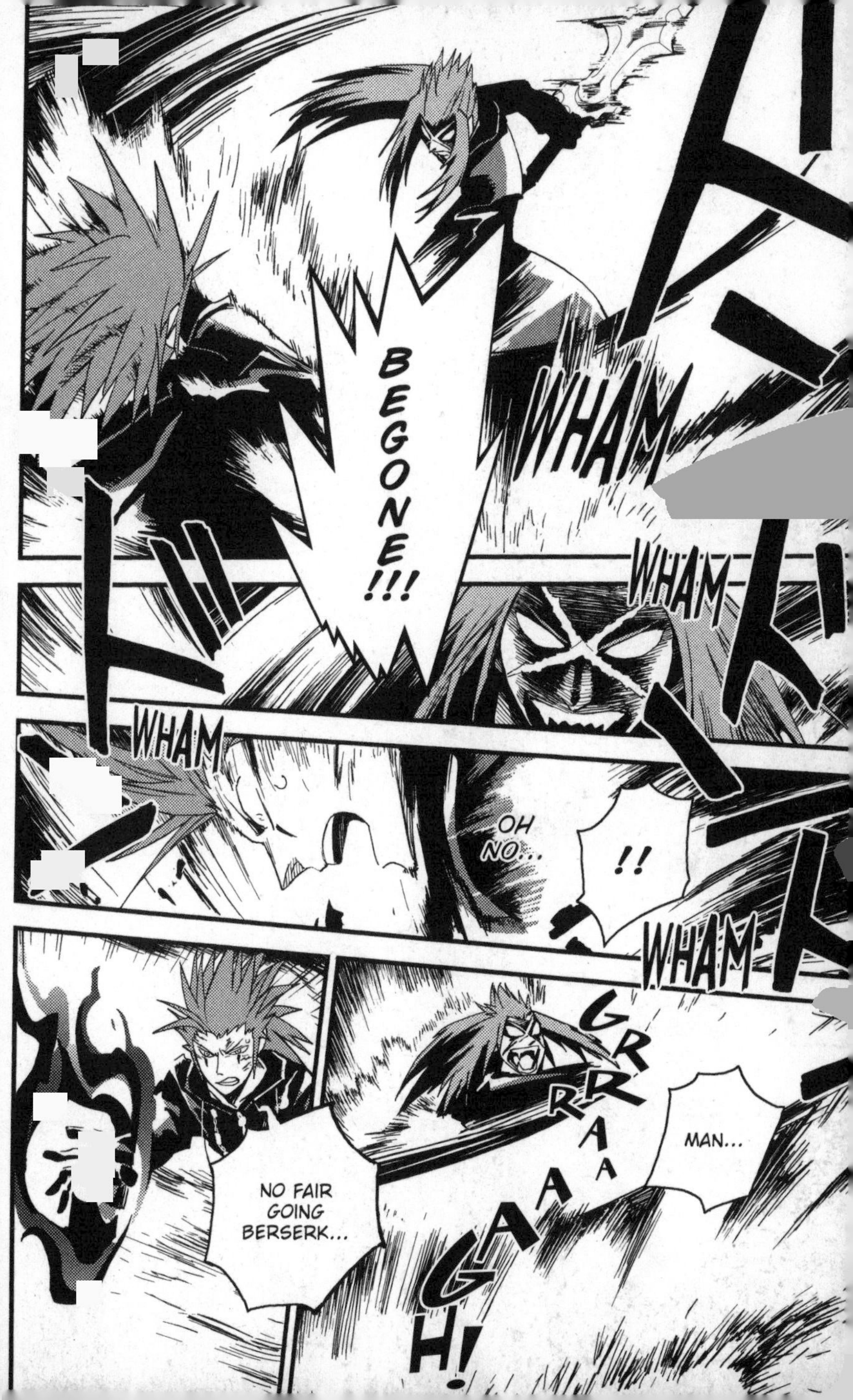
WHAM
BEGONE!!!
WHAM
!!
OH NO...
WHAM
WHAM
GRRRAAAAGH!
MAN...
NO FAIR GOING BERSERK...

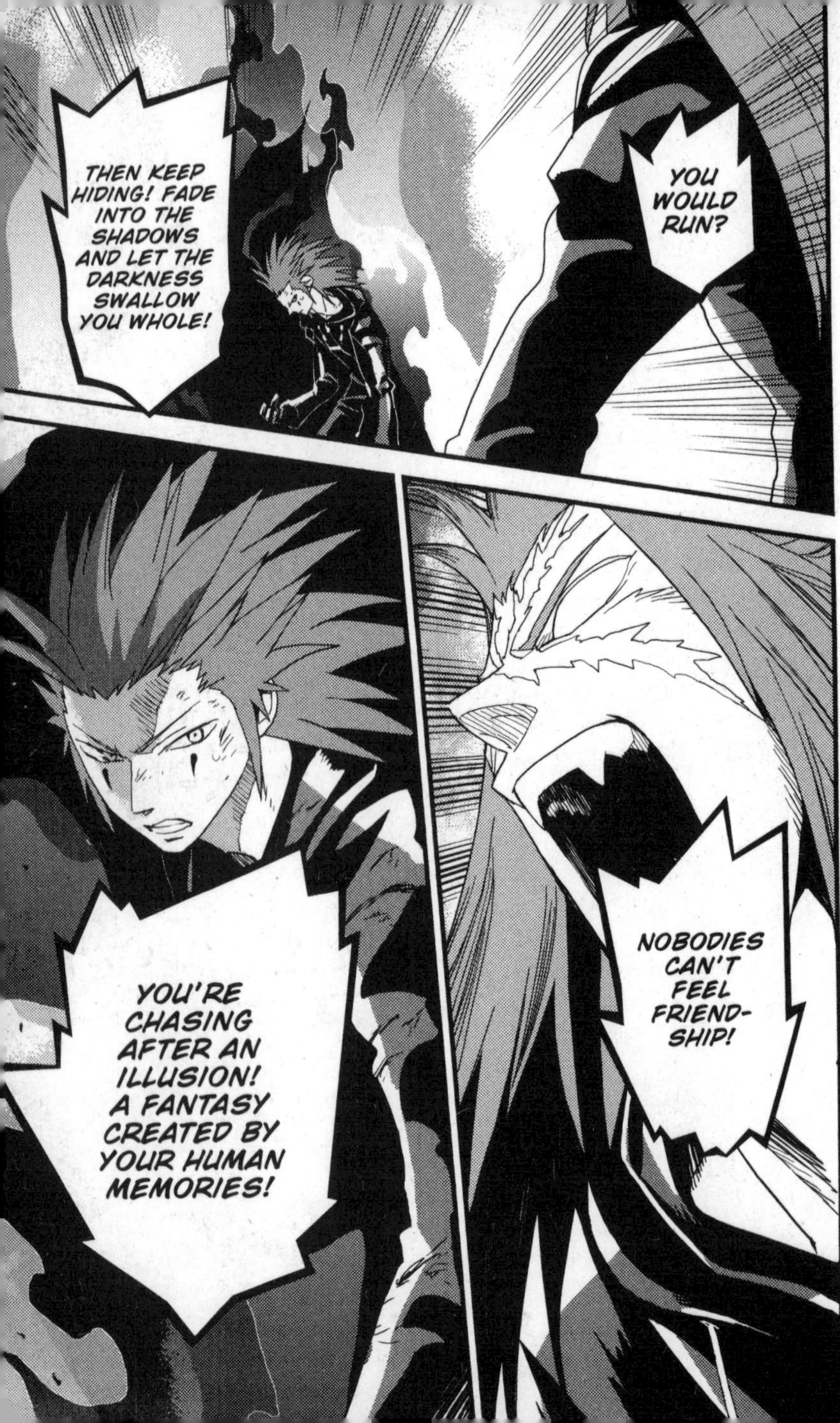
YOU WOULD RUN?
THEN KEEP HIDING! FADE INTO THE SHADOWS AND LET THE DARKNESS SWALLOW YOU WHOLE!
NOBODIES CAN'T FEEL FRIEND-SHIP!
YOU'RE CHASING AFTER AN ILLUSION! A FANTASY CREATED BY YOUR HUMAN MEMORIES!

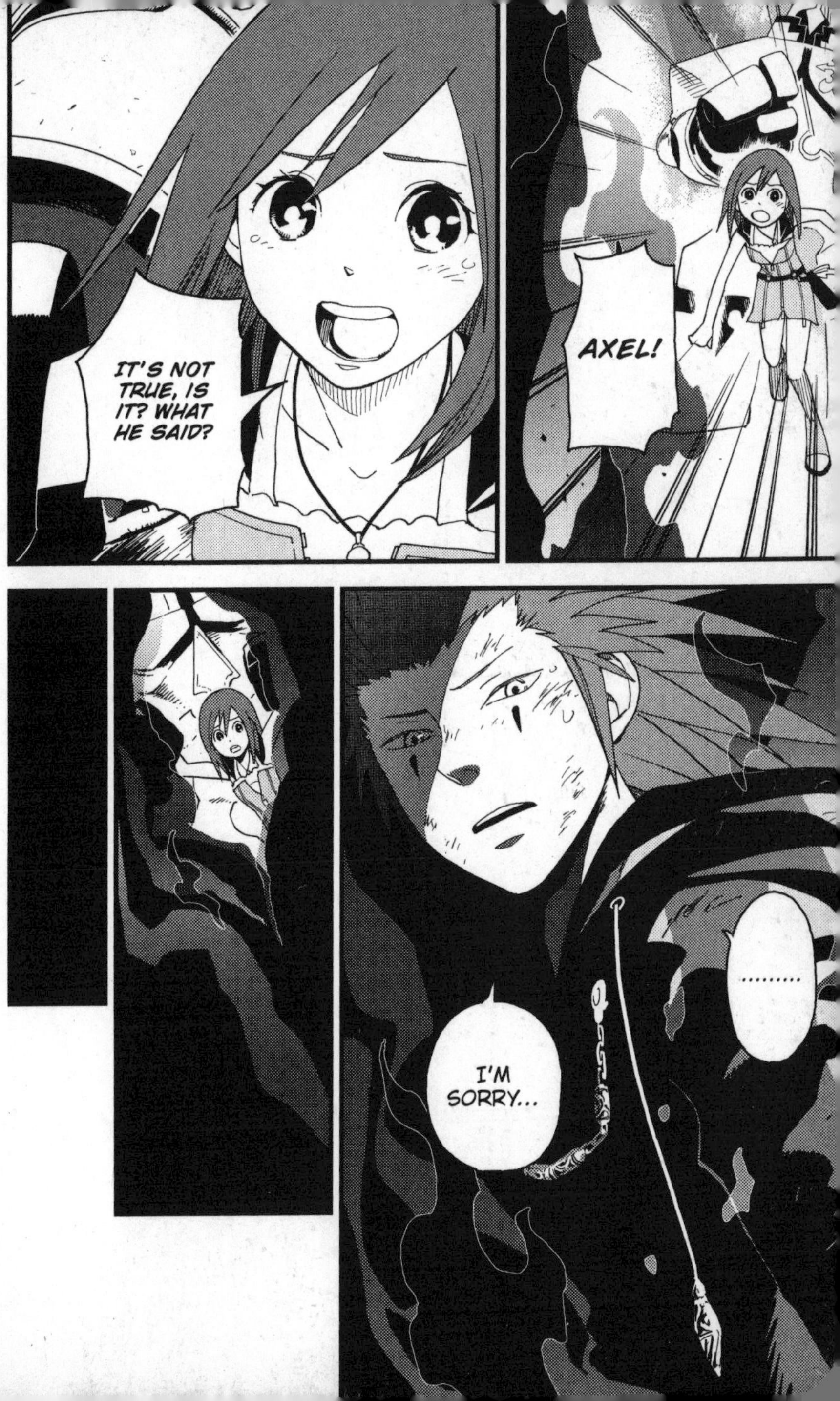
AXEL!
IT'S NOT TRUE, IS IT? WHAT HE SAID?
....
I'M SORRY...

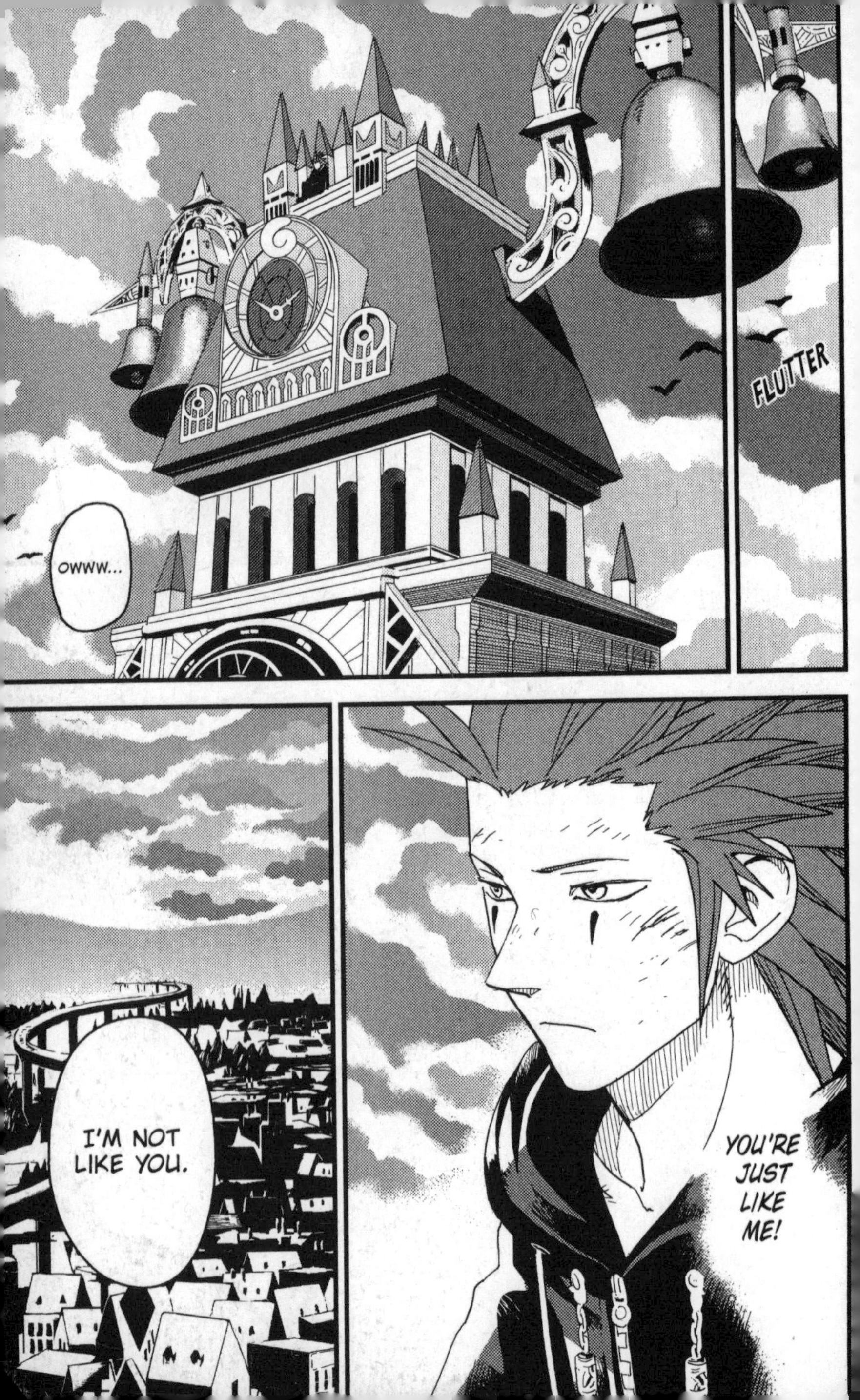
FLUTTER
OWWW...
YOU'RE JUST LIKE ME!
I'M NOT LIKE YOU.

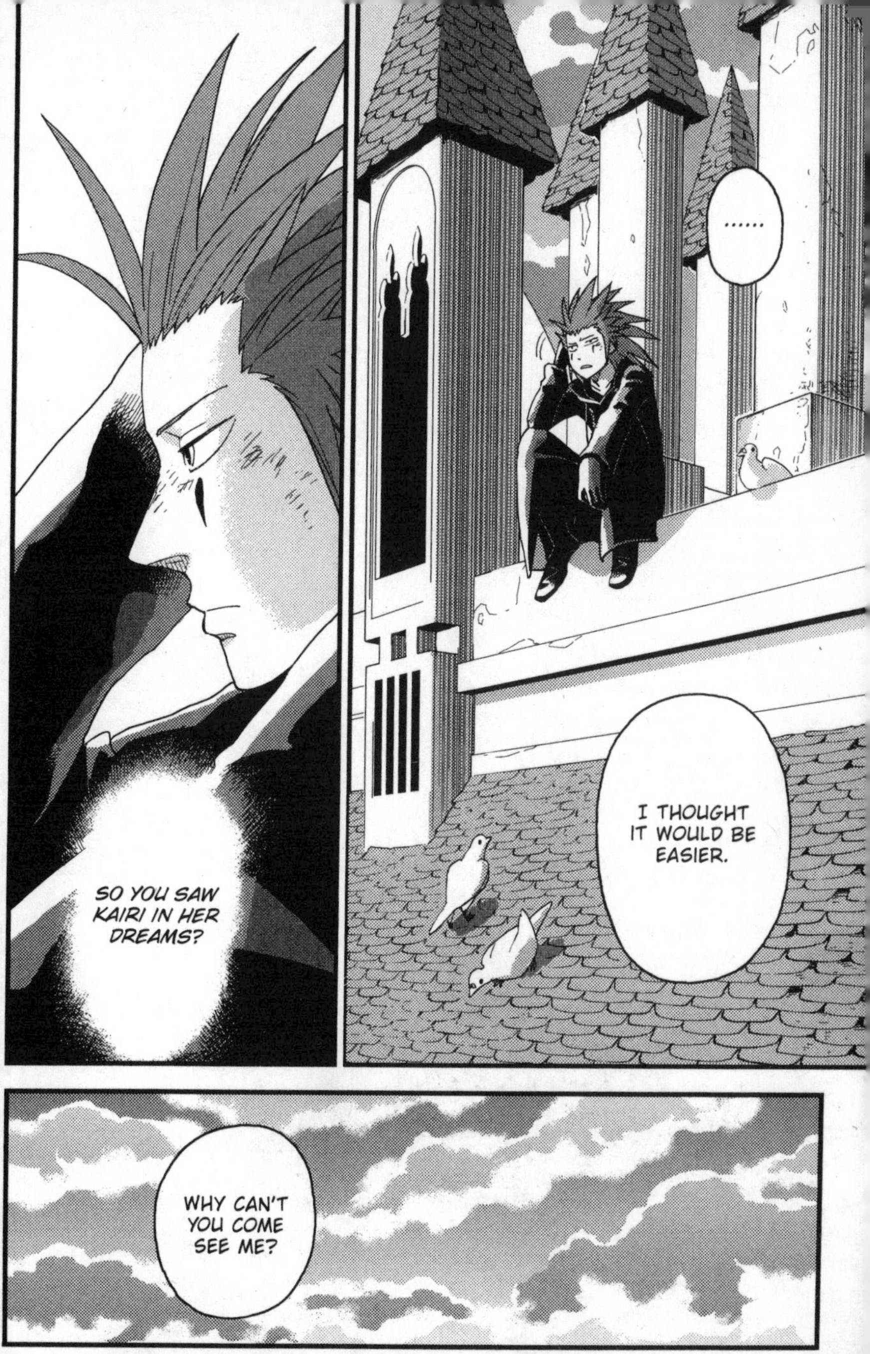
……
I THOUGHT IT WOULD BE EASIER.
SO YOU SAW KAIRI IN HER DREAMS?
WHY CAN'T YOU COME SEE ME?

***To be continued in* KINGDOM HEARTS II ③**

Disney SQUARE ENIX

KINGDOM HEARTS

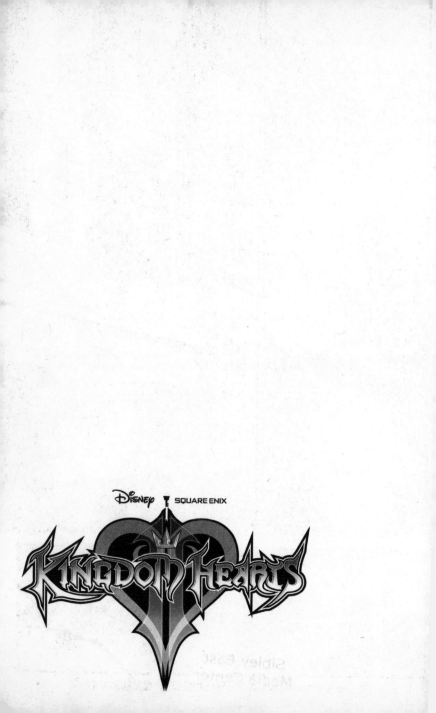

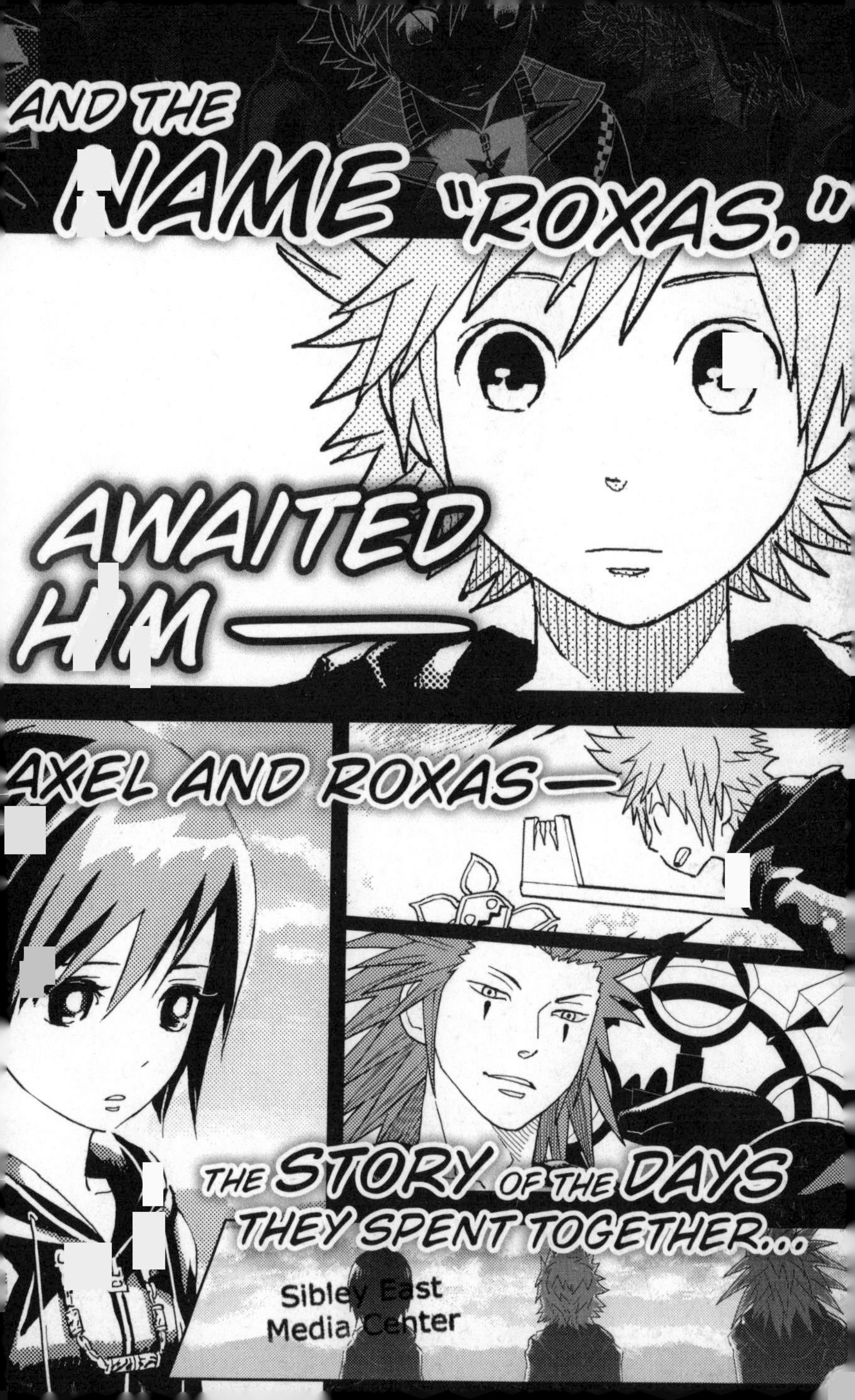
AND THE NAME "ROXAS."
AWAITED HIM—
AXEL AND ROXAS—
THE STORY OF THE DAYS THEY SPENT TOGETHER...

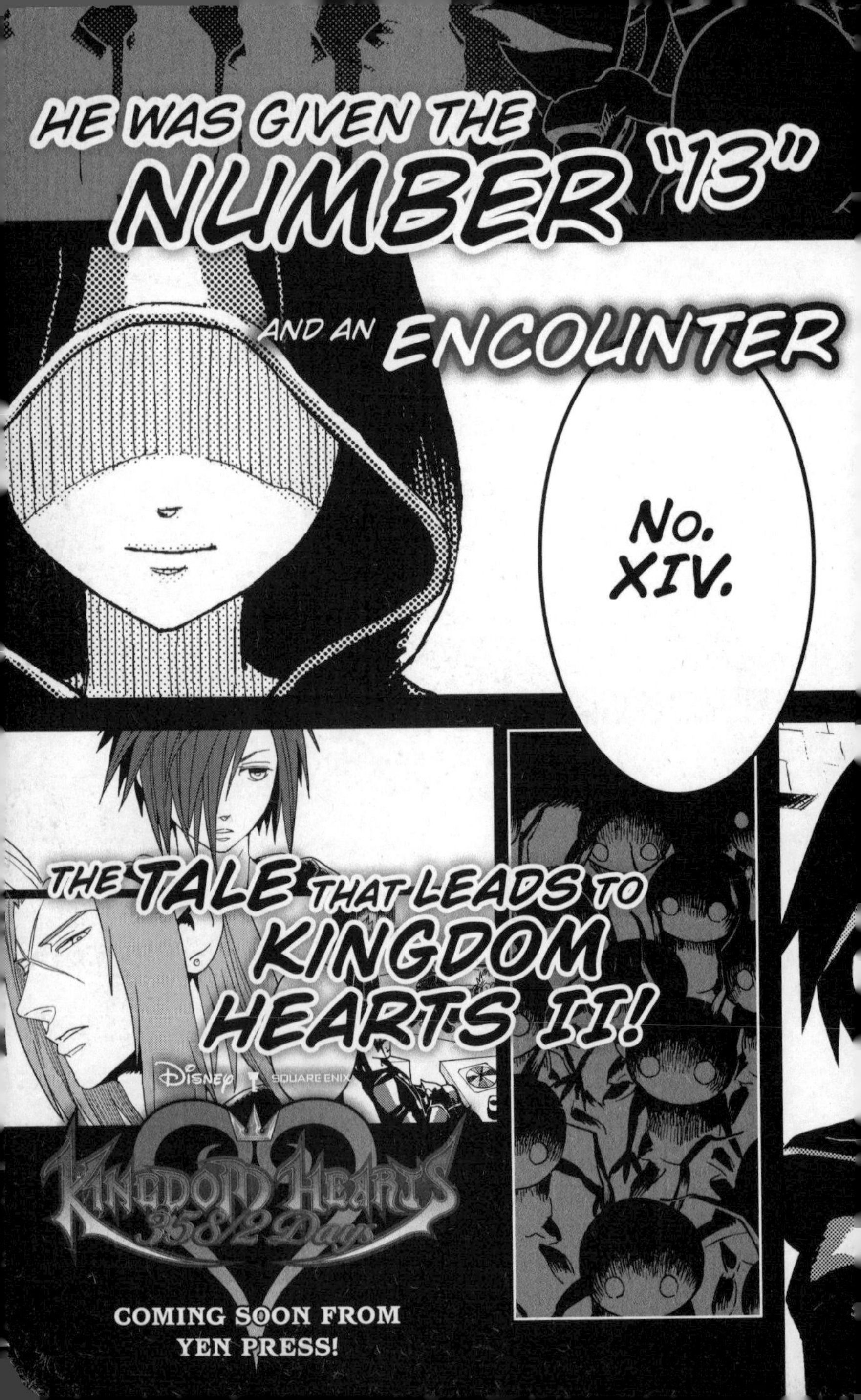
HE WAS GIVEN THE NUMBER "13"
AND AN ENCOUNTER
No. XIV.
THE TALE THAT LEADS TO KINGDOM HEARTS II!
DISNEY SQUARE ENIX
KINGDOM HEARTS 358/2 Days
COMING SOON FROM YEN PRESS!